VICE VERSA

Marjorie Garber

VICE VERSA

Bisexuality and the Eroticism
of Everyday Life

HAMISH HAMILTON · LONDON

HAMISH HAMILTON LTD

Published by the Penguin Group
Penguin Books Ltd, 27 Wrights Lane, London W8 5TZ, England
Penguin Books USA Inc., 375 Hudson Street, New York, New York 10014, USA
Penguin Books Australia Ltd, Ringwood, Victoria, Australia
Penguin Books Canada Ltd, 10 Alcorn Avenue, Toronto, Ontario, Canada M4V 3B2
Penguin Books (NZ) Ltd, 182–190 Wairau Road, Auckland 10, New Zealand

Penguin Books Ltd, Registered Offices: Harmondsworth, Middlesex, England

First published in the United States of America by Simon & Schuster 1995
First published in Great Britain by Hamish Hamilton Ltd 1996
1 3 5 7 9 10 8 6 4 2

Printed in England by Clays Ltd, St Ives plc

A CIP catalogue record for this book is available from the British Library

ISBN 0 241 13448-X

To the memory of Dell Abromson

Acknowledgments

It is a pleasure to acknowledge the many friends and colleagues without whose dedicated assistance this book would not have been possible, chief among them Christina Carlson, Paul Franklin, and Ted Gideonse. To each of them I want to express my gratitude for their relentless ingenuity, their generosity, and their unfailing patience, as well as for their friendship. My thanks as well to Rachel Cohen, Robyn Ochs, and Karen Friedland, who counseled me about historical issues within the bisexual movement, bi political organizations, and the 'zine scene; to the members of the Harvard-Radcliffe Bisexual, Gay and Lesbian Student Association for sharing thoughts and ideas; and to the many friends who were willing to talk with me about the place of bisexuality in their lives, on- or off-the-record.

To my editor Becky Saletan I am enormously grateful, not only for the time and effort she devoted to the book but also for her acute responsiveness in reading it and her collaborative energies in bringing it to its present form. Denise Roy was enormously helpful in making editorial suggestions and in helping to secure text permissions. Beth Vesel convinced me that this was a project worth doing, and that I could do it; her support and encouragement have been crucial throughout. Barbara Akiba and Herrick Wales also provided valuable assistance at an important stage. The Hyder Rollins Fund of the Harvard English Department generously provided funds to help defray the cost of permissions. Many friends on Nantucket, where much of this book was written, contributed immeasurably to it in various ways. I want particularly to thank Mimi Beman and the staff of Mitchell's Book Corner.

Barbara Johnson read every draft of every chapter and made crucial suggestions at each stage. My debt to her increases with every project; I am glad to say that at this point it looks as if it will take a lifetime to pay off.

This book is dedicated to Dell Abromson, my closest childhood friend, who lived a far too short—though, I think, an extraordinarily rich, full, and happy—life. I would have very much liked to know what she thought of the ideas put forward in these pages.

Contents

Introduction: Vice Versa

A man's heterosexuality will not put up with any homosexuality, and *vice versa.*

—Sigmund Freud, "Analysis Terminable and Interminable"[1]

When a woman doesn't identify with a classically female position, she is expected to identify with a classically male one, and *vice versa* in the case of a man.

—Kaja Silverman, Male Subjectivity at the Margins[2]

A very large number of both male and female respondents had made at least one full circle—an affair with a man, then one with a woman, and finally back to a man, or vice versa.

—Philip W. Blumstein and Pepper Schwartz,
"Bisexuality: Some Social Psychological Issues"[3]

As far as I can detect, I have always felt bisexual, strongly and equally attracted to men and women. At certain stages in my life, for psychological reasons, I have felt impelled to love and be loved by a man instead of a woman, or vice versa.

—Colin Spencer, Which of Us Two?[4]

Bisexuality, on the other hand, like gay, lesbian, or straight sexuality, has nothing to do with either vice or virtue.

—Marcia Deihl of the Boston Bisexual Women's
Network, letter to The Boston Globe[5]

Vice versa. From the Latin phrase meaning "with reversal of the regular order, conversely." "Vice" here comes from the same word as "vicinity," or place. Thus vice versa; places turned; contrariwise.

Why call a book about bisexuality *Vice Versa*?[6] Doesn't the very phrase suggest only two possibilities? Male *or* female, gay *or* straight, monogamous *or* nonmonogamous, adolescent *or* mature, normal *or* perverse? What is the force of that "or," that sense of inevitable alternatives? Or is it this very structure of the "versa" that in itself constitutes a "vice"? And where is the place of bisexuality, which, despite or perhaps because of the "bi" in its name, presents itself in the popular imagination as a third choice? Gay, straight, or bi?

Reversal. Mutual exclusiveness. Vice. All these notions, implicit in the expression "vice versa," will be reexamined in the course of this study.

Vice versa. Quite to the contrary.

The world is flat. The sun revolves around the earth. Human beings are either heterosexual or homosexual.

Alexander the Great had both male and female lovers. So did Julius Caesar. So, it turns out, did Sappho. And Socrates. But, it will be contended, the Greeks and the Romans were different from us. They were pagans. They lived so many years ago, and their culture had very different values. Besides, we say, they must have had a preference. If a man and his boy lover went to war together, and the man had a wife at home, wasn't he really responding to social and economic pressures to marry and beget children? Or was he, perhaps, responding to a different set of cultural prejudices in taking the boy as his lover—as he had himself been taken and trained in his youth? Were they, these distant and familiar ancients, really straight or really gay?

James I of England, Shakespeare's king, was married and a father, yet he had famous, indeed notorious, liaisons with men. He called the Duke of Buckingham his "sweet child and wife."[7] And what about Shakespeare himself? Married at eighteen, his wife already pregnant with his first child, he wrote eloquent love sonnets to a young man, the "master-mistress of his passion." Bisexuality (often in recent criticism labeled "homoeroticism," but clearly "hetero" as well) occurs as an important motive and plot device in several of his plays as well—*Twelfth Night, The Merchant of Venice,* and *As You Like It,* to cite the best-known instances, but also in more covert forms in *Othello, Much Ado About Nothing,* and *A Winter's Tale.* In *Othello* in particular the vagaries of sexual jealousy are combined with bisexual desire.

As many scholars have pointed out, men often had sex with other men, and women with other women, without regarding themselves as what we would today call homosexuals. "Bisexuality" is an anachronistic term for early modern Europe, but that does not mean that instances of it are absent from the literary and cultural record. Quite the contrary.

Marie Antoinette, the wife of Louis XVI, was publicly criticized by her husband's political enemies for engaging in lesbian relationships, which were depicted in a series of scurrilous (and fascinating) popular engravings. Likewise, in an eighteenth-century novel like John Cleland's *Fanny Hill*, Fanny has exciting and satisfying sexual relations with other women as well as with men, and the brothel-keeper narrator's desire to code those experiences as "initiation" or a preamble to "real" sex with men doesn't ring true; these pages are among the most erotically provocative of the novel, and it will not do merely to ascribe this fact to men's interest in girl-girl sex. Ask any woman who has read the book.

But these instances belong to a time before the invention of "the homosexual" as a kind of person, a type, a fate. Prior to the nineteenth century —or, some will say, the eighteenth—homosexuality in the Western world was a practice, not an identity. "The nineteenth-century homosexual became a personage, a past, a case history, and a childhood, in addition to being a type of life, a life form, and a morphology, with an indiscreet anatomy and possibly a mysterious physiology. Nothing that went into his total composition was unaffected by his sexuality," writes Michel Foucault in a phrase that has become a familiar part of modern discussions of sexual identity. "The sodomite had been a temporary aberration; the homosexual was now a species."[8]

Sometimes we go backward when we think we are going forward (and vice versa). The multiple specification of "perversions" and variations created not only legal strictures and medical treatments but also concomitant pleasures which were derived, in part, from breaking the rules.

Is bisexuality a "third kind" of sexual identity, between or beyond homosexuality and heterosexuality? Or is it something that puts in question the very concept of sexual identity in the first place? Why, instead of hetero-, homo-, auto-, pan-, and bisexuality, do we not simply say "sexuality"? And does bisexuality have something fundamental to teach us about the nature of human eroticism?

These are the questions this book sets out to explore.

Bisexualities

Everyone is bisexual.

—*Common wisdom*

There is no such thing as bisexuality.

—*Common wisdom*

Bisexuality tends to make otherwise reasonable people particularly nervous.

—Lear's *magazine*[9]

I see that a lot of people are going bisexual this year.

—*Martha Weinman Lear,* The New York Times[10]

To interrogate oneself tirelessly on one's sexual drives seems to me self-destructive. One can be aroused, for example, by the sight of a holly leaf, an apple tree, or a male cardinal bird on a spring morning. As deeply rooted as they are in our sentimental and erotic lives, we must consider that our genitals can be quite thoughtless.

—*John Cheever,* Journals[11]

"I've always known I was bisexual." The speaker was a sixteen-year-old high school student at Cambridge Rindge and Latin High School. The occasion was the school's annual Coming-Out Day, and the announcement by Khadjihah Britton was made to an audience of 250 classmates. Typical for liberal Cambridge, Massachusetts? Perhaps. But across the country, from Berkeley, California, to Minneapolis, Minnesota, to Fort Lauderdale, Florida, more and more young people are declaring themselves to be bisexual. Doing so, says one public-health intern, offers them a chance to resist categorization: Saying you're bisexual "just says you're not yet defined and gives you some freedom."[12] It also describes a social and sexual openness modeled in part on media stars and popular culture, from Madonna to Mick Jagger to Elton John.

"From where I sit it's definitely becoming more chic," reports a twenty-year-old Midwestern market researcher, and the coordinator of a Chicago group for young gays and bisexuals concurs: "The truth is," she says, "they're open to everything."[13] Freedom, openness, chic—one can almost hear the grumblings of Ms. and Mr. Grundys on both the right and the left. *Newsweek,* predictably and plausibly, linked this openness to other ongoing reexaminations of cultural certainty: "[A]t high schools around the country," it reported, "multiculturalism has begun to embrace multisexualism."[14] On the other hand, some gays and lesbians continue to insist that coming out as bisexual is "easier." At Rindge and Latin's Coming-Out Day a young lesbian invoked the shibboleth of "heterosexual privilege" for bis: "After all, you've still got the straight part." And for some, freedom and openness translate into "confusion" at a time when all kinds of identities for teens—job, school, career, even body size and appearance, as well as sexuality—are in the process of construction and revision.

I read these comments on U.S. multiculturalism, "multisexualism," the "cool" new profile of teen bisexuality, and the annual assembly at Cambridge Rindge and Latin as I traveled on a German railroad train going from Munich to Konstanz. Rindge and Latin is a block from where I work; there was something at once defamiliarizing and confirmatory about encountering these voices and images as the train rumbled through the Black Forest. I had spoken on gender and eroticism at Munich; I was on my way to Konstanz, a university located in the city where the Great Schism was debated by clerics in the fifteenth century, and where today the border with Switzerland cuts through the edge of town. My mind was on borders and borderlines.

Back home I picked up a copy of the *New York Times* and found, on its Education page, an article on "a high school club for gay students," as its headline declared. The high school was the selective though public Hunter High, located, as the article noted, "on the sophisticated Upper East Side." The club was the 10 Percent Club, which gets its name from the "notion that as much as 10 percent of society may be gay"—a "notion" found in the 1948 Kinsey Report on *Sexual Behavior in the Human Male*. And the gay students? "This year," the article notes in paragraph twelve, halfway down the page, "no members of Hunter's 10 Percent Club have come out and said they're exclusively gay. 'Everyone's bisexual,'" said the president. "Could that really be true?" the columnist asks.

He gets, of course, predictable answers. It's easier to come out as bi than as gay. "It's easier to say, 'I'm bisexual,'" one member suggests. "You can recognize your feelings but not totally alienate yourself from society." But as the columnist notes later on, with what seems like gentle irony, despite the supposed sexual savvy of today's teenagers, and the fact that "the 10 Percent Club sounds as savvy as you get," "every one of the bisexuals interviewed said they'd never had relations with someone of their own sex."[15]

"I really *have* begun to wonder whether the hetero/homo divide as such is breaking down among [that] generation," says a gay man who teaches at a prestigious California institution. "My 'radar' has proved to be completely ineffectual all semester: One of the most gay-empathetic and at-ease-in-the-classroom men turned out to be straight, raised by a sometimes-lesbian mother, one of the surefire dykes turned out to be dating a guy who had himself previously been dating a guy who preferred to cross-dress as a woman. . . . And if this is happening at as staid an undergraduate environment as [this university], I really do wonder what's evolving elsewhere!"

One thing that clearly *is* evolving is bi-consciousness and bi-visibility. The rock group Living Colour recorded a song entitled "Bi" that included the refrain, "Everybody wants you when you're bi." Lead singer Brett Anderson of the British band London Suede caused something of a stir when he characterized himself as "a bisexual who's never had a homosexual experience."[16]

Dance-pop group Fem 2 Fem, characterized as a "lipstick lesbian" group with a "steamy sex vibe," includes two women described in the press as "straight," one as "gay," and one as "bi."[17] The very existence of this third category, quietly nested in parentheses—"(bi)"—after singer Julie Ann Park's name, gives a visibility and legitimacy to an erotic self-description that has often been regarded as either euphemistic or suspect.

The late rock star Kurt Cobain told the gay and lesbian newsmagazine *The Advocate* that if he had not met and married Courtney Love, he "probably would have carried on with a bisexual lifestyle."[18] He seemed to suggest that bisexuality was, for him and people like him, the inevitable default position, more natural than monosexual restrictiveness. Comedian, entertainer, and *Playboy* cover girl Sandra Bernhard, one of the most striking bisexual celebrities since her almost-namesake Sarah, urges audiences at her cabaret act to avoid consignment to one of three food groups: heterosexuality, homosexuality, bisexuality. "Both men and women can relate to both the man and woman in me,"[19] she declares.

In Rose Troche's lesbian comedy *Go Fish,* a lesbian sleeps with a man. *Grief,* an AIDS-themed film by Richard Glazer, centers on a (bi)sexually conflicted artist played by Alexis Arquette, who was also featured in the bisexual college film *Threesome.* In *Paris, France,* three men and a woman, all writers, bedhop together. If this is the 1994 Lesbian & Gay Film Festival, change is indeed under way. "This refusal to abide by settled categories of sexual identity is all very dizzying, it's all politically incorrect, and it all lends the festival a spark of unpredictability," muses the *Boston Globe.* This is the new bisexuality, which is to say, the old bisexuality—bisexuality as eroticism, "unpigeonholed sexual identity,"[20] *not* bisexuality as the "third" choice between, or beyond, hetero- or homosex.

Everything Old Is New Again

Under the headline "Bisexual Chic," another article in *Newsweek* declared authoritatively that "Bisexuality is in bloom." It quoted a famous female music star, who said one of the greatest loves of her life was a woman—a

Vassar sophomore who had recently begun dating a man after four years of exclusively lesbian relationships—and two psychiatrists with opposing views—"Bisexuality is a disaster for culture and society," one proclaimed, while the other, the president-elect of the American Psychiatric Association, announced, "It is getting to the point where heterosexuality can be viewed as a hangup."[21]

In the same week, *Time,* not to be outdone, described in a piece called "The New Bisexuals" both the triumphs and the trials of this sexual phenomenon, from the biographies of celebrated actresses and writers to the appearance of best-selling novels, memoirs, and attention-grabbing bisex films to, once again, the divided views of the psychiatric community: "It has become very fashionable in elite and artistically creative sub-groups to be intrigued by the notion of bisexuality," said one expert, while another deplored both bisexuality and homosexuality as symptoms of a developmentally troubled childhood. "Bisexuals," declared a third, "generally do not have the capacity to fall in love with one person."[22]

There is nothing surprising in this, you may think. Competition between newsmagazines frequently produces similar stories in similar weeks, and the omnipresence of "bisexual chic" from pop stars to films and talk shows makes it an obvious topic for media notice. As *Newsweek* itself proclaims, with proprietary pride, "the news media have become a confessional for celebrities who are rushing out of their closets to join the new bisexual chic." What may be a little surprising, though, is the dates of these two articles. Both were published in May 1974—roughly twenty years ago.

The female music star with a woman lover was folk singer Joan Baez—and, in *Time*'s version, the very-bisexual Janis Joplin. Among the actresses cited were Tallulah Bankhead and Maria Schneider. Cross out the names and replace them with new ones and you'd have stories fit to print in a newsweekly of today. The psychiatric experts included names still frequently cited in omnibus articles about bisexuality, pro and con: doomsayers Charles Socarides and Natalie Shainess, supporters Judd Marmor of the APA and John Money, the specialist in gender identity at Johns Hopkins University. The obligatory accompanying photographs included a cross-dressed male model with his arms around a man and a woman *(Newsweek)* and a group of "partygoers at a bisexual liberation gathering in a Manhattan apartment."

Nor were the early seventies the first time around for "bisexual chic" as a social and cultural phenomenon even in this century. "Bisexual experimentation" in the twenties has been linked to the popularization of Freud (or "Freudianism"), the advent of World War I, and a general predilection for the daring and unconventional: bobbed hair, short skirts, the rejection of Prohibition and "Victorian" strictures. Novels by Ernest Hemingway, Djuna Barnes, and Sherwood Anderson; plays by Sholem Asch and Édouard Bourdet; the popularity of drag balls (held in such mainstream venues as the Hotel Astor and Madison Square Garden); the vogue among whites and blacks for bisexual Harlem blues songs and singers, the instant success in America of Marlene Dietrich—all of these declared "bisexuality" a sign at once of freedom and transgression.[23]

Why, then, all the fuss about bisexuality in the nineties? (We are speaking here of the *1990s*—although the bisexual lives of such figures as Sarah Bernhardt and Oscar Wilde mark out another period of bisexual "experimentation" and "chic" a century ago.) Is sexuality a fashion—like platform shoes, bell-bottomed trousers, or double-breasted suits—that appears and then disappears, goes underground, only to be "revived" with a difference? Is it that "news," by its very nature, must always be "new" to be noticed? Do we need to keep forgetting bisexuality in order to remember and rediscover it?

There are some important differences between the fascination with bisexuality today and that of twenty years ago. In the seventies, still the period of the self-styled Sexual Revolution, the ostensible objects were pleasure, freedom, and the breaking down of boundaries. Bisexuality and the drug culture promised the experiences of the borderline, the edge, the anti-bourgeois. Bisexuality, and its uneasy sometime-synonym, androgyny, were signs of the times.

Just a few years after Stonewall, when feminism, Gay Liberation, and the Lesbian Nation were beginning to gain visibility and strength, bisexuality looked in part like a crossover tactic, an anything-goes lifestyle in which anyone could play. Twosomes were out; to be a pair was to be square. Communal living, "swinging," "threesomes," group sex—these were the media clichés of the time. To be young and bisexual in the seventies meant in part to find the media and the music industry describing a life that uncannily matched one's own desires, and, as all popular media do, also created them. It was still very dangerous to be out and gay. If you were bisexual, you could be accused then, as now, of seeking what would come to be known as "heterosexual privilege." But what if you really did desire both women and men?

Bisexuals in the 1990s are still sometimes said to be guilty of wanting "heterosexual privilege" (or of getting it whether they want it or not), but the Sexual Revolution is long gone. In place of the dissolution of border-lines, today's cultural politicians offer the strictures of Identity Politics. Borderlines are back: Ethnic, racial, religious, and sexual minorities assert their visibility and, thus, their power. Although action groups like Queer Nation offer a kind of inclusiveness, a fellow-travellers' umbrella under which can cluster lesbian, gay, bi-, transgender, and other groups, subverting static concepts of gender and flaunting practices from sadomasochism to drag, there is still a sense of turf battle, and a certain flavor of moral martyrdom, in the sex wars of the nineties.

The appearance of "biphobia," a word coined on the model of homophobia,[24] suggests that the opposition to bisexuality is a mode of social prejudice. Straight people may stereotype bisexuals as closeted men who deceive their wives with a series of randomly chosen male sex partners, spreading AIDS to an "innocent" heterosexual population, including unborn children. Some gays and lesbians also stereotype bisexuals as self-indulgent, undecided, "fence-sitters" who dally with the affections of same-sex partners, breaking their hearts when they move on to heterosexual relationships.

Despite these stereotypes and resentments, however, bisexuality—and even the by now much-recycled concept of "bisexual chic"—has moved steadily into the mainstream, fueled by music videos, talk shows, sitcoms, and advertising, as well as by sexual practice. In one three-month period in mid-1992, for example, the television presentation during prime time of a three-part British series based on the bisexual marriage of British author and aristocrat Vita Sackville-West and her husband, diplomat Harold Nicolson, coincided with a lead article in *Lear's* about "The Bisexual Potential" (the headline superimposed upon a cover photo of Ivana Trump), a *Playboy* feature story on erstwhile Madonna playmate Sandra Bernhard,[25] a grumpy *Village Voice* piece in the self-styled "Queer Issue" entitled "Bi Any Means Necessary; They Call Themselves Queer Bisexuals and, to the Distress of Many in the Gay Movement, They Want In,"[26] and a three-page spread on bisexuality in *Time* magazine.[27]

New biographies of Marlon Brando, Laurence Olivier, Marlene Dietrich, Leonard Bernstein, and John Cheever stress, with intriguing detail, the element of bisexuality in their makeup and relationships. Susie Bright, editor of the lesbian pro-sex magazine *On Our Backs,* has described herself as a bisexual, or "bisexual lesbian." (As we will see, the wide range of descriptions and self-descriptions qualifying the label "bisexual" these days is indicative of the contestedness of this terrain.) Bi journals and 'zines bid for circulation. Bi hotlines are advertised among the "Adult Phone Services." A series of anthologies, some confessional and autobiographical, others with an academic flavor, has hit the bookstores.

For some time now, television talk shows have featured topics from "Bisexuality and Marriage," "A Homosexual Married to a Heterosexual," and "People Change Sex to Have Sex with Same Sex" (all on "Donahue") to "Marriage and a Family Therapist: The Nature of Couples and Bisexual Relationships" ("Oprah"), and the number of such topics is increasing. Television series like "Dynasty" and "Quantum Leap" and daytime soap operas have featured plots involving bisexuals. In a celebrated prime-time instance on the TV show "L.A. Law," C. J. Lamb, played by sexy Amanda Donohoe, kissed a bemused and befuddled female law associate (Michele Greene) in a parking lot.

The ensuing flap made both Donohoe and The Kiss famous, despite the network's attempt to downplay the eroticism. "I think a lot of young women are very ambiguous about their sexuality," Donohoe remarked. "I mean, we get such a hard time from guys in the first place, is it any wonder?"[28] Told that an NBC spokesperson had denied that C.J. was bisexual, Donohoe retorted, "The network better have the guts to leave C.J.'s sexuality well enough alone. I think it would be disastrous if she started dating a man and never again mentioned her sexual attraction to women."[29] And asked on an NBC press tour which way her character would go the next season, she answered promptly, "Well, both ways, darling." She posed for photographs hand-in-hand with bisexual entertainer Sandra Bernhard, and rumors circulated that she was dating Bernhard, as well as blond Van Halen vocalist Sammy Hagar.[30] "I think her bisexuality should be of paramount importance in terms of her growth," said Donohoe of C.J.'s character and future. "Personally, I'd like to see her battle a few fundamentalist Christians." But by the fall of 1992 she had been written out of "L.A. Law." Before long the show had a new female character: a willowy blond fundamentalist Christian.

Meanwhile the bisexual kiss, a proven audience draw, had moved on to less squeamish and more permissive television territory: On her ABC sitcom, Roseanne and a straight woman friend accompanied the bisexual Nancy (Sandra Bernhard, this time in the cast rather than on the sidelines) and Nancy's new girlfriend Sharon (Mariel Hemingway) to a lesbian bar called Lips. After some initial awkwardness, Roseanne got into the spirit of things, and Sharon kissed her. "Maybe you liked it just a little," Nancy suggested slyly. "Sexuality isn't all black and white. There's a whole gray area. You're afraid a small percentage of you might have been turned on by a woman."

The mainstream success of such advertising campaigns as Calvin Klein jeans and underwear has confounded neat categorical distinctions between straight and gay consumers, and can contribute, in fact, to destabilizing not only the market but also the individual. Photographer Bruce Weber's homoerotic studies of men in Calvin's jeans and briefs "made people wonder about their own sexuality," Weber noted.[31] A male college student who encountered one of the underwear ads confided to his father that he found it disturbing: "It makes a man attracted to another man." But straight and bisexual women also found Calvin's (and Weber's) muscle-y seminude men attractive. The print advertisements, whatever their overt or covert target audience, were being read *bisexually*.

Here, too, was a paradox. The more borders to patrol, the more border crossings. And if, as I believe, the act of crossover is itself, as the word implies, a "transgression," the exciting guilty pleasures of transgressing, of intruding and spying and misbehaving, added to the eroticism of the occasion. With a broad wink to those in the know, the Weber ads barely "passed" as straight—and simultaneously invited trespass *by* straights into an aesthetic (and an erotic) that was, in baring almost everything, clearly also coded gay. But to *call* these ads "bisexual" would, oddly, have robbed them of some of their erotic power, which seemed to inhere in the possibility of transgression. Giving permission to break a rule, as many parents learn, does not always give pleasure, and in fact may take the desired pleasure away. And if luxury items like nameplate boxer shorts and $50-an-ounce perfume are already in the category of "transgression" because of their cost and seductive superfluousness, one more transgression, advertising logic suggests, may make the pleasure even more exquisite, the object even more "necessary."

Take one apparent example of manifest superfluousness in design, the fly front on the boxer shorts Calvin Klein designed for women. When it first appeared on the market, "men's underwear" for women was startling and titillating to some. To others, the "masculine boxer shorts" and "wide-waistband briefs that looked like jockstraps for girls"[32] were the realization of a desire they had forgotten they had ever had. I remember my first set, tops and bottoms in black with a cotton drawstring, and white elastic stitched with the designer's name—a gift from a woman friend. *Time* magazine wondered, in an article on "Calvin's New Gender Benders,"[33] why Klein retained the same design for women as for men, despite key differences in anatomy. "It's sexier with the fly," Klein answered. It was, too. Eighty thousand pairs of women's boxer shorts were sold in ninety days.

To underrate clothing and fashion as political statements would be to refuse to look at history—and to deny ourselves a lot of fun. Twentieth-century designers have played both cautiously and at times outrageously with gender crossover, as numerous "fashions of the nineties" articles reflect. On the brink of a new century, pundits try to predict sexual and social trends of the future through futuristic developments in clothing style. "Fashion has served a more complex function for lesbians and gays than it has for heterosexuals" over the last twenty-five years, according to the gay and lesbian publication *The Advocate.* "After all, has the straight community ever developed an idea such as color-coded handkerchiefs that cue others to the wearer's sexual proclivities?"[34]

"In fashion, at least, the drama of sexual ambiguity has reached its dénouement, taking the skirts and flowing manes at the men's shows in stride,"[35] declared the "Runways" page in the Sunday *New York Times,* announcing that "androgyny, 1980's style, is over"—in case you hadn't noticed. In the 1970s, Mick Jagger and David Bowie could still scandalize an audience with costumes that hinted at the feminine. By the eighties,

Boy George and Annie Lennox had become "fashion's role-reversal models," while designers offered what the *Times* chose to describe as "asexual equality" in clothing, with fabric draped loosely over male and female genitals. But with the much-touted "mainstreaming of gay culture"—a phrase one reads a great deal these days—fashion items like leather pants and ear studs have become de rigueur in the world of cool style, while very short hair for women, and long or very short hair for men, has again come to signify "liberation" and gender defiance without any sense that it is really threatening the order of things. As the *Times*'s Suzy Menkes noted, "It is the idea of breaking a sexual code that is upsetting." And the gym-tightened torsos of open-shirted males and small-boned "waif" females play with sexual codes but don't break them—at least when designers like Gaultier, Versace, Armani, Matsuda, and Paul Smith are in charge.

"What I love about fashion is that it's so tied into psychology and sociology," says Calvin Klein.[36] Fashion photographer Bruce Weber once tried to convince Gianni Versace to design a kilt for male models, but Versace, the master of leather- and bondagewear, demurred: no "skirt" for men in his collection.[37] Meanwhile, in the *Village Voice,* a dominatrix took on Madonna's *Sex* for its failure to distinguish between a dominant and a submissive shoe, the *New York Post* ran a three-part article on dominatrixes and their slaves, and a reporter quipped that "the United States is fast becoming a country in which mainstream readers can be expected to know the difference between a seven-inch and a nine-inch patent-leather heel."[38] Body piercing "went mainstream" when supermodel Christy Turlington displayed a ring in her navel in a London fashion show, and the next day Naomi Campbell did the same. "In our culture, body piercing has origins in the gay scene and fetish scene," said Teena Maree, a Los Angeles piercer who caters to the London club world, "but the origins of body piercing are dotted all over the planet."

Tattoos have also crossed over. "Once the preserve of macho males (and gay men) wanting to tout their virility,"[39] they are now part of the teen scene, the preteen crowd (wash-off-able tattoos were very big for a while among the ten-year-old set), and the high-fashion world. Model Eve Salvini became famous for the tattoo on her bald head, and photographic exhibits of body tattoos have been shown in galleries from Los Angeles to New York. If menswear for women, earrings and skirts for men, navel and nipple rings for everyone, and tattoos on every part of the body, visible and invisible, are now part of the "mainstream," what buttons, envelopes, and borderlines are left to push?

How about "bisexual style"?

In the Harvard student journal *HQ* (no relation to *GQ*), editor Rachel Cohen wrote with droll amusement about the difficulty of being "a visible,

bisexual woman." Crossing a bridge over the Charles River she encountered a man whose "widely belted narrow waist, slicked back hair, impressive sideburns" and general air "proclaim[ed] his identity from one end of
the bridge to the other." She read him, through these signs, as a fellow
member of the "bisexual/gay/homosexual/queer community," and flashed
him a smile of greeting and recognition. He stared past her with a look
she interpreted as saying not "heart-warming bonds of community . . .
stretch supportively between us," as she had hoped, but rather "there is a
straight woman on this bridge who is smiling at me, indicating that she is
so blind that even my careful hours of image-construction have failed to
communicate [to her] the blatantly obvious fact of my sexual orientation."
From this Cohen concludes, not for the first time, that bisexual identity
can be invisible.

How to indicate bisexuality in terms of style? Pink triangles, she noted,
have been taken over as "the province of every liberal-leaning Clinton
supporter." More specifically intended lavender and blue "biangles" seem
to go unrecognized, while items like freedom rings, big black boots, biker
jackets, and short hair all convey multiple messages and have been generally adopted as aspects of hip style. "Cross-dressing is well nigh impossible," and backward-twisted baseball caps declare "prep school" rather
than gender-crossing when worn by college-age women.

Even if these symbols said *something,* they wouldn't say "bisexual."
Should "bi women" wear "short black boots," or "only shave under one
armpit," or wear their biker jackets every other day, or merely carry
around a copy of *Bi Any Other Name* wherever they go? "Nothing short of
a large sign with the word 'BI' inscribed on it in block letters" would
improve her "visi-BI-lity," she concludes, and even that would probably
be interpreted awry. "No, like many people at Harvard, I've got a schizo-
phrenic image and nothing to wear."[40]

As Cohen is the first to admit, this is college humor, not philosophy or
the archaeology of fashion. But the claim that bisexuality is "invisible" in
other realms—statistically, culturally, historically, politically—frames this
sardonic portrait of the bisexual student's dilemma. Visibility is, indeed,
what bi's have said they lacked, for years. And invisibility, as the title of
Ralph Ellison's famous book somberly reminds us, can lead to cultural
disregard—and worse—for any group society decides to overlook, or
look through.

Discovering Bisexuality

"Bisexuality!" wrote Sigmund Freud to his friend Wilhelm Fliess in August
1899. "I am sure you are right about it. And I am accustoming myself to
regarding every sexual act as an event between four individuals."[41] For
Freud, "the innately bisexual constitution of human beings,"[42] or what he
most commonly referred to as the "bisexual disposition," accounted for

internal conflict and consequent neurosis. It also accounted for homosexuality (a "perversion" which Freud felt "scarcely deserves the name," since "it can be traced back to the constitutional bisexuality of all human beings. . . . Psychoanalysis enables us to point to some trace or other of a homosexual object-choice in everyone")[43]—and for some of the stress and strain of a girl's becoming a woman ("an individual is not a man or a woman but always both—merely a certain amount more the one than the other").[44]

Vita Sackville-West, penning the now-celebrated "confession, autobiography, whatever I may call it" that her son discovered after her death locked up in a Gladstone bag,[45] offered, in what she called an "impersonal and scientific spirit" (although we shall see the degree to which she, like Freud, was animated by something other than scientific disinterestedness), "the perfectly accepted theory that cases of dual personality do exist, in which the feminine and the masculine elements alternately preponderate." "I believe," she wrote, "that the psychology of people like myself will be a matter of interest, and I believe it will be recognized that many more people of my type do exist than under the present-day system of hypocrisy is commonly admitted."[46] This was in 1920. Despite a smattering of articles over the years in professional archives like *The Journal of Marriage and the Family, The Journal of Homosexuality, The American Psychologist,* and *The Journal of Counseling and Development,* "people of [her] type"— whom Sackville-West called "dual personalities" and others have called (with varying degrees of admiration and scorn) androgynes, closet gays, swingers, or bisexuals—are still being discovered, "outed," exclaimed over, and explained away in the last decade of the twentieth century. Vita's "present-day system of hypocrisy" is still very much in evidence in many quarters.

It is not in the professional journals, however, or even in gay publications like *The Advocate* and *Out/Look,* but rather in the popular (and even the so-called women's) magazines that some of the most provocative assertions about bisexuality have appeared: *Ms., Lear's, Glamour, Cosmopolitan,* and *Mademoiselle.* Margaret Mead wrote in the pages of *Redbook* in 1975, "The time has come, I think, when we must recognize bisexuality as a normal form of human behavior." Changing traditional attitudes about homosexuality is important, she affirmed, but "we shall not really succeed in discarding the straitjacket of our cultural beliefs about sexual choice if we fail to come to terms with the well-documented, normal human capacity to love members of both sexes."[47]

By "well-documented" Mead meant, in part, attested to over time. She noted that while homosexual relationships between older and younger men in ancient Greece and Sparta are frequently cited, "it is usually left out of account that the older men also had wives and children."[48] The court culture of the European Renaissance, the cluster of artists on the Left Bank in Paris before and after World War I, and the Bloomsbury group in London were all historical contexts in which "innovative men and women were privately but quite frankly bisexual in their relationships."[49] Mead's own account seems to have been prompted at least in part by the recent publication of *Portrait of a Marriage* (1973), which identified specific historical persons, not merely fictional characters, as capable of relating to both men and women sexually and emotionally in a fulfilling way. Presciently throwing down the gauntlet to today's "family values" hardliners, Mead took, as befits an anthropologist, a longer cultural view: "At this time in the history of our earth," she wrote, "there is no social need to press any individual into parenthood. We can free men and women alike to live as persons."[50]

As Gloria Steinem noted, this call to freedom in the 1970s may well have reflected Margaret Mead's own personal history and choices, as well as her research in cultural and cross-cultural anthropology. It is noteworthy, however, that almost twenty years later bisexual activists still cite her words—published, significantly, in *Redbook,* a quintessential "family values" magazine—as cultural authority for bi-pride. In the intervening period, however, the onset of the AIDS epidemic and the consequent suspicion attaching to closeted bisexuals—in practice, closeted bisexual *men* —as potential carriers of the virus led to a radical shift in public perception. The glory years of bisexual chic in the seventies—from David Bowie to Elton John, from *Bisexual Living* (1975) to *The Bisexual Option* (1978) to *Barry and Alice: Portrait of a Bisexual Marriage* (1980)—gave way to a spate of books and articles effectively scapegoating the bisexual man.

Concomitant with this development, and to a certain extent dependent upon it, was the rise of gay and lesbian theory, both an academic and a political movement. To some gay theorists and researchers, attacks on bisexuals were really not very veiled attacks on gay men, who were scapegoated for promiscuity, duplicity, and the supposed immaturity of their lifestyles. By defending bisexual men as gay men, these theorists thus wittingly or unwittingly reinforced one of the bisexual's most self-lamented characterizations: invisibility. Bi men, reappropriated as gay, either ceased to exist as a separate and separable category, or else were put down as closeted, self-hating, or self-ignorant—men who were "really" gay if only they had the courage to say so.

A glance at the medical and sociological literature of the middle eighties will confirm the sense in which "bisexuality" in that period came to mean "one more mode of risky behavior in the age of AIDS." Risky, and thus in some people's view irresponsible, especially in a gay subculture in which multiple sexual encounters were still very much part of social as well as sexual life.

One male gay theorist—a good friend—with whom I discussed my present project, expressed some concern about what a fully theorized bisexuality, described in terms of its omnipresence in literature, culture, and society, would do to the project of gay and lesbian studies, which had worked so hard, and succeeded so well, in describing homosexuality *not* as the "other" of heterosexuality but rather as a locus for cultural critique, social reevaluation, and change. He worried that bisexuality would repolarize hetero- and homosexuality, placing itself conjecturally between them, and usurp the place of radical critique.

I will take up these issues subsequently in more detail, but it is worth saying now that gay and lesbian studies, in an important and path-breaking move to make visible and concrete the culturally repressed (or suppressed) homosexual content of many books, films, aesthetic styles, and individual life stories, has claimed figures like Virginia Woolf, Oscar Wilde, Ernest Hemingway, Cary Grant, the poet H.D. (Hilda Doolittle), the Harlem Renaissance writer Countee Cullen, and King James I of England, and texts like Shakespeare's *Sonnets,* Alice Walker's *The Color Purple,* D. H. Lawrence's novella *The Fox,* James Baldwin's *Giovanni's Room,* and a variety of vampire stories and films from Anne Rice and *The Rocky Horror Picture Show* to *The Hunger* as gay figures and gay texts, even though many of them might more appropriately be described as bisexual. At the very least, such lives and works (like many others that will be discussed here) test the boundaries that purport to separate "bisexuality" from "gay and lesbian."

Other issues raised by therapists, journalists, and bisexuals themselves in analyzing the ambivalent position of bisexuality in today's cultural scene are *nonmonogamy* (less supportively called promiscuity, flightiness, or instability); *maturity and immaturity* (heterosexuals often see bisexuality as a "stage" rather than an achieved condition or lifestyle; gays likewise sometimes scorn bisexuality as a "stage" in the coming-out process of people who are "really" lesbian or gay); *trendiness;* and *"heterosexual privilege."*

No sociological or therapeutic model for describing bisexuality has come to terms with either its erotic power or its stigmatization by both straights and gays. Until recently, the standard scale for measuring homosexuality, heterosexuality, and (inevitably, in the middle) bisexuality was the so-called Kinsey scale, developed by sex researcher Alfred Kinsey in 1948. Kinsey asked respondents to rate themselves along the following continuum:

> (0) Exclusively heterosexual
> (1) Predominantly heterosexual, only incidentally homosexual
> (2) Predominantly heterosexual, but more than incidentally homosexual
> (3) Equally heterosexual and homosexual
> (4) Predominantly homosexual, but more than incidentally heterosexual
> (5) Predominantly homosexual, only incidentally heterosexual
> (6) Exclusively homosexual

As many critics have subsequently pointed out, this "scale," while it avoids censorious moral judgment and thus does an invaluable service for the cause of toleration and social understanding, completely ignores questions of social context, cultural practice (Kinsey's sample was overwhelmingly white and middle class), erotic intensity, physical activity and emotional involvement, and sexual fantasy. It flattens all sexual encounters (or emotional relationships) into two dimensions. Nonetheless, it is the starting point for much discussion of orientation and social-cultural self-placement among homosexuals and bisexuals who have written about the topic; it is not uncommon to read of someone, in a personal memoir rather than a sociological analysis, describing himself or herself as a "Kinsey 3" or a "Kinsey 6." The Kinsey scale is in its format a continuum, not wholly unlike Adrienne Rich's famous "lesbian continuum," which charted female-female relationships from friendship to sexual involvement.

An attempt in 1980 to replace the Kinsey scale with a more multidimensional study produced the Klein Sexual Orientation Grid (KSOG), developed by sex researcher Fritz Klein, as a result, significantly, of a survey conducted in *Forum* (now *Penthouse Forum*) magazine. The implication, presumably, was that respondents would be people who were especially interested in sex, or in analyzing their own sexualities. The KSOG asked respondents to rank themselves in the Past, Present, and Ideal on questions of sexual attraction, sexual behavior, sexual fantasies, emotional preference, social preference, self-identification, and straight/gay lifestyle.

For each of these categories they were to rate themselves by number: 1 for Other Sex Only, 2 for Other Sex Mostly, through 4 for Both Sexes Equally, and all the way to 7, Same Sex Only—a gradient clearly borrowed from the Kinsey scale. The questions about self-identification and lifestyle were to be answered from a scale worded somewhat differently, from 1 Hetero Only to 7 Gay Only. The Klein grid improved on Kinsey's continuum by acknowledging that "sexuality" could concern fantasy as well as behavior, and that sexual orientation and sexual identification (at least for *Forum*'s upscale, largely urban, overwhelmingly Western readers) also included questions of lifestyle. But the Klein grid couldn't account for changes in people's patterns of relationships *over time,* nor for the influence of social and cultural factors that continually shifted the boundaries and definitions of apparent "opposites" like gay/straight, male/female, and sexual orientation/sexual practice. And none of these measures, except within the catchall category of "fantasy," take note of the positive impulse toward perverseness, the erotic appeal of transgression, the desire that itself comes from crossing a boundary.

Like the Kinsey scale, the Klein grid presumed that there were two poles, homo- and heterosexual, and that bisexuals occupied some middle space. Subsequent clinical studies used the KSOG-tested questions concerning bisexual men's contentedness in their marriages, frequencies of orgasms among bi and hetero men, "swinging" among bi and hetero couples, and so on. And some time ago another study proposed a Multidimensional Scale of Sexuality that measures, among other things, people who have switched from hetero- to homosexuality or vice versa, and bisexuals who have encounters with both sexes at the same time or who alternate periods of attraction to men with periods of attraction to women. Terms like "sequential" versus "concurrent" bisexuality are probably helpful additions to a language that is still struggling with linear sequence.

There are also taxonomies of bisexuality itself. A book of essays on the relationship between bisexuality and HIV/AIDS around the world lists "Defense Bisexuality" (defending against homosexuality in societies where it is stigmatized), "Latin Bisexuality" (the insertive role in certain "Mediterranean cultures" is not regarded as homosexual, so that men who participate in same-sex encounters may consider themselves nonetheless heterosexual), "Ritual Bisexuality" (as with the Sambia of Papua–New Guinea, in which younger males fellate older men in order to ingest their "masculinizing" semen, a practice that is part of a rite of initiation, may continue for years, and is apparently replaced by exclusive heterosexuality after marriage),[51] "Married Bisexuality," "Secondary Homosexuality" (more frequently called "situational bisexuality"—sex with same-sex partners in prisons or other single-sex institutions, in public parks or toilets, or for money), "Equal Interest in Male and Female Partners" (so-called true bisexuality), "Experimental Bisexuality," and "Technical Bisexuality" (with partners who may be dressed as members of the other sex, or have had some form of gender reassignment: transsexuals or members of a "third sex" in some cultures).[52]

But what if we were to begin with the category "sexuality" (or "desire") rather than with a binary opposition between homosexual and heterosexual, or same-sex and opposite-sex partners? What if, in an attempt to understand this version of the "third," we were to turn not to a two-dimensional model (the scale, the grid) but rather to a model that incorporated a third dimension, and that also made the question of two-versus-one, or inside/outside, essentially moot? What I propose is a model closer to the so-called Möbius strip, a topological space that can be visualized by pasting together the ends of a rectangular strip after having first given one of the ends a half-twist. It thus has only one side, not two, and, if split down the middle, remains in one piece. Thus we have not a "third" but one space that incorporates the concepts of "two," "one," and "three" (two apparent "sides," illusionistically; one continuous surface, and a third dimension in space). That this is closer to a diagram of bisexuality—that is to say, *sexuality*—than any model of "the middle" (even, as one witty, and hostile, psychologist put it, the "Excluded Middle")[53]—will be an important part of my argument here.

◆

Jealousy, the marriage model, the erotic triangle, the variations in sexual intensity from person to person (sex drive as opposed to sexual orientation or sexual aim), the erotic appeal of transgression, the role of cross-dressing as part of bisexual play, the changing roles of men and women over time, generational differences, the persistence of the fantasy of "falling in love," which is always at odds with steady-state relationships—all of these topics come up whenever bisexuality is addressed. And all of them speak to the question of eroticism—not to one small segment of the population but to most of it.

What sense does it make, after all, to call all of the activities and fantasies around same-and-other-sex relationships by a single name? Is it really appropriate to include in the same general category (1) a man who after ten years of marriage declares that he is gay, moves to San Francisco, and takes up a lifestyle of multiple male partners, phone sex with men, and gay activism; (2) a woman who was politicized by the feminist movement in the seventies and becomes a lesbian because she believes that real intimacy in a patriarchal culture is only possible with other women; (3) a couple who, like Vita Sackville-West and Harold Nicolson in the earlier part of this century, or like *Time* magazine's featured pair and hundreds of others today, remain happily married to one another and each have affairs with members of their own sex; and (4) young men and women who "come out" as bi rather than gay or straight in high school or in college, without passing through a "phase" of gay or straight identity?

I remember an occasion a few years ago at a California conference on Queer Theory when a stunning blonde lesbian college student observed matter-of-factly that one of her most erotic turn-ons was male-male pornography. Many women at the conference (myself included) nodded agreement; more than a few men, older and younger, looked stunned. Is this a sign that patriarchy still controls the sex trade, and thus our most private feelings? Is it evidence, as some women suggested, that gay male lifestyles tend to be more overtly nonmonogamous and experimental, and thus provide a richer field for fantasy? Or is it, as seems to me also profoundly the case, that eroticism and desire are always to some degree transgressive, politically *in*correct? Are women who look at videotapes of men making love as part of their own lovemaking with women classifiable as "bisexual"? And if so, is the case the same for heterosexual couples—or self-identified straight men—who watch lesbian pornography, soft- or hard-core, to spice up their own sex lives? Why, in other words, do we seem so desperately to want this third category, "bisexual," to contain and control those desires, fantasies, and relationships that will not be confined by conventional social mythology and the institution of marriage?

The Pleasures of Disorientation

"Someone who has an ostensible sexual orientation may nevertheless, in a particular relationship, be quite sexually expressive and responsive with someone who is not apparently the 'object' of that orientation," writes critic John Stoltenberg. And again, "Insistence on having a sexual orientation in sex is about defending the status quo, maintaining sex differences and the sexual hierarchy; whereas resistance to sexual orientation regimentation is more about where we need to be going."[54] In 1989, in the midst of a chorus of voices urging "identity politics" as a powerful tool for gay and lesbian liberation, Stoltenberg's was a controversial formulation. Viewed from a somewhat later perspective, and especially from the vantage point of popular culture, the questioning of *"a* sexual orientation" has acquired a certain currency.

"A goodly number of media characters have no definite sexual orientation," says lesbian science fiction fan Barbara Tennison. Why do we *assume* they are straight? Because that is the "recognized norm in our culture." But not only might "undeclared" on-screen characters be gay without "declaring" themselves to be so, it is also the case that "attraction toward members of the opposite sex" does not necessarily exclude "attraction toward one's own sex": "bisexuality is also an option," and, moreover, "it may not be a momentous decision to characters in an SF universe."[55] Quite so.

SF, science fiction, is the utopian (as well as the dystopian) literature of our day. Consider the case of so-called slash lit, amateur fan magazines in which fans imagine explicitly romantic and sexual relationships between male characters in the popular media (for example, Batman and Robin, the Lone Ranger and Tonto, Starsky and Hutch). The term "slash" comes from the diacritical mark used to indicate a fantasized relationship between two male characters: thus *S/H* means a 'zine that concerns itself with a romance between Starsky and Hutch. Because of the work of film theorist Constance Penley, who has studied them for a number of years, the best known of these "fandoms," as they have become known in the world of popular culture, is *K/S,* a series of *Star Trek* fan publications featuring Captain James T. Kirk of the USS *Enterprise* and his half-Vulcan friend Mr. Spock. In one example of *K/S,* Captain Kirk is saluted after an encounter with Mr. Spock with the sweeping proclamation, "Welcome to bisexuality, Captain Kirk, where gender has nothing to do with who you want."[56] The fact that slash's biggest fans are women, and largely, in the early years, heterosexual women, indicates something of the place of erotic speculation and what is often called "the pornographic imagination" as it crosses over hypothetical boundaries of gender and sexuality.

The *K/S* "fandom," as Penley reported, "is almost 100 percent female." When she herself became involved with the group, as what she acknowledges to be "a fan of this fandom,"[57] she was curious to know "what was the sexual orientation of the fans—straight, lesbian, or some of each?"[58] She also posed a related question: Did the fans regard the Spock-Kirk liaison as "homosexual"?

The founding scenario of the genre is a short story in which the half-

Vulcan Spock enters the condition of *pon farr,* a sexual heat suffered every seven years by all Vulcan males, which results in death if the Vulcan does not mate—and mate not with a random partner but with someone "with whom he is already empathetically bonded."[59] Since Kirk and Spock happen to be alone together on a distant planet, Kirk offers himself to Spock as a sexual partner; after they have sex the two discover that they are in fact in love with each other. *K/S* fans, whose rallying cry is the Vulcan philosophy Infinite Diversity in Infinite Combination, have tended, though not without exceptions, to regard the relationship as *"cosmic destiny:* the two men are somehow meant for each other and homosexuality has nothing to do with it."[60]

What Penley argues, quite convincingly, is that this reading of Kirk and Spock as "not homosexual" is not, or not mainly, a result of homophobia (she thinks there may be "some element of homophobia in the wish to keep them heterosexual," but that "it would distress the *K/S* writers a great deal to think that they might be harboring homophobic thoughts"[61]), but rather a by-product (or bi-product?) of the flexibility of fantasy. Having Kirk and Spock together sexually but not "as" homosexuals "allows a much greater range of identification and desire for the women: in the fantasy one can *be* Kirk or Spock . . . and also still *have* (as sexual objects) either or both of them."[62] And why is this? Because psychoanalytically speaking, "the subject, at the level of the unconscious, is bisexual." It is this bisexuality that permits, and indeed encourges, "a great variety and range of identifications . . . even and above all across gender boundaries."[63]

If the sexual imagination is "bisexual," then the surprising appeal to straight as well as lesbian and bisexual women of a male-male popular culture sexual fantasy scenario is not so surprising after all. For it is not "identification" per se but rather "desire" and "fantasy" that structure erotic scenarios—and they do so in ways that, as psychoanalytic theorists have long known, permit the fantasizer to play a number of roles at once. Fantasy is a story; as analysts Jean Laplanche and J.-B. Pontalis point out, the fantasist "cannot be assigned any fixed place in it," and may in fact be "present in the fantasy" in the "very syntax of the sequence" rather than in any one specific position or role.[64]

The bisexual mobility of fantasy. Contemporary examples of this virtual reality of fantasy can doubtless be found every day on the Internet.

Consider the case of "Elizabeth," a Chicago woman in her thirties who sought romance—and sex—on-line. She soon found herself, through the medium of the Usenet list, in deep erotic conversation with James, a Washington, D.C., architect whom she met through a computer news and discussion group called "alt.sex.bondage." Reading a sexy story he put on the net, she contacted him by E-mail, and before long they were in direct and private touch via the Net's Internet Relay Chat. After three weeks of daily contact, James suggested that they meet in person: "We can't leave our bodies out of this anymore," he wrote.

James booked a hotel room in L.A., and they agreed to meet in the hotel bar. The astute reader will already have guessed the punch line: When James turned up, he was a woman named Jessica. After an hour of conversation, during which Elizabeth expressed her surprise and consternation, they went up to the hotel room together and made love. "Our intimacy was real," says Elizabeth in explanation. "I couldn't suddenly pretend just because of gender that it never existed." To do so, she felt, would be lying to herself. "Gender is just a label," she thinks. "Who I have sex with doesn't define me. It's how well I can connect with another person that does." [65]

"Welcome to bisexuality, Captain Kirk, where gender has nothing to do with who you want." From "alt.sex.stories" to "alt.sex.bondage" to "The Flirt's Nook" and "The Romance Connection," from the Usenet to America Online, sex, romance, and courtship today are being pursued, and perused, by computer, situating hundreds of thousands of people at "the locus of desire and technology." [66] Elizabeth, who describes herself as "not a lesbian" and "not a bisexual," found herself in a romantic situation in which gender was not the overriding consideration, and in which "lovemaking," in words as well as in actions, on screen as well as in bed, across the miles as well as across the room, is predicated on fantasy and on the reinvention of the self. "I'm on-line therefore I can become," she says, perhaps only half-jokingly. Her relationship with James/Jessica did not continue at the same hot pace. And Elizabeth conceded some trepidation about her personal safety when she went to a hotel to meet an unknown man. But her experience—a "bisexual" experience in the most direct and also most unexpected way—was for her a matter of personal realization and personal freedom.

Part 1 **Bi Ways**

Culture, Politics, History

Chapter 1

Bi Words

Lots of people think that *bisexual* means *cowardly lesbian*.

—The Advocate, *interview with Sandra Bernhard*[1]

Homosexuality was invented by a straight world dealing with its own bisexuality.

—*Kate Millett,* Flying[2]

Switch-hitter. Swings both ways. Fence-sitter. AC/DC. These and other once-colorful epithets have been frequently used to describe bisexuality in this century. Whether taken from baseball or from electricity, such terms suggest versatility: a batter who *switch-hits* often has a better chance of *getting to first base*—another phrase that has taken on a distinctly sexual tinge in modern times. The *New Dictionary of American Slang* is more specific than any teenager of my adolescence: to "get to first base" involves hugging, kissing, caressing, and so on; to "get to third base" means "touching and toying with the genitals"; and to "get to home plate," or to "score," means "to do the sex act"[3]—assuming, it seems, that there is only one "real" sex act to do.

Switch-hitters, I remember from my days as a Mickey Mantle fan, were as often made as born. To learn to "swing both ways" meant practice and discipline, not just natural talent. Certainly there was nothing suspect about them; they represented a double strength because they maximized their own potential as athletes and strategists. You wanted switch-hitters in your lineup even if by swinging from one side rather than the other the hitter sacrificed a little raw power for artifice and skill.

One of the contributors to the bisexual feminist anthologies *Closer to Home* and *Bi Any Other Name* describes herself as "a nine-time San Francisco Advertising Softball League all-star" who "rather likes the designation 'switch-hitter.' "[4] The newsletter of the Boston Bisexual Women's Network included a list of "Famous Switch-Hitters" (culled, interestingly, from a published book of *Lesbian Lists*[5]) that included Lady Emma Hamilton ("the mistress of both Queen Maria Caroline of Naples and Admiral Nelson"), Natasha Rambova ("wife of silent-screen heartthrob Rudolph Valentino, and sometime lover of [director] Alla Nazimova"), and Edith Lees Ellis, the wife of Havelock Ellis. (Who says feminists don't have a sense of humor?) *Switch Hitter* is also the name of a Cambridge-based 'zine for bi men and women. It's clear from these wry appropriations, though, that "switch-hitter" in a sexual context has not been an automatic term of praise or pleasure.

What about AC/DC, a term used in the past, somewhat disparagingly, to suggest either a failure of sex and gender type or a wishy-washiness about sexual orientation ("he seemed a little AC/DC to me"). Again, it's worth wondering how versatility and adaptability became such bad things. An appliance that works on both alternating current (AC) and direct current (DC) sounds handy, to say the least. Here's what *Brewer's Dictionary of Twentieth-Century Phrase and Fable* says about it: "[T]he expression originated in America by analogy with electrical devices adaptable for either alternating or direct current. It became popular in the UK during the 1960s and early 1970s." *Brewer's* thinks this term may be related to "the sexual imagery of electricity" in the "tradition of 'male' and 'female' connectors in wiring."[6] Plug it in anywhere, and it works.

So on the one hand we have American ingenuity and know-how, and indeed American sporting competitiveness. (Basketball, hockey, and tennis players also work to cultivate their even-handedness.) On the other we have resistance and reticence, sometimes even recoil and repugnance, at the idea that sexual versatility could include the widest range of consensual partners and pleasures. Sex isn't supposed to be an invention, or a sport, or a labor-saving device.

Is it a sensory indulgence, like "having your cake and eating it, too"— yet another phrase that, with its variants, is often applied to the perceived situation of bisexuals? One bisexual woman in a committed monogamous relationship with another woman reports that her partner "felt that choosing a bisexual identity meant that I was declaring my sexual ambiguity— my need to have my cake and eat it, too."[7] What does this maxim mean? Is it the same as "having it both ways"? I don't think so. To have it both ways is to have this *and* that. A married man who also has sex with men or boys could be said to "have it both ways," whether or not that phrase was understood in its most limited anatomical sense. But is he "having his cake and eating it, too"? Who, or what, is the cake here? Here there's a kind of cultural static interference, the original phrase having crossed wires somewhere along the way with "putting the icing on the cake," which means wrapping up a victory beyond doubt, perfecting it, adding the finishing touches.

Is bisexuality the "icing on the cake" of homosexuality? Of heterosexuality? Or is bisexual living and loving the icing on the cake of bisexual feelings, bisexual desire?

The "having your cake" phrase is often understood to have a kind of economic subtext: "you cannot spend your money and yet keep it," one reference book translates rather flatly, offering the additional, and seemingly contradictory analogy, "Ye cannot serve God and Mammon" (Matthew 6:24; Luke 16:13). The combination of the two seems to align God with spending and Mammon with keeping riches, in defiance of the usual assignment of spheres of influence to those competing authorities.

I have always thought "having your cake and eating it, too" meant not only a failure to save and ration pleasure but also a related gluttony or absence of reserve. If the stereotypical bisexual man with a wife and some male lovers on the side is treating his wife like surety or security and his lovers as pleasure, then maybe he *is* having his cake etcetera. That appears to be the point of the phrase when hurled, a little awkwardly (like a custard pie in the face?) as an epithet.

But most bisexuals, needless to say, do not think of themselves as "having it all" in the sense of an easy life. Many describe their isolation or ostracization from the gay or queer community, and their sense of apartness from the world of "heterosexual privilege" in which many gays and lesbians have thought them to be seeking refuge. If "having it all" and "having things both ways" imply repletion and total satisfaction even in the face of contradiction, "having your cake and eating it, too," with its tacit monitory prefix ("you *can't* have...") suggests that retribution, whether from individuals or from society as a whole, is somehow on its way. (So *there.*)

I suspect that some of the animosity toward bisexuals, what the bi movement has come to call "biphobia," is based upon a puritanical idea that no one *should* "have it all." "Choice," itself a contested word in some queer circles, is taken to imply choosing against, as well as choosing with —"not choosing" something as a way of choosing something else. And politically speaking, choosing a *person* rather than a label or category is often seen as denial rather than acceptance. Especially for those who feel they have "no choice" about their sexuality.

What's in a Name?

It is my opinion that while the word *bisexual* may have its uses as an adjective, ... it is not only useless but mendacious when used as a noun.

—John Malone, Straight Women/Gay Men[8]

My feeling is that labels are for canned food.... I am what I am—and I know what I am.

—R.E.M.'s Michael Stipe, discussing
"the whole queer-straight-bi thing" in Rolling Stone[9]

One thing that just about everyone agrees on is that "bisexual" is a problematic word. To the disapproving or the disinclined it connotes promiscuity, immaturity, or wishy-washiness. To some lesbians and gay men it says "passing," "false consciousness," and a desire for "heterosexual privilege." To psychologists it may suggest adjustment problems; to psychoanalysts an unresolved Oedipus complex; to anthropologists, the narrowness of a Western (Judeo-Christian) world view. Rock stars regard it as a dimension of the performing self. Depending on the cultural context it can make (Mick Jagger, David Bowie, Sandra Bernhard) or break (preacher Jim Bakker; congressman Robert Bauman; even briefly, tennis star Billie Jean King) a career.

Talk-show hosts are convinced that "bisexuality" is a cover for unbridled lust, or what bisexual activists prefer to call "nonmonogamy." Never mind that monosexuals, straight and gay, have practiced enthusiastic nonmonogamy for centuries.

"Back-formation" is a term from linguistics that describes the way words and concepts can be constituted retroactively, providing what is in effect a false pedigree in the form of a putative etymology. Strictly speaking, a back-formation is a new word created by removing a prefix or a suffix (or what is thought to be a prefix or a suffix) from an already existing word; thus our singular "pea" comes from subtracting the "s" from the earlier English plural, pease, and the modern slang "ept," rather than the more literally correct "apt," is created by removing the prefix from "inept." This looks harmless enough, but it soon enters the realm of the political by way of an authenticating gesture toward origins. The logic of apparent priority—the illusion of priority produced by back-formation—creates a hierarchy of the "natural," the "normal," or the "original."

What does back-formation have to do with bisexuality? In the broadest and most general sense, it explains why many people regard the "bisexual" as a variant—and often a perverse or self-indulgent variant—of the more "normal" practice of heterosexuality, rather than viewing heterosexuality (or, indeed, homosexuality) as a specific personal or cultural option within a broader field that could be called simply "sexuality." Historically speaking, the word "heterosexual" is a back-formation from "homosexual." Before people began to speak of "homosexuals" as a kind of person, a social species, there was no need for a term like "heterosexual" (literally, sexually oriented toward the [or an] other sex). Both words date in English from around the turn of the century. Neither appears in the first edition of the *Oxford English Dictionary,* the standard reference work, begun in 1879 and completed in 1928. Each makes its first appearance in the *Supplement.*

In English, then, the word "homosexual" dates from around 1897, when the sexologist Havelock Ellis introduced it in his *Studies in the Psychology of Sex* as a coinage of his fellow Victorian sex-writer and Eastern traveler Richard Burton. " 'Homosexual' is a barbarously hybrid word," wrote Ellis, "and I take no responsibility for it." Ellis preferred other, less "hybrid" terms, like "sexual inversion," based upon a notion of congenital and inborn sexual disposition toward persons of one's own sex. He regarded sex as a positive force in human life, whether it took the form of masturbation, oral sex, intercourse, or a variety of other sexual pleasures. Himself married to a bisexual woman, Ellis proposed "trial marriages" before partners made lasting commitments to each other, recognized the pleasures of variety in sexual partners, and offered a critique of the institution of marriage, which he called "rather . . . a tragic condition than a happy condition."

His deprecation of the new word "homosexual" does not reflect a negative attitude toward homosexual behavior, but rather a classically trained scholar's resistance to blending Greek (*homo,* same) and Latin (*sexus*) roots. But the resistance, however philological, is worthy of note. A question of authenticity and origins is being raised here; the naturalizing of the term "homosexual" is made more difficult by its problematical parentage —a parentage which, significantly, is "hetero" rather than "homo." (This is made even more problematic by the apparent homology between the Greek adjective *homos,* meaning "same" and the Latin noun *homo,* meaning "man, human being." The false etymology "man-lover" or "desirer of men" crosses the "true" etymology of "lover or desirer of the same [sex]." The term "het" for a heterosexual person, now in common use among gays, lesbians, queers, and bi's, is yet another example of a back-formation, this one troped on "homo," a disparaging term for a gay or homosexual person. (Quentin Crisp, for example, referred to himself as having become a national institution, one of the "stately homos of England.") For a person who regards himself or herself as part of the mainstream, "het" is a reminder of the way in which the familiar can be defamiliarized, the unmarked term become marked, the "self" turned into someone else's "other."

"Heterosexuality" is, in a way, begotten as a term by its elder sibling, "homosexuality." In fact, the first definition in the *Oxford English Dictionary* betrays some of this anxiety of origin. "Pertaining to or characterized by the normal relation of the sexes," it says, begging the question of the "normal." "Opposite to *homosexual.*" And then, immediately, "Sometimes misapplied, as in quote 1901," the first recorded use of the term, in *Dorland's Medical Dictionary.* In *Dorland,* "heterosexuality" is defined as an "abnormal or perverted sexual appetite towards the opposite sex." This is, indeed, we might say, a "misapplication" if the standard definition posits, without specifying, a "normal" relation "of the sexes." But what significance might there be in the fact that not only does "homosexuality" precede "heterosexuality," but the "abnormal" practice of something called "heterosexuality" precedes its usage in the language as a term for a "normal relation of the sexes"? "Of *the* sexes," implying that the reader knows full well what those sexes are, as well as what would be "normal" for (note the definition does not say "between") them.

Medical dictionaries, like sexologists, are of course always on the lookout for pathologies. Health is not usually defined in them except by its contrary and by its absence. The "normal" itself may be considered in this sense a back-formation from the more interesting and provocative "abnormal."

Hung Up on Labels

Bi-curious attr SWM sks bi-curious SWM for mutual 1st encounter. No gays.

—Now[11]

"There is no such thing as a homosexual person, any more than there is such a thing as a heterosexual person," declared Gore Vidal in 1979 to the readers of *Playboy*. "The words are adjectives, describing sexual acts, not people. Those sexual acts are entirely natural; if they were not, no one would perform them." As for slang terms and labels, "the reason no one has yet been able to come up with a good word to describe the homosexualist (sometimes known as gay, fag, queer, etc.) is because he does not exist. The human race is divided into male and female. Many human beings enjoy sexual relations with their own sex, many don't; many respond to both. The plurality is the fact of our nature and not worth fretting about."[11] More than ten years later, Vidal—who himself avoids all labels, including "bisexual"—genially reiterated his view: "[T]he dumb neologisms, homo-sexual and hetero-sexual, are adjectives that describe acts but never people."[12]

A homosexual, the character Roy Cohn expostulates to his doctor in Tony Kushner's *Angels in America,* is not someone with a specific set of erotic interests, but rather a person without clout.

> ROY: Your problem, Henry, is that you are hung up on words, on labels, that you believe they mean what they seem to mean. AIDS. Homosexual. Gay. Lesbian. You think these are names that tell you who someone sleeps with, but they don't tell you that.
> HENRY: No?
> ROY: No. Like all labels they tell you one thing and one thing only: where does an individual so identified fit in the food chain, in the pecking order? Not ideology, or sexual taste, but something much simpler: clout. Not who I fuck or who fucks me, but who will pick up the phone when I call, who owes me favors. This is what a label refers to. Now to someone who does not understand this, homosexual is what I am because I have sex with men. But really this is wrong. Homosexuals are not men who sleep with other men. Homosexuals are men who in fifteen years of trying cannot get a pissant antidiscrimination bill through City Council. Homosexuals are men who

know nobody and who nobody knows. Who have zero clout. Does this sound like me, Henry?[13]

Cohn, of course, is *not* a bisexual. "Roy Cohn is a heterosexual man who fucks around with guys," he declares. That the occasion of this diatribe is his doctor's attempt to tell him he has AIDS and needs medical attention makes the bravado all the more poignant.

Strong recoil from the word "homosexual" can be found among bisexuals, too, perhaps especially those who are "having their cake and eating it, too." As we will see in greater detail in a subsequent chapter, the writer John Cheever has chronicled in graphic terms his sexual relations with both men and women, all the while enjoying his image as a husband, father, and "squire of Ossining," and vigorously protesting the application of the word "homosexual" to any of his relations with men.

Cheever's son Benjamin, reflecting on this denial of homosexuality years after his father's death, took a generous view. "I think it would be wrong to judge it as dishonesty. Literally, it was a lie, of course, but in some figurative sense it was true. He never considered himself to be a homosexual. I don't mean to split hairs, or to separate my father from those people who do consider themselves to be homosexual, but only to say that this was a word he would not apply to himself, and words were frightfully important to him."[14]

Cheever the son himself prefers the word "bisexual." "Looking back at my father's life, and at his writing, it must seem difficult to believe that I didn't know about his bisexuality, but I didn't even suspect,"[15] he says. His discovery of his father's sexual involvement with men "came in stages," until it seemed "possible that he'd been bisexual almost from day one."[16] Yet the elder Cheever's public stance on homosexuality was unrelentingly harsh. "In public he was an ardent heterosexual, and he told me that homosexuality made men vain, ungenerous, and ultimately ridiculous."[17] To call this attitude "self-hatred" has become fashionable, and it contains more than a kernel of truth. The evidence seems to suggest that John Cheever did not hate himself, or the men he loved, but that he was contemptuous of visibly gay men and especially gay couples.[18] In his letters to male lovers this inconsistency is consistent. He can make mock of an old-young male couple in a gleaming Mercedes, and then unselfconsciously borrow Molly Bloom's ecstatic mantra of sexual affirmation from the close of *Ulysses:* "Call me soon," he writes to one young man. "Call me collect and when the operator asks if I'll accept the charges on a call from _____ I'll say yes, yes, yes, yes."[19]

He recalls a relationship with the composer Ned Rorem (a "former male beauty" who "sucked my cock three times a day for three days"),[20] and, in writing to the same man, congratulates them both on not being homosexual: "Your description of your love for _____ pleased me deeply since it refreshed my sense of that genuineness of heart I so admire in you and made clear the fact that for both of us the love of a woman is without parallel. . . ."[21] And again, six months later, "It all seems quite simple. Neither of us is homosexual and yet neither of us are foolish enough to worry about the matter. If I want your cock or your mouth I know I have only to ask and yet I know that there is so much better for you in life than my love that I can think of parting from you without pain."[22]

If the fictional Cohn and the diarist Cheever are both reacting to the ways in which the word "homosexual" has been stigmatized and marginalized, the word "lesbian," too, has been made to carry derogatory baggage. "Man-hater," a persistent epithet hurled at both feminists and lesbians (as if the two groups were automatically the same), arises whenever male centrality, privilege, and/or desirability are questioned. Bisexuals escape this particular categorical slur, thus inviting resentment from gays and lesbians, since they appear to fall under the catchall category of "hetero-sexual privilege," which includes "man-lovers" (when applied to women; male man-lovers need not apply). In a characteristic asymmetry, "woman-hater" tends in popular parlance to refer to crusty old patriarchs who don't like the idea of female vice presidents, platoon commanders, or department chairmen, rather than to (explicitly) gay men. The element of sexuality only comes in, it seems, when the "hating," so called, is perceived as coming from women.

"Man-hating," like unshaven legs and underarms (again, for women only) are said to be telltale signs of bad, separatist, "radical" feminism. Never mind that most women in Europe, no matter what their politics, prefer not to shave their legs or armpits as a matter of personal style (American myopia and Hollywood glitz creating the illusion of a "norm" that is in fact an abnorm). Or that many American feminists and lesbians *do* choose to shave their legs (who cares?). Or that "man-hating" (give it its Latin name "misandry," and see how the sense of the term alters) is really the Right's and the media's inaccurate version of an aversion to that other buzzword, patriarchy. "Man-hating," like hairy legs, has always been a scare-tactic functioning, with disturbing success, as a way of discouraging feminism and sexual self-empowerment.

But feminism isn't a dress code, a grooming strategy, a (leg-)hair style —or a sexuality.

Then what about the famous rallying cry "Feminism is a theory, lesbi-anism is a practice"? This, indeed, was a sign of its times, the tempestuous late sixties and early seventies.[23] As the editors of *Bi Any Other Name* maintain, "for many, lesbian and gay separatism during the seventies and eighties became a chauvinistic, holier-than-thou way of life, a power-over tool that gave us a rigid party line by which to police one another for political correctness." Yet, as they note, "bisexuals were some of the first men to write gay manifestos and to initiate the men's anti-sexist movement and some of the first women to build the lesbian feminist movement."[24]

In the early seventies, two lesbian authors speculated that some women might be "moving into developing a true bisexuality," because the "aura of radical chic surrounding Lesbians in the women's movement" may have influenced their desire to self-identify as lesbian. In other words, those then identifying as lesbian might include a number of women who, had they known or felt comfortable with the label, might have called themselves bisexual. "Bisexual women who have been caught on both sides and in the middle of the heterosexual/homosexual argument" went largely unheard, they reported, though they might turn out to be "the most important group to speak up in the women's movement on the whole topic of sexuality." And why was this? Perhaps because "bisexual women bring out fears of homosexuality in straight women and also fears of heterosexuality in women who live as Lesbians."[25]

What kind of fears? Political fears—and fears of themselves, of what might be inside them. As so often, fear and desire were the most familiar as well as the strangest of bedfellows.

These days, the suspicion of shifting categories manifests itself in a label like "L.U.G.," for "Lesbian Until Graduation," a description that implies that the former-lesbian has decided to avail herself of heterosexual privilege after leaving the haven of her college years. "She was oh-so-close with her dorm-mates," the magazine *10 Percent* comments sardonically of the typical L.U.G. "But that was then, and this is . . . adulthood."[26]

"Lesbians who sleep with men" has become an expanded and expanding category. "Among self-designated lesbians," notes April Martin, a New York psychologist and author of *The Lesbian and Gay Parenting Handbook,* "there are some who have sex occasionally or even exclusively with men, some who have deep, committed love relationships with men, some whose primary buddies and comrades are men. There are also women who designate themselves as heterosexual with exactly the same patterns."[27] Martin thinks "there is more sexual diversity among women than among men," and that while self-identified lesbians "report attractions to men and sexual activity with men with some frequency," self-identified gay men are "much less likely to report desires to sleep with women, or to act on such desires if they have them."[28]

If women who are frequently attracted to men and frequently have sex with them are "lesbians," then it becomes clear that, in these women's eyes at least, "lesbian" is a cultural and political designation rather than— exclusively—a narrowly drawn sexual one. Not everyone will be happy with this idea, needless to say. But usage tends to follow use, as dictionary-makers, often to their chagrin, acknowledge. "Our clumsy categories of gay, bisexual and straight are political divisions, primarily, much more than descriptive categories," says Martin, who does not want her remarks mistaken as a suggestion that "everyone, deep down, is bisexual, or could be if they wanted to." Rather, since she suspects that absent social bias there would still be people who reported that from their earliest moments they were attracted exclusively to one sex or the other, the question to be posed would be, "What makes those with exclusively homosexual attractions different from those with exclusively heterosexual attractions?"[29] Or, we might add, what makes those with exclusive attractions different from those with inclusive attractions?

What about men? Do they have the same problems with nomenclature that bisexual women do? Not quite, it seems—the triple identity of feminism, lesbianism, and bisexuality has led to more complex definitional and partisan politics. Gay men are often described as less political, more concerned with sex and less with organizing, more into the club scene than women —though this, too, is rapidly becoming an outdated stereotype.

The renewal of "lesbian chic" and "bisexual chic" has focused attention on the sexiness of women in same-sex relationships. It's become a truism of gay and lesbian magazines that lesbian sex has gotten "hotter" in the past several years, which doesn't mean that earlier lesbians didn't have hot sex but that, as lesbian novelist Katherine V. Forrest points out, sexiness is now very much a part of how lesbian writers and filmmakers describe their lives. "We are, in some ways, going through what gay men went through in the '70s," says Forrest. "We're acknowledging our sexuality and exploring it. The success of lesbian erotica is a reflection of that."[30]

The queer movement has also given a viable context to relations, sexual and flirtatious, between gay men and lesbians. Opposite-sex fantasies have been incorporated into some lesbian erotica, like "The Surprise Party," a short story by lesbian writer Pat Califia that describes the abduction of a lesbian by three gay male "policemen" who force her to have sex with them.[31] An article in *Details* reported on gay men who "sometimes sleep with straight women (and vice versa)."[32] "Ask your girlfriend who first made her tingle," says the author, "and five times out of ten it was a homo."

A piece in the British journal *Gay Times* announced that "Sex between gay men and lesbians is coming out of the closet.... Now people talk openly of their opposite-sex-same-sexuality lovers and at the party after the SM Pride March a gay man and a lesbian had sex on the dance floor, but it wasn't heterosexuality. You can tell."[33] As critic Jo Eadie points out, what "you can tell" here above all is that bisexuality is being edited out of consciousness, or disavowed.[34] "Opposite-sex-same-sexuality" enshrines "gay" and "lesbian" as the real, identifying, and in this gay context reassuring sexualities of the participants. That "it wasn't heterosexuality," and that "you" (the insider) can know that and "tell" it, whether to yourself or to like-minded others, is presented as a boundary-keeping consideration, a border guard against permeable and politically dangerous transgression. What if it *were* "heterosexuality"? Would "heterosexuality" have to change? Would it have to be let into the gay-lesbian-queer arena? What if it were *bisexuality?* Would that make the gay man and the lesbian having sex into "bisexuals"? If not, what *is* bisex? And if so, what happens to the titillation of insider-transgression, a licensed and *permitted* boundary-crossing that, paradoxically, enforces the "keep out" sign for unwelcome trespassers?

Labels and labeling are a big issue for many people who, for lack of a better term, call themselves bisexual. The word "label" turns up over and over again in bi publications.[35] At stake are questions of "identity politics" and group solidarity, cultural visibility now and in the past, and the vexed question of bisexuality's fluid nature. Put in terms of a conundrum, we might say: How can something fluid be something solid? How to reconcile a "sexuality" that takes the form of narrative (this then that; this and that; this because of that; this after that) with a "politics" that depends upon solidarity?

At a National Bisexual Conference in 1990, Elizabeth Reba Weise, who would shortly become the editor of a collection of essays on bisexuality and feminism, observed that she was "a bit uncomfortable declaring myself a bisexual. The label doesn't seem as solid as the lesbian label. Because to declare yourself bisexual is to declare, really, that labels don't mean anything. So it seems paradoxical to declare this an identity."[36]

"I dislike labels. My past is heterosexual, my present life is mostly lesbian, and my future is unknown," writes Dvora Zipkin, who characterizes herself, selecting what she regards as the best available choice, as a "bisexual lesbian."[37] Some years ago she joined a women's group in which, in an exercise designed to explore the question of identity, each woman was asked to associate herself with one of four subgroups: Lesbian, Bisexual, Heterosexual, or Choose Not to Label. After some thought she joined Choose Not to Label, and discovered that of the several others in her group some were there because they didn't know to which group they belonged, others because they didn't like labels, and some for both reasons.

A couple of years later, when the exercise was repeated, Zipkin again chose Choose Not to Label, finding herself this time one of only two women in the group, a change that seemed to mark a shift in cultural perspective. Today, if she had to choose, she says she'd pick Bisexual. "It's the closest I can come to who I am. And it's the label with the most flexibility and tolerance for change."[38] Yet she noted ruefully that "it often seems as if both communities—heterosexual and lesbian—are trying to get us bisexuals over to their respective 'side,' consciously or not."[39]

Labels perform different functions for different people. For those who can't make categorical sense of their own desires, who feel there is no place for them in the sexual world, the term "bisexual" comes as a god-send, a moment comparable to the (mislabeled) Ugly Duckling's discovery that "I *am* a swan." "I thought I had to be either gay or straight," one woman told sociologists Martin Weinberg, Colin Williams, and Douglas Pryor when they surveyed members of a San Francisco Bisexual Center. Another reported, "My feelings had always been bisexual. I just did not know how to define them."

"The first time I heard the word, which was not until I was twenty-six, I realized that was what fit for me," said a bisexual man. "I had sexual feelings for both men and women. Up until that point, the only way that I could define my sexual feelings was that I was either a latent homosexual or a confused heterosexual."[40] Several said that discovering Fred Klein's 1978 book *The Bisexual Option* gave them a mirror in which to see themselves. The same was said a bisexual-generation later by many people who came across the 1991 collection *Bi Any Other Name*.

"If there are two terms and you find a third term—there is black, there is white, and there is biracial; there is homosexual, there is heterosexual, there is bisexual—you've at least broken down the dichotomy," says a poet, now married, who has had relationships with both men and women. "That may be transitional, but I think it's a necessary stage in language, in the development of language about these things."

Her present colleagues had no reason to know about her bisexuality. But at lunch one day, one of them spoke out strongly against labels like "multiracial" in the United States. Someone else mentioned sexuality. "And I suddenly felt obliged to say, wait a minute, it does matter whether there is an intermediate term. It does matter whether we're simply talking in dichotomies. And that isn't to say once you have an intermediate term you're stuck with it. But certainly without one you never get beyond a certain place.

"This is part of my vision of things, that once you define a middle, you define a place, it's an expanded middle. And it's a middle that will not keep its terminology. Finally 'bisexual' isn't going to do it either. But it's better than nothing. It's better than what we had, since neither of those things worked."[41]

The bisexuals interviewed in the Weinberg study were not only self-defined as bisexuals but also bisexually identified to the point that they chose to belong to a social association that brought them into contact with others similarly identified. Ninety percent of them, according to the researchers, did not think of themselves as in transition from heterosexual to homosexual or vice versa, but rather as settled in their sexual identity. Yet fully one-quarter of these people still said they were "confused" about their bisexuality, and more than half the women and three-quarters of the men had previously felt confusion.

This was not, they said, because of doubts about their erotic inclinations, but because of pressure from monosexuals, some of them heterosexual, but more of them lesbian or gay. Living in the San Francisco Bay area, "many bisexuals referred to the persistent pressures they experienced to relabel themselves as 'gay' or 'lesbian' and to engage in sexual activity exclusively with the same sex." No one was "*really* bisexual," they were repeatedly told. There was no socially validated role for bisexuals. Bisexuality was "a politically incorrect and inauthentic identity."[42] Hence the founding of the Bisexual Center, and the development of a sense of community.

"The first time I read the word *bisexual,* I knew instantly that that's what I was," observed a young city planner who contributed some thoughts on "the 'b' word" to an essay collection. He recalls once having two crushes, "one on the most handsome boy, and the other on the most beautiful girl in the school." He was then in the third grade. Some twenty years later he began to explore the subject, checking in his university's library catalog, where no books on "bisexuality" were listed. In 1987 he went to Washington to join the March for Lesbian and Gay (and Bisexual) Rights, marching under the National Bisexual Network banner and listening to folksinger Holly Near.[43]

Holly Near herself, with a strong following among lesbians, became a lightning rod for bisexual identity issues when it became known that she was involved with a man. "Because my lover was a man," she wrote in her autobiography *Fire in the Rain, Singer in the Storm,* "I didn't feel comfortable sharing my happiness"[44] with lesbian-feminists. Yet she identified as a lesbian, not a bisexual. "Holly Near," one commentator wrote wryly, "declines to call herself bisexual because, one, she 'doesn't feel like a bisexual,'[45] and two, her lesbianism is 'linked to [a] political perspective' rather than mere 'sexual preference'[46]—unlike, presumably, her bisexuality."[47] How to carve out a political space for bisexuality became a major concern for activists.

Bi Default

toujours gai toujours gai

—*"the song of mehitabel"*[48]

One of the most effective political strategies employed by the lesbian and gay movement was the reclaiming and renaming of homosexuals from the past. *The Gay Book of Days,* for example, is a birthday book, "An Evocatively Illustrated Who's Who of Who Is, Was, May Have Been, Probably Was, and Almost Certainly Seems to Have Been Gay During the Past 5,000 Years."[49]

The more serious and scholarly *Gay/Lesbian Almanac* sports a mock-eighteenth-century subtitle: "A New Documentary, In which is contained, in Chronological Order, Evidence of the True and Fantastical HISTORY of those persons now called LESBIANS and GAY MEN, and of the Changing Social Forms of and Responses to those Acts, Feelings, and Relationships now called Homosexual, in the Early American Colonies, 1607 to 1740, and in the Modern United States, 1880 to 1950."[50] The term "almanac," like "book of days," is suggestive: Entries proceed year by year, covering history as the book of days covered the calendar, putting in place the missing building blocks of an alternative social and cultural story, both "true" and "fantastical."

It is noteworthy that both the calendar and the almanac date from the early eighties, a moment of imaginative political consolidation for gay history. Like dozens of other similar publications of their time, they were designed to restore a lost or neglected past, to shine the spotlight on figures all too recently hidden in darkness, indistinct and unrecognized. But bringing out the homosexuals of the past meant labeling; it also meant, to a certain extent, bracketing bisexuality. "Gay (or bisexual)" and "lesbian (or bisexual)" became, for purposes of political classification, gay and lesbian. The concept of the "default category" was at work.

In computer science, a "default" is a particular value for a variable that is assigned automatically by an operating system and remains in effect unless canceled or overridden by the operator. If you have a word-processing program on your computer, its default setting for line spacing will probably be single space; if you want double spacing you will have to alter the document's format—or, if you want to double space *all the time,* reset the default in the operating system so that the automatic format is double rather than single space. Double space then becomes the "default" setting, or default category. Similarly, in the cultural mainstream, the default category for sexuality is "heterosexual." What the *Gay Book of Days* had done was to reset the default for sexuality as "gay and lesbian." "Bisexual" was subsumed under "gay" or "lesbian" and written out, since the targeted opposition was between "heterosexual" and "not-heterosexual." A binary system is created out of a multiplicity of options. What was most neglected or most stigmatized became the object of scrutiny—and, in these cases, of identification and celebration. Identity politics demanded identities, and identifications.

Thus, *The Gay Book of Days* could list on subsequent pages for the month of April: Henri de Montherlant ("exploring [in his novels] the diffi-cult area of his ambiguous sexuality, exploiting his sexual affairs with women while muffling his even more intense affairs with men"), Madame de Staël ("Madame de Staël liked not only men but . . . women too"), William Shakespeare ("too much is at stake in permitting the greatest poet in the English language to be anything but straight. . . . Still, why would a straight poet write sonnets to a man he called 'the master-mistress of his passion' "), and Ma Rainey ("part of a circle of black lesbians and bisexuals that included Bessie Smith, Jackie 'Moms' Mabley, and Josephine Baker").

In this particular week in April, chosen virtually at random, the historical personages who "almost certainly seem to have been gay" according to the book's title are thus, almost to a man or woman, "bisexual" according to the author's own account. This is a good lesson, not so much in human history (though it is that, too), but in the functioning of classification. "Gay," in 1982 when the first version of the *Gay Book of Days* was published, included "bisexual" and made it, from the point of view of the title, the cover, and the advertising for the book, invisible. Bisexuals *were* gay, because gay was a minority category and often a stigmatized one. Like the "one drop of black blood" that was once said to determine racial identity because white was the favored "majority" category, the same-sex relationships of famous people made them "gay" whether or not they also had opposite sex lovers. Note that they are described in the book's title and subtitle as "gay," not "lesbian," though the author claims with some irritation that that would be like saying "poetess" instead of "poet"; "by 'gay' I simply mean 'homosexual,' male or female."[51]

This, too, is a marker of historical change. Lesbianism began to achieve publishing parity with gay male identity only in the late eighties and nineties. But the author's note about "poetess" (and, he adds, "Negress" and "aviatrix") doesn't include any comparable gesture toward bisexuals. Lesbians, apparently, were at least visible in their invisibility. Bisexuals had not yet achieved even that dubious distinction.

"We must identify the obvious, reclaim our writers, poets, painters and activists," argue bisexual authors Loraine Hutchins and Lani Kaahumanu, who list Anaïs Nin, Colette, Frida Kahlo, Lorraine Hansberry, Walt Whitman, D. H. Lawrence, Langston Hughes, W. Somerset Maugham, Djuna Barnes, Tallulah Bankhead, and Ma Rainey as among those who "have loved both men and women."[52]

"They're always referring to Djuna now as a lesbian, but—she had many lovers, male and female," observed Djuna Barnes's friend, the poet Charles Henri Ford, who lived with Barnes in Paul Bowles's house in Tangier in 1933.[53] "Those who continue to classify the poems of Sappho as 'Lesbian' are missing the point," declared an article in the newsletter of the Boston Bisexual Women's Network. "Sappho's lesbianism does not appear to be a refusal of men, but rather a way of refusing to suppress any sexual preference."[54]

It's easy to mock this tendency to pull role models out of distant and not-so-distant history. But this is the way in which invisible and noncanonical minorities have come to public attention in our time. There is a place for this naming and thematizing in the educational system, even when it goes under the feel-good heading of "self-esteem." It can't replace analysis and subtle interpretation, but it can inspire young people—and older ones—who feel written out of history and culture. At a time of widespread discouragement among "posties" and "Generation X-ers" about the possibility of any viable future, at a time when cultural, ethnic, and political minorities still face discrimination even from elected school boards with normalizing "Christian" agendas, minority role models and visibility are indispensable social tools.

But what sense does it make to call Julius Caesar, Virginia Woolf, or Michelangelo "bisexual"? This claim of a "transhistorical bisexual culture," argue some critics, is historically suspect and neither politically nor philosophically viable. "The bisexual identities we have developed are products of our time and our environment, and were not shared by Alexander the Great or Eleanor Roosevelt."[55] So why ask "whether Tchaikovsky was 'really' gay or 'really' bisexual?"

A further drawback of "reclaiming" in political terms is the way it puts bisexuals in opposition to gays and lesbians, setting up a kind of property dispute or custody battle: Figures in history become sexual-identity role models, displaced from historical context to justify modern (and postmodern) lives.

I think we may delude ourselves a little about how truly "historicized" our notions of cultural identity can ever be. The Alexander the Greats, Vita Sackville-Wests, and Eleanor Roosevelts we muse about are as much the constructions of modern biographers, filmmakers, and novelists as they are the "real," "original," and "historicized" persons who once bore those names. (The test case here is, as so often, Shakespeare, who is clearly reinvented by every generation in its own image.)

But even in the present, the problem of naming preoccupies us. *The Advocate,* a biweekly (not at all the same as a "bi weekly,") describes itself as "The National Gay & Lesbian Newsmagazine." *10 Percent* calls itself "the magazine of lesbian and gay culture," and, during the time of its publication, *Out/Look* identified itself as the "National Lesbian & Gay Quarterly." Despite its self-characterization, *The Advocate* conducted a sex survey in 1994 that asked lots of questions about bisex ("has your sexual attraction to the two genders *shifted* from the past?" "When you have had sexual fantasies while awake, whom have you fantasized about?"), used the phrase "gay or bisexual" in numerous cases ("Have you told any of the following people that you are gay or bisexual?"), and listed "bisexual" as the second choice for self-identification (after "homosexual/gay" and before "heterosexual/straight" and "not sure"), but the questionnaire was advertised in large print as a "Special Mail-In Gay Sex Survey."

The editors of yet another journal, *Out,* describe it as the magazine reflecting the changing "status of gays and lesbians" in the nineties,[56] and refer to it as part of the "gay press," though a note to readers in very tiny type and clearly written by a lawyer disclaims any intentional outing in *Out.* "Readers please note," it says. "Subjects and contributors to OUT magazine are gay, lesbian, bisexual and straight. In the absence of a specific statement herein concerning the sexual orientation or personal practices of any individual mentioned in, or contributing material to, this publication, no inference with respect thereto is intended and none should be implied." This is the sole mention of bisexuality on the editorial page.

Ironically, the same cultural invisibility that led to the creation of such journals was now being practiced, by policy or inadvertence, by the publishers of glossy gay and lesbian newsmagazines. A "magazine" is a storage place, not only for articles and stories, but in a different context for ammunition. In this case those who had the magazines were, once again, patrolling the borders.

Bi Lines

When the *San Francisco Bay Times* added the word "bisexual" to its masthead for the first time (on April Fool's Day, 1991), becoming "The Gay/Lesbian/Bisexual Newspaper & Calendar of Events for the Bay Area," not all its readers were pleased by the change. Letters to the editor, Kim Corsaro, demanded to know her sexual orientation and that of her staff members, "so that we can judge for ourselves if the *SF Bay Times* represents us," according to a letter signed by five lesbians. "For the record," Corsaro wrote, "I am a lesbian. I do not have a bisexual lover." Her staff was made up, she said, of "26 lesbians, 23 gay men, 5 bisexuals and 3 hets." In a satiric response to this situation a group calling itself HUAC (Homosexual Unity and Conformity) showed up in San Francisco's Castro district with a device called an "Acme Bi Detector." Suspected bisexuals ("half-hets") were asked to take a loyalty oath ("I am not now, nor have I ever been a bisexual, a member of any bisexual organization, or offered aid and comfort to bisexuals claiming any part of the Gay/Lesbian Community"). Anyone who collapsed with laughter and could not complete the oath, or who refused to take it, was tagged with a two-way yellow arrow. Those who eluded bi detection and were certified clearly gay or lesbian were awarded a purple star with the number "6" for a top ("pure" gay) Kinsey score.[57]

On the whole, though, gay and lesbian journals and magazines are going seriously mainstream in design, advertising, and editorial style, like other formerly "alternative" publications, while bisexual 'zines (small, individually produced alternative magazines) and newsletters are still produced on a shoestring, and tend to look it. And it is in the pages of these bi-journals, and in the few existing anthologies of bisexual writing, that arguments for reclaiming bisexuals of the past have been made and debated. In this case, however, the sexual dissidents would not be wrested from obscurity, but from gay or lesbian identification.

The bisexual 'zine *Logomotive: A Magazine of Sex & Fun (From a Bisexual Perspective)* offered a page of "bisexual lists," including some seventy-five "famous bisexuals," listed alphabetically from (perpetual favorite) Alexander the Great to (perpetual favorite) Virginia Woolf, including Lord Byron, Queen Christina of Sweden, Ram Dass, Freddie Mercury, Sappho, and St. Augustine. A footnote in small type noted, "The list of bisexual figures is arbitrary. These are people who were known to have relationships with people of genders other than their own, as well as their own. Some have identified as bisexual, others have not labeled themselves, while others still identify with a sexual orientation other than 'bisexual.'"[58] Other "bi lists" were also provided, of bi movies, bi comic books, and bi science-fiction novels, chosen "because they have a bisexual theme, character(s), chapters, story lines or research; or they were written or produced by bisexual(s)." In case the reader was becoming too comfortable with labels, a note from the editor also informs her or him that "we're changing our name." Henceforth the 'zine would be known as *Slippery When Wet,* a title, the editors rather coyly pointed out, still related to "transportation." But the shift to a deliberately erotic double-meaning highlighted another issue relevant to bisexual self-awareness. How to make bisexuality sexy?

It would seem as if bi-sex might have something for everyone, in terms of fantasy, affection, and desire. Yet the politics of organized bisexuality in the nineties, with many of its energies coming out of feminism and a discourse of rights, and cognizant also of the popular demonization of the "bisexual AIDS carrier," the duplicitous married man who was said to have infected his unsuspecting wife and unborn children, in a way militated against sexiness. This the new journals set out to change. The model of the lesbian pleasure journal *On Our Backs,* founded by bisexual-lesbian and "anti-censorship cultural heroine"[59] Susie Bright as a direct challenge to the less pro-sex, more rights-based *Off Our Backs,* led to the founding, or renaming, of other 'zines and journals that let *sex* back in under the big tent of "sexuality," and bisexuality. The San Francisco–based *Anything That Moves,* which began publishing in January 1991 and might be described as the premier regional magazine of the American "bisexual community," adopted the subtitle "Beyond the Myths of Bisexuality," although its name reflects one of the biggest myths of all. Under former editor Karla Rossi, every issue began with a standard editorial, "About our name . . . ":

> Our choice to use this title for the magazine has been nothing less than controversial. That we would choose to redefine the stereotype that "bisexuals will fuck anything that moves," to suit our own pur-

poses has created myriad reactions. Those critical of the title feel we are [perpetuating] the stereotype and damaging our images. Those in favor of its use see it as a movement away from the stereotype, toward bisexual empowerment.

. . . We are challenging people to face their own external and internal biphobia. We are demanding attention, and are re-defining "anything that moves" *on our own terms.*

READ OUR LIPS: WE WILL WRITE OR PRINT OR SAY ***ANYTHING THAT MOVES*** US BEYOND THE LIMITING STEREOTYPES THAT ARE DISPLACED ON TO US.[60]

The sardonic adoption of a negative stereotype as a proudly worn label is consonant with the retrieval of "queer" among gays, lesbians, and others who describe themselves as "gay-affirmative," and also with the insider use of formerly deplored terms like "nigger" (by African Americans only, as in the rap group N.W.A., "Niggers with Attitude") and "fag hag," now occasionally claimed by some women who like hanging out with gay men.

Anything That Moves, as the title for a bisexual magazine, not only puts sex on the front burner, it also makes a deliberate gesture of inclusiveness. Not only the "good" bisexuals, who affirm their monogamy and make bisexuality potentially more acceptable to the mainstream, but all persons who are bisexual or interested in bisexuality are, at least in theory, welcome. As bisexual rights activist Lenore Norrgard, herself a founding editor of the Seattle Bisexual Women's Network newsletter *North Bi Northwest,* has argued, bisexuals "should take to heart the hard lesson the gay movement taught us through trying to present gays as 'normal' "[61]— that is, by excluding "drag queens, bulldykes, and gays of color" in favor of an upscale, relatively unthreatening, largely white male image of yuppie professionals and artists.

The political expediency (and proportional majority) of the "normal gays" position has been articulately maintained by books like Bruce Bawer's *A Place at the Table,* which locates "mainstream gays" (unlike "subculture-oriented gays") in a lifestyle context "indistinguishable from that of most heterosexual couples in similar professional and economic circumstances."[62] His position is in part that ordinary, nonsubculture homosexuals have been overtaken by the subculture, or the two subcultures (the Castro and the gay gentlemen's club). "If the heterosexual majority ever comes to accept homosexuality," Bawer contends, "it will do so because it has seen homosexuals in suits and ties, not nipple clamps and bike pants."[63] I'm assuming that Bawer does not include lesbians under the rubric of "homosexuals" here. The image of women in suits and ties, however stylish on the fashion pages, does not yet seem calculated to reassure "the heterosexual majority" in America's heartland, or even most of its corporate boardrooms.

Anything That Moves is less concerned with the heartland than with the heart, the court, the counseling session, and the bed. In some ways it is joyously less sophisticated than either a tucked-in book like Bawer's or a slick publication like *The Advocate,* full of glossy photographs and media-wise columnists. Like its parent organization, the Bay Area Bisexual Network, the magazine explicitly supports "celibacy, monogamy and non-monogamy as equally valid lifestyle choices" and "free expression of responsible consensual sexual activity." It is a newsletter and an advocacy bulletin board.

Its editorial statement, reprinted, as noted, with every issue, goes on to offer a credo and a philosophy, as well as a critique of labels. In a short space it is admirably clear, fervent, and passionately engaged.

> Bisexuality is a whole, fluid identity. Do not assume that bisexuality is binary or duogamous in nature: that we must have "two" sides or that we MUST be involved simultaneously with both genders to be fulfilled human beings. In fact, don't assume that there are only two genders. Do not mistake our fluidity for confusion, irresponsibility, or an inability to commit. Do not equate promiscuity, infidelity, or unsafe sexual behavior with bisexuality. Those are human traits that cross ALL sexual orientations. Nothing should be assumed about any-one's sexuality—including your own.[64]

> . . . Do not expect a clear-cut definition of bisexuality to jump out from the pages. We bisexuals tend to define bisexuality in ways that are unique to our own individuality. There are as many definitions of bisexuality as there are bisexuals. Many of us choose not to label ourselves anything at all, and find the word "bisexual" to be inade-quate and too limiting.

The gauntlet is thrown down; the question is really who will pick it up, since in its present format and circulation, as an organ of the Bay Area Bisexual Network (BABN), *Anything That Moves* is largely preaching to the converted. Its subscribers, I presume, are mostly bisexuals and what the editors call "bi-positive people whether or not they consider themselves bisexual." The "you" who has false expectations, including "your own" sexuality, is probably not yet reading *ATM.*

ATM, incidentally, is the magazine's own abbreviation of its name. Like PC, which meant "personal computer" to millions before it became cul-tural shorthand for "politically correct," ATM has another meaning in the world of technology and automation—I, for one, can't see these initials without mentally translating them as "automatic teller machine." Perhaps more likely, we have reached a moment of cultural saturation in the world of acronyms, where virtually every possible abbreviation has a double meaning. These particular "tellers" may have different tales, but the curious relationship between name and acronym is oddly and insistently recurrent in the world of bi-politics, as is the tendency to pun on the word "bi" itself.

Consider the Queer Nation Bi Caucus UBIQUITOUS (Uppity Bi Queers United in Their Overtly Unconventional Sexuality), LABIA (Lesbian and Bi [Women] in Action), WRAMBA (Women's Radical Multicultural Bisexual Alliance), BiCEP (the Bisexual Committee Engaging in Politics), BiONIC (Bisexuals Organising Noise, Insurrection & Confrontation), LeBiDo (for lesbians and bi women), and *BiANGLES,* a bisexual 'zine. The Boston Bisexual Women's Network, originally called *BiWoman,* pluralized its name to *BiWomen,* thereby (therebi?) achieving a pun on "by" and "bi" at the same time that it moved from the essentialist ("I Am Woman") to the politico-collective.

Such plays on words, often dismissed as trivial and unserious ("the pun is the lowest form of humor," pundits humorlessly intone), can have important effects. They can change the register of thought, bring repressed or unbidden associations to the surface, or, at the very least, call attention to the name and its component parts, as do the idiosyncratic spellings of many advertised products (Quik, Jell-O, Kleenex). These are examples of verbal condensation and modification that come to function as familiar lower-case words after a time. The more familiar they are, the more the licensers have to defend their trademark from incursion, the more they command the market and the field.

So, too, with sexual shorthand, from S/M to bisex. The "bi" in bisexual plays on words, often irritating in its omnipresence, sells the product. "Bi" seems both user-friendly and deceptively sexless. It has been said that the 1993 march on Washington for Lesbian, Gay, and Bi Equal Rights and Liberation included the word "bisexual" only after it had been abbreviated to "bi" because some people feared that "bisexual" would call too much attention to sex.[65] Scrabble players take note: "Bi" is now in the dictionary as a word that means (*Slang, noun*) a bisexual person or, adjectivally, bisexual.

Long before Freud, ancient dream interpreters saw that the wittiness of subconscious associations was in fact the shortest way to understanding their meanings: "[D]reams become ingenious and amusing because the direct and easiest pathway to the expression of their thoughts is barred."[66] What have been called "switch-words," ambiguous terms that conflate two or more meanings, allow the mind to change tracks (the railway metaphor is deliberate, since the term originates from the turn of the century).[67] And precisely because wordplay has often been dismissed or devalued, it can dare to make suggestions that would be resisted by a more direct or "serious" route. The "bi"-play of bisexual journalists, essayists, and activists can be allowed to go by as just "play."

In being playful it also plays at being suggestive if not downright sexy.

When the doubleness of double meanings in jokes and wordplay is sexual, it is often referred to as a double entendre (lay translation: "How's that again?" or, to give a double entendre for double entendre, "Come again?") —the equivalent of an auditory, sexualized double take. Switch-words, like switch-hitters, suggest the possibility of operating in more than one direction. And bi, we may note, like double, means two. The apparent two-ness of "bisexuality," however refuted and contested by bisexual theorists (as well as nontheoretical bisexuals), invites a language of double meanings. (Of course, once it is allowed to function as the verbal equivalent of a political cartoon, the pun or play on words can criticize any position. One of the least complimentary coinages for bisexual women in the late eighties was "hasbians"—former lesbians who have taken male lovers or who now assert their bisexual identity.)

Sometimes the terminology, however baroque, is not an attempt to be clever but rather to be clear or, alternatively, to be politically correct. The editor of the bisexual anthology *Closer to Home* comments in *ATM* on the names her contributors give themselves: "bi-dyke, bi-lesbian, lesbian-identified bisexual, bi-affectional, lesbian, and formally-lesbian [*sic*— should it be 'formerly lesbian'?] bisexual. Anything but straight."[68] Earnest names rather than easy ones, "bisexual lesbian" and "lesbian-identified bisexual" reveal in their apparent contradictoriness both the political tensions within queer subcultures and the degree to which "bisexual" is, after all, *not* really analogous to, and therefore inconsistent with, "lesbian" or "gay."

The "True Bisexual"

> We demand that it tell us our truth, or rather, the deeply buried truth of that truth about ourselves which we think we possess in our immediate consciousness.
>
> —*Michel Foucault,* The History of Sexuality[69]

In a sexual context so fraught with allegations of falsehood, false consciousness, and fictive identity ("there's no such thing as a bisexual"), the quest to fix and pin down this elusive desiring personage has taken constant refuge in statistics and figures. The bipolar Kinsey scale was part of the problem: Since it had a midpoint between "exclusively heterosexual" (0) and "exclusively homosexual" (6), a real or "true" bisexual was sometimes thought to be a "Kinsey 3," rather than, as Kinsey himself read the scale's continuum, as encompassing Kinsey 1s, 2s, 4s and 5s as well. Was it possible to be "a little bisexual," or was that like being "a little pregnant"? The phrase "true bisexual" began to appear as an index of equal affections —or, alternatively, as a way of restricting the use of "bisexual" from taking over the larger part of the population. But what was the "truth" about true bisexuals?

Performance remains more quantifiable than desire, even when scales try to measure various factors like attraction, fantasies, behavior, "social" and "emotional" preference, and lifestyle. Thus a hard-wired definition was offered to Ensign Vernon E. (Copy) Berg III after he confessed to the U.S. Navy in 1976 that he had had sex with men. Berg first came out as "bisexual," and only later began to describe himself as gay. When he was interviewed by Dr. John Money, a human sexuality expert at Johns Hopkins University, who was to serve as an expert witness at his administrative hearing, he says Money concluded "that the number of orgasms I had had with each sex—which at that point had been about 50–50, men to women—qualified me as a true bisexual."[70] Who could argue with that?

In this quest for the "true bisexual" he, or she, was clearly regarded as either a fabulous beast or an endangered species, and in any case as an exception to the monosexual rule. The burden of proof was on the bisexual to prove that he or she existed. "True" in the phrase "true bisexual" is a scientism, meaning typical or conforming to type ("the horseshoe crab is not a true crab," says my dictionary firmly), but the other meanings of "true," from sincere to authentic to truthful and accurate get pulled along in the semantic slipstream, so that the alternatives to "truth" here are all in the realm of falsehood rather than variation.

But what if we were to turn this truth test around, and see bisexuality as the statistical norm. Can we conceptualize a "true heterosexual," someone who has never been attracted to a person of the same sex? Or a "true homosexual"? These are the Kinsey 0s and 6s, by most accounts a genuine minority of the world's population.

The sexuality of the poet H.D. (Hilda Doolittle) has been the subject of considerable critical discussion, based not on the facts of her life but on the interpretation of those facts.

Freud called her "a perfect bi." Her early affair with Frances Josepha Gregg, her engagement to Ezra Pound, her marriage to Richard Aldington, her long relationship with Bryher (the pen name—or by-name—of writer Annie Winifred Ellerman)—all these establish H.D. as in some sense the paradigmatic bisexual figure among twentieth-century authors. During her analysis with Freud in Vienna in 1934, she reported his phrase excitedly to Bryher in a letter. "He says, 'you have two things to hide, one that you were a girl, the other that you were a boy.' It appears that I am that all-but-extinct phenomenon, a perfect bi-."[71]

A perfect bi. For a passionate collector like Freud, whose beloved antiquities were on display in his consulting room, H.D. was herself a collector's item. Displaying to his admiring literary patient, with her strong interest in the Greek classics, his "favorite" among his antiquities, he held out a little bronze statue of Pallas Athene with one hand "extended as if holding a staff or rod. 'She is perfect,' he said, *only she has lost her spear.*' " [72] The identification of the spearless Pallas with the "castrated" woman of Freud's essays on femininity became a staple of a certain kind of feminist criticism, and H.D.'s assertion in "The Master" that "woman is perfect" is seen as her reply to his slightly patronizing benevolence, her rearming of the phallic woman.

"Well, this is terribly exciting," H.D.'s letter to Bryher continued with what sounds from a distance like both bravado and anxiety, "but for the moment PLEASE do not speak of my own [writing], for it seems the conflict consists partly that what I write commits me—to one sex, or the other, I no longer HIDE. It is not quite so obvious as that—and no doubt, before I leave, we will come to some balance." [73]

For H.D. the crisis appears to have been in part coming out, and in part a question of genre. Her poetry, like that of other Imagists, had been described in the period as "feminine," [74] by which was often meant static, minor, miniaturized, or "passive." In later years she went on to write in epic poetry (traditionally described as a "big," "masculine" form) as well as in fiction. Her prose works, especially the novel and diaries unpublished until after her death, explored issues of desire for women. But the conflict, if it was a conflict, was not a question of either/or. The "balance" she hoped for involved a more complicated acknowledgment of roles. "Not only did I want to be a boy but I wanted to be a hero," she recalled. [75] In fact she had been cast as "the hero" in school plays, admiring the cross-dressed (and bisexual) Sarah Bernhardt in *L'Aiglon.* Her early lover Frances Gregg had shown her some "beautiful photographs of herself in Greek costume; she had been a boy or youth in some play." [76]

Later she dreamt that she was wearing men's evening clothes ("I had been looking at some new pictures of Marlene Dietrich") and that underneath them she wore a "long party-slip that apparently belonged to [a] ballgown. The dream ends on a note of frustration and bewilderment," [77] she reports to Freud. She associates the dream with Ezra Pound, who took her to "school-girl dances" but "danced so badly."

H.D. and Bryher had also consulted Havelock Ellis some ten years previously, and the "sage of sex" suggested that Bryher might well be a boy "escaped into the wrong body." [78] The sexual inversion theories of Ellis and Edward Carpenter's ideas about an "intermediate sex" were part of the couple's sense of who and what they might be. She and Bryher co-starred with Paul Robeson and his wife, Eslanda, in 1930 in a film called *Borderline,* directed by Bryher's husband, Kenneth McPherson, that centered on a love triangle further complicated by interracial questions. Bryher played a lesbian innkeeper with short hair and cigar, while "H.D.'s unglamorized elegance," writes one commentator, "suggests at times a feminized man." [79]

But the "bisexual" label for H.D., despite Freud's imprimatur, did not come easily or without cost.

Here are some observations about her by a scholar analyzing the cultural contributions of American and English expatriate women in the Paris of the first half of the twentieth century (I have italicized key interpretive and evaluative phrases):

> For H.D., the patriarchal and heterosexual features of Modernism constituted *a trap,* forcing her to efface the issue of her own sexual difference, which was *problematically bisexual.* All of H.D.'s writing displays an *uncertainty of sexual identity,* making the writing moment *highly traumatic* for her. The sexual identity out of which they are composed *oscillates between the heterosexual and the homosexual.* She was pulled toward *contradictory worlds*—the paternal and heterosexual world of Modernism (exemplified in her relationships with Ezra Pound and Richard Aldington) and the maternal and homosexual world of Bryher. Ultimately *she was never able to choose* between the two, and the writing moment always brought with it *this crisis of sexual identity.* Had H.D. ever been able *to resolve her own sexual ambivalence, the dual attractions of heterosexuality and homosexuality* that constantly beckoned her, perhaps the writing would have "settled" into one mode or the other. *But the choice was not to be made.*[80]

In each of these formulations, the phrases I have put in italics emphasize H.D.'s apparent failure of self-knowledge, or failure of self-acknowledgment, implicitly described as a failure of nerve. Her problem is that she can't decide which one she is, or that she resists and denies the consequences of that decision. Contrasted to her lover Bryher, characterized in the same account as a strong-minded woman who "knew from adolescence that she was lesbian,"[81] H.D. is continually said to be beset by "*confusion* about her own sexual directions and emotional attachments."[82] "Were the demands of the heterosexual norm antithetical to her creative urges to which her lesbian writing was *the real, honest alternative?*,"[83] the author asks rhetorically.

"Bisexuality" here is, as so often, described as a "confusion" and even a potential dishonesty, a "highly traumatic" oscillation, a "choice" that refuses to be made. This analysis is symptomatic of one way in which claims of bisexuality have been received and read. It is not that it is wrong about H.D., or for that matter that it is right: What is interesting from our current perspective is that the critic's anxieties and political urgencies here all come down on the side of *a* decision and *a* choice, as if bisexuality somehow represented something else. Something threatening.

We might note that a version of the phrase "dual attractions" perhaps coincidentally appears as the title of the sociological account mentioned earlier of bisexual life in the San Francisco of the eighties.[84] The glancing homonym of "dual" and "duel" with its implication of paradox or antithesis, and the idea that bisexuality involves *two* passions, not one, has contributed to the problem. Is what is needed here a kind of Hegelian synthesis, an understanding of the third place as produced by dialectical law? If every thesis elicits its own contradiction, or antithesis, can this conflict of erotic attractions produce a synthesis? Or is the contradiction in fact part of what makes bisexuality erotic, as well as unsettling?

"I had two loves separate," H.D. wrote in a poem about Freud, describing the situation he would call bisexual. Rachel DuPlessis and Susan Stanford Friedman, early pioneers of feminist H.D. scholarship, cite the phrase "two loves separate" from the poem "The Master," a poem in which the speaker instructs "the old man" (Freud) "to explain / the impossible, / which he did."

"Bisexuality" appears in their assessment as something to which H.D. becomes "reconciled": "[F]or H.D.'s lesbianism was not exclusive, neither in her life nor in her texts." They note not only her engagement to Pound and her marriage to Richard Aldington but also the male "lover-companions" who figured largely in her later life.[85] Freud "freed her to explore and acknowledge her lesbian desires," and "connected H.D.'s writer's block to her deep discomfort with her bisexuality." The "impossible" he was asked to explain—and did—was "the absoluteness and totality of her drive toward both sexes."[86] "In print," wrote Friedman and DuPlessis, "H.D. could examine her identity as a tormented heterosexual seeking nonoppressive relationships with men, the culturally approved love objects for women." They go on to say, "In private, however, H.D. explored her passion for women and its relation to her artistic identity."[87] Was the analysis, later described by H.D. in an appreciative *Tribute to Freud,* ultimately "public" or "private"?

Claire Buck, following psychoanalyst Juliet Mitchell, works from the premise that "bisexuality stands as the mark of the instability of sexuality and sexual difference."[88] Since bisexuality "is the sign that masculinity and femininity are not identities, but positions of desire to which the subject has an uncertain and shifting relationship,"[89] the example of H.D.'s life and writing offers an opportunity to explore the centrality of bisexuality to arguments for the constructedness of sexual "identity."

H.D.'s bisexual modernism is in fact sexual postmodernism. The "perfect bi" is not the Kinsey 3, poised neatly and symmetrically between straight and gay, but something, some*one,* both more complex and more elusive. In the familiar phrase from *Some Like It Hot,* uttered at the moment when Osgood learns that the "Daphne" he has proposed to is a man: "nobody's perfect."

"Queer"

How is "bisexual" related to "queer"? British critic Joseph Bristow notes that over the last twenty years bisexuality has sometimes been regarded as "too queer," and at other times "not queer enough." He himself regards the (re)appropriation of "queer" as a phenomenon of style, something he calls, disarmingly, "metrosexual"—that is, largely urban and upper middle class. This is perhaps another way of saying that it is a label of some privilege.

"QUEER IS IN! Gay and lesbian is old, tired and OUT!" declares *Ecce Queer,* a "cool, mac-ed out publication" according to one enthusiastic reader.[90] The accompanying photographs, labeled Lesbian, Gay Man, Queer Boy, and Queer Girl, offer a tongue-in-cheek typology of style and behavior. The Lesbian "disapproves of bisexuality," is "afraid of fashion," and "attends women's music festivals religiously"; her gay male counterpart "buys off the rack, but lies about it," "goes to A-list parties," "thinks 'political action' means writing a check," and "is embarrassed by Dykes on Bikes in the Pride Parade." The Queer Boy "may have actually slept with a woman," and the Queer Girl "may have actually slept with a man." Both of them are described as "totally fabulous" and "definitely having fun," even in the realm of politics, which can also "be fun." This is playfulness and self-irony—"you too can be hip, fashionable, socially and politically conscious" trumpets the text—but it underscores the degree to which bisexuality has become not only mentionable but "fashionable" in the new generation of queers.

Queer chic is now *so* chic in metrosexual circles that the "straight queer" is everywhere to be found. *GQ* sketched out a "Spectrum of Gay Positivity" that ranged from "Active in Gay Causes" (Barbra Streisand, Elizabeth Taylor) to "Appropriating Gay Characteristics" (Markie Mark, Prince), "Professing One's Own Inner Gayness" (Kurt Cobain, Sharon Stone), and "Pretending to Be Gay" (Madonna, certain college students). "Fumbling disclosures of omnisexuality" were viewed as a necessary awkward stage through which the "cultural elite" was passing—part of the price of ultimate social acceptance and assimilation, "until gay culture becomes boringly familiar to Americans, like hip-hop in the suburbs and Protestant-Catholic intermarriage."[91] This will not, it seems safe to say, happen tomorrow. But is what *GQ* dubbed the "queer-is-cool philosophy" a fashion or a sexuality? Or is there any difference?

"Queer" sounds quite different when used as a term for oneself than it does when it is shouted or sneered from the street corner. Its power as an aggressive generalization, a refusal to accept "a minoritizing logic of toleration or simple political interest-representation" in favor of a "resistance to regimes of the normal,"[92] makes the term a powerful theoretical tool for queer theorists. The word's in-your-face qualities, what lesbian playwright Holly Hughes called its "cringe factor,"[93] have contributed to its popularization, against the theoretical grain, by people, especially young people, who are adamantly not interested in "theory."

Yet as many participants in the new sexuality debates stress, "queer" has real drawbacks when specificity and representation are required. It is a postmodern label with roots in fashion and discourse, and an appealing omnipresence in early twentieth-century literary and cultural texts ("You're a queer one, Julie Jordan") that seems to validate the historical existence of "queer people" before the queer movement, and Queer Nation, took off. But despite its value as a political slogan, "queer" is not, finally and fundamentally, an easy political term. Lesbian and gay writers from Terry Castle to Eric Marcus have expressed doubts about its pertinence, since it erodes the very specificity they consider crucial.[94] "The term *queer* has lately become popular in activist and progressive academic circles in part, it seems to me, precisely because it makes it easy to enfold female homosexuality back 'into' male homosexuality and disembody the lesbian once again," writes Castle. "To the extent that 'queer theory' still seems . . . to denote primarily the study of male homosexuality, I find myself at odds with both its language and its universalizing aspirations." "Queer performativity" has its own cultural power among those who know what "performativity" means.[95] For the person in the street (or on the street corner), however, "queer" often remains, culturally and discursively speaking, a matter of style and rhetoric. It's popular with some young people and some academics, but its universalizing impulse is (designedly) at odds with its joyful claim of stigmatization. Precisely because of the ambivalently exclusive mantle of "chic," it's unlikely that "everybody's queer" will replace the cliché "everybody's bisexual" in the near future.

Cultural theorist Jonathan Dollimore thinks "queer" as a term "needs to be reworked." "I really believe," he said, "in cultural practice, that you rework, redefine, distort, play around with" political terms. "Queer could be made a really provocative category," or it could become, as in some sense it has, a "marginal, almost elitist kind of thing. Most people don't know what it means. They just know it's where the action's at. Well, if it stays like that, then it'll just die another factionary death. But it seems to me that it could be reworked, more extensively," to "pick up on 'bisexual' " and other concepts, too.

Wherever one comes out on the question of "queer" versus "lesbian and gay" or indeed "lesbian-gay-bisexual-transgender-s/m," what seems clear is that labels, like slogans, are not only visible but also territorial. They, too, create an in-group and an out-group even, or especially, when their gestures of "inclusion" are seen as preemptive.

Is bisexuality *more* "queer" than gay or lesbian identity? Or less? Is it "in the middle," "wavering,"[96] or at the extremes?

Journalist Eric Marcus describes the scene at gay and lesbian conferences, where "the angry rhetoric of the incessant internecine warfare, the flying dogma, and radical versus mainstream versus conservative political debates" often divide conference-goers. After a three-year debate about whether the Vassar College Lesbian and Gay Alumnae/i organization should add the word "bisexual" to its name he stepped down as president of the group, "exhausted from the intergenerational, cross-cultural, multiracial, bigender, polysexual" conflict—and encountered "queer" as a political label. A new debate had begun.

Marcus doesn't much like "queer," though he acknowledges its useful history and confrontational quality that make it "ideal for militant political slogans like 'We're here, we're queer, get used to it.' " But he finds "queer" overly inclusive. The very fact that it is described as encompassing "gay, lesbian, bisexual, transgender, transvestite," and other persons makes it unappealing to him.

"As a gay man, I'm not all those things," he says. "I don't want to be grouped under the all-encompassing umbrella of queer. I'm not even all that comfortable being grouped with bisexuals, let alone transsexuals, transvestites, and queer straights." He doesn't want to emphasize the "odd-ness" or "otherness" of his existence as an out gay man: "I'd rather em-phasize what I have in common with other people than focus on the differences. The last thing I want to do is institutionalize that difference by defining myself with a word and a political philosophy that set me outside the mainstream."[97]

This is a disarming personal portrait, but it raises some questions about the very inclusiveness Marcus resists. It sounds like he'd like to be in-cluded, but in the "mainstream" rather than the margins. What he "has in common with other people" doesn't seem to function the same way when he's talking about bisexuals and transgendered persons as when he's talk-ing about the "majority of gay and lesbian people" who, he believes, want to merge, as he does, with the "mainstream" (the word appears three times in his discussion).

Ultimately, for Eric Marcus as for many other gays and lesbians, the issue appears to be, at least in part, generational: "[F]or younger queers, who make up the bulk of those who consider themselves queer, being queer is a way to carve out a new path, different from the one created by an older generation of gays and lesbians." But what's especially striking to me here is that, in grouping bisexuals with ("let alone") transsexuals and transvestites, he's implicitly placing bisexuality farther outside the "mainstream" than gay and lesbian identity. By the logic of his categories, bi is not between but beyond the heterosexual-homosexual divide.

If bisexuality is in fact, as I suspect it to be, not just another sexual orienta-tion but rather a sexuality that undoes sexual orientation as a category, a sexuality that threatens and challenges the easy binarities of straight and gay, queer and "het," and even, through its biological and physiological meanings, the gender categories of male and female, then the search for the meaning of the word "bisexual" offers a different kind of lesson. Rather than naming an invisible, undernoticed minority now finding its place in the sun, "bisexual" turns out to be, like bisexuals themselves, everywhere and nowhere. There is, in short, no "really" about it. The question of whether someone was "really" straight or "really" gay misrecognizes the nature of sexuality, which is fluid, not fixed, a narrative that changes over time rather than a fixed identity, however complex. The erotic discovery of bisexuality is the fact that it reveals sexuality to be a process of growth, transformation, and surprise, not a stable and knowable state of being.

Bi Sexual Politics

Politics is the art of the possible.

—Otto von Bismarck

Politics makes strange bedfellows.

—Charles Dudley Warner

"Would coming out as bisexual be easy or hard?" The question is posed by bisexual lecturer and facilitator Robyn Ochs. The occasion is a meeting of the Harvard Bisexual, Gay and Lesbian Student Association convened to discuss bisexuality.

This is a tactic Ochs uses frequently as an icebreaker, a way of beginning a discussion. Not that the group needs to learn to talk with one another—they've been meeting on gay, lesbian, and queer topics for a number of months. But several members of the group think of themselves as bisexual, and others have strong opinions, pro and con, on the subject. Ochs is present to stir up some of those feelings and field questions and comments. She does this, year in and year out, on college campuses and in support groups across the country.

"Would coming out as bisexual be easy or hard?" The students scribble on three-by-five cards; there is a sound of pen-scratching in the room. For a moment it sounds like exam time. Then the answers are read aloud:

> Hard, because a lot of people treat bisexuality as a phase on the way to "complete" homosexuality.
> Hard, because, I'd feel trendy—aarrgh.
> Hard, because dealing with an alternative orientation is extremely difficult in this society.
> Easy, because I'm already out.
> Hard, because people would think I really was gay but could not accept it.

Hard, because I do not feel attracted to ♀.

Hard, because being bi isn't being straight, and not being straight isn't easy.

Hard, because people can't fit you into their preconceived categories.

Easy, because I would know me.

Hard, because I've never had sex with a man.

Hard, because parents and family might not understand.

<u>Easy</u> because you have more choice! (increased pool of applicants).

Easy, probably, because I have already come out as a gay man.

Easy, because straight people wouldn't see you as so different (from homos). [and, on the same card, by the same person:] Hard, because that identity is harder to define than homo.

Hard, because lots of people think bisexual people have to have lots of promiscuous sex with people of both sexes.

Hard, because (1) coming out is hard, (2) with parents—the fact that you *could* live a het life but might choose not to would make your life harder to defend to them.

Hard, because it would involve justifying myself to both the gay and straight communities. Also, my role would be even less clear than it is now. I don't know if my friends could handle it.

Hard, because it's what my father has encouraged me to do since I told him I was gay.

Easy, because I have loving, accepting, cool friends—one of whom is bisexual! (She's very cute, too!)

Hard, because neither straight nor gay communities claim to know what to do with one, or refuse to let one be individual, by wanting to claim one as either/or.

Easy, because it draws less intolerance from straights than being "gay."

As each reply is read there are chuckles of appreciation and recognition, followed by some earnest, sometimes contentious, debate. Not everyone agrees with everyone else. Certainly, not everyone in the discussion is bisexual, and many who are not consider this a relatively unimportant topic—for reasons that some of the "hard to come out as bisexual" respondents have noted on their cards. There is also some slight generational resistance to Ochs's position as discussion leader. For some of these college students, her idea of bisexuality, formed in the feminist movement and through grassroots organizing of support groups, is different from theirs, which depends more on the "gay studies" and "queer theory" movements of the late eighties and the nineties.

One measure of this, beyond the participants' ages, is the fact that the group is itself "bi-sexual," or coeducational. There are about an equal number of men and women, including, for both genders, a significant number (for Harvard) of people of color. They are passionate, articulate, disputatious, impatient, provocative, and engaged. Whatever "bisexuality" is, they find it fairly comfortable to talk about it. And this, too, marks a change.

What is, or are, "the politics of bisexuality"? Just as there is no one way to be bisexual, so there is no single "politics" for bisexuality. There is political bisexuality and resolutely apolitical bisexuality. There are bisexual politics, bisexual politicians, and the "politics of the bisexual movement," which is really in practice many "politics" within many branches of a "movement" that differs from region to region, country to country, and age group to age group. It may be useful, nonetheless, to look at some of these areas in turn, not to establish a definitive bisexual ideology (or "bideology"?), but rather to give some sense of the ways in which bisexuality again eludes convenient categorization and challenges both conventional and unconventional wisdom.

"I'm not sure that because there are people who identify as bisexual there is a bisexual identity," queer theorist Eve Kosofsky Sedgwick told an interviewer in 1991. "*If* 'bisexual' were an important classification," she said, there would be contention about whether figures like Oscar Wilde, Cole Porter, Virginia Woolf, and Eleanor Roosevelt were really bisexual or lesbian and gay. "But the gay and lesbian movement isn't interested in drawing that line."[1]

For reasons of their own, however, some participants in "the *bisexual* movement" *were* interested in drawing such a line. At stake was their own legibility, their visibility in history. Sedgwick's argument draws strength from a traditional politics of opposition: "[T]o the degree that the lesbian and gay movement says people who are bisexual aren't part of this movement, then to that degree a bisexual identity would become more distinct, more necessary, more meaningful." Her phrase, "this movement," recapitulates the gesture of inside-outside, of delimiting a space. That was in 1991. But movements move, and the omnipresence on college campuses of "lesbigay" groups, the increasing self-identification of high school and college students as "bi" rather than gay, lesbian, or even queer, suggests that the torch has been passed. "My goal," declares one longtime campus activist, "is not to appropriate historical figures *away* from lesbians and gay men, but rather, in the act of reclaiming historical figures who had bisexual lives, to rewrite ourselves *into* lesbian and gay history. If we can be proudly claimed once we're dead, we can be proudly claimed while we're alive."[2]

At about the time that Sedgwick was expressing doubts to *Outweek* about "bisexual identity," bisexual activists were planning the second National Bisexual Conference, poet June Jordan was addressing the Stanford University Bisexual, Gay and Lesbian Student Association, and campus organizations all over the country—and in other countries as well—were changing their names from "gay and lesbian" to Bisexual, Lesbian and Gay. There is now a Gay, Lesbian and Bisexual 'Ohana at the University of Hawaii, a Lesbian, Gay and Bisexual Coalition at Cornell, a Lesbian/Bisexual/Gay Alliance at St. Olaf's College in Minnesota, and a Gay/Lesbian/ Bisexual Student Organization at the University of Southern Mississippi.

Catharine Stimpson, former dean of the graduate school at Rutgers University and now an officer of the MacArthur Foundation, says her Rutgers students clearly saw themselves as part of a "bisexual 'Third Wave.'" "They're quite condescending about dividing humanity into heterosexual and homosexual," she observed.[3]

Bisexuals, notes Larry Gross, are "leading the way in [the] latest labeling campaign" among groups claiming "a distinct identity and equal billing" as sexual nonconformists. "No longer willing to be seen as occupying a halfway house in the coming out process, or as being a hybrid category occupying positions one through five on Kinsey's zero-to-six scale of sexual behaviors, women and men who insist that they are attracted to members of both sexes have claimed an independently valid identity."[4]

But it is that very identity which disrupts. Bisexuality unsettles certainties: straight, gay, lesbian. It has affinities with all of these, and is delimited by none. It is, then, an identity that is also *not* an identity, a sign of the certainty of ambiguity, the stability of instability, a category that defies and defeats categorization. What critic Elisabeth Däumer calls "the multiplicity of at times conflicting identifications generated by the bisexual point of view," an "ambiguous position *between* identities," can produce "radical discontinuities between an individual's sex acts and affectional choices, on the one hand, and her and his affirmed political identity on the other."[5] No wonder it makes sexual politicians uncomfortable.

The real question remains: Is bisexuality, even if difficult to define, cognate with the categories of gay and lesbian, insofar as it names a distinct, identifiable minority? Or is it in fact something else, a category so large that, like the proverbial large-print letters on a map, it is really too big to read? If so, what does this say about identity politics and the politics of inclusion and recognition? How can we resist lapsing back into an undifferentiated "humanism" that says "we're all the same," while perpetuating differences in tolerance, visibility, and social acceptance that compel a sense of second-class citizenship?

If bisexuality is another sexual minority, like lesbianism and gayness, or even if it is part of an umbrella category called "queer," then reclaiming role models, however dehistoricized, makes a certain sense, or does a certain kind of cultural work. As was the case with race, religion, and ethnicity, the reclaiming of bisexuals, like the congratulatory category of "firsts" (the first Catholic president of the United States, the first African American on the U.S. Supreme Court, the first female Hollywood film producer, the first Jewish member of the Yale English department), marks a certain kind of social progress.

Legislative attempts to secure civil rights protection for gays and lesbians have been uneven, as has the contestatory matter of "gays in the military"; it is far from clear that most people these days tend to think of sexual or erotic minorities as analogous to ethnic or religious minorities when it comes to representation and the law. But the "first openly lesbian president of the United States," to choose an example I would be surprised to see coming just around the corner, would certainly "make a statement," as they say in the world of style. In the world of substance, such a claimed identity would also have significant cultural consequences. But what about the "first bisexual president"? Would she, or he, have an equal impact? It depends upon how we understand bisexuality.

Bisexual Politicians

The stereotypical "bisexual politician" is the guy who gets caught. Take former congressman Robert Bauman of Maryland, for instance, a conservative father of four and a strong supporter of the Republican right wing who was revealed in 1980 to have solicited sex from male prostitutes. In 1960 Bauman had married "a woman with whom I had a great deal in common. We were both Roman Catholic. We were both very strong conservatives, politically. We were both active in the Nixon campaign. We both worked on the Hill." He and Carol "were very committed to a lot of different things and we loved each other strongly. It was just a match made in heaven."[6]

Twenty-three years later, after he pled nolo contendere to the charges of solicitation, was "exposed" in the public press, and lost his bid for reelection, Bauman was informed by the Catholic Church that his marriage had been annulled. The grounds? "Mistake of person." Since he was "homosexual" throughout the period of his marriage, though he and his wife may not have known about it, he "could not have contracted a valid marriage."[7] It was at that point, he says, that he decided to say he was gay. He began to speak out in public in favor of gay rights, a position he had previously opposed. The American Bar Association, "Good Morning America," and the "Today" show all wanted to hear from him.[8] But the Reagan and Bush administrations had no jobs for a gay ex-congressman, nor would conservative gay Republicans, of whom Bauman says there are many, identify themselves in public as part of a political action committee. "They wouldn't even write checks. They would give cash, so there was no traceable evidence."[9]

Bauman remained in Washington to live near his four children. By his own account his struggle was to come to terms with the concept of homosexuality during the many years when he was married and having sex with men. Nowhere in his self-description does the word "bisexual" appear. Not much is served by asking him to think of himself as bisexual, or even to think of the course of his life as bisexual. Not much except to redraw the lines of inclusion and exclusion—and to tell a story that makes sense of his whole life as he lived and experienced it, including his commitment to the children born of the marriage, whom he clearly does not want to write out of his story.

Another politician who has come under considerable fire for her bisexuality is National Organization for Women president Patricia Ireland. In this case the relationship with a same-sex partner was not, as in Bauman's case, a carefully guarded and initially shameful "secret" only disclosed by increasingly heedless behavior and by alcoholism. Bauman's sex partners during his marriage were often pickups. Ireland's same-sex involvement is one of long standing, and reflects a commitment to a particular individual. But because of her precarious position as the leader of a women's group already labeled "lesbian" by political opponents, Ireland became the target of critiques from both lesbians and straights, inside the women's movement and out of it.

Married since her college days to James Humble, a painter who lives in Miami, Patricia Ireland also has a relationship with a woman who lives in Washington, and who declined to identify herself because she was concerned about losing her job. "Does She Speak for Today's Women?" the *New York Times Magazine* asked pointedly, describing the fact that Ireland "has both a husband and a female companion" as one of the "confounding revelations of her personal life" that have "disturbed women across the ideological spectrum."[10]

"There's still the concept of Mom, Dad, Dick, Jane, Spot, Puff," Ireland remarked. "But there are really all kinds of arrangements people make in their lives."[11] Despite pressure put upon her by *The Advocate,* a gay and lesbian magazine, she refused to label herself as either a lesbian or a bisexual: "What I have described is who my family is, not my sexuality," she said.[12]

Ireland was particularly nettled by the suggestion that she should divest herself of her husband, who helped to support her through law school and has always shown great kindness and consideration as well as love.[13] Bisexual marriage, for Patricia Ireland, was thus doubly political: She ardently defended her right to private adult relationships, including an enduring and sustaining marriage, while sustaining hits from both the straight and the gay communities for the kinds of choices she had made. Interestingly, no one seems to have called her indecisive or irresolute, common put-downs for bisexuals in the public press. Exhortations for her to dissolve her marriage of twenty-five years were made in the name of political correctness rather than of "facing the truth" about herself. As a woman she was faulted more for making a choice, even, or especially, a choice of *two* partners, rather than for lacking the courage to choose.

If we turn from Patricia Ireland to a gender pioneer of an earlier generation, Mattachine Society founder Harry Hay, we find another intriguing mix of politics and sexuality that also led both to a marriage and a highly visible coming out. Hay, born in Britain in 1912, was twenty-six years old, and actively gay, when he courted and married Anita Platky. Like Hay, Platky was a member of the fledgling Communist Party in the United States. They met first at picket lines and demonstrations, after a therapist suggested that Hay stop looking for a "girlish boy" and start looking for a "boyish girl." Anita Platky, tall, dark, and Jewish, "once cast as an Amazon in a stage play,"[14] was attracted to Hay by their common interests in politics and the arts.

Hay told her he had had homosexual relationships but thought their marriage could work, and she wrote him expressing agreement: "Hell, darling, I do want to be with you, work with you, and live with you—start our job of building together, and I can build without attaching paramount importance to sex. I'm pretty sure I can, and you can too. . . . So many of the people getting married these days have not that mutual interest [in political activism] to use as one brick in the foundation."[15]

Perhaps predictably, given the particular category crises of the times, the religious differences between the two (Hay's family was Catholic) stirred more controversy within the family than any perceived sexual incompatibility. Hay's mother at first objected, and later urged him to buy twin beds, though he insisted on a double bed. "The marriage was physically passionate for the first several years,"[16] one chronicler notes, though Hay also began cruising in the public parks, and had a number of more extensive gay affairs during the time of his marriage.

But Communist colleagues, who frowned on homosexuality, regarded the Hays as an ideal young married couple. They adopted two children and started a Leftist nursery school. At their home in Los Angeles, near Silver Lake and Echo Park, Party meetings mixed with family gatherings. In that same house around 1950 the first meetings of the Mattachine Society, the first male homophile organization in the United States, were quietly held.

The Hays' marriage ended in 1951. At the time his wife remarked, "You certainly didn't marry me—you married the Communist Party." Many of his gay friends of the thirties had also married. As his friend James Kepner commented, "In the forties, for many gays who wanted to be socially productive, marriage was a necessity."[17] Hay himself said that he and

Anita "loved each other dearly and had a wonderful time doing anything together." He also said, "If she had been a boy, we would still probably be together."[18]

The forties were a different time, the CPUSA and the Mattachine Society were each (despite present-day animadversions to the contrary) quite different kinds of groups from the National Organization for Women, and Harry Hay, of course, was a man while Patricia Ireland is a woman. The differences between them, in short, outweigh the similarities. Yet both Hay and Ireland, committed to gender and sexuality issues, seem even more different from Robert Bauman than they do from each other.

It is instructive to look at how bisexuality appears, and disappears, in these political lives. Appears, as an experiential mode of being, part of a marriage that works over a not inconsiderable period of time, and that engages friendship and common cultural interests as well as sex and family life. Disappears, as a political concept that does not "play well" in public places, either to the right or the left. Hay, the "founder of the modern gay movement," as he is described, is also a husband and a father, a man who was married for thirteen years. Ireland, the spokeswoman for feminism at a time when so-called new feminists have begun to insist—as old feminists have done for years—that feminism belongs to all women, not just to certain groups, is to all appearances a happily married woman who is also happily paired with another woman.

Tolstoy's oft-quoted truism about families—"Happy families are all alike; every unhappy family is unhappy in its own way"[19]—was never true. Happy families are often happy in their own way, and the on-off switch of happiness and unhappiness is another one of those cultural myths that lead people to think that imperfection is the same thing as dysfunction. If we had a Kinsey scale for happiness, few people would stay at either "pure" end for long. Past "happiness," like past passion, does not evaporate without a trace. Whether that trace is material-palpable, in the form of children, friends, photographs, and memories, or whether it has merely contributed to making the present person more nuanced and realistic about himself or herself, the move to erase it, repudiate it, or "get beyond it" has its dangers. One of the key purposes of studying bisexuality is not to get people to "admit" they "are" bisexual, but rather to restore to them and the people they have loved the full, complex, and often contradictory stories of their lives.

But politicians these days are at risk if they have contradictory lives. Against both human nature and the nature of political advancement politicians have been expected to be role models, a phrase which itself highlights the double fictionality of the expectation: A role is an acted part, a model is a diagram—or a fashion plate. History forgives politicians everything once they are dead, and nothing when they are alive. Perhaps it is for that reason that the few bisexual politicians claimed as role models have been figures from the past—and especially, from the past history of women.

A number of bisexual-feminist writers have chosen anarchist and feminist Emma Goldman as a model, even though Goldman's own writings and speeches, like her relationships, were overwhelmingly heterosexual. Goldman, who married and had many male lovers, was the object of passionate feelings on the part of Almeda Sperry, a fellow anarchist worker and friend who had been a prostitute until she heard Goldman speak on the evils of white slavery. Did the two women have a sexual relationship? Biographer Alice Wexler thinks "that Sperry's sexual feelings toward Goldman were ever reciprocated seems unlikely,"[20] while Lillian Faderman concludes that "their erotic relationship was apparently culminated."[21]

Goldman's "unusual friendship"[22] with Sperry produced a number of explicit and ardent letters. Sperry's experience as a prostitute had left her with "a contempt for men"—"nearly all men try to buy love, if they don't do it by marrying they do it otherwise."[23] The one man she did show some respect for, she wrote to Emma, was, unsurprisingly, Emma's closest friend, Alexander Berkman. When she discovered she was pregnant, she said, if it were "Sash Berkman's baby" she would have it, because *"He* is a *man."* As Candice Falk notes, he was also "Emma's man." "Almeda's fantasy was to possesses the man who had possessed Emma, if she could not have Emma directly."[24]

Falk, like Faderman, thinks Goldman and Sperry did have sex together, though she hedges her bets a little: "[A]lthough it might have been Almeda's fantasy, it seems more likely that the all-encompassing Emma did in fact consummate her attraction for Almeda." Both authors cite a letter from Sperry, unfortunately undated, that declares, "if I only had courage enuf to kill myself when you reached the climax then—then I would have known happiness, for then at that moment I had complete possession of you.... I cannot escape from the rhythmic spurt of your love juice ... my dear whose succulence is sweet and who drips with honey." Whether this is "fantasy" or not, the Goldman-Sperry relationship was clearly "consummated" in their correspondence. Goldman's ongoing and deeply erotic relationship with Ben Reitman, the most important sexual figure in her life, offered both a counterpoint and a counterpoise to her involvement with Almeda Sperry. Her correspondence with Sperry, Falk notes, was "most frequent and intense when Emma's infatuation for Ben was waning," while Almeda represented "an alternative to Emma's helpless infatuation with her 'man.' "[25]

Emma Goldman may have "felt a profound ambivalence about lesbi-

anism as a lifestyle,"[26] but she was unquestionably a champion of homosexuality in principle and of Oscar Wilde in particular, calling Wilde's
prosecutors "miserable hypocrites," and enthusiastically participating in a
verbal "battle royal about inversion, perversion, and the question of sex
variation."[27]

In a letter to lifelong friend Alexander Berkman, Goldman declared that
"the Lesbians are a crazy lot. Their antagonism to the male is almost a
disease with them. I simply can't bear such narrowness."[28] The immediate
object of this critique, lesbian novelist Djuna Barnes, was in fact so unan-
tagonistic to "the male" that she had several affairs with men and might
accurately be described as bisexual. It seems possible that Goldman, in
writing to a male friend of long standing with whom she often discussed
sexual matters, is implicitly comparing her own broadmindedness to the
hypothetical lesbian "narrowness" she singles out for criticism.

In any case, while her status as a "bisexual politician" seems compromised, at best, her sexual politics were liberatory to a younger generation
of activists.[29]

A similar affection and reverence attaches to the figure of Eleanor Roosevelt. Is a First Lady a "politician"? Again, recent history says yes, although
these women are not elected to any office. Roosevelt, who disliked the
term "First Lady," was extremely politically active before, during, and after
the presidency of FDR—it was her activism and intelligence that provoked
her enemies.

"Although she was at the center of a movement of feminists and activists
during her own lifetime, Eleanor Roosevelt has only belatedly been reclaimed by contemporary feminists,"[30] notes Blanche Cook in her biography of Roosevelt. Her reclaiming by lesbians and bisexuals has taken even
longer.

Roosevelt's friendships with two lesbian couples, Esther Lape and Elizabeth Read and Nancy Cook and Marion Dickerman, developed during the
twenties. These relationships, part of a female support network that was
social and cultural as well as political, reminded Roosevelt of her years as
a student at Madame Marie Souvestre's Allenwood School—years which,
as we will later see, were to produce one of the most erotic "lesbian
novels" of this century, Dorothy Strachey Bussy's *Olivia*.

But Roosevelt's collegial friendships with these women caused much
less consternation than her passionate relationships with journalist Lorena
Hickok and with former bodyguard Earl Miller, a man thirteen years
younger than she. As Cook notes, the public record of Roosevelt's life, and
the suppression of numerous letters she exchanged with both Hickok and
Miller, amount to "a calculated denial of ER's passionate friendships."
"Women who love women, and women who love younger men have

understood for generations that it was necessary to hide their love, lest they be the targets of slander and cruelty."[31]

The case of Roosevelt and Hickok, neither of them conventionally "attractive" by the standards of the day,[32] was dismissed by "the most insulting stereotypes"[33] of repression and desperation. Yet this relationship, forged when both women were adults with a rich and nuanced understanding of Washington politics and social life, produced not only a lifelong intimacy but also some remarkable letters, not all of which have been destroyed. Each day they exchanged letters, Roosevelt's often ten or fifteen pages long.

"I wish I could lie down beside you tonight and take you in my arms," she wrote to Lorena Hickok in a letter described by Hickok's own biographer as "particularly susceptible to misinterpretation," since it seemed to express a desire that "could not mean what it appears to mean."[34] Even less susceptible to misinterpretation, and often quoted to illustrate the erotic nature of the relationship, was Hickok's letter to Roosevelt: "Only eight more days.... Most clearly I remember your eyes, with a kind of teasing smile in them, and the feeling of that soft spot just north-east of the corner of your mouth against my lips...."[35] Since Hickok herself transcribed and edited much of their correspondence, burning the originals of many of Roosevelt's letters to her and many more of her own, the record remains partial but suggestive. Cook's balanced and thoughtful biography, which focuses mainly on Roosevelt's schooling, marriage, family, friendships, and political life, not on her sexuality, was instantly famous in some quarters, and notorious in others, because it purportedly outed Roosevelt as a lesbian.

The relationship with Earl Miller, given equal weight in the book, has largely dropped from the gossip circuit, despite the fact that it was much noted and much deplored in Roosevelt's lifetime. Miller, a boxer, gymnast, swimmer, horseman, and former circus acrobat, became an intimate companion, riding, swimming, and playing music with Roosevelt as well as accompanying her to public functions. Friends criticized their easy physical familiarity with one another: his arm around her waist or shoulder, her hand on his knee. Roosevelt's son James thought they might have had an affair.[36] Her friends Nancy Cook and Marion Dickerman described in later years the rumors that Roosevelt had wanted to leave FDR after the 1932 election and marry Earl Miller.[37]

But perhaps because "frumpy older women do not have sex"[38] and relationships between older women and younger men were still publicly taboo, the place of Earl Miller in Eleanor Roosevelt's personal life has tended to be ignored or "dismissed almost without hesitation"[39] as a romantic liaison, transformed instead into suitable mother-son terms. Blanche Cook comments feelingly on "the romance of the closet" as it may have affected both the Hickok and Miller relationships: "[I]ts very secrecy lent additional sparkle to the game of hearts."[40] A relationship with a younger man, like a relationship to a smoking, drinking, poker-playing female reporter who "acted like one of the boys"[41] (but who also, as Cook notes, baked, painted her nails, wore girdles, and dieted) held the First Lady up to potential criticism or ridicule.

But the political energies that found it important to "reclaim" Eleanor Roosevelt for feminism and for lesbianism have tended to regard the romance in her life as bound up with women, not with a woman and a man. To relabel her "bisexual" in a political way may be just to reshuffle the content of the boxes. Yet to fail to take cognizance of her capacity to have loving, erotic relationships, on paper and in person, with both women and men is, once again, to underestimate her qualities, her imagination, and her remarkable will.

Third Parties

Politics is an enterprise both myopic and strabismic: It is nearsighted, and it squints. It does these things not by inadvertence or incapacity but by design, focusing on a cause and a group identity, marking a difference, a borderline, between the "in" and the "out," between "us" and "them."

Slogans, identity cards, party insignia, journals, logos, loyalty oaths—these are the impedimenta of organized politics, whether the group in question is the Republican Party, the Communist Party, or the National Gay and Lesbian Caucus. An "us" needs a "them." The more threatening "they" are, the better for "us." The "King and his Parliament," the "New Dealers," the "rich," the "Jews," "white European men," the rabble who must be taught a lesson, the rebels who must learn their place.

Feminist and bisexual Kate Millett popularized the phrase "sexual politics" in her ground-breaking book of that title first published in 1969. Her book began, tendentiously and powerfully, with close readings of erotic passages of heterosexual sodomy and compelled, violent, but titillating heterosex from novels by Henry Miller and Norman Mailer—passages which are then juxtaposed to the "scathing critique of sexual politics" in the cross-dressed, gender-, race- and class-bending plays of Jean Genet. "Unless the new rebels have truly forsworn the customary idiocy of the old sexual politics, there will be no revolution," she observes about the closing moments of *The Balcony*. "Sex is deep at the heart of our troubles," she argues, paraphrasing Genet, "and unless we eliminate the most pernicious of our systems of oppression, unless we go to the very center of the sexual politic and its sick delirium of power and violence, all our efforts at liberation will land us again in the same primordial stews."[42] If this talk of "revolution" and "liberation" has the whiff of the sixties about it, it is a nice strong scent, somewhere between teen spirit and fresh air.

For Millett, sexual politics are about power, and power differentials, although French philosopher Michel Foucault, whose name would become synonymous with both power and sexual politics for academics of the seventies, does not appear in her pages. But Millett does not lack for other authorities to cite, from Hannah Arendt and Gunnar Myrdal to psychiatrist Robert Stoller and sex researcher John Money.

Having dexterously hooked her reader with juicy passages from Miller and Mailer, the more seductive for their complete political incorrectness, Millett now proceeds, once she has our attention, to lay out her understanding of "a theory of sexual politics" that is "ideological," "biological," "sociological," "class"-based, "economic and educational," concerned with "force," "anthropological" (embracing "myth" and "religion"), and "psychological" in turn. The key word is "patriarchy," not, at that time, as overworn as it would be in subsequent years.

Millett's book is genuinely what its cover proclaims it to be, a "feminist classic" and a "landmark work." What is so noteworthy about it, given the enormous influence the very phrase "sexual politics" has had in our time, is how relatively little the book has to say about homosexuality, lesbianism, and bisexuality. She sees male homosexuality as having inherited the "glamour waning in literary accounts of heterosexuality," which used to "prosper" on the "clandestine and forbidden character" of "star-crossed lovers, adulterers, and those who transgress the boundaries of caste and class."[43] Lesbianism was, she thought, then at a stage where its existence was publicly exploited solely for the titillation of men, whether in the porn flicks of New York's Forty-second Street or in Hollywood's version of *The Fox.* "Whatever its potentiality in sexual politics, female homosexuality is currently so dead an issue that while male homosexuality gains a grudging tolerance, in women the event is observed in scorn or in silence."[44] Recall that this was 1969, the eye of the storm in the Sexual Revolution.

And what of the political prospects for bisexuality? Millett, despite her own life choices, felt that there were none. Bisexuality was a theory invoked by Freud to placate intellectual Victorian ladies who could be assured that they had "masculine" minds: "Standing on the ground of bisexuality, we had no difficulty in avoiding impoliteness. We had only to say: 'This doesn't apply to *you.* You're the exception; on this point you are more masculine than feminine.'"[45] Since "femininity is forcefully prescribed and praised as the mature resolution of the child's bisexual dilemma," Millett says witheringly, "the theory of bisexuality" does not "provide much relief to the individual."[46]

For many years, during the obligatory Freud-bashing that marked some feminist approaches to psychoanalysis, this was the prevailing view not only of Freud (condescending to the "ladies," thinking of sexuality in terms of men) but also of bisexuality as it was advanced by the Freudians: "Despite the hypothesis that we are all, to some degree, bisexual, one is made to grow anxious when males display feminine traits, just as masculine traits are unbecoming to females, evidence of penis envy. It is remarkable how Freudian prescription tends to ignore its own notion of bisexuality or to find symptoms of it as backsliding."[47]

We will have occasion a little later on to look more closely at Freud's ideas about bisexuality and how they relate to his own affections and anxieties as well as to the entire theory of psychoanalysis, of which he considered bisexuality the central tenet or the "main thing." For now, it may be useful to note Millett's disappointment as well as her irritation that "symptoms of bisexuality" could be seen not as advancing a sexual frontier but as "backsliding." It is the "infantilism" argument again. Bisexuality as she understood Freud to be describing it was presexual, therefore not political, whatever the potentiality for another kind of (sexy, disturbing, politicized) bisexuality might be.

So-called third parties in American politics may in point of fact be the fourth or fifth or tenth on the ballot; what makes them "third" is that they challenge the either/or "two-party" system, which is one of the ways we have come to define our democracy.

When a "third party" gets big or strong enough it can displace one of the original two, as the Republican Party did in 1864. (Thomas Jefferson's political party, first organized in 1792, originally called itself the Democratic-Republican Party, a fact it is convenient to forget since it complicates the modern-day sense of opposition between Democrats and Republicans.) The lesson to learn here is that nothing lasts forever, including what seem like "opposites" that define a field of inquiry or knowledge.

What is the "opposite" of bisexual? Monosexual? We have not yet reached a point, though nothing is unimaginable, at which monosexuals, hetero- and homo-, band together to stave off the advancement of bisexuals. If the standard opposition is heterosexual/homosexual, or straight/gay or queer/straight, that slash mark, that virgule, is the fulcrum on which oppositional energies depend. To replace the virgule with an ellipsis, a series of dots (heterosexual . . . homosexual), to replace the opposition with the continuum or, even more disturbingly, to print the words over one another, overlapping, is to challenge the very basis on which a "politics of sexuality" is predicated.

Politics is the art and craft of opposition; of *creating* oppositions in order to make a space, and a constituency, for change or conservation. It's overly simple to say that politics is always binary, but the *language* of politics is binary. The Confederacy versus the Union. The government versus the rebels. The left versus the right. And when a binary politics intersects with a binary notion of sexuality there is no place for bisex, no place for that which destabilizes and disrupts.

A Matter of Pride

In January 1990, organizers of the Northampton, Massachusetts, Lesbian and Gay Pride March voted to remove the word "bisexual" from the march's title, even though the word had been added, in a gesture of inclusion, only a year before. Calling the change "a statement of political affiliation—not a personal rejection of bisexual people," march organizers commented that when bisexuals are listed among the participants, "everything gets watered down and suddenly we all become 'gay people.' "[48] "Why can't you be gay for a day?" one woman asked bisexuals who attended a meeting to protest the January decision. The chief complaint of its proponents was that some lesbian speakers had been turned down the previous year for being too "exclusionary." The new march steering committee, also set up at the same January meeting, required that its members be lesbians or gay men—not bisexuals.

Northampton has been a proud women's community and a magnet for lesbians for many years, since at least the 1970s. There are bed-and-breakfasts just for women, book stores carry lesbian erotica (and one declines to stock any books by men). Guessers say one in ten of the town's thirty thousand women are lesbians, but they are a strong, and sometimes controversial, cultural presence. "It's more an issue of visibility than numbers," says the mayor.[49]

Lesbians in the Northampton area wrote the local gay press with anger and indignation to ask why bisexuals insisted on "attaching" themselves to their community. "Proponents of the inclusion," wrote the Boston gay paper *Bay Windows,* "claim the word would allow for a more diverse and accurate celebration, and that gays and lesbians are being 'biphobic' when they exclude bisexuals. They say excluding them is tantamount to heterosexuals excluding homosexuals. Opponents counter that bisexuality is a different experience [from] homosexuality, and that events such as pride marches should reflect their specifically gay and lesbian history. If bisexuals want to celebrate their differences, they say, let them do it with their own resources and organizations."[50]

"I am beginning to think some Lesbians in the Northampton area are stuck back in the middle '70s," one observer noted,[51] and it seemed clear that generational tensions between seventies women's-movement lesbians and nineties bisexuals and queers had indeed exacerbated, if not entirely caused, the contretemps. On the occasion of the march itself the remarks of lesbian speaker Sarah Dreher were interrupted by what a local newspaper called "a group of self-identified bisexuals." "You just think you should be respected because you're older," Dreher said a "gay boy" told her.[52] When Dreher's speech was reprinted in the newsletter of the Boston Bisexual Women's Network, she was described as a "respected community member and elder." The tension encompassed "queers, gay men, lesbians-who-sleep-with-men, 'lipstick lesbians,' s/m lesbians, transgendered folks," according to one activist who attended the Pride March, but bisexuals were often targeted as the "cause" of the tension. "They were easily separable from lesbians as 'other,' " since they "called themselves by a different name."[53]

The controversy, thus posed, crystallizes the tension between theory and activism. If bisexuality *is* a different experience from homosexuality, as parts of this book will suggest, does it in fact follow that the political interests of bisexuals and homosexuals diverge, or that resources and organizations should be strictly dedicated to advancing the interests of one of these groups? In other contexts, as for example with the transgender community (transvestites, transsexuals, "shemales," and others), the specific nature of each group does not preclude cooperation for common political ends like visibility, cultural recognition, and tolerance, or even— as I have suggested elsewhere—the "right to shop" without interference or disapproval.[54] Do we need to agree that bisexuality is directly analogous to homosexuality in order to argue for a common interest in marching for "pride"?

This may look from outside like a teapot tempest, but feelings ran very high on all sides, as they did on similar "name-change" occasions when the San Francisco *Bay Times* added "bisexual" to its masthead, and when the New England Associaton of Gay and Lesbian Psychologists considered adding "bisexual" to its title. On all of these occasions the protests were led by women. Why should that be?

Is "biphobia in the lesbian/gay community," as one observer claims, an "almost exclusively female phenomenon"?[55] And if so, is that because, as she thinks, "most women have some degree of choice about their sexual orientation and most men don't"—a point about which the Northampton lesbians might well choose to disagree—or is it because the feminist movement of the seventies crossed paths with emergent lesbian separatism in a way that made sexual and emotional relationships between women newly visible and attractive?

Did women become lesbians because of the women's movement? Undoubtedly some did, if by "become lesbians" we mean, experientially rather than existentially, that these women chose to live with other women and to have erotic and domestic relations with them. They chose a partner and a life. And if their choices were inflected by the temper of the times, so, it could be argued, were everyone else's, whether those choices were heterosexual, homosexual, bisexual, celibate, or promiscuous. No one falls in love in the abstract—or, at least, not for long.

Do other people ever change their sexual interests for political reasons? Of course they do. "Normative heterosexuality" is one result of such a bias, the decision to "go straight" for social comfort and economic advantage —the phenomenon that has produced the Lesbian (or Bisexual) Until Graduation—but so is the phenomenon of the "straight queer" and of bisexual or lesbian "chic." In this sense the borderline between fashion and politics is itself permeable, as Leonard Bernstein demonstrated when he hosted the party for Black Panthers that Tom Wolfe memorably dubbed "radical chic"—the parent of all subsequent "chic" coinages.

Politics is more often claimed to have influenced people's sexualities when it comes under the heading of something like "feminist solidarity" and separatism or "free love" than when it coincides with a conventional cultural practice like heterosexual monogamy.

"Free love" in the sixties—and indeed in the 'teens and twenties—was as often a doctrine as a desire. But the doctrine often became the desire, without anyone taking a conscious decision to make it so. It was part of a zeitgeist or a weltanschauung; it was "in the air"; it was a "sign of the times." *Why* you had sex didn't make it less sexual, or more (or less) sexy. As my mother counseled me (to no avail, as it turned out), "It's as easy to fall in love with a rich man as a poor one." So, too, with women who fell in love with women in part as a result of their feminist work. Why not? In women's communities formed on the basis of shared political convictions, love and sex were natural developments.

There are also many persons, female and male, who call themselves bisexual or are interested in bisexuality, who have no use at all for organized sexual politics. "The bisexual movement, as such, leaves me cold, as does much of the political gay movement," remarks radical sex activist Susie Bright, whose writings and performances have nonetheless had a strong political impact.[56] Criticized by her "lesbian elders" when she first announced her bisexuality in the seventies, she maintains: "It's straightforward enough to ask for an end to prejudice. It's preposterous to ask sexual beings to stuff ourselves into the rapidly imploding social categories of straight or gay or bi, as if we could plot our sexual behavior on a conscientious, predictable curve.

"When I was young, I was very hurt by political ringmasters who said they wouldn't talk, fuck or work with me because I was bisexual. Now that I've worked, fucked and talked with them *all,* I'm not hurt anymore, because I know their secret. They desire what they condemn."[57]

Bisexuality and Identity Politics

Turbulent, fleshy, sensual, eating, drinking and breeding,
No sentimentalist, no stander above men and women or apart from them,
No more modest than immodest.

—*Walt Whitman, "Song of Myself"*

"The frequently heard assertion that in a world of genuine equality, where men were nonoppressive and nurturing, everyone would be bisexual," declared poet Adrienne Rich, "blurs and sentimentalizes the actualities within which women have experienced sexuality."

In her classic essay "Compulsory Heterosexuality and Lesbian Existence," written in the late seventies and originally published in 1980, Rich argued with clarity and power that "heterosexuality, like motherhood, needs to be recognized and studied as a *political institution.*"[58] Countering the assumption that it was lesbianism, not heterosexuality, that needed explanation, she forcefully questioned the existence of a "mystical/ biological heterosexual inclination, a 'preference' or 'choice' that draws women toward men." Heterosexuality, she said, was a "man-made institution" that functioned for the benefit and perpetuation of "male power" and patriarchy.[59] Lesbians in history had been occluded both by "the ideology of heterosexual romance" and by a token "inclusion" (in practice a historical erasure) as "female versions of male homosexuality."[60]

To "discover the erotic in female terms: as that which is unconfined to any single part of the body or solely to the body itself,"[61] to recognize that "woman-identification is a source of energy, a potential springhead of female power, violently curtailed and wasted under the institution of heterosexuality"[62]—these were among the objectives of her argument. "Bisexuality" she therefore dismissed as mere sentimentalism, "the old liberal leap across the tasks and struggles of here and now."[63]

That was a decade and a half ago, eons in terms of young people and college generations. Bisexual feminists of a subsequent generation, for whom Rich's phrases "compulsory heterosexuality," "heterosexual privilege," and "the lesbian continuum" have been deeply influential, have sought in her work some forgiveness toward the bisexual life, some way to mitigate the damning accusations of sentimentality and soft liberalism. (It is an index of the times that "liberal" was for Adrienne Rich the manifest opposite of "radical," not, as in a post-Reagan era, of "conservative.")

Bay area bisexual activist Lani Kaahumanu wrote revealingly in 1982 of her previous contempt for bisexuals: "As far as I was concerned they were a bunch of closet cases, not deserving of serious consideration. As a lesbian, I felt superior in some ways and was embarrassed for them. How naive to take the bisexual 'stage' seriously. I was sure they would get over it and 'come out' when they let go of the very real heterosexual privilege they were obviously clinging to. Why else would anyone say they were bisexual?"[64] The "stage" or "phase" argument, as she went on to note, is a matter of semantic one-upmanship. "For most lesbians and gay men, bisexuality is a stage. And for most lesbians, bisexuals and gay men, heterosexuality is a stage."

In fact, of course, all the world's a stage, depending on where we stand to look back, or forward, at the course of our lives. "My political consciousness is lesbian, but my lifestyle is bisexual," wrote Kaahumanu. "All men are not the enemy, just as all women are not my allies."[65] Whatever Adrienne Rich might think of bisexuality and bisexuals now—and there is no reason to think that she has changed her mind—the bisexuality she scorned then was a different bisexuality, a bisexuality that focused on swinging and on opening up marital relations, with no changes in patriar-chal institutions. What, then, are the chief political objections to bisexuality today?

The accusation of "heterosexual privilege" remains, though with the rise of a bisexual movement it is less a blanket indictment than it was. Alan Sinfield, a longtime activist for gay rights issues in Britain, notes that although there is "*political* suspicion of bisexuals among lesbians and gays in the UK," things are changing. "The main recent change," he says, "is that bisexuals are considerably less likely to be seen as reluctant lesbians/gays" unwilling to come out. More difficult to set aside is the sense that bisexuality threatens identity politics, and thus undermines the hard-won gains of gay and lesbian liberation.

Concern about the emergence of an "almost puritanical radical identity politics" among gays and lesbians was expressed by Jonathan Dollimore, cofounder with Sinfield of the University of Sussex program on Sexual Dissidence. "We don't want a new hierarchy," he says, noting "those tyran-nical narratives" that claim " 'you're either one thing or another.' And if you become the other, then when you were the original thing, it was bad faith." "What I would not tolerate," he said thoughtfully and without heat, "is people who then embrace that sort of thing in the exclusionary identity politics mode, saying 'I am now gay,' " as if their whole lives before that were a lie, or didn't count. "I just don't believe that desire works like that." Dollimore has given the matter considerable thought. After many years with a male partner he is now living with a woman, and they recently had a child. Some of the students who flocked to Sussex to study gay culture with him responded with anxiety. "They fought for this identity, they've gone through the trauma of coming out." "I think some of them have felt a sort of betrayal," he said. "They felt let down in some obscure way they can't voice." "I had attracted these students from all over the place to come and work with me as a gay man only to 'cease to be gay' in their eyes." Would he describe himself as bisexual? "At some level we all want to be free of labels and identities," he said. "But that is a luxury. I might call myself a gay person or a bisexual." He is working, he says, "to dislodge the complacencies and the prejudice of other people, and to make visible new forms of sexuality, new forms of desire."

Michèle Barrett, a feminist and professor of sociology at the City Univer-sity, London, suggests that many elements in society and culture today are "so homophobic that in a sense one can forgive an identified gay commu-nity anything in response to that homophobia," but she also notes, regret-fully, that "some of the people who have made sexual politics their life or their work are remarkably coercive in how they relate to people about it." "The policing comes from the straight pro-family lobby," she said, "but I do find distressing the extent to which in contemporary politics the gay lobby, and within recent memory the radical feminist lobby, has taken up a very didactic and judgmental attitude toward people and relationships."

Rather than liberating, some gay liberation rhetoric had become confining, "part and parcel of the desire to corral everybody into boxes."

Biphobia, says Amanda Udis-Kessler, a frequent participant in U.S. bisexual debates, is a "crisis of meaning," based in part on the perceived conflict between a constructionist understanding of sexuality (an understanding that sees sexual categories not as unchanging essences but as fluid positions that alter and develop in response to cultural and epistemological factors) and the insistent realities of oppression and prejudice. Demonstrating in their lives and histories the fact that sexuality is a narrative, not a fixed label, bisexuals threaten the establishment of interest groups based upon "identity" in the narrowest, most essential sense. "People who base their claims to social rights on the basis of a group identity will not appreciate being told that that identity is just a social construct,"[66] observed one critic dryly. Another shrewdly encapsulated the fear that "once we have deconstructed identity" there will be nothing "stable and secure upon which to base a politics."[67] "Lesbians and gay men," says Udis-Kessler, "protective of the essentialist view of sexuality, equate the fluidity and apparent choice-making of bisexuality with that of constructionism and feel a tremor in the structure underlying their lives and identities."[68]

Bisexuality means that your sexual identity may not be fixed in the womb, or at age two, or five. Bisexuality means you may not know all about yourself at any given time. "How does one reify fluidity? How does one make a category of the potential to have either kind of relationship?" Amanda Udis-Kessler accurately notes the mental machinations by which either/or became both/and: "[T]he lore which developed described bisexuals as people who could not be satisfied with either sex, but who had to be involved with both, usually at the same time."[69]

The next step was the stereotype of the bisexual as swinger, the promiscuous, dangerous, nonmonogamous transgressor of boundaries. And, at the same time, as if it were not a logical contradiction, the idea of the bisexual as a fence-sitter, unwilling to commit to either side, rather than a person who walked comfortably through an open gate from one "side" to another. The fence as a boundary and a sign of property ("Keep Out!," "Stay Inside," or "Don't Stray") came to mark the landscape of sexual categories. "Fence-sitter" became yet another disparaging label. But who built the fences? On the open range fences exist because there are *no* natural boundaries. What they signify is not existential difference but the property difference between "mine" and "yours"—or us and them.

Bisexual activists in the nineties have sought to make common cause with Adrienne Rich, or with her voice for feminism.[70] They see the "bi movement" as the successor to the "gay and lesbian movement," which was the successor to seventies feminism, which was in turn derived in part from the strategies, organizing tactics, and moral fervor of the civil rights movement of the sixties. They don't, most of them, think that "everyone is bisexual," or that the "world of genuine equality" so ardently and bitterly put in question by Rich is any closer to realization, or likely to be soon. But the two strands of bisexual thinking, the identity-politics, rights-based arguments for visibility on the one hand and the theoretical, deconstructive, category-questioning arguments for rethinking erotic boundaries on the other are not always easily combined.

Despite resistance—and in some cases rejection—from some gay and lesbian groups (not to mention heterosexuals), bisexuals have been organizing rapidly. The *International Directory of Bisexual Groups* lists hundreds of organizations, networks, clubs, 'zines, and support groups in more than a dozen countries, from Australia, Canada, Costa Rica, and El Salvador to Russia, Sweden, the United Kingdom, and Zimbabwe, as well as in forty-four of the fifty states.

In Britain, theorists have engaged the radical discontinuities of present-day sexual separatism and advocacy as they reflect upon the language in which we talk about sexualities. The use of "same-sex" and "opposite sex," instead of "homosexual" (or gay or lesbian) and "heterosexual," not only avoids historical anomaly when talking about the past but also allows for the articulation of a bisexual presence. What do you call a married man who is having an affair with another man? If you call him "gay," you supply a label that may not meet the specifics of the case. You also erase bisexuality. He becomes either "gay" or "straight." Such binary language will not offer a space for bisexuality because it declines to take temporality into consideration: Bisexuality, as I have suggested, is not an "identity" (or a figure or a trope) but a narrative, a story. Yet the practical necessities of politics require *making* bisexuality into an "identity," at the same time that bisexuality itself, or bisexualities themselves, put in question the viability of a "politics of identity" at all. The result, again in practical terms, has been considerable infighting among gays and lesbians on the one hand and bisexuals on the other, the very existence of which ironically underscores the fact that these secure identities and divisions are already on the way out. To acknowledge this is not to accept defeat but to recognize success.

Politics is always belated. Political movements that think they mark the space of the new are often overtaken by others that render their novelty, urgency, or timeliness both dated and suspect. When these movements pride themselves on their dissidence, they are most likely to be blindsided and indignant. Thus the fulminations of some segments of the Old Left (which preferred to think of itself merely as the Left) at the depredations of the New Left. As some vestiges of the Old Left made a sharp right turn into neoconservatism, the New Left found itself under attack—from the left—by feminists and people of color. This is not idiosyncratic; it is how political change takes place. "I know when I'm being out-lefted," commented cultural critic Gerald Graff cheerfully when challenged by a feminist critique. Is it better to be out-lefted, or left out?

Bisexuality and Human Freedom

> He has told me he likes men as well as he likes women, which seems only natural, he says, since he is the offspring of two sexes as well as two races. No one is surprised he is biracial; why should they be surprised he is bisexual? This is an explanation I have never heard and cannot entirely grasp; it seems too logical for my brain.
>
> —*Alice Walker,* Possessing the Secret of Joy[71]

"I am black and I am female and I am a mother and I am bisexual and I am a nationalist and I am an antinationalist. And I mean to be fully and freely all that I am!" With these words poet June Jordan addressed a gathering of bisexual, gay, and lesbian students in 1991. She was putting it —and herself—on the line.

"Bisexuality invalidates either/or formulation," she declared. "Bisexuality means I am free and I am as likely to want and to love a woman as I am likely to want and to love a man, and what about that? Isn't that what freedom implies? . . . If you are free, you are not predictable and not controllable. To my mind, that is the keenly positive, politicizing significance of bisexual affirmation."[72]

Jordan, who teaches at Berkeley, told her audience at the Stanford University Bisexual, Gay and Lesbian Student Association that she had been asked to address two different Berkeley campus rallies on succeeding days —the first, against racism; the second, for bisexual, lesbian, and gay rights. Four to five hundred people came out to protest against the evils of racism. Fewer than seventy-five turned up the next day to support sexual rights. "There should have been just one rally," she says. "One rally: Freedom is indivisible."

"I need to speak on bisexuality," Jordan insists. "I do believe that the analogy is interracial or multiracial identity. I do believe that the analogy for bisexuality is a multicultural, multiethnic, multiracial world view. Bisexuality follows from such a perspective and leads to it, as well."[73]

June Jordan's claim that the analogy to bisexuality was "interracial or multiracial identity" can be usefully compared to British bisexual activist Jo Eadie's citation of "miscegenation" and "hybridity" as models for a sexual politics of bisexuality. "Miscegenation," literally a sexual relation or marriage between persons of different races, has been offered as a deliberately provocative metaphor for political practice by American feminist Donna Haraway.[74] "Hybridity," originally the breeding of plants or animals of different varieties, species, or races, has been utilized by critic Homi K. Bhabha to describe ways of complicating "cultural differentiation" by introducing "a disturbing questioning of the images and presence of authority."[75] In a practical sense, what both of these terms do is to challenge the merely oppositional us/them terms in which political debate is often framed. In suggesting a model for breaching the boundary, they put the boundaries themselves in question, forming new entities that displace or coexist with old ones.

One of the critiques of "binary thinking" has been that one of the two terms is always hierarchically superior to the other, as in the pairs male/female, black/white, straight/gay. Even in the case of a deliberate, carnivalized reversal of received hierarchies (the claim that black is better than white; female is better than male; gay is better than straight), what develops is often a rigidifying of the boundary. It is clearly a choice of either/or, not both/and. "Bisexual," like "miscegenate" and "hybrid," moves the debate and the issue elsewhere, beyond a conservatizing fantasy of purity,[76] whether that purity is racial, national, gendered, sexual, or erotic. These last two, it is important to insist, are not always the same.

What, then, is a bisexual politics?

First, bear in mind that biphobia is modeled on, and a direct by-product of, homophobia—not just heterosexism, the assumed centrality of opposite-sex partnerships in human relations, but homophobia, a hatred and fear and ignorance manifested against lesbians and gay men. There would be no "biphobia" against a (presumed) minority within a minority unless that minority, the gay and lesbian community, were oppressed by hostile and fearful heterosexuals often overly anxious or overly complacent about their own sexual identities. When homophobia comes to an end, by any combined process of legal remedy, moral regeneration, and social education, biphobia will be easy—by comparison—to eradicate. The primary problem here, let us not forget, is unthinking prejudice against gays, lesbians, *and* bisexuals from people who think they have the right (they often say God gave it to them) to pontificate on matters of human desire.

Second, let us dismiss, as the courts are now beginning to do, the "comfort factor" issue, the claim that has been made, for example, by some in the military that having homosexuals around makes heterosexuals "uncomfortable." This argument, as has often been pointed out, is the same one that was used to maintain segregated armed forces (until blacks were urgently needed for combat), single-sex service academies, and other bastions of separatism that have subsequently been integrated without the world coming to an end. "Because they make me uncomfortable" is not a good reason to justify exclusion. It isn't a good reason for whites and men, and it isn't a good reason for heterosexuals *or* for separatist lesbians and gay men. Once more, the analogy is far from exact: Lesbians who have been oppressed and reviled for years have very good reason to want a "safe space" free from oppression. The hope here, if a somewhat utopian one still, is that the opposite of oppression need not be, or remain, separatism. Bisexual lesbians say they seek inclusion, not a takeover of lesbian communities.

Third, a bisexual politics is in a certain sense neither "sexual" nor a politics. It is about eroticism, which in many of its most powerful manifestations, today and over time, has been determinedly politically *un*correct, depending on scenarios of inequality, power, denial, demand, and desire. Neither love nor lust is politically correct except in a state that regulates (and regulates out) all human choice. Susie Bright is right when she says it's "preposterous" to think that people can assort themselves into "the rapidly imploding social categories of straight or gay or bi, as if we could plot our sexual behavior on a conscientious, predictable curve." And June Jordan is right to say "if you are free, you are not predictable and not controllable," and to claim that "that is the keenly positive, politicized significance of bisexual affirmation."

A bisexual politics, then, is a model for understanding the overlap between political action and sexual desire. For as bisexuality, by its very "existence," unsettles ideas about priority, singularity, truthfulness, and identity, it provides a crucial paradigm—in a time when our culture is preoccupied with gender and sexuality—for thinking differently about human freedom.

Chapter 3

Fatal Attractions

V******s should be pulled out of their coffins and exposed to the light of day but, we repeat but, only by duly authorized personnel wearing rubber gloves, mouth-guards and dental dams, in case of accidental contact.

—*Anna Livia, "Minimax"* [1]

When Paul Verhoeven's 1992 film *Basic Instinct,* in which an ice-pick wielding Catherine Tramell played by Sharon Stone is depicted as a "bisexual serial-murder suspect," [2] was being filmed in San Francisco, activists disrupted the filming. Across the country protesters picketed the film, shouting "Catherine did it" at moviegoers waiting to enter the theaters. In fact, "Catherine Did It!"—exclamation point and all—became the name of the Queer Nation committee formed to protest the film's "homophobia and misogyny." In retaliation, some decried the protest as repressive political correctness: "[P]erhaps the only safe way to portray a psycho killer is as a white, heterosexual American male." [3] Director Verhoeven acknowledged that "a lot of stars didn't want to consider [the part of Catherine] because it was about a bisexual killer," [4] but he maintained, in a bromide that did not endear him to objectors, "I would argue that we are *all* probably born bisexual." [5]

Was *Basic Instinct* "bad for bisexuals"? the *New York Times* described it as "about a detective whose search for the killer of a rock star leads him to a female suspect who is bisexual," while "the plot also involves a lesbian murderer and another female character who may be a lesbian and a killer." [6] The executive director of the Gay and Lesbian Alliance Against Defamation deplored the fact that it "made lesbians and bisexual women threatening murderers [while] the victim is a straight white man." [7] But the gay and lesbian *Advocate* characteristically focused on the film's lesbianism rather than its bisexuality. Calling it "a bad straight movie," the *Advocate*'s critic noted that "every woman in *Basic Instinct* has killed someone; and the trigger for these murderous impulses is clearly identified as lesbian sex." [8] *Commonweal* responded that "the accusation by some gay groups that this movie contributes to homophobia is a canard. Sharon Stone's character is bisexual, but her lesbianism isn't an expression of her suspected murderousness but of her power," described as "the license that wealth, brains, and looks bestow." What made the movie titillating was "the feeling that this woman can and may do *anything.*"[9] Does "anything" include "anything that moves"?

The bisexual magazine *Anything That Moves* came in for a political sideswipe from *The Progressive,* which deplored the way "identity politics" in the *Basic Instinct* protests dispensed with the notion of representation by insisting that only members of a given group could "accurately and unproblematically represent the needs, desires, or experiences" of that group. Citing *ATM*'s own protest in its statement of purpose, "We are tired of being analyzed, defined, and represented by people other than ourselves," *The Progressive* decried this "typical statement" of a view that could only eventuate in "old-fashioned American individualism: Every identity is an island."[10]

Other critiques of the Queer Nation and ACT UP protests were less measured: "How should society respond to unstable and destabilizing groups like this? They have some justice on their side, but they distort and debase our already tattered politics by respecting nobody's rights but their own. . . . Apparently, because of AIDS, none of these values is allowed to count at all."[11]

But how bi was *Basic Instinct?* Two of its woman characters, Catherine, played by Stone, and psychotherapist Beth Garner, played by Jeanne Tripplehorn, have had relationships with both men and women (with the same man, Mike Douglas's detective Nick Curran, and, as it ultimately develops, with each other). Stone's sex scenes are genuinely sexy, enhanced by the perception of danger (the ice pick) and the danger of perception (lesbian lover Roxy's voyeurism). Bisexual triangles abound —Nick-Roxy-Catherine, Nick-Catherine-Beth—as does mimetic desire: "There was this girl I met in college. I slept with her once, she started following me around, copying my clothes, she dyed her hair. . . . It was awful," Catherine tells Nick about the person he will soon identify as Beth. As for Roxy, who is later revealed as a juvenile murderess, "She wanted to watch all the time. . . . She got excited." Nick, no liberal, sneeringly calls her "Rocky," while Catherine shrewdly finds the fantasy behind his contempt: "Would you like her to join us sometime?" Some critics noticed that all the sex scenes were in fact heterosex: "[T]o Verhoeven, a movie in which bisexual women have sex only with men was, if anything, more prurient"[12] because it *was* a male fantasy.

Did the film suggest that bisexuals were amoral, murderous, obsessive —or just sexy and desirable? Different people had different views. Was it pro-sex, pro-powerful woman, or antilesbian and antibi?

Read allegorically rather than mimetically, though, *Basic Instinct* suggests another kind of fantasy: a cultural fantasy that makes interpretative sense of the expedient logic that brought AIDS activists and rights protesters together to challenge it. For buried not too deep beneath its surface, obscured by the fact that its bisexual protagonists were women rather than men, was the familiar story of the bisexual AIDS carrier, the secret, duplicitous, and "passing" sexual outlaw who was the erotic scapegoat of the eighties.

The film is drenched with blood, blood that spills all over the rich bedsheets of the victimized male rock star and later spatters the overweight, sexually wistful cop who ogles Stone and falls victim to Tripplehorn. Tripplehorn herself is protected by a rubber raincoat: The blood gets on him, not on her. Read: latex. Read: condom. Read: danger to the unprotected. The AIDS threat of the film is doubled, as in a bad dream: not only the sexual contact but the ice pick, usually understood as blatantly phallic, readily seen here as a big needle puncturing Stone's unlucky bedmates. Even though the cops confiscate the murder weapon, she has a steady supply. The tangled sexual histories of the protagonists fit in here, too; it's not only the *noir* thriller technique, where everyone has a past that catches up with him (or her), but also the scariest fact of AIDS transmission: "[W]hen a person has sex," U.S. Secretary of Health and Human Services Otis Bowen somberly declared in 1987, "they're not just having it with that partner, they're having it with everybody that partner has had it with for the past ten years."[13] Sex with Catherine leads back to sex with Beth which leads back to Catherine having sex with Beth which leads back to: death. To murder. To murder by bisexuality.

AIDS and the Stealth Bisexual

When Martin Weinberg, Colin Williams, and Douglas Pryor, the researchers of a major study on bisexuality in San Francisco, did their initial fieldwork in 1983, they "did not foresee . . . a development that had tremendous implications for research on sexual preference: the emergence of AIDS."[14] Once they began to understand the magnitude of the crisis, they realized that "large-scale changes in society—disease, death, and additional stigma—could affect sexual preference." They returned to San Francisco in 1988 and interviewed many of their original subjects again.

The specter of the "bisexual AIDS carrier" had become a major demon in the AIDS story by the late 1980s. "The potential role of bisexuals in heterosexual transmission of AIDS has been gravely underestimated," announced the *Atlantic Monthly* in 1987[15] under the provocative subhead, "Bisexual: Is He or Isn't He?" Bisexuals, said *Newsweek* the same year, were becoming the "ultimate pariahs of the AIDS crisis."[16] The emblem of a dangerous and immoral duplicity, a "homosexual *posing* as a heterosexual," the bisexual became, as one analyst reflected, "the epidemic's new *bête noire* . . . a creature of uncontrollable impulses . . . whose activities are invariably covert."[17]

"AIDS Specter for Women: The Bisexual Man," read a headline on the front page of the *New York Times* in 1987, introducing a dramatic article that described bisexuals as "often secret and complex men" who cannot admit their homosexual activities, even—sometimes—to themselves. "The figure of the male bisexual, cloaked in myth and his own secretiveness, has become the bogeyman of the later 1980s, casting a chill on past sexual encounters and prospective ones."[18] The scare words are already in place: specter, bogeyman, not only mythic but "cloaked in myth," lurking on every psychic and erotic street corner to ambush the unsuspecting.

The stereotype of the cheating bisexual husband, "unwilling or unable to control his dangerous double love life,"[19] becomes a natural and inevitable scapegoat for the transmission of AIDS to an "innocent" and unsuspecting population. *Cosmopolitan,* warning its readers about "The Risky Business of Bisexual Love," presented a checklist of clues to help in detecting a bisexual man: "If a man's eyes follow other men, be very cautious." "Be suspicious if he seems intensely interested in how other men dress." "If he looks into another man's eyes for even a microsecond longer than it takes to make socially acceptable eye contact, beware. Heterosexual men do not do it."

The article went on to warn against "men in certain careers," such as the "narcissistic businesses" of "theatre, fashion, the beauty industry, art and design, and fitness. Many bisexuals are also attracted to the helping professions: medicine, social work, counseling." Jobs that involved travel or cash tips, handy for eliminating "clues about their philandering,"[20] were also suspect.

"Wives who know their husbands are bisexual can at least take steps to protect themselves from venereal diseases," *Cosmopolitan* counseled. "Wives who don't know are in mortal danger. More women have contracted the AIDS virus from bisexuals than in any other way," the magazine added darkly, "except sharing needles or having sex with IV drug users." This statistic, no longer true, was regularly used as a way of underscoring the "risky business" of having anything to do with bisexual men. "It is astonishing that so few bisexual men are found out," claims *Cosmo,* "because in general they are highly sexed and often promiscuous. Research shows they have more sex with their wives than the average heterosexual —and more sex with men than the average homosexual!" The exclamation point, like the exclamation, is *Cosmo*'s own.

"Bisexuals Put Women at Risk, Studies Say," declared the *Boston Globe* in 1990 over an article that began "Male bisexuals are posing a measurable risk of AIDS to hundreds of thousands of American women." Although some of those at risk were "female intravenous drug users," most, according to the article, were "heterosexual women" (as if the two female at-risk categories did not overlap). Thus both "bad" women and "good" women, but especially "good" (that is, heterosexual, non-drug-using) women were vulnerable to the AIDS virus through contacts they thought were safe. Moreover, they "might find it impossible to detect their risk, since men who are bisexual . . . may not admit their involvement."[21] It was the era of the stealth bisexual.

When the social scientists conducting the San Francisco study returned to that city in 1988, they found a bisexual community changed in a number of ways—older, more monogamously inclined, strengthened as well as threatened by the presence of mortality in their minds and lives. "AIDS made me look at the real emptiness I experienced having anonymous sex," said one respondent (a woman). A man said: "Commitment and monogamy—the desire for a committed relationship—have gained greater credibility for me because of maturity and aging. And I'm scared of AIDS."[22] Two-thirds of those interviewed on this second go-round had taken the HIV antibody test; 17 percent of the men and 6 percent of the women tested positive. Many retained nonmonogamy as a *value* but were not practicing it, and not only because of AIDS; open relationships, many found, were difficult to sustain or manage. Others, though, had moved in the opposite direction, toward rather than away from openness. Declaring one's bisexuality was even more problematic than it had been, given the "growing belief that bisexuals were carriers of HIV." "The bi male is scapegoated as the door for AIDS into the heterosexual community," one bisexual man commented.[23] "Lesbians, as a result of the AIDS crisis, are more frightened of anyone who touches sperm," said a woman. "They see me as a potential disease spreader."[24]

The researchers had expected a shift in sexual practices, away from "high-risk" behaviors like anal intercourse and toward "safe" practices like masturbation. While they did find that "Jack-and-Jill-off" masturbation parties had replaced swingers' events in some social contexts, masturbation rates did not in fact increase, according to those interviewed. What seemed to be happening was a turn away from sexuality altogether. "Gone was the hedonistic flavor of the early 80s when sex was celebrated and explored." "Instead of a symbol for freedom, unfettered sexuality became associated with death."[25]

Other things had changed, too; the Bisexual Center that had been the focus of the interviewers' research had closed. Its leaders felt that AIDS-related political and social work was more important than what Weinberg, Williams, and Pryor call "propounding the bisexual lifestyle." "As the culture of sexual experimentation in San Francisco receded, the ideological basis for bisexuality virtually disappeared," the researchers remark, leaving open the question of what particular ideology they have in mind.[26] In place of the Center they found the Bay Area Bisexual Network, which had become the focal point for information and organizing in the area, as well as the publisher of *Anything That Moves.*

"Bisexuals don't spread AIDS; unsafe sex spreads AIDS," is the response of bisexual activists to the negative publicity surrounding bisexuality and HIV infection. Ironically, the "invisibility" issue so crucial to bisexuals (the fact that they tend to "disappear" as an identifiable category, reassigned as either "gay" or "straight") was addressed in media terms by the AIDS crisis. Now bisexuals were indeed "visible" in the news. "Finally, 'bisexual' is a word that exists," said one woman, and another noted, "It's a negative not positive visibility." "We wanted recognition. We got it, but suddenly it's like we're lepers," a bisexual man observed. Others, however, drew unexpected strength from the publicity. "Most of the stuff coming out of the media about bisexuality is negative. It makes me feel it's more important than ever to come out about being 'bi.' "[27]

What happened to the "bisexual label" among those interviewed in the Weinberg study? More than one-third of those who had called themselves "bisexual" in 1983 questioned that self-identification in 1988. Some felt more accurately described as gay or lesbian, others "felt they lacked the social skills or the opportunity to develop relationships with both sexes" or thought their "bisexuality was a 'staging ground,' a middle or transitional period,"[28] one now saw herself as heterosexual, and several rejected labeling altogether. "Being around the Bi Center there was a lot of emphasis on labeling. Since leaving, these labels aren't important to me," one explained, while another declared, "The sexual label was a box. It just seemed like there's a set of assumptions about how bi persons are supposed to be."[29]

While the researchers had begun their book with the view that for "the majority of bisexuals" in their sample homosexuality was "added on" to heterosexuality, they seemed to prefer the image of the "anchor" to that of the box. "Once heterosexuals and homosexuals had lifted the anchor of an exclusive sexual preference and experienced sex with both men and women, subsequent changes became easier for them," they assert in their introduction.[30] Changes like "multiple relationships" and "nonmonogamy." But after the new data provided by the second set of interviews, the same researchers offered a speculative shrug of the shoulders about their subjects' "bisexual identity": "[W]ho can say how these people will see themselves in another five years—given that the label 'bisexual' seems to have less of an 'anchoring' effect than those denoting an exclusive sexual preference."[31]

Even as an object of study, then, "bisexuality" proved evanescent, fleeting, hard to pin down, the "scientific" inquiry revealed to be heavily dependent upon the "social" factors. If self-identification was the criterion, what happened when people no longer identified with the category and there was no Center to join? And if an "exclusive sexual preference" was seen as an "anchor," was that a sociological, political, cultural, physiological, or erotic fact of life? Could "nonexclusive" or "inclusive" ever have an "anchoring" effect?

Fluid Exchanges: The Bisexual Vampire

"Continued high-risk behavior among male bisexuals in the AIDS era is believed to reflect their sexual isolation, low social visibility, and limited access to health promotion efforts," noted a 1991 study of bisexuality and

HIV/AIDS around the globe. "They are marginalized, and hence cut off from both mainstream heterosexual and targeted homosexual AIDS prevention campaigns."[32] In reports on bisexuality in places as diverse as Latin America, New Zealand, the Netherlands, Indonesia, India, and sub-Saharan Africa, researchers concluded that "bisexual men throughout the world" who "continue to contract HIV and transmit it to their partners" may "face far more stigmatization and receive far less support from society in general, and from their own social circles, than homosexual men do."[33]

As so often happens, the problem in these cross-cultural studies was in part one of definition, a problem made more difficult by the shifting definitions of bisexuality itself. In Thailand, physical and sexual contact between males and females is much more proscribed than that between members of the same sex. Male Thai bar workers who had sex with both men and women but prefer women think of themselves as heterosexual, not bisexual.[34] In Latin America, "the distinction between active and passive roles" in both sexual intercourse and gender performance "is in fact more important throughout the region than are the medical or scientific definitions of homosexuality, heterosexuality, and bisexuality."[35] Adolescent bisexuality, situational bisexuality, and ritual bisexuality are found in various parts of Africa, from the Yorubas and Hausas of Nigeria to the Azande custom of "marriage with boys" reported some years ago by British anthropologist E. E. Evans-Pritchard.[36] "One should realize," said a report on bisexuality in the Netherlands, "that most bisexual behavior will occur without being labeled as bisexual."[37]

Even to scientists and health-care professionals dedicated to containing the spread of AIDS, and not concerned with moral finger-pointing or blame, the problem posed by bisexuals was that they were everywhere, in every land and culture, but often invisible even to themselves. Given their undetectable ubiquity, it was perhaps inevitable that bisexuals would assume a mythic identity in popular culture.

The "bisexual AIDS carrier" as a secret double agent was a primary villain of the eighties, even more heinous than the out gay man with AIDS, because he (or even sometimes she) could "pass" as straight—and thus pass on the deadly virus to an unsuspecting victim. In popular culture this figure emerged, insistently, in the guise of an overmastering erotic attraction: not aversively, as an identifiable person with AIDS, but covertly, as the era's favorite erotic double agent, the vampire.

"Like Tiresias, the vampire has looked at sex from both sides," observes one critic. "It seems that the vampire is sexually capable of everything." "The bisexuality of the vampire is not only monstrously strange, it is also a very human impulse—an impulse that . . . the vampire has made astonishingly literal."[38] Instead of dying, the bisexual vampire brings death —deliciously masked in pleasure.

◆

The first popular vampire novel in English was *The Vampyr: A Tale,* published in 1819 by Byron's doctor J. W. Polidori, who modeled his hero on the bisexual poet who "felt himself, by his very nature, an anomaly in his own society."[39] "Perverted sexuality,"[40] "suddenly sexual women,"[41] "covert misogyny"[42] are among the more familiar descriptions of Bram Stoker's *Dracula,* about whom one critic remarked with certainty, "The prevailing emotion of the novel is a screaming horror of female sexuality."[43] The vampires of our century have been variously portrayed as devouring women with dangerous heterosexual appetites, homoerotic males, vampire lesbians in masked or unabashedly frank and desiring forms, Jews,[44] racial "others,"[45] and, most recently, bisexuals. They have, in short, insistently incarnated the fears and desires of the times.

The figure of the vampire translates Victorian sexologists' theories of sexual "inversion" into another curious version of normative heterosexuality, by insisting that to want a male must be a feminine desire and to want a woman a masculine desire: As Christopher Craft deftly notes, "the body, quite simply, is mistaken."[46] Sexual inversion "understands homoerotic desire as misplaced heterosexuality"[47] and the vampire story both eroticizes and demonizes these endangered boundaries. In *Dracula,* "the Count's sexuality is double."[48] Freud's friend, the psychoanalyst Ernest Jones, observed that "in the vampire superstition proper the simple idea of the vital fluid being withdrawn through an exhausting love embrace is complicated by more perverse forms of sexuality."[49] But as another commentator remarks, "in *Dracula* women have all the wet dreams."[50]

The mythic creation of female monsters passionately driven by desire who penetrate with their elongated fangs, and disquieting passive and voluptuous male monsters who nurse, feeding their victims with their blood, demonstrates, claims Craft, "the homoeroticism latent in the vampiric threat,"[51] while the classic way of killing a vampire, driving a stake through the heart, is a mode of "phallic correction"[52] that restores powerful penetrative maleness to its proper, order-giving place.

Vampires have also been popularly claimed as lesbian territory. Works like Coleridge's poem "Christabel" and mythic figures from Lilith to Lamia are read as "foremothers of today's female vampire," while a new cult of admiration surrounds Le Fanu's 1871 story "Carmilla," "the most famous and influential lesbian vampire story."[53] Numerous "lesbian vampire novels"[54] appeared in the first half of the twentieth century. Explicit lesbian vampire films, appearing at least as early as *Dracula's Daughter* (1936), became increasingly popular B-flicks in the late sixties and early seventies, the "Golden Age of lesbian vampire movies."[55] Susan Sontag saw the plot of Ingmar Bergman's *Persona* (1965) as the agonized relationship of two women "rendered mythically as vampirism."[56]

"Boy, does Hollywood love those lesbian vampires," commented Vito Russo.[57] But if Russo, a gay man, was becoming weary of lesbian vampires, lesbian readers and audiences were not. Bonnie Zimmerman appreciatively described the attractiveness of lesbianism in contrast with "abnormal, ineffectual" heterosexuality in *Daughters of Darkness,*[58] noted the recurrence of the "distinguished," "glamorous and dangerous vampire" in lesbian fiction,[59] and suggested a connection between the popularity of the lesbian vampire film and the ambivalent response to the feminist movement in the seventies. "Since feminism was not yet perceived as a fundamental threat," Zimmerman argued, "men could enjoy the sexual thrill provided by images of lesbian vampires stealing women and sometimes destroying men in the process."[60] In a campier vein, Charles Busch's *Vampire Lesbians of Sodom* played for five years and 2,024 performances, becoming the longest-running Off-Broadway play in history.[61] It was even suggested that the historical Dracula was a woman.[62]

Where once the "vampire" was an allegorization of unnatural female power in otherwise "normal"-seeming women (domineering schoolmistresses and dominating rich bitches prominent among them) she was now naturalized into a dramatic character, her vampire qualities detectable on the surface, and thus in a way deprived of the power of her secret transgression. "The lesbian has become literalized in contemporary vampire films,"[63] noted critic Sue-Ellen Case. Furthermore, a "proliferation of the undead" had recently begun to replace the lone vampire. "The undead overrun things, proliferate wildly, are like contamination, pollution, a virus, disease—AIDS. Not AIDS as just any disease, but AIDS as it is used socially as a metaphor for same-sex desire among men, AIDS as a construction that signifies the plague of their sexuality."[64] For Case, this meant once again the displacement of the lesbian, "since same-sex desire appears as gay male."

There remained the question of whether vampires were "really" lesbian or just sexually indiscriminate: The editor of a 1993 anthology of lesbian vampire stories wondered "how to distinguish between a lesbian or bisexual vampire and a vampire that simply does not differentiate between male and female prey."[65] But a "lesbian or bisexual vampire" now seemed to have become a positive role model, and questions of the gender and sexuality of the author as well as of the reading or viewing public were part of the discussion.[66] Countess Elizabeth Bathory, allegedly the real model for Bram Stoker's Dracula, is likewise described as being "lesbian or bisexual."[67] The countess, it seems, liked to dress like a man when she carried on her vampiric activities, and had an influential Aunt Klara who was also "a well-known bisexual and lesbian."[68] Is there a difference between "lesbian *or* bisexual" and "lesbian *and* bisexual" (or even "bisexual and lesbian")?

It is interesting to find "bisexual" tucked in here as if it were an acceptable and unproblematic extension of "lesbian." For the erotic and political purposes of the "lesbian vampire" industry, bisexuality is sometimes—though not always—affirmatively queer. The 1970 French film *Le Frisson des Vampires* included a dominant bisexual vampire mistress in leather and chains. In the 1986 *Mark of Lilith,* made in Britain, "Lilia, a white bisexual vampire, meets up with a black lesbian researcher whose perspectives jolt her out of a blindness caused by patriarchy."[69] Even vampire women who seem to have been created largely for the delectation of male audiences can be subversively turned: Consider the fan-cults that have grown up around Theresa Russell in *Black Widow* or even Sharon Stone in *Basic Instinct.* There are lesbian separatist vampires, and bisexual lesbian vampires: The dangerous borderline being protected against in these claims of identity is straight male voyeurism, not bi- or ambisexuality.

"Do you prefer men, is that it? Is it because women are weaker, smaller, and too quickly drained?" an eager female victim demands of Kerry, the titular "Vampire" in Pat Califia's story of that name, set in a leather bar. "As far as I know, James was your last . . . shall we say, completely satisfying experience. . . . Or could it be that you would rather drink your life from a woman . . . yet you refuse to let yourself have me because you would enjoy it too much?"[70] "Be careful. Are you really sure you want some of my blood?" replies Kerry. In the story's context this is a question of love: "When passion returned, she was careful not to bite the other's lips or tongue."[71] This is safe sex among the vampires. "It is only when they become indifferent or vengeful that the undead make their victims like themselves, immortal predators and thus useless and untouchable."[72]

Califia's 1988 book of erotic fiction, *Macho Sluts* (in which "The Vampire" appears) ends with "A Note on Lesbians, AIDS, and Safer Sex" that advises readers in the use of gloves, sex toys, and dental dams. "Many lesbians believe that diseases are only brought into our community by bisexual women," she observes with regret. "Since sex with men is stigmatized in the lesbian community . . . you are likely to get false information. . . . You can try to protect yourself against disease by segregating your sex life, so that you have no intimate contact with bisexual women, IV drug users, recently reformed heterosexual women who are now exclusively lesbian, and any other 'high risk' group. This has the potential to polarize us, and make some women scapegoats."[73]

"We may already be seeing a 'vampirization' of high-risk groups for the disease," noted one observer, citing a heterosexual who told the *New York Times Magazine* that the safe-sex message seemed to be to avoid "intermingling." "People are saying you should sleep only with your own kind."[74]

With bisexuals this advice is particularly useless: Are they a "kind"? What kind of a "kind"? The "kinds" envisaged here may be heterosexuals, homosexuals, intravenous drug users. If the vampire myth is about insiders and outsiders, endogamous and exogamous sexual relations, even, as has been argued, about the threat of interracial sex, then its timeliness and ubiquity today sort with current fears, and current desires.[75] The stigmatization of the bisexual as secretly the "other kind" rather than "your own kind"—the drama of the stealth bisexual—is what makes the

AIDS carrier–vampire connection particularly egregious and pertinent to bisexuality. In the typology of demons from Satan to Dracula it is "passing" that poses the problem: the handsome Satan, the romantic Dracula, the bisexual gay man.

Some of the most visible screen vampires in the 1990s have been male: Gary Oldman in Francis Ford Coppola's film *Bram Stoker's Dracula,* Tom Cruise and Antonio Banderas in Neil Jordan's film of Anne Rice's *Interview with the Vampire.* "Bloodsucking could find its way into the standard foreplay repertoire," observed one of Banderas's fans appreciatively.[76] "In *Nosferatu,*" said Coppola, "Murnau saw the connection between the vampire's diseased blood and plague; people today may see, as we did, the connection with AIDS."[77]

In fact, of course, they have already done so. Yet the very ubiquity of the AIDS connection, Neil Jordan felt, inhibited the screenwriters for *Interview.* "One of the problems the film has had in being made is that they've all tried to treat the book as a metaphor for gay sexuality," he said. Banderas, who had starred as a gay man in Pedro Almodovar's brilliant *Law of Desire* and been featured in a number of the director's other sexually adventurous films, also appeared as Tom Hanks's gay lover in *Philadelphia.*

When asked about the bisexual nature of her vampire immortals, author Rice, who writes "enthusiastic hard-core pornography" under another name, responded, "The imagination is bisexual. . . . Once you're 'out of nature,' to use Yeats's phrase, you see all people as beautiful and you make a bond to people of your own sex as easily as to people of the opposite sex."[78] Although the "eroticism of this story" attracted Jordan, whose *The Crying Game* had its "secret" transvestite heroine, he stressed the fact that *Interview*'s erotic appeal was "not specific"—by which he seemed to mean not specifically gay. "It's about the most bizarre objects of desire, really, isn't it?" As for the blood-lust theme, he saw it as "one of those all-embracing metaphors that mean a lot and a little at the same time."[79]

"Blood is the primary metaphor," said Coppola about his Dracula tale. The dangerous but life-restoring transfusions performed by Dr. Van Helsing, the "blood exchange" that Stoker and Anne Rice both insist are necessary to the making of a new vampire, and the dangerous eroticism of Dracula's thirst for blood in the film all insistently make the point. "Dracula snatches the bloody razor from Harker's hand, and licks it clean with a delicate sweep across his tongue (that Harker doesn't see). He savors it erotically," instructs the screenplay.[80] When the Three Brides begin to make love to Jonathan Harker, the "Middle Bride's mouth and tongue come into frame. She licks and caresses Harker's nipple. Suddenly her white teeth bite his tit. His blood spurts into her red lips like a water fountain." Harker reacts "in ecstasy and pain," and as all three begin to kiss him Dracula enters, furious: "How dare you touch him! When I have forbidden it—This man belongs to me!"[81]

"This man belongs to me!" It is not, directly, a claim made in the name of erotic desire. But the borderline between unlawful lusts is breached by the vampire. This is why *vampire* has come to denote not an identity but a historical progression of stigmatized identities; not a fixed place but a threshold. Indeed the threshold is the very sign of vampire transgression, the line of mortal defense. The claim to possess the vampire is always staked in the wrong place.

What is "covert" or "displaced" in *Dracula,* written in the 1890s, is open in Anne Rice's enormously popular vampire novels published a century later. Before he became a vampire, Rice's Lestat, a young French aristocrat, had had casual sex with women and a passionate intellectual and sexual "conversation" with a young man, Nicolas, whom he later converts to vampirism with disastrous results. After his initiations into the pleasures of vampiric feeding he becomes strongly drawn to the rival vampire leader, Armand. In both literary and cinematic guises, as Rice's Lestat or Tom Cruise's, the vampire Lestat is sexy, winning, and appealingly vulnerable for an immortal. Is Lestat "a bisexual"? Or is he "a vampire that simply does not differentiate between male and female prey"? The fundamental category of difference for vampires is not male/female but mortal/vampire, or living/undead.

"Where Rice excels is in evoking the elusive nature of vampiric sexuality," said the *Houston Post* of her *Vampire Chronicles.*[82] But if vampire desire is elusive, it is also inclusive. In the course of a single volume Lestat has "luscious," "irresistible," "exquisite"[83] encounters with his vampire master, Magnus, who seduces him; with Magnus's elderly manservant; with a young man; with a young woman and her infant; and with his mother, Gabrielle, whom he deliberately transforms into a vampire to keep her from dying. "She was flesh and blood and mother and lover and all things beneath the cruel pressure of my fingers and my lips, everything I had ever desired. . . . We were lovers kissing."[84] Incest in vampiric conquest is just another seductive borderline waiting to be crossed.

Once fully transformed to vampire status, Lestat's mother kills a young man and dresses in his clothes: "[T]o describe it more truly, she became the boy."[85] Is Gabrielle "a bisexual" in the older psychological sense, half-male, half-female? Surely the point is here once again not sexual "identity" but allegorical meaning: The vampire story becomes, at different historical moments, a powerful vehicle for telling another kind of story.

Nor are Rice's vampires alone in their erotic variety. The vampire Miriam in *The Hunger,* played by Catherine Deneuve in the 1983 film (director Tony Scott's first picture), takes Sarah Roberts for her vampire lover after previous partner John Blaylock begins to show the sudden signs of vampire age.[86] Scott artfully packs his cast with vampire overkill. Blaylock, played by sometime-bisexual David Bowie (a preternaturally pale performer, one of whose avatars was "the Thin White Duke"), had to age three hundred years in the course of the film, while Susan Sarandon, cast in the part of Sarah, had earlier fallen prey to the seductions of bisexual Transylvanian hearthrob Tim Curry in the *Rocky Horror Picture Show.*

It is characteristic of the stake particular audiences have in the vampire that, we are told, "a debate has been generated within lesbian circles as to the 'authenticity' of the sex between Deneuve and Sarandon."[87] This doesn't mean, as it first seems that it might, the question of whether the two actually had sex together before the cameras, but rather whether a body double was used in place of Deneuve to film the sex scenes with Sarandon, "a rumor which is often told with considerable disappointment." Deneuve became a lesbian cult figure, and the "100% lesbian" *Deneuve* magazine, "hot and informative . . . a must have!"[88] is today available on newsstands and through catalogs. The quest for "authenticity" in the sex scene may be doomed to failure, but the idea of a "body double" is entirely apt for the vampire figure. Is anyone really there? Who is it we make love with when we make love?

When I say that vampire "identity" is not fixed but (literally as well as figuratively) fluid, I do not mean that lesbian vampires or vampiric sexualized women or gay male vampires have not existed in literature and culture. Vampires, arguably, are everywhere where there are sexual borderlines. But often when the name "vampire" is *not* spoken, when the fangs are not visible and the vampire goes, allegorically speaking, under cover, the power of the figure is much greater. To know that you are entering a world of vampires is to be forewarned. For that reason among others, perhaps the most powerful bisexual vampire film of recent years has been neither *Bram Stoker's Dracula* nor Anne Rice's *Interview* but Cyril Collard's *Savage Nights,* which won four César awards for its handsome young French director three days after he died of AIDS.

The film's protagonist, Jean, has two lovers, Samy, a soccer-playing skinhead who leaves his girlfriend for the handsome, sexy Jean, and Laura, a young girl who bears, perhaps not coincidentally, the name of Petrarch's elusive lady, the classic and prototypical female "beloved." *Savage Nights,* described as the "story of a bisexual film maker who falls for a teen-age actress and has unsafe sex with her without disclosing that he is infected with the AIDS virus," was viewed by millions in France and many more around the world, and became not only a cult film but a subject of furious controversy. Sales of the semiautobiographical novel based on the film grew to almost half a million copies. "With Cyril Collard, AIDS was no longer a question of poetry, hygiene and morality, but of desire and love," announced a front-page article in *Le Monde.* "He conveyed something new—that life with AIDS is still life."[89]

Collard himself began to be discussed in uncannily familiar terms: "Jean, played by Mr. Collard, *looks strong and healthy* [in the film]. And Mr. Collard *has even survived his own death* to become the icon for what is known as the Collard generation." But the "romantic aura" that surrounded him was *"punctured"* by "a report that a young woman whom he is said to have infected with the AIDS virus has died."[90]

Overnight, opinion about Collard began to change. The dead woman's mother thanked the essayist Françoise Giroud, who had made the episode public. "I feel relieved of a heavy secret that I promised my daughter I would never reveal," she said. "It is very serious to portray a mortal act as a hymn to love," declared France's health minister, Philippe Douse Blazy. *Le Monde* deplored the "necrophilic industry" that had promoted the Collard cult after his death, while others pointed out that Collard was himself becoming yet another scapegoat in the quest to find someone or something to blame for AIDS. "He was young, he was handsome, he loved life, but he sowed death," one French writer said.[91]

Collard's seductive on-screen power, palpable as his film continued to circulate through theaters in the months and years after his death, sent a complicated message. He *was* the bisexual vampire, demonized and desired, living and dead, incredibly attractive to men and to women in the film—and in the movie theater. Romane Bohringer, Collard's female costar, tried to lay the controversy to rest by denying him any special status: "He was just a living person, of flesh and bones, that's all," she said. "There are no guilty parties. There are only victims."[92]

Chapter 4

No Scandal in Bohemia

The great artists of the world are never Puritans, and seldom even ordinarily respectable.

—H. L. Mencken, Prejudices[1]

It is not surprising to find bisexuality alive and well in artists' colonies and aesthetic subcultures. In Bohemia and the avant-garde, the standard expectation for artists, writers, and cultural innovators has been a style of living that flouted convention, especially sexual convention. From Bloomsbury to Taos, from Harlem to Hollywood, from Berlin to Paris to Greenwich Village, bisexuality has left its mark on twentieth-century literature, painting, poetry, drama, and music, as well as on that indefinable thing called "culture." What is surprising, and indeed symptomatic, is the degree to which these bisexual lives have been described as everything *but* bisexual: as gay or lesbian, as "experimental," as transgressive for the sake of transgression rather than as the consequence of sexual attraction or desire. Once again invisibility is produced as a startling by-product of omnipresence.

Bloomsbury: "Such Plural Affections"

A sign of the way bisexuality is and is not treated in discussions of Bloomsbury sex life is the curious fact that the index of a modern book on the relationship of Virginia Woolf and Vita Sackville-West has one entry under "lesbianism" that says "and marriage," and another entry under "marriage" that says "*see also* lesbianism," but no entry under "bisexuality."

Yet if any "lifestyle" should be said to typify the lives of the Bloomsberries, it is in fact bisexuality. Woolf and Sackville-West were married women who had sex with women. Harold Nicolson had affairs with men throughout his married life. The painter Duncan Grant was the lover of economist John Maynard Keynes for more than six years, then had an affair with Virginia Woolf's brother Adrian, and spent much of the remainder of his life in a ménage à trois with Woolf's artist sister Vanessa Bell and the writer David Garnett. (Garnett ultimately married Duncan and Vanessa's daughter Angelica.) Keynes himself, as we will note in more detail shortly, was an active and enthusiastic homosexual who was considered by his Bloomsbury friends to be "married"[2] to Grant before his own heterosexual marriage to ballerina Lydia Lopokova. Katherine Mansfield, who married John Middleton Murry, was also bisexual, as was the artist Dora Carrington, known simply as Carrington.

Even Lytton Strachey, arguably the most gay, least bi (and most unimaginably straight) member of the Bloomsbury group, once proposed to Virginia Stephen (who would later marry Leonard Woolf), and lived much of his life with Carrington, who had fallen deeply in love with him. For a while Strachey and Carrington shared a house with Ralph Partridge, whom she subsequently married, and with whom Lytton in turn fell in love (although Ralph was "completely heterosexual," his second wife reports, so that Lytton had to realize that sex with him was a "no go").[3]

One of the most notorious anecdotes of Lytton Strachey's highly quotable life is the story of his appearance before the Hampstead Tribunal to claim exemption from forced military service on the grounds of health and conscience. Suffering from hemorrhoids, he arrived at the Tribunal carrying a small plaid traveling rug and an inflatable air cushion which he promptly blew up and sat upon, covering his knees carefully with the rug. "Tell me, Mr. Strachey," the military interrogator asked, "what would you do if you saw a German soldier attempting to rape your sister?"

Several of his sisters were in the gallery. Strachey briefly turned to look at them, consideringly, and then faced the board to give his answer. "I should try to come between them," he said.[4]

This droll reply, carrying with it all the force of conviction, did not entirely amuse his questioners, though Strachey was ultimately excused from service on medical grounds. As a story about his penchant for triangulation, however, it is perfect. Trying to come between them became, not only for Strachey but also for many of his Bloomsbury associates, a surprisingly satisfying aspect of sexual and social life. The triad, the triangle, the threesome, and the companionable, almost incestuous, recycling of friends into lovers and spouses into confidants is a characteristic of the life shared by many of these "loving friends."[5]

What Vita Sackville-West had characterized as "the most civilized, because the least natural, class of society," and "the more educated and liberal classes" were indeed taking steps, in their private and not-so-private lives, toward the goals she predicted: "the general admission of normal but illicit relations" and "possibly even the reconstruction of marriage." That these cheerfully "unnatural" and deeply loyal friends and colleagues were, on the one hand, delighted to épater les bourgeois and, on the other, seriously committed to the reconstruction of other verities, including the principles of twentieth-century art, fiction, philosophy, mathematics, and economics, makes them all the more appropriate as inadvertent social pioneers. Nothing could have bored them more, or more excited their derision, than the notion of being politically correct.

"How I hate being a girl!" the blond, attractive Carrington wrote to the painter Mark Gertler, one of her first suitors, early in their relationship.[6] Her "boyish figure" had led Lytton Strachey impulsively to embrace her on a country walk; the embrace, far from attracting her, had led Carrington to plot a practical joke in revenge, stealing to his bedside with a pair of scissors to cut off his full and flowing beard. But when he awakened and looked into her eyes, she—unaccountably—fell "violently in love with him," and remained so for the rest of her life.[7]

The odd pair seem to have had a brief and unsuccessful physical relationship,[8] but the life they shared was structured around a series of triangular relations: first Strachey, Carrington, and Gertler, who adored, desired, and briefly slept with Carrington, but whom Strachey found more attractive than Carrington did—"a state of affairs," as Michael Holroyd notes, "that really satisfied no one."[9] Then Strachey, Carrington, and Partridge. "The more deeply in love with her Partridge became, the more Strachey became attracted to him," writes her biographer. "The three fell into a comfortable relationship," and at the Carrington-Strachey Mill House at Tidmarsh "Ralph shared Carrington's bed."[10] The longer the relationship endured, the less comfortable it became. Partridge pressed her to marry him, and she did so, finally, because she feared that her love for Strachey was becoming burdensome to him. She wrote Strachey a painful letter, and he replied the same day that reaffirming his "love for you, even though it is not what you desire, may yet make our relationship a blessing to you. . . . You and Ralph and our life at Tidmarsh are what I care for most in the world." In a tone somewhat reminiscent of the Nicolsons', he addressed the nature of their bond. "You seemed in your letter to suggest that my love for you has diminished as time has gone on: that is not so. I am sure it has increased. It is true that the first excitement, which I always (and I suppose most people) have at the beginning of an affair, has gone off; but something much deeper has grown up instead."[11] "Oh Lytton how difficult things are. I wish I hadn't such plural affections," she wrote to him.[12]

Almost ten years earlier Strachey had considered a marriage of convenience as a way of solving his perpetual financial difficulties. At the time, Lady Ottoline Morrell had helpfully suggested Ethel Sands, a rich lesbian with an exquisite house in Chelsea, as a likely partner.[13] At one point he proposed marriage to Virginia Stephen, realizing the moment that he did so that the whole idea was repugnant to him. ("As I did it, I saw it would be death if she accepted me. . . . I was in terror lest she should kiss me.")[14]

Virginia accepted, but immediately thought better of it. "I managed," he noted with relief, "to get out of it before the end of the conversation." On the next day Virginia "declared that she was not in love with me, and I observed finally that I would not marry her. So things have simply reverted."[15] (By virtually the same post, as it happened, Leonard Woolf was writing to Lytton to announce his own intention to propose to Virginia.) It was some six years later that Lytton first encountered Carrington, at a house party assembled by Virginia's sister Vanessa Bell, and inspired the passion that would last a lifetime.

As Carrington's marriage to Ralph Partridge became complicated first by her affair with his friend Gerald Brenan, then by a lesbian relationship with the American Henrietta Bingham, the beautiful and popular daughter of the ambassador to the Court of St. James's, it became clear that Lytton —likewise engaged with a string of lovers, his unvaryingly male—was permanently bound to her, as she to him.

Carrington wrote to her friend Alix Strachey, Lytton's sister-in-law (and herself bisexual), that she was "much more taken with H. [Henrietta] than I have been with anyone for a long time. I feel now regrets at being such a blasted fool in the past, to stifle so many lusts I had in my youth, for various females." To her lover Gerald Brenan, who was not pleased to receive the confidence, Carrington reflected that "I had more ecstasy with her and no feeling of shame afterwards. I think Henrietta, although she gave me nothing else, gave me a clue to my character. Probably if one was completely Sapphic it would be much easier. I wouldn't be interested in men at all, and wouldn't have these conflicts."[16]

As for Henrietta Bingham, she herself was equally attractive to and attracted by men and women. Bingham had come to Europe in 1921 with her instructor, mentor, and lover, Mina Kirstein, a Smith College English instructor who was the sister of the bisexual ballet impresario Lincoln Kirstein. The two women presented themselves to Freud's friend Ernest Jones for analysis, as he informed Freud with evident pleasure: "An actively homosexual girl came to be analyzed in December. . . . Now her feminine partner who lives with her has come also. They are both well educated and highly intelligent persons . . . so you may imagine that the analytic work is especially interesting."[17] The young John Houseman fell in love with Henrietta and she took him to bed, an occasion he later remembered with "a mixture of embarrassment and pleasure";[18] the ever-helpful Jones was ready with advice for the young suitor on both the sexual techniques and the birth control methods he should use.[19] Mina Kirstein returned to Smith and shortly married, but Henrietta remained for a while in England, enjoying herself. "Although she sometimes had affairs with men," Gerald Brenan reported of his rival, "she was mainly a Lesbian." Later, after her return to Kentucky, Henrietta settled into a long and contented relationship with the tennis champion Helen Hull Jacobs. ("I don't believe I've ever seen Henrietta so settled and happy," her brother Barry wrote to their father, the Judge, in 1935. "She has been leading a wonderfully healthy life, playing tennis and riding every day.")[20]

At the time of their affair, however, Henrietta Bingham described herself accurately to Carrington: "my passions don't last long, but..."[21] Gerald Brenan also noted that "Henrietta changed her lovers often."[22] When the two women first met, Bingham was involved with the sculptor Stephen Tomlin, a friend of Lytton's and Carrington's, a fact which did not prevent her from beginning a relationship with Carrington, while Carrington herself continued to sleep periodically with Brenan. Brenan at first lent them his room in London for their meetings, but gradually grew jealous at the sexual competition. "What I did not then know was that Carrington was basically a Lesbian too and that her affair with Henrietta would affect her physical relations with me.... I would pay dearly for her having met the American girl."[23] "Basically a Lesbian" to him must have meant "hav[ing] more ecstasy," as Carrington impolitically told him, since Brenan was also well aware that this "was the only Lesbian affair" of Carrington's life.[24]

Yet whomever they slept with, or fell passionately in love with, or day-dreamed about, Carrington and Lytton Strachey remained somehow dependent upon each other. Two days before his death at the house they had once shared with Ralph Partridge at Ham Spray, Hungerford, Strachey called out for her, saying, "Carrington, why isn't she here? I want her. Darling Carrington, I love her. I always wanted to marry Carrington and never did."[25] Whatever the truth of this remark, it was for her an extraordinary final gift, one she duly recorded in her commonplace book. A few weeks after Strachey's death from cancer at the age of fifty-one, Carrington, then only thirty-two, committed suicide.

But these are extravagant people, it will be objected—artists, writers, snobs, incestuously involved with one another, and, it might be claimed, irresponsible and self-indulgent. It is characteristic of artists, and of persons who regard themselves as artists, to lead untidy and unconventional lives. What do the foibles of the little world of Bloomsbury have to do with the "realities" of bisexuality and marriage?

Let us consider the situation of another member of the Bloomsbury group who became a public figure of a different order: the economist John Maynard Keynes. In his early forties, Keynes married the ballerina Lydia Lopokova. It was a highly successful marriage, for all that it alarmed and disconcerted some of his Bloomsbury friends—notably Lytton Strachey and Virginia Woolf.

Prior to this attachment, however, Keynes was as well known among his friends for his homosexual affairs—with Duncan Grant, with Sebastian Sprott, and with several other young men, "as well as a certain amount of casual sex"[26]—as he was for his financial acumen and economic wizardry.

A recent biographer, Robert Skidelsky, notes that his precedessor Sir Roy Harrod left out any mention of Keynes's homosexuality in writing of his subject's life, while others took cognizance of it to bolster theories of more widespread instability: "Sir William Rees-Mogg argued that Keynes's rejection of 'general rules,' which his homosexuality reinforced, led him to reject 'the gold standard which provided an automatic control of monetary inflation,' " while political scientist David Marquand offered the opinion that "the 'homosexual culture' in which Keynes lived his early life explained his ambivalent attitude to authority," leading him to hold "outsider values" and "outsider loyalties."[27] A lone footnote in J. C. Gilbert's 1982 study of Keynes and monetary economics pointedly left the issue unresolved, declaring that "whether Keynes's bisexuality is of much relevance is at present an open question."[28]

What is less of an open question is that Keynes *was* bisexual, that he had and enjoyed a robust sexual life with men—and what Bloomsbury referred to as "marriage" with at least two of them—before he met and married Lopokova. "Marriage" in Bloomsbury terms meant "going steady."[29] "You're married to Adrian [Stephen] now, which you weren't before," the young economist wrote to Duncan Grant in December 1910. "I'm feeling very wretched and don't know what I ought to do."[30] The affair with Grant broke up in 1911, and after a few years of relative unattachment and casual affairs Keynes took up with Sebastian Sprott, a Cambridge undergraduate, in October 1920; Bloomsbury soon considered them to be "married."[31] Sprott, like many university-educated homosexuals of the time, was largely attracted to young men of the working class. He explored the boy-bars of Berlin, hired ex-prisoners as domestic help, and later changed his name from Sebastian to Jack, delivering a lecture late in his life on his friendship with the public hangman. But Keynes had different tastes. He was interested in artists rather than in artisans. And he was also, somewhat surprisingly (at least to his old friends), becoming interested in women.

He had had a few flirtations with women—in 1917 and in 1920. In December 1921 he was still very much coupled with Sprott, and the two men spent Christmas at Tidmarsh with Lytton Strachey. But Keynes had in the meantime fallen in love with Lydia Lopokova. "I'm entangled—a dreadful business—and barely fit to speak to," he wrote to Lytton on December 27. Vanessa Bell, to whom he was close (and who was now living with Keynes's former lover Duncan Grant), cautioned him against marrying her, expressing the view that "she'd be a very expensive wife" and "is altogether to be preferred as a mistress." Keynes replied, "You needn't be afraid of marriage, but the affair is very serious."[32] Indeed it was. Keynes canceled his scheduled posting to India. Although Lydia was still officially married to someone else, Bloomsbury took note, with surprise and alarm, of this newest development. "Maynard," as he was known to them, was still seeing Sebastian Sprott. "Maynard is rather mysterious,"

Lytton Strachey wrote to Sprott. "I've only talked to him vaguely (and not very lately) about his states of mind, but I didn't at all gather that he likes you less. I think your Janus-diagnosis is the right one. . . ."[33]

Janus is the patron of doorways and of the month of January; he looks both backward and forward. As we will see later in contemporary novelist Paul Monette's ruminations on "the Janus-face of bi" in his own sexual life, this image suggests a dual identity, perhaps even, to follow the figure literally, a two-faced one, though none of Keynes's friends seem to have accused him of settling for heterosexual respectability in his choice of a new love. Duncan Grant wrote to Vanessa Bell, "As for Maynard, until I see him carrying on with L. I must give up trying to imagine what happens —it beggars my fancy." But as Keynes's biographer points out, this is less a critique of his choice of a woman (a common enough crossover in Bloomsbury) than of his choosing this particular woman.[34] A married ballerina was not, per se, a safe choice, nor was Lopokova a Bloomsbury blue-stocking. In fact, Vanessa, Virginia Woolf, and others were considerably less than hospitable to the two lovers, regarding Lydia as an intrusion on their previous intimacy with "Maynard," and hoping that the affair would end without what Vanessa called "real marriage."[35]

Taos and Santa Fe: "How Untamed and Wild We Are"

The social and artistic milieu of Taos and Santa Fe in the late twenties and thirties can be said to rival Bloomsbury for the unconventionality and incestuousness of its sexual and social arrangements.

Consider the case of one celebrated sometime resident, D. H. Lawrence, whose life and writings intersect with both the literary elite of Bloomsbury and the new artists' colony presided over by wealthy patroness Mabel Dodge Luhan ("the Ottoline of the Golden West")[36] in northern New Mexico. In 1920, two years before he arrived in Taos with his wife, Frieda von Richthofen, Lawrence had published *Women in Love,* a novel in which he disclosed, through the autobiographical character of Rupert Birkin, his "dream . . . of a kind of triangular marriage."[37] Birkin—whom Lawrence's old friend Richard Aldington claimed "could never be mistaken for anyone but Lawrence"[38]—earnestly announces to his friend Gerald Crich that "because the relation between man and woman is made the supreme and exclusive relationship, that's where all the tightness and meanness and insufficiency comes in."

> "You've got to take down the love-and-marriage ideal from its pedestal. We want something broader. I believe in the *additional* perfect relationship between man and man—additional to marriage."
>
> "I can never see how they can be the same," said Gerald.
>
> "Not the same—but equally important, equally creative, equally sacred, if you like."

"I know," said Gerald, "you believe in something like that. Only I can't *feel* it, you see." He put his hand on Birkin's arm, with a sort of deprecating affection. And he smiled triumphantly.[39]

When Gerald dies at the novel's end, Birkin remarks somberly to his wife, Ursula, "he should have loved me. I offered him."

"Aren't I enough for you?" she asked.

"No," he said. "You are enough for me, as far as a woman is concerned. You are all women to me. But I wanted a man friend, as eternal as you and I are eternal."

"It's an obstinacy, a theory, a perversity," she tells him. "You can't have two kinds of love. Why should you?"

"It seems as if I can't," he said. "Yet I wanted it."

"You can't have it, because it's false, impossible," she said.

"I don't believe it," he answered."[40]

In these, the final lines of a novel titled *Women in Love,* Lawrence's protagonist declares his faith in the "two kinds of love" as neither "theory" nor "perversity" but necessity and practice. Aldington, himself bisexual and at one time married to the bisexual poet H.D., noted that Birkin "has all Lawrence's hankering for a 'colony of friends' and for some mystic-sensual relationship with a male friend."[41]

"How did Lawrence deal with his longings for a strong male bond?" biographer Brenda Maddox asks rhetorically, adding, "he was not homosexual in any accepted meaning of the term. But he was troubled much of his life by yearnings for manly love which his marriage, against his hopes, failed to dispel."[42] Maddox takes a "male plus female" view of Lawrence's eroticism. "Lawrence was not, like Forster, a suppressed homosexual who did not have the courage of his desires. He is not so easily categorized. Rather, he was a hypersensitive man unable to bring together the male and female components of his personality, and in the grip of a terror of losing the boundaries of self."[43] The book's dust jacket copy alludes more directly to Lawrence's "plaintive search for a bisexual lover." But among the biography's many references to Lawrence's "homosexual longings," taste for heterosexual sodomy, and that "dream of a triangular marriage, in which his partnership with his wife would be supplemented by the close friendship with a man, a blood brother,"[44] the concept of bisexuality is only allusively invoked.

Maddox regards Birkin's desire for a man as well as a woman in his life as a sign of a desire "less homosexual than infantile"—a desire to "incorporate a father": "[Y]ou can have two kinds of love—when you are a child," she suggests. Yet she notes Lawrence's continuing interest in "male lovers of men" and his quest for what Maurice Magnus described, in a letter to Norman Douglas, as "bisexual types *for himself.*"[45]

At Taos, Lawrence spent much of his time with Clarence Thompson, a "tall, fair and haughty" Harvard drop-out with a theatrical taste in clothes; Mabel Luhan, for one, assumed that their relationship was sexual.[46] Later, in France, he would strike up a similar close friendship with the young Welsh writer Rhys Davies. His friends and critics were divided as to whether he was, or was not, "homosexual."[47] But what lies behind the question? Is it a matter of wanting to know whether Lawrence, often described as "preachy" on the topic of erotic liberty, really practiced what he preached?

In the high altitudes of Taos and Sante Fe bisexual love was often, and exhilaratingly, in the air. Painter Georgia O'Keeffe, married to photographer Alfred Stieglitz, had a number of affairs with women and with men. Among her lovers were the bisexual Mabel Dodge Luhan (then O'Keeffe's hostess) and her husband Tony, a native Pueblo whose demeanor and six-foot presence—dressed in full native costume, turquoise jewelry, and waist-length braids—dazzled visitors at the Luhans' Big House in Taos. When Mabel Luhan was hospitalized for a hysterectomy, Georgia became Tony's scribe, since he could not read or write English. "By exacerbating Mabel's jealousy," biographer Benita Eisler comments in an interesting parenthetical aside, "Georgia paid her back for preferring Tony, for ultimately choosing, as most bisexual women do, a man."[48]

During this first stay at Taos O'Keeffe is also said to have had a sexual relationship with her traveling companion, Beck (Rebecca) Strand, the wife of O'Keeffe's former lover (and Stieglitz protégé) Paul Strand. Beck's letters to her husband are full of her pleasure in being with Georgia, describing a union that was "intact and happy and a miracle of surprise to me." "It's too terrible how untamed and wild we are," she told him with glee. She and Georgia sunbathed in the nude and walked around in the compound without clothes on, flirting periodically with painter John Marin, who was disconcerted by this assault and took himself off to go fishing.

Taos and its surrounding areas drew artists and writers from Lawrence and his wife, Frieda, to the poet Witter Bynner and his wealthy lover, Willard (Spud) Johnson. Convention was not an issue in these pockets of the new Southwest. Many lesbian women, including anthropologists, archaeologists, and photographers, settled in the region and were to be seen, some as couples, at social gatherings hosted by the conservative and the proper. Mary Cabot Wheelright, a transplanted native of Boston, bought a huge ranch at Alcalde, and began to collect the artifacts that would become the Wheelright Museum in Santa Fe. For O'Keeffe, Wheelright was a rival force; Eisler suggests that "to a bisexual woman her open lesbianism was too challenging,"[49] but any strong personality, and especially any strong woman, would probably have had a similar effect.

In a life full of erotic and romantic relationships—the last of them when

the artist was in her late eighties and her companion in his twenties—
Georgia O'Keeffe seems to have had conquest and comfort in mind rather
than gender. The more successful she became the more autocratic she
was in her choices. In this she was no different from any contemporary
celebrity or movie star.

Like many other independent and successful women of her era she was
scornful of feminism though she exemplified many of its ideals and also
many of its excesses.[50] Her bisexuality was not politically based. It was a
matter of who she saw, who she wanted, and what pleasures she could
derive from the encounter. If being an artist freed her from some conventional expectations, or led her to court unconventionality in herself, that
was, in a way, no more than "natural."

Frida Kahlo, another brilliant bisexual painter of the same era, teased and
flirted with O'Keeffe at Stieglitz's gallery, as her husband, the muralist
Diego Rivera, affectionately reported to a mutual woman friend.[51] "Frida
had many girl friends and lesbian friends," said a male acquaintance of
the period. "Her lesbianism did not make her masculine. She was a kind of
ephebe, boyish and emphatically feminine at the same time." Her husband
encouraged her affairs with women, either because he feared not satisfying her own "very strong" sexual desires (he was twenty years older
than she), or because he found the idea of sex between women exciting
—or both. Women's sexual organs, unlike men's, Rivera said, were "all
over the body, and therefore two women together would have a much
more extraordinary experience." Rivera did not, however, readily accept
his wife's heterosexual affairs, though she is said to have preferred men to
women. Among her better-known lovers were Leon Trotsky and the sculptor Isamu Noguchi. Rivera "considered Frida's lesbian affairs a sort of
safety valve," a friend surmised.[52] Meanwhile he himself continued to have
numerous affairs with women.

As with O'Keeffe and Stieglitz, the man's early success and the place of
the woman painter as a protégée (Kahlo was Rivera's third wife, O'Keeffe
was Stieglitz's second; both were aggressively promoted by their artist
husbands) combined with a social and erotic atmosphere that can fairly
be called "bohemian" to foster independence and experimentation in
women already predisposed to go their own way. Is "bisexuality" here an
effect, or a cause, of the complex creative and personal lives of these two
women painters? It is really the wrong question. To seek cause and effect
here is to trivialize and compartmentalize a richness of experience, a
boldness in taking pleasure, and an arrogant neediness that compelled
response. If these bisexual women are exceptions, then their experiences
may usefully drive us to question the usefulness of rules.

Kahlo's paintings—*Two Nudes in a Forest* of 1939 and *Self-Portrait with
Cropped Hair* of 1940, with what her biographer calls the "carnal lips

beneath a slight mustache" that characterize many of her self-portraits—reflect her pan-sexuality; her hetero-, homo-, and autoeroticism; and the intensely eroticized world of her imagination. "That Frida's masculine side became more pronounced in the late forties," writes biographer Hayden Herrera, "is apparent in her self-portrait; she gave her features an ever more masculine cast, making her mustache even darker than it actually was. But there was always a definite androgynous aspect to both Frida and Diego; both were attracted to what they saw of their own gender in their mate."[53] As Frida's health became more fragile over the years—a horrifying collision between a bus and a trolley in her youth left her with a shattered pelvis and a steel bar driven through her body; for the rest of her life she was in and out of hospitals, undergoing some thirty-two operations on her spine and her right foot, and living with constant pain—her intimates were more frequently women, often women who were having affairs with Rivera. "She consoled herself," said the art critic Raquel Tibol, "by cultivating the friendship of women with whom Diego had amorous relations."[54]

What is particularly worth noting here is the periodic shifting of sexual attraction (from men to women, from women to men) and its contingency (women who were Rivera's lovers were eroticized, or made objects of potential conquest, for Kahlo). Kahlo's—and indeed O'Keeffe's—modulation of sexual attentiveness from man to woman, or from woman to man, suggests something of the intrinsically bisexual nature of human relationships when observed over the period of a lifetime. No one relationship, no one orientation, is for them the "real one." What is "real" is what they are doing at the time.

Greenwich Village and Harlem: Chic to Chic

Lillian Faderman's engrossing book about lesbian life in twentieth-century America, *Odd Girls and Twilight Lovers,* devotes a chapter on the 1920s to what she calls "Lesbian Chic"—a title that would itself reappear as a *Newsweek* cover story about the sexy lesbians of the 1990s. Faderman carefully chronicles "experimentation and repression" in the flapper decade, especially as it manifested itself in the progressive, arty, and conveniently marginal subcultures of Harlem and Greenwich Village, where tourists and "experimenters" could go to sample alternative lifestyles, or to come out under cover of a cultural carnival.

What is odd about *Odd Girls*'s treatment of these counterculture lesbians, however, is the consistency with which Faderman discloses that they are more accurately described as bisexual. Her book, published in a gay and lesbian series with the general title "Between Men—Between Women," in fact locates the action in Harlem—and to a certain extent in the Village—in people, and "experiments," that fall between these "betweens." Both uptown and downtown may have been full of lesbians, but "lesbian chic" more often than not turns out to be "bisexual chic."

Actually, Faderman herself comes right out and says so. "The etiology of 'lesbian chic,' the *bisexual experimentation* of the 1920s, has been traced by some social critics to World War I,"[55] she explains in a section called "The Roots of Bisexual Experimentation." The phrase "bisexual experimentation" appears four times in five pages. It describes the desire of young American rebels for "unconventional" and "daring" behavior that could both shock their parents and explore new avenues of sexuality opened up by the then-fashionable figure of Freud. "Bisexuality seemed to address all those goals," allowing voyeurs and "heterosexuals" to play with homosexuality without committing to it. A young woman who developed an erotic interest in another young woman could "consider her experience simply bisexual experimentation, which was even encouraged in certain milieus."[56]

Whether experiment or permanency or something in between, when we come to look more closely at these milieus, we learn that a remarkable number of key figures in Greenwich Village and the Harlem Renaissance were bisexual.

In the Village the sexual revolution of the twenties drew upon the new Freudianism and on sexual pioneer Edward Carpenter's theory of "companionate marriage"[57] to produce a climate in which "free love" for men and women was the ideal, or idealized, form of liberation. In practice, this more often than not meant heterosexual nonmonogamy—and, again in practice, more often for men than for women.[58] The ideal of equality between the sexes remained an ideal—if it was one—though some independent, and independently minded, women like radical anarchist Emma Goldman and free-spirited dancer Isadora Duncan took advantage of the opportunity to enjoy multiple lovers. There were certainly many homosexuals and bisexuals, male and female, in the Village and in Village culture, and the stereotype of the long-haired, sandaled poet, dancer, or musician, so familiar from the fifties and sixties, likewise dates a good bit farther back, at least to the twenties. But "nonmonogamy," that rattling can tied to the tail of bisexuals and bisexuality today, was emphatically a gesture of heterosexual liberation, and, just as much worth noting, was part of a theory of equality, autonomy, and individual independence—no matter how well, or how badly, it worked in practice.

The example of one brilliant figure from the bohemian literary culture of Greenwich Village in the twenties may serve to exemplify the limited usefulness of terms like "homosexual," "lesbian," and "bisexual" when used in an exclusive or exclusionary way.

Poet, playwright, feminist, and political activist Edna St. Vincent Millay, known as "Vincent" to school friends, is described by Lillian Faderman as a woman whose "erotic life" at Vassar, where she attended college, was "exclusively with women." But when she moved to Greenwich Village,

Faderman reports, she came under pressure "to give up exclusive lesbianism" and become "at least bisexual."[59]

Lively, striking, and bold, with "an intoxicating effect on people" according to Edmund Wilson, one of the many male "suitors" who fell in love with her,[60] the red-haired, green-eyed Millay was immensely attractive to men as well as to women. She was probably the model for the sexy lesbian "Lakey" in Mary McCarthy's novel about Vassar classmates, *The Group.* Wilson proposed to her; so did poet Witter Bynner, whom we have already encountered with his male lover as part of the Taos scene. Arthur Ficke, who was already married, fell deeply in love with her. "Her lovers, male and female, were so numerous that they considered holding reunions," writes historian Ann Douglas. "On one occasion, 'Vincent'... generously let two men make love to her at the same time; Edmund Wilson was assigned the top half of her body, John Peale Bishop the lower."[61] A celebrity among artists and intellectuals in the Village, she was active in political causes, championing Sacco and Vanzetti; she "seemed to be the incarnation of what was in the twenties called 'the Jazz Age.' "[62]

In 1922, Millay married Dutch bon vivant Eugen Boissevain, a widower who "combined the virtues of a lover and companion with those of a devoted husband,"[63] according to biographer Jean Gould. Noting that he had lived with his previous wife, Inez Milholland—a feminist who was one of Millay's "college heroines"—in a relationship based on free love, Gould suggested that he may have had a similar arrangement with Millay, a point Faderman also wants to insist upon: "Despite her various attempts to resist, [Millay] appears to have succumbed to the pressure. She married, although it was to a man who, she claimed, left her relatively free to behave as she pleased. She said of her life with her husband that they 'lived like two bachelors.' But to have chosen to live as a lesbian, even in the world of Greenwich Village, was too problematic for her, despite her history of love for other women."[64]

This may be true, or it may be projection, or it may, quite probably, be both. George Chauncey's history of urban gay life in the years before World War II, *Gay New York,* suggests that gays and lesbians were treated by New Yorkers with indifference or curiosity, rather than hostility or fear.[65] The *Gay Book of Days,* which notes that Millay's sexiest poems were addressed to lovers whose genders remained unspecified, and speculates that Millay's life was "most likely a bisexual romp," also observes that it is time for some new biographies of the poet, since the older ones are excessively discreet about her female lovers. Certainly Gould's reference to "the duality of her nature—the conflict between masculine and feminine impulses"—is not a ringing endorsement of Millay's bisexual eroticism, especially since she speculates that "that element" may have "scared off" Witter Bynner. But Gould's book was published in 1969, when authors (and publishers) were still reticent about the homosexual and bisexual lives of their subjects.

One danger here, though one that Faderman, a punctilious historian, carefully avoids, is what might be called the "coulda-shoulda-woulda" school of thought, or in this case the "shouldna-wouldna-couldna" school: If these people had felt they were free to be lesbians or gay men they would not have been bisexual. If bisexuality is regarded as a social compromise, a kind of trimming of one's sails, then it stands to reason, or so the argument goes, that these half-out people really *wanted* to be all the way out. Their bisexuality is a regrettable fact of history, a by-product (or bi-product) of oppression.

For individual persons this may well be true. For others, who chose same-sex and opposite-sex partners, who chose marriage, whether passionate, companionate, or "bachelor," life's complications had their compensations and often their very palpable pleasures. In any case, viewed through the optic of history, "coulda-shoulda-woulda" is, to put it plainly, beside the point. The artists, writers, performers, and intellectuals of the twenties, in Harlem, the Village, Paris's Left Bank, and dozens of other artists' colonies around the world, had vivid lives and loves. To discount their experience, which was to a remarkable degree bisexual, in favor of an imagined utopia of same-sex (or opposite-sex) consistency to which they seldom aspired, is to write out human richness, diversity, pleasure, and loss, replacing them with mere ideology. It is also to lose, in the process, the very flavor of these heady times.

Millay's husband "left her free, to write, to think, and to live and love as she pleased."[66] He ran the house and farm in the country. She lived there with him and wrote her poetry. He also served as her secretary and business manager. The appearance of the fifty-two sonnets that comprised *Fatal Interview,* her eloquently passionate account of a recent love affair, characterized as "the poet's definitive statement on sexual love," stirred renewed speculation about the particulars of her emotional and sexual life, while a press report that she was married and living with "her husband of eight years' standing" disappointed some who expected more, or different, revelations.[67] She had her own loves, as he had his. She was not, perhaps, "in love with him" as she had been in love with Ficke, with others, and "with love itself"[68]—though an old friend like Max Eastman could talk enthusiastically of how the "first flush of their love" led them to sequester themselves alone together in the countryside[69]—but she and Eugen lived together and shared a circle of friends until, in 1949, he died.

Passionate, celebrated, dramatic, Millay, with a busy schedule of poetry readings on college campuses, was under constant pressure to live up to her own reputation. In the fifties, poet Anne Sexton, whose life was equally complicated by male and female lovers, regarded her as both a role model and a blocking figure, old-fashioned yet exemplary in her way. "I am a reincarnation of Edna St. Vincent," she confessed to a friend, acknowledging her "secret fear" of being "like Edna," a "fear of writing as a woman writes. I wish I were a man—I would rather write the way a man writes."[70] But Millay's own experiences, literary and personal, her bisexual love life and her capacity to write passionately about love for both—or all—sexes, may have been more significant to Sexton than she knew, or was willing to see.

"I too beneath your moon, almighty Sex / Go forth at nightfall crying like a cat," Millay announced in a sonnet that concluded "lust is there, and nights not spent alone."[71] Her love poetry is both erotic and ironic: "I could have loved you better in the dark," she will say, "And I wish I did not feel like your mother."[72] Her single best-known lines begin "My candle burns at both ends; / It will not last the night."[73] Why should we seek to locate those burning ends at either pole of the Kinsey scale? The question is not whether she "became heterosexual" when she married or "remained a lesbian" despite her marriage but rather what usefulness these labels can offer when describing a life as complex, erotic, productive, and sexually provocative as hers.

The best response is probably Millay's own, when cornered in the twenties by a poem-writing psychoanalyst inquiring into the source of her constant headaches. Did Millay think she might have, even subconsciously, an "occasional erotic impulse" toward someone of her own sex? he hazarded cautiously. "Oh, you mean I'm homosexual!" replied Millay equably. "Of course I am, and heterosexual too, but what's that got to do with my headache?"[74]

Uptown as well as downtown, some of the most talented and memorable artists "burned their candles at both ends." Among the female blues singers who made Harlem the musical showplace of the twenties were Bessie Smith and Ma Rainey, both bisexual. Bessie Smith, married to Jack Gee in 1923, had sexual relationships with women at least as early as 1926, when she became involved with Lillian Simpson. A gossip item had appeared in a newspaper the year before linking her to male impersonator Gladys Ferguson. Chris Albertson comments on "the wide range of her sexual tastes."[75] Her "Foolish Man Blues," recorded in 1927, posed a disingenuous "puzzle" to which she clearly had some answers for the "two things" she claims not to understand are "a mannish-acting woman, and a skipping, twistin', woman-acting man."

Gertrude (Ma) Rainey, described by Paul Oliver as a "short, dark-skinned, wild-haired, bi-sexual woman,"[76] married Will (Pa) Rainey in 1904 when she was still in her teens, and toured with him. Her "Prove It on Me Blues" put the issue of lesbianism and cross-dressing playfully up front:

> They say I do it,
> Ain't nobody caught me
> They sure got to prove it on me.
> Went out last night
> With a crowd of my friends,

They must've been women
Cause I don't like no men.
It's true I wear a collar and a tie . . .

Other bisexual blues artists included Alberta Hunter, whose marriage in 1919, says Faderman, "gave her a protective coloration—not of heterosexuality, which would have been going too far in favor of conservatism, but of bisexuality"[77] and "Ethel Waters and her lover of many years, Ethel Williams," who "must have believed," since they did not masquerade as exclusively heterosexual, that "in their own sophisticated circles of Harlem, bisexuality was seen as interesting and provocative," even "supersexy."[78]

Even a manifest butch like popular "bull dyker" Gladys Bentley, who wore men's suits both on stage and off, became a singing sensation in a white tuxedo at the Clam House, and married a woman in a civil ceremony in New Jersey, was, according to Faderman, "in reality bisexual."[79] Bentley, whose 250-pound frame, openly lesbian lifestyle, and scandalously parodic song lyrics made her the toast of Harlem, also became a legendary figure in Harlem fiction of the twenties, appearing recognizably as a transvestite entertainer in Carl Van Vechten's *Parties,* in Clement Wood's *Deep River,* and in Blair Niles's 1931 novel of gay male Harlem life, *Strange Brother.* Artist Romare Bearden recalled that when he was growing up in Harlem in those years " 'Gladys Bentley' was a woman dressed as a man. You also had a male performer who called himself 'Gloria Swanson.' So Harlem was like Berlin, where they had such things going on in cabarets at the time."[80]

Later in life, after her celebrity days were over, Bentley wrote an article for *Ebony* called "I Am a Woman Again" in which she recanted her lesbianism—an article that some have claimed she was compelled to write for economic reasons.[81] She reported that she had married journalist J. T. Gibson, although he subsequently denied it. In 1952, Bentley was married in California to a man sixteen years her junior. After she and her husband divorced, she spent her last years as a dedicated worker for the Temple of Love in Christ.

"Bentley's ultimate capitulation to social norms and her subsequent repudiation of lesbian life should not be allowed to overshadow her immense accomplishments,"[82] writes Eric Garber, a cultural historian of lesbian and gay life in Harlem. Fair enough. But do we need to choose only the "real," lesbian Bentley, the Harlem superstar, and ourselves repudiate the last, less professionally visible twenty years of her life? Might the evidence not suggest that economic reasons influenced *both* her early, transvestite lifestyle and her later marriage? And what does it mean to choose one moment, especially the most glamorous moment in a life of complex performances and complex human decisions, and fix on it as the real one?

Bisexuality was part of the club scene for audiences as well as performers, and many Harlem nightclubs "catered to straights and gays together."[83] Faderman documents the uptown travels of "white women who went to Harlem to 'be lesbian,' [who] were sometimes only 'trying it on.' . . . Some of these women considered themselves bisexual."[84] Among them were "Libby Holman, the celebrated singer of the '20s, who was married to a man, [but] nevertheless came to Harlem, where she could not only act as a lesbian but even be outrageously gay," touring nightspots with her lover Louisa Carpenter du Pont Jenney dressed in identical men's suits and hats.[85] Other "women celebrities and high-livers, most of them also married to men but out for a good time with other bisexual females"[86] were Beatrice Lillie, Tallulah Bankhead, Jeanne Eagels, Marilyn Miller, and "Lucille Le Sueur (who later became Joan Crawford)."[87]

For Harlem residents, "liberality toward bisexuality" and a "manifest acceptance of bisexuality among the upper classes" was exemplified by the career of wealthy socialite A'Lelia Walker, who was married several times and surrounded by a crowd of "handsome women and effete men." "Some believed that her various marriages were 'fronts' and her husbands were themselves homosexuals," says Faderman, "but like many of the sophisticated bisexual Harlemites, she felt it desirable to be married, regardless of what she did in her affectional life."[88] "Among Harlem women of wealth or fame, bisexuality was not uncommon, though few would have admitted to exclusive homosexuality."[89]

Here again the implication seems to be that lesbianism was the harder choice, the one to which a woman would have reluctantly to "admit." Bisexuality, by contrast, was easy, sexy, "not uncommon." Faderman never says it is less legitimate. She does, however, leave the door open to a claim that bisexuality is a cover for "exclusive homosexuality."

What is so striking in Faderman's account is the way the word "bisexual" rather than "lesbian" appears repeatedly while the argument seems to regard bisexuality as a halfway point, a tourist's tease, a kind of "experimentation," a seductive attribute ("bisexuality seems to have suggested that a woman was super-sexy"), or a kind of passing. "Among some sophisticated Harlem heterosexuals in the '20s the lesbian part of bisexuality was simply not taken very seriously."[90]

The racy, creative, deliberately provocative and permissive culture that was both the image and the reality of the Harlem Renaissance was, it would appear, remarkable in the omnipresence of bisexual entertainers, writers, artists, tourists, and hangers-on. It was a bisexual culture in the aesthetic as well as the anthropological or subcultural sense of the word. Clearly, bisexuality was as "chic" in Harlem as lesbianism, if chic means fashionable or stylish. By calling the twenties a decade of "lesbian chic,"

Faderman makes an important point about the existence and influence of lesbianism. But in doing so she also has to dismiss bisexuality at the same time that she invokes it. In a subsequent section on the economically hard-pressed thirties, she will evoke the "bisexual compromise" to describe, regretfully, some lesbians' decisions to marry men for economic security. Caught between "experimentation" on the one side and "compromise" on the other, bisexuality once again threatens to become invisible at the very point when it is most powerful and significant.

For whether as experiment, desire, or lifestyle, bisexuality was an intrinsic part of the culture of the twenties, as much an aspect of Harlem or "Jazz Age" life as its music or its progressive magazines. A biography by adopted son Jean-Claude Baker describes Josephine Baker's relationships with women as well as men. Soon to take off for a brilliant career in Paris, the young Josephine had a number of "lady lovers," starting with blues singer Clara Smith, "The Queen of the Moaners" (no relation to Bessie).[91] "Girls needed tenderness, so we had girl friendships, the famous lady lovers, but lesbians weren't well accepted in show business, they were called bull dykers," said Baker's friend Maude Russell, known as "the Slim Princess" in her early years. "I guess we were bisexual, is what you would call it today."[92]

If bisexuality was common among women in Harlem in the 1920s, it was equally so among men. Bisexual men were key figures in the art, publishing, and theatrical worlds of the Harlem Renaissance. The author of *Home to Harlem,* the first Afro-American best-seller, was Claude McKay, "a black man who was himself bisexual,"[93] and who wrote dialect verse and sonnets as well as fiction. *Home to Harlem,* which offered a lively, unbowdlerized look at Harlem life, was denounced by some black intellectuals who felt it gave an unsavory picture of African-American life. W. E. B. DuBois said he felt he needed a bath when he finished reading it.[94] The novel's venturesome hero Jake, "tall, brawny and black,"[95] finds himself at one point in a railroad dining car reading Alphonse Daudet's "Sapho" and humming a version of Bessie Smith's "Foolish Man Blues":

> *And there is two things in Harlem I don't understan'*
> *It is a bulldyking woman and a faggoty man. . . .*

McKay had sexual relations with women as well as many homosexual affairs. He was briefly married in 1914 to a woman he had fallen in love with as a young man in Jamaica, and had a daughter from the marriage whom he never met. "McKay was bisexual, although he had none of the mannerisms of most homosexuals," wrote a former lover, the novelist and critic Josephine Herbst, who was also bisexual, to a friend. Not only did she know about McKay's sexuality from her own experience, she had been told about it by some of his colleagues on the staff of *The Liberator.*[96] "The evidence indicates his primary orientation was toward the homosexual on the spectrum of human sexual relations," notes a recent biographer, and he "probably considered bisexuality normal for himself, if not all mankind."[97]

There was also the poet Countee Cullen, described at a later ceremony renaming the 135th Street Branch of the New York Public Library in his honor as "utterly uncomplicated as a personality."[98] The wedding of Countee Cullen to W. E. B. DuBois's daughter Nina Yolande in 1928 was the social event of the season in Harlem. A thousand sightseers joined guests at the Salem Methodist Episcopal Church, sixteen bridesmaids attended the bride, and canaries sang in gilded cages. Countee Cullen sailed for Europe two months later with the best man, Harold Jackman, and without the bride. Two years later the marriage was dissolved. Cullen and Jackman, intimate friends, were known as "David and Jonathan." Jackman, a handsome junior high school history teacher, was the model for major characters in novels by Carl Van Vechten and Wallace Thurman. As for Cullen, he later married Ida Roberson in 1940, a marriage that was "apparently successful, according to at least one account."[99]

The writer, music critic, and photographer Carl Van Vechten facilitated many careers, including that of Langston Hughes, and "photographed nearly every celebrated black person in America."[100] A white man deeply attracted to black arts and culture, he had an open marriage with his actress wife Fania Marinoff that allowed him to have relationships with men.[101] The Van Vechtens' soirees were famous, bringing together white and black artists, singers, musicians, and writers who partied and talked together into the small hours, attracting the attention of the press, and thus bringing even more curious visitors uptown.

White "experimenters" often saw blacks as sexually "free," while bisexuality and interracial relationships were combined as fashionable transgressions. Nancy Cunard, the flamboyant, defiantly unconventional heiress to a steamship fortune whose anthology, *Negro,* was published in 1934, told her lover, the black composer Henry Crowder, that "she liked lesbians; had enjoyed their company before and hoped to do so again." "My answer," he said, "was that I wanted nothing to do with lesbians or anyone who had anything to do with them. 'In that case,' Nancy replied, 'we had better separate right here.' " But after a brief separation Crowder changed his mind. "Since that time I have met, dined and danced with many lesbians and have had reason to radically change my opinion of them. . . . I think I can now number several lesbians among the best friends I have known in Europe."[102] Many of Nancy's best friends were gay men, and it is said that she had sex with some of them. "Oh, *do* let's try," she urged a dubious prospective partner on board a steamer crossing the channel.[103]

But not all stories of bisexuality in the Harlem Renaissance have an "experimental," upbeat tone. Many record a lifelong struggle with questions of social, cultural, erotic, and racial identities that crossed and recrossed troubled boundaries. While the occasional artist or entertainer like Gladys Bentley stressed her sexual transgressiveness to draw an audience eager for adventure, other bisexuals, gays, and lesbians tried to minimize awareness of their sexual nonconformity. Some did marry to pass as straight, as others tried to pass as white. Films of the 1980s, like Marlon Riggs's *Tongues Untied*, make clear how relatively recently "black and gay" has become a public chant of pride.

Wallace Thurman, coeditor with Hughes and Zora Neale Hurston of the short-lived journal *Fire!!*, published in 1929 a novel called *The Blacker the Berry*, which featured "a black bisexual who is a scoundrel."[104] In the twenties, Thurman, described by critics as a "scandalous bon vivant"[105] who was "also somewhat effeminate"[106] and by Langston Hughes as "a strangely brilliant black boy,"[107] married educator and labor organizer Louise Thompson. She filed for divorce almost immediately, though for technical reasons the divorce was never granted, and she attended him in the incurable ward on Welfare Island where he died at age thirty-two, depressed, alcoholic, and, it is claimed, "riddled with guilt about his sexual ambivalence."[108]

Nella Larsen's 1929 novel *Passing* describes an erotic triangle in which two women with skin light enough to pass as white, one married to a black man and the other to a white man, encounter one another after years apart. Clare, whose husband does not know she is black, falls to her death from an apartment window after he discovers her racial identity. The novel leaves open the question as to whether Clare is a suicide or has been pushed out the window by her friend Irene in a fit of jealousy.

Passing, with its suggestive title, has been read as a novel of veiled lesbian feelings.[109] Admiring Clare herself, Irene also comes to imagine that her husband will desire her, and that Clare's beauty represents a threat to her marriage. In a way, the novel constitutes a classic bisexual plot, where same-sex desire is both transferred imaginatively onto an opposite-sex relationship (her husband will desire Clare, since she does) and also derived from it (since her husband desires Clare, she does). This is a pattern that fits Freud's classic essay on "delusional jealousy," homosexuality, and paranoia, a pattern that, we will see, underlies the "bisexual plot" as it functions both in fiction and in many bisexual lives.

Racial and sexual passing were also issues in the life of writer Jean Toomer, the author of the highly praised 1923 novel *Cane*. Toomer was of mixed racial heritage and classically handsome. The first time he submitted a piece to *The Liberator,* editor Claude McKay dismissed the work of "Miss Toomer" as too long and lacking in unity. Toomer "quickly corrected the gender mistake,"[110] and his work shortly began to appear in the journal. He became a golden figure on the Harlem literary scene and was taken up by the literary lights of Greenwich Village; there was a rumor that he had had an affair with Edna St. Vincent Millay.

Toomer seems to have been particularly attractive to, or attracted by, women who also loved women. The doyenne of Taos, Mabel Dodge Luhan, a friend of Carl Van Vechten's and a longtime resident of Greenwich Village, fell for Toomer and invited him to stay with her and her husband in New Mexico. Luhan, who delighted in triangular seductions, was especially attracted by the fact that he was having an affair with Waldo Frank's wife, Margaret Naumburg: "You see, a man who has a complete and fulfilling sex outlet is made free," she said. "It gives him control."[111] Toomer gradually drifted away from his Harlem colleagues and into a white world. In 1931 he married white novelist Margery Latimer, "an intense feminist, fascinated . . . by civil rights and Afro-Americans, sexual unorthodoxy . . . and Jean Toomer."[112]

The sexuality of the man who was arguably Harlem's most famous writer, poet, novelist, storyteller, and autobiographer—Langston Hughes—has been much debated in the context of black modernism and gay studies. Arnold Rampersad's distinguished biography observes that although "marriage was a dead issue for Langston" by 1948, "he gave his acquaintances no reason, other than his increasing age and relentless bachelorhood, to suppose that he was homosexual." A woman who had known him since 1938 told Rampersad, "Langston may have been bisexual, but I'm willing to take an oath of God that he was not homosexual. I knew other women who had gone out with him and they could not have been deluded, since they were—most of them—healthy, intelligent people."[113]

In Isaac Julien's 1989 film *Looking for Langston,* dedicated to James Baldwin and featuring the work of gay writers like Baldwin, Bruce Nugent, and Essex Hemphill, Hughes's life is framed within a Harlem Renaissance now seen, as Henry Louis Gates, Jr., notes, as "surely as gay as it was Black, not that it was exclusively either of those things."[114] Director Julien appears as the corpse in the casket in the film's opening moments, "identifying" himself with Hughes, though as Gates appropriately insists, it would be reductive to view the film as either "fixing the historical question about Hughes's sex life" or as rendering it "immaterial" because the film is only a fiction.[115] The fixed-unfixed question, close to the heart of both postmodernism and poststructuralism, poses a dilemma for those who want to "know" and for viewers who understand "identity politics" to be a certainty rather than a process. "If *Looking for Langston* is a meditation on the Harlem Renaissance, it is equally an impassioned rebuttal to the virulent homophobia associated with the Black Power and Black Aesthetic Movements."[116]

But the dichotomy of gay and straight does not fit all lives. To transpose Langston Hughes across the boundary from heterosexual to homosexual may serve a crucial political function in legitimating historical black gayness or gay blackness. If "we look for Langston but we discover Isaac,"[117] that is only to say that the past is recuperable through the deliberate appropriations of the present.

Giovanni's Roommate

As we've seen, bisexuality has often been deemed politically incorrect from the point of view of sexual politics. Recent work on black male writers like Langston Hughes, Alain Locke, Countee Cullen, and Claude McKay has made it clear that being black and gay, or black and bisexual, was hardly anomalous but rather both common and commonly concealed in twentieth-century America. But James Baldwin's *Giovanni's Room,* a novel published in 1956 about a white bisexual man's dilemma of choice, appears more than usually off the path of black self-consciousness and affirmation. Baldwin was marginalized from the macho canon of the sixties for being gay—not an image that was desired, or even tolerated, by the nascent Black Power movement. How does bisexuality come to bear the allegorical burden of racial ostracism and self-doubt? This, as we will quickly see, is one of the stories *Giovanni's Room* has to tell.

In what sense is Baldwin's David bisexual? The book is framed by his relationship with Hella, who becomes his fiancée and who has, as the novel begins, left him to return to America. But Hella is always absent from the novel's center. David's relationship with Giovanni begins after she has gone off to Spain to consider his marriage proposal.

The affair with Giovanni, conducted in the manifestly and allegorically closetlike "room" of the title as well as in the context of a louche and very gay Paris, takes over David's life. He is, in the main, unreflectively happy until a letter from Hella announces her impending return and her acceptance of his proposal. Then everything begins to fall apart. He picks up a girl and takes her to bed, hating it, himself, and her. He meets Hella at the station, recognizing with pleasure her hair (now worn "a little shorter"), her tan, and her "wide-legged, boyish stance." [118] He cuts Giovanni out of his life without a word, till they encounter by chance and he sees that Giovanni has been taken over by Jacques, the French queen they both sponge off and despise.

Gradually it dawns on David that his love for Giovanni has made it impossible for him to marry Hella. From their rented house in the south of France he flees to Nice, picks up a sailor, and spends several days with him before Hella appears to accuse him bitterly of not telling her what they both already knew. In the meantime, Giovanni has been imprisoned for killing Guillaume the bar owner, another elderly queen to whom he has in desperation reapplied for work, and who has instead contemptuously used him for sex and then tried to turn him away. The novel is framed by the impending execution of Giovanni, and by Hella's return to America. As for David, he imagines himself doomed to seek out nameless boys, unable to marry or even to fall joyously in love.

"I was thinking, when I told Hella that I had loved her, of those days before anything awful, irrevocable, had happened to me, when an affair was nothing more than an affair. Now, from this night, this coming morning, no matter how many beds I find myself in between now and my final bed, I shall never be able to have any more of those boyish, zestful affairs —which are, really, when one thinks of it, a kind of higher, or anyway, more pretentious masturbation. People are too various to be treated so lightly. I am too various to be trusted. If this were not so I would not be alone in this house tonight. Hella would not be on the high seas. And Giovanni would not be about to perish, sometime between this night and this morning, on the guillotine."[119]

This masterful description, a triumph of the storyteller's withholding art, comes just four pages into the novel. It comes, that is to say, at the beginning, not the end. The novel's business will be accounting for how David—and Hella and Giovanni—have gotten to the place from which their tale begins. The mini-mystery, how Giovanni came to be in prison, and for what crime, and against whom, is only gradually unfolded; it is finally incidental to the story of David's own realization of his . . . what?— his fate, his nature, his choices, his desires?

There is much discussion of gender roles in *Giovanni's Room*. Again the effective device of a first-person narrator allows for revelations both sympathetic and untrammeled. "I invented in myself a kind of pleasure in playing the housewife after Giovanni had gone to work," David reflects. "But I am not a housewife—men never can be housewives."[120] Contrast this with Hella's desperate plea to him: "David, please let me be a woman. I don't care what you do to me. I don't care what it costs. I'll wear my hair long, I'll give up cigarettes, I'll throw away the books. . . . Just let me be a woman, take me. It's what I want. It's *all* I want."[121] That night he leaves her to pick up a sailor in a bar in Nice. It was her independence, her "boyishness," and her resistance that he loved. Once she acquiesces, once they start planning for permanency and children, he feels trapped. Yet earlier he has debated the same issue with Giovanni:

> "I—I cannot have a life with you," I said.
> "But you can have a life with Hella. . . ."
> "Yes," I said wearily, "I can have a life with her." I stood up. I was shaking. "What kind of life can we have in this room?—this filthy little room. What kind of life can two men have together, anyway? All this love you talk about—isn't it just that you want to be made to feel strong? You want to go out and be the big laborer and bring home the money, and you want me to stay here and wash the dishes and cook the food and clean this miserable closet of a room and kiss you when you come through that door and lie with you at night and be your little *girl*. That's what you want. That's what you mean and that's *all* you mean when you say you love me. You say I want to kill *you*. What do you think you've been doing to me?"

"I am not trying to make you a little girl. If I wanted a little girl, I would be *with* a little girl."

"Why aren't you? Isn't it just that you're afraid? And you take *me* because you haven't got the guts to go after a woman, which is what you *really* want."

He was pale. "You are the one who keeps talking about *what* I want. But I have only been talking about *who* I want.

"You know very well," said Giovanni slowly, "what can happen between us. It is for that reason you are leaving me."[122]

Giovanni's distinction between *what* he wants and *who* he wants resonates with the language of many of today's bisexuals, who insist that they fall in love with a person, not a gender.

Bisexuality functions in *Giovanni's Room* as a metaphor for exile, for marginality, for not belonging. But in important ways *Giovanni's Room* is not a bisexual novel. It is a novel in which bisexuality is what might be called an artifact—a device, a result of investigations aimed at other questions. Indeed bisexuality, which seems to be everywhere in this novel, turns out, we might say, finally to be nowhere. Just as David is bisexual, so also is Giovanni, who reminisces about the girls at home in Italy, and particularly about the village girl who became the mother of his stillborn child. "In Italy I had a woman and she was very good to me. She loved me, she loved *me,* and she was always there when I came in from work, in from the vineyards, and there was never any trouble between us, never. I was young then and did not know the things I learned later on or the terrible things you have taught me. I thought all women were like that. I thought all men were like me—I thought I was like all other men. I was not unhappy then and I was not lonely—for she was there—and I did not want to die. I wanted to stay forever in our village and work in the vineyards and drink the wine we made and make love to my girl."[123]

"She loved *me.*" But did he love her? Giovanni does not say. What he does say, repeatedly, is that he loves David. Even Hella can perceive that, though she doesn't yet know the story of their affair. "He was in love with you," she says to David. "Why didn't you tell me that? Or didn't you know it?"[124]

Giovanni is type-cast as the man of nature, the sexy and sexual man of all work, capable of passionate love for men and for women. But David, the novel's paradigmatic bisexual, seems in fact—this is very conspicuous once you notice it—not to like women, or sex with women, at all. In a book suffused with sexuality there are only two explicit sex scenes. Both take place between David and a woman: Sue, the insecure and overweight American girl he picks up to test his heterosexuality after the letter from

Hella, and Hella herself. Both chronicle, quite explicitly, a disgust with the female body. "I realized that I was doing something awful to her and it became a matter of my honor not to let this fact become too obvious," he says of his desperate coupling with Sue. "I tried to convey, through this grisly act of love, the intelligence, at least, that it was not her, not *her* flesh, that I despised."[125] And with Hella, after the first relief of familiarity and comfort, it is the same. The passage in which he describes his repugnance is compelling; I found that I had remembered it, with queasy vividness, from my first reading of Baldwin's book a quarter century ago.

"I don't know, now [writes David], when I first looked at Hella and found her stale, found her body uninteresting and her presence grating. It seemed to happen all at once—I suppose that only means that it had been happening for a long time. I trace it to something as fleeting as the tip of her breast lightly touching my forearm as she leaned over me to serve my supper. I felt my flesh recoil. Her underclothes, drying in the bathroom, which I had often thought of as smelling even rather improbably sweet and as being washed much too often, now began to seem unaesthetic and unclean. A body which had to be covered with such crazy, catty-cornered bits of stuff began to seem grotesque. I sometimes watched her naked body move and wished that it were harder and firmer, I was fantastically intimidated by her breasts, and when I entered her I began to feel that I would never get out alive. All that had once delighted me seemed to have turned sour on my stomach."[126]

The vagina dentata, the devouring womb, is only the most familiar of these visceral images of engulfment and disgust, for which "misogyny" seems too clinical and, these days, too aversively political a term. That the body of a loved one could come to harbor such disgust is a perfectly familiar if unwelcome recognition for many people (straights, gays, and bisexuals alike) who do not intend to cease loving and desiring the person they once chose and now cannot desire. It is surely beside the point to label David as a woman-hater. But it is significant in the way Baldwin crafts his novel that sex with men remains allusive and romantic, sex with women fleshy, flabby, and ultimately ludicrous when it is not terrifying or "grotesque."

We could, if we liked, call David a "sequential bisexual," a man who once loved both men and women (he tells us in the opening pages of the novel about his initiation with a young male classmate, its pleasures and his fears for the future) and now desires only boys. But this kind of vocabulary seems completely inadequate for the delicate precision of a novel, especially a novel as finely wrought as Baldwin's. Dr. Fred Klein's book *The Bisexual Option* describes *Giovanni's Room* as "the internal private hell of the neurotic bisexual," the "nadir of the bisexual's portrait." "In fiction," writes Klein, "the bisexual is more often than not depicted as the villain—the spy or the traitor—or the weak, vacillating neurotic. In *Giovanni's Room* both types are juxtaposed."[127]

This good-for-the-bisexuals-bad-for-the-bisexuals scorekeeping has its place, even if that place is slightly different now from what it was when Klein wrote his book in the seventies. I agree with him that "David's bisexuality is not real," though again, what we mean by "real" may well differ; for Klein, David is in "transition to homosexuality." But it is also worth keeping in mind the way in which bisexuality functions as a screen here for a complex negotiation of racial and cultural issues. In an essay called "Encounter on the Seine: Black Meets Brown," originally published in 1950 as "The Negro in Paris" and then reprinted in the 1955 *Notes of a Native Son* a year before the publication of *Giovanni's Room,* Baldwin offers another triangulation based on race and color. Black, brown, and white function in his essay much in the way straight, bi, and gay function in *Giovanni's Room.* It is not that they correspond, point for point, with one another but rather that two inevitably becomes three.

"They face each other," Baldwin writes, "the Negro and the African, over a gulf of three hundred years—an alienation too vast to be conquered in an evening's good will, too heavy and too double-edged ever to be trapped in speech. This alienation causes the Negro to recognize that he is a hybrid. Not a physical hybrid merely: in every aspect of his living he betrays the memory of the auction block and the impact of the happy ending. In white Americans he finds reflected—repeated, as it were, in a higher key—his tensions, his terrors, his tenderness. Dimly and for the first time there begins to fall into perspective the nature of the roles they have played in the lives and history of each other. Now he is bone of their bone, flesh of their flesh; they have loved and hated and obsessed and feared each other and his blood is in their soil. Therefore he cannot deny them, nor can they ever be divorced.

"The American Negro cannot explain to the African what surely seems in himself to be a want of manliness, of racial pride, a maudlin ability to forgive. It is difficult to make clear that he is not seeking to forfeit his birthright as a black man, but that, on the contrary, it is precisely this birthright which he is struggling to recognize and articulate. Perhaps it now occurs to him that in his need to establish himself in relation to his past he is most American, that this depthless alienation from oneself and one's people is, in sum, the American experience."[128]

"Want of manliness" envisaged as want of racial pride; alienation that turns out to be itself the quintessential American experience; a hybrid state that is more than merely physical; and love and hate and obsession and fear overdetermining the relationship so that "he cannot deny them, nor can they ever be divorced." It does not take much to see that these are key themes for *Giovanni's Room* as well as for Baldwin's reading of race in his time. The figure of marriage, appropriately presented here through the figure of impossible divorce, marks the relationship of the American Negro with white America.

In fact, as the author's introduction makes clear, the completion of *Notes of a Native Son* came about at exactly the same time as the completion of *Giovanni's Room,* and renewed his sense of alienation through the cross-over of gay and black. No sooner had he written the title essay of *Notes of a Native Son* than he "returned to New York, where I finished *Giovanni's Room.* Publisher's Row, that hotbed of perception, looked on the book with horror and loathing, refused to touch it, saying that I was a young *Negro* writer, who, if he published this book, would alienate his audience and ruin his career. They would not, in short, publish it, as a favor to me. I conveyed my gratitude, perhaps a shade too sharply, borrowed money from a friend, and myself and my lover took the boat back to France."[129]

There is always a question, with metaphorical readings, of which is the tenor and which the vehicle—or, in less lit-crit terms, of which things are to be understood as the true subject under discussion, and which is a way of imaging or imagining that subject. Is bisexuality in *Giovanni's Room* then a tenor or a vehicle? Is the novel "about" bisexuality, or, indeed, about gay male identity, or is it "really about" the complicated situation of the mid-century American Negro, a category and a personage apparently unrepresented in the novel?

This is not really a matter of "really," but of "how." *Giovanni's Room* is clearly "about" bisexuality, whether with or without guilt: David's version of bisexuality, or Giovanni's. It sees bisexuality as an impossible position but also as an inevitable one, for reasons that have to do with culture, custom, and economics (David only succeeds in getting money from home by announcing his forthcoming marriage to Hella) as well as desire. Indeed, it sees desire as both implicated in, and produced by, culture, custom, and economic realities, though these are sometimes related by an outlaw rather than an inlaw logic (his engagement to Hella saps his desire for her; the economic privations that confine him to Giovanni's room increase rather than undercut their mutual desire). If "David's bisexuality is not real," as I've agreed with Dr. Klein that it isn't, then its very unreality is what makes it worth discussing. Likewise, if *Giovanni's Room* can be read as a novel about race that contains no persons of color, it can also be read as novel about bisexuality whether or not its protagonists are "really" bisexual. It is not a matter of whether David is a good role model for bisexuals.

Yet the question of role models, minus that inelegant term, did arise in one of the angriest critiques of Baldwin's racial and sexual politics. Eldridge Cleaver's essay on Baldwin in *Soul on Ice,* an essay called "Notes *on* a Native Son."[130] Replacing Baldwin's "of" with "on," and alluding directly to the example of Richard Wright (the author of *Native Son*), Cleaver takes Baldwin to task for his "ethnic self-hatred."[131] Why does Baldwin hate himself, hate his blackness, hate his Negro identity? Because, says Cleaver, he is a homosexual. Or perhaps it is because he hates himself and hates blackness that he has become a homosexual.

Black intellectuals like Baldwin, says Cleaver, "have become their own opposites."[132] The "intellectual sycophant" (for Cleaver, despite his name, does not mince words) "hates what he is" and "becomes a white man in a black body"[133]—a phrase that ringingly recalls the popular description of the transsexual, and before that of the male "sexual invert," as "a woman trapped in a man's body"—the biological "bisexual."

"The black homosexual, when his twist has a racial nexus" has been "deprived . . . of his masculinity" by the white man, he says. Indeed, a writer who is a real "rebel and a man," like Richard Wright, will barely mention homosexuality, and then only in the context of so-called punk-hunting, the chasing down of homosexuals by bands of youths in the black ghettos of America. Wright's novelistic heroes may be "shackled with a form of impotence," but at least they were "strongly heterosexual. Their heterosexuality was implied rather than laboriously stated or emphasized; it was taken for granted, as we all take men until something occurs to make us know otherwise."[134] So: compulsory heterosexuality, "as we all take men until something occurs to make us know otherwise." Something like *what?*

Something, it turns out, like James Baldwin's novels.

James Baldwin's "first love" was "the white man," however he may seek to cover that love with "the perfumed smoke screen of his prose." And this is why Eldridge Cleaver's own "love for Baldwin's vision had become ambivalent."[135] Just how ambivalent this "love" would be, and how implicated in the very language of homosexuality, would become clear in the course of the essay. For Cleaver's is a tale of disappointed love.

Once he "lusted after anything that Baldwin had written."

His lust, indeed, had a scenario, and a curious one: He wanted "to sit on a pillow beneath the womb of Baldwin's typewriter and catch each newborn page as it entered this world of ours."[136] Is Cleaver here the midwife? The father? In any case, the image is that of childbirth, a common enough cliché of male literary creation, but curious—very curious—in the way in which it is pursued. For Cleaver will not, perhaps cannot, leave it alone.

"The case of James Baldwin aside for a moment," Cleaver says with some disingenuousness, since he is not going to leave Baldwin aside, not even for a moment, "it seems that many Negro homosexuals, acquiescing in this racial death-wish, are outraged and frustrated because in their sickness they are unable to have a baby by a white man." Despite the fact that they are "already bending over and touching their toes for the white man, the fruit of their miscegenation is not the little half-white offspring of their dreams." And despite their "intake of the white man's sperm," these black homosexuals produce nothing, or nothing but the incidental pleasure of physical relief, "the unwinding of their nerves."[137]

In this passage the black man becomes the bottom, the white man the top; the white man is the inserter, the black man the insertee, the "passive" recipient of white sex and white culture. Cleaver holds up for ridicule the figure of Rufus Scott in Baldwin's novel *Another Country,* "a pathetic wretch who indulged in the white man's pastime of committing suicide, who let a white bisexual homosexual fuck him in his ass." [138] Tacitly and explicitly Cleaver contrasts himself with Rufus Scott. He is not only a black activist but an activist heterosexual, who prefers the white butch Norman Mailer to the black queen James Baldwin.

Cleaver—the Cleaver of this essay—does not approve of homosexuals. He quotes Norman Mailer: "Driven into defiance, it is natural, if regrettable, that many homosexuals go to the direction of assuming that there is something intrinsically superior in homosexuality, and carried far enough it is a viewpoint which is as stultifying as it is ridiculous, and as anti-human as the heterosexual's prejudice." This is, we may want to recall, the sixties, not the nineties, talking.

"I for one," adds Cleaver with heavy irony, "do not think homosexuality is the latest advance over heterosexuality on the scale of human evolution. Homosexuality is a sickness, just as are baby-rape or wanting to become the head of General Motors."

Forced to choose, he takes the straight white man over the gay black man as his authority. Thus Mailer's analysis in *The White Negro* is "penetrating," he says, while Baldwin's critique of it is "schoolmarmish." [139] Mailer "hits the spot" [140] in his dismissal of homosexuality, while Baldwin's characters "all seem to be fucking and sucking in a vacuum."

Mailer is to be praised for "the solid kernel of truth that he gave us" about the relationship between whites and blacks. Never mind his excessive verbiage: "[A]fter all, it is the baby we want and not the blood of afterbirth." [141] Both the seed and the baby come from Mailer. No wonder Cleaver feels "ambivalent" about his former "love" for Baldwin. In fact, what he evidences is something very like jealousy: Baldwin loves another; loves the white man; does not, somehow, love him. And the language of his revenge is the language he thinks he has rejected, the language of miscegenation and, indeed, of bisexuality.

Cleaver's essay might be described as virulently heterosexual. He equates homosexuality with decadence, and heterosexuality with a Jungian synthesis or convergence of opposites. The paradox as he sees it is that Mailer is a truer heir of Richard Wright than Baldwin, because he extolls "masculinity." [142] The violent and eroticized heterosexual sodomy of a Mailer short story like "The Time of Her Time" (in which a middle-aged white man forces a coolly derisive young white woman to orgasm against her will by taking her from behind) is presumably preferable, because more "masculine," than the romantic and consensual, equally eroticized lovemaking of two men in *Giovanni's Room.*

It may be worth noting that Cleaver wrote many of his essays from prison, where issues of top and bottom and of a black man who might or might not "let a white bisexual homosexual fuck him in his ass" could be said to have certain personal or at least situational relevance. Homosexuality in prison has been a fact of life recognized by experts from Freud to Kinsey to Jean Genet, not to mention the media "discovery" of male-male prison rape as a nouveau scandal of the nineties. Yet Cleaver's own account of his time in jail is distinctly, indeed defiantly, heterosexual. He campaigned for sex-visits for all prisoners, not just the married ones, and put up a centerfold of a white woman in his cell. The guard tore it down. Imprisoned the first time for marijuana use, he was sent up a second time for rape, which he classified an "insurrectionary act." "Rape-on-principle," Maxwell Geismar called it:[143] Cleaver's rage at white women for the ideal of beauty they had come to represent to black men, and his rage at white men for a history of pillage and rape of black women.

His fury at James Baldwin is fueled by this same passion; as with the white pin-up on his cell wall, he finds that he loves what he hates, he hates what he loves, he is not, despite his enormous will to be so, the perfect master of his own desires. If Baldwin "let a white bisexual homosexual fuck him in the ass," Cleaver will not forgive him. Or himself.

The story of Eldridge Cleaver's response to James Baldwin is worth pausing over, not only because of its intrinsic interest, but because it constitutes a useful and timely warning about the dangers of overdetermined affections as they play themselves out in the public sphere. I suggested above that artists and writers, because they are situated both within and on the margins of mainstream culture, are in a unique position to signal experimentation and change. But this position is never occupied without risk. A public that applauds creative nonconformists and dissidents at one moment may revile them at another, and vice versa. Bisexuality, even embedded in a literary text, can provoke symptomatic feelings of jealousy, disappointment, and betrayal—as well as desire. The beloved is not so securely to be known and possessed, after all. And lives, it turns out, are no more politically correct than art.

Bisexuality and Celebrity

I awoke one morning and found myself famous.

—*George Gordon, Lord Byron* [1]

Acting on stage and in front of a camera was a sexual experience for me.

—*Greta Garbo* [2]

"**E**verybody is bisexual," says bisexual poster boy Gore Vidal. "Not that everyone practices it." [3]

Lifestyles of the Rich and Famous

When we are told that legendary screen lover Errol Flynn was bisexual and that he spent "an enjoyable night" with the eighteen-year-old Truman Capote, we tend to shrug it off as Hollywood excess. Capote himself is said to have remarked to Marilyn Monroe, when asked whether he had a good time, "If it hadn't been Errol Flynn, I wouldn't even have remembered it." [4] Flynn, Dietrich, Garland, Tyrone Power, Cary Grant, James Dean—the bisexuals of the Golden Age of Hollywood were as numerous and as omnivorous as the rock-and-pop bisexuals of Glitter and the Sexual Revolution—Bowie, Jagger, Joplin, Elton John—or the postmodern "bisexuals" of MTV and David Letterman—Madonna and Sandra Bernhard.

Is bisexuality just another publicity device for calling attention to the larger-than-life transgressions that make a star a star? Is bisexuality, like Greek or Shakespearean tragedy, something that happens to the great or near-great, who live on a scale with higher highs and more melodramatic lows, an occupational hazard or a professional perk? Something celebrities do because they have the opportunity, the stress, or the need for novelty in private as well as in public life? Do people become stars because they are bisexuals, or do they become bisexuals because they are stars?

"I am bisexual, in some circles famously so." This declaration, one could hardly call it a confession, is that of formerly famous glitter-rock spouse Angela Bowie, the ex-wife of David Bowie, in her 1993 autobiography *Backstage Passes*. "David and I may in fact have been the best-known bisexual couple ever. We were certainly the most famous couple ever to admit and celebrate our bisexuality so publicly. So if you didn't know before, now you do."[5]

For Angela Bowie, bisexuality is her claim to fame. But why should someone be famous for being bisexual?

A scene in Wendy Wasserstein's hit comedy *The Sisters Rosensweig* opens with Geoffrey Duncan, wryly described as an "internationally renowned director and bisexual," entertaining his female lover, her sisters, and their dinner guests with a story. It is apparently a hilariously funny story, since the guests all enter "laughing hysterically," and to indicate that the story is already in progress the scene begins, in medias res, with "So":

"So Danny Kaye supposedly dresses up like a customs inspector at the New York airport, and when Sir Larry comes through, he calls him aside into a special room, strips him buck naked, and inspects every single bloody part of him!"

"Why?" asks Sara, one of the sisters, who has been cast for this exchange in the role of the straight man. "Was he smuggling?"

"Sara," explains Geoffrey, "they were, as we say, 'very close personal friends.'" "Danny Kaye!" exclaims Sara in disbelief. "As in Hans Christian Andersen!" "And then apparently they went off and spent a very warm and funsy night at the Saint Regis." "Has this been documented?" Sara demands. "Who gives a damn?" says Geoffrey.[6]

Celebrity—bisexuality—biography.

The source from which Geoffrey is gleefully quoting—and which does *not,* as it happens, specifically document this by-now-so-well-known story —is Donald Spoto's biography of Laurence Olivier.[7]

> During the stopover at New York's Idlewild Airport, he was stopped by a customs officer who inspected his passport and tickets, inquired in a nearly incomprehensible accent about Olivier's travels and promptly informed him that a body search would be required.... After submitting to the indignities of an inspection of every inch and crevice of his body, Olivier was astonished to see the customs officer step back and slowly remove a complex disguise (a dark wig and a heavily powdered latex mask) and there before the naked Olivier stood Danny Kaye.

(At the risk of sounding like Sara, I can't help wondering whether at this point Kaye burst into a chorus of "the king is in the altogether, the altogether, the altogether ...")

The story itself was featured in virtually every review, together with other details of Olivier's sex life—and the sex lives of his wives. His first wife, Jill Esmond, was a lesbian: "[T]he trauma of the wedding night, as she turned away from her husband with a resolute revulsion for sex, must have caused him to feel not only unattractive and ashamed but also inadequate and incompetent."[8] His second wife, Vivien Leigh, "began to suspect Olivier's sexual ambivalence," both in the triangular relationship he and she developed with actor Peter Finch and "especially in the increasingly frequent visits and almost obsessive attention of Danny Kaye." His third wife prevailed upon him to remove from his autobiography accounts of "the numerous homosexual escapades of his adult life."[9]

Rumor linked Olivier sexually with lifelong friend Noël Coward (Spoto says, in a sentence that is a masterpiece of double negation, that "whether Olivier was disingenuous in his insistence that he never wavered and whether the relationship with Coward was briefly carnal is impossible to ascertain")[10] as well as with reviewer and "Ultimate Fan" Kenneth Tynan. "Sexual intimacy with Tynan might well have been consistent with their mutual admiration," writes Spoto, in the could-have, might-have mode so dear to (some) contemporary biographers—a mode we might call the prurient wishful subjunctive. "Whatever may have transpired privately— and an overtly homosexual affair cannot definitely be established—Tynan's threat a few years later to publish a book about their relationship caused Olivier to become violently upset."[11]

Olivier has been celebrated for years for his cross-gender magnetism, an aspect of his performing self that is in fact characteristic of all the greatest stars of this century. Film director Elia Kazan noted, with approval, his "girlish" quality, by which he meant his ability to "tease and play the coquette";[12] Tynan himself wrote memorably that "Olivier's relationship with his audience is that of a skilled but dominating lover."[13]

Now it turns out that there is a referent to this figure, a ground to this metaphor. Laurence Olivier "was bisexual." Like another celebrated Shakespearean actor, Michael Redgrave,[14] he had affairs with men, with women, with the audience, and with the camera. What does this say about stardom? About living up to one's own legend? About how legends get produced and disseminated? And what do the revelations of the Spoto biography, so gleefully retailed by the buoyant Geoffrey of Wasserstein's play, tell us about the interrelationship of bisexuality and biography in today's mass-market readership?

In a literary era dominated by postmodernism, it is interesting to look at celebrity biographies, for in a way no literary form could be *less* postmodern. These are books that aspire to the condition of the well-made novel, full of "explanations" for why characters act as they do. Many employ the mind-reading techniques so notoriously deployed in Joe McGinnis's book on Ted Kennedy, techniques which are a staple of the genre: he thought to himself, she wondered, their hearts leapt up. What is sought, what is seductive in celebrity biography is a narrative, a coherent, consistent "story"—a true life story—what we might think of as the antithesis of the postmodern.

The postmodern celebrity biography, we might suppose, would be something closer to the Alek Keshishian film *Madonna: Truth or Dare,* with its bold graphics, discontinuous narrative, intrusive camera, alternation of black and white documentary and color concert footage, and post-credits interchange between director and star. Truth—or Dare. While postmodernism might be characterized as opting for the Dare, the celebrity biographies I will be considering, and which constitute a multimillion-dollar business in the United States today, opt for the "truth"—the truth that sells. And what is that truth today? Bisexuality.

The publishing industry seems indeed to have gone in for "bisexual advertising" in a big way, as trumpeted by jacket copy from recent biographies of James Dean, Angela Bowie, Judy Garland ("Many of her lovers were gay men, and she frequently turned to other women for romantic solace"),[15] Marianne Faithfull, Elton John, and others. The jacket flap of *Jagger Unauthorized* by Christopher Andersen promises "the full story of his bizarre relationships with David Bowie, Rudolf Nureyev, Andy Warhol, and one of today's biggest male rock superstars"—who turns out, allegedly, to be Eric Clapton.[16] "Eric and Mick were caught in bed together, it's true," claims an acquaintance. "It was a very narcissistic scene, very ambivalent sexually."[17] The inside flap copy for *Malcolm Forbes, The Man Who Had Everything* by Christopher Winans asserts that "the man who squired Elizabeth Taylor to society functions one evening was not the same man who the next night was racing his motorcycle through the steamy, seedy underworld of New York's downtown streets, a handsome young man clinging tightly to his back."[18] (How can there be *a* biography of a man who is "not the same man"?)

The back cover of *Howard Hughes: The Secret Life* by Charles Higham quotes an excerpt from an advance review: "An outing of the billionaire closet bisexual. . . . Strongly documented . . . a hypnotic portrait of a great American monster,"[19] while the flap promises an account of "Hughes' seduction in his teens by his uncle Rupert, a famed novelist and playwright" after which "Hughes became bisexual, and was later to have affairs with several male stars, including Cary Grant and Tyrone Power." Thus does the copywriter neatly dispose of the question of bisexuality's cause and effect, which has occupied psychotherapists, geneticists, social science researchers, and doomsday prophets for countless hours over time.

"Marlon would openly acknowledge the tie between his bisexuality and his search for meaning in life," the author of *Brando: The Biography* flatly declares. "Rumors linked him with novelist James Baldwin; actors Wally Cox, Christian Marquand, and others; and even Leonard Bernstein and Gore Vidal."[20] Clearly, bisexuality sells books, or is thought to. Is it the bisexuality of the protagonist that attracts the attention of researchers (and media)? Or is it that bisexuals tend also to be especially newsworthy and celebrated in their fields? Either bisexuality makes you a celebrity, or a remarkable number of celebrities are bisexual. Is "bisexuality" here in the position of the subject or of the object?

As the form of my question will suggest, I believe that the answer is "both"—or rather, that it is impossible to distinguish, when it comes to the lives of people who live in the limelight, between object and subject, between desirability and desire.

Many "ordinary" bisexuals—that is to say, unfamous people who have been interviewed by clinicians or talk-show hosts—"explain" their bisexuality by some version of the following rhetorical question: Why should I overlook the erotic possibilities of half the human race? As Woody Allen has more memorably phrased it, according to formerly self-declared "bisexual"—now "gay"—mega-producer David Geffen, "Say what you will about bisexuality, you have a 50 percent better chance of finding a date on Saturday night."[21] Or, as James Dean is said to have remarked to one of his male lovers, "I'm certainly not going to go through life with one hand tied behind my back."[22]

For performers and artists, and arguably for anyone in the media-inflected public sphere, this question of universal attraction cuts both ways. "Good actors," writes one critic, "exist inside a monosexual world. Great performers—an Olivier, a Garbo, a Dietrich, a Chaplin—are often flecked by sexual ambiguity."[23] And in the case of celebrities like these, "sexual ambiguity" and "bisexuality" are not—or rather, not only—pathologized. Childhood adjustment problems, over- or underattentive mothers, over- or underdominant fathers—all of this is grist for the performative mill. "Bisexuality was a Hollywood tradition, one upheld with some style by such stars as Tallulah Bankhead and Marlene Dietrich,"[24] reports Judy Garland's biographer. Singer k.d. lang speaks of "making your sexuality available, through your art, to everyone. Like Elvis, like Mick Jagger, like Annie Lennox or Marlene Dietrich—using the power of both male and female."[25] "Monty's bisexuality was practically legendary," says Bill Gunn, a screenwriter and playwright, about his friend Montgomery Clift. "I think that's what made him so exciting to people in the theater—just about everybody felt they had a chance with him."[26]

Marlene Dietrich's cross-dressing, one of her biographers suggests, "not only capitalizes on an aspect of the actress's bisexual nature; it also enables women in the audience to love her and simultaneously establishes ... an identification with men."[27] Among the extraordinary roster of Dietrich's lovers over a long and gallant career were a number of women, including the Berlin music-hall performer Claire Waldoff, playwright and screenwriter Mercedes de Acosta (who also had an affair with Dietrich's rival Greta Garbo), and Edith Piaf.

"She always admitted to me that she preferred women to men," said Dietrich's secretary Bernard Hall after her death. "She said, 'When you go to bed with a woman, it is less important. Men are a hassle.'" Needless to say, however, the list of her male lovers is a roll call of the famous and the powerful: among them Douglas Fairbanks, Jr., Erich Maria Remarque, Maurice Chevalier, Jean Gabin, John Gilbert (for whom she also competed with Garbo), Michael Wilding, Yul Brynner, Frank Sinatra, Eddie Fisher,

Generals Patton and Gavin—and even, her daughter claims, Adlai Stevenson and Edward R. Murrow.

All great stars are bisexual in the performative mode. Dietrich herself once remarked, "Each man or woman should be able to find in the actress the thing he or she most desires and still be left with the promise that they will find something new and exciting every time they see her again." Her great skill lay in the personification of bisexuality as the performative sign of stardom.

A clever director will deploy these energies on the stage or the screen, in effect quadrangulating triangular desire, as Josef von Sternberg does with the kiss in *Morocco* (Gary Cooper watching Dietrich in top hat and tails) or as Nicholas Ray does with James Dean and Sal Mineo in *Rebel Without a Cause:* "Nick Ray was not averse to using Jimmy's bisexuality to good purpose. The director knew that Sal was homosexual, and encouraged him to explore that part of him that would love Jimmy. At the same time, according to Ray, Jimmy fell in love with Sal."[28]

Whether it is actualized in sexual relationships or remains on the level of elusive attraction, this heightened performative state, this state of being simultaneously all-desiring and all-desired, incarnates in the celebrity the two, sometimes apparently conflicting, definitions of bisexuality: having two genders in one body, and being sexually attracted to members of "both" sexes. I put the word "both" in quotation marks, for the number two seems to me a starting point rather than an endpoint for the enumeration of "the" sexes, or "the" genders.

"He can be masculine and feminine but never neuter," wrote one of Olivier's reviewers, and Kenneth Tynan is famous for remarking that Dietrich had "sex but no particular gender." Photographer Cecil Beaton said of Mick Jagger, a favorite model, that he was "feminine and masculine: a rare phenomenon." "He is sexy, yet completely sexless. He could nearly be a eunuch."[29] Clifton Fadiman wrote of Judy Garland that "she seemed to be neither male nor female."[30] Columnist Joe Hyams asserts that James Dean was "one of the rare stars, like Rock Hudson and Montgomery Clift, who both men and women find sexy."[31] Despite Beaton and Hyams, though, this quality is not "rare"; it is the indefinable extra something that makes a star.

"Bisexuality" for stars often means gender-envy, gender crossover, cross-gender identification. "Mick wanted to *be* Tina Turner," one of Jagger's friends reports. "He told me that when he's performing that's the image he has of himself. He *sees* himself as Tina Turner."[32] Elton John claimed that David Bowie "has always wanted to be Judy Garland."[33] Michael Jackson models his looks on Diana Ross or Elizabeth Taylor.[34] Singer Annie Lennox "did" Elvis on the American Grammy Awards show. Director Josef von Sternberg, in a famous pronouncement, remarked that "I am Miss Dietrich, and Miss Dietrich is me."

But equally often the crossover is in "object" as well as "subject," for performatively bisexuality functions as a "shifter" in grammatical terms, taking love songs addressed from an "I" to a "you" and giving erotic permission to cross gender boundaries. Janis Joplin has been compared to Edith Piaf and Billie Holiday—both, like Joplin herself, bisexual singers —as a powerful "diseuse," or performer of monologues. "To hear Janis sing 'Ball and Chain' just once is to have been laid, lovingly and well," wrote one music critic.[35]

It is no accident that both Marlene Dietrich and Judy Garland developed fanatically loyal followings among gay men. I remember with heart-stopping clarity attending a Garland concert at the Forest Hills stadium in New York late in her career, when the audience called out to the faltering star, "You're a real trouper, Judy." "Talk it, Judy—we don't care." As Garland's biographer notes, "the combination of her turbulent private life, her repertoire of songs about men who got away, and indeed her whole melodramatic persona had made her into something of a camp icon."[36] As for Dietrich, she herself acknowledged the power of the bisexual shifter:

> You could say that my act is divided between the woman's part and the man's part. The woman's part is for men and the man's part is for women. It gives tremendous variety to the act and changes the tempo. I have to give them the Marlene they expect in the first part, but I prefer the white tie and tails myself. . . . There are just certain songs that a woman can't sing as a woman, so by dressing in tails I can sing songs written for men.[37]

Songs such as "I've Grown Accustomed to Her Face," sung without a gender-switch in the pronoun.

In a famous formulation about the "homosexual wishful phantasy of *loving a man*," Freud described how the unconscious proposition "*I* (a man) *love him* (a man)" could be translated into more apparently tolerable conscious forms: "I do not *love* him—I *hate* him," or "I do not love *him*—I love *her*," or "it is not *I* who loves the man—*she* loves him" (for women, "it is not *I* who loves the women—*he* loves them"), or "*I do not love at all*—*I do not love anyone.*"[38] Freud took a rather dismal view of these options; to him, they were signs, respectively, of paranoia, erotomania, delusions of jealousy, or megalomania—but then, we might say, that's show business. These sentiments are the stock-in-trade of pop, rock, blues, and torch songs, where the singer becomes the conduit for the doubly identificatory emotions of her, or his, audience. Doubly identificatory because, once again, the object of identification is both the entertainer and the ventriloquized protagonist of the song.

In another essay, this one on "Hysterical Phantasies and Their Relation to Bisexuality" (1908), Freud theorized that "hysterical symptoms are the expression on the one hand of a masculine unconscious sexual phantasy, and on the other hand of a feminine one,"[39] and followed up this on-the-one-hand/on-the-other-hand formulation with a concrete example of such handiwork: "when a person who is masturbating tries in his conscious fantasies to have the feelings both of the man and of the woman in the situation which he is picturing." We might also want to recall here James Dean's remark about his own bisexuality, "I'm certainly not going to go through life with one hand tied behind my back."

However uncomfortable—or comfortable—the analogy with the masturbating fantasist (or the bondage slave) may make us, this is a good description of the complicit relationship of audience to performing star. In fact, Freud unwittingly sets up such a comparison by framing his essay on fantasy and bisexuality with a reference to the "strange performances with which certain perverts stage their sexual satisfaction, whether in idea or in reality." One particularly memorable case involved a patient who "pressed her dress up against her body with one hand (as the woman), while she tried to tear it off with the other (as the man)."[40]

It is neither a joke nor a mere witticism to suggest that such staged "performances," with their manifestations of bisexual desire and satisfaction, are an important part of the mechanism of stardom for Mick Jagger, David Bowie, or Janis Joplin—as indeed for James Dean and Montgomery Clift. It is not only the "performer," but also the "performance," which can be bisexual, and can derive from the complex deployment of fantasy effects of enormous power and pleasure. Not for the first time we can see that what is perverse in the private individual may be culturally valued in the celebrity. What is pathologized in the clinic is celebrated on the stage and at the box office. In fact, "bisexuality," which is so difficult to pinpoint "in life," is perfectly recognizable as a performative mode.

Marlene Dietrich's daughter Maria Riva explains that in the Dietrich household the phrase "in life" was used to distinguish real life from things that were "movie star" related and therefore unreal.[41] Yet the paradox of Marlene Dietrich was, of course, that the "movie star" *was* real. "I don't ask you whom you were applauding—the legend, the performer, or me," the star confided to the audience attending a Marlene Dietrich retrospective at the Museum of Modern Art in 1953. "I, personally, like the legend."

True Confessions

"Life" is what is sought in biography. But it is precisely in eroticism that the real life/stage life distinction breaks down, as Truman Capote's remark about going to bed with Errol Flynn makes clear. Celebrity loves celebrity itself—loves the simulacrum with real love.

We tend to use the phrase "sex life" either as a shorthand term for the sexual experiences and sexual tastes of an individual over time, as in "his sex life was largely confined to occasional encounters with willing strangers," or else as a euphemism for the considerably less socially acceptable "Gettin' any?" "How's your sex life?" means "How are you doing in bed these days, and who are you doing it with?" Broadly speaking, one sense is diachronic and the other is synchronic—one characterizes, the other particularizes; one looks at sex as a history, the other looks at sex as a story. But can a "sex life" be, or tell, a life story?

In the preface to his one-volume life of Henry James, published in 1985, Leon Edel notes some important changes in the practice of biographical writing over the years that bear upon this question of a "sex life." His original study had been written between 1950 and 1971; the redacted single volume benefited from—or at least responded to—subsequent changes in social attitudes toward privacy and sexuality, what Edel characterized as "the candor which prevails, the freedom we now possess in writing lives to deal with the physical as well as cerebral side of men and women":

> I am not trying to suggest that I have, in my revisions, gone in quest of a "sex life" or even a "love life" for Henry James. . . . What I have been able to do is to discard certain former reticences, to take less advantage of certain "proprieties" I practiced out of respect for sur-viving members of the James family. . . . Selection, taste, tact, and cer-tain decencies still remain: and biographers will have to be judged by the skill with which they adhere to what we humanly want to know rather than load us with gossip and the modern bedroom. We are able to offer a more forthright record of personal relations, of deeper emotions and sexual fantasies, and need no longer wrap indiscretions and adulteries in Victorian gauze. . . . I have accordingly inserted some new passages and an inevitable amount of speculation —the stock-in-trade of all biographers. [42]

Now, this is a fascinating account of a scrupulous scholar's scruples. Edel first observes that biographers now feel freer to talk frankly about items formerly regarded as backstairs gossip. The same, we might say, is true for the media, who used to protect philandering politicians and what were then called "AC/DC" actors and film stars from prying public eyes. His figure is that of unwrapping, removing the layers of gauze, the reticences and proprieties that have in the past cloaked indiscretions and adulteries; there's more truth, apparently, as well as more enterprise, in walking naked. But, he tells us, biographers will still select, still abide by "certain decencies," giving us "what we humanly want to know" rather than te-diously loading us with "gossip and the modern bedroom."

Leaving aside whether this latter is not in fact exactly what we, humanly or inhumanly, want to know, let us consider the method Edel employed for achieving this new and desirable level of candor: not only the insertion of "some new passages" but also "an inevitable amount of speculation, the stock-in-trade of all biographers." Rather than merely subtracting obfusca-tions, then, or even selecting from among available facts, the contemporary biographer will add something: speculation. Instead of revealing the "truth" beneath the gauze, the newly liberated biography, freed from the convention of reticence, replaces concealment with augmentation—good guesses, connecting the dots, speculative fictions. Even if there were a tape recorder or a videocamera set up in the "modern bedroom" (or the "postmodern bedroom," which is to say, any room in the house), it could only suggest, and not define, the elusive and shifting contours of desire. To locate the deeper emotions and sexual fantasies of their subjects, biographers, it seems, have to have a few fantasies of their own.

Some celebrity biographies have taken for granted a certain public awareness of the protagonist's interesting sexuality—indeed, that is one presumptive reason why the book is being purchased, reviewed, read, or in fact written. Malcolm Forbes's biographer chronicles his own research as if he were an investigative reporter. He tells the story of a hapless predecessor who was also working on a biography of Forbes, and "asked him about the rumors that he was bisexual." " 'Christ!' " Malcolm replied. " 'What sort of book is this?' "[43] "The rumors about [Forbes's] sexuality swirled for decades," he reports. "Virtually everybody interviewed for this book raised the question without being prompted." And again, "The question was inevitable. Usually it would surface without coaching within the first five minutes of an interview. Was this book going to mention Malcolm's alleged appetite for young men?" Like Angela Bowie's even less subtle hints about future disclosures ("Maybe Mick is still a little pissed about my appearance on Joan Rivers's show, where I recounted my finding him and my husband in bed together. Well, more on *that* anon"[44]) this is a come-on that predicts the hot stuff that lies ahead. "It didn't take a lot of digging to uncover evidence to back the rumors."[45] At the same time, such a device takes the biographer off the hook; it is not he but those he interviews who bring up the subject.

Historian Daniel Boorstin lamented in the sixties the concomitant rise of "the celebrity"—"a person who is well known for his well-knownness" —and the "pseudo-event"—a staged or incited event, often timed to coincide with the evening news. The typical pseudo-event was, he said, "not a train wreck or an earthquake, but an interview."[46] Since the purpose of the interview is to produce and disseminate celebrity, and since celebrity is found to be bound up in some peculiar fashion with bisexuality, we should not be surprised to find that it is in the pages of magazines like *Interview* and *Rolling Stone* and *The Advocate,* as well as on television interview programs like "20/20," that the attempt is constantly being made to establish bisexuality as a "fact" (a "fact of life"). Yet language can function *as* a sexual act, not just as a way of naming one. That is why explicit sexual vocabularies are so often censored. When sex is discussed, the discussion is itself sexy. Sexual language is never merely descriptive or constative; it is performative. To ask a celebrity for the correct name of his or her sexuality is to attempt to pin it down—as if it were possible to do so—in the constative, and not the performative, mode.

As for bisexuality as the "truth" of a "life," we find that the very stars whose biographers are marketing bisexuality as truth are themselves in a more complex and *narrative* relation to it. Bisexuality, like celebrity, appears as an infinite regress. Bisexuality seems always to be being ascribed, claimed, denied, and disavowed. Thus Boy George, returning to the celebrity spotlight after recording the title song for *The Crying Game,* told *Newsweek,* "I used to say I was bisexual, which is a lie, and I felt really bad about it."

Producer David Geffen, in an article proclaiming him the gay and lesbian *Advocate*'s 1991 Man of the Year, was asked why, in an interview with *Vanity Fair,* he had claimed to be bisexual—an interview that described him as having gone from being "in love with Cher to being in love with Marlo Thomas to being in love with a guy at Studio 54."[47] "It was a big step for me when I said in *Vanity Fair* that I was a bisexual man," he explains. "That was as much as I could do then. This is what I can do now. I'm OK with where I was then and where I am now."[48]

Flamboyant rock star Elton John told *Rolling Stone* in a much-publicized interview in 1976 that he was bisexual. In fact, he confided to interviewer Cliff Jahr, "I think everybody's bisexual."[49] In 1984, on Valentine's Day, he married Renate Blauel, a sound studio recording engineer, after an engagement of four days. "Bisexuality's not a solo proposition," he told the press. "Everyone does some experimenting. I'm not denying anything I've said. But I have a right to make a choice."[50] *People* magazine speculated about whether the new Mrs. John was "a lover or a cover," and at the wedding—attended by numerous celebrities, including drag star Dame Edna Everage—a five-tiered fruitcake was served to the guests.

By 1992, long divorced, Elton had changed his tune. "No longer calling himself bisexual, Elton says he's quite comfortable being gay," *Rolling Stone* now reported.[51]

When David Bowie made *his* famous claim, in an interview with the British journal *Melody Maker* in 1972—"I'm gay and I always have been, even when I was David Jones"—he did so from the (relatively) safe ground of bisexuality. After all, he was married to the equally publicly bisexual Angela, he was the father of one-year-old Zowie (who later changed his name to Joey), and his escapades with women were well known. His word "gay" was *read* by the media as meaning "bisexual," just as Elton John's word "bisexual" was, inevitably, read as meaning "gay." A decade later, in the conservative baby-boomer eighties, Bowie confided to the ever-interested *Rolling Stone* that saying "I was bisexual" was "the biggest mistake I ever made."[52]

Where Elton and David Geffen and Boy George repudiated bisexuality in favor of coming out as gay, Bowie at this point sought to erase or revise it in the "other" direction, toward the straight and narrow, and Jagger followed suit. "In interview after interview he claimed that he had never really taken drugs . . . and that rumors concerning his bisexuality were just that—rumors."[53] The question of which is "worse" in the public mind, to be bisexual or to be gay, is complicated in the case of certain celebrities by the need to be on the cutting edge, where "worse" is "better" and *Bad* is good. How to be on the cutting edge without cutting yourself off?

Folksinger Joan Baez writes in her autobiography, "In 1972 I was talking with a young reporter from a Berkeley paper. He asked me if I was heterosexual. I said simply that if the affair I'd had ten years ago counted, then I was bisexual. I didn't realize what a catch he had when he left my house and tore back up the coast to print his story."

The next day reporters thronging her doorstep were met by a woman friend who was helping Baez with child care after her breakup with her husband. "Just my luck to have a woman greet them at the door in her nightgown," she notes wryly. She also reports the friend's offhand question to her: "Did you tell someone you were a lesbian?"[54] Notice "lesbian," not "bisexual." In 1972, lesbian was the riskier, the more scandalous, thus the more newsworthy category. Even when the term "bisexual" is acknowledged it tends to disappear. Baez writes that she hasn't since had another affair with a woman "or a conscious desire to."[55] *Is* she bisexual? *Was* she? Was she if she said she was? Is the term constative (descriptive) or performative?

Tennis star Martina Navratilova, described by *Time* magazine in 1992 as Aspen's "most famous bisexual,"[56] told Barbara Walters on the television show "20/20" when asked whether she considered herself "bisexual, a lesbian, what?" that she liked both "men and women, but I prefer to be with women." Sports columnist Robert Lipsyte hailed her "description of her bisexuality to Barbara Walters" as "one of the most provocatively intelligent I've heard."[57] But Martina herself, once the target of a palimony suit and now a celebrity lesbian on the fund-raising circuit, had earlier disdained the label, announcing in her autobiography, "I'm not a one-sex person, and yet I hate the term *bisexual*. It sounds creepy to me."

Her ex-lover, former Texas Maid of Cotton Judy Nelson, who had left a doctor husband and two sons to live with Martina, is even more resistant. "Judy believes that the labels of 'heterosexual,' 'homosexual,' and 'bisexual' need to be deemphasized and that the word 'sexual' can stand alone," Nelson's biographer explains, adding, perhaps unsurprisingly, "Judy feels that the label 'lesbian' has a very negative connotation."[58] Judy's new lover is Martina's ex-, best-selling lesbian novelist Rita Mae Brown.

Meanwhile, elsewhere on the tennis circuit, Billie Jean King, who had an affair with hairdresser Marilyn Barnett while still married (as she was until 1985) to former husband Larry King, first told a press conference that she didn't "feel homosexual," and then explained that she hadn't meant to deny the facts of her attachment. "I meant only that I had never lived as a homosexual, in that full life-style, and that when I had the relationship with Marilyn I felt no differently than I ever have. Obviously I must be bisexual. I suspect many people are, only they're not aware of it. I couldn't have sustained the affair with Marilyn and not be bisexual." But for Billie

Jean, since she "felt no differently with Marilyn than I did when I made love to a man," the point she sought to get across was, "please, no labels."[59]

For both King and Navratilova, "bisexual" was the right term and the wrong one at once. This is partly the kind of resistance to labels that leads people to say, for example, that they believe in equal rights for women but that they're not feminists, as if feminism meant something other, something scarier (something more lesbian?) than that. But in the particular case of bisexuality, it is not only phobia but also something about the term's odd relationship to temporality and to performance that is at stake.

The more we look at celebrities and bisexuality, the more it seems as though perhaps *no one* is bisexual, although almost everybody practices it. "Jimmy was neither homosexual nor bisexual," one of James Dean's lovers declared, "I think he was multisexual. He once said that he didn't think there was any such thing as being bisexual."[60]

Gore Vidal once teased an interviewer with the idea that he might in fact be "trisexual." "Why, when young," he asserts, "even an unescorted canteloupe wouldn't have been safe in my company."[61] Here Vidal joins (he would probably rather say, leads) the creative erotic company of bisexual "sexpert" Susie Bright, who told Phil Donahue it didn't matter whether one's partner was "man, woman, or grapefruit," and bisexual painter Larry Rivers, who feelingly describes in his autobiography his teenage sexual relationship with a blue velvet armchair in his mother's living room.

But what would it mean to say that someone "is" bisexual?

Leonard Bernstein declared in 1984 that "although he had been homosexual and heterosexual, he had never been both during the same period."[62] Does that mean that he is never bisexual? Or always bisexual? Clinicians these days tend to characterize bisexuality as either "sequential" or "concurrent," depending upon whether the same-sex/opposite-sex relationships are going on at the same time. But although this will at first seem useful in making gross distinctions, it is finally less clear than it appears. For one thing, what, precisely, is "the same time"? Alternate nights? The same night? The same bed?

Many of James Dean's friends believed that his "homosexual activities ceased" when he came to Hollywood to film *East of Eden;* "the Jimmy we all knew in Hollywood was very much a swinging heterosexual."[63] Yet his biographer acknowledges that his ambiguous sexuality is central to his fame and fascination. Is it helpful to see James Dean as a "sequential" or "serial" bisexual?

Cary Grant lived with fellow actor Randolph Scott in a gay relationship well known in Hollywood circles. He was also erotically involved with Howard Hughes. All three men married—Grant five times—but gossip columnists and the movie star community were well aware of their bisexuality. In the *Hollywood Reporter,* Edith Gwynn described an imaginary party game, of a kind quite common in those days, in which the guests arrived dressed as movie titles: In this fantasy Dietrich was said to have come as *Male and Female,* Garbo as *The Son-Daughter,* and Grant as *One-Way Passage.*[64] As for Howard Hughes, in his prereclusive days, his lovers included, in addition to Grant, Scott, and Tyrone Power, Katharine Hepburn, Ginger Rogers, Gene Tierney, and Olivia de Havilland.[65]

"Lavender marriages" were common in Hollywood—the star-studded liaison of Robert Taylor and Barbara Stanwyck, for example, or, in a slightly different way, the marriage of Judy Garland and Vincente Minnelli. Should we consider such marriages, because of their heterosexually "legitimating" aspects, somehow not "real" marriages? This judgment is occasionally proffered both from the left and from the right—that is, from the direction of gay-affirmative politics (and the controversial "outing" of celebrities) as well as from the direction of family values. The celebrity in question is "really" gay or lesbian; the marriage is a cover or a sham. "Bisexuality" is regarded as an artifact of the closet, of Hollywood public mores, or of patriarchy. But how does this kind of marrying for social position differ from other kinds? From, for example, the quest of older, wealthier men for younger, ever more beautiful wives? So-called trophy wives? Or, for that matter, the collection of "trophy husbands," ever younger and more muscular, by the likes of Judy Garland and Elizabeth Taylor. Is it possible that the artifact here is not "bisexuality" but marriage?

A biography of Rock Hudson, coauthored by the star and published after his death, describes his three-year marriage to Phyllis Gates: "[T]he story that was told and retold until it became canon was that the marriage had been arranged to kill rumors that Rock was homosexual. The question of whether the marriage was real or phony is the central conundrum of Rock Hudson's life. It is still unresolved, and perhaps never can be, for one of the principals is dead and the other is not sure what happened."[66]

Phyllis came to believe that publicist Henry Willson and Universal Studios *did* arrange the marriage to forestall a devastating exposé in *Confidential* magazine, although she knew nothing of it at the time. "Now I don't believe it was genuine," she says. (To complicate things further, Rock, now dead, is said to have told friends that Phyllis was bisexual, something she denies.)[67]

Phony or real, "not sure what happened," still unresolved—the difficulty of narrating the truth of a "sex life" is compounded internally by the conventions of institutions (like marriage and "Hollywood") and externally by the conventions of biography itself. Manipulated by studios, publicists, fan magazines, gossip columnists, rumor, and conscious self-fictionalizing, it seems as if celebrity biography is "Dare" rather than "Truth." "I had heard the rumors about Jimmy," writes James Dean's friend and biographer in the preface to his book. "But I knew the difference between rumor and fact, and I really didn't care what Jimmy did or who he did it with. Even had the rumors been true it wouldn't have mattered."[68]

Even had the rumors been true. "Don't believe those rumors," Madonna winks to her audience as she performs with Sandra Bernhard, and Sandra comes back grinning, a half-beat later, with a reply: *"Believe* those rumors." The exchange is captured on videotape, and featured in *Truth or Dare.*

When the Kinsey report on *Sexual Behavior in the Human Male* was published in 1948, Rock Hudson bought a copy and found it "reassuring."[69] The idea of a sexual continuum, from exclusively heterosexual to exclusively homosexual, appealed to him. He was looking for himself in the Kinsey report, just as Radclyffe Hall's lesbian protagonist Stephen Gordon discovered herself in the pages of her father's copy of Krafft-Ebing. But even in that 804-page repository of facts about sex lives, bisexuality existed, so to speak, between the lines. It was a question not posed as such, an answer that happened by accident. "Bisexuals" in the Kinsey report were the product of a statistical overlap.

Hudson told his cobiographer that he "was attracted to women," but he "preferred to be with men." "He preferred it if they had also slept with women, if they 'had a story.' "[70] The "story," the conquest *over* heterosexuality, the transgressive seduction, is part of what is erotic. Stories are seductive; it is with stories that we fall in love.

"Bisexuality" is not a fixed point on a scale but an aspect of lived experience, seen in the context of particular relations. What is peculiarly postmodern about these celebrity biographies is the way in which bisexuality, though it appears at first to be everywhere—on the jacket blurb, in the headlines, in the index—is, ultimately, not nowhere but elsewhere. Like postmodernism itself, it resists a stable referentiality. It performs.

Truth or Dare—that is to say, constative or performative, the mode of "fact" or the mode of enactment. (A far cry from "Truth or Consequences," the quiz-show hit of the forties and fifties, in which, by a logic of reward and punishment, you "get" what you "deserve.") The public adoption or disavowal of one sexual label or another by a celebrity does not constitute a *description* of a sex life but rather an *event* within it. Just ask anyone in the military who pronounces the sentence, "I am a homosexual." To narrate a sex life is itself a sexual performance; if you could simply and objectively state the truth of a sex life it would cease to be truly sexy. To see an equivalence between celebrity and bisexuality is to attempt to *fix* two terms that are similar only in their naming of a process of self-reinvention, self-transgression. The terms "celebrity" and "bisexuality" can't settle into a happily married couple, because if they did, both partners would immediately cease to be what they are. It would be in effect another lavender marriage.

Celebrities do constantly reinvent themselves. Look at David Bowie. Look at Madonna. Look at Michael Jackson. One of the ways in which they have done this—as these examples will suggest—is by renegotiating and reconfiguring not only their clothes, their bodies, and their hair but also their sexualities. But the cognate relationship between postmodernism and bisexuality merely underscores the fact that *all* lives are discontinuous —a fact well known to biographers.

To shock and to give pleasure: These are the arts of the erotic icon as consummate star. At a "come-as-the-person-you-most-admire" costume party in Hollywood in 1935, Marlene Dietrich went dressed as Leda *and* the Swan. Her escort was "Marlene Dietrich," the young English actress Elizabeth Allen dressed in Marlene's *Morocco* top hat and tails. One of Dietrich's biographers notes that this was "perhaps the ultimate bisexual statement for those who got it."[71] For the sheer diversion of inventive role-playing—and an object lesson in the theatrical joys of self-love—this is an image more arresting than any in Madonna's *Sex.*

Part 2 **Bi-ology**

Science, Psychoanalysis, Psychomythology

Chapter 6

The Secret of Tiresias

I know how it feels to be a woman because I am a woman, and I won't be classified as just a man.

—Guitarist Pete Townshend of the Who [1]

When you come to a fork in the road, take it.

—Baseball manager and philosopher Yogi Berra

Ovid tells the story of Tiresias, who became the victim of a quarrel between the king and queen of the gods because he "knew both sides of love." One day in the forest, Tiresias came upon a pair of snakes coupling. He struck them with his staff, separating them, and was thereupon transformed from a man into a woman. After seven years, he encountered again the same pair of serpents, struck them again, and was restored to male form. Tiresias was asked by the royal couple to say whether man or woman had the most pleasure in sexual love. When he answered, "women," Juno blinded him. Jupiter, unable to reverse this punishment, gave to Tiresias (was it a gift or a curse?) the art to prophesy the future. [2]

Hesiod's earlier Greek version of the myth is even more specific about the increments of pleasure: "Teiresias [this is the usual transliterated Greek spelling] was chosen by Zeus and Hera to decide the question whether the male or female has most pleasure in sexual intercourse: And he said: 'Of ten parts a man enjoys one only; but a woman's sense enjoys all ten in full.' For this Hera was angry and blinded him, but Zeus gave him the seer's power." [3]

Tiresias is perhaps the classical figure most insistently invoked by poets, writers, and gender theorists to describe the paradoxes of bisexuality. Why should this be?

"I Feel Like Tiresias"

Like Tiresias, the vampire has looked at sex from both sides. . . . It seems that the vampire is sexually capable of everything.

—John Allen Stevenson[4]

"I feel like Tiresias, in the weird position of being able to make a direct comparison between two very different forms of sexual pleasure."[5] The speaker is Jan Clausen, a woman who, after many years of a "technically irreproachable" lesbian life, found herself in love with a man. Her article, published in the gay and lesbian magazine *Out/Look,* predictably stirred controversy. The screamer headline read, "What does it mean when a lesbian falls in love with a man?" and Clausen dryly referred to her situation as a "newly 'fallen' state." For her, heterosexuality had suddenly become the new transgression, the new risk, the new erotics of the forbidden. Out of the Eden of sexual and political separatism, into the "identity limbo" of bisexuality, an identification she resists.

"I do not know what 'bisexual' desire would be, since my desire is always for a specifically sexed and gendered individual. When I am with a woman, I love as a woman loves a woman, and when I am with a man, I love as a woman loves a man. So bisexuality is not a sexual identity at all, but a sort of anti-identity, a refusal (not, of course, conscious) to be limited to one object of desire, one way of loving."

After a long relationship with a woman, sex with her male lover "astonishes" her "with its physical directness." Clausen says she felt in a way competitive with her female lover, whose body was the analogue of hers. With a man, "because we don't share the physical being," she feels unique. Yet she still desires women. She now notices femmes more, where once she was only drawn to butches. She is white, and her male lover is black. She wonders why *that* difference doesn't count as much as gender in the eyes of those who categorize her choices. Lesbian sex for her, she says, is comparable to poetry, sex with men more like fiction.

Clausen summons the figure of Tiresias as a sign of her experience of loving both women and men. And, like Tiresias, she cannot resist the invitation to compare.

"Who makes better lovers, men or women? Women?" The questioner in this case was not Jupiter but television–talk show host Phil Donahue, and the answer was supplied by "sexpert" Susie Bright. "When people fall in love and when there's intimacy, it's the most intense thing that's happening, whether it's man, woman, or grapefruit," said Bright, an assured mistress of the sound bite. "And, you know, you're in love and that's all that matters and the simplest touch just drives you crazy."[6]

Mindful of his audience's desire for clarity, Donahue tried to pin his expert down: "Susie Bright, are you . . . You are a—what are you, Susie?

You're—Are you a bisexual or is that—you don't like that word, 'bisexual?' " "I've been in love with both men and women," Bright noted, observing that the audience was much more comfortable discussing "love" (what was it?) and "God" (did He approve?) than sex. "What are the differences between making love with women and with men?" she asked the group at large. "There are differences and they're worth talking about, and as long as we keep being scared and talking about other issues we're never going to get to that."

Donahue, the consummate professional, here interposed with a commercial break (talk shows have their own versions of foreplay), but when he returned it was only Susie Bright who was willing to offer any comparisons, and even then the audience was dissatisfied.

"I'd like to know, which do you prefer?" asked a woman in the audience, "since you just had a baby." "Well, you're not going to get me to say which I prefer," replied Bright. "If I asked you your favorite things to eat or the most beautiful places you've ever been or . . . who was your favorite person in the family, you would probably say, 'Well, I love so-and-so because they did this for me, but this other person just blew me away because they could get to me on a certain level that no one else could.' "

At this complex moment a male audience member rose to accuse Bright of putting down "true heterosexual love and lovemaking," advising her that "It's great. You ought to try it some time. You probably can't." A nonplussed Donahue reminded the man that "She had a baby!" and was put in his place: "Well, that—anybody can have a baby." "Yeah. They can?" asked Donahue. And they were out of time.

The privileged vantage point of the expert, or sexpert, is partly what gives Tiresias his—or her—cachet. What seems to be desired, or desirable, is a kind of erotic comparison shopping—comparison shopping that sometimes goes under the name of "bisexuality." "It's a bisexuality of thought," noted the producer of a television film about transsexual tennis star Renée Richards. "Women, for example, are beginning to wonder what it feels like when a man makes love. That kind of thing."[7]

Even at the level of the TV talk show this curiosity of comparison obtains. A transsexual who had had three sex-change operations—like Tiresias, at seven-year intervals—was quizzed by the perpetually curious Phil Donahue about the range of his experience. "You were born a woman, became a man, went back to a woman, and you're now a man again." One audience member asked whether his brain was now male or female; a caller—doubtless one of many—wanted to know more bluntly about the success of other aspects of the transition. Was he "satisfied now"? "Can you get it up? And what's the story?"[8]

"What's the story?" I want to suggest, *is* the story of Tiresias.

Tiresias figures in many crucial stories told by ancient Greek and Roman authors. The story of his sex change, as we have already seen, is retold by both Hesiod and Ovid. Later in life he will appear as the most famous seer of ancient Greece, regarded by kings and heroes as a wise man. Called on to advise both Oedipus and Pentheus, Tiresias saw his advice to them disregarded, to their ultimate cost. In Sophocles's *Oedipus Rex* and Euripides's *The Bacchae* these headstrong monarchs overrode the insight of the seer. Even after death, Tiresias continued to offer sage advice, counseling Odysseus in the underworld how to return to his home in Ithaca. How have these apparently disparate narratives developed around the same enigmatic and omnipresent figure? What's the story?

"The story of Tiresias—the male seer who spent seven years as a woman —is merely the best-known of many legends depicting men and women who changed sex during the course of their lives," wrote Martin Duberman in 1980, in a discussion of "the bisexual debate." Duberman, who asserts with good humor that he is not and has never been a bisexual, had noted in his diary a year previously that "bisexuals seem to be popping up all over." He observed that "the bisexual idea has come increasingly to be the standard against which all who aspire to be *bona fide* members of the Sexual Revolution must measure themselves."[9]

For Duberman, too, "Tiresias" marked the spot of sexual "anti-identity," of sexual difference *within,* "the bisexual impartiality of the Greeks" (a phrase he cites from Will Durant), which was gradually overtaken by Judeo-Christian homophobia and Cartesian dualism, and which seemed to him to be staging a comeback in 1980. In a world in which a person could only be classified as male *or* female, black *or* white, gay *or* straight, bisexuality simply does not fit. The knowledge of Tiresias, reflected in the many bisexual and androgynous gods of ancient Greece, had come under attack by both gays and straights. Yet "it seems beyond dispute that bisexuality is currrently more visible and assertive than at any previous time." His conclusion: that "human beings will behave sexually as their culture tells them to behave," and that, despite mechanisms of forgetting fostered by controlling interests, such cultural mandates have differed greatly over time.

In his frank and fascinating autobiography, *What Did I Do?*, bisexual painter Larry Rivers ruminates on his several sexual relationships with men in a life that also included two marriages and numerous affairs with women. Rivers notes that "homosexual sex, for me at around twenty-seven, was an adventure, for a while on a par with trying a new position with a woman."[10] His fantasy life, he asserts, whether he was masturbating or having sex with a man, always involved images of women. "I was so convinced of being heterosexual I could be homosexual."[11] He is fond of quoting Gore Vidal's maxim: "There are only homosexual acts, not homosexuals."[12] Yet living in the Greenwich Village of jazz musicians, poets, and painters in the forties, fifties, and sixties he fell in love, he says, with "the world of homosexuals"[13]—and sometimes with homosexuals themselves, both gay men and lesbians. One of his many partners was the woman poet Jean Garrique, who was also a lover of the novelist Josephine Herbst.

But Rivers's most intense relationship with a member of this "world of homosexuals" was his sometime affair with poet Frank O'Hara, and it is in contemplating this relationship with O'Hara that he invokes the situation of Tiresias:

"What brought the physical between us to a 'civilized' conclusion," he recalls, "were the women who slept with me, and their price, which was my (almost) undivided attention. What existed between Frank and me was never matched, and finally had to die. I gave Frank pleasure, I owed him nothing. Fidelity among men in my circle was a subject no one spent a minute thinking about. Because women gave me such sexual pleasure, I owed them something." And here he is reminded of the figure of Tiresias: "I know that women enjoy sex as much as men, and according to Tiresias the Hermaphrodite, even more than men. But back in the fifties I was still carrying the baggage of my Bronx beginnings."[14]

In this rueful look back Rivers does not see *himself* as Tiresias; rather, he invokes the seer as ironical expert on women's pleasure, a pleasure Rivers devalues even as he seeks it out. In transferring or displacing the Tiresian identity away from himself—to "Tiresias the Hermaphrodite"— he preserves the pathos of his feeling for O'Hara ("the closeness of our friendship and all he meant to me was not alleviating my discomfort at being involved with a man") and the callow intensity of his youthful desire for sex with women. He also avoids calling himself bisexual. His passions, as detailed in the autobiography, are omnivorous. Is Rivers one of Masters and Johnson's "ambisexuals," who get equal sexual pleasure from women and men and, indeed, from adventurous sex of any kind? Or is he just a free spirit, responding to the complex eroticism of a heightened artistic and cultural milieu where ideas were as provocative as bodies? What does the figure of Tiresias mean to him?

Perhaps the most celebrated appearance of Tiresias in modern dress (or undress) is T. S. Eliot's "old man with wrinkled female breasts" from his 1922 poem *The Waste Land*—quite possibly the source of Larry Rivers's description of him as a "hermaphrodite."

> *I Tiresias, though blind, throbbing between two lives,*
> *Old man with wrinkled female breasts, can see*
> *At the violet hour*

declares Eliot's disillusioned voyeur of social decay.

> *I Tiresias, old man with wrinkled dugs*
> *Perceived the scene, and foretold the rest—*
> *I too awaited the expected guest.*

The sorry scene of seduction, Eliot's classed-down fable of the typist and the clerk, is witnessed in the weary silence of sexual anomie.

> *(And I Tiresias have foresuffered all*
> *Enacted on this same divan or bed;*
> *I who have sat by Thebes below the wall*
> *And walked among the lowest of the dead.)*[15]

Eliot here brings together the fragments of the Tiresias story from Ovid ("old man with wrinkled female breasts") to Sophocles ("by Thebes below the wall") to Homer ("walked among the lowest of the dead"). Tiresias, who has "foresuffered all," is the wise, resigned looker-on, spectator not participant, somehow both male and female.

The breasts of Tiresias had made a slightly earlier and perhaps even more startling appearance in Guillaume Apollinaire's surrealist play of that name, begun in 1903 but not staged until 1917—a play that Eliot, with his interest in French avant-garde literature, must almost surely have known. In this case Tiresias begins life as a woman, Thérèse, a rebellious wife who declares that she is a feminist and promptly turns into a man, Tiresias. She grows a beard, her breasts (balloons tied to her chest with string) promptly fall off, and she forces her husband to change clothes with her. Her unnamed husband accepts his new gender assignment with equanimity ("Since my wife is a man / It's right for me to be a woman") and sets about learning how to have babies.

He then goes to consult a fortuneteller (a figure very similar to Eliot's Madame Sosotris, "famous clairvoyante . . . the wisest woman in Europe"), who, inevitably, turns out to be Thérèse-Tiresias in disguise. At the close of the play, Thérèse decides to leave public life and return to her husband (bringing back with her, among other artifacts of married life, "three influential ladies whose lover I have become").

Apollinaire's Thérèse/Tiresias is phantasmagorically a transsexual rather than a hermaphrodite. Her breasts come and go with her gender. She changes sex, as does her husband, so that each remains heterosexual. (The "three influential ladies" whose lover she says she has become—if they exist—presumably know her as the male Tiresias.) In this sense Apollinaire's play has more in common with the equally surreal "Nighttown" section of James Joyce's *Ulysses* than it does with *The Waste Land*. Published in the same year as Eliot's poem, *Ulysses* offered yet another image of Tiresias in the encounter of Leopold Bloom with the cross-dressed, gender-crossing figure of the dominatrix Bella/Bello Cohen.

Homer's *Odyssey* placed Teiresias in the underworld, where he advises Odysseus on how to return safely home to his wife and son. In Joyce's novel, "Bella" is identifiable as "Tiresias" through her change of gender in the course of the scene. She also carries an animate, indeed chattily loquacious, version of the mysterious "winnowing fan" that Homer's Teiresias foretold to Odysseus as a sign.[16] Is this Bloom's fantasy? Bloom's nightmare? The overdetermined figure of the modernist Tiresias, working both sides of the street of gender, seems here to incarnate ambivalence, experience, and a certain tawdry pathos.

Equally Tiresian in his gender incarnations and his air of world-weariness is the formidable Dr. Matthew-Mighty-grain-of-salt-Dante-O'Connor in Djuna Barnes's *Nightwood,* yet another modernist masterpiece with Tiresias—and bisexuality—at its heart. *Nightwood* is probably as familiar to today's students of gender, gay studies, and modernism as Eliot's *Waste Land* was to a previous generation of readers. If Eliot's Tiresias is hermaphroditic, Apollinaire's transsexual, and Joyce's at once transsexual, transvestite, and homosexual (since Bella/Bello with her mustache, short hair, and skirt evokes the image of the stereotypical "mannish lesbian" as much as of the "man"), then Barnes's Tiresias is manifestly gay.

In the novel's most famous scene, Dr. O'Connor, a brilliantly conceived and slightly histrionic old queen, is discovered in bed in full woman's makeup, wig, and flannel nightgown. "Doctor, I have come to ask you to tell me everything you know about the night,"[17] confesses Nora, whose desperate passion for the bisexual Robin Vote has driven her to despair. O'Connor, who calls himself "the last woman left in this world, though I am the bearded lady,"[18] replies with prolix parables from his own life, a life which seems, like that of the classical Tiresias, to have spanned several ordinary lifetimes. "In the old days I was possibly a girl in Marseilles thumping the dock with a sailor,"[19] he tells her. What Nora seeks from him is the wisdom she believes must derive from his experience. In this case, too, the modernist Tiresias, like Eliot's, has "foresuffered all / Enacted on this same divan, or bed."

A Shifty Character

But who is Tiresias? In what shape does he appear? How does his own sexuality get conceptualized or overwritten by today's commentators on gender, from high art to pop art to pop talk? We might notice that Tiresias himself has become a shape-shifter in these various invocations. Martin Duberman, as we have seen, seems to regard him as a transsexual while Larry Rivers calls him a "hermaphrodite." Jan Clausen, who "feel[s] like Tiresias," raises the question of "bisexual identity" and "bisexual desire," only to set them aside as terms that seem to reify and restrict rather than to open up the complex possibilities of individual response.

In each case the term "bisexual" is rejected or resisted, even though it is also in some way invoked. For various reasons the authors themselves won't, or don't, call themselves bisexual. So we are left to observe that Tiresias shows up in multiple forms where bisexuality is simultaneously evoked and avoided. It is, I think, not an accident that the word "bisexual" in these instances has both too many meanings and too few adherents. Far from constituting a problem or an obstacle in understanding bisexuality, this elusiveness, this shifting is itself central to the question of bisexuality —central because it demonstrates something crucial about the nature of human desire. Eroticism is what escapes, what transgresses rules, breaks down categories, questions boundaries. It cannot be captured in a manual, a chart, a lab test, or a manifesto. To "be" a bisexual is an impossible use of the copula.

It may seem, therefore, as though the figure of Tiresias is being used to evoke everything *but* bisexuality. Bisexuality here constitutes itself precisely as resistance—the "refusal to be limited to one"—even if that "one" is defined as "bi." And if, as I think is the case, bisexuality is related to *narrative* as transvestism or hermaphroditism is to *image*, then it makes sense that the naming of Tiresias should mark the place of a *story* rather than a *body*. It is not any one state or stage of life but the whole life, the whole life "story" as we like to call it, that is sexualized and eroticized. By its very nature bisexuality implies the acknowledgment of plural desires and change over time.

Despite the contrary example of *Nightwood*, Tiresias seems often, if not always, to be imagined heterosexually: as a man presumed to have had sex with a woman, or as a woman presumed to have had sex with a man. In Ovid's myth, as in many of these modernist rewritings, Tiresias changes sex rather than change partners. His knowledge would seem to be that of his own pleasure as a male or a female.

Is "bisexuality" here really just an alternation of maleness and female-ness, a version of what Freud in his early writings called the "bisexual disposition" of all human beings? Is Tiresias to be read allegorically merely as someone "getting in touch with his feminine side," in the phrase popularly in use among many male-to-female transsexuals?

As it happens, the transsexual, the hermaphrodite, and the homosexual have all been very much part of the history of "bisexuality" as it has evolved in scientific and social discourse. The word "bisexual" first had reference to the copresence of male and female sexual organs (and some-times reproductive capacities) in the same body. Early psychoanalytic writ-ings equated "bisexuality" with hermaphroditism, regarding what we would today call bisexuality—sexual attraction to both men and women —as an aspect of homosexuality, or "sexual inversion."

In cultural terms, with regard in particular to myth and to literature, these conflicting definitions converge on the figure of Tiresias. What is at stake—and it is far from trivial—is the question of whether "bisexuality" has reference to the subject or the object. Perhaps it is in fact the question of whether *any* sexuality has reference to subject or object. Is Tiresias's mysterious knowledge, which makes him so revered and so reviled, gifted with prophecy and afflicted with blindness—is his knowledge finally about his *own* pleasure, or about that of the other?

"The conceptualization of bisexuality in terms of *dispositions,* feminine and masculine, which have heterosexual aims as their intentional corre-lates," says Judith Butler, "suggests that for Freud *bisexuality is the coinci-dence of two heterosexual desires within a single psyche.*"[20] If this were in fact the case, Tiresias would then be an accurate emblem of the bisexual. But this whole matter of "dispositions," as Butler and others have insisted, accepts as a biological given a concept of maleness and femaleness in the human psyche, and a "heterosexual matrix for desire," that has in fact been produced by culture—by cultural prohibitions and sanctions. As Gayle Rubin points out, a notion of normative heterosexuality is part of the social organization of sex and gender: "Gender is not only an identifi-cation with one sex; it also entails that sexual desire be directed toward the other sex. The sexual division of labor is implicated in both aspects of gender—male and female it creates them, and it creates them heterosex-ual."[21]

If, as many gender theorists maintain, to imagine bisexuality heterosexu-ally is to resist the acknowledgment of primary same-sex desire, then this image of the "male" and "female" or "masculine" and "feminine" sides of the personality or the brain needs also to be set aside as imprecise old-think—or, more urgently, as cultural homophobia masking an unwelcome truth about the existence of queer desire.

But to regard the knowledge of Tiresias as "heterosexual" and therefore *not* "gay" or "queer" seems to me to forgo some of the very real pleasures of sexual role-playing. To me, at least, the idea of Vita Sackville-West taking Virginia Woolf off on a secret weekend while dressed as "Julian" has its own distinct and hot erotic appeal. Was "Julian" a third presence in Vita and Virginia's bed? And was he "male" or "female"?

Juno wants to know when *Tiresias* had pleasure. Was it as a man? As a woman? Is this really in part an inquiry into the pleasure of the other, and is the erotic pleasure of bisexuality in part about *being the other,* whether through explicit role-playing, memory, fantasy, or the erotic effect of trans-gression? Do you have your own pleasure or the other's pleasure? Whose pleasure are you having? Was it good for you?

Film critic Linda Williams regards the squabble between the gods in which Tiresias became embroiled as a fable about the catch-22 of the war between the sexes. Since the Greeks constructed pleasure as the opposite of control and self-mastery, "the female loses the game of power if she wins that of pleasure."[22] By *acknowledging* her pleasure, she "loses," even though in *having* pleasure she "wins."

Williams's observations about hard-core pornography constitute a thoughtful allegorical reading of the Tiresias story that links it squarely to bisexuality: "An ideal of bisexuality drives the quest for the knowledge of the pleasure of the other," she suggests. "That one sex can journey to the unknown other and return, satiated with knowledge and pleasure, to the security of the 'self.' While most pornography belies this ideal—like Teiresias, it can only speak from its phallic point of origin—it does speculate that such a journey is possible. Of course it is not, since there is no such thing as a discrete sexed identity who can journey from fixed self to fixed other, and since these identities themselves are constructed in fluid relations to fictional 'others' who exist only in our relation to them. But the impossibility of pornographic knowledge does not prevent the fantasy from flourishing; indeed, it may even encourage it."

British cultural theorist Jonathan Dollimore addresses this issue concretely by describing his pleasure of watching sex videos. "I find if I look at a video of a man and a woman having sex, I very much identify with both positions. I also find that the identification with the woman doesn't correspond precisely with my gay experience where, for example, I might want to be fucked by that man as another man." But when he watches videos "I want to be fucked by that man as a woman—my experience is very strongly with the woman—my desire is going very strongly through the woman. To put it quite simply, there are times when I want the vagina. I'm not just wanting to position myself in the position of the woman as a man. Now, I would not for a minute suggest that this sort of complex connection or fantasy of identification and desire is exclusive to the bisexual. All I know is for me it has been explored most interestingly there."

Did people who were open to this more fluid kind of sexual fantasy make better lovers? Better than they used to be, Dollimore thought, whether or not they were better than other people. Perhaps different, rather than "better." Being able to imagine oneself in many sexual roles permits identification *and* desire to be part of the sexual scenario and the "dynamics of the relationship." It was not just a question of theory, but of pleasure.[23]

What Dollimore calls "the fantasy of identification and desire," what Williams calls "the impossibility of pornographic knowledge," a knowledge rendered not less but more desirable because of its impossibility, is precisely the knowledge of Tiresias.

Is it not indeed likely that for Juno and Jupiter (or for Hera and Zeus), Tiresias himself became a fantasy object of erotic speculation?

If bisexuality, like Tiresias, is often imagined heterosexually, as the copresence or alternation of "male" and "female" selves each desiring an object of the "other" gender, how does this positing of a heterosexual norm change if we imagine that bisexuality is related to a fantasy about knowing the pleasure of the other?

This is a key technique of an erotic novel like Jeanette Winterson's *Written on the Body* (1992) in which the gender of the narrator is boldly declared, on the inside cover of the book jacket, to be "undeclared." "*Written on the Body* is a book for the human condition, a book which recognises love as our most significant achievement. Generous in scope, sumptuous in detail, this is a story told by a vulnerable and subversive Lothario, gender undeclared."

Authors, of course, are not responsible for jacket copy. But the "undeclared" gender of the narrator has been a focus of most reviews of the book. The general consensus of readers has held that the speaker is a woman, and that the love triangle is itself therefore bisexual, although Winterson's deft ploy in withholding this knowledge—if it *is* knowledge —has increased both the erotic power of the book and its commercial sale. Identified only by a pronoun ("I") and its variants ("me," "myself"), explicitly provided with a bisexual past ("I had a lover once, her name was Bathsheba"; "I was in the last spasms of an affair with a Dutch girl called Inge"; "I had a boyfriend once called Crazy Frank"),[24] the narrator of *Written on the Body* is always in erotic dialogue with the reader, describing what "I" want to do with and to "you." "You" has a local referent —the narrator's current mistress, Louise—but it exceeds that referent in dozens of aphoristic, pronoun-steeped sentences: "[I]f you are broken then so am I" and "You are what I know."[25]

What is at work here is the eroticism of the shifter, a technique that can perhaps be best exemplified by returning briefly to Joyce's *Ulysses,* where it is, not incidentally, tied to the identity of Tiresias and of secret knowledge.

"Is me her was you dreamed before?" inquires Bella/Bello Cohen's fan, propounding in *Ulysses* a Tiresian gender riddle of its own: "Was then she him you us since knew? Am all them and the same now we?" Here the pronouns are all "shifters," to use Roman Jakobson's term—words that change their referent with each use, depending upon the context. "Am all them and the same now we"? Which is you, and which is me? Are "them" all now "us"—or "we"? This question of the shifter and the shifting referent is in fact central to an understanding both of Tiresias's sexuality and of his vaunted wisdom. Tiresias himself (or herself) is a shifter, an index not only of sex and gender instability but of the erotic secret of bisexuality. Does the X chromosome or the Y chromosome, the female or the male, mark the spot?

Consider the narrative of one postmodern Tiresias—or rather, the classical Teiresias as envisioned by the contemporary novelist Meredith Steinbach. Steinbach's narrative alternates between third and first person to revisit the mythological scene. "How it was that I, Tereisias, grew to be a man I did not know," one of her chapters begins. "My mother and her maids had often said that it would be so—that little boys turned to men one day most inexplicably." In defamiliarizing the "natural" progression from boy to man, Steinbach, and Teiresias, reopen the questions posed by Freud, to which "bisexuality" was, for him, a crucial answer.

At times the tone of Steinbach's Teiresias resembles that of Mary Renault, a lesbian writer whose books about the classical past enjoyed an unprecedented popularity among gay male readers at a time when mainstream treatments of "healthy" homosexual and bisexual love were few and far between. "The 'female' lover, the eunuch Bagoas, the Persian boy," writes Renault's biographer David Sweetman, "seems to represent for Mary a solution to the problems of gender by being, like T. S. Eliot's Tiresias, of neither, yet of both sexes at once."[26]

What Steinbach imagines is the primal scene of Tiresias's knowledge: "Teiresias is rubbing the astonishment from his eyes with his fists. The gods have called him in to settle an argument." "Zeus puts the question to him: 'Who has the most pleasure in sex? Who receives the most—man or woman—Teiresias?' " " 'Yes,' Hera says softly. 'Tell us, Teiresias, we hear that you've had a dream, and in it you were everything.' "[27]

The story the gods want to hear is the story of his transformation.

I take the liberty of quoting at length because Steinbach's work is not as familiar as Eliot's or Joyce's, and also because Steinbach does something they do not: She imagines Teiresias in the moment that will answer the gods' question. She imagines Teiresias having sex—but with whom?

> Perhaps there was nothing unusual at all in his nighttime experiences and the way he remembered his own tender new breasts, pale there between his two arms. The moment itself a confusion of incident never to be untangled, the product never to be forgotten as long as Teiresias lived. That moment when he was both, seen and seeing, woman and man. Two male eyes looked at him, glistening like agates. Turn around and turn around again, for down under the housing of his ribs a warmth reared up, Teiresias!, seemed to be tucked up, concentrated now into a burning in the pulp of him that radiated out out and away, down the insides of his legs. Then it was as if his sex had been turned inside out. Something fitted itself tightly inside. Back and forth he rooted his hips. Who knew how the realities coincided—which was the polished wood, which the inlaid?
>
> Vertigo—he saw the woman, dark hair full out around the high bones of her face and the slope of her shoulders, luminous, until— vertigo—he saw his own feminine face looking up from between new arms. And—turn about once again—there a dark masculine face, strong at the jaw, the meaty shoulders, a chest broad and covered with softly curling hairs that invited the cheeks and lips, and under the fingertips the long gentle curve of the back. He had never quite seen it this way. Then the pounding, now powerful, now gentle,

driving into that part which Teiresias as a woman came intimately to understand.[28]

The sense of "vertigo" here as man turns into woman then woman into man utilizes the techniques of film editing, the jump cut and shot-reverse-shot, to stress Teiresias's surprise, and also to indicate the split in his subject position: "That moment when he was both, seen and seeing, woman and man." This double seeing, this moment of both seeing and being seen, will lead ultimately to the loss of sight. "He had never quite seen it this way." Afterward, after the experience of seeing "his own feminine face," he will see differently, see with a difference, see the future. Here is another question for us: How is Tiresias's blindness related to his (bi)sexuality?

When we say "Tiresias," which Tiresias do we mean? Ovid's—the man-woman? Or Sophocles's—the blind seer who knows what Oedipus has yet to discover? How is it that the Tiresias who knows about men's and women's pleasure is also the patriarch, the wise old man who can see into the future? How does the fact of Tiresias's wisdom follow from the fact of his shape-shifting, of his sex change? Why should the one be the consequence of the other?

Scholars have sometimes sought to separate Tiresias the blind seer from the Tiresias who has experienced female as well as male pleasure.[29] But the two are the same. What does it mean that in classical Greek and Latin literature the kinkiest figure is also the wisest?

After his blinding, Tiresias becomes the omnipresent and legendary wise man of Greek epic and drama. Wherever there is a crisis of gender, a crossroads in human sexuality, Tiresias is on the scene. Once you look for him, he is everywhere. Like Alfred Hitchcock's famous cameo appearances in his own films, "a kind of visual signature,"[30] the appearances of Tiresias steal the show. He is the walk-on character par excellence, the third actor who always upstages the scene.

In the mythological episode which was to become the founding scenario for psychoanalysis, Sophocles's *Oedipus Rex*,[31] Tiresias is with Oedipus at Thebes, where the tragic truth is discovered: Unwittingly, Oedipus has fulfilled his destiny, has killed his father and married his mother.[32] Fleeing Corinth to avoid the fate ordained him by an oracle, Oedipus meets an unknown man at a crossroads and kills him. Arriving in Thebes, he answers the Sphinx's riddle, saves the land, and marries its widowed queen. A plague afflicts the city. Oedipus vows to punish the criminal whose presence has caused the plague. Tiresias tells him, "You are the one you seek."[33]

Tiresias is there.

Tiresias is also at Thebes at the moment, earlier in Greek history, when the puritanical young King Pentheus scorns the bacchic rites of the god Dionysus, a moment compellingly described in the *Bacchae* of Euripides.

Refusing to pay honor to the god, Pentheus encounters a comely stranger, beardless, fair-skinned, and with flowing hair, who is, though the young king does not know it, Dionysus in disguise. "Your blasphemies have made you blind," says the stranger as he is taken captive. "You do not know who you are." Himself old and blind, ludicrously dressed as a bacchant in fawn skin and ivy, Tiresias tries to warn Pentheus, but the young man resists, is tricked into assuming the dress and wig of a woman, and is killed by his mother, who in her bacchic ecstasy mistakes him for a beast.

Tiresias is there.

And Tiresias is there when another beautiful boy, Narcissus, goes to his fate. No sooner has Ovid told the story of how Tiresias became a blind seer than he recounts, in the same book of the *Metamorphoses,* the cautionary tale of Narcissus, desired by both male and female lovers, who scorned them all out of pride.[34] His mother consulted Tiresias about whether Narcissus would live a full life span and received the enigmatic answer, "If he never knows himself." Narcissus falls in love with his own reflection and does not at first know what he sees. When he finally realizes that "I am he" (*iste ego sum*), he drowns seeking vainly to embrace himself.

In the Narcissus story Tiresias, who has been both man and woman, sees, and sees through, the fate of another quintessentially liminal being, a boy erotically attractive to both men and women, and situated on the threshold of boyhood and manhood. At first apparently so different—one old and wise; one young, foolish, and beautiful—these mirroring figures, Tiresias and Narcissus, may be seen as types of the bisexual, desiring and desired.

Narcissus's appeal is simultaneously to male and female lovers, who choose him not for his gender but for his beauty (and his resistance). Though the story of the nymph Echo's tragic passion is the best known of his conquests, it is the prayer of a rejected *youth,* a young man, that is granted by the goddess of Vengeance and leads to Narcissus's infatuation with himself. By contrast, Tiresias's sexuality is serial, offstage, and implicitly heteroerotic. We never see him in love, we never encounter a story in which he takes a lover. All his wisdom is presented as a given: Somehow, he knows.

The classical poet Callimachus tells yet another story about the blinding of Tiresias. He says that Tiresias surprised the goddess Athena bathing, and saw what was forbidden to be seen: the body of the "virile virgin," an uncanny sight.[35] Tiresias and Athena are both figures "of ambivalent sexual status" who are associated with the linkage of perception and sexuality. Athena is often pictured with both male and female insignia—a lance and a distaff—and the interloper may have seen the goddess as phallic woman, anatomically male and female at once. Or, as Nicole Loraux imagines, he may have seen that she had the body of a woman, yet nonetheless possessed the powers of a man. Which sight would be more secret? Or more uncanny? It is tempting to see this as another version of the discovery of bisexuality, the body of Athena taking the place of the coupling serpents.[36] Can "bisexuality" here be understood *both* morphologically *and* erotically, or must one reading yield power to the other?

Oedipus, Pentheus, Narcissus, Athena. Notice that all of these stories involve versions of the same events: dangerous or unlawful looking, gender-crossing, sexual desire, and bodily transformation. They are in fact all doubled stories, stories at once about the protagonist and the spectator. "You are the one you seek." "You do not know who you are." "If he never knows himself." "I (that one) am he."

The fate of Narcissus, like the fates of Oedipus and Pentheus, is not to recognize himself when he encounters that self in another form. Again the erotics of the shifter are at work, and Tiresias is there.

The Subject Presumed to Know

"When Freud uncovers what can only be called the subject's lines of fate, it is the face of Tiresias that we question before the ambiguity in which his verdict operates," argues the French psychoanalyst Jacques Lacan.[37] In this assertion, Tiresias is explicitly identified with Freud. His interpretation of what a patient tells him is always presented in oblique, suspended form, like Tiresias's prophetic riddles. His power, the power of the analyst, lies precisely in not using the power that is his. In psychoanalytic terms, this permits the functioning of the transference: Thoughts and emotions are "transferred" by the patient from an old scenario (relations with a parent, a sibling, a lover) to a new one (the relationship with the analyst), and are remembered, repeated, worked through. The analyst becomes a third party. Like the third actor of classical Greek drama he, or she, plays many roles.

For Lacan, Freud was himself the object of transference, the *sujet supposé savoir,* the subject who is supposed to know. In his description of psychoanalysis, the psychoanalytic institution becomes the twentieth century's equivalent of the oracle and the seer.

"What does an organization of psychoanalysts mean when it confers certificates of ability," asks Lacan, "if not that it indicates to whom one may apply to represent this subject who is supposed to know?

"Now, it is quite certain, as everyone knows, that no psychoanalyst can claim to represent, in however slight a way, a corpus of absolute knowledge. That is why, in a sense, it can be said that if there is someone to whom one can apply there can be only one such person. This *one* was Freud, while he was alive."

Everyone knows, says Lacan, that no psychoanalyst can know everything.

Except Freud. Because Freud, as the founder of psychoanalysis, was what there was to know. "Freud, on the subject of the unconscious, was legitimately the subject that one could presume to know." Moreover, Lacan insists, "he was not only the subject who was presumed to know. He did know."[38]

What did he know?

He knew what Tiresias knew, for everywhere Tiresias appears turns into a primal scene of psychoanalysis. What Freud knew was narcissism, and the Oedipus complex, and the drama of the speaking dead, and the crossroads of gender and sexuality, the riddle of "masculine" and "feminine." What he knew was what Tiresias knew. And what Tiresias knew was that bisexual knowledge is analytical knowledge, but only from the point of view of blindness.

The analyst's ability to hold up a mirror to the other's failures of self-recognition depends upon his being *presumed* to know. Thus the classic analytic scenario: The wise old man with a beard sits behind the couch, where the patient cannot see him but from where he can see the patient. Physical sight is deemed an obstacle to insight. The blindness of Tiresias is at once a sign of his bisexuality and of his intuition. He is only blind as far as consciousness is concerned; in the unconscious, he sees.[39]

"Since I have been acquainted with the notion of bisexuality," Freud wrote in his *Three Essays on the Theory of Sexuality,* "I have regarded it as the decisive factor, and without taking bisexuality into account I think it would scarcely be possible to arrive at an understanding of the sexual manifestations that are actually to be observed in men and women."[40] And in a letter to his friend Wilhelm Fliess, "Repression and the neuroses, and thus the independence of the unconscious, presuppose bisexuality."[41]

Narcissus, Oedipus, the underworld, and blindness. Tiresias gives us a way of understanding the hidden links between classical myth and Freudian theory, between bisexuality and analytic insight, between desire and disavowal. The scene of Tiresias is uncannily also the "other scene," the scene of the unconscious. Where we find Tiresias is where we find psychoanalysis. And where we find psychoanalysis, we find bisexuality.

Chapter 7

Freud and the Golden Fliess

Immortality, retribution, the entire beyond are all reflections of our psychic internal [world]. *Meschugge?* Psycho-mythology.

—*Letter from Sigmund Freud to Wilhelm Fliess, December 12, 1897* [1]

The ancient gods still exist, because I obtained a few recently, among them a stone Janus who looks at me with his two faces in a very superior manner.

—*Letter from Freud to Fliess, July 17, 1899* [2]

It may perhaps seem to you as though our theories are a kind of mythology and, in the present case, not even an agreeable one. But does not every science come in the end to a kind of mythology like this?

—*Sigmund Freud, "Why War?"* [3]

Psychoanalysis, an art and science born in the last half of the nineteenth century, has tended to cast its stories of human development in the shape of classical myth, from Freud's Oedipus complex to Hélène Cixous's "Laugh of the Medusa." It is indicative of the close relationship between psychoanalysis and classical mythology as modes of explanatory storytelling that when Freud came to discuss the sexual instinct, or drive, in his pathbreaking *Three Essays on the Theory of Sexuality,* he did so by recounting a myth. "The popular view of the sexual instinct," he wrote, "is beautifully reflected in the poetic fable which tells how the original human beings were cut up into two halves—man and woman—and how these are always striving to unite again in love." [4]

The "fable," of course, is Aristophanes's comic account in Plato's *Symposium.* The degree to which it is a "popular view" is augmented by Freud's own editorial excision or repression. Implying in his retelling that the original beings were each half male and half female, Freud goes on to tell us, "It comes as a great surprise, therefore, to learn that there are men whose sexual object is a man and not a woman, and women whose sexual object is a woman and not a man." Yet in Aristophanes's original fable, that is exactly what one would have expected:

> In the beginning we were nothing like we are now. For one thing, the race was divided into three, that is to say, besides the two sexes, male and female, which we have at present, there was a third which partook of the nature of both, and for which we still have a name, though the creature itself is forgotten. For though "hermaphrodite" is only used nowadays as a term of contempt, there really was a man-woman in those days, a being which was half male and half female.
>
> ...[E]ach of these [three sexes] was globular in shape, with rounded back and sides, four arms and four legs, and two faces, both the same, on a cylindrical neck, and one head, with one face one side and one the other, and four ears, and two lots of privates, and all the other parts to match....

These creatures, says Aristophanes, were arrogant and strong, and tried to scale the heights of heaven and rival the gods. So Zeus decided upon a plan: He slit them in half and had Apollo turn each face around toward the side that had been cut. But when "the work of bisection" was complete it left each half with a desperate yearning for the other, and the race began to die out from a longing to be reunited. Zeus felt so sorry for them that he modified his scheme: He moved their sexual organs around to the front and made them "propagate among themselves, the male begetting upon the female," so that if a male and female half came together, the race would be continued, and if male came together with male, each would "obtain such satisfaction as would allow him to turn his attention and his energies to the everyday affairs of life."

The poetic fable to which Freud alludes thus has a rather different character from the heterosexual manifest destiny his use of it implies. In fact, for Aristophanes, heterosexual love, the love of the male for the female, is far from the most admirable or the highest. It is derived from the "hermaphrodite sex," and it leads, often, to excess. "Each of us is forever seeking the half that will tally with himself," he says.

> The man who is a slice of the hermaphrodite sex, as it was called, will naturally be attracted by women—the adulterer, for instance— and women who run after men are of similar descent—as, for instance, the unfaithful wife. But the woman who is a slice of the original female is attracted by women rather than by men—in fact she is a Lesbian—while men who are slices of the male are followers of the male, and show their masculinity throughout their boyhood by the way they make friends with men, and the delight they take in

lying beside them and being taken in their arms. And these are the most hopeful of the nation's youth, for theirs is the most virile construction.

I know there are some people who call them shameless, but they are wrong. It is not immodesty that leads them to such pleasures, but daring, fortitude, and masculinity—the very virtues that they recognize and welcome in their lovers—which is proved by the fact that in after years they are the only men who show any real manliness in public life. . . . They have no natural inclination to marry and beget children, for they would just as soon renounce marriage altogether and spend their lives with one another.[5]

Let us look at this "poetic fable" from the perspective of what it tells us about sexuality, or, to recur to the topic which has led Freud to allude to it, "Deviations in Respect of the Sexual Object" in the larger context of "The Sexual Aberrations." Who are the "aberrants" and the "deviants" here?

The heterosexual lovers in Aristophanes's fable (according to Freud the "original human beings" who were "cut up into two halves—man and woman") are not only derived from the "hermaphrodite sex" (a term used in Freud's own time to describe male and female homosexuals) but are also characterized in terms of nonmonogamous passion and appetite: adulterers and women who run after men. Nowhere in this droll little tale can be found the idealized heterosexual pair with their family values intact. Quite to the contrary, fidelity and strong cultural values seem to repose in same-sex, and especially in male-male, love. "Virility" and "masculinity," likewise, are not conceived as virtues of the heterosexual (or, more properly here, hermaphroditically derived) male lover, but rather seem to be intensifiers describing "persons who act as men should"— pretty much the same spin, with a different result, that is given to those words today. The most virile in Aristophanes's fable is the man who loves men; the most masculine, the man who chooses a male lover. And these are the persons most influential in public life. Freud himself notes that in Greece "the most masculine men were numbered among the inverts."[6]

We should remind ourselves that only men were permitted to participate in public life in Plato's time, so that relationships between men are the only ones capable of political equality and participation in the public sphere. These virile men, derived from the original males, would prefer not to marry and beget children, but do so "in deference to the usage of society." Marriage and the home were private concerns, less elevated though socially necessary for the propagation of race and culture. But Aristophanes concludes that "the happiness of the whole human race, women no less than men," is to be found in the "healing of our dissevered nature by finding each his proper mate."

Freud would return to this "poetic fable" later in his career, when he cited it in "Beyond the Pleasure Principle" to support not a theory of sexuality but an argument about the human instinct for self-preservation —what he calls the "life instincts." He there acknowledges that the Aristophanes story "deals not only with the *origin* of the sexual instinct but also with the most important of its variations in relation to its object"— precisely the point we might have expected him to make in the section of the *Three Essays* on "Deviations in Respect of the Sexual Object," where in fact no mention is made of it. Under the general heading of "The Sexual Aberrations," which include not only "inversion" but also "bisexuality," Aristophanes's fable—or, to describe it more accurately, Plato's story of Aristophanes's fable—was used by Freud to introduce a "popular" notion of heterosexual inevitability.

On the face of it, if one can use so anatomical a figure to characterize so complex a tale of scrambled anatomies, the fable of originary doubleness does not allow for bisexuality at all. The "original" three sexes were male/male, female/female, and male/female. What courtship or "questing and clasping" goes on between them is ostensibly a process of searching for the missing half, which is either male or female, but not interchangeably the one or the other. Halves of originary male/male couples might perhaps marry or beget children under social pressure to do so, as Aristophanes describes it, or in order to engender a second generation of same-sex lovers like themselves.[7] But desire, eros, seems linked here to monosexualism. Indeed, as we have seen, the most promiscuous or indiscriminate figures in this allegorical story appear to be the heterosexuals.

And what of bisexuality? Among the Greeks what we would today call bisexuality was frequently presumed as a version of the norm.[8] It was not an "aberration" or a sign of "deviance" or "degeneracy" except in cases of voracious excess, where not the genders of the partners but the insatiability of the individual might occasion comment. Alcibiades, the Greek general and politician of the late fifth century B.C., was described, with admiration, as having taken husbands from their wives when he was a youth, and wives from their husbands in his later years.[9] Socrates, renowned in Plato's dialogues for his interest in young men, is also said by Xenophon to have visited female prostitutes.[10] The political hero Aristogiton, who assassinated the Athenian tyrant Hipparchus, had a male lover, Harmodius, and also a mistress.[11]

"Women and boys" were frequently mentioned together as interchangeable objects of desire by authors from Theocritus to Meleager to Lucian.[12] In the *Laws,* Plato refers to the sexual restraint of a famous athlete who "never once came near a woman, or a boy either, all the time he was in training."[13] The speaker in this case is an Athenian who deplores all nonprocreative sex, whether with men or with women, as injurious to society; the point here is not that all of ancient Greece spoke with one voice in endorsing bisexual relations, but rather that bisexuality, or ambisexuality, was in many contexts taken for granted. Indeed, as the recurrence of the phrase "women or boys" suggests, if we were to seek a binary distinction here we might well want to place "women and boys" on one side and "men" on the other.

According to Aristophanes (or, rather, Plato), what we today call heterosexuality is a variant rather than a necessary trajectory for human love. Freud attempts to rewrite this story—in accordance with prevailing nineteenth-century sexology—as a story of "inversion," describing "absolute" inverts, who always choose partners of the same sex; "contingent" inverts, who may do so under certain external conditions (like same-sex schools or prisons); and what he calls "amphigenic" inverts, who "lack the characteristic of exclusiveness" and may choose men or women as lovers.[14]

"Amphigenic inverts," whose "sexual objects may equally well be of their own or of the opposite sex," most closely resemble what we would today call "bisexuals," while the category of "contingent inverts," many of whom would turn up for example in a sex survey like the Kinsey report, is today contested terrain, some commentators claiming that they are indeed "bisexual," others, including many of the subjects themselves, disclaiming the "bi" label and describing their experiences instead as experimental or driven by circumstance. "Situational bisexuals" is what Freud's "contingent inverts" are often called today. The prisoner Valentin in *The Kiss of the Spider Woman* is a good example both of such "contingency" and of its unclear boundaries.

Notice that Freud describes amphigenic inverts as persons whose sexuality "lacks the characteristic of exclusiveness." It would be perfectly possible to reverse this statement so as to describe such persons as "possessing the characteristic of inclusiveness." But then they would not be "inverts"; rather, the monosexual and the exclusive heterosexual would then be found "lacking." As we will see, Freud would intermittently ponder this question of erotic "exclusiveness," or what bisexuals call "monosexuality," coming to conclude in a later edition of *Three Essays* that exclusive heterosexuality is "also a problem that needs elucidating."[15]

But this fascinating speculation was a few years away. In his initial attempt to describe sexual "inversion," Freud held, with Wilhelm Fliess and others, that its causes were likely to be biological. The word "amphigenic," significantly, means "born with [or as] both." Following Richard von Krafft-Ebing's terminology, Freud also calls such persons "psychological hermaphrodites."

What is especially striking in this account is that these categories of the amphigenic and contingent invert are *not* what Freud himself describes as bisexuality. "Bisexuality" to him, at least in *Three Essays,* is a separate topic, one that has to do with anatomy, physiology, and hermaphroditism—with, that is to say, biology. "It is popularly believed that a human being is either a man or a woman. Science, however, knows of cases in which the sexual characters are obscured, and in which it is consequently difficult to determine the sex. This arises in the first instance in the field of anatomy. The genitals of the individuals concerned combine male and female characteristics."[16]

"Science," here, is the subject presumed to know. And what science knows is that it is sometimes difficult to know. Compare this opening gambit to a very similar phrase in his late essay on "Femininity" (1933). "When you first meet a human being, the first distinction you make is 'male or female?' and you are accustomed to make the distinction with unhesitating certainty." Again an allegorized "Science" is there to disturb this complacency.

> Science next tells you something that runs counter to your expectations and is probably calculated to confuse your feelings. It draws your attention to the fact that portions of the male sexual apparatus also appear in women's bodies, though in an atrophied state, and vice versa in the alternative case. It regards their appearance as indications of *bisexuality,* as though an individual is not a man or a woman but always both—merely a certain amount more the one than the other.[17]

Are hermaphrodites bisexual? Sometimes. Are bisexuals hermaphrodites? Seldom. Yet this confusion of the physical and the erotic has persisted in the definition of the word "bisexual." It is traceable to a superimposition of metaphor or figure upon referent.

The Story of Hermaphroditus

Ovid's Hermaphrodite, less bisexual than asexual, not made up of two genders but of two halves. Hence, a fantasy of unity. Two within one, and not even two wholes.

—*Hélène Cixous, "Sorties"*[18]

In Ovid's *Metamorphoses,* Hermaphroditus is the child of Hermes and Aphrodite, whose two names are joined in his. Like Narcissus, he is said to have come to the side of a pool, where he encountered a nymph, Salmacis, who desired him. The naive Hermaphroditus resisted her embraces, but she nonetheless pursued him, clung to him, and would not let go. Salmacis prayed to the gods to make them one flesh: "so were these two bodies knit in close embrace: they were no longer two, nor such as to be called, one, woman, and one, man. They seemed neither, and yet both" *(neutrumque et utrumque).*[19]

As was the case with Tiresias, so here again the gods' gift or curse could not be reversed. Hermaphroditus was condemned to this "two-formed" *(biformis)* life. But his prayer was also granted, and the pool henceforth became an enfeebling spring, sapping the virility of any man who bathed in it, making him a "half-man" *(semivir).* It is worth doing the math here; two *(biformis),* in the case of anatomy and sexuality, apparently equals less than one *(semivir).* The lesson, such as it was, would not be lost on later and more censorious generations.

In Ovid's terms, then, the story of Hermaphroditus is closely related to that of Narcissus and, indeed, to that of Tiresias and his transformation. But this cautionary tale, so apparently *un*pleasurable to its hero, has been borrowed in modern times to characterize not the possibility of complex eroticism but the anatomical and biological mingling of male and female.

We should note that ancient Greek rites, like the Egyptians', pay rich homage to hermaphroditic deities. Dionysus, himself a god born from the body of the king of the gods, was worshiped as a deity who crosses the boundaries of gender. His appearance is often "feminine," as it is in Euripides's *Bacchae,* where, as we have seen, he is beardless and wears his hair in ringlets. But his sign is the phallus, whether attached to his body or held aloft as a detached emblem of sexuality and erotic power.

Since the Middle Ages the word "hermaphrodite" has been used in English to designate a human being in whom male and female characteristics are actually or apparently combined. Thus the (usually pejorative) sense of "an effeminate man or a virile woman" coexists with more "scientific" uses, and, inevitably, with "moral" or "ethical" ones as well. The hapless Hermaphroditus of Ovid, whose resistance to sexual dominance by a woman led to his becoming a double-formed half-man, and whose classical representations often connoted the most enviable aspects of divine transcendence and super-sexuality, was cited in the medieval and modern periods as a sign of (1) anatomical anomaly or freakishness, (2) male (or female) homosexuality, (3) effeminacy or weakness, (4) moral inconsistency or self-contradiction, with a hint of hypocrisy, and (5) corruption.

A key issue seemed to be whether one gender or another could be seen to prevail, and also whether the "hermaphroditical" appearance, dress, or behavior was optional or inevitable.[20] A lot seems to have depended on whether sex, or rather human sexuality, was anywhere in the picture. Thus for example the "Epicoene and Hermaphrodite Convents, wherein Monks and Nuns lived together" were deplored, as was "the womanish decking of the persons of some few hermaphrodites." The mythical Sardanapalus of Assyria, whose effete ways apparently did not prevent him from waging heroic battle against the rebelling Medes, was said to have burned himself and his wife on the eve of defeat. "By which act he delivered his subjects from a monstrous Hermaphrodite who was neither true man, nor true woman, being in sexe a man, & in heart a woman." On the other hand, while hermaphroditic *persons* were often to be criticized (if they chose their duality) or pitied (if they had no choice about their condition),[21] nonhuman entities, whether earthworms, angels, or "the calm fresh evening, time's hermaphrodite" might be accepted as part of nature, or even idealized.

Thus, in the case of the hermaphrodite, what we have is a cultural history that makes persons of double sex into an allegory (of fertility, of sexuality, of undifferentiated power, of the irrational, etc.) and an empirical history that discovers such persons and, depending upon the culture and its beliefs, may venerate them as exceptional beings, regard them as freakish, or try, in a way it considers kindly and enlightened, to alter, erase, translate, "normalize," or conceal them. As we will see in a subsequent chapter, the fortunes of the "hermaphrodite" were very similar to the fortunes of the androgyne. Both were idealized in the abstract, exceptionalized in the flesh, and stigmatized when they seemed in any way to encroach upon sexuality.

The Great Antithesis

Tiresias: I am trying to warn you against your unfortunate habit of asking questions, wanting to know and understand everything.

—*Jean Cocteau*, The Infernal Machine[22]

We should finally learn from this Sphinx to ask questions, too.

—*Friedrich Nietzsche*, Beyond Good and Evil[23]

We might say that there are three mythological tropes of bisexuality: as experience (Tiresias), as essence (Hermaphroditus), and as desire (Aristophanes's fable in Plato's *Symposium*). Each of these had its influence upon Freud. But, as we will see, there was a fourth mythological narrative even more crucial than these: the story of Oedipus. What, if anything, might that ur-myth of psychoanalysis tell us about bisexuality?

The familiar Oedipus story begins with the hero killing an old man at a crossroads. The old man is Oedipus's father Laius, who had ordered his newborn son taken to the mountains to die in order to prevent exactly this event. But the "prehistory" of the myth involves a key episode in which the young Laius, received graciously at King Pelops's court, ungratefully repaid his benefactor by abducting Pelops's beautiful son Chrysippus. It is in fact Pelops, seeking reparation for Chrysippus's rape, who calls down the curse on the house of Labdacus, the prophecy of Laius's murder by his own son. The myth of Oedipus thus has its origins in a tale of homosexual seduction—and in Laius's bisexuality.

Laius is described in some accounts as the "inventor" of pederasty.[24]

Other authorities blame him not for his seduction of the boy Chrysippus but for the violation of his host's hospitality. He has been viewed as a "perverse" person, "an active homosexual with sadistic traits"—in short, just the kind of parent upon whom Freud had blamed the neuroses of his patients in his early, and ultimately rejected, "seduction theory." [25]

Sophocles excludes this motif from *Oedipus Rex,* and Freud excludes both the inherited curse and the theme of paternal seduction from his interpretation of the Oedipus myth, though it seems clear that he could have known the story of Laius and Chrysippus from popular nineteenth-century mythological handbooks. This exclusion has attracted the attention of some psychoanalytic commentators, who think Freud may be turning away from dangerous inquiries into his own father's sexual history of extramarital affairs with women. [26]

But there may be another kind of reason why Freud chose not to stress the connection of Oedipus with a lineal curse inherited because of his father's bisexual relations. When Freud came up with the theory of the Oedipus complex, which replaced his earlier "seduction theory," he placed the emphasis of psychoanalysis on infantile sexual *fantasies* rather than on a child's sexual *experiences* with a parent. And when he replaced the innate and originary "bisexual disposition" of biology with the revised cultural understanding of bisexuality in his later works, he once again emphasized fantasy and desire over any merely historical inheritance.

To the end of his life Freud wrestled with the "conundrum" of bisexuality. It might indeed be said that he came back after death as what he liked to call a "revenant" to offer some final views, for in the posthumously published *Outline of Psycho-Analysis* (1938) he returned once again to "the great enigma of the biological fact of the duality of the sexes," still using the term "bisexuality" to describe it:

> We are faced here by the great enigma of the biological fact of the duality of the sexes: it is an ultimate fact for our knowledge, it defies every attempt to trace it back to something else. Psycho-analysis has contributed nothing to clearing up this problem, which clearly falls wholly within the province of biology. In mental life we only find reflections of this great antithesis; and their interpretation is made more difficult by the fact, long suspected, that no individual is limited to the modes of reaction of a single sex but always finds some room for those of the opposite one. . . . This fact of psychological bisexuality, too, embarrasses all our enquiries into the subject and makes them harder to describe. [27]

Antithesis. Duality. Bisexuality. In each of these words the key number is two: two sexes, two sides to the personality, not only an antithesis but a "great antithesis," its magnitude baffling to the scientist, humbling to the social and psychoanalytic observer.

BI-OLOGY: SCIENCE, PSYCHOANALYSIS, PSYCHOMYTHOLOGY

But the "great antithesis" is also described as a "great enigma." This "enigma" of the biological fact of there being two sexes, like the "riddle of femininity" posed in the *New Introductory Lectures on Psycho-analysis*[28] and the "great riddle of sex" with which he terminates "Analysis Terminable and Interminable," has about it a distinct aroma of Sphinx.

Sexing the Sphinx

Long afterward, Oedipus, old and blinded, walked the
roads.   He smelled a familiar smell.   It was
the Sphinx.   Oedipus said, "I want to ask one question.
Why didn't I recognize my mother?"   "You gave the
wrong answer," said the Sphinx.   "But that was what
made everything possible," said Oedipus.   "No," she said.
"When I asked, What walks on four legs in the morning,
two at noon, and three in the evening, you answered,
Man.   You didn't say anything about woman."
"When you say Man," said Oedipus, "you include women
too. Everyone knows that."   She said, "That's what
you think."

—*Muriel Rukeyser, "Myth"*[29]

SOLDIER: You're pale. . . . What's wrong with you? Feel weak?
YOUNG SOLDIER: It's funny . . . I thought I heard a noise. I thought it was him.
SOLDIER: The Sphinx?
YOUNG SOLDIER: No, the ghost.

—*Jean Cocteau, The Infernal Machine*[30]

Artists and writers engaged with issues of sexual orientation seem often to have chosen the Sphinx as an emblem of their own riddles. In 1969 singer David Bowie posed for a photographer in the costume of the Sphinx. Bowie's hands and arms stretched out before him, pink-lacquered fingernails like claws, a huge ring on one finger and a bracelet around the other wrist. An Egyptian headdress framed his face. For this performer of many guises, costumes, roles, and sexualities, the Sphinx is a perfect image.

Others who have claimed the Sphinx as their own include lesbian writer Monique Wittig, who describes an erotic encounter between two sphinxes ("You are face to face with m/e sphinx of clay, as I follow you eyeless grey crouched over m/e. . . .*I* begin to sway before you while you are in suspense. *I* am taken with the desire to enter into the darkness of your body your face your limbs. A hissing is audible. A continuous vibration traverses m/y body . . ."), and Oscar Wilde, the bisexual inventer of modern homosexuality. Wilde's sphinx, in the tradition of French Parnassian poetry, begins as "beautiful and silent," an "exquisite grotesque! half woman and half animal!" By the conclusion of the poem, which took Wilde years to write, she has become a "False Sphinx!," a "loathsome mystery" who "wakes in [him] each bestial sense."

The long history of interpretations of the Sphinx has frequently returned to the question of gender and sexuality. Jungian readings often see the Sphinx as a conflation of animus and anima, male and female;[31] Freudian psychoanalytic readings connect it with sexual difference and castration anxiety: "[T]he small child," writes one analyst, "is familiar with the head and breasts of the mother, but the lower body, always kept covered, represents the Unknown."[32] Psychoanalytic anthropologist Géza Róheim interpreted "the being with the indefinite number of legs" in the Sphinx's riddle as a symbolic embodiment of the primal scene, a fantasy or memory of the "combined body" of mother and father in parental intercourse.[33]

On the occasion of his fiftieth birthday in 1906, Freud's Viennese colleagues presented him with a carefully chosen gift: a medallion that displayed his portrait in profile on one side and, on the other, Oedipus solving the riddle of the Sphinx. The inscription in Greek, from Sophocles's *Oedipus Rex,* read: "He divined the famous riddle and was a most mighty man." The allusion was clearly to Freud as the modern Oedipus.

At the presentation ceremony, there occurred what Ernest Jones calls "a curious incident." Freud became "pale and agitated" when he read the inscription; he "behaved as if he had encountered a *revenant,*" a ghost from the past—"and so he had." He demanded to know who had thought of the passage from Sophocles, and then explained that as a young student at the University of Vienna he had often strolled around the courtyard inspecting the busts of famous professors. He had had the fantasy of seeing his own bust there in the future, and—this was the uncanny thing—he had imagined it inscribed "with the *identical words*" he now saw on the medallion.[34]

The medallion itself, designed by the sculptor Karl Maria Schwerdtner, is worth a closer glance. On the one side is Freud, vigorous, bearded, intense, looking resolutely ahead, the bust cut off conventionally at the shoulder line of his Victorian business suit. On the other side Oedipus, a classical nude with a fillet around his head, beardless, leaning on a staff, placidly confronts a Sphinx with the head of a beautiful pre-Raphaelite woman and the front claws of a lion. This Sphinx, with her escaping tendril of hair and her coin-sharp profile, could have come straight from the pages of Dante Gabriel Rossetti. She is larger in scale than Oedipus, and she, like Freud on the reverse of the medal, appears as a head-and-shoulders bust in profile facing right. Perched on a rock, she looks Oedipus in the eye; the rest of her body, below the shoulder line, is out of the medallion's frame.

There are a few peculiar elements here. For one thing, Oedipus, his head resting on his arm in the conventional gesture of deep thought, is depicted, despite his evident youth, in the riddle's third and last phase ("What goes on three legs in the evening?") because of his staff. The staff as a pictorial element might well have been derived by the sculptor from classical statuary, where a tree stump or other leaning-device is often used to support the frame of the free-standing body. It is also necessary for the pose of deep thought, since Oedipus has to lean on *something* in order to rest his face in his hand. But nonetheless the effect is a little odd, since the scene alludes so directly to the moment of the solution of the riddle, a moment that occurred when Oedipus was in the prime of life. "What goes on four legs in the morning, on two at noon, and on three in the evening?" The presence of the staff, a strong diagonal in the middle of the medallion that like a virgule separates Sphinx-space from Oedipus-space, poses a new question: What does it mean that the Oedipus who solves the riddle of the Sphinx should be standing on three legs rather than two?

An even more striking element of the medallion's design is the fact that, although Freud is clearly intended to be the Oedipus figure of Sophocles's quotation, he is visually twinned not with Oedipus but with the Sphinx. Iconographically the two profile heads, both bearing the unmistakable signs of turn-of-the-century dress and taste, both facing in the same direction, both cut off at the shoulder, are very much more like each other than either is like the full-length Oedipus with his deliberately classicized (un)dress and posture. Yet all of the medallion's "readers," including the Viennese psychoanalysts who commissioned and presented it to their chief, have interpreted the gift as a straightforward illustration of the inscription from Sophocles: Freud is the "mighty man" who "divined the famous riddle."

"Who of us is Oedipus here? Who the Sphinx?" asked Nietzsche.[35] In a sense, paradoxically, it could be said that the "subject presumed to know" is not the person with the answers but the person who poses the questions. Ask anyone who has been in analysis. "Is not the analyst always the Sphinx?"[36] Freud is perhaps most useful to us today not for the way he answered the riddle but for the ways in which he continuously posed and reposed it. And no riddle was posed more often by Freud than the question of bisexuality.

"The Main Thing"

I do not in the least underestimate bisexuality. . . . I expect it to provide all further enlightenment.

—*Letter from Freud to Fliess, March 25, 1898* [37]

And now, the main thing! As far as I can see, my next work will be called "Human Bisexuality." It will go to the root of the problem and say the last word it may be granted me to say—the last and the most profound.

—*Letter from Freud to Fliess, August 7, 1901* [38]

"Bisexuality! You are certainly right about it. I am accustoming myself to regarding every sexual act as a process in which four individuals are involved." [39] This rhapsodic interjection, expressed in a letter to Wilhelm Fliess in August 1899, marks a key moment in Freud's thought. It marks as well the overdetermined and emotionally fraught nature of their relationship, which would come to an acrimonious end.

The "discovery" of human bisexuality as a fundamental fact of life by Freud's close friend Wilhelm Fliess and Freud's own enthusiastic appropriation of the concept are vital developments in the twentieth century's complex rethinking of sexuality, repression, and desire.

During the course of his long career Freud used "bisexuality" as the centerpiece for wide-ranging theories about how culture and the psyche are formed, from the physical (intersexuality, hermaphroditism) to the psychological (homosexuality, "perversion," repression, sublimation, transference). The term was constantly present in his work, as it was in that of his contemporaries in the emerging field of "sexology"—figures like Havelock Ellis and Edward Carpenter, whom we will consider in a later section in the context of "science." For Freud, whose work spans a long and changing period of cultural history, the meaning of bisexuality shifted considerably from the beginning of his career in the late nineteenth century to its end in the midst of preparations for the Second World War. In focusing on Freud here I want to stress the enormous influence, for good and ill, that "Freudian" notions of bisexuality have had for modern culture, and to situate both Freud and "bisexuality," like psychoanalysis, on the permeable borderline between myth and science.

When he first began to think about bisexuality Freud envisioned it as biological, chemical, and anatomical—in any case, innate: "the bisexuality of all human beings." [40] His concept of the "bisexual disposition" in *Three Essays* implied a kind of "infantile unisex" [41]—the child, whose body bore biological traces of both male and female elements, was erotically attracted to both males and females. Only later, through a mechanism of repression, did he or she achieve "maturity" by suppressing one side of the "bisexual disposition" in accordance with (heterosexual) social norms and expectations. "The subject's sexual constitution," he theorized, "which is derived from an initial bisexuality," undergoes repression as a result of childhood experiences and socialization.[42]

This idea—which, as we shall see, derived in large part from Freud's conversations with Fliess—accounted for neurosis: When the repressed other side manifested itself (the "masculine" side of women, the "feminine" side of men) the result was dysfunction and distress.

As will be clear from this short account, the "originary bisexual disposition" was imagined not only as innate and biological but also as intrinsically part of a system at once heterosexual and monosexual. Men would normally grow up to desire women and to repress any leftover "originary" desire for men; for women the reverse would be true. An adult was "bisexual" only in terms of his or her biological makeup. What we would today call bisexuality—sexual attraction to both men and women—was a problem, a symptom of neurosis.

For Freud, however, this description ultimately raised more questions than it answered. Later in his career he changed his ideas about so-called primary bisexuality, regarding it, as Jacqueline Rose nicely puts the case, no longer as "an undifferentiated sexual nature prior to symbolic difference," but rather as "the availability to all subjects [i.e., all persons] of both positions in relation to that difference itself."[43]

In other words, it was not that bisexuality represented a biological or developmental stage prior to "mature" heterosexual desire, but rather that all human subjects were precarious or divided in their sexuality, developing sexual roles and desires as a result of cultural as well as biological factors and "gender imprinting."[44] "Bisexuality" for Freud, then, comes to mean the unfixed nature of sexual identity and sexual object choice.

Fliess had argued that the "bisexual constitution of human beings" was directly related to biology, so that in biological males the "feminine" was normally repressed, and in biological females the "masculine." By 1919, in the essay "A Child is Being Beaten," Freud was taking an opposite position, insisting "that both in male and female individuals masculine as well as feminine instinctual impulses are found, and that each can equally undergo repression and so become unconscious."[45]

Crucial to this more complicated notion of bisexuality is Freud's revised notion of the Oedipus complex, which grounds sexual difference. Also

described by Freud as the "core complex" because he regarded it as the centerpiece of his theory, the "nucleus of neuroses,"[46] the Oedipus complex in its "complete form" includes both the "positive" version of the complex, in which the child (like Oedipus in Sophocles's play) exhibits sexual desire for the opposite-sex parent and rivalry with the parent of the same sex, and the "negative" version, in which the situation is reversed: The child desires the same-sex parent and feels rivalrous with the parent of the opposite sex.

The Oedipus complex and its concomitants in Freudian theory, penis envy and the castration complex, are part of the organizing structure of human desire, creating through the prohibition of incest an unbreakable bond between wish or desire and law. As he writes in *The Ego and the Id* (1923), the "more complete Oedipus complex, which is twofold, positive and negative, is due to the bisexuality originally present in children."

It is in fact "this complicating element introduced by bisexuality that makes it so difficult to obtain a clear view of the facts in connection with the earliest object-choices and identifications, and still more difficult to describe them intelligibly," Freud conceded. "It may even be that the ambivalence displayed in the relations to the parents should be attributed entirely to bisexuality and that it is not . . . developed out of identification in consequence of rivalry."[47]

Retaining the term "bisexuality" and revising its meaning in the direction of psychology and culture, rather than, as formerly, of biology and anatomy, Freud evolved in his later works a much more supple and subtle idea about sexual identity and desire. Culture and language compel a choice, but, as Jacqueline Rose points out, "anyone can cross over and inscribe themselves on the opposite side from that to which they are anatomically destined."[48]

Nor is this crosswalk a one-way street. Individuals are constantly in the process of enacting their sexualities. Sexualities, like the much-debated terms "masculinity" and "femininity"—are not identities but positions of identification, positions that are intrinsically fluid rather than fixed.

Post-Freudian theorists, especially feminist and queer theorists, have offered compelling critiques of some of Freud's views of bisexuality. Hélène Cixous distinguishes between "bisexuality as a fantasy of a complete being," "a fantasy of unity," like Ovid's Hermaphrodite, "less bisexual than asexual," and what she calls "the *other bisexuality*," the "location within oneself of the presence of both sexes," that gives "permission" to multiple desires.[49]

Judith Butler points out that any concept of "primary bisexuality" and its repressions is itself a back-formation from the presumption or imposition of a heterosexual norm. "The effort to locate and describe a sexuality 'before the law' as a primary bisexuality or as an ideal and unconstrained polymorphousness implies that the law is antecedent to sexuality." The concept of breaking the law, or being outside the law, can only be imagined once the idea of a law is in place. Sexuality as it is generally understood today is in fact produced by law—by taboo, by prohibition, and by social and economic motives. Clearly "the law produces *both* sanctioned heterosexuality and transgressive homosexuality." Bisexuality is "not a possibility beyond culture, but a concrete cultural possibility that is refused and redescribed as impossible."[50]

Others who have written about bisexuality recently have tended to set aside Freud's views or to use them—especially his enthusiastic comments in his letters to Fliess—only as epigraphs juxtaposed to more personal or political accounts of present-day bisexual issues. Yet any account of where we are now in terms of bisexual theory, or of bisexual politics or bisexual practice, must take cognizance of Freud's formative role.

By turns brilliant and infuriating, self-doubting and self-assured, Freud is the intellectual forerunner of most modern and postmodern speculations on sexuality—and bisexuality. Popularized, quoted out of context, dehistoricized, and rewritten by followers often less brilliant and more dogmatic than he, "Freud," like "Shakespeare," has become a cultural monolith, indeed himself a myth.

Friendship Terminable and Interminable

Distressing memories succumb especially easily to motivated forgetting.

—*Sigmund Freud,* The Psychopathology of Everyday Life[51]

Blessed are the forgetful: for they get the better even of their blunders.

—*Friedrich Nietzsche,* Beyond Good and Evil[52]

The story of Sigmund Freud's interest in bisexuality, and its foundational relation to his work, cannot be separated from his relationship with Fliess. The two first met in 1887, when Fliess, an ear, nose, and throat specialist in Berlin, attended some of Freud's lectures in Vienna on neuropathology. The two men had similar backgrounds; both were Jews, medical researchers, physicians, and outsiders, intellectually as well as socially, to the professional and personal worlds in which they practiced. In a sense both were intellectual risk-takers, ambitious to revise the paradigms of science. Fliess would become best known for his theory that sexual passion was seated in the nose, and for his idea that periodic cycles of twenty-three and twenty-eight days controlled the physiological lives of men as well as women.

The nasal eroticism theory now seems more outlandish than it did then, at a time when hysteria and the displacement of symptoms from one (usually lower, more intimate) part of the body to another (more seemly and mentionable) was emerging as a key underlying precept of what would become psychoanalysis. The nose, to contemporary racial hygienists, was a distinguishing sign of Jewishness and, according to some schemes, criminality. Its protuberant shape suggested the male genitals (again, an idea that has after a fashion endured, as the popularity of cigarette advertisements featuring the cartoon character "Joe Camel" suggests[53]). In any case, Freud's own ideas of infantile sexuality, the Oedipus complex and its implication of incestuous desire, and the psychological roots of bodily manifestations from paralysis to masochism would not have seemed any more far-fetched. In the context of these ideas, and in an intellectual climate that had already produced speculations on homosexuality as a "third sex" by sexologists like Richard von Krafft-Ebing, Havelock Ellis, and Magnus Hirschfeld, the concept of bisexuality, and of what Freud in his early papers began to call "the bisexual disposition" of all human beings, seems far from extreme.

Fliess, however, regarded it as his own piece of intellectual property, and in the early years of their friendship Freud was careful to acknowledge his proprietorship.

At a meeting between the two men in Breslau in December 1897, Fliess broached to Freud a version of the theory of bisexuality and his controversial association of it with ambidexterity or left-handedness. The experience was a heady one for Freud, as he acknowledged when he returned. "Back home and in harness again, with the delicious aftertaste of our days in Breslau. Bi-bi [bisexuality-bilaterality] is ringing in my ears."[54] As we will see in a later chapter, the analogy with left-handedness was to become a recurrent one in the discourse of sexuality. What is notable here, however, is the palpable sense of discovery, and the concurrent sensation of social, virtually of erotic, pleasure.

The conversation between the two friends at Breslau continued to resonate in their letters. "I do not in the least underestimate bisexuality," Freud assured Fliess on March 15, 1898, "I expect it to provide all further enlightenment," and he adds, "especially since that moment in the Breslau marketplace when we found both of us saying the same thing."[55] Here the exhilaration of intellectual connection suffuses the memory, and carries an authentic sexual charge. For what is clear in the Freud-Fliess correspondence is that sexuality, however scientifically explored and pursued, was not something merely theoretical. It could and did carry over into the terrain of the homosocial, where, perhaps inevitably, the topic under discussion, bisexuality, was acted out.

"What is your wife doing other than working out in a dark compulsion the notion that Breuer [Freud's former collaborator and friend] once planted in her mind when he told her how lucky she was that I did not live in Berlin and could not interfere with her marriage?" he wrote to Fliess in August 1901, after the relationship had cooled. "You take sides against me." "I do not share your contempt for friendship between men," he continued, ostensibly describing a relationship between Breuer and his brother, "probably because I am to a high degree party to it. In my life, as you know, woman has never replaced the comrade, the friend." In fact, Breuer's "male inclination"—Breuer's, mind you, not Freud's— "would," if it were not "so timid," offer "a nice example of the accomplishments into which the androphilic current in men can be sublimated."[56] Freud's views about the relative value of male and female friendships was apparently both long standing and well known; in October 1911, Emma Jung would write to him asking about a rift in his relationship with her husband, entreating that the "dear Herr Professor" should "not count me among the women who, you once told me, always spoil your friendships."[57]

After the "traumatic" end of the friendship with Fliess, Freud wrote to his colleague Sándor Ferenczi about the "withdraw[ing]" of "homosexual cathexis,"[58] and another analytic colleague and friend, Marie Bonaparte, observed in her private notebook that "Martha Freud understood very well that Fliess was able to give her husband something beyond what she could. Fliess, according to Freud, had as passionate a friendship for Freud as Freud had for Fliess."[59] Both the attraction and the rivalry between the men are nicely captured in another passage from Bonaparte's notebook: "As for bisexuality," she wrote, "if Fliess was the first to talk about it to Freud, he could not pretend to priority in this idea of biology. 'And if he gave me bisexuality, I gave him sexuality before that.' That is what Freud told me."

What caused the rift between Fliess and Freud was, on the one hand, Fliess's possessiveness, intellectually and personally, and, on the other, an extraordinary act of "forgetting" on Freud's part. Essentially what he forgot was that he himself had not thought up the bisexual theory on his own.

For some time the two friends had been in the habit of meeting for what they decribed as private "congresses"—a term that itself nicely conflates the public sphere of the professional conference with the intimate one of sexual intercourse. On one of these occasions Freud apparently informed Fliess that he had decided that the neuroses could only be explained if one began with the notion that all human beings are possessed of a bisexual constitution. Fliess replied with astonishment that he had suggested this idea to Freud years before, and that Freud had at the time been highly skeptical.

Ruefully, and with the aim of restoring the friendship, Freud published what amounted to an apology in *The Psychopathology of Everyday Life,* a work which, as he had written Fliess in the letter about the "androphilic current" between men, "is full of references to you—manifest ones, for which you supplied the material, and concealed ones, for which the motivation goes back to you." Here is the passage from *The Psychopathology of Everyday Life:*

> One day in the summer of 1901 [an error for 1900] I remarked to a
> friend with whom I used at that time to have a lively exchange of
> scientific ideas: "These problems of the neuroses are only to be
> solved if we base ourselves wholly and completely on the assumption
> of the original bisexuality of the individual." To which he replied:
> "That's what I told you two and a half years ago at Br. [Breslau] when
> we went for that evening walk. But you wouldn't hear of it then." It
> is painful to be requested in this way to surrender one's originality. I
> could not recall any such conversation or this pronouncement of my
> friend's.[60]

A week later Freud did remember the incident, "which was just as my
friend had tried to recall it to me."

This example of "forgetting" is symptomatic enough in itself, but it is
further compounded by its placement. For the example of Fliess (who of
course goes unnamed here) and the originality of the bisexual theory is
told in the *Psychopathology* as the eleventh, the last in a long series, under
the general heading "The Forgetting of Impressions and Knowledge."
We might perhaps suspect Freud of trying to tuck it into some fairly
inconspicuous spot, since, as he himself confessed in print, the whole
episode was "painful" as well as embarrassing. Immediately after narrating this anecdote, however, he is constrained, since it is the last, to
summarize what his several examples are demonstrating. His summary is
telling:

"Finding fault with one's wife, a friendship which has turned into its
opposite, a doctor's error in diagnosis, a rebuff by someone with similar
interests, borrowing someone else's ideas—it can hardly be accidental
that a collection of instances of forgetting, gathered at random, should
require me to enter into such distressing subjects in explaining them."

We may notice that virtually *all* of these characterizations, which refer
apparently to the several discrete examples one through eleven given
above in Freud's text, also fit, uncannily, the eleventh example, the story
of Fliess and bisexuality (here intended to be summarized only as "borrowing someone else's ideas"). Once described as his "only other,"[61]
whose praise was "nectar and ambrosia" to him,[62] Fliess had become, by
1901, a source of anxiety, rivalry, and competition.

Shortly after this lapse of memory and its apologetic aftermath Freud
had a dream: In it he set out "before my friend" what he described as "a
difficult and long-sought theory of bisexuality." The friend, of course, was
Fliess; the dream, Freud concluded when he wrote it up in his *Interpretation of Dreams,* was an example of wish fulfillment. But what was the
theory? Although he was struck by its being "clear and flawless," the long-
sought theory "was not given in the dream."[63]

This was then not a dream about the content of the theory of bisexuality
but a dream about getting the theory right, and presenting the answer,

triumphantly, to Fliess—who, when he read the dream book in manuscript, must have noted this further sign of competitive rivalry.

Another, more celebrated dream likewise involved Fliess and their scientific rivalry. This was the so-called *Non vixit* dream, in which Freud and Fliess encountered a dead friend, P. Not realizing the friend was dead, Fliess addressed some words to him, at which point Freud intervened to explain that the friend could not understand because *"non vivit"*—he is not alive. But in the dream Freud misspoke, and said *"non vixit"* (he did not live), an error he himself immediately caught in the dream. He then gave P. a piercing look, at which P. grew indistinct and melted away. He had become an apparition, a "revenant"—a ghost who returns. At his disappearance the Freud of the dream "was highly delighted," and concluded that "people of that kind only existed as long as one liked and could be got rid of if someone else wished it."[64]

That this dream can be read as a dream about getting rid of Fliess, as well as (or instead of) the relatively blameless "P." whom he annihilates with a glance, is suggested by Freud's own interpretation. "In point of fact," he asserts, "I am incapable of doing . . . what I did in the dream, of sacrificing to my ambition people whom I greatly value." Indeed, he imagines that he "must have reflected (unconsciously) with regret on the fact that the premature death of my friend P., whose whole life had been devoted to science, had robbed him of a well-merited claim to a memorial." It also struck him "as noticeable" that in the dream "there was a convergence of a hostile and an affectionate current of feeling toward my friend P., the former being on the surface and the latter concealed."[65]

Freud does not read this dream as having any relevance to the question of bisexual theory. But the dispute over a "well-merited claim to a memorial" on the part of a colleague whose life had been devoted to science, and about whom he had to notice a convergence of hostile and affectionate feelings (here in the reverse order of what he detects in the dreamer's relation to P.—affection on the surface, hostility concealed) points with fair clarity to Fliess. Indeed, as we have seen, when a "memorial" to his own scientific accomplishments was presented to him a few years later on the occasion of his fiftieth birthday, his response was to grow pale "as if he had encountered a revenant."[66]

"Since I have become acquainted with the notion of bisexuality I have regarded it as the decisive factor," Freud would declare in his *Three Essays on the Theory of Sexuality,* "and without first taking bisexuality into account I think it would scarcely be possible to arrive at an understanding of the sexual manifestations that are actually to be observed in men and women."[67] So reads the sentence in all editions of *Three Essays* except the first. But something has been deleted, revised—or repressed—here. In the original edition of 1905 the same sentence began, "Since I have become acquainted through Wilhelm Fliess with the notion of bisexuality . . ."

By the time he came to revise *Three Essays* in 1915, Freud had, as in the dream, made his rival disappear.

The more Freud thought about the concept of bisexuality the more it seemed to him the answer to his core problem, repression. Repression, he decided, "is possible only through reaction between two sexual currents." And this was the insight he had gotten from Fliess. As he wrote to him in August 1901, "The idea itself is yours. You remember my telling you years ago, when you were still a nose specialist and surgeon, that the solution lay in sexuality. Several years later you corrected me, saying that it lay in bisexuality—and I see that you are right."

The problem was indeed one of authorship and priority. Strictly speaking, the idea was Fliess's. "So perhaps I must borrow even more from you; perhaps my sense of honor will force me to ask you to coauthor the work with me; thereby the anatomical-biological part would gain in scope." Freud himself would concentrate "on the psychic aspect of bisexuality and the explanation of the neurotic."[68] This "next project," then, would "quite properly unite us again in scientific matters as well."

The collaboration, of course, never took place. Instead, Freud received an angry reply from his friend protesting what seemed to be the appropriation of Fliess's ideas.

The language of propriety and "honor" in the letter of August 1901 discloses both Freud's discomfort and the awkwardness of his position. He needed to put forward a theory of bisexuality as part of his own larger argument about human sexuality, but Fliess was being uncooperative, preferring to wait until his own tabulations were complete. Freud was forced into an increasingly defensive position: "I certainly had no intention," he wrote testily a month later, "of doing anything but working on my contribution to the theory of bisexuality, elaborating the thesis that repression and the neuroses, and thus the independence of the unconscious, presuppose bisexuality." Fliess should know by now—"from the relevant reference to your priority in 'Everyday Life' "—that he, Freud, had no intention of claiming credit. But the "general biological and anatomical aspects of bisexuality" were indispensable, and "since almost everything I know about it comes from you, all I can do is cite you or get an introduction entirely from you."[69]

The tension between the two men grew greater when, in 1904, Fliess read Otto Weininger's book *Sex and Character,* published the previous year. For *Sex and Character* set forth a theory of bisexuality that explained both sexual attraction and repression in terms of the copresence of masculine and feminine elements in all living organisms. Fliess blamed Freud for leaking his ideas about bisexuality to Weininger through a common acquaintance.

"Dear Sigmund," he wrote bitterly to his friend, "I have come across a book by Weininger, in the first biological part of which I find, to my consternation, a description of my ideas on bisexuality and the nature of sexual attraction consequent upon it—feminine men attract masculine women and vice versa."[70]

A complex and perverse figure, Weininger was a self-hating Jew who committed suicide in spectacular fashion, shooting himself to death in the Beethoven House in Vienna. He had strong and eccentric views about gender, sexuality, and race, which were later to influence the eugenic policies of the Nazi regime. Paradoxically, he was also cited admiringly by feminists like Charlotte Perkins Gilman. Freud would later characterize him as a "young philosopher," "highly gifted but sexually deranged."[71] Sensationalized by the suicide of its twenty-three-year-old author, *Sex and Character* quickly became an international best-seller that was ultimately translated into at least sixteen languages.

Weininger's ideas about bisexuality are fascinating and notorious. Human beings, he says, live in a "permanent bisexual condition."[72] There is no such thing as an ideal man or an ideal woman, although we can construct such ideals hypothetically: "[T]he fact is that males and females are like two substances combined in different proportions, but with either element never wholly missing. We find, so to speak, never either a man or a woman, but only the male condition and the female condition."[73]

If, "without any malicious intention," we were to substitute a plus sign for "masculinity" and a minus sign for "femininity," we would be able to account for physiological variation across the gender spectrum: "woman-ish men with strong beards," "masculine women with abnormally short hair who none the less possess well-developed breasts and broad pel-ves."[74]

Sexual attraction thus consists of the coming together of a "complete male" with a "complete female," by a mathematical combination of the male-plus-female elements in a "male" and the female-plus-male elements in a "female." Thus a man who was four-fifths male and one-fifth female would be partnered by a woman who was four-fifths female and one-fifth male, and so on. He offers an anecdote to support his idea of sexual complementarity: "I once heard a bi-sexual man exclaim, when he saw a bi-sexual actress with a slight tendency to a beard, a deep sonorous voice and very little hair on her head, 'There is a fine woman.' 'Woman' means something different for every man or for every poet, and yet it is always the same, the sexual complement of their own constitution."[75]

As these examples will suggest, what Weininger meant by "bisexuality" was something like the copresence of "masculine" and "feminine" charac-teristics in every individual, with the corollary that each seeks its comple-ment.

This sounds plausible enough within the historical context of turn-of-the-century thought. In fact it sounds very much like Aristophanes's fable of the split beings in the *Symposium,* with the difference—common to many biological theories of bisexuality—that it presupposes originary heterosexuality, at least at the level of abstraction. Males are drawn to females, females to males. "Inverts" are anatomically determined; "there is no such thing as a genuine 'psycho-sexual hermaphrodism.' "[76] But since Weininger also believed firmly that male was better than female—that "the male has everything within him" while "the woman can never become a man,"[77] and that, for example, "a female genius is a contradiction in terms"[78]—and since, moreoever, he associated maleness with intellect, memory, science, morality, and Aryanism, and femaleness with falseness, lack of judgment, amorality, hysteria, and Jewishness, his views on primary bisexuality are in a way overwhelmed by his cultural and racial assumptions.

"It is almost an insoluble riddle that woman, herself incapable of love, should attract the love of man," he muses.[79] On the other hand, "Homosexuality in a woman is the outcome of her masculinity and presupposes a higher degree of development." He noted that Catherine II of Russia, Queen Christina of Sweden, and George Sand were among the large number of "highly gifted women and girls" whom he had ascertained to be "partly bisexual, partly homo-sexual," and who "reveal their maleness by their preference either for women or for womanish men."[80]

Weininger's chapter on Judaism must have struck the Jewish physicians Freud and Fliess with special force, if they read it. ("the Jew is always more absorbed by sexual matters than the Aryan"; "no one who has had experience of them considers them loveable"; "the Jew is really nothing because he believes in nothing"; "the most manly Jew is more feminine than the least manly Aryan"; "as there is no real dignity in women, so what is meant by the word 'gentleman' does not exist amongst the Jews.")[81] Yet in their correspondence they do not comment on this racialized consequence of a biological and permanent "bisexuality," nor do they bother to note that Weininger himself had converted, and had been born a Jew. Their outlook here is determinedly universal. They look past, or away from, racial and religious slurs toward a "science" that will transcend cultural difference. Later Freud would quote Weininger's analogy between Jews and women with clinical detachment in a footnote to the "Little Hans" case, pointing out that "the castration complex is the deepest unconscious root of anti-semitism."[82] But at this super-charged moment in the Freud-Fliess relationship the issue between them is Weininger's theft of the idea of "bisexuality," not what he does with it.

Fliess was understandably furious. Since Weininger knew Hermann Swoboda (a pupil of Freud's and the recent author of yet another new book on bisexuality), Fliess told Freud that he had "no doubt that Weininger obtained knowledge of my ideas via you and misused someone else's property. What do you know about it?" he demanded.[83]

Thus directly confronted, Freud responded disingenuously. He did not know Weininger, he claimed, and he had only talked to Swoboda about bisexuality incidentally, in the course of analytic treatment. Owning up supposedly to "everything I know about it," he hypothesized that Weininger could have gotten the idea of bisexuality "elsewhere," tipped off by a casual mention from Swoboda. "The late Weininger," he wrote Fliess, "was a burglar with a key he picked up." Meanwhile, Freud was now finishing his *Three Essays on the Theory of Sexuality,* "in which I avoid the topic of bisexuality as far as possible."[84]

But Fliess was not persuaded. He consulted another friend, Oskar Rie, who told him (correctly) that Freud had seen Weininger's book in manuscript. Moreover, Weininger claimed his idea of bisexuality was "entirely new," so he could not after all have gotten it "elsewhere." Why did Freud not advise him that the idea was really Fliess's? Why had he not warned his friend? And what was Freud doing using the idea of "persistent bisexuality" in his analytic treatment after he had resisted the idea in conversations with Fliess?

Faced with this new information, Freud confessed. He had (again) "forgotten" how much he had talked with Weininger about Swoboda. "In conjunction with my own attempt to rob you of your originality, I better understand my behavior toward Weininger and my subsequent forgetting." He himself, in other words, was the burglar with the key. But of course, he writes pacifically, one can't patent ideas, especially when they are already abroad in the world. "You must admit that a resourceful mind can on its own easily take the step from the bisexual disposition of some individuals to extending it to all of them," even though the idea was Fliess's innovation. "For me personally you have always (since 1901) been the author of the idea of bisexuality." But since the matter had become so vexed, and in order to avoid further misunderstanding and claims of priority, would Fliess kindly read over the remarks on bisexuality in *Three Essays* and change them to his satisfaction? Freud himself could hardly wait "till you have surrendered your biology to the public" to bring forward his own ideas. And really there is "so little of bisexuality or of other things I have borrowed from you in what I say" that a few remarks will suffice, if only Fliess would check to make sure there are no "grounds in them for reproaches later on."[85]

So ends the correspondence, and the friendship. Still angry, Fliess got a friend to publish a pamphlet attacking Weininger, Swoboda, and Freud, which Freud denounced in a letter to Karl Kraus, the Viennese satirist and editor of the witty, acerbic political journal *Die Fackel.* "What we are here concerned with," he wrote self-righteously in January 1906, "is a defense against the overbearing presumption of a brutal personality and the banning of petty personal ambition from the temple of science."[86] To sexologist Magnus Hirschfeld, editor of the Berlin *Yearbook for Sexual Borderline Cases (Jahrbuch für sexuelle Zwischenstufen),* he described the pamphlet as a "disgusting scribble" that "casts absurd aspersions on me," the "phantasy of an ambitious man" who has lost the capacity of judgment. "It is not pleasant," he noted solemnly, "for me to utter harsh words in public about someone with whom I have for twelve years been associated in the most intimate friendship."[87]

In a few years Freud would be referring to Fliess, in a letter to his new confidant Carl Jung, as a "one-time friend" who "developed a dreadful case of paranoia after throwing off his affection for me, which was undoubtedly considerable." Paranoia for Freud could encompass delusions of persecution, erotomania, delusional jealousy, and delusions of grandeur, all linked to a defense against homosexuality.[88] But, he remarked to Jung with a palpable shrug of the shoulder, "one must try to learn something from every experience."[89]

The first phase of Freud's thinking about bisexuality could in a way be said to come to an end with the demise of the relationship with Fliess. The degree to which it was determined by that relationship, and by what some critics have regarded as his emotionally driven overestimation of Fliess's views,[90] may remain a matter for debate. But what is clear is that Freud did not give up bisexuality when he gave up Fliess. Quite to the contrary, as Juliet Mitchell has shrewdly noted, he continued to refine and ponder its meanings. "Like so many of his revolutionary notions ['bisexuality'] originated as a hunch, was questioned, cross-questioned, modified, found wanting, and finally reestablished as an essential concept. In the course of its history it moved from its biological origins to a psychoanalytic meaning. As with 'masculine' and 'feminine', the word remained the same but the significance shifted."[91]

How did it shift? And what does it mean to say that bisexuality is psychologically and culturally rather than anatomically or biologically determined?

To understand this it will be helpful to bear in mind that bisexuality remained for Freud throughout his career a key problem—perhaps *the* key problem, both in theory and in practice. Mitchell aptly calls it "the unsolved figure in the carpet." Like that elusive Jamesian entity, it was for Freud "the general intention of his books: the string the pearls were strung on, the buried treasure"[92] at the same time that it remained, to a certain extent, ironically undescribed and undescried.

At one point early in their relationship Freud had written to his friend Fliess that he expected the concept of bisexuality to provide "all further enlightenment" about human sexual identity and the neuroses.[93] During the course of preparing his account of the "Dora" case—which, although published in 1905, was largely written in 1901, still at the height of the Fliess years—he wrote to his friend that "bisexuality is mentioned and specifically recognized once and for all, and the ground is prepared for detailed treatment of it on another occasion."[94] As we have already noted, he wrote excitedly to Fliess a few years later, "And now the main thing! As far as I can see, my next work will be called 'Human Bisexuality.' It will go to the root of the problem and say the last word."[95]

Freud never came to write a book called "Human Bisexuality," but it is arguable that the entire corpus of his work could be regarded under that title.

At times, he evidences a particular relish in wresting the theory of bisexuality away from Fliess. His sharp put-down of the idea that each biological sex represses the instincts of the other ("with men, what is unconscious and repressed can be brought down to feminine instinctual impulses; and conversely with women")[96] in an essay of 1919, almost twenty years after the Fliess infatuation, ascribes that view to "a colleague with whom I was at the time on friendly terms" and adds, rather tartly and with what may not be perfect truth, "I may say at once that I have always regarded [this theory] as incorrect and misleading."[97]

Fundamentally, however, Freud kept trying to work at, and work out, his own theory. Among the topics to which he returned with particular emphasis are three that have a special bearing on subsequent understandings of bisexuality: the nature of eroticism and bisexual desire; the relationship among three apparent pairs of "opposites" (masculine and feminine, active and passive, and heterosexual and homosexual); and the "problem" of monosexuality.

Object Relations

Freud sometimes speaks of bisexual attraction as an erotic relation of the subject with the "masculine" aspect of a woman or the "feminine" aspect of a man—or a boy. In his account of "inversion" among the ancient Greeks in *Three Essays,* he describes just such an attraction. "It is clear that in Greece, where the most masculine men were numbered among the inverts, what excited a man's love was not the *masculine* character of a boy, but his physical resemblance to a woman as well as his feminine mental qualities—his shyness, his modesty and his need for instruction and assistance." When the boy became a man he was no longer a sexual object for men, but rather took boy lovers himself.

In this instance, then, "the sexual object is not someone of the same sex, but someone who combines the characters of both sexes; there is, as it were, a compromise between an impulse that seeks for a man and one that seeks for a woman, while it remains a paramount condition that the object's body (i.e., genitals) shall be masculine." In 1915, Freud added another sentence as a capstone to this argument: "Thus the sexual object is a kind of reflection of the subject's own bisexual nature."[98]

There is something here to irritate everyone. Many feminists will resist being told that women are naturally shy and modest, just as many gays and lesbians will surely cavil at the idea that "the sexual object is not someone of the same sex." Freud's ancient Greek male citizen, it seems, "really" seeks a feminine partner, or rather, as Freud says, "someone who combines the character of both sexes." His choice is a "compromise"—another red-flag term. But in point of fact his choice is a boy. Not a man, and not a woman. And not a compromise.

Considered from the point of view of eroticism, however, there is some sense in what Freud says, if we can bring ourselves to forgive him for writing in his own time rather than in ours. Indeed in our time superstars, models, and entertainers who "combine the character of both sexes" are among our most desired fantasy objects. *Is* the sexual object "a kind of reflection of the subject's own bisexual nature"? What is the relationship of subject to object?

In an essay published in 1908, "Hysterical Phantasies and Their Relationship to Bisexuality," Freud suggested that "hysterical symptoms are the expression on the one hand of a masculine unconscious fantasy, and on the other hand a feminine one." Such symptoms often had "a bisexual meaning"—that is, they took part in two different stories, or two versions, two perspectives, of the same story. "We need not then be surprised or misled if a symptom seems to persist undiminished although we have already resolved one of its sexual meanings; for it is still being maintained by the—perhaps unsuspected—one belonging to the opposite sex."[99]

In such a case "masculine" and "feminine" fantasies are contesting within the same individual. Freud's example here, one we have had occasion to mention before, is that of a woman who "pressed her dress up against her body with one hand (as the woman) while she tried to tear it off with the other (as the man)." A painting by René Magritte called *Titanic Days* superbly illustrates the conflict. In it a monumental nude woman pushes away a clothed male body which is also, mysteriously, part of her own; her arms thrust at his shoulders, while his hands, likewise seemingly attached to her, fondle her thighs. The 1908 essay may be taken as a kind of middle stage in Freud's thinking about bisexuality, a "halfway house," as Juliet Mitchell puts it, between the concept of originary bisexuality and the more complex notion of the "oscillations and imbalance"[100] of the adult subject.

In Freud's 1920 case study of "Homosexuality in a Woman" he again uses "bisexuality" to describe this kind of doubled attraction. The patient was an eighteen-year-old woman who fell in love with a woman ten years older than herself—a woman whom her parents claimed to be having promiscuous affairs with men and with a married woman friend. This "questionable lady," as Freud dubs her, had become the focus of the younger woman's entire attention: she sent her flowers, waited for her at tram stops, kissed her hand, and even attempted to commit suicide when her father, seeing the two women together, "passed them by with an angry glance."[101] It was not clear whether the women were actually sexually involved—"whether the limits of devoted admiration had already been exceeded or not"—but the parents were seriously "vexed," and brought their daughter to Freud for a "cure."[102]

In writing up the case, Freud seizes on the opportunity to disavow the argument of biological determinism or "physical hermaphroditism"—the old Fliess argument. "Readers unversed in psycho-analysis" will want to know whether the "homosexual girl" had masculine physical characteristics. Freud himself cannot say for certain—"the psycho-analyst customarily forgoes a thorough physical examination of his patients in certain cases" —but he can say that there is often no correlation between physical and psychical "hermaphroditism," though he has to admit that in women "bodily and mental traits belonging to the opposite sex" are more apt to coincide than they are in men. And indeed the patient (who "had her father's tall figure") showed certain "male" characteristics, like good judgment: her "intellectual attributes," "her acuteness of comprehension and her lucid objectivity"—all these could indeed be "connected with masculinity." Still, Freud says, these are not the point. They are "conventional" rather than "scientific" distinctions. What distinguished the young woman's passion was her behavior: "[S]he displayed the humility and the sublime overvaluation of the sexual object so characteristic of the male lover," including "the preference for being the lover rather than the beloved."[103]

We may wonder whether Freud had ever considered the possibility of decoupling these stereotypes, to imagine a lesbian woman who was, as the current phrase has it, "Butch in the streets, femme in the sheets"? Freud's conventional gendering of courtship refuses to see lover and beloved as flexible roles, regarding them instead as opposites. His patient, he concluded, "had thus not only chosen a feminine love-object, but had also developed a masculine attitude toward that object."[104]

Freud's investigation, proceeding along the lines of the Oedipal triangle, detected in the young woman a disappointed desire to have her father's child, a rivalry with the mother who *had* borne him another child—a son —and a rejection of both the love for the father and the feminine role. "She changed into a man and took her mother in place of her father as the object of her love."[105] In so doing she also restored her relationship to the mother, and found "a substitute mother" in the older woman who was the object of her current passion.

Lesbian and queer theorists have found it easy to criticize Freud's attitudes in this case, in which the "problem" was clearly not the girl's but her parents'. She was perfectly content with her passion, and showed no neurotic symptoms; it was her parents who found the relationship intolerable and sent her to the doctor. As in the "Dora" case, where the analyst's position toward a female patient in love with a woman is even more problematic, it is tempting to be sidetracked into an assessment of Freud's shortcomings. If his only way of understanding the woman's sexual attraction to another woman is to assert flat out that "she changed into a man," something is wrong with this picture.

But there are elements of this case which are rather intriguing from a bisexual point of view. For one thing, when Freud decides that he wants to explain his patient's having "foresworn her womanhood" as a result of rivalry and disappointment, he does so at first by invoking a parallel dysfunction in men ("after a first distressing experience" many "turn their backs for ever upon the faithless female sex and become woman-haters") and then segues, without warning, into an anecdotal snapshot of normative bisexuality, a sociocultural version of the earlier biological arguments about vestiges of one sex's anatomy surviving in the opposite sex: "In all of us, throughout life, the libido normally oscillates between male and female objects; the bachelor gives up his men friends when he marries, and returns to club-life when married life has lost its savour."[106]

In 1920, Sigmund Freud was sixty-four years old. He had been married since 1886. As we have noticed in his correspondence with Fliess and in a letter to him from Carl Jung's wife, friendships with men were of vital importance to him. As he wrote to Fliess, "In my life, as you know, woman has never replaced the comrade, the friend." Smack in the middle of his clinical account of "the mystery of homosexuality,"[107] as typified by the case of a young woman, he gives us this homely and *unheimlich* example of "the universal bisexuality of human beings"[108] by describing the "normal" sexual oscillation of a middle-aged man. We may be reminded of the more confessional tone of the letter to Fliess in which he announced the universality of the Oedipus complex: "I have found in my own case, too . . ."[109]

The case of the homosexual woman also suggested to Freud an interpretation of bisexuality which had to do with erotic identification and fantasy. "Her lady's slender figure, severe beauty, and downright manner reminded her of the brother who was a little older than herself. Her latest choice corresponded, therefore, not only to her feminine but also to her masculine ideal; it combined satisfaction of the homosexual tendency with that of the heterosexual one."[110]

This fact, Freud insists, "should warn us not to form too simple a conception of the nature and genesis of inversion, and to keep in mind the universal bisexuality of human beings."[111] In fact, he regards the young woman's choice of love object as a proof of the theory of bisexuality, since "she found in her 'lady' an object which promised to satisfy not only her homosexual trends, but also that part of her heterosexual libido which was still attached to her brother."[112]

So the young woman's "bisexuality" is manifested both as identification and as desire. From a modern lay perspective we might say that it is not really bisexual, since her love object remains in real life a woman, whatever fantasies attach to her identity—or her lover's. But what Freud is working toward here is an understanding of *positions of identification* and *positions of desire*.

In Defense of Substitution

> A woman is, occasionally, quite a serviceable substitute for masturbation. It takes an abundance of imagination, to be sure.
>
> —*Karl Kraus*

Late-twentieth-century interpretations tend to speak of concurrent versus sequential bisexuality. Freud's men's club example is sequential ("the bachelor gives up his men friends when he marries, and returns to club-life when married life has lost its savour")[113] while—in his reading, at least—the woman's choice of love object is, in fantasy, concurrent (the older woman she loves is a "substitute" for both the mother and the brother).

No one, naturally, likes the idea of being a substitute or loving a substitute, least of all whole classes of persons who find themselves often described as imitating what someone else loudly maintains to be the "real thing." For decades, until recently, this has been the situation of gays and lesbians, whose sexualities have been deplored as secondary, parodic, even pathetic, by self-satisfied "straights" whose own notions of romantic love come right out of trash fiction, Hollywood films of a certain era, Valentine's Day cards, *Bride's* magazine, and a calculated misunderstanding of the complicated system once known as "courtly love." Having said this, however, I want to put in what is likely to be an unpopular good word for the mechanism of substitution in erotic life. First of all, there is no "real thing" in that idealized sense. And second, like the theorists' "signifying chain" of associations, substitution can teach desire.

The woman in the case history loves the same person twice: "as a woman" and "as a man." Freud calls this bisexuality, and it is. It is bisexuality from the point of view of the subject rather than the object. It is an acknowledgment of the place of fantasy—what Freud calls "overvaluation" —in all stories of romantic love.

The "Psychogenesis of a Case of Homosexuality in a Woman" was, significantly, Freud's last case history, written much later than the famous cases that made his reputation: "Dora" (1905), "Little Hans" (1909), the "Rat Man" (1909), Schreber (1911), and the "Wolf Man" (1918), the publication of which was delayed for several years because of World War I. In it Freud began to explore both female sexuality and homosexuality in ways that would lead to his controversial papers on the consequences of the anatomical distinction between the sexes (1925), "Female Sexuality" (1931), and "Femininity" (1933). As he changed his mode of presentation, moving away from clinical details and the report of specific dreams and incidents toward a generalized and sometimes prescriptive account of the "little girl," the "woman," and "female sexual life," he inevitably allegorized his narrative, telling a tale that was both no one's and, in his view, everyone's.

Bisexuality remained for him the crux of development and its indwelling mystery. He was convinced in the last years of his life that "bisexuality . . . comes to the fore much more clearly in women than in men,"[114] because women had two sexual organs, the "masculine" clitoris and the "feminine" vagina. Sexual maturation and "normal" femininity, he believed, could only come about if the little girl renounced masturbation, "activity," and her desire for her mother. "The little girl wants to believe that she has given her mother the new baby, just as the boy wants to." "No doubt," he acknowledges, "this sounds quite absurd, but perhaps that is only because it sounds so unfamiliar."[115]

The same libidinal forces are at work in the female and the male child; there is only one libido, and it has both active and passive aims, or sources of pleasure. "Heterosexuality" for women, which Freud significantly equates with "the path to femininity," in fact develops as a result of a series of disappointments, losses, and humiliations.[116]

It was not only Freud's thoughts that were undergoing revision but also the nature and circumstances of his patients. Before the First World War most of Freud's patients were middle-class women, many of them Jewish, from economically comfortable families who were exhibiting symptoms of "hysteria" and were incapacitated to some degree by their symptoms. Their symptoms were "sexual" and traceable to a past traumatic experience. As Elisabeth Young-Breuhl observes, "Desire dammed up seeks a substitute outlet in symptoms, and to hysterics the symptoms constituted their entire sexual lives."[117]

As Freud's patient population changed, as society itself underwent major changes following World War I, the "bisexuality" of women, once seen as the cause of hysteria and repression, was increasingly identified by him as that which enabled women to go into "masculine" professions (like that of psychoanalysis). "Bisexuality" could account for the otherwise inexplicable cultural creativity of women, and their success in the public sphere. It is worth noting that this is not very different from some observations made by the "highly gifted but sexually deranged" Otto Weininger.

Although he would assert with particular tendentiousness that despite "the denials of the feminists" there are no grounds for regarding "the two sexes as completely equal in position and worth," Freud was willing to concede that "the majority of men are also far behind the masculine ideal" and "that all human individuals, as a result of their bisexual disposition," "combine in themselves both masculine and feminine characteristics, so that pure masculinity and femininity remain theoretical constructions of uncertain content." This, too, was a point of view insisted upon by Weininger.

His early theory of bisexuality provided for Freud an axis along which he could plot other apparent opposites. In fact, the detection of them *as* opposites seem to confirm the theory. If elements that could be regarded as "masculine" and "feminine" were both present, bisexuality was, in effect, proven. "We find, then," he wrote with satisfaction, "that certain among the impulses to perversion occur regularly as pairs of opposites." In the case, for example, of sadism and masochism, he was "inclined to connect the simultaneous presence of these opposites with the opposing masculinity and femininity which are combined in bisexuality."[118]

This is how the passage reads in the first edition of *Three Essays,* published in 1905, and also in the second, published in 1910. But by 1915, Freud was rethinking the meanings of terms like "masculinity" and "femininity."

In a revised edition of *Three Essays* that year he added, crucially, a further clause to this last sentence, qualifying his terms. The passage now reads, "We should rather be inclined to connect the simultaneous presence of these opposites with the opposing masculinity and femininity which are combined in bisexuality—a contrast whose significance is reduced in psycho-analysis to that between activity and passivity."

By 1924 this "reduction" had been expanded to a "replacement," so that the final version, as it appears in the canonical *Standard Edition,* described the masculinity and femininity which are combined in bisexuality as "a contrast which often has to be replaced in psycho-analysis by that between activity and passivity."

The layering of editorial changes in this passage may usefully serve as a sign of the apparent shift from biology to culture in Freud's thought. The somewhat apologetic glossing of "masculine" and "feminine" as "active" and "passive" would be a key feature, much derided by feminist critics, of his late essays on "Female Sexuality" (1931) and "Femininity" (1933). "We are accustomed to employ 'masculine' and 'feminine' as mental qualities as well, and have in the same way transferred the notion of bisexuality to mental life," he wrote in "Femininity," in a passage that would become notorious among later feminist critics.

"Thus we speak of a person, whether male or female, as behaving in a masculine way in one connection and in a feminine way in another. But you will soon perceive that this is only giving way to anatomy or to convention. You cannot give the concepts of 'masculine' and 'feminine' *any* new connotation. The distinction is not a psychological one; when you say 'masculine', you usually mean 'active', and when you say 'feminine', you usually mean 'passive.' "[119]

Yet Freud points out that women can be active in numerous ways, while men need to be passive in order to socialize. In nature, he observes, the female of the species is sometimes more aggressive than the male; consider the case of the female spider.[120] "If you now tell me," says Freud in his most urbane and imperturbable manner, "that these facts go to prove precisely that both men and women are bisexual in the psychological sense, I shall conclude that you have decided in your own minds to make 'active' coincide with 'masculine' and 'passive' with 'feminine.' But I advise you against it. It seems to me to serve no useful purpose and adds nothing to our knowledge."[121]

As we have already seen, in the very late *Outline of Psycho-Analysis* (1938), published after his death, Freud returned yet again to "the great enigma of the biological fact of the duality of the sexes," still using the term "bisexuality" to describe it. "No individual is limited to the modes of reaction of a single sex," he wrote there, "but always finds some room for those of the opposite one, just as his body bears, alongside of the fully developed organs of one sex, atrophied and often useless rudiments of those of the other."

> For distinguishing between male and female in mental life we make use of what is obviously an inadequate empirical and conventional equation: we call everything that is strong and active male, and everything that is weak and passive female. This fact of psychological bisexuality, too, embarrasses all our enquiries into the subject and makes them harder to describe.[122]

For reasons different from Freud's, these binary equivalences continue to embarrass. Bisexuality for Freud was sometimes a combination of masculine and feminine characteristics, and sometimes a conflict between them. The combination produced a Leonardo, or an Anna Freud. The conflict produced hysteria, neurosis, "inversion," and dysfunction. But how was one to tell the difference?

If Freud strove to distinguish masculine-feminine from active-passive, the generations that succeeded him have had a hard time distinguishing gender from sexuality, trying to get beyond the idea that gay men were inevitably "feminine" and lesbians "masculine." Where did bisexuality fit into the picture?

Is bisexuality a "combination" or a "compromise," to use two of the many terms Freud sometimes employed to describe it? Is it a middle space between two more "exclusive" positions, as the Kinsey scale would indicate? Or is bisexuality—what Freud on another occasion described as an individual's "full bisexual functions"—the whole of which heterosexuality and homosexuality are themselves compromised parts? Is bisexuality "beyond" homo- and heterosexuality, or "between" them?

For Freud and his colleagues and rivals, this question presented itself in the form of yet another back-formation: "monosexuality."

"A Problem that Needs Elucidating"

Freud's opinion of his associate Wilhelm Stekel, a member of the so-called Wednesday Psychological Society that met every week at the Freud home in Vienna, was that Stekel was "weak in theory and thought"[123]—and this was when the two men were on relatively good terms. After a major break, he called him "an uneducable individual, a *mauvais sujet*," and a "perfect swine." But he also acknowledged that Stekel "has the best nose of any of us for the secrets of the unconscious." "I have often contradicted his interpretations and later realized that he was right," he wrote to Jung. "Therefore we must keep him and distrust him and learn from him."[124]

Stekel was notorious among the Wednesday crowd for his desire to be the midst of every conversation, often inventing a patient afflicted with the disorder of the week—Ernest Jones called this Bunbury figure "Stekel's Wednesday patient"[125]—so as to be able to contribute to the evening's discussion. His clinical studies, collected under the general title *Disorders of the Instincts and the Emotions,* included a volume on masturbation and homosexuality, part of which was translated into English in 1950 under the somewhat misleading title *Bi-Sexual Love.*

Despite its title, Stekel's treatise is not so much a study of bisexuality as it is a critique of other psychoanalysts' views on homosexuality. He begins by deploring those physicians who claim that masturbation causes homosexuality (it would be more accurate, he asserts forthrightly, to say that masturbation causes *sexuality*) and he cites, as epigraphs to various of his chapters, a characteristic aphorism from Nietzsche ("Living—is it not the will to be otherwise than nature is?") and an equally compelling observation from Goethe ("Boy love is as old as the race and therefore it may be said to be part of nature, although against nature"). Like Freud, he recognizes that the category of the "natural" and the "normal," as conceived by the society in which he lives, is in fact one of repression.

What is most useful about Stekel's book, however, derives directly from Freud's critique of him, and that is a tendency to flat assertion of what he clearly regards as spectacular and controversial ideas. *"There is no inborn homosexuality and no inborn heterosexuality. There is only bisexuality,"*[126] he declares (italics, characteristically, in the original). *"There are no monosexual persons!" "All persons are bisexual.* But persons repress either the homosexual or the heterosexual components on account of certain motives or because they are compelled by particular circumstances and consequently act as if they were monosexual." [127] "Every monosexuality is other than normal or natural. *Nature has created us bisexual beings and requires us to act as bisexual beings.*" [128]

As we have seen, many of these views Stekel shared with—or got from—Freud. But his emphasis on the abnormality or unnaturalness of monosexuality highlights, in what are virtually "pop psychological" terms, a consistent if less obvious strain of thought in Freud's own work: the idea that "monosexuality" was itself what Stekel described as "a neurotic trait shared by every normal person."

"All human beings are capable of making a homosexual object-choice and have in fact made one in their unconscious," he wrote in an important 1915 footnote to *Three Essays*. "Indeed," he insisted, "from the point of view of psycho-analysis the exclusive sexual interest felt by men for women is also a problem that needs elucidating and is not a self-evident fact based upon an attraction that is ultimately of a chemical nature." [129]

In other words, not only is homosexual desire as plausible as heterosexual desire, but *any* "exclusive sexual interest," whether heterosexual or homosexual, is a "problem" for analysis.

In his 1920 case study of a homosexual woman Freud is similarly clear: "One must remember that normal sexuality too depends upon a restriction in the choice of object," he cautions. "In general, to undertake to convert a fully developed homosexual into a heterosexual does not offer much more prospect of success than the reverse, except that for good practical reasons it is never attempted." [130]

The tone here is almost jocular, the irony is a social irony. Practical reasons, however "good," are pragmatic, not psychological. Unlike some of his psychoanalytic followers in the next generation, Freud was not a great believer in the possibility of "conversion," either from homosexual to heterosexual or vice versa. The only "conversions" that work, in his estimation, are those that, by "making access to the opposite sex (which had hitherto been barred)" are able to "restore" to formerly exclusive homosexuals their "full bisexual functions." [131]

In other words, homosexuals who have consulted him have "become" bisexuals, not straights. They haven't given up their erotic attraction to same-sex partners. They have added, for reasons that may be erotic or may be "practical," relationships to members of the opposite sex.

Without social pressure and opprobrium, would they have come to him for treatment? Almost certainly not. But does that make their "conversion" bogus? If we are tempted to answer "yes" to that question, we will shortly find ourselves back in the realm of nature rather than culture.

We have noticed that "bisexual" for Freud can mean anything from (1) having two sets of sexual organs to (2) having two psyches, one male and one female to (3) having a precarious and divided sexuality which is fluid rather than fixed with regard to both identification and object. But what about our simpler conventional modern definition—having both male and female lovers?

Freud does come to use the word "bisexual" in something like its modern sense toward the end of his career. In "Analysis Terminable and Interminable," published in 1937, virtually the last paper to appear in his lifetime, he observes genially:

> It is well known that at all periods there have been, as there still are, people who can take as their sexual objects members of their own sex as well as of the opposite one, without the one trend interfering with the other. We call such people bisexuals, and we accept their existence without feeling much surprise about it. We have come to learn, however, that every human being is bisexual in this sense, and that his libido is distributed, either in a manifest or a latent fashion, over objects of both sexes.[132]

Persons he once described clinically as "amphigenic inverts" can now be accepted without surprise or comment. Those who do merit comment are the monosexuals, the ones in the "second and more numerous class" for whom homosexual and heterosexual desires are in conflict, those for whom it is true to say that "A man's heterosexuality will not put up with any homosexuality, and *vice versa*."

Bisexuality and Civilization

When Freud wrote eagerly—and unwisely, given his correspondent's own stake in the project—to Wilhelm Fliess about his plan for a major book on "Human Bisexuality," he perhaps unwittingly predicted not only the *Three Essays* of 1905 and the "Dora" case but also works as diverse as *Civilization and Its Discontents* and "Analysis Terminable and Interminable." For it is in his last and most sweeping accounts of human culture that Freud returns again to the issue with which he began: bisexuality and repression.

In the letter of August 7, 1901, Freud had proclaimed his "chief insight": The bisexuality of the individual was the long-sought answer to "repression, my core problem."[133] In his final essays it is again repression that attracts his attention, but here, fittingly, the emphasis is cultural rather than individual.

Freud notes in *Civilization and Its Discontents* that repression *grounds* civilization. It treats sexual dissidents as if they were a subject population capable of revolt. His language is that of colonial discourse and of a Europe already—in 1930—discernibly under siege. "Civilization behaves towards sexuality as a people or a stratum of its population does which has subjected another one to its exploitation," he writes. "Fear of a revolt by the suppressed elements drives it to stricter precautionary measures. A high-water mark in such a development," he adds with deliberate irony, "has been reached in our Western European civilization."

The quintessential repression, against the "unmistakably bisexual dis-position" of humankind, is the rejection of same-sex love, of "extra-genital satisfactions," and of relationships that do not conform to standards of "legitimacy" and "monogamy"—rejection of, that is, everything that today's gays, lesbians, and bisexuals stand accused of promoting. "Pres-ent-day civilization makes it plain that it will only permit sexual re-lationships on the basis of a solitary, indissoluble bond between one man and one woman, and that it does not like sexuality as a source of pleasure in its own right and is only prepared to tolerate it because there is so far no substitute for it as a means of propagating the human race."

This "extreme picture" is one with major ethical consequences for cul-ture and civilization. "The requirement, demonstrated in these prohibi-tions, that there shall be a single kind of sexual life for everyone, disregards the dissimilarities, whether innate or acquired, in the sexual constitution of human beings; it cuts off a fair number of them from sexual enjoyment, and so becomes the source of serious injustice."[134]

How significant is it that this essay of Freud's, that sets forward a theory of instinct, aggression, destruction, and repression as constituent of what we call "civilization," should contain a lengthy footnote on, precisely, bisexuality?

The footnote underscores the essay's ambivalence about civilization and its discontents, summarizing, once more—as he has done so often—the general argument about bisexuality: that human beings have an "unmistak-ably" bisexual disposition; that they may once have been biologically her-maphrodite, and that "the individual corresponds to a fusion of two symmetrical halves, of which, according to some investigators, one is purely male and the other female"; that "every human being displays both male and female instinctual impulses," and that in psychology such gendered attributes are often translated into attributions of activity and passivity that do not in fact correspond to male and female behavior in the animal kingdom.

> If we assume it as a fact that each individual seeks to satisfy both male and female wishes in his sexual life, we are prepared for the possibil-ity that those two [sets of] demands are not fulfilled by the same object, and that they interfere with one another unless they can be kept apart.[135]

If repression grounds civilization, it is bisexuality, in its many guises, that is being repressed. Repressed for our own good. Bisexuality is that upon the repression of which society depends for its laws, codes, boundaries, social organization—everything that defines "civilization" as we know it.

Androgyny and Its Discontents

At present I am pursuing my mythological dreams with almost autoerotic pleasure.

—*Letter from C. G. Jung to Sigmund Freud, April 17, 1910*[1]

We have been looking at the story of Tiresias and the myths of the Sphinx as ways in which Western literature and culture have posed questions about bisexuality: the aspect of conundrum or riddle, the desire to fix desire, and the sense of delicious transgression in knowing or experiencing or fantasizing the pleasure of the other.

But there is one mythological construct that has been even more directly conflated and confused with bisexuality: androgyny. In the catalog of "psycho-mythologies," none has had a more persistent relation to bisexuality than the androgyne, a figure both male and female, pictured in classical and Renaissance art and literature as a transcendent and harmonious union of opposites.

"Androgyny" is often described by philosophers, poets, and theologians as a state of exalted being, the ideal completion of humanity in a condition of transcendence; as such, the image of wholeness paradoxically utilizes sexual symbols only to leave the body behind, to attain stasis and perfection beyond gender, sexuality, and desire. But at the same time androgyny in the "real world" has come to connote both lack of sexual differentiation in style and appearance—an unmarked physicality so striking as to be marked, as for example in the case of a performer like k.d. lang or Michael Jackson, or of certain female Olympic athletes, or of the character "Pat" on "Saturday Night Live"—and *pansexuality,* a sexiness that presents itself as desiring, and desirable to, many different objects, in many different forms —as in the careers of rock and film stars like Mick Jagger, Elvis Presley, and Marlene Dietrich. In these latter cases, far from being transcended, sex, gender, and sexuality are in the foreground.

What does "androgyny" have to do with bisexuality?

The Androgyne and the Hermaphrodite

Although the two words originally meant the same thing (Latin *androgynus,* hermaphrodite, from Greek *androgunos,* male and female), the difference between an androgyne and a hermaphrodite as the terms are commonly used today is the difference between a synthesis and a hybrid. The hermaphrodite presents insignia of maleness and femaleness at once: Hermaphroditic figures in classical statuary often display both feminine breasts and a penis. The androgyne is more usually characterized as indistinguishably masculine and feminine; with androgynous persons you can't tell, or almost can't tell, whether they are male or female. Thus this fairly typical anecdote from a 1984 issue of *People* magazine: "A psychologist recently asked his 7-year-old nephew, 'Is Michael Jackson a girl or a boy?' The boy thought for a moment before replying, 'Both.' "[2]

We could say that the hermaphrodite is a figure of sex, the androgyne a figure of gender, and the bisexual, at least in modern usage, a figure of sexuality. But since the word "bisexual" has meant "two-sexed" in biological terms, it has often been confused, conflated, or crossed with both "hermaphrodite" and "androgyne." As we have seen, Freud described anatomical hermaphrodites as "bisexual," meaning "having a body at once male and female," and then used the term "psychosexual hermaphrodite" to describe what we would today call a bisexual, a person whose "sexual objects may equally well be of their own or of the opposite sex."

It was, however, Carl Gustav Jung and his followers—from Mircea Eliade to Joseph Campbell—who popularized the cult of the androgyne in this century. For Jung, "bisexuality" meant transcendent union, "wholeness," and its symbol, or "archetype," was the androgyne or hermaphrodite.

"It is a remarkable fact that perhaps the majority of cosmogonic gods are of a bisexual nature," Jung declared in his essay on the "child archetype" in a section titled "The Hermaphroditism of the Child." "The hermaphrodite means nothing less than a union of the strongest and most striking opposites," he contended, and went on to describe, in a passage that underwrites the doctrine of psychic "wholeness" from seventies feminism to the "men's movement" of the nineties, his theory of "bisexuality" as a concordance of opposites.

> As civilization develops, the bisexual primordial being turns into a
> symbol of the unity of personality, a symbol of the self, where the
> war of opposites finds peace. In this way the primordial being be-

comes the distant goal of man's self-development, having been from the very beginning a projection of his unconscious wholeness.[3]

Jung's disciple Erich Neumann uses "bisexual" in a similar way to denote male and female coexisting in one form.[4] Thus, in a characteristic passage, Neumann describes the "bisexual symbol of creation" in the ancient Aztec symbol of the sacred spring, where "the flowing, fecundating water is masculine, but the spring as a whole is a uterine symbol of the childbearing feminine earth." (Both the romantic, ecstatic prose and the division of male and female into fecundating and bearing roles are identifying marks of Jungian discourse; modern examples persist in latter-day Jungians like Robert Bly and Camille Paglia.)

"Man's imagination has been preoccupied with this idea over and over again on the high and even the highest levels of culture," Jung declared, citing examples drawn from late Greek culture, from Gnosticism, and from the tradition of Christ's androgyny.[5] The "Gospel according to the Egyptians in the second epistle of Clement," for example, looked forward to a time "When the two shall be one, the outside as the inside, and the male with the female neither male nor female."

This concept of the ubiquity of androgyny through the history of the world's cultures is an aspect of Jung's theory of archetypes, which in turn depends upon his notion of the "collective unconscious." Broadly speaking, the "collective unconscious" is exactly what it sounds like: an "unconscious" that is "universal," unchanging, and "identical in all individuals," an unconscious that "does not develop individually but is inherited." This was both his modification of and his debt to Freud, and Jung sought to distinguish it from the "personal unconscious" that was the signal discovery of psychoanalysis:

> While the personal unconscious is made up essentially of contents which have at one time been conscious but which have disappeared from consciousness through having been forgotten or repressed, the contents of the collective unconscious have never been in consciousness, and therefore have never been individually acquired, but owe their existence exclusively to heredity. Whereas the personal unconscious consists for the most part of *complexes,* the content of the collective unconscious is made up essentially of *archetypes.*[6]

To what extent is this romantic and mystical fantasy of the wellsprings of myth a projection of the unconscious of the investigators? Third-world psychiatrist Frantz Fanon offered a telling critique of the "collective unconscious," describing it as "purely and simply the sum of prejudices, myths, and collective attitudes of a given group," the result of "the unreflected imposition of a culture."[7]

> European civilization is characterized by the presence, at the heart
> of what Jung calls the collective unconscious, of an archetype: an
> expression of the bad instincts, of the darkness inherent in every ego,
> of the uncivilized savage, the Negro who slumbers in every white
> man. And Jung claims to have found in uncivilized peoples the same
> psychic structure that his diagram betrays. Personally, I think that
> Jung has deceived himself. . . . All the peoples he has known—
> whether the Pueblo Indians of Arizona or the Negroes of Kenya in
> British East Africa—have had more or less traumatic contacts with
> the white man.[8]

In short, "Jung has confused instinct and habit." "In the collective unconscious of *homo occidentalis,* the Negro—or, if one prefers, the color
black—symbolizes evil, sin, wretchedness, death, war, famine." But "the
collective unconscious is not dependent upon cerebral heredity," as Jung
claimed. Rather, it is acquired, imposed, "projected," in the terms of that
psychoanalytic mechanism: "When European civilization came into contact
with the black world, with those savage peoples, everyone agreed: Those
Negroes were the principle of evil." There is therefore no reason to be
surprised when, for example, an Antillean "relives the same fantasies as a
European"—it is from Europeans that he or she has derived the "archetypes" of the "collective unconscious."[9]

Jung, says Fanon, "wanted to go back to the childhood of the world, but
he made a remarkable mistake. He went back only to the childhood of
Europe."[10] And as with Jung himself, so with those who followed him.
Thus in her study of the "myths and rites of the bisexual figure in classical
antiquity," French scholar Marie Delcourt, citing Jung, finds striking paral-
lels between Greek and Latin "two-fold gods," and correlates them with
later manifestations of female saints in men's clothing. But although her
claims are universal—"Hermaphrodite is an example of *pure myth,* conceived in the mind of man as he groped to find his place in the world"—
she nonetheless excludes some materials from comparison: "As for the
bisexual figures in Oriental religions, they are too numerous and too
strange to be included here; they require a special study."[11]

Others have pointed out that Jung "rarely acknowledges that cultures
may differ" with respect to psychological attributes assigned by his own
culture.[12] He is interested in similarities, not differences. His schema, like
those of his followers, is a totalizing and "universal" structure. His examples are drawn in the main not from case studies but from the world's
mythologies, all passed through the alembic of his own preconceptions
and prejudices. They yield "universal" readings which are *his.* The difficulty would come when he tried to apply these universal principles to
actual persons.

Animadversions

The *anima* to Jung is the unconscious feminine side of a man, and the *animus* the corresponding masculine side of a woman. The androgyne or hermaphrodite (for this purpose he uses the two terms interchangeably) represent the ideal integration of masculine and feminine in the psyche of the individual, a state he calls "wholeness" or "individuation."

> Wholeness consists in the union of the conscious and unconscious personality. Just as every individual derives from masculine and femi- nine genes, and the sex is determined by the predominance of the corresponding genes, so in the psyche it is only the conscious mind, in a man, that has the masculine sign, while the unconscious is by nature feminine. The reverse is true in the case of a woman. All I have done in my *anima* theory is to rediscover and reformulate this fact. It has long been known.[13]

One of the pitfalls of this view, beyond the romantic uniculturalist dream of the "collective unconscious" and the theory of archetypes, was the notion that "masculine" and "feminine" traits were both given and universal, and that the relation between the conscious and the uncon- scious is always heterosexual. For Jung, as for his followers, "masculine" and "feminine" were known—and unchanging—quantities. One had only to look (admittedly through spectacles of one's own manufacture) and one would see.

What complicated the theory still further was the fact that, although it was designed to foster wholeness intrapsychically, in the individual, Jung had to concede that "in practice, however, it is not so simple, because as a rule the feminine unconscious of a man is projected upon a feminine partner, and the masculine unconscious of a woman is projected upon a man. The elucidation of these problems," he observed dismissively, "is a special branch of psychology and has no part in a discussion of the mytho- logical hermaphrodite"[14]—to which he preferred to return.

Part of the problem was Jung's insistence on abstractions. The anima, the animus, the persona, the shadow, the wise old man—to list the most fundamental of his "archetypes"—were "out there" somewhere in the collective unconscious: timeless, universal, eternal, unchanging. Within such a grand scheme, the human body and its desires necessarily took a back seat. Actual, biological hermaphrodites, for example, were not archetypes but monsters; only the idealization was attractive.

Likewise actual men and women in touch with their anima or animus had an unfortunate propensity to be unappealing. "Since masculine and feminine elements are united in our human nature," Jung declared in a cranky and tendentious piece called "Woman in Europe," "a man can live in the feminine part of himself, and a woman in her masculine part. None the less the feminine element in man is only something in the background, as is the masculine element in woman. If one lives out the opposite sex in oneself one is living in one's own background, and one's real individuality suffers. A man should live as a man and a woman as a woman." So much for "androgyny" in real life as opposed to mystical theory.

Woman's nature, Jung declared, is one of "moods and emotions"; what comes to her from the unconscious is "assuredly not real reasonableness" but rather "a sort of *opinion*" that lays claim to being absolute truth. "A woman who takes up a masculine profession is influenced by her unconscious masculinity" in a way that she may not notice but that everyone else does. "She develops a kind of rigid intellectuality based on so-called principles, and backs them up with a whole host of arguments which always just miss the mark in the most irritating way." In the worst case scenario these opinions can grow into a "demonic passion that exasperates and disgusts men," and smothers "the charm and meaning of her femininity." She "may even become frigid," or develop an "aggressive, urgent form of sexuality that is more characteristic of a man," or—especially "in Anglo-Saxon countries"—she may develop "optional homosexuality in the masculine role."[15] What is the potential cure for these dangerous ills? To avoid the runaway animus, the dominance of the "contrasexual element," "there is a quite special need for the woman to have an intimate relationship with the other sex."

Heterosexuality is the remedy—the remedy for both "bisexuality" (the copresence of "masculine" and "feminine" elements in the psyche) and "optional homosexuality" (a fascinating phrase that implies, through the hypothetical availability of other "options," a bisexuality in the modern sense). While this is not a surprising conclusion, given the general premises of Jung's views of the sexes, it is slightly more startling to remind ourselves that he more than once put this remedy into practice.

Jung's affairs with two female patients, Sabina Spielrein and Toni Wolff, have been much commented upon in recent histories of the psychoanalytic movement.[16] Both Spielrein and Wolff became colleagues as well as patients; Wolff assisted him with his research until Emma Jung registered a protest, and later came virtually to be a member of the household in the period around 1916 as Jung's own mental condition became prey to hallucinations and episodes of depersonalization for which her presence was a calming anodyne.[17] As for Spielrein, who became a psychoanalyst herself, she has been convincingly described as the model for the concept of the "anima," the inner feminine voice Jung describes as "the woman within me"[18] and also, like Rumpole of the Bailey describing his wife, as "She who must be obeyed."[19] At once a muse and a temptress, the anima was for him initially a figure that inspired deep distrust as well as desire: "What the anima said seemed to me full of a deep cunning." "The anima might then have easily seduced me into believing that I was a misunderstood artist." "The insinuations of the anima, the mouthpiece of the unconscious, can utterly destroy a man."[20] When Jung broke off the relationship in 1918–19, he felt that he was coming out of "the darkness"; he received a letter from the person he describes as "that esthetic lady" and found that "the letter got on my nerves. It was far from stupid, and therefore dangerously persuasive."[21]

Animosity

Jung's notion of the male animus in women is manifestly a back-formation from his personal vision, or rather audition, of anima as the "woman within." "My conclusion was that she must be the 'soul,' in the primitive sense, and I began to speculate on the reasons why the name 'anima' was given to the soul. Why was it thought of as feminine? Later I came to see that this inner feminine figure plays a typical, or archetypal, role in the unconscious of a man, and I called her the 'anima.' The corresponding figure in the unconscious of woman I called the 'animus.' "

The anima, in other words, was not a mere abstraction but something between an erotic fantasy and a hallucination. As John Kerr neatly observes, the idea of the "anima" had from the first "a romantic application, and this may in part explain its enduring popularity as a concept"[22]— falling in love became a matter of finding the person of the opposite sex who incarnated one's own other, or inner, self. The word "anima" has a pleasant ring (Jung's naive speculation on the gendering of nouns—"Why was it thought of as feminine?"—does not pause over the corresponding question of why philosophers and artists are thought of as male) but the "animus" has—can it be altogether an accident?—a slightly more menacing connotation. "An animating motive; a feeling of animosity; bitter hostility or hatred. See synonyms at *enmity*," suggests my dictionary, which also lists Jung's specialized definition ("In the psychology of Carl Jung, the masculine inner personality, as present in women").[23]

When a man gives way to the dominance of the anima inside him, something very familiar appears to happen: Like the "effeminate" man of the Renaissance or some versions of the nineteenth-century "invert," he "becomes" a woman:

> Men can argue in a very womanish way, too, when they are anima-possessed and have thus been transformed into the animus of their own anima. With them the question becomes one of personal *vanity* and *touchiness* (as if they were females); with women it is a question of *power,* whether of truth or justice or some kind of "ism"—for the dressmaker and hairdresser have already taken care of their vanity.[24]

Yet man is "forced to develop his feminine side, to open his eyes to the psyche and to Eros"—a "task he cannot avoid, unless he prefers to go trailing after woman in a hopelessly boyish fashion, worshipping from afar but always in danger of being stowed away in her pocket." Still, it was an undoubted fact that "the masculinity of the woman and the femininity of the man *are* inferior."[25]

In short, while purporting to conflate binaries in mystic unity, Jung in fact establishes them even more definitively as complementary opposites. For him, female and male are analogous to Eros and Logos, and although he gestures away from the profound implications of this division ("I used Eros and Logos merely as conceptual aids to describe the fact that women's consciousness is characterized more by the connective quality of Eros than by the discrimination and cognition of Logos"),[26] Jung is firmly convinced of the unchanging truths of gender stereotypes. Thus it is altogether fascinating to watch him establish, with firm faith in his own rationality, a capricious certainty on the part of *women* ("it consists of *opinions* instead of reflections, and by opinions I mean a priori assumptions which lay claim, as it were, to absolute truth") that everywhere characterizes his *own* practice. As he remarks, "Such assumptions, as everyone knows, can be extremely irritating."[27]

Here, then, was the paradox: For Jung and his adepts, "androgyny" was *only* imaginable as a theoretical construction. The androgyne was an "idea," an "ideal," a "vision," a "doctrine," a "mind," or a state of mind—anything but a concrete reality. Once it *became* a reality—walking down the street hand in hand with its mirror twin, capitalizing on sexual ambiguity to seduce and entrance an audience—it was sullied, misinterpreted, and not what they meant at all.

Androgyny and Bisexuality

For Freud, as we noticed, homosexuality was a kind of bisexuality. But Jung insists that homosexuals erroneously try to live out on the literal level a mode of being that is properly one of the spirit and the symbol. This is his critique of Freud's bisexual theory: that it is predicated on the personal rather than the transcendent. "The crucial difference between bisexuality and androgyny," according to Jungian analyst June Singer, is that "bisexuality, in common parlance, refers to acting out maleness and femaleness in sexual behavior. But Jung seems to imply that bisexuality in the contemporary Western world is an expression, usually misunderstood, of a natural but unconscious thrust toward androgyny."[28] As a student of folklore and mythology as well as of comparative religion, Jung knew of societies in which erotic bisexuality (as well as transvestism and transsexualism) were central to culture. But his emphasis was always on the intrapsychic. "Jung regarded bisexuality as an archetypal element in the collective unconscious that surfaced under certain conditions in normative cultural practice," notes Singer. "Acceptance of the bisexual—or rather, androgynous—potential has been an absolute requirement for admission as a full member of the adult community in some societies."

Notice the effortless ease with which Singer inserts the correction: "bisexual—or rather, androgynous." Bisexuality as a term is elided, crossed out, or crossed over. One anthropological example she gives is that of penile subincision among Australian aborigines, a rite that gives the young initiates a "penis-womb." The others are all instances of ritual cross-dressing: The young male novices of the Masai, the Nuba, and the Nandi of Africa dress in female clothing, while girls undergoing initiation among the Sotho of South Africa wear male dress.[29] The contested term "bisexuality" here is thus exemplified by cross-gender practices rather than by sexual ones.

This desire to purge "androgyny" of the sexual implications of "bisexuality" has been a recurrent and symptomatic goal of many of its adherents in this century. How to respond "if they ask me my identity" but "I am the androgyne"[30] wrote poet Adrienne Rich in 1972, some ten years before she came to deplore, in "Compulsory Heterosexuality and Lesbian Existence," the "sentimental," "liberal," and "frequently heard" assertion that in a world of perfect equality "everyone would be bisexual."[31]

In the early seventies, "androgyny" was enjoying a certain vogue. Carolyn Heilbrun's book *Toward a Recognition of Androgyny* had been published in 1973, and had inspired a major forum on "Androgyny: Fact or Fiction" at the Modern Language Association's annual meeting.[32] Heilbrun's book had a specific, and specifically delineated, political goal: "Androgyny seeks to liberate the individual from the bounds of the appropriate," it announced. "Androgyny suggests a spirit of reconciliation between the sexes; it suggests, further, a full range of experience open to individuals who may, as women, be aggressive, as men, tender."[33] The rhetoric of agency here is suggestive: Androgyny "seeks" and "suggests" social change. Androgyny was a belief structure, a world view—a view that some would soon regard as utopian, and then, inevitably, as a snare and a delusion. But first there was the stage of infatuation.

It was in these early, heady days that eager enthusiasts like Paglia (whose *Sexual Personae*, with its telltale Jungian title and obsession with neopaganism, is a hodgepodge of watered-down Nietzsche and warmed-over Jung)[34] began writing mini-histories of the androgyne as cultural role model. More skeptical observers, many but not all of them feminists, noted that the androgynous idea could be "intrinsically reactionary rather than liberating,"[35] since it ignored historical process and elevated instead "a static image of perfection, in eternity."[36]

That static image came, of course, most directly and notably from Jung, as well as from scholars sympathetic to his views, like Joseph Campbell, whose best-selling books *The Hero with a Thousand Faces* and *The Masks of God* made much of the androgynous, mythic experience of the hero and the ubiquity of androgyny in world religion. Norman O. Brown, too, was routinely cited, for example to emphasize the key role of androgyny in mystical texts from the Kabbala to Jakob Böhme to Nikolay Berdyayev. The latter's claim, "The great anthropological myth which alone can be the basis of an anthropological metaphysic is the myth about the androgyne," is approvingly quoted by Heilbrun and gives some sense of the mid-century appetite for grand ideas and totalizing worldviews.

It is striking, in retrospect, how intellectually dependent the feminist interest in "androgyny" was upon the formulations of male scholars with a bent for right-wing views and a manifest resistance to the political and intellectual achievements of women. Nor did this go unnoticed by feminists themselves; almost immediately thoughtful critics began to take note of the fact that historically the concept of the androgyne had been very often that of "the masculine completed by the feminine," taking for granted women's basic inferiority, and blithely assuming that "it is impossible for the female vessel to contain masculine intelligence and spirituality, while it is not only possible but natural for the masculine vessel to be filled and fulfilled by feminine emotion and physicality."[37] They noted that Jung and Neumann, in particular, considered it "urgently important for the men in our patriarchal society to recognize the feminine within themselves before the untrammeled combination of masculine science and masculine aggressiveness destroys us all," but "they do not at the same time look forward with joy to woman's realization that within her lie masculine qualities of intellect and aggression." Indeed, such a recognition, and the integration of those qualities, was regarded as "a risky business, fraught with peril."[38]

No less a figure than James Hillman, the director of the Jungian Institute in Zurich, warned that "analytical psychology"—that is, the work of the Jungians—is "willy-nilly continuing a very ancient tradition of denying woman soul and casting the images of this soul into shadow."[39] Other critics noted that the entire concept depended not only on a static image of *perfection,* but also on relatively static notions of what "masculine" and "feminine" were all about, and what those words meant when they were applied to "man" and "woman." It began to seem as if "androgyny" was not, after all, a formula for social change.

Mary Daly, the fiery radical-feminist theologian, was among those who first welcomed, and then thought better of, the androgynous ideal. Initially, in a book called *Beyond God the Father,* she had urged her readers to strive toward "psychic wholeness, or androgyny."[40] Shortly, however, Daly reversed herself and in her own phrase "recanted," excoriating the word as a "confusing term," a "semantic abomination," "John Travolta and Farrah Fawcett-Majors Scotch-taped together."[41] (On some occasions in her speaking rounds Daly rhetorically Scotch-taped other pairs, like John Wayne and Brigitte Bardot, but the already hyphenated Fawcett-Majors, then the centerpiece of the quite nontheological "Charlie's Angels," served her purpose best, and survived into the published version.)

Why was Daly angry? Fundamentally she saw androgyny as a betrayal, a false promise based on a false premise. "Feminist theorists have gone through frustrating attempts to describe our integrity by such words as *androgyny,*" she reported bitterly. "Experience proved that this word, which we now recognize as expressing pseudowholeness in its combination of distorted gender descriptions, failed and betrayed our thought. The deceptive word was a trap. . . . When we heard the word echoed back by those who misinterpreted our thought we realized that combining the 'halves' offered to consciousness by patriarchal language usually results in portraying something more like a hole than a whole. Thus *androgyny* is a vacuous term which not only fails to represent richness of be-ing. It also functions as a vacuum that sucks its spellbound victims into itself. Such pseudowholeness," she concluded with spirit—and with truth—"characterizes all false universalisms (e.g., humanism, people's liberation)."[42]

As Catharine Stimpson was shortly to worry, "androgyny" as an ideal could also displace the more disturbing fact of homosexuality in political and academic discourse, offering the fantasy of a union of "masculine" and "feminine" traits in a securely heterosexual context. Men should be "caring" and do the dishes; women could have professional careers. The "sensitive man" and the "woman-who-could-have-it-all" emerged as new idealizations, and, on the surface at least, were imagined within the context of the old social ideal of marriage and the family. What they did in bed was not discussed.

Even when its adjacency to gay culture was remarked, the relationship of the androgyne to gay and lesbian sensibility was not stressed. Heilbrun's book begins and ends with Virginia Woolf, whose "androgynous vision" was to be central to most feminist discussions of androgyny in the period. Woolf wrote her own version of the Platonic fable in *A Room of One's Own,* a passage widely and approvingly quoted by many seventies feminists:

> In each of us two powers preside, one male, one female; and in the man's brain, the man predominates over the woman, and in the woman's brain, the woman predominates over the man. The normal and comfortable state of being is when the two live in harmony together, spiritually cooperating. If one is a man, still the woman part of the brain must have effect; and a woman also must have intercourse with the man in her. Coleridge perhaps meant this when he said that a great mind is androgynous. . . . It is when this fusion takes place that the mind is fully fertilized and uses all its faculties.[43]

The Coleridge quotation, too, was omnipresent in the literature, always cited as a free-floating dictum or doxa, rather than as a reflection on Coleridge's own life, affections, or desires. Woolf, Coleridge, and, inevitably, Shakespeare ("the type of the androgynous," in Woolf's phrase) were the androgynes of choice: androgynes, so to speak, above the neck.

◆

One thing the advocates of "androgyny" insisted upon, however, was that it was not the same as bisexuality. We might bear in mind here Freud's useful dictum that where there is resistance, there is emotional paydirt.

Thus Carolyn Heilbrun, reflecting on her book's success, attempted to clarify her terms to exclude the erotic: "As I used the word androgyny, it did not mean hermaphrodite, nor did it mean bisexual or homosexual. I have learned that far more people than we once thought are bisexual, and that we are going to have to learn to be comfortable with that idea in the future. But bisexuality was not what I was writing about."[44]

Feminist critic Barbara Charlesworth Gelpi likewise drew a line: "At the outset I should define the way in which I am using the term 'androgyny.' By it I refer to a psychic unity, either potential or actual, conceived as existing in all individuals. My remarks do not directly apply to physical bisexuality or to lesbianism or homosexuality."[45]

"Bisexuality is by no means the same as androgyny," June Singer insisted in *Androgyny: The Opposites Within,* and in a second edition of her book, published a decade later, she reiterated her disclaimer with a vehemence that seemed to suggest a profound personal discomfort:

> *Androgyny* came out at a time when ambiguous sexuality was one of the shockers of the popular culture. Male rock stars appeared as caricatures of the most offensive female features, ranging from the heavily made up whore-types all the way to the most ridiculous sissified images. Meanwhile, on the streets, fashion favored the ubiquitous blue jeans, and the body's trend was to litheness and leanness, long hair and heavy shoes, so that the sex of a young person was often difficult to determine from the rear and one was thankful for a mustache or a beard when the person turned around, to resolve the mystery. For many, androgyny came to mean a hopeless and hapless confusion of the sexes. This was the furthest possible departure from the actual intent of the book.[46]

There were thus really two kinds of androgyny, the good kind, which was spiritual, mythic, "archetypal," and productive of intrapsychic oneness, and the bad kind, which was physical, sexy, and disturbing, and which was likely to lead to bisexuality, group sex, the "hapless confusion of the sexes," and the "superabundance of erotic possibilities" for which Eliade disparaged the work of decadent authors from Oscar Wilde to Théophile Gautier and A. C. Swinburne.[47] Since the entire superstructure of "androgyny" and the theory of archetypes was fundamentally a binary system (masculine/feminine, soul/shadow, etc.) this was not really a surprise. What was surprising, a little, was the vehemence with which this separation into good and bad—or, as its defenders preferred to put it, into true and false concepts of androgyny—was maintained.

In a famous passage in "Notes on 'Camp' " Susan Sontag had described the androgyne as "certainly one of the great images of Camp sensibility," instancing the "thin, flowing, sexless bodies in Art Nouveau prints and posters" and the "haunting, androgynous vacancy behind the perfect beauty of Greta Garbo."[48] Singer took Sontag to task for her "mistaken" description of the androgyne as a term that could be applied to "effete young men who wore foppish clothes or to women with boyish figures and facade."

Camp, Sontag had suggested, "draws on a mostly unacknowledged truth of taste: The most refined form of sexual attractiveness (as well as the most refined form of sexual pleasure) consists in going against the grain of one's sex. What is most beautiful in virile men is something feminine; what is most beautiful in feminine women is something masculine." (This passage bears a striking resemblance to Jacques Lacan's observation that *"virile* display in the human being itself seem[s] feminine."[49])

Furthermore, Sontag had shrewdly added, "allied to the Camp taste for the androgynous is something that seems quite different but isn't; a relish for the exaggeration of sexual characteristics and personal mannerisms. For obvious reasons, the best examples that can be cited are movie stars."[50]

To Singer this description of androgyny was dangerously wrong, precisely because it regarded the androgyne as a figure of "transitory style": transitory rather than eternal and timeless. The ideal of androgyny had to be protected against fashion, fad, and confusion. Definitions like Sontag's, Singer complained (echoing Eliade), recalled the "tasteless novels" of Wilde and Gautier, the "morbid interest in sexual flagellation" of the Marquis de Sade and Swinburne, the "vampire passion" of *Salomé* and the "celebration of Lesbian love" in Baudelaire—in short, all that is of most interest to today's interpreters of queer culture.

It was for this reason, too, that Singer argued so vehemently against conflating androgyny with bisexuality. "Bisexuality is a fad now," she quotes a young man as saying to her. "I'm not so sure it has to do with sexual behavior as much as it does with empathizing with people. Even more [this was the Jungian point], I believe it has to do with one's attitude toward oneself. If you try to act it out, there's a confusion; neither you nor the others know exactly who you are. You don't go anywhere. It just loses its edge."[51]

The "edge" could only be kept sharp, it seemed, by lack of use.

"A Perfectly Natural Alternative"

When it came to her own clinical practice, however, Singer took a different tack. She had to acknowledge that "In the context of androgyny, bisexuality would seem to be a perfectly natural alternative through which some people might express their sexuality," and that "free-flowing intimacy may be expressed wherever it may be attracted; with members of one's own sex, with members of the opposite sex, or, a third alternative, with members of both."[52] To paraphrase Ti-Grace Atkinson, androgyny might be the theory, but bisexuality was often the practice.

She instances the case of Mr. A, a married man who "had become obsessed with the feeling that if he were to give way to his desire for sex with a man, that he would somehow cross over into the land of no return. He would no longer be a heterosexual; he would become a homosexual." Mr. A, she says, "was convinced that when you cast your lot in with the heterosexual community you necessarily excluded yourself from the company of homosexuals, and vice versa."[53]

Is it too much to hope that A here stands for Androgyne? That this little case study is an allegory of androgyny and its discontents?

"At this point," Singer reports, "it was necessary to consider the bisexual potential." "Bisexuality," she informs the reader, "is no stranger to those who experience their sexuality as polyvalent and who enjoy a variety of sexual experimentation for its own sake. But bisexuality as a possible form of enduring relationships, to be taken seriously in the context of love and to be the basis of serious commitment, has yet to find many outspoken supporters." Nonetheless, as a clinician, "I raised the question of bisexuality with Mr. A."[54]

Mr. A, it seems, was not displeased by this suggestion. "Freed of the feeling that any homosexual experience at this time would make a 'homosexual' out of him, he considered risking an exploration of this aspect of his nature." At this point Singer's normally workmanlike prose explodes into the treacly lyricism we have come to recognize as the true Jungian note. To do justice to her account I will have to quote it at length:

> It was as though he had entered into the mythic world, the wild forested mountains near Thebes which had once harbored the fabled maenads, companions of Dionysus. Those women had left their homes for a season of worship of the half-man half-woman god, for revelry and joy, and sometimes for destruction. So, too, was Mr. A enchanted by the god of bisexuality and the bisexuality of the god. He felt his own bisexuality the more because he saw his life as demanding only the masculine functioning, at work and at home. He saw his wife as a woman who filled all the feminine stereotypes, and who demanded that he take the masculine role. He felt he could not do this. The idea of sexual relations with her became more and more repugnant to him, as he longed to rest and live out his own grace and beauty, and especially his passivity, in the arms of a man.[55]

What does "bisexuality" mean in this remarkable passage? It seems to mean, according to Singer, that "he *became* the feminine side of his nature." It does not seem to mean that he had sex with his wife and with men during the same time period, although we are told that "healing began for Mr. A" when he realized that he didn't need to play "a one-sided role." He had a long talk with his wife. Their sex life together improved in ways that remain unspecified. "The question of what label to put on his sexuality became less important to him." He stopped his compulsive drinking.

What ultimately happened to Mr. A? It is not so easy to tell. "He became more conscious of the ebb and flow of energies, the need for experiencing both kinds of movement: that which was active, progressive, and tended toward order; and that which was passive, regressive, and tended in the direction of creative chaos."[56]

Any bets on which is the "masculine" and which the "feminine" energy? And so on to the case of Ms. B, who left her husband of five years to live with a woman, who "discovered in her female lover all the well-disciplined, self-activating qualities that women as a rule expect from men," who reminded Singer of "the practices of the Amazons of ancient legend," and about whom Singer asked herself the question, "Was Ms. B really a homosexual?"[57]

And then to Mr. C, a shy Southern boy who got in with a gay crowd at college and developed a fixation on black men as sex partners, then subsequently, when on a business trip, went with a gay friend to a private club where "anything goes," and shortly thereafter emerged as a heterosexual. "In his case, his excursion into homosexuality had been a step in his psychological and sexual development. This is not to say that homosexuality is necessarily to be equated with immaturity, or heterosexuality with maturity. But in Mr. C's case, the progression was a developmental one."[58] Inevitably, Singer is again reminded of "an archetypal association," this time with "an ancient ritual" of hermaphrodite boy dancers "that is still practiced today on the streets of Old Delhi."[59]

It is instructive to compare this with the equally vatic language of a critic like Paglia, in this case (the passage is pretty much chosen at random) describing Shakespeare's character Rosalind in *As You Like It*: "Rosalind's hybrid gender and perpetual transformations are the quicksilver of the alchemical Mercurius, who had the rainbow colors of the peacock's tail. Jung says Mercurius as quicksilver symbolizes 'the "fluid," i.e., mobile, intellect.'. . . . The Philosopher's Stone or hermaphroditic *rebis* of alchemy often has wings, which Jung interprets as 'intuition or spiritual (winged) potentiality.' Both masculine and feminine, Rosalind is a Mercurius of swift, sovereign intelligence. Speed as hermaphroditic transcendance [*sic*]; we see this in Vergil's Amazon Camilla and Giambologna's ephebic Mercury in ecstatic flight."[60]

In Paglia's effusion, as in Singer's (slightly) more restrained prose, the alchemical and mystical elements of Jungian psychology are offered as explanations—or, more precisely, are juxtaposed to the matter under discussion as if they are self-explanatory.

For Singer, "the androgyne consciously accepts the interplay of the masculine and feminine aspects of the individual psyche. One is the complement of the other, in the same sense that the active, probing sperm is the complement of the waiting, yielding ovum."[61] The active-passive dichotomy against which Freud had advised his audience in "Femininity" as well as in long footnotes to *Three Essays* and *Civilization and Its Discontents*[62] is here unabashedly reinstated as the natural, because biological, relation between the sexes.

"Androgynes are rarer than unicorns,"[63] a self-described radical feminist mused ruefully in the aftermath of the androgyny boom. The same figure, at the same time, was striking other like-minded critics, who were perhaps remembering that the only way to catch a unicorn was said to be with a female virgin.[64] "If the homosexual is an outlaw of many cultures, the androgyne is their unicorn," wrote Catharine Stimpson in the early seventies. The androgyne, she argued, was "nothing more, or less, than an idea," or more precisely the sum of two ideas, the idea of the feminine and the idea of the masculine.[65] Writing from a position within the nascent gay and lesbian liberation movements, she wondered how the then-fashionable idea of androgyny could translate into political action. More concretely, she worried that the pursuit of the fantasmatic "androgyne" could deflect necessary attention away from the danger of stereotypes like "masculine" and "feminine" and from the fact of homosexuality, and the lives of homosexuals. Androgyny as it was then being debated by feminist critics and enshrined in literary works like Ursula LeGuin's *The Left Hand of Darkness* was, she thought, in fact a way of avoiding or resisting homosexuality.

Even for heterosexual feminists, the ideal of androgyny had serious political as well as philosophical limitations, since its normative image was male rather than female, the image of an enriched and empathetic man in touch with his "feminine" sensibilities, rather than the more socially disruptive figure of the "male-identified," "masculinized," aggressive or assertive woman. Stimpson thus refuted Heilbrun's claim that androgyny was about women; in practice, and historically, she claimed, it had almost always been about men. That this assertion (which is made by many other feminists in the period, Gelpi prominent among them) has some basis in fact may be seen in the new avatars of androgyny in the 1990s, where Jungian theories, with or without the androgyne name, survive most prominently in the rhetoric of the "men's movement" and of many male-to-female cross-dressing groups.

Moreover, the classical notion of androgyny as it derived from Jung, Plato, and the anthropological view of world religion was intrinsically heterosexual. "As the concept of androgyny has developed historically," observed one critic, "it insists on heterosexual pairing, on the couple, and thereby denies both promiscuity or multiple relations and non-heterosexual relations. . . . In a culture like ours that until very recently saw each female as the personal property of some male, multiple relations and bisexual and homosexual choices can be liberating behaviors."[66]

If this sounds like a call to arms of exactly the kind most feared and caricatured by the far right, it also offers a shrewd observation about the dynamics of cultural history. The "liberating behaviors" of bisexuality and its most frequently criticized possibilities (multiple relations, promiscuity, homosexual choices) were the practical affects and effects of the doctrine of androgyny as espoused by centrist feminists, despite or because of their insistence that androgyny had nothing to do with sex or sexiness, that it was just about equality and "wholeness."

And the more these "behaviors" were resisted, even on the lofty theoretical level, the more appealing they became. "What would happen sexually once social and psychic unity exists cannot be predicted," one essay noted calmly. "Bisexuality and homosexuality may or may not increase; but certainly more natural, less fearful sexual relationships (of whichever kind) could be expected. Becoming an androgynous human being and living in an androgynous society would definitely influence the way we relate sexually, but in developing the new concept of androgyny we are definitely using it in a cultural rather than a physical sense."[67]

So the philosophy that was not about sexuality was going to turn out to be about sexuality after all.

Strange Bedfellows

The split between "good" and "bad" androgyny remains in place today, in part for strategic reasons. If the women's movement of the seventies and the spiritualist side of feminism were strongly influenced by Jung, then two of the most Jungian of present-day gender groups, as I have noted, are the "men's movement" and certain cross-dressers and transgenderists. It is probably not an accident that both kinds of groups—and they may well regard themselves as strange bedfellows—are predominantly concerned with "the feminine side" in men, rather than the "masculine side" in women. Nor will it come as a surprise that the official rhetoric of some of these groups insists upon heterosexuality, despite the fact that in private many individuals connected with them will acknowledge their own sexual experimentation—and, indeed, their bisexuality.

"As my obsession with WOMAN grew it finally occurred to me that maybe I should undertake psychotherapy à la Jung," writes "men's movement" guru Sam Keen artlessly in his best-selling book *Fire in the Belly: On Being a Man.* "Perhaps if I got to know my feminine side I would not be so dependent upon women for my pleasure and succor. But therapy seemed only to push me deeper into the arms of WOMAN. For several introspective years I juggled the predicates of gender and wondered constantly: Am I receptive, nurturing, intuitive, sensuous, yielding—'feminine' enough? Am I initiatory, decisive, rational, aggressive—'masculine' enough?"[68]

For Keen, as for feminist Catharine Stimpson, the story of androgyny is also a myth: "the unisex myth." In the sixties, he says, "a generation of hippie men tuned in, turned on, dropped out, became softer, and wore long hair. Among the more affluent, unisex haircuts and boutiques became the rage. Across town in the financial district, the new working woman practiced her oppposite but equal style of unisex. She bought a briefcase, and began power-dressing."

"In the world of psychology some believed that the unisex myth was manifesting Carl Jung's belief in the androgyny of men and women. In Jungian analysis, to become whole, men must discover their feminine side —their 'anima,' or soul. To become whole, women must explore their 'animus,' or worldly and aggressive side. . . . The end of the process is that each man and woman must first consummate an inner marriage between the masculine and feminine before he or she can relate realistically to a member of the opposite sex."[69]

Ultimately Keen came to question the usefulness of these labels. "In my judgment, we would gain much clarity if we ceased using the words 'masculine' and 'feminine' except to refer to the stereotypes of the genders that have been historically predominant. Far better to remain with the real mystery of man and woman than the false mystification of the masculine and the feminine."

As for "the unisex myth," he reported that it seemed again to be losing points on the "Dow Jones Mythic Index," in favor of a renewed interest in "the uniqueness of the sexes" and "the differences between the genders." But Keen retained some nostalgia. "What remains appealing about the idea is that, if we are androgynes, then we already bear the other within ourselves."[70]

If we are androgynes. We may notice, once again, the determined heterosexism of this approach to androgyny. Keen's explorations, he reports, came in the wake of the breakup of his first marriage, and he devotes much space to acquainting the reader with the pleasures of his second. Whether preoccupied with WOMAN or women, real mysteries or false mystifications, for the "men's movement," and for Keen, androgyny is not apparently about getting in touch with your *homosexual* side. At least not overtly.

"We are white, college-educated, heterosexual men," Mark Gerzon confesses. "We are quick to talk about sex and slow to discuss intimacy. . . .

We allude frequently to being real, red-blooded, all-American men, and sometimes we even make fun of 'queers.' . . . Yet we feel increasingly vulnerable."[71] In his analysis of "the changing face of American manhood" Gerzon seeks to replace five old "archetypes of masculinity" (the Frontiersman, the Soldier, the Expert, the Breadwinner, and the Lord) with five new "emerging masculinities" (Healer, Companion, Mediator, Colleague, and Nurturer). "The human qualities they symbolize transcend sexual identity," he insists. "To heal, nurture, or mediate is neither a masculine nor a feminine role," so that "unlike the old archetypes, which were for men only, the emerging masculinities are not."[72] The earnestly gendered ungendering of this last assertion demonstrates the Jungian double bind at its most incorrigible.

In an attempt to avoid putting off his lay readers, Gerzon calls "archetype" a "stodgy word,"[73] yet he still persists in using it. "Our task, as Jung argues," he says, "is not to deny these images or archetypes but to become conscious of them." "Each of the masculine archetypes described in this book," he notes, "requires the denial of the feminine. Each depends on denying the independent creative power of womanhood (its so-called masculine side) and on denying the tender, vulnerable dimension of manhood (its so-called feminine side). . . . Spirituality in a man does not require denial of the feminine. On the contrary, it is an affirmation of femininity as an essential part of ourselves."[74]

The other major national movement to retain and work within the Jungian categories of masculine and feminine "wholeness" is the cross-dressing and transgender community. Diverse and complex, this community, or group of communities, including everything from transsexuals to passing and recreational cross-dressers to drag queens and S/M groups, does not speak with a single voice. But many male to female cross-dressers I have talked with describe their interest in "getting in touch with the feminine side" of themselves. By "feminine" they often mean "softer," more demonstratively emotional; concerned with clothing, makeup, fabrics, and aesthetic detail; engaged with music and the arts; social, interpersonal, nonaggressive.

The brochure for Fantasia Fair, an annual gathering of cross-dressers in Provincetown, Massachusetts, invites attendees to "Live the Fantasy!" to "Turn your Dream into Reality!" to "Live 'en femme' for 10 days." Issued by the Human Outreach & Achievement Institute, sponsor of the event, the brochure asks—and answers—the crucial question: "Who's it for? Crossdressers, Crossgenderists, Transsexuals, Androgynes."

Cross-dressers are not necessarily "androgynes," but many strive for, and base their personal and genealogical self-understanding upon, a concept of androgyny. An article by Holly Boswell in the *TV/TS Tapestry, A*

Journal for All Persons Interested in Crossdressing & Transsexualism, laid out the familiar argument for the benefit of a particular population.

> Therapists today acknowledge that andro-gyny—one's personal blending of so-called masculine and feminine traits—is the healthiest model for self-actualization and fulfillment. This entails a process of transcending social conditioning in order to more fully become uniquely ourselves. C. G. Jung called this process *individuation,* and recognized that a reconciliation with one's inner contrasexual energy (the feminine *anima* in men, and the masculine *animus* in women) was the key to *wholeness.*

"While many people have androgynous potential, the tradition of a *third sex* involves a minority within which these tendencies are much more pronounced," she concludes, listing among the "truly transgendered" the *berdache* of native North America, the shamans of Siberia, the *mahu* of Polynesia, and the Amazons—all familiar figures not only in the cultural genealogies of cross-dressers but also in high-culture mythographic accounts of the Jungian archetypes.[75]

A box on the bottom of the page highlights the message: "Androgyny . . . is the healthiest model for self-actualization. . . ." Actually the text in the box reads "androgeny." *Tapestry* not infrequently has typos of this sort (its staff is dedicated but overworked). In this case, however, the misspelling is suggestive, since the "gyn" which means "woman" has been displaced by a "gen," the sign of genealogy, and androgyny itself has disappeared to be replaced by a word modeled on the male hormone "androgen." The transgender community is necessarily very much up on its hormones, so the slip, which we might call a new version of hormone replacement therapy, is perfectly "natural." But it is also telling.

Tri-Ess, the Society for the Second Self, is a national support group for heterosexual cross-dressers and their spouses or partners. The membership form asks applicants to enroll on the "honor system" (the phrase is in quotation marks in the original), only applying for full membership if you are in fact a heterosexual cross-dresser. The Membership Pledge and Agreement sets forth the purpose of the society: "the assistance of its members in developing, understanding, accepting, and attaining confidence in the expression of the feminine side of their personalities." The pledge concludes with this avowal: "In seeking membership I acknowledge that I believe in the full expression of my personality, both masculine and feminine."

Masculine and feminine, but not "straight and gay." Gay cross-dressers and transsexuals can become "Friends of Tri-Ess," at a reduced rate. No mention is made of lesbians. It is fascinating to imagine what Carl Jung would have made of this development, a perfectly logical if literal transposition of his ideal categories into concrete and visible terms.

Tri-Ess is the exception rather than the rule for cross-dressing organizations. Its stringency is almost surely based in part on a desire to escape further stigmatization-through-stereotype. (The assumption that all cross-dressers are gay and that all gays are sexually promiscuous is still made by a vast number of people in this country.) But many other cross-dressers and transgenderists are, of course, both pro-sex and gay affirmative. Strikingly, many are also bisexual—bringing the two parts of that much-disputed term back into synchrony with one another.

In my travels around the United States and in Europe, meeting with members of the transgender community, I have encountered a significant number of transgenderists who described themselves as bisexual in the usual modern sense of the term; they had love affairs with both men and women, or they desired to do so. One was a married therapist who himself cross-dressed and ran a large organization that served cross-dressers. Another was Francis Vavra.

Francis Vavra is a female to male cross-dresser whose husband cross-dresses as a woman. Francis is also a bisexual, and sees a relationship between gender identity(ies) and sexuality. "I have always led a dual existence in my inner life," Francis says, "always felt physically attracted to boys/girls, men/women throughout my life, as well as feeling I personally was both genders (both at separate and the same time)." Francis came out publicly as a bisexual and a cross-dresser virtually simultaneously, and began to go to strip shows, women's dance clubs, and other gatherings where there was physical contact with women. Francis has speculated much more, inwardly and in conversations with a therapist, on cross-dressing than on sexuality. "My sexuality," says Francis, "is a quite natural part of my being."

> I've always felt balanced and whole, even when emphasizing one gender or sexual choice over the other, because I am always cognizant of both at the same time, but it is always other people who seem to want me to "choose" which I am, or to stay as one (straight/gay, female/male). I rebel against that, as I am truly both. I do notice a more extreme "shift" whenever I fully cross-dress (with mustache, etc.) as Francis, versus my femme self, when I more readily drift back and forth in my inner feelings of gender, and bi-attractions. I have been noticing "bi-movies" lately, where I am equally attracted to (and can therefore identify with) both the hero and heroine.[76]

This last remark goes to the heart of the question of desire. Some therapists and analysts would hold that attraction is the opposite of identification. Thus feminist film theorists in the seventies argued, following Laura

Mulvey, that (implicitly, straight) women had to become imaginative "transvestites" or gender-crossers in order to watch responsively films made (by men, for largely male audiences) that placed women in the position of the looked-at, the gazed-upon: the object.

For lesbians, critics countered, this problem did not arise, or arose differently. Lesbians could watch "straight" films with heterosexual love plots and find a direct relation between the camera's eye and their own specular pleasure. Yet the subject-object structure remained, and could apparently only be modified, not contravened, by making "sex objects" more interesting and active subjects. The viewer still got to "choose." Francis's self-description, however, explodes this whole question of "identification" by acknowledging that erotic positions are (potentially always) doubled: vice versa. Attraction and identification for Francis are both available positions, and not always antithetical ones, even in the moment of looking.

In fact, as we have already noted in the context of "bisexual advertising," consciously targeted populations are never the only ones to respond to provocative visual images. Gay (and bisexual) men in the fifties could appreciate Marlon Brando and James Dean playing "straight" roles designed to allure female audiences and, in the nineties, find amusement and erotic pleasure in magazine layouts advertising perfume, cologne, and underwear. Straight (and bisexual) women derive pleasure from looking at buffed-up gay male bodies on display.

"Dr. Garber," asked Geraldo Rivera, after hearing Francis's story and contemplating photographs of Francis and husband Roxanna together, both cross-dressed, on a program devoted to the phenomenon of "women who dress as men," "Dr. Garber, does Francis really want to be a man?" Francis was one of five cross-dressers featured on the show; I, because I had written a book on cross-dressing, was invited to serve as the "expert." And "expert" to Geraldo and his producers meant reading the minds and motives of the panelists, who evidently could not be trusted to know themselves. The "expert," as always, was the person presumed to know. Thus I was "Dr. Garber," a technically accurate but functionally misleading mode of address (since my degree is in English literature, not in medicine or psychology) while the panelists were addressed by their first names.

"I don't know," I answered. "Ask Francis."

This was clearly the wrong answer from the point of view of "expertise," though it did give Francis a chance to say what s/he thought. (No, s/he didn't "want to be a man." She liked who and what s/he was. "S/he," incidentally, was Francis's own preferred choice of pronoun.) Geraldo and his audience clearly wanted Francis to "choose" between polarities *they* saw as real, and mutually exclusive. They did not want anyone to stake out a position that called those poles into question. Or, rather, they wanted someone to do exactly that, so that they could have the pleasurable experience of simultaneously enjoying and resisting it. Their position as audience was one of scandalous pleasure, scandalous disapproval, and, in some ways most eroticized of all, scandalous superiority. (Interestingly, several older women in the audience spoke admiringly of the panelists' lifestyles. The only strong objection, apart from one family-values hardliner, came from young women in short skirts and off-the-shoulder blouses who couldn't understand why their onstage counterparts didn't want to look like *them*.)

Androgyny on the Borderlines of Sex

"Feathers! Androgyny! The Folies-Bergère Reopens" announced a headline in the Arts section of the *New York Times*. When the long-running Paris music hall closed in December 1992, its once-risqué specialty of topless dancers in feathers seemed to many in show business to be over the hill rather than over the top. But less than a year later Parisians as well as tourists were again packing the seats. The lure? "Sexual ambiguity, bizarre physical types, unlikely voices, abrupt passages from the surreal to near-slapstick, and a trademark tango." What is described as "an androgynous young Berber on a white horse with a startling—sometimes shattering—soprano voice" set the tone, which was said to have been inflected, as well, by the magic realism of Gabriel García Marquez and the fantasmatic transvestites and dwarfs of Federico Fellini.[77]

In this context, "androgyny," 1990s style, suggests not only camp on the runway but also sex, as well as "sexual ambiguity." The most celebrated of modern performers have been described as androgynous—and sexy. Their crossover looks are part of their appeal. This is not at all the same thing as "getting in touch with your female (or male) self," or, as one Jungian cultural anthropologist put it, "the reconciliation of the masculine and feminine sides of the human being."[78] When it comes to the sexual come-on of "androgyny," reconciliation has (almost) nothing to do with it. From Boy George to the performer who used to be called Prince, the unsettling nature of gender uncertainty is itself an erotic borderline.

"Most of the new androgynous women," noted an article in the gay and lesbian magazine *Out/Look* on pop, folk, rock, and punk singers like Michelle Shocked, Tracy Chapman, Phranc, k.d. lang, and the Indigo Girls, "constructed their songs and their images with a sexual ambiguity that at times verged on camp." But, the article went on to ask, "is it lesbian music?"[79] Good question. Phranc, who wears her hair in a flat-top, sang the story in the early nineties: "Androgyny is the ticket or at least it seems to be. Just don't wear a flat-top and mention sexuality, and girl you'll go far, you'll get a record contract and be a star." Michelle Shocked was at the time "rumored to be involved with a man" (the rumors turned out to be true, but what was more to the point was that this information had gossip status) while memories of Holly Near, who "hid her bisexuality in order to appeal to a women's music audience" were fresh in the minds of both lesbians and bisexual activists. "We've made the world safe for androgyny in the charts," noted Deidre McCalla, a singer and songwriter.

Does "androgyny" in show business have more power if the androgynous performer comes out as straight, or as bi—or if she or he artfully conceals or resists disclosing a sexual preference? Is fantasy, in other words, more powerful in the absence of too much corroborating "fact" (whether the fact takes the form of "rumor" or substantive evidence)? The look may be androgynous, but that hardly suggests that its performer is an androgyne—or a bisexual. Yet all too commonly the terms are confused and conflated.

With "androgyny" several different sets of ideas and associations are put in play: sexy gender indeterminacy situated on an exciting borderline; unthreatening, perhaps even asexual gender indeterminacy, situated on a merely puzzling borderline; and spiritual transcendence that elides the borderline altogether.

A k.d. lang fan reports, "I took one look at k.d. and I said to myself: is that a guy or a girl? There was something about her attitude that I liked."[80] Another bisexual woman reported *her* dream about k.d. lang: "I had never been particularly attracted to that androgynous look before, but now I'm most attracted to a person whose sex is not known at first glance, regardless of that person's sex."[81]

Without the borderline, without the edge, though there may be sex, there is no sexiness.

Pat Riley, short, chunky, bespectacled, dressed in chinos and a cowboy shirt buttoned up to the neck, is not your usual sex symbol. The joke about Pat is gender indeterminacy: Is Pat male or female? Actually, Pat doesn't look very male—or, for that matter, very female either. "Pat's Theme" ends with the triumphant refrain, "It's time for androgyny— here's Pat."

Pat's life story in paperback is a wonderful experiment in pronoun suppression: We learn, for example, that Pat's proud parents, Fran and Jean, divorced when Pat was very young. "But Dad moved next door." (Which one is Dad?) Neither parent remarried "(even though Jean did run off with some idiot for a short time)."[82] Is the "idiot" male or female, straight or gay? Is Jean? Who knows? Who cares?

The account of the marriage and divorce is immediately followed by Pat's eighth-grade science project, which was conducted, inevitably, on the topic of "asexual reproduction," a subject the teacher judges too distant from Pat's own thoughts and life experiences to get a good grade. And so on to the social dancing class, with pictures of Pat dancing with first a male and then a female partner (both are taller than Pat). Clippings from the school newspaper, and Pat's own account, emphasize that the class encouraged them not "to automatically take partners of the opposite sex."

Pat takes a lover, "Chris." And when Chris, inevitably, jilts Pat for someone else, the someone else is an equally androgynous "Terry." (Pat winds up in a relationship with "Adrian.") Pat's favorite entertainer, needless to say, is Michael Jackson; Pat's first stage role, Peter Pan.

"Is Pat bisexual?" someone asked me. It's hard to know (and, you may say, harder to care). Pat's puppet alter ego, Little Pat, insists that "I only date puppets of the opposite sex." But the comedy here crosses over, if gingerly, from androgyny to homo- and bisexuality.

To compare Pat to Dil, the character played by Jaye Davidson in Neil Jordan's *The Crying Game,* is to compare . . . what? Apples and oranges? Chalk and cheese? Dil is sexy, erotic, feminine, seductive; Pat is deliberately constructed to be none of these things (though, sexual taste being as variegated and perverse as it is, I'd guess there's a sexy-Pat fan club out there somewhere). Dil looks like a gorgeous woman, or, if your eye is good and your experience is wide enough, like a gorgeous transvestite. Later, when Fergus cuts off her hair and dresses her in her dead boyfriend's cricket sweater and flannels, Dil looks even more like a girl. She doesn't really pass successfully. But Fergus is in these terms a sexual innocent. So imagine his consternation when she takes off her clothes and he sees her body, and her penis.

Innumerable men of my acquaintance—admittedly, straight men, and, as it happens, white men, and, as it happens, middle-aged men—told me that director Neil Jordan had used a body double for this scene. The naked body, the body with the penis, was not, they said, the body of the person who had been on-camera in the previous scenes. In other words, they were in the grip of what Freud would call "disavowal." Their problem was the same as Fergus's: They had come to desire that which, once they "knew" what it was, they "knew" they didn't desire. Or did they? The split between mind and body, or knowledge and desire, was so extreme for these men that they preferred to believe that the trick was in the technology rather than in their own psyche and libido.

In this climactic scene, where Dil bares all and Fergus turns away, repulsed by his own desire, Dil is, specularly, momentarily, an androgyne, male and female at once. And Fergus? Is he, because he is attracted to Dil as well as to (other) women, a bisexual? For that matter, was Dil's former boyfriend, the soldier who gets seduced and betrayed by Miranda Richardson as an IRA operative, a bisexual?

And what about my male friends, with their disavowal and their desires? They are not "bisexuals," at least not as a result of this one instance of misreading. But their attraction to Dil is not a false move. (There is no "false" in erotic attraction, just as there is no "no" in the unconscious.) We might say that they are responding "bisexually" in a performative sense, responding to gender cues and miscues, responding to the "woman" produced by artifice and artifact, responding, in short, to the performance of femininity, made more emphatic and more erotic by its situation on the edge or borderline. What this mistake which is not a mistake tells us about bisexuality, or the erotics of bisexual attraction, is that we edit out and rationalize away many of the erotic moments in our lives because they do not conform to our outward assessment of ourselves. Call this repression or sublimation or (what is one of its least salubrious defense mechanisms) homophobia; by whatever name, it is a refusal to acknowledge the place of desire.

That kind of refusal seems to me to be at work in Sally Potter's 1993 film *Orlando,* which received generally glowing press notices and much commentary on its "androgynous hero." Androgyny was Potter's preferred term, though the novel, and the life stories on which it was based, concerns itself much more with bisexuality: Vita Sackville-West, as we have seen, was the prototype of the contented bisexual woman.

But Potter's film, which she repeatedly declared to be only loosely based on Woolf's *Orlando,* stresses gender rather than sexuality. Orlando as a pretty young man (played by a rather vapid Tilda Swinton) doesn't have sex; Orlando as a pretty young woman (played by a slightly more animated Tilda Swinton) does, but only with a rambunctious and banally Byronic American boy (pop star Billy Zane). No homosex; no bisex. As Caryn James noted in the *New York Times,* "the delicate Ms. Swinton looks nothing like Sackville-West, whom Woolf once lovingly described as 'mustachioed.' "[83] A bland and inoffensive androgyny, in other words, is substituted for ambiguous, ambivalent, transgressive sexuality.

Orlando's voice-over in the Elizabethan scenes describes himself as possessing "the feminine appearance to which every young man of the time aspired." The final episode, which takes Orlando beyond Woolf's "real time" stopping point of 1928 to Potter's "real time" in the 1990s, is once again counterpointed by Orlando's voice, this time describing the "slightly androgynous" appearance that "females aspired to" in our own age. "Man or woman, Orlando is ever in sexual fashion," a reviewer comments astringently.[84] But is it sex? Or just gender?

By all accounts the high point of the film comes near its beginning, with the brilliant casting of the magnificent, flaming homosexual queen Quentin Crisp as Queen Elizabeth to Swinton's boy Orlando. In one of those coincidences that are too perfect to be coincidences, the article in the *New York Times* ended with warm words of praise for the film ("Ms. Potter's extraordinary film promises not to fade, or wither, or grow old" —echoing the command given by Crisp-Elizabeth to Swinton-Orlando at the beginning of the film). This was followed by a half-inch filler ad of the kind used throughout the newspaper to "justify" columns of type. The insert ad, in capital letters, read simply, CAMP, A PLACE TO DREAM: GIVE TO THE FRESH AIR FUND.[85]

The whole film, arguably, needed to be sent to Camp. Jane Marcus railed against the absence of a gay sensibility: "Does Sally Potter have any idea what *Orlando* means to readers, what for decades Orlando's slippery sexuality has meant? How dare she represent Orlando as merely a straight white Englishwoman?"[86] (Complaining that she wanted to apologize to the art house audience "who had clearly come to see a gay film," Marcus also averred that "it was so embarrassing I had to apologize to my husband," thereby striking a note of bisexual equity that might well come across to some as a claim of heterosexual privilege.)

But what did Potter think her film was about?

At a discussion at the University of Sussex after a screening of the film Potter said she wanted Orlando to find "something essential" about herself, "something transcendent," since Virginia Woolf had clearly intended Orlando to be an "innocent, essential human self."[87] Something essential; something transcendent. This is the androgyne as humanist hero. There is no bisexuality in Potter's Orlando, because there is no sexuality.

The real question about "androgyny" is how it comes to mean both sexlessness and sexiness at once. What's sexy about crossover gender cues, or sexual misreading, or undecipherable gender? How can people who are also attracted to exaggeratedly "male" or "female" figures be turned on by persons of uncertain, or transgressively double-signed, gender and sexuality? For the two are hardly mutually exclusive. Fans of k.d. lang can also be fans of Julia Roberts or Kelly McGillis; fans of Boy George or David Bowie may take erotic pleasure in the performances of Clint Eastwood or Sylvester Stallone. Indeed, one of the commonest realizations produced by work on drag, cross-dressing, and transvestite representation is that exaggerated "maleness" may cross over into the realm of "femininity" (Stallone, with his doe eyes and his sleekly tended body is in fact a good example) and that the reverse (vice versa) may be true for exaggerated "femaleness" (Mae West).

If bisexuality is related to androgyny, it is not related by similitude or analogy (thus it does not automatically follow that persons who are "in the middle" sexually are attracted to figures who cross gender lines or confound gender stereotypes), but rather by a different kind of mechanism.

Perhaps the clearest way of answering the question about androgyny and sexiness is to begin by analyzing androgyny as a metaphor. A metaphor, as we have noted, consists of two parts: the word being used figuratively (the vehicle) and the idea that it is meant to convey (the tenor). Androgyny is sexy when it is the vehicle (the physical form or performance we see) and not sexy when it is the tenor (the idea or idealization). When the performance is androgynous, it is frequently erotic, and its eroticism is often bisexual, appealing both to men and to women.

"Mick Jagger was the first performer to appeal to *both* sexes—heterosexual males as well as females and gays," said one of his friends from the early days, with an interesting gloss on the word "both." "He could arouse both sexes like no one before, or since."[88] "Bisexuality and androgyny," said another Jagger acquaintance from the seventies, were "not only accepted" but "encouraged."[89]

The 1960s and 1970s, like the 1890s of Oscar Wilde and Aubrey Beardsley, demonstrated once again that androgyny—at least the "bad" androgyny, the bad-boy or bad-girl androgyny—could be sexy. In this sense, "androgyny" connoted transgressive sexuality (boys and men with long hair and makeup, women with very short hair or shaved heads, crossover clothing from jeans to dresses for men). It could lead to "bi-lib"; it could lead to gender misreading and mistaking. It was exciting in part because it was a violation of one's parents' certainties about gender and gender roles, and in part because reading—the interpretation of signs—is always exciting. It was exciting, in other words, because it was uncertain. It connoted risk.

When "androgyny" was not the vehicle of a metaphor but its tenor, however—when it denoted something like "wholeness" or "integration" of the personality—it was determinedly *un*sexy. It meant, or was said to mean, or was said *only* to mean, stasis, not movement, and union, not desire. In other words, not lack but fullness.

At the turn of the century, the word "androgyne" meant a certain kind of male homosexual who might also refer to himself as a "female impersonator," although he had nothing to do with the professional stage. Later it came to suggest a kind of undifferentiated gender, of the kind that in the sixties was called "unisex." A glance at the career of "unisex," now mostly employed either to describe haircuts, sweatshirts, lumber jackets, and other ungendered clothing, or to indicate that there is only one rest room on the premises to be used by male and female alike, will suggest how the "sex" has dropped out over the years.

Basically, what is wrong with "androgyny" as a term in and of itself and as a synonym for "bisexuality" is that it tries to take the sex out of gender. "The androgyne," writes Mircea Eliade, "is considered superior to the two sexes just because it incarnates totality and hence perfection."[90] The androgyne is idealized as a perfect, completed, serenely self-satisfied being, like Edmund Spenser's Hermaphrodite Venus, covered with a veil:

> *But sooth it was not sure for womanish shame,*
> *Nor any blemish, which the worke mote blame;*

> *But for, they say, she hath both kinds in one,*
> *Both male and female, both vnder one name:*
> *She syre and mother is her selfe alone,*
> *Begets and eke conceiues, ne needeth other none.*
>
> —*The Faerie Queene* 4:10–41

"Ne needeth other none." This was the real point. The androgyne, Jung's integrated personality, was self-sufficient, a being at rest, secure and serene within herself or himself. He or she needed no one else.

That this was an impossible and indeed a dangerous ideal became clear in the case of America's favorite "androgynous hero," Michael Jackson, an entertainment personality as famous for his apparent sexlessness as for his spectacular (and sexy) style—"the mythic, androgynous Jackson" as he was described by *Vanity Fair*.[91] Androgynes *are* myths, or, as we prefer to call them these days, "cultural icons." But a human being, even a "reclusive man-child with no known history of romantic relationships" who "prefers to live a fantasy life in the company of children"[92] will almost surely cross over that artificial barrier between "good androgyny" and "bad androgyny."

We might recall Jung's emphasis, in "The Psychology of the Child Archetype," on what he called "the hermaphroditism of the child": "the archetype of the child, which expresses man's wholeness. . . . The 'eternal child' in man is an indescribable experience, an incongruity, a disadvantage, and a divine prerogative."[93] If, as Sam Keen insists, the "wild man" so important to the "men's movement" has "many names, many faces," among them "*homo ludens,* the playboy, the *puer aeternis,* Peter Pan,"[94] then Jackson would seem to be an uncanny enactment of that fantasy hero, the inner child of maleness.

In the case of Jackson, the initial mistake, the belief that Jackson himself could be like a Jungian archetype, timeless, unchanging, eternal, and transcendent, led inevitably to what (the well-named) *Vanity Fair* called a "Nightmare in Neverland."

Jackson lives at Neverland Ranch. In my book *Vested Interests,* I suggested that his eternal youth, his gender-crossing style, and his popularity with children made him the Peter Pan for our time—almost the first male Peter since the part was originally written by James Barrie for a young actress. In the midst of the controversy surrounding Jackson's relationship with a young boy, a Hollywood studio chief was quoted as saying that Jackson never had real film potential. "He doesn't have a distinct persona that translates into movies," the executive claimed. "I think he would have been a very good Peter Pan. Other than that, I don't know what you do with him."[95]

In effect, Michael Jackson had gone from being Peter Pan to being James Barrie—from the eternal child to the man who surrounds himself with children. And the consequences have been shattering—not only for Jackson and those with whom he has been personally involved but also for his fans. "After a quarter-century of alternately adoring and pitying Michael Jackson," wrote columnist Derrick Z. Jackson (no relation), "I find myself in a limbo as odd as his androgyny and race-erasing. . . . If he has abused children he should get serious jail time and serious therapy. But a part of me, the child in me, prays that he didn't do it."[96]

Michael Jackson's unexpected marriage to Lisa Marie Presley, daughter of "the King," shifted media attention from his alleged interest in boys to his newly affirmed and institutionally validated "heterosexuality," though the press tended to treat this as the most neon of lavender marriages. No one, to my knowledge, claimed Jackson as "a bisexual." The borderline he had crossed in the public eye was not between an imagined homo- and a presumptive heterosexuality, but rather between androgyny and sexuality. Despite, or perhaps, because of, the manifest erotic content of his brilliant stage performances, the public wanted Jackson to remain aloof from mere sexual behavior. The marriage was a palliative, a public relations coup, and a dynastic sensation. What it wasn't—what it couldn't be, what no actual sexual relationship or set of relationships *could* be—was a way of putting Michael Jackson's idealized androgyny back together again.

Chapter 9

Ellis in Wonderland

The omnipresent process of sex, as it is woven into the whole texture of
our man's or woman's body, is the pattern of all the process of our life.

—*Havelock Ellis*, The New Spirit

Every artist writes his own autobiography.

—*Ellis*, The New Spirit

There are two fundamental meanings to "bisexuality"—and they are, at
least on the face of things, at variance with each other. The first has to do
with the subject, the second with the object, or objects, of desire.

Our modern sense of a person "sexually attracted to members of both
sexes"—the person who "is" bisexual, or is "a bisexual"—is the later one.
The earlier, on which the modern meaning is uneasily propped, is "of two
sexes," or "having both sexes in the same individual"—a sense that derives from nineteenth-century ideas about biology, botany, evolution, and
animal behavior ("a flower which possesses stamens and pistils is bisexual"[1]) but also from myth, fable, and religion.

Thus in the early nineteenth century the poet Samuel Taylor Coleridge
could write of "the very old tradition of the *homo androgynus*—that
is, that the original man . . . was bi-sexual."[2] "Bisexual" is the preferred
nineteenth-century term. The seventeenth century said "bisexed" or even
"bisexous," for "of both sexes," again with dual reference to natural history[3] and religion.

> *Our bisexed Parents, free from sin,*
> *In Eden did their double birth begin.*[4]

Notice that in this couplet "bisexed" and "free from sin" were equated
with one another. Here, as in Coleridge's recollection that "the original

man" was thought of as "bi-sexual," there is in fact a kind of Gnostic memory of an original double state, analogous to Plato's famous fable of the doubled and split human beings in the *Symposium.*

Bisexual in this sense means undivided, perfect, prefallen. According to this rather restricted use of the term, to be "bisexual" was to be above or beyond human sexuality, to transcend it. "Bisexuality" was the origin, but it was also, at least in an idealized sense, the goal.

The teleology of science, of course, implied a quite different sense of progress. "The sexes" evolved over time; a rose or a snail might be bisexual, but a human being, of a higher evolutionary order, was male or female, not both. Or so one might think.

In fact, however, nineteenth-century science suggested that human beings were constitutionally bisexual. They possessed a "latent bisexuality" or an "originary bisexual disposition," evidence for which could be found in the vestigial symmetries of male and female bodies: male breasts, the homology of the penis and the clitoris, the labia and the scrotum. Charles Darwin and his followers pointed out that the ancestors of the vertebrates were hermaphrodites, and that vertebrates, too, were hermaphroditic in embryo, and sometimes "bisexual" in their physical manifestations.[5]

"Bisexuality" in this sense of biological two-in-one-ness became generally recognized as a "fact." At the same time, speculative thinkers from the sexologist Karl Heinrich Ulrichs to the philosopher Arthur Schopenhauer were noting the "bisexuality of the human individual."[6]

It was a short step from these observations to a psycho-sexual theory about the nature of desire. Ulrichs, himself a homosexual (or as he would have described himself, an "Urning," "Uranian," or "invert"), suggested that an innate bisexuality, analogous to Plato's fable, explained sexual inversion, and this view was amplified by writers like Edward Carpenter and, most signally, Havelock Ellis. In fact, when we come to examine the theories of these students of sexuality who immediately preceded Freud, it becomes all the more astonishing that Wilhelm Fliess could have convinced Freud for so long that he, Fliess, had a patent on the idea of bisexuality. For bisexuality, in all its several meanings, was very much "in the air."

Carpenter's theories of sexuality, as expressed in a work like the 1895 *Love's Coming of Age* and the 1908 collection *The Intermediate Sex,* imagined the possibility of an almost metaphysical union: "Nature," he wrote, "does not always keep her two groups of ingredients—which represent the two sexes—properly apart."[7] He felt "that there were many signs of an evolution of a new human type that would be *median* in character, neither excessively male nor excessively female," as Jeffrey Weeks notes, and that bisexuality might thus become a social and cultural norm.[8] In a late work he explored the bisexual nature of the poet Percy Bysshe Shelley. His *Love's Coming of Age* offered what would become an influential theory of "companionate marriage," based not on sexual fidelity, which he considered secondary, but on a "freer, more companionable, and less pettily exclusive relationship" that went beyond the initial "sex-glamor"[9] of youthful attraction.

Equally influential, and equally compelling, were the arguments of Havelock Ellis. Beginning in 1896 and later in his path-breaking *Psychology of Sex,* Ellis maintained that "inversion" was "a psychic and somatic development on the basis of a latent bisexuality."[10] Psychic *and* somatic. Inversion, or homosexuality, was something that occurred both in the mind and in the body. It was congenital,[11] and it had reference to a prior state in the history of the organism—a state that Ellis and others called "bisexuality."

The "invert" was part male, part female, or rather part "masculine" and part "feminine." The male invert's "feminine" side desired men; the female invert's "masculine" side desired women. Thus human sexuality could still be imagined according to a heterosexual model. It was "bisexuality" that produced homosexuality. Indeed, the two terms were often used as virtual equivalents.

Ellis's immediate predecessor, Richard von Krafft-Ebing, had likewise contended that bisexuality, understood in this medico-historical light, demonstrated the innateness of homosexuality: "Careful investigation of the so-called acquired cases makes it probable that the predisposition also present here consists of a latent homosexuality, or at least bisexuality," he wrote in 1892.[12]

The argument for innateness was a politically liberal one then, as in some ways it is today. Inversion was not to be regarded as a matter of choice (and therefore, potentially, of criminality or vice) but rather of "disposition," a term that, like its modern counterpart "orientation," invokes the weight not only of science, but of nature.

Indeed, Ellis also claimed that heredity was a factor—again anticipating genetic theories about sexual identity that would be put forth a century later. "This hereditary character of inversion," he asserted, "is a fact of great significance." "I can have no doubt concerning the existence of the tendency."[13] Nearly 39 percent of his cases had "inverted relatives"; similar figures were reported, he said, by other researchers, like L. S. A. M. von Römer and Magnus Hirschfeld. (We might compare this with the genetic studies of the late twentieth-century researchers to be discussed in Chapter 12, like Michael Bailey and Richard Pillard, or Dean Hamer, who tracked the family histories of gay male twins or brothers in another attempt to prove that a tendency to homosexuality could be inherited.)

The bisexual as we might describe him or her today, the person attracted to both men and women, was, in accordance with this same logic of the body, described in early sexological literature as a "psychosexual hermaphrodite."[14] Where the body led, the mind, and the desires, would follow.

◆

Bisexuality, in the sense of two-sexes-in-one-body, thus "explained" same-sex attraction by explaining it away. It was not the same sex to which we were attracted; it was the "opposite" sex as identified by the "masculine" (or "feminine") component inside our apparently female (or male) selves. Heterosexuality was preserved at the same time that science found a place, and an apparent origin, for the "invert."

We might notice here once again how discussions of bisexuality tend to drift toward discussions of homosexuality (or "inversion"). This is in fact a general tendency in the literature of sexology. Bisexuality is insistently named, but only as a disposition or predisposition. In practice it tends to disappear, or to be hidden under other terms. Thus, although he noted the new modern use of "bisexual" to describe "those persons who are attracted to both sexes," and found it more "convenient" than the cumbersome "psychosexual hermaphrodite,"[15] Ellis was in a way more concerned with distinguishing between homosexuality and inversion than he was with defining a "bisexuality" that addressed the desire for both men and women. This was at least in part because he preferred to define "homosexuality" as including persons whose attraction to their own sex was "of a slight and temporary character"—persons who today might be included under the broadest characterization of "bisexual."

The gradual merging of the two meanings of bisexuality was accomplished by the first decades of the twentieth century, as Ellis would note in the later editions of his *Studies in the Psychology of Sex.* "By bisexuality it is possible to understand not only the double direction of the sexual instinct but also the presence of both sexes in the same individual."

Though we may think of this "double-sexed" notion of bisexuality as quaint and out of current use, it is worth noting works like *Napoleon— Bisexual Emperor,* published in 1972, in which a medical doctor contends that excessive activity of the pituitary gland "during the period of his greatest ascendancy" and an "Organ Inferiority associated with his feminine build and hypogonadism" may have led to Napoleon's "fear of love, women and marriage" as well as to an exaggeration of male-linked traits like "strength, power, cruelty and coarseness."[16] A biological explanation, however idiosyncratic, could still be offered in the late twentieth century to account for issues of "history" and "destiny."

"Uncertainty and Doubt"

Ellis saw clearly that the "simplest of all possible classifications" was the grouping of all sexually functioning persons into three divisions: the heterosexual, the bisexual, and the homosexual—a classification that is still in use today. Yet he found this tripartite division of "no great practical use." Why? Because "the bisexual group is found to introduce uncertainty and doubt."[17]

And what does Ellis mean by "uncertainty and doubt"? He means, in effect, that the category when looked at closely tends either to expand (to include many if not most heterosexuals and homosexuals) or to disappear (since it is not discretely separable from the other two categories):

> Not only a large proportion of persons who may fairly be considered heterosexual have at some time in their lives experienced a feeling which may be termed sexual toward individuals of their own sex, but a very large proportion of persons who are definitely and markedly homosexual have had relationships with persons of the opposite sex. The social pressure, urging all persons into the normal sexual channel, suffices to develop such slight germs of heterosexuality as homosexual persons may possess, and so to render them bisexual.

Bisexuality is thus both an artifact of "social pressure" in the direction of normative heterosexuality and a behavioral fact of life. It characterizes the feelings of both "persons who may fairly be considered heterosexual" and "persons who are definitely and markedly homosexual." (The distinction between these two formulations—"may fairly be considered"; "are definitely and markedly"—itself suggests the disequilibrium between a socially sanctioned identity and an outlaw sensibility, where heterosexuality, even or especially presumptive heterosexuality, is the default category, the unmarked term.)

Furthermore, although the "uncertainty and doubt" in this passage are those of the social scientist seeking functional classifications, these terms are entirely symptomatic of the elusiveness of "bisexuality" as a concept. They bear in fact a startling resemblance to some of the terms of opprobrium heaped upon bisexual individuals from Ellis's time to ours: allegations of duplicity, psychological instability, immaturity, passing, or a "transitional phase."

Ellis himself had no such judgmental views. Convinced of the congenital nature of inversion, he also believed that there was a continuum of sexual behavior on which what were sometimes considered the "perversions" could be charted as exaggerations of normal or average tendencies. He resisted, whenever he could, the prescriptive idea of the "normal." For him, bisexuality and ambisexuality, the first attested to by latent organic signs and the second by undifferentiated infantile desires, helped to demonstrate the legitimacy of homosexuality and other tabooed practices.[18]

"Embryologists, physiologists of sex and biologists generally," he wrote, "not only accept the idea of bisexuality, but admit that it probably helps to account for homosexuality. In this way the idea may be said to have passed into current thought. We cannot assert that it constitutes an adequate explanation of homosexuality, but it enables us in some degree to understand what for many is a mysterious riddle, and it furnishes a useful basis for the classification not only of homosexuality, but of the other mixed or intermediate sexual anomalies in the same group."[19]

This "group" included physical hermaphroditism, eunuchoidism, and transvestism or cross-dressing, all potentially to be regarded, in his view, as aspects of latent bisexuality, even though many such persons are not, and were then known not to be, homosexual. Thus, "to place the group of homosexual phenomena among the intermediate groups on the organic bisexual basis is a convenient classification," though hardly "a complete explanation." Perhaps, Ellis speculates, it is rather a matter of glands, or "internal secretions"—metabolic chemical processes that affect the body and the mind. Homosexuality, or "sexual inversion," could "fairly be considered a 'sport,' or variation, one of those organic aberrations which we see throughout living nature."[20]

So much for "organic" or "latent" bisexuality. But when he comes to consider bisexuality as a set of sexual practices rather than an organic blueprint, "the bisexual group is found to introduce uncertainty and doubt." The uncertainty and doubt of the investigator have over time been projected onto the psyche of the subject. How can you be sure you are— or recognize—a bisexual when bisexuality is a category that undoes the notion of category itself?

"Two Odd People"

It would be interesting to know to what degree, if any, Ellis reflected on the "uncertainty and doubt" that these "superficial" and unscientific (but apparently inescapable) classifications introduced into his own life. A scholar and researcher, even one who came to be known as the "Sage of Sex," need not inevitably be deflected from the path of disinterested investigation by the vicissitudes of biographical detail. Still, just as it is worth noting that many of the biologists of the 1980s and 1990s who are tracing potential genetic links between genes or brain tissue and gay (male) identity are themselves gay men, looking through electron microscopes at themselves, so it is at least of some passing interest that Havelock Ellis was married to a woman who, he came to believe, was a "congenital sexual invert"—a woman whom he never ceased to love, and with whom he lived (and apparently had sex) intermittently in the course of a long career of mutually sanctioned affairs. Her death left him for a while convinced that his own life was over. (It was not; he fell in love again and spent the time until his death with Françoise Delisle, who invented as her surname an anagram of his).

Havelock Ellis and Edith Lees Ellis, a novelist, playwright, and highly successful performer on the American lecture circuit, had agreed to have no children, and to be economically independent of one another. Ellis had previously had a passionate (but possibly unconsummated) relationship with the feminist writer Olive Schreiner, who found that in her private life she craved sexual domination of a kind Ellis was not prepared to provide. His admiration for Edith encompassed, indeed as part of her charm, her boyish qualities. As a schoolgirl she had been compared in her appearance to Byron, and was encouraged to act in productions of Shakespeare, "playing the chief male parts."[21] One of her particular successes was Romeo, a part that may have come unconsciously to mind when Ellis wrote later, in his autobiography, about his feelings when he learned that his wife was having an affair with a former classmate, "Claire."

He was not jealous, he insists, "But, after all, I was human. There remained beneath the surface the consciousness of a flaw in the ideal of married love I had so far cherished, and a secret wound of the heart, 'not so deep as a well nor so wide as a church door,' but enough to kill that conception of mutual devotion in marriage."[22]

Casting himself here as Mercutio and Edith as Romeo, he sustains a "secret wound 'not so deep as a well,'" inflicted perhaps by accident, but nonetheless fatal. "We were destined to work out a larger and deeper conception of love, but that beautiful conventional conception had for us been killed. Even my strong sense of justice could scarcely have long tolerated so one-sided a sexual freedom in marriage. It might be true that I was exclusively heterosexual and she was not, and that therefore there was no demand on me to go outside marriage for love. But it was also true that the very qualities in her nature which made her largely homosexual were qualities which, fortifying as they might be to our comradeship, were inimical to the purely feminine qualities of sweetness and repose which a man seeks in a woman and therefore opposed in our case to a strict conjugal fidelity. And so it proved."

These words were written, of course, long after the fact of the affair with "Claire," or the more intense subsequent affair with "Lily," or the "numerous intimate relationships with women" he says Edith had throughout her life.[23]

"I knew," he declares, "for she had told me everything, of the sentimental and sometimes passionate attraction which from early school-life up to a few years before marriage she had experienced for girl friends. I knew that when a schoolgirl the resulting relationships had sometimes possessed a slight but definite sensuous character, though it had not found that experience in later adult friendships with women. I knew that such feelings were common in young girls. But at that time I had no real practical knowledge of inborn sexual inversion of character. In the essay I had written on Walt Whitman in *The New Spirit* I had passed over the homosexual strain in Whitman, in a deprecatory footnote, as negligible. I am sure that if I ever asked myself whether there was a homosexual strain in Edith, I answered it similarly. I was not yet able to detect all those subtle traits of an opposite sexual temperament as surely planted in her from the beginning as in Whitman. . . . The masculine traits were, indeed, not obvious in Edith any more than the feminine traits in Whitman; most people, I believe, failed to see them, and I cannot too often repeat that she was not really man at all in any degree but always woman, boy, and child, and these three, it seemed, in equal measure."[24]

Woman, boy, and child. The Victorian penchant for eroticizing and conflating these three roles, as evidenced in the success of a play like *Peter Pan* and in the music hall cult of the "principal boy" (a beautiful young woman dressed like a beautiful young man), surely colors Ellis's own attraction here. The reader of Ellis's *Autobiography* is left to conjecture whether the "boy" as well as the "woman" had some erotic appeal for the husband.

He evokes the same image in his description of Edith's relationship with Lily, who was to die a year after the affair began and haunt her lover ever after through spectral revisitations. "Edith," he says, "was indefatigable, as she always was, in her devotion and endlessly inventive in a lover's attentions. At such time she had all the air and spirit of an eager boy, even the deliberate poses and gestures of a boy, never of a man, and on one side of her, deeply woman-hearted as she was, it was more than a pose, with her restless activity and her mischievousness and her merry, ringing laugh, which suited so well with her well-shaped, compact head and her short, curly hair."[25]

Ellis seems to have participated helpfully in arranging some of the assignations between Edith and Lily, which were hindered by the watchfulness of Lily's elder sister. "On one occasion I gave up my studio at Hawkes Point for the day, to enable them to picnic quietly there. It was but rarely, indeed, that they could spend the night together and that Lily would hurry to Carbis with her little nightdress at a late hour when she had almost been given up."[26]

"You *are* two odd people!" Claire had said to Edith, with a smile, when told that Ellis could be trusted with the truth of their relationship.[27] For Ellis there seemed to be something at stake in calling Edith odd, and himself even: even-tempered, "exclusively heterosexual," with a "strong sense of justice." And there is a marked and remarkable resistance in his assertion, twice made, that however "boyish" Edith might have been, "she was not really man at all in any degree," that she "never" had the poses and gestures "of a man."

Woman, child, boy—in all of these ways Edith Ellis could be his opposite, for "man" is the conventional "opposite" to each of these terms in turn. He could imagine her to be a boy, could permit her to be a woman, could indulge and flirt with her as a child. But she could not be a "man" to him, for then she would be not the "opposite sex" but the same.

By inverting inversion, by marrying and loving a woman whom he could imaginatively see as a boyish lover of other women, Havelock Ellis took upon himself both the role of the dispassionate investigator and the role of the passionate subject of investigation. "A man who is attracted to boys may be brought to love a boyish woman," he writes in another context, citing the early sexual pioneer Albert Moll. "In the case of bisexual individuals, or of youthful subjects whose homosexuality is not fully developed, it is probable that this method is beneficial."[28] If Ellis was "exclusively heterosexual," he was not without curiousness and curiosity. He thought more about sex than most people, and perhaps did less about it. "Bisexuality" for him was an unstable analytic category; it may also have been a space of fantasy, speculation, and transferential desire.

One of Ellis's biographers takes the position that Edith Ellis was not really a lesbian or a "congenital invert" but rather a woman disappointed in the sexual side of her marriage. "If I am right, the argument in Havelock Ellis's mind, when he first gave his blessing to Edith and Claire, was that he had not succeeded in satisfying Edith sexually, though he had succeeded in establishing a spiritual love-relationship with her which had brought both of them great benefit. He could not demand that she should not receive from a woman what he was unable to give her himself."[29] As for Edith's own choice of a woman for her lover, she did it, he opines, in part to save her husband's pride.

Writing in the 1950s, shortly after the publication of the second Kinsey report (on *Sexual Behavior in the Human Female*), the biographer Arthur Calder-Marshall evokes Kinsey's famous rating scale—a scale which, as we will see shortly in some detail, produces "bisexuality" only as a statistical overlap.

"According to Kinsey standards which reckoned homosexual attachment from 0 for no homosexual attachments to 6 for no heterosexual attachment, Edith's at this time would have been a Kinsey-rating of 4. She was not, that is to say, a totally inverted person. She was making the transition, rather later than most people, because of her prematurity and her unfortunate childhood, from adolescence to the adult sexual pattern. And then, because of Havelock Ellis's own limitations, she lapsed."[30]

This is a rather extraordinary passage of cultural analysis, viewed from the standpoint of today. Like Ellis, Calder-Marshall regards lesbianism (or same-sex attraction in general) as a transitional phase, something Edith might have grown out of were her husband not both sexually inadequate to her needs and excessively convinced of the truth of his own theories. He seeks to contextualize Ellis just as we might seek to contextualize him, in the frame of the moment from which he writes:

"At that time nobody knew very much about the causes of what is usually called homosexuality, but which he preferred to call sexual inversion. Even to-day it is debatable whether it is entirely congenital, entirely environmental or combinations of the two. Havelock Ellis decided that there were two types of homosexuality, one congenital sexual inversion and one pseudo-homosexuality. What seems more likely is that there is a large number of intermediates, who are more easily classified in terms of the curable and the incurable. Roughly speaking the curable lie more fully in the Kinsey-ratings 1 to 3 and the incurable from 4 to 6. Edith Ellis wanted to be cured, and from a nondominant man like Ellis she felt no noticeable physical repulsion. On the other hand, Ellis's conviction that she was an incurable sexual invert and his lack of desire to cure her thrust her back on a path which she had already traversed. She felt that he was making her a sexual invert because he had not got the sexual potency to make her normal."[31]

"She felt he was using her for his work, was making her into a Lesbian in order to find out the feminine side of the business instead of helping her out of her troubles."[32] The "troubles," the "form of emotional expression which she had been growing out of," are Calder-Marshall's view, and perhaps not an entirely objective one, since he is convinced that some "inverts" are "curable" and some "incurable." Edith, he thought, "wanted to be cured."[33]

The language of "cure" echoes Ellis's own, though he was skeptical that true inverts ever wished for it ("Hirschfeld," he says, "remarks that the inverts 'cured' by hypnotism were either not cured or not inverted"[34]). The moral edge in "lapse" may mark Calder-Marshall's own view of homosexuality, but he, too, looks at bisexuals and does not see them. For him, as in a way for Ellis, they are "intermediates" who can either be cured or not—that is to say, they may be nudged back over the line to normal heterosexuality, or they may "lapse" back into the adolescent homosexual affections out of which they should, by now, have grown. "Intermediates" are curable or incurable, depending on where they fall on the Kinsey scale. What is not imagined is that they might remain, or prefer to remain, just where and how they are.

"I ask myself," writes Calder-Marshall with a first-person obtrusion unusual in a biographer, acknowledging his own deep curiosity about the matter, "I ask myself why, if Havelock was right in his initial diagnosis that Edith was a congenital sexual invert attracted only to women, she should at the age of fifty-five have been taxing her husband . . . about sexual infidelity, to which she should have been utterly indifferent."

To this question, posed in these terms, there can be no suitable reply. Calder-Marshall's Edith is a woman waiting for her husband to realize that she desires him, and meanwhile patiently biding her time in "a number of physical relationships with women, which satisfied the side of her nature which Havelock did not satisfy." She was in effect a situational or "environmental homosexual,"[35] like the schoolboy (or schoolgirl), the soldier, or the prisoner; what Freud would later call, in more mystificatory terms, a "contingent invert." Only instead of a boarding school or a barracks or a prison she had a marriage.

"From his point of view, the brief story of their marriage was that their spiritual love was so deep that it survived her infidelities with many women and his far smaller number of intimate friendships with women. . . . From her point of view, I think that the brief story of their marriage was that Edith loved his calm, heroically accepting spirit so much that she accepted the limitations he dictated before marriage; no children, separate establishments, long absences. . . . She tried to provoke him to virility, but when he gave his blessing to her affair with Claire, she accepted what she took to be a confession of impotence. She resented Amy [a woman with whom Ellis had an affair] so fiercely because it did not fit in with her theory of impotence. . . . She felt in love with Lily and after Lily's death had a number of physical relationships with women, which satisfied the side of her nature which Havelock did not satisfy. He on his side had a number of mildly erotic friendships with women, none of which harmed the spiritual love, which Havelock emphasized was the most important. But when Margaret Sanger appeared and Havelock fell in love with her—as he was careful to emphasize, *only* in a spiritual sense—the balance of Edith's mind went, though she still preserved above everything her love for Havelock."[36]

What is "preserved above everything" here is Edith's essential heterosexuality. If this reads like a film noir narrative of the forties, full of loyalty, suspense, and unthinking betrayal, it also suggests, and perhaps for that very reason, the need for a "story" to explain, or explain away, the varieties of sexual pleasure.

"The bisexual group is found to introduce uncertainty and doubt," Ellis wrote in his great and controversial volume on *Sexual Inversion,* a study that made him at once the Dr. Ruth and the Ann Landers of his day. Every day he received visits and letters from people who preferred to bring their problems to the Sage of Sex rather than to the doctor or the priest. "While therefore the division into heterosexual, bisexual, and homosexual is a useful superficial division, it is scarcely a scientific classification," he concluded. It therefore seemed best to him "to attempt no classification at all."[37]

This classification that is not a classification, that is above all "not scientific," has in the course of this century become the norm. Gay, straight, or bi are the sexual identities made available in both the public and the clinical press. Kinsey's famous seven-point scale, established with the explicit intention of replacing the unsatisfactory distinctions among heterosexuals, homosexuals, and bisexuals with a more accurate continuum from "exclusively heterosexual" (0) to "exclusively homosexual" (6), in fact expanded the middle ranges that connoted some degree of bisexuality without ever mentioning the word.

As Paul Robinson observes, Kinsey "was clearly unaware that from a theoretical standpoint a seven-way breakdown differed in no significant respect from a three-way breakdown." Both involved the same basic assumption: "that at some point differences of degree became differences of kind."[38] Respondents could choose to describe themselves, for example, as "predominantly heterosexual, only incidentally homosexual" (1), or as "predominantly homosexual, but more than incidentally heterosexual" (4), or even as "equally heterosexual and homosexual" (3). Categories 0 and 1 corresponded roughly to "heterosexual," categories 5 and 6 to "homosexual," and categories 2 through 4 to "bisexual."

But the word "bisexual" vanished, although the concept (or the "fact") remained omnipresent and pervasive. The Kinsey scale mapped out what Ellis had observed: that the bisexual group introduced uncertainty and doubt. In the interest of "scientific classification," bisexuality had disappeared—and was everywhere.

Chapter 10

Standard Deviations

What you don't know would make a great book.

—*Sydney Smith,* Lady Holland's Memoir

Everything happens to everybody sooner or later if there is time enough.

—*George Bernard Shaw,* Back to Methuselah

When an interviewer asked Dr. Wardell Pomeroy, coauthor of the Kinsey report, what made someone bisexual, he replied that it was the wrong question. "You should ask, 'Why isn't everybody?'"[1]

If "Why isn't everybody?" means, "Why doesn't everyone have erotic relationships with both men and women?," then the answers are not far to seek: repression, religion, repugnance, denial, laziness, shyness, lack of opportunity, premature specialization, a failure of imagination, or a life already full to the brim with erotic experiences, albeit with only one person, or only one gender.

But "Why isn't everybody?" is still the wrong question. Gore Vidal's distinction between essence and practice points up yet another paradox in the definition and discussion of bisexuality. Is it the potential to have sexual feelings for members of both sexes? Or the potential to act on them? Or the acting, the sex, itself? This explains in part why statistics about bisexuals vary so spectacularly, from the 10 percent of an *Essence* magazine poll (based on people who called themselves bisexual) to the original Kinsey report's figure of 15 percent (for both men and women)[2] to bisexual activist and therapist Maggi Rubenstein's whopping 80 percent, a figure she deduces from the number of people who've had, or say they've had, same-sex fantasies, feelings, or dreams.[3]

A disparity of 70 percent, even allowing a certain margin for error, is enough to give one pause. The claim that practically everyone is bisexual, like the (equally frequently made) claim that no one is, suggests that the concept of bisexuality is being asked to do a lot of cultural work here. It might be more fruitful to pose a version of the same question in Freud's almost equally droll and nonjudgmental terms: "[F]rom the point of view of psycho-analysis the exclusive sexual interest felt by men for women is also a problem that needs elucidating."[4]

Those who discount bisexuality as a fiction tend to argue that bisexuals are "really" homosexuals who won't or can't admit it—a view espoused by some gay and lesbian separatists, and supported by a number of psychoanalysts and psychologists like Irving Bieber[5] and John Malone. "The self-accepting homosexual," Malone declared in 1980, "feels no need to claim the title of bisexual." The word "bisexual," he thought, might have some use as an adjective, but "it is not only useless but mendacious when used as a noun."[6] So either everyone is or no one is. This is finally a distinction without a difference.

The quest for a universal, like the need to articulate a norm, masks an anxiety about difference and displaces it onto a theory of origins. "One sometimes hears," writes feminist Mariana Valverde, "that bisexuality is superior to both the conformity of exclusive heterosexuality and the narrowness of exclusive homosexuality. In other words, this approach legitimizes bisexuality in the same way that conservative thought legitimizes exclusive heterosexuality, i.e., by reference to a myth of what is 'natural.'" On the other hand, bisexuality can function in cultural terms as a mode of resistance, by putting in question the duality on which our notions of sexual "normalcy" are based. "Although bisexuality, like homosexuality, is just another deviant identity, it also functions as a rejection of the norm/deviance model."[7]

Is bisexuality then the most conservative or the most radical of ideas about human sexuality? The most "natural"? Or the most "perverse"?

Kinsey's Sliding Scale

As the Kinsey researchers clearly saw, "pure" heterosexuality and "pure" homosexuality were abstractions rather than experiential realities for many ordinary Americans, however they might choose to classify themselves. In fact, the only way the dichotomy was maintained was by placing "all persons who are exclusively heterosexual in a heterosexual category, and all persons who have any amount of experience with their own sex, even including those with the slightest experience, in a homosexual category." "It would be as reasonable to rate all individuals heterosexual if they have any heterosexual experience, and irrespective of the amount of homosexual experience which they may be having."[8] The split between straight and gay was an artifact of religious and cultural bias, not a "scientific" referential reality. Bisexuality, or rather some combination of homosexual and heterosexual experiences and responses, was more accurately reflective of human experience. Or so the researchers found.

Published in 1948 by Alfred C. Kinsey, Wardell Pomeroy, and Clyde C.

Martin under the title *Sexual Behavior in the Human Male,* this account of America's sexuality scandalized the very populace whose activities were under scrutiny, exposing a real divide between what people did and what they thought others should—and should not—do. The Kinsey report's observations on bisexuality are humane, thoughtful, nonjudgmental, and frequently eloquent—in their way a model for the narrative of social science reporting.

What does the first Kinsey report, *Sexual Behavior in the Human Male,* have to say about bisexuals? First, that the category includes *almost half the population.* Of those surveyed, 46 percent had engaged in both heterosexual and homosexual activities, or reacted to persons of both sexes, during their adult lives. Second, that the term used to describe this group was both inaccurate and inexact.

"It is rather unfortunate," the Kinsey authors remark, "that the word 'bisexual' should have been chosen to describe this intermediate group. The term is used as a substantive, designating individuals—persons; and the root meaning of the word and the way in which it is usually used imply that these persons have both masculine qualities and feminine qualities within their single bodies. We have objected to the use of the terms 'heterosexual' and 'homosexual' when used as nouns which stand for individuals. It is similarly untenable to imply that these 'bisexual' persons have an anatomy or endocrine system or other sorts of physiologic or psychologic capacities which make them partly male and partly female, or of the two sexes simultaneously.

"As applied to human and sexual behavior," the researers note with some firmness, "the term indicates that there are individuals who choose to have sexual relations with both males and females; and until it is demonstrated, as it certainly is not at the present time, that such a catholicity of taste in a sexual relation is dependent upon an individual containing within his anatomy both male and female structures, or male and female capacities, it is unfortunate to call such individuals bisexual. Because of its wide currency, the term will undoubtedly continue in use among students of human behavior and in the public in general. It should, however, be used with the understanding that it is patterned on the words 'heterosexual' and 'homosexual,' and, like them, refers to the sex of the partner, and proves nothing about the constitution of the person who is labelled bisexual."[9]

The suppositions of turn-of-the-century sexologists from Havelock Ellis and Richard von Krafft-Ebing to the early Sigmund Freud are here summarily dismissed as having no demonstrable basis in fact. Furthermore, the construction of the intermediate category of the "bisexual" seems clearly based upon a prior binary assumption about sexuality. The Kinsey authors see clearly that the hypothetical division of the world of sexual beings into two groups, heterosexual and homosexual, creates a potentially false dichotomy and, in consequence, a misunderstanding—and underestimation—of the importance of "bisexuality" in human sexual life:

> Concerning patterns of sexual behavior, a great deal of the thinking done by scientists and laymen alike stems from the assumption that there are persons who are "heterosexual" and persons who are "homosexual," that these two types represent antitheses in the sexual world, and that there is only an insignificant class of "bisexuals" who occupy an intermediate position between the other groups. It is implied that every individual is innately—inherently—either heterosexual or homosexual.[10]

This was in 1948; it may be argued that we have made virtually no progress since that time in understanding bisexuality's place in sexual and cultural life.

But the Kinsey report does more than document behavior and query the genealogy of terms. By emphasizing, much as Freud does, the repressive role that culture has played in policing sexuality, *Sexual Behavior in the Human Male* argues, in effect, for an understanding of human sexuality that sets aside presuppositions about the "normal" and the "healthy." Without social pressure to conform and societal disapproval of "deviance," the number of bisexuals in America and elsewhere would be, they suggest, even larger.

"If homosexual activity persists on as large a scale as it does, in the face of the very considerable public sentiment against it and in spite of the severity of the penalties that our Anglo-American culture has placed upon it through the centuries, there seems some reason for believing that such activity would appear in the histories of a much larger portion of the population if there were no social restraints," the report observes. "The very general occurrence of the homosexual in ancient Greece, and its wide occurrence today in some cultures in which such activity is not as taboo as it is in our own, suggests that the capacity of an individual to respond erotically to any sort of stimulus, whether it is provided by another person of the same or of the opposite sex, is basic in the species. That patterns of heterosexuality and patterns of homosexuality represent learned behavior which depends, to a considerable degree, upon the mores of the particular culture in which the individual is raised, is a possibility that must be thoroughly considered before there can be any acceptance of the idea that homosexuality is inherited, and that the pattern for each individual is so innately fixed that no modification of it may be expected within his lifetime."[11]

"Heterosexuals" and "homosexuals" may both be culturally produced categories, representing "learned behavior" rather than "natural" essence. If this is so, then, as the Kinsey scale itself suggests, there are really no boundaries except those ordained by custom. More like a rheostat than an on-off switch, the Kinsey scale, like the color spectrum, charts a series of variations which by convention are divided into discrete "colors" or "sexualities."

As for the allegation that homosexuals and bisexuals are dysfunctional neurotics (remember, this is 1948, on the eve of the McCarthy witch-hunts and only a few years after the U.S. government first officially declared that homosexuality was incompatible with military service),[12] the report's authors again questioned the pattern of cause and effect. "It is," they wrote, "a considerable question whether these persons have homosexual histories because they are neurotic, or whether their neurotic disturbances are the product of their homosexual behavior."[13] If a practice is outlawed, and one who practices it declared an outlaw, doesn't society in effect create "neurosis" through its own blindness and intolerance?

The Kinsey authors were deeply skeptical of what they called "attempts to identify the biologic bases of homosexual activity" precisely because of the crossover factor: the presence in their study of so many individuals who had both homosexual and heterosexual experiences or responses, "in exactly the same period of time, or even simultaneously in the same moment." It was, in fact, the evidence of bisexual behavior and feelings, even or especially at a time when such behavior and feelings were publicly under attack by politicians, the Pentagon, the medical establishment, and the media, that convinced the Kinsey authors of the existence of a sexual *continuum,* and led them to promulgate the famous "Kinsey scale":

"It should be emphasized that it is one thing to account for an all-or-none proposition, as heterosexuality and homosexuality have ordinarily been taken to be. But it is a totally different matter to recognize factors which will account for the continuum which we find existing between the exclusively heterosexual and the exclusively homosexual history."[14] In effect, what the Kinsey report established—and what may have shocked mainstream America most of all—was not the existence of significant numbers of *homosexuals* but rather the overwhelming presence of *bisexuals* and *bisexuality* in American life.

Survey after survey has suggested this conclusion. As Barbara Ehrenreich observes, commenting on a 1989 study by researchers affiliated with the National Academy of Sciences, "either 'bisexuality' is a very common condition, or another artificial category concealing the overlaps." "What heterosexuals really fear," she shrewdly deduces, "is not that 'they'—an alien subgroup with perverse tastes in bedfellows—are getting an undue share of power and attention, but that 'they' might well be us."[15]

It may be said that this, too, the Kinsey authors foresaw. "It is a characteristic of the human mind that it tries to dichotomize in its classification of phenomena," they wrote in their follow-up volume, *Sexual Behavior in the Human Female,* a text generally noticed more for its revelations about female orgasm than for its latitude in matters bi- and homosexual. To many people—and, they might have added, especially to many Americans in the outwardly conformist 1950s—"Things either are so, or are not so. Sexual behavior is either normal or abnormal, socially acceptable or unacceptable, heterosexual or homosexual; and many persons do not want to believe that there are gradations in these matters from one to the other extreme."[16]

Thus, while the word "bisexual" does not appear anywhere on the fabled "Kinsey scale," Kinsey and his colleagues find almost nothing *but* bisexuality when they come to analyze their results. "It should again be pointed out," they assert in the volume on the *Human Female* (dedicated, in impassive, depersonalized social-science-ese, to "the nearly 8000 females who contributed the data on which this book is based"), "that it is impossible to determine the number of persons who are 'homosexual' or 'heterosexual.' It is only possible to determine how many persons belong, at any particular moment, to each of the classifications on a heterosexual-homosexual scale."[17]

And who were Kinsey's subjects? They were 5,940 "white, non-prison" women[18] and "about 5,300" white men. The 915 women interviewed who had prison experience were excluded because their sexual histories would have "seriously distorted" the calculations, and the 934 nonwhite women because the sample was too small to enable competent comparison of subgroups (this was, after all, 1953). Likewise in the *Male* study, the researchers concluded that "the story for the Negro male cannot be told now, because the Negro sample . . . is not yet sufficient for making analyses comparable to those made here for the white male."[19] The occupational breakdown for the female study is worth glancing at. It includes such professions as berry picker, circus rider, cigarette girl, dean of women, male impersonator, Salvation Army officer, soda jerker, taxi dancer, and taxi driver, while the husbands of the female subjects go alphabetically from "abortionist" to "Y.M.C.A. staff," with pauses along the way for occupations like bootlegger, missionary, psychiatrist, poet, pimp, and thief. For a snapshot of middle-class white America in the postwar period, there is no better, or more revealing, source.

The Kinsey scale included both "overt experience" and "psychologic response," and it found that 8 to 10 percent of married women, 11 to 20 percent of unmarried women, and 14 to 17 percent of previously married women reported such "homosexual" responses in the period between their twentieth and thirty-fifth years. Taking into consideration the varying numbers of individuals in each group, the accumulative incidence of such responses for women was 28 percent. This was much lower than the percentage for men (50 percent, according to Kinsey's calculations in the *Human Male* volume) despite the conventional wisdom, disproved by their data, that women had more homosexual responses and contacts than men.

This false opinion they ascribed to the permissibility of open affection between women, and also to the recurrent male fantasy of watching two women making love, so that "wishful thinking" on the part of "heterosexual males" may have upped the estimates. "Psychoanalysts," they add in their typical, matter-of-fact way, "may also see in it an attempt among males to justify or deny their own homosexual interests."[20]

As for those interests, they are reflected, write the Kinsey people a generation before "homosociality" became a word to reckon with in academic gender studies, in male institutions like "cafes, taverns, night clubs, public baths, gymnasia, swimming pools," as well as in "specifically homosexual magazines and organized homosexual discussion groups." American culture, it appears, is designed for bisexual living, if by "bisexual" we mean, as Kinsey does, the complex of "responses" and "contacts" to which their subjects testified.

Yet even as they engaged in them—and perhaps, as contemporary gender theory argues, as the price of such engagement—Americans condemned such practices. In impressively liberal terms the report notes that "particularly in our Judeo-Christian culture" some kinds of sexual behavior "are condemned by religious codes, public opinion, and the law because they are contrary to the custom of the particular culture or because they are considered intrinsically sinful or wrong, and not because they do damage to other persons, their property, or the security of the total group."[21] Do as I say, not as I do, was how the Kinsey report read American morality.

Without explicitly saying so, the sex researchers from Indiana in effect accused American moralists of provincialism, noting (in a move that presages scientific researcher Simon LeVay, and that today's sociobiologists and evolutionary psychologists might do well to bear in mind) that "the existent mammalian species have managed to survive in spite of their widespread homosexual activity" and that in some Muslim and Buddhist cultures sexual relations between men are widespread even though "these are also cultures in which the institution of the family is very strong."[22] They do not here use the word "bisexuality," but that is clearly what they are describing. Indeed, in the *Human Female*'s sole mention of the term, Kinsey lays out the options of sequential or concurrent bisexuality: "Sometimes their homosexual and heterosexual responses and contacts occur at different periods in their lives; sometimes they occur coincidentally."[23]

Kinsey also saw erotic potential in what might be called crossover technique, the lovemaking skills of homosexuality adding excitement and pleasure to heterosexual sex. "Most males are likely to approach females as they, the males, would like to be approached by a sexual partner," while "females in their heterosexual relationships are actually more likely to prefer techniques which are closer to those which are commonly utilized in homosexual relationships."

Women, the report declared, enjoy "generalized emotional stimulation" before touching, "physical stimulation of the whole body" before specifically genital contact, and attention to the clitoris and the labia minora carried through to orgasm. Most sex manuals of the sixties and even the seventies repeated this information about women's continuum of pleasure from emotion to orgasm—a view challenged by some sex-positive bisexual and lesbian groups in the late eighties and nineties, with their emphasis on S/M, following on the affirmative model of gay male sex, with its possibilities for chance encounters and multiple, sometimes anonymous, partners. But Kinsey's 1953 view still seems in a way visionary, especially when he suggests, with laconic and perhaps unconscious wit, that it is "quite possible for males to learn enough about female sexual responses to make their heterosexual contacts as effective as females make most homosexual contacts." With perseverance and skill a man may, perhaps, learn to make love to a woman as "effectively" (or pleasurably) as women make love to one another.[24]

Incidentally, this is a comment often made about bisexual lovers, both men and women: that the erotic attention paid to a partner of one's own sex often makes the bisexual more attentive and responsive to the pleasures of a heterosexual partner. When I asked a (heterosexual) friend what he thought the special appeal of one longtime gay man was to his present female partner, my friend answered, as if it were a commonly acknowledged fact, that gay men made better lovers. "She just comes and comes."

Notice that the Kinsey reports do not say "men" and "women," but rather "males" and "females," "persons" and "individuals." (They certainly never say anything as provocative as "she just comes and comes.") Like the deliberately dry twin titles, *Sexual Behavior in the Human Male* and *Sexual Behavior in the Human Female,* words like "male" and "female" stress the animal-behavior roots of the studies (Kinsey himself was an entomologist, who signed his letters "Alfred Kinsey, professor of zoology")[25] and deeroticize the juicy information contained in all those bland-looking tables and graphs. Nevertheless, the first report was a best-seller when it appeared. The publisher ordered a sixth printing within ten days of its initial appearance; 185,000 copies, a staggering number for the times, were in print. Someone was reading—or at least buying—the "Kinsey report," and it wasn't only zoologists.

One of the first readers, as we have noted, was film star Rock Hudson, who bought a copy of *Sexual Behavior in the Human Male* when it first came out in 1948, and discussed it with his gay friends Mark Miller and George Nader. What they found there—and they were far from alone in doing so—was the first validation of their existence by "a respected scientist, an impartial observer."[26] For Hudson, the Kinsey statistics were, as we saw, "reassuring." That "males do not represent two discrete populations, heterosexual and homosexual," that most men fall in between exclusive homosexuality and exclusive heterosexuality, that more than one man in three had some homosexual experience—this was not news to him about himself, but it was news about the world, and the country, he lived in.

Up Close and Personal

The popularity of *Sexual Behavior in the Human Male* and its sequel, *Sexual Behavior in the Human Female,* prepared the way for a whole new sex information industry in America. This new industry sought to gratify the barely suppressed wish for prurient details, names, and faces, elicited by the deadpan Kinsey voice and the camouflaging of all those sexy men and women—masturbating, petting, and attending burlesque shows, having orgasms, multiple partners, and sex with animals—under the colorless terms "males" and "females" and the relentless march of columns of figures.

Now these hidden individuals were brought forward and given presence and voice, whether in their narrative responses to survey questions or in their appearances on television talk shows. Some wrote books about their lives, and in those books they told anecdotes rather than gave statistics. In the wake of the Sexual Revolution, hard upon *Time*'s and *Newsweek*'s (first) discovery of the "new bisexuals" in 1974 and television interviewer Barbara Walters's weeklong discussion of bisexuality on a program aptly called "Not for Women Only" in 1975, there appeared books like *Bisexual Living* (1975), *View from Another Closet: Exploring Bisexuality in Women* (1976), *The New Couple: Women and Gay Men* (1979), *Barry and Alice: Portrait of a Bisexual Marriage* (1980), and, after the AIDS crisis had come to stigmatize bisexual men in the eighties, *When Husbands Come Out of the Closet* (1989).

A woman in her fifties, "the wife of a doctor, the mother of two children, very keen on tennis and golf" who was also a lay Freudian analyst was interviewed in the pages of *Vogue* magazine in May 1974 on the subject of her bisexuality. "The world is pretty bisexual now," she observed. "I think the problem now is to make it as unimportant as what one had for dinner." Asked her opinion about whether there was "anything genetic about exclusive homosexuality or heterosexuality? ... or, for that matter, bisexuality?" she replied that she thought it was learned, not innate. Why the questioner thought she would have expertise on this matter is not clear.

Bisexuality (1977), by Charlotte Wolff, a respected psychiatrist who described herself as bisexual, traced some mythological and psychoanalytic views of the topic but focused on her interviews with some 150 male and female bisexuals, located through advertisements in the *Gay News, Spare Rib, Time Out,* and the journal of the transvestite-transsexual Beaumont Society. She also appended some tables in good post-Kinsey style, charting the answers to questions like "Is bisexuality an advantage creatively?" ("socially?" "emotionally?" "mentally?") and "present desires to be of the opposite sex."

Psychiatrist Fred Klein's book *The Bisexual Option* (1978), aimed at the popular market and described on the back of the paperback as "present[ing] in clear prose the candid voices of self-avowed bisexuals," discussed "the myth of the bisexual's nonexistence" and proposed a new continuum, spanning the distance between neurotic and healthy, that (just like the heterosexual-homosexual continuum) seemed to collapse in the direction of the two outer poles. Profiles of "four neurotic bisexuals: Nora, Walter, Ann, Donald" are followed by profiles of three healthy ones, Harold, Hazel, and Jane. Perhaps predictably, the neurotics tell better stories. (I like the one about "Ann," one of whose most satisfying male lovers was a cross-dresser who was considering taking hormones to develop breasts for her. His fantasy was to be a lesbian; after Ann declined his offer, she went to see a therapist who told her to try a woman, which she did, with pleasant results. Klein concluded that her bisexual identity was less secure than her need to be hurt and her low self-image.)

Klein's subtitle, *A Concept of One Hundred Percent Intimacy,* will suggest the pop-psych niche for which it was designed, but the book is thoughtful and the prose is, as promised, clear. But Klein also writes in another voice, the voice of the medical professional. (Indeed, in some of his scholarly publications he is known as Dr. *Fritz* Klein.[27]) Klein, Hal Wells, Ph.D. (author of *Bisexual Living*), Jean Schaar Gochros, Ph.D. (author of *When Husbands Come Out of the Closet*), and other therapists were the experts—or as bisexual erotic pundit Susie Bright would later call herself, the "sexperts")—while their clients or interview subjects provided the data. This position of authority was subsequently to become an obligatory (and often thankless) part of every television talk show, from "Geraldo" to "Larry King Live." The television format was more conducive to the success of banality; the expert was *supposed* to be the "straight man" (or woman), as I learned from my own talk-show experiences. The rest of the cast, the ones who talked about their sex lives, had all the good lines.

The talk shows did not *replace* books of popular psychology, but rather *staged* them; the experts were often chosen because they had already written a book about the subject. But the elusive aura of "science" or expertise, marked in those professional initials (Ph.D., M.D., M.S.W.) and in the talk-show hosts' insistent iteration of professional titles, was in part the legacy of Kinsey and the public's need to *know.*

Of course, the media marriage counselor or sex expert had long been a staple of the popular press, providing counseling and a version of therapy for those unwilling, or unable, to consult more private oracles. (Tiresias, as we have seen, performed this function for Jupiter and Juno.) While many recent television programs have presented bisexual marriages as interesting rather than disastrous arrangements, the advice column—a kinder, gentler, earlier, and more female version of the take-no-prisoners talk radio and the blow-dried TV talk show of today—more often than not viewed bisexuality as a marital catastrophe.

For years a regular feature in the *Ladies' Home Journal* offered advice for readers whose marriages were in trouble under the general title "Can This Marriage Be Saved?" Early in 1982 the magazine grappled with the problem of bisexuality as it was seen to threaten a marriage. "Ginger had no idea that Tom was leading a double life. What happens when a woman finds out her husband is having an affair—with a man . . . ?" Under the headline "My Husband Is Bisexual," the *Journal* explored Tom and Ginger's relationship, in an irresistible tabloid style that brought the reality of the question home.

" 'I don't see how Tom and I can stay together,' said Ginger, 38, with a toss of her long, satiny blond hair," the article began. She had had "no inkling my husband was homosexual," or rather "bisexual, since we do make love," until they went together to see Tom's psychologist. There Tom blurted out the truth: "You're the only woman I've ever loved, and I care for you deeply. But I'm bisexual."

After she got over her initial shock, Ginger began to think over their relationship, remembering that "he was extremely sensitive, which is what attracted me to him" when they were teenagers, and that "maybe my parents had been right, that I should never have married Tom in the first place." The couple had been married for almost twenty years and had two teenage children. Now she was having to face the fact of his ongoing sexual relationship with Harry, "a bachelor who got Tom his present job."

Since "Can This Marriage Be Saved?" routinely begins by announcing that the names of those described have been changed to conceal their identities, we might spare a moment to speculate on the phrase that has proverbially come to connote male pseudonymous identity and indiscriminateness, "every Tom, Dick, and Harry." In choosing to name the male protagonists of this tale "Tom" and "Harry," the columnist tacitly acknowledges the "Dick" that comes between them. But Tom's own account of his need for "male companionship" is quite discreet. He ascribes his bisexual desires not to the sexiness of men but to other factors: his own sexual inexperience, his sense of inadequacy as a lover, the disapproval of the marriage on the part of Ginger's socially conscious parents, his own over-protective and underaffectionate family, his early sexual relationship with an older gay man, Ginger's "compulsive talk" and "empty chatter," and his "trouble keeping up with Ginger's sexual demands." (All this in two pages.) His feelings for Harry were those of gratitude, he said.

The marriage counselor, fulfilling the expert's role, was optimistic. "After eight months of therapy," he reported, "Tom made his choice. His relationship with Ginger had improved so much that he was no longer threatened by her, and he therefore lost his reason for seeking homosexual contact." Tom and Ginger had moved to another state "to make a break with Tom's past life."[28]

Readers might perhaps be pardoned for wondering whether bisexuality was really the chief problem in this marriage, or whether "saving" it was after all a good idea, but that was Tom and Ginger's business, not anyone else's. What is worth noting here, though, is that "saving" the marriage in this case meant getting rid of its bisexual component—something the expert was able to wish away by posing Tom's situation as a "choice" between sex with men and sex with Ginger, and indirectly blaming Ginger for Tom's same-sex desires.

But if the *Journal*'s expert regarded "saving" a marriage as a matter of the bisexual partner's choosing between loving men and loving women, this was not the inevitable opinion. Another couple, this one contemplating marriage, addressed the same problem—the man's bisexuality—in the pages of *Cosmopolitan* that same year, in an article that asked, with its italics firmly in place, "Is there *any* hope, then, for wedded bliss with a bisexual?" Several of the couples they interviewed "said definitely yes." And here, significantly, sex—what might be called bi-sex, the pleasure of sleeping with a bisexual person—was definitely part of the picture.

Mark, "a stockbroker in his early thirties who moonlights as a pianist in small, avant-garde night clubs," was dating Ann, who worked for a San Francisco security company and was "aware of the dearth of acceptable men for someone at her professional level." Mark "tried to signal Ann that he was bisexual through his actions rather than words," finally setting up a confrontation where Ann sat on one side of a table "nervously sipping a tequila sunrise" while across from her Mark and his "best friend," Peter, toyed with wine spritzers and Peter "gently caressed Mark's neck." After a painful two weeks Ann called Mark, they got together and made love, and Mark decided he wanted to marry Ann. As for Ann, she "is beginning to realize that a lasting relationship will require a significant change of attitude on her part."[29]

Note that here it is the monosexual woman, not the bisexual man, who is contemplating changes. Bisexual men are "more attractive, sexier, and virtually every city in the country is *swarming* with them," another woman says. And sex with them is great. "In bed bisexual lovers offer both sensitivity and a new realm of uninhibited exploration. They're used to giving *and* receiving during sex, which can't help doubling *your* fun." Other couples consulted said they had ground rules—they didn't want to meet each other's lovers or talk about any affairs.

But this was before AIDS awareness became part of the picture for such couples. By 1988 another traditional women's magazine, *Woman's Day*, could set itself to tell the "shocking truth" about the marriage of Barbara and Tim—"My Husband's Other Lovers Were Men"—and describe both the breakup of the marriage and the "clues" that might teach a woman "How to Identify a Bisexual Male."[30] The "lay" person was no longer presented as an "expert" on her own life. Instead, she had to be taught to read her partner(s). "I never thought that bisexuality or AIDS or divorce would touch my life," said Barbara. "I'm from the Midwest. I grew up in the 50s. I guess you'd say I'm a traditional, conventional person."

◆

In these journals the allure of "science" (or its morganatic partner, "social science") has latterly come to replace the chatty, cozy intimacy of the magazine advice column, which seemed to talk about *one* relationship at a time in a way that generalized or even universalized its story. The "sex survey," which could, as Kinsey demonstrated and others have since tried to emulate, become a crossover best-seller, generalizing deductively from statistics rather than inductively (or seductively) from anecdotes, became in its turn a regular feature. Perhaps because upscale, soft-sell erotic magazines were thought to have a special appeal for the sexually adventurous, studies of bisexuality took their cues, and their evidence, from glossies: *Forum* magazine, as we have already noted, produced the data used for the Klein Sexual Orientation Grid, and thus became the basis for Klein's book on *The Bisexual Option*. The *Playboy* Readers' Sex Survey of January 1982—"the largest sex survey ever conducted and tabulated"—was the source for a report on the behavior patterns and sexual identity of bisexual men that found, as might be expected (and as Kinsey et al. had already in effect demonstrated) that many more men were bisexual than claimed to be. Approximately two-thirds of the men who reported adult homosexual experiences called themselves not bisexual but heterosexual—one in eight had bisexual experience, but only one in twenty-two described himself as "a bisexual." Nor was this just a marker of change over time, of men who had, as the phrase goes, "grown out of" their bisexual "phase." Of those who said they had had sex with men as adults and that future same-sex encounters were not "off-limits," only 39 percent called themselves bisexual; the rest asserted that they were straight.[31]

The dates and source of this study hint at its function: Part of the researchers' concern was reliably to identify susceptibility to sexually transmitted diseases, especially AIDS. What may have seemed playful to *Playboy* had in the intervening years become deadly serious, and a failure to self-identify as bisexual had epidemiological as well as psychological and political effects. The study points up some of the failings of the Kinsey report when it comes to self-classification. "People do not naturally think of their own sexual behavior as lying on a continuum," the researchers concluded. "They do label themselves in discrete categories, and they are affected by the labels they choose." Moreover, even the concept of "passing," often used to describe the behavior of married bisexuals, seemed limited in usefulness: "[M]ost of the men who identified themselves as 'heterosexual' probably neither think of themselves as 'passing' or 'in denial' but, rather, chose, from a sexual script that offered only two labels, the one that fit best. People pigeonhole themselves into socially defined categories, and 'bisexual' is not one of them."[32]

This may pinpoint the danger of a study that takes ten years to complete, since "bisexual" in the nineties has become a much more recognizable label, thanks in part to the work of bisexual organizations across the country as well as to films from *Basic Instinct* to *Threesome* and *Three of Hearts*. But whether *Playboy*'s readers would self-identify as bi in greater numbers remains a question. A ninety-question sex survey of 2,400 readers conducted jointly by *Mademoiselle* and *Details* and reported in *Mademoiselle* in June 1993 asked, among other things, whether respondents had ever had a sexual experience with a member of their own sex, whether their partners had, whether they had ever taken part in a threesome (this question was part of a boxcar series that also included videotaping, the use of a dildo, having sex with much older or younger partners, body piercing, S&M, and using food for sexual purposes—apparently *Mademoiselle*'s anatomy of kink) and how their sex lives would change if it weren't for AIDS. They were also asked if they were "heterosexual? bisexual? homosexual?" with the sequence of terms suggesting that bi was in the middle, not at the outer edge of experiment and experience.

And what did the survey disclose about people who read *Mademoiselle* or *Details* and take time to fill out surveys in popular magazines? "You are an overwhelming heterosexual group in action (only three of you [women] describe yourself as homosexual)" the author comments breezily, "but your fantasy life is another matter." Eighteen percent of "you" have sexual fantasies about both men and women. Only 7 percent of women had had a threesome, "but 21 percent of the men have engaged in three-way sex (that 7 percent of you must be very busy)."[33] How many are bisexual? *Mademoiselle* doesn't bother to say.

In an article four months earlier, however, *Mademoiselle* took cognizance not only of "the era of the baby dyke" but also of what it headlined as "one of the hottest issues among lesbians of any age"—bisexuality.[34] Without benefit of survey the article chronicled prejudice against bisexuals from within the new young lesbian community (bisexuality is merely "convenient" [i.e., heterosexually privileged], a blueprint for rejection, a refusal to come out, a vantage point for using lesbians as "sex toys"). It also quoted one woman's mother as constantly "correcting her" when the daughter said she was gay: "You're not gay, you're bisexual." (Relatives of the notorious Menendez brothers, who shot their parents at point-blank range in their Beverly Hills mansion, would exhibit a similar squeamishness when it came to Erik Menendez's sexuality, as Dominick Dunne reported: "The words 'gay' and 'homosexual' were of so fearful a nature to most members of the Menendez family with whom I spoke that they were unable to deal with them. Whenever the subject arose in conversation, I was immediately corrected with the word 'bisexual,' as if that lessened the shame for them.")[35] Here the generational divide—gay is worse, bi is worse, gay is better, bi is better—is clear. And here, too, the powerful, forward-pointing language of the trend ("hottest," "new style," "next generation") can be seen overtaking the more static format of the survey, with its painstaking chart of behavior over time.

◆

The so-called Battelle study, a report on the findings of scientists at the Battelle Human Affairs Research Centers in Seattle, Washington, published by the Alan Guttmacher Institute in March 1993, was much ballyhooed in the press for its findings that only 1 percent—not, as Kinsey had maintained, 10 percent—of American men were "exclusively homosexual."[36] Gay groups, who had come to rely on the 10 percent figure as a baseline, assuming in fact a much larger number in the closeted population, deplored the finding, and gay and lesbian journals like the one itself called *10 Percent* discounted the Battelle methods of face-to-face interviews given by female researchers as unlikely to yield reliable results. Why would a closeted gay man open up to intrusive questioning by a woman social scientist?

The Battelle study, however, was interesting for reasons quite different from those that caught the media's attention. The study attempted to determine the prevalence of vaginal, anal, and oral sex among a sampling of men twenty to thirty-nine years of age. The researchers began with certain assumptions: that religion (especially "conservative religion") promotes a "more restrictive sexual ideology," so that men who called themselves religious were less likely to have had nonvaginal sex or many partners; that education, conversely, increased the likelihood of anal and oral sex and of multiple partners because it "reflects the degree to which an individual is open to new ideas and nontraditional values"; that age and marriage or partnership might be reasonably expected to correlate positively with sexual experience, so that older, married respondents would have had more and more different kinds of sex; and that race and ethnicity, for reasons not wholly clear to the researchers, were often important determinants for the sexual experiences of adult men. On this last point it is worth noting that "race" to the Battelle scientists was an either/or proposition, "white" or "black." A footnote explains that "white includes all men not classified as black (white, Asian or Pacific Islander, Native Americans and nonblack Hispanics)." Likewise the category of "religion" was broken down into Conservative Protestant, Other Protestant, Catholic, and Other or None. Jews, Muslims, pantheists, and atheists were thus all lumped together in the last, default group. This seems sufficiently odd to raise some worries about what the researchers thought they were measuring, and is indicative of the way another key binary was handled. For the men interviewed for this study were asked to describe their sexual orientation in the following way:

In reponse to the question "During the last 10 years, what would you say that your sexual activity has been?" they could answer (1) exclusively heterosexual, (2) mostly heterosexual, (3) evenly heterosexual and homosexual, (4) mostly homosexual, or (5) exclusively homosexual. Bisexuality thus appears as an overlap of hetero- and homosexuality, splitting the difference, so to speak, between apparently recognizable established cate-gories. Yet of the study's five possibilities for self-description, three de-scribe bisexual lives. We are told, for example, that "Education was positively related to having had same-gender activity but not to exclusive homosexual activity."[37]

The report notes that the figures for same-sex activity may be slightly lower than that of other recent studies, but that "none is close to the 10% figure that persists from Kinsey's study." A 1991 study of men and women, the authors note, had estimated that "three percent have not been sexually active as adults, 91–93 percent have been exclusively heterosexual, 5–6 percent have been bisexual and less than 1 percent have been exclusively homosexual."[38] This is the only place in the article about the Battelle findings that the word "bisexual" appears. It is never used to describe their own research.

One reason for this, or at least one effect of it, may be to avoid the stigmatization of the bisexual-as-AIDS-carrier that was so prevalent in the sociomedical literature of the eighties. A principal aim of the Battelle study was to determine risks of HIV or other sexually transmitted diseases (STDs) among various sectors of the population. Each section of the report comments on this question, weighing the risks of AIDS transmission for each group and each sexual behavior. Thus we learn that conservative Protestant men are the least likely to have performed or received oral sex; that Hispanics are more likely to have had anal intercourse but least likely to have had oral sex; and that only 20 percent of men aged twenty to thirty-nine have engaged in anal intercourse (a figure that correlates, they say, with two other recent studies of sexually active heterosexual men and women).

But the absence of questions that directly address bisexual identity is again indicative of the problem social science encounters when attempting to tabulate such a fluid category. Consider, for example, Masters and John-son's famous report on sexuality in the sixties, *On Sex and Human Loving*. "Masters and Johnson," it turns out, are in fact a threesome: Eleven books usually said to have been authored under that joint name are officially credited to William H. Masters, Virginia E. Johnson, and Robert C. Kolodny, who is described as "their longtime colleague" on the book jacket of their latest work.[39] But despite this promising triangulation, none of the three in fact had a fraction as much as Kinsey to say on the subject of bisexuality, to which the six-hundred-page *On Sex* report devotes all of three pages. They do, however, find space to acknowledge that it certainly does present a problem for the sex analyst: "The nature of bisexuality remains very much a puzzle at the present time. There are no good leads on what "causes" bisexuality, and the varied patterns of bisexual biographies wreak havoc with many theories about the origins of sexual orientation."[40]

This is perfectly true, and justly problematic for the researchers. To seek a "cause" and an "origin" implies an etiology, like that of an illness. Why not seek instead the cause and origin of monosexuality, which seems much more peculiar, since it excludes a whole class of persons from being the potential objects, and subjects, of erotic love. Having cataloged in the briefest terms (remember, three pages out of six hundred) the likeliest circumstances to produce bisexual behavior, sexual experimentation, group sex, and a "bisexual philosophy" developed "as an outgrowth of their personal belief systems," by which Masters-Johnson-and-Kolodny seem to mean the "woman's movement" (the quotation marks in this case are theirs), they go on to include situational bisexuals in prison and the military, "heterosexual" male-male prostitutes, frequenters of public rest rooms and the tearoom trade, and their own coinage, "ambisexuals," who fit the characterization wryly adopted as a title by the editors of the bisexual journal *Anything That Moves*.

The most suggestive thing they have to say about bisexuality is the last: "It is very possible that as more is learned about this subject our understanding of the complexities of human sexuality will be improved." As flabby a sentiment as this seems to be, it acknowledges the fact that sex researchers may have been looking at the question backwards, or, as the title of *this* book suggests, *Vice Versa*. Bisexuality is not the puzzle. The puzzle is sexual exclusiveness.

Yet such signals go unheeded by contemporary sex researchers, who continue to attempt to pigeonhole sexuality. The 1993 *Janus Report* (named, sad to say, after its chief researchers, not after the two-faced god) describes itself as the successor to Kinsey and to Masters and Johnson. The *Janus* researchers found that "the number of persons who had engaged in homosexual acts either frequently or ongoing almost equally identify themselves as homosexual or bisexual."[41] But they reported the same problem that had been commented upon by Kinsey: how to define "homosexual" and "bisexual"—a rather fundamental issue. For as they point out, if they tabulate not only "ongoing" and "frequent" homosexual encounters but also "occasional" ones, the figure for "homosexuals" rises from 4 percent of men and 2 percent of women (according to their own study) to 22 percent of men and 17 percent of women, "much larger than most estimates." The *Janus Report*'s response is not to recode these people with occasional or frequent homosexual experiences as bisexual, but rather to leave out the "occasional" data altogether when compiling their statistics. In this way they are able to generate a table that shows a fairly low sexual "self-identification" as bisexual (5 percent for men, 3 percent for women), but without also offering a table for behavior, much less one for fantasies and dreams.

A 1994 report on *Sexual Behaviour in Britain*—perhaps symptomatically sold in bookstores, when it first came out, with an accompanying insert of "Errata"—informed readers that more than half of the men who had had a same-sex sexual partner in the last five years also had an opposite-sex sexual partner, while for women the figure went as high as three-quarters. This "high prevalence of bisexual behaviour" was documented by studies in Britain, in the United States, in France, and in Norway. The French figures were 82 percent for men and 78 percent for women, the Norwegian figures 83 percent and 75 percent. In other words, an astoundingly high proportion of men and women reporting "same-gender" sexual practice also reported "opposite-gender" practices.[42] You might have thought this would be major news, and that bisexuality would therefore rate at least a chapter, or a subsection, of its own in the over-four-hundred-page report. Yet this information is in fact contained in three pages of a long chapter entitled "Sexual Diversity and Homosexual Behaviour," and seems largely of interest to researchers for its implications for disease prevention. In the entire volume, subtitled "The National Survey of Sexual Attitudes and Lifestyles," bisexuality rates a scant five pages.

As for the much-heralded *Sex in America,* which purported to be "the most comprehensive, revealing report on our sexual behavior today and its surprising implications," it, too, blithely conflates "homosexual and bisexual," offering pie charts and bar graphs to show the percentage of Americans interviewed who identified themselves as "either homosexual or bisexual," and thus rendering bisexuality statistically invisible yet once more.[43]

The *America* researchers did allow for same-sex desire, behavior, and/or identification, and dutifully map the overlaps ("more people find others of the same gender sexually attractive than have homosexual sex"; of the 8.6 percent of women interviewed who acknowledged same-sex feelings or experiences "a substantial proportion of these women [13 percent] do not consider themselves lesbians even though they both desire other women and have had sex with women").[44] But for these researchers, as for Masters and Johnson and others, the problem presents itself as how to define "homosexual":

> People often change their sexual behavior during their lifetimes, making it impossible to state that a particular set of behaviors defines a person as gay. . . . Does a man who left his wife of twenty years for a gay lover count as homosexual or heterosexual? . . . Does the married woman who had sex with her college roommate a decade ago count? Do you assume that one homosexual experience defines someone as gay for all time?[45]

Despite these excellent questions and others in the same spirit, they continue to quest not for bisexuality but for "homosexuality," all the while expressing frustration that it is not where they seek to find it: "[W]e cannot so simply say that a person is or is not gay."

Even less simply, apparently, can they say that someone is (or is not) bisexual. Of the study's four references to bisexuality, two are to the catchall "homosexual or bisexual" category, and the other two, equally predictably, are in the chapter on AIDS, and warn against dangerous characters like the "bisexual man living on Long Island who secretly traveled to New York City and had sex with men. He became infected with HIV and infected his wife." "To examine the spread of HIV from infected gay men to men who have sex with women and men, we need to know with whom the bisexual men will have sex as well as where they live."[46] Bisexuality, when it appears at all explicitly in this study, appears—precisely because of its "secret" (i.e., undocumented) nature—as a threat to health rather than as a way of living and loving.

Is bisexuality a "sexual attitude," a "lifestyle"—or a "sexuality"? As Fred Klein and others have pointed out, it has not been regarded as a "culture" in the contemporary sense of "gay and lesbian culture" since the days of Oscar Wilde. But as many others have noted, bisexuality as a lived practice was historically foundational to many cultures, from ancient Greece to parts of twentieth-century New Guinea. How to reconcile its ubiquity and invisibility, how to define its status, is a problem that science has traditionally approached through developmental models of the individual or of the society.

But in doing so scientists and social scientists have necessarily separated out "sexual orientation" as if it were a category distinct from, rather than cutting across, criteria such as hair color, body size, musculature, wealth, social position, and other traits well known to novelists and ad executives as constitutive of eroticism. (If gentlemen prefer blondes, it does not necessarily follow that blondes prefer gentlemen. To rule out money as an erotic attribute—innate or acquired—is to fly in the face of history.)

The seeming solidity of "homosexual" and "heterosexual" as scientifically measurable categories—in contrast to "bisexual," too diffuse and hard to define—has thus determined the shape of social science sexual surveys around the invisibility of bisexuality. The same is true, as we are about to see, of the biological sciences. But, as biologist Ruth Hubbard notes, "the use of the phrase 'sexual orientation' to describe only a person's having sex with members of their own gender or the other sex obscures the fact that many of us have other strong and consistent sexual orientations—toward certain hair colors, body shapes, racial types. It would be as logical to look for genes associated with these orientations as for 'homosexual genes.' "[47]

Chapter 11

The Return to Biology

Whether or not we find what we are seeking
Is idle, biologically speaking.

—*Edna St. Vincent Millay, "I Shall Forget You Presently"*

Over Sexed

"Dear Ann Landers," wrote "A Concerned Father in Ukiah, California,"

> My teenage son came home the other day with a story that floored
> me. One of his high school teachers is teaching the students that
> there are five sexes in the human race—male, female, homosexual,
> bisexual, and asexual. . . .
>
> I told my son that the teacher is wrong, that there are only TWO
> sexes, male and female, and the other categories are sexual practices.
>
> Ann, I'm disturbed by this misinformation. . . . What do the experts
> say about this? Do they claim there are five sexes nowadays? Things
> are changing so fast that it's hard to keep up.

Rising to the occasion, Ann Landers hastened to set the record straight.

"There are only two sexes—male and female. Recent studies indicate
that homosexuality, bisexuality and asexuality are not the result of something that has gone wrong with the sex organs, but rather a biochemical-
genetic alteration that no one has been able to explain."[1]

This exchange, printed under the pedagogically disturbing but culturally reassuring headline "Teacher Needs to Learn Lesson—There Aren't
Five Sexes," is a fairly characteristic signpost of the increasing desire to
categorize and "explain" the vagaries of human sexuality in popular terms.
What is sometimes called sexual preference (implying a choice) and sometimes called sexual orientation (implying a destiny) are in this schoolroom
example—at least as reported, third hand, by the teenager's father—
equated with "sex." "Sex" (biology) and "gender" (sociology, anthropology, and culture) are here silently and unhelpfully conflated. The result is

to "save" heterosexuality, pointedly not listed as one of the "sexes," as the "natural" province of the first two delineated "sexes," male and female. Ann Landers's reply, addressing in telescoped terms both the list of five sexes and the implied critique, asserts that bi-, homo-, and asexuality are not "wrong" but different. They aren't wrong; but they aren't sexes.

This would seem perfectly straightforward, so to speak, in the everyday commerce of the newspaper advice page and perhaps even self-evident, if there had not appeared three months later in the respected journal *The Sciences* an article by geneticist Anne Fausto-Sterling, called "The Five Sexes," with the provocative subhead, "Why Male and Female Are Not Enough."[2]

Fausto-Sterling describes the legal erasure and medical reassignment of intersexed persons, those whose bodies are, biologically, anatomically, or chemically, a mixture of male and female.

The deep commitment of Western culture to the idea that there are only two sexes, exemplified in the limitations of language (Fausto-Sterling has to have recourse to *s/he* and *his/her* to describe some of her subjects) and law (over the past century rights and obligations like the vote, the military draft, marriage, and private, consensual sex have all been governed by state or national laws about males and females), has led to a cultural resistance to openly intersexed individuals, called by Fausto-Sterling "herms" (true hermaphrodites, with one testis and one ovary), "merms" (male pseudohermaphrodites, with testes, some aspects of female genitalia, but no ovaries), and "ferms" (female pseudohermaphrodites, with ovaries and some aspects of male genitalia but no testes).

Doctors have translated the bodies of such persons into some semblance of "normality," reclassifying children who, as they grew older, developed sexual characteristics (an organ on a "female" that looks more like a penis than a clitoris; a "male" with an X and Y chromosome who develops breasts, and begins to menstruate) that marked them as other than they had at first been regarded. "The aims of the policy," she stresses, "are genuinely humanitarian, reflecting the wish that people be able to 'fit in' both physically and psychologically. In the medical community, however, the assumption behind the wish—that there be only two sexes, that heterosexuality alone is normal, that there is one true model of psychological health—have gone virtually unexamined."[3]

It is almost as if, in the story of the Ugly Duckling, veterinary intervention (and concomitant counseling) had translated the undiagnosed cygnet into a cosmetic mallard for his (or her?) own good.

"Hermaphrodites," Fausto-Sterling asserts with eloquence, "have unruly bodies. They do not fall naturally into a binary classification; only a surgical shoehorn can put them there. But why should we care if a 'woman,' defined as one who has breasts, a vagina, a uterus and ovaries and who menstruates, also has a clitoris large enough to penetrate the vagina of another woman? Why should we care if there are people whose biological equipment enables them to have sex "naturally" with both men and women? The answers seem to lie in a cultural need to maintain clear distinctions between the sexes. Society mandates the control of intersexual bodies because they blur and bridge the great divide. Inasmuch as hermaphrodites literally embody both sexes, they challenge traditional beliefs about sexual difference: they possess the irritating ability to live sometimes as one sex and sometimes as another, and they raise the specter of homosexuality."[4]

Of homosexuality—or of bisexuality? "To have sex 'naturally' with both men and women." This geneticist's fearless and provocative vision of a society, perhaps many generations from now, in which "sexuality is something to be celebrated for its subtleties and not something to be feared or ridiculed" opens the door not only to a fuller acceptance of homosexuality but also to the inclusion of bisexuals, transgenderists, and others who do not neatly fit into older preconceptions of social "normality."

Needless to say, such a visionary view of science and society did not go unchallenged. A briefer version of Fausto-Sterling's article appeared on the op-ed page of the *New York Times* under the title "How Many Sexes Are There?" and elicited a predictable range of commentary. One letter writer asked, plaintively, "What is it about human sexuality that leads people to engage in extraordinarily fuzzy thinking?"[5] British geneticist Winston Holt's book on *The Sexual Continuum* was cited to suggest that "each of us to some degree is both heterosexual and homosexual, and therefore bisexual," and Alfred Kinsey was quoted as saying that "The only abnormal sex act is the one you can't do."[6] *Times* readers were also reminded that "Native Americans believe that there are four sexes: men who love women, men who love men, woman who love women and women who love men; and since men who love men and women who love women are fewer in number, they must be blessed by the gods."[7] (This cross-cultural point is one often made in bisexual 'zines and newsletters.)

What is especially striking about this cultural moment, however, is the way in which the 1990s seem to be re-creating the 1890s. Biologistic arguments explaining homosexuality are again in force, in contention, and in vogue; studies of hereditary family linkages are once again being undertaken, as they were a hundred years ago, in quest of an answer to the riddle of human sexuality that can be grounded in ascertainable "fact" —in science rather than in cultural influence. And once again, as was the case a hundred years ago, the quest for the biological truth of homosexuality, and thus of heterosexuality, is foundering on another inconvenient "fact"—the fact of bisexuality as a mode of human behavior. For bisexuality queers the pitch, messes up the neat double columns of figures: straight and gay.

Bi for biology, from *bios,* life. Bi for bisexuality, from *bis,* two.

The Question of Bi-ology

Biology is back. After decades of disfavor as an explanation for homosexual behavior (what used to be called, with finger-pointing disparagement, "homosexual tendencies"), biology is now making a major comeback. The "gay gene," the "gay brain," and the biological imperative—not a "lifestyle choice" but a DNA blueprint, a "fact" of life—are now the focus of studies by clinicians and investigators.[8] The politics of these new (or rather, renewed) claims has, in effect, come full circle. As the *Wall Street Journal* noted, "the discovery of a definitive biological cause of homosexuality could go a long way toward advancing the gay-rights cause. If homosexuality were found to be an immutable trait, like skin color, then laws criminalizing homosexual sex might be overturned."[9] Same-sex marriage, job protection, antidiscrimination in housing laws—all of these could hinge on the redefinition of homosexuality as biologically caused rather than socially and culturally chosen.

Dr. Paul Cameron, the chairman of the Family Research Institute, a conservative lobbying group that sails under the slogan "Scientists Defending Traditional Family Values," offered the following political advice to gay-rights activists: "If I were a gay-rights manager, I'd say, 'Guys, whatever we do, we have to make them believe we were born that way.' If they can get a majority of Americans believing it, they're home free."

But the political stakes for gays and lesbians are complex: If science can "prove" that homosexuality isn't a choice, what is to prevent its being repathologized and either "cured" or therapeutically aborted after prenatal testing disclosed the presence of the "gay gene"? Tying the rights discourse to science opens the possibility of devaluing choice as somehow illegitimate. It also tacitly reaffirms the either/or nature of the heterosexual-homosexual split. What would happen if the "gay gene" were detected in routine testing of heretofore impeccably heterosexual men and women? Would that mean they were "really" gay? Would it suggest that they should be therapeutically resocialized as gay in order to be true to their genes?

"A biological explanation of homosexuality simultaneously explains heterosexuality," write Michael Bailey and Richard Pillard in an article welcoming Simon LeVay's research on the brain as good news for gays and lesbians. They note that "homophobia remains the one form of bigotry that respectable people can express in public," and suggest that the scientific study of the origins of sexual orientation will open up public debate and lead to breakthroughs of "self-discovery."[10] To track the genetic origins of homosexuality, they claim, is no more stigmatizing than to seek out the genetic causes of traits like extroversion or intelligence, which are regarded as positive rather than negative qualities. (How dubiously uncontroversial such other quests would prove was demonstrated by the clamorous reception of Richard Herrnstein and Charles Murray's *The Bell Curve*.)

The quest for a "scientific" explanation (or should that be scientific "explanation"?) of homo- and heterosexuality has been much on the minds of gender critics, as well as of biological scientists, in recent years. "Nobody knows how sexual orientation is in fact determined," Mariana Valverde observed in 1987, insisting that one reason for this failure is that almost all research to date had concentrated on finding "the causes" of homosexuality "as if heterosexuality had no cause."[11] Research like that of Bailey and Pillard, LeVay, and Dean H. Hamer attempts to redress that unequal balance, but in doing so it creates a new one. By seeking to resist ambiguity, their research models inevitably write out bisexuality.

The old biology of nineteenth-century sexologists (and, subsequently, the racial "hygienics" of Nazism, a "scientific" view that saw homosexuals as genetically flawed and logically subject to extermination) had maintained that homosexuals could be recognized by certain stigmata, from beard-lessness and "limp wrists" in men to enlarged clitorises and short haircuts in women. By this biological logic, Jewish men, for example, were associated with women and with homosexuals; they were "oriental," "soft," high-voiced, degenerate, circumcised (and thus already self-castrated), and extravagant of gesture. According to sexologist Richard von Krafft-Ebing, the most identifiable "sexual inverts" were congenital, and could be recognized by the high voice, small waist, and wide pelvis in men, or, conversely, by the low voice, small breasts, and narrow pelvis in women.[12] Thus the form of the body represented the "inverted" desire: If a man desired a man, he would, according to this theory of "ideal" congenital sexual inversion, look not like a man but like a woman. Heterosexuality was thereby retained as the model. A male-female pair was envisaged, even if the "male" was a lesbian in trousers or the "female" a man in skirts.

The diagnosis of homosexuality as a perversion with biological roots and clinical and behavioral symptoms (women who wore trousers, smoked, chose not to marry; men who as children played with dolls and grew up to be hairdressers, ballet dancers, or interior decorators) was set aside by liberal psychology and psychoanalysis.

Thus Freud's initial insistence on the "bisexual disposition" of all human beings was grounded in an early faith in biology. By "bisexual," Freud meant a wide range of things, from what we would call explicit homosexuality to same-sex friendship, identification with the "opposite sex," cross-gender behavior (men acting "effeminate"; "masculine" women), the undifferentiated tissues of the embryo, and the vestigial presence in the adult of tissues and organs of what, once again, he and his successors would call the "opposite sex." But Freud's early attempts to find a biological and anatomical basis for what he variously characterized as the "bisexual disposition," the "bisexual constitution," and the "bisexual organization" of all human beings bears a striking resemblance to recent claims, almost a hundred years later, that again seek an answer in biology.

"We're mixed bags, all of us," declared a professor directing research on androgens and women's health.[13] Yet even when modern science confronts the fact that "the borders between classic maleness and femaleness are much grayer than people realized," with the increasing awareness that male sex hormones like testosterone play a crucial part in women's bodies, the implications go unexplored. "Male Hormone Molds Women, Too, in Mind and Body," announced the *New York Times.* "What society says is normal and what is normal for women can be very different," observes another medical researcher. "Women can have a full beard and still be breast-feeding."[14]

But though the debate about how androgens affect the brains as well as the bodies of women has begun to heat up—are androgenized women in fact "more mathematical, more aggressive, more sexually active, more enamored of guns and computers"?[15]—it does not seem to include the suggestion that the "mixed bags" might (bio)logically include "mixed" desires. That is to say, bisexual desires.

"The theory of bisexuality," Freud wrote, "has been expressed in its crudest form by a spokesman of the male inverts: 'a feminine brain in a masculine body.' But we are ignorant of what characterizes a feminine brain." Krafft-Ebing, he says, also puts forward such a theory, one perhaps not quite so crude: that "every individual's bisexual disposition endows him with masculine and feminine brain centres as well as with somatic organs of sex." And here, too, Freud is skeptical: "But what has just been said of masculine and feminine brains applies equally to masculine and feminine 'centres' " within the brain.[16]

Later gender theorists, like the psychoanalyst Robert J. Stoller, would challenge this on the basis of new scientific research even as they praised Freud's vision: "the brain is female," Stoller asserted, "in that *in both sexes* feminine behavior results if male hormones are not added."[17] And the media fanfare surrounding Simon LeVay's 1991 research on the hypothalamus revisits this territory of the "sexual brain" with the object of demonstrating that homosexuality is biologically produced.

According to LeVay—who examined the brains of forty-one men and women, many of them gay men who died of AIDS, and included no lesbian women in his research sample—the hypothalamus, the "part of the brain that produces sexual feelings," is much smaller in gay men than in straight men. As a result, he claims, it is possible to argue for a genetic and biological basis to male homosexuality. Gay men may after all be born rather than made. Even hairdressers and flower arrangers, he provocatively told the gay and lesbian newsmagazine *The Advocate,* might be biologically determined, identifiable by the size of their hypothalamic nuclei.[18] (Questions of larger and smaller size are not unfamiliar in sex discourse, as the *Advocate* headline "And How Big Is Yours?" wryly conceded.)

What advantage was there in grounding sexuality in biology? Hadn't some gay people objected to the idea that they were programmed for life by their brain structure? LeVay, himself a gay man, offered a by now familiar political analogy with the civil rights movement of the sixties. If gay identity were innate rather than chosen, genetic rather than optional and capricious, biological rather than behavioral, laws restricting equal opportunity for homosexuals would be prohibited by the courts. Surveys had shown, LeVay noted, that people were more tolerant of gays and lesbians when they thought they "were born that way" than when they thought it was "a lifestyle choice."

LeVay returns not only to biology but, in fact, to sociobiology. His remarks are characteristically full of analogies to male lions, lesbian seagulls, and the evolutionary strategies of the mammalian male animal, whose promiscuity is seen as ensuring the propagation of the species; hence gay men are living out a biological dictum for multiple partners which is inhibited in straight men by "the reluctance of women to be promiscuous." Thus, with the return to biology, the liberal move of Freud and his followers appears to have come full circle.

But what place has *bisexuality* in a medical research project like Simon LeVay's? If the hypothalamus of gay men is smaller than that of straight men, what size hypothalamus should bisexuals have? Are they to be imagined, like the furnishings of Goldilocks's third bear, to be neither too big nor too small, but just right—middle-sized glands for the excluded middle of sexual orientation? Might bisexuals have even smaller hypothalamuses than gay men—or larger ones, even, than straights? Or would medical science support the convictions of those psychologists and psychiatrists who think bisexuality is a mirage? Are all hypothalamuses either gay or straight? Is there such a thing as a "bi brain"? And if not, how do we account for bisexuality? The many political critiques of LeVay's study, which took him to task for everything from removing sexual desire from the realm of culturally constructed behavior to facilitating a eugenic campaign to eliminate homosexuals in utero, do not focus on this key question.

Critics of LeVay's research pointed out that (1) his hypothesis claimed a symmetry based upon the object of attraction, with those attracted to men (gay men and heterosexual women) having smaller hypothalamic nuclei than those attracted to women (heterosexual men and lesbians), but because his study contained no brain tissue from lesbians he was unable to test that part of his hypothesis; that (2) according to his own data the *range* of sizes of hypothalamic nuclei was virtually the same for homosexuals and heterosexuals, with some homosexuals having larger nuclei than many heterosexuals, and some heterosexuals having smaller nuclei than many homosexuals, so that "though the groups showed some difference as groups, there was no way to tell anything about an individual's sexual orientation by looking at his hypothalamus";[19] and that (3) since all his subjects were cadavers, there was no way of verifying the range or extent of their sexual behaviors.

This last point is the most relevant to charting bisexuality. LeVay describes his subjects as follows: "[N]ineteen subjects were homosexual men who died of complications of acquired immunodeficiency syndrome (AIDS) (one bisexual man was included in this group). Sixteen subjects were presumed heterosexual men; six of these subjects died of AIDS and ten of other causes. Six subjects were presumed heterosexual women. One of these women died of AIDS and five of other causes."[20]

The word "presumed" in the phrase "presumed heterosexual men" is marked by a footnote: "Two of these subjects (both AIDS patients) had denied homosexual activity. The records of the remaining 14 patients contained no information about their sexual orientation; they are assumed to have been mostly or all heterosexual on the basis of the numerical preponderance of heterosexual men in the population [A. C. Kinsey, W. B. Pomeroy, C. E. Martin, *Sexual Behavior in the Human Male* (Saunder, Philadelphia, 1948)]."

This strikes me as extraordinary "scientific" information. LeVay's category of "heterosexual men," the functional basis of his comparison study ("A Difference . . . Between Heterosexual and Homosexual Men") turns out to be almost entirely based on inference, guesswork, or statistical percentages drawn from a social science study which, however prestigious or canonical in the field, was completed more than forty years ago. To "presume" that the percentages remain the same over time, and that Kinsey's percentages are authoritative enough in 1991 to allow the "assumption" of heterosexuality in fourteen men about whose sexual orientation in fact nothing is known, seems not only stunningly inexact but also to be positing the very thing that LeVay wants to prove: namely, that homosexuality and heterosexuality are biological, perhaps innate, rather than social and cultural. For if "homosexuality" and "heterosexuality"—or, to use Kinsey's much less problematic terms, homosexual and heterosexual *behavior*—were in fact substantially produced or altered by cultural factors, we would have no reason to think that 1948's "numerical preponderance" would hold today.

Then there is the matter of the AIDS patients who "had denied homosexual activity"—itself a phrase of some interest, since it seems to imply that the investigators or doctors attending on the case initially "presumed" them homosexual—and of the "one bisexual man" who was included, by LeVay, in his homosexual sample. Why not include him, with equal logic, in the *heterosexual* group? Or indeed in *both* groups? "Homosexual" here becomes in effect a "default" category meaning "anything but straight."

Either LeVay regarded bisexuality as a euphemistic cover for gay identity, so that a "bisexual" in the terms of his study was really a gay man who had not come out to himself or to others, or else he hypothesized that having any sexual interest in men, even if he also had a sexual interest in women, would affect a man's hypothalamus in ways that would make him look, under the microscope, more gay than straight. In either case, bisexuality as a scientifically determinable category once again disappears, is subsumed. The "bisexual individual" is counted among the homosexual men "for statistical purposes," while the "presumed heterosexuals," about whose sex lives in fact nothing is known, are counted among the straights.

LeVay begins his paper in *Science* by noting that sexual orientation has traditionally been studied on the level of psychology, anthropology, or ethics,[21] with the clear implication that he is going to move the discourse in the direction of biological evidence, of ascertainable scientific fact. He ends it by reviewing problems in interpreting his data, including the fact, already noted above, that his "ability to make correlations between brain structure and the diversity of sexual behavior that undoubtedly exists within the homosexual and the heterosexual populations" was limited— one might use a stronger word—by the "use of postmortem material." Dead men tell no tales.

The telltale word here is "undoubtedly" ("the diversity of sexual behavior that undoubtedly exists"), a word that, casually introduced into the text, becomes in effect the paper's bisexual ghost (here, there, and everywhere)—or, if you like, the bisexual skeleton in its half-opened closet. For what can this undoubted diversity of behavior be, in the context of an article that is only concerned with the sexual object (men or women) and not with the sexual aim (oral, anal, or genital sex)[22]—what can this "diversity" be except bisexuality? How much "diversity" makes a straight into a gay, or a gay into a straight, according to the either/or logic of LeVay's classification?

LeVay himself, challenged to explain how "a 40-year-old guy who's married and with children" can one day come out as gay, compares the gayness of such men to other genetic traits, like that for adult diabetes, that do not manifest themselves until later in life. "Their sexuality is probably just as genetically loaded as are kids' who realize they are gay when they are 12 years old."[23] Thus, for LeVay, such instances of sequential bisexuality are indices of a kind of latency; these men are genetically homosexual, not bisexual, although their homosexuality may not be apparent to them early on. Bisexuality here disappears into a kind of genetic false consciousness.

In the contrary case, that of a person who had early sexual experiences with same-sex partners and then switched to exclusive other-sex relations (the "it's a phase" or boys-will-be-boys theory of bisexuality, Freud's "contingent inverts"), should we expect that the hypothalamus would give the answer "straight"? And what is to be said about the individual, male or female, who is genetically programmed for gayness but dies before the program kicks in? Would the gland of such a person disclose this future identity? Would he or she be "really" *potentially* gay? LeVay's study had at least six variables: gay/straight, male/female, died of AIDS/died of other causes. Bisexuality here would be an inconvenient further complication, whether the size of the hypothalamus is a product of innate genetic design or, as has also been conjectured, a result of lived experience as a gay—or straight—person.

Furthermore, the absence of lesbians from his study makes the question of bisexuality's place even more acute. LeVay subsequently apologized for perpetuating "the tradition of ignoring women in biomedical research," explaining that he couldn't find "brains of women whose sexual orientation is known," since that information doesn't usually appear on medical charts. Because so many of his subjects were gay men with AIDS, their sexuality became part of their etiology of disease. They were "known" to be gay. The women, by contrast, were apparently "known" to be straight. But how do we "know"? How much gay sex, or straight sex, makes a person gay or straight? Bear in mind, once more, the specter of the "bisexual AIDS carrier," that bogeyman of the eighties, whose secret life was said to be itself a cause of infection, and whose personality was conjectured to be duplicitous, cowardly, self-indulgent, or self-hating. Were any of them among the AIDS casualties in LeVay's study? If so—or even if not—would he mark them down as "gay"?

"This way of categorizing people obscure[s] the hitherto accepted fact that many people do not have sexual relations exclusively with one or the other sex," biologist Ruth Hubbard observes trenchantly, reflecting on the nineteenth-century turn of inquiry by which "homosexuality stopped being what people did and became who they were."[24] At what point does the politics of identity, necessary for the attainment of equal rights, come into conflict with the political incorrectness of human desire?

Some people are only attracted to redheads, or to people with muscular bodies, or to rich people. Do we call them roussophiles, or biceptophiles, or plutophiles? Do we examine their brains or their genes for the cause? When a young and beautiful woman marries an elderly and wealthy husband we may call her a fortune-hunter or a trophy wife or a society matron, but we do not, usually, describe her as having a perversion, or as choosing a way of life contrary to the will of God—at least not to her face. Indeed, the Bible might well be called in as evidence for sanctioning just such an arrangement. What if the same woman has previously been married to a man her own age, or if a woman who marries a blond had previously married a man with black hair? Is she to be questioned closely about why she has changed her mind?

But blond hair and black hair do not affect the economic structure, it will be objected. They do not enforce the institution of marriage and patriarchy, so there is no real analogy to be made. Well, then, what if a white woman marries a black man? We used to have a name for this unlawful practice—miscegenation. But black-white marriages are no longer against the law, at least in the United States, and while many people, black and white, may privately question it even today, "intermarriage"— between blacks and whites, between Christians and Jews—has become a much more culturally accepted practice now than it was fifty years ago. The term for such arrangements these days is not "intermarriage" or "mixed marriage" or "miscegenation" but "marriage."

Why do we resist the idea that erotic life is all part of the same set of pleasures, that there is only one sexuality, of which the "sexualities" we have so effectively and efficiently defined are equally permissible and gratifying aspects?

Because to do so would threaten the social structures on which "civilization" and "society" are built. And because much modern eroticism depends, in part, precisely upon transgression, upon the sensation or perception of daring, of breaking a law or flaunting a taboo. Like Robert Frost's famous definition of free verse as "playing tennis with the net down," what used to be called "free love" (extramarital, nonmonogamous, ambisexual) needs rules to break.

Gay Genes

Simon LeVay, who has now given up science for a career in adult education at the West Hollywood Institute of Gay and Lesbian Education, gave the media the "gay gland." Other reseachers—Michael Bailey and Richard Pillard in one study, Dean H. Hamer and associates at the National Cancer Institute in another—have given us the "gay gene." Hamer's investigation, results of which were published in *Science* in July 1993 (two years after LeVay's research appeared in the same journal), examined forty pairs of gay brothers and determined that identical pieces of the end tip of the X chromosome (inherited from the mother) appeared in thirty-three pairs to predispose them genetically to homosexuality. Again, the immediate nonscientific fallout was political, and the findings were once more appropriated to a discourse of rights.

If homosexuality was proven to be largely inborn, gay people would be protected by the courts from discrimination. The same fears—of experimentation to eliminate potential homosexuals from the population, in this case by gene therapy—and the same doubts—about drawing a firm distinction between gay and straight—were voiced. Anne Fausto-Sterling, who had been critical of earlier attempts to study human behavior through genetic research, praised the caution of Hamer's conclusions, which allowed for an interplay of the genes, the brain, and the environment in the molding of human behavior. As for LeVay, the *New York Times* described him as "ecstatic." He was quoted as calling Hamer's results "the most important scientific finding ever made in sexual orientation."[25]

Once again, though, the question of bisexuality might be said to complicate the equation, if not to queer the results. What Hamer's team did was to scrutinize the life histories of 114 men who identified themselves as homosexual. They then discovered a surprising number of homosexual males on the maternal side of the family, and, turning to brothers as most likely to be genetically linked, scrutinized their X chromosomes through a procedure known as linkage mapping. It was this procedure that revealed the surprising consonance of DNA markers on the tip of the X chromosome.

How did the study know these men were gay? Because they said so. No men who said they were heterosexual—or bisexual—were included, and although a parallel study of lesbians (again, self-identified) is under way, no results have yet appeared. "Sexual orientation is too complex to be determined by a single gene," said Hamer. But if the presence or absence of this genetic marker indicates either a direct relationship to sexual object choice or (as is also conjectured) a "temperamental" predisposition to homosexuality, what is the status of the bisexual? Is he to be thought of as resisting (heroically or perversely) the message of his genes when he has relationships with women? Should genetic factors be thought of as options or as limits? We are once again here on the terrain of the "natural" and the "original."

Hamer and his team of researchers at the National Cancer Institute begin their paper on genetics and male homosexuality with a stylish reference to homosexuality as a "naturally occurring variation," thus whisking it under the big tent of Darwinism. Their study of forty pairs of homosexual brothers, like Michael Bailey and Richard Pillard's earlier twins study, "recruited" subjects "through advertisements in local and national homophile publications."[26]

They end with a cautionary note on medical ethics that looks forward to Jonathan Tolins's play *The Twilight of the Golds,* in which a couple is told that genetic testing has proven their unborn child will be gay. Should they have the child or abort it and try again for a straight one?

"We believe," writes Hamer and his colleagues with admirable directness, "that it would be fundamentally unethical to use such information to try to assess or alter a person's current or future sexual orientation, either heterosexual or homosexual, or other normal attributes of human behavior."[27] The zinger here is "other normal attributes," which closes the parentheses begun by "naturally occurring variation" to establish that both in the language of biology and in the language of psychology homosexuals are as "normal" and "natural" as hets.

But who are Hamer's either/or homo- and heterosexuals? Using the Kinsey scale of 0 to 6, Hamer finds that his straights are very straight (Kinsey 0s and 1s) and his gays are very gay (Kinsey 5s and 6s) in self-identification, attraction, and fantasy. "Only the sexual *behavior* scale gave a small overlap between the two groups largely because of adolescent and early adult experiences" (my emphasis).[28] So at least a small number of persons said one thing about their sexuality(ies) and did another. Yet by discounting these early experiences as insignificant, the researchers were able to conclude that sexual orientation was a "dimorphic rather than a continuously variable trait." That is, they were able to omit consideration of bisexuality. ("Dimorphic" means existing or occurring in two distinct forms.) "Heterosexuals" who had had sex with men, and "homosexuals" who had had sex with women, were part of this "dimorphic" sample.

Furthermore, when participants were asked about their family histories, they were requested to rate their male relatives as "either definitely homosexual" or "not definitely known to be homosexual (heterosexual, bisexual, or unclear)." Checking with the relatives in question, researchers confirmed these opinions, except for one person who said he was asexual and two who refused to answer. (The total number of participants and relatives in the study was 166.) In this context, then, bisexual was determined to mean, for statistical purposes, "not homosexual," rather than "homosexual." Thus, while the default category for LeVay was homosexual, for Hamer it is "not homosexual."

Hamer et al. were, perhaps deservedly, rather defensive about this flattening out of the sample: "[D]escribing individuals as either homosexual or nonhomosexual," they declare, "while undoubtedly overly simplistic, appears to represent a reliable categorization of the population under study." Here is the word "undoubtedly" again, a word that in the narrative of LeVay's hypothalamic study played the role of the bisexual ghost. We could say that it does the same in Hamer's gene study, for what is "undoubtedly overly simplistic" is in fact the elimination of bisexuality as a category of analysis. To prove a point about the scientific relationship of homosexuality to genetics it is apparently necessary to remove distractions like "bisexual," "asexual," or the extremely provocative "unclear."

In other words, in the interests of science, bisexuality has been made to disappear. But not completely.

In their peroration, which we have already noted to be both hortatory and political in tone, Hamer et al. suggest a broadening of linkage studies beyond "males who self-identified as predominantly or exclusively homosexual" to include "individuals who identify as bisexual or ambisexual." Self-identification rather than behavior thus becomes the key to the scientific analysis of sexual orientation. What does this tell us about the relationship of ideas to acts?

◆

By taking self-description as the ground of fact, rather than tracing sexual contacts as systematically as it traced family trees and DNA markers, Hamer's study may be said to repeat what it finds: that men who say they are gay are gay. The *Times* qualifies its own noncommittal response to the news ("Report Suggests Homosexuality Is Linked to Genes") by raising the question of "ambiguity," but in what might be regarded as the wrong place. "So far the study has been limited to men who said they were gay, eliminating the ambiguity that would come from considering the genes of men who called themselves heterosexual." The real "ambiguity" here is, we may say, itself ambiguous, doubly located in the careful phrasing of "men who *said* they were gay . . . men who *called themselves* heterosexual" and in the intrinsic ambiguity of sexuality and eroticism especially when regarded over the span of a lifetime. The "bi" at the center of "ambiguity" is more than just a coincidental felicity for my argument; rather, it is a linguistic tag, like the genetic tag at the end tip of the chromosome, indicating a potential and posing a question. Is it possible to "eliminate ambiguity," or desirable to do so? What does science mean when it claims to know the truth about sexual desire? Does X really mark the spot?

Many of the scientists who are conducting studies on genetics and gay identity are, like Simon LeVay, themselves gay. This should not in itself suggest bias, any more than does the heterosexual identity of past sex researchers, but it does suggest a certain overdetermination of interest. Like so many researchers, in any discipline, scientific or humanistic, they are looking to find themselves. The popular response to their work has been a response consonant with identity politics. Whether "good news" or "bad news" for gays, it affirms essential identities rather than fluid constructions. Should we now look forward to a cadre of bisexual scientists searching for a bi gland, a bi gene, or, perhaps, a bisexually identified male research subject with a small hypothalamus and an unmarked X chromosome? Or vice versa?

Off the Charts

The social scientists' quest to locate sexualities on a quantifiable continuum and the geneticists' attempt to fix and determine gay identity through the microscope have in common a desire to *see:* to see clearly who is gay, who is straight, and who might cross those boundaries without showing or knowing it. Since the discourse of rights, at least in the United States, depends upon the identity of personhood—the U.S. constitution protects only persons, not acts—bisexuals have, following the lead of gays and lesbians in quest of civil rights, sought to establish themselves as a visible and definable group. Just as some gays believe that scientific evidence of their existence will aid them in their quest for equal treatment under the law, so some bisexuals seek a parallel equality through visibility: The model here clearly is identity politics, which has enabled not only interest-group lobbying but also historical self-awareness and individual pride for African Americans; women; Asian, Latino, and Native Americans; and, in the past decade, gays and lesbians.

But bisexuality will not readily fit this model. Defining the set as broadly as possible for both political and humane reasons as those who have or have had any degree of attraction to men and to women, bisexual activists and organizers come up, for example, against the real differences between what social scientists call "concurrent" and "sequential" bisexual behavior.

If "sequential" bisexuals are categorized as "really" gay or "really" straight depending on the nature of their present relationships ("coming out to themselves" on the one hand or "going straight" and getting beyond an adolescent "phase" on the other) then not only the definition of "bisexuality" but also those of "homosexuality" and "heterosexuality" are at stake.

For "homo" and "hetero" define themselves as opposites, however social science instruments like the Kinsey scale and the Klein grid keep demonstrating that such "purity" is a cultural artifact. And identity politics as well as science has an interest in keeping them opposite. To add "bisexuality" as a third category here is not in fact to refine the terms of analysis but instead to expose the radical limitations of rights-based arguments when linked to a concept of fixed identity. This is one reason why "reclaiming" historical personages and contemporary celebrities as bisexual rather than gay—Oscar Wilde, Virginia Woolf, David Bowie, Martina Navratilova—has stirred such a fuss in both the gay and the bisexual communities.

Biologists don't see bisexuality through their instruments and social scientists only see it as a composite of elements. Yet it exists, in other mammals as well as in humans, in ordinary people as well as in the famous, in adults as well as in children. If the subjects of social science analysis come uncannily to life in the talk-show medium, provoking the inevitable discussion of whether they are being used by the media or are using it for their own ends, the dispassionate categories of the Kinsey scale have likewise been taken over by today's gay and bisexual activists.

As bisexual writer Amanda Udis-Kessler notes, "phrases such as 'one in ten' and 'Kinsey 6' are probably as ingrained in queer culture as Judy Garland, Oscar Wilde, leather, *Desert Hearts,* Provincetown and Ferron."[29] In choosing "Kinsey 6" (or "Kinsey 3," defined as "equally heterosexual and homosexual") as a T-shirt slogan mode of self-identification, the successors of Kinsey's abstract "males" and "females" reclaim the territory of the survey, infusing it with personality, irony, and wit. But in giving life to these abstractions they also give them reality. To think in terms of categories is to categorize. It is no accident that gay and lesbian visibility gave rise to "gay and lesbian chic" as well as to campaigns to liberalize or repress gay and lesbian rights.

Thus, when a scale making use of the terms "concurrent" and "sequential" bisexuality came to the attention of a bisexual feminist writer, she was quick to "predict" that this "new jargon" would "find its way into many a bi circle."[30] No matter that the terms were not new;[31] a new use would be found for them in mirroring and "scientifically" validating their existence. Like Rock Hudson reading the Kinsey report, like Simon LeVay charting the biology of gay identity, bisexuals also seek to read the face of nature, to find themselves already written there.

Ultimately, however, the object of scrutiny will escape even the most vigilant and searching eyes. Bisexuality undoes statistics, confounds dimorphism, creates a volatile set of subjects who will not stay put in neat and stable categories. No calipers will fit the shape of desire, which remains, thankfully, unquantifiable by even the most finely tested instruments.

Chapter 12

On the Other Hand

> **ambisextrous**, a. *humorous*. [Blend of AMBIDEXTROUS, *a*, and SEX, *sb.*] AMBISEXUAL, *a*.
> **ambisexual**, *a*. [f. AMBI + SEXUAL *a*.] Of both sexes, bisexual; sexually attracted by or attractive to persons of either sex.
> **ambisinistrous**, *a*. [f. Latin *amb(i)*- both + *sinister* = left + OUS = AMBILAEVOUS. As it were, left-handed on both sides; the opposite of *ambidexter*.
>
> —*Three successive entries in the* Oxford English Dictionary[1]

The letter writer who asked rhetorically, in response to Anne Fausto-Sterling's essay in the *New York Times,* "What is it about human sexuality that leads people to engage in extraordinarily fuzzy thinking?" went on to urge a comparison with the "less emotive" topic of "handedness." "Most people would concede that there are two types of hands, a right and a left," he claimed, questioning whether persons with missing or extra fingers would alter our typology, suggesting that there "aren't really two types of hands but at least six kinds."[2]

Now, as it happens, this "less emotive" comparison bears an uncanny resemblance to a highly charged exchange between Sigmund Freud and his friend Wilhelm Fliess on the subject of bisexuality and handedness, which is in turn connected to a persistent analogy between left-handedness and homosexuality—or ambidexterity and bisexuality.

Modern analogies between left-handedness and gay identity crop up with startling regularity. The *Times* op-ed page, for example, ran two articles on a single day, each of which offered a (rather offhand) version of the same comparison. Chandler Burr, claiming that "scientists concluded years ago that sexual orientation was not chosen," says they did so "basically the same way they concluded that left-handedness is not chosen, through common sense. Left-handers tell us they don't choose to be left-handed. Aspects of left-handedness, like homosexuality," he adds, "almost universally appear in early childhood."[3]

Biologist Ruth Hubbard, in an excerpt from her book *Exploding the Gene Myth,* quotes gay journalist Randy Shilts, who had said that a biological explanation of homosexuality "would reduce being gay to something like being left-handed, which is in fact all it is."[4] Hubbard comments with characteristic forthrightness, "This argument is not very convincing. Until the latter half of this century, left-handed people were often forced to switch over and were punished if they continued to favor their 'bad' hand. Grounding difference in biology does not stem bigotry."[5]

The comparison seems almost to have become conventional, something of a cliché. Ensign Vernon (Copy) Berg III, later to be a major figure in Shilts's book on gays in the military, was initally described in a 1976 article in *Time* magazine as "an avowed bisexual." His father, Commander Vernon Berg, Jr., a Protestant chaplain, told *Time,* "Some people are born left-handed and some right-handed. In our family we accept people as they are."[6] And tennis star Martina Navratilova, in an autobiography published in 1985 (before her nineties lesbian celebrity), scoffed, "I've been labeled 'the bisexual defector' in print. Want to know another secret? I'm even ambidextrous. I don't like labels. Just call me Martina."

In his book *The Course of Life* (1906), Wilhelm Fliess, whose theory of the inborn bisexual disposition of human beings was so signally to influence Freud, included a long chapter "On the Significance of Ambidextrous Symmetry," including sixty-seven case histories linking left-handed persons with the psychological and physical characteristics of the opposite sex. For Fliess, ambidexterity and bisexuality were not really separable from left-handedness and homosexuality.

Sexologist Havelock Ellis had likewise observed in his study of *Sexual Inversion,* "In the majority of adult bisexual persons it would seem that the homosexual tendency is stronger and more organic than the heterosexual tendency. Bisexuality would thus in a large number of cases be comparable to ambidexterity," which some experts had found to occur "most usually in people who are organically left-handed."[7]

Ellis makes no comment, here, about his own handedness. The point is raised in a general way as a preface to the recounting of specific autobiographical histories—histories which, as it turns out, are in fact "homosexual autobiographic statements" provided to him by "inverts" themselves.

But in Ellis's *own* autobiography we do learn something of interest along these lines. Describing his "muscular awkwardness" and lack of skill at games as a child, he provides the following explanation: "I was, I believe, naturally left-handed; I have never been able to throw a ball with my right hand, and though I have never written with my left hand, my right-handed use of the pen was always the despair of my teachers."[8]

Naturally left-handed, but, doubtless after the fashion of the day, constrained to write with his right, Ellis was then himself ambidextrous, a condition he compares artlessly to bisexuality just before embarking on his highly detailed catalog of case histories of inverts. Elsewhere in the autobiography, as we have seen, he comments directly on his own "exclusive heterosexuality" and his wife's "boyishness" and sexual affairs with women.

Sometimes ambidexterity is just ambidexterity, as a cigar is just a cigar. But in a man who has no difficulty understanding, in the same autobiography, that his mother's shy protestation "I did not mean you to see that"— on the occasion of his observing her urinating on a path in the London Zoological Gardens—"could not be taken at face value," and in fact could be understood clearly as "I meant you to see that" or even "I loved you to see that,"[9] for a man capable of this degree of subtlety in reading, it is perhaps possible to imagine that something is "left" out of his account. So, too, as we will see, with Fliess and Freud.

Bi-Bi Baby

As we have noted, the passionate friendship between Sigmund Freud and Wilhelm Fliess may account for the heady tone of Freud's letter dated December 1897. "Back home and in harness again," he wrote, "with the delicious aftertaste of our days in Breslau. Bi-bi is ringing in my ears."[10]

"Bi-bi" was bisexuality-bilaterality, Fliess's theory of a connection between bisexuality and left-handedness.

"What I want now," Freud continued in his letter, "is plenty of material for a mercilessly severe test of the left-handedness theory; I have needle and thread ready." Here he refers to a test commonly used to see if a person is left-handed.

In the winter of 1897–98, Freud explored, with fascinated self-absorption, his own reluctance to accept the left-handedness theory. "It is of great interest to me," he wrote to Fliess, "that you are so affected by my still negative attitude to your interpretation of left-handedness. I shall try to be objective, for I know how difficult that is. . . . If I had a disinclination on personal grounds, because I am in part neurotic myself, this disinclination would certainly have been directed toward bisexuality, which, after all, we hold responsible for the inclination to repression. It seems to me that I object only to the permeation of bisexuality and bilaterality that you demand."

Perhaps, he speculates, Fliess's own interest in Freud's attitude toward the theory of bisexual bilaterality is personal. "I had the impression, furthermore, that you considered me to be partially left-handed; if so, you would tell me, since there is nothing in this bit of self-knowledge that might hurt me. It is your doing if you do not know every intimate detail about me; you have surely known me long enough. Well, then, I am not aware of any preference for the left hand, either at present or in my childhood; rather I could say that years ago I had two left hands. There is only one thing I would have you consider: I do not know whether it is always obvious to other people which is their own right and left and where right and left are in others."

His own "infamously low capacity" for visualizing things spatially, he says, may be related to this defect. In other words, if he appears left-handed (bisexual) to Fliess, that may be because he is unsure or confused about which is his left (homosexual) and which his right (heterosexual) side, or, even more importantly, "where right and left are in others" (Fliess, for example).

"This is how it appears to me," he sums up his reasoning, with one of those disarming flashes of self-analytic insight so characteristic of him. "But I know very well, indeed, that it nevertheless may be otherwise, and that the aversion to your conception of left-handedness I have so far felt may rest on unconscious motives. If they are hysterical," he writes, equably, "they certainly have nothing to do with the subject matter, but merely latch onto a catchword, for example, that I have been up to something that one can only do with the left hand. In that case the explanation will turn up someday, God knows when."[11] Was Freud thinking here of Rousseau's famous description of reading as an activity to be pursued with one hand while masturbating with the other? Or of the belief in many cultures that the left hand was unclean, unfit to carry food to the mouth, because it is the one with which one wipes one's bottom?[12] What can he have been "up to" that "one can only do with the left hand"?

In his authorized biography, Freud's fellow analyst Ernest Jones regards the question of left-handedness as a kind of joke, a sign of Fliess's intellectual possessivenesss. He remarks that Fliess "falsely accused" Freud of being left-handed and that Freud "jocularly" replied with the pleasantry about having two left hands. Jones is ironic and definitive: Fliess "mistook Freud's hesitancy" on the left-handedness hypothesis "for a sign of doubt about the great theory of bisexuality, with which it was in Freud's mind connected, and which, as we shall see, was a very sacred topic."[13]

But in fact the bi-bi theory deserves more than a knowing snicker here, on the one hand, so to speak, because of Freud's later observations in the case of Leonardo da Vinci about the relationship of left-handedness to homosexuality and artistic genius, and on the other hand because of the strikingly parallel ways in which society has attempted to "cure," "correct," or "convert" left-handers, homosexuals, and bisexuals.

◆

Almost a year after the original "bi-bi" conversation, Freud was still thinking about his friend's theory. "Leonardo—no love affair of his is known—is perhaps the most famous left-handed person. Can you use him?" he wrote to Fliess on October 9, 1898.[14] And much later, after the end of the friendship, he himself determined to "use" Leonardo as the subject of a book. Exploring in the mode of psychoanalytic biography (he conceded that his fellow analysts might accuse him of writing a "psychoanalytic novel") Leonardo's attachment to his mother, his autoeroticism and narcissism (introduced here for virtually the first time as an analytic term),[15] his homosexuality, and his scientific and artistic passion, Freud produced a theory of androgyny, originary bisexuality—and left-handedness.

Many mythological deities, for example those of Egypt and of classical Greece, he noted, combine male and female sexual characteristics as the only "worthy representation of divine perfection." The phallic mother—the child's fantasy of the mother with a penis, the sign of completeness and perfection—is a psychoanalytic version of this ideal. Leonardo, the illegitimate child of a beloved mother, may have repressed his early erotic attachment to her, and displaced it onto boys like himself (autoeroticism; narcissism). In the homosexual man this is in fact an adjustment away from an unacceptable heterosexual desire: "By repressing his love for his mother he preserves it in his unconscious and from now on remains faithful to her. While he seems to pursue boys and to be their lover, he is in reality running away from the other women, who might cause him to be unfaithful."[16]

Thus one type of homosexual man (Freud is careful to say that this is only one of many possible paths to homosexuality) is originally a bisexual whose conversion to monosexuality (in this case, desire for boys and men) is traceable to excessive and repressed desire for a woman (his mother).

Freud concedes that little is known about Leonardo's actual sexual relationships, but notes that he "took only strikingly handsome boys and youths as pupils" and, moreover, looked after them "just as a mother nurses her children."[17] "Leonardo was enabled to live in abstinence and to give the impression of being an asexual human being,"[18] avoiding neurosis, however, by sublimating his eroticism into his work. A later relationship with his father and then with a noble patron ("father-substitute"), Freud hypothesizes, might have provided more occasion for displacement, in this case from painting to scientific investigation, and back.

But what of his left-handedness? What part does that attribute play in Freud's admiring diagnosis of an androgynous, non-neurotic artist-scientist? In fact, it functions to confirm it: "The tendency of biological research to-day is to explain the chief features of a person's organic constitution as being the result of the blending of male and female dispositions, based on [chemical] substances. Leonardo's physical beauty and his left-handedness might be quoted in support of this view."[19]

Thus biology, which, like psychoanalysis, deals not with the "instincts" (or, as later translators would render this term, the "drives") but with the body, offers an apparently corroborating opinion. Leonardo was beautiful and left-handed; therefore he may well have been homosexual; or rather, as the left-handedness theory would in fact maintain, bisexual.

It is significant that in 1910, when Freud had split with Fliess and was already characterizing him in his letters to other male colleagues as "paranoid" (which meant, in the terms of Freud's own psychoanalytic writings of the period, "homosexual"),[20] he was still teased enough by the left-handedness idea to slip it into the tail end of his essay.

The exact nature of Leonardo's ambidexterity was in fact a topic of dispute among da Vinci scholars of the time, with some maintaining that he possessed equal facility with both hands, and others that he drew with his right hand and painted with his left, so that he was not truly ambidextrous.[21] But what is especially telling here is that left-handedness and ambidexterity are not only linked but identified, or perhaps even confused with one another, as deviations from the right-handed norm. In just the same way scientific investigators of Freud's day, whether they were sexologists or psychoanalysts, have tended to link and conflate homosexuality with bisexuality. As we will see, this tendency persists in some quarters today.

Left Out

Sinister (unfavorable, unlucky) is the Latin word for "left"; the French *gauche* has come to mean "awkward" or "inept." By contrast "right" is *dexter* (dextrous, skillful) in Latin, *droit* (as in "adroit") in French. Likewise the German *linkish,* clumsy, is related to "links" (left). Italian *mancino* connotes not only a left-handed person but also a thief, and this socio-etymology of left and right is also found in many non-European language systems. In the Bantu languages, just to give one example, the name for left frequently implies bad luck, or inferiority.[22] The word "left" itself comes from Celtic *Lyft,* meaning "weak" or "broken."

Left-handedness has long been a topic of cultural fascination for writers and thinkers from Plato to Darwin, from Sir Thomas Browne to Carlyle, from Benjamin Franklin to William James. The Bible and early Egyptian tomb writings explicitly mention practices permitted for the right hand and forbidden for the left. Ecclesiastes locates the wise man's heart at his right hand and the fool's at his left (10:2) and the parable of the sheep and the goats divides nations at the Last Judgment between the sheep, on the right hand of God, who will go to His kingdom, and the "cursed" goats, on the left, destined for everlasting fire (Matthew 25:31–36).

Ancient Greeks and Romans, Navahos and Zunis, Maoris and the natives of Maui have depended on the left-right distinction to delineate mythological and religious beliefs. In many societies, although not in all, left-handedness has over the years been popularly associated with superstition, witchcraft, and uncleanness.

Left and right have also been aligned with gender. Right-handedness has often been linked with maleness and creativity, left-handedness with femaleness and destruction.[23] Galen, following Anaxagoras, contended that boys were produced by the right testicle and ovaries and girls by the left.[24] Aristotle cites the pairs left and right, male and female, in the Pythagorean Table of Opposites, and links the left parts of the body with the female ("moister" and "hotter"), the right with the male.[25] The birth of Eve from Adam's left side was said to portend the fall.

Nor are ideas about the sinister left-hander only a matter of antiquated folk belief. Clinical researchers have joined mystics in seeking to "explain" the history of the sinister left hand. In 1903, a few years before Fliess's study was published, the Italian criminologist Cesare Lombroso viewed left-handedness as a sign of degeneracy, claiming left-handers were disproportionately represented among criminals, psychopaths, and mental defectives.[26] A 1934 monograph on handedness by Dr. Ira S. Wile noted that "just as pariahs and untouchables should use only the left hand for contact with impurities, many others would reserve it for use exclusively in the excretory areas. The left hand is the unclean hand."[27] And in 1946, after the end of World War II, and at the inception of what would come to be known, disparagingly, as "Momism," an American professor of psychiatry, Abram Blau, contended that left-handedness, or, as he preferred to call it, "sinistrality," was "nothing more than an expression of infantile negativism" traceable to—and blameable on—neglect or rejection by the mother.[28]

Blau quotes with approval a psychiatric profile of the typical left-hander, the "sinistral personality": "He is overmeticulous in dress and social manner, devotes an excessive care to the collection of useless articles, is either brutal or coldly aloof"[29] (a description uncannily similar to stigmatizing stereotypical profiles of a certain kind of gay man of the same period), and he insists that sinister laterality, willful left-handedness, is not inherited but chosen, a preference, not an orientation.

"There is absolutely no evidence to support the contention that dominance, either in handedness or in any other form, is a congenital predetermined human capacity . . . the theory of heredity must be put down as erroneous." Therefore the left-hander is an inexplicable deviant, defying received custom and social wisdom: "Why a small percentage of the human race persists in using the left or unconventional hand, despite taboos and rigid social barriers imposed by society to prevent such usage, has long been a challenging problem to scholar and scientist."[30]

Anyone who has encountered late-twentieth-century diatribes about homo- and bisexuality as capricious lifestyle choices that outrage "family values" will recognize this tone of evangelical contempt. Perhaps it is worth noting that slang terms for left-handed are often related to slang terms for homosexual or gay; in Australia, a left-hander is a "molly-dooker," from the same word as "molly-house," a place where effeminate homosexual men congregated ("dooker" from "dukes," as in "put up your dukes").[31] The conventional terms "straight" and "bent" for heterosexual and homosexual are likewise both directional and evaluative.[32]

Scientific investigators over the years have made the same hypothetical assumptions, questioning whether left-handedness might be either *caused by* a pathological condition or a *marker* for some underlying pathology. The list of possible suspects is long: mental retardation, autism, schizophrenia, alcoholism, dyslexia, bedwetting, criminality, blond hair, artistic creativity, exceptional verbal abilities, and homosexuality have all been linked with the sinister fact of left-handedness.[33] One modern investigator has suggested that left-handers live shorter lives—some nine years shorter than righties.[34]

Some recent studies have stressed a possible relationship between testosterone and left-handedness, suggesting, according to one researcher, that lesbians ought to be more likely to be left-handed.[35] (Is this the place for me to say that I myself am left-handed, or, more accurately, bilateral: write and play tennis left, bat and throw right?)

In one study, in which subjects were "recruited from a local homosexual organization" in Canada, the claim was made that the rate of lesbians who were either left- or mixed-handed was 69 percent of the group, more than four times the rate found among heterosexual women.[36] In a comparison study of one hundred heterosexual and ninety-four homosexual men in London, the results likewise demonstrated that there were in fact "an overabundance of left-handers among male homosexuals,"[37] a finding that has, it is claimed, been confirmed by later studies.

However, as with Freud and Fliess, and, indeed, with Leonardo, "left-handers" are not quite what they appear. For "left-handers" here turn out to mean "those who are not consistently or strongly right-handed." The binary nature of the study in effect erases mixed- or both-handedness. "In other words," as one researcher blithely explains, "the non-right-handed group consisted of both left- and mixed-handed individuals."[38] Ambidexterity was not a category available for the respondents' use. It is not at all clear whether "homosexual" in these same studies meant in fact "not consistently or strongly heterosexual," rendering the bisexual as invisible and uncounted as the ambidextrous.

We may recall that Fliess's discussion of the psychosexual relationship of handedness and sexuality was called "On the Significance of Ambidextrous Symmetry." Actually, ambidextrousness plays a part in some of the most canonical discussions of left and right in Western culture. Talmudic scholars, for example, argue about whether the Hebrew phase *itter yad yemino* in key biblical passages (Judges 3:15, 20:16) means "left-handed" or "ambidextrous."[39]

Plato puts forth a strong argument in favor of ambidexterity, regarding the preference for the right hand as a piece of cultural superstition ascribed to "the folly of nurses and mothers." "Nature," he says, "makes the members on both sides broadly correspondent; we have introduced the difference between them for ourselves by our improper habits." To avoid this unnecessary limitation in human capacity, founded merely on "foolishness," "officers of both sexes" should be employed in training young people, "so that all our boys and girls may grow up ambicrural and ambidextrous, their native endowments suffering no preventable distortion through acquired habit."[40]

The analogy to a theory of originary bisexuality is clear enough. Acquired habit, foolishness, "the folly of nurses and mothers" ("Momism" *avant la lettre?*) have led, Fliess might have argued, to the "distortion" of the human capacity to love and desire both sexes, thus restricting and repressing our natural gifts. What is "improper" is the idea of a difference between right- and left-handedness, between heterosexuality and homosexuality. The "native endowment" is bisexuality, which undergoes repression with a consequent loss for the individual and the culture.

History records a significant number of famous bisexual ambidextrals, from Alexander the Great, who had both male and female lovers and was said to have discovered in his travels a tribe that was exclusively left-handed, to Lord Robert Baden-Powell, the "skirt-dancing" founder of the Boy Scout Movement, who lived with a beloved fellow soldier, married late in life, and, himself ambidextrous, was saluted by an Ashanti chieftain with a left-handed greeting, described as proper for heroes. Baden-Powell later adopted the left-handed secret handshake for his Boy Scouts (who have, nonetheless, steadfastly refused to admit homosexuals as scoutmasters or as members of scouting troops).[41]

It was Baden-Powell who wrote—and signed with both hands—the introduction to a book by the founder of the Ambidextral Culture Society, John Jackson, a layman who may perhaps be seen as one in a series of turn-of-the-century British enthusiasts. Jackson's Society, founded in 1905 to combat pagan prejudice against the equal use of both hands, stood behind its slogan "Justice and Equality for the Left Hand."[42] (Jackson was also an advocate of Upright Penmanship to avoid the necessity of a right-handed slant in cursive writing, a reform that would have been a great boon to me in the second grade.)

Baden-Powell, like Plato before him, contended that ambidexterity was beneficial in warfare, and thus, in effect, patriotic. The painter Edwin Landseer, who had taught drawing to the left-handed Queen Victoria, was one of many other prominent persons who supported the ambidextrists. But the left-handed liberation movement was not without its detractors. An eminent physician of the period took the podium to inveigh, in a lecture called "Dexterity and the Bend Sinister," against the "taint of fad-dism" among the Ambidextrists, claiming that "some of those who pro-mote it are addicted to vegetarianism, hatlessness or anti-vaccination and other aberrant forms of belief."[43]

This was the period in British and American history that also saw socie-ties organized to promote ideas like temperance, phonetic spelling, women's suffrage, and the authorship of "Shakespeare's" plays by Sir Fran-cis Bacon. It is easy to mock such zealous amateurs, but none of these ideas has disappeared, and it might be argued that one or two of them have even achieved respectability.

Part 3 Bi Laws

Institutions of ''Normal Sex''

Chapter 13

Normal Schools

It gives you a queer feeling if, late in life, you are ordered once again to write a school essay.

—*Sigmund Freud,*
"Some Reflections on Schoolboy Psychology"[1]

My emotion at meeting my old schoolmaster warns me to make a first admission: it is hard to decide whether what affected us more and was of greater importance to us was our concern with the sciences that we were taught or with the personalities of our teachers.

—*Freud,*
"Some Reflections on Schoolboy Psychology"[2]

In English preparatory and public schools romance is necessarily homosexual.

—*Robert Graves,* Good-bye to All That

Normal III

The word "normal" comes from a Latin term meaning perpendicular or at right angles. By the nineteenth century, it had come to mean regular or usual, done by the rule or on the square, not deviating from the common type or standard. In modern chemistry and physics, "normal" has a specific technical application having to do with statistical averages or means. But over time the word has also taken on a moral and quasi-medical status that confuses the "average" or "mean" with the right, true, or appropriate.

Normal schools, from the French *école normale* (model school), were training schools for teachers, usually for the elementary grades. At a conference held a few years ago in the town of Normal, Illinois, the site of Illinois State University—a former teachers' college—participants joked that by gathering in "Normal, IL" they had found the perfect site for the topic under discussion, feminism and psychoanalysis. The town got its name from the college.

The first question Geraldo Rivera asked me when I appeared on his television show as a designated "expert" to talk with several women who dressed as men was "Dr. Garber, is this normal?" It might not be usual, I replied, but it was perfectly "normal." Normal, I suggested, was not a useful term. Geraldo seemed to regard this as equivocation, but the cross-dressers on the show hastened to agree. The form of his question emphasized the sense in which "normal" in the late twentieth century has become a kind of sociocultural back-formation from the dreaded "abnormal."

As for "abnormal" ("deviating from the ordinary rule or type; contrary to rule or system; irregular, unusual, aberrant"), it is another nineteenth-century coinage with a fascinatingly various history, from "anomalous" to the depreciatory "abnormous." "Few words," comments the *Oxford English Dictionary,* "show such a series of pseudoetymological perversions." In other words, "abnormal" is itself an abnormal word, exhibiting and acting out "perversions" by unreliably shifting its spellings and forms.

One significant consequence of the idea of bisexuality for Freud and psychoanalysts following him was a recognition that what was regarded as "normal" heterosexual behavior was in fact the result of cultural conditioning rather than the dictates of some biologically mandated or divinely ordained human nature.

"Psycho-analysis," Freud wrote in *Three Essays,* "considers that a choice of an object independently of its sex ... is the original basis from which, as a result of restrictions in one direction or another, both the normal and the inverted types develop." "Normal" and "inverted" were merely received terms, not judgments. "Indeed, libidinal attachments to persons of the same sex play no less a part as factors of normal mental life ... than do similar attachments to the opposite sex."[3] "Normal sexuality too depends upon a restriction in the choice of object," he insisted. "All human beings are capable of making a homosexual object-choice and have in fact made one in their unconscious." Yet to become "normal" rather than "ill" a person learns to restrict his or her desires in accordance with the expectations of others. And nowhere are those expectations more rigid than in the context of adolescence.

In a lecture delivered to students at the University of Zurich in 1922, C. G. Jung addressed what he called "the love problem of a student" with typical confidence in the truth of his own opinions. "Homosexual relations between students of either sex are by no means uncommon," he told his student audience, although he judged them less common "among us, and on the continent generally" than in those countries where boy and girl students are strictly segregated from one another. "I am speaking here," he assured them, "not of pathological homosexuals who are incapable of real friendship and meet with little sympathy among normal individuals, but of more or less normal youngsters who enjoy such a rapturous friendship that they also express their feelings in sexual form."[4]

More or less normal youngsters. Which is it—more, or less? "With them it is not just a matter of mutual masturbation, which in all school and college life is the order of the day," but of a higher kind of friendship, a friendship "in the classical sense of the word," and especially a friendship between an older man and a younger. "A slightly homosexual teacher," it seems, "often owes his brilliant intellectual gifts to his homosexual disposition." But "the more homosexual a man is, the more prone he is to disloyalty and to the seduction of boys." "A friendship of this kind naturally involves a special cult of feeling, of the feminine element in a man. He becomes gushing, soulful, aesthetic, over-sensitive, etc.—in a word, effeminate, and this womanish behavior is detrimental to his character."

It seems that we have moved, effortlessly and unresistingly under Jung's tutelage, from the contemplation of "homosexual relations between students of either sex" to sex between men. And just as such sexual relations take place between "more or less normal" students, with the conventional phrase "more or less" covering over the apparent fact that some are more and some are less "normal" in his view, so Jung's contemplation of sexual relations between male teachers and male students is also inflected with a "more or less"—the "slightly homosexual" teacher and the "more homosexual" one. Plainly for him, less is more. The "more homosexual" a teacher is, the more he becomes like a woman: gushing, soulful, oversensitive, and so on.

What then about relations between academic women? Here, says Jung, age difference is not so important, because what is central is "the exchange of tender feelings" and of "intimate thoughts." "Generally," he says, "they are high-spirited, intellectual, and rather masculine women who are seeking to maintain their superiority and to defend themselves against men. Their attitude to men is therefore one of disconcerting self-assurance, with a trace of defiance. Its effect on their character is to reinforce their masculine traits and to destroy their feminine charm. Often a man discovers their homosexuality only when he notices that these women leave him stone-cold."[5]

Despite Jung's insistent idealization of archetypal androgyny in myths and legends, the phenomenon of "feminine" men and "masculine" women in real life clearly throws him off-balance. To be self-assured with men is enough, apparently, to destroy "feminine charm." It is all too clear here exactly who is disconcerted and who is left stone-cold.

But what does Jung have to say about bisexuality in the context of "the love problem of a student"? Unsurprisingly, it is at this point in Jung's address that the rhetoric of the "normal" returns, we may say with a vengeance. "Normally," he says, "the practice of homosexuality is not prejudicial to later heterosexual activity. Indeed, the two can even exist side by side. I know a very intelligent woman who spent her whole life as a homosexual and then at fifty entered into a normal relationship with a man."

"Normally" those who practice homosexuality can become "normal" if they give it enough time. That "the two"—homosexuality and heterosexuality—"can even exist side by side" is, once again, the bisexual premise that underlies Jung's airier notions of cosmic oneness.

The Crush

Romance now rears its head shyly and pretty innocently in the shape of the "crush," the "pash," the "having a thing about."

—*Arthur Marshall*, Giggling in the Shrubbery

Since through my destiny that flaming desire forces me to speak which has forced me to sigh always, you, O Love, who arouse me to it, be my guide, and show me the way, and tune my rhymes to my desire.

—*Petrarch*, Rime Sparse[6]

Is a "crush" real love?

Sometimes it's better. There's nothing like that sensation of tingling hyper-awareness through your whole body, the physical sensation of heightened sensibility—heart literally beating faster—whenever the beloved person is near, the unchallenged idealization of the longed-for object, who never disappoints because he or she is never really known. Nor is it only a pleasure accessible to the very young. "I love having crushes," says lecturer on bisexuality Robyn Ochs, who is in her thirties. "They are one of the great pleasures of life, and I welcome them. However, I rarely act on my attractions."[7]

The crushes, pashes, and "things" described in a book called *Giggling in the Shrubbery* (a companion volume on boys' schools is called *Whimpering in the Rhododendrons*)[8] are British rather than American, though similar "smashes," "flames," "raves," and "spoons" could be found on both sides of the Atlantic.[9] The time is the thirties and forties. The former pupils are perhaps selective in their recollections—or selected for what they did, and did not, recall. "No instances of actual sexual involvement are reported or anything even vaguely physical," the editor reassures us. "A horrified revulsion might well have been the result of amatory dilly-dallyings, for these affairs were on an altogether higher plane."[10] Nonetheless, some of the recollections in *Giggling* are fascinating. How high the plane is, and how absent the "dilly-dallyings," the reader may decide.

In that all-female society we were subject to strange "Pashes." There was a cult to declare oneself devoted to a member of staff, or another girl. Our Headmistress encouraged the belief that sex was filthy, and the very thought or mention of it was degrading, praising the love between David and Jonathan above all. Marriage was a last resort for the lower orders and more stupid people.[11]

An account of convent-school life:

We had "crushes" on each other—my mother at the Convent many years earlier called them "pashes"—when you were small you had a crush on either a prefect, the head girl, or the games' captain (or even a nun). When I arrived at the top of the school I found that small girls had crushes on me. We also had V.B.F.'s and B.F.'s—"very best friends" and "best friends," there was a subtle difference. . . .

I don't really know even now if any of these crushes or friendships had lesbian overtones—we certainly knew nothing of that specifically. . . . I can remember creeping out of my room in the middle of the night and visiting [a girl] in her bed in her room, where we used to lie close together and talk; I enjoyed these visits, but don't really recall having any particular sexual feelings.[12]

I like the "really" that qualifies the final sentiment here. Another respondent had this to say:

We were very innocent about sex. Some girls used to get "pashes" on older girls, but all it amounted to was gazing at them in chapel and writing notes to tell them how wonderful they were. I do remember a rumour that the girls at one school were not allowed hairbrushes with handles, and although we all laughed knowingly at this, we did not discuss with each other what the reason might be. We never saw any men, except the odd job man . . . , our Headmaster/priest, a man who taught us national dancing, and a pianist called Raymond, whom we all dubbed weedy and feeble (our most damning insult). Although we were mostly attractive girls, training for a career on the stage and going to parties in the holidays, we didn't miss the opposite sex. I was eighteen when I left and never wished that we were co-ed. In my time there were two older girls who were rumoured to have "done it," but we never knew for sure.[13]

There's much rich lore here, from the hairbrushes with handles to the uncorroborated but erotically powerful rumor that the two older girls had "done it." But what strikes me most about this account is the story of the "pashes" on older girls. "All it amounted to" was "gazing at them in chapel" and "writing notes to tell them how wonderful they were." Readers of Dante and Petrarch, take note. Those poets, too, gazed on their unattainable ladies in church, fell instantly in love, and wrote of their desire and their pain. I make no claims for the literary merit of the notes passed in an English girls' school. But the "pashes" themselves, and the structure of longing described in this casual reminiscence, are a version of the same structure that, in heterosexual terms, determines the fate of the sonnet tradition and thus of love poetry in Italian, French, and English. The former student's deprecatory gestures ("we were very innocent about sex"; "all it amounted to was") mask the pain, the ecstasy, and the seriousness of the moment. A "pash," after all, is a little passion. And to the passionate, no passion is little. By minimizing and trivializing these same-sex moments in erotic careers that may then go on to become predominantly heterosexual, we not only consent to a setting-aside of adolescent homoeroticism as a miscast rehearsal for the "real thing," but we also vastly underestimate the strength of passion and desire that comes with first love.

A school-friendship is termed by Italian girls a "flame" *(fiamma),* notes Havelock Ellis. "In every college the 'flame' is regarded as a necessary institution. The relationship is usually of a markedly Platonic character, and generally exists between a boarder on one side and a day-pupil on the other."

A survey conducted by Italian researchers in the 1890s among "the pupils of Normal Schools," with students aged from twelve to twenty, suggested that the binary opposition at work here—the eroticized boundary—was not, for situational reasons, that between male and female, nor yet between older and younger girls, but rather between the outside and the inside, the boarders and the day students. "The boarders are most inflammable, but it is the day-pupils who furnish the sparks."[14]

Some 60 percent of students were said to have had "flame" relationships during their schooldays. One, who "had herself aroused very numerous 'flames,' " reported that boarders sometimes fell in love with day students even before meeting them, on the basis of their reputations for elegance or beauty. "The beloved, unconscious of the tumult of passions she has aroused, goes into school, not knowing that her walk, her movements, her garments are being observed from stairs or dormitory corridor."[15]

A former boarder was being shown over the college on the day of her arrival when her companion ran up to her, "embracing me, closing my mouth with a kiss, and softly caressing my hair. I gazed at her in astonishment, but experienced a delicious sensation of supreme comfort. Here began the idyll!" The kisses aroused in her new feelings: "I felt that they were not like the kisses of my mamma, my papa, my brother, and other companions; they gave me unknown sensations; the contact of those moist and fleshy lips disturbed me." They proceeded to exchange letters "and the usual rights and duties of 'flames.'"

But flames were exclusive, unlike friendships, and therefore contained the possibility of jealousy. This student was afraid of her flame's "Othello-like jealousy." "She would suffocate me, even bite me." For her own part she was afraid of "losing her," a fear she artlessly confessed to the headmistress one day, culminating this confession by "throwing myself in her arms." It is perhaps not surprising under the circumstances that the headmistress's smile, which "went through my heart," immediately convinced her "how silly I was, and what a wrong road my companion was on. From that day I could no longer endure my flame." The "wrong road" seems to have led to sexual activity for the ardent and impetuous lover ("Later I heard that she had formed a relationship which was not blessed by any sacred rite"). On the other hand, or the other road, the student's own passion, now neatly transferred to the headmistress, remained safely "Platonic"—at least as far as she reports.[16]

Did "flames" generally lead to sex? It depends on who you ask, and also on what you think "sex" is—whether, for example, it's really different in kind, or just in degree, from caresses, kisses, hand holding, and embraces. One woman insisted that she had known of only a single definite homosexual relationship during her time at school, and "the couple in question were little liked."[17] Ellis himself maintains that, while there is "an unquestionable sexual element" in the "flame" relationship, it does not follow that the girls involved are expressing "real congenital perversion of the sex-instinct"—that is, they aren't lesbians in his sense, because they "cease to feel these emotions" when they leave college "to enter social life." How he knows what they feel, as opposed to what they do, is hard to say. Entering social life undoubtedly meant entering the world of marriage, a change of venue motivated at least as much by social as by erotic concerns.

But in fact one of his points is to establish the legitimacy of these feelings, which he does, somewhat irritatingly to modern gay sensibilities, by insisting on their transience. Normal schools *are* normal, Ellis claims. "There is no reason to suppose that women teachers furnish a larger contingent of perverted individuals than other women."[18]

Since a normal school is a teachers' college, the researchers had the opportunity of consulting a number of former students who were now teachers. One, who "had never herself been either the object or the agent in one of these passions" but had had "ample opportunity of making personal observations" described the typical "flame" as "exactly like a love-relationship," with a dominant lover and a shy or obstinately reluctant beloved passing through courtship stages from mute adoration to presents of flowers and little messages conveyed by third parties to a letter of declaration and eventual acceptance. The teacher regarded this as being "like" a love relationship rather than in fact being one. Ellis himself calls the flame a *"love-fiction, a play of sexual love"* (the italics are his), and the Italian researchers concur, describing the letters exchanged between "flames" as a kind of masturbation, or "intellectual onanism." Another former student feels sure that heterosexuality prevents "flaming": "I can say that a girl who is in love with a man never experiences 'flame' emotions for a companion."[19] But what does this say except that if she is in love with someone she is not—at this moment—in love with anyone else?

The presumption of a kind of progress from homosexual to heterosexual love, the implication that school-love is "puppy love," ignores both the intensity of those feelings and their recapitulation of just those stages of passion, suffering, and exaltation that we have come to regard as the true hallmarks (enshrined indeed in the sentiments often found on Hallmark greeting cards) of "being in love." The Italian researchers produced a list of characteristics that distinguished "flames" from ordinary friendships. The list is worth scrutinizing because it is a typology of love—any love, but especially what we call "romantic," by which we often mean "adolescent," love.

1. the extraordinary frequency with which, even by means of subterfuges, the lovers exchange letters;
2. the anxiety to see and talk to each other, to press each other's hands, to embrace and kiss;
3. the long conversations and the very long reveries;
4. persistent jealousy, with its manifold arts and usual results;
5. exaltation of the beloved's qualities;
6. the habit of writing the beloved's name everywhere;
7. absence of envy for the loved one's qualities;
8. the lover's abnegation in conquering all obstacles to the manifestations of her love;
9. the vanity with which some respond to "flame" declarations;
10. the consciousness of doing a prohibited thing;
11. the pleasure of conquest, of which the trophies (letters, etc.) are preserved.[20]

Those exemplary heterosexual "Italian" lovers Romeo and Juliet, and Shakespeare's other mooning adolescents from Orlando to the Navarrese lords in *Love's Labour's Lost*, exhibit identical symptoms.

Despite its "apparently non-sexual nature," Ellis says of the flame, "all the sexual manifestations of college youth circle around it, and in its varying aspects of differing intensity all the gradations of sexual sentiment may be expressed." But was this true only in Italy? Quite the contrary. In England " 'raves,' 'spoons,' etc." seemed to flourish in boarding schools and colleges, despite institutional attempts to discourage any "morbid" or "unhealthy" feelings.

"From what I have been told by those who have experienced these 'raves' and have since been in love with men," writes a woman who was familiar with the girls' colleges of the period, "the emotions called forth in both cases were similar, although in the case of the 'rave' this fact was not recognized at the time." Like Ellis, she presumes that these "raves" are a stage for most young women, though she knows of girls who have left school and have even had "numerous flirtations with the opposite sex," girls "who cannot be accused of inversion" since they have "all the feminine and domestic characteristics" and yet maintain these passionate romantic friendships.[21]

The existence and persistence of romantic friendships between women in past as well as present times are, thanks to recent scholarship, no surprise.[22] But what this data on "The School-Friendships of Girls" also insists upon, and what is very often itself dismissed in the same way that Ellis is thought to dismiss female-female passion, is the indistinguishability of kinds of erotic love.

The fact is that we *learn* to love. We *learn* to desire. We "model," to use the social scientists' word, our erotic feelings. Some of these young women became (or remained) heterosexuals; some became (or remained) lesbians. The heterosexuals—the "normal" graduates of the "normal schools"—were, some 60 percent of them by the Italian doctors' study, emotionally and perhaps even experientially bisexual. They loved women; then they loved men. Not necessarily "instead." Perhaps, in fact, "because."

Ellis's female correspondent tells a fascinating anecdote about two young women, A. and B., who met at a girls' college and were instantly attracted. Both already had "raves," one on a man ("an actor she had lately seen") and the other on a married woman. They "lived for one another." They "became inseparable." The "sexual element" in their relationship was "certainly marked." Although at the time they were "both quite ignorant" of sexual matters, "they indulged their sexual instincts to some extent." Their intense relationship continued for three or four years, and after ten years "they are both exceedingly fond of each other, although their paths in life are divided and each has since experienced love for a man." The correspondent feels she must add that "A. and B. are both attractive girls to men and women" and that "B. especially appears always to have roused 'rave' feelings in her own sex, without the slightest encouragement on her part."[23]

It is hard to know whether to take this last at face value. In my experience the rousing of strong erotic feelings on a continuous basis is hardly ever done without encouragement, however unconscious or "slight." But never mind; lucky B. Would we say that A. and B. are heterosexuals, since they have "experienced love for a man"? Lesbians, even self-denying lesbians? Bisexuals? These seem like categories imposed from without, to assort and regiment relationships and feelings that A. and B., whoever they were (and whether or not, as I incline to suspect or perhaps just to hope, the correspondent was in fact one of them), were able to manage very adeptly on their own.

Goodbye to All That?

> In this environment there is nothing unnatural about the attraction exercised by a small boy over an elder one. A small boy is the nearest approach possible to the feminine ideal. Indeed a small boy at a Public School has many of the characteristics that a man would hope and expect to find in a woman. He is small, weak, and stands in need of protection. He is remote as a woman is, in that he moves in a different circle of school life, with different friends, different troubles, different ambitions. He is an undiscovered country. The emotion is genuine and usually takes the elder boy by surprise.
>
> —*Alec Waugh*, Public School Life: Boys, Parents, Masters

> When I was a child, I spake as a child, I understood as a child, I thought as a child: but when I became a man, I put away childish things.
>
> —*I Corinthians 13:10*

"In English preparatory and public schools," wrote the poet and mythographer Robert Graves, "romance is necessarily homosexual. The opposite sex is despised and treated as something obscene. Many boys never recover from this perversion. For every born homosexual, at least ten permanent pseudo-homosexuals are made by the public school system; nine of those ten as honourably chaste and sentimental as I was."[24]

Graves's description of early-twentieth-century upper- and upper-middle class English boys'-school life in his autobiographical memoir *Goodbye to All That* testifies to an idealization of love among schoolboys that corresponds to the "crushes" and "pashes" of girls. Words like "romance" and "honourably" suggest a code of courtly love.

"Pseudo-homosexual," in this context, is not the same as the postmodern phenemenon of the so-called Straight Queer, or Queer Straight, the heterosexual who thinks it's cool to be taken for gay. "Pseudo-homosexual" here is a technical term, introduced in the period by the sexologist Iwan Bloch to describe persons who have homosexual relations because they are in same-sex situations with no access to members of the other sex.[25]

Bloch describes in his survey of English history "an occasional apparent increase in homosexuality" that is driven by fashion and dissolute life styles, a "real epidemic increase in homosexual tendencies, which are sometimes manifested in a slight and uncertain fashion but, at other times, are strongly roused and can lead to an apparent perversion of natural feeling." "Pseudo-homosexuality" was especially to be found in England among "sailors, schoolboys and university students, mine and street workers, footballers, athletes, members of certain men's and boys' associations and the like"—in short, a large percentage of the male population. "Lack of intercourse with women, and especially indulgence in alcohol, here play an important part," Bloch adds, as does the English men's club, and "the intensive cultivation of games," so like the "cult of homosexuality" among the sport-loving ancient Greeks.[26]

So the male-bonding society of English life, at virtually all social levels, is conducive to "pseudo-homosexuality." How is the "pseudo" kind distinguishable from the real thing? Presumably because pseudo-homosexuals turn out to be (also) heterosexuals—that is, bisexuals. Or what current sociology likes to describe as "sequential bisexuals"—people who have sex with same- and opposite-sex partners at different times in their lives.

Freud, as we've seen, called such persons "contingent inverts," who under certain circumstances like "inaccessibility of any normal sexual object" and "imitation" are "capable of taking as their sexual object someone of their own sex and of deriving satisfaction from sexual intercourse with him" (no mention of "her").[27] Inaccessibility of opposite sex partners and "imitation" (or "fashion") were key parts of Bloch's scheme, which he later renamed "secondary homosexuality."[28] Today such persons are more frequently described as "situational bisexuals," or, more accurately, as engaging in situational bisexuality.

Fascination with the phenomenon of "pseudo-homosexuality" was widespread. Magnus Hirschfeld enumerated three classes of what he called "spurious inverts" (male prostitutes and blackmailers; good-natured or pitying souls who permitted themselves to be loved; and the inmates of same-sex schools, barracks, or prisons),[29] while Havelock Ellis made short work of this attempt at classification, remarking that "every one of Hirschfeld's three classes may well contain a majority of genuinely homosexual or bisexual persons," and that the question was rather one of a degree of feeling than of a kind.

Presuming that "the basis of the sexual life is bisexual," he noted that some people have homosexual feelings so strong that they persist even in the presence of potential heterosexual love-objects, while in others the homosexual responses are "eclipsed" by heterosexual desire. "We could not, however, properly speak of the latter as any more 'spurious' or 'pseudo' than the former," Ellis declared roundly.[30] Desire was desire— there was nothing spurious or "pseudo" about it, despite the situation or "contingency" that had given it rise. The body could respond, the heart could break.

Words like "pseudo" and "spurious," evoking as they do a rhetoric of the real and the fake, the original and the copy, may remind us that in some quarters homosexual desire (and gay culture from butch to drag) has been dismissed out of hand as an imitation of the real thing.[31] Yet in fact it would be as possible to call *all* eroticisms "pseudo" as to deny that any of them are. What are the hallmarks of the real when it comes to human feelings? Do we judge by outcome (marriage, a long-term relationship, a suicide attempt)? By the teleology of personal history (a broken engagement followed by a marriage to someone else, a straight relationship followed by a gay one)? Is the "real" the last—or the lost?

Whether the ground of the genuine is considered to be that of homosexuality or of heterosexuality, a term like "pseudo-homosexual" (and its biologically inflected cognate, "pseudo-hermaphrodite"—Krafft-Ebing's term for what we now call bisexuals) suggests by implication a kind of false consciousness. The subject must not really know himself or herself, otherwise he or she would be straight or gay. Graves's description contrasts the "pseudo-homosexual" with the "born" homosexual (Freud's "absolute invert"), again following the lead of contemporary sex theorists for whom "inversion" was inborn and perhaps even hereditary. The "pseudo-homosexual," like the "contingent invert," will turn, or return, to heterosexuality once the opportunity presents itself.

Yet as Graves implies, the "pseudo-homosexual" was the usual rather than the exceptional case in the same-sex public school. The "pseudo" was in fact the "normal." If one is "born" and the other is "made," the distinction would often manifest itself only after the fact.

The ironies of a homophobic culture whose most exclusive enclaves and institutions for self-replication were literal hotbeds of homosexuality have not been lost on the products of this schooling system. Alan Sinfield notes that middle-class same-sex schools got started in England in the late nineteenth century as a way of separating young men from the distractions of women.[32] "The parting of boys from the women who were generally dominant in their childhood, and subjecting them to systematic brutalization, were not the incidental price of 'a good education': *they were the point.*"[33]

"If all persons guilty of Oscar Wilde's offences were to be clapped in gaol, there would be a very surprising exodus from Eton and Harrow, Rugby and Winchester, to Pentonville and Holloway," observed W. F. Stead in 1895, in response to Wilde's conviction and sentencing: "But meanwhile public school boys are allowed to indulge with impunity in practices which, when they leave school, would consign them to hard labour."[34] As Sinfield trenchantly observes, "Public schools were crucial in the development of homosexual identity because, despite the official taboo, they contributed, in many instances, an unofficial but powerful cultural framework within which same-sex passion might be positively valued."[35]

The rhetorical invocation of Greek models of *paideia* and an in-house hierarchy that required younger boys to "fag" for older ones virtually guaranteed that compliance with the system would lead to crushes, "raves," and fierce affections. As one correspondent wrote to Havelock Ellis, "no one can have passed through a public-school and college life without constantly observing indications of the phenomenon in question. It is clear to me that in a large number of instances there is no fixed line between what is called distinctively 'friendship' and love; and it is probably the influence of custom and public opinion that in most cases finally specializes the physical passion in the direction of the opposite sex."[36]

In this observer's opinion, then, what was "made"—what was, in Graves's borrowed phrase, "pseudo"—was in fact *heterosexuality.* Custom and public opinion weighed in on the side of the "opposite sex"—of the normal as it was normally understood. It was these factors that led the public-school or college boy to "specialize"—that is, to become, as a practical matter, a heterosexual rather than a bisexual person.

Specialization implies a narrowing down of the field. In its biological sense, which is probably meant here, "specialized" also means adapted or modified to suit its environment—something clearly accomplished by the overt cultural conditioning of the school scenario, however mixed its covert messages. But if the heterosexual is a specialist, the bisexual may perhaps be thought of as a generalist. And it is against this generalization that it is possible to love and desire and make love to persons of *both* sexes, that the conformist codes of eroticism in the same-sex institution, whether it be a school, a camp, or a prison, are most inexorably (and most deliciously) set.

It begins to become clear that "normalization" is as much a function of narration as of experience. The struggle to tell, or to edit and censor, the schoolgirl's or schoolboy's sexual and sentimental autobiography runs up against the fear (desire?) of a return of the repressed. Robert Graves tells the story of his school years at Charterhouse in a tone at once easy and offhand. "In my fourth year I fell in love with a boy three years younger than myself, who was exceptionally intelligent and fine-spirited. Call him Dick. . . . I was unconscious of any sexual desire for him, and our conversations were always impersonal. This illicit acquaintance did not escape comment, and one of the masters, who sang in the choir, warned me to end it. . . . Finally the Headmaster took me to task for it. I lectured him loftily on the advantage of friendship between elder and younger boys, citing Plato, the Greek poets, Shakespeare, Michelangelo and others, who had felt as I did. He let me go without taking any action."[37]

"My boys are amorous, but seldom erotic," the headmaster of Charterhouse had announced innocently to a group of his fellow headmasters. Graves, assessing the passions of his schooldays, agrees with this distinction between " 'amorousness' (by which he meant a sentimental falling in love with younger boys) and eroticism, or adolescent lust. The intimacy that frequently took place was very seldom between an elder boy and the object of his affection—that would have spoiled the romantic illusion—but almost always between boys of the same age who were not in love, but used each other as convenient sex instruments."[38] On one occasion, for example, Graves and a boxing partner both exerted themselves with exceptional vigor, and his opponent refused to go down for the count. "I discovered that he, like myself, was conscious of Dick watching the fight."[39]

"I went through one of the worst quarters of an hour of my life on Dick's account," he reports. "When the master who sang in the choir warned me about exchanging glances with Dick in chapel I had been infuriated. But when one of the choir-boys told me that he had seen the master surreptitiously kissing Dick once, on a choir-treat, I went quite mad. Without asking for any details or confirmation, I went to the master and told him that unless he resigned, I would report the matter to the Headmaster—he already had a reputation in the school for this sort of thing and kissing boys was a criminal offense."[40] The master vigorously denied the charge, and Dick, sent for, corroborated his friend's story. The master collapsed, promised to resign by the end of the term, and thanked young Graves for not going to the headmaster; a year later, in 1915, he was killed in the war. Dick meanwhile confessed that he had not been kissed at all, but saw that Graves was in a jam and helped him out. "It must," he concludes without much remorse, "have been some other member of the choir!"[41]

"Poetry and Dick were still almost all that really mattered,"[42] Graves recalls of this period in his life. But from this point, the memoir sets out on a tale of normalization. Graves left school, entered the army, began a distinguished war career, and moved, in tentative but deliberate stages, toward heterosexuality. In 1919, convalescing at Oxford, he "fell in love with Marjorie, a probationer nurse, though I did not tell her so at the time. My heart had remained whole, if numbed, since Dick's disappearance from it, yet I felt difficulty in adjusting myself to the experience of woman love."[43]

Not too long after that he married Nancy Nicholson, a feminist who objected to the presence of "obey" in the marriage service, wore trousers upon occasion, cut her hair short, and kept her name. He met her when she was only sixteen but already a very decided personality. She wanted, and subsequently had with him, four children, two boys and two girls.

"She had her way exactly," Graves reports in a passage startling for its juxtapositions and characteristic in its lack of emphasis, "but began to regret her marriage, as a breach of faith with herself—a concession to patriarchy. She wanted somehow to be dis-married—not by divorce, which was as bad as marriage—so that she and I could live together without any legal or religious obligation to do so." And then without pause he adds, "I met Dick again, for the last time, and I found him disagreeably pleasant. He was up at Oxford now, about to enter the diplomatic service, and so greatly changed that it seemed absurd to have ever suffered on his account. Yet the caricature likeness to the boy I had loved persisted."[44]

Invoked thus as a revenant, "greatly changed," already apparently expunged from Graves's erotic imagination, Dick disappears from the narrative, and ultimately Nancy does, too. (She and Graves subsequently divorced and he married again, producing another four children with his second wife.) But Dick's disappearance leaves a trace—the trace of an erasure.

In real life Dick was a man by the name of G. H. Johnstone, known to his friends as "Peter." The nickname was given him by Graves, and had been his pet name for his own younger brother. In the 1929 edition of *Good-bye to All That* Graves reported receiving news of a court case that linked Peter Johnstone to a "certain proposal" made to a corporal in a Canadian regiment. "This news," he wrote, "was nearly the end of me. I decided that [Johnstone] had been driven out of his mind by the war." In short, "It would be easy to think of him as dead."[45]

According to his nephew and biographer, Richard Perceval Graves, it was this news that initially shocked Robert Graves into resolute heterosexuality. "Robert was relieved to recall his fleeting love affair with Marjorie. It proved to him that although, like many young men, he had gone through what he now described as a 'pseudo-homosexual' phase, his natural instincts were heterosexual."

In his remarks on schoolboy "pseudo-homosexuality" in the 1927 edition of his memoirs, Graves had written originally, "Many boys never recover from this perversion. I only recovered by a shock at the age of twenty-one. For every one born homo-sexual there are at least ten permanent pseudo-homo-sexuals made by the public school system. . . ."[46] But the shock of Dick's brush with the law is edited out of the revised edition of 1957. The personal reminiscence, "I only recovered by a shock at the age of twenty-one," is deleted from the passage, so that it now read "Many boys never recover from this perversion. For every one born homosexual . . ." (In the years between editions, the hyphen in homosexual had also disappeared, so that the word "homosexual" integrated itself as an identity, while Graves had removed himself from its immediate vicinity.)

The changes, it is reasonable to think, took place for reasons that may be prudential rather than prudish. "I wonder how my publishers escaped a libel action," Graves speculates in the Prologue to the 1957 edition. By this time he was a poet, a scholar and translator of classical literature, and a famous man. And the fifties were a time less hospitable to sexual frankness and homosexual reminiscences than the more open-minded twenties. Still, we are perhaps entitled to see his progress from pseudo-homosexual to paterfamilias as a story, at least in part, of being scared straight.

Officially Normal

> And let the reader refuse to be shocked for one further and even more important reason. We are dealing with young men who are in a state of transition. In most cases these odd manifestations of the spirit seem but temporary. . . . We become normal when we go down.
>
> —*Terence Greenidge,* Degenerate Oxford?[47]

"It was not natural that men of different characters and tastes should be intimate," reflects a Cambridge dean in E. M. Forster's posthumously published novel *Maurice,* "and although undergraduates, unlike school-boys, are officially normal, the dons exercised a certain amount of watch-fulness, and felt it right to spoil a love affair when they could."[48]

In *Maurice,* the story of a young man, not unlike Forster himself, coming to terms with his homosexuality in the public-school and university cul-ture of England before World War I, the word "normal" functions as an index of prohibited desire. Maurice is in love with his Cambridge friend Clive Durham, with whom he has worked out, after their departure from the university, a largely platonic, deeply passionate arrangement. Their families know each other; they spend Wednesdays and weekends together, though not in the same bed, or even as it turns out in the same bedroom. Maurice, says his mother indulgently, "is a regular old bachelor."[49]

Regular. Normal. "Officially normal." The dean's sociological assump-tions have built into them an empirical skepticism, since "officially nor-mal" in effect means potentially "abnormal," and the love affairs the dons love to spoil are frequent enough to be both recognized and pleasurably thwarted. Furthermore, what is "normal" for university students is appar-ently "abnormal" for schoolboys, for whom the abnormal is, by implica-tion, the norm. Like the regular old bachelor, the schoolboy is permitted his same-sex affections. To officialdom, as personified by the dean (who sends Maurice down), this is a borderline whose limits are known and respected.

"Male and female! Ah wonderful!" a schoolmaster had enthused to the boy Maurice, informing him of the mysteries of marital sex (for Maurice, as a boy without a father, was deemed in need of manly education). "You can't understand it now, you will some day, and when you do understand it remember the poor pedagogue who put you on the track."

"I think I shall not marry," replied the young Maurice immediately, to which his genial benefactor responded by inviting "you and your wife to dinner with my wife and me" ten years later. The cross-generational gesture of intimacy has its intended effect. "Maurice was flattered and began to contemplate marriage."[50]

Ten years later Maurice has long ceased his contemplation, but for Clive Durham it is a different matter. "Against my will I have become normal. I cannot help it," he writes Maurice from Greece, the ironic site of his return to heterosexuality.[51] "There had been no warning—just a blind alteration of the life spirit, just an announcement, 'You who loved men, will henceforward love women. Understand or not, it's the same to me.' "[52] Now he goes for drives and notices women, who notice him back. "How happy normal people made their lives!"[53] When the time comes for him to confront the skeptical and loving Maurice, Clive repeats in person his avowal in the letter ("I have become normal,—like other men")[54] and promptly falls in and then out of love with Maurice's look-alike sister Ada in the course of a turbulent hour.

"We love each other and know it," insists Maurice, but Clive replies determinedly, "If I love anyone it's Ada." He adds, "I take her as a random example," a qualification that understandably fails to mollify Maurice. But Clive thinks to himself that he has "found in her the exact need of his transition." "She was the compromise between memory and desire."[55]

Like most compromises, this one soon fails to satisfy, and he concludes as he walks out the door that "he would not marry Ada—she had been transitional,"[56] but the clinical term matches his obsessive iteration of "normal" as a self-diagnosis that is also a self-fulfilling and finally self-satisfied prophecy. In retrospect, or rather in his own cryptoamnesic retrospect, Clive Durham turns out to be "normal" after all. He marries Anne Woods, stands for Parliament, and becomes a priggish young squire with prematurely thinning hair. And what of Maurice? He is pursued by the specter of the normal, and therefore of marriage. Confronted with the suggestion that Ada might replace him in Clive's affections, he loses his temper: "Except on one point his temperament was normal, and he behaved as would the average man who after two years of happiness had been betrayed by his wife."[57] Clive is the "wife" in this artless figure. To keep Clive, or at least to keep from losing him completely, Maurice declares, with perfect untruthfulness, his own intentions.

> "The fact is I'm hoping to be married," said Maurice, the words flying from him as if they had independent life.
> "I'm awfully glad," said Clive, dropping his eyes. "Maurice, I'm awfully glad. It's the greatest thing in the world, perhaps the only one—"

Why does Clive drop his eyes, a common gesture of shyness and flirtation in women—at least women in literature? Maurice's declaration reassures him, renders moot and invisible their previous passion. Or: Maurice's declaration pains him; he is lying when he says he is glad.

His eyes rose. "Oh, Maurice. I'm so glad. It's very good of you to tell me—it's what I've always wished for you."

"I know you have."[58]

Clive is pleased by Maurice's news "because it rounded off his own position. He hated queerness, Cambridge, the Blue Room [the study in which they exchanged kisses and ideas about Greek philosophy at Clive's family home], certain glades in the park were—not tainted, there had been nothing disgraceful—but rendered subtly ridiculous." Since his own marriage to Anne he had "thought of confessing to her about Maurice," but their sex life was always conducted in silence. "Despite an elaborate education, no one had told her about sex."

"It was always without a word. . . . So much could never be mentioned. He never saw her naked, nor she him. They ignored the reproductive and the digestive functions. So there would never be any question of this episode of his immaturity"—that is, any mention of Maurice. "It was unmentionable. It didn't stand between him and her. She stood between him and it, and on second thoughts he was glad."[59]

Clive feels "purified" by Maurice's avowal, and in a burst of emotion— "Dare he borrow a gesture from the past?"—kisses his friend's hand.

He rushes to tell Anne of Maurice's intention, making for himself a threesome of their two twosomes, since the couple immediately begin to conspire with Maurice for the success of his (nonexistent) courtship. "There was to be a laughing open secret about this girl in town, who had almost accepted his offer of marriage but not quite. It didn't matter how ill he looked or how queerly he behaved, he was officially a lover, and they interpreted everything to their satisfaction and found him delightful."[60] Clive's own "normality" is shored up by Maurice's against the "queerness" he wants so much to repudiate.

Deeply unsettled by Clive's kiss (which he finds both "trivial and prudish"),[61] Maurice flees to London and a consultation with a hypnotist. "When he was shut into the [hypnotist's] waiting room with *Punch* the sense of the normal grew stronger. . . . He wanted a woman to secure him socially and diminish his lust and bear his children."[62] "I shall make suggestions to you which will (we hope) remain and become part of your normal state when you wake," says the hypnotist soothingly.[63] But any progress Maurice might make toward this "normal state" is abruptly curtailed, at least in the hypnotist's view, by his subsequent erotic involvement with Clive's gamekeeper Alec Scudder. "By pleasuring the body Maurice had . . . confirmed his spirit in its perversion and cut himself off from the congregation of normal man."[64]

Alec Scudder, we should note, is the one manifest bisexual in Forster's novel, writing in a letter to Maurice that "It is natural to want a girl, you cannot go against human nature. . . . I have never come like that to a gentleman before." (He also writes menacingly that *"I know about you and Mr. Durham"*—the emphasis in the letter is his—leading Maurice to take fleeting pleasure in the fact that "Clive hadn't quite kept out of the mud after all.")[65] But for Scudder, as for Maurice, the relationship between the men is not just sex, but love.

The question of the "normal" arises once more when Maurice goes to Southampton to see Scudder off to the Argentine on a ship called the *Normannia*—the name suggests not only "Norman" but "normal" and "man," and it is the path not taken for Scudder, despite Maurice's despairing conviction that "when he got out to his new life he would forget his escapade with a gentleman and in time he would marry." "No amount of insight would prevent the *Normannia* from sailing"[66]—but it sails without Alec.

At the dock, waiting to say goodbye, Maurice finds himself greeted by the clergyman from Scudder's parish, and once again thrust back into the emotional condition of a schoolboy. " 'Now this is very kind of you,' said the clergyman. . . . He spoke as one social worker to another, but Maurice thought there was a veil over his voice." "How come you to know so precisely when his boat sailed?" Maurice "tried to reply—two or three normal sentences would save him—but no words would come, and his underlip trembled like an unhappy boy's." "The trembling spread all over his body and his clothes stuck to him. He seemed to be back at school, defenceless."

What did the clergyman know? Maurice had once assumed "that a white-faced parson in a cassock could never have conceived of masculine love," but now he "feared and hated" his clerical companion, who goes on to remark darkly that Scudder "has been guilty of sensuality." There is an ominous pause. "With women," he continues. "I have reason to believe that he spent that missing night in London."[67]

"What sort of man is that keeper of yours," Maurice asks Clive with superb nonchalance. "Straight?" He trembled as he asked this supreme question.

"Scudder?" replies Clive. "A little too smart to be straight. However, Anne would say I'm being unfair. You can't expect our standard of honesty in servants, any more than you can expect loyalty or gratitude."[68]

At the novel's close, as Maurice announces his passion for Alec and disappears, never to be seen or heard of again, Clive, who has been editing political broadsides, turns back to his work: "He waited for a little in the alley, then returned to the house, to correct his proofs and to devise some method of concealing the truth from Anne."[69]

The last note is thus what would become a cliché about bisexuals, the married man's deception of his wife. Clive has disavowed Maurice, yet we are led to believe, by Forster's visionary and slightly overripe prose, that the emotional melody lingers on. Maurice, like the beloved schoolboy in Robert Graves's memoir, becomes a revenant, an ever-returning ghost of passion past. "To the end of his life Clive was not sure of the exact moment of [Maurice's] departure, and with the approach of old age he grew uncertain whether the moment had yet occurred. The Blue Room would glimmer, ferns undulate. Out of some eternal Cambridge his friend began beckoning to him, clothed in the sun, and shaking out the scents and sounds of the May term."[70]

Chapter 14

Erotic Education

It is well known how easily erotic wishes develop out of emotional relations of a friendly character, based upon appreciation and admiration (compare Molière's "Kiss me for the love of Greek"), between a master and a pupil, between a performer and a delighted listener, and especially in the case of women.

—*Sigmund Freud, "Group Psychology and the Analysis of the Ego"* [1]

The pupil and the master exchanged a longish glance in which there was a consciousness of many more things that are usually touched upon, even tacitly, in such a relation.

—*Henry James, "The Pupil"* [2]

I expect you'll be becoming a schoolmaster, sir. That's what most of the gentlemen does, sir, that gets sent down for indecent behavior.

—*Evelyn Waugh, Decline and Fall* [3]

We Are All Greeks

The quest for a classical education, for a firm grounding in the Greek and Roman classics, has lately provoked much nostalgia among gloomy traditionalists who regard something they call "multiculturalism" as the enemy of something they call "culture." Earlier in this century T. S. Eliot could memorably encapsulate and inadvertently parody some of these arguments in a dialogue he imagined taking place between a naive student and a wise teacher: Why should we study the classics, asks the student, brashly, when we know so much more than they did? Precisely, replies the teacher with satisfaction. And they are what we know. [4]

This is not the place to address the complexities of the current debate about the literary canon and the so-called culture wars. And in any case, the reader may well be thinking, this turf war within academia, whether it is a global struggle or a minor skirmish, seems to have nothing to do with our topic, bisexuality. Precisely, we might reply with satisfaction. Bisexuality is what we do not want to know—about the past, about historical understandings of that elusive and irresistible entity called "love"— and about those personages, created of bits and pieces of learning, misprision, cultural bricolage, and DNA, whom it pleases us to call "ourselves."

As classicists and humanists have, for the most part, acknowledged, the Greek and Roman classics are not without their pitfalls when it comes to creating an unquestionably heterosexual society. One of the early scenes of *Maurice,* rendered indelibly comic in both the film and the novel, is the moment in the dean's translation class when one of the youthful translators stumbles on a suspect passage. "Mr. Cornwallis observed in a flat toneless voice: 'Omit: a reference to the unspeakable vice of the Greeks.'"[5]

Clive, still in the first fine flush of his undergraduate zeal, condemns this to Maurice as "hypocrisy," an activity of censoring for which the pedagogue should be fired. "I regard it as a point of pure scholarship. The Greeks, or most of them, were that way inclined, and to omit it is to omit the mainstay of Athenian society." To cap off this summary judgment he asks Maurice carelessly, but clearly expecting an affirmative answer, "You've read the *Symposium?*"[6]

For another Cambridge undergraduate of the period, E. M. Forster's friend Lytton Strachey, reading the *Symposium* had been a revelation. He read it in his schoolboy years, he said, "with a rush of mingled pleasure and pain," filled with "surprise, relief, and fear to know that what I feel now was felt 2,000 years ago in glorious Greece."[7] Strachey's love affairs at school were "almost certainly platonic and inconclusive," says his biographer—and the relationship between Plato with a capital P and highly charged "platonic relationships" with a small p is part of a cultural history of emotion we have tended to gloss over, if not forget. "Platonic relationships" are powerful in part because they are unconsummated—they stretch out the tension, the expectation, the hope, the small pleasures of eye contact and half-smile. To consummate them, however devoutly that consummation may be wished, is in some sense to bring them to an end, because the pleasure is in the waiting, in the denial or the pretense of denial of desire. And the go-between for many such relationships has been, as it was in Clive and Maurice's case, Plato, or rather, "Plato," a book, a living remnant of the "classical past."

That books can be dangerous is nothing new, of course; this same Plato, or one version of him, is famous for warning against the dangers of poetry. Literary theorist Jonathan Dollimore, who writes on sexual dissidence and perversion, remarked in measured tones during a conversation "my whole fascination with homoeroticism began when I started reading books." He is not sure "whether that means that books corrupted me—and that's my preferred narrative—or whether it's the fact that books liberated some potentiality, which I think is more likely the truth." "But," he says, "I love the idea that books corrupted me! The great books."[8]

The great books. Precisely. They are what we know. "Isn't it really rather dangerous to let boys read Plato if one is desirous that they should accept conventional moralities?" wondered A. C. Benson, the biographer of aesthete Walter Pater, at the end of the last century.[9] And philosopher Allan Bloom, a teacher of Plato lamenting the falling-off of what he regarded as true intellectual engagement in the universities of post-sixties America, complained that "It is much more difficult today to attach the classic books to any experience or felt need the students have."[10] Cultural critics have sometimes noticed an irony here. As one observed, while "the likes of Dinesh D'Souza, . . . William Bennett and . . . Camille Paglia," ardent defenders of "cultural literacy and curricular correctness," have seen the classics of ancient Greece and Rome as "a bulwark against a whole host of pretenders large and small: post-this and post-that, multiculturalism, feminist theory, women's studies, and, more recently, lesbian and gay studies," in fact "the texts and theories they so vigorously promote have been at the forefront of queer theory and lesbian and gay studies."[11]

Classical Greek protocols of education regularly incorporated relations between boys (*paides*) and men (*erastes*), from whose tutelary and philosophical engagements we derive not only our word *paideia,* the title of a much-honored book on the ideals of Greek culture,[12] but also the word "pederasty," a much-dishonored term for erotic relations between adult men and children.

Modern terms like "homosexual," "lesbian," and "bisexual" are anachronistic when used to describe erotic relations in the classical world. Even "same-sex" and "opposite-sex," less historically inaccurate, are not really good terms, because as many scholars have recently emphasized, the sociosexual world of classical antiquity was organized by "social gender," not by anatomy. The crucial distinctions for men were not between "homosexual" and "heterosexual" but between inserter or penetrator and insertee.

In classical Athens an adult man could penetrate any social inferior—a boy, a woman, a foreigner, a slave of either sex—but would regard it as shameful to be penetrated. As a boy grew older he underwent a change in sexual role, from *paides* or *eromenos* (beloved) to *erastes,* lover, though this change was not instantaneous but gradual, passing through the stage of *neaniskoi,* young men in the middle years of fifteen to twenty-five, who were both active and passive.[13] A grown man when he married might have sexual relations with both *paides* and women.

"Non-educational, vulgar love affairs" between boys and men were guarded against by Athenian law,[14] but consensual relations were not outlawed if the lover were old enough and well chosen as a mentor rather than just a figure of physical desire.

Though it has often been suggested that the Greeks "were not *erastai* all their lives,"[15] but oriented their adult sexuality predominantly toward relations with women, whether the women were wives, concubines, courtesans, or prostitutes, many scholars now argue that in practice things did not work out quite so simply, and that relationships between grown men and both boys and women persisted through the adult lives of male citizens. In any case, ancient Greek education, on which our idealized notions of a "classical education" depends, allowed for, and indeed encouraged, spiritual and philosophical relationships between grown men and boys.

"The Greeks were certainly bisexual, in the sense that when they were boys they were loved by a man, while in the first years of their own adulthood they preferred to make love to adolescent boys," declares one scholar of the ancient world. "Later in life they chose women, and even when they were married they were allowed to have their boy lovers." The Romans, too, it is said, "felt that it was normal for a man to have sexual relations with other men as well as with women."[16]

Gore Vidal comments on our discomfort in encountering so fluid a concept of the "normal" among the ancients:

> It is an underlying assumption of twentieth-century America that human beings are either heterosexual or, through some arresting of normal psychic growth, homosexual, with very little traffic back and forth. To us, the norm is heterosexual; the family is central; all else is deviation, pleasing or not depending on one's own tastes and moral preoccupations. Suetonius reveals a very different world. His underlying assumption is that man is bisexual and that given complete freedom to love—or perhaps more to the point in the case of the Caesars, to violate—others, he will do so, going blithely from male to female as fancy dictates. . . . It is an odd experience for a contemporary to read of Nero's simultaneous passion for both a man and a woman. Something seems wrong. It must be one or the other, not both.[17]

But is "bisexual" really the appropriate term? "In the case of classical Athens," David Halperin points out, "erotic desires and sexual object-choices in antiquity were generally not determined by a typology of anatomical sexes (male versus female), but rather by the social articulation of power (superordinate versus subordinate)." The distinction between homosexuality and heterosexuality "had no meaning for the classical Athenians; there were not, so far as they knew, two different kinds of 'sexuality,' two different structured psychosexual states or modes of affective orientation, but a single form of sexual experience which all free adult males shared—making due allowance for variations in individual tastes, as one might for individual palates."[18]

This is not to say that "all Greek men must have felt such indifference," but rather to observe that, on the evidence of many ancient documents, Greek commentators were reluctant "to predict, in any given instance, the sex of another man's beloved merely on the basis of that man's past sexual behavior or previous pattern of sexual object choice."[19] Although scholars sometimes described "the cultural formation underlying this apparent refusal by Greek males to discriminate categorically among sexual objects on the basis of anatomical sex" as a "bisexuality of penetration" or a "heterosexuality indifferent to its object."[20] Halperin contends that it makes more sense not to think of it as a "sexuality" in the modern sense at all.

Difficult as it may be to conceptualize from a twentieth-century perspective supersaturated with the language of "homo-" and "heterosexuality," modern and postmodern notions of "sexual identity" are anachronistic when applied to the ancient Greeks. There were thus no "homosexuals" in classic Athens, but there were no "heterosexuals" (or, indeed, in a modern sense, "bisexuals") either.

In any case, the inconvenient fact is that eroticism, *eros* in its broadest sense, was a constitutive aspect of ancient teaching and learning, as well as of Greek and Roman texts from Plato to Martial. Bloom writes wistfully about a loss in today's classrooms of "the enthusiasm and curiosity of young Glaucon in Plato's *Republic,* whose *eros* makes him imagine that there are splendid satisfactions in store for him about which he does not wish to be fooled and for knowledge of which he seeks a teacher." Here is what Glaucon's teacher, Socrates, tells him about the all-encompassing nature of love.

> It does not become a lover to forget that all adolescents in some sort sting and stir the amorous lover of youth and appear to him deserving of his attention and desirable. Is not that your "reaction" to the fair? One, because his nose is tiptilted, you will praise as piquant, the beak of another you pronounce right royal, the intermediate type you say strikes the harmonious mean, the swarthy are of manly aspect, the white are children of the gods divinely fair, and as for honey-hued, do you suppose the very word is anything but the euphemistic invention of some lover who can feel no distaste for sallowness when it accompanies the blooming time of youth?[21]

It is the absence of this "blooming time of youth," that Bloom-as-Socrates regrets in the mute inglorious Glaucons of his own time, indifferent as they seem to be to philosophy and the liberal arts, spouting instead "nothing but cliches, superficialities, the material of satire."[22] "The refinement of the mind's eye that permits it to see the delicate distinctions among men, among their deeds and their motives, and constitutes real taste, is impossible without the assistance of literature in the grand style."[23] And that grand style is to be found above all in the Greek and Roman classics.

"We are all Greeks," claimed the English Romantic poet Shelley in his preface to *Hellas.* In a disquisition on love in ancient Greece he protested against the concealment of homoeroticism in ancient poetry by the editors and translators of his time.[24] The first English translation of the *Symposium,* published in two parts in 1761 and 1767, had boldly and simply changed the genders of key figures—much as editors of Shakespeare's sonnets would do in the same period, for the same reasons. Thus the Greek word *eromenos,* meaning "male beloved," became "mistress," and the "army of lovers" that would have its historical counterpart in the famous Theban Band of warrior-companions becomes, by implication, a bevy of knights and ladies. The word "boy" in Greek was simply translated as "maiden" or "woman," thus making same-sex love invisible to the non-Greek reading eye.[25] As the example of the Greek tutor in *Maurice* suggests, even when one could read Greek after a fashion, one was often encouraged or instructed to avert one's eyes from the quite literally "unspeakable vice of the Greeks."

In Germany, classical scholarship was held in such high esteem that frank translations, and indeed "learned essays on Greek pederasty," did appear during the course of the nineteenth century, helping "to pave the way for the German homosexual emancipation movement that was born with the twentieth century."[26] Some decades later Allan Bloom would note with approval the "use of Plato" in Thomas Mann's *Death in Venice,* in which the pederastic obsession of the old man Aschenbach for a beautiful young boy on the beach is brought sharply to his own consciousness by his memory of quotations from the *Phaedrus,* "probably one of the things Aschenbach was supposed to have read as a schoolboy." "Plato had been incorporated into the Greek tradition," writes Bloom, "but its content, discourse on the love of a man for a boy, was not supposed to affect him." That it *does,* that Aschenbach's eroticism is stirred and confirmed by classical example, seems to Bloom a sign of intellectual health. "Plato's respectable dialogue is the intermediary between Aschenbach's good conscience and his carnality," he writes. Unlike fellow conservatives William Bennett and Roger Kimball, Bloom *is* able to read what the classics he promotes have to say. "Plato found a way of expressing and beautifying, of sublimating, perverse sexuality."[27] To sublimate is not only "respectable" but beautiful: It is, and Bloom is quite right here, the way of the teacher. We are all Greeks.

FANTASIES OF BISEXUALITY

(Clockwise from top left) Three in a bed: cover of *Genre* magazine, 1992. The deceiving bisexual husband from a pulp fiction novel of 1946 (note the wife's prominently displayed wedding and engagement rings). Sex unlimited: photograph chosen by *Mirabella* magazine illustrating an article on bisexuality, 1994.

BISEXUAL BLOOMSBURY

Vita Sackville-West (*top left and right*) and
Harold Nicolson each had relationships with
same-sex partners in the course of their long
and happy marriage. Among Vita's lovers were
Rosamund Grosvenor (pictured, *above*, with Vita,
Harold, and Lord Sackville), Violet Trefusis (*middle
right*), and Virginia Woolf (*right*).

Painter Dora Carrington fell in love with Lytton Strachey, whose erotic preference was emphatically for men. The pair (pictured, *above*, with Strachey's brother, James, at right) lived together for years, even when Carrington married another painter, Ralph Partridge. Among Strachey's friends was the economist John Maynard Keynes, whose several love affairs with men—including artist Duncan Grant—were followed by his marriage to Russian ballerina Lydia Lopokova (*middle*). Strachey and Keynes are pictured (*below*) with philosopher Bertrand Russell.

TAOS: THE WILD WEST?

Painter and photographer Georgia O'Keeffe, married to Alfred Stieglitz, had brief affairs with a number of women, including Beck Strand (pictured, *top left*, with O'Keeffe), and Taos doyenne Mabel Dodge Luhan *(above)* whose relationships with men and women were legendary. Luhan's husband, Native American Tony Luhan *(middle right)*, was a charismatic figure in Taos society. Painters Frida Kahlo and Diego Rivera *(top right)* spent time in Taos, as did D. H. Lawrence and his wife, Frieda *(bottom right)*. Kahlo's affairs with women interested Rivera; Lawrence's relationships with young men may or may not have been sexual, though Mabel Dodge Luhan thought—or hoped?—they were.

HARLEM BI DAY AND NIGHT

(Clockwise from top left) Blues legends Gertrude "Ma" Rainey and Bessie Smith, pictured with her husband, Jack Gee. Writers Jean Toomer and Claude McKay. Yolande DuBois, daughter of sociologist and writer W. E. B. DuBois, with poet Countee Cullen during their brief but celebrated marriage (six months later Cullen left for Europe with the best man). Poet Langston Hughes and his friend, the writer Wallace Thurman; both had erotic relationships with men as well as women.

DOMESTIC BLISS?

(From the top) Cary Grant and Randolph Scott; Rock Hudson and Phyllis Gates; Judy Garland and Vincente Minnelli.

BI HIMSELF

Mick Jagger.

CELEBRITY THREES

(From the top) Madonna and Sandra Bernhard visit David Letterman; Marlene Dietrich with actresses Suzy Vernon (left) and Imperio Argentina; James Dean with Dick Davalos and Julie Harris on the set of *East of Eden*.

BI HERSELF

Janis Joplin.

PROFESSORS OF DESIRE

(Clockwise from top) Sigmund Freud
and best friend Wilhelm Fleiss; sexual
inversion experts Edith Lees Ellis and
Havelock Ellis; Alfred Kinsey
interviewing a female subject.

(From the top) A complex Oedipus: Laurence Olivier as Oedipus Rex. Medallion struck for Freud's fiftieth birthday, showing a bust of Freud on one side and Oedipus and the Sphinx on the reverse. Tiresias reports on his sex change to Jupiter and Juno (engraving after Hendrik Goltzius, c. 1615).

LITERARY BI LINES

(From the top) Oscar Wilde and lover Lord Alfred Douglas; Wilde's wife, Constance; writers W. H. Auden, Christopher Isherwood, and Stephen Spender; schoolboys Robert Graves (left) and G. H. "Peter" Johnstone at Charterhouse.

BI SOCIETY

(Clockwise from top left) Edna St. Vincent Millay, Nancy Cunard, H.D., Djuna Barnes.

BISEXUAL MARRIAGES

(Clockwise from top right)
Mary and John Cheever;
Leonard and Felicia Bernstein;
Paul and Jane Bowles;
cross-dressed married couple
Francis Vavra (left) and
Roxanna Rochette.

THE SHORTEST DISTANCE BETWEEN TWO
POINTS IS A TRIANGLE

Peter Finch, Glenda Jackson, and Murray Head in
Sunday, Bloody Sunday, 1971.

TRAUMATIC TRIANGLES

(Clockwise from top left) Shirley MacLaine, Audrey Hepburn, and James Garner in *The Children's Hour*, 1962; Hertha Thiele inspects her classmates' secret pin-up collection in *Maedchen in Uniform*, 1931; Maggie Smith, Robert Stevens, and Jane Carr in *The Prime of Miss Jean Brodie*, 1969; Sandy Dennis, Keir Dullea, and Anne Heywood in *The Fox*, 1968.

THREE'S COMPANY

(Clockwise from top left) Michael York, Liza Minnelli, and Helmut Griem in *Cabaret,* 1972; Mitchell Lichtenstein, Winston Chao, and May Chin in *The Wedding Banquet,* 1993; Richard E. Grant, Maria de Medeiros, and Fred Ward in *Henry and June,* 1990; Lara Flynn Boyle, Josh Charles, and Stephen Baldwin in *Threesome,* 1994.

WHAT IS A PAIR?

(From the top) The divided self: René Magritte's *Titanic Days (Les Jours gigantesques)*, 1928; Vincent van Gogh, *Shoes*, 1887; Janet Rickus, *Three Pears*, 1993.

◆

We are all Greeks. That claim of heritage was also an erotic claim in the life and writings of Shelley's friend and contemporary Lord Byron, the most famous bisexual of his time. At school at Harrow much of Byron's emotional life centered on his relations with younger boys, some of whom were described in the poems he wrote when he left Harrow for Cambridge University. "From the very first," Louis Crompton notes, "Byron's biographers were forced to take note of his large number of schoolboy favorites and the intensity of his passion for them."[28] John Cam Hobhouse, a lifelong friend who "undoubtedly knew more about Byron's bisexuality than anyone else of whom we have any record,"[29] scribbled in the margin of a biography published a few years after the poet's death that "the principal cause & motive of all these boyish friend[ships]" seemed to have been ignored or glossed over.

Byron's early poetry reflects his interest in both women and boys. The schoolboy verses may have been enhanced, in a literary way, by his reading of Greek and Latin classical literature in which love of boys was a common topic. With the publication of *Childe Harold's Pilgrimage,* which made him famous overnight, his bisexuality became part of his official poetic persona, for the volume contained his love poems to John Edlestone, the poems "To Thyrza," and a series of poems inspired by a brief affair with Constance Spencer Smith. One critic warned him against the fate of Orpheus (who was killed by the Bacchantes after he turned to the love of boys, having lost his beloved Eurydice for a second time), and Crompton notes the irony of the praise bestowed upon the poems to Edlestone as ideal expressions of love. "The paradox reveals how deep the need was in his personality to assert his identity as a bisexual."[30] As if to confirm this, Byron's next affair would be with Lady Caroline Lamb, a woman whose pleasure was to appear at his door in the costume of a male page.

Yet like the timid translators of Greek, Byron often chose the path of gender bowdlerization in his writing. He changed the genders in his poems, he made autobiographical notes that were ambiguous in their reference, he wrote letters in which the name and gender of the beloved were concealed by a code name.[31] In short, in literary terms, he passed as a heterosexual: a textual heterosexual.

Now what I want to suggest here is that the history of rewriting, encoding, and editing the "classics" in order that they should tell an orderly tale, which is to say, most often a tale with a heterosexual ending, has been repeated, compulsively, in the history of the protocols of *modern* education in England and America. The "secret" identity of Plato's *Phaedrus* and other paradigmatically "homosexual" texts has been a schoolboy's—and schoolgirl's—open sesame for years, as is clear in a book like Mary Renault's *The Charioteer,* where the *Phaedrus* has the same effect upon young Laurie as the *Symposium* had on the youthful Lytton Strachey. "Greek love" has been a familiar euphemism, if it is a euphemism, for a long time.

But the heritage of same-sex and opposite-sex eroticisms as both independently and collectively describing the nature of *eros,* like the story of Greek education as taking cognizance and advantage of the fundamental erotic nature of the pedagogical relation, is a story that not everyone wants to hear. As many of the texts we are about to examine make evident, the story that is preferred, the story that is routinely told and ostensibly believed, is the story of "experimentation," "infatuation," "substitution," and "conversion," in which same-sex relationships among students, or erotic tensions between students and teachers of the same sex, are explained as not real, not serious, not permanent.

It is worth noting that the rewriting that takes place can be "gay" or "straight." We begin with the "end" of the story, and retell it so that it "comes out right," producing, as if inevitably from the materials of a life, the person we (think we) are now. Freud called this "secondary revision" when he came to talk about how dreams work: It imposes a plausible narrative of continuity and logic over the heterogeneity of thoughts—and desires.

But why should we set aside the feelings, heterosexual or homosexual, that overwhelm us just at the time when we are "coming out" to ourselves as sexual persons, as people who have bodies and fantasies and desires? To call such feelings, as Havelock Ellis at one point tries to do, merely "love-fictions" or the "play of sexual love" is to hide from ourselves. It is simply emotional hypocrisy.

Something quite crucial is being *looked through* rather than *looked at,* described as part of one or another kind of erotic love, as if there were only two—as if life, like digital technology, were indisputably binary: gay *or* straight, male *or* female, immature *or* mature, child *or* adult. How many people, looking at themselves and the course of their lives, see only one or the other? What is forgotten, repressed, erased, or denied here, once again, is the bisexuality of a lifetime: the capacity to love, to desire, to be in love with, to be obsessed with, men and women, boys and girls, same- and opposite-sex lovers, whether that love is physically realized or remains, perhaps even more powerfully, in the realm of desire. To call such desire if it is not acted upon "unfulfilled" or "disappointed" is, as I have already suggested, the most mistaken of notions. It is this very potential for loving, and for falling "in love," that makes education possible.

A few important points seem to me to need making here, all of which have a direct bearing on bisexuality and pedagogy. First, that very often in such schoolboy and schoolgirl stories the erotic object is the *institution,* so that pedagogy and eroticism are natural, rather than unnatural, concomitants of one another; it is that very naturalness that requires them to be declared, *ex cathedra,* unnatural and out of bounds. By "institution" I mean here both the teacher and the school: Mr. (or Ms.) Chips and Alma Mater. The passion of returning alumni and alumnae is based as much upon fantasy as upon memory—a fact that has not been lost on institutional fund-raisers. What is learned in school is something between knowledge and desire, and often the desire, in Freud's phrase the "overestimation of the object," is necessary so that learning can take place.

Second, a related point, that the teacher's role as transferential object of the student's affections can be quite independent of his or her gender or sexuality, just as the analyst can stand in for either mother or father in the patient's psychoanalytic transference. The erotic center of the attraction is somewhere between wanting to *be* the teacher and wanting to *have* him or her. Thus for example the schoolboys in the film *Dead Poets Society* want desperately to *be* the young Mr. Keating, and thus are driven to revive the long-defunct Dead Poets Society he founded. But they also want to *have* Mr. Keating, whom they address unselfconsciously (at his invitation) as "O Captain My Captain," a borrowing from Walt Whitman with erotic undertones the film does not wish (or bother) to explore. A good teacher, Keating knows that the best way to get them to fall in love with poetry is to get them to fall in love with his own passion for it. Keating's own "heterosexuality" is certified by the photo of his girlfriend on the desk of his study, an image that effectively comes between him and the emotionally needy student who drops in to consult him. For all of its avuncular nature, however, the scene between them is highly charged, and leads, however circuitously, to the boy's flouting of his father's wishes in favor of his teacher's, and thus to his suicide. There need not (necessarily) be any *sex* between teachers and students for there to be lots of *eroticism*.

A third point, perhaps at the present time the most contestatory, is that while particular *characters* and *sexual practices* in the best-known school narratives may be importantly identified as lesbian or gay, and scandals of revelation and self-knowledge in these narratives may likewise be structured around lesbian or gay identity, the *plots* in which they are contained are very often *bisexual* plots, *whether or not there is a "bisexual" character in the text.* By "school narratives" I mean those works, from *The Charioteer* and *A Separate Peace* to *Maedchen in Uniform, Tea and Sympathy,* and *Brideshead Revisited,* in which "coming of age" often seems virtually the same as "coming out," and where the deep passions of students for one another or for their teachers is honestly acknowledged and explored. Gay film historian Parker Tyler, who deplored the film of *Tea and Sympathy* (in which a gay-seeming "straight" boy is saved from a life of self-doubt or worse by being taken to the dormitory housemother on whom he has a crush), wrote quite accurately that the "real" homosexuality of the film was "the statutory ambisexed sadism of the schoolboys" rather than the allegations of effeminacy against the long-haired, musically inclined hero. "What is an old-fashioned academic institution," he insists, "is made to appear in *Tea and Sympathy* as a baseless 'criminal conspiracy.' "[32]

The reason this will be viewed in some quarters as contestatory is that it may seem to unmake a newly recognized genre, and appear in so doing to critique or challenge advances in gay, lesbian, or queer canon recovery, or even to make gayness or lesbianism "disappear" just at the point when they have finally been accorded long-denied recognition. That is very far from my intention. But it seems to me crucial to read these novels, stories, and films within the context of the heterosexualizing world of which they are themselves a sometimes unwilling but never oblivious part. That all schools are "normal schools"—that is, schools that teach teaching and schools that teach "normality"—means, as every school narrative knows full well, that to talk about schooldays is to talk about the "abnormal" as the norm.

Three into Two Won't Go

In the introduction to a collected volume of her plays, Lillian Hellman describes herself as a model for Mary, the schoolgirl in *The Children's Hour*. Mary spreads a rumor about her female teachers' "unnatural" relations after furtively reading Théophile Gautier's erotic bisexual novel *Mademoiselle de Maupin*. Hellman "reached back" into her childhood "and found the day *I* finished *Mlle de Maupin;* the day *I* faked a heart attack; the day *I* saw an arm get twisted. And I thought again of the world of the half-remembered, the half-observed, the half-understood."[33] Like Mrs. Mortar and Martha Dobie, Hellman comments in her personal manuscript notes on the play, Mary is "abnormal."[34] In fact the word "abnormal" in reference to all three characters appears frequently throughout the notes, always denoting "incompleteness, ambiguity, and marginality."[35]

Was Hellman in her own mind "abnormal"? The speaker of the "Julia" section of *Pentimento* confesses to "the love I had for her, too strong and too complicated to be defined as only the sexual yearnings of one girl for another. And yet certainly that was there."[36] But when a male acquaintance accuses the two women of having a lesbian relationship ("everybody knew about Julia and me") she slaps him in the face, turns over the table, and goes home. In her memoir *An Unfinished Woman* Hellman quotes with evident pride Ernest Hemingway's remark: "So you have *cojones,* after all. I didn't think so upstairs. But you have *cojones,* after all."[37] Lillian Hellman was determined to make her mark among the male authors and playwrights without being labeled, as assertive women often were, a "mannish lesbian." "Throughout her life," as one critic points out, "Hellman worked to construct the public myth of her aggressive heterosexuality, a myth that far overshadows the suggestions of bisexuality that occasionally surface in her memoirs."[38]

Yet *The Children's Hour* is bisexual, not because any of its characters is
—though my candidate for "the" bisexual in the plot would be Martha,
who confesses to her friend Karen that "I have loved you the way they
said" and is thus generally described as a lesbian—but rather because it
sets up a dynamic of choice between living with a man and living with a
woman.

Karen Wright and Martha Dobie are friends who run a boarding school
for girls. Dr. Joseph Cardin is Karen's long-term boyfriend, and shortly
after the play begins, he officially becomes her fiancé. When Martha asks
whether this means that "we won't be taking our vacation together," Karen
replies, "Of course we will. The three of us."

Martha had been looking forward to it being "just you and me—the
way we used to at college," but Karen is, as Hellman's stage direction says,
"cheerful," or, we might even say, oblivious, in her revision of the plan:
"Well, now there will be three of us. That'll be fun, too."[39] Martha is not
so sure.

What she is quite sure about is that "The three of us can't live together"
—but she is referring to a different triad, a group of three *women:* Karen,
Martha, and Martha's overbearing and ineffectual aunt, Lilly Mortar, a former actress who has been giving elocution lessons at the school. It is Mrs.
Mortar who first mentions the unmentionable, Martha's jealousy of Joe, in
retort to the suggestion that the younger women will pay her to leave:

> MRS. MORTAR: Every time that man comes into this house, you have a
> fit. It seems like you just can't stand the idea of them being together.
> God knows what you'll do when they get married. You're jealous of
> him, that's what it is.
> MARTHA: I'm very fond of Joe, and you know it.
> MRS. MORTAR: You're fonder of Karen, and I know that. And it's unnatu-
> ral, just as unnatural as it can be. You don't like their being together.
> You were always like that even as a child. If you had a little girl friend,
> you always got mad when she liked anybody else. Well, you'd better
> get a beau of your own now—a woman of your age.[40]

"Unnatural" is this play's code word for lesbian desire. When a third
threesome, the spiteful schoolgirl Mary Tilford and her two roommates,
come to discuss this conversation, which the roommates have overheard,
they focus on the meaning of the term:

> PEGGY: Well, Mortar said that Dobie was jealous of them, that she was
> like that when she was a little girl, and that she'd better get herself a
> beau of her own because it was unnatural, and that she never wanted
> anybody to like Miss Wright and that was unnatural. . . .
> MARY: What'd she mean Dobie was jealous?
> PEGGY: What's unnatural?

EVELYN: Un for not. Not natural.
PEGGY: It's funny, because everybody gets married.
MARY: A lot of people don't—they're too ugly.[41]

Mary, it seems, subscribes to the "can't get a man/becomes a man-hater" school of antifeminist, or antilesbian, rhetoric. What does she know about lesbian love? Whatever she's read in *Mademoiselle de Maupin,* a novel which has been described as "lesbian-themed"[42] but which could equally well be called "bisexual," since its heroine delights in having both a male and a female lover, and says so quite explicitly near the close: "My dream would be to have each sex in turn, and to satisfy my dual nature: man today, woman tomorrow."[43] The audience is led to think that Mary's own libidinous imagination has been stirred by her reading, that her fantasies of the two schoolmistresses together are a fiction concocted through reading a fiction.

But before she comes to tell her story to her doting and credulous grandmother, repeatedly invoking as she does so the key words "jealous" and "unnatural," Mary's own threesome is disbanded. Mary is the bad apple. "You and Evelyn never used to do things like this," Karen tells them. "We'll have to separate you three." Three threesomes, in each case volatile, unstable. But as unstable as they are, it is only when the triad is disrupted that catastrophe ensues. What does the man think? Dr. Cardin is not only Karen's fiancé but also Mary Tilford's relative. He broaches the question of his forthcoming marriage in a conversation with Martha that uses Mary as a straw-third, a way of introducing the subject of three.

CARDIN: Listen, friend, I'm marrying Karen, but I'm not writing Mary Tilford into the contract. *(Martha moves slightly. Cardin takes her by the shoulders and turns her around to face him again. His face is grave, his voice gentle)* Forget Mary for a minute. You and I have got something to fight about. Every time anything's said about marrying —about Karen marrying me—you— *(She winces)* There it is. I'm fond of you. I always thought you liked me. What is it? I know how fond you are of Karen, but our marriage oughtn't to make a great deal of difference—
MARTHA *(pushing his hands from her shoulders):* God damn you. I wish—*(She puts her face in her hands. Cardin watches her in silence, mechanically lighting a cigarette. When she takes her hands from her face, she holds them out to him. Contritely)* Joe, please, I'm sorry. I'm a fool, a nasty, bitter—
CARDIN *(takes her hands in one of his, patting them with his other hand):* Aw, shut up. *(He puts an arm around her, and she leans her head against his lapel. They are standing like that when Karen comes in. . . .)*

MARTHA *(to* Karen, *as she wipes her eyes):* Your friend's got a nice shoulder to weep on.[44]

Once the damaging accusation of "sinful sexual knowledge" between the two women is made, and Mary's grandmother impulsively (imperiously? sedulously? disastrously?) advises all her friends to withdraw their daughters from the Wright-Dobie school, the dimly chivalrous Dr. Cardin proposes that "the three of us"[45] leave the New England town of Lancet (Hellman's names are carefully chosen; this is a surgical knife that cuts both ways) and move to, of all places, Vienna, Freud's home town, where, it turns out, Cardin has done his medical training. But Karen is convinced that three into two won't go, that "It won't work . . . the two of us together." She suspects that he suspects her, that he thinks there may be truth in the story of lesbian love. Goaded by her, he asks the question, which is enough to convince her that he would always harbor doubts, despite her firm denial ("No. Martha and I have never touched each other"). In short, she lures him into giving her up. The end comes swiftly: Martha's confession ("I did love you. I do love you. I resented your marriage; maybe because I wanted you; maybe I wanted you all along; maybe I couldn't call it by a name . . . I've never loved a man. I never knew why before. Maybe it's that")[46] and suicide; Mrs. Mortar's verdict on finding the dead body ("It seems so queer—in the next room";)[47] Mrs. Tilford's arrival, recantation —her granddaughter has admitted the false accusation—and quest for absolution.

But Martha's suicide is not the only thing that can't be "fixed" here, can't be restored to the way it was. Even had she lived, as she does in the heterosexualized 1936 film version *These Three,* the arrangement so carefully cultivated by all three parties would not be recuperable. Its eroticism comes in fact from its unspoken nature, from the way in which erotic tension develops, triangularly, from unacted-upon desires. The moment the phrase "the three of us" is spoken as a reality, as an explicit arrangement for the future rather than a pleasurably "accidental" arrangement of the present, the erotics of the situation are arrested and contravened. Once again, we are looking at a structure of intense affinity, exciting "latency," and open-ended, because unmentioned and unmentionable, desire. Consummation here—either the happy ending of a Karen-Martha union with the inconvenient Joe out of the way, or a genuine ménage à trois, is not to be wished. What is to be wished, as Martha says quite clearly, is that things could have gone on as they were before.

"My Crush Was Not a Joke"

Life was meant to be lived, and curiosity must be kept alive. One must never, for whatever reason, turn his back on life.

—*Anna Eleanor Roosevelt*, Autobiography

"How should I have known," writes Dorothy Strachey Bussy in her introduction to *Olivia,* an erotic girls' school novel of uncommon affective power, "what was the matter with me? There was no instruction anywhere. The poets, it is true (for even then I frequented the poets), had a way of talking sometimes which seemed strangely to illuminate the situation. But this, I thought, must be an illusion or an accident. What could these grownup men and women with their mutual love affairs have in common with a little girl like me? My case was so different, so unheard of. Really, no one had ever heard of such a thing, except as a joke. Yes, people used to make joking allusions to 'school-girl crushes.' But I knew well enough that my 'crush' was not a joke. And yet I had an uneasy feeling that, if not a joke, it was something to be ashamed of, something to hide desperately."[48]

Olivia is a good example of what Blanche Wiesen Cook has called "the European boarding-school genre that dominated lesbian literature before the 1950's."[49] The heroine falls in love with Mlle Julie, and desires her—never more than when she watches her kiss the naked shoulder of another woman. The 1931 German film *Maedchen in Uniform* (based on Christa Winsloe's play *The Child Manuela*) divides its powerful women into butch and femme, with the male-identified headmistress enlisted on the side of heterosexual prohibition, while Fräulein von Bernberg, whom every girl desires, reciprocates the young heroine's homoerotic feelings enough to cause trouble for everyone concerned. Is this really not love? It is hard to imagine erotic feelings any more intense than these.

In the film, young Manuela, introduced to the boarding school world as a latecomer, is immediately told by her new schoolmates that everyone is in love with Fräulein von Bernberg. Such is the power of fantasy, suggestion, and abandonment; no sooner does her brusque relation leave her at the school than she is offered a new object of desire. When she herself encounters the famous Fräulein on the stairs, she is, needless to say, already more than half "in love." Notice, though, that when Manuela arrives at the dormitory room in her all-girl school, her roommates eagerly display a secret wall of male pin-ups: film stars and other fantasy lovers. The ground of eroticism here is a presumptive heterosexuality, the secret passion for *men,* which is no sooner articulated in the film than it disappears virtually without a trace. The triangular structure of desire, refracted off that pin-up wall, enables the "normal school" passion for Fräulein von Bernberg.

Manuela, who will become the teacher's favorite, has no male pin-ups; her passion marks its own difference in its (apparent) willingness to proceed directly, without interpolation, to the teacher as object of desire. But in fact her own desire is refracted off the "normalizing" desire of her schoolmates, who find no inconsistency in pinning up one thing and pining for another. Manuela thus retraces the "bisexual" triangle in an oblique, foreshortened, and abbreviated form. Desire functions by means of just such interpolations; the smallest pleasures are, in many ways, the most acutely, even unbearably, pleasurable. That was certainly the case with *Olivia,* and with Dorothy Strachey Bussy.

"This account of what happened to me during a year that I spent at a school in France seems to me to fall into the shape of a story," Bussy notes in her introduction to *Olivia.* "Its truth has been filtered, transposed, and, maybe, superficially altered, as is inevitably the case with all autobiographies." It is the story of "the year when I first became conscious of myself, of love and pleasure, of death and pain, and when every reaction to them was as unexpected, as amazing, as *involuntary* as the experience itself."[50]

This, then, is a true account, however filtered and fictionalized. What is the truth it seeks to tell?

"Love has always been the chief business of my life, the only thing I have thought—no, felt—supremely worth while, and I don't pretend that this experience was not succeeded by others. But at the time I was innocent, with the innocence of ignorance. I didn't know what was happening to me. I didn't know what had happened to anybody."[51]

"I don't pretend that this experience was not succeeded by others." What sets this powerful story of love apart is that it is the *first.* But that does not make it less real. It may make it more so. "For after that first time there was always part of me standing aside, comparing, analysing, objecting: 'Is this real? Is this sincere?' . . . Was this stab in my heart, this rapture, really mine or had I merely read about it? For every feeling, every vicissitude of my passion, there would spring into my mind a quotation from the poets."[52]

Dorothy Strachey Bussy had attended Les Ruches, the French school run by the charismatic Marie Souvestre until it was forced to close by the onset of the Franco-Prussian War. The sister of the biographer Lytton Strachey and also of James Strachey, who with his wife, Alix, became the English translators of Freud, Dorothy Strachey was a member of a remarkable family. A sister, Joan Pernel Strachey, became principal of Newnham College, Cambridge; Philippa and Marjorie Strachey also had distinguished careers in politics, education, and the arts. Her mother, Lady Strachey

(Jane Maria Grant), was instrumental in arranging for Marie Souvestre to set up her new school in England, and helped her to find students among the most liberal intellectual circles of the period. Dorothy became later in life the translator and friend of André Gide. She was the wife of the French painter Simon Bussy, whom she married in 1903—and the author of what has been celebrated as one of the great "lesbian novels," *Olivia,* a novel that was written in 1933 when she was sixty-eight years old, and which contains a remarkable portrait of Marie Souvestre as the beloved and longed-for Mlle. Julie.

What does it mean that a married woman should write one of the most evocative lesbian novels of our time and describe it in the introduction as her "autobiography"? It means two things: that we vastly underestimate the role of bisexual feelings in our lives, and that we need to take seriously the legitimacy of the "crush" as real love.

The novel is dedicated to the "beloved memory" of Virginia Woolf. Its delectable accounts of boarding-school passion have made it a modern favorite among lesbian readers.[53] "Many women, including Bussy (speaking in the voice of Olivia), appear to have found a more complete love as an adolescent than they were ever to find with a man," suggests one lesbian critic.[54] Diana Fuss makes a similar move in a footnote to an excellent chapter on hysteria in girls' boarding schools. "Strachey's marriage by no means discredits the importance of *Olivia* as an autobiographical 'lesbian novel,'" Fuss insists. "If anything it may lend a certain poignancy to the unmistakable (and at times unrelenting) tone of nostalgia that drives this narrative from start to finish. As with Virginia Woolf, Dorothy Strachey's sexuality defies easy, quick, or simplistic categorization."[55]

It is precisely this defiance of "easy, quick, or simplistic categorization" that I am here claiming as the proper and extensive realm of bisexuality. The middle-aged woman writing in the voice of a schoolgirl is so compelling that many readers presume her story to be the work of someone only recently a child, with a child's clear and absolute passion: "I knew well enough that my 'crush' was not a joke."

The school on which the fictional Les Avons in *Olivia* was based was Marie Souvestre's Les Ruches, attended not only by Dorothy Strachey and her sister Elinor, but also by Natalie Barney and other daughters of American and European liberal thinkers, women who were, like Barney, to go on to make names for themselves as artists, intellectuals, and salon hostesses— as well as sexual nonconformists. (Barney became one of the most famous lesbians of postwar Paris.) When the Franco-Prussian War forced Mademoiselle Souvestre, the daughter of French philosopher and novelist Emile Souvestre, to close down Les Ruches, she opened another school outside London.

To this progressive school, Allenwood, which was to educate generations of remarkable women, Dorothy Strachey came as a teacher of Shakespeare. And in 1899, at the age of sixteen, Eleanor Roosevelt arrived as a student, and became at once one of Marie Souvestre's favorites, seated by her side at dinner, and devoted—like Olivia—to the dynamic, soft-voiced, witty, and brilliant Mademoiselle Souvestre, who was almost seventy at the time.

Teacher and student traveled alone together to France, Belgium, and Germany, and with another student to Rome. After Roosevelt left Allenwood the two women exchanged warm letters until the time of Mlle. Souvestre's death, and she noted in her memoirs that she kept those letters with her, like the letters from her father, wherever she went. All her life Eleanor Roosevelt kept her teacher's portrait on her desk.

During the time that Roosevelt was at Allenwood she was "everything," according to one schoolmate. "She was beloved by everybody. Saturdays we were allowed a sortie into Putney which had stores where you could buy books, flowers. Young girls have crushes and you bought violets or a book and left them in the room of the girl you were idolizing. Eleanor's room every Saturday would be full of flowers because she was so admired."[56] She was herself the object of crushes, not resented but in fact rather admired because of her special status as Mlle. Souvestre's chosen companion.

When *Olivia* was anonymously published in 1948 by Leonard and Virginia Woolf's Hogarth Press a classmate from Allenwood sent Eleanor Roosevelt a copy, urging it upon the former First Lady as "a little book" which "I think may be of interest." "It is quite short and so would not take up much of your valuable time."[57] Roosevelt replied thanking her, and expressing her pleasure in the book. "I am glad you liked *Olivia*," the classmate, Marjorie Bennett Vaughn, wrote in her next letter. "It seemed to take me back so far!" On Roosevelt's honeymoon trip to Europe in the summer of 1905 she and Bennett had shared memories of Mlle. Souvestre, who died in March of that year. Traveling with her husband to sites she had first visited with her teacher "brought home the loss, and made me long for her more than once."[58] The gift of *Olivia* more than forty years later thus recalled a time of former intimacy between students, as well as between student and teacher.

But Eleanor Roosevelt herself was not an Olivia. Blanche Cook notes that she was "very specific about her own feelings toward Marie Souvestre,"[59] and identifies her instead in the character of Laura, Mademoiselle Julie's favorite, the "awkward," "badly dressed," but "clever" and "intellectually superior" student possessed of "every kind of excellence," of whom Olivia is at first jealous and then fond. "Do you love her?" the impassioned Olivia asks Laura. "Oh," says Laura, "you know I do. She has been the best part of my life. . . . She has opened my eyes to all I like best in the world, showered me with innumerable treasures."

"And tell me this, Laura. Does your heart beat when you go into the room where she is? Does it stand still when you touch her hand? Does your voice dry up in your throat when you speak to her? Do you hardly dare raise your eyes to look at her, and yet not succeed in turning them away?"

"No," said Laura. "None of that."[60]

Transfer Credits

I had a crush on her—no, I was in love with her.

—Lianna

Olivia speaks of her feelings as a "school-girl crush," though she is quite sure that her "crush is not a joke." What happens when those same strong feelings develop between a student and a teacher who are both adults? The question is explored perceptively in John Sayles's 1983 film *Lianna*. Lianna, the wife of a college documentary film instructor, takes an evening course with a woman professor of child psychology and has an affair with her, to the consternation of her best friend and the dismissive and spiteful satisfaction of her chronically unfaithful husband. Her precocious thirteen-year-old son is more blasé: "So my old lady's a dyke—big deal," he says to her, and is told to watch his language: "I'm not your old lady, I'm your mother." At the end of the film Lianna's lover has left her to return to another woman, but we are given to believe that she now considers herself to be, in her own word, "gay." The best friend, Sandy, reports that she "said it wasn't new—that she'd always felt that way," and one of the film's loveliest sequences has Lianna walking down the street, smiling to herself, as she suddenly notices that every woman she sees is sexy and intriguing.

Lianna's predilection for falling in love with teachers is an engrained one; she is a repeat offender. She married her husband, her former English teacher, after her freshman year of college, leaving school to do so. "I started out as an English major," she tells Ruth in the early moments of their courtship. "Started out—what did you wind up as?" "A wife." But even this student-teacher relationship was not her first, as we learn during the seduction scene in Ruth's apartment. Like many mutually engineered seductions this one draws for its fantasy material and its permission to transgress on a story of earlier sexual initiation. Sitting on the couch next to Ruth (the two women get closer each time the camera takes a fresh look), Lianna tells the story of her first crush, on a camp counselor. She and her bunkmate used to follow the counselor at night to a beach where she met her boyfriend, a lifeguard, and watched them make love. ("I couldn't believe her breasts," she says.) Then they'd go back to their bunk, get in bed, and pretend to be the counselor and the lifeguard. "I had a crush on her—no, I was in love with her." This is the moment for Ruth to kiss Lianna. And then they are in bed.

"Do you sleep with a lot of women?" asks Lianna. "A lot?" says Ruth. "No —I've been doing it for a while, though." Ruth has also been married, for "one whole year. It was just a mistake. We said I'm sorry to one another and went on to other things." Is Ruth bisexual? The word is never spoken in the film.

Dick, Lianna's husband, tells her that whether or not she gets custody of the children will depend on "whether you're a true convert to the fold." Clearly he, like Lianna, sees this as an either/or proposition. Sitting the children down to tell them about Lianna's same-sex affair he edges gently into the topic only to have Spencer identify it all too clearly: "You mean like homos?"

> DICK: When this happens between women . . .
> SPENCER: They're called lesbians.
> DICK: Yes—but let's not use that word.

At least "that word" is spoken in order to be barred from being spoken. Spencer can say lesbian, homo, and dyke. Lianna can say gay, even if she giggles with embarrassment when she says it. She is (inevitably) reading *The Well of Loneliness,* the 1928 lesbian classic, and there is a terrific scene at the library card catalog as she thumbs through a reference drawer mumbling to herself "Ledbetter—Lermontov—LESBIAN!" A startled middle-aged woman next to her looks up, and quickly looks away. No one says bisexual, and no one much thinks of it, except perhaps for Ruth when she's trying to explain to Lianna why she never thought things would get serious between them: "Sometimes women—straight women—they'll have an affair just to see what it feels like." But even here Ruth says "straight," just as Lianna will come to declare herself "gay." Is this another place where bisexuality, like the navel of the dream, disappears?

When Lianna tells her husband she's had an affair, he asks curtly, "Was it the man of your dreams?" "It wasn't a man," says Lianna. Dick is both relieved and amused. "You've come a long way from Alberta." When he learns the affair was with "Professor Brennan" ("I always thought there was something fishy about her") he immediately sees the point:

> DICK: So you're still fucking your teachers.
> LIANNA: So you're still fucking your students.
> DICK: At least they're the right sex.

Even her friend Sandy, the football coach's wife, who is also taking Ruth Brennan's night class, has seen this coming: "I think you have a crush on her," she says to Lianna as they leave class early on, before anything has happened. But she doesn't mean a "real" crush, like the one a football player had on her. She means a transferential crush on a teacher—as if that were a different thing.

That "pashes," or "raves," or crushes on teachers are somehow exempt from "real" sexuality has been a persistent normalizing claim. The flip side of this, that teachers who sleep with their students can be charged with sexual harassment, is also on exhibit in *Lianna;* not only is Dick having an affair with a graduate student (he has sex with her in the sandbox at a wild English department party while bearded pedagogues inside sip earnestly at their chablis), but he—and, it seems, many of his colleagues—have married former students, who immediately become typists and research assistants rather than objects of fantasy and lust. But the relationship of Lianna and Ruth is different; Sandy can't quite believe in its existence: "Professor Brennan?" she says to Lianna in puzzlement. "An affair—you mean like a love affair?"

Even Ruth's other affair, with a woman named Jan, has its academic frame. She announces to the night-school class that she has to leave town (it appears, rather belatedly in the film, that she is a visiting professor whose permanent job is elsewhere) to consult with the head of her department. Lianna wants to know if this story is a cover for her planned visit to Jan, but it turns out that Jan *is* the head of the department—something Lianna has apparently never really imagined. For her, department heads are mostly male, and women, except for Ruth, mostly the less professionally empowered partners.

"You're the only person I've ever been in love with," Lianna says to Ruth just before they separate. And she has told her husband she wants to fall in love—not, she emphasizes, fall in love again. What she felt for him, she thinks, isn't love. But what about that camp counselor? Was it just self-dramatization (or fantastic seduction technique) that led Lianna to say "I had a crush on her—no, I was in love with her"? When she and her friend from camp were playing the-counselor-and-the-lifeguard in bed, they both played both parts.

As the great novels of erotic teacher transference demonstrate, the classroom is one place where same-sex desire is often opened for the adolescent lover. Let me insist, though: Transference on a teacher is *bisexual,* which is to say that it does not necessarily correlate with the student's ordinary sexuality or sexual orientation. That many great teachers have *been* bisexual—have loved, and had love affairs with, both men and women—is a slightly, but only a slightly, different story.

Let me emphasize once again: What I am calling erotic education— which is to say, virtually *all* education—is "bisexual" in a structural sense, as a property of institutions, not of persons. "Bisexuality" in the pedagogical context does not refer to a characteristic of individuals but of relations, a complex interplay of desire, identification, power, and hierarchy. My claim is not that students or teachers become "bisexuals," but that they are involved in, indeed often pleasurably complicit with, a structure of teaching and learning that is itself "bisexually" erotic. This is not the same as the often empty assertion that "everybody's bisexual." Whether we think of ourselves as bisexual, heterosexual, lesbian, gay, or in any other "sexual" way, we live in a bisexual culture, whose bisexuality is written so large that, like the largest letters on the map, we cannot always read it.

Chemistry in the Classroom

The lay public . . . will doubtless seize upon this discussion of transference-love as another opportunity for directing the attention of the world to the serious danger of this therapeutic method. The psycho-analyst knows that he is working with highly explosive forces and that he needs to proceed with as much caution and conscientiousness as a chemist. But when have chemists ever been forbidden, because of the danger, from handling explosive substances, which are indispensable, on account of their effects?

—*Sigmund Freud, "Observations on Transference-Love"*[61]

"I have enough gunpowder in this jar to blow up this school," said Miss Lockhart in even tones.

She stood behind her bench in her white linen coat, with both hands on a glass jar three-quarters full of a dark grey powder. The extreme hush that fell was only what she expected, for she always opened the first science lesson with these words and with the gunpowder before her, and the first science lesson was no lesson at all, but a naming of the most impressive objects in the science room. Every eye was upon the jar.

—*Muriel Spark,* The Prime of Miss Jean Brodie[62]

Freud's somewhat testy remarks about the importance and the danger of transference-love are inadvertently and deliciously echoed by the description of Miss Lockhart in *The Prime of Miss Jean Brodie,* and then fended off, a little jealously, by Miss Brodie herself. "I leave her to her jars and gases. They are all gross materialists, these women in the Senior school."[63]

Transference—or, as some analysts write portentously, "the transference"—is the actualization of unconscious wishes by "transferring" wishes from the past, often love or hate for the parents, to a new scenario, like the relationship between an analyst and a patient. The phenomena of transference—the positive and negative feelings produced—have the effect of "making the patient's hidden and forgotten erotic impulses immediate and manifest."[64] In other words, the patient can "fall in love" with the analyst; the student can fall in love with the teacher. When it happens the other way around, it is called "countertransference." In either case the powder keg can indeed blow up in the chemist's face. Perhaps it is not an accident that we talk about love and sex as "good chemistry."

What has transference to do with bisexuality? In the case of the classroom, or even the analytic session, really quite a lot. For the analyst or teacher of either gender can be made to stand in for the parent of either gender. "To say the 'transference' is to Freud as mother does not altogether satisfy me," wrote bisexual poet H.D. (Hilda Doolittle). "He had said, 'And—I must tell you (you were frank with me and I will be frank with you), I do *not* like to be the mother in transference—it always surprises and shocks me a little. I feel so very masculine.'" H.D. asked him "if others had what he called this mother-transference on him. He said ironically and I thought a little wistfully, 'O, *very* many.'"[65]

Miss Brodie's students, who found the plain Miss Lockhart "beautiful"[66] when surrounded by her jars and gases, found Miss Brodie sexy in complicated ways. The "Brodie girls" were "different" from the other girls at Marcia Blaine School, as the repressive headmistress Miss Mackay declares. "There is always a difference about Miss Brodie's girls and the last two years I may say a *marked* difference." And the difference had at least in part to do with sex. "The year to come was in many ways the most sexual year of the Brodie set, who were now turned eleven and twelve; it was a crowded year of stirring revelations. In later years, sex was only one of the things in life. That year it was everything."[67]

Miss Brodie herself is the heroine of a heterosexual drama, the apex of an erotic triangle. For as in the English theater school we noted above, there are only a few men at Marcia Blaine: "One of these was Mr. Gordon Lowther, the singing master for the whole school, Junior and Senior. The other was Mr. Teddy Lloyd, the Senior girls' art master. They were the only men on the staff. Both were already a little in love with Miss Brodie, for they found in her the only sex-bestirred object in their daily environment, and although they did not realise it, both were already beginning to act as rivals for her attention."[68] Lloyd, the married, one-armed art master, becomes at Miss Brodie's instigation the painter—and lover—of some of her girls; Lowther, the duller dog of the two, courts her assiduously, then marries the more conventional chemistry mistress.

It is Teddy Lloyd, however, who stirs the girls' imaginations, though it is with Lowther that Miss Brodie actually has what they always call, solemnly, "sexual intercourse." With Lloyd she has something far more exciting: a kiss. Or rather, as in *The Children's Hour,* the report of a kiss, triangulated through a third party. "Monica Douglas . . . claimed that she had seen Mr. Lloyd in the act of kissing Miss Brodie. She was very definite about it in her report to the five other members of the Brodie set. There was a general excited difficulty in believing her." "I *saw* them, I tell you." "They didn't see me . . . I just turned and ran away."

"Was it a long and lingering kiss?" Sandy demanded, while Jenny came closer to hear the answer.

Monica cast the corner of her eye up to the ceiling as if doing mental arithmetic. Then when her calculation was finished she said, "Yes it was."

"How do you know if you didn't stop to see how long it was?"

"I know," said Monica, getting angry, "by the bit that I did see. It was a small bit of a good long kiss that I saw, I could see it by his arm being round her, and—"

"I don't believe all this," Sandy said squeakily, because she was excited and desperately trying to prove the report true by eliminating the doubts. "You must have been dreaming," she said.[69]

In *The Children's Hour,* Mary Tilford's report of a kiss between two women is presented as a spiteful fantasy; there is no keyhole in the door through which Mary claims to have watched them. The heterosexual kiss that Monica describes likewise seems like a "dream." In fact Sandy wants so much to have witnessed it herself that she tries an "experimental re-enactment," opening the door, gasping, and retreating in a flash. "On her fourth performance" she is surprised by Miss Brodie herself, who wonders aloud what she is doing. "Only playing," says Sandy.[70]

The primal scene for the Brodie set is their heroine's lost lover, Hugh Carruthers, who "fell like an autumn leaf" on Flanders Field. Sandy and Jenny collaborate in the composition of a melodrama about Hugh (beginning with the fantasy premise that "he had not been killed in the war, that was a mistake in the telegram")—a story whose publication they agree to defer until "our prime." "Do you think Miss Brodie ever had sexual intercourse with Hugh?" said Jenny. "I don't think they did anything like that," said Sandy. "Their love was above all that."[71] Whether Hugh, who is said to have been killed a week before the armistice, ever existed outside of this collective narrative fantasy is a question the book, and the Maggie Smith film, leave unanswered.

As for Miss Brodie, she is herself the architect of her own transferential substitutions, predicting that one girl will be famous for sex, another for mathematics, a third for spying, and so on, and attempting to engineer an affair between Rose Stanley and Teddy Lloyd. " 'I am his Muse,' said Miss Brodie, 'but I have renounced his love in order to dedicate my prime to the young girls in my care. I am his Muse but Rose shall take my place.' "[72]

Sandy, who in fact ends up sleeping with Lloyd, is furious at both Miss Brodie's obstinacy and her obtuseness. She "perceived that the woman was obsessed by the need for Rose to sleep with the man she herself was in love with; there was nothing new in the idea, it was the reality that was new. She thought of Miss Brodie eight years ago sitting under the elm tree telling her first simple love story and wondered to what extent it was Miss Brodie who had developed complications throughout the years, and to what extent it was her own conception of Miss Brodie that had changed."[73]

She is also jealous. Why doesn't Miss Brodie see Sandy herself as an erotic figure, a sexual star? And why, above all, does Teddy Lloyd, who is having an affair with Sandy, paint all the Brodie girls as if they were "one big Miss Brodie"?[74] "Sandy thought, too, the woman is an unconscious Lesbian. And many theories from the books of psychology categorised Miss Brodie, but failed to obliterate her image from the canvases of one-armed Teddy Lloyd."[75]

Oh, those unconscious Lesbians. Sandy, who as an adult (and a convert to Catholicism, holding court for the press in her convent cell) writes a best-selling book of pop-psychology, "The Transfiguration of the Commonplace," may be onto something—but what is an "unconscious Lesbian"? A repressed spinster? A self-deluded, self-denying heterosexual? Miss Brodie says she lives for her girls, but she doesn't have sex with them. She has sex with the tedious Mr. Lowther. Whose unconscious is really being explored here, anyhow?

It is not a matter of lesbianism but of transference-love.

The Professor of Desire

Professors rarely speak of the place of eros or the erotic in our classrooms. Trained in the philosophical context of Western metaphysical dualism, many of us have accepted the notion that there is a split between the body and the mind. Believing this, individuals enter the classroom to teach as though only the mind is present, and not the body.

—*bell hooks,* Teaching to Transgress[76]

It is precisely because I believe it is not possible to neatly separate the sexual from other sorts of relations that I find the movement to bar the sexual from pedagogy not only dangerous but supremely impractical.

—*Jane Gallop, "Feminism and Harassment Policy"*[77]

Jane Gallop is a Distinguished Professor of English at the University of Wisconsin-Milwaukee. She is also a major feminist theorist. In the early seventies she was an outspoken lesbian; she and her longtime boyfriend, photographer and filmmaker Dick Blau, have a seven-year-old son. Gallop is frank about the relationship of eroticism and pedagogy, viewing "crushes on professors as a form of transference—the endowing of new people in our lives with the emotional significance our parents once held for us," in the words of an appreciative cover story in the academic news-and-gossip-magazine *Lingua Franca*. "When students develop crushes, as they frequently do, she thinks it best to talk about them openly, looking upon infatuation as an analyst looks upon transference: an instrument of understanding if acknowledged, a block to learning if not."[78]

Why was Gallop the subject of a magazine cover story? Because she had been accused of sexual harassment by two lesbian graduate students—and exonerated of that charge by the university. Perhaps inevitably *Lingua*

Franca's fair-minded and largely favorable report began by invoking Miss Brodie:

> If she is prudent, a professor won't speak too much in public about any feelings of identification or desire a student has stirred in her. Especially not now, when everyone is at such pains to avoid eroticizing the classroom. Better for an academic to err in the direction of a selfless, sexless schoolmarm than in that of a Miss Jean Brodie, triangulating her passions through the bodies of her girls. A prudent professor won't look too closely at the relationship whose potential for immoderation and transference German academics acknowledge by calling their thesis advisers *Doktor-Vaters*.
>
> But Jane Gallop, the feminist theorist and literary critic, is not especially prudent.[79]

One reason this story made news, of course, was its man-bites-dog angle, more recently exploited to the maximum by Michael Crichton's novel *Disclosure* and the film based on it. The woman in power is accused of being the harasser, in this case with a double twist, since Gallop, who "has slept with men and women" (even this frank article can't for some reason say *bisexual*) was accused by two lesbians, one of whom faulted her for "pretending to a fashionable lesbianism."[80] Gallop *had* been a lesbian, "publicly and politically," in the early seventies. On one public occasion she quipped that her "sexual preference was graduate students"—a tactic to bring usually unacknowledged classroom dynamics into the open. When she and a female graduate student, who had been pressing her to regard their relationship as equal, not teacher-student, engaged in a highly public kiss in a local lesbian bar, some students nearby regarded it as a "performance," some as "humorous," and one felt sure that anyone not present at the time would "miss the point" of what had taken place. Gallop was clear about her own understanding: "I wanted the other graduate students at the bar to think about the erotics of the relation between teacher and student." Part of her job as a teacher, she felt, was "to make students feel uncomfortable, to ask them questions they don't necessarily want to face."[81]

The same graduate student, who describes herself as having been "smitten" by Gallop's books and reputation as a theorist even before she took her seminar, had interviewed her mentor for a publication called *Composition Studies: Freshman English News*—not precisely the place one might expect a lively exchange about the relationship between the pleasures of writing and of having sex. But there in fact it is, with Gallop drawing the analogy in terms of pleasure, resistance, and the crossing of thresholds, and the graduate student pressing her about her own concerns: "Well, speaking of sex and writing, where does your view of teaching as a form of seduction fit in?"[82]

The kiss left a bad taste in everyone's mouth. The student not only pressed sexual harassment charges but also wrote about her complaints in the *Lesbian and Gay Studies Newsletter*. At a conference Gallop convened on pedagogy, students leafleted and several invited speakers themselves felt harassed, caught in "an atmosphere of intimidation," as one put it. The real issue seemed to some to be Gallop's power as a "distinguished professor" (the only woman holding that rank at UW-M) and the students' ambivalence about a strong, sexy woman who was witty, very smart, and a "bad-girl" feminist as well as an internationally admired literary theorist.

As for sexual harassment, Gallop herself is ambivalent, noting that many "men in their fifties who are married to someone who was their student twenty or thirty years ago" doubt that harassment really exists. "When sexual harassment sounds like sex, then what you get is a situation where everybody officially says it's bad, but everybody does it." Other women members of the faculty agree, though they support, as Gallop does not, the university's policy prohibiting consensual amorous relationships between teacher and student: "There are a lot of faculty in [my] department," said one, "men and women, who are married to former students. So the policy becomes really interesting to enforce" among people who "have not only done this but don't see much wrong with it or think this is just the way it's always been done."[83]

The way it's always been done. What's striking here is the heterosexism of this "normalization" in marriage. Just as bisexuality becomes invisible if it is parsed into "really straight (but experimenting)" or "really gay (but afraid to admit it)," so prohibited amorous relationships between teacher and student become invisible as code violations if they have a "happy ending" in marriage. Looked at backward, with twenty-twenty hindsight, these are courtships and romances, not transgressions. But what if the partners are of the same sex? And is that not, as we have been seeing, to a large extent "the way it's always been done"?

" 'Raves' on teachers are far commoner than between two girls," a woman friend told Havelock Ellis. "In this case the girl makes no secret of her attachment, constantly talking of it and describing her feelings to any who care to listen." The school setting, the "normal school," in fact provides the crossing or meeting point between two different though related kinds of idealizations. Raves or crushes on schoolmates—the captain of the field hockey team, the class president, the head cheerleader, the camp counselor-in-training—have a transferential aspect to them; the admired object is grander, older, more celebrated, often desired by others.

But the crush on a teacher, whether of the same or the other sex, *is* transference. And transference is at the heart of pedagogy. That is why it is so difficult to talk about it. And that is why sexual harassment is always a lurking possibility whenever strong teaching is taking place. Desire—transference and countertransference, the student for the teacher, the teacher sometimes for the student—is not an accidental or a perverse effect, but an intrinsic part of the process.

Scenes of instruction are potentially *always* scenes of seduction. It is only that we learn to resist them, or to hold them in abeyance or turn them to other account, often generating as we do so an excess of emotion that works its way into the learning process itself. A good teacher learns this, too.

Telling Tales Out of School

We have been looking at various ways in which the intrinsic, if often repressed or denied, eroticism of education affects learning "bisexually." Love for a same-sex schoolmate, bunkmate, teammate, or teacher is often coded as "normal" if it abides by certain protocols of expectation, and if it is regarded by the participants and/or their elders as temporary and transitional. In deciding that such feelings are "just a phase," society plays a central role in the recoding or repositioning of those youthful feelings. It is "normal," this interpretation suggests, to "grow out of it," to stop feeling "normal" same-sex desire and begin to feel "normal" desire for the opposite sex. By invoking the convenient concept of the "phase," people often try to minimize the importance of early love.

When we turn to the so-called transference, the erotics of pedagogy and of the institution, we can see the virtual ubiquity of romantic relationships between students and teachers—not only in the highly specific locale of the same-sex boarding school but also in other clearly tutelary and mentoring contexts more familiar, perhaps, to many people from college, university, night-school for adults. Here again such romances, as much of literature and literary history attests, are not barriers to learning but spurs to it. The danger of crossing the borderline eroticizes both the line and the learning process.

What is "normal" here is to deny or repress the erotic content of the pedagogical relation. The danger of acknowledging it directly is not just "sexual harassment" (heterosexual teachers have often slept with their students and occasionally married them either before or after the fact) but rather that a too-frank acknowledgment of desire can impede, rather than augment, the possibility of transferential learning. It is this "normalization," this automatic sublimation, that Jane Gallop set out to challenge.

In the next chapter we will come to the ultimate "normalization" of the story of maturation through schooling, the idea that it is "normal" to reach a settled sexual identity, and that that "identity" is either heterosexual or homosexual. The claim that bisexuality is "immature" is closely related to this assumption that maturity means choosing between those ostensibly polar alternatives. In the ideal, or rather, normatively idealized telling of the story, of course, there is in fact no choice; everybody is happily and unquestioningly heterosexual. I will here call the narrative passage from same-sex to opposite-sex love a "conversion narrative" to stress both the familiar crossover to "full" heterosexuality and the frequently evangelical sense that accompanies it. Nowhere in this passage—the experience of same-sex school love, the recoding of it as a "phase," the transferential relation between teacher and student, and the final "stabilization" of a sexual identity—is there apparently a place for bisexuality as a reality.

The "truth," as we shall see, depends upon the nature of the telling, the "narrative" as much as the "conversion." Before the reader beats me to it, let me say here that my own sense-making desire has surely had a hand in the way I retell these tales—"tales," as the saying used to go, "out of school."

Chapter 15

"It's a Phase"

And, as he journeyed, he came near Damascus: and suddenly there shined round about him a light from heaven . . .

And the Lord said unto him, Arise, and go into the street which is called Straight . . .

—*The Acts of the Apostles, 9:3, 11*

Narratives of Conversion

As we have seen, the word "conversion" seems to recur with great frequency to describe changes, or supposed changes, in people's sexual orientation. The word, recalling Paul's experience on the road to Damascus, calls up something that happens when one is already on a road, producing an inner change of direction, a *re*orientation, a turn. As Freud memorably put it, "In general, to undertake to *convert* a fully developed homosexual into a heterosexual does not offer much more prospect of success than the reverse, except that for good practical reasons the latter is never attempted." [1] And in the film *Lianna,* Lianna's chronically unfaithful husband tells her that whether or not she gets custody of the children depends on "whether you're a true *convert* to the fold." As this last example will illustrate, conversion sometimes carries with it the implication of indoctrination or membership in a cult—that is, if the "faith" or "fold" to which one is said to have been converted is anathema to the observer. For Freud's "good practical reasons," this is less likely to be the case with "converts" to heterosexuality than with "converts" to lesbianism or homosexuality.

The appeal of the conversion metaphor lies in part in its narrative clarity: I was this, but now I'm that. I was blind, but now I see. The mutual exclusivity of the two moments, figured as blindness and truth, would seem to preclude the possibility of calling these life stories "bisexual." But, as with most cases of blindness and insight, the truth may be slightly more complicated.

One further convenience of some conversion stories—convenient, that is, for the convert—is the instant invalidation of an inconvenient past. There was "before," and then there is "now." Apparently, if you believe in conversion, the two stages need not have anything to do with each other. The fact that several mid-level figures in the Watergate scandal underwent highly publicized conversion experiences, becoming "born again" and dedicating themselves to the pursuit of sectarian virtue, was widely seen as an appropriate cleansing gesture that wiped the moral and ethical slate clean. For related reasons conversions in prison are not uncommon, nor do I mean to imply that they are false or insincere. But conversion is, to use an overworked word, "binary." It draws a line. It is not interested in questioning the existence, or the moving nature, of the borderline.

We have already taken note, in the foregoing chapters, of some stories that could be characterized as conversions, for example, Robert Graves's decision to marry and to remove from his thoughts—and his autobiography—disquieting details about adult homosexual behavior on the part of a boy he had once loved. In E. M. Forster's novel, Maurice goes so far as to consult a doctor who might perhaps be able to "change" him—and this quest for medical or psychoanalytic transformation from gay to straight is one of the most familiar twentieth-century narratives of conversion, an article of secular faith among many who came to think of the medical profession as a kind of magical priesthood. But as with other forced conversions in history, these "conversions," as in the case of Maurice, are not always successful, nor are they without consequences and unpleasant side effects. How many psychiatrists does it take to change a lightbulb? the familiar joke asks. The answer, of course, is "One. But it has to really want to change."

Can one convert to bisexuality? A send-up of the whole conversion experience surfaced not too long ago in the form of a button declaring the wearer to be a "born-again bisexual." More seriously, there are many persons who have written memoirs or appeared on talk shows to explain how they used to think of themselves as gay or straight and now think of themselves as bisexual. But the nature of these personal adjustments does not, by and large, present itself as an exclusion or denunciation, or a rewriting of the whole personal narrative. Rather it tends to take the form of inclusiveness, what a formerly gay man now involved with a woman described as "finding the other half of the human race attractive." It was not that he had lost his interest in men—not at all. But he was now involved with a woman.

"I know now I'm bisexual," a woman may say. Or, "I know now I'm a lesbian." (She is less likely to utter a sentence like, "I know now I'm straight.") But these are not conversions. Conversions are not rheostats but on-off switches. They are often, in the lay world, motivated by considerations we could call political: solidarity, heterosexual privilege, a decision, more often taken in the past than now, that certain life activities, like having children, belong to a world that is hetero- rather than homosexual. Or they could indeed be motivated by issues of faith, by a belief that homosexuality and bisexuality are against God's law. These days conversion narratives are closely related as well to the whole question of sexual labels and of categories of identity.

What I am primarily interested in here, though, are not conversions but conversion *narratives*—the way the story is told *as* a conversion. The conversation narrative from Paul to Augustine to Malcolm X has a familiar and honored place in Western culture and letters. But *sexual* conversion narratives have a particular appeal. They suggest both a quest for self-knowledge and a mode of self-discipline and self-discovery, together with some unavoidable and intriguing transgressive sexual detail. For one of the things that makes conversion stories "sell" is the way they permit, indeed require, the convert to have previously wallowed in sin, or mud. As with Satan in *Paradise Lost,* it is the "bad" characters that are the most engrossing. Virtue, however virtuous, is by definition narratively a little dull: monogamy and domesticity, however pleasurable to the monogamous and the domestic, make less good reading than more various and variable adventures, whether hetero-, homo-, or bisexual in nature. As we will see in the cases of both poet Stephen Spender and novelist Paul Monette, it is the sexual *mis*adventures that a good storyteller can turn to the best account in describing his adventures.

The classic sexual conversion narratives can go either from straight to gay, or from gay to straight. I will look here at selected sexual conversion narratives, not in order to endorse the terms in which they are framed but in order to illustrate how the conversion frame has made bisexuality disappear from the narrative. In these narratives, as Freud's mention of "good practical reasons" implies, the apparent symmetry between the gay-to-straight and the straight-to-gay conversions is skewed by the institutions of normative heterosexuality, particularly marriage. People's erotic investment in the institution of marriage cannot be underestimated, whether that investment is positive or negative. We will look more closely at marriage as an institution in the next chapter. For the moment, we will focus on its *narrative* function.

Phased In

The tickling narrative, unlike the sexual narrative, has no climax.

Is the tickling scene, at its most reassuring, not a unique representation of desire and, at its most unsettling, a paradigm of the perverse contract? Does it not highlight, this delightful game, the impossibility of satisfaction and of reunion, with its continual reenactment of the irresistible attraction and the inevitable repulsion of the object, in which the final satisfaction is frustration?

—*Adam Phillips,* On Kissing, Tickling, and Being Bored [2]

The basic pattern of the sexual "it's a phase" plot is usefully if gingerly laid out by the 1982 Robert Towne film *Personal Best,* whose executive producer, it is interesting to note, was bisexual-on-his-way-to-being-gay David Geffen. Mariel Hemingway plays Chris Cahill, a "third-rate hurdler" with her father for a coach. She catches the eye of pentathlete Tory Skinner (Patrice Donnelly) at the Olympic Trials in Eugene, Oregon, and after the almost obligatory seduction scenes of (1) crying on Tory's shoulder, (2) smoking pot with her side by side on the floor of her apartment, and (3) arm-wrestling her to a draw (a contest provoked by Tory's taunt or tease that Chris isn't competitive enough) the two women become lovers.

Tory persuades her reluctant coach to allow Chris to work out with the track team, and Chris soon becomes his favorite. We see scenes of his massaging her legs for muscle cramp, and before long he has offered her a full scholarship if she'll stay in town over the summer and work with him. The catch? She is to begin training for the pentathlon, and thus to begin direct competition with Tory. Tory is less than pleased, and also less than thrilled that Chris allows herself to flirt innocently with a young boy at a party. Chris apparently knows so little about (hetero)sex that she doesn't get the point of a masturbation joke when one of the other women tells it in the steam room. The love scenes between the two women, while they constitute the only erotic moments in the film, turn on the question of "tickling," something Chris says she has learned by practicing on her brothers.

When Tory gives Chris a mistaken piece of advice about high-jumping (Did she do it on purpose? Was her unconscious acting out?) Chris blows out her knee, is out of the Pan-Am Games, and goes home with the coach, who is determined to separate Chris and Tory, and who starts to make a pass at the recumbent Chris while she lies on his bed nursing her knee and eating ice cream. Again, though, Chris simply doesn't get it—he's her coach, not her lover, and she can't see that the two roles could combine. So he backs off, goes off with the team to the Games, and tells her to work out in the swimming pool. Where, of course, she finds a man.

Not just any man but, as it turns out, an ex-Olympic champion, although she bench-presses more than he does (but maybe that's because he's mesmerized by staring at her crotch as she spots him at the free weights). In any case, she and Denny soon apparently become lovers, though the film omits any sex scene between them. Still, a track teammate who asks her "What's got into you, girl?" gets her wordless gesture of an answer (to which, to her credit, the teammate replies, "Is that all?").

The what's-got-into-you theme is further played out in the one scene where we do see Chris and Denny in (or more accurately, on) the bed. He gets up to use the bathroom and she goes with him. She wants to hold his penis when he urinates; she's always wanted to pee standing up. He is reluctant, embarrassed, and acquiescent. "I can't," he says, and "this isn't going to work." But Chris is determined to make it work: She runs the tap, and voilà! Thus the phallic woman who can do it all, and have it all, including Olympic-level competitiveness, has metamorphosed from the weepy teenager of the opening scenes who disappoints her dad.

As for the affair with Tory, Denny reveals that he knew about it all the time—"the two most beautiful girls in San Luis Obispo; it wasn't a secret" —and that he doesn't care (he says this three times, for emphasis), he just wants Chris to be truthful with him. "There's nothing to tell," she says, looking into his eyes. "We don't see each other anymore—ever." But they do, of course, reconcile on the track, despite Coach Tingloff's continuing attempt to keep them apart. Chris wishes Tory luck, then sacrifices her own best race to allow her ex-lover to qualify for the Moscow Olympic Games along with her. But the Games, of course, have already been boy- cotted by the United States, so the two women (and another teammate) are, as a sports announcer says, "all dressed up with no place to go." On the medal stand Tory, who never shows any resentment, admits that Chris's boyfriend is "awfully cute—for a guy."

So much for the plot. So far it charts a "typical" conversion from what is often called experimentation, or a schoolgirl crush, to a supposedly more "mature" heterosexual relationship with a man. Chris "grows out of" her lesbian romance, and recodes it (without loss, in this fairy-tale account) as what she previously called it: "friends."

But this reading ignores a good deal of what little eroticism the plot contains. For this bisexual conversion narrative is really a family romance. One of its mysteries for the viewer is why the "transitional" love affairs are sexier than the apparently real or final one. Let's try again.

If we look at *Personal Best* in terms of its interpersonal relations, we can see that its Oedipal triangles are showing. Chris has two pairs of "parents," her biological mom and dad (with dad, as we've noted, doubling as coach) and the pair that succeed them, Tory and Coach Tingloff. Ultimately she rejects both, as she "has to," according to the developmental model, on her way to individuation and heterosexual romance. In the film's opening scenes we see her father badgering her ("I want to know exactly what was bothering you about your trail leg") and then manifesting quiet fury at the news that she will be leaving him for another coach. ("How much is he giving you? A full ride—tuition? How much?" "Nothing." *"Nothing?"*) Chris's all-but-invisible mother tries to intervene and is quickly shut up by her husband. This is the last we see of either of them in the film.

The second triangle of Tory, Tingloff, and Chris develops from a mirroring lesbian dyad, identification mingling with desire in Tory's love. "If I had what you had—speed, strength, flexibility . . ." she breathes. Some critics may not be happy with the characterization of the Tory-Chris bond as mother and child, and I want to emphasize here that I am speaking of positions in a structure, not of sexual role-playing, although at least twice we see Tory acting protectively like a mother toward Chris: first in the cry-on-your-shoulder scene, and then when Chris develops food poisoning at a track meet in Colombia. Tory sends for medical help, then sits up all night with her sick lover, who insists that she not leave her even to get some rest for the next day's competition. Unsurprisingly Chris, fully rejuvenated, wins; the exhausted Tory messes up, and the coach sides with Chris.

Although we have previously seen a jealous Chris watching horseplay between Tory and Tingloff (in fact Tory, as we've noted, intervened to force Tingloff to accept Chris in the first place) a shift has taken place: Now the new "father" wants the child for himself. It's now Tory who's jealous, at a party where she gets drunk and on the playing field. The coach wants Chris to work out at the men's gym, where he, not Tory, will spot her. Tory reads this, correctly, as the beginning of the end. "Maybe we should see other people," she suggests painfully to Chris. But Chris still doesn't get it. "Jesus Christ, Tory, we're friends." "Yeah—we may be friends—but every once in a while we also fuck each other." We may note that she does not say "tickle."

For Chris the relationship with Tory does not have a sexual name (she calls her a "roommate" when Denny asks her about her past), although we find out that they have been living together for three years. If this is a "phase," and the film seems to want us to think that it is, it is not just a fleeting moment.

On the other hand, a sexual relationship with the coach, even though it might be said to mark heterosexual "progress," is also "impossible" because it would be incestuous. The team is like a family. When he oversteps the bounds, having brought the injured Chris back to his apartment, he sees immediately what the costs are and backs away.

Indeed, Chris seems singularly unconscious of the sexual designs others have upon her, childishly soaking up the coaching and care lavished on her by both Tory and Tingloff but never acknowledging her own sexual part in either relationship. This is a countertransferential rather than a transferential romance. And it is one that instates healthy heterosexuality as fraternal rather than parental.

Recall that Chris learned about "tickling" by playing with her brothers, and getting paid for it. At the film's final track meet, the 1980 Olympic Trials, again held in Oregon and thus a return and recap of the opening scenes, when Chris has apparently blown her chances, a track official tells her "your brother" is here and wants to see you. The "brother" is Denny, whose words of wisdom (don't compete with other people, compete with yourself) are fairly characteristic of his unthreatening and even banal presence. Despite the "brother" label, which is really there in order to mark its own limitations, Denny is exogamous and other. He is not a member of the track team—he's switched to water polo. A relationship with him violates no other bonds, which may be one reason why he is so curiously anerotic in the film.

All of the erotic energies of *Personal Best,* and its often-inventive camera play (lingering on the women's long, muscular legs as they run in the sand dunes or on a rapid-fire sequence of female high-jumpers' spread legs and tucked buttocks as they slither expertly over the bar), are focused on women's bodies, and quite specifically on the perfect muscle tone of its two female stars. Men fare less well. The frontal nude shot of Denny on his way to the toilet presents the male body as vulnerable rather than eroticized, while Coach Tingloff, even with his cutely dated Mick Jagger haircut, is set up as the desirer more than the desired. As so often in life, so also in this film, once the powerful and elusive teacher figure shows his desire he becomes both ludicrous and disempowered.

First phased in, then phased out, and finally unfazed, bisexuality in *Personal Best* is a way of explaining how beautiful blond girls who wear makeup can have sex with other women. Tory, who doesn't wear makeup, is the real lesbian. Chris is something else. Is she a bisexual? Or just someone who doesn't yet know that the sexual narrative has a climax? If three years with Tory hasn't taught her, she hasn't been paying much attention.

Phased Out

One of the commonest pieces of common wisdom about bisexuality is the idea that it is "just a phase," an exploratory mode, a by-product of adolescent horniness, opportunism, and experimentation rather than a mature, adult, and sustainable way of living one's sexual life. Films like *Personal Best* are able to have things both ways without really challenging the status quo: Mariel Hemingway's on-screen affair with the darkly handsome, self-assured female sprinter Patrice Donnelly is titillating enough for a cross-over audience, but a real man comes along to steer her in the right direction in the nick of time.

Actress Hemingway's reappearance as a (small-) screen lesbian in the

1994 television episode where she kissed Roseanne in a gay bar may well have been calculated by the TV producers to recall for aging boomers her 1982 coming out in *Personal Best,* even though that coming out, like the ground hog's in February, was succeeded by a lengthy disappearance from the queer scene. As the stripper date of on-and-off-screen bisexual Sandra Bernhard, Mariel Hemingway was much more sexy and self-confident than she had been in Robert Towne's film.

It was sitcom character Roseanne in fact who found herself caught in the middle, enjoying the kiss more than she was quite comfortable admitting, and unwilling to allow her overcurious husband to appropriate the event, as she described it to him, as a spur for his own sexual fantasies. His hope, he said to her, was that she in fact *might* be gay—"just a little gay"—gay, or rather bisexual, enough to mobilize his own desires. She turned the tables on him by describing, not the kiss and her reaction to it, but *her* fantasies of male-male sex. Turned off, he turned the light out and settled back to a grumpy sleep.

"Just a phase"—it's what many parents say and hope when their children tell them they're gay, lesbian, or bisexual. But bisexuals are also accussed of going through a "phase" by many gays and lesbians, who consider that there are really only two poles, straight and gay. Once they grow up, the idea seems to be, they will know which one they are. Until that time they are waffling, floundering, vacillating, faking, posturing, or being misled by dangerous acquaintances. Bisexuality thus gets defined as intrinsically immature, as, in a way, the very sign of immaturity, and bisexuals are urged by many gays, as well as many straights, to put away childish things.

Converting Oscar Wilde

It is highly appropriate that he is remembered with a window. He is neither in nor out.

—*Oscar Wilde's grandson Merlin Holland,
on the stained-glass window mounted in Westminster Abbey in Wilde's honor*[3]

In some conversion narratives, such as the one discussed above, homosexuality functions as a "phase," while marriage provides the narrative goal. In others, the marriage comes first, as a "blindness" that is transcended by the discovery that one is "really" gay.

One nicely contestatory example of this might be that of Oscar Wilde, this century's paradigmatic founding figure of gay style, wit, culture, and sensibility. There will be people who insist that Wilde was always gay despite his passionate courtship and boastfully successful early days of marriage.[4] Richard Ellmann's magisterial life of Wilde, aided by unerring hindsight, takes a balanced view of the young husband's ardor, reminding the reader that "His mind had other recesses, from which he drew 'The Sphinx' and later *The Picture of Dorian Gray* and *Salome,*" and that "latent was a darker possibility, that some place would have to be found in this marriage for low aesthetic as well as for high aesthetic, for sphinxes and gamy savors as well as for stately conversations and rapturous orthodox couplings." Reading Joris-Karl Huysmans's decadent novel *À Rebours,* Wilde was especially taken, we are told, with a passage describing a homosexual experience, which "summoned him towards an underground life totally at variance with his aboveboard role as Constance's husband." [5]

Wilde's affair with Robert Ross at Oxford was apparently his first homosexual experience; Ross was seventeen when they met.[6] Again Ellmann locates a turning point: Wilde "was now able to make his experience of marriage and countermarriage the center of his career in prose. Homosexuality fired his mind." [7] As for Constance Wilde, she "suspected her husband's reorientation only once, and that was not until 1895, when she came back to the house unexpectedly." [8]

"Reorientation" is Ellmann's word, and a quietly provocative move. If "sexual orientation" is our omnibus euphemism for gender-directed desire, used in deliberate preference to a phrase like "sexual preference," which seems to imply choice, then what is a "reorientation"? A conscious or unconscious choice? A change in one's sexual "nature"? A culturally inflected shift? Or merely a neutral avoidance of explanation?

Whatever it means, "reorientation" would seem to imply a prior "orientation." After Wilde's notorious affair with Lord Alfred Douglas, culminating in his trial and imprisonment, his wife considered divorcing him, but he "wished at all costs to prevent the parting from wife and children which would follow a divorce." [9] Though Constance Wilde changed her name and her sons' from Wilde to Holland, she visited him in prison and wrote to him weekly after his release from prison and subsequent exile in France. He proposed living with her and the two boys. Meanwhile he visited a female prostitute without enjoyment, "the first these ten years, and it shall be the last," but instructed his friend, the poet Ernest Dowson, to "tell it in England, where it will entirely restore my reputation." [10]

Gore Vidal evinces some amusement at the various retellings of the Wilde saga. "In the four decades since the Second World War, Wilde has gradually become more and more a victim-hero of a hypocritical society whose most deeply cherished superstitions about sex were to be violently shaken, first, by the war, where the principal secret of the warrior male lodge was experienced by millions on a global scale and, second, by Dr. Alfred C. Kinsey, who reported that more than one-third of the triumphant

Butch Republic's male population had participated in the tribal mysteries," he wrote in a review of Ellmann's biography. "As a result, Oscar Wilde ceased to be regarded as a criminal; he had been nothing worse than maladjusted to a society that was not worth adjusting to." As for Ellmann's version of Wilde's story, with its graphic accounts of his sex life and his death, Vidal judged that it "may suit altogether too well the AIDSy Eighties."[11]

"My feeling about Oscar Wilde," says Jonathan Dollimore, who has written about Wilde extensively and perceptively,[12] "is that clearly he was bisexual, and there is a sense in which I do deplore that representation of Wilde as living entirely in bad faith in relation to his wife. "Ten years ago, one would've wanted to talk about him exclusively as gay. Now, I think, is precisely the time to rethink Wilde's message." What he continued to feel about Wilde, however, is that Wilde had had an experience of conversion that was revelatory to him as an individual and as an artist.

Dollimore readily speaks of his own initial discovery of gay sexuality as "a classic conversion narrative. Because I'd never fantasized about that. I never desired it. When it happened it was just an incredible transformation." "I can remember," he says, "sitting down and thinking, look, if that degree of radical transformation in my sexual life is possible, where I become the unthinkable, anything is possible."

"So for me, that was a conversion. It changed everything. And my life is still structured in relation to that revolutionary event. So I can understand the conversion narrative. What I would not tolerate, and what I would tease and be quite aggressive to is people who then embrace that sort of thing in the exclusionary identity politics mode. You know, of saying: 'I am now gay. My whole life is that story.' I just don't believe that desire works like that."

Oscar Wilde, he says, "had that kind of conversion narrative that I was talking about. And one of the things I've argued in relation to Wilde is the tremendous power of that experience, when you identify yourself as having deviant desires. And what a tremendous energy that gives you in terms of social critique. The deviant desire of sensationality is his legacy. That is the way that Wilde resonates endlessly to me."[13]

Unless we restrict our definition of bisexuality to mean only the mythical "perfect bi," who desires men and women equally, Wilde *was* bisexual in his experience. His "sexual preference" became young men, and his marriage seems clearly to have been motivated at least in part by social and pecuniary concerns. But to use gay/straight here as an on-off switch is to underestimate both Wilde and the complexity of human sexuality. To say that Wilde was homosexual and not bisexual is to make a statement more indebted to politics than to biography. It is seductive, but it is not true.

Yet since Wilde's genius lay in inventing himself as an apostle of perversity, of transgression as such, to "reclaim" him as bisexual *instead of* gay would be merely to repeat the gesture of fragmentation and compartmentalization, the gesture of essentializing, that is contrary to his own practice and thought. The need for a word describing such transgressive self-invention has led to the currency of the word "queer." The danger, however, is that "queer" may become yet another essentialized identity or political faction, replacing, in a way quite un-Wildean, a brilliant transgressive style with an essential unchanging "sincerity."

The Double Conversion of Stephen Spender

The contention that the bisexual life is a lie, against which Dollimore argues in the case of Wilde, would also come to color the controversy between novelist David Leavitt and his source, fictional model and bête noir, Stephen Spender.

Spender's autobiography *World Within World* was originally published in 1951. American novelist David Leavitt revived interest in it when he borrowed aspects of its plot for a novel of his own, published in 1993. The novel, *While England Sleeps,* led Spender to institute a lawsuit, alleging breach of copyright and the violation of his "moral right" to his own work. Leavitt's publisher settled out of court without admission of liability, agreeing not to sell the novel in its originally published form anywhere in the world. Leavitt, who had conceived of his book as an homage to Spender, and had initially (until deterred by his American publisher) intended to cite the poet by name on the dedication page, agreed to delete the passages that had given offense.

David Leavitt is a gay novelist, and *While England Sleeps* is largely the story of the love and sexual passion of its hero, Brian Botsford, for the working-class young man, Edward Phelan, he first meets at a political gathering and then invites to live with him. Basically what Leavitt undertakes to do is to supply a story that revises and elaborates on Spender's 1951 account, an account written with what the author then called "certain inevitable reticences."[14] Botsford, like the young Spender, also has a concurrent affair with a woman, the lively and free-spirited Philippa Archibald, whom he has reluctantly agreed to meet at the urging of a financially generous aunt. To his surprise, Philippa is sexy, not dreary. She takes him to bed, he begins to see and sleep with her regularly (deceiving the docile and faithful Edward, with whom he continues to share his flat), and in a key scene in the novel he proposes marriage to her and is rejected. "Has it occurred to you," she says, "that you might be happier in a homosexual relationship? . . . I think you only thought you were happy with me, Brian. I could tell you weren't."[15]

At this point he realizes that he really loves Edward, but of course it is too late. Edward has left for Spain, and dies a painful death from typhoid fever in Brian's helpless arms. The symptoms of his illness are described in a way that makes clear the present-day analogy to AIDS.

Edward is the novel's emotional center, haunting the narrator long after his death. Although Brian's subsequent relationship with another gay man is briefly mentioned (it lasts for twenty-two years before his lover finally leaves him for a young male dancer), there is no question that the tenderness, the eroticism, and the truth of feeling all focus on this lost and near-perfect passion. Philippa reappears briefly toward the end of the novel as a brittle, crop-haired society woman who speaks "brightly" and opens her mouth "not so much in a smile as a rictus."[16] For good measure it turns out that the source of Edward's troubles at the hands of the Communists in Spain, and thus the real agent of his tragic death, was Philippa's "ideologically promiscuous" Aunt Dot. The phrase "ideologically promiscuous" is Philippa's.

Philippa's vapidity is established early on; Leavitt's lesbians (of whom there are several in the novel) are far more likable than his straight women. After she and Brian first have sex together, she tells Brian that his inexperience shows (it's "fairly well known—that you're homosexual") but hastens to tell him that it doesn't matter to her. "I for one don't perceive sexuality as something rigid. I'm sure under the proper circumstances I could very happily make love to a woman, and will."

" 'As far as I'm concerned,' Philippa said, 'love occurs between people, not genders. Why limit ourselves? It's 1936; it's practically the future.' "[17] This consummate cliché of bisexuality, so frequently found in identity-exploring essays of the 1990s (the future?), is offered as a chirpy bedside banality, and Brian's own pillow talk, if more earnest, is even less deft. "I always intended to end up with a woman—no, not intended, that's not what I mean. What I mean is, I always felt it was my *destiny* that I should fall in love with a woman. Which is not to say there's anything wrong with love between men—only I always suspected it wasn't the end of the road for me. Do you understand?"[18]

What the reader quickly comes to understand is that Philippa is right, that Brian is self-deluded or trammeled by his desire for social respectability, and that what ultimately happens to him (a fading career as a Hollywood screenwriter, blacklisting, his lover's desertion, prostate surgery) is all somehow a consequence of that failure of nerve or self-knowledge that made him, however briefly, choose the flighty Philippa over the serious, loyal, and sexually thrilling Edward.

When Spender expressed his displeasure at the preempting and rewriting of his life story, Leavitt lashed out at him in political terms that echo the novel: "In sharp contrast to *World Within World*," he said, "my hero, once he arrives in Spain, never doubts where his loyalties must lie. And where Spender renounced his homosexuality in favor of what he called 'the normal'—he married twice—Botsford ends up uninhibitedly and unapologetically gay."[19] "Renouncing" and "loyalties" taken together make a strong statement, especially when Leavitt goes out of his way to quote, in the same brief article, E. M. Forster's famous accolade to friendship: "[I]f I had to choose between betraying my country and betraying my friend, I hope I should have the guts to betray my country."[20] Leavitt thus describes Spender's marriages as a renunciation, in the sense that a defector "renounces" his citizenship.

Bisexuality for Leavitt would be a kind of treason. Or is this renunciation rather a kind of unnecessary sacrifice, the timid Spender "renouncing" pleasures the "uninhibited" Botsford feels free to enjoy? In any case, Spender's two marriages are described as a kind of compensatory overkill, their plurality substituting for his real—that is, homosexual—desire.

Does one renounce a sexuality? Can one really renounce a desire?

As it happens, the word "renounce" had itself appeared in Spender's *World Within World,* where he had used it not in reference to homosexuality but to heterosexuality, which he does indeed, as Leavitt had charged, call "a normal way of life." "Since a relationship of the highest understanding can be between two people of the same sex," he wrote there, "some who have experienced this relationship renounce a normal way of life." This seems on the face of things an affirmation of the enduring same-sex bonds that some of his close friends, like Christopher Isherwood and W. H. Auden, had formed with other men, and if Leavitt would forgive him the use of the word "normal" (used here, pretty clearly, as Freud uses it, to mean "what most people expect," rather than "what I approve of") he might find the liberal sentiments here espoused acceptable if he were charitably inclined. But liberalism is not what he is looking for. He is looking for something more like solidarity and consistency. He wants Spender to come out as gay. And when Spender fails to do so, he sees him as hiding behind heterosexual privilege.

But the passage in which Spender discusses renunciation is not in fact concerned with either homosexuality or heterosexuality but rather with his own sexuality, which journalist James Atlas summarily characterized in the *New York Times* as one of "sexual confusion." "The author's sexual confusion," Atlas says, "is never far from the surface. The conflict between Mr. Spender's attraction to men and his desire to lead a normal domestic life—he married twice—is one of his primary themes."[21]

What is the relationship between "sexual confusion"—Atlas's lay diagnosis—and bisexuality?

To answer this we will need to look at a few key passages in the autobiography, of which only a portion is cited by Atlas. But before doing so it might be useful to recapitulate some of the facts of Spender's life as he tells them in his autobiography, and as subsequent friends and commentators have described them.

As a young man Spender, like his friends Auden and Isherwood, was homosexual. His love affairs, like theirs, were with young men, often men of a lower (and therefore exotic) class. At the age of twenty-five, while deeply involved with a man called Tony Hyndman, with whom he had lived and traveled through Europe and whom he calls "Jimmy" in the autobiography, he had an affair with the psychoanalyst Muriel Gardiner, who had been twice married and had a child.

Spender wrote to Isherwood in the fall of 1934 about his relationship with Muriel Gardiner:

> About the change. I don't feel in the least on a high horse about it; as a matter of fact, I absolutely agree with your saying that it is mostly a business of time, place and circumstance. It affects me so little that it has not even made any difference to my relationship with Tony. It has rather improved it on the whole. I think I am certainly fonder of him than I could be of any woman I know of. But as I find sleeping with a woman more satisfying, it also means that our relationship isn't something we tire of when we tire of it sexually. Anyhow, directly one writes about all this, one writes badly.[22]

A few months later he wrote Isherwood again in the same vein. "I don't feel a bit altered by my new life. Please don't imagine so....I admire Tony & feel as I always did about him."[23]

During the period of the affair with Gardiner, Spender divided his time between Vienna and London, unwilling to "abandon"[24] Hyndman. The social and other gaps between them lent "some element of mystery which corresponded almost to a difference of sex," he wrote. "I was in love, as it were, with his background, his soldiering, his working-class home."[25] The fact that his liaison with Gardiner began at a time when Hyndman was in the hospital and the two men were Gardiner's guests in Vienna made the relationship even more complicated. "What we faced was the knowledge that there might be a real inability on my part to choose; which was different from saying that circumstances made it impossible for me to do so....Something which we called my 'ambivalence' for ever kept unsleeping watch between us, like a sword."[26]

Ultimately, Gardiner married someone else, a fact that did not really surprise him. Nonetheless, he decided to separate from Hyndman, and each man took a flat of his own.

In the autumn of 1936, Spender met Inez Pearn at a luncheon party. A few days later he proposed to her, and they were married three weeks after that. In *World Within World,* he reflected on why he had acted so rashly. He was still on the rebound from Gardiner. He had begun to find friendships fragile and work inadequate compensation for solitude. And his attraction to Inez made him worry that someone else would propose to her before he did. "Marriage seemed the only solution."[27]

Before we leap to the conclusion that this is the defensive and closeted response of a gay man who can't face the consequences of his gay identity, we might ask ourselves how often this same sentiment has motivated marriages (and quite successful marriages at that) between persons whose sexual history and desires are straight rather than gay. In any case, Spender writes in his autobiography that "it would be true to say that we 'adored' one another."[28]

Stephen and Inez Spender were married for three years. Much of Spender's energy at that time was taken up with politics, and a good deal of his time was spent in Spain, some of it in a desperate attempt to save Hyndman, who had enlisted in the International Brigade. He felt responsible for having persuaded Hyndman to join the Communist Party and, by breaking with him and marrying Inez, for Hyndman's decision to enlist. But his marriage, however imperfect, "seemed to me the centre of my life."

Occasionally, on returning home, he'd stop outside the house, and "the feeling that she was in the flat upstairs was one of intoxicating wonder." When he realized that his wife was in love with someone else, he was full of despair. "There were hours when I simply became a prey to the most stupefying anger and jealousy."[29] I cite this only to reinforce Spender's own view that this was a passionate relationship, not merely a conventional arrangement.

Spender and Inez separated in the summer of 1939. In his autobiography, Spender characterizes his initial reaction as resembling the madness of drug addicts undergoing withdrawal. He decided never again to make himself vulnerable to such pain. Like others who have felt this way, however, Spender came to change his mind. In April 1941 he married the pianist Natasha Litvin, a marriage that would last more than fifty years and produce two children. In the beginning, he was haunted by guilt over the failure of his relationships with Hyndman, Gardiner, and Inez. "One day, Natasha said to me: 'From now on there is no question of blame. There is only us,' and this was the faith . . . on which our marriage was founded."[30]

The story of his life, as Spender describes it, is a story of homosexual and heterosexual relationships, of emotional commitments to both men and women, and ultimately of a marriage that had endured over time.

This fulfilled and happy life James Atlas did not hesitate to describe as one of "sexual confusion."

The passage that Atlas quotes to buttress his contention comes from *World Within World.* The initial topic under discussion, a very modern-sounding one, is same-sex relationships and psychosexual labels. Let me here quote the passage, italicizing the sentence that Atlas uses to support his claim of "sexual confusion":

> I have come to wonder whether many contemporaries in labelling themselves do not also condemn themselves to a kind of doom of being that which they consider themselves in the psychological text-book. For example, *I suspect that many people feel today that a conception of friendship which can be labelled homosexual, on account of certain of its aspects, excludes normal sexual relationships; and conversely that the heterosexual relationship should preclude those which might be interpreted as homosexual.* As a result of this tendency to give themselves labels, people feel forced to make a choice which, in past times, was not made. It also follows that since a relationship of the highest understanding can be between two people of the same sex, some who have experienced this relationship renounce a normal way of life.

In the past, he points out, so-called abnormal relationships often took place alongside "normal" ones. "Men labeled themselves less and adjusted themselves more." Shakespeare, he notes, declared his love for a man in his sonnets, but also urged him to marry and father children. Even in the middle sonnets, where the poet's ardor is "less disinterested," he talks of his mistress as well. Never is the notion put forth that the poet and his male lover belong "to a world of men of a third sex," as is "characteristic of much literature in the twentieth century."

Nevertheless, Spender determined "to try to go beyond those qualities which isolated me from commonly shared human experience, towards the normal. Here when I use the term 'normal,' I mean that which is generally considered to be so. It is true, of course, that what is 'normal' for the individual is simply to conform with his own nature. But what I am concerned with here, is adjusting my acceptance of my own nature to the generally held concept of the normal, though this may be a rarely attained ideal."[31]

In a rather sardonic portrait of Spender written for the *New Yorker,* Ian Hamilton describes the tone of this analysis as "a near comic-pomposity." "The Spender self can be explored by way of three paramount, lifelong preoccupations," he declares, "fame, sex, and politics. In each of these areas irresolution struck deep."[32] Irresolution, indecisiveness, even "betrayal"; these are not-so-coded code words for bisexuality. However comically earnest or irresolute Spender's attempt to think through these issues may seem from a later perspective, it lays out questions that are still very much in contention today. If we were to dismiss all such lucubrations out of hand we would be left with nothing but sound bites.

When he speaks of a "world of men of a third sex" Spender is specifically referring to the work of pioneers like Magnus Hirschfeld, who founded the Institute for Sexual Science in Berlin in 1919, and sought through institutional means to challenge that section of the German Criminal Code which set out punishments for homosexual acts between men. Spender's friend Christopher Isherwood, who lived in a room adjacent to the institute during his first years in Berlin and socialized with its "patients or guests, whichever you chose to call them," notes that despite periodic beatings by supporters of the growing Nazi party, Hirschfeld "was even allowed to present the grievances of the Third Sex in a speech to some members of the Reichstag."[33]

For Isherwood, the discovery of other members of his "tribe," and the realization that he could no longer regard homosexuality as "a private way of life discovered by himself and a few friends"[34] came first as an unwelcome, and then as an increasingly proud truth. For Spender these categories, institutes, and societies seem to have compelled a parallel self-examination, resulting in a different set of truths about himself.

Spender's account of the "normal" is manifestly a pre–gay liberation concession to public assumptions about homo- and heterosexuality. If he were writing his autobiography now he might or might not have a different view of the trade-offs involved. But his concern to historicize sexual labels produces what seems like a description of normative *bisexuality,* a choice (to use Wallace Stevens's useful phrase) "not between, but of." "Normal" and "abnormal," in his terms, are socially and not medically or theologically constructed concepts. Shakespeare's sonnets speak in the voice of a persona who articulates both homosexual and heterosexual passions. Is this really a description of "sexual confusion"? The tone as well as the content of the passage say otherwise.

Spender himself gives his feelings a slightly different psychological description, what he and Gardiner had called "ambivalence." In the technical language of psychoanalysis, ambivalence means having simultaneous feelings of love and hatred toward the same object.[35] It is a powerful and not a wishy-washy feeling; it is not the same as being "unable to make up one's mind."

After Hyndman, Spender had concluded that he could not live with a man. In fact, his relationship with Hyndman had led him "to discover a need for women." He still needed male friendship, but in order to "identivy my own work and development, even the need for women." He grew "vividly aware of an ambivalence in my attitudes towards men and women.

Love for a friend expressed a need for self-identification. Love for a woman, the need for a relationship with someone different, indeed opposite, to myself." These needs "seemed to some extent to be mutually exclusive, so that whilst I was with a friend it might seem that I had renounced a whole world, of marriage, of responsibilities, and I had been received into another where everything was understood, where work, ideas, play and physical beauty corresponded in the friend's life with my own." But with women, "instead of reflecting and being reflected by my physical-spiritual comrade, I had entered into the wholeness of a life outside me, giving to the woman that in myself which was not contained in her, and taking from her what was not in me."[36]

This self-analysis, too, it would be easy to dismantle in terms of gender-stereotyping and a refusal of desire, if we were determined to tear the passage apart rather than learn from it. Why separate identification from desire? Why decide that women were somehow "other," were *not* to be located on the emotional map as comrades who shared work, play, and ideas? Isn't Spender here revealing exactly the kinds of prefeminist and pregay consciousness that makes a novelist like David Leavitt long to rewrite his life as it should have been?

I don't think he is. Or rather, I don't think his sense of the divisions or ambivalences in his life are importantly different from the reasonings of any person asked to explain why he or she has come to a crossroads, has faced a choice. Recall the "mystery"—"almost a difference of sex"—introduced by the gaps of class and interest in his relationship with "Jimmy." Eroticism in Spender's own terms—whatever it might be in another person's—seemed linked to the perception or fantasy of such differences.

One of the things we have noticed about bisexuality over and over again is that it reveals a structure of desire in which gender becomes an example of, rather than the defining case of, erotic difference—or, indeed, erotic sameness or mirroring. The structure "X is *like* me (is female; is blond; is long-haired; is poor; likes Bach) therefore I desire [him or her]" is functionally indistinguishable from the structure "X is *unlike* me (is male; is dark; is short-haired; is rich; likes heavy-metal) therefore I desire [him or her]." Both kinds of statements are rationalizations after the fact. When Spender writes of two simultaneous but overlapping needs, he is describing a general case of perceived emotional and erotic choice.

Toward the end of *World Within World* he returns once more to this question. "There was disillusionment as well as joy in finding in another exactly what I was myself, for I found evil as well as good." In retrospect, he finds his relationships with women to be the hardiest, because "in the relationship of opposites there remained always the mystery of an unknown quantity."[37]

If you talk to many people today who describe themselves as bisexual, you will often hear some version of the same division or doubling of

desires. Sex with a same-sex partner offers mirroring; sex with an opposite-sex partner offers complementarity. We have already encountered
several versions of this story, and we will certainly encounter more. The
"two needs...existing side by side" are what Martin Weinberg and
his colleagues call in their sociological study of bisexuality "dual attraction."

But on the other hand, many bisexuals do not see their desires falling
so neatly into two types. One lawyer I interviewed said, "I actually think
that most of what people say about their sexual experience is just ridiculous fantasy, so I never take it seriously." Does he think they lie? "They're
saying something at that moment that needs to be said and has an emotional truth to it in their own minds. But I've heard so many people
describe their sexual biographies and their sexual histories in ways that I
knew had only the vaguest relationship to the facts."

"I'm attracted physically to lots of different people," he said. "But I tend
to find people erotically appealing in their specificity on a very individual
basis. Somebody presents himself to one as an integrated individual, not
first and foremost as a man or as a woman. What makes a particular person
sexy may be something that's related to their gender but may also not—it
might be their ideas, the way they talk, the way they walk, the way their
body moves." And sex itself, "sexuality and the particular erotic practices"
between people, is always "very customized."

Gay writers want to defend Stephen Spender's homosexuality by attribut-
ing his marriage to Natasha to social comfort and conformism. And it
would be social conformism if it were dependent on forgetting the past—
something the very existence of a memoir like *World Within World* directly contravenes. Spender's friend David Plante said "the gay-rights people" see him "simply in terms of his homosexuality.... So they are
simplifying Stephen. All they see is the stereotype: a homosexual man
married to a heterosexual woman. So they say Stephen is false to the
marriage, false to homosexuals."[38] In wanting to see Spender as *either* gay
or straight, his choices as *either* deluded *or* genuine, *either* socially induced *or* truly sexual, all these missionary positions seek to convert a
bisexual life into a monosexual one.

The most obvious point to be made is that Spender's life and choices
occurred at a different historical moment from Leavitt's. Leavitt, in conceiving of his novel as an "homage" to Spender, indeed initially saw Spender
as a path-breaker, one who *enabled* Leavitt's own wider choices and
greater openness. But now Stephen Spender is the old guard, and David
Leavitt's supporters are the young turks with a political agenda that seems
moral and incontrovertibly right to them.

The mutual misunderstandings here are in part based on the fundamental inequalities of heterosexual and homosexual rights today. If there had, for example, been the possibility of gay marriage, if the choice of a partner with full economic and social rights and recognition were not limited by law, Spender would have been faced with a different set of choices. If, instead of being unlawful in England in his youth, homosexuality had been a freely available, socially tolerated option, the young Spender might have chosen to live with a man, or to have continuing erotic relationships with men, as indeed his friends Isherwood and Auden did despite the law. Or he might have chosen a woman, as he did. But we should not discount the erotics of the unlawful; riskiness and perversity have their own compelling appeal. If *heterosexuality* were suddenly declared unlawful, there would without question spring up an underground of closet heterosexuals who found opposite-sex partners thrilling because forbidden. But no time machine can catapult Spender, or any of the rest of us for that matter, back to the future. And in the meantime he has lived a life.

Janus

> I loved him sincerely and, when he told me that the love of women was a terrible thing, I believed him.
>
> —*Vaslav Nijinsky on Serge Diaghilev, whom he left to marry Romola de Pulszki* [39]

Paul Monette is best known as the author of poignant and eloquent memoirs and fiction about gay men and the AIDS crisis. A poet as well as a novelist, Monette was also, for a period after his graduation from Yale, a prep school English teacher, living among adolescent boys. Graduated from Yale, he at first careened, he says, "from celibacy to obsession." Then, as a resident teacher at the Sutton Hill School, a Connecticut prep school for boys with the "aura of a penal colony" that was "run by retired colonels and defrocked monks," he allowed himself to be seduced by a good-looking junior with a girlfriend at home in New Jersey.

Closeted and afraid, he had gone through Andover and Yale watching his every move, turning his crushes on other men into friendships rather than sexual relationships. "Asexual to a fault, too timid even to sweat," he recalls, he should by rights have wound up as "the graying head of an English department in a second-rate boys' school." "Of course I'd be master in one of the senior dorms—forming 'special friendships with the humpy ones, steeling myself to stay away from backrubs.' "[40] What saved him from "the schoolmaster's fate"? Only coming out, he says, and meeting his lover, Roger.

His coming-of-age story, *Becoming a Man,* charts Monette's life story up until the time he meets Roger Horwitz, the lover whose illness and death from AIDS he describes so movingly in *Borrowed Time.* Its dramatic culmination, then, will be his first meeting with Roger at a dinner party on

Beacon Hill, chronicled in the last three pages of the book ("I'd found the right one at last").[41] Readers of the best-selling *Borrowed Time* will have anticipated this happy ending, however bittersweet in its aftermath, and hoped for a narrative resolution to the almost picaresque adventures of the hero, a hapless if deftly self-dramatizing sexual naif in a time before gay liberation or queer theory.

Monette excels at finding the small details that illuminate larger issues. When he turns his attention, in *Becoming a Man,* to his own experiences with bisexuality, he is frank in admitting his own ambivalence. "I've never quite understood the double Janus face of bi—Janus, the Roman god of gates and doors, especially closets. I've met too many who kept the truth from their women and used their men like hookers. . . . I try not to be gayer-than-thou about bi. Mostly I fail."[42]

The double Janus face of bi. We might recall Freud's letter to his friend Fliess about the "stone Janus" in his collection of antiquities "who looks at me with his two faces in a very superior manner."[43] As Monette points out, the attitude of superiority is, or at least was, often manifested by those on the "gayer-than-thou" side, for whom "the truth" was gay identity, and the Janus face nothing more or less than two-facedness, duplicity, false consciousness. But "gayer-than-thou" is a relatively recent product of hard-won and precarious gay liberation. Most of Monette's memoir charts gay-ness as something everything conspires to try to "cure."

The general outlines of the plot are not unlike Forster's *Maurice:* self-ignorance, self-discovery, repression, sexual awakening, a threat of exposure leading to consultation with a therapist, an attempt to "go straight," and the ultimate encounter with "the right one at last." It is in the context of this rather familiar narrative structure that Monette presents his adventures with women, what he describes as "this heterosexualizing marathon."[44]

First there comes the scare: a half-unwilling affair with Greg, a cocky junior at a second-rate prep school where Monette is a resident English master. "I knew we were right in the heart of darkness, teacher molesting student,"[45] he recalls, though it was Greg who initiated the relationship and called the shots. When, almost inevitably, Greg's attitude changed from adoration to something like blackmail, Monette, although initially supported by a school establishment that assumed the student must be lying, moved first to a coed school (of better quality), then to "a part-time gig at a women's junior college," and then, via a job as a decorator and a variety of gay encounters in Boston, to a shrink. "I'd like to be straight," he tells him. Privately he had reservations: "How would I ever teach myself not to eroticize men? It was as deeply rooted in me as the fact of gender itself." The word "teach" is not an inadvertent choice: The teacher had become, again, the good student. "It was like enrolling in a graduate course in self—with a reading list and deadlines, as well as a chance to show off in class to an approving teacher. Another shot at another A."[46]

Students of conversion narratives take note: Monette does not say "How would I teach myself to desire women?" but rather "How would I teach myself *not to* eroticize men?" Conversion requires negation.

The word "heterosexual" now begins to appear in the memoir with aggressive self-mockery, as he hurls himself into the "heterosexualizing marathon" with Emma, with Julia, with Sally, with Alida, with Ellen: "As soon as I understood I might be a closet heterosexual, every encounter with Emma became freighted with the possibility of romance.... Calls poured in all week from friends who'd seen us together, whom Julia had dazzled as much as she'd dazzled me. It was the most heterosexual I'd ever felt."[47] After an auto accident, provoked, he thinks, by his attraction to his young male passenger, he goes eagerly to bed with his female lover: "[E]ven that night I wanted another lesson in heterosex."[48]

He becomes, in short, a caricature of what he calls "galloping, rampant manhood," reporting each heterosexual conquest with self-declared "self-satisfaction"[49] to his shrink. "I see now," Monette reflects from the other side of this crisis, "how tenaciously he was questioning my whole commitment to straighthood, what an evasion it was of my confronting my shame at being queer."[50] This is the view from *now,* the present tense of the memoir, when "becoming a man" has resolved itself as "being queer." But what about *then?*

Then, the key words were "normal" and "bisexual," offered up in awkward juxtaposition.

"I was doing the wild thing at last—the *normal* thing. I strutted around all day in a swoon of self-satisfaction," Monette reports of his heterosexual sleeping-around days. The italicized "normal" is his.

What did the therapist think? "If I wanted to be bisexual, fine, but the male half of me needed to be workable and satisfying, not tortured and self-denying." "Of *course* I was bisexual," a female friend tells him, "prodding me to have it both ways,"[51] whereupon he meets Pip, a young architect, and takes him home to bed, the first man he's been with in months. "After we came, we sat up half the night talking about what 'bi' meant. We both decided that our overriding instinct was for the normal thing with women." He continues to see Pip and a woman named Sally: "What better way to find out how bi I was than to have one of each?"[52] Sally is officially the girlfriend of an architect named Justin, who initiates a threesome and later invites Monette to Vermont: "[O]f course I'd gone upcountry for one reason only and that was to get it on with Justin. Was it because I was angry at Sally? Or had I finally decided Justin and I were comrades under the skin, since he was embracing rather than running from his bi instincts?"[53]

He also takes up, at the same time, with a new woman, Ellen: "I'd spend the weekend at Ellen's hoping the bi confusion would go away." "Thinking about Ellen," he writes in his journal, "I think: well, perhaps I can bring it off after all, our sex life is pretty 'normal' now, whatever that means. Not exciting, but that's because I don't believe in myself yet to *make* it exciting. And thinking: all right, it's a together and complete relationship, but what about my need to be alone, what about my love of the poses and smut and daring of getting a man, what about pure *desire* . . ."[54]

Monette and Ellen spend some time on the beach in Truro, where she meets "a man in his sixties, a designer from Montreal" who observes casually, "Your lover's a homosexual, I believe." Monette feels betrayed, paranoid, and "read": "I 'looked' queer, even with a woman on my arm."[55] Furthermore Ellen admits to this casual acquaintance that "she loved me even though the sex wasn't very good," confirming his qualified view of their "normal" sex life in the journal. Indeed, his female lovers seem to love him because, rather than in spite of, his queerness: "I even love the faggot in you," says Julia (with what he regards as some degree of calculated flattery). "I don't think he's anything to be ashamed of. I just think he's becoming superfluous."[56]

But, as it turns out, Julia is wrong. The memoir ends with Monette's first meeting with Roger, "the right one at last." Monette's memoir is thus an account of a failed conversion: More zealous even than his therapist, Monette throws himself into the "heterosexualizing marathon" with all the energy of denial—and of the good student. The only "normal" thing he learns, however, is how to undervalue women. He shapes his irony as if it were directed at himself ("from the vantage of life outside the closet it's too easy to scathe and ridicule. I see the manic posturing and the agonized self-doubt . . ."), but the women come off as loyal and sweet, handy to have about at the time, lacking somehow in an irony of their own: "I have to force myself to remember that it wasn't just more wasted time, loving those women. That they were the ones who finally broke the ice skin that sealed me among the living dead. That I couldn't have ever opened myself to Roger or any other man if the women of '72 and '73 hadn't been there first. Unjudging and tender, taking their own risks in the open country of the heart, no kiss ever a waste of time."[57]

Whose time is it that he worries about wasting in the first words of this passage and the last? Was "no kiss ever a waste of time" for *them,* even though he has to keep reminding himself "that it wasn't just more wasted time"? The women were sturdy little tugboats, ice breakers, clearing the way for Roger and real love.

Was Paul Monette ever "bisexual"?

Monette is a good test case. He is a gay man. He writes, thinks, lives— and will die—from that perspective. He is *not* a bisexual. Or is he? If he was bi once does he then become a member of a group that should be conceptually, or statistically, thought of as bisexual? In other words, does "bisexual" here denote a category of persons who have at one time or another loved, and made love with, members of both sexes? Or is "bisexuality" here an artifact of the conversion narrative? It is impossible to know whether Monette's relations with women were *produced* by being forced or *ruined* by being forced. Perhaps without the pressure to become "normal" he would have had no sexual relations with women. Or perhaps he would have been freer to enjoy them. But that is to imply that sexuality can occur outside of history. What Monette's narrative teaches us is what Spender's, in a different way, also teaches us: Bisexuality marks the spot where all our questions about eroticism, repression, and social arrangements come to crisis.

Chapter 16

Family Values

She was married, true; but if one's husband was always sailing round Cape Horn, was it marriage? If one liked him, was it marriage? If one liked other people, was it marriage? And finally, if one still wished, more than anything in the whole world, to write poetry, was it marriage? She had her doubts.

—*Virginia Woolf,* Orlando

"I don't understand why things can't go back to normal at the end of the half-hour like on *The Brady Bunch.*"
"Because Mr. Brady died of AIDS."

—*from the film* Reality Bites

It's not another woman, but another man that has Carrie Fisher crying all the way to court. The actress is splitting up with agent Bryan Lourd, who is the father of her 20-month-old daughter, because he's seeing a man.

—*"Names and Faces,"* The Boston Globe [1]

The question of bisexuality and marriage is high on most people's curiosity list whether they doubt the existence of the category "bisexual" or affirm it. Do bisexuals have monogamous marriages? If so, in what sense are they "bisexual"? If not, in what sense are they "marriages"?

The association of bisexuality with nonmonogamy is so pervasive that the *Boston Phoenix* once refused to accept personals ads from bisexuals, saying that its ads were for people looking for "long-term, monogamous relationships." (Local bisexuals organized a successful phone calling and publicity campaign to persuade the paper to change its policy.) But as many bisexuals today have tried to insist, in the face of persistent media misunderstanding, the question of monogamy versus nonmonogamy is completely separate from the question of monosexuality versus bisexuality. We might think of such dedicated nonmonogamists as playboy Porfirio Rubirosa, basketball star Magic Johnson, heiress Doris Duke, or even actress Elizabeth Taylor, who is perhaps better described as a "serial monogamist," with eight marriages to her credit (or debit) to date.

There are many ways in which monogamy and nonmonogamy affect marriages, even or perhaps especially when the partners are self-declared monosexuals. The ballyhoo that has surrounded bisexual nonmonogamy is partly a result of that rather clunky term's being used by social scientists and bisexual activists (it is hard to imagine Taylor, or for that matter Magic Johnson, making such a big deal about what used to be called sleeping around). But bisexual nonmonogamy also conjures images of sexual betrayal (a feeling common to the partners of mono- and bisexuals, and addressed later in this book) and of, most latterly and pointedly, the spread of AIDS and other sexually transmitted diseases to unsuspecting and faithful partners (usually, as the story is told, wives of men who are secret bisexuals emerging from the connubial closet).

And for many partners of the newly uncloseted, the question: Was our marriage therefore a sham? What, after all, is a marriage?

What Is a Marriage?

I say we will have no moe marriage.

—Hamlet, Act III, scene i, line 147

"Matrimony," says the dictionary, is "the act or state of being married; marriage." Derived, it seems, from Middle English, and thence from the Old French *matrimoine,* from Latin *matrimonium,* from *mater, matr-,* mother. To be married, to participate in a rite of matrimony, is, apparently, to be officially, culturally situated to become a mother.

And what about matrimony's cognate, patrimony? Again derived from Middle English and from Old French, *patrimoine,* from *pater, patr-,* father, an apparently identical structure. What does my modern dictionary have to say about patrimony?: "a. An inheritance from a father or other ancestor. b. An inheritance or a legacy, heritage. c. An endowment or estate belonging to an institution, especially a church."

So "matrimony" is marriage (with the implication of impending motherhood), and "patrimony" is inheritance. The "father" in patrimony is, in effect, the dead or bequeathing father, the lineal father, he who provides the heritage, whether it is in the form of lands, name, stocks and bonds, or philosophy.

It would be naive to ask how these two words, so apparently similar in structure and etymology, came to diverge in meaning. After all, however out of fashion they are as terms of opprobrium or idealization, "patriarchy" and "matriarchy" are cognate terms: rule by fathers (or men), rule by mothers (or women). "Paternal" and "maternal," or, for that matter, "patricide" and "matricide," are apparently equivalent, differing only as to the gender of the parent. Although "matronymics" are somewhat less common than "patronymics" in Western culture, the idea is the same: the name is inherited from the maternal or paternal ancestor. But in the nonequivalence of patrimony and matrimony we encounter, I believe, a crux of some significance for ideas of sex and gender, desire and partnership, social freedom and economic control. And this nonequivalence is of the greatest importance in the rethinking of the place of bisexuality in our cultural past—and cultural future.

The asymmetry between mothers and fathers implied by this etymological excursus has prompted many social commentators to wonder whether the institution of marriage is still appropriate for today's changing sexual roles. "Marriage no longer serves women very well," wrote feminist Katha Pollitt. "There isn't any way, in our modern, secular society, to reconnect marriage and maternity. We'd have to bring back the whole 19th century: restore the cult of virginity and the double standard, ban birth control, restrict divorce, kick women out of decent jobs, force unwed pregnant women to put their babies up for adoption on pain of social death, make out-of-wedlock children legal nonpersons." Much though not all of this, I have to say, reminds me not of the nineteenth century but of the surburban 1950s, where the cult of virginity and the stigmatization of unwed mothers was, at least rhetorically, in full force, and many women were reluctant to divorce and lacked decent jobs. Divorcée, with or without the adjective "gay," is not a term one hears much these days, but in the fifties it was everywhere, and it meant something between risqué, cheerfully amoral, and "available." These days, "if women can support themselves, they don't need to marry for what was politely called security but was, to put it bluntly, money. If single women can have sex in their own homes, the respect of friends and interesting work, they don't need to tell themselves that any marriage is better than none. Why not have a child on one's own? Children are a joy; many men are not."

Pollitt's conclusion proposes the demystification of marriage as the inevitable middle-class ideal. "Instead of trying to make women—and men— adapt to an outworn institution, we should adapt our institutions to the lives people actually lead" by offering single mothers the options of parental leave, day care, flexible schedules, and pediatricians with evening hours.[2] In the meantime, the number of single mothers by choice is increasing dramatically, and includes 11.3 percent who have some college education, and 8.3 percent of women in professional and managerial jobs —not to mention the movie stars and other public figures for whom these material concerns are presumably not a factor. Marriage used to be a prelude to childbearing; now the child often comes either before or instead of the marriage.

◆

The outcry over gays in the military right after President Bill Clinton's inauguration in 1993 led to a number of thoughtful reflections on the troubled and often disingenuous relationship between gays and lesbians and social institutions. None was more reasoned or more heartfelt than that of *New Republic* editor Andrew Sullivan, in an essay entitled "The Politics of Homosexuality." Sullivan linked the right to marry with the right to serve as defining categories of citizenship. "If the military ban deals with the heart of what it is to be a citizen," he wrote, "the marriage ban deals with the core of what it is to be a member of civil society."[3] And since "the heterosexuality of marriage is civilly intrinsic only if it is understood to be inherently procreative; and that definition has long been abandoned in civil society," the prohibition of gay marriage functions solely as a sign of public disapproval. Emotionally, Sullivan contends, marriage is "characterized by a kind of commitment that is rare even among heterosexuals." That many gays and lesbians have formed and will continue to form such long-term attachments is clear, and the question of whether all gay people want to live in committed relationships is hardly relevant. To give them the right to do so legally does not diminish "the incentive for heterosexuals to do the same."

Why, in other words, should gay marriage threaten straight marriage, unless, as an institution, it is already threatened? Sullivan, no radical, speaks in the language of humanism: "[T]he vast majority of us—gay and straight—are brought up to understand that the apex of emotional life is found in the marital bond." Yet if gay people are denied that bond, their committed relationships are inherently unequal, socially as well as in the eyes of the law. "Their relationships are given no anchor, no endpoint, no way of integrating them fully into the network of family and friends." Life partners have to be continually described in terms of euphemisms (like "life partners"). "The brave attempt to pretend that gay people don't need marriage," says Sullivan, comes at considerable emotional and social cost. The two issues—gays in the military and gay marriage—seek to legislate not "private tolerance" but "public equality."

Thus, paradoxically, some of the most vocal upholders of the ideal of marriage today are gays and lesbians. Gay historian John Boswell revealed, to some readers' consternation, that as early as the eighth century some churches performed ceremonies sanctifying same-sex unions.[4] When "Doonesbury" cartoonist Garry Trudeau featured this information in his comic strip two Illinois newspapers promptly dropped the strip.[5] The advent of "domestic partners" legislation to enable gay and lesbian couples to register their relationships and to gain access to some of the material benefits afforded in our culture to married persons (health insurance, common custody of children, certain aspects of inheritance) as well as a measure of social recognition and visibility has raised fascinating questions about the very nature of marriage.

Marriages of Convenience

In common parlance, the expression "bisexual marriage" can mean several quite different things: the open relationship, in which one or both partners have sexual relations with members of their own sex as well as with their spouse, and the so-called marriage of convenience, in which the partners agree to wed for pragmatic rather than erotic reasons. We might bear in mind that until fairly recently *most* marriages were in this sense "marriages of convenience" in that they were as much about property, inheritance, and alliance as about romantic love. Romantic love seemed for a long time in human history antithetical to marriage; hence, for example, the medieval "courtly love" triad of wife, husband, and troubadour-lover. "The poet," wrote C. S. Lewis in a description that has still not been surpassed, "normally addresses another man's wife, and the situation is so carelessly accepted that he seldom concerns himself much with her husband: his real enemy is the rival."[6] In a courtly love manual like that of the twelfth-century author Andreas Capellanus, for example, "no rule is made clearer than that which excludes love from the marriage relation. . . . Conjugal affection cannot be 'love' because there is in it an element of duty or necessity."[7] Our relatively modern notion that love and marriage go together like a horse and carriage in effect makes the horse synonymous with the cart.

Marriages of convenience between gay (or bisexual) men and lesbians (or bisexual women) were common in the Hollywood of the studio system era, where nervous executives were eager that their stars mirror the values of mainstream America. And conjugal arrangements made by gay and lesbian or bisexual people who found the fact of marriage convenient are part of every era.

The poet H.D., whom Freud called a "perfect bi," was courted by Ezra Pound, then married to classical scholar Richard Aldington, but her most enduring partner was the historical novelist Bryher, whose original name was Annie Winifred Ellerman. Bryher, the daughter of millionaire shipping magnate John Ellerman and herself a lifelong lesbian, was also married, first to the publisher Robert McAlmon then later to the novelist Kenneth McPherson.

Bryher's father had disapproved of her wandering life, and faced with the prospect of losing his financial support, she proposed to McAlmon. "He wanted to go to Paris to meet Joyce but lacked the passage money. I put the problem before him and suggested that if we married my family would leave me alone. I would give him part of my allowance, he would join me for occasional visits to my parents, otherwise we would lead strictly separate lives."[8]

"MacAlimony" was the nickname McAlmon acquired perhaps inevitably as a result of his lucrative divorce settlement with Bryher.[9] Opinions differ on whether or not he wanted or achieved a sexual component to their marriage. Kenneth Lynn thinks "there is reason to believe that he developed a genuine attraction to his wife, both intellectually and physically, and that her spurning of him was the experience that intensified as nothing else in his later life ever would his childhood conviction that the world was against him."[10] When McAlmon's friend William Carlos Williams flatly stated that the McAlmon-Bryher marriage had remained unconsummated, McAlmon broke off their friendship. Novelist Kay Boyle maintained that McAlmon had been duped by Bryher, in a one-sided ploy enabling her to continue the relationship with H.D.[11] Whatever the sexual facts about the McAlmon-Bryher marriage, it was certainly at one point convenient for both of them. When it became inconvenient, they divorced.

Bryher, who seems never seriously to have questioned her lesbianism, nonetheless married again. Her marriage to Kenneth McPherson, described in one account as a liaison that "served to screen H.D., whose affair with McPherson H.D. wished to hide from her husband, Richard Aldington,"[12] was another "marriage of convenience." But for whom were these marriages principally convenient?

"In Fear. Gay Soldiers Marry for Camouflage," read the headline in the *New York Times.* The article described a common ploy in today's armed forces: "marriages of convenience with partners of the opposite sex, who may also be gay."[13] Hundreds, perhaps thousands of gay servicemen and women were said to have contracted such "convenience marriages." In one case a lesbian Marine corporal married her best friend, a gay male Marine corporal; the maid of honor at the ceremony was her girlfriend, the best man, his boyfriend. When the wife decided not to reenlist, she "no longer needed the marriage" and divorced her husband. Sometimes the spouses are civilians. Marriage confers material benefits in the form of added pay, health insurance, and even lowered car insurance, since young married men are deemed to be at lower risk for accidents than single ones. The "sham marriages" include a lot of attentive details, since the government checks up: "My husband would send me flowers at work on Valentine's Day or show up at the office for lunch," one married lesbian reported. Partners observe each other's birthdays and anniversaries, and often attend military functions together, even though many do not share living quarters. Keeping up appearances is stressful, and many would like to end what some characterize as a "charade."

But, as the article also points out, marriages of convenience are often entered into as well by heterosexuals, including heterosexuals in military service who do it for the perks. As for the sham attentiveness, from birthday and Valentine's Day celebrations to formal social functions, many a quietly dysfunctional heterosexual marriage preserves precisely these amenities as a sign of its "success."

There are also many people who marry for reasons of citizenship. Some male soldiers stationed overseas have married foreign women for money, permitting the wife to become a U.S. citizen. After she is naturalized, the couple often divorce, and the woman brings her family to the States.

The poet W. H. Auden entered into such a "passport marriage" with Erika Mann, the daughter of novelist Thomas Mann. In 1935, Mann, who had appeared in *Maedchen in Uniform,* ran a satirical cabaret critical of the Nazis and was threatened with the loss of her German citizenship. She asked Christopher Isherwood to marry her so as to provide her with a British passport. Mann had previously been married to an actor who became a Nazi sympathizer and eventually directed the Berlin State Theater, but she was, it was said, "largely lesbian by inclination"[14]—someone who met her for the first time during that period remarked that "she was nine-tenths a man—I mean no pun [on her name]."[15]

Isherwood "felt honored, excited, amused," he said—but "reluctantly said no." He told Mann the marriage would cause difficulties with his family, which was true enough, in a complicated way. His mother still wanted grandchildren, and "would have been horrified by such a marriage of convenience." His lover Heinz might well have been put in danger by Isherwood's marriage to someone who had been declared "a public enemy of the Third Reich." And he himself, he had to confess, had a "rooted horror of marriage."

Isherwood "shrank from marrying Erika," he said, "lest somebody, somewhere, might suspect him of trying to pass as a heterosexual." He thought of marriage as "the sacrament of the Others," and even found marriages between heterosexuals slightly distasteful. When his "basically homosexual friends got married—declaring that they were really bisexual, or that their wife was 'someone who understands,' " he "expressed sympathy but felt disgust," he said, noting that "many of these would start having sex with men on the side, while still maintaining that marriage alone is meaningful and that homosexuality is immature—i.e., disreputable, dangerous, and illegal."[16] He could not bring himself to marry Erika, but he asked whether he could put the idea to Auden. When he did so, Auden wired back one word: "Delighted."

Auden was at the time teaching at the Downs School at Colwall in Herefordshire, England, and living in a nearby cottage, sharing his rooms with a fellow teacher. When a long-awaited envelope of Erika's photographs arrived, he tore the package open eagerly and announced to his housemate, "There is my wife." At the registry office where he went to get the marriage license he knew neither his future wife's age nor her name, since she had previously been married and divorced, but the license was granted nonetheless. The elderly clerk, said Auden dryly, "would have married me to the poker."[17]

After the ceremony he drove Erika back to her hotel, and wrote to Stephen Spender, "I didn't see her till the ceremony and perhaps I shall never see her again. But she is very nice."[18] But in fact, after his initial amusement at the situation, Auden came to admire her and, her brother thought, to take the relationship a little more seriously. In 1936 he dedicated a book of poems to her, and wrote to a friend, "Since I saw you I've married (for passport reasons) Erika Mann, Thomas' daughter, who is a wonderful person."[19] He paid a visit to the Mann family in Switzerland and met the novelist. In 1939, when Auden and Isherwood visited the Manns and Erika in Princeton, New Jersey, Thomas Mann asked them to join the family for a photograph for *Time* magazine. "I know Mr. Auden's your son-in-law," said the photographer. "But Mr. Isherwood—what's his relation to your family?" "Family pimp," said Mann promptly, in German, a language the photographer, alone of the group, did not speak.[20] As for Auden, he apparently had fond enough memories of the married state to seek it again in his later years, proposing marriage to philosopher Hannah Arendt in 1970, a month after the death of her husband. In a letter to Mary McCarthy following Auden's death in 1973, Arendt remembered this as an appeal for help, sadly noting her own refusal "to take care of him when he came and asked for shelter."[21]

The bisexual marriage of convenience for "passport reasons" gets a double reverse twist in Ang Lee's film *The Wedding Banquet* (1993), in which a gay real estate entrepreneur, a naturalized American born in Taiwan, marries a Chinese painter and part-time waitress who wants to get her green card so she can remain in the States. Wai Tung (Winston Chao) lives happily with his lover, Simon (Mitchell Lichtenstein), in Greenwich Village, but his parents, eager to have a grandchild, keep asking him when he will marry. When they decide to fly to New York from Taiwan to meet the bride, the "fiction" of an engagement becomes "reality," and Wai Tung arranges to marry Wei Wei (May Chin). Wei Wei is attracted to him, though she knows about Simon. At the wedding banquet of the title (offered as a gesture of respect by the owner of a Chinese restaurant who feels indebted to Wai Tung's father, a Taiwanese general), the bride and groom get drunk, shed their clothes in compliance with their friends' boisterous insistence, and consummate the marriage, with the inevitable plot result: Wei Wei becomes pregnant, and the parents stay on in New York to await the birth of the child.

Like all marriages of convenience, this is really a marriage of inconvenience. Wei Wei can't cook, but she provides her new in-laws with exquisite meals concocted by Simon. And Simon himself grows restive with the arrangement. The film's dénouement, in which the canny General presents to Simon the ceremonial gift of money that is the traditional gift to a new in-law (and which we have earlier seen him earmark for the daughter-in-law, Wei Wei), links tradition and innovation, recognizing the gay marriage that has previously been erased, like the apartment's "tell-tale gay accouterments,"[22] in expectation of the parents' arrival.

Married to a Talk Show

Janine Walker and Ken Baldwin are engaged. Janine says that Ken is her prince and that she is now looking for her princess.

—*Oprah Winfrey, "The Oprah Winfrey Show"*[23]

Some "bisexual marriages" involve a commitment to monogamy, others do not. The same could be said of heterosexual marriages. "I'm committed to a relationship with this person," said Eve Diana, a bisexual woman featured on the "Donahue" show. Eve said she was very visible in the gay community, had had a number of relationships with women, and now was committed to a monogamous marriage. "It has nothing to do with bisexuality." How had her husband reacted to the news that she was bisexual? "A lot of guys would have dropped the salad fork and been out of there," offered Phil Donahue. "I guess it's my good fortune not to know which is the salad fork," replied Eve's husband equably.[24]

In the annals of superstition, dropping a fork means that a woman will shortly pay a call. Dropping a knife means that the visitor will be a boy or man. Or at least that's the way it goes in America. In other parts of the world, the opposite expectation holds: A knife indicates the visit of a member of the female sex; a fork, one of the male sex.[25] So Donahue's offhand remark—and John's reply—had an unwitting pertinence. The expected guest would be male *or* female: The fork was bisexual.

Finding the typical bisexual couple is like finding a typical heterosexual or a typical Republican: The more you collect clichés, the more the individuals seem to escape them. But talk shows being what they are, the vast majority of "married bisexuals" interviewed before studio audiences are not, like Eve Diana, committed to a monogamous relationship.

Tyrone and Tony were guests on "The Ricki Lake Show" when the subject was bisexuality. Tyrone was married and had two children, but he now lived with Tony. When Tony announced that he was gay, not bi, the audience applauded. "It's okay to be gay but not to be bisexual?" Ricki asked them. The problem seemed to be Tyrone's marriage and children, especially when it turned out that Tony had first moved in with the married couple. After a few years Tyrone's wife, who had declined to appear on the program, moved out. Tyrone, who seemed quite young, said he had lived with his wife for ten years and with Tony for five, three of which overlapped. Again the audience booed. "I have a wife and two kids and I have a lover," he said to them without heat. "I have no problem with this. If you do, that's your problem." They did, and it was.

The problem seemed to be that Tyrone was having too good a time.

"Having his cake and eating it too" was, inevitably, the way some expressed it. He insisted that his wife had options and chose from among them. He talked about his closeness with his children. He identified himself as Tony's lover. Why wasn't he conflicted? What *was* his problem?

Viewers seem to have both fascination and condemnation for those who, in one way or another, are "having it both ways." And hosts sometimes stumble over themselves trying to figure out what questions to ask.

A "Donahue" program of the early eighties brought together several married couples in which the husband was bisexual; in one case the wife was also a therapist. Tina knew Richard was gay when she married him, didn't she?

"Yes," Tina acknowledged, "I knew it the day I met him that he was bisexual. Because we met at a group called the Bisexual Center in Southern California."[26]

"I am not gay and I am not really totally straight," Richard told the studio audience. "I think I have been bisexual all my life. . . . Why can't I have a marriage same as anyone else? It may be slightly altered to suit my needs or to make me happy, but just because it doesn't fit into everyone else's norm doesn't mean I have to scrap the rest of my life."

Callers and the audience, predictably, disagreed, labeling the spouses of bisexuals "very unself-confident" and lacking "pride in themselves" (the epidemic of therapyspeak among lay persons, and the cult of "self-esteem," is not the least of the sins of popular culture). Tina added fuel to the audience's ire by announcing calmly that she and her husband were looking for "another man to be married to," a "third person with an equal share in our relationship." The Sharrards, Tina confided, had sex once a day with one another, "which is plenty for me." If her husband "wanted to go out and have more" that was "fine" with her. "I bend over backwards," said another panelist, "to try to make Roger's life as pleasant as possible."

"I was told a person is either gay or not, no middle of the road," said one caller. "You were told wrong," replied Tina, the therapist. "Pardon me?" asked the startled caller. "You were told wrong. That is a social prejudice that is not true. There are a lot of bisexual people in the world." The caller persevered: But couldn't the "gay partner" have been happy in a gay relationship? To this Richard Sharrard answered, "I have been in relationships where for a while I was in a totally gay relationship or a totally straight relationship and I always felt like something was missing." "Being bisexual," he said, "you don't quite fit into either world."

The audience's sense of surprise that such marriages existed, or could work, was palpable. But the show ended with the virtually obligatory division of the house, with Donahue asking whether "this is none of anybody else's business and you are happy for them" or "this is wrong and they should be faithful to one person regardless of their sexuality." Predictably, the nays had it.

◆

The usually unflappable Oprah Winfrey had an awkward moment of her own in interviewing Janine Walker, the engaged woman who was also "looking for her princess."

> OPRAH: Does being in love with a woman feel the same as being in love with a man?
> JANINE WALKER: No.
> OPRAH: It doesn't. See, I thought that was a stupid question.

After the station break Janine got to explain what she meant. A sexual relationship with a woman could include friendship, "verbalization," "playfulness," trips to the mall, and jokes about men. "So it's like a friendship-love affair," hazarded Oprah. "Right," said Walker. "I'm not out for promiscuous sex."

This is one version of the stories bisexual women tell about sex with other women. But there is another version, a version that focuses more directly and frankly on the pleasures of same-sex eroticism. Men have hard bodies, women have soft ones. Men are "different," women are "same." Men are bigger, women are smaller. Why choose?

Bisexuality doesn't mean "that you want to have sex with a man and two women," Walker insisted. "A lot of men have the fantasy of having sex with two women at the same time. And they see the term 'bisexual' and they think that that's what it means. . . . It's not what it means."

Or at least it isn't exactly what it means. Consider another relationship involving two women and a man. Nina and David Hartley live in a threesome with "Bobbie," with whom they sometimes have sex. David and "Bobbie" were a couple for eighteen years, but "Bobbie" didn't want to have children; then David met Nina, who does. The two women say they're not jealous of each other. "I consider her my more-than-sister, my wife," said "Bobbie." Phil Donahue, whose guests they were, quipped, "That'll thrill the Mormons."[27]

But "Bobbie" persisted. "I've got a wife instead of being one," she said, adding that any woman who'd been a wife would know what she meant.

Bi-gamy

A member of a sexual threesome reports his and his partners' experience when they went to a swingers' conference in 1978, "and the director didn't know how to handle a threesome. Really, think about that: swinging is couples. Finally, he worked out a deal for us to stay with a couple. They explained us to their children as Mormons."[28]

The Mormon religion is known for its attention to what have been described in the popular press as family values: heterosexuality, togetherness, abstention from drugs, alcohol, and even caffeine. In one respect, of course, Mormons have not always been consistent with today's family values credo, since the history of the church includes male polygamy, a practice abandoned as church doctrine only relatively recently, and then as the price of Utah's joining the union of states. Polygamy, a practice that not only quite literally enforced patriarchy but also tended to provide a man with an abundance of children (vital for farming and other family pursuits) and a convenient domestic labor force of wives, is the manifest opposite of monogamy, perhaps the greatest "family value" of them all.

"Male nature being polygamous, the restoration of all things demanded a sanctification of that polygamy, rather than an abolishment of a nature that could not be corrected," Harold Bloom writes in his study of Mormonism, *The American Religion*. Bloom, who regards this assessment as "truthful and realistic," notes with equanimity the "erudite arithmetic" by which scholars have debated whether Brigham Young had twenty-seven or fifty-five wives, and whether Joseph Smith "had managed eighty-four marriages within the three years before his murder."[29] "Good clean or unclean fun," Bloom calls this scholarly speculation, in the puckish tones that sometimes make him sound like an academic Gore Vidal.

With all the fuss about bisexuals espousing nonmonogamy as a style of life, and the consequently perceived threat to the institution of marriage, it is fascinating to note the persistence of the "bisexual Mormon" as a dramatic character type in American dramas of public and private life. Is it because of the background of "polygamy" and the lay assumption about what that might mean that the figure of the bisexual Mormon recurs with some surprising frequency in contemporary explorations of bisexuality and marriage? I am thinking here of Joe Pitt, the married Mormon politico who leaves his wife to take a male lover in Tony Kushner's *Angels in America,* and also of Senator Brigham Anderson, the moral center of Allen Drury's 1957 novel *Advise and Consent,* later made into an Otto Preminger movie starring Don Murray as the upright and principled married senator with a secret in his past.

Drury's Senator Anderson is the senior senator from Utah, "one of the rising young men of the country," "born into a prominent family in Salt Lake City, high in the councils of the Church," and looking forward with confidence to "a life of ever more satisfying and worthwhile public service."[30] His name and the state he represents clearly recall Brigham Young, one of the founders of the religion also known as the Church of Jesus Christ of Latter Day Saints. Anderson is no saint, but he is a thoughtful self-reliant personality, who had "in general been much luckier than most at avoiding the more unpleasant aspects of human living."[31] That is, until he ran afoul of a Senate confirmation hearing in which there were to be no holds barred.

Drury's novel is one of those thick-textured products of the late fifties, over six hundred pages of small print (even the dust jacket calls it "massive"), that endeavors to give a full if not fully rounded portrait of both its characters and the Washington governmental culture of which they were a part. Thus we read in depth of Brig Anderson's teen years, his time at Stanford, and the unsettling encounter with a fraternity brother who "only once . . . dared to take a long gamble and ask quietly, 'It isn't easy, is it?' " as they sat opposite one another at a little San Francisco bar south of Market Street. But "this particular friend had problems Brigham Anderson suspected and didn't want to get involved with," so he stared him down amiably and changed the subject. He "enjoyed" the girls he met "sufficiently so that he was pretty sure he didn't want what his fraternity brother wanted."[32]

With these plain hints the novelist nudges his hero into the war in the Pacific.

> Through it all, however, he still remained essentially untouched, though there were many who would have wished otherwise and some who made it very plain to him. Not always did this come in conventional context. Quite often he found, first with surprise and then with his usual calm acceptance of life, it would be fellow officers or enlisted men, many of them married, to whom his unfailing kindness and decency seemed to indicate possibilities they felt they must test out, apparently with the idea that it probably wasn't true, but wouldn't it be wonderful for them if it were.[33]

And did Anderson respond? "With one exception," we are told, "something always held him back." Until one fateful day in Honolulu.

> Very late in the war, returned to Honolulu for two months' rest, he had been lying on the beach one afternoon when someone deliberately came over and lay down beside him on the sand. For the better part of an hour they lay there hardly moving, hardly looking at one another. . . . Suddenly the whole surging loneliness of the war, his own tiredness and questioning of himself, the burdens of so much agony everywhere in the world, the need for a little rest and a little peace without fighting any more with himself or anybody, had seemed unbearable, and like two children in a trance they had returned to the hotel together and from then on for nearly a month they were never apart for long. Any other time, any other place, he knew it would never have happened; but many things like that happened in war, he had observed, and no one noticed and no one cared. For four weeks he was happy. . . . Then for reasons which he could never analyze exactly, but which he became convinced later were probably sound, he became suspicious, and with suspicion came jealousy and, for a time, an agony of heart such as he never

> hoped to undergo again. . . . He asked to be returned to the front . . .
> they saw one another for the last time, looked, and looked away. He
> knew then that they would never be together again, but he knew also
> that in all probability few things for either of them would ever again
> be as deep.[34]

The gelid prose here should not obscure the point: Without any noun or
pronoun to indicate the gender of his partner, Brigham Anderson's affair
with a fellow soldier, his emotional release and sexual jealousy, are carefully set out as this hero's Achilles' heel. His return to the States and to
Utah, his time in Stanford Law School, and a letter from the still ungendered and unidentified friend are then accounted for. "He kept it for a day
and a night, read it many times, thought of replying, started to jot down
the address, and then changed his mind, finally tore it up completely. . . .
But it hurt still, and hurt badly. . . . He never heard again, even though
there was a time after he first became nationally prominent when he was
afraid he might hear, in some way that might be detrimental to him. But
he never did."[35]

At this point he begins to build a political career in earnest, and to seek
in earnest for a wife. "One night in Provo he met a shy, plain girl who
seemed to like him; in six months time he was convinced he liked her
too, and by the end of the year they were married. . . . He did his best
sincerely to make Mabel Anderson happy, and for the most part he succeeded. Sometimes old memories would return like a knife, but he was
sure she never knew it, and he put them aside ruthlessly and concentrated
on his home and career."[36]

The tone of *Advise and Consent* reads today like that of a Harlequin
romance, but the crisis that will bring down Brigham Anderson is established in forebodings worthy of Greek tragedy. What is the sound of one
shoe dropping? Neither "bisexuality" nor "homosexuality" are mentioned
here; there is the whiff of a gay bar in the frat brother's long look and half-
uttered proposition, and the full-blown fantasy of an *Advocate* classified
ad in the pick-up-turned-once-in-a-lifetime-love-affair on the beach.

It is clear from these passages that his love for his wife is part of the
world of patriotism, religion, duty, politics, and ambition.[37] The "perfectly
genuine happiness" and then the "agony of heart" he enjoyed with his
lover in Hawaii is prompted by a different scenario. His wife, he has to
conclude, "is one of those good people who are also, in spite of all their
earnest efforts, basically dull."[38] "The episode in Hawaii," as he thinks of
it, remains central to his understanding of himself; "nothing ever again
induced in him quite that combination of restlessness, uncertainty, impulse, and desire." "For all its pain, and for all that it was not exactly the
sort of thing you would want to discuss in Salt Lake City, he did not
regret that it had happened." But "there were ten thousand reasons, of
reputation, family, home, and career why it should not be revived."[39]

In Otto Preminger's film, the one homosexual episode in Brig Anderson's life is revealed through the machinations of a wimpy and ambitious left-wing senator, Fred Van Ackerman (played with conviction by George Grizzard), a kind of rising McCarthy of the left. Van Ackerman has come into possession of a photograph that "incriminates" Anderson by revealing his long-ago affair, and arranges for Mabel Anderson to find it. The soldier-lover is depicted as a hunky gay hustler whose dates are managed by a eunuchoid pimp with a pink satin double bed—the apparent opposite of the straight-living Anderson. The scene in which Brig confronts him in a New York gay bar is a masterpiece of period melodrama. Overcome by a combination of despair, nobility, and self-hatred, fearing exposure for his family, Anderson slits his throat in his Senate office.

In the novel the situation is considerably more complicated. Anderson asks his wife to throw away some old army uniforms, in the pocket of one of which is the telltale photograph and its suggestive inscription (never quoted in the text). The photo, in a manila envelope, is placed by a cleaning woman on Anderson's desk with some other papers; grabbing up all the papers to go to work, he inadvertently takes it with him. The envelope falls out of his car and into the curious hands of a Supreme Court Justice, who immediately recognizes its value as blackmail and hands it over to the majority leader of the Senate. When Anderson, the chairman of a key Senate confirmation committee, refuses to rubber-stamp the president's choice for secretary of state (who has been a member of a Communist cell and lied about it under oath), the president asks for and gets the photo, and forwards it to the ruthless Senator Van Ackerman, the leader of COMFORT, the Committee on Making Further Offers for a Russian Truce. Van Ackerman holds a televised rally in which he speaks Joe McCarthy's familiar words. "I have here in my hand," he says, the "documented proof" that Anderson is "not morally fit."[40] His plan is to reveal the truth about Anderson at a speech to the Senate.

As word spreads throughout Washington of what Brigham Anderson did in Honolulu, Anderson's wife gets an anonymous phone call followed by a crude but explicit note: "Composed of pasted letters clipped from a newspaper, its message was quite explicit enough, even for Mabel, who was not very sophisticated about such matters, or indeed about much of anything." "It happened; it happened," he tells her, "I went off the track."[41] Her response is all too familiar in the context of the partner betrayed by a bisexual spouse: *"How can I ever be sure again?"* "He felt then as though the world had ended," and she quickly moves to take the words back ("I didn't mean that, . . . I didn't, I didn't, I didn't,"[42] yet in fact she *does*). To cap things off, Anderson receives a phone call from "a voice he had never thought, and never wanted, to hear again" explaining that "they looked me up," "they offered me money, an awful lot of money," and "I told them what they wanted to know."[43]

Here Drury repeats the curious ungendering of this lover from the past, who is only described as "the voice," never as "he" or "him," in the account of their extensive conversation. The voice is by turns plaintive, apologetic, desperate, sad. "I would have helped you," says Anderson, and the voice says, "I never meant to hurt you." When Anderson shoots himself in his office after writing out a full account of the case, he realizes, "in one last moment of rigid and unflinching honesty," that "it was not only of his family that he was thinking as he died. It was of a beach in Honolulu on a long, hot, lazy afternoon."[44]

In other words, the bittersweet ending of the Brigham Anderson story in Drury's *Advise and Consent* confirms, rather than backs away from, the sincerity of this long-ago passion. Mabel Anderson, the loyal Mormon wife, is consistently undercut: She is good but "basically dull," painfully sincere, not quick on the uptake, capable of being managed by deft displays of simulated sexual desire.[45] Among the reasons Anderson gives for never again seeking a relationship with a man are "reputation, family, home and career," but also "self-preservation, obligation to society, integrity, and *self-denial.*"[46] The true loves of his life are his small daughter and his lost lover, both captured in images of blissful happiness in the ocean waves.

Perhaps significantly, the heroic Brig Anderson, "that nice guy that everybody liked so much," is contrasted in Drury's novel with Fred Van Ackerman, described as "that twisted little man from Wyoming."[47] "Why should I bother trying to find out what's in that queer little mind?" asks a senator sunbathing at the solarium atop the New Senate Office Building, a place that, with its "atmosphere of a gymnasium, redolent of steam, disinfectant, sweat, and nakedness," made Anderson "think of things he didn't want to think of."[48] Anderson may be the noble bisexual, but Ackerman is the twisted queer.

As for the long-ago lover, the voice on the telephone, he comes to gendered life only in Anderson's dying reverie ("a lost boy was crying on the telephone") and in his own, answering suicide: "[A] tall young man with haunted eyes got drunk in a shabby café in a little town in Indiana and jumped off a bridge. There were no papers on his body and nobody knew who he was."[49]

The relationship between Louis Ironson, a gay man in Tony Kushner's *Angels in America, Part Two: Perestroika,* and Joe Pitt, his bisexual Mormon lover, founders on Louis's discovery that Joe, a law clerk, has ghostwritten court decisions that Louis regards as "legal fag-bashing"— decisions that say that "homosexuals . . . are *not* entitled to equal protection under the law."[50] " 'Have you no decency, sir? At long last? Have you no sense of decency?' Who said that?" he challenges Joe. The quotation, which he describes as "the greatest punchline in American history," is Joseph Welch's famous rebuke of Senator Joseph McCarthy in the Army-McCarthy hearings. He is equally shocked to discover that Joe is a Mormon.

Why *is* Kushner's baffled bisexual hero, like Allen Drury's, conceived as a Mormon? Joe's Mormonism is a centerpiece of Kushner's *Angels* diptych. In *Part One: Millennium Approaches,* he is introduced as a dutiful husband with a wife he humors, calls "buddy," and cuts out of the important questions in his life, little things like his sexuality and his political aspirations. Harper Pitt retaliates by taking pills and seeing visions, but her instincts about her husband are sound:

> HARPER: I heard on the radio how to give blowjobs.
> JOE: What?
> HARPER: You want to try?
> JOE: You really shouldn't listen to stuff like that.
> HARPER: Mormons can give blowjobs.[51]

From a phone booth in Central Park Joe calls his mother to say he's a homosexual (an assertion his mother finds "ridiculous"), and then he confronts his wife. "I knew this when I married you. I've known this I guess for as long as I've known anything, but . . . I thought maybe that with enough effort and will I could change myself. . . . I have no sexual feelings for you, Harper. And I don't think I ever did."

In *Part Two: Perestroika,* Harper and Joe have a postcoital conversation:

> HARPER: When we have sex. Why do you keep your eyes closed?
> JOE: I don't.
> HARPER: You always do. You can say why, I already know the answer.
> JOE: Then why do I have to . . .
> HARPER: You imagine things. Imagine men.
> JOE: Yes.[52]

By making Joe Pitt a Mormon, the playwright dramatizes and thematizes a modern crisis of belief which has at its root the conundrum of sexuality. Mormonism suits Kushner's dramatic purposes in part because it is an "American religion" as well as one that believes in angels and in personal salvation. And Kushner, like Allen Drury, places his principled and conflicted Mormon in telling juxtaposition to the double duplicity of Senator McCarthy and his disciples, for Joe Pitt is Roy Cohn's protégé. When he tells the hospitalized Cohn, dying of AIDS, that he has left his wife for a man, Cohn's indignant response is predictable to everyone but Joe: "You're with a man? Now you listen to me," he says. "I want you home. With your wife. Whatever else you got going, cut it dead."[53]

The image of the "bisexual Mormon," with its intrinsic sense of oxymoron, becomes a powerful paradigm for the condition of conflict and choice.

But what happens when this fictional construct begins to speak in his or her own words?

"Although brought up Mormon," says self-described bisexual Christopher Alexander, "I managed to avoid some of the highly significant anti-homosexual messages that many in the Mormon Church, as well as in other churches, transmit."[54] He had sexual experiences with women and with men in high school, called himself "gay," had secret crushes on lesbians, and met Teresa when he was in college. "Teresa knew that I wasn't particularly promiscuous or sexually active with many other men, but unlike her I was nonmonogamous."[55] The couple became active in a group called Affirmation: Gay and Lesbian Mormons, after attending the Lesbian and Gay Freedom Day Parade in San Francisco. Subsequently Alexander had a serious relationship with a man, began to be concerned about AIDS, married Teresa, and became the general coordinator of Affirmation, where some members expressed dissatisfaction with the fact that a Mormon gay and lesbian group was being directed by a married bisexual man. "He doesn't count, he's bisexual," some coworkers complained. Nonetheless Alexander persevered ("by this time I was much more secure with my identity as a bisexual") and began conducting workshops on bisexuals with AIDS, as well as a support group for bi's and heterosexuals. He met a man at the International AIDS conference in 1987 and began a romantic relationship with him. The three of them—Teresa, Christopher, and his new lover, Martin—spent a great deal of time together until Martin's death. "Sometimes Martin attended workshops with me when I spoke about bisexuality. Once he and Teresa even spoke on a panel together." Chris Alexander believes that "more people could make bisexuality work in their lives if they didn't restrict their views of themselves into one sexual category."[56]

Alexander's is an unusual story but not a spectacular one, especially as he tells it. "Getting comfortable with myself as a bisexual has been a lifelong process," he notes. Tony Kushner and Allen Drury both use the figure of a bisexual Mormon to underscore the apparent impossibility of a middle ground between marriage and same-sex eroticism. But in the far more banal precincts of what it pleases us to call "real life," that theoretically impossible middle ground, or overlapping territory, is the space where some Mormons, and many other people, choose to live.

Cat House

What *is* the "American religion"? Is it Mormonism, as Harold Bloom suggests? Or puritanical sexuality and its strange but inevitable bedfellow, the return of the repressed?

The plot of *Advise and Consent*—buried love for a male companion returns to wreak havoc on a married male protagonist—resembles, in many ways, the plot of Tennessee Williams's play *Cat on a Hot Tin Roof.*

And, as in the hospital stage set in *Angels in America,* the central prop for the stage set of *Cat on a Hot Tin Roof* is a bed: "a big double bed which staging should make a functional part of the set as often as suitable, the surface of which should be slightly raked to make figures on it seen more easily." The room in which it sits, like the house that is now "the home of the Delta's biggest cotton-planter," once belonged to a gay couple, "the original owners of the place, Jack Straw and Peter Ochello, a pair of old bachelors who shared this room all their lives together."[57]

So Tennessee Williams's brilliant mid-fifties analysis of modern marriage will be set on a stage in which the "original" marriage is gay. Straw and Ochello's relationship "haunts" the play as Williams suggests that it should. Next to theirs, the marriage of Maggie the Cat, whose voice "sometimes drops low as a boy's" so that "you have a sudden image of her playing boys' games as a child," and ex-football hero, current alcoholic, and self-suspecting "queer" Brick Pollitt, seems like a structure of lies.

What is a marriage? Character after character in *Cat* thinks a marriage is sex and children. "I want to ask you a question, one question," Big Mama says to Maggie. "D'you make Brick happy in bed?" "Why don't you ask if he makes *me* happy in bed?" Maggie retorts. (In the bowdlerized 1958 film version, starring Paul Newman and Elizabeth Taylor, the phrase "in bed" is discreetly cut, and the question becomes not one of sexual pleasure but of ineffable and indefinable "happiness.") "Something's not right!" Big Mama—who is, after all, *Brick's* mama—insists. "You're childless and my son drinks!" The stage direction tells us that *"She turns at the door and points at the bed."* "When a marriage goes on the rocks, the rocks are *there,* right there!"[58]

What is "not right" in the marriage of Maggie and Brick, we will shortly discover, has something to do with Brick's relationship with his childhood buddy Skipper, with whom Maggie has had an affair. Skipper is dead, and now Brick can't stand to be around Maggie. Maggie insists the affair was just her way, and also Skipper's, of getting closer to Brick. "We made love to each other to dream it was you, both of us!"[59]

In Maggie's eyes Brick and Skipper were the couple, and she the triangulating third, the odd one out: "Why I remember when we double-dated in college, Gladys Fitzgerald and I and you and Skipper, it was more like a date between you and Skipper. Gladys and I were just sort of tagging along as if it was necessary to chaperone you!—to make a good public impression—"[60] For Brick this is "naming it dirty," taking the "one great true thing" in his life, the friendship with Skipper, and sullying it. "I married you, Maggie. Why would I marry you, Maggie, if I was—?" The missing word, the word "queer" and indeed the explicit term "sodomy," are not supplied until act two, when they come out in a conversation between Brick and his father, Big Daddy.

For Maggie the *"unconscious* desire" (both the emphasis and the Freudian vocabulary are hers) was only on Skipper's side. When she said to him,

"SKIPPER! STOP LOVIN' MY HUSBAND OR TELL HIM HE'S GOT TO LET YOU ADMIT IT TO HIM!" (here the level of volume is indicated by the playwright's capitalization in the script), he first ran away, then tried with her sexual complicity "to prove that what I had said wasn't true." Now Brick won't touch her, and she wants sex and children. She has even been to a gynecologist to get checked out. Her tiresome sister-in-law, as she is too well aware, already has five "no-neck monsters" and is expecting a sixth. The "problem" Maggie faces is thus squarely posed to her by Brick in the last moments of act one: How is she "going to have a child by a man that can't stand you"? "That's a problem," she says, "that I will have to work out."

Brick's unhappiness has landed him not only with a drinking problem but also, most recently, with a broken ankle, sustained when he tried to jump hurdles at the high school in the middle of the night. The broken ankle and the crutch it necessitates position him squarely in the role of this very Freudian play's Oedipus—"swollen foot," castration complex, and all. That his parents are called, in what I take to be a "typical" Southern locution, Big Daddy and Big Mama, only reinforces the almost-cartoonlike, and yet very powerful, Oedipalization of the story. We are only a step away from the surreally cruel-and-kind families of Edward Albee's plays, who literally dismember their children in the course of what they call love.

But it is not these unmistakable Oedipal markers but another aspect of the Oedipal triangle that is most germane to the question of bisexuality. That aspect is the so-called primal scene, the traumatic event witnessed, remembered, or fantasized by the child, which functions as a source of later dysfunction. *Cat on a Hot Tin Roof* uncovers the events of Brick's relationship with Skipper, a relationship he refuses to call "queer," and establishes it as "the inadmissible thing Skipper died to disavow," to quote once again from Williams's extremely specific directorial instructions. The question, with which we will want to engage in a moment—is whether the admission of the inadmissible, and the acknowledgment of that which has been disavowed, marks Brick as "a homosexual" and his marriage as either a social fiction or, as it is sometimes interpreted, a veiled transvestite bond.

At the close of the play Maggie announces her pregnancy to a startled family gathering, and then turns down the lamp in the bedroom and prepares "to make the lie true." In order to do this she hurls Brick's crutch over the railing and locks up his liquor cabinet, painstakingly described by Williams as a piece of furniture that functions as a closet ("a very complete and compact little shrine to virtually all the comforts and illusions behind which we hide from such things as the characters in the play are faced with"[61]): The two gestures are versions of the same.

The scene that unveils the "primal scene" is itself an exchange between an apparently weak son and an apparently powerful father. "You started drinkin' when your friend Skipper died," says Big Daddy, himself dying of cancer, though he hasn't yet been told. *"Silence for five beats,"* Williams instructs (that's a very long silence onstage). *"Then Brick makes a startled movement, reaching for his crutch."* "What are you suggesting?" It seems that according to his brother and sister-in-law, "there was something not right exactly in your—"

" 'Not right'?"

"Not, well, exactly *normal* in your friendship with—."

The word "normal," as so often, triggers a firestorm, but not of the usual kind. "Normal?" says Brick. "No!—It was too rare to be normal, any true thing between two people is too rare to be normal. Oh, once in a while he put his hand on my shoulder or I'd put mine on his, oh, maybe even, when we were touring the country in pro-football an' shared hotel-rooms we'd reach across the space between the two beds and shake hands to say goodnight, yeah, one or two times we—"

> BIG DADDY: Brick, nobody thinks that that's not normal!
>
> BRICK: Well, they're mistaken, it was! It was a pure an' true thing and that's not normal![62]

Football hero Brick is a prime example of someone exhibiting what has been called homosexual panic. His closeness to Skipper makes him de-spise, or seem to despise, homosexuality, "ducking sissies," "queers," and "fairies." When he and Skipper discovered that a pledge to their fraternity "did a, *attempted* to do a, unnatural thing," he tells Big Daddy furiously, they threw him off campus, and when last heard of he was in North Africa. He is outraged (or is he?) that big Daddy seems to think "me an' Skipper did, did, did—*sodomy!*—together" (but it's *he* who makes the suggestion, not Big Daddy. In *whose* "unconscious desires" is this thought lurking, we might ask, even if only to be disavowed?). Maybe, he speculates angrily, that's why he and Maggie have been put in the bedroom previously occu-pied by Straw and Ochello, a room in which "that pair of old sisters slept in a double bed where both of 'em died."[63]

So much smoke—can there really be no fire? It's Maggie's fault, he says. "Y'know, I think that Maggie had always felt sort of left out because she and me never got any closer together than two cats on a—fence humping." So Maggie worked on Skipper, "poured in his mind the dirty, false idea that what we were, him and me, was a frustrated case of that ole pair of sisters that lived in this room, Jack Straw and Peter Ochello!—He, poor Skipper, went to bed with Maggie to prove it wasn't true, and when it didn't work out, he thought it *was* true!" And he became a drunk. And he died.

Big Daddy is a good psychiatrist; Williams makes him one. *"Big Daddy has listened to this story, dividing the grain from the chaff,"* he tells us. *"Now he looks at his son."* And asks the inevitable analyst's question. Not How did that make you feel? but the *other* analyst's question: What did you leave out? And "out," indeed, it comes. What Brick has left out is the long-distance call from Skipper, the last time the two men spoke together, "in which he made a drunken confession to me and on which I hung up!"

Tennessee Williams is a master of the guilty-secret-buried-in-the-past. In *A Streetcar Named Desire,* Blanche Dubois's discovery of her young husband in bed with a boy leads her to tell him he disgusts her, and thus provokes his suicide. The film version of *Streetcar* has Blanche confessing guilt for her husband's death, but characteristically omits the cause. Is the guilty secret really homosexuality or bisexuality? It seems pointless to wrangle over this—in both *Cat* and *Streetcar* the man is married and feels divided desires.

Cat on a Hot Tin Roof tells two contradictory stories about Brick's sexuality, one in the stage directions and author's notes, the other in the dialogue. One says that the contestatory "truth" over which the characters wrangle is that Brick is really "a homosexual"; the other says that he "can't be" (isn't—mustn't be). Neither version leaves interpretative space for acknowledging that his love for Skipper and his marriage with Maggie can both be "true." Bisexuality, which is one way of describing the trajectory of his experiences, is only imagined as a lie, whatever the "truth" may be.

The film version of *Cat* further erases this possibility, together with the eroticization of Brick's past relationship with Skipper. None of the "sissy"-"fairy"-"queer" language survives the transition to film, nor does the hand-holding with Skipper in the hotel room. Maggie certainly doesn't refer to the two boys as "dating" each other in high school, nor does she turn out to have actually had sex with Skipper. Instead, her marital purity is preserved; she says she was afraid she might lose both of them if she went through with the seduction. And speaking of seductions: Brick's recuperative heterosexuality is in full force at the end of the film, when it is he, not Maggie, who does the inviting to the bedroom and declares his intention of making the fantasy child a real one. Having patched things up with Big Daddy, who is the film's replacement as a lost love object for the largely ignored Skipper, Brick himself drops the crutch and tells his wife to lock the door. Elia Kazan persuaded the playwright to change the original version for Broadway, making Big Daddy a larger presence in the last act and rendering Maggie more likable. The film thus culminates in the restoration of son to father and father to son, indicated by Brick's renewed willingness to call his father Big Daddy, a term he earlier disavowed.

Interestingly, this reinstatement of the father as the central grounding figure in the movie version of a bisexual drama can also be found in Steven Spielberg's presentation of Alice Walker's *The Color Purple.* Walker ends the novel on a utopian bisexual note, leaving Celie and her formerly abusive husband "Mr." sewing together on the porch, both thinking about Shug Avery, the woman they both love. But Spielberg adds an entirely fabricated father from whom Shug Avery is estranged (in the novel, her father is unknown), who happens to be the local preacher, and with whom she is reconciled in a joyous coming together of the frequenters of the juke joint and the congregation of the church. The film—no surprise— also glosses over the sexual relationship between Shug and Celie, presenting it as a warm friendship. Thus, at the end of both *Cat on a Hot Tin Roof* and *The Color Purple,* an anguished or idealized bisexuality is erased, and a father figure commands center stage. Where the original works explore questions of sexual ambivalence and discovery with subtlety and quiet subversiveness, the films erase what is unsettling or creative about them by means of this return to the paternal ordering principle. No consideration of bisexuality, marriage, and family values can fail to note this return of the patriarchs on the site of buried bisexuality. The films are perhaps miniaturized versions of what the institution of marriage is designed to reproduce.

Chapter 17

Marriages of Inconvenience

A marriage so free, so spontaneous, that it would allow of wide excursions of the pair from each other, in common or even in separate objects of work and interest, and yet would hold them all the time in the bond of absolute sympathy, would by its very freedom be all the more poignantly attractive, and by its very scope and breadth all the richer and more vital —would be in a sense indestructible.

—*Edward Carpenter*, Love's Coming-of-Age [1]

"Bisexual marriage" has been a topic of considerable fascination in the tabloid, talk-show, and pop-psychology worlds, since it seems to some observers to pose an internal contradiction. If a marriage is defined as an exclusive and exclusionary sexual and social relationship between two people, with a strong economic basis and a public vow of fidelity ("forsaking all others"), then how can it be bisexual?

The confusion, as lesbian activist Ann Northrop points out, stems from the fact that "bisexuality is misunderstood as meaning simultaneous relationships." [2] In part for prurient reasons—the desire to imagine that *someone* is having all these sexual adventures—bisexual people who announce themselves as bisexual and who are also married, whether to other bisexuals or to monosexuals, get a lot of flack.

Part of the problem with the concept of "bisexual marriage" is semantic. Does it mean "marriage between bisexuals," "marriage to a bisexual," or a kind of "marriage," like that contracted as a publicity stunt by Roseanne Arnold, her former husband, Tom, and their assistant, Kim Silva, that stretches the boundaries, and the meaning, of the term "marriage" itself? Or does it mean being married to two people simultaneously, one of each sex? In Sidney Lumet's *Dog Day Afternoon* (1975), Al Pacino starred in the true-life story of a bank robber driven to distraction by his two wives: Angie, the mother of his children, and Leon, a gay man he married in a Greenwich Village "white wedding" with cross-dressed bridesmaids. The bank robber, "Sonny," wound up in the penitentiary, according to the end-credits; Angie went on welfare; and Leon had a sex-change operation.

Some people marry, and then decide or discover that they are bisexual. Some people marry and then decide or discover they are gay, remaining married for a variety of reasons from the much maligned "heterosexual privilege" to the desire to "keep the family together" for their own sake or their children's, to the simple fact that they like or enjoy their spouse's company. Other people marry knowing they are bisexual, or that one partner is bisexual. Some bisexual marriages are more visible than others, and some bisexual persons have been particularly committed to marriage as an institution—or to their own marriages, whether those marriages were convenient or (occasionally) inconvenient.

Let us look at three different models for how "bisexual marriage plots" might be told.

In the 1978 film *A Different Story,* a gay man and a lesbian share living quarters. Albert (Perry King) has been the kept lover of a famous conductor; Stella (Meg Foster) is involved in a lesbian relationship with a closeted schoolteacher who is terrified of being found out. (The scriptwriters have clearly amused themselves by raiding classic love narratives. "Stella" and her lesbian lover "Phyl"—in this case, short for "Phyllis"—owe their names to Sir Philip Sidney's sonnet sequence *Astrophel and Stella;* Albert is the male original of Marcel's elusive, and bisexual, beloved Albertine in Marcel Proust's *Remembrance of Things Past.*) Stella and Albert fall in love, marry, and have a child. Albert's newfound heterosexuality is clinched (in the audience's eyes) by his having an extramarital affair with a beautiful female model. The climactic discovery scene—Albert's lover is in the shower and Stella opens the door to expose her rival—comes as something of a surprise to the audience, since we are led to share Stella's expectation that Albert has returned to having sex with men.

Predictably, *A Different Story* was criticized for reinforcing the idea that "gays can go straight" and "that their homosexuality is expendable."[3] The film, in short, was viewed as a progress narrative. While the plot as a whole can be called bisexual, the progress from gay to straight nevertheless erases the concept of bisexuality.

In *Making Love,* a 1982 film starring Kate Jackson, Michael Ontkean, and Harry Hamlin, the "progress" goes in the other direction: not from gay to straight, but from straight to gay. Zack, a Beverly Hills doctor (Ontkean), has an affair with Bart, a successful writer (Hamlin), and wants to leave his marriage, but Bart isn't interested in commitment; Zack leaves his wife anyway, goes off to New York, and finds a boyfriend. It was, noted Vito Russo dryly, "the first time in commercial film that a serious gay couple were permitted a happy ending. Hollywood thinks that's radical and that's its mistake. If that's all a film is about, it's boring."[4] Too straight for gays, too gay for straights, agreed most gay critics.

The film indeed used all the familiar clichés of the time: the bisexual husband as gay deceiver, the wife's desperate attempt to save the marriage at all costs. "I'm married, Bart. It's not as if *I'm* gay," Zack protests before falling into bed with him. Alarmed by Zack's moody silence, his wife, Claire, coaxes him to speak:

> CLAIRE: Zack, whatever it is, I'm your wife and I love you.
> ZACK: I've had desires I've been repressing and they're starting to surface. I find that I'm attracted to men. I've got to stop denying it.
> CLAIRE: What are you telling me? That our whole marriage is a lie?

When Claire suggests that Zack see a shrink he insists that he isn't ill and won't "change." "All right then, we'll accept it," she announces bravely, but this is not what Zack wants either. "I don't want a double life," he says.

Once again, bisexuality is normalized out of existence. Marriage is either real or a lie; life should not be double.

In contrast, Barry Kohn and Alice Matusow subtitled their 1980 book "Portrait of a Bisexual Marriage," a title clearly intended to echo Nigel Nicolson's very successful 1973 account of the lives of his parents, Harold Nicolson and Vita Sackville-West, both bisexuals, in *Portrait of a Marriage.* Barry and Alice were writing, as they explained, in the context of the late seventies' "movement for sexual liberation. People are beginning to affirm their right to sexual self-determination," and, as a result, "more and more people are talking about bisexuality."[5]

"What is different about us is that our marriage is no longer based on traditional notions of monogamy, fidelity, and heterosexuality," they explain in their introduction. "We are both bisexual, we are open about this with each other, but we continue to view our marriage as the primary relationship in our lives."

It was Barry who first "came to terms" with his bisexuality, and came out to Alice, who then began to explore her own sexual feelings. He "wasn't going to change"[6]—a phrase Alice, in her chapters of the book, repeats more than once. She responded by getting a vibrator, reading *Rubyfruit Jungle,* and having sex with a close woman friend and a male rolfer. They consulted therapists. Barry was told by his therapist that he could be "cured" and by his male lover that he was gay. It was only when he discovered the existence of support groups for "bisexual and gay married men" that he began to feel less like an anomaly. Over Alice's initial objections, he began a support group of his own.

He is quite clear in his own mind that he is bisexual. "While I have had sex with other women and men, Alice pleases me more sexually than any other person."[7] After years of fantasizing about anal sex, he confesses the fantasy to Alice, and they add it to their sexual repertoire. But "even though my experience with anal sex has shown me that sexual activity with women and men can be almost interchangeable," he also values the differences. "I would not want to miss the unique experience of vaginal intercourse with a woman, any more than I would want to give up the pleasure of touching and losing myself in the largeness of a man's body and the power of his muscles."[8]

Meanwhile Alice was going through Dr. Elisabeth Kübler-Ross's stages of mourning for her marriage: denial, depression, bargaining, and acceptance.[9] She began to have erotic as well as emotional relationships with women, and overcame stereotypes about lesbianism and female beauty.[10]

The book they wrote together, alternating chapter by chapter, presents itself as a success story: they lived on a tree-lined street, they had a red station wagon and a seven-year old son; he was a lawyer and she was a psychiatric social worker. This was bisexuality as the American Dream. It ended in 1987 when Barry Kohn died of AIDS.

Let us now consider four notable "bisexual marriages," each of which has attracted considerable attention because of the identity of the participants and because, in at least two cases, a bisexual writer of very considerable skill has written journal entries about the experience that greatly enrich our sense of how such marriages work—and fail to work. In two of the four marriages discussed here only one partner is bisexual—by far the more common situation in bisexual marriage. In the other two cases, something like Edward Carpenter's utopian model for companionate marriage may, at least provisionally, have been approached. The first two cases are those of composer Leonard Bernstein and author John Cheever; the third, the marriage of Paul and Jane Bowles; and the fourth, the most celebrated "bisexual marriage" of the century, that of Vita Sackville-West and Harold Nicolson.

The Musical Man of All Trades

Take heart again girls: handsome Leonard Bernstein, the musical man of all trades, is still very eligible. This corner the other morning had him married to Felicia Montealegre, television's No.1 dramatic actress. 'Taint so. They were once engaged but the romance stopped short of the altar.

—*Gossip column in the* Pittsburgh Press, *January 7, 1950*

It's hard to know at this distance how tongue-in-cheek this arch gossip item intends to be. Perhaps all its double meanings are inadvertent. "Musical" is early slang for "homosexual," and "man of all trades," in a gay context, self-explanatory. But Bernstein is portrayed as an "eligible" bachelor and not a "confirmed" one. His movie-star good looks and his international celebrity made him an undeniable catch. The "romance" here described as having "stopped short of the altar" had done so, in fact, several years before, with an engagement made and then broken in 1947.

When the couple did marry, in 1951, it was after a lengthy set of exchanges about the nature of the marriage commitment.

The marriage of Leonard Bernstein and Felicia Montealegre Cohn, which took place after a number of delays and second thoughts, offers a good example of the kinds of tensions and decisions within which complicated and thoughtful people often decide to plot their lives. Bernstein was music's wunderkind, glamorous and sexy, with a history of relationships with men and many friends in New York's homosexual arts community. Felicia, the Catholic granddaughter of a rabbi, had an extremely successful acting career. As Nora in Henrik Ibsen's *A Doll's House,* that paradigmatic exploration of a woman's role in marriage, she was seen by millions. At the time of their marriage she was perhaps better known than her husband.

Leonard Bernstein's early sex life is by almost any criteria appropriately described as bisexual. During his college years he told his friend Mildred Spiegel that he didn't know which sex he would choose—"the pendulum was swinging back and forth."[11] To another friend he noted in 1939 that he had "met a wonderful girl. I'm about to have a sex life again. That's encouraging."[12] At the same time he was very attracted to men. Several of his composer-mentors were homosexuals, including Aaron Copland and Marc Blitzstein. As their friendship grew, he wrote to Copland regularly about his adventures with men and women, letters the appreciative Copland described as "just the kind I love to get: The 'I miss you, I adore you' kind, while sailors and marines flit through the background in a general atmosphere of moral decay."[13]

"My French has picked up enormously," wrote Bernstein expansively, "what with the Marquise and Alphand and my new friendy-wendy, Prince Chavchavadze. All very confusing. . . . What to do? I know—marry my new girl-friend—she's lovely—my dentist's daughter. . . . My love to Farley Granger. Can you fix me up?" And again, "I'm as confused as ever, what with my new friend [a married man, the tenor from his friend Paul Bowles's avant-garde opera] and my new girl-friend, whom I am afraid to involve unfairly."[14]

From the vantage point of her own affair with married lover Richard Hart, which intervened between her first engagement to Bernstein in 1947 and their eventual marriage in 1951, Felicia had written Bernstein, "Lenny dear, wait till you fall in love, deeply wonderfully in love, before you get married. Anything else is second best and you'll be cheating yourself and someone else."[15]

The child of traditional, observant Jews, Bernstein was, says biographer and friend Humphrey Burton, "an old-fashioned family man," despite his worldliness, who "desired to please his own parents and obey the Hebrew scriptures by going forth and multiplying. He trembled uncontrollably at the marriage ceremony, but he went through with it; it was one of the most difficult and important decisions of his life."[16] As for Felicia, who had endured the breakups and reunions, Burton first poses the question and then answers it: "Did Felicia marry Bernstein knowing he was bisexual? The answer must be that she knew about his past but she thought she could change him."[17] They were erotically attracted to one another, and he had never, after all, been exclusively gay. They were married in September 1951; by early spring Bernstein could tell his piano teacher Helen Coates proudly, "WE ARE PREGNANT."[18] Their daughter Jamie was born in 1953; their son, Alexander, in 1955, and their daughter Nina in 1962.

There followed two decades of marriage, during which Bernstein, in the midst of a brilliant career as composer, conductor, and celebrity, had occasional homosexual encounters, but none that impinged upon or threatened his life with Felicia and their children. Once Jamie Bernstein, working as a guide at Tanglewood for the summer, heard rumors about her father's homosexual past, but Bernstein, consulted, denied that the stories were true, calling them merely the jealous inventions of ill-wishers. Then in 1971 he met Tom Cothran, the music director of a San Francisco radio station, and fell in love with him. Over the next five years Cothran became a member of his family circle, and ultimately the cause of his departure from the household.

"Close friends had assumed for some time that his marriage was based on friendship rather than physical attraction," says biographer Burton,[19] but a friend reported that he burst into tears when confiding that he had lost sexual interest in his wife after her mastectomy. "He was facing a crisis about his sexuality," reports Burton. "He was finding his craving for the love of young men more and more difficult to suppress."[20] Times and mores were changing—this was now the seventies, and Bernstein himself, hosting a party for the Black Panthers, became the somewhat embarrassed source of Tom Wolfe's famous phrase "radical chic." And he was contemplating his own mortality, considering "how to divide the time I have left."[21] Should he change the way he lived? His wife discovered a love letter to Bernstein from a man. Someone called to tell her that her husband and his assistant were having an affair; it seemed as if their unspoken covenant, that he would be discreet and protect the home, was being breached. In 1976 he left Felicia for Cothran. *Newsweek* called it a "trial separation,"[22] and Felicia told *People,* "We hope to reconcile."[23]

A few months later Bernstein did go back to Felicia, but before long her illness returned, this time as cancer of the lung, and she died in 1978. Bernstein himself lived for another twelve years. His last lover, aspiring novelist Mark Adams Taylor, was twenty-eight years old when they met in 1989. Taylor reported that Bernstein was "notorious for the scores of young men he had had." "I was beyond belief seduced," he said, but "it was not merely sex." Bernstein, by this time a grandfather, was seventy-one years old. He told Taylor that he loved him, and also that he had loved his wife.

"Passionately?" asked Taylor (he was, after all, only in his twenties).

"Everyone I love, I love passionately," said Bernstein.[24]

Over a Cheever

"Did you ever fall in love with another man?" Susan Cheever asked her father, John Cheever, in 1977, when she was a writer for *Newsweek*.[25] Cheever had just published his novel *Falconer,* which contains explicit descriptions of homosexual relationships in a style that represented a significant departure from his usual urbane reticence.

"The possibility of my falling in love with a man seems to me to exist," Cheever replied. "Such a thing could happen. That it has not happened is just chance. But I would think twice about giving up the robustness and merriment I have known in the heterosexual world."

This lofty reply apparently struck the young reporter as an evasion, for she pursued him. "Well, have you ever had a homosexual experience?"

"My answer to that," he responded, "is, well, I have had many, Susie, all tremendously gratifying, and all between the ages of 9 and 11." If language were a polygraph test, this affectional vocative—*Susie*—would read as a needle blip, a sign that the speaker was not telling the whole truth. As indeed, his daughter, and the world, would soon know.

"Few people knew of his bisexuality," Cheever's son Ben would write in the introduction to John Cheever's journals, published in 1990, eight years after his death. "Very few people knew the extent of his infidelities."[26] One of the more curious aspects of the John-Cheever-Was-a-Bisexual revelations is the degree to which they were managed by his family, or more accurately by his children, two of whom—Susan and Ben—are writers themselves.

The publication of John Cheever's journals came about at his own request. In early 1980, three years after the interview with *Newsweek,* he brought one of his looseleaf notebooks to his son and asked him to read it. As Benjamin Cheever did so, tears ran down his father's cheeks. They agreed that there was much in the journal that would be of interest to young writers. They also agreed that the journals could not be published till after John Cheever's death. Cheever was worried that the family might find publication difficult. His son said he thought they could take it.

After John Cheever's death, Robert Gottlieb, his friend and editor from the *New Yorker,* selected the portions of the journals that were to appear, first in the magazine, and then, a larger selection, in book form. Gottlieb's principle of selection was, he said, "to follow the line of Cheever's inner life as he wrote it down day after day, year after year," and "to reflect, in proportion, the conflicts and the satisfactions of the thirty-five or so years that these journals represent." The idea was to show a writer at work, thinking, weighing, debating with himself. "Repetitions were kept to a minimum, except where they seemed to reflect obsessions that had to be acknowledged."

Of these "obsessions," sexuality was perhaps the chief. Cheever talks of it most often as "homosexuality," but that is in part because he is writing from within the other camp, writing as a man with a wife and three children, unable in many ways to imagine a life without that heterosexual frame. The word "bisexuality" appears only once in the published journal entries, and, significantly, it describes not Cheever's situation but that of a nameless young man in a therapy group, a young man whose companions —all but Cheever—declare this identity to be "phony." Benjamin Cheever can refer matter-of-factly to his father's bisexuality in introducing the journals to a new readership in 1991, but bisexuality is not really available to Cheever himself as a "lifestyle" choice, though in fact it quite accurately describes how he chose to live his life. Does his bisexuality require its own invisibility? Cheever tends to regard himself, at least in the journals, as both a "real" and a "fictional" character, constantly in transition. Does choosing bisexuality for him mean not recognizing that he is who he is and maintaining always the fiction that he is "becoming" (or "coming out") as something or someone different?

The journal entries that follow are testament to a life lived in constant engagement with the question of the erotic, and with its attendant pleasures and fears. Cheever regularly alternates feelings of bodily well-being with feelings of intense personal loneliness. The totality of his pleasures —in words, in nature, in his children, in his own body, in the attentions of and to the bodies of others—is recorded in these pages, which are not unselfconscious (he is too much a writer for that) but rather mercilessly self-revealing, even when what they reveal is self-deception.

There is less consistency than truth in these observations. At one moment we may find him convinced that "I am gay. I am gay," writing that "I believed that my homosexuality had been revealed to me and that I must spend the rest of my life unhappily with a man. I clearly saw my life displayed as a sexual imposture." At the next he wakes up "thinking of scrambled eggs, and it is revealed to me that any sustained sentimental life with a man who is not my brother or my son is highly taxing and quite impossible." Of a few things he is quite certain: that men of his generation were trained to fear homosexuality, and especially homosexuality in themselves; that he often loves and desires his wife, with whom, he frequently claimed in his journals, he constantly discussed divorce;[27] and that being loved, and particularly being loved by a younger person, a protégé or protégée, is for the narcissistic writer a necessity, an unexpected joy, and a gift.

Cheever was born in 1912. These journal entries, all of which address the question of bisexuality and eroticism, begin when he was forty-seven years old. The last entries, made the year he died, were thus written at the age of seventy.

> That was the year everybody in the United States was worried about homosexuality. They were worried about other things, too, but their

other anxieties were published, discussed, and ventilated while their anxiety about homosexuality remained in the dark: remained unspoken. Is he? Was he? Did they? Am I? Could I? seemed to be at the back of everyone's mind. [1959]

I spend the night with C. [a man], and what do I make of this? I seem unashamed, and yet I feel or apprehend the weight of social strictures, the threat of punishment. But I have acted only on my own instincts, tried, discreetly to relieve my drunken loneliness, my troublesome hunger for sexual tenderness. Perhaps sin has to do with the incident, and I have had this sort of intercourse only three times in my adult life. I know my troubled nature and have tried to contain it along creative lines. It is not my choice that I am alone here and exposed to temptation, but I sincerely hope that this will not happen again. I trust that what I did was not wrong. I trust that I have harmed no one I love. The worst may be that I have put myself into a position where I may be forced to lie.[28] [1960]

It is my wife's body that I most wish to gentle, it is into her that I most wish to pour myself, but when she is away I seem to have no scruple about spilling it elsewhere. I first see X at the edge of the swimming pool. He is sunbathing, naked, his middle covered by a towel.... I do not like his voice, his mind; I probably will not like his work. I like only that he seems to present or offer himself as a gentle object of sensual convenience. And yet I have been in this country a hundred times before and it is not, as it might seem to be, the valley of the shadow of death. And, whatever the instinctual facts are, there is the fact that I find a double life loathsome, morbid, and anyhow impossible.[29] [1962]

To use the word "love" to describe the relationships between men is inappropriate. There is, under the most exhaustive scrutiny, no trace of sexuality in these attachments. We are delighted to look into one another's faces, but below the neck there is nothing to be observed. We are happy and content together, but when we are separated we never think of one another. These bonds are as strong as any that we form in life, and yet we can pick them up and put them down with perfect irresponsibility. We do not visit one another in the hospital and when we are apart we seldom write letters, but when we are together we experience at least some of the symptoms of what we call love.[30] [1963]

I see the uneasy—and I think uncurable—paradox with which I must live. Would I sooner nuzzle D.'s bosom or squeeze R.'s enlarged pectorals? At my back I hear the word—"homosexual"—and it seems to split my world in two.... It is ignorance, our ignorance of one another, that creates this terrifying erotic chaos.[31] [1966]

I brood on the lack of universality of our sexual appetites. A loves his wife and no one but her. B loves young women, and when these are scarce he makes out with men who impersonate youth. C likes all comely women between the ages of twelve and fifty including all races. D likes himself, and jacks off frequently. He also likes men who resemble him sufficiently to make the orgasm narcissistic. E likes both men and women, depending on his moods, and I don't know whether he is the most tragic or the most natural of the group. None of them share, at any discernible level, the desires of the others. They share customs, diets, habits of dress, laws, and governments, but naked and randy they seem to be men from different planets.[32] [1968]

In *Esquire,* a piece on the New Homosexuality. I don't know what to make of it. The claim is that once guilt is overcome the eccentricities of the old-fashioned homosexual will be overcome. Men who love men will be manly and responsible citizens. They claim that an androgynous life can be completely happy, but I have never seen this.[33] [1969]

[In a clinic for treatment of his alcoholism:] During group analysis a young man talks about his bisexuality and is declared by everyone in the group but me to be a phony. I perhaps should have said that if it is phony to have anxieties about bisexuality I must declare myself a phony.[34] [1975]

I am highly susceptible to romantic love. . . . Yesterday I experienced that intoxicating arrogance of the self-declared alien, the sexual expatriate. I am unlike you, unlike any of you. . . . I am queer, and happy to say so. At the same time, the waitress is so delectable that I could eat her hands, her mouth.[35] [1977]

Lonely, and with my loneliness exacerbated by travel, motel rooms, bad food, public readings, and the superficiality of standing in reception lines, I fell in love with M. in a motel room of exceptional squalor. . . . We wrote love letters for three months, and when we met again we tore at each other's clothes and sucked each other's tongues. We were to meet twice again, once to spend some hours in a motel and once to spend twenty minutes naked before a directors' lunch I had to attend. I was to think of him for a year, continually and with the most painful confusion. I believed that my homosexuality had been revealed to me and that I must spend the rest of my life unhappily with a man. I clearly saw my life displayed as a sexual imposture. . . . I was determined not to have this love crushed by the stupid prejudices of a procreative society. Lunching with friends who talked about their tedious careers in lechery, I thought: I am gay. I am gay. I am at last free of all this. This did not last for long.[36] [1978]

I think that H. [Hope Lange, with whom Cheever had a decade-long affair[37]] is in the East, and how much I love her . . . How simple and powerful it all seems. We were meant to love each other. . . . I have known this marvellous feeling before—known it with other girls, known it with men, known it with that wife who refuses these days to let me enter her bedroom. It seems to me quite as natural as walking.[38] [1980]

I am thoroughly happy with M., and I believe he feels the same way with me, and it is a happiness that I have never known before. I look, quite naturally, for its limitations, and when my great, dear friend gestures toward a field of golden leaves I admire the lightness but I have no wish to write a poem, as I would with a girl. This is not a lack but it is a difference, and I do feel strongly that we both have work to do. Parting with M. is extremely sweet, but in the morning I wake in the arms of an imaginary girl.[39] [1980]

This last entry testifies to the particular pleasures of the state of "being in love," as distinct from merely loving, or being loved. That feeling of super-awareness, of the air, of nature, of sound, of the radical condition of merely being alive that a love affair brings, at least in its early stages, is effectively captured by Cheever in his journals time after time. His observations here are unselfconsciously gendered (he and M. "both have work to do," not a remark he ever makes in these terms about his wife, a poet). The disavowal of the impulse to write poetry for a man (the muse, it seems, remains a woman) is coupled with a poetic allusion—parting with M., like Romeo's parting with Juliet, is sweet sorrow. But where Romeo wishes that the two lovers could say good-night till it be morrow, Cheever himself wakes on the morrow in the arms of "an imaginary girl."

By turns ludicrous, self-pitying, and intensely moving, John Cheever's journals are evidence of a life in which the erotic has a place of unsurpassed importance, whatever the cost in other human relations:

So, at the mortal risk of narcissism, I am that old man going around and round the frozen duck pond in my hockey skates, stopping now and then to exclaim over the beauty of the winter sunset. And I am he who can be seen in the early summer morning, pedalling my bicycle to Holy Communion in a High church where they genuflect and use the Cranmer prayer book. I am also he whose loud cries of erotic ecstasy can be heard through the walls of the Millstream Motel. "You can't go on living like this," says my lover. I'm not quite sure what is meant.[40] [1981]

In 1981, Cheever was again taken to the hospital, this time for the removal of a cancerous kidney. His male lover came to pick him up and take him home, arriving twenty minutes late: "One of the disadvantages of homosexual love is waiting for a man. Waiting for a woman seems to be destiny, but waiting for one's male lover is quite painful."[41]

In 1982, still ailing, he is driven to a ceremony where he receives a medal; the male lover and Cheever's family are all in attendance. Two days later he is having sex with another man.

> I ask R. to come for a visit. He is a pleasant young man about whose way of life, whose friends, I know nothing and can imagine nothing. Carnally the drive is very ardent, and we end up in a heap of brush before lunch. I find my orgasm very gratifying and very important. ... but I seem in my ardor to have pulled my chest out of line. This is quite painful.[42]

John Cheever died on June 18, 1982.

When Susan Cheever came back to the subject of her father in print after his death, her then-tentative questions, and his then-evasive answers, had undergone a significant change. "For decades my father had been wrestling with his own lusts," she wrote. "He found his desires unacceptable —and so did the society he lived in."[43] The two contests he fought with his wife and with alcoholism were joined, perhaps in part motivated, by a third. "My father's sexual appetites were one of his major preoccupations, and his lust for men was as distressing to him as his desire for women was self-affirming and ecstatic. The journals contain argument after argument with himself on the subject of homosexuality." Cheever, she said, loved men but disliked homosexuals, whom he thought of as "limp-wristed, lisping men" who "run gift shops, [and] sell antiques." "He was terrified that his enjoyment of homosexual love would estrange him from the natural world, from the pure and anchoring influence of his family, from the manly pleasures he also loved. He had been brought up in a world and in a religion that rejected homosexuality absolutely."[44]

The journal entries as we have looked at them do not entirely support this view. Many of the passages recording sex or love shared with men could be described, to use Susan Cheever's own phrase, as "self-affirming and ecstatic." Likewise, the "pleasures of the natural world" are afforded him, as we have seen, by the very physical sense of well-being that is the state of "being in love" regardless of the gender of the beloved.

But the daughter deals with her father's "ambivalence"[45] and its cultural and historical situation straightforwardly, sympathetically, and without distracting pathos. "My father had had his share of heterosexual affairs, but when he began to give in to his love for other men, he was more confused and self-condemning than he had ever been. The sexual freedom of the

1960s made matters worse. He had spent fifty years suppressing his homo-sexual longings and his bawdy obsession with sex in all its forms. Now all around him other writers were coming out of the closet. John Rechy's *City of Night* and James Baldwin's *Giovanni's Room* were just two of the novels dealing specifically and graphically with homosexual life. I think this made him even more determined to keep his secret."[46] And again, "I think it was partly his fear of his own desires that kept my father drinking, and I think his anxiety over his sexual ambivalence also kept him married. As long as he was the Ossining squire, the father of three, the dog-loving, horseback-riding, meadow-scything, long-suffering husband, there could be no doubt in the public mind about his sexual preferences, and perhaps less doubt in his own."[47]

Susan Cheever also puts her father's experiences in context. His tenure as writer-in-residence at the University of Iowa's Writer's Workshop intro-duced him to "groupies" when he was sixty years old and he "talked endlessly about his heterosexual popularity." "He was never alone. Spe-cifically, he was never, or rarely, alone in bed."[48] After a disastrous experi-ence as a visiting professor at Boston University he signed himself into the Smithers Alcoholism Rehabilitation Unit in 1975, and gave up drinking. He regained control of some dimensions of his life, but "his longing for love from other men increased."[49]

In 1976 he wrote *Falconer,* a novel that is focused on a "tender homo-sexual love affair." Its protagonist is a man who is a heroin addict, and whose "marriage is a travesty of marriage vows."[50] "What about the hetero-sexual world?" Susan Cheever had asked him in the *Newsweek* interview. "Women who don't know what a kind and generous and loving man you are might be upset by your portrait of the bitch-wife Marcia in *Falconer."* *Falconer*'s author demurred at this, claiming the interviewer was "putting a narrowness on it" he hadn't intended. "I don't really have any message on women." And what about his marriage? "Well, it's been extraordinary," the interviewee replied. "That two people of our violent temperament have been able to live together for nearly 40 years as we have seems to me a spendid example of the richness and diversity of human nature . . . and in this 40 years there's scarcely been a week in which we haven't planned to get a divorce."

"But in *Falconer* you seem to be saying that the salvation of men is in their relationship with other men."

"No, I don't feel that at all. I think the salvation of men and women is in men and women. I think the salvation of men and women is in men, women and children."[51]

After the publication of this novel, and then of *The Stories of John Cheever,* a collection that won him a number of prestigious literary awards, he again embarked upon a career as a visitor to university campuses, and it was on one of those trips that he met "Rip" (as some of the journal entries call him), "the young writer who would be his close friend, lover, and confidant for the rest of his life."[52]

"Rip," whose name in published journals was changed to "M.," was married, as was Cheever. Each worried about the effect of his relationship on the other's marriage. They became companions as well as lovers, although Susan Cheever says she didn't know they were lovers until she read the journals after her father's death. "I guess what surprised me most was that I hadn't already known. Looking back now, it seems to me that my father's relationship with Rip, for all its painfully obvious problems, was as sweet and satisfying a source of love as love could be for him. His marriage to my mother was not particularly satisfactory, his children were gone, and his mistresses were old or in California. He also saw himself in Rip."[53]

Here it is perhaps worth interjecting another contextual note, one that some readers may find irrelevant. In their prefatory discussions both Susan Cheever, the author of the posthumous memoir, and Benjamin Cheever, whose introduction serves as a preface to the *Journals,* briefly touch upon their own divorces and remarriage. Benjamin Cheever reports that he initially read some pages of the journals when he "had left my first wife and come to stay with my parents."[54] He has since remarried; Susan Cheever has been twice married and twice divorced.

These children's balanced accounts of their father's stubbornness, self-indulgence, and periodic bouts of self-pity come in the context of a world in which changing one's mind, or changing one's life, had become something different from what it had been before. If homosexuals were stigmatized in the America of John Cheever's youth, so was divorce. Yet nowhere in the journals does it seem as if really choosing a gay life was what John Cheever wanted. He wanted, in a sense, what he had; the luxury of too much and not enough, the paradox of a choice that was, because he made it so, not really a choice.

Nowhere is it written that bisexuals, and bisexuality, have to be likable. Cheever, a magnificent writer, comes across in his journal entries—not only the ones about sex, but also the entries about colleagues, and work, and family—as often spoiled, pettish, narrow, WASPy, and waspish. His infidelities gain spice because they are infidelities. Love for him, in the sense of ecstatic love, romance, is something that not only can, but perhaps must, exist outside marriage. But he does love—and fall in love. His account of his passions, the grand and the trivial, the female and the male, have in the *Journals* as profound a ring of truth as his pat disclaimer in the *Newsweek* interview rings of falsehood.

"Right after he died," Benjamin Cheever told an interviewer, "I was particularly angry about his homosexual affairs. He'd been so adamant in his public dislike of homosexuality.

"Now, I think you have to take the people you love the way you find them. I loved my father. He was bisexual. But his bisexuality didn't give him only grief. It gave him joy as well. Yes, I was surprised to discover that my father was capable of cold-blooded hypocrisy. But I have discovered also that his hypocrisy was an attempt to be better than he was."[55]

"Misbehaving with Some Girl or Man"

One of the most remarkable literary marriages of the twentieth century was the marriage between the American writers Paul and Jane Bowles. A revival of interest in Paul Bowles's work, following the Bernardo Bertolucci film made from his novel *The Sheltering Sky* and the publication of his letters and photographs, has coincided with a rediscovery of Jane Bowles's novels, like *Two Serious Ladies,* by a new generation of feminist and lesbian readers.

Paul Bowles was equally gifted as a composer and a writer. His friends and sponsors included Aaron Copland, Virgil Thompson, Djuna Barnes, Gertrude Stein, Claude McKay, and Tennessee Williams, among many others, and his letters make fascinating reading. Perhaps, he wrote impishly to a friend at age nineteen, he "can still be normal (by that I mean either hetero or homo) but if not, then I must wander down life seeking something to fall definitely in love with." But he suspects that whatever it is, it will be "some sort of a vice. There can never be any love, any affection, even any satisfaction 'in my life.' Whatever is to please me must be a vice. True, really. Being beaten, for instance. A Vice. But how enjoyable. Burning woods. How exquisite. Biting myself for the pain. All more enjoyable than misbehaving with some girl or man."[56]

In another exuberant letter to the same friend he asked, rhetorically, "can a person who is totally heterosexual be indulgent toward the amiable perversions? . . . I think not. It is only the individuals who find every vice amusing enough to indulge in it who can be truly sympathetic with the others. . . . Moi, I should like to know intimately all forms of pleasure. . . . As of course under vices I list either heterosexual or otherwise indulgence. Any form—a vice."[57] He has been reading Verlaine, and André Gide, who will become a friend.

But the openness to experience here is not only an affectation. He wrote to Aaron Copland in 1933 to complain that returning to America had curtailed his sex life. "Where in this country can I have 35 or 40 different people a week, and never risk seeing any of them again? Yet in Algeria, it actually was the mean rate."[58]

When an old girlfriend buttonholed him and "went on to say when would we be married," he found that he was indifferent to say the least. "I discovered that I no longer desired to amuse myself with her in any manner. It was an ordeal. Long kisses for an hour, and finally it was over. Comme il serait dangereux d'aimer les jeunes filles, comme on aime les garçons; plusieurs par jour! On serait déja en prison quelque part! [How dangerous it would be to love girls the way one loves boys: several a day! We would already be off in prison somewhere!]"[59] This letter, likewise written to Copland, assumes a commonality of interest in boys, but it also reflects what was surely a prevailing double standard. Bedding boys was easy, and, at least in North Africa, where Bowles had been living, without consequences. Bedding girls, middle-class girls, was something else again.

And when Bowles himself does marry, he drops the information, off-hand, in a letter to editor Dorothy Norman: "I thought I would get married so I did, and we started off for various parts of the world, as you might expect."[60] The woman he married, Jane Auer, was lively, eccentric, and brilliant. Tennessee Williams would call her "the most important writer of prose fiction in modern American letters," and Truman Capote, who wrote appreciatively of "her boyish clothes and schoolgirl's figure" and her role as "the eternal urchin, appealing as the most appealing of non-adults," called her "that modern legend named Jane Bowles."[61]

Jane Bowles's biographer, Millicent Dillon, writes of Bowles's "uncertainty about her own sexuality and about what choice she would make of that sexuality, assuming she had a choice."[62] She refused to go to bed with Paul Bowles when they were dating (when they first met, on a trip to Harlem with Erika Mann, she clearly preferred to speak to Mann, and he "didn't find her endearing").[63] But they were attracted to each other, and in 1938 they were married. Some friends assumed it was a marriage of convenience, others claimed her mother had pressured her to marry. Bowles himself said they used to fantasize about getting married, then say, "It's terrible to be tied," and "then somehow that changed into, 'Why don't we? Let's.'" "From fantasy to actuality is often a much shorter distance than one imagines," he reflected.[64]

"The marriage," writes Millicent Dillon, "broke apart sexually" in 1940, in the wake of Jane's lesbian relationships and increased involvement in "bohemian" life. She dressed in boy's clothes, and she was often out at night. "Paul tried to persuade her to renew their sexual relationship, but she said she did not want to. She did not want to discuss it. Eventually he gave up trying. In a way it was a relief to him. At least, he felt, it would be the end of having to wait up night after night, wondering what she was doing, whom she was with, whether she'd been hurt.

"Changed, the marriage would go on. Their sexual life together was ended, but the devotion between them would now be sealed through their creative lives."[65] This judgment, arrived at with the cooperation of Paul Bowles ("without whom there would have been no book—or certainly not this book"[66]) may raise the question again: What is a marriage? In this case a marriage between a bisexual man and a lesbian was reinvented so as to last a lifetime.

In the course of her nomadic and often extravagant life Jane Bowles had affairs with Helvetia Perkins, Renée Henry, the Princess Martha Ruspoli de Chambrun, a woman in Tangier named Cherifa, and a number of women who appear in her biography under pseudonyms. As Dillon notes, a sexual mystique seemed to always attach to her, and rumors of her lesbian lovers were many. "I always say right away that I'm Jewish and a lesbian," she said to Marguerite McBey.[67] Did she have affairs with men? That, too, says

Dillon, is "part of the sexual mystique about her," but though many men found her attractive she remained, in her own way, faithful to the marriage, and to Paul. She told Dione Lewis that she knew he wouldn't mind if she had affairs with women, but that "he would be very hurt if she had an affair with a man."[68] Another friend, Roberta Bobba, stressed the importance of the relationship: "I knew some gay women who were married, who did it for family pressure or for the sake of appearances. But Jane really took on the role of the wife. She didn't do it for form's sake."[69]

Many years later, after Jane Bowles's death, Paul Bowles wrote to documentary filmmaker Regina Weinrich (who would make the film about him, *Paul Bowles: The Complete Outsider*) to protest that he was not holding back any information about himself. "As to my sex life," he wrote, "it has always been largely imaginary; what few 'relationships and intimacies' there were are all recounted in the Autobiography. I think what people really want to know is: With whom have you been to bed? To answer that, it would be necessary to have known their names."[70]

The "misapprehensions that have accrued around the Bowles myth" include the idea, held by many, "that his relationship with his wife was . . . less than devoted." As Michael Upchurch points out, the letters dispel that myth fairly clearly and directly, focusing on Bowles's affection for "Janie" and on his solicitude and distress when a stroke afflicted her in 1957 and set off a round of hospitalizations that lasted until her death sixteen years later, in 1973, when she was fifty-six.

Why does the "Bowles myth" *require* this notion of a marriage that is not really a marriage? Does its openness disqualify it as "marriage"? If all marriages had to pass a "sex test," how many would quietly fail?

Like the better-known "bisexual marriage" of Harold Nicolson and Vita Sackville-West, the Bowleses' marriage was a marriage between two individuals of great self-possession and strong will. And like the Nicolsons' marriage, it was a marriage contracted by two people committed to each other, "even if it did stretch the definition of marriage as most people see it."[71]

The Convenience of Inconvenience

Nigel Nicolson's *Portrait of a Marriage,* the story of his parents, the diplomat Harold Nicolson and the writer Vita Sackville-West, was first published in 1973—eleven years after his mother's death and five years after his father's. Violet Trefusis, the woman with whom Sackville-West had been in love, was also dead; she had died the previous year. Their deaths, wrote Nicolson, made possible the publication of Sackville-West's autobiography. "Let no reader condemn in ten minutes a decision I have pondered for ten years," he cautioned in his introduction. "A few of my parents' friends expressed misgivings, but most confirmed my growing conviction that in the 1970s an experience of this kind need no longer be regarded as shameful or unmentionable, for the autobiography was written with profound emotion, and has an integrity and validity of universal significance."[72]

In retrospect, what is most jarring here is Nicolson's calm confidence that the 1970s had ushered in a period of tolerance and acceptance. More than twenty years later intolerance and repression have revived as "respectable" and even "religious" points of view, displayed under the banners of *soi-disant* "family values" and the broadly condemnatory (and illogical) rubric of a kind of anerotic "patriotism," whether American or (as hypocritically trumpeted in the scandal-plagued cabinet of John Majors) British. Listen to the conviction with which Nicolson sets forth his parents' case:

> It is the story of two people who married for love and whose love deepened with every passing year, although each was constantly and by mutual consent unfaithful to the other. Both loved people of their own sex, but not exclusively. Their marriage not only survived infidelity, sexual incompatibility and long absences, but it became stronger and finer as a result. Each came to give the other full liberty without inquiry or reproach. Honour was rooted in dishonour.[73]

There is a curious anachronism to this declaration. Words like "honor" and "dishonor" have today been largely banished to the realm of military engagements—or encounters between rival gangs. We seldom meet them in the context of marriage, at least once the ceremony itself is concluded. And the carping moralists of today's pop pulpits (from think tank to talk show) will surely query the appropriateness of "honor" to describe a marriage grown "stronger and finer" by infidelity. His parents' love for each other, their son writes, "made out of a non-marriage a marriage that succeeded beyond their dreams." How can a marriage that was, in Nicolson's own phrase, "superficially a failure because it was incomplete" be held up as a paragon? How can the book that tells its story declare itself, unashamedly, "a panegyric of marriage"? How did a bisexual marriage become such a success?

Let us begin with the thing that above all sets the marriage of Nicolson and Sackville-West apart, which is not the bisexuality of the partners but the underlying and primary infidelity that preceded any sexual liaison for Sackville-West: her passion for a house. As the female descendant of a family entailed in the male line, Sackville-West would never inherit her beloved family seat of Knole, the Elizabethan house in which she was brought up. Knole would remain her principal passion, her "primary relationship" (to use the jargon of modern sociology's analysis of bisexual lifestyles)—the unattainable beloved whose loss, whose unavailability to the lover, underlies and structures all her other needs and desires. ("As the wedding day drew near," Nigel Nicolson remarks, "Vita felt no qualms, except about leaving Knole.")[74] In the shadow of this privileged passion, a passion that was as unlawful as any homosexual and/or extramarital infidelity (since by the law's own terms it was impossible that a woman should ever inherit), came Vita Sackville-West's love for Harold Nicolson, and for Violet Trefusis, and for Geoffrey Scott, and for Virginia Woolf.

To mention Knole ("Oh my lovely Knole," as Sackville-West apostrophizes it longingly early in her autobiography)[75] is to allude to the question of class, which it would be silly to dismiss as irrelevant here. Both upper- and lower-class persons are, in literature at least, often permitted excesses and adventures which the middle-class reading public delights in denying itself. In America, which pretends to have no social class structure, these wistful projections are even more vivid, only we tend to make kings and queens of our film and pop stars, dynasties of our capitalists, philanthropists, and political families from Rockefeller to Kennedy and Roosevelt. Indeed, a number of such people have gone on to marry "real" royalty—the marriage of Grace Kelly to Prince Rainier of Monaco comes to mind, as, in the opposite direction, does that of Jacqueline Kennedy to shipping magnate Aristotle Onassis. Modern-day readers of Virginia Woolf often regard her unproblematically as if she were a middle-class feminist challenging the establishment rather than a privileged member of a privileged society, someone who, for example, found it easy to say that she didn't much like Jews (even though she married one). The Nicolsons didn't like Jews or "coloured people" either—a point on which their two sons vigorously disagreed with them.[76] They felt themselves to inhabit a world that was at once highly selective and unquestionably special.

With Vita and Harold, as critics democratically refer to them, the pleasures of nonconformity are a little bit noblesse oblige, though it's quite unfashionable to say so. It's not for nothing that Vita begins her autobiographical memoir with an account of her grandfather Lord Sackville's liaison with Pepita, a beautiful Spanish dancer, with whom he had seven illegitimate children, one of whom was Sackville-West's mother. Nor is it atypical of her to remark that her lover Violet Keppel's mother "was the King's mistress (which added a touch of romance to Violet)" even before their affair proper began.[77] The issue is not snobbism, though snobbery, too, can be eroticizing, since it sets up insiders against outsiders in a calculus of desire, but rather something much more like entitlement. Vita Sackville-West, quite simply, felt entitled to love and live as she pleased. This is one reason she has become something of a heroine to some readers (and public broadcasting television audiences) today.

Thanks to a highly successful dramatization of "Portrait of a Marriage" in 1992—another sign of nineties "bisexual chic" that did not necessarily translate into social acceptance for unfamous living bisexuals—the facts of the story are well known. Sackville-West and Nicolson were married in 1913, and in the course of the next several years their two sons were born. Vita began her affair with Violet Keppel (an affair that could reasonably be described with the overworked word "tempestuous") in April 1918. A little more than a year later, in June 1919, Violet married Denys Trefusis, insisting, however, that "their marriage would be in name only; they would have no sexual relations whatever,"[78] and continued to press Vita to "elope" with her. (In frustration Harold wrote to his wife, "Why do you imagine that there is nothing between eloping with Violet and cooking my dinner?")[79] When the two women did elope to Amiens together they were followed, in comic-opera style, by their two husbands in a two-seater airplane. The relationship between them continued, off and on, until the autumn of 1921, when Violet returned to Denys. Vita and Harold remained married—and happily married, despite subsequent affairs for both—until Vita's death in 1962.

Growing up "as much like a boy as possible," longing for trousers or a kilt (both of which she would later sport), Vita recalls herself as a plain but clever child. Certainly she was clever about love, if her retrospective understanding is any evidence. Meeting Violet Keppel when she was twelve and Violet ten, she says she "treated her with unvarying scorn, my one piece of really able handling, which kept her to me as no proof of devotion would have kept her."[80] The two young girls became fast friends, Violet gave her a ring and a kiss, and Vita promptly fell in love with another woman. Her first affair, conducted during the same time as her courtship by and engagement to Harold Nicolson, was with Rosamund Grosvenor. "Men didn't attract me," she writes, "I didn't think of them in what is called 'that way.' Women did. Rosamund did." Soon they were "living on terms of the greatest possible intimacy." "I realized vaguely that I had no business to sleep with Rosamund, and I should certainly never have allowed anyone to find it out, but my sense of guilt went no further than that." The relationship, however, was "almost exclusively physical." Rosamund, who was to be a bridesmaid at her wedding, was, Vita notes, "quite stupid." "She always bored me as a companion."[81]

Not so Harold, the "best actual *playmate* I had ever known," with his "brilliant cleverness."[82] When he asked her to marry him she agreed. "It never struck me as wrong that I should be more or less engaged to Harold, and at the same time very much in love with Rosamund." Furthermore, her passion for Rosamund grew stronger during the course of her engagement. ("I loved Harold from that day on," she writes, "but I continued my liaison with Rosamund. I say this with deep shame.")[83] As for her relationship with Harold, it was "so fresh, so intellectual, so unphysical." "Some men seem to be born to be lovers, others to be husbands." Harold belonged to the latter category. Indeed, when they did marry and went to Florence on their honeymoon they lived in the same cottage Vita had shared with Rosamund eighteen months before, a fact she describes as "one of the things I am most ashamed of in my life," since it was not only disloyal to Rosamund 'but also showed a great want of delicacy.[84] Still, she did it. Harold offered "sheer joy of companionship," without the complications of too much eroticism: "It was all open, frank, certain and although I never knew the physical passion I had felt for Rosamund, I didn't really miss it."[85]

> I seem to be incapable of fidelity, as much then as now. But, as a sole justification, I separate my loves into two halves: Harold, who is unalterable, perennial, and *best;* there has never been anything but absolute purity in my love for Harold, just as there has never been anything but absolute bright purity in his nature. And on the other hand stands my perverted nature, which loved and tyrannized over Rosamund and ended by deserting her without one heart-pang, and which now is linked irremediably with Violet.[86]

The tone of delighted "bad-girl" pleasure is as palpable as the insistence on temporality: love for Harold is "unalterable and perennial," love for Violet "irremediable"—though in fact it would come to an end. But what is perhaps most striking in Vita's self-analysis is her Manichean (or faux Manichean) view of herself as part good angel (matched by Harold's "absolute bright purity") and part bad ("my perverted nature"). "I regret that the person Harold married wasn't entirely and wholly what he thought of her, and that the person who loves and owns Violet isn't a second person, because each suits each."[87]

"Violet had struck the secret of my duality," she wrote in her memoirs, recalling the events of April 18, 1920, that "changed my life."[88] The story of the seduction—for it was, at least in her account, quite clearly a seduction—makes seductive reading. The two women were alone at Long Barn, the Nicolsons' country cottage. Harold was in London. Vita had just acquired a set of male clothing ("breeches and gaiters"—"like the women-on-the-land were wearing") and in the "unaccustomed freedom" they offered she jumped, climbed, vaulted over gates, and "felt like a schoolboy on holiday." Violet followed her, "never taking her eyes off me." That evening they talked until two in the morning—or rather, Vita talked. "Violet only listened—which was skilful of her. . . . She was far more skilful than I. I might have been a boy of eighteen, and she a woman of thirty-five. She was infinitely clever—she didn't scare me, she didn't rush me, she didn't allow me to see where I was going; it was all conscious on her part, but on mine it was simply the drunkenness of liberation—the liberation of half my personality."

Violet lay on the sofa, Vita "sat plunged in the armchair." Violet took her hands "and parted my fingers to count the points as she told me why she loved me. I hadn't dreamt of such an art of love." "She appealed to my unawakened senses," wrote Vita. "She pulled me down until I kissed her

—I had not done so for many years. Then she was wise enough to get up and go to bed; but I kissed her again in the dark after I had blown out our solitary lamp." Vita spent a sleepless night, restless with excitement. It was not until more than a week later, having arranged to go together (and without Harold) to Cornwall, that they finally went to bed. Pausing on the journey at Plymouth, they "went to the nearest hotel," and were told there was only one room. "It seemed like fate."[89]

No one, I think, who has ever had an affair involving danger and risk (and what else is an affair?) can fail to be affected by the eroticism of this account. The absent husband, so present in his wife's thoughts ("I told her how all the gentleness and all the femininity of me was called out by Harold alone, but how towards everyone else my attitude was completely otherwise");[90] the sense of liberation and carnival conferred by boys' clothes, the tantalizing touch, the deferred pleasure even more pleasurable for being deferred, the accident of there being only one room at the hotel so that circumstances conspired to bring about the fulfillment of their mutual desire.

Violet's great coup, as Vita instantly saw, was to set free the "boy" in her —the same "boy" she had employed as an alter ego in the sprawling historical novels she wrote in her early teens. The masquerade in boys' clothes would continue to be a trigger for erotic pleasure in their relationship; thus was born the figure of "Julian," Vita in triumphant disguise, who "looked like a rather untidy young man, a sort of undergraduate, of about nineteen," and who, having strolled from Hyde Park Corner to Bond Street smoking a cigarette, took Violet in a taxi to the train station, and from there to a lodging house in Orpington and to bed. ("The landlady was very benevolent and I said Violet was my wife.")[91] Julian recurs throughout the correspondence of Vita and Violet, and makes occasional appearances in the memoirs. "Once we got to Paris . . . we led the same life we had led before, of cafés, theatres, and 'Julian.' " "Sometimes I saw people I knew, and wondered what they would think if they knew the truth about the slouching boy," and in particular "if they would recognize the silent and rather scornful woman they had perhaps met at a dinner-party or a dance." It's clear that danger and risk were themselves part of the sexual excitement: "I never appreciated anything so much as living like that with my tongue perpetually in my cheek, and in defiance of every policeman I passed."[92] Nigel Nicolson notes that the risks were in a way greater for Violet than for Vita, since Violet was not in disguise and was thus perfectly identifiable as the companion of the "slouching boy" in cafés, thé dansants, and rooming houses. "Violet was herself a fashionable society girl, a little scatter-brained it was generally considered, but not vicious, and here she was in company with this disreputable boy in public places where at any moment she, or both, might be recognized."[93]

"You could do anything with me," wrote Violet to Vita, "or rather Julian could. I love Julian overwhelmingly, possessively, exorbitantly. For me he stands for emancipation, for all liberty, for youth, for ambition, for attainment."[94]

But meanwhile, what of Harold and that perfect marriage? At first Harold Nicolson knew nothing of the particulars of the affair, regarding Violet as an old friend of his wife's with whom she was spending, quite reasonably and naturally, a lot of time while he toiled at his job in the foreign office. Vita had a certain gift for dissimulation and, more to the point, of self-justification. But as the stakes got higher—as Denys Trefusis proposed to Violet, as news of the two women now spending four months together in Monte Carlo became irresistible to society gossips in London and Paris— both Harold and Denys began to see Vita's and Violet's relationship as a potential threat. "Horrible thought what friends Denys and Julian would be!" Violet wrote flirtatiously to Vita. "They would be in open competition for [me]."[95]

What makes a marriage? Sex? Friendship? Trust? Understanding? Children? A commonality of taste and interest?

By the time Vita and Harold's sons were born, it was clear that for both of them marital sex had lost much of its appeal. Both in fact were more sexually attracted to members of their own sex than they were to each other. Vita's son writes that "she had no concept of any moral distinction between homosexual and heterosexual love, thinking of them both as 'love' without qualification."[96] And Harold, too, though he was not given to grand passions as was his wife, came to prefer "incidental" relationships with men to sex with his wife. "With his strong sense of duty (much stronger than Vita's) he felt it to be less treacherous to sleep with men in her absence than with other women."[97] This is a point of view often expressed by people in bisexual marriages. But the Nicolsons' was a "bisexual marriage" in an unusually complete way, since both of them had same-sex partners. "It was fortunate that they were both made that way," Nigel Nicolson notes without emphasis. "If only one of them had been, their marriage would probably have collapsed. Violet did not destroy their physical union; she simply provided the alternative for which Vita was unconsciously seeking at the moment when her physical passion for Harold, and his for her, had begun to cool."[98]

"Is it that I am not amorous enough? How can I even think such things!" Harold wrote to Vita in September 1918, at the beginning of the Violet affair. "And against me I have that little tortuous, erotic, irresponsible and unlimited person. I don't hate her. No more than I should hate opium if you took it."[99] Harold, his son acknowledges, preferred to avoid confrontations with unpleasant truths. (As evidence of this he cites, quite pertinently, Nicolson's minimizing, in his biographies of Verlaine and Swinburne, the homosexuality of the former and the masochism of the latter.[100]) Vita, a more volatile personality by nature, did, she said, "hate" Denys Trefusis,[101] and regarded him in a highly particular way as a sexual rival. After his marriage to Violet, a marriage Vita herself could have prevented had she stayed in London as Violet had begged her to do, she was frantic with erotic jealousy. Staying alone in a small hotel in Paris, she sought out Violet on her honeymoon. "I took her there, I treated her savagely, I made love to her, I had her, I didn't care, I only wanted to hurt Denys, even though he didn't know of it."[102] She then went to Switzerland with Harold, while Denys and Violet continued on their honeymoon journey. When the two couples returned (separately) to England, Vita told her mother about the affair, and before long she and Violet were en route to Paris and Monte Carlo together. She remarks rather drolly that when she and Trefusis "met at a grotesque interview in London" and he asked her "how much money I should have to keep Violet and myself on if we went away," she felt "like a young man wanting to marry Violet and being interviewed by her father."[103] It should I think be emphasized that she *liked* this role, even as she found it "grotesque." The swashbuckling heir of the Sackvilles that she would have been had she been male, and as Virginia Woolf would make her in the character of Orlando, suited both her romantic personality and her passion.

As the editor of Violet's letters to Sackville-West neatly observes, "Violet relied on sex to gain intimacy, and Vita used intimacy to achieve sex."[104] "If you desired it," Vita wrote, "I would have humiliated my flesh for you. I'd have submitted to what seems to me the supreme horror—I'd have had a child to give you pleasure."

"When we married," Vita wrote to Harold two years before her death, in 1960, "you were older than I was, and far better informed. I was very young, and very innocent. I knew nothing about homosexuality. I didn't even know that such a thing existed either between men or between women. You should have told me. You should have warned me. You should have told me about yourself and warned me that the same sort of thing was likely to happen to myself. It would have saved us a lot of trouble and misunderstanding. But I simply didn't know."[105]

What she "didn't know" had more to do with the power of passion than with the mechanics of sex—she had after all been sleeping with Rosamund Grosvenor throughout her engagement with Harold. But the relationship with Violet was different. At the end of 1922 she wrote to her husband, "Not for a million pounds would I have anything to do with Violet again, even if you didn't exist, you whom I love fundamentally, deeply and incurably. Oh yes, I know you will say, 'But you loved me then, and yet you went off with her.' It's quite true. I did love you, and I always loved you, all through those wretched years, but you know what infatuation is, and I was mad."[106] The difference, as Harold himself once admitted, was between loving and being "in love." Some twenty years later, when Violet reappeared in her life having left France for wartime England, Vita wrote her the following:

> We simply could not have this nice, simple, naif, childish connexion without its turning into a passionate love-affair again. . . .
> You are an unexploded bomb to me.
> I don't want you to explode.
> I don't want you to disrupt my life. . . .[107]

On the day the nature of her infatuation with Violet first became clear to her Vita wrote at length in her autobiography:

> I keep thinking that Harold, if he ever reads this, will suffer so, but I ask him to remember that he is reading about a *different person* from the one he knew. . . . I know of no truthful record of such a connection—one that is written, I mean, with no desire to appeal to a vicious taste in any possible readers. . . .

She was even then convinced that the real problem was in society's misconception of the nature of "normal" and "natural" human relations, and in the institutionalization of a wholly inadequate and antiquated concept of marriage.

> [A]s centuries go on, and the sexes become more nearly merged because of their increasing resemblances, I hold the conviction that such connections will to a very large extent cease to be regarded as merely unnatural, and will be understood far better, at least in their *intellectual* if not in their physical aspect. . . . I believe then that the psychology of people like myself will be a matter of interest, and I believe it will be recognized that many more people of my type do exist than under the present-day system of hypocrisy is commonly admitted. . . .
> The first step in the direction of such candour must be taken by the general admission of normal but illicit relations, and the facilitation of divorce, or possibly even the reconstruction of marriage. Such advance must necessarily come from the more educated and liberal classes. Since "unnatural" means "removed from nature," only the most civilized, because the least natural, class of society can be expected to tolerate such a product of civilization.[108]

Class and education would help to dispel the fiction of a "natural" heterosexuality, to establish the "illicit" (homosexuality, bisexuality, even the illegitimate union of her famous grandparents) as "normal." "The most civilized, because the least natural" class must take the lead.

What did the Nicolsons, that model and "most civilized," if "least natural" couple, think of marriage? That it was itself both "unnatural" and the "greatest of human benefits," something that "must be based on love guided by intelligence."[109] After the end of the affair with Violet each sometimes brought a lover home to Long Barn to join the same weekend party. "Vita is absolutely devoted to Harold," wrote Lady Sackville, Vita's mother, in her diary, "but there is nothing whatever sexual between them, which is strange in such a young and good-looking couple. She is not in the least jealous of him."[110] Vita herself wrote that "ninety-nine people out of a hundred, if they knew all about us, would call us wicked and degenerate" but that in her opinion no one was less so: "our two lives, inside and outside, are rich lives."[111]

" 'Trust,' " their son wrote, "in most marriages, means fidelity. In theirs it meant that they would always tell each other of their infidelities, give warning of approaching emotional crises, and, whatever happened, return to their common centre in the end."[112] "I think that is really the basis of our marriage, apart from our deep love for each other," wrote Vita to Harold shortly before her death, "for we have never interfered with each other, and strangely enough, never been jealous of each other."[113]

For Violet Trefusis, too, marriage ultimately meant a kind of happiness, although her husband, Denys, died early, of consumption, in 1929. "Marriage," she wrote in her own autobiography, "can be divided into two categories: those that begin well and end badly, those that begin badly and end well. Mine came (roughly) under the latter heading." After a year of turmoil they established a life together in France: "The same things made us laugh. We quarrelled a lot, loved not a little. We were more to be envied than pitied."[114] Violet, like Vita, became a successful novelist, and also a lively figure in the intellectual society of Paris. No more than her lover was she barred by the strength of their extraordinary passion from the tasks and opportunities of the life she ultimately chose.

After the grand passion with Violet, Vita had numerous other affairs with women, including Mary Campbell, who was living at the time in the gardener's cottage at Long Barn with her husband, Roy, a poet; Hilda Matheson, talks director at the BBC, at whose invitation the Nicolsons gave their BBC broadcast on the meaning of marriage; and Virginia Woolf.

Nigel Nicolson regarded it as "a travesty of their [Vita and Virginia's] relationship to call it an affair," since "the physical element in their friendship was tentative and not very successful, lasting only a few months, a year perhaps."[115] This nicety may turn on one's definition of an affair, though the son's opinion here seems to mirror the mother's. "I am scared to death of arousing physical feelings in her, because of the madness," Vita wrote to Harold in August 1926. "Besides, Virginia is not the sort of person one thinks of in that way. There is something incongruous and almost indecent in the idea. I *have* gone to bed with her (twice), but that's all. Now you know all about it, and I hope I haven't shocked you. My darling, you are the one and only person for me in the world."[116]

We should bear in mind here that Vita is writing to her husband, and may have reason to minimize the importance of the erotic relationship with Woolf. Feminist scholars have pointed to playful and sexy letters from Woolf to Sackville-West entreating her to "throw over your man."[117] "Honey, dearest," one letter reads, "don't go to Egypt please. Stay in England. Love Virginia. Take her in your arms. . . ."[118] If, as Mitchell Leaska noted, Vita "had a tendency, perhaps even a talent, for coming between husbands and wives,"[119] moved by the attractions of danger and by the challenge to her own sexual power, Woolf, too, could turn sexual jealousy into an erotic force. Or perhaps it is just that her more erotic experiences occurred in and with language, and that their affair was in a sense lived most fully in the pages of *Orlando,* aptly described by Nigel Nicolson, in the most frequently quoted sentence of his book, as "the longest and most charming love letter in literature."

In any event, Virginia Woolf wrote to Sackville-West just days before they went to bed together, "In all London you and I alone like being married."[120] And they did. Woolf, whose own arrangement with her husband accommodated her sexual indifference ("she has never lived with anyone but Leonard, which was a terrible failure, and was abandoned quite soon," Vita reported to Harold),[121] gained strength and pleasure from her marriage, Leonard's intelligence and care, and their work together. Shortly after Virginia Woolf's suicide, the deeply distressed Sackville-West wrote to Nicolson: "I was thinking 'How queer! I suppose Hadji [her pet name for Nicolson] and I have been about as unfaithful to one another as one well could be from the conventional point of view, even worse than unfaithful if you add in homosexuality, and yet I swear no two people could love one another more than we do after all these years."

"It *is* queer, isn't it? It does destroy all orthodox ideas of marriage?" The final question mark, apparently out of place yet perfectly placed, is her own.[122]

All marriages are unorthodox in their own ways. Some admit their unorthodoxy more directly than others, and some, often to their own cost, keep secrets. But marriage is an institution, and sexual desire, though we like to think of it as directly and unproblematically linked to "love and marriage," is a willful, inconsistent, and often ungovernable entity. How can a structure, like marriage, contain a force, like eroticism? Imperfectly, if at all. We might say that *all* marriages are bifurcated between the wild and the tame, between the adventurous and the routine, between passion and obligation. Bisexual marriages only make explicit, literal, and racy what is emotionally the case for any long-range commitment that is tied to a structure. The "choice" between a male and a female lover seems more extreme, more extravagant, more transgressive, perhaps, than the other kinds of choices, fantasied and acted-upon, that confront partners in every marriage. But precisely because partners in bisexual marriages have to face the paradoxes of their desires, they have sometimes come to terms with themselves, their partners, and their marriages in a particularly thoughtful way. What these bisexual marriages exemplify is less the paradox of bisexuality than the imperfect fit between the stability of marriage and the unruliness of sexual desire.

Part 4 Bi Sex

The Erotics of the Third

Erotic Triangles

If triangles had a god, he would have three sides.

—*Charles de Secondat, Baron de Montesquieu,*
Lettres Persanes[1]

Our entire sense of what it means to be "in love" with someone is based upon the assumption of exclusivity, the assumption that what is "natural" for lovers is to pair up, preferably in the heat of passion and for life. Logic and language would seem to suggest that couples, whether heterosexual, homosexual, or even bisexual, make their appearance in narratives of love and desire—like the animals on Noah's ark—two by two. But as many commentators have noticed, the basic unit of the couple is, paradoxically, not two but three.

Famous couples tend to appear in threes, in what the tabloids call "love triangles." Arthur, Guinevere, and Lancelot; Scarlett, Rhett, and Ashley; "Shakespeare," the dark lady, and the rival poet; Archie, Betty, and Veronica; Helen, Menelaus, and Paris; Tristan, Isolde, and King Mark—these are the models for how we think of great love.

The fundamental romantic courtship narratives of Western culture, and of many other cultures as well, are stories of how the lover "won" the beloved from a rival or tragically failed to do so. It is as though love can only be born through an obstacle. This would explain the centrality of adultery in Western literature. The obstacle, or rival, could take many forms, play many roles: If, for example, the lover were a man, the rival might be another man, a woman, a possessive (or incestuous) parent, a religious or instructional figure who functions in loco parentis as an object of alternative desire, a career or other vocation that interferes with the completion or fulfillment of the courtship, or—a particularly popular choice, at least until recently—God. The same options would obtain if the lover were a woman.

It is more than twenty years now since critic René Girard drew attention to the key role of rivalry in the functioning of romantic love plots. What

Girard called "triangular desire," and later "mimetic desire" (a desire that is provoked by the rival's desire rather than by the supposed love object itself) was, he felt, present in romantic literature from *Don Quixote* to the present day. Love is mediated, not a straight line but a triangle. "Triangular desire is the desire which transfigures its object."[2] The courtly lover, the snob, the child, all love what someone else loves—*because* someone else loves. It is through the other's desire that we consider something or someone desirable. We learn desire, and we learn to desire, by imitating another's desire. Girard quotes a key passage from Proust's *Remembrance of Things Past:* "In love, our successful rival, that is our enemy, is our benefactor. To a person who aroused in us only an insignificant physical desire, he adds an immense prestige and value, which we immediately recognize."[3]

The triangle, he explains, is only a model, or rather a "whole family of models." "The triangle is no *Gestalt*. The real structures are intersubjective. They cannot be localized anywhere; the triangle has no reality whatever; it is a systematic metaphor, systematically pursued."[4] So what is being described is a relationship, a set of positions that define one another. The mediator brings together two spheres of possibilities, of which the rivals are each representative. The result is a growing "ambivalence of desire,"[5] in which passion and hatred, love and jealousy, are mutually constituted and feed on one another. "We can have no . . . doubts about the priority of the Other in desire,"[6] writes Girard. What my rival desires I may come to desire, *because* he or she desires it. In other words, desire is produced by competition and rivalry, not by the innate qualities of the person who is desired. The great heterosexual romances are thus rendered possible, in Girard's analysis, by the importance of the other *man* for the male lover.

While the literary romances Girard studies are generally heterosexual, he acknowledges that his model might also explain "at least some forms of homosexuality." It is Proust who serves as Girard's transitional case: Homosexuality in Proust could be regarded as "a gradual transferring to the mediator of an erotic value which in 'normal' Don Juanism remains attached to the object itself."[7]

Feminist critic Eve Kosofsky Sedgwick took up Girard's invitation to look at the relationship between homosexuality and triangular desire, with results Girard perhaps had not expected. For what she found is not that Girard's model can *extend* from heterosexuality to homosexuality but that it is precisely homosexuality that *explains* heterosexuality. Sedgwick describes Girard's formative insight clearly in her own study of triangular desire, *Between Men:* "[I]n any erotic rivalry, the bond that links the two rivals is as intense and potent as the bond that links either of the two rivals to the beloved. . . . In fact, Girard seems to see the bond between rivals in an erotic triangle as being even stronger . . . than anything in the bond between either of the lovers and the beloved. And within the male-centered novelistic tradition of European high culture, the triangles Girard traces are most often those in which two males are rivals for a female; it is the bond between males that he most assiduously uncovers."[8]

As she notes, Girard's schema of the triangle draws strongly both on contemporary anthropological work (notably Claude Lévi-Strauss's observations on "the traffic in women" in preliterate societies) and on Freud, whose famous articulation of the "Oedipal triangle," the young child caught in the middle, so to speak, between love for the mother and rivalry with the father, became the foundation of modern psychoanalysis. And, as Sedgwick also notes, since such formulations, whether Girard's, Freud's, or those of the folk tales on which both depend for corroborative evidence, are "transhistorical," they posit an unchanging human subject relatively unshaped by culture and history.

Sedgwick herself took the Girardian scheme a key step further, calling attention, as does her book's title, to relations "between men," and in the process offering a nuanced, sophisticated, and vastly influential paradigm for what would become "Gay Studies."[9] She noted in passing that neither Girard nor Freud gender their erotic triangles—or rather, what amounts to virtually the same thing, that they assume the triangle to consist of two men in competition for the same woman. She cited, especially, anthropologist Gayle Rubin's work, which links "patriarchal heterosexuality" to the traffic in women by analyzing Lévi-Strauss's description of that traffic ("The total relationship of exchange which constitutes marriage is not established between a man and a woman, but between two groups of men, and the woman figures only as one of the objects in the exchange, not as one of the partners").[10] Sedgwick redirected attention to the "homosocial" and "homosexual" bonds men form with each other, and the ways in which those bonds have been historically coded as "virile" or "effeminate," depending upon prevailing concepts of class, gender, and power.

Drawing upon interpretative moves made by Michel Foucault and Jacques Lacan, Sedgwick proposed to rearticulate the erotic triangle, treating it "not as an ahistorical, Platonic form, a deadly symmetry from which the historical accidents of gender, language, class and power detract, but as a sensitive register precisely for delineating relationships of power and meaning, and for making graphically intelligible the play of desire and identification by which individuals negotiate with their societies for empowerment."[11] In short, she redrew the erotic triangle to show that it was not symmetrical. Because males and females do not, historically, have equivalent cultural power in most societies, and because, whatever the prevailing rhetoric of "opposites" or "complementarity" (the "opposite sex," the "other half") "one gender is treated as a marginalized subset rather than an equal alternative to the other," bonds between men will be seen as different from bonds between women, and same-sex bonds will be valued (and evaluated) differently.

From this set of key insights has developed a rich field of inquiry, helping to account, just to take one example, for the relative "invisibility" of lesbianism vis-à-vis male homosexuality in the nineteenth century: Because men traditionally have more social and economic power, male homosexuality is more threatening than female homosexuality, and thus becomes visible to the law. In a similar way, male homosocial bonds have often been formed in a way that attempts to fend off the perceived threat of homosexuality. Men's clubs and boy scout troops have been bastions of "male bonding" but not, at least in terms of public policy, advocacy groups for male-male erotic relations. To secure male homosocial desire, male homo*sexual* desire becomes stigmatized and vilified, creating a (comparably) safe space for relations between men. By this reading, heterosexuality becomes a necessary backformation of male-male desire.

Sedgwick's "asymmetrical" erotic triangle thus was a new and improved version (or rather, the old and "original" patriarchal version, now newly brought into view) of Girard's relatively schematic and symmetrical triangle, which, in turn, was a tracing of Freud's Oedipal triangle transposed, so to speak, onto the "traffic in women" triangle of Lévi-Strauss. (Are you still with me?) The three points remained the same: two men and a woman. The woman might be fantasmatic or hypothetical (for example, the entirely suppositious woman upon whom the narrator of Shakespeare's sonnets urges the "fair youth" of the early sonnets to beget future children as copies of himself) or she might be emblematic of some abstract quality or entity (for example, Helen of Troy, Marlowe's "face that launched a thousand ships," either idealized as in Homer or more compromised and ironized in Shakespeare's *Troilus and Cressida*). But however "symmetrical" or "asymmetrical" its gender and power relations might be, the conventional triangle pairs, or pits, two men with and/or against each other in (apparent) quest of a woman.

The Other Woman

Girard pointed out the role of the rival in creating desire as value. Sedgwick asked, what is the designation "rival" covering up? Terry Castle and other lesbian critics now began to ask, What is this whole set of triangles rendering invisible? In the classic triangle of two men and a woman, what disappears is the other woman.

Castle, one of the most powerful and suggestive of today's lesbian critics, offers praise of Sedgwick and a strong reading of her argument together with an equally strong critique. If, as Castle paraphrases Sedgwick's argument, "the male-female-male 'erotic paradigm' is endlessly repeated in canonical English literature "precisely as a way of fending off the destabilizing threat of male homosexuality," and if "the triangular male-female-male figure returns at the conclusion of each story—triumphantly reinstalled—as a sign both of normative (namely, heterosexual) male bonding and of a remobilization of patriarchal control," then, Castle wants to know, "within such a totalizing scheme, with its insistent focus on relations 'between men,' what place might there be for relations between women?"[12]

Plainly this is a rhetorical question. Equally plainly, the answer is, in Castle's reading of Sedgwick, some version of "none." Castle observes astringently that "an entire category of women—lesbians—is lost to view."[13] Quite literally. We might note that, in the reproduction of Manet's *Déjeuner sur l'herbe,* which was used on the cover of Sedgwick's book, one of the two naked women is cropped out. Where Manet had painted two (clothed) men and two (naked) women, the viewer now sees only a threesome.

To demonstrate her point, Castle constructed yet another triangle. In effect she flips over or unfolds the Girard-Sedgwick triangle, rotating it on one of its sides to form an adjacent triangle the third point of which is female, not male. "One of the terms from the original triangle now occupies the 'in between' or subjugated position of the mediator." Next to the "normative" male-female-male triangle she has thus placed its mirror opposite: female-male-female.

Moreover, just as the threat to patriarchal culture was inherent in the possibility that the two male terms might "hook up directly, so to speak, replacing the heterosexual with an explicitly homosexual dyad," so, Castle suggests, the two female terms might merge directly, shifting "from homosocial to *lesbian* bonding." The male term would then drop out, having no other male left with which (or with whom) to bond.

Castle goes on to propose a definition for lesbian fiction that is based upon the functioning of such a triangular structure, describing as "the underlying principle of lesbian narrative itself" the fact that "for female bonding to 'take,' as it were, male bonding must be suppressed." (This immunosuppressive language is not an accident; Castle, like Sedgwick, chooses her words with care.) By "male bonding" she means, as she explains, "male homo*social* bonding," since "lesbian characters in novels can, and do, quite easily coexist with male homo*sexual* characters."[14]

What is the usefulness of such a principle? asks Castle. For one thing, she says, it allows the interested reader to identify the two settings in which such plots of lesbian desire are likely to flourish: "the world of schooling and adolescence (the world of premarital relations) and the world of divorce, widowhood, and separation (the world of postmarital relations). In each of these mimetic contexts," Castle observes, "male erotic triangulation is either conspicuously absent or under assault."[15]

But in point of fact, as she quickly goes on to acknowledge, male erotic figures are not always or even often missing from these works. In fact, "the central lesbian bond may be undermined or broken up, usually by having one of the principals die ... get married ... or reconcile herself in some other way with the erotic and social world of men."

Thus, borrowing a pair of terms from critic Nancy K. Miller, she says that these novels and other works concerned with adolescence exhibit " 'dysphoric' lesbian counterplotting," depicting "female homosexual desire as a finite phenomenon—a temporary phase in a larger pattern of heterosexual *Bildung*." Postmarital lesbian fiction, by contrast, is " 'euphoric' lesbian counterplotting," because the same-sex relationship follows rather than precedes the opposite-sex one. "Typically in such novels, it is the very failure of the heroine's marriage or heterosexual love affair that functions as the pretext for the conversion to homosexual desire."[16]

So a plot is dysphoric if it ends in heterosexuality, and euphoric if it ends in lesbianism. The plot to which it is counter is the so-called marriage plot, the story told over and over in eighteenth- and nineteenth-century English fiction, and for which the opening sentence of Jane Austen's *Pride and Prejudice* has come, however ironically, to stand: "It is a truth universally acknowledged, that a single man in possession of a good fortune must be in want of a wife."

Castle deploys the terms "dysphoric" and "euphoric" with a shadow of the same mordant humor as a way of making an important political point. There are, she seeks to point out, major works of fiction, at least in the twentieth century, that emphasize erotic relationships "between women," and that give pleasure to the readers when such relationships are seen as lasting and fulfilling.

All three of these readers of Western literature—Girard, Sedgwick, and Castle—presume that what they are explaining is the erotic couple. Girard explains romantic love as triangular desire; Sedgwick sees the relations between the male rivals as the point of a structure in which they seem to compete for a woman; Castle sees relations between women as what Sedgwick and Girard leave out and what she wants to celebrate by eliminating the male mediator.

But what do all three analyses of coupling instate as *constitutive* of the dynamics of their pairs? Triangularity. In other words, bisexuality. In all three cases, it is bisexual triangularity that provokes, explains, and encompasses both heterosexuality and homosexuality. While all three analysts appear to privilege the couple, they *all* prove only that the shortest distance between two points is a triangle.

Romancing the Structure

Let me offer a final reading of triangularity to underscore the nature of this point—a reading that comes in at an angle, so to speak, to this progression of variations on the theme of erotic rivalry. The diagram of the triangle produced by Shoshana Felman in her reading of Edgar Allan Poe's "Purloined Letter" is one that stresses positions in a structure rather than innate or intrinsic identities. Felman is describing psychoanalyst Jacques Lacan's method of reading Poe's story, and his way of investigating the question of "what repeats"—how the notion of the "repetition compulsion," as described by Freud in *Beyond the Pleasure Principle,* functions in "The Purloined Letter" both at and below the level of conscious action.

Poe's story, of course, is itself a story of erotic rivalry: the Queen has a lover, whose existence is unknown to the King; the Minister purloins an incriminating letter that would reveal the Queen's infidelity; Dupin, the detective, deduces the letter's place of concealment, and purloins the letter in turn, restoring it to the Queen. (No mention, incidentally, is ever made of the gender of the Queen's correspondent.)

As Felman notes, "the primal scene" is the scene of the initial theft in the Queen's boudoir; the second scene, the repetition, is the theft of the letter from the Minister by Dupin in the Minister's hotel.

> What constitutes repetition for Lacan [Felman writes] is not the mere thematic resemblance of the double *theft,* but the whole structural situation in which the repeated theft takes place: in each case, the theft is the outcome of an intersubjective relationship between three terms; in the first scene, the three participants are the King, the Queen, and the Minister; in the second, the three participants are the police, the Minister, and Dupin. . . . What is repeated, in other words, is not a psychological act committed as a function of the individual psychology of the character, but three functional *positions in a structure* that, determining three different *viewpoints,* embody three different relations to the act of seeing.[17]

In other words, the triangles of Girard, Sedgwick, and Castle all reveal erotic desire as dependent on one's position in a triangular structure, a structure that replicates itself with the addition of each new participant. In *Gone With the Wind,* Scarlett O'Hara falls in love with Ashley Wilkes in part because he is engaged to his cousin Melanie Hamilton; Rhett Butler's passion for Scarlett originates with his knowledge of her passion for Ashley. Théophile Gautier's novel *Mademoiselle de Maupin* offers two interlocking and alternative triangles involving the same person, since it is not clear whether the mysterious and seductive "Théodore" is a woman or a man: the narrator D'Albert, his fiancée Rosette, and "Théodore" constitute a triangle, but is it a triangle of two men and a woman, or of two women and a man? In either case the position of "rival" circulates among the key players. In one of Ferenc Molnár's plays a husband disguises himself as a guard and seduces his own wife, who later reveals that she has seen through the deception from the beginning. The husband thus acts out his jealousy and his own divided wishes (that he should prove right in suspecting her; that his suspicion should have no cause) while the wife's fidelity and infidelity are both confirmations of his fantasies. But with whom has she been unfaithful? This husband wanted triangularity so much that he played two parts. The only person he could bear to lose her to was himself.

Girard, Sedgwick, and Castle may themselves be imagined as constituting three points of a triangle. Each has his or her "angle," describing the fundamental patterns of affinity and rivalry, love and hatred, that inform (1) heterosexual, (2) gay male, and (3) lesbian plots in literature. Each offers a valuable way of reading anew not only a subset of great works but virtually all mimetic literature in the Western tradition, from the Greek classics to the present day. But each of these "angles" is finally *binary,* offering an either/or choice *between*—between the rival and the beloved. Which is which? they enable us to ask. Yet if we take the erotic triangle seriously we will see that the choice, in poet Wallace Stevens's terms, is "not between, but of."

Conquest or seduction—"winning"—is often an aphrodisiac as powerful as the specific charms of the beloved himself or herself. In fact, it is frequently impossible to tell the difference. When we say that we want to be loved "for ourselves," what "selves" do we have in mind?

No one, of course, wants to be told that they have fallen in love, not with a person, but with a structure. It's like the idea of the "unconscious," so unwelcome to so many. We like to think we are in control, if not of our entire lives, then at least of our emotions and affections. To have an unconscious that wants and desires things quite different, and often at variance from, those things we think and say we want is disquieting, to say the least. Likewise with "love," the most desirable of all human qualities. We invest a lot of emotional capital in the idea of "true love": "the real thing," marriages "made in heaven," and the "perfect couple." Yet our greatest love stories are, as we have already noted, narratives of triangularity.

The Logic of the Third

As we look at how erotic triangles work in practice, several things begin to become clear, not only about triangular structures but also about people's fantasies about bisexuality. It appears that some people, like some literary and dramatic characters, get involved in erotic triangles:

- because they (consciously or unconsciously) like the structure. What is eroticized for them is the *triangle,* more than any of its elements. Whether this is because they prefer courtship to marriage or partnership, the process of seduction to the fact of having (or having been) seduced, or (relative) complexity rather than (relative) simplicity, competition gets their juices running. Uncertainty is exciting to them, as is turning it, however briefly, to certainty.

- because they like the position of the "third," the one who interrupts—what is often, in terms of the Oedipal triangle and in the specular terms of film, the position of the child. This is not to say that the "third" person will necessarily be younger, more innocent, or in any other way more "childlike" than the other two. The child is the one who watches, who listens, who claims the right to intervene. With this as with any other motive for triangularity, more than one can play, but only one can be in this (or any other) position *at a time.*

- because they like to change positions, especially across gender and sexuality borderlines. It might seem as if this were a game that two could play as well or better than three, but with two there are only a pair of positions to choose from; switching them still affords the same relationship, or relationships: boy-girl, master-slave, yes-no, vice-versa. The permutations of three are both more numerous and more flexible. This is another version of the logic of the third. The third (or fourth, or fifth, for "three" is here a marker that means more than two) opens up the dyad toward the world. The classical theater of Sophocles saw this with the third actor, who could play many different roles in the course of a single play.

Triangular structures, in other words, are not always a misfortune, an accident, or a halfway point between "here" and "there," or, in the case of bisexuality, between "him" and "her." Sometimes they are sought out, consciously or unconsciously, *because* they are triangular. Furthermore, the function of the triangle in a plot—fictional, dramatic, cinematic, biographical—can be different from its function in motivating a character or individual. The triangular play can, for example, mirror an ambivalence present in the plot elsewhere, an ambivalence that may not be consciously registered *as* ambivalence. It may, that is to say, mark the difficulty of making a choice, or, more significantly, the difficulty of telling "right" from "wrong," "friend" from "enemy," even "self" from "not-self" or "other." It can thus be thematic or symptomatic with respect to the story as a whole, rather than—or in addition to—one of its characters. Again, for these purposes a "story" can be a novel, a play, a biography or autobiography, or someone's dream. The function is the same.

◆

We may recall that Freud was presented with an honorific medallion in 1906, a year after the publication of three of his most original and controversial works, the *Three Essays on the Theory of Sexuality,* the "Dora" case, and *Jokes and Their Relationship to the Unconscious.* In the same year his erstwhile friend Wilhelm Fliess at long last published his own theory of bisexuality in a book called *The Course of Life: Foundation of Exact Biology.*

Freud had complained in his final letter to Fliess two years before that until the topic of bisexuality, which Fliess so jealously guarded as his own, was officially released to the public, "I can do nothing, not even finish the *Jokes,* which in a crucial point is partially based on the theory of sexuality."[18] What was that crucial point? What does a joke have to do with sexuality—or with bisexuality?

It proceeds by the logic of the third.

A smutty joke, says Freud, is the intentional mention of sex and sexuality in speech. Taking for granted the heterosexuality of the social world, he notes that "smut is ... originally directed towards women and may be equated with attempts at seduction."[19] But if a third person is present, there is a barrier to instant gratification. As in the case of a tendentious joke, a smutty joke "calls for three people": the one who makes the joke, the second who is its sexual or hostile object, and the third, in whom the joke produces pleasure. "Here at last we can understand what it is that jokes achieve in the service of their purpose. They make possible the satisfaction of an instinct (whether lustful or hostile) in the face of an obstacle that stands in its way."[20]

What makes a joke work, as he insists, is the participation of the *third person*—not the duality of two but the triangulation of three. "The psychical process in jokes is accomplished between the first person (the self) and the third (the outside person), and not ... between the self and the person who is the object." And a riddle, he says, is a kind of joke which requires greater intellectual effort, and which therefore produces not laughter but thought.[21] It, too, proceeds by the logic of the third.

Thirdness on stage or screen is often an element of comedy. The situation that enables the comedy of the third party is a familiar one, an adaptation of a stock device of stage and screen farce from Richard Brinsley Sheridan's *School for Scandal* to the television sitcom "Three's Company." For reasons that have ostensibly nothing to do with sex or sexuality, three people—two men and a woman or two women and a man—find themselves in a bedroom, apartment, dorm room, or housetrailer. The comic confusions, interactions, and permutations that follow all depend upon double entendres, innocent sexiness, and sexy "innocence."

This setup is a version of that Hollywood staple, the unmarried couple forced to spend a night together in the same room, which provides the impetus for comedy and romance in films from *It Happened One Night* (1934) to *Sylvia Scarlett* (1935), where the sexual comedy is further complicated by Katharine Hepburn's masquerade as a man; *Queen Christina* (1933), in which Greta Garbo in dashing male attire gets into a curtained and canopied bed with John Gilbert; and *I Was a Male War Bride* (1949) where Cary Grant disguises himself as a woman.

It is not an accident that these last three examples involve cross-dressing and mistaken gender identity, together with fleeting threats of same-sex erotic attraction. The third party here is present and absent at once in what might be called the party of the second part: Garbo as boy, Garbo as queen. Even though there are only two people involved, the triangle is imaginatively in place and in play, and the transgressive erotic send-up, going to bed with a same-sex partner and finding yourself in bed with a partner of the opposite sex, itself eroticizes the more conventional relation, bringing danger and daring "safely" into the bed space. In a way it's a version of the Total Woman scenario, in which the housewife dresses up for her husband in leather-and-chains (or French maid apron-and-garters) —the defamiliarization of the familiar sex partner makes the encounter more exciting as a story. In terms of Hollywood films, of course, it's also a way of talking about gay or lesbian sexuality without appearing to do so.

Explicit bisexual triangles can take a variety of erotic shapes. In one version, a person clearly identifiable as bisexual is positioned at the triangle's apex. Thus for example Catherine Bourne in Hemingway's *The Garden of Eden,* Bob Elkin (Murray Head) in *Sunday, Bloody Sunday,* and Catherine Tramell (Sharon Stone) in *Basic Instinct* each has a male lover and a female lover. But as these examples suggest, the outcome can vary, and almost always the missing side of the triangle is filled in by some kind of relationship. In other words, this is not a binary, either/or "choice of Hercules" between virtue and pleasure or even a three-forked "choice of Paris" among love goddesses. The triangle *is* a triangle, not a V. And it's the connections among the "other" partners that need articulating. Like the missing "fourth wall" in proscenium theater, where the illusion is of an audience looking in on a reality that doesn't look back, this third leg or side of the triangle is more active and more determinative than it may at first appear.

As we will see in greater detail in Chapter 20, "Threesomes," Catherine Bourne's husband and her lover themselves become lovers, and ultimately plan to marry, as the excluded Catherine first burns her husband's writings and then flees up the French coast. *Sunday, Bloody Sunday*'s rivals, Glenda Jackson and Peter Finch, both more urbane and complex than their mutual lover, the young sculptor Elkin, find themselves awkwardly trading condolences on a Hampstead street when he leaves them both for career advancement in America. It's too quick a move to see this as merely the Old World versus the New World, but nor will it do merely to say, as many did at the time, that the bisexual man was unable to make a commitment and constitutionally unfaithful. Vito Russo had it right when he observed that audiences at the time wanted "romantic stability" in its characters: "The ability to make a choice is seen as a necessity. Elkin chooses both men and women, and that is against the rules: it is no choice rather than a new choice."[22]

As for *Basic Instinct,* where the triangular structure pits Nick (Michael Douglas) first against the out lesbian Roxy (Leilani Sarelle) and then against the closeted, bisexual therapist Beth (Jeanne Tripplehorn), it is the missing side, the fact of a previous relationship between Beth and Catherine, that makes the plot spin. Beth and Nick have been lovers before the film begins (incidentally, or perhaps not so incidentally, violating another sexual taboo, that which forbids sex between therapists and their patients). The affair between Nick and Catherine doubles the triangles (Nick-Catherine-Roxy; Nick-Catherine-Beth), and once the flamboyantly tough and sexy Roxy, who "likes to watch" (or whom Catherine likes to have watch) when Catherine takes men to bed, is killed in a car chase with Nick, attention focuses on the more dangerous, because not so easily detected, second triangle in which two of the women are bisexual.

Even when a bisexual triangle looks obvious it may have hidden angles. The 1993 *Three of Hearts,* about a lesbian named Connie (Kelly Lynch), her bisexual girlfriend Ellen (Sherilyn Fenn), and Joe, the male escort (William Baldwin) whom Connie hires to get her lover back, offers itself as a love triangle for the nineties, with the gorgeous Baldwin, accurately described by Janet Maslin as "the film's principal love object"[23] and first seen naked in a bathtub talking phone sex to a client, predictably falling in love with the woman he is hired to win over. The triangle's active sides would thus seem to be Connie-Ellen and Joe-Ellen. In fact, though, we see more intimacy between Connie and Joe than between any other pair: the lesbian registered nurse and the male escort who seeks a way out of "the life" seem made for each other, comedically speaking. In fact, we see Joe clowning and flirting with Connie as they sit together on her bed, and Joe making love in bed with Ellen. We never see Connie and Ellen, except in Connie's lovingly preserved, obsessively rewatched videos. Hollywood skittishness? Perhaps. But the effect is to let the Connie-Joe relationship take over the film, especially since it ends with them companionably walking together, his arm around her shoulder, as she commiserates with him on Ellen's elusiveness. The penultimate citation of *The Graduate* (Joe running down the street after Ellen's taxi, yelling, "Ellen! Ellen!" like Dustin Hoffman hollering "Elaine! Elaine!" at the church door) can hardly fail to be tongue-in-cheek, especially when Connie comments that *she* could have caught that cab in high heels. Which of course she never wears, except for "cross-dressed" events like her sister's wedding. Does Joe really *want* to catch the cab, and the rather conventional Ellen inside it? No matter. *Three of Hearts* leaves him with Connie. Good choice.

Erotic Substitutions

Love and sex play often depend upon projection, role playing, and a shifting deployment of identifications and desires, whether the sexuality in question is "straight" or "gay." In Anchee Min's extraordinary memoir of political and emotional education in the last years of China under Mao, *Red Azalea,* a young girl from Shanghai finds herself on a work farm in the country, sharing a bunk bed with her female Party secretary, Yan. The two women, though they "betrayed no intimacy in public," become close, and talk "about everything, including that most forbidden subject— men."[24] During the Cultural Revolution sex outside of marriage could be punished by death, and homosexual love was a counterrevolutionary crime. One night Yan discloses that she has a secret—she is in love with a man. Anchee Min offers to be her personal messenger to Leopard Lee. She is well educated and begins at Yan's request to rewrite and enhance her letters to Leopard. Like Cyrano de Bergerac, she will become an erotic go-between. Because of her role as amanuensis, Min can rejoice, "Her intimacy belonged to me."[25]

Making an excuse—"I did not have enough blankets and was afraid of catching cold"—she joins Yan in bed and gives her the letter. Yan is overcome with pleasure. "Her face flushed. She read and reread the letter. She whispered that it was the best thing she had ever read. She said she did not know I was so talented. She pressed her cheek against mine." She asks how Leopard Lee would react after reading the letter. "I told her that he would fall in love with her. She told me to repeat what I had just said and I did. She whispered, How can you be sure? I whispered back, If I were a man, I would."[26] In bed, Yan turns away, and murmurs, "Too bad you are not a man." "What would you do if I were? I asked. She turned back to face me and said she would do exactly what I had described in the letter."[27]

Although both women still place their ostensible focus on Leopard Lee, their affair with each other is clearly already taking place, deriving some of its erotic impetus from projection and substitution. Hitching a ride to see Leopard and deliver the letter supposedly written by Yan, Min is "as excited . . . as if I were going to meet my own lover."[28] His response is nervous and cool, and though she delivers four letters to him in two months he never writes back. Yan remains lovesick, and Min continues to share her bed by making excuses about the cold weather, delivering further letters every few weeks. When Yan goes off for intensive political training, where she will again see Leopard, Min is afraid she will lose her, but predictably the opposite happens. Yan returns cured. "It's all over and it never happened," she says, and her eager suitor says, "Now I wish you were a man."[29]

The scene of actual lovemaking is a scene of double substitution, the "substitute" coming to substitute for the "original" and to be unveiled as the real object of passion: "I asked if to her I was Leopard. She enveloped me in her arms. She said there never was a Leopard. It was I who created Leopard. I said it was an assignment given by her. She said, You did a very good job."[30] "The moment I touched her breasts I felt a sweet shock. . . . *I did not know what role I was playing any more: her imagined man or myself.*"[31] It is beside the point here to ask which she "really" is or which Yan "really" wants: What they want is what they get, what they get is what they want. They are lovers, and the figure of Leopard has been a crucial mediating figure for their desire.

Later Yan does become Leopard's lover, and Min watches through the draperies as they make love in her parents' house. She had volunteered to stand guard for the couple. "I knew the way she moved when she was aroused and could not help herself from pulling me closer and closer to her, pressing me, pasting me to her skin, leaving teeth marks on my shoulders. I wanted to be an observer, to observe Leopard doing what I have and have not done."[32]

When she sees them together, "I tried to stop my desire. The desire to watch them. The desire to watch my other self—Yan . . . I was in Yan. It was three instead of two people on the porch."[33] Afterward Yan calls her in. "She embraced me and said, I am sorry to do this, but I just have to. I think we are now ready to go on with our own lives." Then Yan and Leopard make love again. "She kissed him deeply. She was showing this to me. She was doing it to me."[34] Later she will reflect, "I had never thought of having her only to myself until the moment I saw Leopard touch her."[35]

Min's life changes dramatically when she is invited to compete for a role in *Red Azalea,* a film about the life of Madame Mao, Jiang Ching. She is duped by a rival and fails to get the part, but as "set clerk" for the film she meets the man known only as the Supervisor. "His fingers were fine and smooth like a woman's." In opera costume "the makeup made him look femininely handsome. . . . Was he a man or a woman? He seemed both. He was grotesquely beautiful."[36] Even the head of the film's lighting crew thinks the Supervisor is "more beautiful than a woman. He asked, Why are you a man? You shouldn't be a man—you ruin your looks when you dress like a man."[37]

Although the Supervisor is married and lives in Beijing, he and Min become lovers in the Peace Park next to the crematorium, a place where "lonely men and women gather each night to experience the essence of drama," masturbating as they watch the couples in secret. "They know they will be shot if caught—so do we. They regard this moment as their last performance—so do we. The fright sweetens the mood."[38] He has guessed she's had a lover before, though he is startled to hear that it was a woman. "If it was love I shared with Yan, it was ambition I shared with the Supervisor," she notes.[39] But she longs for his return.

In the precarious world of revolutionary politics, things take yet another unexpected turn. The film production is denounced and dissolved, and Min is summoned to Beijing for a screen test as Red Azalea, replacing her former rival. Clearly this is the Supervisor's doing, though she protests to her jealous colleagues that she knows no one in Beijing and would be happy to remain as set clerk for the good of the Party. Briefly she becomes a celebrity, as the Supervisor confesses to her in bed that he himself identifies with Jiang Ching. Both of them had played Nora in productions of Ibsen's *A Doll's House*. Now Anchee Min will become the embodiment of Comrade Jiang Ching and the Supervisor—another erotic substitution. But before her part can be filmed, Mao dies, rumors circulate that he was killed by his wife, Jiang Ching, and both Min and the Supervisor are suddenly on the losing side. "We held each other. I felt Yan."[40]

Falling in Love with a Couple

We can get a very good sense of the complex pleasures of the erotic triangle from a film like *Henry and June* (1992), which tells the story of writer Henry Miller; his sexy, "Junoesque" wife, June; and erotic diarist Anaïs Nin, who had a brief but intense affair with Miller in the Paris of the thirties. Two intersecting triangles dominate the action: one comprised of Nin, her husband, Hugo, and Miller; the second of Nin, Miller, and June.

The film sets up these triangles as Oedipal. Nin is the wide-eyed, insatiably curious child who is forever opening doors or parting curtains only to glimpse tangled, naked bodies behind them. Actress Maria de Medeiros, with her round, white face and deep black eyes, is the perfect receptor, and the perfect intruder. She follows Miller to a bordello full of statuesque, naked women, and watches him climb the stairs behind a prostitute. Before long she has persuaded Hugo to go to the same bordello with her, to watch an "exhibition" of two women making love. She and Hugo go on a bicycle ride with Henry and June; when Henry and June stop off to make exuberant love against a tree, she is all eyes again. Every night, lying in bed with her husband, she writes in her diary. Writes first what she sees, and then, as her experiences widen, writes what she does.

Henry's novel is all about June, so that when June first appears, Anaïs is already in love with her. Throughout the film Nin's erotic crush on June is structured as the goal, the place we never see her get to. In the book version, a redaction of the famous diaries to highlight the "Henry and June" portions, the romance with June is much more explicit, less elusive. Compiled by her husband-in-bigamy and literary executor Rupert Pole, the diary selections end purposefully with a bisexual tease: "So Henry is coming this afternoon, and tomorrow I am going out with June," but the real unattainable quest object in the diaries is the psychoanalyst, a "great, sincere man" who tries to convince her that eroticism and sentiment can sometimes coexist, and about whom she writes, with unforgettable bathos, "the awareness that transference is an artificially stimulated emotion inspires me with more mistrust than ever. If I doubt genuine manifestations of love, how much more do I doubt this mentally aroused attachment." [41]

In the film, though, compared to her passion for the elusive June, Nin's affair with Miller, despite its intense passion and physicality, seems almost like a substitution or a transitional event; he is in Paris, June is back in the States with her lesbian lover, Jean. "I've done the wildest things, the foulest things—but I've done them superbly," June will tell her when they visit a lesbian bar together. "I feel innocent now." This paradoxical combination of wildness, foulness, and innocence will become Anaïs's ideal condition, and one she largely achieves by the film's end. When Anaïs looks at June she suddenly sees a flashback of the key scene from *Maedchen in Uniform,* where the girls at a boarding school are kissed goodnight by Fräulein von Bernberg, with whom they are all in love. Again Anaïs feels like the child; June has for her tremendous sexual authority. "Do you love women?" she asks. "What do you mean?" June asks, teasingly. "What about Jean?" The next day June is off to New York, leaving Anaïs unsatisfied and eager.

This kind of film-within-film citation is a staple of modern cinema, and is often used in bisexual-themed films to point up an irony in an existing relationship or to shadow an unexpressed desire for a different one (as it does, for example, in *Making Love*). The earlier film, especially if it exists in a different tonal register from the present one, in this case *Maedchen's* dramatic black and white expressionism juxtaposed to the multicolor lushness of *Henry and June,* has the cinematic effect of dream or fantasy. But what is especially interesting here is that although the comparison to *Maedchen in Uniform* is also made in the diary, the film *reverses the roles* of teacher and student. In Nin's diary the comparison with *Maedchen* is made by June, and she, not Anaïs, is "the worshipful girl Manuela." "Why does June want to think me strong and herself a passionate child beloved by the teacher?" Nin asks rhetorically. It is June, not Anaïs, who there seems to need protection. [42]

"I want to fuck her like a man," Anaïs says to Hugo in bed. She is speaking of June; she wants him to pretend he is making love to her. She herself can imagine, in the course of their lovemaking, that she is in Hugo's position (fucking her like a man) and in June; desire and identification, she learns, are alternative sites of pleasure for her, and there is no reason why she can't have both.

The affair with Henry begins backstage at a nightclub—Henry tears her clothes off while, onstage, Hugo "sits in" at the conga drums. The film segues from her erotic pleasure with Henry to her erotic pleasure with Hugo. "I love you, Henry." "I love you, Hugo." The same substitution, with an added increment of danger and pleasure, takes place during Mardi Gras, when Henry, uncharacteristically, can't get an erection. Anaïs wanders through the streets, and is wordlessly taken by a half naked man wearing blue body makeup and a carnival mask who has followed her into an alley. "I love you, Pussywillow," he says at the end, using the incongruous pet-name Hugo has for her, thus signing his name to the deed. "My first infidelity to Henry was with my own husband." As another variation on the Marabel Morgan "Total Woman" approach to spicing up a marriage, this ploy works wonders. The balance shifts from Henry to Hugo: Now they will seek sexual adventure together.

And so on to the bordello, where the *patronne* indicates that they should choose the two women who will make love in front of them. Anaïs, of course, chooses a woman who looks like June, and one who looks like herself. The lovemaking takes place in front of a mirror, making it seem as if there are two couples. When the women pause to ask if Anaïs and Hugo want something different, Anaïs speaks her desire: "Yes. Stop pretending to be a man." She wants to see, not a man and a woman, but herself having sex with June. The blond prostitute looks up from her activity and says, "Would you like to join us?" Hugo in his dinner jacket, Anaïs in her smart dinner dress exchange glances. They would. They don't. Soon Anaïs will return to the bordello alone, where we see her drinking with the June look-alike while the record player plays Josephine Baker's "J'ai deux amours." Baker's two loves, "mon pays et Paris," are left to stand in eloquent counterpoint to Nin's more immediate and carnal "deux amours," Henry and June.

The full effect of the bisexual triangle of Henry, June, and Anaïs is deferred in the film by June's absence from Paris. In its place the other bisexual triangle—Hugo, Anaïs, and Henry—assembles in bed together, not to have sex but to read, inevitably, about June. The scene is a modern reworking of the typical French farce. Henry, having finished writing his book, cycles over to Anaïs's house, is let in by the maid, and goes to Anaïs's study where he makes love to her. Hugo arrives and is detained in the kitchen by the maid, who towels his hair dry from the rain and heats a baguette for him, offering it for him to take whole in his mouth (an inescapably phallic and comic scene, presumably reversing the genders of an activity going on in the room above). Hugo is thus both the baby and the cuckolded husband. When he finally announces himself to his wife ("Pussywillow, I'm home") Anaïs reacts quickly, rushing him away from her door with the excuse that Henry is inside, sleeping—he has "been up all night" finishing his book. In a few moments Henry, looking a little worse for wear, tries to tiptoe down the stairs and make his escape, but he is called into the adjacent bedroom by Hugo. "Come and join us," Hugo says, echoing the blond prostitute in the bordello's lesbian scene. They are reading the pages of Henry's novel, with audible cries of admiration and pleasure. Henry, trapped, perches himself gingerly on the bed beside them. When the maid enters with drinks and sees the threesome in bed, she crosses herself as she leaves the room.

June (Uma Thurman), who has all this time been back in New York, now returns, remarking in her wonderful smoky voice with its slightly uncertain lower-class accent as she embraces Anaïs, "I don't know who I came back for." But June is prepared only to be the apex of the triangle, not a subsidiary element. She and Anaïs are at last in a bedroom together, and removing their negligees, when, negligently, it would seem, Anaïs lets slip the fact that she and Henry are sleeping together, by observing that they needn't worry about Henry interrupting them: Once he falls asleep nothing can wake him. The resulting altercation effectively ends any chance of the audience getting to watch the "real" love scene between the women, as June storms out with the perfect bisexual version of "a plague on both your houses": "I'm the wrong woman for you, Henry. I'm the wrong woman for *you,* Anaïs." We are not quite in the realm of Abbott and Costello's old joke routine about "Who's on first, What's on second, I-Don't-Know-Who's on third," but we are not so far away either.

Anaïs Nin's diaries are constantly bringing to the surface this insistent triangulation of desire. "Is it June or Henry I am jealous of?"[43] she asks early on, and Henry describes the whole scenario: "It seems to me that from the very moment when you opened the door and held out your hand, smiling, I was taken in, I was yours. June felt it, too. She said immediately that you were in love with me, or else I with you. But I didn't know myself that it was love. I spoke about you, glowingly, without reserve. And then June met you and she fell in love with you."[44] We need to remember that this is really Nin, not Henry—or June—speaking; the diary is her account, and has been widely described as either a work of fiction or of sexual fantasy. But as a fantasy structure, whether or not it is literally accurate to the facts, Nin's diary tells truths. Nin changes places, plays roles: "I want to possess June. I identify myself with the men who can penetrate her." With her husband, too: "Hugo bears down on me, and I instinctively obey Henry's whispered words. I close my legs about Hugo, and he exclaims in ecstasy, 'Darling, darling, what are you doing? You're driving me wild. I've never felt such joy before!'" Substitution and trans-ferential desire *are* her desires. "Everything Henry had said about [June] was true." When her psychoanalyst "imagine[s] the end of my subjection to Henry and June," she concludes that he is jealous. But she remains drawn to him, especially when she sees "the sensual modulation of his mouth, the possibility of savagery."[45]

Diary and diarist together form a dyadic structure, a closed circle. Nin's "marriage" to the diary, which, as we've noted, she takes to bed with her each night, making a third in the bed with her husband, needs the constant interruption and exposure of a reader constituted as a lawful/unlawful espial, a privileged voyeur. The opening scene of the film *Henry and June* features a lustful male publisher (bearded, in loco psychoanalyst) who is aroused by reading Nin's account of her life. In the diary excerpts he is a novelist and publisher's assistant (without a beard), and although he is working with her on her critical study of D. H. Lawrence, it is reading *his* novel that turns *her* on. In both cases the sexual interaction with him, in which she is self-described as inexpert, unimaginative, and ultimately magnanimous to the point of condescension, sets the pattern for her erotic awakening by Henry and June and her concomitant and pleasure-giving deception of her husband. After the incident with the publisher's assistant she "tell[s] the story to Hugo partially, leaving out my activity, extracting the meaning of it for him and for me."[46] Hugo, as we've seen, reacts to her fantasizing in bed about having sex with another man by crying out in ecstasy, "Darling, darling, what are you doing? You're driving me wild. I've never felt such joy before!"

Interestingly, though, he can't stand June. "Hugo admits he is jealous. From the very first minute they hated each other." His jealousy takes a predictable tack; he decides that June has "a mannish neck, a mannish voice, and coarse hands," and that her strength "is like that of a man." "Does she think that with her woman's sensibility and subtlety she can love anything in you that I have not loved?" he asks—or rather, Nin reports him as asking.[47] Thus Anaïs's feelings ("by the end of the evening I was like a man, terribly in love with her face and body") are permitted to be "like a man," but June's make her "mannish." On the other hand (or is it the same hand?) we hear that June has ended her relationship with Jean back in Brooklyn because "Jean was too masculine."[48] Anaïs, with her lace collars, rose-colored dresses, and little black jackets, is certainly femme enough. A male cousin and admirer assures her that even though she desires June she is "not a lesbian, because I do not hate men—on the contrary."[49]

In a way, Anaïs's greatest pleasure is in deferral and substitution. But she also participates in another structure that is familiar in some sexual triangles, and in many people's lives: She falls in love with a couple. I think this must be very common, especially for adolescents and others relatively inexperienced in love. The couple has such glamour; they have, after all, succeeded in winning that most desirable of objects, each other. Their life affords a glimpse of intimacy and sexiness, just inaccessible enough to make them seem irresistible. And then they repay the admiration in some measure, flattered and warmed by the attention. Soon it becomes possible, or seems to become possible, to win, perhaps, just a little bit of special attention from the one, or from the other. Before you know it they are competing for your affection. If you are persistent and like taking risks, you may find yourself involved with one of them, or even with both. Not a few erotic triangles begin this way—and not a few divorces. But the initial emotion here is bisexual. It is the couple that attracts.

Jealousy

Jealousy and envy imply a third presence; object, subject, and a third person toward whom the jealousy or envy are directed. These two "vices" are therefore triangular.

—*René Girard,* Deceit, Desire, and the Novel[1]

Don't talk to me about gay pride or bi pride. Love has no pride—that's the banner the real world marches under.

—*Susie Bright,* Susie Bright's Sexual Reality[2]

The classic triangular story of displaced desire becomes a centerpiece of the unauthorized Calvin Klein biography, *Obsession,* appearing to explain, according to the authors, a shift in Klein's relationship with his future wife, Kelly Rector. For months their relationship had been companionable and romantic but not sexual, his biographers report. Klein, formerly married, had since that time been largely involved with gay men. At a party in Los Angeles the pair were introduced to actor Warren Beatty, whom Calvin Klein had long found attractive, according to friends. And, if the biographers are to be credited, "it was Beatty whom Kelly credited as turning a platonic romance into an authentic love affair."[3]

Beatty, it is said, began to flirt with Kelly Rector at the party, called her the next day, and went to bed with her. Klein was jealous—but of whom? " 'It was as if,' said an intimate of Calvin's, 'by having Kelly, he'd have a piece of Warren.' "[4] I put this remark in double quotes because it is presented in the Klein biography with no more identification than "an intimate says." There is no corroborating footnote, no editorial apparatus to further identify or authorize the quote. Yet for our present purposes it does not matter much whether "an intimate" said so, in so many words, or not, nor need we know who the "intimate" was. What he or she intimated to the biographers, or, if one is more skeptical about evidence, what the biographers sought and "found," is the bisexual triangle at work:

I do not love *him,* I love her. Transferential desire. "Soon after the Warren Beatty incident," Kelly is said to have told friends, Calvin made his first sexual approach to her, and they ended up in bed. From that time, though her friends protested to her, "But he's *gay,*" they were a couple. Three years later they were married.

Jealousy can sometimes be a cover for a more complex passion, often a denial of same-sex attraction, as in Nella Larsen's *Passing,* or, in a more explicitly gay context, the male triangulation of Mary Renault's *The Charioteer.* But jealousy is also, as every analysis of jealousy admits, a complex passion in its own right. It can constitute, as well as camouflage, a passion. Is it then the motor or the brake?

"The year 1985 is an exciting year," rejoiced a social scientist who studies jealousy. "It is the year that jealousy 'came out of the closet'!"[5]

What did she mean by this provocative remark? She went on to explain. "Nancy Friday wrote her personal experience in the popular book *Jealousy; Psychology Today* came out with a survey and report called 'The Heart of Jealousy'; and finally there is the written culmination of my work." In a move that appears not itself entirely devoid of the emotion under debate she then added, "Frankly, it's about time people started sharing their experiences of jealousy with each other."

That jealousy should "come out of the closet" suggests that one of its hidden stories is, precisely, homosexuality. This was Freud's point in a much-discussed essay of 1922. Nancy Friday herself, writing indeed from the depth of "her own frankly revealed experiences,"[6] describes her conversation with a friend, a sexy, married, male therapist who had had numerous girlfriends. He is, in fact, the person to whom she will dedicate her own jealousy book.

"How does it feel to lose a good woman to another man?" she asks him.

"I remember one," he says. "I lost her to another analyst. I had the strangest fantasy. That I was going down on him, the guy she'd left me for. Isn't that crazy?"

"In Freud's paper," Friday reminds him, "he writes that the man's fantasy of sharing his woman with another man suggests the major emotion is between the two men."

"That's bullshit," her friend responds, perhaps predictably (doctors make the worst patients). "Freud's interpretation has nothing to do with me." Certainly he's had fantasies of his wife "making it with the delivery boy and other 'low-lifes'" (the designation in quotation marks is Friday's). "Didn't you identify with those men? Didn't you imagine yourself one of them?"

"That's different. I see plenty of that in my practice; it's a whole different story. That's wanting to introject a male model so men can know how to be men."

"Doesn't that include a sense of wanting to be close to the other man, at least in fantasy? In a way that the world forbids in reality?"

"Sure. That's fine. But that isn't queer or gay. It's more like the Greek idea of us men together, learning how to be men and reinforcing our masculinity. . . . It's all in the service of reinforcing their heterosexuality, ultimately. That's not what Freud said. My fantasy, that's not homosexual."

"I never used the word 'homosexual,' " says Nancy Friday.[7]

"After decades of banishment to popular magazines and advice columns, jealousy and envy, as complex interpersonal emotions, have certainly emerged as legitimate topics of scientific inquiry." So declares Peter Salovey, the editor of a social science volume on jealousy and envy published in 1991 that contains essays by social and clinical psychologists and sociologists.[8] A version of this claim is frequently made in other books on the topic published by psychologists around this time.[9] Jealousy had become a legitimate object of research.

It might seem fitting for the greedy eighties to have produced a social science discourse of jealousy and envy in the nineties, but as several scholars note, the turning point for jealousy studies was not in fact the nineties, when some of these studies appeared collected in book form, but rather a series of academic meetings of psychologists in 1977, when researchers like Eugene Mathes discovered "that I was not the only person doing research on jealousy."[10]

The legitimation and quantification of jealousy as an academic object of inquiry, it seems, arose from competition for sex (in the seventies) rather than money (in the eighties). The expansion of premarital sexual activity, which became "nearly universal in the United States"[11] according to one study, led in turn to a sense that sexual freedom should also exist within marriage, and books on "open marriage" began to appear on the market.[12] Had jealousy become outdated? Apparently not. The Interpersonal Jealousy Scale,[13] the Self-Report Jealousy Scale and the Projective Jealousy Scale,[14] the Chronic Jealousy and Relationship Jealousy scales,[15] the Interpersonal Relationship Scale (IRS),[16] and the Multidimensional Jealousy Scale (MJS),[17] among several others, now joined Rubin's Love Scale of 1970,[18] based on a concept of romantic love as a combination of attachment, caring, and intimacy, as ways of quantifying and describing modern love and (consequent) modern jealousy, or "romantic jealousy."

The questions posed by jealousy researchers were often ingenious. Mathes and his colleagues, for example, conducted a "real-life study" that involved calling people up and asking them if it was all right to date their partners, a study admiringly described by another psychologist as "very clever" and requiring "a lot of courage to do."[19] The scales, however, tended to be unreflectively heterosexual, posing situations like "I don't think it would bother me if my partner flirted with someone of the opposite sex" (to be rated on a scale from "absolutely false" to "absolutely true"), or "If someone of the opposite sex lit up at the sight of my partner, I would become uneasy."[20]

Is there any reason to think these findings would be different if the respondents were gay or lesbian and their partners were of the same sex?

In 1989 it could still be reported that "very little research has been done on jealousy differences between partners with homoerotic and partners with heteroerotic orientations."[21] Jealousy was often a factor in gay and lesbian, as in heterosexual, relationships. "Jealousy may be a greater problem for gay male couples than for lesbian couples, as gay men generally have more sex partners than heterosexual men and women or lesbians,"[22] one study suggested, while another reported that gay men seemed to be *less* jealous than heterosexual men, perhaps because they had many sex partners.[23] Lesbian women, researchers speculated, "may particularly fear that the beloved will seek a heterosexual relationship to escape the stigma and stresses associated with lesbian relationships."[24] It's worth pointing out that all of these studies were published in the seventies or early eighties; it takes a long time for social science statistics to make their way into print, and in the meantime numerous factors, from AIDS to outing to lesbian and bisexual chic, have altered the situation.

Swingers, group sex, and group marriage also came in for survey attention by jealousy researchers, and here, too, the findings were disparate—and fascinating. Husbands rather than wives tended to initiate swinging, but once a couple started to swing the wives enjoyed it at least as much as the husbands[25]—especially because many of the men, apparently, felt inhibited by perceived comparisons with other men.[26] Despite attempts to control jealousy by setting up ground rules for extramarital relationships —much like the ground rules set up by the bisexuals in the *Dual Attraction* study—many swingers (up to a third of those who had tried it) dropped out because of jealousy.[27] Yet they regarded themselves as less jealous than nonswingers. Partners in group marriages showed more commitment to the nonsexual aspects of relationships, like child rearing and work, but "indications are that romantic jealousy is a significant problem in communes in general and especially in group marriages,"[28] where single individuals were often kept out in favor of couples to reduce jealousy. In other words, three was seen as a more dangerous number than four.

Perhaps the most intriguing single piece of information about comparative jealousy concerned "androgyny," described in the standard terms of the 1974 Bem Sex-Role Inventory[29] as the capacity to perform either masculine or feminine sex roles. Androgynous men were found to be *more* jealous than other men, while androgynous women were *less* jealous than other women—or androgynous men.[30] Why? "It is not at all clear," report the researchers.[31]

Since the Bem scale asks individuals to rate themselves on "feminine" characteristics like "cheerful," "childlike," "compassionate," and "affectionate" and also on "masculine" characteristics like "aggressive," "ambitious," "analytical," and "acts like a leader," we may perhaps think of it as more a sign of its times than as an authoritative inventory of truths about gender, sex, or sexuality. My guess is that the relationship to jealousy has as much to do with self-perception ("self-esteem" in today's omnipresent jargon) as it has to do with "masculinity" or "femininity," except insofar as researchers and therapists tend to define "femininity" in terms of mirroring and dependency. If "feminine subjects (male or female) reported that their self-esteem was more affected by their partners' actions than that of other subjects," it makes sense that the "feminine" and "androgynous" people surveyed were both more dependent and, thus, more prone to jealousy. But the reasoning seems circular: Jealousy comes to define an aspect of "femininity," which is then supposedly dislocated from female persons and allowed to circulate freely among men and women. When it manifests itself, the jealous person is often found to be possessive, clinging, controlling: feminine. Acting like a woman. Even though male batterers are often said to be jealous of their partners' real or fantasied lives.

How does *bisexuality* figure within this economy of jealousy?

One cognitive theory of jealousy described a triangular relationship between "a person, P," "his or her beloved, B," and "a rival, R." Several studies suggested that "the most devastating event that can happen to P is sexual intercourse between R and B." Why? Because "it signals the worst: P has most certainly lost B to R." But is P automatically jealous? It depends upon his or her values. "If P values monogamy, exclusivity, and fidelity, R's presence is more threatening than if P values individual freedom or sharing. In fact, if P values individual freedom or sharing, P may evaluate R's presence as positive/benign because R's presence gives B a chance to be sexually free, P a chance to be sexually free (what is good for the goose is good for the gander, or vice versa), and P a chance to share B with R."[32]

Let me pause here just for a moment on the goose and the gander (or vice versa). (The usual phrase is "sauce for the goose . . . ," which is indeed usually taken to mean "good for," though its referent might as well be culinary as alimentary. Is the goose eating the sauce, or being eaten with it?) The P-B-R triangle seems to imply the participation of at least one goose and one gander; if P is male then B is female and, by implication but not explicitly stated, R, the rival for B's attention, is male. Of whom is P more jealous, if he or she *is* jealous—B or R, the beloved or the rival? Various surveys appear to suggest that it is B, who has betrayed P's trust.[33]

Yet another psychologist, addressing the question of "homosexual" elements in cases of "heterosexual" jealousy, notes "the jealous individual's exaggerated preoccupation with the rival. One has the impression that the rival is much more important to the jealous individual than to the partner."[34] Without benefit of alphabet, this psychologist stressed the aspect of emotional overinvestment that characterizes the peculiar erotic power of the third person in the sexual triangle. Freud called such overinvestment "sexual overvaluation," and described it as "the origin of the peculiar state of being in love."[35] We always fall in love with a fantasy, and it is sometimes as easy to fantasize about the rival, who is so desirable that he or she might take away the beloved, as it is about the more familiar and "known" beloved. "Extensive clinical experience of various types of jealousy," observed Freud's friend and biographer Ernest Jones, "has shown that, far from being a response to an objective situation, jealousy is more often an attitude dictated from within by certain motives and, strange to say, often indicates a repressed wish for the betrayal.... This is especially true of persons with a bisexual disposition, who therefore wish to play both a male and a female part in the triangular situation."[36] Triangulation is progressive and associative as well as mimetic or imitative. If we desire what the rival desires, we also sometimes desire the rival because of his or her desire.

On one occasion when I was discussing bisexuality with a group, I mentioned the painter Larry Rivers, whose autobiography, *What Did I Do?*, described his relationships with a number of male and female lovers. "Larry Rivers?" a woman in the audience remarked. "My mother knew him. She always said he was trisexual. He'd try anything."

Trisexuality in these venturesome terms is part of the scenario of the "open marriage" and the nonmonogamous lifestyle often associated in the popular imagination with bisexuals. How does jealousy function in such relationships? Isn't one of the principal risks of bisexuality the constant presence of sexual jealousy?

Susie Bright, for one, clearly thinks so. "Jealousy," she maintains in an essay called "BlindSexual," "is the great equalizer":

> Security and exclusivity—promises broken as often as they are offered—are high on every lover's list of demands. I despise jealousy. I control it only with discipline; it is like a skin I cannot shed.
>
> I search for the lovers who won't consider my bisexuality a *de facto* threat, who will not fear that to love me is to be in perpetual competition with their sex. That fear is the true reaction to bisexuality, not political epithets. Accusing a bisexual of being a traitor reveals one's desperate, and quite human, fear of rejection. I can barely accept that feature in myself.

> Let me be honest with you, and let me be shameful, as it seems so essential to my discipline: I don't want to hear that *you're* bisexual either, especially just after you've fucked me blind. Don't tell me who you "are." I'm a mere mortal, jealous and vulnerable, and I might fall for you in a big way. Show me what you can do. If you succeed in blinding me, I will follow you, potentially, into loss, betrayal, into the fire walk. It will be personal; it will not necessarily be principled. In the moment after orgasm, this is what is memorable. And for many moments after.[37]

Here it is, direct and unadorned. Bisexuality is linked in people's minds with jealousy because it brings home the fact that no one can be considered safe. Everyone is a potential erotic rival. Under heterosexuality or homosexuality half the world, at least, seems unavailable for sexual betrayal. Now, every time your partner goes out with the boys (or the girls), you have to begin to wonder what else might be going on. Paranoia here threatens to become pandemic.

This is one reason therapists and talk-show hosts (the two classes are usually but not always distinct from one another, as witness "Sonya Live" and Dr. Joyce Brothers) ask so frequently whether bisexuals, or, even more often, their partners, are jealous. It's partly projection: Monosexual fears about jealousy and erotic betrayal seem to be realized and actualized in the spectacle, or specter, of a person attracted to both men and women. "Nonmonogamous bisexuality adds fluidity," writes one bisexual woman. "Trust not as in, 'I will love you forever' or 'I will never love anyone but you'—promises that can very easily fall apart—but trust as in 'I will be honest with you.' "[38] Not so easy; nothing is more difficult than giving up control.

Yet bisexuals in fact *don't* seem particularly jealous. It may be self-selection; persons who are especially prone to jealousy might be thought of as avoiding life situations that provoke those feelings, though the unsalubrious example of obsessional stalkers, chronic spouse-beaters, and other possessive out-of-control controlling types, whether heterosexual, homosexual, or bisexual, would seem to give the lie to so easy a Darwinian answer.

One question that is almost always asked is whether individuals are more jealous of the same-sex or opposite-sex relationships of their partners. Is a woman more jealous of her male partner's lover if that lover is a woman, or another man? Again, talk shows have reveled in this question, asking pointedly, as Geraldo did, what happens "When the Other Man is a Woman."[39] In this case, all the guests were women who had "left a marriage for a lesbian lifestyle."

Martin Weinberg, Colin Williams, and Douglas Pryor's *Dual Attraction,* the study of bisexuals in San Francisco in the eighties, includes a brief chapter on "Jealousy" that undertakes to "explore how successful bisexuals were at nonmonogamous relationships," and focuses on the question of whether "primary partners" were "more jealous of an 'outside' partner of their own sex." In their surveys, the primary partners *were:* The logic, as they interpreted it, was "that a person of the same sex as themselves could meet similar needs and thus replace them."[40] While this study's findings usually strike me as unsurprising, this one did surprise me a little.

Weinberg et al. cite examples of the opposite response as well—for example, a man who said of his partner, "I don't know if the term 'jealous' is correct here, she just felt at a complete loss having to compete with a *male!*"[41] Perhaps my own feelings are based on the combination of media accounts and my personal experience. Certainly in fictionalizations of bisexual "betrayal" (or the coming out stories of married and closeted bisexuals and gays) part of the partners' distress seems to come from being blindsided. In the Ira Levin play *Deathtrap,* later made into a movie with Michael Caine and Christopher Reeve, the blindsiding includes the audience. Playwright Sidney Bruhl appears to be jealous of the writing of the younger man, Clifford Anderson, whom we, and Bruhl's wife, think he's never met. It soon turns out, however, that Anderson and Bruhl are lovers. They conspire to kill Bruhl's wife; after her death the literary rivalry develops for real, with expectable but diverting results.

How did the bisexuals studied by Weinberg and his colleagues deal with jealousy? Largely by setting ground rules that offered control—or the illusion of control. The specificity of the rules seemed less important than their existence. How many outside partners there were, whether or not the secondary partners were introduced to the primary partner, how much time could be spent with them, where the nonprimary partners met, whether the outside partner was same-sex or opposite sex, whether pickups and casual sex were permitted—all of these were negotiated. Decisions about the last of these questions, and about several others, clearly changed with the advent of AIDS in the community, as the study showed.

"The common stereotype is that 'bisexual equals nonmonogamous,'" says Karen F., editor of the 'zine *Bi-Girl World.* "In my experience, this is not necessarily true, though bisexual people as a whole seem to be more sexually open and experimental, which may or may not lead to nonmonogamy.

"Personally, I've always felt emotionally monogamous, especially in the longest-term relationship I've had—my current one, with a woman—but to tell the truth, I've never, ever (with men or with women) been able to be sexually monogamous.

"My current relationship demands this bifurcation—it is nonsexual. My partner, whom I love very much, has never been terribly interested in sex, and we reached an agreement fairly early on, and fairly loosely termed, that I could sleep with other people, as long as it didn't interfere with our relationship (that is, a boy and I didn't 'fall in love'). For the most part, over the course of our four-and-a-half-year relationship, this has worked out *all right,* but not perfectly. I've found the quick fling—the one-night stands—to have been the most acceptable to my partner. I didn't talk about them in detail, and then I never really got involved with the person. They've been with men and women, and—interestingly—the gender of the flingee hasn't made much of a difference—to me or my partner. The longer-term, more involved affairs have proved far more difficult for both of us. There have been three of these—all with men. I regret each and every one of these affairs, and now vow not to get involved with a man in such a way again.

"So—I've come to terms with what I have now—a close, intense, long-term relationship with a woman, with possible brief sexual encounters with men and women with whom I do not get emotionally involved on the side. A strange arrangement, perhaps, but one that somehow suits me. I'm so accustomed to this arrangement that it feels normal to me—in fact, I can barely imagine what it must be like having a traditional sexual relationship, say, with a man.

"On the other hand, a part of me yearns for 'normalcy'—either in the form of being married to a decent man (a long shot at this point) or in having a great, sexually fulfilling relationship with a slightly more stable woman. Both these possibilities occasionally cross my mind, but I don't really make any efforts to pursue them. I'm reasonably happy for now, I figure. . . . It looks like I—and certain other bi people I know—just don't jibe with current American culture. Oh well."[42]

Law professor Brian Ford echoes Karen F.'s assessment of bisexuality as encouraging a healthy realism and open-mindedness. He sees a larger sense in which "the idea of bisexuality" might be useful in "undoing the rut we've got ourselves into with identity problems," whether "racial identity" or "gender identity." The *concept* of bisexuality, he suggests, "unsettles ideas about priority, singularity, and truthfulness."[43]

He cautions against "endowing the bisexual with a special wisdom or special potential. It seems to me you can be totally, utterly unimaginative about your bisexuality and utterly stuck in the same way that you can be as a straight person or a gay person." But "managing a relationship with another person involves both a utopian and a pragmatic element, and there's no use pretending that there's just one or the other."

Bisexuality is "a figure for having those things at the same time, together." For example, "you're involved with a woman and you say, 'actually I'm bisexual.' It doesn't mean that you're in the mode of betraying, but it could mean that you're acknowledging the specificity and specialness of a particular relationship and also acknowledging the impossibility of fusion. There is something left out—in some ways human relationships will disappoint the utopian ideal.

"You can never know the whole person—you can never know any other whole person. If I was a man involved with a woman, even if I know she's only attracted to men, the idea that I could therefore, as one particular man, know that I knew her whole erotic life, would be ridiculously presumptuous. I don't think it's any more true in fact of the situations of bisexuals. But when you acknowledge that you have an interest in, or you see yourself as entertaining the possibility of being involved with the other gender, it makes very overt to the person you're involved with that they are not engaging the whole erotic you."

Love for the beloved is sometimes complicated by unconscious feelings of love for the rival. This point, later to be crucial to Girard and also to Sedgwick, was one of the central assertions of a short paper entitled "Some Mechanisms in Jealousy, Paranoia and Homosexuality" delivered by Sigmund Freud in 1921—the paper of which Nancy Friday cheerfully reminded her resolutely "heterosexual" analyst friend. Freud subdivides jealousy into three kinds, one "normal" and the other two pathological. His "three layers or grades of jealousy" are (1) *competitive* or normal, (2) *projected,* and (3) *delusional.* "Normal jealousy," he points out at once, is by some people "experienced bisexually. That is to say, a man will not only feel pain about the woman he loves and hatred of the man who is his rival, but also grief about the man, whom he loves unconsciously, and hatred of the woman as his rival; and this latter set of feelings will add to the intensity of his jealousy."[44]

We should recall that Freud is writing here from a clinical perspective, not—or rather not primarily—from the point of view of literature. Thus his observations both anticipate the readings of literary critics and reinforce them from the side of empirical experience.

Projected jealousy, unlike competitive jealousy, stems from guilt. It is "derived in both men and women either from their own actual unfaithfulness in real life or from impulses toward it which have succumbed to repression"—in other words, from actual or fantasied infidelity. Married people in particular are subject to this kind of temptation, and Freud, himself a married man, notes that "social convention has wisely taken this universal state of things into account," allowing for third-party flirtation (or what he calls "little excursions in the direction of unfaithfulness") within marriage. The result, via triangulation, is usually to reawaken feelings for the original partner: "[T]he desire that has been awakened by the new object find[s] satisfaction in some kind of return to faithfulness to the original object." So "a flirtation may be a safeguard against actual infidelity." But jealous people miss the point of this helpful psychic mechanism. The jealous person "projects his own impulses to faithlessness on to the partner to whom he owes faith," making himself feel better by comparison. "In the treatment of a jealous person like this, one must refrain from disputing with him the material on which he bases his suspicions; one can only aim at bringing him to regard the matter in a different light."[45]

In a curious piece of indirection, Freud here does cite a literary text in support of his observations, and, moreover, what we might regard as the classic case, Shakespeare's *Othello*. But the footnote in which he does so mentions neither Othello nor Iago, both of whom exhibit a degree of jealousy that can fairly be called paranoid. Rather, he quotes a couplet from Desdemona's "Willow" song in Act IV ("I call'd my love false love; but what said he then? . . . If I court moe women, you'll couch with moe men")[46] in which a *woman* accuses her *lover* of infidelity, rather than a husband accusing his wife. It seems as if the mechanism of reversal, projecting jealousy onto the object instead of the subject, is acting itself out in Freud's text.

It is with delusional jealousy, though, that we really approach Othello's (and indeed Iago's) case. Like projected jealousy, delusional jealousy has its roots in repressed impulses toward unfaithfulness, says Freud, "but the object in these cases is of the same sex as the subject." Regarding it, as he does other cases of paranoia, as "an attempt at defence against an unduly strong homosexual impulse," Freud therefore sets out the formula for delusional jealousy: "*I* do not love him, *she* loves him!" Here the position of the "rival" speaks, or speaks back, attempting to redirect the lover's attention.

Freud, as we have seen, regarded homosexuality as something that had an "origin" for the individual—both a psychic and, in some cases, an organic predisposition or cause. In the "jealousy" paper he quickly summarizes the factors he has already identified: attachment to the mother, narcissism, fear of castration, and seduction. To these he will now add "a new mechanism leading to a homosexual object-choice," jealousy of rivals in youth, that through repression undergoes a reversal, "so that the rivals of the earlier period became the first homosexual love-objects." As he notes, this is the opposite of paranoia, in which the person previously loved becomes the hated persecutor. But what is most interesting is that "this new mechanism of homosexual object-choice—its origin in rivalry which has been overcome and in aggressive impulses which have become repressed" has in his clinical observation "led only to homosexual attitudes which did not exclude heterosexuality and did not involve a *horror feminae.*" In other words, it is bisexual.

Love Is Blinds

Jealousy is as old a stand-by in fiction and drama as love itself, from which it is hardly separable. When Alain Robbe-Grillet, a "new novelist," chose *La Jalousie* as title for his third novel, he seemed to be following a well-worn tradition. . . . There are several recurrent "motifs." . . . The most noticeable is the device of slatted blinds, called "jalousies," installed in all the windows. . . . "Blinds" would have fitted the story just as well as a title.

—*Germaine Brée, Introduction to La Jalousie*[47]

The triangle of desire is an isosceles triangle. Thus desire always increases in intensity as the mediator approaches the desiring subject.

—René Girard, Deceit, Desire, and the Novel[48]

"Of all the objects of hatred, a woman once loved is the most hateful." So wrote Max Beerbohm in *Zuleika Dobson*. It is easy for love to turn into hate, or hate into love—far easier than it is for those extremely strong feelings to go away.

In *Othello,* perhaps the most famous of all tragedies of erotic jealousy, Iago's passionate (erotic) feelings toward Othello are at least as strong as the feelings he has toward Desdemona, and the compounding of love and hatred that he feels is completely characteristic of triangular desire. This "reversal of affect"—the disquieting ease with which "love" turns into "hate" and "hate" into "love"—is a phenomenon that many lovers will recognize from their own experience, and it is a staple of revenge tragedy.

Othello's jealousy of his friend Cassio is exacerbated on the one hand by the fact that Cassio overtly played the role of mediator in the courtship of Desdemona (he "came a-wooing" with Othello, Desdemona recalls, and Othello tells Iago that he "went between us very oft"[49]) and on the other hand by Cassio's handsome appearance and sophisticated manners, which Iago as well as Othello come to admire and envy ("He hath a daily beauty in his life / That makes me ugly").[50] The Othello-Desdemona-Cassio triangle, in which Othello acknowledges desire for Desdemona and re-presses or sublimates desire for Cassio—so that it is easy for him to imagine Desdemona choosing Cassio over himself—is thus succeeded by the triangle Iago-Othello-Desdemona, in which Iago's thwarted love for Othello manifests itself as hatred, and leads to his fictive (re)construction of the original triangle, Othello-Desdemona-Cassio.

Othello's love for Cassio turns to hatred, as, for a tragic moment, does his love for Desdemona. Iago, thwarted in his own desire, makes hatred serve the purpose of love. That his feelings toward Othello *are* a kind of erotic passion may be seen clearly as in the appalling scene, perhaps the play's most powerful, when he enacts with Othello a version of a marriage. Convinced by Iago of Desdemona's unfaithfulness, Othello vows revenge, sinking to his knees:

> OTHELLO: Now by yond marble heaven,
> In the due reverence of a sacred vow
> I here engage my words.
> IAGO: Do not rise yet. [*Iago kneels.*]
> Witness, you ever-burning lights above,
> You elements that clip us round about,
> Witness that here Iago doth give up
> The execution of his wit, hands, heart,

> To wrong'd Othello's service! Let him command,
> And to obey shall be in me remorse,
> What bloody business ever. [*They rise.*]

Seconds later Othello will say, "Now art thou my lieutenant," to which Iago replies, "I am your own for ever."[51] The heavily freighted language here ("witness," "engage" "sacred vow," the giving of "hand" and "heart," and especially the word "obey," the wife's commitment in the Anglican marriage rite until the early part of this century) and the stage picture in which Iago contrives that the two men kneel side by side, produce this onstage enactment of a bigamous male-male "marriage": "I am your own forever."

Othello is one of a triad of Shakespearean plays that take sexual jealousy as the prime incentive for potentially tragic action; the other two are *Much Ado About Nothing* and *The Winter's Tale*. In each case an erotic triangle develops, and a husband or husband-to-be is duped into believing that his lady is unfaithful. And in each case a bond between the man and his closest male friend, underestimated as a source of pleasure and anxiety, coexists with, and seems almost to produce, a suspicion of the woman's infidelity. Is the lover jealous of the woman or the man?

Erotic negotiations in these three plays are accomplished, for good and ill, through triangulation, and every interaction among the triad of lover, beloved, and rival or mediator is complicated by erotic feelings. Indeed, in their own ways these plays are exemplars of what I have called "the bisexual plot," which can function equally in fiction, drama, film, history, or personal narrative. The participants, whether or not they are "bisexual" or "bisexuals," interact with one another in a triangular relation that is animated by erotic tension, competition, repositioning, and mimetic or rivalrous desire on both same-sex and opposite-sex sides.

The Bisexual Plot

In tragic life, God wot,
No villain need be! Passions spin the plot.

—*George Meredith*, Modern Love[1]

I earlier called *The Children's Hour* a "bisexual plot" although it is never clear what the erotic relations among Karen, Martha, and Joe really are, because what makes it work *as* a plot is the bisexual tension among the major characters. Freud's essay on jealousy allows for a very similar reading of *Othello,* where again, for my purposes, it matters less whether Iago (or Othello, for that matter) is or is not "homosexual" than that the relationships among Iago, Othello, Desdemona, and Cassio are all, in brilliant and complicated ways, sexualized.

We have had occasion, as we considered the ways in which bisexuality is discussed, represented, and misrepresented in popular conceptions, to notice a number of distinguishing characteristics of the bisexual plot: The "phase," which can be "outgrown" on the way to safely heterosexual (or sometimes gay or lesbian) "maturity"; the mode of "indecisiveness" or "confusion"; the rivalry between a man and a woman, both erotically interested in, and interesting to, a third party; a love relationship with a couple, in which jealousy and rivalry are transmuted into some version of "having it all," or else directed at winning away one member of the couple as one's own lover. Very often, as we have already seen and as we will see again when we come to consider "threesomes," the erotic tension is greatest when it is not acted upon. (This is a mistake filmmakers often make; in trying to actualize sexual feelings and put them on the screen, they sometimes dissipate rather than heighten the eroticism produced by triangulation. We will be able to observe a couple of instances of this in the discussion below.)

The bisexual plot, as I conceive it, is a mode of erotic triangulation in which one person is torn between life with a man and life with a woman. I want to look now at two classic instances of this kind of plot and to note, as we look at them, how once again bisexuality is looked through rather than looked at, reinterpreted, and appropriated to tell another kind of story—pulled, that is to say, to one side or the other of the (perceived) erotic binary, and read as either "really" straight or "really" lesbian or gay. Bisexuality, once again, is everywhere and nowhere, a dangerously fluid mode of desiring that must, by both characters within the plot and critics regarding it, somehow be made to disappear.

"The Famous Phase"

It was a "phase," this taste for evening-calls from collegians and newspaper-men, and would consequently pass away with the growth of her mind.

—Henry James, The Bostonians[2]

Henry James's novel *The Bostonians,* published in 1886, has long been read as a book about the concept of "romantic friendship" between women and issues of lesbian desire. The story of Olive Chancellor, Verena Tarrant, and Basil Ransom, a classic triangle, begins with Olive "taking up" Verena as her companion and protégée, and ends with Basil taking her away. Olive and Verena's relationship is a prime example of the so-called Boston marriage, an arrangement, common in late-nineteenth-century New England, that united two otherwise unmarried women in a mono-gamous relationship based on shared cultural, social, and political interests.

"Whether these unions sometimes or often included sex we will never know," wrote Lillian Faderman, "but we do know that these women spent their lives primarily with other women, they gave to other women the bulk of their energy and attention, and they formed powerful emotional ties with other women."[3] Faderman deftly summarizes the tendency of mid-twentieth-century critics, many of them men, to read *The Bostonians* as a triumph of nature over the unnatural, of Basil's (and Verena's) hetero-sexuality against Olive's lesbianism, which is itself characterized as "per-verse sexuality"[4] and as a "mental malady."[5] Basil Ransom rescues Verena from an "unnatural union,"[6] allowing her to seek fulfillment instead in a "natural" and "normal" heterosexual marriage.

A more recent trend among critics, equally well summarized by Terry Castle, has been to deny that lesbianism is really at the center of the novel at all. "The theme is about something else,"[7] asserted Walter F. Wright flatly in 1962. Castle cites Jean Strouse's biography of Alice James, the novelist's sister (who herself was part of a "Boston marriage"), which warns that it would be "a great mistake" to "read lesbianism into *The Bostonians,*"[8] and clinches her case by quoting critic Tony Tanner, who insisted in his analysis of the novel that "to consider it as a study of lesbianism" would be both "irrelevant and limiting."[9] Yet other critics, she notes, do credit Olive's existence as a lesbian, but only to denounce her as a "horrid,"[10] "twisted,"[11] and "unnatural"[12] figure who "hates men"[13] and wants to ruin Verena's life.

In her own fine treatment of the novel Castle puts a reverse spin on these interpretations, insisting on the reality of Olive's lesbianism and its "heroic"[14] character. She calls *The Bostonians* "the first and perhaps the most haunting 'lesbian tragedy' in modern English and American literature," and regards "Olive Chancellor (potentially) as the first lesbian tragic heroine."[15]

What many of these modern interpretations share is a focus on Olive, the complex protagonist. "James has already shown his sympathy for her,"[16] Castle points out, even before her rivalry and loss make her a "tragic" figure. But if *The Bostonians* can be classified, as Castle, following Jeanette Foster, seeks to do, as a "lesbian novel,"[17] and if "James's female critics have tended on the whole to treat the lesbian theme in *The Bostonians* with more equanimity than their male counterparts have, even those most sympathetic to Olive,"[18] it may be worth noting that though Olive is a "lesbian," Verena, by the same kind of reading, may be deemed a "bisexual." Why not call *The Bostonians,* then, a "bisexual novel"? Or, with less of a sense of essentialist labeling, a novel with a bisexual plot? If part of Castle's argument is to point out that Olive becomes, in critical terms, a "haunting" or "apparitional lesbian," one whose sexuality is often overlooked or looked through, it is also the case that James's criticism has allowed her to usurp discussions of the novel more or less for herself. "Horrid" or "heroic," Olive Chancellor runs away with the novel.[19] In the 1984 film, starring Vanessa Redgrave, Christopher Reeve, and Madeleine Potter, Redgrave does the same.

Olive's interest in a close relationship with a young woman is established at the outset.

> She had an immense desire to know intimately some *very* poor girl. This might seem one of the most accessible of pleasures; but in point of fact, she had not found it so. There were two or three pale shop-maidens whose acquaintance she had sought, but they had seemed afraid of her, and the attempt had come to nothing. She took them more tragically than they took themselves; they couldn't make out what she wanted them to do, and they always ended up by being odiously mixed up with Charlie. Charlie was a young man in a white overcoat and a paper collar; it was for him, in the last analysis, that they cared much the most. They cared more for Charlie than about the ballot.[20]

If we are on the lookout for ghosts, "Charlie" is a good candidate. He is only a rhetorical figure of speech, a preparatory sketch for one point of the triangle, but while Verena is no pale shop-girl, and Basil is no Charlie, this scenario will repeat itself in the most important relationship of Olive Chancellor's life.

She found in Verena, says James, "what she had been looking for so long—a friend of her own sex with whom she might have a union of soul. It took a double consent to make a friendship, but it was not possible that this intensely sympathetic girl would refuse."[21] "'Will you be my friend, my friend of friends, beyond every one, everything, forever and forever?'" she asks.[22] Verena, we are told with wonderful dryness, "had also dreamed of a friendship, though it was not what she had dreamed of most."[23] Has she, like the shop-girls, also dreamt of a "Charlie"?

In any case, a "Charlie" immediately presents himself upon the scene. No sooner has Olive invited Verena to live with her, and (mis)quoted a phrase from Goethe which she translates as "Thou shalt renounce, refrain, abstain!" than a visitor arrives, interrupting the moment.

" 'Oh, well, I guess I can abstain!' Verena answered with a laugh. And she got up rather quickly, as if by taking leave she might give a proof of what she meant. Olive put out her hands to hold her, and at this moment one of the *portières* of the room was pushed aside, while a gentleman was ushered in by Miss Chancellor's little parlour-maid."[24]

It is Basil Ransom. Verena tries to leave—it is her belief that "in the highest social walks it was the custom of a prior guest to depart when another friend arrived"[25]—but of course neither Olive nor Basil wants her to go. "The three stood there together in the middle of the long, characteristic room, and for the first time in her life, Olive Chancellor chose not to introduce two persons who met under her roof." *"Must* she go, Miss Olive," asks Ransom, and to Verena, "Do you flee before the individual male?"[26]

How does three turn into two, or a triangle into a line? This is the agonized geometry of James's novel, not the less agonizing for its domestic setting and the gentle or not-so-gentle irony directed at each of the three major characters.[27] The interruptive nature of the third is immediately established by Ransom. "There is one statement I will venture to advance," he says equably. "I am quite as fond of you as you are of each other!" " 'Much he knows about that!' said Verena, with a side-long smile at Olive Chancellor."[28]

But Verena cannot entirely hide her interest in young men. As Olive exacts a doomed promise from her never to marry she follows it with a description of the "phase" she sees her young friend as going through. The "phase" is not homo- but heterosexuality, and Olive's description of it *as* a phase is, as James frankly notes, an "optimistic contention" on her part. "I am not in the least afraid of your marrying a repulsive man," she declares. "Your danger would come from an attractive one."

"I'm glad to hear you admit that some *are* attractive!" Verena exclaimed, with the light laugh which her reverence for Miss Chancellor had not yet quenched. "It sometimes seems as if there weren't any you could like!"

"I can imagine a man I should like very much," Olive replied, after a moment. "But I don't like those I see. They seem to me poor creatures." . . . The end of the colloquy was that Verena, having assented, with her usual docility, to her companion's optimistic contention that it was a "phase," this taste for evening-calls from collegians and newspaper-men, and would consequently pass away with the growth of her mind, remarked that the injustice of men might be an accident or might be a part of their nature, but at any rate she should have to change a good deal before she should want to marry.[29]

Thus when a young Harvard student, Henry Burrage, begins to court her, "Verena saw him with Olive's full concurrence." "It had now been quite agreed between them that no artificial limits should be set to the famous phase."[30] The courtship finally comes to nothing (Burrage is a "Charlie" both in Olive's and in the dated British slang sense of the term),[31] but the real danger to Olive lies ahead, after Basil Ransom comes to Marmion and stays a month.

"I don't want to marry him," Verena tells Olive, but she confesses, "I like him better than any gentleman I have seen." "Olive had had her suspicions, her terrors, before; but she perceived now how idle and foolish they had been, and that this was a different affair from any of the 'phases' of which she had anxiously watched the development."[32]

It is one of the minor but delicious ironies of James's novel that Verena is in fact more daring in her ideas about marriage than Olive. Her father, the oleaginous Mr. Tarrant, "had been for a while a member of the celebrated Cayuga community, where there were no wives, or no husbands, or something of that sort."[33] "Cayuga" is a fictional name for the Oneida community, which flourished from 1848 to 1879, a religious group in central New York State whose members believed in "complex marriage" —a practice their critics renamed "free love." Verena, whose experiences are called "queer" three times by Olive in a single sentence ("this was queerer than anything she had dreamed of, and the queerest part was that the girl herself didn't appear to think it queer"),[34] grew up among "people who disapproved of the marriage-tie," and "talked of the marriage-tie as she would have talked of the latest novel—as if she had heard it as frequently discussed." This breeziness gives the relatively staid Olive vertigo, and she closes her eyes "in the manner of a person waiting till giddiness had passed."

[T]hough Olive had no views about the marriage-tie except that she should hate it for herself—that particular reform she did not propose to consider—she didn't like the "atmosphere" of circles in which such institutions were called into question. She had no wish now to enter into an examination of that particular one; nevertheless, to make sure, she would just ask Verena whether she disapproved of it.

"Well, I must say," said Miss Tarrant, "I prefer free unions."

Olive held her breath an instant; such an idea was so disagreeable to her. Then, for all answer, she murmured, irresolutely, "I wish you would let me help you!"[35]

As James's droll comparison of "the marriage-tie" to the latest novel makes clear, Verena is merely parroting the convictions of her parents' friends when she endorses "free unions." She is not imminently contemplating nonmonogamy. Nonetheless, Olive is placed in the ironic position of the advocate of exclusive marriage, as, indeed, her subsequent proposal to Verena will emphasize. When she entreats her pressingly, "Promise me not to marry!"[36] her entreaty is, in effect, nothing less than a proposal of marriage. In fact, in cooler, more collected moments Olive herself can see that: "I see it was my jealousy that spoke—my restless, hungry jealousy. . . . I don't want your signature; I only want your confidence—only what springs from that. I hope with all my soul that you won't marry; but if you don't it must not be because you have promised me."[37]

This is, of course, a more devious double-bind even than the original proposal, though Olive does not necessarily intend it as such. She substitutes what might be called a "free union" for her previous offer of a kind of marriage; not the "signature" or the vow but Verena's free choice will seal their relationship. " 'Don't promise, don't promise!' she went on. 'I would far rather you didn't.' "[38] James notes this with his usual astringency: "Her manner of repairing her inconsistency was altogether feminine; she wished to extract a certainty at the same time that she wished to deprecate a pledge."[39] It is at this point that Olive and Verena have their first conversation about the "phase" of heterosexual courtship.

Olive wants exclusivity. Her socialite sister Mrs. Luna remarks to Basil, about Verena's courtship by Henry Burrage, "Olive stands between them —she wants to keep her in the single sisterhood; to keep her, above all, for herself."[40] Henry's mother concurs. "I dare say," she says to Olive, "you don't like the idea of her marrying at all; it would break up a friendship which is so full of interest (Olive wondered for a moment whether she had been going to say 'so full of profit') for you."[41] And again: " 'You may ask me,' added Mrs. Burrage, smiling, 'how you can take a favourable view of a young man who wants to marry the very person in the world you want most to keep unmarried!' This description of Verena was of course perfectly correct, but it was not agreeable to Olive to have the fact in question so clearly perceived."[42]

The battle between, or among, Olive, Verena, and Basil Ransom is then in one sense a battle of the couple against the triangle. But which is the couple and which the third? Olive's searing jealousy at learning that Verena has been secretly corresponding with Basil leads the artless Verena to respond in familiar terms: "[I]t is strange of you to doubt me, to suppose I am not more *wedded* to all our old dreams than ever."[43] The magic word has its effect; at the end of the scene (and the end of the chapter) occurs one of the most quietly powerful erotic moments of the novel:

Olive "looked at Verena fixedly, felt that she was stirred to her depths, that she was exquisitely passionate and sincere, that she was a quivering, spotless, consecrated maiden, that she really had renounced, that they were both safe, and that her own injustice and indelicacy has been great. She came to her slowly, took her in her arms and held her long—giving her a silent kiss."[44]

Whew! Had James elected to end his chapter here, the effect would have been remarkable enough. But he adds a disconcerting coda in the form of a cold little final sentence: "From which Verena knew that she believed her." Immediately the reader's attention and emphasis shift from Olive to Verena, leaving Olive's hyperbole, like that of so many other undefended, ardent lovers, male and female, teetering on the edge of bathos. And the early scene at Olive's house in which Basil interrupts a tête-à-tête between women will be repeated later in the novel when he arrives importunately at the cottage at Marmion, on Cape Cod. Again an interruptive third makes the shape of the triangle all too clear. "She stared at him in sudden horror; for the moment her self-possession completely deserted her. . . . nothing . . . could mitigate the odious fact of his being there. He could only let her take it in, let her divine that, this time, he was not to be got rid of."[45] Even the "unsophisticated" Miss Birdseye sees the point when Basil tells her he is determined to come down.

"I am afraid I shall spoil it, Miss Birdseye."

"Oh, well, a gentleman," murmured the ancient woman.

"Yes, what can you expect of a gentleman? I certainly shall spoil it if I can."[46]

In what sense is it reasonable to call *The Bostonians* a "bisexual novel," or a novel with a "bisexual plot"? Verena does respond to the attentions of both men and women. Her relationship with Olive might be compared, with appropriate historical caveats, to the tutorial relationship of the ancient Greeks, the pedagogical and erotic relationships between an older (male) lover an a younger (male) beloved.[47] We have already noted that

Olive's fantasy structure involves a critical *in*equality between the partners ("She had an immense desire to know intimately some *very* poor girl"), in this case a difference of class or wealth, as well as a difference in age. Verena's youth and naïveté, as well as her unfortunate parentage, give Olive an opportunity for tutelary dominance: "[S]he had lain awake all night thinking of it, and the substance of her thought was that if she could only rescue the girl from the danger of vulgar exploitation, could only constitute herself her protectress and devotee, the two, between them, might achieve the great result."[48]

Bear in mind that it was just about the time when James's novel was written (it was first published in serial form in 1885–86 in the *Century Magazine*) that the modern categories of "homosexuality" and "heterosexuality" were being invented to describe types of persons. "Prior to this time," as sociologist Paula Rust sums up the issue raised by recent gender scholarship, "a person's sexual self was not defined in terms of the sex of her or his partner. Sexuality was structured and described primarily in terms of class, age, and gender role rather than genital sex."[49] Any blanket assertion like this can of course be challenged, and exceptions cited. But in looking at sex and courtship in *The Bostonians* it is surely worth noting the importance of "class, age, and gender role" in the "union" of Olive and Verena. Olive literally buys, or rather rents, Verena from her parents on an annual basis. "She crossed over to her desk and wrote Mr. Tarrant a cheque for a very considerable amount. 'Leave us alone—entirely alone —for a year, and then I will write you another.' "[50] And where Olive's commitment to the relationship is manifestly passionate and indeed unmistakably erotic (however she fails to see that fact herself), Verena's is much more based on comfort, circumstance, opportunity, and a desire to learn. Does this make it an unequal partnership, or an unnatural one? Ask yourself how many marriages—heterosexual marriages—are contracted on this basis even today.

"Are they very much united, the two ladies?" Basil asks the guileless Miss Birdseye. "She tells her everything. *Their union* is so close," comes the reply.[51]

"Union" is the word that repeatedly describes the relationship. Verena's "share in *the union* of the two young women was no longer passive, purely appreciative; it was passionate, too, and it put forth a beautiful energy."[52] "Verena was not to be trusted for an hour. She had sworn to her the night before, with a face like a lacerated angel, that her choice was made, that *their union* and their work were more to her than any other life could ever be."[53]

When Olive learns from Verena that Basil wants to marry her she tries to ignore "her personal loss . . . *their blighted union*," in favor of the public or political question, Verena's "defection from their standard." But her outburst is only readable in terms of sexual jealousy:

> Olive flung herself over on the couch, burying her face in the cushions, which she tumbled in her despair, and moaning out that he didn't love Verena, he never had loved her, it was only his hatred of their cause that made him pretend it; he wanted to do that an injury, to do it the worst he could think of. He didn't love her, he hated her, he only wanted to smother her, to crush her, to kill her— as she would infallibly see that he would if she listened to him. It was because he knew that her voice had magic in it, and from the moment he caught its first note he had determined to destroy it. It was not tenderness that moved him—it was devilish malignity.[54]

This passionate passage, so redolent of erotic pain, draws upon that locus classicus of sexual jealousy, Shakespeare's *Othello,* for some of its evocative power. Basil's "devilish malignity" owes something to the critic Samuel Taylor Coleridge, who famously remarked that Iago was the quintessence of evil, with no motive, only "motiveless malignity" for his deeds. Othello observes at the last of his tormentor, "If that thou be'st a devil, I cannot kill thee."[55] The handkerchief Othello gave to Desdemona, the loss of which becomes the spurious proof of her infidelity, is described as having "magic" in its web.[56] And the tragic end of Shakespeare's play acts out the scenario that Olive, in her anguish, imagines: "[H]e didn't love her, he hated her, he only wanted to smother her . . . to kill her." If these echoes seem faint, they are also insistent. Olive's distraction, which lasts for a period of "lamentable weeks,"[57] becomes "tragic," to recur to Terry Castle's epithet (which is also F. O. Matthiessen's and indeed Henry James's),[58] through its recapitulation of an old and familiar scenario.

Verena's choice, at the end of the novel, does not seem to her a choice but rather an inevitability, though she is willing to see it as "treachery" from Olive's point of view. "It was simply that truth had changed sides. . . . She loved, she was in love; she felt it in every throb of her being. It was always passion, in fact; but now the object was other. Formerly she had been convinced that the fire of her spirit was a kind of double flame, one half of which was responsive friendship for a most extraordinary person, and the other pity for the sufferings of women in general. Verena gazed aghast at the colourless dust into which, in three short months . . . such a conviction could crumble."[59]

Let us then ask again: What sense does it make to call Verena "bisexual" here? Her commitment to Olive and their "union" has never had quite this visceral tang, this "throb" of feeling. And the term "bisexual" is manifestly anachronistic to the period. If homosexuals and lesbians were just then in the process of being "invented" as types of sexual persons, bisexuals were merely a glimmer in the eye of Havelock Ellis. But people love in many ways, and the discovery of a new range of feelings does not discredit earlier ones. Was Verena's relationship with Olive and the woman's movement merely a "phase"?

One of the most consistent criticisms of bisexuals voiced today and over the last two decades has been that they are "sexual opportunists, fickle lovers, traitors, political cowards, or fence-sitters."[60] When Verena comes to the realization that her feelings for Basil Ransom constitute a kind of "treachery" to Olive, and when her commitment to marry Ransom leads her to abandon a public career as a feminist orator, she is vulnerable to many of these same critiques. She is indeed, it might be thought, choosing "heterosexual privilege" and the role of a domestic helpmate over what is sometimes called a "woman-identified" life. "It was always passion, in fact; but now the object was other." Olive Chancellor, having structured her sexuality as a mode of political activism, tries, as we have seen, to separate the personal from the political. But the two are not separable.

Much energy has been expended in trying to decide whether *The Bostonians* is a novel primarily about politics (feminism; "power";[61] Southern "chivalry") or primarily about sexuality ("incipient Lesbianism" and "unnatural friendship";[62] "a normal relationship in a society so sick";[63] a "phallic melodrama";[64] a "lesbian novel"). It is not just that the two terms are metaphors for one another; they are the same. It is partly for this reason that the novel's bisexual plot has the force that it has.

Those critics who read the novel as a defense of "the heterosexual basis of human existence" as over against Olive's "homosexuality" (defined uncompromisingly as "the biological evidence of a rigid self-centeredness that has blinded itself to the heterogeneous character of reality")[65] will rejoice, with Irving Howe, to find that "Ransom wins."[66] But Leon Edel is closer to the truth when he points out that Olive and Basil are "mirror-images": "[T]hose who have read the novel as 'lesbian' tend to see Ransom in a better light than James represents him—for they read him in the belief that he is rescuing Verena from Olive's depravity. The truth is that James has little respect for either."[67] Note that Edel assumes, from the vantage point of 1962, that "those who have read the novel as 'lesbian'" are automatically repelled by Olive's passion. More than thirty years later the pendulum has swung, and the critics most interested in *The Bostonians* (and most interesting to read on it) are lesbian critics, or critics willing to credit the truth and dignity—even "heroism"—of lesbian desire. "At no point," lesbian feminist Judith Fetterley notes, "does James even faintly suggest that he is writing a novel about the abnormal, the unnatural, the perverse, or that the drama of the story resides in pitting the forces of health and sanity against those of depravity."[68]

As I have tried to suggest, I think character-based advocacy in the criticism of fiction, whether it decides that "Ransom wins" or that Olive is a heroine, tends at best to locate in the novel a point of view already fixed in the interpreter's mind. Howe would presumably admire the book less if Ransom lost, if what he describes as a "struggle between ideologies that are not equally in opposition to the natural and the human" had wound up with Olive and Verena living together in contented union. Judith Fetterley reads the novel as in part a manifestation of mimetic desire (Basil desires Verena because Olive wants her)[69] and also as James's version of the "eternal triangle": "[A] man and a woman struggle for the love and the possession of another woman, and the man wins, and the question is why."[70] Her answer, in a complex, nuanced discussion, is that "it is he alone who is capable of arousing her sexually." And she deplores this fact, in terms consistent with her own political stance: "If women respond to male sexuality only when it is expressed in terms of power, aggression, and sadism, then the force of their sexuality is set squarely against their emancipation. . . . Women are doomed to be masochists whose only mode of experiencing pleasure is in the midst of pain."[71]

What do we learn about bisexuality if we see this as a bisexual plot? We learn that issues of power are central in sexuality, but complexly so. For it is possible to be genuinely sexually aroused by that which disempowers you.

Likewise, it is possible, as we have already seen in our examination of teacher-student relations, to have an erotic relationship with an institution. Both Olive and Basil try to get Verena to do just that, but his institution (call it patriarchy, call it marriage, call it romantic love, call it heterosexuality) is more familiar.

The extent to which this novel deserves to be called "bisexual" is the extent to which bisexuality constitutes one important narrative in the double bind of female sexuality. Bisexuality in *The Bostonians* is really an effect—an effect of the difficulty of satisfying women's desire with regard to power and pleasure. Verena's sexuality cannot be divorced from her circumstances. The two sexualities that are to be found in her are both "real" in that they represent two competing erotic spheres, two competing narratives for her future. Olive longs to label one of them a "phase," but the strategy fails of its object. Verena is won over by her own desire to be won. Not Basil's maleness but his disregard for her resistance is what inspires her passion.

Olive's name may link her with Shakespeare's Olivia in *Twelfth Night,* a noblewoman and heiress who falls in love, unwittingly, with a woman in disguise and then with her twin brother. "You are betroth'd both to a maid and man," he explains to her, "But Nature to her bias drew in that,"[72] heterosexualizing her choice in the nick of time. Olive is also, as several feminist critics have noted, a forerunner of Dorothy Strachey Bussy's title character in *Olivia,* a novel of a schoolgirl's passion for her teacher.[73] But Basil's full name means "king's ransom," and it is left to the reader to decide whether what he accomplishes represents a mere exchange of commodities, or a fancied redemption from sin. In James's famous and equivocal final sentence in the novel the word "union," previously used to describe the relationship between Verena and Olive—and, it is interesting to note, again suggested in the 1990s as a term for same-sex relationships that the law will not dignify as "marriage"—is used to describe her impending marriage to Basil as she flees the lecture hall in tears. "It is to be feared that with the union, so far from brilliant, into which she was about to enter, these were not the last she was destined to shed."[74]

Out-Foxed

I am sure the grapes are sour.

—Aesop, The Fox and the Grapes

One of the most frequently cited of all fictional narratives about bisexuality, and still one of the most powerful, is D. H. Lawrence's novella *The Fox,* published in 1923.

The Fox tells the story of two young women, March and Banford, who have set up housekeeping together on a farm during the period of World War I. "The two girls were usually known by their surnames," the opening sentence declares, and it is several pages before we learn that March's other name is Nellie, several more before Banford is referred to as Jill.

March, like many women in wartime Britain, works the land and does most of the outdoor work, wearing men's breeches, coat, and cap. She had learned carpentry and joinery in evening classes so that she could "be the man about the place," and Lawrence tells us that "she looked almost like a graceful, loose-balanced young man," but "her face was not a man's face, ever." Banford, "a small, thin, delicate thing with spectacles" was "the principal investor, for March had little or no money." Her father had set her up on the farm "because it did not look as if she would marry."[75]

The two women, "neither of them young: that is, they were near thirty,"[76] struggle against hardship. They keep fowls and ducks, but they sell both of the heifers they began with, one because it runs away, and the other because it is expecting a calf, and without a man about the place they "panic." (Lawrence never has a particularly light hand with symbolism, and the heifers can be fairly enough equated with their luckless owners.) The chickens and ducks are prey to the fox of the title, with whom March develops a mystical bond: "[H]e knew her. She was spell-bound—she knew he knew her. So he looked into her eyes, and her soul failed her. He knew her, he was not daunted."[77] Again, the appeal of the predator.

After three years of living together March and Banford "were apt to become a little irritable with one another, tired of one another"[78] so they welcome the young soldier, Henry Grenfel, who drops in on them and stays. Banford initially thinks of him as a younger brother, but in the course of the narrative he becomes clearly identified with the fox. "To March he was the fox. Whether it was the thrusting forward of his head, or the glisten of fine whitish hairs on the ruddy cheek-bones, or the bright, keen eyes, that can never be said: but the boy was to her the fox, and she could not see him otherwise." "He was identified with the fox—and he was here in full presence. She need not go after him any more."[79]

Henry immediately develops an interest in March, and determines to marry her. She is at first startled by his proposal but also attracted, acquiescent; Banford, predictably, is furious. The household becomes tense: "[T]hey sat each one at the sharp corner of a triangle, in obstinate remoteness."[80]

March, for her part, feels torn between her affection for Banford and the sheer animal energies of the boy. There are agonized bedtime scenes when Banford wants her to come to their room and Henry urges her to stay with him by the fire. At night he sometimes eavesdrops outside their door. The sensuality of Lawrence's tale is not less powerful for being sometimes obliquely phrased; Henry is very much the male animal ("the youth, setting before the fire in his uniform, sent a faint but distinct odour into the room, indefinable, but something like a wild creature"),[81] elemental, hating to be balked, hating Banford.

"He was in the devil of a temper, feeling he had been insulted.

"Banford's eyes were red, she had evidently been crying. But her manner was more remote and supercilious than ever. . . ."

"March seemed to flourish in this atmosphere. She seemed to sit between the two antagonists with a little wicked smile on her face, enjoying herself. There was even a sort of complacency in the way she laboriously crocheted, this evening."[82]

In the midst of this turmoil Henry kills the fox. March touches his dead body with a wonder that is clearly sexual. ("White and soft as snow his belly: white and soft as snow. She passed her hand softly down it. And his wonderful black-glinted brush was full and frictional, wonderful. She passed her hand down this also, and quivered.")[83] In many ways this is the most explicit erotic encounter in the story.

The erotic temperature goes up further when March appears one night in a dress, startling Henry into thinking of her body and her vulnerability. "She was soft and accessible in her dress. The thought went home in him like an everlasting responsibility." (Butch in the streets, femme in the sheets?) He had been excited by her in her boy's clothes, but this is a different sensation. "Strangely, suddenly, he felt a man, no longer a youth. . . . He felt a man, quiet, with a little of the heaviness of male destiny upon him."[84] He leads her outside, leaving Banford weeping in the house, and persuades her to agree to the marriage, though she feels that she "must go back to Jill."[85]

"Do you wish you were with Miss Banford? Do you wish you'd gone to bed with her?" he asked, as a challenge.

She waited a long time before she answered: "No," she said at last. "I don't wish that."

"And do you think you would spend all your life with her—when your hair goes white, and you are old?" he said.

"No," she said without much hesitation. "I don't see Jill and me two old women together."[86]

Henry's hatred of Banford is quite palpable, and his rage at her role as a blocking agent is uncontained: "You're a nasty little thing," he thinks, as he watches her, "frail thing she was, but with that devilish little certainty which he so detested in her." "I hope you'll be paid back for all the harm you've done me for nothing."[87]

The resolution of the plot comes quickly. Henry, having left the farm to rejoin his regiment, receives a letter from March breaking off the engagement. He isn't real to her when he isn't around. "I love Jill and she makes me feel safe and sane," she writes. Impetuously he gets a leave from his captain and bicycles to the farm, where he finds the engine of fate in the form of a tree about to be felled. Banford's parents have come for a visit, and in their plain sight he cuts down the tree, angling it so that its branch strikes Banford, killing her. "He was glad, he had won."[88]

But though March does marry him, "she could not quite accept the submergence which his new love put upon her," and the passivity he requires of her is impossible for her to achieve. "Something was missing." "He wanted to make her submit, yield, blindly pass away out of all her strenuous consciousness. He wanted to take away her consciousness, and make her just his woman." "She wanted some goal, some finality—and there was none. Always this ghastly reaching, striving for something that might be just beyond. Even to make Jill happy. She was glad Jill was dead."[89]

"Sometimes he thought bitterly that he ought to have left her. He ought never to have killed Banford. He should have left Banford and March to kill one another.

"But that was only impatience and he knew it. He was waiting, waiting to go west."[90]

The novel ends with the two of them staring at the horizon from a cliff in West Cornwall, waiting for the time when they can leave for Canada, where he has lived and has a job waiting. " 'If only we could go soon!' he said, with pain in his voice."[91]

The echo of Milton's *Paradise Lost* in this last tableau is hardly accidental —as I've noted, Lawrence's symbolism is often laid on with a trowel. But the emotional honesty of his portrait is underscored by this description of the early days of the marriage. It would have been easy to end the story at Henry's moment of triumph, with a clear-cut "victory": "He had won." Compare this to Irving Howe's verdict on *The Bostonians*: "Ransom wins."

In fact, Henry Grenfel seems in his callow, roughhewn way quite similar to the much smoother-mannered Basil Ransom in James's novel. Consider a passage like this, describing Verena Tarrant's response to Ransom:

> She said no more, but all her face entreated him to let her off, to spare her; and as this look deepened, a quick sense of elation and success began to throb in his heart, for it told him exactly what he wanted to know. It told him that she was afraid of him, that she had ceased to trust herself, that the way he had read her nature was the right way (she was tremendously open to attack, she was meant for love, she was meant for him), and that his arriving at the point at which he wished to arrive was only a question of time.[92]

"Ransom wins." "He had won." Or, as Vito Russo remarks about the film version of *The Fox,* "Lesbianism loses."

"A tree falls between Jill's legs, killing her, and Ellen goes off into the sunset" with the importunate youth, who has, in the film version, mysteriously been renamed Paul. Russo is droll: "One lesbian is killed, the other cured." But American critics were confused at the dénouement. Martin Gottfried, writing in *Women's Wear Daily,* expressed disbelief that Paul would be attracted to Ellen ("the bulldyke") over Jill ("the female lesbian"). "How," he asked, "could the feminine one be the real lesbian?"[93] We may think this a particularly pertinent debate to wage within the pages of a journal called *Women's Wear Daily.* But it is worth noting that Russo insists that Ellen is a lesbian, albeit one who gets "cured" by film's end. The word "bisexual" does not appear in his discussion.

The 1968 Mark Rydell film, starring Anne Heywood as Ellen, Keir Dullea as Paul, and (perhaps inevitably) Sandy Dennis as the dithery, bespectacled Jill, made explicit some of the moments of sexual tension in the novel: the two women are seen having sex in their bedroom, Ellen and Paul have a tryst in an abandoned cabin, and "we see Ellen masturbating in front of a mirror, enjoying heterosexual fantasies."[94] This was, after all, 1968, supposedly the height of the Sexual Revolution. Dr. Fred Klein, who features *The Fox* in his book *The Bisexual Option* as an exemplar of "the bisexual in the arts," is unenthusiastic about the portrait of March (whom he always calls "Ellen," a name that appears in the film but not in Lawrence's text): "[T]he negative aspect of bisexuality is strongly emphasized," he laments, "when her indecisiveness concerning her bisexuality is followed by death. Bisexuality is seen as an ambiguous state that cannot survive. A choice has to be made—give up either the male or the female sexual object and its corollary, relinquish the inner woman or man. . . . the female object was killed and thereby her inner masculinity."[95]

This is a prime example of what might be called "image-conscious" criticism, the same genre that objects to negative stereotyping of African Americans, Native Americans, Jews, or gays in literature or film. Yet what is more disturbing about Dr. Klein's analysis is that it seems so much at variance with the novel, however it may fit the film. "In the novella," he writes, "Ellen is ambivalent in her desires, and though seen as strong in a number of aspects—especially in her relationship with Jill—she ends up as a passive, unhappy, and self-acknowledged failure. But the negative aspect of bisexuality is strongly emphasized. . . ." and so on.

In Lawrence's novella, however, Nellie March is by any measure the most sympathetic character presented. Her "indecisiveness" is naturalized; she is not choosing between abstract sexualities but between persons, one apparently "safe" and the other apparently dangerous. But which, in fact, is which? And which mode—safety or danger—does she prefer? When she calmly observes that she doesn't imagine growing old with Jill Banford, it is not "lesbianism" but Jill whom she contemplates.

Despite the insistence of its symbolic motifs (or perhaps, to be fair, because of them), Lawrence's version of *The Fox* is both powerful and moving. Its glimpse of the two women's domestic life together is convincing, and the sly, self-confident, and presuming boy is as disturbing to the reader as he is to March—or, for that matter, to Banford. It is, in fact, a very sexy story, however unfairly we may think lesbianism is treated. By my reading, at least, if anybody "wins," it's Nellie, not because she gets the prize of heterosexuality (marriage, het sex, or "heterosexual privilege") but because she's in many ways the strongest character of the three.

"They sat each one at the sharp corner of a triangle, in obstinate remoteness." In *The Fox,* the erotic triangle is clearly in view. In this case it is the triangle that *produces* eroticism to begin with. Relations between March and Banford have become routinized and dull, while the boy Grenfel hones his passions on Banford's growing fear and resentment, listening at the women's bedroom door as the spying child does in Lillian Hellman's *Children's Hour,* constituting himself the third who interrupts and disrupts. Basil Ransom's complacent sentiment, "What can you expect of a gentleman? I certainly shall spoil it if I can," is entirely apt for Henry, whose questionable table manners and status as a gentleman are bitterly attacked by Banford.

Lawrence, whose "dream of a triangular marriage"[96] with both a wife and a close male friend we have already noticed, had a perhaps more complicated and aversive response to the triangle produced by two women and a man. And his chthonic energies and elemental portraits are ripe for a kind of Jungian either/or analysis of "male" and "female." But to look at *The Fox,* in either its novel or film versions, as bad-for-bisexuals (as some recent bisexual commentators have done) is to consider, not too curiously, but not curiously enough.

◆

Reviewers of the Rydell film were virtually unanimous in their conviction that by taking an inexplicit story about sexual desire and making it blatantly explicit—Ellen masturbating before a mirror, Jill and Ellen in bed together—the film actually loses something of the story's suggestive power and force. Pauline Kael deplored the film's explicitness as an aesthetic, and, perhaps by extension, an erotic loss: "[I]f it's all spelled out, if everyone is sexually aware," then "you no longer need symbolism," she lamented.[97] In general, critics tended to see the film as "about" lesbianism rather than "about" bisexuality. Kael, who described the "triangle" in the Rydell film as "pretty much *The Children's Hour* in a woodsy setting," was criticized for dumping on lesbians when she asked rhetorically in her *New Yorker* column, "If March is a swinger like this, if she isn't afraid of sex with men, what's she doing in the woods playing house with that frumpy little Jill?"[98] Renata Adler regarded the film as being about both Banford's lesbianism (Sandy Dennis is "the more feminine, frail, and ultimately lesbian" of the two women) and March's "dissatisfaction" ("one gets the point that she is dissatisfied and lonely many long seconds before her naked scene with the bathroom mirror ends"). The fox, Adler thought, because it is killed by Paul, "seems to represent lesbianism,"[99] likewise killed off at the end. The Catholic journal *Commonweal,* assessing the film as offensively "oddball" and "sick," skated around the tricky question of sexualities altogether, describing the two women's "not-too-happy-arrangement": "March is the unhappier of the two, and more frustrated—which is the point, no doubt, of the masturbation scene."[100] No doubt.

Stanley Kauffmann, who had hoped that even "stripped of Lawrence's ambiguity and dark powers," the film "could still have been a moving, eccentric sex triangle," found Sandy Dennis "a ham" and suggested that Keir Dullea had been cast only because he looked like a fox. Still, he thought, Anne Heywood's March projected a "credibility that homosexuality and heterosexuality exist and contend in her."[101] Like "Ransom wins," this image of "contention" suggests a tug-of-war or an either/or solution. Either March's "homosexuality" (equated with her love for Jill) or her "heterosexuality" (equated with her attraction to Paul) will win the contest for her soul. One of these alternatives must be right. That she might genuinely be attracted to both Jill and Paul—that "homosexuality" and "heterosexuality" might not only "exist" but *co*exist in her—is not envisaged by these critics as a viable option.

Newsweek offered a classic evasion: "Miss Heywood's situation is spelled out as clearly as AC-DC, with an onanistic interlude added as a study aid."[102] Only one major review, Judith Crist's, used the word "bisexuality," and did so in a universalizing move that begs, even as it raises, the question: "Anne Heywood, who plays the girl who is desired by both male and female, is sheer perfection in a stunning portrayal of a woman torn by the bisexuality that obsesses us all."[103] In other words, once again "everybody's bisexual." Whether or not we agree with this para-psychoanalytic sentiment, it is a suggestive voicing of the temper of the late sixties. Either "everybody's bisexual" or March needs to make a choice between hetero- and homo-sex. Her "situation" is either allegorically universal or untenably conflicted.

Why is it that in 1968 lesbianism was more generally visible and nameable than bisexuality in *The Fox*? Was it because lesbianism is so clearly the "other," the not-self, and therefore readily demonized? Or was it because bisexuality—since it was not so easily regarded in the mainstream press as "them" not "us"—posed an even more palpable threat? Conversion, sexual fluidity, the capacity to attract and to be attracted by members of both sexes—these are genuinely dangerous attributes. It is perhaps fitting that the *Saturday Review* characterized Anne Heywood as "astonishingly like the young Garbo."[104]

Let me close, for the sheer pleasure of it, with some words from Greta Garbo herself on the question of bisexuality, "confusion," sexual secrets, and "double desire." Garbo had many male and many female lovers. ("Famously," writes Richard Schickel, "she lured [Cecil] Beaton across the line into a brief, and on his part, impassioned, heterosexual affair.")[105] But, as I hope will be clear from these excerpts from a Garbo autobiography dictated to a friend, the "bisexual plot," when it concerns an actress or a screen "legend," can sometimes have a cast of one.

> I dreamed many times about a mature man with experience who would have the vigor of a boy but an adult's polished methods. Strangely enough, I also dreamed about women of my mother's age who were ideal lovers. These dreams came superimposed on one another. Sometimes the masculine element was dominant, sometimes the feminine one. At other times I wasn't sure. I saw a female body with male organs or a male body with female ones. These pictures, blended together in my mind, occasionally brought pleasure but more often pain. I can use only one word to describe my sexual attitudes: confusion. . . . I don't think I could ever live with either a man or a woman for a long time. Male and female are attractive to my mind, but when it comes to the sexual act I am afraid. In every situation I need a lot of stimulation before I am conquered by the forces of passion and lust. But confusion, before and after, is the dominant factor. When I was with a young girl I dreamed about a young man, and the reverse. . . .
>
> To make up for my sexual shortcomings, or, if you wish, my double

desire, I had a tremendous urge to act on the stage or in films. . . . What is more, and however foolish it might sound, acting on stage and in front of cameras was a sexual experience for me . . . for me it was a sheer sexual experience, and my complete secret. Maybe this pure emotional experience mixed with deep sexual satisfaction is the basis of my creativity.[106]

Chapter 21

Threesomes

We switch partners daily
We play as we please.
Twosy beats onesy
But nothing beats threes.

—*"Two Ladies,"* Cabaret[1]

Four chairs, side by side. Seated in the middle, two attractive young women, Helene and Vicki, holding hands. Flanking them on either side, looking very much alike, are two slim, handsome young men with pony-tails, Brad and John, both dressed similarly, in black shirts and jeans. Brad is Helene's husband; John is Vicki's fiancé. The two women are also lovers. The topic for the day, announced talk-show host Ricki Lake, was "couples who are bisexual and wouldn't have it any other way."

Brad did not, he said, feel threatened by his wife's other relationship. Or, as it turned out, her relationships, in the plural, for after a station break (the obligatory tease of broadcast sex discussions) the foursome onstage were joined by a fifth, Justine, identified as another of Helene's friends and lovers. The introduction of this fifth figure, breaking up the symmetry and quiet, confident balance onstage, was—I had to assume—a strategic ploy to shift the classical into the baroque, the even into the uneven, perhaps (even) the odd. They were all quite appealing, articulate, and smart. There was no way they could be easily dismissed as "losers," though the audience tried. "Are you going to be bisexual for the rest of your life, or is this a phase?" one audience member asked. "How can I know?" Helene replied, reasonably. "We took the initiative to cross this line, and you haven't," she said at one point. John and Brad both, repeat-edly, made the point that if they weren't troubled by the bisexuality of the women they loved, no one else should be either.

Inevitably, the discussion quickly came around to sexual threesomes. "Do you watch?" Ricki asked Brad. "I have," he answered, after a moment. "He does," said Vicki promptly. The audience took a breath. Sometimes, it developed, all three had sex together. Brad's participation, he stressed, was not voyeurism. It wasn't that the prospect of two women together turned him on. Their marriage was loving, mutually trustful, and open, though only Helene, not Brad, sought relationships outside the marriage, and hers were only with women, not with other men.

We have said that love and hatred are in effect two sides of the same strong emotion, and that the affect can switch from one to the other much more readily than it can be made to disappear altogether. If someone disappoints or betrays us in love, we will "hate" them sooner than be indifferent to them. In the same way, another apparent paradox holds true: that the flip side of erotic jealousy is the threesome. In this case, too, the lover gets to gratify both fears and desires: The fear that a partner will be unfaithful is related to a desire to be unfaithful oneself as well as to the desire to know and therefore control the other's infidelity.

Often people equate bisexuality with triangles, and even with sexual threesomes. "Bisexuality is misunderstood as simultaneous relationships," as lesbian activist Ann Northrop observed to Phil Donahue. It is not so much a misunderstanding as a willful mis-taking, a preference for believing that bisexuals are promiscuous, "unable to commit," or only satisfied when they have "both at once," whatever "at once" may be taken to mean. While it is obvious that, to many bisexuals, this image of "both at once" is inaccurate, the image of "three in a bed" seems to satisfy *someone's* fantasy. But it is not always clear that the fantasy belongs to the person identified as bisexual.

Just as the most common negative stereotype of bisexuality is probably sexual betrayal, so the most common "positive" or sexually exciting stereotype is probably "swinging" and having multiple partners for sex. As Helene and Brad both insisted to Ricki Lake's audience, however, Helene was not promiscuous, nor were her woman partners just sex-mates. They were friends, they had met at work (it turned out two of the women were dancers, though what kind was not specified), they had breakfast together, they hung out, they talked.

This "Henry and June" triad of two women and a man, so close to the heterosexual male fantasy of watching two lesbian lovers (and perhaps intervening in their lovemaking), would seem to be the most familiar kind of threesome, appearing as it does in numerous popular cultural forms. It is something of a surprise, therefore, to find that in the Weinberg, Williams, and Pryor study of bisexuals in San Francisco in the 1980s "the two most common gender combinations were primarily male biased; either three men or two men and a woman."[2] Approximately half of the men and women who responded to the Weinberg questionnaire had participated in a threesome in the last twelve months, with a median frequency of two to three times a year, and the frequency of swinging or group sex, reported by 40 percent of the respondents, was about the same, two or three times a year. But these respondents, as we have noted, were self-identified bisexuals, members of an organization called the Bisexual Center, located in a city the survey-takers described as "a natural laboratory for the sexual."[3] For a city with so large a gay male population the all-male threesomes make statistical sense, but even if the participants are all bisexuals this conformation does not readily strike us as an instance of "bisexuality."

Two men and a woman together, however, are clearly "bisexual." But they are also more culturally threatening than two women and a man, a triad that connotes "mastery" and manliness (to men), but also voluptuous excess. Arguably the master of pleasurable guilt, in this as in so many other situations, is Philip Roth's Alexander Portnoy, whose one experience with a threesome was memorable enough to recount to his psychiatrist.

It seems that Portnoy and his girlfriend, whom he has nicknamed The Monkey, are traveling in Italy and decide to fulfill a recurrent fantasy by picking up a woman:

> Doctor, I ask you, who was it that made the suggestion in the first place? Since the night we met, just who has been tempting whom with the prospect of yet another woman in our bed? . . . The fact is that it was The Monkey herself, speaking her high-fashion Italian, who leaned out of our rented car and explained to the whore what it was we wanted and how much we were willing to pay. . . . We had imagined it beforehand in all its possibilities, dreamed it all out loud for many, many months now, and yet I am dumbstruck at the sight of The Monkey's middle finger disappearing up into Lina's cunt.
>
> I can best describe the state I subsequently entered as one of unrelieved *busy-ness.* Boy, was I busy! I mean there was just so much to do. You go here and I'll go there—okay, now you go here and *I'll* go there—all right, now she goes down that way, while I head up this way, and you sort of half turn around on this. . . . and so it went, Doctor. . . .

When the woman departs The Monkey accuses Portnoy of corrupting her, at the same time that she berates him for not taking full advantage of the sexual opportunity. His ill-judged retort, "I couldn't always fight my way *past* you," brings on a fresh torrent of accusations: "I am not a lesbian! Don't you dare call me a lesbian! Because if I am, *you made me one!*"[4]

Now, Roth is—to put it mildly—not a particularly gay-affirmative writer, and *Portnoy's Complaint,* one man's American (Wet) Dream, is hardly a bisexual novel. To my mind, however, it is a very good novel—I still laugh out loud at some parts of it—and well worth unpacking to see what, if anything, this frenzied one-night stand can tell us about the relationship of threesomes to bisexuality. "The Monkey was by then the one with her back on the bed, and I the one with my ass to the chandelier (and the cameras, I fleetingly thought)."

The Three-Body Solution

Writer Michael Szymanski's autobiographical article about his "second coming out"—formerly as a gay man, now as a bisexual—was illustrated on the cover of *Genre* with a full-color photo of two men and a woman in bed together. The man in the center stared moodily and sexily out at the camera; his two partners lay upside down with their eyes closed, curled against him, each one resting in the crook of one of his arms. All three were deeply tanned. This picture said quite clearly that it was about the author-surrogate, the only "subject" in the composition. So did the full-page photograph that illustrates the text. The three lovers were upright this time, standing in a balletic triangle, the second man and the woman each holding one of the "author's" hands. The woman looked at us with defiant possessiveness; the second man locked eyes with the man in the middle. They were slim, shapely, and naked.

Syzmanski's prose offers the scenario of a threesome: "From my earliest fantasies, I imagined being sandwiched between a man and a woman." "I dreamed of a tough, muscular body breathing down on me and a supple, lithe, hairless body in front."[5] But in the context of his article it's evident that though he's erotically attracted to both men and women, he's been involved with either a man or a woman at any given time, not with both in a sexual threesome. At the time of the article he was dating a woman and shunned by many in his West Hollywood gay community. They couldn't hold hands in public; his gay friends were "voyeuristically fascinated." An "ex-editor-in-chief of a gay magazine" warned Syzmanski that he couldn't write for him anymore "unless I was more discreet about *her*." Syzmanski's "problem" was not multiple simultaneous partners but "biphobia," unthinking prejudice against a sexually fluid identity, and the gay community's "heterophobia," to use a term employed by one of his gay friends to describe his own resistance. The semiotics of "bisexuality," however, required something an ordinary still photograph couldn't reproduce: time. Thus the prurient shorthand, the fantasy standing in for "reality": three in a bed.

A similar kind of visual shorthand was used by *Mirabella* to illustrate an excerpt from the Weinberg, Williams, and Pryor study on bisexuality. The magazine article's title, "Tangled Lives," was symptomatic of its ambivalence; purporting to press the envelope of fixed notions of sexual identity, and underlying that "daring" move with its cover tease, "Are We All a Bit Bi?" *Mirabella* nonetheless chose to depict bisexuality as a tangle of sexy, well-muscled bodies. Here the problem of time was solved by the use of superimposed images. The result, in a beautifully erotic photograph, was what looked like an action photo or series of movie-still frames of men and women making love. A woman's breast, and another woman's buttocks (or the same woman's buttocks photographed at a different moment in the sequence) are the only clearly visible sexual body parts. (By contrast, on the cover of *Genre,* the one visible nipple is male.) The same man appears twice in the composition, though a third, apparently different male figure (he has straighter hair) crouches at the bottom of the frame. This is bi-sex by MTV repackaged for the upscale, middle-aged, but ever-young consumer.

Mirabella, despite its feature articles on male authors, artists, and computer gurus, is still largely a "woman's magazine," filled with ads for "turnaround cream" and features called "beauty news." That may be one reason why in the "Tangled Lives" photograph the men are coded as "background" to the women's "foreground," by the angle of the female faces and the placement of the women's bodies parallel to the picture plane. One woman's face, in its angle and expression, is uncannily like that of the bisexual male "author" in the autobiographical *Genre* piece. Again the message is one of thoughtful reflection: "I am contemplating my bisexuality," as that bisexuality is acted out, fantasylike, through the writhing entangled figures. Michelangelo's "Last Judgment," recently cleaned and stripped of some of its censoring loincloths, comes—albeit very briefly—to mind. Bisexuality in this rendering means having a lot of sex. And even though one of Michael Syzmanski's gay male friends floated the hypothesis that "gay men turn straight because they can't compete in the high-pressure world of buffed bodies and hot looks" ("It's a lot easier to find a woman because then you can let yourself go and don't have to look so good"),[6] these multiple bi-bodies are gorgeous. Bisexuality on this level also means having a lot of sexiness. Interestingly, the heterosexual press most commonly uses the image of two women and a man. The gay/lesbian press most commonly shows two men and a woman.

In a book described as the "first systematic exploration of sexual threesomes," therapist Arno Karlen, a frequent guest on television talk shows, reports on his interviews with fifty subjects who have participated in threesomes at one point or another in their lives. Karlen distinguishes threesomes from "swinging," which he characterizes dismissively as "the adulterous equivalent of a package tour."[7] In a sociological study of swingers, 93 percent were white, two-thirds were middle class, the majority were Republicans or independents, and over 30 percent were conservatives.[8] Swingers, he thinks, are often joiners, part of a "hotbed of Middle American banality,"[9] interested in "clubs and planned events and conventions," where "the atmosphere is often that of a horny Rotary Club."[10]

"Unlike swingers, people who have had threesomes fit no mold," thinks Dr. Karlen.[11] One of his subjects, a woman psychologist in her early thirties, describes it as "a sacred communal thing, sharing with a friend. With one partner, there's love between two people; when you open it up, there are three. Maybe you can't love the whole world, but the door creaks open for a minute when you can love without jealousy or possessiveness."[12] "I think the question of threes is vitally important," said another woman. "If you love someone, it's wonderful seeing them pleased, and the only way to watch is with a third person. It's as if one's own self is extended. Anyway, I like to be the mistress rather than the wife."[13]

A man added this perspective: "To me the special pleasure in a threesome wasn't in me screwing one and then the other, but that all three people were interrelated. It was especially exciting if the two women had homosexual relations. By the way, none of the girls had a homosexual history. Our threesomes were an introduction for all of them. For anyone, getting close to your erotic nature involves homosexuality. I never had a triangle with another man; I almost did back in those days, but I realized my prejudice against it."[14]

The word "homosexual" crops up frequently in Karlen's *Threesomes,* as in the suggestion that "threesomes don't involve homosexual contact, but it is potential in the situation,"[15] or in the therapist's assertion that "many women enter threesomes primarily to have a homosexual experience."[16] In this almost-four-hundred-page book on sexual threesomes, however, "bisexual" is, yet again, conspicuous by its virtual absence.

There are occasional personal narratives, spoken by interview subjects, in which the word appears: "Maria is bi, but Connie isn't,"[17] or, from Connie herself, "I never looked at it as a threesome, since I'm not bi and had no romantic involvement with Maria."[18] A male interview subject said the woman he was living with "was bisexual and had been in threesomes before,"[19] while a man who has lived in a "three-way marriage" for ten years with his wife and another woman recalled that "At one point in the revolutionary sixties, another prof and I decided we should be bisexual; we thought that logically it should be natural. We started kissing, and it didn't work. We just giggled and laughed and gave it up."[20]

Nowhere, though, does the therapist himself acknowledge bisexuality as a viable and useful term. When "bisexuality" appears in Karlen's own narrative voice it is in quotation marks; he clearly has his doubts about its existence. He declares that "in some circles, the word *bisexual* is used often and loosely; for a woman it carries no stigma and may even raise her status";[21] he describes a college campus "where feminism, lesbianism, and 'bisexuality' were widely espoused and conferred high status."[22] Again, the quotation marks are his.

"Two to three times more men than women have homosexual experience," he reports, "yet the majority of threesomes involve two women. When two-male triads do occur, the men usually take turns with the woman or pleasure her simultaneously, without homosexual contact. I have heard of occasional male-male sex in orgiastic threes and groups, but not one account of the warm lovemaking many women exchange in such situations. If there is, as a few people claim, increasing male 'bisexuality' in threes and groups, the people I've talked to haven't been part of it or seen it." [23]

Here then is an "expert" on three-person relationships, most involving at least one male and one female partner, and many involving sexual contact between same-sex partners as well as opposite-sex eroticism, who will describe bisexuality only as a phantom proposition, someone else's idea of what is going on.

Why does he avoid the term? Karlen's doubts seem to be based on his rejection of Freudian drive or "instinct" theory ("We are, it says, 'bisexual' by nature" but "today few reseachers think of instinct so simplistically"). [24] "Identification and projection are components of many sex behaviors, homosexual and heterosexual, and should be distinguished from homo-eroticism," [25] he says. "Power" and "intimacy" are the goals he thinks his subjects aim for. "Many threesomes are actually attempts to control jealousy by keeping the competition in sight and more or less in control" while "the gift of a third partner is often a gesture of primacy and power." [26]

Ménages à trois

"In love, I agree with you, a couple is not ideal," Jim (Henri Serre) remarks to the elusive and imperturbable Catherine (Jeanne Moreau) in François Truffaut's 1962 film classic about a ménage à trois, *Jules and Jim*. *Jules and Jim* plays a crucial if cameo role in the 1994 collegiate comedy *Threesome,* also a film about a ménage—or at least a dormitory suite—à trois. As the object of study in Eddy's "French cinema" class (the only class any of the three roommates ever seem to attend), Truffaut's film, never explicitly named, is nonetheless central to *Threesome*'s erotics, especially in its idyllic scenes in the countryside (Southern California here standing in, as it does so often in so many contexts, for the south of France).

But is *Jules and Jim* a bisexual film? Surely not. The whole point of the film would seem to be that Jim and Jules (Oskar Werner) compete for Catherine, and share her, whereas in *Threesome*—if I may continue for a moment to compare small things with great—the erotic trail is a round-robin: Stuart wants to sleep with Alex (mistakenly assigned to his dorm room because of her name) who wants to sleep with Eddy (the third roommate) who, it turns out, would rather sleep with Stuart, though he ultimately has sex with both, and indeed the three of them have sex with one another, though Alex is positioned tastefully(?) in the heterosexual middle. It seems pretty clear that what really turns them on and binds them together *is* the threesome. After some false starts sexual jealousy is resolved, in a way that is clearly temporary, by excluding and indeed rather cruelly rejecting all outsiders (Alex's boyfriend, Stuart's girlfriend,

Eddy's match-made date with a gay man) in favor of endogamous loyalty to the other two insiders—and by all three of them periodically rollicking and sleeping in the same bed. Such are the joys of youth.

Jules and Jim, by contrast, presents two young men, one blond and one dark, one Austrian and one French, one tall and one short, one deft with women but reluctant to settle down and one awkward with women but eager to marry. Both fall in love with a statue that looks like Catherine, and then (when they meet her) with Catherine herself. Jules, the blond, awkward Austrian, marries Catherine but cannot keep her. "She thinks that in a couple only one person need be faithful," explains Jules to his friend, revising his earlier naive opinion that it is always and only the husband who can play around after marriage, while the wife must not stray. Jim becomes Catherine's lover, and plans to marry her with Jules's approval, since Jules wants above all not to lose her completely.

There is a plan, in the event short-lived, for the three of them to live together. As aficionados of the film will recall, Jim and Catherine die when she drives them purposefully off a bridge, and Jules is left to mourn them. At the beginning and the end of the film the two men are compared by the narrator to Don Quixote and Sancho Panza, another mismatched but inseparable pair. "The friendship of Jules and Jim had no equivalent in love," says a voice-over at the end. "They accepted their differences. Everyone called them Don Quixote and Sancho Panza."

Now as it happens, Don Quixote and Sancho Panza are the very figures with whom René Girard begins his account of triangular desire. "Chivalric passion defines a desire *according to Another,* opposed to this desire *according to Oneself* that most of us pride ourselves on enjoying. Don Quixote and Sancho borrow their desires from the Other in a movement which is so fundamental and primitive that they completely confuse it with the will to be Oneself."[27] Although Don Quixote's mediating authority is literary (a book of chivalric romance) and Sancho's is oral (the ideas of Don Quixote) this difference matters far less than the fact that, though each is sure his desires are his own, they are actually only his own insofar as they are derived from someone else.

This is a hard pill to swallow, even in these days of Prozac, for anyone who insists on control and on the knowable and governable self. In the case of Truffaut's film, Jules and Jim—note that their names alone are in the title, as if it were a love story between them, like *Romeo and Juliet*—date the same women, partner each other in boxing, shower side by side in the gym. There are offhand but clearly not accidental citations of Oscar Wilde, Shakespeare, and Proust (Jim's longtime girlfriend's name is Gilberte; one of Catherine's lovers is named Albert), not to mention Stendhal's *The Red and the Black,* another of Girard's proof texts (Jim's fictional name in his autobiographical novel is Julien; his favorite teacher's name was Sorel). The framing of *Jules and Jim* between parenthetical mentions of Don Quixote and Sancho thus establishes it as not only a film about erotic rivalry but also as that which it clearly means to be, a work in the grand European tradition of love narratives.

But bisexual? Despite those sweaty moments in the gym, there seems to be nothing going on between Jules and Jim. If their idealization of Catherine looks a little too much like choosing an object over a subject (she's a statue come to life, a statue they first saw on a slide projected by Albert), she quickly proves that she has a vitality—and a will—of her own. Their first adventure together after she and Jules become a couple (he has to caution his smooth-talking friend—"not this one, Jim"—as the two men go up the stairs to join her) features Catherine cross-dressed as "Thomas," with an "Our Gang" cap, a pencil-drawn mustache that would later resurface in Madonna's "Justify My Love," and that most familiar of gender-testing accessories, a lighted cigar. True, Jules later agrees to have Jim move in with them, many years later when the marriage of Jules and Catherine has become merely a formal union. But whatever sexual attraction there might be between the two men is downplayed to the point of invisibility. The *film* is readable as gay or bi, with its cultural and visual markers from adjoining shower stalls to Oscar Wilde. But the *characters* are less visibly ambisextrous. Nonetheless, what I want to claim here is that such a love trio is latently, but importantly, bisexual, precisely because it activates the three sides of the triangle. It is a relationship among three people, animated by sexual desire. If the narrator wants to claim that "the friendship of Jules and Jim had no equivalent in love," it is in part because we have constructed "love" in such a way as to exclude their kind of friendship. What makes their relationship work is the presence of the three partners.

"A Triangle of Pure Love"

Truffaut's *Jules and Jim* was based on a novel by Henri-Pierre Roché published in Paris in 1953. The character Jules is inspired by Roché's friend, the German-Jewish writer Franz Hessel, that of Kate (the film's Catherine) by Franz's wife, art student Helen Grund Hessel, and Jim by Roché himself. Described by a sympathetic critic as "one of the century's more turbulent love triangles,"[28] and—by Roché himself—as *"un pur amour à trois,"* the relationship lasted for about a dozen years. When, in 1942, Roché heard that Hessel had died after being twice incarcerated in a German concentration camp, he wrote in his journal, "How we counted on having the leisure to continue one day our eternal conversation. We didn't write each other, see each other, out of fear of and pity for Hln [Helen]—and we truly thought that with her love for risk-taking and for the absolute, God would call her before [calling] us.... Hln's violence, and her revolver, were always between us."[29]

In fact, this was not the only *amour à trois* that bound the two men.

"Franz and I have the same taste in women, but we desire different things from them and not for a moment do I think there has ever been any rivalry between us,"[30] Roché wrote in his journal in 1906; among the women they shared were the painter Marie Laurencin, the Countess Reventlow, Franziska, and Euphemia Lamb, an Englishwoman who had been a model for the artist Augustus John.

Roché's novel is faithful to the details of the *ménage à trois*—except that he radically alters its ending. The death of Kate and Jim in the car driven into the Seine replaces the death of Jules after his incarceration in the camps. Mourning "the leisure to continue one day our eternal conversations," Roché rewrites the history of the threesome so that it is Hessel—the first to die—who survives and mourns. As for Roché himself, he repeats the pattern in a triad with his young lover, American actress Beatrice Wood, and the avant-garde painter Marcel Duchamp: "The three of us," writes Wood in her autobiography, "were something like *un amour à trois;* it was a divine experience in friendship."[31] "I am convinced," says a modern scholar who works on Duchamp, "that Roché was in love with Duchamp (as so many men were)." Wood, he says, reported that although Duchamp "was in no way 'homosexual,' he probably had sex with men more than once in his life. Roché is probably one of them."[32]

If there is a "last word" to be spoken about bisexuality in the *Jules and Jim* triad, though, perhaps it should be Truffaut's. When he read Roché's novel, the director reports, "I had the feeling that I had before me an example of something the cinema had never managed to achieve." In his view " 'the public' are unable to make an emotional choice between the characters, because they are made to love all three of them equally. It is that element, that anti-selectivity, which struck me most forcibly in this story which the editor presented as 'a triangle of pure love.' "[33] "Unable to make an emotional choice," placed in a situation of "anti-selectivity," "made to love all three of them equally": In Truffaut's cinematic imagination the erotic transference or projection develops not, or not only, as an aspect of Jules's love for Jim—or Jim's love for Jules-and-Catherine—but rather as a result of an encounter *with the threesome.* The rhetorical elements of indecision and compulsion in his assessment ("unable"; "made to love") here mark a realm of pleasure—a pleasure not the less acute for granting permission to view bisexually, or to take bisexual satisfactions. It is perhaps not an accident that the rhetorical elements Truffaut so clearly saw could make a brilliant film—indecision, compulsion, "anti-selectivity" —are the very same elements that have often been said to characterize what is wrong with bisexuality as a lived practice. There is a lesson to be learned here about both sex and love.

That's Entertainment

A quite different kind of ménage à trois was imagined by playwright Joe Orton in the same years—a bisexual triangle animated not by idealized love but by opportunistic desire. Orton's 1964 bed-sit comedy farce *Entertaining Mr. Sloane* brought bisexuality center stage in a brilliant rewrite of Tennessee Williams interlarded with bits of the mystical Edward Albee "missing baby" plot, the sixties' savage send-up of the Family Oedipus. Its title character, the bisexual and cheerfully amoral Sloane, takes up residence in the house of the forty-one-year-old Kath, who shares the house with her elderly father. In the opening moments of the play Kath confides to him that her "husband," "a mere boy," was "killed in tragic circumstances." The echo of Blanche Dubois is clear, though Orton famously tried to distance his female characters from "your Tennessee Williams drag queens."[34]

It takes Sloane only a minute to winkle out of Kath the fact that she is unmarried and has had a baby out of wedlock. He himself, he confides to her, was brought up in an orphanage. In moments she is stroking his "delicate skin." He will be both the baby and, by play's end, the father of the child.

Kath's brother Ed, whom Orton described as "a man who was interested in having sex with boys. . . . the most ordinary man in the world,"[35] finds Sloane equally fascinating, and Sloane, for his part, finds Ed as easy as Kath to satisfy with invented details of his early life. The mythical orphanage had "just boys" in it ("ideal" says Ed), Sloane reports himself interested in swimming and in bodybuilding ("Good. Good. Stripped?"), and Ed cannot resist asking whether he likes to wear leather next to his skin. "Eddie is a great deal tougher than Sloane," Orton wrote to Broadway director Alan Schneider. "Sloane is the ambiguous figure, not Eddie." The play, he said, was "Not a play about two women and a boy," but "about a man, a woman, and a boy. Very, very important."[36]

"Young, compliant, bisexual, murderous when threatened,"[37] Sloane is the perfect object of desire. Before long both Kath and Ed are having sex with him, and Sloane is running the household. Ed's past is strikingly, and surely deliberately, reminiscent of Brick Pollitt's in Williams's *Cat on a Hot Tin Roof,* but the female interloper who came between him and his beloved friend in the unfallen past was his sister, not his wife. In fact, the "boy" of the opening scene's conversation was, it turns out, Ed's "mate":

> I had a matie. What times we had. Fished. Swam. Rolled home pissed at two in the morning. We were innocent, I tell you. Until she came on the scene. (*Pause.*) Teaching him things he shouldn't 'a done. It was over . . . gone . . . finished. (*Clears his throat.*) She got him to put her in the family way that's what I always maintain. Nothing was the same after. Not ever. A typical story.[38]

Equally typical, and superbly well plotted (Terence Rattigan, no slouch himself, compared the style of *Sloane* to William Congreve and Oscar Wilde),[39] is the way Sloane's ascendancy becomes his comeuppance. As the audience soon discovers, Sloane is not only a first-rate con man and accommodating bed partner but also a murderer who has escaped the law, and when his identity becomes clear to Kath and Ed's crusty old father, and the father threatens him with exposure, Sloane kills him. It dawns on the brother and sister that they now have him at their mercy, and they strike a bargain—the same bargain Demeter made with Pluto over Persephone: "Perhaps we can share you." Six months with Ed, then six months with Kath, who has, she says, "a bun in the oven," and doesn't want to lose the father of her child (again). "Perfect, Eddie," she says with satisfaction. "It's very clever of you to have thought of such a lovely idea!"[40]

"In Orton's plays," John Clum points out, "masculine men are bisexual."[41] "You scatter your seed along the pavement without regard to age or sex,"[42] says the policeman Truscott to Dennis in *Loot*. For that matter, in *What the Butler Saw,* the cross-dressed Geraldine, pretending to be a boy, tells Dr. Rance defiantly, "I must be a boy. I like girls."[43] Clum wonders "whether Orton's insistence on bisexuality wasn't the result of his fear that audiences would tie homosexuality to the effeminacy he despised."[44] John Lahr speculated that this reflected an ambivalence in Orton's own life, reflecting "the split in his own sexual nature": *"Entertaining Mr. Sloane* is the most blatantly autobiographical of plays."[45] But Alan Sinfield suggested that Orton was avoiding something: " '[W]e're all bisexual really' is the commonest evasion. Hal and Dennis [in *Loot*] are said to be indifferent to the gender of their partners. . . . it was not how Orton lived, or others that he knew."[46]

Sinfield, writing in 1990, regarded the playwright as being "stuck in the Orton moment," the pre–Gay Liberation sixties, and "jumping clear" rather than "engaging with" sexual stereotypes as a way of advancing "gay self-understanding." Many of Orton's characters, he wrote then, "show an untroubled practice of homosexuality . . . but none of them is apparently *a homosexual."* At the time—the Sinfield moment?—this was cause for complaint. Orton, says Sinfield, "refused nature, depth and sincerity at least partly because, although he felt an intuitive opposition to the prevailing sexual ideology, he had difficulty conceiving a positive view of the homosexual." Yet in the process, and perhaps precisely because he was "out of step with that reforming tendency," Orton provided the theater with some of its most powerfully transgressive bisexual characters. He was not writing about characters, or only about characters, but instead about interactions; he positioned bisexuality as a norm. With hindsight this seems, at least to me, a quite perspicacious (even if inadvertent) "revolutionary" move.

Life Is a Cabaret

> "I want you for my wife."
> "What would your wife want with me?"

With this hoary joke (why are all unfunny jokes described as "hoary"?) the emcee of the Kit Kat Klub introduces the notion of sexual ambivalence in

Bob Fosse's brilliant film version of *Cabaret* (1972). Joel Grey is himself the master of sexual ceremonies, traversing the entire terrain from "male" to "female" and "straight" to "gay" in the course of his musical numbers. He is "bisexual" in the sense that he pairs and preens onstage with just about anyone, including a troupe of "girls" who may well be transvestite boys. (At least one is, we learn in the famous urinal scene.)

But the film's paramount off-cabaret-stage bisexual is Brian Roberts, the young writer played by Michael York, and the latest permutation of the original "Christopher Isherwood" figure from Isherwood's *Berlin Stories*. York, who had appeared two years previously as the resourceful and uninhibitedly bisexual hero of Harold Prince's black comedy *Something for Everyone* (1970), brought to the role of Brian a version of what I have called the "repertory effect." Audiences had seen him as a bisexual before; they would readily think of him as a bisexual now.

In his autobiography, *Accidentally on Purpose,* York swiftly disposes of the suggestion that he might himself be bi or gay in a single urbane paragraph. In his teenage years, as his voice was beginning to change, "I became aware of the full significance of the homosexual alternative. Although my father had expressed his intolerance of this sexual persuasion now newly legalized, I certainly experimented with it, briefly and unsuccessfully, pressured as much by curiosity as by others to explore this classical ideal. It was not for me. Subsequently, though, many of my dearest friends were homosexual and I was given many professional opportunities to understand and portray their kind." For young York, however, "women now became the exclusive object of desire."[47]

"Their kind" as a reference to homosexuals as a group reflects the title of Christopher Isherwood's *Christopher and His Kind,* a memoir of the decade of the thirties, in which "Christopher Isherwood" and his sexual adventures are described in a book "as frank and factual as I can make it, especially as far as I myself am concerned."[48] Isherwood was indeed homosexual, delightedly so, but the "Isherwood" of *Goodbye to Berlin* was far more reticent about his sexuality than the memoirist of *Their Kind* almost forty years later. It is not that "Christopher Isherwood" leaves no clues; he spends the summer on Ruegen Island in the company of beautiful blond German boys who are principally interested in bodybuilding, and he decides not to disabuse the innocent Natalia Landauer about his supposed affair with Sally Bowles because "doing so would only have involved a long heart-to-heart talk for which I simply wasn't in the mood. And, at the end of all the explanations, Natalia would probably have found herself quite as much shocked as she was at present, and a good deal more jealous."[49]

Still, "Christopher" is relatively sexless in *Goodbye to Berlin*. The famous sentence that was to provide a title for John van Druten's stage play of the Berlin stories, "I am a camera with its shutter open, quite passive, recording, not thinking," offered a camouflage of spectatorship. In a 1975 interview Isherwood acknowledged that he had created a problem for subsequent stage and screen adapters of his work: "[W]hat *is* it about Chris? Why doesn't he do something about this very available, attractive girl?" At the time, though, homosexuality was so daring a topic that it might have overshadowed the other stories he was telling. "If I had made the 'I' a homosexual, especially in *those* days, I would have made him overly-remarkable, and he'd have gotten in the way of the other characters." As a result, he decided to play down some of the details of his actual relationship with Jean Ross, the original Sally Bowles: "[H]ow, at one time I had no money, we actually shared our room and slept in the same bed, and, of course, the relations between my boy friends and her!" Such details would have produced "comedy" but at a "cost," since "it's not what the book is *about*."[50]

Nevertheless, I want to suggest that this question of sexuality, and its crossing of borders from "homosexual" to "heterosexual" (and from the pair to the threesome) *is* in fact exactly "what the book is *about*" insofar as we can ever say what a book is about. "About" here, in its various permutations of meaning from "directly concerning" to "circling around," draws a nice if deliberately imprecise sketch of the ways in which sexuality and bisexuality function in the story of the Christopher Isherwood–Cliff Bradshaw–Brian Roberts character as he negotiates the transition from the thirties to the seventies and the page to the stage and screen.

Isherwood recalls that his relationship with Jean Ross, the model for Sally Bowles, was that of "brother and sister." Their relationship was "asexual but more truly intimate than the relationships between Sally and her various partners in the novel, the plays, and films." They even thought of having sex together, though Jean never tried to seduce him. "What a pity we can't make love," she said one rainy, depressing afternoon, "there's nothing to do." He "agreed that it was and there wasn't." Nonetheless they shared a bed at least once "because of some financial or housing emergency." And Jean knew Christopher's "sexmates," but "showed no desire to share them," although he says he "wouldn't have really minded."[51] The wish here is not "father to the deed," as the old saying has it, but a substitute for it. Once again there is no "no" in the unconscious. Christopher, the third-person narrator of Isherwood's stories and memoirs, gets his sexmates and himself into bed with Jean Ross not by slipping between the bedsheets but by slipping the thought casually onto a sheet of paper. "He wouldn't have really minded."

In fact, he rather seems to like the idea.

To say that the Christopher-Sally relationship is dyadic and "incestuous" (brother to sister, mother to son, sexual outlaw to sexual outlaw) and that the boyfriends each brings in (to the room, to the bed, to the story) represent the "world out there" (functioning in this role like Sophocles's third actor), is merely to resituate the complexities of love and desire as the most central and important of human plots. As he tells the story, they are the couple, however "asexual" their relationship in practice. Their lovers and pickups are interruptions—often welcome, highly courted interruptions, but interruptions nonetheless.

Still, the question of Chris-Cliff-Brian's elusive sexual identity is not peripheral but central.

If Christopher is not sexually interested in Sally, then her sexual posturings "are played out to a narrator for whom it is only theater." He appreciates her moves, but only as performance, and in fact as a kind of performance from which he is nominally detached or estranged. Sally's ineptness then makes a double kind of sense: "[W]hat should be sexy is only 'sexy.'" And this quality of "sex-in-quotation-marks," as Linda Mizejewski points out, ironizes heterosexuality, replacing it with camp.[52] We might say that Christopher wears his rue with a difference. When the Sally of the Berlin stories works the room at a local café, the Lady Windermere (named for a comedy of manners by Oscar Wilde), Christopher notes her lack of business acumen about sex: "She wasted a lot of time making advances to an elderly gentleman who would obviously have preferred a chat with the barman." The tone of sexual schadenfreude here is palpable; he is pleased that she tries, and pleased that she fails. Her failure is an index of his success, or the success of "his kind." Indifference, in fact, makes a difference. Christopher is subtly competitive, rather than merely appreciative or amused by Sally's adventuring with men.

This only faintly limned bisexual triangle—the narrator is himself not angling for the attentions of the elderly gentleman in the Lady Windermere—becomes more apparent and more dramatically crucial in the 1972 film *Cabaret,* where Sally and Brian compete for the sexual and financial favors of the German playboy baron Max.

But it took a long time for Brian to come out. "Christopher," as we've seen, was disarmingly reticent about his sexuality, and especially about his homosexuality. John van Druten's stage play, *I Am a Camera*—written by a gay playwright fully cognizant of the possibilities—displaced the question of dangerous sexuality onto Sally Bowles, permitting her (especially when played by the "boyish" Julie Harris) to traverse the territory from androgyny to promiscuity. Sally's phallic double entendres—alluding to her landlady's bosom, she observes, "I say, Fräulein Schneider's got a big one, hasn't she?"[53]—contribute to the coding of her extravagant and unaccountable behavior as gay male,[54] while the "real" gay male in the story, played in the film version for added spice for those in the know by bisexual actor Laurence Harvey, became Chris, a "confirmed bachelor," wedded to his writing.

"Confirmed bachelor," when uttered as Harvey does in voice-over in the opening moments of the film as a statement about himself, fairly begs to be tested, or, as they say in the airline business, reconfirmed.

"Confirmed" itself quietly implies the opposite, "in doubt" (otherwise why does it need confirmation?), while the use of "confirmed bachelor" as a euphemism for gay man equally quietly erases the specter of another man or men in the erotic picture. The opposite of "confirmed" in this sense is "eligible," which means ripe for marital picking. If the confirmed bachelor is not married (to a woman) he is, by social definition, alone. But the larger social surround of "confirmed bachelor"—fussiness, wealth, society connections—implies the whole spectacle of the "gay gentleman," that useful personage Cole Porter called "The Extra Man":

> *I'm an extra man, an extra man,*
> *I've got no equal as an extra man,*
> *I'm handsome, I'm harmless, I'm helpful, I'm able,*
> *A perfect fourth at bridge or a fourteenth at table.*
> *You will find my name on ev'ry list,*
> *But when it's missing, it is never missed.*[55]

The Chris of *I Am a Camera* does not, of course, travel in such moneyed circles. His confirmation as a bachelor is a defensive and elusive gesture, one that begs to be challenged, as it is, by the scatty charms of Sally Bowles. In what Linda Mizejewski calls "Chris's only heterosexual move in the film," he pounces on Sally one evening after drinking too much wine and lamenting about his work. She has offered an affectionate hug, he responds with what used to be called a "pass," suggesting that "despite his writer's block, he is not entirely impotent."[56] In fact, through the act of making a pass, he passes: passes as heterosexual, then passes up the opportunity. His seriousness about his writing is offered, not entirely convincingly, as the reason he doesn't have a sex life, with Sally or anyone else.

One spectator who was not convinced was Harold Prince, the producer and director who mounted the stage musical *Cabaret,* with a book by Joe Masteroff, in 1966—the same Harold Prince, incidentally, who would cast Michael York as the enterprisingly bisexual hero of *Something for Everyone.* "We gotta put balls on the guy," Prince declared. "If he shacks up with the girl, he's gotta sleep with her!"[57] So Chris Isherwood, confirmed bachelor, became Cliff Bradshaw, red-blooded heterosexual. When the stage musical was revived in 1987, after the enormous success of Bob Fosse's film, Cliff acknowledged that he was bisexual, and was followed around on the stage by an interested German named Gottfried. But this was a back-formation from the film. Celebrated Berlin music hall performer (and Kurt Weill widow) Lotte Lenya, who costarred in the original stage production, remembered that there was no possibility Cliff could have been conceived, in 1966, as anything but straight.[58] The kinky sex stuff and decadent gender ambiguity were displaced onto a new character, the emcee of the cabaret, making Joel Grey an instant international star.

Fosse's *Cabaret* was the fourth in a series of theatrical transformations of Isherwood's Berlin stories, but the first to present its male lead as bisexual, a choice that Isherwood himself decried as "fundamentally anti-gay in attitude." He regarded the Brian Roberts character played by Michael York as offensively "off-again, on-again."⁵⁹ By this time, of course, it was the seventies, and the gay liberation movement had begun to change the public image of homosexuals.

Liza Minnelli, now cast as Sally Bowles, was a camp icon, immediately recognizable, as Isherwood observed, as "every inch Judy Garland's daughter."⁶⁰ The gay male audience—and the lesbian audience, too—was thus in a way secured and acknowledged. Rather than a wanna-be, this Sally Bowles was a show-stopper, her camp associations, already in place from the Hal Prince musical, now way out in the open. When she sang the title song, lamenting the fate of her friend Elsie who fell prey to pills and liquor, the audience was invited to think about Garland's rise and fall, and the ringing decision to go "like Elsie" when her own time comes draws cheers of affirmation from the moment of pathos.

How does Brian Roberts's bisexuality work in *Cabaret?* How does it reflect and refract Minnelli's status as female drag queen and cult star, and the emcee's gleeful ambisexuality, all framed against the encroaching backdrop of what Susan Sontag once called "fascinating fascism"?⁶¹

For one thing, since Minnelli *is* a gay icon, when Brian falls in love with her he may be seen as *more* gay rather than less. Paradoxically, his "heterosexuality" confirms his "homosexuality."

For another, Brian's bisexuality makes the erotic triangle the primary unit of desire.

The film opens with the symptomatic bisexual joke from the emcee: "I want you for my wife." Punchline: "What would your wife want with me?" A slippage in language here is what makes the joke work. The female addressee assumes that he wants to pair her with or give her to his wife. A preposition becomes a proposition: What is the word "for" for?

Shortly we will encounter this problem of the promiscuous preposition in other contexts. Brian Roberts teaches English to German-speakers in order to support himself, and his pupil Fritz Wendel has some trouble with his prepositions. "We do not sleep on each other," he tells Brian about his friend Sally Bowles, to whom he will introduce Brian. "That is correct, 'on'?" "With," says Brian with an indulgent half-smile. Language learners are so charmingly naive in their mistakes, we see him reflecting. The language becomes defamiliarized, literalized, and, ultimately, eroticized, since it is a stranger, an intruder, disrupting the familiar. Consider the following, which comes hard upon Fritz's confusion of "on" and "with."

Sally tries to seduce Brian, with a clumsiness that is both off-putting and endearing, placing his limp and inert hand on her breast. He is polite but plainly uninterested. "Well, do you sleep with girls, or don't you?" she asks, clearly regarding this as a rhetorical question. Again there is a pause, and a semantic slippage, as she realizes that this is a question that can be taken as something other than a sexual come-on. "Oh—you don't," she says after a moment. By this time he has escaped from the bed and is busy at the other end of the room, adjusting the record player. "Well, if you insist—I don't sleep with girls. Or, to be absolutely accurate, I've gone through the motions three times—all of them disastrous."

Sally is quick to regroup, offering comfort now that she sees that his rejection is not of her specifically but of women as sexual partners in general. "Friends are much harder to find than lovers. Besides, sex always screws up a friendship anyway." Immediately the film segues into another fragment of a language lesson between Brian and Fritz. We hear Fritz reciting conscientiously, "He would have been," "She would have been," "We would have been..." This linguistic sequence, a conjugation in the so-called conditional perfect, defines the plot, both in terms of its condition contrary to fact and its elements of wish-fulfillment and ultimate reversal or failure. And the completely expectable and unremarkable rote progression from "he" to "she" to "we," the fundamental architecture of verb conjugation, will turn out to chart Brian Roberts's erotic adventures —as well as those of the third partner in the film's sexual threesome, the wealthy and handsome German baron Maximilian Von Heune (Helmut Griem).

He would have been, she would have been, we would have been... *what?* Rich, happy, married, lovers? Max is a new character in the Isherwood-derived plot, replacing an American named Clive who had become Sally's lover and Sally and Christopher's lavish if short-lived benefactor in Isherwood's novel and its previous stage and screen adaptations. Max's nationality and rank make him the film's "protofascist," the upscale version of the Nazi thugs and beautiful Aryan Hitler youth we encounter elsewhere on the changing German scene. "Maximilian's heterosexuality conceals his homosexuality; Brian's homosexuality conceals his heterosexuality," observes psychoanalyst Stephen Bauer.[62] In practice, both men are bisexual.

No sooner has Brian gone to bed with Sally, in a scene in which he first comforts her for her father's failure to appear at an appointed rendezvous, than Max turns up to disrupt what looks like a heterosexual "cure." "Obviously those three girls were just the wrong three girls," the delighted Sally had commented, and Brian, equally delighted, chimed in on the last few words. The absent threesome ("the wrong three girls") have been apparently replaced by a present twosome. But not for long.

So Sally meets the handsome Max, discovers he is rich, and brings him to the Kit Kat Klub, where he tells her and Brian, "I think it is my duty to corrupt you, agreed?" Brian is testy, his sexual success apparently under threat. Does Sally think she'll get a film job from Max "in exchange for a little infidelity"? When Max wakes them in the morning by bringing a bottle of champagne and three glasses to their bedroom, the erotic triangle is established, though not yet fully sexualized. Max's seduction of Brian will occupy the next several scenes.

Throughout *Cabaret* the musical numbers performed onstage at the Kit Kat Klub provide a counterpoint for events in the "real world" offstage. Thus we hear the emcee's voice-over, "Berlin makes strange bedfellows these days," introducing the musical number "Two Ladies" as we see Sally, Brian, and Max riding in the back of Max's limousine. The strange bedfellows in Berlin are clearly aristocrats and Nazis as well as same-sex lovers. The film uses sexual "decadence" in a complex way to indicate what is happening politically in Germany, and the emcee's raucous devolution toward transvestism and unorthodox sexual partnering discloses the secret of sexual ambivalence at the heart of Nazism. "Two Ladies" will comment on both sets of "strange bedfellows," but, as Linda Mizejewski observes, Brian's bisexuality poses a problem, because "his own sexual ambiguity fails the narrative demand for an either/or political positioning, a clear distinction between (secretly female) monstrous fascism and cleancut (heterosexual) antifascism."[63] He is positioned as the outside observer, an American (no longer an Englishman, as in the earlier versions) in prewar Berlin, who sees what is happening to Germany and rejects it. How then can he fall for Max? Even if Sally is flawed, and even if Helmut Griem is more conventionally beautiful than Liza Minnelli, Brian's seduction by Max after his initial suspicion and resistance marks his temporary acquiescence to fascinating fascism, however deceptively personalized. Here the social myths of the "bisexual as fence-sitter" and the "bisexual as promiscuous deviant" are played out against a national-political backdrop.

Yet what does the audience want? Clearly, we want to see it all.

"Some have one," croons the emcee. "Some have two. Some have . . . two ladies—and he's the only man." On the Kit Kat stage, strobe lights accentuate the rapid-fire change of positions and persons, as huge bedsheets billow and bodies pop up and down. It's a great stage number, with its recurrent refrain of "the two-for-one":

> *We switch partners daily*
> *We play as we please*
> *Twosey beats onesey*
> *But nothing beats threes.*
> *I sleep in the middle—I left—and I right—*
> *But there's room on the bottom if you drop in some night.*

When Brian and Sally accompany Max to his ancestral estate, who sleeps where becomes a logistical question. There's a teasing little scene between

Brian and Max in Max's dressing room when he alludes in passing to his wife, thus diminishing the seriousness or at least the exclusiveness of any claim he might stake on Sally. "Are you still married?" Brian asks. "Very much so," replies Max. But his wife lives elsewhere, and has her own life and interests, "involved with culture and the arts." "We have quite a special relationship." He tosses Brian a sweater from his own collection, and Brian takes off his shirt, revealing Michael York's trim, hairless, boyish body. "I was right. Blue is your color." Things are getting sexy between them.

Who is the third in this ménage à trois? In the evening, Max, Sally, and Brian dance together. The drunken party scene begins with Sally dancing alone, then Max joins her. We can see that Brian doesn't know who he's jealous of—and doesn't quite know that he's jealous. They pull him into the dance, and Brian's head is in the center as the camera frames the scene. But he's drunk, and he passes out, leaving Sally and Max to go off together. Brian is thus in the third position, the position of the child, watching and fantasizing as his parents put him to bed and go off to their own. But Sally has been in that position, too. Max remarks to Brian on an earlier occasion that it's much more peaceful when the child—Sally—is taking a nap.

Perhaps because seducing Sally seems like a contradiction in terms— she appears never to resist sexual opportunity, though in fact we never see her in bed with anyone but Brian—the narrative focuses on the progress of Max and Brian's affair. They exchange glances of sexual complicity in a Bavarian beer garden where a terrifyingly earnest and beautiful Hitler youth sings "Tomorrow Belongs to Me." We see them, irritable and clearly preoccupied with their relationship, in the backseat of Max's car. And then we see the blowup between Brian and Sally, provoked by sexual tension and sexual jealousy.

Maximilian, says Sally defiantly, is a real man. "He's suave and he's divinely sexy and he really appreciates a woman." Unlike you, she implies, with the subtlety of a sledgehammer. She wants Brian to know that his own heterosexual success is by contrast provisional and tentative, that he doesn't measure up.

"Screw Maximilian," he retorts, goaded. "I do," says Sally, clearly intending to play her trump card.

"So do I," says Brian, after a deadly little pause. Sally is furious. This is a game she cannot play, much less hope to win. "You two bastards," she hisses. "Two, two?" Brian shoots back. "Shouldn't that be three?" The scene segues to a grinning emcee Joel Grey cross-dressed in a chorus line at the Kit Kat Klub. And Max decamps, leaving them a short note and a little cash.

Two, two, shouldn't that be three? There are "good" threesomes and "bad" threesomes in *Cabaret,* as there are "good" and "bad" bisexuals. The "best" threesome is the most conventional and the most temporary, the triad of Sally, Brian, and the baby she is expecting, which might be

Brian's and might be Max's. Brian proposes marriage, they share a fantasy of life in a Cambridge country cottage, and Brian, hatted, shirtless, with a necktie flung around his neck and a cigar in his teeth, a manifest, self-parodic caricature of phallic "manliness" draped in overcompensating signifiers, drunkenly toasts . . . not the three of them, but "me and the baby." The omission is significant and in symbolic terms costly. Before long Sally has an abortion without consulting him, and the dream is over. Brian leaves Berlin, while Sally and the emcee, whose "secret femininity"[64] is the secret of nascent Nazi Germany, become the couple who remain: a woman who acts like a drag queen and a man who is made up like a woman.

The film thus counterposes two views of "bisexuality." The first is gender crossover, the second transgressive or inclusive desire. But in the context of Fosse's *Cabaret* they amount to the same thing, though Brian's bisexuality, and indeed Maximilian's, are held at a deliberate distance from camp, drag, and effeminacy. Does Brian's sexuality merely reinscribe indecision? Is he somehow not man enough to be heterosexual, as Sally taunts him in their fight? But the "divinely sexy" Max who "really appreciates a woman" turned out to be bisexual, too. Or does Brian merely lack the courage to admit he is gay? Does one swallow make a summer, or one heterosexual affair make a bisexual? And is Sally, so close to a misogynistic caricature of the ridiculous "seductive" female, really "a woman" at all? Jean Ross's daughter says that her mother always claimed the Sally Bowles character was based not on her but on a man, a friend of Isherwood's. Isherwood himself notes that the name "Bowles" came from Paul Bowles, the American writer and composer, himself (as we have seen) bisexual and married to another extraordinary bisexual writer, Jane Bowles.

In one sense Brian's bisexuality is not so much a personal characteristic as it is a cultural symptom, a sign of the times. But then a sign of which times? The decadent, morally ambivalent thirties? Or the decadent, morally ambivalent seventies? Brian's bisexuality marks both the difference and the similarity between the time period the film is *describing* and the time period in which it was *made*. Bisexuality in 1972 was "chic," as we have seen. And sexy, as Michael York's role in *Something for Everyone,* set in Bavarian Germany, had demonstrated.

The "drive to be both sexes" that film theorist Gaylyn Studlar detects in the cinematic collaboration of Marlene Dietrich and Josef von Sternberg suggests a different kind of "bisexuality," one that allows "the mobility of multiple, fluid identifications"[65] while it flirts dangerously and transgressively with the preoedipal. Such a drive is clearly present in almost all the major erotic players of *Cabaret,* a film that pays constant homage to Dietrich.

Film theorists use the concept of identification here to indicate the position of the spectator. "Multiple, fluid identifications" are those that permit the viewer to "identify," as the term is often popularly used, with more than one character on the screen: for example, both with Brian and with Sally, rather than one or the other. "Bisexual spectatorship" becomes the successor to early and influential theories, notably those of Laura Mulvey and Mary Ann Doane, that regarded "the gaze" in classic film as male. Men looked; women were the looked-at. Men were subjects, women were objects, and usually sexual objects. Men were active, women passive recipients of the gaze. What happened when the woman looked back, as Dietrich powerfully did, or even looked first, holding the man—or woman —by her own gaze, became the topic of conversation by these same theorists, and others.

Mulvey's "transvestite" spectator, the woman who had to transform herself imaginatively into a man in order to view the film from its normative perspective, was further expanded and modified by the logic of bisexuality, which suggested not only the multiple and mobile "fluid identifications" but also the oscillation between positions of identity and desire. In a way this is a version of Freud's description of the thought process of paranoia ("I a man love you a man"; "I do not love him, I hate him"; "I do not love him, I love her") where the successive transformations make the underlying and unacceptable thought ("I a man love you a man") more tolerable on a conscious level. The paranoia that underlies Nazism is thematically congruent, here, with the erotic permutations and combinations gleefully exhibited by the emcee in the Kit Kat Klub.

Taking Turns

On the way she said, "Your wife is wonderful and I'm in love with her."

She was sitting beside him and David did not look to see if she blushed.

"I'm in love with her too," he said.

"I'm in love with you also," she said. "Is that all right?"[66]

This exchange is not, as it might at first seem, taken from a contemporary television talk show on bisexuality and marriage, but rather from Ernest Hemingway's posthumously published novel *The Garden of Eden*. Written between 1946 and his death in 1961, *The Garden of Eden* is a brilliant and powerfully erotic account of the marriage of David and Catherine Bourne, young Americans living on the Côte d'Azur in the 1920s, and their relationship with a woman called Marita, whom they pick up in a café in Cannes and bring back to live with them.

Strictly speaking, it is Catherine who picks her up. Catherine is the book's most transgressive figure, a "girl" who is also a "boy"—and who wants to be the "boy" in bed. "Her hair was cropped as short as a boy's. It was cut with no compromises." " 'You see,' she said. 'That's the surprise. I'm a girl. But now I'm a boy too and I can do anything and anything and anything.' "[67] In bed with David before Marita enters the picture, she makes love to him:

> He lay there and felt something and then her hand holding him and searching lower and he helped with his hands and then lay back in the dark and did not think at all and only felt the weight of the strangeness inside and she said, "Now you can't tell who is who can you?"
>
> "You're Catherine."
>
> "No, I'm Peter. You're my wonderful Catherine. You're my beautiful lovely Catherine. You were so good to change. Oh thank you, Catherine, so much. Please understand. Please know and understand. I'm going to make love to you forever."[68]

David, a writer, finds himself both excited and terrified by this role reversal, by the physical fact of being taken.

> During the night he had felt her hands touching him. And when he woke it was in the moonlight and she had made the dark magic of the change again and he did not say no when she spoke to him and asked the questions and he felt the change so that it hurt him all through and when it was finished after they were both exhausted she was shaking and she whispered to him, "Now we have done it. Now we have really done it."
>
> Yes, he thought. Now we have really done it.

"Don't worry, David. I'm your good girl come back again," she tells him in the morning, pressing her breasts against his chest. "She changes from a girl into a boy and back to a girl carelessly and happily," David reflects.[69] "He thought what will become of us if things have gone this wildly and this dangerously and this fast?"[70]

The book insists upon Catherine's erotic pleasure, and shares that pleasure with the reader. The following conversations in bed all take place within two pages, and a single night:

> "Do you think it would be fun if I went back to being a boy again? It wouldn't be any trouble."
>
> "I like you the way you are now."
>
> "Should I make love this time as a girl and then do it?
>
> "You're a girl. You are a girl. You're my lovely girl Catherine."
>
> "Now can I be a boy again?"
>
> "Why?"

"Just for a little while."

"Why?"

"I loved it and I don't miss it but I'd like to be again in bed at night if it isn't bad for you. Can I be again? If it's not bad for you?"

"I'll only be a boy at night and won't embarrass you. Don't worry about it please." [she says]

"All right, boy."

"I lied when I said I didn't have to."

"Now you change [she says]. Please. Don't make me change you. Must I? All right I will. You're changed now. You are. You did it too. I did it to you but you did it. Yes you did. You're my sweet dearest darling Catherine. You're my sweet my lovely Catherine. You're my girl my dearest only girl. Oh thank you thank you my girl—"[71]

David and Catherine have just been married. They wear the same clothes —unisex striped pullovers and shorts—and, at Catherine's insistence, have the same haircut, a boy's high crop, artificially lightened. David's anxiety is fueled by lack of difference (he'd like his hair shorter than hers; he doesn't want to kiss her "if you're a boy and I'm a boy")[72] and by something that might even be called defensive masculinity or homophobia, were not those terms so leaden and the book so exquisitely deft. David: "We can't be the same." Catherine: "Yes we could if you'd let us." David: "I really don't want to do it."[73] He is afraid he will disappear. "In the night it was very dark."

"David?"

"Yes."

"How are you girl?"

"I'm fine."

"Let me feel your hair girl . . . It's cut so full and has so much body and it's the same as mine. Let me kiss you girl. Oh you have lovely lips. Shut your eyes girl. . . . Just be my girl and love me the way I love you."[74]

Remember that the speaker here is Catherine, the "girl" is David. (Remember, too, that this is a novel by Ernest Hemingway.) It is time for the entry of the third "girl," Marita, who admires Catherine's boyish haircut and slacks. "Look who I brought to see you," says Catherine. Marita has had her hair cut, too. "Whose girl is she?" asks David. "Don't be rough. She's nobody's." "Tell me straight." "All right. She's in love with us both unless I'm crazy." "You're not crazy." "Not yet maybe."[75] By the novel's end Catherine *will* be crazy, and will have destroyed out of jealousy the only drafts of David's stories—the final and unforgiveable transgression.

"I love you," says Marita. "You don't fall in love with two people at once," David replies. But is it true? Whose girl *is* she? Catherine picks her up, and seems to want to give her to David. "She's your girl and I'm your girl." "How can you lose with two girls?" she tells him.[76] But Marita's ideas are a little different. "I'm going to be Catherine's too."

> "I don't go in for girls," Catherine said. It was very quiet and her voice did not sound right either to herself or to David.
> "Don't you ever?"
> "I never have."
> "I can be your girl, if you ever want one, and David's too."[77]

Soon Catherine and Marita are kissing in the car ride back from Nice, with intensely pleasurable results ("I said I couldn't drive if she did that so we stopped. I only kissed her but I know it happened with me")[78] and the threesome is established: "You kiss her too," says Catherine to David, and, somewhat to his surprise, he does. Marita moves into a room down the hall, to which both Catherine and David pay visits, though not without ambivalence. "Catherine feels terribly," says Marita. "Please be kind to her." "The hell with both of you," David says.[79]

Catherine tells David that it's just a phase. "I know I'll get over it as well as I know anything. . . . I couldn't stand it if you went away. I don't want to be with her. It's only something that I have to do. . . . Ever since I went to school all I ever had was chances to do it and people wanting to do it with me. And I never would and never did. But now I have to." David says nothing. "Anyway she's in love with you and you can have her and wash everything away that way."[80]

Now, Hemingway's novel, as erotically well imagined as it is, does not escape from all the clichés of straight male fascination with lesbian sex. Though *The Garden of Eden* begins with Catherine, its center of gravity quickly shifts over to David, the gifted American expatriate writer. The significance of the book's title kicks in, with Catherine quite explicitly cast in the part of Lilith, Adam's legendary first wife, who was created at the same time as her husband and refused to be considered his inferior; David's nickname for Catherine is "Devil," she grows progressively "darker" through an obsession with sunbathing, and she is finally, like her mythic predecessor, expelled from Eden. Marita, whose nickname is "Heiress," inherits the husband—and the world.

When Catherine goes crazy and burns David's manuscripts, then flees up the coast to Biarritz, Marita falls in love with David ("No matter what I'm always your girl. Your good girl who loves you").[81] David thus is able to replace his out-of-control first wife with a sexy but finally quite tame and uxorious second wife, only lacking the proper documents to make it official ("Are we the Bournes?" "Sure. We're the Bournes. It may take a while to have the papers. But that's what we are. Do you want me to write it out?")[82] Even the respectable French hotelkeeper's wife prefers Marita, making up the bed in her room for two the moment Catherine takes off for good.

David is thus established as both victim and victor of the erotic triangle. "He did not have to examine his conscience to know that he loved Catherine nor that it was wrong to love two women and that no good could ever come of it. He did not yet know how terrible it could be. He only knew that it had started."[83]

The triangle itself has, so to speak, been tilted on its side: Where once Catherine was at its apex, as seducer and sexual magnet, David comes in the course of the novel swiftly to replace her, and in so doing to replace an outlaw eroticism with an in-law one, a queer relationship that is increasingly, if doubly, straight. Yet plainly much of the excitement comes from erotic jealousy, competition, and mimetic desire. Catherine drinks too much at lunch and Marita puts her (or takes her?) to bed; David is told not to come in till she's asleep. When he does he finds her awake and eager to make love.

Does anyone feel guilty? "Everybody is happy now," Catherine says once she's confessed kissing Marita, and invited David to kiss her, too. "We've shared all the guilt."[84] David reflects that "it was wrong to love two women" but decides to ride it out. "We're going to take turns," Catherine says. "You're mine today and tomorrow. And you're Marita's the next two days. My God, I'm hungry. This is the first time I've been hungry in a week."[85]

The pleasure in sexual role-playing and role reversal in *The Garden of Eden* is not new. In another late novel by Hemingway, *Islands in the Stream,* a husband fantasizes the same kind of play with his wife, and again she is the initiator:

> "Should I be you or you be me?"
> "You have first choice."
> "I'll be you."
> "I can't be you. But I'll try."[86]

The addition of the bisexual element to the plot of *The Garden of Eden* allows for a freer play of eroticism among three persons, and also strategically positions the husband as dominant even when he is the passive partner, since, after the first provocative moments of lesbian passion, it is David Bourne and not Catherine (or even Marita) who becomes the object of competition and desire.

Many of the details of *The Garden of Eden* correspond to facts and fantasies in Hemingway's own life. His mother dressed him and his sister Marcelline as twins of the same sex. At the age of three at Christmastime the young Ernest worried that Santa Claus might not know that he was a boy.[87] Some childhood photos show him in girlish clothes with very short hair, others in boys' clothes with hair of a length more usual for girls. Next to a photograph of Ernest in a flowery hat and ankle-length gown his mother wrote "summer girl." She noted that "the two big children [Ernest and Marcelline] were then always dressed alike, like two little girls."[88]

In "The Last Good Country," one of the Nick Adams stories, Nick's sister cuts her hair short with a scissors: "It's very exciting," she says. "Now I'm your sister but I'm a boy."[89] In *A Farewell to Arms,* Catherine Barkeley wants to cut her hair short and urges Frederic Henry to let his hair grow, so that they will be "just alike." "Oh darling, I want you so much I want to be you too." "You are. We're the same one," he replies.[90]

Much later Hemingway would write in his diary about his fourth wife, Mary:

> She has always wanted to be a boy and thinks as a boy without ever losing any femininity. If you should become confused on this you should retire. She loves me to be her girls [*sic*], which I love to be, not being absolutely stupid. . . . In return she makes me awards and at night we do every sort of thing which pleases her and which pleases me. . . . Mary has never had one lesbian impulse but has always wanted to be a boy. Since I have never cared for any man and dislike any tactile contact with men . . . I loved feeling the embrace of Mary which came to me as something quite new and outside all tribal law.[91]

The diary entry insists on keeping identification distinct from desire. Mary Hemingway wants to be a boy but retains all her femininity. Hemingway himself loves to be her girl. Mary is, he wants to stress, definitely not a lesbian, as he himself is definitely not homosexual. It's just that they like playing sex games that make gender and/or gendered sex play (penetration? top and bottom roles?) things that are up for grabs.

I can't help wondering: Are the "awards" that Mary gives him rewards —or Oscars?

Chapter 22

Vice Verses

"Can you explain," I asked my colleague, "how you have so completely
expunged a line in a poem that you claim you know so well?"

—*Sigmund Freud*, The Psychopathology of Everyday Life [1]

The great poet, in writing himself, writes his time.

—*T. S. Eliot, "Shakespeare and the Stoicism of Seneca"*

In Hemingway's short story "The Sea Change," a young man and a young
woman meet in a Paris café to discuss the fact that she has taken another
woman as her lover. The story, superbly economical and pointed in itself,
is also a sketch for *The Garden of Eden.*

"If it was a man—" he says.

"Don't say that. It wouldn't be a man. You know that. Don't you trust
me?" she asks.

He replies by quoting, with earnest inexactitude and the manifest rem-
nants of an expensive Ivy League education, a fragment of Alexander
Pope's *Essay on Man:*

"Vice is a monster of such fearful mien," the young man said
bitterly, "that to be something or other needs but to be seen. Then
we something, something, then embrace." He could not remember
the words. "I can't quote," he said.

"Let's not say vice," she said. "That's not very polite."

"Perversion," he said. [2]

"I'd like it better if you didn't use words like that," the woman says.
"There's no necessity to use a word like that." "What do you want me to
call it?" "You don't have to call it. You don't have to put any name to it."
"That's the name for it."

If "vice" is not nice, then "perverse" may be nicer. This change of label, which we might call vice-perversa, shifts the register from morality to normality, from the ethical or religious to the psychological or psychoanalytic. But as Jonathan Dollimore has pointed out, "the real conservative is the pervert." One does not so much "become a pervert" as remain one, despite attempts to sublimate, repress, or deny desires. "It is sexual perversion, not sexual 'normality,' which is the given in human nature."[3] As, indeed, the remainder of Hemingway's story, and its history, will suggest.

Much of this short story is in dialogue—the mood is as much Dorothy Parker (or J. D. Salinger) as Hemingway. The question arises as to whether the woman is going away for good. "I'll come back. I told you I'd come back. I'll come back right away." After a brief moment of resistance ("No, you won't. Not to me.") he agrees: "That's the hell of it, you probably will." "Go on, then."

> "Go on," his voice sounded strange to him.
> "And when you come back tell me all about it." His voice sounded very strange.

The erotic frisson of the "strange" becomes the overriding emotion of the scene. The "girl," as Hemingway describes her throughout, leaves quickly, and the man senses himself to be "a different man," a "different-looking man," "quite a different man" from the person he was before he told her to go.

"Vice," he remarks to the barman, contemplating his own image in the glass door and the mirror behind the bar, "is a very strange thing, James."

"Strange," like "different," appears three times at the end of this very short story, describing the man's distinctive response to his own emotional state. "Strange" echoes as well, if only half-audibly, in the glancing Shakespearean allusion of the title, "a sea change / Into something rich and strange." The experience of "vice," however first blocked or resisted ("'then we something, something, then embrace.' He could not remember the words") is itself exciting, even transforming, in a complicated Dorian Gray kind of way.

> The young man saw himself in the mirror behind the bar. "I said I was a different man, James," he said. Looking into the mirror he saw that this was quite true.
> "You look very well sir," James said. "You must have had a very good summer."[4]

Late in his life Hemingway told Edmund Wilson that he had written "The Sea Change" as a result of a three-hour conversation with Gertrude

Stein about lesbian sex. "I was so sold on her theory that I went out that night and fucked a lesbian with magnificent result," he wrote to Wilson, adding with satisfaction, "we slept well afterwards."[5] At other times he claimed to have overheard a conversation between a couple at a bar on the Riviera—"and I knew the story too too well."[6] Authors' memories of these primal scenes of inspiration are notably unreliable, and Hemingway's tales of origin often seem more than ordinarily suspect—he was a great embellisher. But if the anecdote about Gertrude Stein is true, or even if it's something Hemingway concocted to share with Wilson, it suggests the familiar sexiness of the lesbian pair for the proudly "heterosexual" male onlooker.

Whatever Hemingway's feelings about tactile contact with men, he was fascinated by lesbians, and he had lively and sometimes contestatory relations in the free-wheeling Paris of the twenties not only with Gertrude Stein and Alice B. Toklas but also with Sylvia Beach and Adrienne Monnier, Bryher, Djuna Barnes, and the doyenne of Paris lesbian life, the beautiful and extravagant Natalie Barney. The name of his impotent hero in *The Sun Also Rises,* Jake Barnes, was in part an inside joke, a play on the names of Djuna Barnes and the rue Jacob where Natalie Barney held her famous salons.[7] Lady Brett Ashley in that novel is another elusive, powerful, and dominating close-cropped woman, a sexually powerful precursor of the Catherine of *The Garden of Eden.* Catherine's willful manuscript burning also corresponds to an incident in Hemingway's life, when his first wife, Hadley, packed the manuscripts, typescripts, and carbon copies of all the writing he had done in Europe in a single valise that was then promptly stolen from her train compartment. He couldn't believe she had packed even the carbons. "Hadley had made the job complete," he wrote bitterly to Ezra Pound.[8] Hadley herself was devastated. Pound and Lincoln Steffens each advised Hemingway, with what Pound acknowledged to be "cold comfort," to try to write the stories over again, as David Bourne ultimately succeeds in doing.[9]

In the novel, it indeed becomes clear, Catherine's jealousy is not about David's sex life but about his writing, which bores her and which Marita likes to read. "Has he ever shown you his [press] clippings, Heiress?" she asks Marita. "I think he reads them by himself and is unfaithful to me with them."[10] The ultimate catastrophe, the writer's ultimate nightmare, the burning of the stories, is a nightmare from which David is permitted to awake by remembering them verbatim once his new "marriage" is in place. "Not a sentence was missing and there were many that he put down as they were returned to him without changing them. . . . He wrote on a while longer now and there was no sign that any of it would ever cease returning to him intact."[11]

So a novel that seems to be about the erotic pleasures of bisexuality turns out to be about the high calling of the writer.

But what happens when the most canonical English writer of them all turns out to be bisexual?

Over the Top

You're the top!
You're the Colosseum.
You're the top!
You're the Louvre Museum.
You're a melody from a symphony by Strauss,
You're a Bendel bonnet,
A Shakespeare sonnet,
You're Mickey Mouse.

—*Cole Porter*

Two things seem clear: first, that the narrative of Shakespeare's sonnets is bisexual, and second, that scholars have gone to considerable lengths to avoid naming them as such. After centuries in which the big question was whether or not the sonnets could be read, or had to be read, as homosexual (or, to use the more appropriate terms for the period, "sodomitical" or even "pederastic") we are still dancing around the question of "bisexuality" in a sequence of poems that seems unmistakably to describe the speaker's passionate involvement and erotic feelings about both a "fair youth" and a "dark lady." Why? What does this avoidance have to do with the centrality of bisexual feelings, attractions, and behavior in human sexuality?

"William Shakespeare was almost certainly homosexual, bisexual, or heterosexual. The sonnets provide no evidence on the matter." So scholar Stephen Booth blithely declares in an appendix to his edition of the sonnets—an appendix titled, with equal authorial insouciance, "Facts and Theories About Shakespeare's Sonnets." Is Shakespeare's sexuality a fact or a theory?

Despite Booth's pretended (or real) agnosticism about his poet's sexual inclinations and practices, and despite the fact that he remands this question to the last few small-type pages of a very long and weighty edition, rather than addressing the question, as hypothetically he might, in the preface that begins the book, the matter of whether Shakespeare was homosexual, bisexual, or heterosexual has been the besetting conundrum among lay readers at least since the time of Oscar Wilde. "With this key Shakespeare unlocked his heart," the poet William Wordsworth wrote of the sonnets, to which Robert Browning replied curtly, "If so, the less Shakespeare he."

◆

The "plot" of the 154 sonnets as we now arrange and read them begins with the poetic speaker addressing the "fair youth." Sonnets 1 through 17 and the much-debated sonnet 20 ("A woman's face with Nature's own hand painted / Hast thou, the master-mistress of my passion") praise his beauty and urge him to marry and have children. Sonnets 1 to 126 are all written to the young man, and contain poetry that has often been described as homoerotic and seems at least to a modern sensibility to be so unequivocally. Puns on "prick" and "will" (both the poet's name and a slang term for male and female sexual organs) have excited critics' attention and sometimes their censure.

Later in the sequence a "Dark Lady" appears, and stirs the poet's desire. It appears from the narrative of the sonnet sequence that the young man and the Dark Lady become sexually involved with one another, so that an erotic triangle develops. In several sonnets, notably 129, which begins "Th' expense of spirit in a waste of shame / Is lust in action," the heterosexual relationship with the lady is described in terms that are passionate, painful, and far from idealizing. Sonnet 144, "Two loves I have of comfort and despair" sets out the two points of the triangle ("The better angel is a man right fair, / The worser spirit a woman color'd ill"), but as early as sonnet 42 the triangular tension is present:

> *That thou hast her, it is not all my grief,*
> *And yet it may be said I lov'd her dearly;*
> *That she hath thee is of my wailing chief,*
> *A loss in love that touches me more nearly.*

The "plot" (for we can only call it so inferentially, despite many scholars' desire to read the sequence like a novel) also includes a rival poet who himself admires and writes about the fair youth. So there are *two* rivals, and two triangles, one ostensibly concerned with poetry and the other with sexuality. As for the fair youth, who figures in both, he is thought by various commentators to be Shakespeare's patron, or a noble friend, or, as we will see, even, less convincingly, a boy player in his company. The initials W.H. from the sonnets' dedication ("To the Onlie Begetter of These Insuing Sonnets Mr. W.H.") might, it has been suggested, stand for William Herbert, third Earl of Pembroke, or (transposed) for Henry Wriothesley, third Earl of Southampton (or, in Oscar Wilde's fictional account, for the invented boy player, "Willie Hughes").

Editor Booth complains that "on grounds of its vocabulary—though not of its final statement," sonnet 20, the "master-mistress" sonnet, "has been carelessly cited as evidence of its author's homosexuality,"[12] and directs the reader of his edition to a long discussion on the meaning of "lover" and "love" throughout the sonnets, stressing that "lover" was a "sexually neutral" term. It is "logical and just," he maintains, to "take the abundant examples of the word 'lover' used without suggesting 'paramour' as evidence against automatically assuming Shakespeare is talking about a real or imaginary homosexual relationship," though it is "logical but foolish" to insist that "lover" *has* to mean only "friend" when the context seems clearly amatory.[13] Hallett Smith in the *Riverside* edition is, if possible, even more definitive: "The attitude of the poet toward the friend is one of love and admiration, deference and possessiveness, but it is not at all a sexual passion. Sonnet 20 makes quite clear the difference between the platonic love of a man for a man, more often expressed in the sixteenth century than the twentieth, and any kind of homosexual attachment."[14] Booth's edition was published in 1977, the *Riverside Shakespeare* in 1974.

Very much earlier in the history of the sonnets' reception, however, editors alarmed at the idea that "Shakespeare, a husband, a father, a moral man, addressed a hundred and twenty-six *Amorous* Sonnets to a *male* object!"[15] arranged the sequence in a way that obscured the gender of the "boy" and "friend" to whom they were, ostensibly, written. The standard edition of the *Sonnets* until Edmond Malone's 1780 text was that of John Benson, who changed the order, gave titles to individual sonnets, and altered some pronouns to make the beloved seem to be female rather than male. Malone's crucial and defining edition, which still governs editorial choices today, restored the sequence and in so doing disclosed the "potential sodomite"[16] behind them.

Immediately lines of defense began to be drawn. It was contended that the rhetoric of male-male friendship in the Renaissance used love terms to describe what were really nonsexual relationships (the fabled "platonic love," without the Plato); that the young man in the sonnets was Shakespeare's patron, therefore not a sexual love object; that the sonnets were really replies to other poets' sonnets, so that any innovations, like changing the gender of the beloved, were really just raising the ante or trumping the other guy's ace, a matter of literary competition or invention rather than of biography; and that there was no revealing original sequence at all, but rather, as Benson had claimed, just a random group of poems that could be put together in any order.

Malone was the first editor to suggest that the "beloved" of the sonnets was male. His edition of 1821, which included these criticisms in a commentary by John Boswell, Jr., affixed to the poems and plays, introduced the dramatis personae of the Shakespeare sonnet sequence as we know it today: the poet, the young man, the rival poet, and the dark lady.

The outcry against the idea of a "homosexual," pederastic, or sodomitical Shakespeare was motivated at least in part by patriotism and national pride. The universal Bard, the spirit of the age and "all time," could not have been a homosexual—could he? One eighteenth-century scholar suggested, in two long and lengthy volumes, that Queen Elizabeth herself was the patron and beloved.[17] (Other scholars have since proposed that the Virgin Queen was a man.) Commentator George Steevens regretted the wordplay around "prick" in sonnet 20: "It is impossible to read this fulsome panegyrick, addressed to a male object, without an equal measure of disgust and indignation."[18] Malone responded with an opinion that has become canonical: "[S]uch addresses to men, however indelicate, were customary in our author's time, and neither imported criminality nor were esteemed indecorous."

By the early nineteenth century the reaction had set in with a vengeance. The poet Coleridge, writing in his journal to his infant son Hartley on the date of his christening, assures him "how impossible it was for a Shake-speare not to have been in his heart's heart chaste." The troublesome twentieth sonnet, which addresses the beloved as "the master-mistress of my passion"—a term explained away with uncommon ingenuity by numerous critics from Malone on—is likewise, despite any evidence to the contrary, devoid of "desire against nature"—"its possibility seems never to have entered even his imagination."[19]

Later Coleridge would reassert his position even more strongly: "It seems to me that the sonnets could only have come from a man deeply in love, and in love with a woman; and there is one sonnet which, from its incongruity, I take to be a purposed blind."[20] The "one sonnet," again, was the notorious twentieth. Coleridge, whose friendship with William Wordsworth was so close that it has itself been described as "homo-erotic,"[21] thus went out of his way to establish Shakespeare as heterosex-ual—that is, as definitively *not homosexual.* The "master-mistress" sonnet was merely a feint, a "purposed blind," the exception that proved the rule.

Others felt called upon to make the same emphatic declaration, again circling around the twentieth sonnet with fastidious unease. Either they wished Shakespeare "had never written" the sonnets[22] or they were con-vinced, volubly and elaborately convinced, that the sonnets could not mean what they seemed to say. The allegation "that Shakespeare was perverse in his morals," a "subversive mis-statement" that permitted "per-verse persons to cite Shakespeare as their exemplar,"[23] was based, it was claimed, on misreading. "The master-mistress of my passion" thus meant not "the man I am in love with and desire" but "the person about whom I am writing my poem." If Shakespeare was, to use Ralph Waldo Emerson's phrase, a "representative man," the exemplar of "the poet," and the para-mount source of national cultural pride, he could not—could he?—be homosexual.

So much for the heterosexual Shakespeare, a back-formation, as Peter Stallybrass rightly points out, from the intolerable threat of a homosexual or sodomical Shakespeare. But the latter had, of course, his own parti-sans, of which Oscar Wilde was the most influential and the chief. When Wilde published his "Portrait of Mr. W.H." (1889), a short story in which the "effeminate" Cyril Graham, himself always cast in girls' parts in plays, discovers that "the true secret of Shakespeare's Sonnets" was that they were written to the boy actor "Willie Hughes," his enemies gloated. In a lifetime of deliberately calculated offenses Wilde had finally done the one unpardonable thing: he had maligned the name of Shakespeare.

Frank Harris, Wilde's friend and biographer, "as heterosexual as a man can be"[24] according to Richard Ellmann, tried to discourage Wilde from writing up his theory of Shakespeare's attraction to boys, "because he could see Shakespeare only in his own, womanizing image." However accurate this is as a portrait of the randy Harris, it typified one reaction to the claim that Shakespeare could be a lover of boys. Samuel Butler's 1899 edition of the sonnets observed that no one seriously interested in "such a man as Shakespeare ... can even begin to read the Sonnets without finding that a story of some sort is staring them in the face." Butler, a noted satirist, Homeric scholar, and translator, the author of *The Way of All Flesh* and of *Erewhon* as well as an amateur biologist who offered some telling critiques of Darwin, was thus proposed in his *Shakespeare's Sonnets Reconsidered* (1899) a revised sequence and a frank appraisal.

"There the sonnets are; there is no suppressing them; they are being studied yearly more and more, and will continue to do so, in spite ... of the strongest act of parliament that can be framed to prevent people from reading them. Therefore they should be faced for better or worse. . . . And furthermore, what we think of Shakespeare himself must depend not a little on what we think of the Sonnets."[25]

What he called "Shakespeare's grave indiscretion" was, he thought, a fault of youth and boisterous times. ("Mr. W.H. must have lured him on— as we have Shakespeare's word for it that he lured him on still more disastrously later. It goes without saying that Shakespeare should not have let himself be lured, but the age was what it was, and I shall show that Shakespeare was very young.")[26] In any case, Butler is in a magnanimous mood, "considering the perfect sanity of his later work" and "the fact that the common heart, brain, and conscience of mankind holds him foremost among all Englishmen as the crowning glory of our race": *"Tout savoir, c'est tout comprendre*—and in this case surely we may add—*tout pardonner."*[27]

But this is not quite Butler's last word on the subject—indeed, as distasteful as it is, it might be said that he cannot bring himself to leave the question alone. Introducing his edition, which will present a sequence of sonnets reordered to tell the story Butler thinks must be there, he adds this final reflection, comparing Shakespeare's sonnets to the *Iliad* of Homer:

"One word more. Fresh from the study of the other great work in which the love that passeth the love of women is portrayed as nowhere else save in the Sonnets, I cannot but be struck with the fact that it is in the two greatest of all poets that we find this subject treated with the greatest intensity of feeling. The marvel, however, is this, that whereas the love of Achilles for Patroclus depicted by the Greek poet is purely English, absolutely without taint or alloy of any kind, the love of the English poet for

Mr. W.H. was, though only for a short time, more Greek than English. I cannot explain this.

"And now, at last, let the Sonnets speak for themselves."[28] Which in fact they are not quite permitted to do, since they are presented in Butler's revised and jimmied order. Butler himself, a brilliant and imaginative writer in many respects, was not shy about proposing bold hypotheses: His *The Authoress of the Odyssey* (1897) defends the proposition that the *Odyssey* was written by a woman. "Those who pass the riddle of the Sonnets over in silence," he concluded, "tacitly convey an impression that the answer would be far more terrible than the facts would show."[29] Shakespeare was an essentially moral and virtuous man who had made a youthful and passionate mistake. "Let us, then, face the truth, the whole truth, but let not either speech or silence suggest, as is now commonly done, a great deal more than the truth concerning him."[30]

Half a century later W. H. Auden, of all people, put down the efforts of the hypothetical "homosexual reader" who was "determined to secure our Top-Bard as a patron saint of the Homintern" and thus to ignore both the "unequivocally sexual" sonnets to the Dark Lady and the fact that Shakespeare was "a married man and a father."[31] Since Auden wrote these words in an introduction to the popular Signet edition of the sonnets, used by thousands of college students since its publication in 1964, the line was drawn, the more so since the author of these words was himself well known as a homosexual. Yet as Joseph Pequigney notes, Auden seems to have taken the opposite view in his private conversations. Composer Robert Craft describes in his memoirs an evening spent at the home of Igor Stravinsky and his wife, in which Auden purportedly said, in words very similar to those he used in the Signet, that "it won't do just yet to admit that the top Bard was in the homintern."[32] ("Homintern," for the information of post–Cold War readers, is a term modeled on the Soviet "Comintern"—in Auden's usage a wry acknowledgment that some people believed in an international homosexual conspiracy.) The issue was the same, whether Auden in fact counted himself on the yes or no side: To say publicly that Shakespeare was, or might have been, homosexual—had, or might have had, male lovers—was dangerous in 1964. The "top Bard" had to be above rebuke, which meant that he had to be heterosexual.

Words like homosexual and heterosexual, as we have noted, are anachronistic when used to describe sixteenth-century relationships. Not only the terms but the implications of exclusivity or preference are, strictly speaking, inappropriate for the period. Alan Bray, whose *Homosexuality in Renaissance England* (1982) remains the starting-point for many scholars' investigations of same-sex eroticism in the period, notes the official blindness to such relationships when they didn't interfere with governing agencies. "So long as homosexuality was expressed through established social institutions, in normal times the courts were not concerned with it; and generally this meant patriarchal institutions—the household, the educational system, homosexual prostitution and the like. . . . So long as homosexual activity did not disturb the peace or the social order, and in particular so long as it was consistent with patriarchal mores, it was largely in practice ignored."[33] As Bray points out, "this was not tolerance," but rather "a reluctance to recognize homosexual behaviour" and to associate it firmly with what was regarded as "the fearful sin of sodomy."[34]

The result for the individual was an incentive *not* to identify his (or her) sexual encounters with what we would today call a "sexuality," "sexual orientation," or "sexual preference." The policy of official indifference "made it possible for the individual to avoid the psychological problems of a homosexual relationship or a homosexual encounter, by keeping the experience merely casual and undefined,"[35] writes Bray. And, we might add, nonexclusive. For apparently many, or even most, early-modern "homosexuals" were "bisexuals." G. S. Rousseau describes what he regards as a shift at the end of the seventeenth century "from the old-style bisexual sodomite who held a male on one arm and female on the other while kissing both, to the new-style sodomite who was exclusively homocentric and male oriented."[36]

Yet seldom does the word "bisexual" appear in current analyses of Shakespeare's sonnets, and this, I think, has less to do with fidelity to the cultural and historical circumstances of their composition than it does with the role the sonnets have come to play in today's discourse of gay sexuality.

As so often, the questions being asked by scholars have, in a way, as much to do with their own time as with Shakespeare's. Recent readers have been less skittish than some of their predecessors and, increasingly, more interested in the homoeroticism of the sonnets, partly for political or "identity politics" reasons.

Shakespeare, in short, or at least the Shakespeare of the sonnets, has become in some quarters a gay author. The sonnets are seen to make visible patterns of "male homosexual discourse," and to do so, precisely, in the authoritative voice of the "top Bard." One of the strongest modern readings of the sonnets is one that elects to use them "to illustrate, in a simplified because synchronic and ahistorical form . . . some of the patterns traced by male homosocial desire" in a way that will frame more extended discussions of male-male relations in later fiction. Why choose the sonnets to explore this question? Because they have been "populariz[ed] as homosexual documents" by artists like Wilde, Gide, and Pasolini. And their "popularization" is to no small degree made possible by the fact that they are written by Shakespeare.

◆

The identification of the speaker of the sonnets as a man in love with a man, who describes in the course of the sequence the sexual relationship between them and its physical consummation, has gradually gained currency, at least in certain circles, in our own century. Joseph Pequigney's *Such Is My Love,* published in 1985, broke new ground in declaring, firmly and unapologetically, his intention to "prove that the poet carnally enjoys him as well as her, and uncover a sexual basis for the rivalry with the second poet."[37] Bruce Smith, in *Homosexual Desire in Shakespeare's England,* is less interested in the question of consummation than in the relationship between male bonding and homosexual desire: "[W]hat is important is not whether particular poems and particular passages 'prove' that Shakespeare the man did or did not have sexual relations with a certain other man but how the sonnets as poems insinuate sexual feeling in the bonds men in general made with one another in early modern England."[38]

The acute and perceptive Jonathan Goldberg is typically frank (it is tempting to say that "he comes out swinging," although this would give quite a wrong impression), dismissing Pequigney's book as offering "banalizing and dehistoricized . . . readings . . . of what it calls homosexuality in the sonnets," though he praises him for not shirking the fact that they are concerned with sexuality at all, and excoriating the "formidable" Joel Fineman for reading the sonnets as about the "invention" of heterosexuality "in terms of invidious distinction between a narcissistic homosexuality and a misogynistic heterosexuality that is claimed at least to recognize alterity."[39] Smith describes Fineman's argument less gnomically but to the same point: "Shakespeare uses the *rhetoric* of Platonizing homosexual desire to create a thoroughly heterosexual subjectivity."[40]

Although modern literary scholars often insist that they are avoiding "ahistorical, Platonic form[s]" in favor of nuanced "relationships of power and meaning,"[41] the tidal pull of Shakespeare's sonnets, like the equally strong force of his plays, has been to compel a presentist reading, inadvertently following Ben Jonson's prescient memorial claim that Shakespeare was "not of an age but for all time."

In a bow to the "ahistorical" and Platonic she elsewhere critiques, gay studies pioneer and novel critic Eve Kosofsky Sedgwick begins her analysis of eighteenth- and nineteenth-century English literature with what she elects to call a "deracinated" reading (that is, one displaced from its accustomed environment, literally, "uprooted" or "pulled up by the roots") of Shakespeare's *Sonnets,* arguably the locus classicus of the erotic triangle in all of English literature.

Despite her animadversions about ahistorical reading in Girard,[42] Sedgwick opts for a "dehistoricizing context" and a "simplified because synchronic and ahistorical form" in which to illustrate, through the sonnets, "some of the patterns traced by male homosocial desire."[43] She reads the sonnets as a story: "a relatively continuous erotic narrative" involving four characters—the poet, a fair youth, a rival poet, and a dark lady. Acknowledging, perhaps with a modernist's excessive confidence in the archival murkiness (or at least the murky archives) of the past, the "irrecoverable" nature of "the sexual context of that period," she sees that the early sonnets in which the poet addresses a young man and urges him to marry while professing his own love for him are "heterosexual" in that they socialize the youth toward marriage, procreation, and carrying on his family name. To urge him to marry and to have children is not to deny the speaker's own love for him. "Mine be thy love, and thy love's use their treasure," or, as Sedgwick paraphrases, "you can have women and *still* keep loving me."

In terms of institutions like marriage, the family, and so on (what Sedgwick calls "a structure of institutionalized social relations"), it makes a certain paradoxical sense that the fair youth sonnets should be thus categorized as "heterosexual." But it is nonetheless striking that she never calls them bisexual, despite the sentiment "you can have women and *still* keep loving me."

As for the last group of sonnets, in which the speaker expresses tormented jealousy because of the fair youth's involvement with his mistress, here the erotic triangle shows the speaker "plunging into heterosexual adventure with an eye to confirming his identification with other men" and exhibiting "a desire to consolidate partnership with authoritative males in and through the bodies of females."[44] Sedgwick does not paraphrase this as "you can have *men* and still keep loving me." She does, however, maintain that it is "less radically threatening" to "have contact with other men through a rivalry with a male beloved"[45] than to do so in a triangular relationship that includes a woman.

Where is bisexuality in this nuanced account? The word appears only in a citation from G. Wilson Knight that refers to an idealization of androgyny and in the evocation of the *shaman* or person "halfway between" male and female, both images it is relatively easy for Sedgwick to set aside as not pertinent to her reading. Yet bisexuality in the strong sense of the term, as a description of a desiring sensibility that includes both (some) men and (some) women, though it is weighted with important differences between men and women, straights and gays, suggests the possibility of another kind of reading, what could be called a postmodern reading but also—and this is *not* paradoxical, I would claim—an early modern reading, one that is cumulative and even episodic rather than continuous and given.

Bisexuality, the radically *discontinuous* possibility of a sexual "identity" that confounds the very category of identity, in which sexual passion elects its subjects and objects across these defining (and self-defining) boundaries, can find its authorization in the sonnets, whose very form, continuous and discontinuous at once (closed fourteen line units, tightly rhymed, with unbridgeable spaces for interpretative fantasy between one sonnet and the next), draws a diagram of its own. The triangles, it appears, are drawn by connecting the dots. But each connection is a reader's, or editor's, own narrative supplement.

What is true for literature in general is even more true in the case of Shakespeare: that the evidence of art is appealed to as corroboration for human experience. Nowhere is this more common, or perhaps more necessary and valuable, than in decoding the mysteries of human sexuality. Late-twentieth-century readers of Shakespeare have thus often returned to history in order to claim its relevance to a newly transcendent Shakespeare, a Shakespeare who speaks to "our" concerns as pertinently as an earlier age of scholars presumed that he did for theirs. The Shakespeare of the late twentieth century grapples in his plays with questions of race, gender, and social status, and with economic history. And in both the plays and the sonnets he is increasingly seen to be aware of same-sex desire, whether or not that desire and its concomitants are thought to shed light on his own biography.

But the bisexual plot of the sonnets is still regarded as telling some other story, a story of hetero- or of homosexuality, or (washing one's hands of the whole thing) a story of "literary quality" rather than mere "curiosity about the biographical mystery."[46] The more rich and complex the discourses of sexuality become, the more the forest tends to be obscured by the trees. As Edgar Allan Poe suggested in "The Purloined Letter," the letters can be written so large on a map that the name of the continent is invisible; only the smaller print can be read. So, too, with bisexuality: It encompasses too much; it does not try to resolve contradictions but to accept them. It tells, we might say, *too* many stories, when what is so ardently desired is "the real story."

As we have seen, one modern critic wittily describes the first series of sonnets, to the young man, as "heterosexual," because they urge him to marry and have children.[47] Another cleverly characterizes the dark lady sonnets as sodomitical because they describe nonprocreative erotic practices.[48] A third claims that despite the "homosexual thematic" of the sonnets addressed to the young man, "the specific virtue of this ideal, homosexual desire is *not* to be erotic," while in the sonnets addressed to the dark lady, which evince "a desire for that which is not admired," the reader encounters "a heterosexual desire that is strikingly erotic,"[49] and concludes that "Shakespeare in his sonnets invents the poetics of heterosexuality."

Amid all of these ingenious and enlightening critical maneuverings no one wants to comment on the obvious—that the sonnets describe a bisexual triangle. No one but Joseph Pequigney, whose chapter on "the bisexual soul" builds on some passages from Freud about divided gender, and who is principally interested in validating the relationship between the speaker and the young man. The venerable G. Wilson Knight had observed in the context of the sonnets that "Poetry is itself a bisexual awareness, or action," by which he meant an almost Jungian concordance of opposites. But even he was speaking of the speaker and the fair youth ("a completed unit . . . sees its soul-state reflected in a physical embodiment of its own unity"),[50] not of the triangular relationship of speaker, youth, and dark lady.

Why avoid the obvious? *Because* it is obvious? Or because a bisexual Shakespeare fits no one's erotic agenda?

Bisexual Shakespeares

Shakespeare gives the greatest width of human passion.

—*T. S. Eliot, "Dante"*[51]

In fact, there are two versions of the "bisexual Shakespeare," only one of which has been welcomed with open arms, so to speak, by the reading public. The "good" bisexual Shakespeare is the Shakespeare of the World Soul, the Shakespeare who uncannily understands human motivations and desires, male and female, so perfectly that it seems as if he must somehow *be* both man and woman.

It was Coleridge who memorably described Shakespeare's "androgynous" mind at the beginning of the nineteenth century. "Shakespeare becomes all things, yet ever remaining himself." But it would be a mistake to view this opinion wholly as a romantic and universalizing notion from a previous century. Virginia Woolf chose to elaborate on Coleridge's phrase in *A Room of One's Own,* describing "Shakespeare's mind as the type of the androgynous, of the manly-womanly mind."[52] And French feminist and poststructuralist critic Hélène Cixous writes of "Shakespeare, who was neither man nor woman but a thousand persons" in the same essay in which she argues that "there is no invention of any other I, no poetry, no fiction without a certain homosexuality (the I/play of bisexuality)."[53]

But where Cixous may perhaps imagine her phantasmatic Shakespeare to be a sexual as well as a platonic being, many other commentators have wished to hold the Shakespeare biography at a distance, the better to enjoy his universality. Keats declared that "Shakespeare led a life of allegory; his works are the comments on it."[54] *"He hadn't any history to record,"* Mark Twain remarked with satisfaction,[55] and Emerson wondered in his *Journals,* "Is it not strange that the transcendent men, Homer, Plato, Shakespeare, confessedly unrivaled, should have questions of identity and genuineness raised respecting their writings?"[56] The less that is known of his biography, the more he becomes both Godlike and everyman.[57]

Freud offered another version of the "good" bisexual Shakespeare, the Shakespeare who saw equally into the life of men and women, when he endorsed the idea that "Shakespeare often splits a character up into two personages, which, taken separately, are not completely understandable, and do not become so until they are brought together once more into a unity."[58] His examples are Macbeth and Lady Macbeth. "Together they exhaust the possibilities of reaction to the crime, like two disunited parts of a single psychical individuality, and it may be that they are both copied from a single prototype."[59] This notion of bisexuality owes a great deal to the "two sexes in one body" idea derived from nineteenth-century science. Freud's Shakespeare draws upon his own knowledge of human nature to split one individual's response into two gendered halves.

So the "manly-womanly" Shakespeare who was "neither man nor woman" sees into the heart of things. But does he have sex?

The other bisexual Shakespeare, the Shakespeare who might, like the speaker of the sonnets, have had passionate sexual relationships with both men and women, is a less universal, and less universally welcome, figure. It is true that the bisexual Shakespeare has made sporadic appearances in popular fictionalized accounts, for example in Sidney Cunliffe-Owen's 1933 novel *The Phoenix and the Dove*. There we encounter Elizabeth Vernon, the Dark Lady, explaining the workings of destiny to her new husband, the Earl of Southampton (a marriage arranged by the Queen, who knows that her unborn child is as likely to be Shakespeare's as Southampton's):

> "He may be like you," she said, "and still not be your child. Will made himself so much a part of you. When he thought of a child, it was of your child. The idea of your child absorbed him. When he was with me, he had you in his thoughts, because I was your mistress."
>
> "Say what you like [Southampton replies sturdily], it will be my child. Before he loved you, I had come to you in such a night of passion as he could never know. He is too wise to be so wholly passionate. But in that glorious moment of our love, we created life. I am sure of that."
>
> "He would speak just as strongly if he were here [rejoins the Dark Lady]. He loved me too. He could not help it. He broke your friendship for it. No. In the body, the child will be his or yours and none of us will ever really know. But mystically the child is shared. He is the fruit of both your loves. Will's mind, your body, producing the perfect thing, through me, the instrument of your double strength. He will be what your friendship would have been, could you have possessed one another. Do you remember the sonnet of Will's to you . . . in which he called you the 'master mistress of his passion'?"
>
> Harry nodded, and she went on, speaking very earnestly. "That was the apotheosis of your love, and showed its limits. He tries to think

of you in that sonnet as a woman, because he realises that a woman is necessary to complete the perfection which he senses in you. . . .

"Will thought I had bespelled him into faithlessness to you; you think that you have fallen unwillingly into my toils; yet I have been the helpless victim of both of you, unable not to give myself to both of you in turn. . . .

"Will sucked me dry, as he sucked you dry. . . . Now he is with the Queen. . . . He is the Vampire of Souls."⁶⁰

In this remarkable novel Queen Elizabeth is described in dark ways the author will never quite spell out. He calls her "two-natured," and the inference is that she is a physical hermaphrodite. So the bisexual Shake-speare meets the hermaphrodite Queen, who offers him, in the words of the wistful Dark Lady, "the completeness of the two-fold life, which is the least so great a nature as his required. We ordinary women are content with men, and you common men are content with women; but he is a giant, and so is she."

Next to this triumph of literary solemnity, more contemporary efforts pale, though Anthony Burgess's potboiler *Shakespeare* (1970) offers the arch observation that "Will would not be shocked by evidence of homo-sexuality [among Southampton's circle]: he may have been inclined to it himself; he was, after all, a member of the theatrical profession,"⁶¹ and John Mortimer's British television series cast Tim Curry, the bisexual vam-pire heartthrob of the *Rocky Horror Picture Show,* in the title role of the Bard. In the novel version of Mortimer's biographical fantasia, described as a "witty, bawdy, irreverent look at the life Shakespeare *might* have led while he was writing his plays,"⁶² a boy actor in Shakespeare's company offers his thoughts on the playwright's sexuality:

> It is true that in one of the poems he wrote to Hal [Henry Wriothesley, Third Earl of Southampton, identified in Mortimer's novel with "Hal the Horse-thief"], Shakespeare spoke of that addition which doting nature bestowed upon his patron (whom he there called his "Master-Mistress") whereby he was defeated of the enjoyment of his beloved who, he agrees, was "prickt" out for women's pleasure. Some may think this verse closes the door on all speculation; but I, who know the stir and scandal caused when these same sonnets first became public, think this may be a verse added to silence those who might suspect that Hal, though "prickt," was not thereby placed beyond the full reach of him whose passion is therein made clear. On the other side I must agree that Shakespeare, unlike his teacher Marlowe, would rather lie with a girl or a woman if one could be had, and although he may have been bewitched by some boys, he never, by a nod, a wink, or a hand to the waist, far less to the buttock, made me

a suggestion when I was young and parted as [i.e., cast in the part of] all his Fairest ladies. This I find most strange.[63]

A photograph of Curry, the erstwhile "sweet transsexual from Transvestite Transylvania" now tricked out in a "poet shirt" and a doublet, adorns the cover of Mortimer's *Will Shakespeare*. Clearly there is some hankering after a sexy bisexual Shakespeare after all. But by and large modern Shakespeare critics have far preferred their Shakespeare to be either straight or gay, either the heir of Emerson or of Wilde. Unlike the Dark Lady of Cunliffe-Owen's novel, they would rather not share him.

Having begun this discussion of bisexual triangularity in Shakespeare's sonnets with a lyric from Cole Porter, let me end with another, noting as I do so that Porter himself, a married gay man, might be described as bisexual according to at least some definitions.[64] The Porter songs that I want to take note of here, in what some readers will surely see as a scandalously lowering juxtaposition to the "top Bard," are ones that establish a triangular structure of desire as both the nature of love and the surest way to provoke a lover's admiration. In "Ace in the Hole" from the musical *Let's Face It* (1941) a worldly wise young woman prompts her two friends on how to keep their boyfriends interested. The obvious solution: make them jealous.

> *If about some boy you're silly*
> *But he won't give in,*
> *Tell him you just talked to Lili*
> *And she's lending you Errol Flynn.*
> *If his head's as thick as mutton,*
> *And he just can't get your slant,*
> *Say you talked to Barb'ra Hutton*
> *And she's sending you Cary Grant.*

If he's "still unable" her advice is to say Carole Lombard "is sending you Gable." The point, driven home by the song's refrain, is to "always have an ace in the hole," keeping it in "some secluded but accessible place." The deliberately classed-down rhymes here (thick as mutton–Barb'ra Hutton, unable-Gable) are partly a reflection of the dramatic character who sings them, and partly an arch derogation of the competitive game of love.

An even better known Porter song, this one from *Can-Can* (1953), touts the benefits of love on the rebound.

> *It's the wrong time and the wrong place,*
> *Though your face is charming, it's the wrong face,*

518

> *It's not her face but such a charming face*
> *That it's all right with me.*

Substitution becomes a mode of seduction—and seduction a technique of substitution. The lyric goes on to stress the eroticism of loss and to express a rueful resistance to being attracted that paradoxically results in a heightened response:

> *You can't know how happy I am that we met,*
> *I'm strangely attracted to you.*
> *There's someone I'm trying so hard to forget,*
> *Don't you want to forget someone too?*

This last line, with its transferential pathos, is sheer genius—and likely to work. To call a quatrain like this "Shakespearean" will surely raise the ire and the eyebrows of many, but the intricacy and experimentation of Porter's verse-making and his zest for the odd challenge of making the old story of romantic love new often produce lyrics—and music—that seem perfectly to embody, and at the same time to go beyond, the sensation of being "in love" as his audiences understood it. Even in formalist terms there are some comparisons to be made: the deployment, in particular, of brilliant passages of feminine rhyme (a rhyme of two syllables of which the second is unstressed—as in "passion"-"fashion" and "pleasure"-"treasure"—used throughout Shakespeare's sonnet 87, pointedly in the "master-mistress" sonnet 20 with its nice history of gender and sexuality crossovers, and intermittently to telling effect in many others) is a hallmark of Porter's style, as in the verse from "You're the Top" ("Colosseum"-"Louvre Museum"; "Bendel bonnet"-"Shakespeare sonnet"). Richard Rodgers called "It's All Right With Me" his favorite Porter song, noting that "all of us in the business of writing songs are only too aware of the near impossibility of making a new approach to a love situation by means of words and music."[65]

While trying to avoid what is sometimes called "Fluellenism," after Shakespeare's comic Welshman who found unlikely but to him convincing symmetries between Alexander the Great and the young Henry V ("There is a river in Macedon, and there is also moreover a river at Monmouth . . ."),[66] I want quietly to suggest that these two men of the theater made it their business to imagine love, desire, jealousy, and loss. Indeed it was their business to do so. And if Shakespeare's "sugared sonnets among his private friends," as his contemporary Francis Meres called them, were not, like his plays, caviar for the general, still they did circulate, and circulate still, among readers whose curiosity is, inevitably, doubly directed at the "author's" life and at their own.

Renaissance scholars like Roland Greene and Nancy Vickers have argued convincingly that the sixteenth-century love sonnet was an instrument of global culture, spreading across the known world with the energies of European exploration and discovery. Vickers's meticulous discussions of modern love songs that are today dispersed with electronic ease across the boundaries of space and time, reaching literally millions of viewers and listeners, suggest that rock concerts, MTV videos, and commercials for Coke and Pepsi featuring mega–pop stars like George Michael, Madonna, and Michael Jackson use global technology to reach audiences and convey social and erotic messages in a way strikingly analogous to the dispersal of Petrarchan sonnets four hundred years ago. Petrarch in his own time was not "high culture"—nor, of course, were Shakespeare's plays, banished to the outskirts of the city, and drawing a rowdy crowd that included prostitutes and peddlers as well as aristocrats. Shakespeare's sonnets, by the time they appeared, did participate in a cultural fashion that had become popular among the elite, though his own play *Love's Labour's Lost* mocks the sonnet craze as a pastime for idle self-indulgent juveniles who don't know much about love.

"Everybody Wants You When You're Bi"

Cole Porter served the first half of the twentieth century uncommonly well as one of its principal, wittiest, and most professionally adept chroniclers of love in song. His intellectual attraction to innuendo and double meanings was doubtless increased by his participation in the world of homosexual culture and by his uncloseted but married status. The phenomenon that we have already noted in love lyrics sung by global pop stars, the capacity to shift genders and to become "bisexual" in their erotic appeal, is everywhere in his songs. From explicit commentary ("Let's praise the masculinity of Dietrich's new affinity";[67] "Georgia Sand, dressed up like a gent, / Georgia Sand, what do you represent?")[68] to droll social assessment ("I should like you all to know, / I'm a famous gigolo, / And of lavender my nature's got just a dash of it. / As I'm slightly undersexed, / You will always find me next / To some dowager who's wealthy rather than passionate")[69] he teases the boundaries of "normal" sexuality and social mores. Like his more flamboyant contemporary, Noël Coward, whose song "Mad About the Boy," written originally for four female characters to sing in praise of a beautiful male movie star, instantly became transformed (or rather decoded) into a gay cliché,[70] Porter wrote songs that spoke to several overlapping audiences at once. To say that they "passed" as straight love songs is to underestimate and underrate them.

To seek the equivalent of this witty, teasing, and deliciously evasive sexual skirmishing in our own time we will need to transpose it. For "sexual ambiguity" is not a secret in today's pop music world; rather, it is a commodity. Madonna's famous "bisexuality," George Michael's protected privacy, and the complicated story of Michael Jackson are all news. British alternative rocker Morrissey is described effusively on his appearance at a

Greenwich Village music store: "He's elusive. He's a looker. He's sexually ambiguous. And he's hot."[71]

But the intricate rhyming and sly double meanings, the stress on *language* as the place of sexual and erotic play, is as likely to surface in today's music lyrics as it is in the personalities of performers. The sexual innuendo that is part of how love and sex poetry work from medieval love lyrics ("O Western Wind") to the blues ("Banana in Your Fruit Basket," "Sam—the Hot Dog Man," "My Stove's in Good Condition," "My Pencil Won't Write No More") is alive and well in modern-day pop, rock, and rap. The very doubleness of meaning, as we have noted, is itself sexy, connoting a shared—if open—secret. And a sign of the changing times is the appearance of explicitly bisexual pop songs—not only songs that can be understood bisexually, but songs that are "about" bisexuality.

"Don't try to tell me that you're an intellectual / Because you're just another boring bisexual" taunt the Dead Milkmen in a song that mocks the pretensions of black-clad "poetic" youth. Bisexuality here is "bisexual chic," an affectation, a cultural style. "You'll dance to anything," runs the refrain, which does not mean to speak only about footwork.

Bisexuality in fact is all over the place in contemporary music. It does not have to be inferred or decoded—it is on the surface. And by being there it puts the theme of erotic jealousy and the sexual triangle in a whole new place. For jealousy works by comparison, competition, betrayal, and loss. By demystifying the triangle, and demonstrating that all of its points are desiring subjects as well as desired objects, these bisexual songs endorse "tension and passion" as the ends as well as the means of erotic play and sexual desire.

Look at the lyrics to a song called "Bi" by Living Colour, a song with the insistent and joyful (or rueful?) refrain, "Everybody wants you when you're bi."

> *There's a category if you're straight or gay,*
> *You're a wild card gambler if you like it both ways.*

the lyric declares.

> *Everybody wants you when you're bi,*
> *Looking at the girls, eyeing all the guys,*
> *Everybody loves you when you're bi,*
> *The tension and the passion is doubly amplified.*

Now the verse shifts into the realm of example, here an example with an unexpected sting:

> *My lover told me that she's bi, well, I hate that she's bi,*
> *I wanted to scream, there were tears in my eyes,*

> *She said, "Baby, baby, don't you cry,*
> *'Cause the one I'm with you've been seeing on the side."*

And again to the refrain,

> *Everybody wants you when you're bi,*
> *Feeling all the girls, touching all the guys,*
> *Everybody loves you when you're bi.*

With another example from life experience and the common wisdom of his peers,

> *Well, a friend of a friend of a friend told me,*
> *Everybody's messed up with their sexuality,*

the singer decides,

> *Well, a friend of a friend of a friend told me,*
> *I need a closet big enough to live in,*
> *I need a closet for the whole world to live in.*

and then returns to an extended version of the refrain,

> *Everybody wants you when you're bi,*
> *Loving all the girls, and loving all the guys,*
> *Everybody needs you when you're bi,*
> *And the tension and the passion's doubly amplified.*
> *Everybody wants you*
> *Everybody needs you*
> *Everybody likes you*
> *Everybody loves you*
> *Everybody, yes*
> *Everybody,*
> *Everybody,*
> *Everybody,*
> *Everybody*
> *Everybody loves you*
>
> *Bi!*
> *Licking all the girls*
> *Licking all the guys*
> *Everybody's fucked up with their sexuality*
> *They like it both ways*
> *Like it both ways,*
> *Bi!*

"Everybody wants you when you're bi." However ironic, this claim carries a certain truth; in fact, it is likely to be ironic only because it is, ironically, true. The closet big enough for the singer to live in becomes in the next line "a closet for the whole world to live in." It is not completely impertinent here to quote Donne, whose lover tells his beloved that they will "build in sonnets pretty rooms" to make their "little room / An everywhere."

Two erotic triangles are sketched in "Bi." The first is the triangle of the singer, his lover, and the "one [she's] with." No sooner does he protest her involvement with another woman ("I hate that she's bi") than it turns out he has another reason for concern: "the one I'm with you've been seeing on the side." What's the difference between heterosexual and bisexual nonmonogamy? Between principle and hypocrisy? The story, like the triangle, has (at least) three sides.

Then there is the less defined but equally notable triangle that produces common wisdom: "A friend of a friend of a friend told me / Everybody's messed up with their sexuality." Since the singer is presumably a friend of the "friend of a friend of a friend," the infinite regress suggests a series of interlocking triangles each joined at least at one point. Like the sobering medical mathematics that calculates how many people you "have sex with" every time you have sex with one person who has had sex with others, the suggestion here is ultimately that of having sex with "everybody," who, after all, "wants you," "needs you," and "loves you." Except for the phrase "wild card gambler" in the first verse there is no manifest AIDS awareness in "Bi," which is much more interested in present-tense "looking," "eyeing," "feeling," "touching," and "licking." (All of these but perhaps the last has its counterpart in sonnet language, which, as Joel Fineman has pointed out, tends to be obsessed with the "I" in "eyeing.")[72] Unlike a song like Book of Love's "Pretty Boys and Pretty Girls," widely assumed to be about bisexuality, in which despite his bisexual erotic dreams the lead singer says "sex is dangerous / I don't take my chances," "Bi" wants to celebrate the play of sexualities.

Desire is everywhere in "Bi"—to "like it both ways" is to have an infinity of friends who can become lovers. "Getting together with the girls, laughing with the guys"—these activities, which sound like same-sex rather than mixed-sex gatherings, produce erotic "tension" and "passion" which are, like the music itself, "doubly amplified," which is to say not merely doubled but redoubled and multiplied. "Getting together" and "laughing" become "Loving all the girls, and loving all the guys."

Whether bisexuality is a sexual option, a style choice, or a fundamental human possibility, this song is clear about the way in which "bi" confounds the concept of sexual categories. "There's a category if you're straight or gay," but "if you like it both ways" no category will contain you. Thus the closet becomes the whole world, and "everybody" is your potential lover. "Liking it both ways" doesn't here primarily mean, as it sometimes does, a choice among genital, anal, and oral sex (the so-called erotic aim), but rather a choice of partner (the "erotic object"). Still, the sense of an expanded sexual range clearly encompasses what you do as well as who you do it with.

Epilogue:
Between or Among?

Reading Between the Lines

"*B*etween is properly used of two," wrote Samuel Johnson in his dictionary in 1755, "and *among* of more." Ever the realist, he added, "But perhaps this accuracy is not always preserved." Indeed it is not. The American dictionary-maker Noah Webster observed "that *between* is not restricted to *two.*" The editor of the Oxford English Dictionary, Sir James A. H. Murray, surveyed past practice from the vantage point of 1888 and reported, "In all senses *between* has been, from its earliest appearance, extended to more than two." He concluded, as William Safire notes, that "*between* is still the only word available to express the relation of a thing to many surrounding things severally and individually, *among* expressing a relation to them collectively and vaguely." Wordsmith Safire himself generally prefers *between* for two, and *among* for more than two, but says he would "feel more comfortable with 'the battle between Japan, Europe, and America' because it is a battle between Japan and Europe, between Europe and America, and between Japan and America."[1]

Is bisexuality a relationship *between* or *among*? As we have seen, those who confuse or conflate bisexuality with nonmonogamy, and nonmonogamy with group sex, tend to think of it as a tangle of bodies or body parts. This is not only because the fantasy of three-in-a-bed is exciting (a *Details* magazine sex survey reports that threesomes are men's top sexual fantasies, with 60 percent of men dreaming about them, though only 25 percent had taken part in one; the corresponding figures for women were 40 percent and 13 percent)[2] but also because of the difficulty of visualizing or conceptualizing bisexuality except as triadic, triangular, kinetic, or peripatetic.

According to some definitions, though obviously not those of self-identified bisexuals, a person who used to be straight and is now with a same-sex partner or partners is gay, and a person who used to be gay and is now with an opposite-sex partner or partners is straight. This "law of the excluded middle" excludes bisexuality, which, in some people's minds, must be concurrent or simultaneous in order to be real. "Sequential" bisexuality is just wishy-washy hetero- or homosexuality, and "situational" bisexuality (in same-sex schools, prisons, the armed services, or the locker room) is just fooling around or making do.

A three-dimensional diagram of bisexuality, or, as I have already suggested, a Möbius strip, comes closer to drawing this undrawable line. The following description, in actuality that of a shoelace, will give a sense of the in-and-out-ness of the Möbius path:

> In its rewinding passing and repassing through the eyelet of the thing, from outside to inside, from inside to outside, *on* the external surface and *under* the internal surface (and vice versa when this surface is turned inside out . . .), it remains the "same" right through, between right and left, shows itself and disappears *(fort/da)* in its regular traversing of the eyelet, it makes the thing sure of its gathering, the underneath tied up on top, the inside bound on the outside, by a law of stricture.[3]

Like the lace, bisexuality is neither the "inside" nor the "outside" but rather that which creates both.

If the Shoe Fits

This description of a shoelace, or a laced shoe, comes from a discussion of a painting by Van Gogh that has often been described as a "pair" of shoes. "What is a pair?" asks the author. "What is a pair in this case?" "Let us suppose for example two (laced) right shoes or two left shoes." "What would they [i.e., art critics] have done, try to imagine it, with two shoes for the same foot, or with a shoe even more solitary than these two here?" What if we consider "the hypothesis that they do not make a pair"? If not, what can we call them? The author suggests "an argument of the two-shoes, rather than of the pair, rather than of the couple (homo- or hetero-sexual). Bisexuality of the double in two shoes."[4]

The author of this engaging little discussion is philosopher Jacques Derrida, and his rumination on the shoes of Van Gogh returns insistently to the term "bisexual," meaning both "symbolically associated with both sexes," in this case by being "elongated solid or firm on one surface, hollow or concave on the other"[5] and also "capable of being worn by a man or a woman," but most of all "paired" in an unexpected or nontraditional way. "A pair of shoes is more easily treated as a *utility* than a single shoe or two shoes which aren't a pair. The pair inhibits at least, if it does not prevent, the 'fetishizing' movement, it rivets things to use, to 'normal' use.... It is perhaps in order to exclude the question of a certain use-lessness, or of a so-called perverse usage, that [previous commentators] denied themselves the slightest doubt as to the parity or pairedness of these two shoes."[6]

Which is the left and which is the right? It depends upon where you fix the point of definition. "The other (left?) shoe, on the right side of the picture (how should we orient ourselves to talk about them?) is more right/straight, narrow, strict, less open. In short, what one would in the past have called more masculine."[7] But if we describe the shoes as one would in a theater, in terms of "stage right" and "stage left," then left is right, and right is left.

"I find this pair, if I may say so, gauche. Through and through. Look at the details, the inside lateral surface; you'd think it was two left feet. Of different shoes. And the more I look at them, the more they look at me, the less they look like an old pair. More like an old couple."[8]

The hypothesis that it is a pair makes possible not only "normalcy" but also narrative and identity. "Since it is a pair ... there must be a subject." "If there is a pair then a contract is possible, you can look for the subject, hope is still permitted."[9] If it is a pair, a couple, a left-and-right, heterosex-ual rather than bisexual, the story can be written: They belong to a man of the city, or a woman of the fields. But if they are "two shoes," whom does the shoe fit?

What Is a Pear?

"Three Pears," a painting by American artist Janet Rickus, presents just that: three pears on a cloth-covered table. One is a comice pear, golden yellow and conical; one an Anjou, stubbier, with a tight green skin; the third is a red pear, deep vermilion in color. There they stand, side by side, in a row, touching. The green one is in the middle, between the other two. The red pear leans jauntily to the right. They have a lot of personality, these pears. Do any of them make a pair?

Look closely at the painting and you will see that you can pair them up, if you want to. The Anjou and the red pear are stubbier in shape; the comice is the odd pear out. But the comice and the red pear, warm-hued, both lean to the right, while the cool green pear in the middle stands upright. In attitude or comportment, then, the two outside pears are paired, the gold and the red. The one in the middle is the one outside. But couldn't we say, on third thought, that the comice and the Anjou are classically "pear-shaped," while the red pear, perhaps because it is posed at an angle (or in profile?) seems less conventionally curved and rounded? So perhaps it is the two on the left, the comice and the Anjou, that are the pair of pears.

Three pears. Or three pairs. If we were looking for an allegory of bisexuality we might take this image into account. Compare it to the cover design for a book of sociological and medical essays on bisexuality and AIDS in which, against a background of black, a white silhouette of a man in a business suit stands between a red silhouette of another man, identically dressed, and a red silhouette of a woman in a knee-length dress. The white silhouette holds the hands of the other two. His wrists are fully visible where theirs are hidden behind his. The picture tells its story. He is gendered, he is the man in the middle, and he is in control. He is "the bisexual."

The pears, the pairs of pears, tell a more complicated narrative. They will not stay paired. Like the "bisexual" shoes that are or are not a pair, whose story would be so much more explicable, so much more "useful," if they were a pair, a man's pair or a woman's pair, these pairs of pears are perverse. There are, for one thing, three of them, three pairs, a threesome not a pair. But the pear in the middle is only placed there, it would seem, by accident—or by the paradoxical "accident" of a perfect design.

Notes

Introduction: Vice Versa

1. Sigmund Freud, "Analysis Terminable and Interminable," *The Standard Edition of the Complete Psychological Works of Sigmund Freud* (hereafter referred to as *SE*), trans. James Strachey (London: The Hogarth Press and the Institute of Psychoanalysis, 1937), 23:244.

2. Kaja Silverman, *Male Subjectivity at the Margins* (New York: Routledge, 1992), p. 203.

3. *Journal of Social Issues,* vol. 33, no. 3 (1977), p. 36.

4. Colin Spencer, *Which of Us Two?* (New York: Viking, 1990), p. 259.

5. Marcia Deihl, cofounder of the Boston Bisexual Woman's Network, letter to the *Boston Globe,* August 13, 1993.

6. In the course of my research on this book I was interested to discover that *Vice Versa* had been chosen as the title of a "magazine for gay gals" published in 1947 by a lesbian who used the pseudonym "Lisa Ben" (an anagram for lesbian). Ben produced the magazine on her typewriter, making ten carbon copies of each of the nine issues, and distributed them to her friends, who passed them on to *their* friends. "I called it *Vice Versa,*" she said, "because in those days our kind of life was considered a vice. It was the opposite of the lives that were being lived—supposedly—and understood and approved of by society. And vice versa means the opposite. I thought it was very apropos. What else could I have called it?" Very similar reasons have prompted my own use of the title, which I am delighted to share with Lisa Ben. (Lisa Ben, "Gay Gal," in *Making History: The Struggle for Gay and Lesbian Equal Rights, 1945–1990, an Oral History,* ed. Eric Marcus [New York: HarperCollins, 1992], pp. 8–9).

7. G. P. V. Akrigg, ed., *The Letters of James VI and I* (Berkeley and Los Angeles: University of California Press, 1964), p. 431.

8. Michel Foucault, *The History of Sexuality,* vol. 1, trans. Robert Hurley (New York: Vintage Books, 1980), p. 43. For more on "homosexuality" as a late-nineteenth-century concept, see Jonathan Ned Katz, *Gay/Lesbian Almanac: A New Documentary* (New York: Harper & Row, 1983); David M. Halperin, *One Hundred Years of Homosexuality and Other Essays* (New York: Routledge, 1990); and George Chauncey, Jr., "From Sexual Inversion to Homosexuality," *Salmagundi,* vol. 38, no. 59, pp. 114–46. For a good discussion of and critique of claims for eighteenth-century "homosexuality," see Alan Sinfield, *The Wilde Century: Effeminacy, Oscar Wilde and the Queer Moment* (London: Cassell, 1994), pp. 37–40.

9. "Bisexuality: Having It All," *Lear's,* May 1992, p. 55.

10. Martha Weinman Lear, "Ted & Mary & Archie & Fido," *New York Times,* September 30, 1990, p. 14.

11. John Cheever, *The Journals of John Cheever* (New York: Alfred A. Knopf, 1991), p. 347.

12. Troix Bettencourt of Boston Area Gay and Lesbian Youth, quoted in David

Gelman with Debra Rosenberg, "Tune in, Come Out," *Newsweek* International Edition, November 15, 1993, p. 44.

13. George Hohagen and Carrie Miller, cited in Gelman and Rosenberg, "Tune in, Come Out," pp. 44–45.

14. Gelman and Rosenberg, "Tune in, Come Out," p. 44.

15. Michael Winerip, "In School," *New York Times,* February 23, 1994, p. B7.

16. Jim Sullivan, "Melodrama Gives British Band Suede Its Sheen," *Boston Globe,* October 8, 1993, p. 61.

17. Jim Sullivan, "The Scene," *Boston Globe,* Calendar, May 19, 1994, p. 25.

18. Cited in *The Advocate,* May 27, 1994, p. 79.

19. To Cathleen McGuigan, *Newsweek,* April 30, 1984.

20. Matthew Gilbert, "Out of the Pigeonhole," *Boston Globe,* May 29, 1994, p. A7.

21. "Bisexual Chic: Anyone Goes," *Newsweek,* May 27, 1974, p. 90.

22. "The New Bisexuals," *Time,* May 13, 1974, p. 79.

23. Lillian Faderman, *Odd Girls and Twilight Lovers: A History of Lesbian Life in Twentieth-Century America* (New York: Columbia University Press, 1991), pp. 63–65.

24. Biphobia is often said to be the coinage of San Francisco bi-activist Maggi Rubenstein.

25. *Playboy,* August 1992.

26. Gabriel Rotello, "Bi Any Means Necessary; They Call Themselves Queer Bisexuals and, to the Distress of Many in the Gay Movement, They Want In," *Village Voice,* June 30, 1992, p. 37.

27. "Where Do Bisexuals Fit In? Are They Straight or Gay, or a Category unto Themselves?" *Time,* August 17, 1992, pp. 49–51.

28. Jennet Conant, "The Devil in Miss Donohoe," *Redbook,* February 1992, p. 70.

29. Jeff Yarborough, "Amanda Donohoe," *Interview,* vol. 21, no. 9 (September 1991), p. 113.

30. Conant, "The Devil in Miss Donohoe," p. 70.

31. Steven Gaines and Sharon Churcher, *Obsession: The Lives and Times of Calvin Klein* (New York: Birch Lane/Carol Publishing Group 1994), p. 296.

32. Ibid., p. 297.

33. Ibid., p. 298.

34. "Homo Couture," *The Advocate,* October 6, 1992.

35. Suzy Menkes, "Guys and Dolls to End an Era," *New York Times,* February 21, 1993, Style section, p. 5.

36. Gerri Hirshey, "The Snooty Dame at the Block Party," *New York Times Magazine,* October 24, 1993, p. 142.

37. Ibid., p. 144.

38. William Grimes, "Tracking the Styles of One Painful Year: *Ouch!* That Felt Good," *New York Times,* December 28, 1992, p. B1.

39. Suzy Menkes, "Fetish or Fashion?" *New York Times,* November 21, 1993, Styles of the Times section, pp. 1 and 9.

40. Rachel Cohen, "visi-BI-lity," *HQ,* vol. 2, no. 1 (December 1, 1992), p. 16.

41. Sigmund Freud, *The Ego and the Id* (1923), *SE* 19:33n.

42. Sigmund Freud, "Autobiographical Study" (1925), *SE* 20:36.

43. Ibid., p. 38.

44. Sigmund Freud, "Femininity" (1933), *SE* 22:114.

45. Nigel Nicolson, *Portrait of a Marriage* (New York: Atheneum, 1973), p. vii.

46. Ibid., p. 106.

47. Margaret Mead, "Bisexuality: What's It All About?" *Redbook,* January 1975, p. 29.

48. Ibid.

49. Ibid., p. 31.

50. Ibid.

51. Gilbert Herdt, *Guardians of the Flutes: Idioms of Masculinity* (New York: McGraw-Hill, 1981); Gilbert Herdt, "Fetish and Fantasy in Sambian Initiation," in *Ritual* *of Manhood: Male Initiation in New Guinea* (Berkeley: University of California Press, 1982).

52. Michael W. Ross, "A Taxonomy of Global Behavior," in *Bisexuality and HIV/ AIDS: A Global Perspective,* ed. Rob Tielman, Manuel Carballo, and Aart Hendriks, (Buffalo: Prometheus Books, 1991), pp. 21–26.

53. Edmund Bergler, "The Law of the Excluded Middle," in *Homosexuality: Disease or Way of Life?* (New York: Collier, 1956). In Bergler's view any heterosexual behavior on the part of someone who also had homosexual contacts was suspect, and bisexuality itself was "an out and out fraud." He assumes that men who say they are bisexual have only "lustless mechanical sex" with women.

54. John Stoltenberg, *Refusing to Be a Man: Essays on Sex and Justice* (Portland, Ore.: Breitenbush Books, 1989), p. 106.

55. Barbara Tennison, "Strange Tongues," *Terra Nostra Underground* (1990), p. 1.

56. Gayle Feyrer, "The Cosmic Fuck," in *The Cosmic Collected* (self-published), pp. 11–12. Cited in Henry Jenkins, *Television Poachers: Television Fans and Participatory Culture* (New York: Routledge, 1992), p. 186.

57. Constance Penley, "Feminism, Psychoanalysis, and the Study of Popular Culture," in *Cultural Studies,* ed. Lawrence Grossberg, Cary Nelson, and Paul Treichler (New York: Routledge, 1992), p. 491.

58. Ibid., p. 483.

59. Ibid., p. 485. The story, "The Ring of Soshern," probably written before 1976, circulated in manuscript and was finally published in 1987 in the anthology *Alien Brothers.* Its author, like that of many *K/S* stories, is pseudonymous.

60. Ibid., p. 487.

61. Ibid.

62. Ibid., p. 488.

63. Ibid., p. 489.

64. Jean Laplanche and Jean-Bertrand Pontalis, "Fantasy and the Origins of Sexuality" (1964; trans. 1968); reprinted in *Formations of Fantasy,* ed. Victor Burgin, James Donald, and Cora Kaplan (London and New York: Methuen, 1986), p. 26.

65. Montieth M. Illingworth, "Looking for Mr. Goodbyte." *Mirabella,* December 1994, p. 111.

66. Ibid., p. 108.

Chapter 1: Bi Words

1. Lily Burana, "Sandra Bernhard, Acting Lesbian," *The Advocate,* December 15, 1992, p. 70.

2. Kate Millett, *Flying* (originally published in 1975), quoted in Charlotte Wolff, *Bisexuality* (London: Quartet Books, 1977), p. 50.

3. Robert L. Chapman, *New Dictionary of American Slang* (New York: Harper & Row, 1986), p. 163.

4. Beth Elliott, notes on contributors, in Elizabeth Reba Weise, ed., *Closer to Home: Bisexuality and Feminism* (Seattle: Seal Press, 1992), p. 322. Notes on contributors for *Bi Any Other Name,* ed. Loraine Hutchins and Lani Kaahumanu (Boston: Alyson Publications, 1991), p. 373.

5. *BiWomen: The Newsletter of the Boston Bisexual Women's Network,* vol. 8, no. 5 (October/November 1990), p. 4; Dell Richards, *Lesbian Lists: A Look at Lesbian Culture, History, and Personalities* (Boston: Alyson Publications, 1990).

6. *Brewer's Dictionary of Twentieth-Century Phrase and Fable* (Boston: Houghton Mifflin, 1992), p. 3.

7. Diane Anderson, "Living with Contradictions," in *Closer to Home,* ed. Weise, p. 171.

8. John Malone, *Straight Women/Gay Men* (New York: Dial Press, 1980), p. 181.

9. *Rolling Stone,* October 20, 1994, quoted in *The Advocate,* November 15, 1994, p. 95.

10. *Now,* vol. 7, no. 47 (August 4–10, 1988), p. 59.

11. Gore Vidal, "Sex Is Politics," *Playboy,* January 1979. Reprinted in Gore Vidal, *United States: Essays 1952–1992* (New York: Random House, 1993), p. 550.

12. Gore Vidal, "The Birds and the Bees," *The Nation,* October 28, 1991. Reprinted in Vidal, *United States,* p. 612.

13. Tony Kushner, *Angels in America, A Gay Fantasia on American Themes. Part One: Millennium Approaches* (New York: Theatre Communications Group, 1992), p. 45.

14. Benjamin Cheever, ed., *The Letters of John Cheever* (New York: Simon and Schuster, 1988), p. 326.

15. Ibid., p. 327.

16. Ibid., p. 300.

17. Ibid.

18. See for example, ibid., pp. 335–36.

19. Letter dated May 24, 1977, ibid., p. 337.

20. Letter dated May 25, 1977, ibid., p. 338.

21. Letter dated August 28, 1977, ibid., p. 340.

22. Letter dated February 9, 1977, ibid., p. 341.

23. Ti-Grace Atkinson, in a speech delivered at Columbia University. Quoted in Sydney Abbott and Barbara Love, *Sappho Was a Right-On Woman: A Liberated View of Lesbianism* (New York: Stein & Day, 1972), pp. 119–21.

24. Hutchins and Kaahumanu, *Bi Any Other Name,* p. xxiv.

25. Love and Abbott, *Sappho Was a Right-On Woman,* pp. 156–57.

26. "Name Game," *10 Percent,* no. 6 (January/February 1994), p. 11.

27. April Martin, "Fruits, Nuts, and Chocolate: The Politics of Sexual Identity," *The Harvard Gay and Lesbian Review,* vol. 1, no. 1 (Winter 1994), p. 11.

28. Ibid., p. 12.

29. Ibid., p. 14.

30. Victoria A. Brownworth, "No Mystery," *The Advocate,* May 17, 1994, p. 52.

31. Pat Califia, *Macho Sluts* (Boston: Alyson Publications, 1988), p. 216.

32. Jeff Yarbrough, "The Conde Nast Publications Owe Their Glitz, Glamour, and Gloss to the Gay Aesthetic," *The Advocate,* March 10, 1992, p. 36.

33. Graham McKerrow, *Gay Times,* January 1993, p. 29. Cited in Jo Eadie, "Activating Bisexuality: Towards a Bi/Sexual Politics," in *Activating Theory: Lesbian, Gay, Bisexual Politics,* ed. Joseph Bristow and Angelia R. Wilson (London: Lawrence & Wishart, 1993), p. 151. See also, in the same volume, Clare Hemmings, "Resituating the Bisexual Body," pp. 118–39.

34. Eadie, "Activating Bisexuality," p. 150.

35. For example: Lise Kreps and Gwen Riles, "Hi, My Name Is Bi; Or the Labels Discussion," *North Bi Northwest,* vol. 1, no. 2 (April/May 1989); Lucy Friedland, "Are You Suffering from the BLA's? The Bisexual Label Avoidance Syndrome," *North Bi Northwest,* vol. 3, no. 1 (February/March 1990); Susanna Trnka, "A Question of Labeling," *North Bi Northwest,* vol. 4, no. 3 (June/July 1991); Lucy Friedland and Liz A. Highleyman, "The Fine Art of Labeling: The Convergence of Anarchism, Feminism, and Bisexuality," in *Bi Any Other Name,* ed. Hutchins and Kaahumanu, pp. 285–98; M. S. Montgomery, "An Old Bottle for Old Wine: Selecting the Right Label," *North Bi Northwest,* vol. 4, no. 3 (June/July 1991).

36. Quoted in Sarah Murray, "Bisexual Movement Comes Out Strong," *BiWomen,* vol. 8, no. 5 (October/November 1990), p. 6. Excerpted from an article that first appeared in the *San Francisco Examiner,* August 1990.

37. Dvora Zipkin, "Why Bi?" in *Closer to Home,* ed. Weise, pp. 55–56.

38. Ibid., p. 57.

39. Ibid., p. 65.

40. Martin S. Weinberg, Colin J. Williams, and Douglas W. Pryor, *Dual Attraction: Understanding Bisexuality* (New York: Oxford University Press, 1994), pp. 28–29.

41. Interview with the author, March 1994.

42. Weinberg, Williams, and Pryor, *Dual Attraction,* p. 35.

43. Matthew LeGrant, "The 'B' Word," in *Bi Any Other Name,* ed. Hutchins and Kaahumanu, pp. 207–209.

44. Cited in Carrie Wofford, "The Bisexual Revolution: Deluded Closet Cases or the Vanguard of the Movement?" *Outweek,* February 6, 1991, p. 37.

45. Holly Near, *Fire in the Rain, Singer in the Storm* (New York: William Morrow, 1990), quoted in Beth Elliott, "Holly Near and Yet So Far," in *Closer to Home,* ed. Weise, p. 233. Elliott notes that this phrase is "quoted in just about every article, review, or interview about the book" (Elliott, "Holly Near and Yet So Far," p. 252, n. 3).

46. Interview by Carol Stocker, "So Near, Yet So Far," *Boston Globe,* August 27, 1990; Elliott, "Holly Near and Yet So Far," p. 252.

47. Elliott, "Holly Near and Yet So Far," p. 233.

48. Don Marquis, *archy and mehitabel* (Garden City, N.Y.: Doubleday, 1927).

49. Martin Greif, *The Gay Book of Days 1982* (New York: Carol Publishing Group, 1989).

50. Jonathan Ned Katz, *Gay/Lesbian Almanac* (New York: Harper & Row, 1983).

51. Greif, *The Gay Book of Days 1982,* p. 12.

52. Loraine Hutchins and Lani Kaahumanu, "Who Are We? Establishing and Reclaiming the Bisexual Community," *Anything That Moves,* Spring 1991, p. 19.

53. Ibid., p. 19; Jeffrey Miller, ed., *In Touch: The Letters of Paul Bowles* (New York: Farrar, Straus & Giroux, 1994), p. 557.

54. Ginette Paris, from *Pagan Meditations* (Dallas: Spring Publications, 1986), pp. 39–43. Excerpted as "Who Was Sappho?" in *BiWoman: The Newsletter of the Boston Bisexual Women's Network,* vol. 4, no. 5 (October/November 1986), p. 6.

55. Amanda Udis-Kessler, "Whose Culture Is It Anyway?" *Anything That Moves,* Spring 1991, p. 8.

56. Michael Goff and Sarah Pettit, "The Voyage Out," editorial, *Out,* July 1993, p. 6.

57. Gary North and Karla Rossi, "Bi Visibility in Gay Community Takes 'Dramatic' Turn," *Anything That Moves,* Spring 1991, pp. 13–15; Kim Corsaro, "Bisexuality in the Gay/Lesbian Community: The Controversy Continues," *San Francisco Bay Times,* May 1991.

58. *Logomotive: A Magazine of Sex & Fun (From a Bisexual Perspective),* pp. 3 and 40.

59. Description from the back cover of *Susie Bright's Sexual Reality: A Virtual Sex World Reader* (Pittsburgh and San Francisco: Cleis Press, 1992).

60. *Anything That Moves,* no. 7, Spring, 1994, editorial inside front cover.

61. Lenore Norrgard, "Can Bisexuals Be Monogamous?" in *Bi Any Other Name,* ed. Hutchins and Kaahumanu, p. 283.

62. Bruce Bawer, *A Place at the Table: The Gay Individual in American Society* (New York: Poseidon Press, 1993), p. 34.

63. Ibid., p. 51.

64. *Anything That Moves,* no. 7, Spring 1994, editorial inside front cover.

65. Robyn Ochs, "Biphobia: It Goes More Than Two Ways," in *Bisexual Identities: The Psychology and Politics of an Invisible Minority,* ed. Beth Firestein (San Francisco: Sage, forthcoming).

66. Sigmund Freud, *The Interpretation of Dreams* (1900), *SE* 4:298n.

67. Sigmund Freud, "Fragment of an Analysis of a Case of Hysteria" (1905), *SE* 7:65n.

68. Elizabeth Reba Weise, "Closer to Home," in *Anything That Moves,* no. 4, 1992, p. 33.

69. Michel Foucault, *The History of Sexuality,* vol. 1, trans. Robert Hurley (New York: Vintage Books, 1980), p. 69.

70. Eric Marcus, ed., *Making History: The Struggle for Gay and Lesbian Equal Rights 1945–1990, an Oral History* (New York: HarperCollins, 1992), p. 285. For more on Copy Berg, see Randy Shilts, *Conduct Unbecoming: Gays and Lesbians in the U.S. Military, Vietnam to the Persian Gulf* (New York: St. Martin's Press, 1993).

71. Letter to Bryher, November 24, 1934, Beinecke Rare Book Library, Yale University. Cited by Rachel Blau DuPlessis and Susan Stanford Friedman, " 'Woman Is Perfect': H.D.'s Debate with Freud," *Feminist Studies,* vol. 7, no. 3 (Fall 1981), pp. 407–16.

72. H.D., *Tribute to Freud* (New York: New Directions, 1974), p. 69, italics in the original.

73. Letter to Bryher, November 24, 1934, Beinecke Rare Book Library, Yale University.

74. Shari Benstock, *Women of the Left Bank* (Austin: University of Texas Press), p. 317. Benstock cites O.W. Firkin as a principal voice of this view.

75. H.D., *Tribute to Freud,* p. 120.

76. Ibid., p. 186.

77. Ibid., pp. 180–81.

78. Letter to Bryher, February 14, 1919; letter from Bryher to H.D., March 20, 1919, Beinecke Rare Book Library, Yale University; Andrea Weiss, *Vampires and Violets: Lesbians in the Cinema* (London: Jonathan Cape, 1992), p. 20.

79. Weiss, *Vampires and Violets,* p. 18.

80. Benstock, *Women of the Left Bank,* pp. 312, 321, and 332.

81. Ibid., p. 312.

82. Ibid., p. 315.

83. Ibid., p. 334.

84. Weinberg, Williams, and Pryor, *Dual Attraction.*

85. DuPlessis and Friedman, " 'Woman Is Perfect,' " pp. 407–30. Susan Stanford Friedman and Rachel Blau DuPlessis, " 'I Had Two Loves Separate': The Sexualities of H.D.'s *Her,*" *Montemora,* vol. 8 (1981), pp. 7–30.

86. DuPlessis and Friedman, " 'Woman Is Perfect,' " pp. 424–25.

87. Friedman and DuPlessis, "Sexualities," p. 9.

88. Claire Buck, *H.D. and Freud: Bisexuality and a Feminist Discourse* (New York and London: Harvester Wheatsheaf, 1991), p. 11; Jacques Lacan and the École Freudienne, *Feminine Sexuality,* ed. and trans. by Jacqueline Rose and ed. by Juliet Mitchell (New York: W. W. Norton, 1982), p. 21.

89. Buck, *H.D. and Freud,* still following Mitchell and Rose, p. 11.

90. Karen F., note to the author.

91. David Kamp, "The Straight Queer," *Gentleman's Quarterly,* July 1993, pp. 95–99.

92. Elisabeth D. Däumer, "Queer Ethics; or, the Challenge of Bisexuality to Lesbian Ethics," *Hypatia,* vol. 7, no. 4 (Fall 1992), p. 104, citing Michael Warner, "Introduction: Fear of a Queer Planet," *Social Text,* vol. 19, no. 16.

93. "Identity Crisis: Queer Politics in the Age of Possibilities," *Village Voice,* June 30, 1992, p. 27.

94. Terry Castle, *The Apparitional Lesbian: Female Homosexuality and Modern Culture* (New York: Columbia University Press, 1993), pp. 12–13. "The term *queer* has lately become popular in activist and progressive academic circles in part, it seems to me, precisely because it makes it easy to enfold female homosexuality back 'into' male homosexuality and disembody the lesbian once again. . . . To the extent that 'queer theory' still seems . . . to denote primarily the study of male homosexuality, I find myself at odds with both its language and its universalizing aspirations."

95. Derived both from "performance" in the sense of theatrical representation and "performative" speech-acts ("with this ring I thee wed"), which, according to the typology of J. L. Austin (*How to Do Things with Words,* Harvard UP, 1975), not only describe but *do.* "Performativity" in the latter sense became important to the deconstructive understanding of how language works, "dislinking" cause and effect, the signifier and the world. (Austin himself, having introduced the term in his Norton lectures at Harvard in 1955, subsequently rejected the idea of a "performative" as opposed to a "constantive" utterance.) In its present uses in literary criticism, gender discourse and queer theory, especially when not assimilated wholly into the theatrical concept of "performance," "performativity" has been constructively deployed as a way of "understanding the obliquities among *meaning, being,* and *doing.*" Eve Kosofsky Sedgwick, "Queer Performativity: Henry James's *The Art of the Novel,*" *GLQ* vol. 1, no. 1. (1993). See Sedgwick's article for a nuanced discussion of the problematics of the term, and Judith Butler's essay "Critically Queer," in the same issue of *GLQ,* published in a slightly different form in her *Bodies That Matter: On the Discursive Limits of Sex* (New York: Routledge, 1993). Butler's *Gender Trouble: Feminism and the Subversion of Identity*

(New York: Routledge, 1990) and "Performative Acts and Gender Constitution: An Essay in Phenomenology and Feminist Theory," in Sue-Ellen Case, ed., *Performing Feminisms: Feminist Critical Theory and Practice* (Baltimore: Johns Hopkins University Press, 1990) are among the most influential recent discussions of "performativity." See also the collection of English Institute essays, *Performativity and Performance,* ed. Andrew Parker and Eve Kosofsky Sedgwick (New York: Routledge, 1995).

96. This term, introduced by E. L. Pattullo in "Straight Talk About Gays," *Commentary,* December 1992, is rightly demolished by Bruce Bawer, who notes that "a small minority of people are genuinely bisexual." They are not "waverers" in Pattullo's sense, because they are not potentially either straight or gay; they are and always will be attracted to both sexes in roughly equal measure, and would fare best psychologically in a society in which they could settle down with whomever they loved, male or female, without feeling socially or legally pressured in either direction. See Bawer, *A Place at the Table,* p. 107.

97. Eric Marcus, "What's in a Name?" *10 Percent,* vol. 1 (Winter 1993), pp. 14–15.

Chapter 2: Bi Sexual Politics

1. Carrie Wofford, "The Bisexual Revolution: Deluded Closet Cases or the Vanguard of the Movement?" *Outweek,* February 6, 1991, p. 36.

2. Robyn Ochs, letter to the author, November 23, 1994.

3. Eloise Salhoz, "The Power and the Pride," *Newsweek,* June 21, 1993, p. 58.

4. Larry Gross, *Contested Closets: The Politics and Ethics of Outing* (Minneapolis: University of Minnesota Press, 1993), p. 123.

5. Elisabeth D. Däumer, "Queer Ethics; or, the Challenge of Bisexuality to Lesbian Ethics," *Hypatia,* vol. 7, no. 4 (Fall 1992), p. 98.

6. Robert Bauman, "The Conservative Congressman," in *Making History: The Struggle for Gay and Lesbian Equal Rights, 1945–1990, an Oral History,* ed. Eric Marcus (New York: HarperCollins, 1992), p. 357.

7. Ibid., p. 363.

8. Ibid., p. 364.

9. Ibid., p. 365.

10. Jane Gross, "Does She Speak for Today's Women?" *New York Times Magazine,* March 1, 1992, p. 15.

11. Ibid., p. 16.

12. Ibid., p. 53.

13. Ibid., p. 54.

14. Stuart Timmons, *The Trouble with Harry Hay: Founder of the Modern Gay Movement* (Boston: Alyson Publications, 1990), p. 98.

15. Quoted in ibid., p. 100.

16. Ibid., p. 118.

17. Ibid., p. 96.

18. Ibid., p. 99.

19. Leo Nikolaevich Tolstoy, *Anna Karenina,* trans. Joel Carmichael (New York: Bantam Books, 1960; reprinted 1981), p. 1.

20. Alice Wexler, *Emma Goldman: An Intimate Life* (New York: Pantheon Books, 1984), p. 182.

21. Lillian Faderman, *Odd Girls and Twilight Lovers: A History of Lesbian Life in Twentieth-Century America* (New York: Columbia University Press, 1991), p. 34; Almeda Sperry to Emma Goldman, quoted in Blanche Wiesen Cook, "Female Support Networks and Political Activism," *Chrysalis,* no. 3 (Autumn 1977), p. 57; Emma Goldman to Alexander Berkman in Richard Drinnon and Anna Maria Drinnon, eds., *Nowhere at Home: Letters from Exile of Emma Goldman and Alexander Berkman* (New York: Holt, Rinehart & Winston, 1984), pp. 132–33.

22. Candace Falk, *Love, Anarchy, and Emma Goldman* (New York: Holt, Rinehart and Winston, 1984), p. 169.

23. Almeda Sperry to Emma Goldman, August 8, 1912, Boston University Libraries.

24. Almeda Sperry to Emma Goldman, October 21, 1912, Boston University Libraries; and Falk, *Love, Anarchy, and Emma Goldman,* p. 172.

25. Falk, *Love, Anarchy, and Emma Goldman,* p. 177.

26. Blanche Wiesen Cook, "The Historical Denial of Lesbianism," *Radical History Review,* vol. 20 (Spring/Summer 1979), p. 56.

27. Emma Goldman, *Living My Life* (Salt Lake City: Peregrine Smith, 1982), p. 269.

28. Faderman, *Odd Girls and Twilight Lovers,* p. 34; Almeda Sperry to Emma Goldman, quoted in Cook, "Female Support Networks and Political Activism"; Emma Goldman to Alexander Berkman in Drinnon and Drinnon, eds., *Nowhere at Home,* pp. 132–33.

29. Bisexual activist Liz Highleyman cites Goldman's influence on her own coming of age as "an anarchist, a bisexual, and a sex radical." Lucy Friedland and Liz A. Highleyman, "The Fine Art of Labeling," in *Bi Any Other Name,* ed. Loraine Hutchins and Lani Kaahumanu (Boston: Alyson Publications, 1991), p. 290. Kaahumanu uses a phrase attributed to Goldman as the title of her article on a bisexual dance that enlivened the BiWEST "networking, coalition building, strategizing" conference in San Diego. ("Emma was right," she comments. "There has to be a balance of fun and politics." Lani Kaahumanu, "If I Can't Dance I Won't Join Your Revolution," *Anything That Moves,* vol. 7 [Spring 1994], p. 20.)

30. Blanche Wiesen Cook, *Eleanor Roosevelt,* vol. 1, *1884–1933* (New York: Viking, 1992), p. 8.

31. Ibid., p. 13.

32. Joseph P. Lash, *Love, Eleanor: Eleanor Roosevelt and Her Friends* (Garden City, N.Y.: Doubleday, 1984), p. 126, cited in ibid., p. 441.

33. Cook, *Eleanor Roosevelt,* vol. 1, *1884–1933,* p. 477. Cook cites especially Faber's biography of Hickok.

34. Doris Faber, *The Life of Lorena Hickok: ER's Friend* (New York: William Morrow, 1980), p. 176.

35. Quoted in ibid., p. 152, and discussed in Cook, *Eleanor Roosevelt,* vol. 1, *1884–1933,* p. 479.

36. James Roosevelt with Bill Libby, *My Parents: A Differing View* (Chicago: Playboy Press, 1976), pp. 110–11.

37. Cook, *Eleanor Roosevelt,* vol. 1, *1884–1933,* p. 446; Kenneth Davis, *FDR: The New York Years, 1928–1933* (New York: Random House, 1985), pp. 329–30.

38. Cook, describing a stereotype she believes influenced Joseph Lash's interpretation of the Miller-Roosevelt friendship "in mother-and-son terms." Cook, *Eleanor Roosevelt,* vol. 1, *1884–1933,* p. 441; Lash, *Love, Eleanor,* p. 123.

39. Cook, *Eleanor Roosevelt,* vol. 1, *1884–1933,* p. 13.

40. Ibid., p. 14.

41. Lash, *Love, Eleanor,* p. 126.

42. Kate Millett, *Sexual Politics* (New York: Ballantine Books, 1969; reprinted 1978), p. 30.

43. Ibid., p. 471.

44. Ibid., p. 471n.

45. Sigmund Freud, "Femininity" (1933), *SE* 22:116–17.

46. Millett, *Sexual Politics,* p. 270.

47. Ibid., p. 277.

48. Chris Nealon, "Northampton Debates Bisexual Question," *Gay Community News,* April 1, 1990, p. 6.

49. Barbara Kantrowitz and Danzy Senna, "A Town Like No Other," *Newsweek,* June 21, 1993, p. 56.

50. *Bay Windows,* May 3, 1990, p. 2.

51. Bet Power, "Who Gets to 'Belong' in the Lesbian Community, Anyway?" *Gay Community News,* April 15–21, 1990, p. 3.

52. In a letter to the editor of *Off Our Backs,* Dreher decried the "strong lesbian-hating element beneath the cries for 'inclusion,'" and quoted a "male acquaintance from another community" who had remarked, "This is one of the most misogynist gay communities I've ever seen." *Off Our Backs,* November 1991, p. 24.

53. Robyn Ochs, letter to the author, November 23, 1994.

54. See Marjorie Garber, *Vested Interests: Cross-Dressing and Cultural Anxiety* (New York: Routledge, 1992).

55. Eridani, "Is Sexual Orientation a Secondary Sex Characteristic?" in *Closer to Home: Bisexuality and Feminism,* ed. Elizabeth Reba Weise (Seattle: Seal Press, 1992), p. 173.

56. Susie Bright, "BlindSexual," in *Susie Bright's Sexual Reality: A Virtual Sex World Reader* (Pittsburgh and San Francisco: Cleis Press, 1992), p. 151. "Radical sex activist" is her own self-description, from the Introduction, p. 15.

57. Ibid., p. 152.

58. Adrienne Rich, "Compulsory Heterosexuality and Lesbian Existence," originally published in *Signs: Journal of Women in Culture and Society,* vol. 5, no. 4 (1980), pp. 631–60; reprinted in *Powers of Desire: The Politics of Sexuality,* ed. Ann Snitow, Christine Stansell, and Sharon Thompson (New York: Monthly Review Press, 1983), p. 182.

59. Rich, "Compulsory Heterosexuality," in *Powers of Desire,* ed. Snitow et al., pp. 182–83.

60. Ibid., pp. 189 and 193.

61. Ibid., p. 193.

62. Ibid., p. 199.

63. Ibid., p. 182.

64. Lani Kaahumanu, "Biphobic: 'Some of My Best Friends Are,'" *Plexus,* June 1982, p. 4.

65. Ibid., p. 5.

66. Steven Epstein, "Gay Politics, Ethnic Identity: The Limits of Social Constructionism," *Socialist Review,* vol. 93, no. 4 (May/August 1987), p. 22.

67. Diana Fuss, *Essentially Speaking: Feminism, Nature and Difference* (New York: Routledge, 1989), p. 104.

68. Amanda Udis-Kessler, "Present Tense: Biphobia as a Crisis of Meaning," paper presented to the BiPOL Bisexuality Conference, June 22, 1990. Copyright Amanda Udis-Kessler. See Amanda Udis-Kessler's related essay, "Bisexuality in an Essentialist World," in *Bisexuality: A Reader and Sourcebook,* ed. Thomas Geller (Hadley, Mass.: Times Change Press, 1990), pp. 51–63.

69. Udis-Kessler, "Bisexuality in an Essentialist World," pp. 59–60.

70. See for example, Rebecca Kaplan, "Compulsory Heterosexuality and the Bisexual Existence: Toward a Bisexual Feminist Understanding of Heterosexism," in *Closer to Home,* ed. Weise, pp. 269–90, and Kathleen Bennett, "Feminist Bisexuality: A Both/And Option for an Either/Or World," in *Closer to Home,* ed. Weise, pp. 205–31.

71. Alice Walker, *Possessing the Secret of Joy* (New York: Harcourt Brace Jovanovich, 1992), p. 170.

72. June Jordan, "A New Politics of Sexuality," *The Progressive,* July 1991, p. 13; reprinted in June Jordan, *Technical Difficulties* (New York: Vintage, 1994), pp. 187–93.

73. June Jordan, "A New Politics of Sexuality," address to the Bisexual, Gay and Lesbian Student Association at Stanford University, April 29, 1991; reprinted in adapted form in *The Progressive,* July 1991, pp. 12–13.

74. See Donna Haraway, "A Manifesto for Cyborgs: Science, Technology and Socialist Feminism in the 1980s," in *Feminism/Postmodernism,* ed. Linda J. Nicholson (London: Routledge, 1990), and Donna Haraway, "Situated Knowledges: The Science Question in Feminism and the Privilege of Partial Perspective," in *Simians, Cyborgs and Women* (London: Free Association Books, 1991).

75. Homi K. Bhabha, "Signs Taken for Wonders: Questions of Ambivalence and Authority Under a Tree Outside Delhi, May 1817," in *Europe and Its Others: Proceedings of the Essex Conference on the Sociology of Literature,* 2 vols., ed. Francis Barker et al. (University of Essex, 1985), pp. 98–99.

76. Eadie aptly cites anthropologist Mary Douglas's *Purity and Danger* (London: Routledge, 1966) as the modern locus classicus of the argument about a policed borderline between pollution and purity, with its now-celebrated dictum, "dirt is matter out of place."

Chapter 3: Fatal Attractions

1. Anna Livia, "Minimax," in *Daughters of Darkness: Lesbian Vampire Stories,* ed. Pam Keesey (Pittsburgh and San Francisco: Cleis Press, 1993), p. 235.

2. Scott Harris and Miles Corwin, "Opposition to Film 'Basic Instinct' Rises," *Los Angeles Times,* March 21, 1992, p. B3.

3. Brian D. Johnson, "Killer Movies," *Maclean's,* March 30, 1992, p. 51.

4. Hilary de Vries, *Los Angeles Times,* Calendar, March 15, 1992, p. 3.

5. Johnson, "Killer Movies," p. 51.

6. Julie Lew, "Gay Groups Protest a Film Script," *New York Times,* May 4, 1991, p. 11.

7. Richard Jennings, quoted in ibid., pp. 11ff.

8. David Ehrenstein, "*Basic Instinct:* This Is a Smart, Hot, Sexy Commercial Film?" *The Advocate,* April 21, 1992, p. 87.

9. Richard Alleva, "Dying of Heat: Verhoeven's *Basic Instinct,*" *Commonweal,* April 24, 1992, p. 20.

10. L. A. Kauffman, "Queer Guerillas in Tinseltown," *The Progressive,* July 1992, p. 37.

11. John Leo, "The Politics of Intimidation," *U.S. News and World Report,* April 6, 1992, p. 24.

12. Lynn Hirschberg, "Say It Ain't So, Joe!" *Vanity Fair,* August 1991, p. 78.

13. Otis R. Bowen, statement on AIDS, 1987. See Bowen, "In Pursuit of the Number One Public Health Problem (AIDS)" in *Public Health Reports* May–June 1988, v. 103, n. 3, pp. 211–12.

14. Martin S. Weinberg, Colin J. Williams, and Douglas Pryor, *Dual Attraction: Understanding Bisexuality* (New York: Oxford University Press, 1994), p. 6.

15. In Katie Leishman, "Heterosexuals and AIDS," *Atlantic Monthly,* February 1987, p. 48.

16. *Newsweek,* July 13, 1987.

17. Jan Zita Grover, "AIDS: Keywords," in *AIDS: Cultural Analysis, Cultural Criticism,* ed. Douglas Crimp (Cambridge, Mass.: MIT Press, 1988), p. 21.

18. Jon Nordheimer, "AIDS Specter for Women: The Bisexual Man," *New York Times,* April 3, 1987, p. 1.

19. *Newsweek,* July 13, 1987. Cited in Robyn Ochs, "Bisexuality: The Media Versus Reality," 1993 (unpublished).

20. Susan Gerrard and James Halpin, quoting sociologist Pepper Schwartz, "The Risky Business of Bisexual Love," *Cosmopolitan,* October 1989, pp. 204–205.

21. Richard A. Knox, "Bisexuals Put Women at Risk, Studies Say," *Boston Globe,* June 22, 1990, p. 57.

22. Weinberg, Williams, and Pryor, *Dual Attraction,* p. 259.

23. Ibid., p. 274.

24. Ibid., p. 280.

25. Ibid., pp. 208 and 204.

26. Ibid., p. 213.

27. Ibid., p. 215.

28. Ibid., pp. 225 and 228.

29. Ibid., p. 228.

30. Ibid., p. 8.

31. Ibid., p. 229.

32. Rob Tielman, Manuel Carballo, and Aart Hendriks, eds., *Bisexuality and HIV/ AIDS: A Global Perspective* (Buffalo, N.Y.: Prometheus Books, 1991), p. 9.

33. Susan M. Kegeles and Joseph A. Catania, "Understanding Bisexual Men's AIDS Risk Behavior: The AIDS Risk-Reduction Method," in ibid., p. 147.

34. Wiresit Sittitrai, Tim Brown, and Sirapone Virulrak, "Patterns of Bisexuality in Thailand," in ibid., pp. 97–117.

35. Richard G. Parker and Oussama Tawil, "Bisexual Behavior and HIV Transmission in Latin America," ibid., p. 61.

36. Tade Akin Aina, "Patterns of Bisexuality in Sub-Saharan Africa," in ibid., p. 83. See also E. E. Evans-Pritchard, *Man and Woman Among the Azande* (London: Faber & Faber, 1974), p. 37.

37. Theo G. M. Sandfort, "Bisexuality in the Netherlands: Some Data from Dutch Studies," in *Bisexuality and HIV/AIDS,* ed. Tielman, Carballo, and Hendriks, p. 79.

38. John Allen Stevenson, "A Vampire in the Mirror: The Sexuality of *Dracula,*" *PMLA,* vol. 103, no. 2 (March 1988), p. 146.

39. Louis Crompton, *Byron and Greek Love* (Berkeley: University of California Press, 1985), p. 237. "It now seems possible to argue," says Crompton, "that Byron's bisexuality was far more central to his experience and personality than his biographers have been willing to grant" (ibid., p. 236; see also pp. 8–9, 210–15, 236–38, 242–43, and passim). Doris Langley Moore suggested, in an essay on "Byron's Sexual Ambivalence," that "bisexuality may be at times a less bearable state than homosexuality, since, whatever fulfillment is attained, the lover in some strange spirit of contradiction is liable to feel that he is being false to his nature." Langley Moore, *Lord Byron: Accounts Rendered* (London: John Murray, 1974), p. 456. On Polidori, see also Paul West's novel, *Lord Byron's Doctor* (Chicago: University of Chicago Press, 1989).

40. C. F. Bentley, "The Monster in the Bedroom: Sexual Symbolism in Bram Stoker's *Dracula,*" *Literature and Psychology,* vol. 22 (1972), p. 105.

41. Phyllis A. Roth, "Suddenly Sexual Women in Bram Stoker's *Dracula,*" *Literature and Psychology,* vol. 27 (1977), pp. 113–21.

42. Thomas B. Byers, "Good Men and Monsters: The Defenses of *Dracula,*" *Literature and Psychology,* vol. 31 (1981), p. 29.

43. George Stade, quoted in Francis Ford Coppola and James V. Hart, eds., *Bram Stoker's Dracula: The Film and the Legend* (New York: Newmarket Press, 1992). See Stade, "Dracula's Women," *Partisan Review,* vol. 53, no. 2 (1986), pp. 201–15.

44. See, for a brief summary, Jules Zanger, "A Sympathetic Vibration: Dracula and the Jews," *English Literature in Transition 1880–1920,* vol. 34, no. 1 (1991), pp. 33–44. The notorious "blood libel" all too readily became part of the vampire mythology. Max Schreck's portrayal of Dracula in F. W. Murnau's 1922 film *Nosferatu* has obvious and disturbing affinities to anti-Semitic depictions of Jews in the period.

45. See for example, Stephen D. Arata, "The Occidental Tourist: *Dracula* and the Anxiety of Reverse Colonization," *Victorian Studies,* vol. 33, no. 4 (Summer 1990), pp. 621–45.

46. Christopher Craft, " 'Kiss Me with Those Red Lips': Gender and Inversion in Bram Stoker's *Dracula,*" *Representations,* vol. 8 (Fall 1984), p. 114. Craft notes the persistent "equivocation about the relationship between desire and gender" (p. 108) in works like Sheridan Le Fanu's "Carmilla" and Bram Stoker's *Dracula.*

47. Ibid., p. 115.

48. Ibid., p. 125.

49. Bodily fluids are substituted or inverted, red for white, with blood substituting for both milk and semen, as psychoanalyst Ernest Jones had suggested in his classic work on nightmares. "A nightly visit from a beautiful or frightful being, who first exhausts the sleeper with passionate embraces and then withdraws from him a vital fluid," Jones observes, is a tip-off to the analyst, since "in the unconscious mind blood is commonly an equivalent for semen." Ernest Jones, "On the Vampire," in *Vampires: Lord Byron to Count Dracula,* ed. Christopher Frayling (London: Faber & Faber, 1991), p. 411.

50. John Allen Stevenson, "A Vampire in the Mirror: The Sexuality of *Dracula,*" *PMLA,* vol. 103, no. 2 (March 1988), p. 146.

51. Craft, " 'Kiss Me with Those Red Lips,' " p. 122.

52. Ibid., p. 124.

53. Keesey, *Daughters of Darkness,* pp. 8 and 9.

54. See for example, Lillian Faderman, *Surpassing the Love of Men* (New York: William Morrow, 1981), pp. 341–46.

55. Keesey, *Daughters of Darkness,* p. 13. This was the period of *Countess Dracula* (1972) and *Daughters of Darkness* (1971). Hammer Studio's trilogy of what became known as "sexploitation" films—*The Vampire Lovers* (1970), *Twins of Evil* (1971), and *Lust for a Vampire,* the last of these set in the almost-obligatory venue of a girls' finishing school (1971)—set the standard for the genre, Andrea Weiss. *Vampires and Violets: Lesbians in the Cinema* (London: Jonathan Cape, 1992), p. 88. Roger Vadim's *Blood and Roses* (1960) and Joseph Larraz's *Vampyres* (1974) also featured what would become in some eyes "the perennial lesbian vampire routine." Vito Russo, *The Celluloid Closet,* revised edition (New York: Harper & Row, 1987), p. 255.

56. Susan Sontag, "Persona," *Sight and Sound,* vol. 36, no. 4 (Autumn 1967), p. 191.

57. Russo, *The Celluloid Closet,* p. 255.

58. Bonnie Zimmerman, "Daughters of Darkness: Lesbian Vampires," *Jump Cut,* no. 23–24 (March 1981), pp. 23–24.

59. Bonnie Zimmerman, *The Safe Sea of Women: Lesbian Fiction 1969–89* (Boston: Beacon Press, 1990).

60. Zimmerman, "Daughters of Darkness: Lesbian Vampires," p. 23.

61. *Out,* February/March 1994, p. 16.

62. Raymond T. McNally, *Dracula Was a Woman: In Search of the Blood Countess of Transylvania* (New York: McGraw-Hill, 1983).

63. Sue-Ellen Case, "Tracking the Vampire," *Differences: A Journal of Feminist Cultural Studies,* vol. 3, no. 2 (Summer 1991), p. 15.

64. Ibid., p. 16.

65. Keesey, *Daughters of Darkness,* p. 15.

66. Ibid., p. 16.

67. McNally, *Dracula Was a Woman.*

68. Keesey, *Daughters of Darkness,* p. 13, citing McNally, *Dracula Was a Woman.*

69. Keesey, *Daughters of Darkness,* p. 239.

70. Pat Califia, "The Vampire," in *Macho Sluts* (Boston: Alyson Publications, 1988), pp. 253 and 260.

71. Ibid., p. 182.

72. Ibid., p. 260.

73. Ibid., pp. 292–93.

74. Stevenson, "A Vampire in the Mirror," p. 148; Peter Davis, "Exploring the Kingdom of AIDS," *New York Times Magazine,* May 31, 1987, pp. 32–35.

75. Stevenson, "A Vampire in the Mirror," pp. 139ff.

76. Marilyn Bethany, "Banderas Plays On," *Premiere,* March 1994, p. 72.

77. Francis Ford Coppola, "Finding the Vampire's Soul," in *Bram Stoker's Dracula,* ed. Francis Ford Coppola and James V. Hart, p. 5.

78. Susan Ferraro, "Novels You Can Sink Your Teeth Into," *New York Times Magazine,* October 14, 1990, p. 67. Anne Rice writes contemporary fiction under the name Anne Rampling and pornography as A. N. Roquelaure.

79. Janet Maslin, "Meditation on Vampires, by Way of John Milton," *New York Times,* October 28, 1993, pp. C15 and C20.

80. Coppola and Hart, *Bram Stoker's Dracula,* p. 51.

81. Ibid., pp. 55–56.

82. Blurb to the paperback edition of Anne Rice's *The Vampire Lestat* (New York: Ballantine Books, 1985).

83. Rice, *The Vampire Lestat,* pp. 111, 90, and 119.

84. Ibid., pp. 157 and 169.

85. Ibid., p. 171.

86. Whitley Strieber, *The Hunger* (New York: Avon Books, 1981).

87. Weiss, *Vampires and Violets,* p. 98.

88. Shocking Gay Pride Catalog 1994 (mail order), San Antonio, Texas.

89. Thomas Sotinel, quoted in Alan Riding, "Discovering a Film Idol's Feet of Clay," *New York Times,* April 28, 1994, p. C24.

90. Ibid., p. C20, emphasis added.

91. Dominique Janet, in ibid.

92. Ibid.

Chapter 4: No Scandal in Bohemia

1. H. L. Mencken, *Prejudices,* First Series (London: Penguin, 1965), p. 198.

2. The phrase is James Strachey's, from a letter to his brother Lytton, dated August 26, 1909. Robert Skidelsky, *John Maynard Keynes: Hopes Betrayed 1883–1920* (New York: Penguin, 1994), p. 238.

3. Frances Partridge, quoted in Gretchen Holbrook Gerzina, *Carrington: A Life* (New York: W. W. Norton, 1989), p. 154.

4. Michael Holroyd, *Lytton Strachey: A Biography* (Harmondsworth: Penguin, 1989), pp. 618–29.

5. See for example, David Gadd, *The Loving Friends: A Portrait of Bloomsbury* (New York: Harcourt Brace Jovanovich, 1974).

6. Holroyd, *Lytton Strachey,* p. 636.

7. Ibid., pp. 634–35.

8. Ibid., p. 646; and Gerzina, *Carrington,* p. 90.

9. Holroyd, *Lytton Strachey,* p. 639.

10. Gerzina, *Carrington,* p. 154.

11. Lytton Strachey to Carrington, May 20, 1921, in Holroyd, *Lytton Strachey,* p. 820.

12. Dora Carrington to Lytton Strachey, British Library, Strachey Collection. Quoted in Mary Ann Caws, *Women of Bloomsbury: Virginia, Vanessa, and Carrington* (New York: Routledge, 1990), p. 129.

13. Holroyd, *Lytton Strachey,* p. 504.

14. Lytton Strachey to Leonard Woolf, February 19, 1909, in ibid., p. 404.

15. Lytton Strachey to Leonard Woolf, February 20, 1909, in ibid., p. 406.

16. Dora Carrington, *Carrington: Letters and Extracts from Her Diaries,* ed. David Carrington (London: Jonathan Cape, 1970). See also Sallie Bingham, *Passion and Prejudice* (New York: Applause Books, 1991), p. 199.

17. Ernest Jones to Sigmund Freud, in Bingham, *Passion and Prejudice,* p. 196.

18. Susan E. Tifft and Alex S. Jones, *The Patriarch: The Rise and Fall of the Bingham Dynasty* (New York: Summit Books, 1991), pp. 89–90; John Houseman, *Run-Through: A Memoir* (New York: Simon & Schuster, 1972), pp. 55–56.

19. Bingham, *Passion and Prejudice,* p. 200.

20. Tifft and Jones, *The Patriarch,* pp. 128–29.

21. Carrington to Alix Strachey, undated, in Gerzina, *Carrington,* p. 210.

22. Bingham, *Passion and Prejudice,* p. 198.

23. Ibid.

24. Ibid.

25. Gerzina, *Carrington,* p. 293.

26. Skidelsky, *Hopes Betrayed,* p. 128.

27. Ibid., pp. xv-xvi; Sir William Rees-Mogg, *The Times* (London), November 10, 1983; David Marquand, *Encounter,* April 1984.

28. J. C. Gilbert, *Keynes's Impact on Monetary Economics* (London, Boston: Butterworth Scientific, 1982), 16n; Skidelsky, *Hopes Betrayed,* p. xxii.

29. Robert Skidelsky, *John Maynard Keynes, the Economist as Savior 1920–1937* (New York: Allen Lane/Penguin Press, 1994), p. 140.

30. Letter from J. M. Keynes to Duncan Grant, December 17, 1910, in ibid., p. 256.

31. Skidelsky, *The Economist as Savior,* p. 35.

32. J. M. Keynes to Lytton Strachey, December 27, 1922; Vanessa Bell to J. M. Keynes, January 1, 1922; J. M. Keynes to Vanessa Bell, January 6, 1922, in Skidelsky, *The Economist as Savior,* p. 93.

33. Lytton Strachey to Sebastian Sprott, June 6, 1922, in Skidelsky, *The Economist as Savior,* p. 101.

34. Duncan Grant to Vanessa Bell, January 25, 1922, in Skidelsky, *The Economist as Savior,* pp. 100–101.

35. Letter from Vanessa Bell to Roger Fry, October 29, 1922, in Skidelsky, *The Economist as Savior,* p. 116.

36. Brenda Maddox, *D. H. Lawrence: The Story of a Marriage* (New York: Simon & Schuster, 1994), p. 312.

37. Ibid., p. 227.

38. Richard Aldington, introduction to D. H. Lawrence's *Women in Love* (New York: Viking Press, 1960), p. xi.

39. Lawrence, *Women in Love,* p. 344.

40. Ibid., p. 472.

41. Aldington, introduction to *Women in Love,* p. xii.

42. Maddox, *D. H. Lawrence,* p. 12.

43. Ibid., p. 203.

44. Ibid., p. 227.

45. Maurice Magnus, letter to Norman Douglas, October 28, 1920, Beinecke Rare Books and Manuscript Library, Yale University, quoted in Maddox, *D. H. Lawrence,* p. 269.

46. Lois P. Rudnick, *Mabel Dodge Luhan: New Woman, New Worlds* (Albuquerque: University of New Mexico Press, 1984), p. 216; Maddox, *D. H. Lawrence,* p. 352.

47. "In Davies's judgment, as indeed in the view of Bynner in Santa Fe, Lawrence was not homosexual. Unlike both [Giuseppe] Orioli and Aldington, each of whom later declared the belief that Lawrence's rage stemmed from a refusal to admit his homosexuality, Davies considered that Lawrence's mining background, with its strong emphasis on virility and comradeship, had forced him to mask the deeply feminine side of his nature with a false masculinity." Maddox, *D. H. Lawrence,* p. 450.

48. Benita Eisler, *O'Keeffe and Stieglitz, an American Romance* (New York: Doubleday, 1991), p. 398.

49. Ibid., p. 459.

50. Ibid., p. 488.

51. Hayden Herrera, *Frida: A Biography of Frida Kahlo* (New York: Harper & Row, 1983), p. 198.

52. Jean van Heijenoort, quoted in ibid., pp. 198–99.

53. Herrera, *Frida,* p. 370.

54. Ibid.

55. Lillian Faderman, *Odd Girls and Twilight Lovers: A History of Lesbian Life in Twentieth-Century America* (New York: Columbia University Press, 1991), p. 63, emphasis added.

56. Ibid., p. 67.

57. Edward Carpenter, *Love's Coming of Age* (New York: Mitchell Kennerley, 1911), p. 122.

58. See Ellen Kay Trimberger, "Feminism, Men and Modern Love: Greenwich Village, 1900–1925," in *Powers of Desire: The Politics of Sexuality,* ed. Ann Snitow, Christine Stansell, and Sharon Thompson (New York: Monthly Review Press, 1983), pp. 130–52.

59. Faderman, *Odd Girls and Twilight Lovers,* p. 86.

60. Edmund Wilson, *The Shores of Light: A Literary Chronicle of the Twenties and Thirties* (New York: Farrar, Straus & Young, 1952).

61. Ann Douglas, *Terrible Honesty: Mongrel Manhattan in the 1920s* (New York: Farrar, Straus and Giroux, 1995), p. 48.

62. Sandra M. Gilbert and Susan Gubar, eds., *The Norton Anthology of Literature by Women: The Tradition in English* (New York: W. W. Norton, 1985), p. 1554.

63. Jean Gould, *The Poet and the Book* (New York: Dodd, Mead, 1969), p. 162.

64. Faderman, *Odd Girls and Twilight Lovers,* p. 87.

65. George Chauncey, *Gay New York: Gender, Urban Culture, and the Making of the Gay Male World 1890–1940* (New York: Basic Books, 1994).

66. Gould, *Poet and the Book,* p. 189.

67. Ibid., p. 208; p. 202.

68. Ibid., p. 280.

69. Max Eastman, "My Friendship with Edna Millay," in *Great Companions: Critical Memoirs of Some Famous Friends* (New York: Farrar, Straus & Cudahy, 1959), p. 103.

70. Anne Sexton to W. D. Snodgrass, October 6, 1958, Linda Gray Sexton and Lois Ames, eds., *Anne Sexton: A Self-Portrait in Letters* (Boston: Houghton Mifflin, 1977), p. 40, cited in Diane Wood Middlebrook, *Anne Sexton: A Biography* (Boston: Houghton Mifflin, 1991), pp. 92–93.

71. "I too beneath your moon, almighty Sex," in *Norton Anthology of Literature by Women,* ed. Gilbert and Gubar, pp. 1567–68.

72. Edna St. Vincent Millay, "Rendezvous," in *Norton Anthology of Literature by Women,* ed. Gilbert and Gubar, p. 1566.

73. Edna St. Vincent Millay, "First Fig," in *Norton Anthology of Literature by Women,* ed. Gilbert and Gubar, p. 1555.

74. Max Eastman, "My Friendship with Edna Millay," in *Great Companions,* p. 91.

75. Chris Albertson, *Bessie* (New York: Stein & Day, 1972), p. 116.

76. Paul Oliver, liner notes to *Ma Rainey: The Complete 1928 Sessions in Chronological Order,* Document Records, 1993.

77. Faderman, *Odd Girls and Twilight Lovers,* p. 75.

78. Ibid.

79. Ibid., p. 72.

80. Romare Bearden, interview with Jervis Anderson, quoted in Anderson, *This Was Harlem 1900–1950* (New York: Farrar, Straus & Giroux, 1981), p. 169.

81. Eric Garber, "Gladys Bentley: The Bulldagger Who Sang the Blues," *Out/Look,* Spring 1988, pp. 52–61.

82. Ibid., p. 61.

83. Faderman, *Odd Girls and Twilight Lovers,* p. 73.

84. Ibid., pp. 70–71.

85. Ibid., p. 71.

86. Ibid.

87. Ibid. In "Harlem Nights," *The Advocate,* March 26, 1991, p. 55, Faderman cites Milt Machlin's *Libby* as a source for these bisexual "high livers."

88. Faderman, *Odd Girls and Twilight Lovers,* p. 76.

89. Ibid., p. 74.

90. Ibid., p. 75.

91. Jean-Claude Baker and Chris Chase, *Josephine: The Hungry Heart* (New York: Random House, 1993), p. 38; Daphne Duval Harrison, *Black Pearls: Blues Queens of the 1920s* (New Brunswick, N.J.: Rutgers University Press, 1988), p. 242.

92. Baker and Chase, *Josephine,* p. 64.

93. Faderman, *Odd Girls and Twilight Lovers,* p. 69.

94. Wayne F. Cooper, foreword to Claude McKay, *Home to Harlem* (1928; reprinted, Boston: Northeastern University Press, 1987), p. xviii.

95. McKay, *Home to Harlem,* p. 3.

96. Josephine Herbst to Harold Cruse, November 18, 1968, Josephine Herbst papers, Yale University, in Tyrone Tillery, *Claude McKay: A Black Poet's Struggle for Identity* (Amherst: University of Massachusetts Press, 1992), pp. 12 and 186. For more on Herbst's bisexuality, see also Elinor Langer, *Josephine Herbst* (Boston: Northeastern University Press, 1994).

97. Wayne F. Cooper, *Claude McKay, Rebel Sojourner in the Harlem Renaissance: A Biography* (Baton Rouge: Louisiana State University Press, 1987), p. 75.

98. Charles S. Johnson, "Countee Cullen Was My Friend," September 12, 1951, quoted in Stephen H. Bronz, *Roots of Negro Racial Consciousness. The 1920's: Three Harlem Renaissance Authors* (New York: Libra Publishers, 1964).

99. Bruce Kellner, ed., *The Harlem Renaissance: A Historical Dictionary for the Era* (New York: Methuen, 1987), p. 89.

100. Ibid., p. 368.

101. Thadious M. Davis, *Nella Larsen, Novelist of the Harlem Renaissance: A Woman's Life Unveiled* (Baton Rouge: Louisiana State University Press, 1994), p. 325.

102. Henry Crowder, from his unpublished autobiography, written in the mid-1930s with the help of journalist Hugo Speck, quoted in Anne Chisholm, *Nancy Cunard* (New York: Alfred A. Knopf, 1979), p. 133.

103. Chisholm, *Nancy Cunard,* p. 163.

104. Faderman, *Odd Girls and Twilight Lovers,* p. 69.

105. Kellner, *Harlem Renaissance,* p. 354.

106. David Levering Lewis, *When Harlem Was in Vogue* (New York: Vintage, 1982), p. 236.

107. Langston Hughes, *The Big Sea* (New York: Alfred A. Knopf, 1940), p. 235.

108. Kellner, *Harlem Renaissance,* p. 357.

109. See Deborah McDowell, introduction to *"Quicksand" and "Passing"* (New Brunswick, N.J.: Rutgers University Press, 1986), pp. xxiii–xxvi; Judith Butler, "Passing, Queering: Nella Larsen's Psychoanalytic Challenge," in *Bodies That Matter* (New York: Routledge, 1993), pp. 167–86.

110. Lewis, *When Harlem Was in Vogue,* p. 58.

111. Letter from Mabel Dodge Luhan to Jean Toomer, n.d., in ibid., p. 73.

112. Ibid., p. 267.

113. Frances Wills Thorpe to Arnold Rampersad, in Rampersad, *The Life of Langston Hughes,* Vol. 2: *1941–1967: I Dream a World* (New York: Oxford University Press, 1988), p. 149.

114. Henry Louis Gates, Jr., "Looking for Modernism," in *Black American Cinema,* ed. Manthia Diawara (New York: Routledge, 1993), p. 202.

115. Ibid., p. 204.

116. Ibid., pp. 202–203.

117. Ibid., p. 202.

118. James Baldwin, *Giovanni's Room* (New York: Dell, 1956), p. 158.

119. Ibid., p. 10.

120. Ibid., p. 116.

121. Ibid., pp. 213–14.

122. Ibid., pp. 188–89.

123. Ibid., pp. 182–83.

124. Ibid., p. 212.

125. Ibid., p. 133.

126. Ibid., p. 209.

127. Fred Klein, *The Bisexual Option: A Concept of One Hundred Percent Intimacy* (New York: Arbor House, 1978), p. 184.

128. James Baldwin, "Encounter on the Seine: Black Meets Brown," in *Notes of a Native Son* (1955; reprinted, New York: Beacon Press, 1984), pp. 122–23. Originally published as "The Negro in Paris," in *The Reporter,* June 6, 1950.

129. Baldwin, "Introduction to the New Edition," *Notes of a Native Son,* pp. x–xi.

130. Eldridge Cleaver, "Notes on a Native Son," in *Soul on Ice* (New York: Delta, 1968), pp. 97–111.

131. Ibid., p. 101.

132. Ibid., p. 102.

133. Ibid., p. 103.

134. Ibid., p. 106.

135. Ibid., pp. 99, 100, and 98.

136. Ibid., p. 97.

137. Ibid., p. 102.

138. Ibid., p. 107.

139. Ibid., p. 98.

140. Ibid., p. 109.

141. Ibid., p. 98.

142. "Baldwin's essay on Richard Wright reveals that he despised—not Richard Wright, but his masculinity. He cannot confront the stud in others—except that he must either submit to it or destroy it. And he was not about to bow to a *black* man. Wright understood the truth of what Norman Mailer meant when he said '. . . for being a man is the continuing battle of one's life, and one loses a bit of manhood with every stale compromise to the authority of any power in which one does not believe.' "

143. In an introduction to Cleaver, *Soul on Ice,* p. xii.

Chapter 5: Bisexuality and Celebrity

1. George Gordon, Lord Byron, entry in memoranda after the publication of the first two cantos of *Childe Harold's Pilgrimage.* Cited in Thomas Moore, *Life of Lord Byron* (London: J. Murray, 1847), chapter 14.

2. In Antoni Gronowicz, *Garbo* (New York: Simon & Schuster, 1990), p. 63.

3. Richard Grenier, "Gore Vidal: What It's Like to Be Talented, Rich, and Bisexual," *Cosmopolitan,* November 1975, p. 167; Hector Arce, *The Secret Life of Tyrone Power* (New York: William Morrow, 1979), p. 187.

4. Charles Higham, *Errol Flynn: The Untold Story* (New York: Doubleday, 1980), p. 227.

5. Angela Bowie with Patrick Carr, *Backstage Passes: Life on the Wild Side with David Bowie* (New York: G.P. Putnam's Sons, 1993), p. 18.

6. Wendy Wasserstein, *The Sisters Rosensweig* (New York: Harcourt Brace Jovanovich, 1993), Act I, scene 4, pp. 49–50.

7. Donald Spoto, *Laurence Olivier: A Biography* (New York: HarperCollins, 1992). The account of the customs officer ruse can be found on page 246.

8. Ibid., p. 60.

9. Ibid., p. 223; p. 230.

10. Ibid., p. 61.

11. Ibid., p. 323.

12. Kenneth Tynan, *The Sound of Two Hands Clapping* (New York: Holt, Rinehart & Winston, 1975), p. 130.

13. Kenneth Tynan, *Othello: The National Theatre Production* (originally published New York: Stein & Day, 1966; reprinted in Tynan, *Profiles* [London: Nick Hern/ Walker, 1989], p. 205).

14. See Michael Redgrave, *In My Mind's I: An Actor's Autobiography* (New York: Viking Press, 1983); Rachel Kempson, *A Family and Its Fortunes* (London: Duckworth, 1986).

15. David Shipman, *Judy Garland: The Secret Life of an American Legend* (New York: Hyperion, 1993).

16. Christopher Andersen, *Jagger Unauthorized* (New York: Delacorte Press, 1993), p. 167.

17. John Dunbar, quoted in ibid., p. 167.

18. Christopher Winans, *Malcolm Forbes: The Man Who Had Everything* (New York: St. Martin's Press, 1990).

19. Charles Higham, *Howard Hughes: The Secret Life* (New York: G. P. Putnam's Sons, 1993).

20. Peter Manso, *Brando: The Biography* (New York: Hyperion, 1994), pp. 91 and 164.

21. Paul Rosenfield, "David Is Goliath," *Vanity Fair,* March 1992, p. 162.

22. Jonathan Gilmore, in Joe Hyams, *James Dean: Little Boy Lost* (New York: Warner Books, 1992), p. 80.

23. Michael Billington, "Lasciviously Pleasing," in *Olivier in Celebration,* ed. Garry O'Connor (New York: Dodd, Mead, 1987), p. 72.

24. Shipman, *Judy Garland,* p. 137.

25. Leslie Bennetts, "k. d. lang Cuts It Close," *Vanity Fair,* August 1993, p. 144.

26. Robert LaGuardia, *Monty: A Biography of Montgomery Clift* (New York: Primus, Donald I. Fine, 1988), p. 181.

27. Donald Spoto, *Blue Angel: The Life of Marlene Dietrich* (New York: Doubleday, 1992).

28. Hyams, *James Dean,* p. 209.

29. Andersen, *Jagger Unauthorized,* p. 139.

30. Clifton Fadiman, *Holiday* magazine, "in the first weeks of 1952"; Shipman, *Judy Garland,* p. 399.

31. Hyams, *James Dean,* p. 209.

32. Andersen, *Jagger Unauthorized,* pp. 127–28.

33. Susan Crimp and Patricia Burstein, *The Many Lives of Elton John* (New York: Birch Lane Press, 1992), p. 96.

34. J. Randy Taraborrelli, *Call Her Miss Ross: The Unauthorized Biography of Diana Ross* (New York: Birch Lane Press, 1989), p. 407.

35. Richard Goldstein, quoted in Ellis Amburn, *Pearl: The Obsessions and Passions of Janis Joplin* (New York: Warner Books, 1992), p. 129.

36. Shipman, *Judy Garland,* pp. 399–400.

37. Art Buchwald, "La Dietrich Great Anywhere She Goes," *International Herald Tribune,* December 13, 1959; Spoto, *Blue Angel,* pp. 268–69.

38. Sigmund Freud, "Psycho-analytic Notes on an Autobiographical Account of a Case of Paranoia" (1911), *SE* 12:63–65.

39. Sigmund Freud, "Hysterical Phantasies and Their Relation to Bisexuality" (1908), *SE* 9:165.

40. Ibid., p. 166.

41. Maria Riva, *Marlene Dietrich* (New York: Alfred A. Knopf, 1993).

42. Leon Edel, *Henry James: A Life* (New York: Harper & Row, 1985), pp. xi–xii.

43. Winans, *Malcolm Forbes,* p. 19.

44. From the author's statement on the first page of the book, signed in longhand "Angela Bowie"—thus by implication an especially "personal" and "direct" communication.

45. Winans, *Malcolm Forbes,* pp. 18, 19, and 141.

46. Daniel J. Boorstin, *The Image: A Guide to Pseudo-Events in America* (New York: Atheneum, 1961; reprinted, 1987).

47. Paul Rosenfield, "David Is Goliath."

48. Brendan Lemon, "David Geffen," *The Advocate,* December 19, 1992, p. 38.

49. Cliff Jahr, "Elton's Frank Talk . . . the Lonely Love Life of a Superstar," *Rolling Stone,* October 7, 1976.

50. Crimp and Burstein, *Many Lives of Elton John,* p. 223.

51. *Boston Globe,* March 4, 1992, quoting a *Rolling Stone* interview with Philip Norman, author of *Elton John: The Biography* (Harmony Books, 1992).

52. Kurt Loder, "Straight Time," *Rolling Stone,* May 12, 1983; Henry Edwards and Tony Zanetta, *Stardust: The David Bowie Story* (New York: McGraw-Hill, 1986), p. 393.

53. Andersen, *Jagger Unauthorized,* p. 376.

54. Joan Baez, *And a Voice to Sing With* (New York: New American Library, 1987), pp. 81–82.

55. Ibid., p. 82.

56. *Time,* December 14, 1992, p. 55.

57. Robert Lipsyte, "Connors the Killer Is Really Just a Child," *New York Times,* September 6, 1991, p. B12.

58. Sandra Faulkner with Judy Nelson, *Love Match: Nelson vs. Navratilova,* introduction by Rita Mae Brown (New York: Birch Lane Press, 1993), p. 75.

59. Billie Jean King with Frank Deford, *Billie Jean* (New York: Viking Press, 1982), p. 27.

60. Hyams, *James Dean,* p. 79.

61. Grenier, "Gore Vidal," p. 184.

62. Joan Peyser, *Bernstein: A Biography* (New York: Ballantine Books, 1987), p. 301.

63. Hyams, *James Dean,* p. 209.

64. Charles Higham and Roy Moseley, *Cary Grant: The Lonely Heart* (Sevenoaks, Kent: New English Library, 1989), p. 81.

65. Higham, *Howard Hughes,* pp. 67–70, 76–78, 89–90, 93–94.

66. Rock Hudson and Sara Davidson, *Rock Hudson: His Story* (New York: William Morrow, 1986), p. 97.

67. Ibid., p. 89.

68. Hyams, *James Dean,* p. 2.

69. Hudson and Davidson, *Rock Hudson,* p. 57.

70. Ibid.

71. Steven Bach, *Marlene Dietrich: Life and Legend* (New York: William Morrow, 1992).

Chapter 6: The Secret of Tiresias

1. In Timothy White, *Rock Lives: Profiles and Interviews.* A headline in the *Boston Globe* reported this news in the rather Joycean phrase "Who's Townshend Says He's Bisexual" (November 8, 1990).

2. Ovid, *Metamorphoses* 3.323–31. "Venus huic erat utraque nota. / nam duo magnorum viridi coeuntia silva / corpora serpentum baculi violaverat ictu / deque viro factus (mirabile) femina septem / egerat autumnos; octavo rursus eosdem / vidit, et 'est vestrae si tanta potentia plagae' / dixit, 'ut auctoris sortem in contraria mutet, / nunc quoque vos feriam.' percussis anguibus isdem / forma prior rediit, genetivaque venit imago."

3. Hesiod, *The Homeric Hymns and Homerica,* trans. Hugh G. Evelyn-White (Cambridge, Mass.: Harvard University Press, 1977). "Teiresias" is the transliterated Greek spelling. I have consistently used that spelling when citing from Greek texts, or from scholars who themselves cite from the Greek, and "Tiresias" when citing from Latin texts or from modern English.

4. John Allen Stevenson, "A Vampire in the Mirror: The Sexuality of *Dracula,*" *PMLA,* vol. 103, no. 2 (March 1988), p. 146.

5. Jan Clausen, "My Interesting Condition," *Out/Look,* vol. 2, no. 3 (Winter 1990), p. 13.

6. "The Difference between Men and Women from People Who Have Slept with Both," "Donahue," transcript #3205, national feed date May 14, 1991.

7. Linda Yellen, producer of *Second Serve,* quoted in "Invasion of the Gender Blenders," *People,* April 23, 1984, p. 99.

8. "My Husband-to-Be Is a Transsexual and My Mother Is Upset," "Donahue," transcript #3405, national feed date February 18, 1992.

9. Martin Duberman, "The Bisexual Debate," in *Readings in Human Sexuality,* ed. Chad Gordon and Gayle Johnson (New York: Harper & Row, 1980), p. 183.

10. Larry Rivers with Arnold Weinstein, *What Did I Do? The Unauthorized Biography of Larry Rivers* (New York: HarperCollins, 1992), p. 227.

11. Ibid., p. 233.

12. Ibid., p. 235.

13. Ibid., p. 222.

14. Ibid., p. 236.

15. T. S. Eliot, *The Waste Land,* in *T. S. Eliot: The Complete Poems and Plays, 1909– 1950* (New York: Harcourt, Brace & World, 1952), lines 217–20, 228–30, and 243–46.

16. Homer, *The Odyssey,* trans. E. V. Rieu, revised D. C. H. Rieu (London: Penguin, 1991), Book II, lines 126–27.

17. Djuna Barnes, *Nightwood* (New York: Harcourt, Brace & Co., 1937; reprinted, New Directions, 1961), p. 79.

18. Ibid., p. 100.

19. Ibid., pp. 90–91.

20. Judith Butler, *Gender Trouble: Feminism and the Subversion of Identity* (New York: Routledge, 1990), pp. 60–61.

21. Gayle Rubin, "The Traffic in Women: Notes on the 'Political Economy' of Sex," in *Towards an Anthropology of Women,* ed. Rayna R. Reiter (New York: Monthly Review Press, 1975), p. 180.

22. Linda Williams, *Hard Core: Power, Pleasure, and the "Frenzy of the Visible"* (Berkeley: University of California Press, 1989), pp. 152 and 287.

23. Conversation with the author, May 1994.

24. Jeanette Winterson, *Written on the Body* (London: Jonathan Cape, 1992), pp. 16, 21, and 92.

25. Ibid., pp. 125 and 128.

26. Mary Renault's biographer David Sweetman notes that "the 'female lover,' the eunuch Bagoas, the Persian boy . . . seems to represent for Mary a solution to the problems of gender by being, like T. S. Eliot's Tiresias, of neither, yet of both sexes at once." *Mary Renault: A Biography* (New York: Harcourt, Brace & Co., 1993), p. 294.

27. Meredith Steinbach, "Two Chapters from *Teiresias*," *TriQuarterly,* vol. 71 (Winter 1985), pp. 198–99.

28. Ibid., pp. 200–201.

29. See for example, Nicole Loraux, *Les expériences de Tirésias: Le féminin et l'homme grec* (Paris: Gallimard, 1989), pp. 1–26.

30. Donald Spoto, *The Dark Side of Genius: The Life of Alfred Hitchcock* (New York: Ballantine Books, 1983), p. 105.

31. Sigmund Freud, *The Interpretation of Dreams* (1900), *SE* 4:261–64.

32. Psychoanalyst Géza Róheim suggested that Oedipus and Tiresias are aspects of the same person, and that both are versions of the child who gazes upon the primal scene. "The dialogue they carry on is a dialogue between *repression* (Oedipus) and the *return of the repressed* (Tiresias). The 'bisexuality of the seer,' the bisexuality of Tiresias, derives from his witnessing the coupling that makes male and female into one. And the riddle of the Sphinx is the 'composite being consisting of a combination of mother and father' in the sex act. Thus, 'if Oedipus is the man who sees the Sphinx and understands' the riddle, that is, the primal scene, we must assume that Tiresias the seer and Oedipus the wise are really the same person. Like Tiresias, Oedipus becomes blind and like Tiresias he is transported bodily from this world." Róheim, *The Riddle of the Sphinx, or Human Origins,* trans. R. Money-Kyrle (London: Hogarth Press and Institutes for Psychoanalysis, 1934), p. 21; Róheim, "Tiresias and Other Seers," *The Psychoanalytic Review,* vol. 33. no. 3 (July 1946), pp. 315–17.

33. Sophocles, *Oedipus Rex,* 360ff., in David Grene's translation the passage is rendered, "I say you are the murderer of the king / whose murderer you seek." *Oedipus the King,* in *Sophocles I: Oedipus Rex, Oedipus at Colonus, Antigone,* ed. David Grene and Richmond Lattimore (Chicago: University of Chicago Press, 1954), p. 26.

34. Ovid, *Metamorphoses,* 3.353–55. "multi illum iuvenes, multae cupiere puellae; sed fuit in tenera tam dura superbia forma, / nulli illum iuvenes, nullae tetigere puellae."

35. A. W. Bulloch, ed., *Callimachus, the Fifth Hymn* (Cambridge and New York: Cambridge University Press, 1985).

36. Nicole Loraux, *Les expériences de Tirésias,* p. 255.

37. Jacques Lacan, "The Direction of the Treatment and the Principles of Its Power" (originally published 1958) in *Écrits: A Selection,* trans. Alan Sheridan (New York: W. W. Norton, 1977), p. 236.

38. Jacques Lacan, "Of the Subject Who Is Supposed to Know, Of the First Dyad, and Of the Good," in *The Four Fundamental Concepts of Psycho-Analysis,* trans. Alan Sheridan (New York: W. W. Norton, 1981), p. 232.

39. ". . . hysterically blind people are only blind as far as consciousness is concerned; in their unconscious they see." Sigmund Freud, "The Psycho-Analytic View of Psychogenic Disturbance of Vision," *SE,* 11:212.

40. Sigmund Freud, *Three Essays on the Theory of Sexuality* (1905), *SE* 7:220.

41. Letter from Sigmund Freud to Wilhelm Fliess, September 19, 1901, in *The Complete Letters of Sigmund Freud to Wilhelm Fliess 1887–1904,* ed. and trans. Jeffrey Moussaief Masson (Cambridge, Mass.: Harvard University Press, 1985), p. 450.

Chapter 7: Freud and the Golden Fliess

1. *The Complete Letters of Sigmund Freud to Wilhelm Fliess 1887–1904,* ed. and trans. Jeffrey Moussaief Masson (Cambridge, Mass.: Harvard University Press, 1985), p. 286.

2. Ibid., p. 361.

3. Sigmund Freud, "Why War?" (1933), *SE* 22:211.

4. Sigmund Freud, *Three Essays on the Theory of Sexuality* (1905), *SE* 7:136.

5. Plato, *Symposium,* trans. Michael Joyce, in *Plato: The Collected Dialogues,* ed.

Edith Hamilton and Huntington Cairns (Princeton, N.J.: Princeton University Press, 1961), pp. 542–44.

6. Freud, *Three Essays,* p. 144.

7. So David F. Greenberg speculates, in *The Construction of Homosexuality* (Chicago: University of Chicago Press, 1988), p. 146.

8. See for example, Eva Cantarella's *Bisexuality in the Ancient World,* trans. Cormac Ó'Cuilleanáin (New Haven: Yale University Press, 1992). "For the Greeks and Romans . . . homosexuality was not an exclusive choice. Loving another man was not an option falling outside the norm, a different or somehow deviant decision. It was just one part of the experience of life: the manifestation of an impulse which could be either a matter of feelings or of sexuality; during one's lifetime this would alternate and interweave (sometimes simultaneously) with the love of a woman" (p. vii). Much of Cantarella's book consists of examples of such bisexual relationships in Greek and Roman history, philosophy, and literature, as well as in the structures of pedagogy and citizenship.

9. Diogenes Laertius, *Lives and Opinions of Eminent Philosophers,* trans. C.D. Yonge (London: George Bell and Sons, 1891), p. 72; Michel Foucault, *History of Sexuality,* vol. 2: *The Uses of Pleasure,* trans. Robert Hurley (New York: Viking Press, 1985).

10. Xenophon, *The Works of Xenephon,* trans. H. G. Dakyms (London: Macmillan, 1890–97), *Memorabilia,* vol. 3, no. 11, pp. 121–22.

11. Eva Keuls, *The Reign of the Phallus: Sexual Politics in Ancient Athens* (New York: Harper & Row, 1985), p. 194.

12. Greenberg, *Construction of Homosexuality,* pp. 144–45.

13. Plato, *Laws,* trans. A.E. Taylor, in *Plato: The Collected Dialogues,* ed. Edith Hamilton and Huntington Cairns (Princeton, N.J.: Princeton University Press, 1961), p. 1405.

14. Freud, *Three Essays on the Theory of Sexuality,* pp. 136–37.

15. Ibid., pp. 145–46.

16. Ibid., p. 141.

17. Sigmund Freud, "Femininity" (1933), *SE* 22:114.

18. Hélène Cixous, "Sorties," in Cixous and Catherine Clément, *The Newly Born Woman,* trans. Betsy Wing (Minneapolis: University of Minnesota Press, 1986), p. 84. Originally published as *La Jeune Née* (Paris: Union Générale d'Éditions, 1975).

19. Ovid, *Metamorphoses* 4:284–89. "Sic ubi complexu coierunt membra tenaci / nec duo sint et forma duplex, nec femina dici / nec puer ut possit, neutrumque et untrumque videntur," 4:377–79.

20. OED lists, among other citations, these: "Another likewise was found of sixteene yeeres of age, a very Hermaphrodite of doubtless sex between both." "An hermaphrodite may purchase according to that sexe which prevaileth."

21. Again from the OED: "Henry the Eighth was a kind of Hermaphrodite in Religion," "He acts the Hermaphrodite of Good and Ill, But God detests his double Tongue and Will," "A race of moral Hermaphrodites."

22. Jean Cocteau, *The Infernal Machine,* in *The Infernal Machine and Other Plays,* trans. Albert Bermel (New York: New Directions, 1963), p. 87.

23. Friedrich Nietzsche, *Beyond Good and Evil: Prelude to a Philosophy of the Future,* trans. Walter Kaufmann (1886; reprinted New York: Vintage Books, 1966), part 1, sect. 1, p. 9.

24. George Devereux, "Why Oedipus Killed Laius: A Note on the Complementary Oedipus Complex in Greek Drama," *International Journal of Psycho-analysis,* vol. 34 (1953), pp. 132–41.

25. Marianne Krüll, *Freud and His Father,* trans. Arnold Pomerans (New York: W. W. Norton, 1986), p. 62.

26. Marie Balmary, *Psychoanalyzing Psychoanalysis: Freud and the Hidden Fault of the Father,* trans. Ned Lukacher (Baltimore: Johns Hopkins University Press, 1982), pp. 6, 27, and 37; Krüll, *Freud and His Father,* p. 62; Devereux, "Why Oedipus Killed Laius."

27. Sigmund Freud, *An Outline of Psycho-Analysis* (1937), *SE* 23:188.

28. Freud, "Femininity," p. 116.

29. Muriel Rukeyser, 1973, in *The Muriel Rukeyser Reader,* ed. Jan Heller Levi (New York: W. W. Norton, 1994), p. 252.

30. Cocteau, *The Infernal Machine,* p. 9.

31. See for example, Helmut Remmler, *Das Geheimnis der Sphinx* (Olten: Walter Verlag, 1988).

32. Theodore Thass-Thiemann, "Oedipus and the Sphinx: The Linguistic Approach to Unconscious Fantasies," *Psychoanalytic Review,* vol. 44 (1957), pp. 10–33.

33. Géza Róheim, *The Riddle of the Sphinx, or Human Origins,* trans. R. Money-Kyrle (London: Hogarth Press and Institutes for Psycho-analysis, 1934). See Peter Rudnytsky, *Freud and Oedipus* (New York: Columbia University Press, 1987) for a thoughtful consideration of nineteenth- and early-twentieth-century readings of the myth and Sophocles' play.

34. Ernest Jones, *The Life and Work of Sigmund Freud,* ed. and abridged by Lionel Trilling and Steven Marcus (New York: Basic Books, 1961), pp. 243–44.

35. Nietszche, *Beyond Good and Evil,* sec. 1.

36. Rudnytsky, *Freud and Oedipus,* p. 335.

37. Letter from Sigmund Freud to Wilhelm Fliess, March 15, 1898, in Masson, *Complete Letters of Sigmund Freud,* p. 323.

38. Letter from Sigmund Freud to Wilhelm Fliess, August 7, 1901, in Masson, *Complete Letters of Sigmund Freud,* p. 448.

39. Letter from Sigmund Freud to Wilhelm Fliess, August 1, 1899, in Masson, *Complete Letters of Sigmund Freud,* p. 364.

40. Letter from Sigmund Freud to Wilhelm Fliess, December 6, 1896, in Masson, *Complete Letters of Sigmund Freud,* p. 212.

41. Juliet Mitchell, *Psychoanalysis and Feminism* (New York: Vintage Books, 1975), p. 51.

42. Sigmund Freud, *The Interpretation of Dreams* (1900), *SE* 5:606.

43. Jacqueline Rose, "Introduction-II," in Jacques Lacan and the École Freudienne, *Feminine Sexuality,* ed. and trans. by Jacqueline Rose and ed. by Juliet Mitchell (New York: W. W. Norton, 1982), p. 49n.

44. "The establishment of an unambiguous and unquestioned gender identity." Robert J. Stoller, "Facts and Fancies: An Examination of Freud's Concept of Bisexuality," in *Women and Analysis: Dialogues on Psychoanalytic Views of Femininity,* ed. Jean Strouse, (New York: Grossman Publishers, 1974).

45. Sigmund Freud, "A Child is Being Beaten" (1919), *SE* 17:202.

46. Ibid., p. 193.

47. Sigmund Freud, *The Ego and the Id* (1923), *SE* 19:33.

48. Rose, "Introduction-II," p. 49.

49. Hélène Cixous, "Sorties," in Cixous and Clément, *The Newly Born Woman,* pp. 84–85.

50. Judith Butler, *Gender Trouble: Feminism and the Subversion of Identity* (New York: Routledge, 1990), p. 74, 75.

51. Sigmund Freud, *The Psychopathology of Everyday Life* (1901), *SE* 6:147.

52. Friedrich Nietzsche, *Beyond Good and Evil,* trans. Helen Zimmern (London: Allen & Unwin, 1967), sec. 4, subsec. 217.

53. See Marjorie Garber, "Joe Camel, an X-rated Smoke," *New York Times,* March 20, 1992, A33.

54. Letter from Sigmund Freud to Wilhelm Fliess, December 29, 1897, in Masson, *Complete Letters of Sigmund Freud,* p. 290.

55. Letter from Sigmund Freud to Wilhelm Fliess, March 15, 1898, in Masson, *Complete Letters of Sigmund Freud,* p. 303.

56. Letter from Sigmund Freud to Wilhelm Fliess, August 7, 1901, in Masson, *Complete Letters of Sigmund Freud,* p. 447.

57. Letter from Emma Jung to Sigmund Freud, October 30, 1911, in *The Freud/Jung Letters: The Correspondence between Sigmund Freud and C. G. Jung,* ed. William McGuire, trans. Ralph Mannheim and R. F. C. Hull, Bollingen Series XCIV (Princeton, N.J.: Princeton University Press, 1974), p. 452.

58. Letter from Sigmund Freud to Sándor Ferenczi, October 6, 1910. Quoted in Ernest Jones, *Sigmund Freud: Life and Work* (New York: Basic Books, 1954–57), vol. 2, p. 92.

59. Marie Bonaparte, unpublished notebook. Cited in Masson, *Complete Letters of Sigmund Freud,* p. 3.

60. Freud, *Psychopathology of Everyday Life,* pp. 143–44.

61. Letter from Sigmund Freud to Wilhelm Fliess, May 21, 1894, in Masson, *Complete Letters of Sigmund Freud,* p. 73.

62. Letter from Sigmund Freud to Wilhelm Fliess, July 14, 1894, in Masson, *Complete Letters of Sigmund Freud,* p. 87.

63. Freud, *Interpretation of Dreams,* p. 331.

64. Ibid., pp. 421–22. John Kerr, *A Most Dangerous Method: The Story of Jung, Freud, and Sabina Spielrein* (New York: Alfred A. Knopf, 1993), p. 80, also notes the relevance of these dreams to Freud's competitiveness with Fliess over the bisexual theory.

65. Freud, *Interpretation of Dreams,* pp. 422–23.

66. Jones, *Life and Work of Sigmund Freud,* pp. 243–44.

67. Freud, *Three Essays on the Theory of Sexuality,* p. 220.

68. Letter from Sigmund Freud to Wilhelm Fliess, August 7, 1901, in Masson, *Complete Letters of Sigmund Freud,* p. 448.

69. Letter from Sigmund Freud to Wilhelm Fliess, September 19, 1901, in Masson, *Complete Letters of Sigmund Freud,* p. 450.

70. Letter to Freud, July 20, 1904, in Masson, *Complete Letters of Sigmund Freud,* p. 463.

71. Freud, "Analysis of a Phobia in a Five-Year-Old Boy" (1909), *SE* 10:36n.

72. Otto Weininger, *Sex and Character* (London: William Heinemann, 1903), p. 7.

73. Ibid., p. 8.

74. Ibid., p. 17.

75. Ibid., p. 80.

76. Ibid., p. 45.

77. Ibid., p. 188.

78. Ibid., p. 189.

79. Ibid., p. 251.

80. Ibid., p. 66.

81. Ibid., pp. 311, 304, 321, 306, and 308.

82. Freud, "Analysis of a Phobia," p. 36n.

83. Letter to Freud, July 20, 1904, in Masson, *Complete Letters of Sigmund Freud,* p. 463.

84. Letter from Sigmund Freud to Wilhelm Fliess, July 23, 1904, in Masson, *Complete Letters of Sigmund Freud,* p. 464.

85. Letter from Sigmund Freud to Wilhelm Fliess, July 27, 1904, in Masson, *Complete Letters of Sigmund Freud,* pp. 466–68.

86. Jones, *Life and Work of Sigmund Freud,* p. 206.

87. Ibid.

88. Sigmund Freud, "Psycho-analytical Notes on an Autobiographical Case of Paranoia" (1911), *SE* 12:59–65.

89. Letter from Sigmund Freud to Carl Gustav Jung, February 17, 1908, in McGuire, *Freud/Jung Letters,* p. 121.

90. For example, see Masson, *Complete Letters of Sigmund Freud,* p. 460.

91. Juliet Mitchell, *Psychoanalysis and Feminism* (New York: Vintage Books, 1974), pp. 47–48.

92. Henry James, "The Figure in the Carpet," in *The Figure in the Carpet and Other Stories,* ed. Frank Kermode (London: Penguin Books, 1986), p. 398.

93. Letter from Sigmund Freud to Wilhelm Fliess, March 15, 1898, in Masson, *Complete Letters of Sigmund Freud,* p. 303.

94. Letter from Sigmund Freud to Wilhelm Fliess, January 30, 1901, in Masson, *Complete Letters of Sigmund Freud,* p. 434.

95. Letter from Sigmund Freud to Wilhelm Fliess, August 7, 1901, in Masson, *Complete Letters of Sigmund Freud,* p. 448.

96. Freud, "A Child is Being Beaten," p. 201.

97. Ibid., p. 200.

98. Freud, *Three Essays on the Theory of Sexuality,* p. 144.

99. Sigmund Freud, "Hysterical Phantasies and Their Relation to Bisexuality" (1908), *SE* 9:152.

100. Mitchell, *Psychoanalysis and Feminism,* p. 52.

101. Sigmund Freud, "The Psychogenesis of a Case of Homosexuality in a Woman" (1920), *SE* 18:147.

102. Ibid., p. 150.

103. Ibid., p. 154.

104. Ibid.

105. Ibid., p. 158.

106. Ibid.

107. Ibid., p. 170.

108. Ibid., p. 157.

109. Letter from Sigmund Freud to Wilhelm Fliess, October 15, 1897, in Masson, *Complete Letters of Sigmund Freud,* p. 272.

110. Freud, "Homosexuality in a Woman," p. 156.

111. Ibid., p. 157.

112. Ibid., p. 160.

113. Ibid., p. 158.

114. Sigmund Freud, "Female Sexuality" (1931), *SE* 21:227–28.

115. Ibid., p. 239.

116. Ibid., pp. 235–43. Elisabeth Young-Bruehl makes this point very clearly in her introduction to *Freud on Women: A Reader* (New York: W. W. Norton, 1990), p. 40.

117. Young-Bruehl, *Freud on Women,* p. 5.

118. Freud, *Three Essays on the Theory of Sexuality,* p. 160.

119. Freud, "Femininity," p. 114.

120. Here Freud anticipates novelist Manuel Puig, whose *Kiss of the Spider Woman* would footnote the belief in "the essentially bisexual nature of our original sexual impulse" as set forth in the "Three Essays on the Theory of Sexuality." Puig, *Kiss of the Spider Woman,* trans. Thomas Colchie (New York: Vintage, 1991), p. 151.

121. Freud, "Femininity," p. 115.

122. Freud, *An Outline of Psycho-Analysis,* p. 188.

123. Peter Gay, *Freud, a Life for Our Time* (New York: W. W. Norton, 1988), p. 214.

124. Letter from Sigmund Freud to C. G. Jung, November 11, 1909, in McGuire, *Freud/Jung Letters,* p. 259.

125. Ernest Jones, *Free Associations: Memoirs of a Psycho-Analyst* (New York: Basic Books, 1959). cited in Gay, *Freud,* p. 213.

126. Wilhelm Stekel, *Bi-Sexual Love,* trans. James Van Teslaar (New York: Emerson Books, 1950), p. 41.

127. Ibid., p. 27.

128. Ibid., p. 28.

129. Freud, *Three Essays on the Theory of Sexuality,* pp. 145–46.

130. Freud, "Homosexuality in a Woman," p. 151.

131. Ibid.

132. Freud, "Analysis Terminable and Interminable" (1937), *SE* 23:243–44.

133. Letter to Sigmund Freud to Wilhelm Fliess, August 7, 1901, in Masson, *Complete Letters of Sigmund Freud,* p. 448.

134. Sigmund Freud, *Civilization and Its Discontents* (1930), *SE* 21:104–105.

135. Ibid., pp. 105–106n.

Chapter 8: Androgyny and Its Discontents

1. *The Freud/Jung Letters: The Correspondence Between Sigmund Freud and C. G. Jung,* ed. William McGuire, trans. Ralph Mannheim and R. F. C. Hull, Bollingen Series XCIV (Princeton, N.J.: Princeton University Press, 1974), 186J, p. 307.

2. "Invasion of the Gender Blenders," *People* April 23, 1984, p. 97.

3. Carl Jung, "The Psychology of the Child Archetype," in *The Archetypes and the Collective Unconscious,* trans. R. F. C. Hull, 2nd ed., Bollingen Series XX (Princeton, N.J.: Princeton University Press, 1968), pp. 173 and 175.

4. Neumann describes the "bisexuality" of the Terrible Goddess in Melanesia (who was "either female or of indeterminate sex"), the primordial Mayan gods known as "Lord and Mistress of the Two" who "were regarded as bisexual," and, most central to Paglia and most clearly related to Jung's fascination with alchemy, the figure of Mercury, whose "bisexuality" points to "the corresponding male-female uroboric nature of the Archetypal Feminine." Erich Neumann, *The Great Mother: An Analysis of the Archetype,* trans. Ralph Mannheim, 2nd ed., Bollingen Series XLVII (Princeton, N.J.: Princeton University Press, 1963), pp. 173, 181–82, 198, and 329.

5. Some examples: Gnostic literature uses the androgyne as an emblem of salvation. In the Gospel of Thomas it is "when the two become one," the Kingdom of God is at hand (*Logion* 22: pl. 85, vs. 20–31). In Genesis, God created Adam in his own image, "male and female," before taking Eve from Adam's body. The androgynous union of male and female is likewise described in the Kabbalah as a mode of transcendence. In Hindu mythology both the Upanishads and the Puranas describe the separation of the Supreme Self, "originally bisexual, into male and female." (Alan Watts, *The Two Hands of God: The Myths of Polarity* [New York: Collier Books, 1969], pp. 75 and 80.)

6. Carl Jung, "The Concept of the Collective Unconscious," in *The Archetypes and the Collective Unconscious,* p. 42.

7. Frantz Fanon, *Black Skin, White Masks,* trans. Charles Lam Markmann (New York: Grove Weidenfeld, 1967), pp. 188 and 191.

8. Ibid., p. 187.

9. Ibid., pp. 190–91.

10. Ibid., p. 190.

11. Marie Delcourt, *Hermaphrodite: Myths and Rites of the Bisexual Figure in Classical Antiquity,* trans. Jennifer Nicholson (London: Studio Books, 1961), pp. xii–xiii.

12. Christine Downing, *Myths and Mysteries of Same-Sex Love* (New York: Continuum, 1989), p. 111.

13. Jung, "The Psychology of the Child Archetype," pp. 173 and 175.

14. Ibid., p. 177.

15. Carl Jung, "Woman in Europe," in *Civilization in Transition,* trans. R. F. C. Hull, 2nd ed., Bollingen Series XX (Princeton, N.J.: Princeton University Press, 1970), pp. 118–19.

16. See John Kerr's excellent study, *A Most Dangerous Method: The Story of Jung, Freud, and Sabina Spielrein* (New York: Alfred A. Knopf, 1993).

17. Ibid., p. 503.

18. Carl Jung, *Memories, Dreams, Reflections,* rev. ed. (New York: Pantheon, 1973), pp. 185–87.

19. Kerr, *A Most Dangerous Method,* p. 503.

20. Jung, *Memories, Dreams, Reflections,* p. 187.

21. Ibid., p. 195. For all of these references I am indebted to Kerr's book.

22. Kerr, *A Most Dangerous Method,* pp. 502–503.

23. *American Heritage Dictionary of the English Language,* 1973.

24. Carl Jung, *Aion,* in *Psyche and Symbol,* ed. Violety S. de Laszlo (Garden City, N.Y.: Doubleday, 1958), p. 13.

25. Jung, "Woman in Europe," pp. 125 and 127.

26. Jung, *Aion,* p. 13.

27. Ibid.

28. June Singer, *Androgyny: The Opposites Within* (Boston: Sigo Press, 1976), p. 23.

29. Mircea Eliade, *Rites and Symbols of Initiation* (New York: Harper Torchbooks, 1965), p. 26.

30. Adrienne Rich, "The Stranger," in *Diving into the Wreck: Poems 1971–72* (New York: W. W. Norton, 1973).

31. Adrienne Rich, "Compulsory Heterosexuality and Lesbian Existence" (originally published 1980), in *Blood, Bread, and Poetry: Selected Prose 1979–1985* (New York: W. W. Norton, 1986), p. 34.

32. Carolyn G. Heilbrun, *Toward a Recognition of Androgyny* (New York: Alfred A. Knopf, 1973).

33. Ibid., p. x.

34. For an enlightening discussion of neopaganism in Jung and his followers, see Richard Noll, *The Jung Cult: Origins of a Charismatic Movement* (Princeton, N.J.: Princeton University Press, 1994), pp. 76–80, 103–108.

35. Cynthia Secor, "The Androgyny Papers," *Women's Studies,* vol. 2 (1974), pp. 139–41.

36. Ibid., p. 164.

37. Barbara Charlesworth Gelpi, "The Politics of Androgyny," *Women's Studies,* vol. 2 (1974), p. 152.

38. Ibid., p. 158.

39. James Hillman, "Anima," *Spring,* 1973, p. 116.

40. Mary Daly, *Beyond God the Father: Toward a Philosophy of Women's Liberation* (Boston: Beacon Press, 1973).

41. Mary Daly, *Gyn/Ecology: The Metaethics of Radical Feminism* (Boston: Beacon Press, 1978), p. xi.

42. Ibid., pp. 387–88.

43. Virginia Woolf, *A Room of One's Own* (New York: Harcourt, Brace & World, 1929), p. 102. For a nuanced and useful discussion of this question in the seventies, see Elaine Showalter's chapter "Virginia Woolf and the Flight into Androgyny" in *A Literature of Their Own: British Women Novelists from Bronte to Lessing* (Princeton, N.J.: Princeton University Press, 1977), pp. 263–97. Quoting Woolf's equally famous dictum "one must be woman-manly or man-womanly," Showalter writes that "In many respects Woolf is expressing a class-oriented and Bloomsbury-oriented ideal—the separation of politics and art, the fashion of bisexuality" (p. 288).

44. Carolyn Heilbrun, "Further Notes Toward a Recognition of Androgyny," *Women's Studies,* vol. 2 (1974), p. 144.

45. Gelpi, "The Politics of Androgyny," p. 151.

46. Singer, *Androgyny,* p. ix.

47. Eliade reproves these authors for taking the figure of androgyny too literally. They were, he complained, concerned not with a "wholeness and fusion of the sexes but with a superabundance of erotic possibilities. Their subject is not the appearance of a new type of humanity in which the fusion of the sexes produces a new unpolarized consciousness, but a self-styled sensual perfection, resulting from the active presence of both sexes in one" (Mircea Eliade, *Mephistopheles and the Androgyne,* p. 100). The "active presence of both sexes in one" is late Freudian, not Jungian, bisexuality. As for the "superabundance of erotic possibilities," this was the very thing "androgyny" sought to hold at arm's length, rather than, as so often happened in practice, in its arms. The same critique was offered by Marie Delcourt's *Hermaphrodite,* first published in France in 1956. Seeking "to catch a glimpse of the original significance of androgyny" through a reading of Greek and Latin legends, Delcourt likewise dismissed what she saw as the tendency to "reduce the two-fold god to an effeminate adolescent, a curiosity in which is to be seen no more than a meaningless trifle, designed to pander to pleasures of the most limited and circumscribed kind." Delcourt, who makes the by-now familiar equation of bisexual, hermaphrodite, and androgyne, insisted that "careful examination of the concepts which are at the origin of the myth discovers no erotic component" (Delcourt, *Hermaphrodite,* p. xii).

48. Susan Sontag, "Notes on 'Camp,'" in *Against Interpretation* (New York: Farrar, Straus & Giroux, 1966; reprinted, 1986), p. 279.

49. Jacques Lacan, "The Signification of the Phallus," in *Écrits: A Selection,* trans. Alan Sheridan (New York: W. W. Norton, 1977), p. 291.

50. Susan Sontag, "Notes on 'Camp,' " p. 279.

51. Singer, *Androgyny,* p. 12.

52. Ibid., p. 206.

53. Ibid., pp. 204–206.

54. Ibid., p. 206.

55. Ibid., p. 207.

56. Ibid., p. 208.

57. Ibid., p. 210.

58. Ibid., p. 214.

59. The passage she cites is from Miguel Serrano, *The Serpent of Paradise: The Story of an Indian Pilgrimage* (London: Routledge & Kegan Paul, 1974), pp. 19–20.

60. Camille Paglia, *Sexual Personae: Art and Decadence from Nefertiti to Emily Dickinson* (New Haven: Yale University Press, 1990), p. 210.

61. Singer, *Androgyny,* p. 15.

62. Sigmund Freud, *Three Essays on the Theory of Sexuality* (1905), *SE* 7:219–20; *Civilization and Its Discontents* (1930), *SE* 21:105–106; "Femininity" (1933), *SE* 22:115.

63. Secor, "The Androgyny Papers," p. 163.

64. *Le Bestiare Divin de Guillaume, clerc de Normandie,* thirteenth century. *Benét's Reader's Encyclopedia,* ed. Katherine Baker-Siepmann (New York: HarperCollins, 1948; reprinted, 1987) p. 1011.

65. Catharine R. Stimpson, "The Androgyne and the Homosexual," *Women's Studies,* vol. 2 (1974), pp. 242–43.

66. Secor, "The Androgyny Papers," p. 162.

67. Nancy Topping Bazin and Alma Freeman, "The Androgynous Vision," *Women's Studies,* vol. 2 (1974), p. 186.

68. Sam Keen, *Fire in the Belly: On Being a Man* (New York: Bantam Books, 1981), p. 13.

69. Ibid., p. 213.

70. Ibid., pp. 213–14.

71. Mark Gerzon, *A Choice of Heroes: The Changing Face of American Manhood* (Boston: Houghton Mifflin, 1982), pp. 1 and 2.

72. Ibid., p. 262.

73. Ibid., p. 4.

74. Ibid., p. 229.

75. Holly Boswell, "Reviving the Tradition of Alternative Genders," *Tapestry,* vol. 66 (Winter 1993–94), pp. 44–45.

76. Francis Vavra, letter to the author, February 9, 1993.

77. Roger Cohen, "Feathers! Androgyny! The Folies-Bergère Reopens," *New York Times,* September 30, 1993, p. C13.

78. Justine McCabe, quoted in Peter Engel, "Androgynous Zones," *Harvard Magazine,* January–February 1985, p. 26.

79. Arlene Stein, "Androgyny Goes Pop," *Out/Look,* no. 12 (Spring 1991), pp. 26–33.

80. Danielle Bragmann, in ibid., p. 26.

81. Diane Anderson, "Living with Contradictions," *Closer to Home: Bisexuality and Feminism,* ed. Elizabeth Reba Weise (Seattle: Seal Press, 1992), p. 171.

82. Julia Sweeney and Christine Zander, *It's Pat! My Life Exposed* (New York: Hyperion, 1992), p. 19.

83. Caryn James, "'Orlando,' Like Its Hero(ine), Is One for the Ages," *New York Times,* June 6, 1993, p. 17.

84. Ibid., p. 23.

85. *New York Times,* June 6, 1993, p. 23.

86. Jane Marcus, "A Tale of Two Cultures," *Women's Review of Books,* vol. 11, no. 4 (January 1994), p. 11.

87. Reported by Rebecca L. Walkowitz in a letter to the author, June 1993.

88. Phil May, quoted in Andersen, "Living with Contradictions," p. 68.

89. John Dunbar, in Andersen, "Living with Contradictions," p. 167.

90. Eliade, *Rites and Symbols of Initiation,* p. 26.

91. Maureen Orth, "Nightmare in Neverland," *Vanity Fair,* January 1994, p. 72.

92. Ibid.

93. Jung, "The Psychology of the Child Archetype," pp. 144 and 145.

94. Keen, *Fire in the Belly,* p. 100.

95. Dana Kennedy, "Time to Face the Music," *Entertainment Weekly,* December 17, 1993, p. 30.

96. Derrick Z. Jackson, "Say It Ain't So, Michael," *Boston Globe,* December 15, 1993, p. 23.

Chapter 9: Ellis in Wonderland

1. Asa Gray, *Structural Botany* (New York: Ivison, Blakeman & Taylor, 1880), vol. 3, p. 191, cited in *Oxford English Dictionary* (Oxford: Oxford University Press, 1971).

2. Samuel Taylor Coleridge, *Aids to Reflection* (1848), vol. 1, p. 204, *OED.*

3. Sir Thomas Browne, *Pseudodoxia Epidemica,* "That the whole species or kinds should be bisexous," p. 149, *OED.*

4. Sylvester, *Du Bartas* (1608), p. 267, *OED.*

5. See Havelock Ellis, *Studies in the Psychology of Sex,* vol. 2, *Sexual Inversion* (New York: Random House, 1910; reprinted, 1936), part 2, pp. 310–414.

6. Ibid., p. 311; Arthur Schopenhauer, *The World as Will and Idea,* cited in Sigmund Freud, *Three Essays on the Theory of Sexuality* (1905), *SE* 7:134.

7. Edward Carpenter, *The Intermediate Sex,* 9th ed. (1908; reprinted, London: Allen & Unwin, 1952), p. 17.

8. Jeffrey Weeks, *Coming Out: Homosexual Politics in Britain from the Nineteenth Century to the Present* (London: Quartet, 1977), p. 75.

9. Edward Carpenter, *Love's Coming-of-Age: A Series of Papers on The Relations of the Sexes* (Manchester: Labour Press, 1896), pp. 100 and 101.

10. Ellis, *Sexual Inversion,* p. 312.

11. "Probably not a very large number of people are even aware that the turning in of the sexual instinct toward persons of the same sex can ever be regarded as inborn, so far as any sexual instinct is inborn," wrote Ellis in the Preface to the First Edition of the *Psychology of Sex,* p. vi.

12. Richard von Krafft-Ebing, *Psychopathia Sexualis,* 7th ed., trans. Franklin Klaf (New York: Stein & Day, 1965), p. 187.

13. Ellis, *Sexual Inversion,* p. 265.

14. The term is Krafft-Ebing's. Ellis uses it in early editions of the *Studies in the Psychology of Sex,* but later "willingly reject[s] it in favor of the simpler and fairly clear term," bisexuality, "now more generally employed" (*Sexual Inversion,* p. 88n).

15. Ellis, *Sexual Inversion,* p. 4.

16. Frank Richardson, *Napoleon—Bisexual Emperor* (New York: Horizon Press, 1972), pp. 56 and 89.

17. Ellis, *Sexual Inversion,* p. 88.

18. Ibid., pp. 79–80, 310–17; Paul Robinson, *The Modernization of Sex* (New York: Harper & Row, 1976), pp. 8–9.

19. Ellis, *Sexual Inversion,* pp. 314–15.

20. Ibid., pp. 315–17.

21. Havelock Ellis, *My Life, Autobiography of Havelock Ellis* (Boston: Houghton Mifflin, 1939), p. 257.

22. Ellis, *Sexual Inversion,* p. 310.

23. Ibid., p. 387.

24. Ibid., p. 309.

25. Ibid., pp. 387–88.

26. Ibid., p. 387.

27. Letter from Edith Ellis to Havelock Ellis, February 14, 1893, quoted in ibid., p. 311.

28. Ibid., p. 330.
29. Arthur Calder-Marshall, *Havelock Ellis, a Biography* (London: Rupert Hart-Davis, 1959), p. 137.
30. Ibid., p. 138.
31. Ibid., p. 140.
32. Arthur Calder-Marshall, *The Sage of Sex: A Life of Havelock Ellis* (New York: G. P. Putnam's Sons, 1959), p. 138.
33. Ibid., p. 140.
34. Ellis, *Sexual Inversion*, p. 330.
35. Calder-Marshall, *Havelock Ellis*, p. 147, citing Edward Carpenter and John Addington Symonds.
36. Ibid., pp. 329–30.
37. Ellis, *Sexual Inversion*, pp. 88–89.
38. Robinson, *Modernization of Sex*, pp. 73–74.

Chapter 10: Standard Deviations

1. Pomeroy, quoted in Susan Barron, "Bisexuality: Having It All," *Lear's*, vol. 8, no. 5 (May 1992), p. 84.
2. See Jay P. Paul, "The Bisexual Identity: An Idea Without Social Recognition," *Journal of Homosexuality*, vol. 9, nos. 2 and 3 (Winter 1983–Spring 1984), p. 51.
3. Maggi Rubenstein, *Plexus*, August 1987, p. 6.
4. Sigmund Freud, *Three Essays on the Theory of Sexuality* (1905), *SE* 7:146n.
5. I. Bieber, H. J. Dain, P. R. Dince, M. G. Drellich, H. G. Grand, R. H. Gundlach, M. W. Kramer, A. H. Rifkin, C. B. Wilber, and T.B. Bieber, *Homosexuality: A Psychoanalytic Study* (New York: Basic Books, 1962).
6. John Malone, *Straight Women/Gay Men: A Special Relationship* (New York: Dial Press, 1980) pp. 179 and 181.
7. Mariana Valverde, *Sex, Power, and Pleasure* (Philadelphia: New Society Publishers, 1987), pp. 113 and 115.
8. Alfred C. Kinsey, Wardell B. Pomeroy, Clyde E. Martin, and Paul H. Gebhard, *Sexual Behavior in the Human Female* (Philadelphia: W. B. Saunders, 1953), p. 469.
9. Alfred C. Kinsey, Wardell B. Pomeroy, and Clyde E. Martin, *Sexual Behavior in the Human Male* (Philadelphia: W. B. Saunders, 1948), pp. 656–57.
10. Ibid., p. 637.
11. Ibid., pp. 659–60.
12. Randy Shilts, *Conduct Unbecoming: Lesbians and Gays in the U.S. Military, Vietnam to the Persian Gulf* (New York: St. Martin's Press, 1993), pp. 16–17.
13. Kinsey et al., *Sexual Behavior in the Human Male*, p. 600.
14. Ibid., p. 661.
15. Barbara Ehrenreich, "The Gap Between Gay and Straight," *Time*, May 10, 1993, p. 76.
16. Kinsey et al., *Sexual Behavior in the Human Female*, p. 469.
17. Ibid., p. 472.
18. Ibid., p. 43.
19. Kinsey et al., *Sexual Behavior in the Human Male*, pp. 6–7.
20. Kinsey et al., *Sexual Behavior in the Human Female*, pp. 475–76.
21. Ibid., p. 477.
22. Ibid., p. 482.
23. Ibid., p. 458.
24. Ibid., p. 468.
25. David Halberstam, *The Fifties* (New York: Villard Books, 1993), p. 278.
26. Rock Hudson and Sara Davidson, *Rock Hudson: His Story* (New York: William Morrow, 1986), p. 57.
27. One of the key collections of essays on bisexuality, coedited by Fritz Klein, M.D., and Timothy J. Wolf, M.D., has appeared under three different titles: as a special issue of the *Journal of Homosexuality* (vol. 11, nos. 1 and 2 [Spring 1985]), as a separate volume called *Bisexualities: Theory and Research* (New York: The Haworth Press, 1985),

and as the much more lively sounding, but in fact identical, *Two Lives to Lead: Bisexuality in Men and Women* (New York and London: Harrington Park Press, 1985).

28. Betty Hannah Hoffman, "Can This Marriage Be Saved?" *Ladies' Home Journal,* September 1982, pp. 10–17.

29. Catherine McEver, "The Bisexual Lover," *Cosmopolitan,* April 1982, p. 116.

30. Dianne Hales, "My Husband's Other Lovers Were Men," *Woman's Day,* September 13, 1988, pp. 76ff.

31. Janet Lever, David E. Kanouse, William H. Rogers, Sally Carson, and Rosanna Hertz, "Behavior Patterns and Sexual Identity of Bisexual Males," *Journal of Sex Research,* vol. 29, no. 2 (May 1992), pp. 141–67.

32. Ibid., pp. 164 and 165.

33. Carin Rubenstein, "Sexual Response: Generation Sex," *Mademoiselle,* June 1993, pp. 130–35.

34. "Women in Love," *Mademoiselle,* March 1993, p. 180.

35. Dominick Dunne, "Menendez Justice," *Vanity Fair,* March 1994, p. 118.

36. John O. G. Billy, Koray Tanfer, William R. Grady, and Daniel H. Klepinger, "The Sexual Behavior of Men in the United States," *Family Planning Perspectives,* vol. 25 (1993), pp. 52–60.

37. Ibid., p. 58.

38. T. W. Smith, "Adult Sexual Behavior in 1989: Number of Partners, Frequency of Intercourse and Risk of AIDS," *Family Planning Perspectives,* vol. 28 (1991), pp. 102–107.

39. William H. Masters, Virginia E. Johnson, and Robert C. Kolodny, *Heterosexuality* (New York: HarperCollins, 1994), hardcover book flap.

40. William H. Masters, Virginia E. Johnson, and Robert C. Kolodny, *Masters and Johnson on Sex and Human Loving,* expanded edition (Boston: Little, Brown, 1985), p. 373.

41. Samuel J. Janus and Cynthia L. Janus, *The Janus Report on Sexual Behavior* (New York: John Wiley & Sons, 1993), p. 70.

42. Kaye Wellings, Julia Field, Anne M. Johnson, and Jane Wadsworth, with Sally Bradshaw, *Sexual Behaviour in Britain: The National Survey of Sexual Attitudes and Lifestyles* (London: Penguin, 1994), pp. 211–13.

43. Robert T. Michael, John H. Gagnon, Edward O. Laumann, and Gina Kolata, *Sex in America: A Definitive Survey* (Boston: Little, Brown, 1994), pp. 176 and 178. The complete results of the *Sex in America* study were reported in a simultaneously published scholarly volume, *The Social Organization of Sexuality: Sexual Practices in the United States,* by Edward O. Laumann, John H. Gagnon, Robert T. Michael, and Stuart Michaels (Chicago: University of Chicago Press, 1994). In this volume, too, "bisexual" is a term hard to come by. The authors do note, however, "the importance of the life course in viewing issues such as the gender of sex partners as a dynamic process" (p. 312) in a section called "The Mixture of Same- and Opposite-Gender Sex Partners," observing, in additional, that "while the numbers . . . are very small, it appears that, whereas two-thirds of the women who consider themselves to be homosexual report at least some minimal level of sexual attraction to men, a much smaller minority of the men who report attraction to men but none to women do not consider themselves to be homosexual" (p. 313). The discussion of these issues is situated, predictably, in a chapter entitled "Homosexuality."

44. Michael et al., *Sex in America,* pp. 174 and 177.

45. Ibid., p. 172.

46. Ibid., pp. 208 and 212.

47. Ruth Hubbard, "False Genetic Markers," *New York Times,* August 2, 1993, p. A15.

Chapter 11: The Return to Biology

1. Ann Landers, "Teacher Needs to Learn Lesson—There Aren't Five Sexes," *Miami Herald,* December 21, 1992, p. 2C.

2. Anne Fausto-Sterling, "The Five Sexes," *The Sciences,* March/April 1993, pp. 20–24. A briefer version of this article appeared on the *New York Times* op-ed page under the title "How Many Sexes Are There?" (*New York Times,* March 12, 1993, p. A29).

3. Fausto-Sterling, "The Five Sexes," p. 22.

4. Ibid., p. 24.

5. Steve Wolfe, letter to the *New York Times,* March 26, 1993, p. A12.

6. Gary Fairmount Filosa, letter to the *New York Times,* March 26, 1993, p. A12.

7. Ibid.

8. Simon LeVay, "A Difference in Hypothalamic Structure Between Heterosexual and Homosexual Men," *Science,* vol. 253 (August 30, 1991), pp. 1034–37.

9. David J. Jefferson, "Science Besieged: Studying the Biology of Sexual Orientation Has Political Fallout," *Wall Street Journal,* August 12, 1993, p. 1.

10. Michael Bailey and Richard Pillard, "Are Some People Born Gay?" *New York Times,* October 17, 1991, p. A21.

11. Mariana Valverde, *Sex, Power, and Pleasure* (Philadelphia: New Society Publishers, 1987), p. 112.

12. Richard von Krafft-Ebing, *Psychopathia Sexualis,* 7th ed., trans. Franklin Klaf (New York: Stein & Day, 1965), pp. 221–22.

13. Robert A. Wild, quoted in Natalie Angier, "Male Hormone Molds Women, Too, in Mind and Body," *New York Times,* May 3, 1994, p. C13.

14. Roger S. Rittmaster, quoted in ibid.

15. Angier, "Male Hormone Molds Women, Too," p. C13.

16. Sigmund Freud, "Three Essays on the Theory of Sexuality" (1905), *SE* 7:140. The "spokesman of the male inverts" is Karl Heinrich Ulrichs.

17. Robert J. Stoller, "Facts and Fancies: An Examination of Freud's Concept of Bisexuality," in *Women and Analysis: Dialogues on Psychoanalytic Views of Femininity,* ed. Jean Strouse (New York: Grossman Publishers, 1974), p. 345.

18. Joe Dolce, "And How Big Is Yours?" *The Advocate,* June 1, 1993, p. 40.

19. Ruth Hubbard and Elijah Wald, *Exploding the Gene Myth* (Boston: Beacon Press, 1993), p. 96.

20. LeVay, "A Difference in Hypothalamic Structure," p. 1035.

21. Ibid., p. 1034.

22. LeVay mentions the possibility that his sample may be unrepresentative, since gay male AIDS patients might be thought of as belonging to a "subset of gay men, characterized, for example, by a tendency to engage in sexual relations with large numbers of different partners or by a strong preference for the receptive role in anal intercourse," but he refutes this by noting that "the majority of homosexual men who acquired HIV infection during the Multicenter AIDS Cohort Study reported that they took both the insertive and the receptive role in intercourse, and the same is likely to be true of the homosexual subjects in my study" ("A Difference in Hypothalamic Structure," p. 1036). This is the only mention of sexual roles or aims in the paper, and it is clearly intended to be discounted rather than counted as a differential factor.

23. Dolce, "And How Big Is Yours?" p. 40.

24. Hubbard and Wald, *Exploding the Gene Myth,* p. 94.

25. Natalie Angier, "Report Suggests Homosexuality Is Linked to Genes," *New York Times,* July 16, 1993, p. A12.

26. Dean H. Hamer, Stella Hu, Victoria L. Magnuson, Nan Hu, Angela M. L. Pattatucci, "A Linkage Between DNA Markers on the X Chromosome and Male Sexual Orientation," *Science,* vol. 261, no. 5119 (July 16, 1993), p. 321; J. Michael Bailey and Richard C. Pillard, "A Genetic Study of Male Sexual Orientation," *Archives of General Psychiatry,* vol. 48 (1991), pp. 1089–96.

27. Hamer et al., "Linkage Between DNA Markers," p. 326.

28. Ibid., pp. 321–22.

29. Amanda Udis-Kessler, "Appendix: Notes on the Kinsey Scale and Other Measures of Sexuality," in *Closer to Home: Bisexuality and Feminism,* ed. Elizabeth Reba Weise (Seattle: The Seal Press, 1992), p. 316.

30. Ibid., p. 317.

31. In their article on "The Multidimension Scale of Sexuality," authors Braden Robert Berkey, Terri Perelman-Hall, and Lawrence A. Kurdek cite J. P. Paul's use of "sequential bisexual" and "contemporaneous bisexual" in 1984, and G. Zinik's terms "serial" and "concurrent" in 1985. See *Journal of Homosexuality*, vol. 19, no. 4 (Winter 1990), p. 68; J. P. Paul, "The Bisexual Identity: An Idea Without Social Recognition," *Journal of Homosexuality*, vol. 9, nos. 2–3 (1983–1984), pp. 45–63; G. Zinik, "Identity Conflict or Adaptive Flexibility? Bisexuality Reconsidered," in Fritz Klein, M.D., and Timothy J. Wolf, M.D., *Two Lives to Lead: Bisexuality in Men and Women* (New York and London: Harrington Park Press, 1985), pp. 7–18.

Chapter 12: On the Other Hand

1. *The Oxford English Dictionary*, 2nd ed. (Oxford: Clarendon Press, 1989), vol. 2, p. 222.

2. Steve Wolfe, letter to the *New York Times*, March 12, 1993, p. A29.

3. Chandler Burr, "Genes vs. Hormones," *New York Times*, August 2, 1993, p. A15.

4. David Gelaman with Donna Foote, Todd Barrett, and Mary Talbot, "Born or Bred?" *Newsweek*, February 24, 1992, pp. 46–53.

5. Ruth Hubbard, "False Genetic Markers," *New York Times*, August 2, 1993, p. A15; Ruth Hubbard and Elijah Wald, *Exploding the Gene Myth* (Boston: Beacon Press, 1993), pp. 94–95.

6. "The Bisexual and the Navy," *Time*, February 2, 1976, p. 49.

7. Havelock Ellis, *Studies in the Psychology of Sex*, vol. 2, *Sexual Inversion* (New York: Random House, 1910; reprinted, 1936) p. 288. In a footnote, Ellis quotes Biervliet's "L'homme droit et l'homme gauche" from the *Revue philosophique*, October 1901: "It is here shown that in the constitution of their nervous system the ambidextrous are demonstrably left-sided persons; their optic, acoustic, olfactory, and muscular sensitivity is preponderant on the left side."

8. Havelock Ellis, *My Life, Autobiography of Havelock Ellis* (Boston: Houghton Mifflin, 1939), p. 57.

9. Ibid., pp. 85–86. The incident became a primal scene for the "uralagnia" and theory of "Undinism" he would claim in later life.

10. Letter from Sigmund Freud to Wilhelm Fliess, December 29, 1897, in *The Complete Letters of Sigmund Freud to Wilhelm Fliess 1887–1904*, ed. and trans. Jeffrey Moussaief Masson (Cambridge, Mass.: Harvard University Press, 1985), p. 290.

11. Letter from Sigmund Freud to Wilhelm Fliess, January 4, 1898, in Masson, *Complete Letters of Sigmund Freud*, pp. 292–93.

12. See for example, E. W. Lane, *Manners and Customs of the Ancient Egyptians* (London: Charles Knight, 1837), vol. 1, p. 200: "When a fowl is placed whole upon the tray, two persons, using the right hand alone, perform the operation together. Many of the Arabs will not allow the left hand to touch food excepting when the right is maimed. ..."

Vol. 1, p. 283: "It is a rule with the Muslims to honour the right hand above the left: to use the right hand for all honourable purposes, and the left for actions which, although necessary, are unclean. ..."

13. Ernest Jones, *The Life and Work of Sigmund Freud*, ed. and abridged by Lionel Trilling and Steven Marcus (New York: Basic Books, 1961), pp. 203–204.

14. Letter from Sigmund Freud to Wilhelm Fliess, October 9, 1898, in Masson, *Complete Letters of Sigmund Freud*, p. 331.

15. A footnote added in 1910 to *Three Essays on the Theory of Sexuality* had similarly described "inverts" as "proceed[ing] from a narcissistic basis, and look[ing] for a young man who resembles themselves and whom *they* may love as their mother loved *them*." The sentiments expressed here are very similar to those in the Leonardo essay, which was written during the same time period. It is of some interest that the footnote continues to argue for the *bisexuality* of these "alleged inverts": "[W]e have frequently found that alleged inverts have been by no means insusceptible to the charms of women, but have continually transposed the excitation aroused by women on to a male object. They have thus repeated all through their lives the mechanism by which their inversion arose. Their compulsive longing for men has turned out to be determined by their ceaseless flight from women" (*Three Essays on the Theory of Sexuality* [1905], *SE* 7:145n). This passage closely resembles one in the Leonardo essay quoted above (Freud, "Leonardo da Vinci, and a Memory of His Childhood" [1910], *SE* 11:100), with the perhaps significant difference that Freud does not use the term "invert" for his admired Leonardo.

16. Freud, "Leonardo da Vinci," p. 100.

17. Ibid., p. 102.

18. Ibid., p. 132.

19. Ibid., p. 136.

20. See for example the Schreber case ("Psycho-analytic Notes on an Autobiographical Account of a Case of Paranoia" [1911], *SE* 12:9–82). "My erstwhile friend Fliess," he wrote to Jung, "developed a beautiful paranoia after he had disposed of his inclination, certainly not slight, toward me" (Freud to Jung, February 17, 1908). As Peter Gay points out, "whatever he might tell Jung, he was laboring to analyze his sentiments for Fliess rather than Fliess's sentiments for him" (*Freud, a Life for Our Time* [New York: W. W. Norton, 1988], p. 275).

21. Ira S. Wile, *Handedness: Right and Left* (Boston: Lothrop, Lee and Shepard, 1934), p. 12; Dmitri Merejkowski, *The Romance of Leonardo da Vinci* (New York: Modern Library, 1928), p. 618.

22. Alice Werner, "Note on the Terms Used for 'Right Hand' and 'Left Hand' in the Bantu Languages," *Journal of the Royal African Society*, vol. 4 (1904), pp. 112–16. Cited in Lauren Julius Harris, "Left-Handedness: Early Theories, Facts, and Fancies," in *Neuropsychology of Left-Handedness*, ed. Jeannine Herron (New York: Academic Press, 1980), p. 52.

23. Wile, *Handedness*, p. 37; Robert Hertz, "Le préeminence de la main droite. Étude sur la polarité religieuse," *Revue philosophique de la France et de l'étranger*, vol. 68 (1909), pp. 553–80.

24. Galen (Claudius Galenus), *On the Usefulness of the Parts of the Body (De usu partium)*, 2 vols., trans. Margaret Tallmadge May (Ithaca, N.Y.: Cornell University Press, 1968), vol. 1, p. 57. See also R. E. Siegel, *Galen's System of Physiology and Medicine* (Basel, Switzerland: S. Karger, 1968), pp. 224–30, and R. E. Siegel, *Galen on Psychology, Psychopathology, and Functions and Diseases of the Nervous System* (Basel, Switzerland: S. Karger, 1973), pp. 123–24. For Anaxagoras, see G. Lloyd, "Right and Left in Greek Philosophy," in *Right and Left: Essays on Dual Symbolic Classification*, ed. R. Needham (Chicago: University of Chicago Press, 1973), pp. 167–86. William Harvey, citing Aristotle, rejected Anaxagoras' theory, although he notes that Aristotle does believe that the blood on the right side of the body, and the right side itself, was more perfected than the left. But since Aristotle did not believe that the testicles played any role in fecundating the sperm, he denied that a child's sex could be influenced by sidedness (Harvey, *Prelectiones anatomie universalis*, [Lectures on the Whole of Anatomy], [originally published 1616], ed. and trans. G. Whitteridge [Edinburgh and London: E. & S. Livingstone, 1964], p. 194).

25. Aristotle, *Metaphysics*. See also Lloyd, "Right and Left," p. 171. E. S. Forster, *The Works of Aristotle*, vol. 7, *Problemata* (Oxford: Clarendon Press, 1927), Book 32, ch. 7, p. 961a.

26. Cesare Lombroso, "Left-Handedness and Left-Sideness," *North American Review*, vol. 177 (1903), pp. 440–44.

27. Wile, *Handedness*, p. 235.

28. Abram Blau, *The Master Hand: A Study of the Origin and Meaning of Right and Left Sideness and Its Relation to Personality and Language* (New York: American Orthopsychiatric Association, 1946).

29. Ives Hendrick, *Facts and Theories of Psychoanalysis* (New York: Alfred A. Knopf, 1941).

30. Blau, quoted in Michael Barsley, *The Other Hand* (New York: Hawthorne Publishers, 1966), pp. 208–209.

31. Ibid., p. 46.

32. Harris, "Left-Handedness," p. 57.

33. See for example the studies in Stanley Coren, ed., *Left-Handedness: Behavioral Implications and Anomalies* (Amsterdam and New York: North-Holland, 1990).

34. Ibid.

35. Stanley Coren, *The Left-Hander Syndrome: The Causes and Consequences of Left-handedness* (New York: The Free Press, 1992), p. 200.

36. C. M. McCormick, S. F. Witelson, and E. Kinstone, *Psychoneuroendocrinology,* vol. 1 (1990), pp. 69–76.

37. Coren, *Syndrome,* p. 201. The study is reported in J. Lindesay, *Neuropsychologia,* vol. 25 (1987), pp. 965–69.

38. Coren, *Syndrome,* p. 200.

39. Judges 3:15: "But when the children of Israel cried unto the Lord, the Lord raised them up a deliverer, Ehud the son of Gera, a man lefthanded." Judges 20:16: "Among all this people there were seven hundred chosen men lefthanded; every one could sling stones at an hair breadth, and not miss."

40. Plato, *Laws,* 7:794–95, trans. A. E. Taylor, in *Plato: The Collected Dialogues,* ed. Edith Hamilton and Huntington Cairns, Bollingen Series LXXI (Princeton, N.J.: Princeton University Press, 1961), pp. 1366–67.

41. On Baden-Powell, see Tim Jeal, *The Boy-Man: The Life of Lord Baden-Powell* (New York: William Morrow, 1990), and John Jackson, *Ambidexterity or Two-Handedness and Two-Brainedness* (London: Kegan, Paul, Trench, Tribner and Co., 1905), p. xii.

42. John Jackson, *Ambidexterity* (London: Kegan Paul, 1905), quoted in Coren, *Syndrome,* p. 60.

43. Sir James Creighton-Browne, "Dexterity and the Bend Sinister," *Proceedings of the Royal Institution of Great Britain,* vol. 18 (1907), pp. 623–52.

Chapter 13: Normal Schools

1. Sigmund Freud, "Some Reflections on Schoolboy Psychology" (1914), *SE* 13:241. Written for a collective volume in celebration of the fiftieth anniversary of the Leopoldstädter Kommunalreal-und Obergymnasium in Vienna, popularly known as the "Sperlgymnasium," which Freud had attended between the ages of nine and seventeen (1865–73).

2. Ibid., p. 242.

3. Sigmund Freud, *Three Essays on the Theory of Sexuality* (1905), *SE* 7:145–46, fn. 1 (added in 1915).

4. Carl Gustav Jung, "The Love Problem of a Student," in *Civilization in Transition,* 2nd ed., trans. R. F. C. Hull, Bollingen Series XXII (Princeton, N.J.: Princeton University Press, 1970), p. 107. The editors suggest that the lecture was "probably" delivered in December 1922. The English translation, originally published as "The Love Problem of the Student," was translated from an unpublished German manuscript in *Contributions to Analytical Philosophy* (London and New York, 1928).

5. Jung, "Love Problem of a Student," p. 108.

6. *Petrarch's Lyric Poems: The "Rime Sparse" and Other Lyrics,* trans. and ed. Robert M. Durling (Cambridge, Mass.: Harvard University Press, 1976), poem 73, p. 168.

7. Interview with the author, February 1994.

8. Arthur Marshall, *Whimpering in the Rhododendrons: The Splendours and Miseries of the English Prep School* (London: Collins, 1982).

9. The phenomenon of "smashing" in the new women's colleges in New England was identical in its nature to the English schoolgirls' raves. In both cases middle- and upper-class young women and adolescent girls were placed in single-sex communities with a strong reforming ethos. Martha Vicinus, "Distance and Desire: English Boarding School Friendships," *Signs: Journal of Women in Culture and Society,* vol. 9, no. 4 (1984), p. 604.

10. Arthur Marshall, *Giggling in the Shrubbery* (London: Collins, 1985), p. 158.

11. Ibid., p. 163.

12. Ibid., pp. 163–64.

13. Ibid., p. 166.

14. Obici and Marchesini, *Le "Amicizie" ai Collegio* (Rome, 1898), cited in Havelock Ellis, "The School-Friendships of Girls," Appendix to *Studies in the Psychology of Sex,* vol. 2, *Sexual Inversion* (New York: Random House, 1910; reprinted, 1936), p. 368.

15. Ibid., pp. 369–70.

16. Ibid., pp. 371–73.

17. Ibid., p. 371.

18. Ibid., p. 374.

19. Ibid., pp. 368, 373, and 370.

20. Obici and Marchesini, *Le "Amicizie" ai Collegio,* cited in ibid., p. 370.

21. Ellis, *Sexual Inversion,* p. 379.

22. See Lillian Faderman's *Surpassing the Love of Men: Romantic Friendship and Love Between Women from the Renaissance to the Present* (New York: William Morrow, 1981) as well as her *Odd Girls and Twilight Lovers: A History of Lesbian Life in Twentieth-Century America* (New York: Columbia University Press, 1991). Male romantic friendships also flourished, of course, and have been discussed in school memoirs like those of Terence Greenidge and in biographies like Michael Holroyd's *Lytton Strachey* (Harmondsworth: Penguin, 1989).

23. Ellis, *Sexual Inversion,* p. 380.

24. Robert Graves, *Good-bye to All That* (1929; revised 1957; New York: Doubleday Anchor, 1989), p. 19.

25. Iwan Bloch, *The Sexual Life of Our Time, in Its Relation to Modern Civilization* (1907; trans. M. Eden Paul, New York: Allied, 1927). See also Ellis, *Sexual Inversion,* p. 83n.

26. Iwan Bloch, *Sexual Life in England, Past and Present,* trans. William H. Forstern (London: Francis Aldor, 1938), pp. 388–89.

27. Freud, *Three Essays on the Theory of Sexuality,* p. 137.

28. Iwan Bloch, *Die Prostitution* (Berlin: Louis Marcus, 1912), Bd. i, 103.

29. Magnus Hirschfeld, *Die Homosexualität des Mannes und des Weibes* (Berlin: Louis Marcus, 1914), chap. 7.

30. Ellis, *Sexual Inversion,* pp. 86–87.

31. The most cogent discussion of this view can be found in Judith Butler's *Gender Trouble: Feminism and the Subversion of Identity* (New York: Routledge, 1990), esp. pp. 120–24.

32. Alan Sinfield, *The Wilde Century: Effeminacy, Oscar Wilde and the Queer Moment* (London: Cassell, 1994), p. 64.

33. Ibid., p. 65.

34. Cited in ibid.

35. Ibid., pp. 65–66.

36. Quoted in Ellis, *Sexual Inversion,* p. 82.

37. Graves, *Good-bye to All That,* p. 48.

38. Ibid., p. 40.

39. Ibid., p. 50.

40. Ibid., p. 57.

41. Ibid., p. 58.

42. Ibid., p. 56.

43. Ibid., p. 248.

44. Ibid., p. 296.

45. Robert Graves, *Good-bye to All That* (London: Jonathan Cape, 1929), p. 220.

46. Ibid., pp. 40–41.

47. Terence Greenidge, *Degenerate Oxford? A Critical Study of Modern University Life* (London: Chapman & Hall, 1930), pp. 90–91.

48. E. M. Forster, *Maurice* (New York: Signet, 1973), pp. 77–78. *Maurice* was, as Forster declared on the dedication page, "Begun 1913, finished 1914. Dedicated to a happier year." The author's "terminal notes" are dated 1960; the first hardcover edition (W. W. Norton) appeared in 1971.

49. Ibid., p. 109.

50. Ibid., p. 15.
51. Ibid., p. 113.
52. Ibid., p. 116.
53. Ibid., p. 117.
54. Ibid., p. 124.
55. Ibid., p. 122.
56. Ibid., p. 128.
57. Ibid., p. 130.
58. Ibid., p. 169.
59. Ibid., pp. 170 and 159.
60. Ibid., p. 199.
61. Ibid., p. 179.
62. Ibid., p. 174.
63. Ibid., p. 176.
64. Ibid., p. 209.
65. Ibid., pp. 211–13.
66. Ibid., p. 228.
67. Ibid., pp. 232–33.
68. Ibid., p. 220.
69. Ibid., p. 242.
70. Ibid.

Chapter 14: Erotic Education

1. Sigmund Freud, "Group Psychology and the Analysis of the Ego" (1921), *SE* 18:139. Freud cites Molière, *Les femmes savantes,* 3.5: "Quoi! monsieur sait du grec! Ah! permettez, de grâce, / Que, pour l'amour du grec, monsieur, on vous embrasse."

2. Henry James, "The Pupil," in *Great Short Works of Henry James,* ed. Dean Flower (New York: Harper Perennial, 1966), p. 313.

3. Evelyn Waugh, *Decline and Fall* (Boston: Little, Brown, 1929), prelude.

4. T. S. Eliot, "Tradition and the Individual Talent," in *Selected Essays* (1932; New York: Harcourt, Brace & World, 1960).

5. E. M. Forster, *Maurice* (New York: Signet, 1973), p. 50.

6. Ibid.

7. Michael Holroyd, *Lytton Strachey: A Biography* (London: Penguin, 1971).

8. Interview with the author, May 1994.

9. Alan Sinfield, *The Wilde Century: Effeminacy, Oscar Wilde and the Queer Moment* (London: Cassell, 1994), p. 65.

10. Allan Bloom, *The Closing of the American Mind* (New York: Simon & Schuster, 1987), p. 61.

11. Ann Pelligrini, "Long Before Stonewall," review of Eva Cantarella, *Bisexuality in the Ancient World, Women's Review of Books,* vol. 10, no. 12 (September 1993), p. 29. See for example Michel Foucault, *The History of Sexuality,* trans. Robert Hurley (New York: Vintage Books, 1980); David M. Halperin, *One Hundred Years of Homosexuality and Other Essays* (New York: Routledge, 1990); John J. Winkler, *The Constraints of Desire: The Anthropology of Sex and Gender in Ancient Greece* (New York: Routledge, 1989).

12. Werner Wilhelm Jaeger, *Paideia* (Oxford: Blackwell, 1946).

13. Eva Cantarella, *Bisexuality in the Ancient World,* trans. Cormac Ó'Cuilleanáin (New Haven: Yale University Press, 1992), p. 32. "All of this," notes Cantarella, "meant, obviously, that they could not make good lovers. The law recognised and, so to speak, codified their particular status, taking care to prevent them seducing their younger companions."

14. Ibid., p. 36.

15. Cantarella notes and challenges this contention, page 40 citing, for example, J. Henderson, *The Maculate Muse: Obscene Language in Attic Comedy* (New Haven: Yale University Press, 1975), pp. 204ff.

16. Cantarella, *Bisexuality in the Ancient World,* pp. 216–17.

17. Gore Vidal, "The Twelve Caesars," *The Nation* (1959), reprinted in Gore Vidal, *United States: Essays 1952–1992* (New York: Random House, 1993), p. 525.

18. David M. Halperin, "Is There a History of Sexuality?" in *The Lesbian and Gay Studies Reader* ed. Henry Abelove, Michèle Aina Barale, and David M. Halperin (New York: Routledge, 1993), p. 420. A similar argument is advanced in the title essay of Halperin's *One Hundred Years of Homosexuality and Other Essays* (New York: Routledge, 1990), and in the Editors' Introduction to *Before Sexuality: The Construction of Erotic Experience in the Ancient Greek World,* ed. David M. Halperin, John J. Winkler, and Froma I. Zeitlin (Princeton, N.J.: Princeton University Press, 1990).

19. Halperin, "Is There a History of Sexuality?" p. 428 n. 24.

20. Ibid., p. 421. On "bisexuality," Halperin cites Paul Veyne's phrase "un bisexualité de sabrage," in "La famille et l'amour sous le Haut-Empire romain," *Annales (E.S.C.),* vol. 33 (1978), pp. 50–55, and Ramsey MacMullen's critique of Veyne in *Historia,* vol. 32 (1983), pp. 484–502. Other scholars who use the term "bisexuality" to describe ancient sexual practices include Luc Brisson, "Bisexualité et méditation en Grèce ancienne," *Nouvelle revue de psychanalyse,* vol. 7 (1973), pp. 27–48; Alain Schnapp, "Un autre image de l'homosexualité en Grèce ancienne," *Le Débat,* vol. 10 (1981), pp. 107–17, and Lawrence Stone, "Sex in the West," *The New Republic,* July 8, 1985, pp. 25–37. For the case for "Greek homosexuality," see K. J. Dover, *Greek Homosexuality* (Cambridge, Mass.: Harvard University Press, 1978).

21. Plato, *Republic,* 5:474, trans. Paul Shorey, in *Plato: The Collected Dialogues,* ed. Edith Hamilton and Huntington Cairns, Bollingen Series LXXI (Princeton, N.J.: Princeton University Press, 1961), pp. 713–14.

22. Bloom, *Closing of the American Mind,* p. 60.

23. Ibid., p. 61.

24. Percy Bysshe Shelley, "A Discourse on the Manners of the Ancient Greeks Relative to the Subject of Love," in *The Platonism of Shelley,* ed. James A. Notopolous (Durham, N.C.: Duke University Press, 1949), p. 407.

25. Floyer Sydenham, *The Banquet: A Dialogue of Plato Concerning Love* (London: W. Sandby, 1761); Louis Crompton, *Byron and Greek Love: Homophobia in 19th-Century England* (Berkeley: University of California Press, 1985), pp. 87–88.

26. Crompton, *Byron and Greek Love,* p. 86.

27. Bloom, *Closing of the American Mind,* pp. 236–37.

28. Crompton, *Byron and Greek Love,* p. 80.

29. Ibid., p. 81.

30. Ibid., p. 195.

31. Ibid., p. 66.

32. Parker Tyler, *Screening the Sexes: Homosexuality in the Movies* (1972; New York: Da Capo Press, 1993), pp. 246–47.

33. Lillian Hellman, introduction to *Four Plays by Lillian Hellman* (New York: Random House, 1942), p. viii.

34. *The Lillian Hellman Collection at the University of Texas,* comp. Manfred Triesch (Austin: University of Texas Press, 1968), pp. 102–104.

35. See Mary Titus, "Murdering the Lesbian: Lillian Hellman's *The Children's Hour,*" *Tulsa Studies in Women's Literature,* vol. 10, no. 2 (Fall 1991), p. 219.

36. Lillian Hellman, *Pentimento: A Book of Portraits* (Boston: Little, Brown, 1973), p. 114.

37. Lillian Hellman, *An Unfinished Woman* (Boston: Little, Brown, 1969), pp. 102–103.

38. Titus, "Murdering the Lesbian," p. 226.

39. Lillian Hellman, *Six Plays by Lillian Hellman* (New York: Random House, 1979), p. 15.

40. Ibid., pp. 19–20.

41. Ibid., p. 27.

42. Terry Castle, *The Apparitional Lesbian: Female Homosexuality and Modern Culture* (New York: Columbia University Press, 1993), p. 63.

43. Théophile Gautier, *Mademoiselle de Maupin,* trans. Joanna Richardson (Harmondsworth: Penguin Books, 1981), p. 330.

44. Hellman, *Six Plays,* p. 22.

45. Ibid., p. 64.

46. Ibid., p. 72.

47. Ibid., p. 73.

48. Dorothy Strachey Bussy, *Olivia* (1949; New York: Arno Press, 1975).

49. Blanche Wiesen Cook, " 'Women Alone Stir My Imagination': Lesbianism and Cultural Tradition," *Signs: Journal of Women, in Culture and Society,* vol. 4, no. 4 (1979), pp. 727–28.

50. Bussy, *Olivia,* p. 8.

51. Ibid., pp. 8–9.

52. Ibid., p. 9.

53. See for example Terry Castle's excellent discussion in *The Apparitional Lesbian,* and Diana Fuss's equally admirable account in *Identification Papers* (New York: Routledge, 1995).

54. Martha Vicinus, "Distance and Desire: English Boarding School Friendships," *Signs: Journal of Women in Culture and Society,* vol. 9, no. 4 (1984), p. 609.

55. Fuss, *Identification Papers.*

56. Corinne Robinson, unpublished memoirs; Cook, " 'Women Alone Stir My Imagination,' " p. 116.

57. Cook, " 'Women Alone Stir My Imagination,' " p. 119.

58. Ibid., p. 173.

59. Ibid., p. 120.

60. Bussy, *Olivia,* pp. 57–58.

61. Sigmund Freud, "Observations on Transference-Love" (1912), *SE* 12:170–71.

62. Muriel Spark, *The Prime of Miss Jean Brodie* (New York: Penguin, 1961), p. 110.

63. Ibid., p. 157.

64. Sigmund Freud, "The Dynamics of Transference" (1912), *SE* 12:108.

65. H.D., *Tribute to Freud* (New York: New Directions, 1974), p. 147.

66. Spark, *Prime of Miss Jean Brodie,* p. 37.

67. Ibid., p. 65.

68. Ibid., p. 71.

69. Ibid., pp. 74–75 and 76.

70. Ibid., p. 77.

71. Ibid., p. 34.

72. Ibid., p. 176.

73. Ibid., p. 175.

74. Ibid., p. 150.

75. Ibid., p. 176.

76. bell hooks, *Teaching to Transgress: Education as the Price of Freedom* (New York: Routledge, 1994), p. 191.

77. Jane Gallop, "Feminism and Harassment Policy," *Academe,* September–October 1994, p. 23.

78. Margaret Talbot, "A Most Dangerous Method: The Pedagogical Problem of Jane Gallop," *Lingua Franca,* January/February 1994, p. 27.

79. Ibid., p. 1.

80. Ibid., p. 32.

81. Ibid., p. 35.

82. Ibid., p. 34.

83. Ibid., p. 39.

Chapter 15: "It's a Phase"

1. Sigmund Freud, "The Psychogenesis of a Case of Homosexuality in a Woman" (1920), *SE* 18:151.

2. Adam Phillips, *On Kissing, Tickling, and Being Bored: Psychoanalytic Essays on the Unexamined Life* (Cambridge, Mass.: Harvard University Press, 1993), pp. 10, 11.

3. Merlin Holland, quoted in *Newsweek,* February 27, 1995, p. 21.

4. "It's so wonderful when a young virgin . . ." he began a honeymoon confidence to his friend Robert Sherard, who quickly hushed him up (Richard Ellmann, *Oscar Wilde* [New York: Alfred A. Knopf, 1988], p. 250).

5. Ibid., pp. 246, 252, and 253.

6. Ibid., p. 277.

7. Ibid., p. 281.

8. Letter from Otho Holland (Lloyd) to Arthur Ransome, February 28, 1912, *The Letters of Oscar Wilde,* ed. Rupert Hart-Davis (London: 1962).

9. Ellmann, *Oscar Wilde,* p. 486.

10. Hart-Davis, *Letters,* p. 766.

11. Gore Vidal, "Oscar Wilde: On the Skids Again," in *At Home: Essays 1982–1988* (New York: Vintage Books, 1988), p. 206.

12. See Jonathan Dollimore, *Sexual Dissidence: Augustine to Wilde, Freud to Foucault* (Oxford: Clarendon Press, 1991).

13. Interview with the author, March 1994.

14. Stephen Spender, *World Within World: The Autobiography of Stephen Spender* (London: Hamish Hamilton, 1951), p. viii.

15. David Leavitt, *While England Sleeps* (New York: Viking Penguin, 1993), p. 172.

16. Ibid., p. 278.

17. Ibid., p. 140.

18. Ibid.

19. David Leavitt, "Did I Plagiarize His Life?" *New York Times Magazine,* April 3, 1994, p. 37.

20. E. M. Forster, *What I Believe* (London: Hogarth Press, 1939).

21. James Atlas, "Who Owns a Life? Asks a Poet, When His Is Turned into Fiction," *New York Times,* February 20, 1994, p. E14.

22. Letter from Stephen Spender to Christopher Isherwood, October 21, 1934, in *Letters to Christopher: Stephen Spender's Letters to Christopher Isherwood 1929–1939,* ed. Lee Bartlett (Santa Barbara, Calif.: Black Sparrow Press, 1980), pp. 67–68.

23. Letter from Stephen Spender to Christopher Isherwood, January 18, 1935, Bartlett, *Letters to Christopher,* p. 72.

24. Spender, *World Within World,* p. 196.

25. Ibid., p. 184.

26. Ibid., p. 197.

27. Ibid., p. 205.

28. Ibid., p. 208.

29. Ibid., p. 260.

30. Ibid., p. 280.

31. Ibid., pp. 67–68.

32. Ian Hamilton, "Spender's Lives," *The New Yorker,* February 28, 1994, pp. 76 and 79.

33. Christopher Isherwood, *Christopher and His Kind* (New York: Farrar, Straus & Giroux, 1976), pp. 15 and 18.

34. Ibid., p. 26.

35. See for example Sigmund Freud's "Dynamics of the Transference" (1912), *SE* 12:106–107, but also the case studies of "Little Hans" ([1909], *SE* 10:5–149) and the "Rat Man" ([1909], *SE* 10:191). Coined as a term originally by Eugen Bleuler, ambivalence is fundamental to the work of Melanie Klein and Karl Abraham, among analysts of the period.

36. Spender, *World Within World,* pp. 185–86.

37. Ibid., p. 318.

38. Hamilton, "Spender's Lives," p. 84.

39. An entry from Nijinsky's notebooks, as cited in Alan Riding, "Nijinsky's Notebooks Are Published, Unexpurgated," *New York Times,* January 24, 1995, p. C13. (An

English translation of Nijinsky's notebooks is forthcoming from Farrar, Straus, & Giroux.)

40. Paul Monette, *Becoming a Man: Half a Life Story* (New York: Harcourt Brace Jovanovich, 1992), p. 173.

41. Ibid., p. 276.

42. Ibid., p. 118.

43. Letter from Sigmund Freud to Wilhelm Fliess, July 17, 1899, in *The Complete Letters of Sigmund Freud to Wilhelm Fliess 1887–1904,* ed. and trans. Jeffrey Moussaief Masson (Cambridge, Mass.: Harvard University Press, 1985), p. 361.

44. Monette, *Becoming a Man,* p. 240.

45. Ibid., p. 195.

46. Ibid., p. 233.

47. Ibid., pp. 235 and 238.

48. Ibid., p. 241.

49. Ibid., p. 242.

50. Ibid., p. 249.

51. Ibid., pp. 240 and 251.

52. Ibid., pp. 251 and 252.

53. Ibid., p. 259.

54. Ibid., p. 260.

55. Ibid., p. 261.

56. Ibid., p. 239.

57. Ibid., p. 243.

Chapter 16: Family Values

1. Susan Bickelhaupt, "Names and Faces," *Boston Globe,* April 4, 1994, p. 31.

2. Katha Pollitt, "Bothered and Bewildered," *New York Times,* July 22, 1993, p. A23.

3. Andrew Sullivan, "The Politics of Homosexuality," *The New Republic,* May 10, 1993, p. 37.

4. John Boswell, *Same-Sex Unions in Premodern Europe* (New York: Villard Books, 1994).

5. Frank Rich, "Straight at Stonewall," *New York Times,* June 19, 1994, p. 17.

6. C. S. Lewis, *The Allegory of Love: A Study in Medieval Tradition* (London: Oxford University Press, 1936; reprinted, 1968), pp. 2–3.

7. Andreas Capellanus, *De Arte Honeste Amandi,* ed. E. Trojel (Havniae: In Libraria Gadiana, 1892), p. 153; Lewis, *Allegory of Love,* pp. 35–36.

8. Bryher, *The Heart to Artemis: A Writer's Memoirs* (New York: Harcourt, Brace & World, 1962), p. 201.

9. Edward N. S. Lorusso, introduction to Robert McAlmon, *Village* (1924; Albuquerque: University of New Mexico Press, 1990), p. vii.

10. Kenneth Lynn, *Hemingway* (New York: Simon & Schuster, 1987), p. 195.

11. Lorusso, introduction to *Village,* pp. vii–viii.

12. Shari Benstock, *Women of the Left Bank: Paris 1900–1940* (Austin: University of Texas Press, 1986), p. 312.

13. Eric Schmitt, "In Fear, Gay Soldiers Marry for Camouflage," *New York Times,* July 12, 1993, p. A10.

14. Humphrey Carpenter, *W. H. Auden: A Biography* (London: George Allen & Unwin, 1981), p. 175.

15. Austin Wright, in ibid., p. 177.

16. Christopher Isherwood, *Christopher and His Kind* (New York: Farrar, Straus & Giroux, 1976), pp. 206–207.

17. Carpenter, *W. H. Auden,* p. 17.

18. Brian Finney, *Christopher Isherwood: A Critical Biography* (London: Faber & Faber, 1979), p. 120.

19. Letter from Golo Mann to Humphrey Carpenter, in Carpenter, *W. H. Auden,* pp. 186, 187.

20. Isherwood, *Christopher and His Kind,* pp. 207–208.

21. Carol Brightman, ed., *Between Friends: The Correspondence of Hannah Arendt and Mary McCarthy, 1949–1975* (New York: Harcourt, Brace & Co., 1995), p. 343.

22. Stephen Holden, "A Union of Convenience Across a Cultural Divide," *New York Times,* August 4, 1993, p. C18.

23. "The Oprah Winfrey Show," transcript #8618, national feed date October 25, 1986.

24. "Donahue," transcript #3648, national feed date January 21, 1993.

25. Claudia de Lys, *A Treasury of American Superstitions* (New York: Philosophical Library, 1948), p. 232. De Lys explains the disparity as follows: "From a two-pronged fork, feminine symbol, evolved the three-pronged fork, masculine symbol. Therein lies the confusion in the superstition, that in some parts of the world the dropping of a fork refers to a man, whereas in other places, where the change never took place, it still refers to a woman, and remains the feminine symbol."

26. "Donahue," transcript #08224, national feed date August 22, 1984.

27. "Swinging and Threesomes," "Donahue," transcript #3134, national feed date February 4, 1991.

28. Harold Bloom, *The American Religion: The Emergence of the Post-Christian Nation* (New York: Simon & Schuster, 1992), pp. 108–109.

29. Ibid., pp. 188–89.

30. Allen Drury, *Advise and Consent* (London: Collins, 1960), pp. 293 and 295.

31. Ibid., p. 298.

32. Ibid., p. 300.

33. Ibid., pp. 300–301.

34. Ibid., p. 302.

35. Ibid.

36. Thus, for example, we are told that he returned to Salt Lake City to find "his older sisters married, his older brother in the Church, his younger sisters coming along, his parents, if possible, even more the unshakable pillars of society than they had been." Ibid., p. 301.

37. Ibid., p. 305.

38. Ibid., p. 307.

39. Ibid., p. 452.

40. Ibid., p. 447.

41. Ibid., p. 449 and 450.

42. Ibid., p. 453.

43. Ibid., p. 264.

44. "Of late there had been at times a growing boredom that he had not always quite concealed, though he never let it get out of hand. Nonetheless Mabel knew and there had been an increasing number of arguments about it, usually not very serious and turned off with a joke and a kiss and sometimes a small gift or a night out." "And then with a sudden contrition he had told her how much he loved her and done things she fiercely enjoyed to prove it." Ibid., p. 306.

45. Ibid., p. 307, emphasis added.

46. Ibid., p. 464.

47. Ibid., p. 460.

48. Ibid., p. 433.

49. Ibid.

50. Tony Kushner, *Angels in America, A Gay Fantasia on American Themes. Part Two: Perestroika* (New York: Theatre Communications Group, 1992), p. 110.

51. Tony Kushner, *Angels in America, A Gay Fantasia on American Themes. Part One: Millennium Approaches* (New York: Theatre Communications Group, 1992), p. 27.

52. Kushner, *Perestroika,* p. 106.

53. Ibid., pp. 85–87.

54. Christopher Alexander, "Affirmation: Bisexual Mormon," in *Bi Any Other Name,* ed. Loraine Hutchins and Lani Kaahumanu (Boston: Alyson Publications, 1991), p. 193.

55. Ibid., p. 194.

56. Ibid., p. 197.

57. Tennessee Williams, *Cat on a Hot Tin Roof* (1955; New York: New American Library, 1985), p. xiii.

58. Ibid., p. 37.

59. Ibid., p. 43.

60. Ibid., p. 44.

61. Ibid., p. xv.

62. Ibid., p. 90.

63. Ibid., p. 86.

Chapter 17: Marriages of Inconvenience

1. Edward Carpenter, *Love's Coming-of-Age* (Manchester: Labour Press, 1896), p. 103.

2. "Bisexuals Discriminated Against by Gays and Heterosexuals," "Donahue," transcript #3648, national feed date January 21, 1993.

3. Vito Russo, *The Celluloid Closet: Homosexuality in the Movies,* rev. ed. (New York: Harper & Row, 1987), p. 231.

4. Ibid., p. 272.

5. Barry Kohn and Alice Matusow, *Barry and Alice: Portrait of a Bisexual Marriage* (Englewood Cliffs, N.J.: Prentice-Hall, 1980), p. 190.

6. Ibid., p. 78.

7. Ibid., p. 122.

8. Ibid., p. 123.

9. Elisabeth Kübler-Ross, *On Death and Dying* (New York: Macmillan, 1969), pp. 38–137.

10. Kohn and Matusow, *Barry and Alice,* pp. 130–32.

11. Humphrey Burton, *Leonard Bernstein* (New York: Doubleday, 1994), p. 49.

12. Kenneth Ehrman, quoted in ibid.

13. Burton, *Leonard Bernstein,* p. 109.

14. Ibid., pp. 107–108.

15. Ibid., p. 108. Letter from Felicia Monteleagre, dated "Thursday 27."

16. Burton, *Leonard Bernstein,* p. 211.

17. Ibid.

18. Ibid., p. 216.

19. Ibid., p. 434.

20. Ibid.

21. To Paul Hume, ibid.

22. *Newsweek,* November 8, 1976.

23. *People,* November 25, 1976.

24. Burton, *Leonard Bernstein,* p. 507.

25. *Newsweek,* March 14, 1977. Reprinted in *Conversations with John Cheever,* ed. Scott Donaldson (Jackson: University Press of Mississippi, 1987), p. 124.

26. John Cheever, *The Journals of John Cheever* (New York: Alfred A. Knopf, 1990), p. ix.

27. Christina Robb, "Cheever's Story," *Boston Globe Magazine,* July 6, 1980, reprinted in Donaldson, *Conversations with John Cheever,* p. 222.

28. John Cheever, *Journals,* p. 143.

29. Ibid., p. 172.

30. Ibid., p. 191.

31. Ibid., pp. 213–14.

32. Ibid., pp. 245–46.

33. Ibid., p. 257.

34. Ibid., p. 299.

35. Ibid., pp. 343–44.

36. Ibid., pp. 346–47.

37. Marian Christy, "Benjamin Cheever—A Son in the Shadow," *Boston Globe,* December 25, 1988, p. A14.

38. John Cheever, *Journals,* p. 356.

39. Ibid., p. 366.

40. Ibid., pp. 371–72.

41. Ibid., p. 378.

42. Ibid., p. 394.

43. Susan Cheever, *Home Before Dark* (1984; New York: Bantam, 1991), p. 172.

44. Ibid., p. 174.

45. Ibid., pp. 175 and 176.

46. Ibid., p. 176.

47. Ibid.

48. Ibid., p. 186.

49. Ibid., p. 199.

50. Ibid., pp. 202–203.

51. Donaldson, *Conversations,* pp. 124–25.

52. Susan Cheever, *Home Before Dark,* pp. 206–207.

53. Ibid., p. 209.

54. John Cheever, *Journals,* p. vii.

55. Christy, "Benjamin Cheever."

56. Letter from Paul Bowles to Bruce Morissette, February 20, 1930, in *In Touch: The Letters of Paul Bowles,* ed. Jeffrey Miller (New York: Farrar, Straus & Giroux, 1994), p. 39.

57. Letter from Paul Bowles to Morissette, February 22, 1930, in Miller, *In Touch,* p. 42.

58. Letter from Paul Bowles to Aaron Copland, Summer 1933, in Miller, *In Touch,* p. 117.

59. Letter from Paul Bowles to Aaron Copland, September 2, 1933, in Miller, *In Touch,* p. 124.

60. Letter from Paul Bowles to Dorothy Norman, April 1938, in Miller, *In Touch,* p. 162.

61. Truman Capote, introduction to *My Sister's Hand in Mind: An Expanded Edition of the Collected Works of Jane Bowles* (New York: The Ecco Press, 1977), p. v. The quotation from Williams appears on the book's back cover.

62. Millicent Dillon, *A Little Original Sin: The Life and Work of Jane Bowles* (New York: Holt, Rinehart & Winston, 1981), p. 47.

63. Ibid., p. 37.

64. Ibid., p. 50.

65. Ibid., p. 80.

66. Ibid., p. xii.

67. Ibid., p. 352.

68. Ibid., p. 128.

69. Ibid., p. 328.

70. Letter from Paul Bowles to Regina Weinreich, November 8, 1983, in Miller, *In Touch,* p. 521.

71. Michael Upchurch, "The Great Unknown," *New York Times Book Review,* June 26, 1994, p. 27.

72. Nigel Nicolson, *Portrait of a Marriage* (New York: Atheneum, 1973), pp. viii–ix.

73. Ibid., p. ix.

74. Ibid., p. 95.

75. Ibid., p. 9.

76. Ibid., p. 230.

77. Ibid., p. 23.

78. Ibid., p. 159.

79. Letter from Harold Nicolson to Vita Sackville-West, June 9, 1919, ibid., p. 162.

80. Nicolson, *Portrait of a Marriage,* p. 22.

81. Ibid., pp. 29–30.

82. Ibid., p. 28.

83. Ibid., p. 35.

84. Ibid., p. 38.

85. Ibid., p. 39.

86. Ibid., p. 34.

87. Ibid., p. 39.

88. Ibid., p. 103.

89. Ibid., pp. 104–107.

90. Ibid., p. 104.

91. Ibid., p. 110.

92. Ibid., p. 116.

93. Ibid., p. 152.

94. Letter from Violet Keppel to Vita Sackville-West, October 14, 1918, ibid., p. 152.

95. Ibid., p. 153.

96. Nicolson, *Portrait of a Marriage,* p. 135.

97. Ibid., p. 137.

98. Ibid.

99. Letter from Harold Nicolson to Vita Sackville-West, September 10, 1918, ibid., p. 142.

100. Nicolson, *Portrait of a Marriage,* p. 140.

101. Ibid., p. 108.

102. Ibid., p. 114.

103. Ibid., p. 117.

104. Mitchell A. Leaska, *The Letters of Violet Trefusis to Vita Sackville-West,* ed. Mitchell A. Leaska and John Phillips (New York: Penguin, 1991), p. 49.

105. Nicolson, *Portrait of a Marriage,* p. 136.

106. Letter from Vita Sackville-West to Harold Nicolson, December 8, 1922, ibid., p. 180.

107. Leaska and Phillips, *Letters of Violet Trefusis,* p. 51.

108. Nicolson, *Portrait of a Marriage,* pp. 105–106.

109. Ibid., p. 190; BBC radio broadcast, 1929, in ibid., pp. 189–90.

110. September 23, 1923, in Nicolson, *Portrait of a Marriage,* p. 188.

111. Ibid., p. 187.

112. Ibid., p. 188.

113. Ibid., pp. 231–32.

114. Violet Keppel Trefusis, *Don't Look Round* (New York: Viking, 1992); Nicolson, *Portrait of a Marriage,* p. 181.

115. Nicolson, *Portrait of a Marriage,* p. 207.

116. Letter from Vita Sackville-West to Harold Nicolson, August 17, 1926, ibid., p. 206.

117. Letter from Virginia Woolf to Vita Sackville-West, n.d., 1927, in *The Letters of Virginia Woolf,* ed. Nigel Nicolson and Joanne Trautmann (New York: Harcourt Brace Jovanovich, 1975–77), vol. 3, p. 393; Blanche Wiesen Cook, " 'Women Alone Stir My Imagination': Lesbianism and the Cultural Tradition," *Signs: Journal of Women in Culture and Society,* vol. 4, no. 4 (1979), p. 727.

118. Letter from Virginia Woolf to Vita Sackville-West, July 18, 1927, in Nicolson and Trautmann, *Letters,* vol. 3, p. 397. Blanche Wiesen Cook minced no words in attacking the premise that the marriage defined Vita's life, and that the relationship with Woolf, as she paraphrased the view of some male biographers, "involved neither love nor lust" (Blanche Wiesen Cook, " 'Women Alone Stir My Imagination,' " pp. 727–28). Regarding Nicolson's *Portrait* as not an "adequate biography" of Vita ("though written with love . . . it occasionally resembles a complaining letter from an irate son whose mother was too often removed"), she reserved her harshest words for Quentin Bell, Woolf's nephew and curator, himself the author of a biography. "Having reluctantly accepted the reality of Virginia Woolf's lesbian friendship with Vita Sackville-West, . . .

Quentin Bell explains that they could not have been very satisfying relations." He concludes: "There may have been—on balance I think that there probably was—some caressing, some bedding together. But whatever may have occurred between them of this nature, I doubt very much whether it was of a kind to excite Virginia or to satisfy Vita" (Quentin Bell, *Virginia Woolf: A Biography* [New York: Harcourt Brace Jovanovich, 1975], vol. 2, p. 119).

119. Mitchell A. Leaska, introduction to *The Letters of Vita Sackville-West to Virginia Woolf,* ed. Louise DeSalvo and Mitchell A. Leaska (New York: William Morrow, 1985), p. 31.

120. *The Letters of Virginia Woolf,* ed. Nigel Nicolson and Joanne Trautmann (London: The Hogarth Press, 1975–80), vol. 3, p. 221.

121. Letter from Vita Sackville-West to Harold Nicolson, August 17, 1926, Nicolson, *Portrait of a Marriage,* p. 206.

122. Cited in Suzanne Raitt, *Vita and Virginia: The Work and Friendship of V. Sackville-West and Virginia Woolf* (Oxford: Clarendon Press, 1993), p. 5.

Chapter 18: Erotic Triangles

1. Montesquieu, *Lettres Persanes,* no. 59 (1721).

2. René Girard, *Deceit, Desire, and the Novel: Self and Other in Literary Structure,* trans. Yvonne Freccero (Baltimore: Johns Hopkins University Press, 1990), p. 17.

3. Ibid., p. 2.

4. Ibid.

5. Ibid., p. 40.

6. Ibid., p. 46.

7. Ibid., p. 47.

8. Eve Kosofsky Sedgwick, *Between Men: English Literature and Male Homosocial Desire* (New York: Columbia University Press, 1985), p. 21.

9. The timeliness and power of Sedgwick's intervention can be seen in the titles of books like Emma Donoghue's *Passions Between Women: British Lesbian Culture 1668–1801* (London: Scarlet Press, 1993), and the Columbia University Press series of books on gay and lesbian topics entitled "Between Women, Between Men."

10. Claude Lévi-Strauss, *The Elementary Structures of Kinship* (Boston: Beacon, 1969), p. 115; quoted in Gayle Rubin, "The Traffic in Women: Notes Toward a Political Economy of Sex," in *Toward an Anthropology of Women,* ed. Rayna Reiter (New York: Monthly Review Press, 1975), pp. 157–210.

11. Sedgwick, *Between Men,* p. 27.

12. Terry Castle, *The Apparitional Lesbian: Female Homosexuality and Modern Culture* (New York: Columbia University Press, 1993), pp. 67–73.

13. Ibid., p. 71.

14. Ibid., p. 84.

15. Ibid., p. 85.

16. Ibid., pp. 85–86.

17. Shoshana Felman, "On Reading Poetry: Reflections on the Limits and Possibilities of Psychoanalytical Approaches," in *The Purloined Poe: Lacan, Derrida, and Psychoanalytic Reading,* ed. John P. Muller and William J. Richardson (Baltimore: Johns Hopkins University Press, 1988), pp. 144–45.

18. Letter from Sigmund Freud to Wilhelm Fliess, July 27, 1904, in *The Complete Letters of Sigmund Freud to Wilhelm Fliess 1887–1904,* ed. and trans. Jeffrey Moussaief Masson (Cambridge, Mass.: Harvard University Press, 1985), p. 468.

19. Sigmund Freud, "Jokes and Their Relation to the Unconscious" (1905), *SE* 8:97.

20. Ibid., p. 101.

21. "A joke loses its effect of laughter even in the third person as soon as he is required to make an expenditure on [sic] intellectual work in connection with it. The allusions made in a joke must be obvious and the omissions easy to fill; an awakening of conscious intellectual interest usually makes the effect of the joke impossible. There is an important distinction here between jokes and riddles" (ibid., p. 150).

22. Vito Russo, *The Celluloid Closet: Homosexuality in the Movies,* rev. ed. (New York: Harper & Row, 1987), p. 210.

23. Janet Maslin, "Love in a New York Isosceles Triangle," *New York Times,* April 30, 1993, p. C16.

24. Anchee Min, *Red Azalea* (New York: Pantheon Books, 1994), p. 99.

25. Ibid., p. 107.

26. Ibid., pp. 108–109.

27. Ibid., p. 110.

28. Ibid., p. 113.

29. Ibid., p. 127.

30. Ibid., pp. 128–29.

31. Ibid., p. 129, emphasis added.

32. Ibid., p. 202.

33. Ibid., p. 217.

34. Ibid., p. 221.

35. Ibid., p. 266.

36. Ibid., pp. 235–36.

37. Ibid., p. 256.

38. Ibid., p. 264.

39. Ibid., p. 267.

40. Ibid., p. 302.

41. Anaïs Nin, *Henry and June* (San Diego, New York, London: Harcourt Brace Jovanovich, 1989), pp. 199 and 195.

42. Ibid., p. 270.

43. Ibid., p. 57.

44. Ibid., p. 62.

45. Ibid., p. 68, 58, 14, 268, and 269.

46. Ibid., p. 10.

47. Ibid., p. 18.

48. Ibid., p. 22.

49. Ibid.

Chapter 19: Jealousy

1. René Girard, *Deceit, Desire, and the Novel: Self and Other in Literary Structure,* trans. Yvonne Freccero (Baltimore: Johns Hopkins University Press, 1990), p. 12.

2. Susie Bright, *Susie Bright's Sexual Reality: A Virtual Sex World Reader* (Pittsburgh and San Francisco: Cleis Press, 1992), p. 152.

3. Steven Gaines and Sharon Churcher, *Obsession: The Lives and Times of Calvin Klein* (New York: Birch Lane/Carol Publishing Group, 1994), p. 318.

4. Ibid.

5. Kathleen Fullerton Bernhard, *Jealousy: Its Nature and Treatment* (Springfield, Ill.: Charles C. Thomas, 1986), p. xi.

6. Nancy Friday, *Jealousy* (New York: Bantam, 1991), publisher's blurb to the paperback edition.

7. Ibid., pp. 282–83.

8. Peter Salovey, ed. *The Psychology of Jealousy and Envy* (New York and London: The Guilford Press, 1991), p. xi.

9. See for example Eugene W. Mathes, *Jealousy: The Psychological Data* (Lanham, Md.: University Press of America, 1992), pp. xi–xiii.

10. Ibid., p. xi.

11. Ibid. cites M. Hunt, *Sexual Behavior in the 1970s* (New York: Dell, 1975).

12. N. O'Neill and G. O'Neill, *Open Marriage* (New York: Avon, 1972).

13. Eugene Mathes and Nancy Severa, "Jealousy, Romantic Love and Liking: Theoretical Considerations and Preliminary Scale Development," *Psychological Reports,* vol. 49, pp. 23–31. Initially presented as a paper at the 49th Annual Meeting of the Midwestern Psychological Association, Chicago, Ill., 1977.

14. R. G. Bringle, S. Roach, C. Andler, and S. Evenbeck, "Measuring the Intensity of Jealousy Reactions," *Catalog of Selected Documents in Psychology,* vol. 9, pp. 23–24. Originally presented as a paper, "Correlates of Jealousy," at the 49th Annual Meeting of the Midwestern Psychological Association, Chicago, Ill., 1977.

15. G. L. White, "Jealousy and Partner's Perceived Motives for Attraction to a Rival," *Social Psychology,* vol. 39 (1981), pp. 660–68; G. L. White, "Comparison of Four Jealousy Scales," *Journal of Research in Personality,* vol. 18 (1984), pp. 115–30.

16. R. B. Hupka and B. Bachelor, "Validation of a Scale to Measure Romantic Jealousy." Paper presented at the Annual Meeting of the Western Psychological Association, San Diego, Calif., 1977.

17. M. Pfeiffer and P. T. P. Wong, *Multidimensional Jealousy and Unrequited Love,* unpublished manuscript, Trent University, Peterborough, Ontario, 1987.

18. Z. Rubin, "Measurement of Romantic Love," *Journal of Personality and Social Psychology,* vol. 16 (1970), pp. 265–73.

19. Bem Allen, foreword to Mathes, *Jealousy,* p. ix.

20. From the Interpersonal Jealousy Scale. The questions are presented in an appendix to Gregory L. White and Paul E. Mullen, *Jealousy: Theory, Research, and Clinical Strategies* (New York and London: The Guilford Press, 1989), p. 297.

21. White and Mullen, *Jealousy,* p. 121.

22. Ibid., p. 121; S. S. Brehm, *Intimate Relationships* (New York: Random House, 1985).

23. P. C. Larson, "Gay Male Relationships," in *Homosexuality as a Social Issue,* ed. W. Paul, J. D. Weinrich, J. C. Gonziorek, and M. E. Hotveldt (Beverly Hills, Calif.: Sage Publications, 1982); White and Mullen, *Jealousy,* p. 121.

24. White and Mullen, *Jealousy,* p. 121; V. Morris, "Helping Lesbian Couples Cope with Jealousy," *Women-in-Therapy,* vol. 1 (1982), pp. 27–34.

25. L. G. Smith and J. R. Smith, "Co-Marital Sex. The Incorporation of Extra-Marital Sex into the Marriage Relationship," in *Critical Issues in Contemporary Sexual Behavior,* ed. J. Money and J. Zubin (Baltimore: Johns Hopkins University Press, 1973), pp. 391–408.

26. D. Denfeld, "Dropouts from Swinging, the Marriage Counselor or Informant," in *Beyond Monogamy,* ed. J. R. Smith and L. G. Smith (Baltimore: Johns Hopkins University Press, 1974), pp. 260–67; G. D. Bartell, "Group Sex Among Mid-Americans," *Journal of Sex Research,* vol. 6 (1970), pp. 113–30.

27. C. A. Varnia, "An Exploratory Study of Spouse Swapping," in *Beyond Monogamy,* ed. Smith and Smith, pp. 214–29; White and Mullen, *Jealousy,* p. 122.

28. White and Mullen, *Jealousy,* p. 123; L. L. Constantine and J. M. Constantine, "Sexual Aspects of Multilateral Relations," in *Beyond Monogamy,* ed. Smith and Smith, pp. 268–90; R. M. Kanter, *Commitment and Community: Communes and Utopias in Sociological Perspective* (Cambridge, Mass.: Harvard University Press, 1972); J. W. Ramey, "Communes, Group Marriage and the Upper Middle Class," in *Beyond Monogamy,* ed. Smith and Smith, pp. 214–29.

29. Sandra Bem, "The Measurement of Psychological Androgyny," *Journal of Consulting and Clinical Psychology,* vol. 42 (1974), pp. 155–62; Sandra Bem, "Sex-Role Adaptability: One Consequence of Psychological Androgyny," *Journal of Personality and Social Psychology,* vol. 4 (1975), pp. 634–43.

30. D. Amstutz, *Androgyny and Jealousy,* unpublished doctoral dissertation, Northern Illinois University, 1982; White and Mullen, *Jealousy,* p. 124.

31. White and Mullen, *Jealousy,* p. 124.

32. Eugene W. Mathes, "A Cognitive Theory of Jealousy," in *Psychology of Jealousy and Envy,* ed. Salovey, pp. 57–59.

33. Ibid.

34. Hildegard Baumgart, *Jealousy: Experiences and Solutions,* trans. Manfred Jacobson and Evelyn Jacobson (Chicago: University of Chicago Press, 1990), p. 308.

35. Sigmund Freud, "On Narcissism: An Introduction" (1914–16), *SE* 14:88.

36. Ernest Jones, *Hamlet and Oedipus* (New York: W. W. Norton, 1949; reprint 1976), p. 117.

37. Susie Bright, "BlindSexual," in *Susie Bright's Sexual Reality,* pp. 156–57.

38. Susanna Trnka, "A Pretty Good Bisexual Kiss There . . ." in *Closer to Home: Bisexuality and Feminism,* ed. Elizabeth Reba Weise (Seattle: Seal Press, 1992), p. 107.

39. "Geraldo," transcript #520, national feed date September 13, 1989.

40. Martin S. Weinberg, Colin J. Williams, and Douglas Pryor, *Dual Attraction: Understanding Bisexuality* (New York: Oxford University Press, 1994), p. 108.

41. Ibid., p. 109.

42. Karen F., letter to the author.

43. Interview with the author, March 1993. "Brian Ford" is a pseudonym.

44. Sigmund Freud, "Some Neurotic Mechanisms in Jealousy, Paranoia and Homosexuality" (1922), *SE* 18:223.

45. Ibid., p. 224.

46. William Shakespeare, *Othello, The Riverside Shakespeare* (Boston: Houghton Mifflin, 1974), 4.3.55–57.

47. Germaine Brée, introduction to Alain Robbe-Grillet, *Jealousy (La Jalousie)* (New York: Grove Press, 1959).

48. Girard, *Deceit, Desire, and the Novel,* p. 83.

49. Shakespeare, *Othello,* 3.3.71, 100.

50. Ibid., 5.1.19.

51. Ibid., 3.3.460–69, 479–80.

Chapter 20: The Bisexual Plot

1. George Meredith, *Modern Love,* sonnet 43, in *The Poetry of George Meredith,* ed. Phyllis B. Bartlett (New Haven: Yale University Press, 1978).

2. Henry James, *The Bostonians* (1886; New York and London: Penguin, 1986), p. 154.

3. Lillian Faderman, *Surpassing the Love of Men: Romantic Friendship and Love Between Women from the Renaissance to the Present* (New York: William Morrow, 1981), p. 190.

4. F. W. Dupee, *Henry James* (New York: William Sloane Associates, 1951), p. 152.

5. Louis Auchincloss, *Reading Henry James* (Minneapolis: University of Minnesota Press, 1975), p. 42. Faderman, *Surpassing the Love of Men,* pp. 191–95.

6. Robert McLean, "*The Bostonians:* New England Pastoral," *Papers in Language and Literature,* no. 7 (1971), p. 374.

7. Walter F. Wright, *The Madness of Art: A Study of Henry James* (Lincoln: University of Nebraska Press, 1962), pp. 94 and 95.

8. Jean Strouse, *Alice James: A Biography* (Boston: Houghton Mifflin, 1980), p. 250.

9. Tony Tanner, *Henry James: The Writer and His Work* (Amherst: University of Massachusetts Press, 1985), p. 53.

10. Edmund Wilson, "The Ambiguity of Henry James," *Hound and Horn,* vol. 8 (April–June 1934), p. 396. This and many other telling quotations about sexuality and *The Bostonians* are collected by Judith Fetterly in the beginning of her essay on the novel in *The Resisting Reader* (Bloomington: Indiana University Press, 1978), pp. 102–107.

11. Tanner, *Henry James,* p. 54.

12. Irving Howe, "Introduction to *The Bostonians,*" in *Critical Essays on Henry James: The Early Novels,* ed. James W. Gargano (Boston: Hall, 1987), pp. 154–69.

13. Tanner, *Henry James,* p. 54.

14. Terry Castle, *The Apparitional Lesbian: Female Homosexuality and Modern Culture* (New York: Columbia University Press, 1993), pp. 174, 176, and 177.

15. Ibid., pp. 178–79.

16. Ibid., p. 174. The terms "euphoric" and "dysphoric" are taken from Nancy K. Miller, *The Heroine's Text: Readings in the French and English Novel 1722–1792* (New York: Columbia University Press, 1980), when, as Castle notes, marriage is described as "euphoric" destiny for the heroine—in marked contrast to its use in Castle's lesbian paradigm.

17. Ibid., p. 151; Jeannette Foster, *Sex Variant Women in Literature,* 3rd ed. (Tallahassee, Fla.: Naiad Press, 1985), p. 15.

18. Castle, *Apparitional Lesbian,* p. 264, n. 13.

19. "For better or for worse," writes Judith Fetterley, *"The Bostonians* is finally Olive Chancellor's book." Fetterley, *The Resisting Reader,* p. 118.

20. James, *Bostonians,* p. 62.

21. Ibid., p. 101.

22. Ibid., p. 102.

23. Ibid., p. 103.

24. Ibid., p. 107.

25. Ibid.

26. Ibid., p. 109.

27. Any "heroic" reading of Olive will have to contend with James's intermittent and often devastating irony at her expense. To give two brief examples: of a relatively banal remark of Verena's about the suffering of Joan of Arc at one of their early meetings: "This was so prettily said that Olive could scarcely keep from kissing her" (p. 106). Of Verena's casual observation, in response to a quotation in German, that she did not know the language and would like to learn it: " 'We will work at it together— we will study everything,' Olive almost panted" (p. 107). Basil and Verena are treated with equal irony at other points in the text.

28. James, *Bostonians,* pp. 112–13.

29. Ibid., p. 154.

30. Ibid., p. 179.

31. A chump, a dupe.

32. James, *Bostonians,* p. 366.

33. The woolliness here is Mrs. Tarrant's, for the voice recalling this fact is hers (ibid., p. 93).

34. James, *Bostonians,* pp. 104–105.

35. Ibid., p. 105.

36. Ibid., p. 149.

37. Ibid., p. 151.

38. Ibid., p. 152.

39. Ibid., p. 153.

40. Ibid., p. 261.

41. Ibid., p. 301.

42. Ibid., p. 302.

43. Ibid., pp. 297–98, emphasis added.

44. Ibid., p. 298.

45. Ibid., p. 355.

46. Ibid., p. 354.

47. For more on the erotics of Greek pedagogy, see Chapter 14, "Erotic Education," and Eva Cantarella, *Bisexuality in the Ancient World,* trans. Cormac Ó'Cuilleanáin (New Haven: Yale University Press, 1992), pp. 17–53.

48. James, *Bostonians,* p. 104.

49. Paula C. Rust, "The Politics of Sexual Identity: Sexual Attraction and Behavior among Lesbian and Bisexual Women," *Social Problems,* vol. 39, no. 4 (November 1992), p. 367.

50. James, *Bostonians,* p. 176.

51. Ibid., p. 227.

52. Ibid., p. 178.

53. Ibid., p. 394.

54. Ibid., p. 369.

55. *Othello,* 3.4.69.

56. Ibid., 5.2.287.

57. James, *Bostonians,* p. 371.

58. Matthiessen writes of James's attitude toward Olive that "He does not satirize her, he sees her as essentially tragic" (*The American Stories and Novels of Henry James,* ed. F. O. Matthiessen, [1947; New York: Alfred A. Knopf, 1964], pp. xix–xx). Consider also James's description of the scene in the Music Hall waiting room: "beside her, prostrate, fallen over, her head buried in the lap of Verena's mother, the tragic figure of Olive Chancellor" (James, *Bostonians,* p. 424).

59. James, *Bostonians,* pp. 374–75.

60. Rust, "Politics of Sexual Identity," p. 368.

61. The "true subject of *The Bostonians* is not love but power," Fetterley, *The Resisting Reader,* p. 131.

62. Charles. R. Anderson, "James' Portrait of the Southerner," *American Literature,* vol. 27 (1955), p. 310.

63. McLean, *"The Bostonians:* New England Pastoral," p. 381.

64. Fetterley, *The Resisting Reader,* p. 119.

65. William McMurray, "Pragmatic Realism in *The Bostonians,"* *Nineteenth Century Fiction,* vol. 16 (March 1962), p. 341.

66. Irving Howe, introduction to *The Bostonians* (New York: Random House, 1956), p. xxvii.

67. Leon Edel, *Henry James: The Middle Years* (Philadelphia: Lippincott, 1962), p. 141.

68. Fetterley, *The Resisting Reader,* p. 113.

69. Ibid., p. 146.

70. Ibid., p. 117.

71. Ibid., p. 150.

72. William Shakespeare, *Twelfth Night, The Riverside Shakespeare* (Boston: Houghton Mifflin, 1974), 5.1.260–63.

73. See for example Castle *Apparitional Lesbian,* who also notes that "Olivia is one of Stephen Gordon's middle names" in Radclyffe Hall's *Well of Loneliness* (1928), and that Virginia Woolf uses the name in "Chloe liked Olivia," *A Room of One's Own* (1929).

74. James, *Bostonians,* p. 433.

75. D.H. Lawrence, *The Portable D.H. Lawrence,* ed. Diana Trilling (1947; New York: Viking Press, 1969), pp. 219, 220, and 219.

76. Ibid., p. 219.

77. Ibid., p. 223.

78. Ibid., p. 222.

79. Ibid., pp. 119 and 234.

80. Ibid., p. 258.

81. Ibid., p. 234.

82. Ibid., p. 258.

83. Ibid., p. 265.

84. Ibid., p. 276.

85. Ibid., p. 279.

86. Ibid., pp. 282–83.

87. Ibid., pp. 270–71.

88. Ibid., p. 299.

89. Ibid., pp. 300, 304, and 306.

90. Ibid., p. 304.

91. Ibid., p. 305.

92. James, *Bostonians,* p. 358.

93. Vito Russo, *The Celluloid Closet: Homosexuality in the Movies,* rev. ed. (New York: Harper & Row, 1987), p. 164.

94. Fred Klein, *The Bisexual Option: A Concept of One Hundred Percent Intimacy* (New York: Arbor House, 1978), p. 182.

95. Ibid., p. 182.

96. Brenda Maddox, *D. H. Lawrence: The Story of a Marriage* (New York: Simon & Schuster, 1994), p. 227.

97. Pauline Kael, "The Current Cinema," *The New Yorker,* February 10, 1968, p. 102.

98. Ibid., p. 100.

99. Renata Adler, "Lawrence's Novella Is Intelligently Treated," *New York Times,* February 8, 1968, p. 36.

100. *Commonweal,* March 5, 1968, p. 656.

101. Stanley Kauffmann, "Three for the Road," *The New Republic,* vol. 158 (March 9, 1968), p. 24.

102. *Newsweek,* February 19, 1968, p. 92.

103. Cited approvingly in Klein, *The Bisexual Option,* p. 183. Klein notes that this was the only review he found that mentioned bisexuality, "so, although there are only three characters, it is the bisexual one who does not exist."

104. Arthur Knight, "SR Goes to the Movies," *Saturday Review,* February 10, 1968, p. 40.

105. Richard Schickel, "The Legend as Actress," in Antoni Gronowicz, *Garbo* (New York: Simon & Schuster, 1990), p. 461.

106. Gronowicz, *Garbo,* pp. 62–63.

Chapter 21: Threesomes

1. "Two Ladies," from *Cabaret,* music by John Kander, lyrics by Fred Ebb.

2. Martin S. Weinberg, Colin J. Williams, and Douglas W. Pryor, *Dual Attraction: Understanding Bisexuality* (New York: Oxford University Press, 1994), p. 68.

3. Ibid., p. 6.

4. Philip Roth, *Portnoy's Complaint* (New York: Bantam, 1978), pp. 151–55.

5. Michael Szymanski, "Bisexuality: My Second Coming Out," *Genre,* vol. 8 (October/November 1992), p. 38.

6. Ibid., p. 39.

7. Arno Karlen, *Threesomes: Studies in Sex, Power, and Intimacy* (New York: William Morrow, 1988), p. 67.

8. Ibid., p. 73.

9. Ibid., p. 77. Here he paraphrases anthropologist Gilbert Bartell, in *Group Sex* (New York: Wyden, 1971).

10. Karlen, *Threesomes,* p. 67.

11. Ibid., p. 79.

12. Ibid., p. 111.

13. Ibid., p. 55.

14. Ibid., p. 128.

15. Ibid., p. 83.

16. Ibid., p. 205.

17. Ibid., p. 184.

18. Ibid., p. 194.

19. Ibid., p. 217.

20. Ibid., p. 154.

21. Ibid., p. 207.

22. Ibid., p. 211.

23. Ibid., p. 237.

24. Ibid., p. 206.

25. Ibid., p. 244.

26. Ibid., p. 203.

27. René Girard, *Deceit, Desire, and the Novel: Self and Other in Literary Structure,* trans. Yvonne Freccero (Baltimore: Johns Hopkins University Press, 1990), p. 4.

28. Carlton Lake and Linda Ashton, *Henri-Pierre Roché: An Introduction* (Austin, Tex.: Harry Ransom Humanities Research Center, 1991), p. 9.

29. Ibid., p. 150.

30. December 17, 1906, ibid., p. 152.

31. Beatrice Wood, *I Shock Myself: The Autobiography of Beatrice Wood,* ed. Lindsay Smith (San Francisco: Chronicle Books, 1985), p. 25.

32. Paul B. Franklin, personal communication to the author.

33. François Truffaut, "Henri-Pierre Roché Revisited," trans. Katherine C. Foster, introduction to Roché, *Jules and Jim,* trans. Patrick Evans (London: Pavanne, 1987), p. 1.

34. Letter from Joe Orton to Michael White, July 14, 1967, quoted in John Lahr, *Prick Up Your Ears: The Biography of Joe Orton* (New York: Vintage, 1987), p. 247.

35. Lahr, *Prick Up Your Ears,* p. 187.

36. *Plays and Players,* August, 1965, quoted in ibid., p. 289.

37. John M. Clum, *Acting Gay: Male Homosexuality in Modern Drama* (New York: Columbia University Press, 1992), p. 137.

38. Joe Orton, *Entertaining Mr. Sloane,* in *The Complete Plays* (New York: Grove Weidenfeld, 1976), p. 114.

39. Terence Rattigan, quoted in Lahr, *Prick Up Your Ears,* p. 203.

40. Orton, *Entertaining Mr. Sloane,* p. 149.

41. Clum, *Acting Gay,* p. 125.

42. Orton, *Entertaining Mr. Sloane,* p. 244.

43. Ibid., p. 413.

44. Clum, *Acting Gay,* p. 126.

45. Lahr, *Prick Up Your Ears,* p. 189.

46. Alan Sinfield, "Who Was Afraid of Joe Orton," in *Sexual Sameness: Textual Differences in Lesbian and Gay Writing,* ed. Joseph Bristow (London: Routledge, 1992), p. 182. Originally published in *Textual Practice,* Summer 1990, p. 4.

47. Michael York, *Accidentally on Purpose: An Autobiography* (New York: Pocket Books, 1991), p. 59.

48. Christopher Isherwood, *Christopher and His Kind* (New York: Farrar, Straus & Giroux, 1976), p. 1.

49. Christopher Isherwood, *Goodbye to Berlin* (London: The Hogarth Press, 1939), p. 254.

50. Norman McLain Stoop, "Christopher Isherwood: A Meeting by Another River," *After Dark,* vol. 7 (1975), p. 62.

51. Isherwood, *Christopher and His Kind,* p. 63.

52. Linda Mizejewski, *Divine Decadence: Fascism, Female Spectacle, and the Makings of Sally Bowles* (Princeton, N.J.: Princeton University Press, 1992) , pp. 60–61.

53. John Van Druten, *I Am a Camera* (New York: Dramatists Play Service, 1955), p. 24.

54. See Mizejewski, *Divine Decadence,* p. 86.

55. Cole Porter, in *The Complete Lyrics of Cole Porter,* ed. Robert Kimball (New York: Da Capo Press, 1992), p. 115. The song was apparently unused in *Wake Up and Dream,* 1929.

56. Mizejewski, *Divine Decadence,* p. 137.

57. Frank Marcus, "Ich Bin Ein Berliner," *Plays and Players,* May 1968, p. 15.

58. Interview with Lotte Lenya by George Voskovec, 1972, videotape, Lincoln Center for the Performing Arts, Billy Rose Theatre Collection, New York Public Library; Mizejewski, *Divine Decadence,* p. 213.

59. Stoop, "Christopher Isherwood: A Meeting by Another River." Linda Mizejewski's excellent book *Divine Decadence* is my source for this quotation and for much else in my history of the stage productions of *Cabaret* and its predecessors.

60. David J. Gehrin, "An Interview with Christopher Isherwood," *Journal of Narrative Technique,* vol. 2 (1972), p. 147.

61. Susan Sontag, "Fascinating Fascism," *The Susan Sontag Reader* (New York: Farrar, Straus & Giroux, 1982), pp. 305–25.

62. Stephen F. Bauer, "Cultural History and the Film *Cabaret,*" *Psychoanalytic Study of Society,* vol. 12 (1988), pp. 193–94.

63. Mizejewski, *Divine Decadence,* p. 219.

64. Ibid., p. 218.

65. Gaylyn Studlar, *In the Realm of Pleasure: Von Sternberg, Dietrich, and the Masochistic Aesthetic* (Chicago: University of Illinois Press, 1988), p. 35.

66. Ernest Hemingway, *The Garden of Eden* (New York: Macmillan, 1986), p. 98.

67. Ibid., pp. 14–15.

68. Ibid., p. 17.

69. Ibid., p. 31.

70. Ibid., pp. 20–21.

71. Ibid., pp. 55 and 56.

72. Ibid., pp. 81 and 67.

73. Ibid., p. 176.

74. Ibid., p. 86.

75. Ibid., p. 100.

76. Ibid., p. 103.

77. Ibid., p. 105.

78. Ibid., p. 113.

79. Ibid., p. 116.

80. Ibid., p. 114.

81. Ibid., p. 245.

82. Ibid., p. 243.

83. Ibid., p. 132.

84. Ibid., p. 111.

85. Ibid., p. 170.

86. Ernest Hemingway, *Islands in the Stream* (New York: Charles Scribner's Sons, 1970), p. 344.

87. James R. Mellow, *Hemingway: A Life Without Consequences* (Boston: Houghton Mifflin, 1992), p. 11. For a recent reading of gender in Hemingway, see Nancy R. Comley and Robert Scholes, *Hemingway: Genders: Rereading the Hemingway Text* (New Haven: Yale University Press, 1994).

88. Kenneth S. Lynn, *Hemingway* (New York: Simon & Schuster, 1987), pp. 38 and 41.

89. Ernest Hemingway, *The Nick Adams Stories* (New York: Charles Scribner's Sons, 1972), p. 112.

90. Ernest Hemingway, *A Farewell to Arms* (New York: Charles Scribner's Sons, 1929), p. 299.

91. Mary Welsh Hemingway, *How It Was* (New York: Alfred A. Knopf, 1976), pp. 369–70.

Chapter 22: Vice Verses

1. Sigmund Freud, *The Psychopathology of Everyday Life* (1901), *SE* 6:16.

2. Ernest Hemingway, "The Sea Change," in *The Short Stories of Ernest Hemingway* (New York: Collier/Macmillan, 1987), pp. 398–99. Pope's lines read: "Vice is a monster of so frightful mien / As to be hated needs but to be seen; / Yet seen too often, familiar with her face, / We first endure, then pity, then embrace" (*An Essay on Man,* Epistle 2, ll. 217–20).

3. Jonathan Dollimore, *Sexual Dissidence: Augustine to Wilde, Freud to Foucault* (Oxford: Clarendon Press, 1991), p. 176.

4. Hemingway, "Sea Change," p. 401.

5. Letter from Ernest Hemingway to Edmund Wilson, November 16, 1933, in *Ernest Hemingway: Selected Letters,* ed. Carlos Baker (New York: Charles Scribner's Sons, 1981), p. 400.

6. Paul Smith, *A Reader's Guide to the Short Stories of Ernest Hemingway* (Boston: G. K. Hall, 1989), p. 224; James R. Mellow, *Hemingway: A Life Without Consequences* (Boston: Houghton Mifflin, 1992), p. 400.

7. Kenneth S. Lynn, *Hemingway* (New York: Simon & Schuster, 1987), p. 323.

8. Letter from Ernest Hemingway to Ezra Pound, January 23, 1923, in Baker, *Ernest Hemingway: Selected Letters.* See also Mellow, *Hemingway: A Life Without Consequences,* pp. 208–13.

9. Letter from Ezra Pound to Ernest Hemingway, January 27, 1923, in Mellow, *Hemingway: A Life Without Consequences,* pp. 209 and 210.

10. Ernest Hemingway, *The Garden of Eden* (New York: Macmillan, 1986), p. 215.

11. Ibid., p. 247.

12. Stephen Booth, ed., *Shakespeare's Sonnets* (New Haven: Yale University Press, 1977), p. 163.

13. Ibid., p. 432.

14. Introduction to the Sonnets, *The Riverside Shakespeare* (Boston: Houghton Mifflin, 1974), p. 1746.

15. George Chalmers, *A Supplemental Apology* (London: Egerton, 1797), p. 55.

16. Peter Stallybrass, "Editing as Cultural Formation: The Sexing of Shakespeare's Sonnets," *Modern Language Quarterly*, vol. 54, no. 1 (March 1993), p. 93. For other important recent work on the sonnets, see Margreta de Grazia, "The Scandal of Shakespeare's Sonnets," *Shakespeare Survey* (forthcoming); Gregory W. Bredbeck, *Sodomy and Interpretation: Marlowe to Milton* (Ithaca, N.Y.: Cornell University Press, 1991), pp. 167–80; and Bruce R. Smith, *Homosexual Desire in Shakespeare's England: A Cultural Poetics* (Chicago: University of Chicago Press, 1991), pp. 228–70.

17. George Chalmers, *An Apology for the Believers in the Shakespeare Papers* (London: Egerton, 1797) and *Supplemental Apology*.

18. In Edmond Malone, ed., *The Plays and Poems of William Shakespeare* (London, 1821), vol. 20, p. 241. Steevens's view is one of "the Corrections and Illustrations of Various Commentators" included in the volume, appearing first in the edition of 1780. Malone's reply was first printed in the 1790 edition.

19. T. M. Raysor, ed., *Coleridge's Miscellaneous Criticism* (Cambridge, Mass.: Harvard University Press, 1936), p. 455.

20. Samuel Taylor Coleridge, *Table Talk* (London: J. Murray, 1835) vol. 2, p. 178.

21. Stallybrass, "Editing as Cultural Formation," p. 99. I am indebted to Stallybrass's excellent article for the Coleridge readings here.

22. Henry Hallam, *Introduction to the Literature of Europe in the Fifteenth, Sixteenth, and Seventeenth Centuries* (London: J. Murray, 1847), p. 264.

23. Walter Thomson, *The Sonnets of William Shakespeare and Henry Wriothesley* (Oxford: Blackwell, 1938), pp. 2–3.

24. Richard Ellmann, *Oscar Wilde* (New York: Alfred A. Knopf, 1988), p. 297. As always, so definitive a statement irresistibly suggests the possibility of questioning it.

25. Samuel Butler, ed., *Shakespeare's Sonnets* (London: Longmans, Green, 1899), p. 85.

26. Ibid., p. 70.

27. Ibid., p. 87.

28. Ibid., p. 122.

29. Ibid., p. 86.

30. Ibid., pp. 121–22.

31. W. H. Auden, introduction to *The Sonnets,* ed. William Burton (New York: New American Library, 1964), pp. xxix–xxxiii.

32. Robert Craft, *Stravinsky: Chronicle of a Friendship, 1948–1971* (New York: Alfred A. Knopf, 1972), p. 257; Joseph Pequiney, *Such Is My Love: A Study of Shakespeare's Sonnets* (Chicago: University of Chicago Press, 1985), pp. 79–80.

33. Alan Bray, *Homosexuality in Renaissance England* (Boston: Gay Mens' Press, 1982), p. 74.

34. Ibid., p. 76.

35. Ibid.

36. G. S. Rousseau, *Perilous Enlightenment* (Manchester: Manchester University Press, 1991), p. 142.

37. Pequiney, *Such Is My Love,* p. 4.

38. Bruce R. Smith, *Homosexual Desire in Shakespeare's England,* p. 231.

39. Jonathan Goldberg, *Sodometries* (Stanford, Calif.: Stanford University Press, 1992), p. 257.

40. Bruce R. Smith, *Homosexual Desire in Shakespeare's England,* p. 270.

41. Eve Kosofsky Sedgwick, *Between Men: English Literature and Male Homosocial Desire* (New York: Columbia University Press, 1985), p. 27.

42. Ibid.

43. Ibid., p. 29.

44. Ibid., pp. 38 and 39.

45. Ibid., p. 40.

46. *Riverside Shakespeare,* p. 1748.

47. Sedgwick, *Between Men,* p. 35.

48. Valerie Traub, "Sodomy and Women's Pleasure," paper delivered at a panel of the Shakespeare Association of America, April 1993, p. 7.

49. Joel Fineman, *Shakespeare's Perjured Eye: The Invention of Poetic Subjectivity in the Sonnets* (Berkeley: University of California Press, 1986), pp. 17–18.

50. G. Wilson Knight, *The Mutual Flame: On Shakespeare's Sonnets and the Phoenix and the Turtle* (London: Methuen, 1955), pp. 36–37.

51. T. S. Eliot, "Dante" (1929), in *Selected Essays* (New York, Harcourt, Brace & World, 1932; reprinted, 1960).

52. Virginia Woolf, *A Room of One's Own* (New York: Harcourt Brace Jovanovich, 1981), p. 99.

53. Hélène Cixous, "Sorties," in Cixous and Catherine Clément, *The Newly Born Woman,* trans. Betsy Wing (Minneapolis: University of Minnesota Press, 1986), pp. 122 and 84.

54. Letter from John Keats to George and Georgiana Keats, December 21, 1817, in *The Selected Letters of John Keats,* ed. Lionel Trilling (Garden City, N.Y.: Doubleday Anchor Books, 1956), p. 103.

55. Mark Twain, "Is Shakespeare Dead?" in *What Is Man? And Other Essays* (New York and London: Harper Brothers, 1917), p. 324.

56. Ralph Waldo Emerson, *The Journals and Miscellaneous Notebooks of Ralph Waldo Emerson,* ed. Ralph H. Orth and Alfred R. Ferguson (Cambridge, Mass.: Harvard University Press, 1971), vol. 9, p. 184.

57. For more on this desire not to know too much about Shakespeare's life, see Marjorie Garber, *Shakespeare's Ghost Writers: Literature as Uncanny Causality* (New York and London: Methuen, 1987), pp. 1–27.

58. Sigmund Freud, "Some Character-Types Met With in Psycho-analytic Work" (1916), *SE* 14:323.

59. Ibid., p. 324.

60. Sidney Cunliffe-Owen, *The Phoenix and the Dove: A Novel* (London: Rich & Cowan, 1933), pp. 242–44. My thanks to Michael Dobson and Nicola Watson for reminding me of Cunliffe-Owen's novel.

61. Anthony Burgess, *Shakespeare* (London: Jonathan Cape, 1970), p. 128.

62. John Mortimer, *Will Shakespeare* (London: Coronte Books/Hodder and Stoughton, 1977), title page.

63. Ibid., p. 113.

64. In 1919, Porter married socialite Linda Lee Thomas, described in society columns of the day as the most beautiful woman in America, and in fashion magazines as one of the most beautiful women in the world (Stephen Citron, *Noel and Cole: The Sophisticates* [New York: Oxford University Press, 1993], p. 500). The couple had separate bedrooms and Linda knew of Porter's sexual interest in men. Theirs has been described as "essentially a sexless relationship" in which Linda was the "beard" enabling Porter to pass as straight (p. 53), but the Porters shared tastes in music, art, decoration, and the social world, and they were compatible and devoted in many ways. The marriage grew strained when the Porters moved to Hollywood, notes one biographer. "Linda had always known and accepted Cole's sexual preferences but it was impossible for her to witness daily the more flamboyant side of his homosexuality which life in California brought out" (p. 143), including hordes of chorus boys in the pool each afternoon. (Perhaps inevitably, rumors of lesbianism "would often be whispered" about her [p. 158].) Nonetheless, Linda Porter nursed Cole through his catastrophic riding accident, and the Porters remained married and living together, in the main happily, until her death in 1942. They are buried side by side in Cole's family plot in Peru, Indiana.

65. Citron, *Noel and Cole,* p. 309.

66. William Shakespeare, *Henry V,* 4. 7. 25–27.

67. "Let's Not Talk About Love," from *Let's Face It* (1941), *The Complete Lyrics of Cole Porter,* ed. Robert Kimball (New York: Da Capo Press, 1992), p. 306.

68. "Georgia Sand," written for *Nymph Errant* (1933), dropped during the London run. Kimball, *Complete Lyrics,* p. 160.

69. "I'm a Gigolo," from *Wake Up and Dream* (1929), Kimball, *Complete Lyrics,* p. 114.

70. For *Words and Music* (1932), see Citron, *Noel and Cole,* pp. 318–20.

71. Susan Bickelhaupt, "Names and Faces," *Boston Globe,* May 3, 1994, p. 66.

72. Fineman, *Shakespeare's Perjured Eye.* Even for the very modern-sounding sexual "licking" we might think, if briefly, of Cunliffe-Owen's vampirish bisexual Shakespeare.

Epilogue: Between or Among?

1. William Safire, "Betwixt Among and Between," "On Language," *New York Times Magazine,* September 12, 1993, pp. 28–30.

2. "Love Rules: The 1994 *Details* Survey on Romance and the State of Our Unions," *Details,* May 1994, p. 110.

3. Jacques Derrida, *The Truth in Painting,* trans. Geoff Bennington, and Ian McLeod (Chicago: University of Chicago Press, 1987), p. 299.

4. Ibid., pp. 259, 261, 265, 333, 265, and 334.

5. Ibid., p. 269.

6. Ibid., p. 333.

7. Ibid., pp. 278–79.

8. Ibid., p. 278.

9. Ibid., p. 282.

Index

Permissions

Photo Credits

Fantasies of Bisexuality: cover of *Genre* magazine: cover courtesy of Genre Publishing; photo from *Mirabella:* Tom Carabasi

Bisexual Bloomsbury: Vita Sackville-West, early 1920s. © Nigel Nicholson; Vita Sackville-West, 1934: National Portrait Gallery; Rosamund Grosvenor, Vita Sackville-West, Harold Nicholson, and Lord Sackville: © Nigel Nicholson; Violet Trefusis: © Nigel Nicholson; Virginia Woolf: © Nigel Nicholson; Dora Carrington, Lytton Strachey, and James Strachey: The Lytton Strachey Trust; John Maynard Keynes and Lydia Lopokova: Dr. Milo Keynes; John Maynard Keynes, Lytton Strachey, and Bertrand Russell: Dr. Milo Keynes

Taos: Georgia O'Keeffe with Beck Strand: Beinecke Rare Book and Manuscript Library, Yale University; Mabel Dodge Luhan: Beinecke Rare Book and Manuscript Library, Yale University; Tony Luhan: Beinecke Rare Book and Manuscript Library; Yale University; Frida Kahlo and Diego Rivera: *Mexican Folklore;* D. H. and Frieda Lawrence: Laurence Pollinger Ltd. and the Estate of Frieda Lawrence Ravagli

Harlem Bi Day and Night: Gertrude "Ma" Rainey: Frank Driggs Collection; Bessie Smith and her husband, Jack Gee: Frank Driggs Collection; Jean Toomer: Beinecke Rare Book and Manuscript Library, Yale University; Claude McKay: Beinecke Rare Book and Manuscript Library, Yale University; Yolande Du Bois and Countee Cullen: Countee Cullen Harold Jackman Memorial Collection, The Atlanta University Center Woodruff Library; Langston Hughes with Wallace Thurman: The Atlanta University Center Woodruff Library

Mick Jagger: Cecil Beaton

Domestic Bliss?: Cary Grant and Randolph Scott: Harvard Theater Collection; Rock Hudson and Phyllis Gates: Wide World Photo; Judy Garland and Vincente Minnelli: Wide World Photo

Celebrity Threes: Madonna, Sandra Bernhard, and David Letterman: Wide World Photo; Marlene Dietrich, Suzy Vernon, and Imperio Argentina: British Film Institute Stills, Posters, and Designs; James Dean, Richard Davalos, and Julie Harris: David Loehr Collection

Janis Joplin: Robert Seidemann

Professors of Desire: Sigmund Freud and Wilhelm Fleiss: A. W. Freud et al./Mark Paterson; Edith Lees Ellis and Havelock Ellis: The British Library; Alfred Kinsey and female subject: Photo by Dellenbeck

Psychomythologies: Freud medallion: A. W. Freud et al./Mark Paterson; Laurence Olivier as Oedipus Rex: John Vickers, London; Tiresias engraving: after Hendrik Goltzius, © British Museum

Literary Bi Lines: Oscar Wilde and Lord Alfred Douglas: William Andrews Clark Memorial Library; Constance Wilde: Roger-Viollet; W. H. Auden, Christopher Isherwood, and Stephen Spender: National Portrait Gallery; Robert Graves: Charterhouse School; G. H. "Peter" Johnstone: Charterhouse School

Bi Society: Edna St. Vincent Millay: Mishkin, Courtesy of Special Collections, Vassar College Libraries; Nancy Cunard: Curtis Moffat, © Man Ray Trust ARS/ADAGP 1995; H.D.: Beinecke Rare Book and Manuscript Library, Yale University; Djuna Barnes: © Man Ray Trust ARS/ADAGP 1995

Bisexual Marriages: Mary and John Cheever: © David Gahr; Leonard and Felicia Bernstein: Wide World Photo; Paul and Jane Bowles: Archive Photos; Francis Vavra and Roxanna Rochette: Robert Pritchard

Stills from *Sunday, Bloody Sunday:* The Kobal Collection

Traumatic Triangles: still from *The Children's Hour:* The Kobal Collection; still from *The Prime of Miss Jean Brodie:* Archive Photos; still from *Maedchen in Uniform:* The Kobal Collection; still from *The Fox:* Archive Photos

Three's Company: still from *Cabaret:* Archive Photos; still from *The Wedding Banquet:* Archive Photos; still from *Henry and June:* Copyright © by Universal City Studios, Inc. Courtesy of MCA Publishing Rights, a Division of MCA Inc.; still from *Threesome:* The Kobal Collection

What Is a Pair?: René Magritte, *Titanic Days (Les Jours gigantesques):* Private collection; van Gogh, *Shoes:* The Baltimore Museum of Art: The Cone Collection, formed by Claribel Cone and Miss Etta Cone of Baltimore, Maryland, BMA 1950.302; Janet Rickus, *Three Pears:* Courtesy of Janet Rickus

KU-360-953

0 100 200 300 400 500 600 700 miles

Territorial boundaries are those at 1945

● Chungking

AYAS

BHUTAN

R Brahmaputra

Chindwin R.

R. Salween

CHINA

L

Dhaka

● Mawlaik

B U R M A

Chittagong

Sagaing

Nyaungu ● Mandalay   *Shan*
        Myingan   *Highlands*

Akyab   Taunggyi

      Yenangyaung

          ● Loikaw

Irrawaddy R.   Pyinmana

F R E N C H

Sittang R.

Henzada   Pegu
      Rangoon

S I A M

I N D O

S O U T H

Moulmein

C H I N A

C H I N A

*Andaman
Is.*

S E A

● Mergui

Saigon

*Isthmus
of Kra*

*Nicobar
Is.*

Singora

Jitra

Alor Star   Kota Baharu

Georgetown   Sungei Pattani
Penang I.   Butterworth

Kuala   M A L A Y A
Lumpur

S U M A T R A

▼ Singapore

THE GLASS PALACE

THE
GLASS PALACE

AMITAV GHOSH

HarperCollins*Publishers*

HarperCollins*Publishers*
77–85 Fulham Palace Road,
Hammersmith, London W6 8JB

www.**fire**and**water**.com

Published by HarperCollins*Publishers* 2000
3 5 7 9 8 6 4

This novel is entirely a work of fiction. The names,
characters and incidents portrayed in it are the work
of the author's imagination. Any resemblance to actual
persons, living or dead, events or localities
is entirely coincidental

A catalogue record for this book is
available from the British Library

ISBN 0 00 226102 2

Set in PostScript Linotype Meridien by
Rowland Phototypesetting Ltd,
Bury St Edmunds, Suffolk

Printed and bound in Great Britain by
Clays Ltd, St Ives plc

To my father's memory

CONTENTS

Acknowledgments

pp. 15–16: adapted from W. S. Desai: *Deposed King Thebaw of Burma in India, 1885–1916*, Bharatiya Vidya Series, Vol 25, Bharatiya Vidya Bhavan, Bombay, 1967 (appendix VII, p. 119)

p. 89: adapted from, Patricia Herbert, *The Hsaya San Rebellion (1930–1932) reappraised*, Monash Univ., Melbourne, 1982 (p. 5)

p. 349: from Majjhima Nikaya [adapted from *The Buddhist Tradition in India, China and Japan*, ed. W. T. de Bary, Vintage, New York, 1972; p. 27]

p. 350: from Samyutta Nikaya [adapted from *The Buddhist Tradition in India, China and Japan*, ed. W. T. de Bary, Vintage, New York, 1972; p. 16]

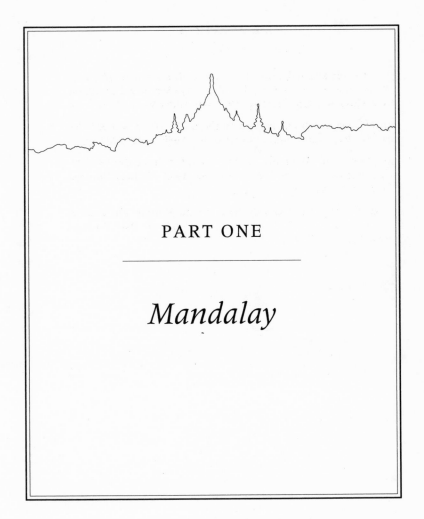

PART ONE

Mandalay

One

There was only one person in the food-stall who knew exactly what that sound was that was rolling in across the plain, along the silver curve of the Irrawaddy, to the western wall of Mandalay's fort. His name was Rajkumar and he was an Indian, a boy of eleven – not an authority to be relied upon.

The noise was unfamiliar and unsettling, a distant booming followed by low, stuttering growls. At times it was like the snapping of dry twigs, sudden and unexpected. And then, abruptly, it would change to a deep rumble, shaking the food-stall and rattling its steaming pot of soup. The stall had only two benches, and they were both packed with people, sitting pressed up against each other. It was cold, the start of central Burma's brief but chilly winter, and the sun had not risen high enough yet to burn off the damp mist that had drifted in at dawn from the river. When the first booms reached the stall there was a silence, followed by a flurry of questions and whispered answers. People looked around in bewilderment: What is it? *Ba le?* What can it be? And then Rajkumar's sharp, excited voice cut through the buzz of speculation. 'English cannon,' he said in his fluent but heavily accented Burmese. 'They're shooting somewhere up the river. Heading in this direction.'

Frowns appeared on some customers' faces as they noted that it was the serving-boy who had spoken and that he was a *kalaa* from across the sea – an Indian, with teeth as white as his eyes and skin the colour of polished hardwood. He was standing in the centre of the stall, holding a pile of chipped ceramic bowls. He was grinning a little sheepishly, as though embarrassed to parade his precocious knowingness.

3

His name meant Prince, but he was anything but princely in appearance, with his oil-splashed vest, his untidily knotted *longyi* and his bare feet with their thick slippers of callused skin. When people asked how old he was he said fifteen, or sometimes eighteen or nineteen, for it gave him a sense of strength and power to be able to exaggerate so wildly, to pass himself off as grown and strong, in body and judgement, when he was, in fact, not much more than a child. But he could have said he was twenty and people would still have believed him, for he was a big, burly boy, taller and broader in the shoulder than many men. And because he was very dark it was hard to tell that his chin was as smooth as the palms of his hands, innocent of all but the faintest trace of fuzz.

It was chance alone that was responsible for Rajkumar's presence in Mandalay that November morning. His boat – the sampan on which he worked as a helper and errand-boy – had been found to need repairs after sailing up the Irrawaddy from the Bay of Bengal. The boatowner had taken fright on being told that the work might take as long as a month, possibly even longer. He couldn't afford to feed his crew that long, he'd decided: some of them would have to find other jobs. Rajkumar was told to walk to the city, a couple of miles inland. At a bazaar, opposite the west wall of the fort, he was to ask for a woman called Ma Cho. She was half-Indian and she ran a small food-stall; she might have some work for him.

And so it happened that at the age of eleven, walking into the city of Mandalay, Rajkumar saw, for the first time, a straight road. By the sides of the road there were bamboo-walled shacks and palm-thatched shanties, pats of dung and piles of refuse. But the straight course of the road's journey was unsmudged by the clutter that flanked it: it was like a causeway, cutting across a choppy sea. Its lines led the eye right through the city, past the bright red walls of the fort to the distant pagodas of Mandalay hill, shining like a string of white bells upon the slope.

For his age, Rajkumar was well-travelled. The boat he worked on was a coastal craft that generally kept to open waters, plying the long length of shore that joined Burma to Bengal. Rajkumar had been to Chittagong and Bassein and any number of towns and villages in between. But in all his travels he had never come across thoroughfares like those in Mandalay. He was accustomed to lanes and alleys that curled endlessly around themselves so that you could never see beyond the next curve. Here was something new: a road that followed a straight, unvarying course, bringing the horizon right into the middle of habitation.

When the fort's full immensity revealed itself, Rajkumar came to a halt in the middle of the road. The citadel was a miracle to behold, with its mile-long walls and its immense moat. The crenellated ramparts were almost three storeys high, but of a soaring lightness, red in colour, and topped by ornamented gateways with seven-tiered roofs. Long straight roads radiated outwards from the walls, forming a neat geometrical grid. So intriguing was the ordered pattern of these streets that Rajkumar wandered far afield, exploring. It was almost dark by the time he remembered why he'd been sent to the city. He made his way back to the the fort's western wall and asked for Ma Cho.

'Ma Cho?'

'She has a stall where she sells food – *baya-gyaw* and other things. She's half-Indian.'

'Ah, Ma Cho.' It made sense that this ragged-looking Indian boy was looking for Ma Cho: she often had Indian strays working at her stall. 'There she is, the thin one.'

Ma Cho was small and harried-looking, with spirals of wiry hair hanging over her forehead, like a fringed awning. She was in her mid-thirties, more Burmese than Indian in appearance. She was busy frying vegetables, squinting at the smoking oil from the shelter of an upthrust arm. She glared at Rajkumar suspiciously: 'What do you want?'

He had just begun to explain about the boat and the repairs and wanting a job for a few weeks, when she interrupted him. She began to shout at the top of her voice, with her eyes closed: 'What do you think – I have jobs under my armpits, to pluck out and hand to you? Last week a boy ran away with two of my pots. Who's to tell me you won't do the same?' And so on.

Rajkumar understood that this outburst was not aimed directly at him: that it had more to do with the dust, the splattering oil and the price of vegetables than with his own presence or

5

with anything he had said. He lowered his eyes and stood there stoically, kicking the dust until she was done.

She paused, panting, and looked him over. 'Who are your parents?' she said at last, wiping her streaming forehead on the sleeve of her sweat-stained *aingyi*.

'I don't have any. They died.'

She thought this over, biting her lip. 'All right. Get to work, but remember you're not going to get much more than three meals and a place to sleep.'

He grinned. 'That's all I need.'

Ma Cho's stall consisted of a couple of benches, sheltered beneath the stilts of a bamboo-walled hut. She did her cooking sitting by an open fire, perched on a small stool. Apart from fried baya-gyaw, she also served noodles and soup. It was Rajkumar's job to carry bowls of soup and noodles to the customers. In his spare moments he cleared away the utensils, tended the fire and shredded vegetables for the soup pot. Ma Cho didn't trust him with fish or meat and chopped them herself with a grinning short-handled *da*. In the evenings he did the washing-up, carrying bucketfuls of utensils over to the fort's moat.

Between Ma Cho's stall and the moat there lay a wide, dusty roadway that ran all the way around the fort, forming an immense square. Rajkumar had only to cross this apron of open space to get to the moat. Directly across from Ma Cho's stall lay a bridge that led to one of the fort's smaller entrances, the funeral gate. He had cleared a pool under the bridge by pushing away the lotus pads that covered the surface of the water. This had become his spot: it was there that he usually did his washing and bathing – under the bridge, with the wooden planks above serving as his ceiling and shelter.

On the far side of the bridge lay the walls of the fort. All that could be seen of its interior was a nine-roofed spire that ended in a glittering gilded umbrella – this was the great golden *hti* of Burma's kings. Under the spire lay the throne room of the palace, where Thebaw, King of Burma, held court with his chief consort, Queen Supayalat.

Rajkumar was curious about the fort but he knew that for those such as himself its precincts were forbidden ground. 'Have you ever been inside?' he asked Ma Cho one day. 'The fort, I mean?'

'Oh yes.' Ma Cho nodded importantly. 'Three times, at the very least.'

'What is it like in there?'

'It's very large, much larger than it looks. It's a city in itself, with long roads and canals and gardens. First you come to the houses of officials and noblemen. And then you find yourself in front of a stockade, made of huge teakwood posts. Beyond lie the apartments of the Royal Family and their servants – hundreds and hundreds of rooms, with gilded pillars and polished floors. And right at the centre there is a vast hall that is like a great shaft of light, with shining crystal walls and mirrored ceilings. People call it the Glass Palace.'

'Does the King ever leave the fort?'

'Not in the last seven years. But the Queen and her maids sometimes walk along the walls. People who've seen them say that her maids are the most beautiful women in the land.'

'Who are they, these maids?'

'Young girls, orphans, many of them just children. They say that the girls are brought to the palace from the far mountains. The Queen adopts them and brings them up and they serve as her handmaids. They say that she will not trust anyone but them to wait on her and her children.'

'When do these girls visit the gateposts?' said Rajkumar. 'How can one catch sight of them?'

His eyes were shining, his face full of eagerness. Ma Cho laughed at him. 'Why, are you thinking of trying to get in there, you fool of an Indian, you coal-black kalaa? They'll know you from a mile off and cut off your head.'

That night, lying flat on his mat, Rajkumar looked through the gap between his feet and caught sight of the gilded hti that marked the palace: it glowed like a beacon in the moonlight. No matter what Ma Cho said, he decided, he would cross the moat – before he left Mandalay, he would find a way in.

*   *   *

Ma Cho lived above the stall in a bamboo-walled room that was held up by stilts. A flimsy splinter-studded ladder connected the room to the stall below. Rajkumar's nights were spent under Ma Cho's dwelling, between the stilts, in the space that served to seat customers during the day. Ma Cho's floor was roughly put together, from planks of wood that didn't quite fit. When Ma Cho lit her lamp to change her clothes, Rajkumar could see her clearly through the cracks in the floor. Lying on his back, with his fingers knotted behind his head, he would look up unblinking, as she untied the aingyi that was knotted loosely round her breasts.

During the day Ma Cho was a harried and frantic termagant, racing from one job to another, shouting shrilly at everyone who came her way. But at night, with the day's work done, a certain languor entered her movements. She would cup her breasts and air them, fanning herself with her hands; she would run her fingers slowly through the cleft of her chest, past the pout of her belly, down to her legs and thighs. Watching her from below, Rajkumar's hand would snake slowly past the knot of his longyi, down to his groin.

One night Rajkumar woke suddenly to the sound of a rhythmic creaking in the planks above, along with moans and gasps and urgent drawings of breath. But who could be up there with her? He had seen no one going in.

The next morning, Rajkumar saw a small, bespectacled, owl-like man climbing down the ladder that led to Ma Cho's room. The stranger was dressed in European clothes: a shirt, trousers, and a pith hat. Subjecting Rajkumar to a grave and prolonged regard, the stranger ceremoniously raised his hat. 'How are you?' he said. *'Kaisa hai? Sub kuchh theek-thaak?'*

Rajkumar understood the words perfectly well – they were what he might have expected an Indian to say – but his mouth still dropped open in surprise. Since coming to Mandalay he had encountered many different kinds of people, but this stranger belonged with none of them. His clothes were those of a European and he seemed to know Hindustani – and yet the cast of his face was neither that of a white man nor an Indian. He looked, in fact, to be Chinese.

Smiling at Rajkumar's astonishment, the man doffed his hat again, before disappearing into the bazaar.

'Who was that?' Rajkumar said to Ma Cho when she came down the ladder.

The question evidently annoyed her and she glared at him to make it clear that she would prefer not to answer. But Rajkumar's curiosity was aroused now, and he persisted. 'Who was that, Ma Cho? Tell me.'

'That is . . .' Ma Cho began to speak in small, explosive bursts, as though her words were being produced by upheavals in her belly. 'That is . . . my teacher . . . my Sayagyi.'

'Your teacher?'

'Yes . . . He teaches me . . . He knows about many things . . .'

'What things?'

'Never mind.'

'Where did he learn to speak Hindustani?'

'Abroad, but not in India . . . he's from somewhere in Malaya. Malacca I think. You should ask him.'

'What's his name?'

'It doesn't matter. You will call him Saya, just as I do.'

'Just Saya?'

'Saya John.' She turned on him in exasperation. 'That's what we all call him. If you want to know any more, ask him yourself.'

Reaching into her cold cooking fire, she drew out a handful of ash and threw it at Rajkumar. 'Who said you could sit here talking all morning, you half-wit kalaa? Now you get busy with your work.'

There was no sign of Saya John that night or the next.

'Ma Cho,' said Rajkumar, 'what's happened to your teacher? Why hasn't he come again?'

Ma Cho was sitting at her fire, frying baya-gyaw. Peering into the hot oil, she said shortly, 'He's away.'

'Where?'

'In the jungle . . .'

'The jungle? Why?'

'He's a contractor. He delivers supplies to teak camps. He's away most of the time.' Suddenly the ladle dropped from her grasp and she buried her face in her hands.

Hesitantly Rajkumar went to her side. 'Why are you crying, Ma Cho?' He ran a hand over her head in an awkward gesture of sympathy. 'Do you want to marry him?'

She reached for the folds of his frayed longyi and dabbed at her tears with the bunched cloth. 'His wife died a year or two ago. She was Chinese, from Singapore. He has a son, a little boy. He says he'll never marry again.'

'Maybe he'll change his mind.'

She pushed him away with one of her sudden gestures of exasperation. 'You don't understand, you thick-headed kalaa. He's a Christian. Every time he comes to visit me, he has to go to his church next morning to pray and ask forgiveness. Do you think I would want to marry a man like that?' She snatched her ladle off the ground and shook it at him. 'Now you get back to work or I'll fry your black face in hot oil . . .'

A few days later Saya John was back. Once again he greeted Rajkumar in his broken Hindustani: '*Kaisa hai? Sub kuchh theek-thaak?*'

Rajkumar fetched him a bowl of noodles and stood watching as he ate. 'Saya,' he asked at last, in Burmese, 'how did you learn to speak an Indian language?'

Saya John looked up at him and smiled. 'I learnt as a child,' he said, 'for I am, like you, an orphan, a foundling. I was brought up by Catholic priests, in a town called Malacca. These men were from everywhere – Portugal, Macao, Goa. They gave me my name – John Martins, which was not what it has become. They used to call me João, but I changed this later to John. They spoke many many languages, those priests, and from the Goans I learnt a few Indian words. When I was old enough to work I went to Singapore, where I was for a while an orderly in a military hospital. The soldiers there were mainly Indians and they asked me this very question: how is it that you, who look Chinese and carry a Christian name, can speak our language? When I told them how this had come about, they would laugh and say, you are a *dhobi ka kutta* – a washerman's dog – *na ghar ka na ghat ka* – you don't belong anywhere, either by the water or on land, and I'd say, yes, that is exactly what I am.' He laughed, with an infectious hilarity, and Rajkumar joined in.

One day Saya John brought his son to the stall. The boy's name was Matthew and he was seven, a handsome, bright-eyed child, with an air of precocious self-possession. He had just arrived from Singapore, where he lived with his mother's family and studied at a well-known missionary school. A couple of times each year, Saya John arranged for him to come over to Burma for a holiday.

It was early evening, usually a busy time at the stall, but in honour of her visitors, Ma Cho decided to close down for the day. Drawing Rajkumar aside, she told him to take Matthew for a walk, just for an hour or so. There was a *pwe* on at the other end of the fort; the boy would enjoy the fairground bustle.

'And remember –' here her gesticulations became fiercely incoherent – 'not a word about . . .'

'Don't worry,' Rajkumar gave her an innocent smile. 'I won't say anything about your lessons.'

'Idiot kalaa.' Bunching her fists, she rained blows upon his back. 'Get out – out of here.'

Rajkumar changed into his one good longyi and put on a frayed *pinni* vest that Ma Cho had given him. Saya John pressed a few coins into his palm. 'Buy something – for the both of you, treat yourselves.'

On the way to the pwe, they were distracted by a peanut-seller. Matthew was hungry and he insisted that Rajkumar buy them both armloads of peanuts. They went to sit by the moat, with their feet dangling in the water, spreading the nuts around them, in their wrappers of dried leaf.

Matthew pulled a piece of paper out of his pocket. There was a picture on it – of a cart with three wire-spoked wheels, two large ones at the back and a single small one in front. Rajkumar stared at it, frowning: it appeared to be a light carriage, but there were no shafts for a horse or an ox.

'What is it?'

'A motorwagon.' Matthew pointed out the details – the small internal-combustion engine, the vertical crankshaft, the horizontal flywheel. He explained that the machine could generate almost as much power as a horse, running at speeds of up to eight miles an hour. It had been unveiled that very year, 1885, in Germany, by Karl Benz.

'One day,' Matthew said quietly, 'I am going to own one of these.' His tone was not boastful and Rajkumar did not doubt him for a minute. He was hugely impressed that a child of that age could know his mind so well on such a strange subject.

Then Matthew said: 'How did you come to be here, in Mandalay?'

'I was working on a boat, a sampan, like those you see on the river.'

'And where are your parents? Your family?'

'I don't have any.' Rajkumar paused. 'I lost them.'

Matthew cracked a nut between his teeth. 'How?'

'There was a fever, a sickness. In our town, Akyab, many people died.'

'But you lived?'

'Yes. I was sick, but I lived. In my family I was the only one. I had a father, a sister, brothers . . .'

'And a mother?'

'And a mother.'

Rajkumar's mother had died on a sampan that was tethered in a mangrove-lined estuary. He remembered the tunnel-like shape of the boat's galley and its roof of hooped cane and thatch; there was an oil lamp beside his mother's head, on one of the crosswise planks of the hull. Its flickering yellow flame was dulled by a halo of night-time insects. The night was still and airless, with the mangroves and their dripping roots standing thick against the breeze, cradling the boat between deep banks of mud. Yet there was a kind of restlessness in the moist darkness around the boat. Every now and again, he'd hear the splash of seed pods arrowing into the water, and the slippery sound of fish, stirring in the mud. It was hot in the sampan's burrow-like galley, but his mother was shivering. Rajkumar had scoured the boat, covering her with every piece of cloth that he could find.

Rajkumar knew the fever well by that time. It had come to their house through his father, who worked every day at a warehouse, near the port. He was a quiet man, who made his living as a *dubash* and a *munshi* – a translator and clerk – working for a succession of merchants along the eastern shore of the Bay of Bengal. Their family home was in the port of Chittagong, but his father had quarrelled with their relatives and moved the family away, drifting slowly down the coast, peddling his knowledge of figures and languages, settling eventually in Akyab, the principal port of the Arakan – that tidewater stretch of coast where Burma and Bengal collide in a whirlpool of unease. There he'd remained for some dozen years, fathering three children – of these the oldest was Rajkumar. Their home was on an inlet that smelt of drying fish. Their family name was Raha, and when their neighbours asked who they were and where they came from they would say they were Hindus from Chittagong. That was all Rajkumar knew about his family's past.

Rajkumar was the next to fall sick, after his father. He had returned to consciousness to find himself recovering at sea, with his mother. They were on their way back to their native Chittagong, she told him, and there were just the two of them now – the others were gone.

The sailing had been slow because the currents were against them. The square-sailed sampan and her crew of *khalasis* had fought their way up the coast, hugging the shore. Rajkumar had recovered quickly, but then it was his mother's turn to sicken. With Chittagong just a couple of days away she had begun to shiver. The shore was thick with mangrove forests; one evening, the boatowner had pulled the sampan into a creek and settled down to wait.

Rajkumar had covered his mother with all the saris in her cloth bundle, with longyis borrowed from the boatmen, even a folded sail. But he'd no sooner finished than her teeth began to chatter again, softly, like dice. She called him to her side, beckoning with a forefinger. When he lowered his ear to her lips, he could feel her body glowing like hot charcoal against his cheek.

She showed him a knot on the tail end of her sari. There was a gold bangle wrapped in it. She pulled it out and gave it to him to hide in the waist knot of his sarong. The *nakhoda*, the boat's owner, was a trustworthy old man, she told him; Rajkumar was to give him the bangle when they reached Chittagong – only then, not before.

She folded his fingers around the bangle: warmed by the fiery heat of her body, the metal seemed to singe its shape into his

13

palm. 'Stay alive,' she whispered. *'Beche thako*, Rajkumar. Live, my Prince; hold on to your life.'

When her voice faded away Rajkumar became suddenly aware of the faint flip-flop sound of catfish burrowing in the mud. He looked up to see the boatowner, the nakhoda, squatting in the prow of the sampan, puffing on his coconut-shell hookah, fingering his thin, white beard. His crewmen were sitting clustered round him, watching Rajkumar. They were hugging their sarong-draped knees. The boy could not tell whether it was pity or impatience that lay behind the blankness in their eyes.

He had only the bangle now: his mother had wanted him to use it to pay for his passage back to Chittagong. But his mother was dead and what purpose would it serve to go back to a place that his father had abandoned? No, better instead to strike a bargain with the nakhoda. Rajkumar took the old man aside and asked to join the crew, offering the bangle as a gift of apprenticeship.

The old man looked him over. The boy was strong and willing, and, what was more, he had survived the killer fever that had emptied so many of the towns and villages of the coast. That alone spoke of certain useful qualities of body and spirit. He gave the boy a nod and took the bangle – yes, stay.

At daybreak the sampan stopped at a sand bar and the crew helped Rajkumar build a pyre for his mother's cremation. Rajkumar's hands began to shake when he put the fire in her mouth. He, who had been so rich in family, was alone now, with a khalasi's apprenticeship for his inheritance. But he was not afraid, not for a moment. His was the sadness of regret – that they had left him so soon, so early, without tasting the wealth or the rewards that he knew, with utter certainty, would one day be his.

It was a long time since Rajkumar had spoken about his family. Among his shipmates this was a subject that was rarely discussed. There were many among them who were from families that had fallen victim to the catastrophes that were so often visited upon that stretch of coast. They preferred not to speak of these things.

14

It was odd that this child, Matthew, with his educated speech and formal manners, should have drawn him out. Rajkumar could not help being touched. On the way back to Ma Cho's, he put an arm round the boy's shoulders. 'So how long are you going to be here?'

'I'm leaving tomorrow.'

'Tomorrow? But you've just arrived.'

'I know. I was meant to stay for two weeks, but Father thinks there's going to be trouble.'

'Trouble!' Rajkumar turned to stare at him. 'What trouble?'

'The English are preparing to send a fleet up the Irrawaddy. There's going to be a war. Father says they want all the teak in Burma. The King won't let them have it so they're going to do away with him.'

Rajkumar gave a shout of laughter. 'A war over wood? Who's ever heard of such a thing?' He gave Matthew's head a disbelieving pat: the boy was a child, after all, despite his grown-up ways and his knowledge of unlikely things; he'd probably had a bad dream the night before.

But this proved to be the first of many occasions when Matthew showed himself to be wiser and more prescient than Rajkumar. Two days later the whole city was gripped by rumours of war. A large detachment of troops came marching out of the fort and went off downriver, towards the encampment of Myingan. There was an uproar in the bazaar; fishwives emptied their wares into the refuse heap and went hurrying home. A dishevelled Saya John came running to Ma Cho's stall. He had a sheet of paper in his hands. 'A Royal Proclamation,' he announced, 'issued under the King's signature.'

Everybody in the stall fell silent as he began to read:

> To all Royal subjects and inhabitants of the Royal Empire: those heretics, the barbarian English kalaas having most harshly made demands calculated to bring about the impairment and destruction of our religion, the violation of our national traditions and customs, and the degradation of our race, are making a show and preparation as if about to wage war with our state.

15

They have been replied to in conformity with the usages of great nations and in words which are just and regular. If, notwithstanding, these heretic foreigners should come, and in any way attempt to molest or disturb the state, His Majesty, who is watchful that the interest of our religion and our state shall not suffer, will himself march forth with his generals, captains and lieutenants with large forces of infantry, artillery, elephanterie and cavalry, by land and by water, and with the might of his army will efface these heretics and conquer and annex their country. To uphold the religion, to uphold the national honour, to uphold the country's interests will bring about threefold good – good of our religion, good of our master and good of ourselves and will gain for us the important result of placing us on the path to the celestial regions and to Nirvana.

Saya John pulled a face. 'Brave words,' he said. 'Let's see what happens next.'

After the initial panic, the streets quickly quietened. The bazaar reopened and the fishwives came back to rummage through the refuse heap, looking for their lost goods. Over the next few days people went about their business just as they had before. The one most noticeable change was that foreign faces were no longer to be seen on the streets. The number of foreigners living in Mandalay was not insubstantial – there were envoys and missionaries from Europe; traders and merchants of Greek, Armenian, Chinese and Indian origin; labourers and boatmen from Bengal, Malaya and the Coromandel coast; white-clothed astrologers from Manipur; businessmen from Gujarat – an assortment of people such as Rajkumar had never seen before he came here. But now suddenly the foreigners disappeared. It was rumoured that the Europeans had left and gone downriver while the others had barricaded themselves into their houses.

A few days later the palace issued another proclamation, a joyful one, this time: it was announced that the royal troops had dealt the invaders a signal defeat, near the fortress of Minhla. The English troops had been repulsed and sent fleeing across the border.

16

The royal barge was to be dispatched downriver, bearing decorations for the troops and their officers. There was to be a ceremony of thanksgiving at the palace.

There were shouts of joy on the streets, and the fog of anxiety that had hung over the city for the last few days dissipated quickly. To everyone's relief things went quickly back to normal: shoppers and shopkeepers came crowding back and Ma Cho's stall was busier than ever before.

Then, one evening, racing into the bazaar to replenish Ma Cho's stock of fish, Rajkumar came across the familiar, white-bearded face of his boatowner, the nakhoda.

'Is our boat going to leave soon now?' Rajkumar asked. 'Now that the war is over?'

The old man gave him a secret, tight-lipped smile. 'The war isn't over. Not yet.'

'But we heard . . .'

'What we hear on the waterfront is quite different from what's said in the city.'

'What have you heard?' said Rajkumar.

Although they were using their own dialect the nakhoda lowered his voice. 'The English are going to be here in a day or two,' he answered. 'They've been seen by boatmen. They are bringing the biggest fleet that's ever sailed on a river. They have cannon that can blow away the stone walls of a fort; they have boats so fast that they can outrun a tidal bore; their guns can shoot quicker than you can talk. They are coming like the tide: nothing can stand in their way. Today we heard that their ships are taking up positions around Myingan. You'll probably hear the fireworks tomorrow . . .'

Sure enough, the next morning, a distant booming sound came rolling across the plain, all the way to Ma Cho's food-stall, near the western wall of the fort. When the opening salvoes sounded, the market was thronged with people. Farm wives from the outskirts of the city had come in early and set their mats out in rows, arranging their vegetables in neat little bunches. Fishermen had stopped by too, with their night-time catches fresh from the river. In an hour or two the vegetables would wilt and the fish eyes would begin to cloud over. But for the moment everything was crisp and fresh.

17

The first booms of the guns caused nothing more than a brief interruption in the morning's shopping. People looked up at the clear blue sky in puzzlement and shopkeepers leant sidewise over their wares to ask each other questions. Ma Cho and Rajkumar had been hard at work since dawn. As always on chilly mornings, many people had stopped off for a little something to eat before making their way home. Now the hungry, mealtime hush was interrupted by a sudden buzz. People looked at each other nervously: what was that noise?

This was when Rajkumar broke in. 'English cannon,' he said. 'They're heading in this direction.'

Ma Cho gave a yelp of annoyance. 'How do you know what they are, you fool of a boy?'

'Boatmen have seen them,' Rajkumar answered. 'A whole English fleet is coming this way.'

Ma Cho had a roomful of people to feed and she was in no mood to allow her only helper to be distracted by a distant noise.

'Enough of that now,' she said. 'Get back to work.'

In the distance the firing intensified, rattling the bowls on the benches. The customers began to stir in alarm. In the adjoining marketplace a coolie had dropped a sack of rice and the spilt grain was spreading like a white stain across the dusty path as people pushed past each other to get away. Shopkeepers were clearing their counters, stuffing their goods into bags; farm wives were tipping their baskets into refuse heaps.

Suddenly Ma Cho's customers started to their feet, knocking over their bowls and pushing the benches apart. In dismay, Ma Cho turned on Rajkumar. 'Didn't I tell you to keep quiet, you idiot of a kalaa? Look, you've scared my customers away.'

'It's not my fault . . .'

'Then whose? What am I going to do with all this food? What's going to become of that fish I bought yesterday?' Ma Cho collapsed on her stool.

Behind them, in the now-deserted marketplace, dogs were fighting over scraps of discarded meat, circling in packs around the refuse heaps.

Two

At the palace, a little less than a mile from Ma Cho's stall, the King's chief consort, Queen Supayalat, was seen mounting a steep flight of stairs to listen more closely to the guns.

The palace lay at the exact centre of Mandalay, deep within the walled city, a sprawling complex of pavilions, gardens and corridors, all grouped around the nine-roofed hti of Burma's kings. The complex was walled off from the surrounding streets by a stockade of tall, teak posts. At each of the four corners of the stockade was a guard-post, manned by sentries from the King's personal bodyguard. It was to one of these that Queen Supayalat had decided to climb.

The Queen was a small, fine-boned woman with porcelain skin and tiny hands and feet. Her face was small and angular, the regularity of its features being marred only by a slight blemish in the alignment of the right eye. The Queen's waist, famously of a wisp-like slimness, was swollen by her third pregnancy, now in its eighth month.

The Queen was not alone: some half-dozen maidservants followed close behind, carrying her two young daughters, the First and Second Princesses, Ashin Hteik Su Myat Phaya Gyi and Ashin Hteik Su Myat Phaya Lat. The advanced condition of her pregnancy had made the Queen anxious about her children's whereabouts. For the last several days she had been unwilling to allow her two daughters even momentarily out of her sight.

The First Princess was three and bore a striking resemblance to her father, Thebaw, King of Burma. She was a good-natured, obedient girl, with a round face and ready smile. The Second

19

Princess was two years younger, not quite one yet, and she was an altogether different kind of child, very much her mother's daughter. She'd been born with the colic and would cry for hours at a stretch. Several times a day she would fly into paroxysms of rage. Her body would go rigid and she would clench her little fists; her chest would start pumping, with her mouth wide open but not a sound issuing from her throat. Even experienced nurses quailed when the little Princess was seized by one of her fits.

To deal with the baby, the Queen insisted on having several of her most trusted attendants at hand at all times – Evelyn, Hemau, Augusta, Nan Pau. These girls were very young, mostly in their early teens, and they were almost all orphans. They'd been purchased by the Queen's agents in small Kachin, Wa and Shan villages along the kingdom's northern frontiers. Some of them were from Christian families, some from Buddhist – once they came to Mandalay it didn't matter. They were reared under the tutelage of palace retainers, under the Queen's personal supervision.

It was the youngest of these maids who had had the most success in dealing with the Second Princess. She was a slender ten-year-old called Dolly, a timid, undemonstrative child, with enormous eyes and a dancer's pliable body and supple limbs. Dolly had been brought to Mandalay at a very early age from the frontier town of Lashio: she had no memory of her parents or family. She was thought to be of Shan extraction, but this was a matter of conjecture, based on her slender fine-boned appearance and her smooth, silken complexion.

On this particular morning Dolly had had very little success with the Second Princess. The guns had jolted the little girl out of her sleep and she had been crying ever since. Dolly, who was easily startled, had been badly scared herself. When the guns had started up she'd covered her ears and gone into a corner, gritting her teeth and shaking her head. But then the Queen had sent for her and after that Dolly had been so busy trying to distract the little Princess that she'd had no time to be frightened.

Dolly wasn't strong enough yet to take the Princess up the steep stairs that led to the top of the stockade: Evelyn, who was sixteen and strong for her age, was given the job of carrying her. Dolly followed after the others and she was the last to step into the guard-post – a wooden platform, fenced in with heavy, timber rails.

Four uniformed soldiers were standing grouped in a corner. The Queen was firing questions at them, but none of them would answer nor even meet her eyes. They hung their heads, fingering the long barrels of their flintlocks.

'How far away is the fighting?' the Queen asked. 'And what sort of cannon are they using?'

The soldiers shook their heads; the truth was that they knew no more than she did. When the noise started they'd speculated excitedly about its cause. At first they'd refused to believe that the roar could be of human making. Guns of such power had never before been heard in this part of Burma, nor was it easy to conceive of an order of fire so rapid as to produce an indistinguishable merging of sound.

The Queen saw that there was nothing to be learnt from these hapless men. She turned to rest her weight against the wooden rails of the guard-post. If only her body were less heavy, if only she were not so tired and slow.

The strange thing was that these last ten days, ever since the English crossed the border, she'd heard nothing but good news. A week ago a garrison commander had sent a telegram to say that the foreigners had been stopped at Minhla, two hundred miles downriver. The palace had celebrated the victory, and the King had even sent the general a decoration. How was it possible that the invaders were now close enough to make their guns heard in the capital?

Things had happened so quickly: a few months ago there'd been a dispute with a British timber company – a technical matter concerning some logs of teak. It was clear that the company was in the wrong; they were side-stepping the kingdom's customs regulations, cutting up logs to avoid paying duties. The royal customs officers had slapped a fine on the company, demanding arrears of payment for some fifty thousand logs. The Englishmen had protested and refused to pay; they'd carried their complaints to the British Governor in Rangoon. Humiliating ultimatums had followed. One of the King's senior ministers, the Kinwun Mingyi, had suggested discreetly that it might be best to accept the terms; that the British might allow the Royal Family to remain in the palace in Mandalay, on terms similar to those of the Indian princes – like farmyard pigs in other words, to be fed and fattened by their masters; swine, housed in sties that had been tricked out with a few little bits of finery.

The Kings of Burma were not princes, the Queen had told the Kinwun Mingyi; they were kings, sovereigns, they'd defeated the Emperor of China, conquered Thailand, Assam, Manipur. And she herself, Supayalat, she had risked everything to secure the throne for Thebaw, her husband and step-brother. Was it even imaginable that she would consent to give it all away now? And what if the child in her belly were a boy (and this time she was sure it was): how would she explain to him that she had surrendered his patrimony because of a quarrel over some logs of wood? The Queen had prevailed and the Burmese court had refused to yield to the British ultimatum.

Now, gripping the guard-post rail the Queen listened carefully to the distant gunfire. She'd hoped at first that the barrage was an exercise of some kind. The most reliable general in the army, the Hlethin Atwinwun, was stationed at the fort of Myingan, thirty miles away, with a force of eight thousand soldiers.

Just yesterday the King had asked, in passing, how things were going on the war front. She could tell that he thought of the war as a faraway matter, a distant campaign, like the expeditions that had been sent into the Shan highlands in years past, to deal with bandits and dacoits.

Everything was going as it should, she'd told him; there was nothing to worry about. And so far as she knew, this was no less than the truth. She'd met with the seniormost officials every day, the Kinwun Mingyi, the Taingda Mingyi, even the *wungyis* and *wundauks* and *myowuns*. None of them had so much as hinted that anything was amiss. But there was no mistaking the sound of those guns. What was she going to tell the King now?

The courtyard beneath the stockade filled suddenly with voices.

Dolly stole a glance down the staircase. There were soldiers milling around below, dozens of them, wearing the colours of the palace guard. One of them spotted her and began to shout – the Queen? Is the Queen up there?

Dolly stepped quickly back, out of his line of sight. Who were these soldiers? What did they want? She could hear their feet on the stairs now. Somewhere close by, the Princess began to cry, in short, breathless gasps. Augusta thrust the baby into her arms – here, Dolly, here, take her, she won't stop. The baby was screaming, flailing her fists. Dolly had to turn her face away to keep from being struck.

An officer had stepped into the guard-post; he was holding his sheathed sword in front of him, in both hands, like a sceptre. He was saying something to the Queen, motioning to her to leave the cabin, to go down the stairs into the palace.

'Are we prisoners then?' The Queen's face was twisted with fury. 'Who has sent you here?'

'Our orders came from the Taingda Mingyi,' the officer said. 'For your safety Mebya.'

'Our safety?'

The guard-post was full of soldiers and they were herding the girls towards the steps. Dolly glanced down: the flight of stairs was very steep. Her head began to spin.

'I can't,' she cried. 'I can't.' She would fall, she knew it. The Princess was too heavy for her; the stairs were too high; she would need a free hand to hold on, to keep her balance.

'Move.'

'I can't.' She could hardly hear herself over the child's cries. She stood still, refusing to budge.

'Quickly, quickly.' There was a soldier behind her; he was prodding her with the cold hilt of his sword. She felt her eyes brimming over, tears flooding down her face. Couldn't they see she would fall, that the Princess would tumble out of her grip? Why would no one help?

'Quick.'

She turned to look into the soldier's unsmiling face. 'I can't. I have the Princess in my arms and she's too heavy for me. Can't you see?' No one seemed to be able to hear her above the Princess's wails.

'What's the matter with you, girl? Why're you standing there? Move.'

She shut her eyes and took a step. And then, just as her legs were starting to give way she heard the Queen's voice. 'Dolly! Stop!'

'It's not my fault.' She began to sob, her eyes pressed tightly shut. Someone snatched the Princess from her arms. 'It's not my fault. I tried to tell them; they wouldn't listen.'

'It's all right.' The Queen's voice was sharp but not unkind. 'Come on down now. Be careful.'

Weeping in relief, Dolly stumbled down the steps and across the courtyard. She felt the other girls' hands on her back, leading her down a corridor.

Most of the buildings in the palace complex were low, wooden structures, linked by long corridors. The palace was of relatively recent construction, just thirty years old. It was closely modelled on the royal residences of earlier Burmese capitals, at Ava and Amarapura. Parts of the royal apartments had been transported whole after the founding of Mandalay, but many of the smaller outlying buildings were unfinished and still unknown, even to the palace's inhabitants. Dolly had never before been in the room she was led to now. It was dark, with damp, plastered walls and heavy doors.

'Bring the Taingda Mingyi to me,' the Queen was screaming at the guards. 'I will not be kept prisoner. Bring him to me. Right now.'

An hour or two went slowly by; the girls could tell from the direction of the shadows under the door that morning had changed into afternoon. The little Princess cried herself out and fell asleep across Dolly's crossed legs.

The doors were thrown open and the Taingda Mingyi came puffing in.

'Where is the King?'

'He is safe, Mebya.'

He was a stout man with oily skin. In the past, he'd always been ready with advice but now the Queen could not get a single clear answer out of him.

'The King is safe. You should not worry.' The long, drooping hairs that sprouted from his moles shook gently as he smiled and showed his teeth.

He produced a telegram. 'The Hlethin Atwinwun has won a famous victory at Myingan.'

'But those were not our guns I heard this morning.'

'The foreigners have been halted. The King has dispatched a medal, and decorations for the men.' He handed her a sheet of paper.

She didn't bother to look at it. She had seen many telegrams over the last ten days, all filled with news of famous victories. But the guns she'd heard that morning were not Burmese, of this she had no doubt. 'Those were English guns,' she said. 'I know they were. Don't lie to me. How close are they? When do you think they will reach Mandalay?'

He wouldn't look at her. 'Mebya's condition is delicate. She should rest now. I will return later.'

'Rest?' The Queen pointed to her maids, sitting on the floor. 'The girls are exhausted. Look.' She pointed to Dolly's red eyes and tear-streaked face. 'Where are my other servants? Send them to me. I need them.'

The Taingda Mingyi hesitated, and then bowed. 'Mebya. They will be here.'

The other maids arrived an hour later. Their faces were sombre. The Queen said nothing until the guards had shut the doors. Then everyone clustered tightly around the new arrivals. Dolly had to crane her head to catch what they were saying.

This was what they said: the British had destroyed the fort at Myingan with immaculate precision, using their cannon, without losing a single soldier of their own. The Hlethin Atwinwun had surrendered. The army had disintegrated; the soldiers had fled into the mountains with their guns. The Kinwun Mingyi and the Taingda Mingyi had dispatched emissaries to the British. The two ministers were now competing with one another to keep the Royal Family under guard. They knew the British would be grateful to whoever handed over the royal couple; there would be rich rewards. The foreigners were expected to come to Mandalay very soon to take the King and Queen into captivity.

The invasion proceeded so smoothly as to surprise even its planners. The imperial fleet crossed the border on 14 November, 1885.

25

Two days later, after a few hours of shelling, British soldiers took possession of the Burmese outposts of Nyaungbinmaw and Singbaungwe. The next day, at Minhla, the fleet came under heavy fire. The Burmese garrison at Minhla was a small one, but it resisted with unexpected tenacity.

The British forces were armed with the latest breech-loading rifles. Their artillery support consisted of twenty-seven rapid-firing machine guns, more than had ever before been assembled on the continent of Asia. The Burmese could not match this firepower. After an exchange of fire that lasted several hours, the British infantry was sent ashore.

There were some ten thousand soldiers in the British invasion force and of these the great majority – about two-thirds – were Indian sepoys. Among the units deployed at Minhla there were three battalions of sepoys. They were from the Hazara Regiment and the 1st Madras Pioneers. The Indians were seasoned, battle-hardened troops. The Hazaras, recruited from the Afghan border, had proved their worth to the British over decades of warfare, in India and abroad. The 1st Madras Pioneers were among the most loyal of Britain's foot soldiers. They had stood steadfastly by their masters even through the uprising of 1857, when most of northern India had risen against the British. The Burmese defenders of Minhla stood little chance against these sepoys, with their newly manufactured British equipment and their vastly superior numbers. The dogged little defence force dissolved when the redoubt was charged.

The aftershock of the collapse at Minhla was felt a long way upriver. At Pakokku the garrison melted away; at Nyaungu, near the great, pagoda-covered plain of Pagan, Burmese gunners spiked their own cannon after firing a few shots. At Mygingan, which was under the command of the Hlethin Atwinwun, the defenders were forced to abandon their positions after a bombardment that lasted several hours. A few days later, without informing King Thebaw, the Burmese army surrendered.

The war lasted just fourteen days.

Three

For two days after the bombardment of Myingan, Mandalay was strangely, almost eerily quiet. Then the rumours started. One morning a man went running through the marketplace, past Ma Cho's stall. He was shouting at the top of his voice: foreign ships had anchored off the shore; English soldiers were marching towards the city.

Panic struck the market. People began to run and jostle. Rajkumar managed to push his way through the crowd to the adjoining road. He could not see far: a cloud of dust hung over the road, drummed up by hundreds of racing feet. People were running in every direction, slamming against each other and pushing blindly at anything that came their way. Rajkumar was swept along in the direction of the river. As he ran, he became aware of a ripple in the ground beneath him, a kind of drumbeat in the earth, a rhythmic tremor that travelled up his spine through the soles of his feet.

The people in front of him scattered and parted, pushing up against the sides of the road. Suddenly he was in the front rank of the crowd, looking directly at two English soldiers mounted on brown horses. The cavalrymen were waving people away with drawn swords, clearing the road. The dust had made patterns on their polished boots. Looming behind them was a solid mass of uniforms, advancing like a tidal wave.

Rajkumar darted to the side of the road and pressed himself against a wall. The crowd's initial nervousness melted as the first squad of soldiers marched past with their shouldered rifles. There was no rancour on the soldiers' faces, no emotion at all. None of them so much as glanced at the crowd.

'The English!' someone said, and the words went quickly from mouth to mouth, growing louder and louder until they became a kind of murmured cheer. But as the vanguard passed and the next squad came into view, an amazed silence descended on the spectators: these soldiers were not English – they were Indians. The people around Rajkumar stirred, as though moved to curiosity by the sight of an Indian in their midst.

'Who are these soldiers?' someone said.

'I don't know.'

It struck Rajkumar suddenly that he hadn't seen any of the usual Indian faces in the bazaar all day: none of the coolies and cobblers and shopkeepers who always came there every day. For a moment this seemed odd, but then he forgot about it and was once again absorbed in the spectacle of the marching sepoys.

People began to ask Rajkumar questions. 'What are these soldiers doing here?'

Rajkumar shrugged. How was he to know? He had no more connection with the soldiers than did they. A group of men gathered around him, crowding in, so that he had to take a few backward steps. 'Where do the soldiers come from? Why are they here?'

'I don't know where they come from. I don't know who they are.'

Glancing over his shoulder, Rajkumar saw that he had backed himself into a blind alley. There were some seven or eight men around him. They had pulled up their longyis, tucking them purposefully up at the waist. The sepoys were just a short distance away, hundreds, perhaps thousands of them. But he was alone in the alley – the only Indian – out of earshot, surrounded by these men who were clearly intent on making him answer for the soldiers' presence.

A hand flashed out of the shadows. Taking a grip on his hair, a man pulled him off the ground. Rajkumar swung up a leg and dug it back, aiming his heel at his assailant's groin. The man saw the kick coming and blocked it with one hand. Twisting Rajkumar's head around, he struck him across the face with the back of his fist. A spurt of blood shot out of Rajkumar's nose. The shock of the blow slowed the moment to a standstill. The arc of blood seemed to stop in its trajectory, hanging suspended in the air, brilliantly translucent, like a string of garnets. Then the crook of an elbow took Rajkumar in the stomach, pumping the breath out of him and throwing him against a wall. He slid down, clutching his stomach, as though he were trying to push his insides back in.

Then, suddenly, help arrived. A voice rang through the lane. 'Stop.' The men turned round, startled.

'Let him be.'

It was Saya John, advancing towards them with one arm in the air, looking oddly authoritative in a hat and coat. Tucked snugly into the palm of his upraised hand was a small, blunt-nosed pistol. The men backed away slowly and once they'd gone, Saya John slipped the pistol into his coat pocket. 'You're lucky I saw you,' he said to Rajkumar. 'Didn't you know better than to be out on the streets today? The other Indians have all barricaded themselves into Hajji Ismail's compound, at the foot of Mandalay hill.'

He held out a hand and helped Rajkumar to his feet. Rajkumar stood up and wiped the blood off his throbbing face. They walked out of the alley together. On the main road soldiers were still marching past. Rajkumar and Saya John stood side by side and watched the triumphal parade.

Presently Saya John said: 'I used to know soldiers like these.'

'Saya?'

'In Singapore, as a young man I worked for a time as a hospital orderly. The patients were mainly sepoys like these – Indians, back from fighting wars for their English masters. I still remember the smell of gangrenous bandages on amputated limbs; the night-time screams of twenty-year-old boys, sitting upright in their beds. They were peasants, those men, from small countryside villages: their clothes and turbans still smelt of woodsmoke and dung fires. "What makes you fight," I would ask them, "when you should be planting your fields at home?" "Money," they'd say, and yet all they earned was a few annas a day, not much more than a dockyard coolie. For a few coins they would allow their masters to use them as they wished, to destroy every trace of resistance to the power of the English. It always amazed me: Chinese peasants would never do this – allow themselves to be used to fight other people's wars with so little profit for themselves. I would look into those faces and I would ask myself: what would it be like if I had something to defend – a home, a country, a family – and I found myself attacked by these ghostly men, these trusting boys? How do you fight an enemy who fights from neither enmity nor anger, but in submission to orders from superiors, without protest and without conscience?

'In English they use a word – it comes from the Bible – *evil*. I used to think of it when I talked to those soldiers. What other word could you use to describe their willingness to kill for their masters, to follow any command, no matter what it entailed? And yet, in the hospital, these sepoys would give me gifts, tokens of their gratitude – a carved flute, an orange. I would look into their eyes and see also a kind of innocence, a simplicity. These men who would think nothing of setting fire to whole villages if their officers ordered, they too had a certain kind of innocence. An innocent evil. I could think of nothing more dangerous.'

'Saya,' Rajkumar shrugged offhandedly, 'they're just tools. Without minds of their own. They count for nothing.'

Saya John glanced at him, startled. There was something unusual about the boy – a kind of watchful determination. No excess of gratitude here, no gifts or offerings, no talk of honour, with murder in the heart. There was no simplicity in his face, no innocence: his eyes were filled with worldliness, curiosity, hunger. That was as it should be.

'If you ever need a job,' Saya John said, 'come and talk to me.'

Just before sunset the occupying troops withdrew from the fort. They carried away cartloads of booty from the palace. To the astonishment of the townsfolk, they left without posting pickets around the fort. For the first time that anyone could remember the gateways of the citadel stood open and unguarded.

The soldiers marched back the way they had come but through streets that were now empty. As the tramp of their feet faded away an uneasy quiet descended on the city. Then, with the suddenness of a night-time eruption in a chicken-coop, a group of women burst out of the fort and came racing over the funeral bridge, their feet pounding a drum roll on its wooden surface.

Ma Cho recognised some of the women. They were palace servants; she had seen them going in and out of the fort for years, stepping haughtily down the road in their slippered feet, their longyis plucked daintily above their ankles. They were running now, stumbling through the dust without a thought for their clothes. They were carrying bundles of cloth, sacks, even furniture; some were bent over like washerwomen on their way to the river. Ma Cho ran out into the street and stopped one of the women. 'What are you doing? What's happened?'

'The soldiers – they've been looting the palace. We're trying to save a few things for ourselves.' The women disappeared and all was quiet again. Presently the shadows around the fort began to stir. There were ripples of activity in the darkness, like the fluttering of moths in the recesses of a musty cupboard. People crept slowly out of the dwellings that surrounded the citadel. Advancing to the walls they peered distrustfully at the empty guard-posts. There were no soldiers anywhere in sight, nor even any sentries from the palace guard. Was it really possible that the gates had been left unguarded? A few people stepped on the bridges, testing the silence. Slowly, walking on the balls of their feet, they began to advance towards the far bank of the eighty-foot moat. They reached the other side and went creeping to the gates, holding themselves ready to run back at the slightest check.

It was true: the guards and sentries were all gone. The palace was unguarded. The intruders slipped through the gates and vanished into the fort.

Ma Cho had been watching undecided, scratching her chin. Now she picked up her sharp-bladed da. Tucking the wooden handle into her waist she started towards the funeral bridge. The fort's walls were a blood-red smear in the darkness ahead.

Rajkumar ran after her, reaching the bridge abreast of a charging crowd. This was the flimsiest of the fort's bridges, too narrow for the mass that was trying to funnel through. A frenzy of jostling broke out. The man beside Rajkumar found himself stepping on air and dropped over the side; a wooden plank flipped up, tipping two women screaming into the moat. Rajkumar was younger than the people around him and lighter on his feet. Slipping through the press of bodies, he went sprinting into the fort.

Rajkumar had imagined the fort to be filled with gardens and palaces, richly painted and sumptuously gilded. But the street he now found himself on was a straight and narrow dirt path, lined with wooden houses, not much different from any other part of the city. Directly ahead lay the palace and its nine-roofed spire – he could see the gilded hti flashing in the darkness. People were pouring down the street now, some carrying flaming torches. Rajkumar caught a glimpse of Ma Cho rounding a corner in the distance. He sprinted after her, his longyi tucked tight around his waist. The palace stockade had several entrances, including doorways reserved for the use of servants and tradespeople. These were set low in the walls, like mouseholes, so that no one could pass through them without bowing. At one of these small door-ways Rajkumar caught up again with Ma Cho. The gate was quickly forced. People began to tumble through, like water over the lip of a spout.

Rajkumar stayed close behind Ma Cho as she elbowed her way to the entrance. She heaved him in and then squeezed through herself. Rajkumar had the impression of having fallen upon a perfumed sheet. Then he rolled over and found that he was lying on a bed of soft grass. He was in a garden, within reach of a sparkling canal: the air was suddenly clear and cool, free of dust. The orientation of the palace's gateways was towards the east: it was from that direction that ceremonial visitors approached, walk-ing down the formal pathway that led to the great glass-tiled pavilion where the King held court. On the western side of the stockade – the side that was closest to the funeral gate – lay the women's quarters. These were the halls and apartments that now lay ahead of Ma Cho and Rajkumar. Ma Cho picked herself up and hurried, panting, in the direction of a stone archway. The doors of the main chamber of the women's palace lay just beyond, yawning open. People stopped to run their fingers over the doors' jade-studded panels. A man fell on his knees and began to pound the slats of wood with a rock, trying to knock out the ornaments. Rajkumar ran past, into the building, a couple of steps behind Ma Cho. The chamber was very large and its walls and columns were tiled with thousands of shards of glass. Oil lamps flared in sconces, and the whole room seemed to be aflame, every surface shimmering with sparks of golden light. The hall was filled with a busy noise, a workmanlike hum of cutting and chopping, of breaking wood and shattering glass. Everywhere people were intently at work, men and women, armed with axes and das; they were hacking at gem-studded *Ook* offering boxes; digging patterned gemstones from the marble floor; using fish-hooks to pry the ivory inlays from lacquered sadaik chests. Armed with a rock, a girl was knocking the ornamental frets out of a crocodile-shaped zither; a man was using a meat cleaver to scrape the gilt from the neck of a *saung-gak* harp and a woman was chiselling furiously at the ruby eyes of a bronze *chinthe* lion. They came to a door that led to a candlelit anteroom. There was a woman inside, standing by the latticed window in the far corner.

Ma Cho gasped. 'Queen Supayalat!'

The Queen was screaming, shaking her first. 'Get out of here. Get out.' Her face was red, mottled with rage, her fury caused as much by her own impotence as by the presence of the mob in the palace. A day before, she could have had a commoner imprisoned for so much as looking her directly in the face. Today all the city's scum had come surging into the palace and she was powerless to act against them. But the Queen was neither cowed nor afraid, not in the least. Ma Cho fell to the floor, her hands clasped over her head in a reverential *shiko*.

Rajkumar dropped to his knees, unable to wrench his gaze away. The Queen was dressed in crimson silk, in a loose garment that billowed over her hugely distended stomach. Her hair was piled in lacquered coils on her tiny, delicately shaped head; the ivory mask of her face was scarred by a single dark furrow, carved by a bead of sweat. She was holding her robe plucked above her ankle and Rajkumar noticed that her legs were encased in a garment of pink silk – stockings, an article of clothing he had never seen before. The Queen glared at Ma Cho, lying on the floor in front of her. In one hand, Ma Cho was holding a brass candlestand with a chrysanthemum pedestal.

The Queen lunged at the prostrate woman. 'Give that to me; where did you get it? Give it back.' Leaning stiffly over her swollen stomach, the Queen tried to snatch away the candlestand. Ma Cho eluded her hands, pushing herself backwards, crab-like. The Queen hissed at her: 'Do you know who I am?' Ma Cho offered her yet another respectful genuflection, but she would not part with her candlestand. It was as though her determination to cling to her loot was in no way at odds with her wish to render due homage to the Queen.

Just one day earlier the crime of entering the palace would have resulted in summary execution. This they all knew – the Queen and everyone who had joined the mob. But yesterday had passed: the Queen had fought and been defeated. What purpose was to be served by giving her back what she had lost? None of those things was hers any more: what was to be gained by leaving them to the foreigners to take away?

Through all the years of the Queen's reign the townsfolk had hated her for her cruelty, feared her for her ruthlessness and courage. Now through the alchemy of defeat she was transformed in their eyes. It was as though a bond had been conjured into existence that had never existed before. For the first time in her reign she had become what a sovereign should be, the proxy of her people. Everyone who came through the door fell to the floor in a spontaneous act of homage. Now, when she was powerless to chastise them, they were glad to offer her these tokens of respect; they were glad even to hear her rail at them. It was good that they should shiko and she berate them. Were she meekly to accept her defeat none would be so deeply shamed as they. It was as though they were entrusting her with the burden of their own inarticulate defiance.

Rajkumar's eyes fell on a girl – one of the Queen's maids. She was slender and long-limbed, of a complexion that was exactly the tint of the fine *thanaka* powder she was wearing on her face. She had huge dark eyes and her face was long and perfect in its symmetry. She was by far the most beautiful creature he had ever beheld, of a loveliness beyond imagining.

Rajkumar swallowed to clear his throat, which was suddenly

swollen and dry. She was in the far corner of the room with a group of other girls. He began to work his way towards her along the wall.

She was an attendant, he guessed, perhaps nine or ten years old. He could tell that the bejewelled little girl beside her was a Princess. In the corner behind them lay a heap of richly coloured cloths and objects of brass and ivory. The girls had evidently been busy salvaging the Queen's possessions when they were interrupted by the mob.

Rajkumar looked down at the floor and saw a jewelled ivory box lying forgotten in a corner. The box had a gold clasp and on its sides were two small handles, carved in the shape of leaping dolphins. Rajkumar knew exactly what he had to do. Picking the box off the ground, he ran across the room and offered it to the slender little girl.

'Here.'

She wouldn't look at him. She turned her head away, her lips moving silently as though in a chant.

'Take it,' said one of the other girls. 'He's giving it to you.'

'Here.' He thrust the box at her again. 'Don't be afraid.'

He surprised himself by taking hold of her hand and placing it gently on the box. 'I brought it back for you.'

She let her hand rest on the lid. It was as light as a leaf. Her lowered eyes went first to the jewelled lid and then travelled slowly from the dark knots of his knuckles to his torn and dirt-spattered vest and up to his face. And then her eyes clouded over with apprehension and she dropped her gaze. He could tell that her world was ringed with fear so that every step she took was a venture into darkness.

'What's your name?' Rajkumar said.

She whispered a couple of inaudible syllables.

'Doh-lee?'

'Dolly.'

'Dolly,' repeated Rajkumar. 'Dolly.' He could think of nothing else to say, or as much worth saying, so he said the name again louder and louder, until he was shouting. 'Dolly. Dolly.'

He saw a tiny smile creep on to her face and then Ma Cho's voice was in his ear. 'Soldiers. Run.' At the door, he turned to

35

look back. Dolly was standing just as he'd left her, holding the box between her hands, staring at him.

Ma Cho tugged at his arm. 'For what are you staring at that girl, you half-wit kalaa? Take what you've got and run. The soldiers are coming back. Run.'

The mirrored hall was echoing with shouts. At the door, Rajkumar turned back to make a gesture at Dolly, more a sign than a wave. 'I will see you again.'

Four

The Royal Family spent the night in one of the furthest outbuild-
ings in the palace grounds, the South Garden Palace, a small
pavilion surrounded by pools, canals and rustic gardens. The next
day, shortly before noon, King Thebaw came out to the balcony
and sat down to wait for the British spokesman, Colonel Sladen.
The King was wearing his royal sash and a white *gaung-baung*,
the turban of mourning.

King Thebaw was of medium height, with a plump face, a thin
moustache and finely shaped eyes. As a youth he had been famous
for his good looks: it had once been said of him that he was the
handsomest Burman in the land (he was in fact half Shan, his
mother having come to Mandalay from a small principality on
the eastern border). He'd been crowned at the age of twenty and
in the seven years of his reign had never once left the palace
compound. This long confinement had worked terrible ravages
on his appearance. He was only twenty-seven but looked to be
well into middle age.

To sit on the throne of Burma had never been Thebaw's personal
ambition. Nor had anyone in the kingdom ever imagined that the
crown would one day be his. As a child he had entered into the
Buddhist boy's customary novitiate in the monkhood with an
enthusiasm unusual in one of his birth and lineage. He had spent
several years in the palace monastery, leaving it just once, briefly,
at the behest of his father, the august King Mindon. The King had
enrolled Thebaw and a few of his step-brothers in an English school
in Mandalay. Under the tutelage of Anglican missionaries Thebaw
had learnt some English and displayed a talent for cricket.

But then King Mindon had changed his mind, withdrawing the princes from the school and eventually expelling the missionary. Thebaw had returned gladly to the monastery on the palace grounds, within sight of the water-clock and the relic house of the Buddha's tooth. He had proceeded to earn distinction in scriptural study, passing the difficult *patama-byan* examination at the age of nineteen.

King Mindon was perhaps the wisest, most prudent ruler ever to sit on the throne of Burma. Appreciative though he was of his son's gifts, he was equally aware of his limitations. 'If Thebaw ever becomes king,' he once remarked, 'the country will pass into the hands of foreigners.' But of this there seemed to be little possibility. There were forty-six other princes in Mandalay whose claims to the throne were as good as Thebaw's. Most of them far exceeded him in ambition and political ability.

But fate intervened in the familiar guise of a mother-in-law: Thebaw's happened to be also his step-mother, the Alenandaw Queen, a senior consort and a wily and ruthless exponent of palace intrigue. She arranged for Thebaw to marry all three of her daughters simultaneously. Then she shouldered him past his forty-six rivals and installed him on the throne. He had no choice but to assent to his accession: to accept was an easier alternative than to refuse, and less potentially lethal. But there was a startling new development, something that threw everybody's calculations off kilter: Thebaw fell in love with one of his wives, his middle Queen, Supayalat.

Of all the princesses in the palace, Supayalat was by far the fiercest and most wilful, the only one who could match her mother in guile and determination. Of such a woman only indifference could have been expected where it concerned a man of scholarly inclination like Thebaw. Yet she too, in defiance of the protocols of palace intrigue, fell headlong in love with her husband, the King. His ineffectual good nature seemed to inspire a maternal ferocity in her. In order to protect him from her family she stripped her mother of her powers and banished her to a corner of the palace, along with her sisters and co-wives. Then she set about ridding Thebaw of his rivals. She ordered the killing of every member of the Royal Family who might ever be considered a

38

threat to her husband. Seventy-nine princes were slaughtered on her orders, some of them new-born infants, and some too old to walk. To prevent the spillage of royal blood she had had them wrapped in carpets and bludgeoned to death. The corpses were thrown into the nearest river.

The war too was largely of Supayalat's making: it was she who had roused the great council of the land, the Hluttdaw, when the British began to issue their ultimatums from Rangoon. The King had been of a mind for appeasement; the Kinwun Mingyi, his most trusted minister, had made an impassioned appeal for peace and he was tempted to give in. Then Supayalat had risen from her place and gone slowly to the centre of the council. It was the fifth month of her pregnancy and she moved with great deliberation, with a slow, shuffling gait, moving her tiny feet no more than a few inches at a time, a small, lonely figure in that assembly of turbaned noblemen.

The chamber was lined with mirrors. As she approached its centre, an army of Supayalats seemed to materialise around her; they were everywhere, on every shard of glass, thousands of tiny women with their hands clasped over their swollen waists. She walked up to the stout old Kinwun Mingyi, sitting sprawled on his stool. Thrusting her swollen belly into his face, she said. 'Why, grandfather, it is you who should wear a skirt and own a stone for grinding face powder.' Her voice was a whisper but it had filled the room.

And now the war was over, and he, the King, was sitting on the balcony of a garden pavilion, waiting for a visit from Colonel Sladen, the spokesman of the conquering British. The evening before, the colonel had called on the King and informed him, in the politest and most discreet language, that the Royal Family was to be transported from Mandalay the next day; that His Majesty would do well to use the remaining time to make his preparations.

The King had not stepped out of the palace in seven years; he had not left the vicinity of Mandalay in all his life. What were his preparations to be? One might as well try to prepare for a journey to the moon. The King knew the colonel well. Sladen had spent years in Mandalay as a British emissary and had often visited the palace. He was fluent in Burmese and had always shown himself to be correct in his manners, at times affable and even friendly. He needed more time, the King had told Sladen, a week, a few days. What could it matter now? The British had won and he had lost: what difference could a day or two make?

The afternoon was well advanced when Colonel Sladen came walking up the path that led to the South Garden Palace, a pebbled trail that meandered between picturesque pools and goldfish-filled streams. The King stayed seated as Colonel Sladen approached.

'How much time?' said the King.

Sladen was in full dress uniform, with a sword hanging at his waist. He bowed regretfully. He had conferred at length with his commanding officer, he explained. The general had expressed his sympathy but he had his orders and was bound by the responsibilities of his position. His Majesty must understand; left to himself he, Sladen, would have been glad to make accommodations, but the matter was not in his hands, nor anyone else's for that matter . . .

'How much time then?'

Sladen reached into his pocket and pulled out a gold watch. 'About one hour.'

'One hour! But . . .'

A guard of honour had already been formed at the palace gates; the King was being waited on.

The news startled the King. 'Which gate?' he enquired in alarm. Every part of the palace was charged with portents. The auspicious, ceremonial entrance faced east. It was through these gates that honoured visitors came and departed. For years British envoys to Mandalay had been consigned to the humble west gate. This was a grievance of long standing. Sladen had waged many battles with the palace over such fine points of protocol. Would he now seek to exact revenge by forcing the King to exit the palace by the west gate? The King directed an apprehensive glance at the colonel and Sladen hastened to reassure the King. He was to be allowed to leave by the east gate. In victory the British had decided to be generous.

40

Sladen looked at his watch again. There was very little time now and a vitally important matter had yet to be settled: the question of the entourage that was to accompany the Royal Family into exile.

While Sladen was conferring with the King, other British officers had been busy organising a gathering in a nearby garden. A large number of palace functionaries had been summoned, including the Queen's maids and all other servants still remaining on the grounds. King Thebaw and Queen Supayalat looked on as the colonel addressed their servants.

The Royal Family was being sent into exile, the colonel told the assembled notables. They were to go to India, to a location that had yet to be decided on. The British Government wished to provide them with an escort of attendants and advisors. The matter was to be settled by asking for volunteers.

There was a silence when he finished, followed by an outburst of embarrassed coughs, a flurry of awkward throat-clearings. Feet were shuffled, heads lowered, nails examined. Mighty wungyis shot sidelong glances at powerful wundauks; haughty myowuns stared awkwardly at the grass. Many of the assembled courtiers had never had a home other than the palace; never woken to a day whose hours were not ordered by the rising of the King; never known a world that was not centred on the nine-roofed hti of Burma's monarchs. All their lives they had been trained in the service of their master. But their training bound them to the King only so long as he embodied Burma and the sovereignty of the Burmese. They were neither the King's friends nor his confidants and it was not in their power to lighten the weight of his crown. The burdens of kingship were Thebaw's alone, solitude not the least among them.

Sladen's appeal went unanswered: there were no volunteers. The King's gaze, that mark of favour once so eagerly sought, passed unchecked over the heads of his courtiers. Thebaw remained impassive as he watched his most trusted servants averting their faces, awkwardly fingering the golden *tsaloe* sashes that marked their rank.

This is how power is eclipsed: in a moment of vivid realism, between the waning of one fantasy of governance and its

41

replacement by the next; in an instant when the world springs free of its mooring of dreams and reveals itself to be girdled in the pathways of survival and self-preservation.

The King said: 'It does not matter who comes and who does not.' He turned to Sladen: 'But you must come with us, Sladen, as you are an old friend.'

'I regret this is impossible, Your Majesty,' answered Sladen. 'My duties will detain me here.'

The Queen, standing behind the King's chair, directed one of her flinty glances at her husband. It was all very well for him to express fine sentiments, but it was she who was eight months pregnant, and saddled moreover with the care of a colicky and difficult child. How was she to cope without servants and attendants? Who was going to calm the Second Princess when she had one of her raging tantrums? Her eyes scanned the assembly and settled on Dolly, who was sitting on her heels, braiding leaves of grass.

Dolly looked up to see the Queen glaring at her from her place on the pavilion balcony. She gave a cry and dropped the leaves. Had something happened? Was the Princess crying? She jumped to her feet and hurried towards the pavilion, followed by Evelyn, Augusta and several of the others.

Sladen breathed a sigh of relief as the girls came up the steps of the pavilion. Some volunteers at last!

'So you're going?' he said, as the girls hurried past, just to make sure.

The girls stopped to stare; Evelyn smiled and Augusta began to laugh. Of course they were going; they were orphans; they alone of the palace retainers had nowhere else to go, no families, no other means of support. What could they do but go with the King and Queen?

Sladen glanced once again at the assembly of courtiers and palace servants. Was there no one else present who would accompany the King? A single shaky voice answered in the affirmative. It belonged to an official of advanced age, the Padein Wun. He would go if he could bring along his son.

'How much time left?'

Sladen looked at his watch. 'Ten minutes.'

Just ten more minutes.

The King led Sladen into the pavilion and unlocked a door. A wedge of light fanned into the darkened room, igniting a firefly display of gold. The world's richest gem mines lay in Burma and many fine stones had passed into the possession of the ruling family. The King paused to run his hand over the jewelled case that held his most prized possession, the Ngamauk ring, set with the greatest, most valuable ruby ever mined in Burma. His ancestors had collected jewellery and gemstones as an afterthought, a kind of amusement. It was with these trinkets that he would have to provide for himself and his family in exile.

'Colonel Sladen, how is all this to be transported?'

Sladen conferred quickly with his fellow officers. Everything would be taken care of, he reassured the King. The hoard would be transported under guard to the King's ship. But now it was time to leave; the guard of honour was waiting.

The King walked out of the pavilion, flanked by Queen Supayalat and her mother. Halfway down the meandering path the Queen turned to look back. The Princesses were following a few paces behind with the maids. The girls were carrying their belongings in an assortment of boxes and bundles. Some had flowers in their hair, some were dressed in their brightest clothes. Dolly was walking beside Evelyn, who had the Second Princess on her hip. The two girls were giggling, oblivious, as though they were on their way to a festival.

The procession passed slowly through the long corridors of the palace, and across the mirrored walls of the Hall of Audience, past the shouldered guns of the guard of honour and the snapped-off salutes of the English officers.

Two carriages were waiting by the east gate. They were bullock-carts, *yethas*, the commonest vehicles on Mandalay's streets. The first of the carts had been fitted out with a ceremonial canopy. Just as he was about to step in, the King noticed that his canopy had seven tiers, the number allotted to a nobleman, not the nine due to a king.

He paused to draw breath. So the well-spoken English colonels had had their revenge after all, given the knife of victory a final little twist. In his last encounter with his erstwhile subjects he

43

was to be publicly demoted, like an errant schoolchild. Sladen had guessed right: this was, of all the affronts Thebaw could have imagined, the most hurtful, the most egregious.

The ox-carts were small and there was not enough room for the maids. They followed on foot, a ragged little procession of eighteen brightly-dressed orphan girls carrying boxes and bundles.

Several hundred British soldiers fell in beside the ox-carts and the girls. They were heavily armed, prepared for trouble. The people of Mandalay were not expected to sit idly by while their King and Queen were herded into exile. Reports had been heard of planned riots and demonstrations, of desperate attempts to free the Royal Family.

The British high command believed this to be potentially the most dangerous moment of the entire operation. Some of them had served in India and an incident from the recent past weighed heavily on their minds. In the final days of the Indian uprising of 1857, Major Hodson had captured Bahadur Shah Zafar, the last of the Mughals, on the outskirts of Delhi. The blind and infirm old emperor had taken refuge in the tomb of his ancestor, Humayun, with two of his sons. When it came time for the major to escort the emperor and his sons back into the city, people had gathered in large numbers along the roadside. These crowds had grown more and more unruly, increasingly threatening. Finally, to keep the mob under control, the major had ordered the princes' execution. They had been pushed before the crowd and their brains had been blown out in full public view.

These events were no more than twenty-eight years in the past, their memory freshly preserved in the conversation of messes and clubs. It was to be hoped that no such eventuality would present itself now – but if it did it would not find King Thebaw's escort unprepared.

Mandalay had few thoroughfares that could accommodate a procession of this size. The ox-carts rumbled slowly along the broader avenues, banking steeply round the right-angled corners. The city's streets, although straight, were narrow and unpaved.

Their dirt surfaces were rutted with deep furrows, left by the annual tilling of the monsoons. The ox-carts' wheels were solid, carved from single blocks of wood. Their rigid frames seesawed wildly as they ploughed over the troughs. The Queen had to crouch over her swollen stomach to keep herself from being battered against the sides of the cart.

Neither the soldiers nor their royal captives knew the way to the port. The procession soon lost its way in the geometrical maze of Mandalay's streets. It strayed off in the direction of the northern hills and by the time the mistake was discovered it was almost dark. The carts wound their way back by the light of oil-soaked torches.

During the daylight hours the townsfolk had been careful to keep away from the streets: they had watched the ox-carts go by from windows and rooftops, at a safe distance from the soldiers and their bayonets. As dusk gathered, they began to trickle out of their homes. Reassured by the darkness, they attached themselves to the procession, in small and scattered groups.

Dolly looked very small when Rajkumar spotted her. She was walking beside a tall soldier, with a small cloth bundle balanced on her head. Her face was grimy and her *htamein* was caked with dust.

Rajkumar still had a few small things that he had found in the palace the night before. He went hurrying to a shop and exchanged them for a couple of handfuls of palm-sugar sweets. He wrapped the sweets in a banana leaf and tied the packet with string. Sprinting back, he caught up with the procession as it was making its way out of the town.

The British fleet was moored just a mile or so away, but it was dark now and the going was slow along the rough and uneven roads. With nightfall, thousands of Mandalay's residents came pouring out. They walked alongside the procession, keeping well away from the soldiers and their moving pools of torchlight.

Rajkumar sprinted ahead and climbed into a tamarind tree. When the first ox-cart came into view he caught a glimpse of the King, just visible through the tiny window. He was sitting straight-backed, his eyes fixed ahead of him, his body swaying to the cart's lurching motion.

Rajkumar worked his way slowly through the crowd until he was within a few feet of Dolly. He kept pace, watching the soldier who was marching beside her. The man turned his eyes away for a moment, to exchange a word with someone behind him. Rajkumar saw his chance: he darted through to Dolly and pressed his banana leaf packet into her hand.

'Take it,' he hissed. 'It's food.'

She stared at him, in uncomprehending surprise.

'It's the kalaa boy from yesterday.' Evelyn jogged her elbow. 'Take it.'

Rajkumar raced back into the shadows: he was no more than ten feet from Dolly, walking beside her, shrouded by the night. She picked the packet open and stared at the sweets. Then she held the packet up in her hands, offering it to the soldier who was marching beside her. The man smiled and shook his head, in friendly refusal. Someone said something in English, and he laughed. Several of the girls laughed too, Dolly included.

Rajkumar was astonished, even angry. What was Dolly doing? Why was she giving these hard-won tidbits to the very men who were leading her into captivity and exile? But then, slowly, his initial sense of betrayal turned to relief, even gratitude. Yes, of course, this was what one must do; Dolly was doing exactly what had to be done. What purpose would it serve for these girls to make a futile show of resentment? How could they succeed in defiance when the very army of the realm had succumbed? No, better by far to wait, and in the meanwhile to smile. This way Dolly would live.

Half a mile from the port, the soldiers formed a cordon across the road to hold the crowd back. People began to climb trees and gather on rooftops, looking for vantage points. Unexpectedly Rajkumar came upon Ma Cho sitting on a tree-stump. She was weeping, and between sobs, telling anyone who would listen the story of her encounter with the Queen the night before.

Rajkumar tried to console her by running a hand gently over her head. He had never seen an adult cry like this before. What was she weeping for? He glanced up, as though looking for an answer on the faces around him. It was not till then that he noticed that many others were crying too. He had been so intent on keeping pace with Dolly that he had paid little attention to the people around him. Now, looking on either side, he could see that every face was streaked with tears.

Rajkumar recognised several people from the looting of the night before. He recalled how they had hacked at the furniture and dug up the floors. Now those very men and women were lying prostrate with grief, mourning the loss of their King and sobbing in what looked like inconsolable sorrow.

Rajkumar was at a loss to understand this grief. He was, in a way, a feral creature, unaware that in certain places there exist invisible bonds linking people to one another through personifications of their commonality. In the Bengal of his birth those ties had been sundered by a century of conquest and no longer existed even as memory. Beyond the ties of blood, friendship and immediate reciprocity, Rajkumar recognised no loyalties, no obligations and no limits on the compass of his right to provide for himself. He reserved his trust and affection for those who earned it by concrete example and proven goodwill. Once earned, his loyalty was given wholeheartedly, with none of those unspoken provisions with which people usually guard against betrayal. In this too he was not unlike a creature that had returned to the wild. But that there should exist a universe of loyalties that was unrelated to himself and his own immediate needs – this was very nearly incomprehensible.

An anguished murmur ran through the crowd: the captives were moving, alighting from their ox-carts, entering a ship. Rajkumar jumped quickly into the branches of a nearby tree. The river was far away and all he could see was a steamer and a line of tiny figures filing up a gangplank. It was impossible to tell the figures apart. Then the ship's lights went out and it disappeared into the darkness.

Many thousands kept vigil through the night. The steamer's name was *Thooriya*, the sun. At daybreak, when the skies lightened over the hills, it was gone.

Five

After five days on the Irrawaddy the *Thooriya* slipped into the Rangoon river in the near-darkness of late evening. It anchored at mid-river, a good distance from the city's busy dockside.

At first light the next day the King went up on deck, carrying a pair of gilded binoculars. The glasses were of French manufacture, a prized heirloom that had once belonged to King Mindon. The old King had been much attached to the binoculars and had always carried them with him, even into his Audience Hall.

It was a cold morning and an opaque fog had risen off the river. The King waited patiently for the sun to scorch away the mist. When it had thinned a little he raised his glasses. Suddenly, there it was, the sight he had longed to see all his life: the towering mass of the Shwe Dagon pagoda, larger even than he had imagined, its hti thrusting skywards, floating on a bed of mist and fog, shining in the light of the dawn. He had worked on the hti himself, helped with his own hands in the gilding of the spire, layering sheets of gold leaf upon each other. It was King Mindon who had had the hti cast, in Mandalay; it had been sent down to the Shwe Dagon in a royal barge. He, Thebaw, had been a novice in the monastery then, and everybody, even the seniormost monks, had vied with each other for the honour of working on the hti.

The King lowered his binoculars to scan the city's waterfront. The instrument's rims welled over with a busy mass of things: walls, columns, carriages and hurrying people. Thebaw had heard about Rangoon from his half-brother, the Thonzai Prince. The town was founded by their ancestor, Alaungpaya, but few members of their dynasty had ever been able to visit it. The British had seized the town before Thebaw's birth, along with all of Burma's coastal provinces. It was then that the frontiers of the Burmese kingdom were driven back, almost halfway up the Irrawaddy. Since then the only members of the Royal Family who had been able to visit Rangoon were rebels and exiles, princes who had fallen out with the ruling powers in Mandalay.

The Thonzai Prince was one such: he had quarrelled with old King Mindon and had fled downriver, taking refuge in the British-held city. Later the Prince had been forgiven and had returned to Mandalay. In the palace he was besieged with questions: everyone wanted to know about Rangoon. Thebaw was in his teens then and he had listened spellbound as the Prince described the ships that were to be seen on the Rangoon river: the Chinese junks and Arab dhows and Chittagong sampans and American clippers and British ships-of-the-line. He had heard about the Strand and its great pillared mansions and buildings, its banks and hotels; about Godwin's wharf and the warehouses and timber mills that lined Pazundaung Creek; the wide streets and the milling crowds and the foreigners who thronged the public places: Englishmen, Cooringhees, Tamils, Americans, Malays, Bengalis, Chinese.

One of the stories the Thonzai Prince used to tell was about Bahadur Shah Zafar, the last Mughal emperor. After the suppression of the uprising of 1857 the British had exiled the deposed emperor to Rangoon. He'd lived in a small house not far from the Shwe Dagon. One night the Prince had slipped off with a few of his friends and gone to look at the emperor's house. They'd found him sitting on his veranda, fingering his beads. He was blind and very old. The Prince and his friends had meant to approach him but at the last minute they had changed their minds. What could you say to such a man?

There was a street in Rangoon, the Prince had said, that was named after the old emperor – Mughal Street. Many Indians lived there: the Prince had claimed that there were more Indians than Burmese in Rangoon. The British had brought them there, to work in the docks and mills, to pull rickshaws and empty the latrines. Apparently they couldn't find local people to do these jobs. And indeed, why would the Burmese do that kind of work?

In Burma no one ever starved, everyone knew how to read and write, and land was to be had for the asking: why should they pull rickshaws and carry nightsoil?

The King raised his glasses to his eyes and spotted several Indian faces, along the waterfront. What vast, what incomprehensible power, to move people in such huge numbers from one place to another – emperors, kings, farmers, dockworkers, soldiers, coolies, policemen. Why? Why this furious movement – people taken from one place to another, to pull rickshaws, to sit blind in exile?

And where would his own people go, now that they were a part of this empire? It wouldn't suit them, all this moving about. They were not a portable people, the Burmese; he knew this, very well, for himself. He had never wanted to go anywhere. Yet here he was, on his way to India.

He turned to go below deck again: he didn't like to be away from his cabin too long. Several of his valuables had disappeared, some of them on that very first day, when the English officers were transporting them from the palace to the *Thooriya*. He had asked about the lost things and the officers had stiffened and looked offended and talked of setting up a committee of inquiry. He had realised that for all their haughty ways and grand uniforms, they were not above some common thievery.

The strange thing was that if only they'd asked he'd gladly have gifted them some of his baubles; they would probably have received better things than those they'd taken – after all, what did they know about gemstones?

Even his ruby ring was gone. The other things he didn't mind so much – they were just trinkets – but he grieved for the Ngamauk. They should have left him the Ngamauk.

On arriving in Madras, King Thebaw and his entourage were taken to the mansion that had been made over to them for the duration of their stay in the city. The house was large and luxurious but there was something disconcerting about it. Perhaps it was the contingent of fierce-looking British soldiers standing at the gate or perhaps it had something to do with the crowds of curious onlookers who gathered round its walls every day. Whatever it was, none of the girls felt at home there.

Mr Cox often urged the members of the household to step outside, to walk in the spacious, well-kept gardens (Mr Cox was an English policeman who had accompanied them on their journey from Rangoon and he spoke Burmese well). Dolly, Evelyn and Augusta dutifully walked around the house a few times but they were always glad to be back indoors.

Strange things began to happen. There was news from Mandalay that the royal elephant had died. The elephant was white, and so greatly cherished that it was suckled on breast-milk: nursing mothers would stand before it and slip off their blouses. Everyone had known that the elephant would not long survive the fall of the dynasty. But who could have thought that it would die so soon? It seemed like a portent. The house was sunk in gloom.

Unaccountably, the King developed a craving for pork. Soon he was consuming inordinate amounts of bacon and ham. One day he ate too much and fell sick. A doctor arrived with a leather bag and went stomping through the house in his boots. The girls had to follow behind him, swabbing the floor. No one slept that night.

One morning Apodaw Mahta, the elderly woman who supervised the Queen's nurses, ran outside and climbed into a tree. The Queen sent the other nurses to persuade her to climb down. They spent an hour under the tree. Apodaw Mahta paid no attention.

The Queen called the nurses back and sent Dolly and the other girls to talk to Apodaw Mahta. The tree was a *neem* and its foliage was very dense. The girls stood round the trunk and looked up. Apodaw Mahta had wedged herself into a fork between two branches.

'Come down,' said the girls. 'It's going to be dark soon.'

'No.'

'Why not?'

'I was a squirrel in my last birth. I remember this tree. This is where I want to stay.'

Apodaw Mahta had a pot belly and warts on her face. 'She looks more like a toad than a squirrel,' Evelyn whispered. The girls screamed with laughter and ran back inside.

U Maung Gyi, the interpreter, went out and shook his fist at her. The King was going to come down from his room, he said, and he was going to bring a stick to beat her with. At that Apodaw Mahta came scurrying down. She'd lived in the Mandalay palace for a very long time and was terrified of the King.

Anyone could have told her that the last thing in the world the King was likely to do was to run out into the garden and beat her with a stick. He'd never once stepped out of the house in all the time they'd been in Madras. Towards the beginning of their stay he had once asked to visit the Madras Museum. This had taken Mr Cox by surprise and he had said no, quite vehemently. After that, as though in protest, the King had refused to step out of the house.

Sitting in his room, with nothing to do, curious fancies began to enter the King's mind. He decided to have a huge gold plate made in preparation for the birth of his new child. The plate would weigh several pounds and it would be set with one hundred and fifty of his most valuable rubies. To pay for the plate, he began to sell some of his possessions. The household's Tamil employees served as his emissaries.

Some of these employees were spies and Mr Cox soon found out about the sales. He was furious. The King was wasting his wealth, he said, and what was more, he was being cheated. The servants were selling his things for a fraction of their value.

This made the King even more secretive in his dealings. He handed Dolly and Evelyn expensive jewellery and asked them to arrange to have it sold. The result was that he got even lower prices. Inevitably the Englishmen found out through their spies. They declared that the King couldn't be trusted with money and enacted a law appropriating his family's most valuable properties.

A mutinous quiet descended on the mansion. Dolly began to notice odd little changes in Evelyn and Augusta and her other friends. Their shikoes became perfunctory; they began to complain about sore knees and refused to stay on all fours while waiting on the Queen. Sometimes when she shouted at them they would scowl back at her.

One night the Queen woke up thirsty and found all her maids asleep beside her bed. She was so angry she threw a lamp at the wall and slapped Evelyn and Mary.

Evelyn was very upset. She said to Dolly: 'They can't hit us and beat us any more. We don't have to stay if we don't want to.'

'How do you know?' Dolly said.

'Mr Cox told me. He said we were slaves in Mandalay but now we're free.'

'But we're prisoners, aren't we?'

'Not us,' said Evelyn. 'Only Min and Mebya' – meaning the King and Queen.

Dolly thought about this for a while. 'And what about the Princesses?'

Now it was Evelyn's turn to think.

'Yes,' she said at last. 'The Princesses are prisoners too.'

That settled the matter as far as Dolly was concerned. Where the Princesses were, she would be too: she couldn't imagine what they would do without her.

One morning a man arrived at the gate saying he'd come from Burma to take his wife back home. His wife was Taungzin Minthami, one of the Queen's favourite nurses. She had left her children behind in Burma and was terribly homesick. She decided to go back with her husband.

This reminded everyone of the one thing they'd been trying to forget, which was that left to themselves they would all rather have gone home – that none of them was there because he or she wanted to be. The Queen began to worry that all her girls were going to leave so she began to hand out gifts to her favourites. Dolly was one of the lucky ones, but neither Evelyn nor Augusta received anything.

The two girls were furious at being passed over and they began to make sarcastic comments within the Queen's hearing. The Queen spoke to the Padein Wun, and he took them into a locked room and beat them and pulled their hair. But this made the girls even more resentful. Next morning they refused to wait on the Queen.

The Queen decided that the matter had passed beyond resolution. She summoned Mr Cox and told him that she wanted to send seven of the girls back to Burma. She would make do by hiring local servants.

Once the Queen had decided on something there was no

question of persuading her to change her mind. The seven girls left the next week: Evelyn, Augusta, Mary, Wahthau, Nan Pau, Minlwin, and even Hemau, who was, of all of them, the closest to Dolly in age. Dolly had always thought of them as her older sisters, her family. She knew she would never see them again. On the morning of their departure she locked herself into a room and wouldn't come out, even to watch their carriage roll out of the gates. U Maung Gyi, the interpreter, took them to the port. When he came back he said the girls had cried when they'd boarded the ship.

A number of new servants were hired, men and women, all local people. Dolly was now one of last remaining members of the original Mandalay contingent: it fell on her to teach the new staff the ways of the household. The new ayahs and maids came to Dolly when they wanted to know how things were done in the Mandalay palace. It was she who had to teach them how to shiko and how to move about the Queen's bedroom on their hands and knees. It was very hard at first, for she couldn't make herself understood. She would explain everything in the politest way but they wouldn't understand so she would shout louder and louder and they would become more and more frightened. They would start knocking things over, breaking chairs and upsetting tables.

Slowly she learnt a few words of Tamil and Hindustani. It became a little easier to work with them then, but they still seemed strangely clumsy and inept. There were times when she couldn't help laughing – when she saw them trying out their shikoes, for example, wiggling their elbows and straightening their saris. Or when she watched them lumbering around on their knees, huffing and puffing, or getting themselves tangled in their clothes and falling flat on their faces. Dolly could never understand why they found it so hard to move about on their hands and knees. To her it seemed much easier than having to stand up every time you wanted to do something. It was much more restful this way: when you weren't doing anything in particular you could relax with your weight on your heels. But the new ayahs seemed to think it impossibly hard. You could never trust them to carry a tray to the Queen. They would either spill everything as they tried to get across the room, or else they would creep along so slowly that it would take them half an hour to get from the door to her bed. The Queen would get very impatient, lying on her side and watching her glass of water move across the room as though it were being carried by a snail. Sometimes she would shout, and that would be worse still. The terrified ayah would fall over, tray and all, and the whole process would have to be resumed from the start.

It would have been much easier of course if the Queen weren't so insistent on observing all the old Mandalay rules – the shikoes, the crawling – but she wouldn't hear of any changes. She was the Queen of Burma, she said, and if she didn't insist on being treated properly how could she expect anyone else to give her her due?

One day U Maung Gyi caused a huge scandal. One of the Queen's nurses went into the nursery and found him on the floor with another nurse, his longyi pulled up over his waist. Instead of scurrying off in shame he turned on his discoverer and began to beat her. He chased her down the corridor and into the King's bedroom.

The King was sitting at a table rolling a cheroot. U Maung Gyi lunged at the nurse as she went running in. She tripped and grabbed at the tablecloth. Everything flew into the air: there was tobacco everywhere. The King sneezed and went on sneezing for what seemed like hours. When he finally stopped he was angrier than anyone had ever seen him before. This meant still more departures.

With the head nurse thinking herself to be a squirrel and another gone home to Burma, the Queen now had very few dependable nurses left. She decided to get an English midwife. Mr Cox found one for her, a Mrs Wright. She seemed pleasant and friendly enough, but her arrival led to other problems. She wouldn't shiko and she wouldn't go down on her hands and knees while waiting on the Queen. The Queen appealed to Mr Cox but the Englishman came out in support of Mrs Wright. She could bow, he said, from the waist, but she needn't shiko and she certainly wouldn't crawl. She was an Englishwoman.

The Queen accepted this ruling but it didn't endear Mrs Wright to her. She began to rely more and more on a Burmese masseur who had somehow attached himself to the royal entourage. He was very good with his hands and was able to make the Queen's pains go away. But the English doctor found out and made a huge fuss. He said that what the masseur was doing was an affront to medical science. He said that the man was touching Her Highness in unhealthy places. The Queen decided he was mad and declared that she would not send the masseur away. The doctor retaliated by refusing to treat her any more.

Fortunately the Queen's labour was very short and the delivery quick and uncomplicated. The child was a girl and she was named Ashin Hteik Su Myat Paya.

Everyone was nervous because they knew how badly the Queen had wanted a boy. But the Queen surprised them. She was glad, she said: a girl would be better able to bear the pain of exile.

For a while Mandalay became a city of ghosts.

After the British invasion, many of the King's soldiers escaped into the countryside with their weapons. They began to act on their own, staging attacks on the occupiers, sometimes materialising inside the city at night. The invaders responded by tightening their grip. There were round-ups, executions, hangings. The sound of rifle-fire echoed through the streets; people locked themselves into their homes and stayed away from the bazaars. Whole days went by when Ma Cho had no call to light her cooking fire.

One night Ma Cho's stall was broken into. Between the two of them, Rajkumar and Ma Cho succeeded in driving the intruders away. But considerable damage had already been caused; lighting a lamp, Ma Cho discovered that most of her pots, pans and utensils had been either stolen or destroyed. She let out a stricken wail. 'What am I to do? Where am I to go?'

Rajkumar squatted beside her. 'Why don't you talk to Saya John?' he suggested. 'Perhaps he'll be able to help.'

Ma Cho snorted in tearful disgust. 'Don't talk to me about Saya John. What's the use of a man who's never there when you need him?' She began to sob, her hands covering her face.

Tenderness welled up in Rajkumar. 'Don't cry, Ma Cho.' He

ran his hands clumsily over her head, combing her curly hair with his nails. 'Stop, Ma Cho. Stop.'

She blew her nose and straightened up. 'It's all right,' she said gruffly. 'It's nothing.' Fumbling in the darkness, she reached for his longyi, leaning forward to wipe the tears from her face.

Often before, Ma Cho's bouts of tears had ended in this way, with her wiping her face on his thin cotton garment. But this time, as her fingers drew together the loose cloth, the chafing of the fabric produced a new effect on Rajkumar. He felt the kindling of a glow of heat deep within his body, and then, involuntarily, his pelvis thrust itself forward, towards her fingers, just as she was closing her grip. Unmindful of the intrusion, Ma Cho drew a fistful of cloth languidly across her face, stroking her cheeks, patting the furrows round her mouth and dabbing the damp hollows of her eyes. Standing close beside her, Rajkumar swayed, swivelling his hips to keep pace with her hand. It was only when she was running the tip of the bunched cloth between her parted lips that the fabric betrayed him. Through the layered folds of cloth, now wet and clinging, she felt an unmistakable hardness touching on the soft corners of her mouth. She tightened her grip, suddenly alert, and gave the gathered cloth a probing pinch. Rajkumar gasped, arching his back.

'Oh?' she grunted. Then, with a startling deftness, one of her hands flew to the knot of his longyi and tugged it open; the other pushed him down on his knees. Parting her legs she drew him, kneeling, towards her stool. Rajkumar's forehead was on her cheek now; the tip of his skinned nose thrust deep into the hollow beneath her jaw. He caught the odour of turmeric and onion welling up through the cleft between her breasts. And then a blinding whiteness flashed before his eyes and his head was pulled as far back as it could go, tugged by convulsions in his spine.

Abruptly, she pushed him away, with a yelp of disgust. 'What am I doing?' she cried. 'What am I doing with this boy, this child, this half-wit kalaa?' Elbowing him aside, she clambered up her ladder and vanished into her room.

It was a while before Rajkumar summoned the courage to say anything. 'Ma Cho,' he called up, in a thin, shaking voice. 'Are you angry?'

'No,' came a bark from above. 'I'm not angry. I want you to forget Ma Cho and go to sleep. You have your own future to think of.'

They never spoke of what happened that night. Over the next few days, Rajkumar saw very little of Ma Cho: she would disappear early in the morning, returning only late at night. Then, one morning, Rajkumar woke up and knew that she was gone for good. Now, for the first time, he climbed the ladder that led up to her room. The only thing he found was a new, blue longyi, lying folded in the middle of the room. He knew that she'd left it for him.

What was he to do now? Where was he to go? He'd assumed all along that he would eventually return to his sampan, to join his shipmates. But now, thinking of his life on the boat, he knew he would not go back. He had seen too much in Mandalay and acquired too many new ambitions.

During the last few weeks he'd thought often of what Saya John's son, Matthew had said – about the British invasion being provoked by teak. No detail could have been more precisely calculated to lodge in a mind like Rajkumar's, both curious and predatory. If the British were willing to go to war over a stand of trees, it could only be because they knew of some hidden wealth, secreted within the forest. What exactly these riches were he didn't know but it was clear that he would never find out except by seeing for himself.

Even while pondering this, he was walking quickly, heading away from the bazaar. Now, looking around to take stock of where he was, he discovered that he had come to the whitewashed facade of a church. He decided to linger, walking past the church once, and then again. He circled and waited, and sure enough, within the hour he spotted Saya John approaching the church, hand in hand with his son.

'Saya.'

'Rajkumar!'

Now, standing face to face with Saya John, Rajkumar found himself hanging his head in confusion. How was he to tell him about Ma Cho, when it was he himself who was responsible for the Saya's cuckolding?

It was Saya John who spoke first: 'Has something happened to Ma Cho?'

Rajkumar nodded.

'What is it? Has she gone?'

'Yes, Saya.'

Saya John gave a long sigh, rolling his eyes heavenwards. 'Perhaps it's for the best,' he said. 'I think it's a sign that the time has come for this sinner to turn celibate.'

'Saya?'

'Never mind. And what will you do now, Rajkumar? Go back to India in your boat?'

'No, Saya.' Rajkumar shook his head. 'I want to stay here, in Burma.'

'And what will you do for a living?'

'You said, Saya, that if I ever wanted a job I was to come to you. Saya?'

One morning the King read in the newspapers that the Viceroy was coming to Madras. In a state of great excitement he sent for Mr Cox.

'Is the Viceroy going to call on us?' he asked.

Mr Cox shook his head. 'Your Highness, I have not been informed of any such plan.'

'But protocol demands it. The Kings of Burma are the peers of such sovereigns as the kings of Siam and Cambodia and of the emperors of China and Japan.'

'I regret, Your Highness, that it is probably too late to effect a change in the Viceroy's itinerary.'

'But we must see him, Mr Cox.'

'The Viceroy's time has already been spoken for. I am sorry.'

'But we wish to find out what the Government plans to do with us. When we came here, we were told that this was not to be our permanent residence. We are eager to know where we are to live and when we are to go there.'

Mr Cox went away and came back a few days later. 'Your Highness,' he said, 'I am glad to be able to inform you that the matter of a permanent residence for you and your family has finally been resolved.'

'Oh?' said the King. 'And where is it to be?'

'A place by the name of Ratnagiri.'

'What?' The King stared at him, nonplussed. 'Where is this place?'

'Some hundred and twenty miles south of Bombay. An excellent place, with fine views of the sea.'

'Fine views?'

The King sent for a map and asked Mr Cox to show him where Ratnagiri was. Mr Cox indicated a point somewhere between Bombay and Goa. The King was thoroughly alarmed to note that the place was too insignificant to be marked on the map.

'But we would rather be in a city, Mr Cox. Here in Madras. Or Bombay. Or Calcutta. What will we do in a small village?'

'Ratnagiri is a district headquarters, Your Highness, not a village by any means.'

'How long are we to remain there? When will we be allowed to return to Burma?'

Now it was Mr Cox's turn to be nonplussed. It had not occurred to him that the King still harboured hopes of returning to Burma.

Mr Cox was a kindly man, in his gruff way. 'Your Highness,' he said, in a quiet and gentle voice, 'you must prepare yourself to be in Ratnagiri for some time, a considerable time I fear. Perhaps . . .'

'Perhaps for ever?'

'Those were not my words.' Mr Cox coughed. 'Not at all. Those words were not mine. No, I must insist, they were not . . .'

The King rose to his feet abruptly and went to his room. He did not step out again for several days.

They left Madras a month later on a steamer called the *Clive*. The voyage was very different this time around. They sailed along the coast with the shore rarely out of sight. They went through the Palk Straits, with the northern tip of Ceylon visible on the left, and the southernmost point in India, Cape Comorin, in view on the right.

Four days after leaving Madras the *Clive* nosed into a wide and sunlit bay. There were cliffs at either end of the bay, a sweeping beach and a meandering river. The town was on a hill, above the bay; it was so thickly blanketed with coconut palms that very little could be seen of it.

They spent the night on the steamer and went ashore the next morning. The *Clive* pulled in beside a jetty that reached a long way out into the shallow bay. Carriages were waiting for them at the far end, near a fishing village. The King was greeted with a gun salute and a guard of honour. Then the carriages set off in single file down a narrow, tree-shaded path. There were red-tiled houses on either side, with gardens of mango trees and areca palms. There were policemen everywhere, holding back the people who'd gathered to watch. They passed a bazaar and a grey-walled gaol and a line of police-barracks. The road ended at a large, two-storeyed bungalow set inside a walled garden. It was on a bluff above the town, overlooking the bay. It was called Outram House.

The King went in first and climbed slowly up the stairs. He came to a large bedroom and went inside. The room was furnished with a desk, a bed and three armchairs. It opened on to a small balcony that faced westwards, towards the sea. The King walked very slowly round the room. He toyed with the slatted wooden shutters, scratched at a rosette of candlewax and ran a finger over a half-effaced mark on the wall, crumbling the flaking plaster between finger and thumb. There was a faintly musty smell in the room and a tracing of mildew on the wall. He tried to mark these things in his memory for he knew they would fade in time and a day would come when he would want to remember them – the vividness of his first encounter with the site of his captivity, the sour mildewed smell of it and the roughness of its texture upon the skin.

Downstairs Dolly was running across the garden with the First Princess, chasing a lizard of a bright red colour. This was different from the mansion in Madras, much smaller but more welcoming. Here one could run and play hide-and-seek between the trunks of leaning coconut palms. She came to a mango tree whose branches reached all the way up to a window on the top floor of the bungalow. Perhaps that would be her room, her window, with twigs scratching against the glass.

A bell began to ring in a temple, somewhere in the town below. She stopped to listen, looking down the slope of the garden, across the canopy of coconut fronds, towards the wide sparkling bay. She could smell drying fish and incense. How bright it was, how peaceful. Everything seemed so safe here, behind these high stone walls.

The King heard the bells too. He stepped out on to the balcony of the upstairs bedroom. The whole town lay spread out below, framed by the sweep of the bay and the two steep promontories on either side. The view was magnificent, just as Mr Cox had said. He went back into the bedroom. He sat in one of the armchairs and watched the ghostly shadows of coconut palms swaying on the room's white plaster walls. In this room the hours would accumulate like grains of sand until they buried him.

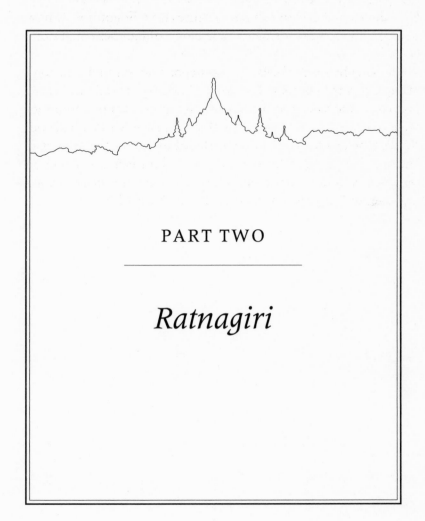

PART TWO

Ratnagiri

Six

For Rajkumar and Saya John the busy time of year was when the rivers rose. Every few weeks they would load a cargo of sacks, crates and boxes on to one of the Irrawaddy Steamship Flotilla's riverboats: shuddering, paddle-wheeled steamers, captained, more often than not, by Scotsmen, and crewed mainly by Chittagong khalasis, such as Rajkumar had himself once sought to be. With the weight of the engorged river behind them, they would go shooting downstream from Mandalay at such speeds as to put the flotilla's itineraries to rout. At sunset, when it was time to pull into shore, they would frequently find themselves anchoring beside some tiny river-bank hamlet that consisted of nothing more than a few thatched huts, clustered around a police station parade ground.

No matter how small the village, a fair would materialise instantly around the anchored steamer: hawkers, food vendors, boat-borne shopkeepers, sellers of fried snacks and distillers of country liquor would come hastening with their wares, delighted by the unexpected netting of this great shoal of customers. Sometimes news of the steamer's arrival would filter through to a travelling troupe of entertainers. At nightfall, to the accompaniment of a concert of rain-bred croaking, puppeteers' screens would come alive above the banks and the gaunt, twitching outlines of the Bodaw and the Bayin, the Minthami and the Minthagyi, the Natkadaw and the Nan Belu would loom out of the darkness, as large and as familiar as the shadows on the moon.

Saya John liked to travel first-class, in a cabin: his business was flourishing and he had money to spare. He had moved into a large house on Mandalay's 33rd Street – a dwelling that housed Rajkumar as well as everyone else who was in any way connected with his business. The British occupation had changed everything: Burma had been quickly integrated into the Empire, forcibly converted into a province of British India. Courtly Mandalay was now a bustling commercial hub; resources were being exploited with an energy and efficiency hitherto undreamt of. The Mandalay palace had been refurbished to serve the conquerors' recondite pleasures: the west wing had been converted into a British Club; the Queen's Hall of Audience had now become a billiard room; the mirrored walls were lined with months-old copies of *Punch* and the *Illustrated London News*; the gardens had been dug up to make room for tennis courts and polo grounds; the exquisite little monastery in which Thebaw had spent his novitiate had become a chapel where Anglican priests administered the sacrament to British trooops. Mandalay, it was confidently predicted, would soon become the Chicago of Asia; prosperity was the natural destiny of a city that guarded the confluence of two of the world's mightiest waterways, the Irrawaddy and the Chindwin.

Saya John was earning rich profits now, ferrying supplies and provisions to teak camps. Although not a man who had a great craving for luxuries, he felt it necessary to grant himself a good night's sleep when he was setting out on one of his supply expeditions. A cabin on the first-class deck of an Irrawaddy steamship was, after all, but a small indulgence.

As for Rajkumar, he spent his shipboard nights on the lower deck. Some of the crew were boys his own age, whose job it was to hang over the bows of the vessel, plumb line in hand, just as he himself had once done, watching for shifting sandbanks and calling out the depths, '*Ek gaz; do gaz, teen gaz . . .*' With them he would slip into his own Chittagong tongue, and when the steamer lay at rest, they would rouse him from his deckside mat and take him over to land, to show him the places where boatmen went at night.

When it came time to go ashore, the next day, Rajkumar would be red-eyed and Saya John fresh, heartily breakfasted and eager to get his cargo unloaded, to be on his way to the camp where he was headed. The first part of the journey was usually by ox-cart.

They would breast rivers of mud as they went creaking towards the distant mountains.

When everything went as planned, these journeys would end at some tiny inland hamlet, with a team of elephants waiting to relieve them of their cargo, leaving them free to turn back. But all too often they would arrive at their roadhead only to learn that the camp ahead could spare no elephants; that they would have to find their own porters to carry their cargo into the mountains. Then Rajkumar too had to yoke a basket to his back, a wickerwork *pah* with a deep cover and a forehead-strap. To his particular charge would fall the small bespoke luxuries that were specially ordered by the forest Assistants who ran the timber camps – cigars, bottles of whisky, tins of canned meat and sardines, once even a crystal decanter sent up by Rowe & Co., the big Rangoon department store.

They would set off at daybreak with Saya John leading a long line of porters and Rajkumar bringing up the rear; they would climb sideways, like mules, along the rain-sodden paths, digging the edges of their feet into the red, purchaseless mud. It was a ritual with Saya John, a kind of superstition, always to start these journeys in European clothes: a sola topee, leather boots, khaki trousers. Rajkumar went barefoot, like the porters, wearing nothing but a vest, a longyi and a farmer's wide-brimmed hat.

But no matter how much care he took, Saya John's costume never survived long intact: the undergrowth would come alive as they passed by, leeches unfurling like tendrils as they awoke to the warmth of the passing bodies. Being the most heavily clothed in the party, it was Saya John who invariably reaped the richest of these bloody harvests. Every hour or two he would call a halt. The trails were lined with thatched bamboo shelters, erected at regular intervals by the timbermen. Sitting huddled beneath the dripping thatch, Saya John would reach into his bags to retrieve the tarpaulin-wrapped packet in which Rajkumar had packed his matches and cheroots. Lighting a cheroot he would draw deep until a long, glowing tip had formed. Then he would go over his body, burning off his leeches, one by one.

The thickest clusters of leeches were gathered always along the fissures of the body, where cloth chafed on skin: the folds and

67

creases would guide the creatures to their favourite destinations – armpits, the groin, the cracks between legs and buttocks. In his shoes Saya John would sometimes find scores of leeches, most of them clinging to the webbed skin between the toes – to a leech the most prized of the human body's offerings. There were always some that had burst under the pressure of the boot, leaving their suckers embedded in the flesh. These were the sites that were most likely to attract fresh attacks, from insects as well as leeches; left unattended they would fester, turn into foul-smelling, deep-rooted jungle sores. To these spots Saya John would apply *kow-yok* – a tar-like touch of red tobacco, smeared on paper or cloth. The poultice would fasten itself so tightly to the skin as to stay attached even when immersed in water, drawing out the infection and protecting the wound. At each stop Saya John would shed an article of clothing, and within the space of a few hours he would be dressed like Rajkumar, in nothing more than a longyi and a vest.

Almost invariably they would find themselves following the course of a *chaung*, a rushing mountain stream. Every few minutes a log would come hurtling through the water, on its way down to the plain. To be caught in mid-stream by one of these hurtling two-ton projectiles was to be crippled or killed. When the path switched from one bank of the chaung to the other, a lookout would be posted to call out the intervals between logs so that the porters would know when it was safe to cross.

Often the logs came not singly but in groups, dozens of tons of hardwood caroming down the stream together: when they hit each other the impact would be felt all the way up the banks. At times a log would snag, in rapids or on the shore, and within minutes a tangled dam would rise out of the water, plugging the stream. One after another logs would go cannoning into one another, adding to the weight of the accumulated hardwood. The weight of the mass would mount until it became an irresistible force. Then at last something would give; a log, nine feet in girth, would snap like a matchstick. With a great detonation the dam would capsize and a tidal wave of wood and water would wash down the slopes of the mountain.

'Chaungs are the tradewinds of teak,' Saya John liked to say.

In the dry season, when the earth cracked and the forests wilted, the streams would dwindle into dribbles upon the slope, barely able to shoulder the weight of a handful of leaves, mere trickles of mud between strings of cloudy riverbed pools. This was the season for the timbermen to comb the forest for teak. The trees, once picked, had to be killed and left to dry, for the density of teak is such that it will not remain afloat while its heartwood is moist. The killing was achieved with a girdle of incisions, thin slits, carved deep into the wood at a height of four feet and six inches off the ground (teak being ruled, despite the wildness of its terrain, by imperial stricture in every tiny detail).

The assassinated trees were left to die where they stood, some-times for three years or even more. It was only after they had been judged dry enough to float that they were marked for felling. That was when the axemen came, shouldering their weapons, squinting along the blades to judge their victims' angles of descent.

Dead though they were, the trees would sound great tocsins of protest as they fell, unloosing thunderclap explosions that could be heard miles away, bringing down everything in their path, rafts of saplings, looped nets of rattan. Thick stands of bamboo were flattened in moments, thousands of jointed limbs exploding simul-taneously in deadly splinter blasts, throwing up mushroom clouds of debris.

Then teams of elephants would go to work, guided by their handlers, their *oo-sis* and *pe-sis*, butting, prodding, levering with their trunks. Belts of wooden rollers would be laid on the ground, and quick-fingered *pa-kyeiks*, specialised in the tying of chains, would dart between the elephants' legs, fastening steel harnesses. When finally the logs began to move such was the friction of their passage that water-carriers would have to run beside them, dousing the smoking rollers with tilted buckets.

Dragged to the banks of chaungs, the logs were piled into stacks and left to await the day when the chaungs would awaken from the hibernation of the hot season. With the first rains, the puddles along the streams' beds would stir and stretch and join hands, rising slowly to the task of clearing away the debris accumulated over the long months of dessication. Then, in a matter of days, with the rains pouring down, they would rear up in their beds, growing hundreds-fold in height: where a week before they had wilted under the weight of twigs and leaves, they would now throw two-ton logs downstream like feathered darts.

Thus would begin the logs' journey to the timberyards of Rangoon: with elephants nudging them over the slopes into the frothing waters of the chaungs below. Following the lie of the land they would make their way from feeder-streams to tributaries, until they debouched finally into the engorged rivers of the plains.

In years of bad rain, when the chaungs were too feeble to heft these great weights, the timber companies' profits plummeted. But even in good years they were jealous, punishing taskmasters – these mountain streams. At the height of the season a single snagged tree could result in a pile-up of five thousand logs or even more. The servicing of these white waters was a science unto itself, with its own cadre of adepts, special teams of oo-sis and elephants who spent the monsoon months ceaselessly patrolling the forest: these were the famed *aunging* herds, skilled in the difficult and dangerous arts of clearing chaungs.

Once, while sheltering beside a dying and girdled trunk of teak, Saya John gave Rajkumar a mint leaf to hold in one hand and a fallen leaf from the tree in the other. Feel them, he said, rub them between your fingers.

Teak is a relative of mint, *tectona grandis*, born of the same genus of flowering plant, but of a distaff branch, presided over by that most soothing of herbs, verbena. It counts among its close kin many other fragrant and familiar herbs – sage, savoury, thyme, lavender, rosemary and most remarkably holy basil, with its many descendants, green and purple, smooth-leaved and coarse, pungent and fragrant, bitter and sweet.

There was a teak tree in Pegu once, with a trunk that measured one hundred and six feet from the ground to its first branch. Imagine what a mint's leaf would be like if it were to grow upon a plant that rose more than a hundred feet into the air, straight up from the ground, without tapering or deviation, its stem as straight as a plumb-line, its first leaves appearing almost at the top, clustered close together and outspread, like the hands of a surfacing diver.

The mint leaf was the size of Rajkumar's thumb while the other would have covered an elephant's footprint; one was a weed that served to flavour soup while the other came from a tree that had felled dynasties, caused invasions, created fortunes, brought a new way of life into being. Yet even Rajkumar, who was in no way inclined to indulge the far-fetched or the fanciful, had to admit that between the faint hairiness of the one and the bristling, coarse-textured fur of the other, there was an unmistakable kinship, a palpably familial link.

It was by the bells of their elephants that teak camps made themselves known. Even when muted by rain or distance, the sound could always be counted on to produce a magical effect on a line of porters, lengthening their pace and freshening their step.

No matter how long he had walked or how tired he was Rajkumar would feel a surging in his heart when a camp loomed suddenly into view – a forest clearing with a few thatch-roofed huts clustered around a *tai*, an elongated wooden house on stilts.

Teak camps were always the same and yet they were all different, no two camps ever being built in the same place, from one season to the next. The initial felling of the forest was done by elephants with the result that the clearings were invariably scarred with upturned trees and ragged pits.

A tai stood at the centre of each campsite and it was occupied always by the forest Assistant, the company officer in charge of the camp. To Rajkumar's eye these tais were structures of incomparable elegance: they were built on wooden platforms, raised some six feet off the ground on teakwood posts. Each was endowed with several large rooms, one leading into another, and ending finally in a wide veranda, always so oriented as to command the best possible view. In a camp where the forest Assistant was served by an industrious *luga-lei*, the veranda of the *tai* would be sheltered by a canopy of flowering vines, with blooms that glowed like embers against the bamboo matting. Here would sit the Assistant of an evening, with a glass of whisky in one hand and a pipe in another, watching the sun go down across the valley and dreaming of his faraway Home.

They were distant, brooding men, these Assistants. Before going to see them Saya John would always change into European clothes, a white shirt, duck trousers. Rajkumar would watch from a distance as Saya John approached the tai to call out a greeting, with one hand resting deferentially on the bottom rung of the ladder. If invited up he would climb the ladder slowly, placing one foot carefully after the other. There would follow a flurry of smiles, bows, greetings. Sometimes he would be back in a matter of minutes; sometimes the Assistant would offer him a whisky and ask him to stay to dinner.

As a rule the Assistants were always very correct in their manner. But there was a time once when an Assistant began to berate Saya John, accusing him of having forgotten something he had ordered. 'Take that grinning face out of here . . . ,' the Englishman shouted, 'I'll see you in hell, Johnny Chinaman.'

At the time Rajkumar knew very little English but there was no mistaking the anger and contempt in the Assistant's voice. For an instant Rajkumar saw Saya John through the Assistant's eyes: small, eccentric and erratically dressed, in his ill-fitting European clothes, his portliness accentuated by the patched duck trousers that hung in thick folds around his ankles, with his scuffed sola topee perched precariously on his head.

Rajkumar had been in Saya John's service three years and had come to look up to him as his guide in all things. He found himself growing hot with indignation on his mentor's behalf. He ran across the clearing to the tai, fully intending to haul himself up the ladder to confront the Assistant on his own veranda.

But just then Saya John came hurrying down, grim-faced and sombre.

'Sayagyi! Shall I go up . . . ?'

'Go up where?'

'To the tai. To show that bastard . . .'

'Don't be a fool, Rajkumar. Go and find something useful to do.' With a snort of annoyance, Saya John turned his back on Rajkumar.

They were staying the night with the *hsin-ouq*, the leader of the camp's oo-sis. The huts where the timbermen lived were well to the rear of the tai, so placed as not to interrupt the Assistant's view. These structures were small, stilt-supported dwellings of one or two rooms, each with a balcony-like platform in front. The oo-sis built the huts with their own hands, and while they were living in a camp, they would tend the site with the greatest diligence, daily repairing rents in the bamboo screens, patching the thatch and building shrines to their *nats*. Often they would plant small, neatly fenced plots of vegetables around their huts, to eke out the dry rations sent up from the plains. Some would rear chickens or pigs between the stilts of their huts; others would dam nearby streams and stock them with fish.

As a result of this husbandry teak camps often had the appearance of small mountain villages, with family dwellings clustered in a semi-circle behind a headman's house. But this was deceptive for these were strictly temporary settlements. It took a team of oo-sis just a day or two to build a camp, using nothing but vines, freshly-cut bamboo and plaited cane. At the end of the season, the camp was abandoned to the jungle, only to be conjured up again the next year, at another location.

At every camp it was the hsin-ouq who was assigned the largest hut, and it was in these that Saya John and Rajkumar usually stayed. Often when they were at camp, Saya John and Rajkumar would sit on the huts' balconies, talking late into the night. Saya John would smoke cheroots and reminisce – about his life in Malaya and Singapore and his dead wife.

The night when Saya John was berated by the Assistant, Rajkumar lay awake a long time, staring at the flickering lights of the tai. Despite Saya John's admonitions, he could not put aside his indignation at the Assistant's behaviour.

Just as he was drifting off to sleep, Rajkumar heard someone crawling out to the balcony. It was Saya John, armed with a box of matches and a cheroot. Rajkumar was suddenly awake again and just as angry as he had been earlier in the evening.

'Sayagyi,' Rajkumar blurted out, 'why didn't you say something when that man was shouting like that? I was so angry that I wanted to go up to the tai to teach him a lesson.'

Saya John glanced across the clearing to the Assistant's tai, where a light was still shining. The Assistant's silhouette was clearly visible, outlined against the thin cane walls; he was seated in a chair, reading a book.

'You have no business to be angry, Rajkumar. In his place you would be no different, perhaps worse. What amazes me is that more of them are not like this one.'

'Why, Sayagyi?'

'Think of the kind of life they lead here, these young Europeans. They have at best two or three years in the jungle before malaria or dengue fever weaken them to the point where they cannot afford to be far from doctors and hospitals. The company knows this very well; it knows that within a few years these men will be prematurely aged, old at twenty-one; and that they will have to be posted off to city offices. It is only when they are freshly arrived, seventeen or eighteen, that they can lead this life, and during those few years the company must derive such profit from them as it can. So they send them from camp to camp for months on end with scarcely a break in between. Look at this one: I am told he has already had a bad bout of dengue fever. That man is not much older than you, Rajkumar – maybe eighteen or nineteen – and here he is, sick and alone, thousands of miles from home, surrounded by people the likes of whom he has never known, deep inside a forest. And look at him: there he is, reading his book, with not a trace of fear on his face.'

'You are far from home too, Sayagyi,' said Rajkumar. 'And so am I.'

'But we are not so far as he is. And left to ourselves none of us would have been here, harvesting the bounty of this forest. Look at the oo-sis in this camp; look at the hsin-ouq, lying on his mat, dazed with opium; look at the false pride they have in their skill as trainers of elephants. They think, because their fathers and their families have all worked with elephants, that no one knows their animals as they do. Yet until the Europeans came none of them had ever thought of using elephants for the purposes of logging. Their elephants were used only in pagodas and palaces, for wars and ceremonies. It was the Europeans who saw that tame elephants could be made to work for human profit. It was they who invented everything we see around us in this logging camp. This entire way of life is their creation. It was they who thought of these methods of girdling trees, these ways of moving logs with elephants, this system of floating them downriver. Even such

74

details as the structure and placement of these huts, the plan of the tai, the use of bamboo thatch and rattan – it was not the oo-sis with their hoary wisdom who thought of these things. All of this came from the minds of men like this one sitting in this tai – this boy who is not much older than you.'

The merchant thrust a finger at the silhouetted figure in the tai. 'You see that man, Rajkumar?' he said. 'That is someone you can learn from. To bend the work of nature to your will; to make the trees of the earth useful to human beings – what could be more admirable, more exciting than this? That is what I would say to any boy who has his life before him.'

Rajkumar could tell that Saya John was thinking not of him, his luga-lei, but of Matthew, his absent son, and the realisation bought a sudden and startling pang of grief. But the pain lasted only an instant and when it had faded Rajkumar felt himself to be very much the stronger, better prepared. He was here, after all, in this camp – while Matthew was far away in Singapore.

Seven

In Ratnagiri there were many who believed that King Thebaw was always the first to know when the sea had claimed a victim. He spent hours on his balcony every day, gazing out to sea with his gold-rimmed glasses. Fishermen had learnt to recognise the distinctive twin flashes of the King's binoculars. Returning to the bay, of an evening, they would look up in the direction of the hilltop balcony, as though for reassurance. Nothing happened in Ratnagiri, people said, but the King was the first to know of it.

Yet, the King himself was never seen after that first day when he rode up from the harbour with his family. The royal coaches were a familiar sight around town, with their teams of dappled horses and their moustachioed coachman. But the King never went out in them, or if he did, it was impossible to tell. The Royal Family had two *gaaris* – one an open trap and the other a brougham with curtained windows. There were rumours that the King was sometimes hidden inside the brougham, but no one could be sure because of the heavy velvet curtains.

The Princesses, on the other hand, were seen around town three or four times every year, driving down to the Mandvi jetty or to the Bhagavati temple, or to the houses of those British officials whom they were permitted to visit. The townsfolk knew them all by sight – the First, Second, Third and Fourth Princesses (the last was born in Ratnagiri, in the second year of the King's exile).

In their early years in India, the Princesses usually dressed in Burmese clothes – aingyis and htameins. But as the years passed their garments changed. One day, no one quite remembered when, they appeared in saris – not expensive or sumptuous saris, but the simple green and red cottons of the district. They began to wear their hair braided and oiled like Ratnagiri schoolgirls; they learned to speak Marathi and Hindustani as fluently as any of the townsfolk – it was only with their parents that they now spoke Burmese. They were pleasant-looking girls and there was something about them that was very direct and unaffected. When they drove through the streets they neither averted their gaze nor looked away. There was a hunger in their eyes, a longing, as though they yearned to know what it was like to walk through the Jhinjhinaka bazaar, to dawdle at the shops and bargain for saris. They sat alert and upright, taking everything in, and occasionally asking questions of the coachman: Whose sari shop is that? What sort of mangoes are those on that tree? What kind of fish is that hanging in that stall over there?

Mohan Sawant, the coachman, was a local boy, from an impoverished hamlet down by the river. He had dozens of relatives in town, working as rickshaw-pullers, coolies and tonga-wallahs: everyone knew him.

When he came down to the bazaar, people would seek him out: 'Give the Second Princess these mangoes. They're alphonsos from our garden.' 'Give the little girl a handful of this dried kokum. I saw her asking you about it.'

The Princesses' eyes touched everyone they lit upon. They were children: what had they done that they should live like this? Why should they be prevented from visiting local families; from forming friendships with Marathi children of good education? Why should they grow to womanhood never knowing any company other than that of their servants?

Once or twice a year the Queen would ride out with her daughters, her face a white mask, stern and unmoving, her lips stained a deep, deathly mauve by her cheroots. People would crowd into the streets to look at her as she rode by, but she never seemed to notice anyone or anything, sitting as straight as a rod, her face stern and unmoving.

And then there was Miss Dolly, with her long, black hair and her chiselled face, as beautiful as a fairytale princess. Over the years, all the others who had accompanied the Royal Family to

77

Ratnagiri had drifted slowly away – the maidservants and royal relatives and household officials. Only Miss Dolly stayed.

The King knew what people said of him in Ratnagiri, and if he was alarmed by the powers attributed to him, he was also amused and not a little flattered. In small ways he tried to do his duty by the role that had been thrust on him. Sometimes women would stand on their roofs, holding high their newborn children in the hope of attracting the imagined benedictions of his gaze. He would keep his glasses trained on these credulous mothers for several minutes at a time. It seemed a very small thing to ask for and why should he not grant those things that were in his power to give?

And the fact was that not everything that was said about him was untrue. The matter of the boatmen, for example: every day, when he stepped on the balcony at dawn, he would see the square white sails of the fishing fleet pasted across the bay like a string of stamps. The boats were *horis*, deep-hulled catamarans with single outriggers, from the fishing village of Karla at the mouth of the river. In the evenings, with the sun growing ever larger as it dipped towards the horizon, he would see the same boats tacking before the wind as they slipped into the bay. He was never aware of counting the boats that set sail in the morning, but somehow he always knew exactly how many there were. One day, when the catamarans were far out to sea, he saw a sudden squall sweeping down on them. That evening, when the fleet was straggling back, he could tell that the number wasn't right, that one was missing.

The King sent for Sawant: he knew that the fishing village was not far from the hamlet where the boy's family lived. Sawant was not yet a coachman at this time: he was fourteen and still just a syce, a groom.

'Sawant,' said the King, 'there was a storm at sea.' He explained what had happened. Sawant went hurrying down the hillside, and the news reached the fishing village before the boats were home. Thus began the legend of Ratnagiri's watchful king.

From the vantage point of his balcony, the King had the best seaward view of anyone in the district: it was only natural that he should see certain things before others. Down on the bay, not far from the jetty, there stood a small boathouse, a thatched shed adjoining a godown. There was a story attached to the boathouse. It was said that a British general, Lord Lake, had once ridden into Ratnagiri, with a unit of crack troops known as the Royal Battalion. This was after a long campaign in which several native rulers had been put to rout. His Lordship was in high spirits and one night, after a long evening of merry-making, he'd organised a boat-race for his officers. Boats had been commandeered from the local fisherfolk and the officers of the Royal Battalion had gone wallowing across the bay in canoes and dug-outs, paddling furiously, cheered on by their soldiers. According to legend, His Lordship had won by a full length.

Subsequently it had become something of a tradition among the officialdom of Ratnagiri to go sculling on the bay. Other stations in India afforded diversions such as pigsticking and polo: the bay was Ratnagiri's sole offering. Over the years the boathouse had acquired its own small pantheon of rowing heroes and sailing legends. The best-known of these concerned one Mr Gibb, a rowing blue from Cambridge and a district official of great repute. Mr Gibb was so expert an oarsman that he had been known to steer his long, slim racing shell through the bay's narrow and turbulent channel, out into the open sea. It was the King who had observed the first performance of this amazing feat; it was through him that Ratnagiri had come to learn of it.

It was to the King too that the inhabitants of Ratnagiri looked for reliable information on the coming of the monsoons. One morning each year he would wake to see a faint but unmistakable deepening in the colour of the line that bisected his window. That smudge on the horizon, as fine as a line of antimony on an eyelid, would grow quickly into a moving wall of rain. Perched high on the hill, Outram House would mark the monsoon's first landfall; rain would come smashing into the balcony; it would seep under the door and through the cracks in the shuttered windows, gathering inches deep under the King's bed.

'Sawant! The rains are here. Quick. Seal the shutters, put out the buckets and take everything off the floor.'

Within minutes the news would flow down the hillside. 'The

King has seen the rains.' There would be a great stir below; grand-mothers would rush to remove their pickles from the sun, and children would run cheering from their houses.

It was the King also who was the first to spot the steamers when they headed into the bay. In Ratnagiri, it was the comings and goings of these vessels that marked the passage of time, much as cannon-shots and clock-towers did in other district towns. On mornings when a steamer was expected people would congregate in large numbers at the Mandvi jetty. Fishing boats would slip into the bay at dawn, with cargoes of dried fish. Traders would ride in on ox-carts that were loaded with pepper and rice.

No one awaited the steamers' arrival more impatiently than King Thebaw. Despite warnings from the doctor he had not been able to curb his craving for pork. Since there was none to be had in Ratnagiri, consignments of bacon and ham were shipped to him every week from Bombay; from Goa came spicy Portuguese *choriço* sausages, peppered with chillies.

The King tried, as best he could, to battle this unseemly longing. He thought often of his distant predecessor, King Narathihapati of Burma, famously a glutton for pork. For the infamy of aban-doning his capital to the armies of Kubilai Khan, Narathihapati had earned the immortally shameful title 'The King who ran away from the Chinese'. His own wife and son had handed him the poison that was to end his life. A love of pork was not a good portent in a king.

The King usually spotted the steamer when it was still far out to sea, an hour or so from the jetty. 'Sawant! The boat!' Within minutes the coachman would be on his way, in the brougham.

The carriage became the steamer's harbinger. No longer did people have to wait all day on the jetty: the brougham's descent gave them ample warning of the steamer's arrival. In this way, the burden of marking the days passed slowly from the steamers to the black coach with the peacock crest: it was as though time itself had passed into Thebaw's keeping. Unseen on his balcony Thebaw became the town's guardian spirit, a king again.

* * *

The year Dolly turned fifteen there was an outbreak of the plague along the coast. Ratnagiri was particularly hard hit. Fires burnt night and day in the crematorium. The streets emptied. Many people left town; others locked themselves into their houses.

Outram House was situated at a good distance from the sites of the outbreak, far enough from the principal centres of population to be safe from the contagion. But as terror spread through the district it became evident that this isolation was not without its own perils: Outram House found itself besieged by neglect. The bungalow had no sewerage and no water supply. The toilets had to be emptied daily of nightsoil, by sweepers; water had to be carried up in buckets, from a nearby stream. But with the outbreak of the plague, the sweepers stopped coming and the coolies' water-buckets lay upturned beside the kitchen.

It was Dolly who usually served as the intermediary between the compound's staff and the Royal Family. By default, over the years, more and more of the household's everyday duties had fallen on her. It was no easy job to deal with the scores of people who worked in the compound – the bearers, grooms, gardeners, ayahs, cooks. Even at the best of times Dolly had trouble finding servants and persuading them to stay. The trouble was that there was never enough money to pay their salaries. The King and Queen had sold almost everything they'd brought over from Mandalay: their treasure was gone, all except for a few keepsakes and mementos.

Now, with the town stilled by the fear of disease, Dolly had a taste of what it would mean to manage the house without help. By the end of the first day, the toilets were giving off an unbearable stench, the tanks were running empty and there was no water with which to wash or bathe.

The only servants who remained were the half-dozen who lived on the estate, Sawant among them. Sawant had risen quickly from the position of syce to that of coachman and his stolidity and cheerfulness had conferred a certain authority on him, despite his youth. In moments of crisis, it was to him that everyone turned.

For the first couple of days, with Sawant's help, Dolly managed to make sure that the tanks in the Queen's bedroom were kept filled. But there was no water for the King and the toilets were very nearly unusable. Dolly appealed to Sawant, 'Do something, Mohanbhai, *kuchh to karo.*'

'Wait.'

Sawant found a solution: if the Queen were to allow the household's workers to build temporary shelters around the walls of the compound, then they too would be safe from the contagion. They would return and, what was more, they would always be on hand to do their jobs. No more would messengers have to run back and forth between the compound and the town, summoning this cook or that ayah; no more would there be any talk of quitting. They would become a self-contained little village, up on the hill.

Dolly gave his arm a grateful squeeze. 'Mohanbhai!' For the first time in days she felt able to breathe again. How dependable he was, always ready with a solution. What would they do without him?

But now, how to get the Queen's consent? She was always complaining about how small the compound was, how cramped, how much like a gaol. What would she say to the prospect of having the entire staff move up from town? But time was running out. Dolly went to the Queen's door. 'Mebya.'

'Yes?'

Dolly raised her head off the floor and sat back on her heels. 'The servants have stopped coming because of the sickness in town. In a day or two they will escape to the countryside. No one will remain in Ratnagiri. Soon there will be no water in the house. The toilets will run over. We will have to carry the filth down the hill ourselves. Mohanbhai says, why not let the others build a few rooms around the compound, beyond the walls? When the fear is past they will leave. This will solve everything.'

The Queen turned away from the kneeling girl to look out of the window. She too was weary of dealing with servants – wretches, ungrateful wretches, what else could you say of them? The more you gave them the more they seemed to want – yes, even the good ones, like this girl Dolly. No matter what they received there was always something else, some other demand – more clothes, another necklace. And as for the rest, the cooks and sweepers and ayahs, why did they seem harder to find with every passing year?

You had only to step outside to see thousands of people standing about, staring, with nothing better to do than loiter by the roadside. And yet when it came to finding servants you would think you were living in a world of ghosts.

And now, with this sickness spreading, they were sure to perish in their thousands. And what then? Those who were willing to work would become even rarer – like white elephants. Better have them move while there was still time. It was true what the girl said: it would be safer to have them on the hill, well away from town. Otherwise they might well carry disease into the compound. And there would be advantages to offset the unsightliness. They would be available to be called upon whenever necessary, night or day.

The Queen turned back to Dolly. 'I have decided. Let them build their shelters on the hill. Tell Sawant to let them know that they can go ahead.'

Within days a *basti* arose around the compound, a settlement of shacks and shanties. In the bathrooms of Outram House, water began to flow; the toilets were clean again. The settlers in the basti daily thanked the Queen. Now it was her turn to be deified: overnight she became a guardian goddess, a protector of the unfortunate, an incarnate *devi* who had rescued hundreds from the ravages of the plague.

After a month the outbreak subsided. There were some fifty families living around the compound now. They showed no signs of returning to their old homes in the congested lanes of the town: it was far nicer on the breezy hill. Dolly talked the matter over with the Queen and they decided to let the settlers stay. 'What if there's another epidemic?' the Queen said. 'After all, we don't know that it's really over yet.'

The Princesses were delighted to have the shacks remain: they had never had playmates their own age before. Now they had dozens. The First Princess was eight, the youngest three. They spent their days running around the compound with their new friends, discovering new games. When they were hungry they would run into their friends' shacks and ask for something to eat; in the afternoons, when it was too hot to play outside, they would fall asleep on the mud floors of the palm-thatched shanties.

Four years later there was another outbreak of the plague. More people moved up the hill. Just as Sawant had predicted, the basti around the compound became a little village in its own right, with winding lanes and corner shops. No longer did the dwellings consist solely of shacks and shanties: tiled houses began to appear, one by one. But the little settlement had no provisions for sewage and no other facilities. When the breeze turned, a smell of excrement and refuse engulfed Outram House, wafting up from the ravines on the far side of the bluff.

An English district official became concerned about the Princesses' education and arranged for the hiring of an English governess. Only one of the Princesses showed any aptitude for study, the youngest. It was she and Dolly who profited the most from the governess's stay. They both became quickly fluent in English and Dolly even began to paint with watercolours. But the governess didn't last long. She was so outraged by the conditions of the Royal Family's captivity, that she fell out with the local British officials. In the end she had to be sent back to England.

The Princesses were older now, and so were their playmates. Sometimes the boys would tweak the girls' pigtails and brush up close against them as they were running around the compound. It fell to Sawant to take on the role of their defender and champion. He would go storming off into the basti, only to return with bruises on his face and cuts on his lip. Dolly and the Princesses would gather round in silent awe: without asking they knew that his wounds had been acquired in their defence.

Sawant was by this time a tall, swarthy young man with a deep chest and a trimmed black moustache. He was not just a coachman now but a gatekeeper as well. In that capacity he had been allotted the guardroom beside the gate to use as his own. The room was small, with just a single window and a string bed, and its only adornment was a picture of the Buddha – a token of Sawant's conversion, under the King's influence.

In the normal course Sawant's room was forbidden to the girls, but they could scarcely stay away when he lay inside, nursing wounds that had been acquired on their behalf. They would find ways of slipping in, unnoticed, with plates of food and packets of sweets.

84

One hot July afternoon, entering Sawant's room on a household errand, Dolly found him asleep on his string bed. He was naked but for a white loincloth, a cotton *langot*, knotted between his legs. Seating herself beside him she watched his chest, undulating with his breath. Thinking to wake him she reached for his shoulder, but her hand dropped instead to his neck. His skin was slippery, covered with a thin film of moisture. She ran her forefinger down the centre of his chest, through the puddle of sweat that had gathered in the declivity, to the spiral pit of his navel. A line of fine hair snaked downwards, disappearing into the damp folds of his cotton langot. She touched the filaments with the tip of her finger, brushing them backwards, against their grain, pushing them erect. He stirred and opened his eyes. She felt his fingers on her face, tracing the shape of her nose, pushing ajar her lips, grazing the tip of her tongue, following the curve of her chin down to her throat. When he reached her neckline, she stopped his hand.

'No.'

'You touched me first,' he challenged her.

She had no answer. She sat still as he fumbled with her strings and clasps. Her breasts were small, late-developing, tipped with tiny, blooming nipples. There were prickly calluses on his coachman's hands, and the ridges of his palms scraped hard against the soft tips of her breasts. She put her hands on his sides and ran them down the cage of his ribs. A lock of hair came loose at her temple, and drops of sweat went circling down the strands, dripping slowly off the end, on to his lips.

'Dolly, you are the most beautiful girl in the world.'

Neither of them knew what to do. It seemed impossible that their limbs could be made to fit together. Their bodies slipped, fumbled, scraped. And then, suddenly, she felt the kindling of a great flame of pain between her legs. She cried out aloud.

He unrolled his cotton langot and dried her blood with it, swabbing it from her thighs. She took hold of one end of the cloth and wiped the red stains from his empurpled glans. He reached between her legs and patted her pubis clean. They sat back on their heels, facing each other, their knees thrust between each other's legs. He spread the wet, white cloth over their knitted limbs: the sunburst of her blood was flecked with the opacity of his semen. They stared at the vivid cloth in silent amazement: this was their handiwork, the banner of their union.

She returned the next day and for many days afterwards. Her bed was in a dressing room on the upper floor. In the adjoining bedroom slept the First Princess. Beside Dolly's bed there was a window, and outside, within easy reach, stood a mango tree. Dolly took to slipping out at night and climbing back before dawn.

One afternoon, in Sawant's room, they fell asleep, sweating on the damp string of his bed. Then a scream filled the room and they sprang awake. It was the First Princess, standing over them, eyes blazing, hands on hips. In the heat of her anger she was transformed from a twelve-year-old girl into a woman.

'I was wondering, and now I know.'

She ordered Dolly to dress, to leave the room. 'If I ever see you alone again together, I will go to Her Majesty. You are servants. You will be thrown out.'

Sawant, all but naked, fell to his knees, clasping his hands together. 'Princess, it was a mistake, a mistake. My family, they depend on me. Open your heart, Princess. It was a mistake. Never again.'

From that day on, the eyes of the First Princess followed them wherever they went. She told the Queen that she had seen a burglar climbing up the mango tree. The tree was cut down and bars were installed in the window frames.

It came to be decided that the Bombay newspapers would be delivered to Outram House, along with the King's shipments of pork. The first batch was found to carry reports on a subject of absorbing interest: a narrative of the European tour of King Chula-langkorn of Siam. This was the first time an Asian monarch had travelled to Europe on a state visit. The tour lasted several weeks and through that time no other interest existed for King Thebaw.

In London King Chulalangkorn stayed at Buckingham Palace. He was welcomed into Austria by the Emperor Franz Joseph; befriended in Copenhagen by the King of Denmark; feted in Paris by the President of France. In Germany Kaiser Wilhelm stood waiting at a railway station until his train rolled in. King Thebaw read the reports over and over again, until he knew them by heart.

It was not so long ago that Thebaw's great-grandfather, Alaungpaya, and his grandfather, Bagyidaw, invaded Siam, crushed her armies, unseated her rulers, and sacked Ayutthaya, her premier city. In the aftermath, the defeated nobles had chosen a new ruler and Bangkok had become the country's new capital. It was because of the kings of Burma, because of Thebaw's ancestors, because of the Konbaung dynasty, that Siam had its present dynasty and its ruling king.

'When our ancestor, the great Alaungpaya, invaded Siam,' Thebaw said to his daughters one day, 'he sent a letter to the King of Ayutthaya. There was a copy in the Palace archives. This is what it said: *"There is no rival for our glory and our karma; to place you beside us is to compare the great Galon of Vishnu with a swallow; the sun with a firefly; the divine hamadryad of the heavens with an earthworm; Dhatarattha, the Hamsa king with a dung beetle."* That is what our ancestor said to the King of Siam. But now they sleep in Buckingham Palace while we lie buried in this dungheap.'

There was no denying the truth of this. With the passing of the years Outram House had grown ever more to resemble the surrounding slums. Tiles had blown away and had not been replaced. Plaster had crumbled from the walls, baring great swathes of brick. Branches of peepul had taken root in the cracks and grown quickly into sturdy young saplings. Inside, mildew had crept upwards from the floor until the walls looked as though they had been draped in black velvet. Decay had become the Queen's badge of defiance. 'The responsibility for the upkeep of this house is not ours,' she said. 'They chose this to be our gaol, let them look after it.'

Newly arrived Collectors sometimes talked of razing the basti and moving the servants back to town. The Queen would laugh: how besotted they were, these men, in their arrogance, to imagine that in such a land as India they could hold a family imprisoned in isolation on a hill. Why the very soil would revolt against it!

The rare visitors who were allowed to call were shocked by the sight of the basti, the smell of waste and excrement, by the pall of woodsmoke that hung thick in the air. Often they descended from their carriages with looks of stunned surprise on their faces, unable to believe that the residence of Burma's last King had become the nucleus of a shantytown.

The Queen greeted them with her proud, thin-lipped smile. Yes, look around you, look at how we live. Yes, we who ruled the richest land in Asia are now reduced to this. This is what they have done to us, this is what they will do to all of Burma. They took our kingdom, promising roads and railways and ports, but mark my words, this is how it will end. In a few decades the wealth will be gone – all the gems, the timber and the oil – and then they too will leave. In our golden Burma where no one ever went hungry and no one was too poor to write and read, all that will remain is destitution and ignorance, famine and despair. We were the first to be imprisoned in the name of their progress; millions more will follow. This is what awaits us all: this is how we will all end – as prisoners, in shantytowns born of the plague. A hundred years hence you will read the indictment of Europe's greed in the difference between the kingdom of Siam and the state of our own enslaved realm.

Eight

The Irrawaddy was not the only waterway that Saya John used. His work often took him farther east, down the Sittang river and into the Shan highlands. A day's journey inland from the river-bank town of Pyinmana, there stood a village called Huay Zedi. Many years before, when the teak companies first started to explore this stretch of forest, Huay Zedi was itself a temporary teak camp like any other. But with the passing of the years the annual camps had migrated higher and higher up the slopes so that the business of providing them with supplies had become increasingly difficult. In time, because of the advantages of its location, on the sloping hinge where the mountains joined the plain, Huay Zedi became a kind of roadhead for the highlands. Many of the loggers and elephant trainers who accompanied the company into that previously unpopulated region chose to settle in and around this village.

Very few of the oo-sis, pe-sis and pa-kyeiks who lived in Huay Zedi were Burman by origin: some were Karen, some Karenni, some Pa-O, some Padaung, some Kadu-Kanan; there were even a few families of Indian *mahouts*, elephant trainers from Koraput, in the eastern Ghats. The inhabitants of the village kept to them-selves and had little to do with plainspeople; Huay Zedi was a place that was entire unto itself, a part of the new cycle of life that had been brought into being by teak.

The village stood just above a sandy shelf where a chaung had strayed into a broad, meandering curve. The stream was shallow here, spread thin upon a pebbled bed, and through most of the year the water rose only to knee-height – a perfect depth for the villagers' children, who patrolled it through the day with small crossbows. The stream was filled with easy prey, silver-backed fish that circled in the shallows, dazed by the sudden change in the water's speed. The resident population of Huay Zedi was largely female: through most of the year the village's able-bodied males, from the age of twelve onwards, were away at one teak camp or another up on the slopes of the mountain.

The settlement was ringed with immense, straight-limbed trees, growing thickly together to form a towering wall of foliage. Hidden behind this wall were vast flocks of parakeets and troupes of monkeys and apes – white-faced langurs and copper-skinned rhesus. Even commonplace domestic sounds from the village – the scraping of a coconut-shell ladle on a metal pot, the squeaking wheel of a child's toy – were enough to send gales of alarm sweeping through the the dappled darkness: monkeys would flee in chattering retreat and birds would rise from the treetops in an undulating mass, like a wind-blown sheet.

The dwellings of Huay Zedi differed from those of teak camps only in height and size – in form and appearance they were otherwise very alike, being built of identical materials, woven bamboo and cane, each being similarly raised off the ground on shoulder-high teakwood posts. Only a few structures stood out prominently against the surrounding greenery: a timber bridge, a white-walled pagoda and a bamboo-thatched church topped by a painted teak-wood cross. This last was used by a fair number of Huay Zedi's residents, many of whom were of Karen and Karenni stock – people whose families had been converted by followers of the American Baptist missionary, the Reverend Adoniram Judson.

When passing through Huay Zedi, Saya John stayed usually with the matronly widow of a former hsin-ouq, a Karenni Christian, who ran a small shop from the vine-covered balcony of her tai. This lady had a son, Doh Say, who became one of Rajkumar's closest friends.

Doh Say was a couple of years older than Rajkumar, a shy, gangling youth with a broad, flat face and a cheroot-stub nose. When Rajkumar first met him, he was employed as a lowly *sin-pa-kyeik*, an assistance to a pa-kyeik, a handler of chains: these were the men who dealt with the harnessing of elephants and the towing of logs. Doh Say was too young and too inexperienced to be allowed to do any fastening himself: his job was simply to heft the heavy chains for his boss. But Doh Say was a hard and earnest worker and when Rajkumar and Saya John next returned they found him a pa-kyeik. A year later he was already a pe-si, or back-rider, working with an aunging herd, specialising in the clearing of streams.

At camp, Rajkumar would attach himself to Doh Say, following on his heels, occasionally making himself useful by lighting a fire or boiling a pot of water. It was from Doh Say that Rajkumar learnt to brew tea the way that oo-sis liked it, thick, bitter and acid, beginning with a pot that was already half stuffed with leaves and then replenishing it with more at every filling. In the evenings he would help Doh Say with the weaving of cane walls, and at night he would sit on the ladder of his hut, chewing betel and listening to the oo-sis' talk. At night the herd needed no tending. The elephants were hobbled with chain-link fetters and let loose to forage for themselves in the surrounding jungle.

It was lonely at the camp, and Doh Say would often talk about his sweetheart, Naw Da, a girl in her early teens, slender and blooming, dressed in a tasselled white tunic and a homespun longyi. They were to be married as soon as Doh Say was promoted to the rank of oo-si.

'And what about you?' Doh Say would ask. 'Is there a girl you're thinking of?'

Rajkumar usually shrugged this off, but once Doh Say persisted and he answered with a nod.

'Who is she?'

'Her name is Dolly.'

This was the first time that Rajkumar had spoken of her and it was so long ago now that he could scarcely recall what she'd looked like. She was just a child, and yet she had touched him like no one else and nothing before. In her wide eyes, saturated with fear, he had seen his own aloneness turned inside out, rendered visible, worn upon the skin.

'And where does she live?'

'In India I think. I don't know for sure.'

Doh Say scratched his chin. 'One day you'll have to go looking for her.'

Rajkumar laughed. 'It's very far.'

'You'll have to go. There is no other way.'

It was from Doh Say that Rajkumar learnt of the many guises in which death stalked the lives of oo-sis: the Russell's viper, the maverick log, the charge of the wild buffalo. Yet the worst of Doh Say's fears had to do not with these recognisable incarnations of death, but rather with one peculiarly vengeful form of it. This was anthrax, the most deadly of elephant diseases.

Anthrax was common in the forests of central Burma and epidemics were hard to prevent. The disease could lie dormant in grasslands for as long as thirty years. A trail or pathway, tranquil in appearance and judged to be safe after lying many years unused, could reveal itself suddenly to be a causeway to death. In its most virulent forms anthrax could kill an elephant in a matter of hours. A gigantic tusker, a full fifteen arms' length off the ground, could be feeding peacefully at dusk and yet be dead at dawn. An entire working herd of a hundred elephants could be lost within a few days. Mature tuskers were valued in many thousands of rupees and the cost of an epidemic was such as to make itself felt on the London Stock Exchange. Few were the insurers who would gamble against a disease such as this.

The word anthrax comes from the same root as anthracite, a variety of coal. When anthrax strikes human beings it shows itself first in small pimple-like inflammations. As these lesions grow little black dots become visible at their centres, tiny pustules, like powdered charcoal: thus the naming of the disease. When anthrax erupts on an elephant's hide the lesions develop a volcanic energy. They appear first on the animal's hindquarters; they are about the size of a human fist, reddish-brown in colour. They swell rapidly and in males, quickly encase the penis sheath.

The carbuncles are most numerous around the hindquarters and as they grow they have the effect of sealing the animal's anus. Elephants consume an enormous amount of fodder and must defecate constantly. The workings of their digestive systems do not stop with the onset of the disease; their intestines continue to produce dung after the excretory passage has been sealed, the unexpurgated fecal matter pushing explosively against the obstructed anal passage.

'The pain is so great,' said Doh Say, 'that a stricken elephant will attack anything in sight. It will uproot trees and batter down walls. The tamest cows will become maddened killers; the gentlest calves will turn upon their mothers.'

They were at a camp together once when an epidemic struck. Saya John and Rajkumar were staying, as was their custom, with the camp's hsin-ouq, a small, stooped man with a shoelace moustache. Late one evening Doh Say burst in to tell the hsin-ouq that an oo-si was missing: it was thought that he had been killed by his own elephant.

The hsin-ouq could make no sense of this. This elephant had been in its oo-si's care for some fifteen years and had not been known to cause trouble before. Yet just before his death the oo-si had led his mount away from the herd and shackled her to a tree. She was now standing guard over his corpse and would not let anyone approach. None of this was as it should have been. What had gone wrong? Late as it was, the hsin-ouq headed into the jungle, with Doh Say and a few others. Saya John and Rajkumar decided to go with them.

It so happened that the Assistant who was in charge of the camp was away for a couple of days, staying in the company's chummery in Prome. In his absence there were no firearms in the camp. The oo-sis were armed only with flaming torches and their customary weapons, spears and das.

Rajkumar heard the elephant from far away. The noise grew very loud as they approached. Often before Rajkumar had been amazed at the sheer volume of sound that a single elephant could produce: the trumpeting, the squeals, the flatulence, the crashing of saplings and undergrowth. But this was something other than the usual feeding-time racket: there was a note of pain that pierced through the other accustomed sounds.

They arrived on the scene to find that the elephant had cleared a large space around itself, flattening everything within reach. The

93

dead oo-si lay under a tree, battered and bloody, just a yard or two from the elephant's chain-shackled feet.

Saya John and Rajkumar watched from a distance as the hsin-ouq and his men circled around the angry cow, trying to determine what had gone wrong. Then the hsin-ouq gave a cry and raised his hand to point at the animal's rump. Dim though the torchlight was, Rajkumar could tell that there were swellings on the elephant's rear, an angry red in colour.

Immediately the hsin-ouq and his men turned around and plunged headlong into the forest, racing back the way they had come.

'Sayagyi, what is it? Why are they running?'

Saya John was hurrying through the undergrowth, trying to keep the oo-sis' torches in sight. 'Because of anthrax, Rajkumar.' Saya John flung the word breathlessly over his shoulder.

'What, Saya?'

'Anthrax.'

'But, Saya, why don't they try to rescue the corpse?'

'No one can approach the creature now for fear of contagion,' said Saya John. 'And in any case they have more pressing things to think of.'

'More pressing than their friend's body?'

'Very much more. They could lose everything – their animals, their jobs, their livelihood. The dead man gave up his life in an effort to keep this elephant from infecting the rest. They owe it to him to get the herd out of harm's way.'

Rajkumar had seen many epidemics come and go – typhoid, smallpox, cholera. He had even survived the outbreak that had killed his family: to him disease was a hazard rather than a danger, a threat that had to be lived with from day to day. He found it impossible to believe that the oo-sis would so easily abandon their comrade's corpse.

Rajkumar laughed. 'They ran as if a tiger was after them.'

At this Saya John, usually so equable and even-tempered, turned on him in a sudden fury. 'Be careful, Rajkumar.' Saya John's voice slowed. 'Anthrax is a plague and it was to punish pride that the Lord sent it down.'

His voice slowed and deepened as it always did when he was

quoting the Bible: *'And the Lord said unto Moses and unto Aaron, Take to you handfuls of ashes of the furnace, and let Moses sprinkle it toward the heaven in the sight of Pharaoh. And it shall become small dust in all the land of Egypt, and shall be a boil breaking forth with blains upon man, and upon beast, throughout all the land of Egypt.'*

Rajkumar could understand only a few words of this but the tone of Saya John's voice was enough to silence him.

They made their way back to camp to find that it had emptied. Doh Say and the others had departed with the evacuated herd. Only the hsin-ouq remained, to wait for the Assistant. Saya John decided to stay on in order to keep him company.

Early next morning they returned to the site of the accident. The infected elephant was quieter now than before, dazed by pain and weakened by its struggle with the disease. The swellings had grown to pineapple size and the elephant's hide had begun to crack and break apart. As the hours passed the lesions grew yet larger and the cracks deepened. Soon the pustules began to leak a whitish ooze. Within a short while the animal's hide was wet with discharge. Rivulets of blood-streaked pus began to drip to the ground. The soil around the animal's feet turned into sludge, churned with blood and ooze. Rajkumar could no longer bear to look. He vomited, bending over at the waist, hitching up his longyi.

'If that is what this sight has done to you, Rajkumar,' Saya John said, 'think of what it must mean to the oo-sis to watch their elephants perish in this way. These men care for these animals as though they were their own kin. But when anthrax reaches this stage the oo-sis can do nothing but look on as these great mountains of flesh dissolve before their eyes.'

The stricken elephant died in the early afternoon. Shortly afterwards the hsin-ouq and his men retrieved their comrade's body. Saya John and Rajkumar watched from a distance as the mangled corpse was carried into the camp.

'And they took ashes of the furnace,' Saya John said, softly, under his breath, *'and stood before Pharaoh; and Moses sprinkled it up toward heaven; and it became a boil breaking forth with blains upon man, and upon beast. And the magicians could not stand before Moses because*

of the boils; for the boil was upon the magicians, and upon all the Egyptians . . .'

Rajkumar was eager to be gone from the camp, sickened by the events of the last few days. But Saya John was proof against his entreaties. The hsin-ouq was an old friend, he said, and he would keep him company until the dead oo-si was buried and the ordeal ended.

In the ordinary course of things, the funeral would have been performed immediately after the body's retrieval. But because of the forest Assistant's absence, there arose an unforeseen hitch. It was the custom for the dead to be formally released from their earthly ties by the signing of a note. Nowhere was this rite more strictly observed than among oo-sis, who lived their lives in daily hazard of death. The dead man's note of release had still to be signed and only the Assistant, as his employer, could sign it. A messenger was dispatched to the Assistant. He was expected to return the next day with the signed note. It only remained to wait out the night.

By sunset the camp was all but deserted. Rajkumar and Saya John were among the few who remained. Rajkumar lay awake a long time on the hsin-ouq's balcony. At the centre of the camp's clearing, the tai was blazing with light. The Assistant's luga-lei had lit all his lamps and in the darkness of the jungle there was an eerie grandeur to the empty tai.

Late at night Saya John came out to the balcony to smoke a cheroot.

'Saya, why did the hsin-ouq have to wait so long for the funeral?' said Rajkumar on a note of complaint. 'What harm would have resulted, Saya, if he had buried the dead man today and kept the note for later?'

Saya John pulled hard on his cheroot, the tip glowing red on his glasses. He was so long silent that Rajkumar began to wonder whether he had heard the question. But just as he was about to repeat himself Saya John began to speak.

'I was at a camp once,' he said, 'when there was an unfortunate accident and an oo-si died. That camp was not far from this one, two days' walk at most, and its herds were in the charge of our host – this very hsin-ouq. The accident happened at the busiest time of year, towards the end of the rains. The season's work was nearing its close. There were just a few stacks left when a very large log fell askew across the banks of the chaung, blocking the chute that was being used to roll the stacked teak down to the stream. The log wedged itself between two stumps, in such a way as to bring everything to a halt: no other logs could be rolled down until this one was moved.

'The Assistant at that camp was a young man, perhaps nineteen or twenty years old, and his name, if I remember right, was McKay – McKay-*thakin* they called him. He had been in Burma only two years and this was his first season of running a camp on his own. The season had been long and hard and the rain had been pouring down for several months. McKay-thakin was proud of his new reponsibility and he had driven himself hard, spending the entire period of the monsoons in the camp, never giving himself any breaks, never going away for so much as one weekend. He had endured several bad bouts of fever. The attacks had so weakened him that on certain days he could not summon the strength to climb down from his tai. Now with the season drawing to a close, he had been promised a month's leave, in the cool comfort of the Maymyo hills. The company had told him that he was free to go as soon as the territory in his charge was cleared of all the logs that had been marked for extraction. With the day of his departure drawing close, McKay-thakin was growing ever more restless, driving his teams harder and harder. The work was very nearly completed when the accident happened.

'The jamming of the chute occurred at about nine in the morning – the time of day when the day's work draws to a close. The hsin-ouq was at hand and he immediately sent his pa-kyeiks down to harness the log with chains so that it could be towed away. But the log was lodged at such an awkward angle that the chains could not be properly attached. The hsin-ouq tried first to move it by harnessing it to a single, powerful bull, and when this did not succeed he brought in a team of two of his most reliable cows. But all these efforts were unavailing: the log would not budge.

97

Finally, McKay-thakin, growing impatient, ordered the hsin-ouq to send an elephant down the slope to butt free the obstinate log.

'The slope was very steep and after months of pounding from enormous logs, its surface was crumbling into powder. The hsin-ouq knew that it would be very dangerous for an oo-si to lead an elephant into terrain of such uncertain footing. But McKay-thakin was by now in an agony of impatience and, being the officer in charge, he prevailed. Against his will, the hsin-ouq summoned one of his men, a young oo-si who happened to be his nephew, his sister's son. The dangers of the task at hand were perfectly evident and the hsin-ouq knew that none of the other men would obey him if he were to order them to go down that slope. But his nephew was another matter. "Go down," said the hsin-ouq, "but be careful, and do not hesitate to turn back."

'The first part of the operation went well, but just as the log sprang free the young oo-si lost his footing and was stranded directly in the path of the rolling, two-ton log. The inevitable happened: he was crushed. His body was unscarred when it was recovered, but every bone in it was smashed, pulverised.

'This young oo-si, as it happened, was much loved, both by his peers and by his mount, a gentle and good-natured cow by the name of Shwe Doke. She had been trained in the company's aunging herds and had been in his charge for several years.

'Those who know them well claim to be able to detect many shades of emotion in elephants – anger, pleasure, jealousy, sorrow. Shwe Doke was utterly disconsolate at the loss of her handler. No less saddened was the hsin-ouq, who was quite crushed with guilt and self-reproach.

'But worse was still to come. That evening, after the body had been prepared for burial, the hsin-ouq took the customary letter of release to McKay-thakin and asked for his signature.

'By this time McKay-thakin was not in his right mind. He had emptied a bottle of whisky and his fever had returned. The hsin-ouq's entreaties made no impression on him. He was no longer capable of understanding what was being asked of him.

'In vain did the hsin-ouq explain that the interment could not be deferred, that the body would not keep, that the man must have his release before his last rites. He pleaded, he begged, in his desperation he even attempted to climb up the ladder and force his way into the tai. But McKay-thakin saw him coming and came striding out, with a glass in one hand and a heavy-bored hunting rifle in the other. Emptying one barrel into the sky, he shouted: "For pity's sake can you not leave me alone just this one night?"

'The hsin-ouq gave up and decided to go ahead with the burial. The dead man's body was interred as darkness was gathering.

'I was staying the night, as always, in the hsin-ouq's hut. We ate a sparse meal and afterwards I stepped outside to smoke a cheroot. Usually a camp is full and bustling at that time of day: from the kitchen there issues a great banging of tin plates and metal pots and the darkness is everywhere pierced by the glowing tips of cheroots, where the oo-sis sit beside their huts, savouring their last smoke of the day and chewing a final quid of betel. But now I saw, to my astonishment, that there was no one about; I could hear nothing but frogs and owls and the feathery flapping of great jungle moths. Absent also was that most familiar and reassuring of a camp's sounds, the tinkling of elephants' bells. Evidently, no sooner had the soil been tamped down on the dead man's grave than the other oo-sis had begun to flee the camp, taking their elephants with them.

'The only elephant that was still in the camp's vicinity was Shwe Doke, the dead man's mount. The hsin-ouq had taken charge of his nephew's riderless elephant after the accident. She was restless, he said, and nervous, frequently flapping her ears and clawing the air with the tip of her trunk. This was neither uncommon nor unexpected, for the elephant is, above all, a creature of habit and routine. So pronounced an upheaval as the absence of a long-familiar handler can put even the gentlest of elephants out of temper, often dangerously so.

'This being the case, the hsin-ouq had decided not to allow Shwe Doke to forage through the night, as was the rule. Instead he had led her to a clearing, some half-mile's distance from the camp and supplied her with a great pile of succulent treetop branches. Then he had tethered her securely between two immense and immovable trees. To be doubly sure of keeping her bound he had used, not the usual lightweight fetters with which elephants are shackled at night, but the heavy iron towing chains

99

that are employed in the harnessing of logs. This, he said, was a precaution.

'"A precaution against what?" I asked. By this time his eyes were dulled by opium. He gave me a sidelong glance and said, in a soft, slippery voice: "Just a precaution."

'There now remained in the camp only the hsin-ouq and me and of course, McKay-thakin in his tai. The tai was brightly lit, with lamps shining in all its windows, and it seemed very high, perched on its tall, teakwood stilts. The hsin-ouq's hut was small in comparison and much closer to the ground, so that standing on its platform I had to tilt my head back to look up at McKay-thakin's glowing windows. As I sat staring, a low, reedy wail came wafting out of the lamplit windows. It was the sound of a clarinet, an instrument the thakin sometimes played of an evening to while away the time. How strange it was to hear that plaintive, melancholy music issuing forth from those shining windows, the notes hanging in the air until they became indistinguishable from the jungle's nightly noise. Just so, I thought, must a great liner look to the oarsmen of a palm-trunk canoe as it bears down on them out of the night, with the sounds of its ballroom trailing in its wake.

'It had not rained much through the day, but with the approach of evening clouds had begun to mass in the sky, and by the time I blew my lamp out and rolled out my mat there was not a star to be seen. Soon the storm broke. Rain came pouring down and thunder went pealing back and forth across the valleys, echoing between the slopes. I had been asleep perhaps an hour or two when I was woken by a trickle of water, leaking through the bamboo roof. Rising to move my mat to a dry corner of the hut, I happened to glance across the camp. Suddenly the tai sprang out of the darkness, illuminated by a flash of lightning: its lamps had gone out.

'I was almost asleep again when, through the chatter of the rain I heard a tiny, fragile sound, a distant tinkling. It was far away but approaching steadily, and as it drew nearer I recognised the unmistakable ringing of an elephant's bell. Soon, in the subtle tensing of the hut's bamboo beams, I could feel the animal's heavy, hurrying tread.

'"Do you hear that?" I whispered to the hsin-ouq. "What is it?"

'"It is the cow, Shwe Doke."

'An oo-si knows an elephant by its bell: it is by following that sound that he locates his mount every morning after its night-long foraging in the forest. To do his job well a hsin-ouq must know the sound of every animal in his herd; he must, if the need arises, be able to determine the position of all his elephants simply by concentrating on the ringing of their bells. My host was a hsin-ouq of great ability and experience. There was not, I knew, the slightest likelihood of his being mistaken in his identification of the approaching bell.

'"Perhaps," I ventured, "Shwe Doke was panicked by the storm; perhaps she managed to break loose of her fetters."

'"If she had broken loose," the hsin-ouq said, "the chains would still be dragging on her feet." He paused to listen. "But I hear no chains. No. She has been freed by a human hand."

'"But whose could that hand be?" I asked.

'He silenced me abruptly, with a raised hand. The bell was very close now and the hut was shivering to the elephant's tread.

'I started to move towards the ladder but the hsin-ouq pulled me back. "No," he said. "Stay here."

'The next moment the sky was split by lightning. In the momentary glare of that flat sheet of light, I saw Shwe Doke, directly ahead, moving towards the tai, with her head lowered and her trunk curled under her lip.

'I jumped to my feet and began to shout in warning: "Thakin; McKay-thakin . . ."

'McKay-thakin had already heard the bells, felt the tremor of the elephant's approaching weight. A flame flickered in one of the tai's windows and the young man appeared on the veranda, naked, with a lantern in one hand and his hunting rifle in the other.

'Ten feet from the tai Shwe Doke came to a standstill. She lowered her head as though she were examining the structure. She was an old elephant, trained in the ways of the aunging herd. Such animals are skilled in the arts of demolition. It takes them no more than a glance to size up a dam of snagged wood and pick a point of attack.

101

'McKay-thakin fired just as Shwe Doke began her charge. She was so close now that he could not miss: he hit her exactly where he had aimed, in her most vulnerable spot, between ear and eye.

'But the momentum of Shwe Doke's charge carried her forward even as she was dying on her feet. She too hit the tai exactly where she had aimed, at the junction of the two cross-beams that held it together. The structure appeared to explode, with logs and beams and thatch flying into the air. McKay-thakin was catapulted to the ground, over Shwe Doke's head.

'Such is the footwork of the skilled aunging elephant that it can balance its weight on the lip of a waterfall, perch like a crane upon a small mid-stream boulder, turn in a space that would trip a mule. It was with those small, practised steps that Shwe Doke turned now, until she was facing the Assistant's prone body. Then, very slowly, she allowed her dying weight to go crashing down on him, head first, her weight rolling over in a circular motion, in a technically perfect execution of the butting manoeuvre of the aunging elephant – an application of thrust so precise as to be able to cause a ten-thousand-ton tangle of teak to spring undone like a sailor's knot. McKay-thakin's lantern, which had been sputtering beside him, went out and we could see nothing more.

'I threw myself down the hut's ladder with the hsin-ouq close behind me. Running towards the tai I stumbled in the darkness and fell, face first on the mud. The hsin-ouq was helping me up when a bolt of lightning split the sky. Suddenly he let go of my hand and unloosed a hoarse, stammering shout.

'"What is it?" I cried. "What did you see?"

'"Look! Look down at the ground."

'Lightning flashed again and I saw, directly ahead of me, the huge scalloped mark of Shwe Doke's feet. But beside it was a smaller impression, curiously shapeless, almost oblong.

'"What is it?" I said. "What made that mark?"

'"It is a footprint," he said, "human, although crushed and mangled almost beyond recognition."

'I froze and stayed exactly where I was, praying for another bolt of lightning so that I would be able to ascertain for myself

102

the truth of what he had said. I waited and waited but an age seemed to pass before the heavens lit up again. And in the meanwhile it had rained so hard that the marks on the ground had melted away.'

Nine

In 1905, the nineteenth year of the King's exile, a new District Collector arrived in Ratnagiri. The Collector was the district's administrative head, the official who was ultimately responsible for dealing with the Burmese Royal Family. The job was an important one and the officials who were appointed to this post were almost always members of the Indian Civil Service – the august cadre of officials who administered Britain's Indian possessions. To join the Indian Civil Service candidates had to pass a difficult examination that was held in England. The overwhelming majority of those who qualified were British, but there were also among them a small number of Indians.

The Collector who arrived in 1905 was an Indian, a man by the name of Beni Prasad Dey. He was in his early forties, and an outsider to the Ratnagiri region: he was a Bengali from Calcutta, which lay diagonally across the map of India, at the other end of the country. Collector Dey was slim and aquiline, with a nose that ended in a sharp, beak-like point. He dressed in finely-cut Savile Row suits and wore gold-rimmed eyeglasses. He arrived in Ratnagiri accompanied by his wife, Uma, who was some fifteen years his junior, a tall, vigorous-looking woman, with thick, curly hair.

King Thebaw was watching from his balcony when Ratnagiri's officialdom gathered at the Mandvi jetty to receive the new Collector and his young wife. The first thing he noticed about them was that the new Madame Collector was dressed in an unusual garment. Puzzled, he handed his binoculars to the Queen. 'What's that she's wearing?'

The Queen took a long look. 'It's just a sari,' she said at last.

'But she's wearing it in the new style.' She explained that an Indian official had made up a new way of wearing a sari, with odds and ends borrowed from European costume – a petticoat, a blouse. She'd heard that women all over India were adopting the new style. But of course everything came late to Ratnagiri – she herself had never had an opportunity to look into this new fashion at first hand.

The Queen had seen many Collectors come and go, Indian and English; she thought of them as her enemies and gaolers, upstarts to be held in scant regard. But in this instance she was intrigued. 'I hope he'll bring his wife when he comes to call. It'll be interesting to see how this kind of sari is worn.'

Despite this propitious beginning the Royal Family's first meeting with the new Collector came close to ending in disaster. Collector Dey and his wife had arrived at a time when politics was much on people's minds. Every day there were reports of meetings, marches and petitions: people were being told to boycott British-made goods; women were making bonfires of Lancashire cloth. In the Far East there was the war between Russia and Japan and for the first time it looked as though an Asian country might prevail against a European power. The Indian papers were full of news of this war and what it would mean for colonized countries.

It was generally not the King's custom to meet with officials who came to Outram House. But he had been following the Russo-Japanese war very closely and was keen to know what people thought of it. When the new Collector and his wife came to call, the King's first words were about the war. 'Collector-sahib,' he said abruptly, 'have you seen the news? The Japanese have defeated the Russians in Siberia?'

The Collector bowed stiffly, from the waist. 'I have indeed seen reports, Your Highness,' he said. 'But I must confess that I do not believe this to be an event of any great significance.'

'Oh?' said the King. 'Well, I'm surprised to hear that.' He frowned, in a way that made it clear that he wasn't about to let the subject drop.

The night before Uma and the Collector had been briefed at length on their forthcoming visit to Outram House. They'd been told that the King was never present at these occasions: it was the Queen who would receive them, in the reception room on the ground floor. But they'd entered to find the King very much present: he was dressed in a crumpled longyi and was pacing the floor, smacking his thigh with a rolled-up newspaper. His face was pale and puffy, and his wispy grey hair was straggling unkempt down the back of his neck.

The Queen, on the other hand, was exactly where she was meant to be: sitting rigidly upright on a tall chair, with her back to the door. This, Uma knew, was a part of the set order of battle: visitors were expected to walk in and seat themselves on low chairs around Her Highness, with no words of greeting being uttered on either side. This was the Queen's way of preserving the spirit of Mandalay protocol: since the representatives of the British were adamant in their refusal to perform the shiko, she in turn made a point of not acknowledging their entry into her presence.

Uma had been told to be on her guard in the reception room, to look out for delinquent sacks of rice and stray bags of dal. This room was sometimes used as an auxiliary storeroom and several unwary visitors were known to have come to grief in its hidden pitfalls: it was not unusual to find heaps of chillies hidden under its sofas and jars of pickles stacked on its bookshelves. On one occasion a beefy superintendent of police had sat down heavily on the spiny remains of a dried fish. Another time, ambushed by a powerful whiff of pepper, a venerable old district judge had sneezed his false teeth clear across the room. They had fallen clattering at the Queen's feet.

These reception-room stories had caused Uma much apprehension, prompting her to secure her sari with an extravagant number of clips and safety-pins. But on entering the room she'd found its effects to be not at all as expected. Far from being put out, she felt oddly comforted by the familiar fragrances of rice and mung dal. In any other setting Queen Supayalat, with her mask-like face and mauve lips, would have seemed a spectral and terrifying figure. But the odours of domesticity seemed to soften her edges a little, adding an element of succour to her unyielding presence.

Across the room, the King was smacking his newspaper loudly

on his palm. 'Well, Collector-sahib,' he said, 'did you ever think that we would live to witness the day when an Eastern country would defeat a European power?'

Uma held her breath. Over the last few weeks the Collector had conducted many heated arguments on the implications of a Japanese victory over Russia. Some had ended in angry outbursts. She watched anxiously now as her husband cleared his throat.

'I am aware, Your Highness,' the Collector said evenly, 'that Japan's victory has resulted in widespread rejoicing among nationalists in India and no doubt in Burma too. But the Tsar's defeat comes as no surprise to anyone, and it holds no comfort for enemies of the British Empire. The Empire is today stronger than it has ever been. You have only to glance at a map of the world to see the truth of this.'

'But in time, Collector-sahib, everything changes. Nothing goes on for ever.'

The Collector's voice grew sharper. 'May I remind Your Highness that while Alexander the Great spent no more than a few months in the steppes of central Asia, the satrapies he founded persisted for centuries afterward? Britain's Empire is, by contrast, already more than a century old, and you may be certain, Your Highness, that its influence will persist for centuries more to come. The Empire's power is such as to be proof against all challenges and will remain so into the foreseeable future. I might take the liberty of pointing out, Your Highness, that you would not be here today if this had been pointed out to you twenty years before.'

The King flushed, staring speechlessly at the Collector. It fell to the Queen to answer for him. She leant forward, digging her long, sharp fingernails into the arms of her chair. 'That is enough, Mr Collector,' she said. 'Enough, *bas karo.*' There was a moment of stillness in which the only sound was that of the Queen's nails, raking the polished arms of her chair. The room seemed to shimmer as though the floor had given off a sudden haze of heat.

Uma was seated between Dolly and the Second Princess. She had listened to her husband's exchange with the King in dismayed silence, sitting frozen in her place. On the wall ahead of her was a small watercolour. The painting was a depiction of a landscape at sunrise, a stark red plain dotted with thousands of mist-wreathed pagodas. Suddenly, with a clap of her hands, Uma uttered a loud cry. 'Pagan!'

The word had the effect of an explosion in a confined space. Everyone jumped, turning to look in Uma's direction. She raised a hand to point. 'On the wall – it's a picture of Pagan, isn't it?'

The Second Princess was sitting next to Uma. She seized eagerly on this diversion. 'Yes – that is it. Dolly can tell you – she painted it.'

Uma turned to the slim upright woman on her left. Her name was Dolly Sein, she recalled: they had been introduced on the way in. Uma had noticed that there was something unusual about her, but she'd been too busy concentrating on protocol to give the matter any further thought.

'Did you really paint that?' Uma said. 'Why, it's wonderful.'

'Thank you,' Dolly said quietly. 'I copied it from a book of prints.' Their glances crossed and they exchanged a quick smile. Suddenly Uma knew what it was that she'd been struck by: this Miss Sein was perhaps the loveliest woman she'd ever set eyes on.

'Madame Collector,' the Queen tapped a knuckle on the arm of her chair, 'how did you know that was a picture of Pagan? Have you had occasion to visit Burma?'

'No,' Uma said regretfully. 'I wish I had but I haven't. I have an uncle in Rangoon and he once sent me a picture.'

'Oh?' The Queen nodded; she was impressed by the way the young woman had intervened to save the situation. Self-possession was a quality she'd always admired. There was something attractive about this woman, Uma Dey; the liveliness of her manner was a welcome contrast to her husband's arrogance. If not for her presence of mind she would have had to order the Collector out of the house and that could only have ended badly. No, this Mrs Dey had done well to speak when she did.

'We would like to ask you, Madame Collector,' the Queen said, 'what is your real name? We have never been able to accustom ourselves to your way of naming women after their fathers and husbands. We do not do this in Burma. Perhaps you would not object to telling us your own given name?'

'Uma Debi – but everyone calls me Uma.'

'Uma?' said the Queen. 'That is a name that is familiar to us. I must say, you speak Hindustani well, Uma.' There was a note of unfeigned appreciation in her voice. Both she and the King spoke Hindustani fluently and this was the language she preferred to use in her dealings with officials. She had found that her use of Hindustani usually put the Government's representatives at a disadvantage – especially the Indians. British civil servants often spoke Hindustani well and those who didn't had no qualms about answering in English. The Indians, on the other hand, were frequently Parsis or Bengalis, Mr Chatterjee this or Mr Dorabjee that, and they were rarely fluent in Hindustani. And unlike their British counterparts they were hesitant about switching languages; it seemed to embarrass them that the Queen of Burma could speak Hindustani better than they. They would stumble and stutter and within minutes she would have their tongues tied in knots.

'I learnt Hindustani as a child, Your Highness,' Uma said. 'We lived in Delhi for a while.'

'*Achha?* Well, now we would like to ask something else of you, Uma.' The Queen made a beckoning gesture. 'You may approach us.'

Uma went over to the Queen and lowered her head.

'Uma,' the Queen whispered, 'we would like to examine your garments.'

'Your Highness!'

'As you can see, my daughters wear their saris in the local style. But I prefer this new fashion. It is more elegant – the sari looks more like a htamein. Would it be too great an imposition to ask you to reveal the secrets of this new style to us?'

Uma was startled into laughter. 'I would be glad to, whenever you please.'

The Queen turned stiffly to the Collector. 'You, Collector-sahib, are no doubt impatient to be on your way to the Cutchery and the many pressing tasks that await you. But may I ask if you will permit your wife to remain with us a little longer?'

The Collector left, and in defiance of the initial auguries of disaster, the visit ended very amicably, with Uma spending the rest of the afternoon in Outram House, chatting with Dolly and the Princesses.

The Collector's house was known as the Residency. It was a large bungalow with a colonnaded portico and a steep, red-tiled roof. It stood on the crest of a hill, looking southward over the bay and the valley of the Kajali river. It was surrounded by a walled garden that stretched a long way down the slope, stopping just short of the river's gorge.

One morning Uma discovered a narrow entrance hidden behind a thicket of bamboo at the bottom of her garden. The gate was overgrown with weeds but she was able to open it just wide enough to squeeze through. Twenty feet beyond, a wooded out-crop jutted out over the valley of the Kajali river. There was a peepul at the lip of the gorge, a majestic old tree with a thick beard of aerial roots hanging from its gnarled grey branches. She could tell that goats came to graze there: the earth beneath the tree's canopy had been cropped clean of undergrowth. She could see trails of black droppings leading down the slope. The goatherds had built themselves a platform to sit on by heaping earth and stones around the peepul's trunk.

Uma was amazed by the view: the meandering river, the estu-ary, the curve of the bay, the windswept cliffs – she could see more of the valley from here than from the Residency on top of the hill. She returned the next day and the day after. The goat-herds came only at dawn and for the rest of the day the place was deserted. She took to slipping out of the house every morning, leaving the door of her bedroom shut, so that the servants would think she was still inside. She would sit in the peepul's deep shade for an hour or two with a book.

One morning Dolly surprised her by appearing unexpectedly out of the peepul's beard of hanging roots. She'd called to return some clothes that Uma had sent over to Outram House – petticoats and blouses, for the Princesses to have copied by their tailors. She'd waited in the drawing room of the Residency while the servants went looking for Uma. They'd looked everywhere before giving up: memsahib wasn't at home, they said, she must have slipped out for a walk.

'How did you know I was here?'

'Our coachman is related to yours.'

'Did Kanhoji tell you?' Kanhoji was the elderly coachman who drove Uma around town.

'Yes.'

'I wonder how he knew about my secret tree.'

'He said he'd heard about it from the herdsmen who bring their goats here in the morning. They're from his village.'

'Really?' Uma fell silent. It was odd to think that the goatherds were just as aware of her presence as she was of theirs. 'Well, the view's wonderful, don't you think?'

Dolly gave the valley a perfunctory glance. 'I've grown so used to it I never give it a thought any more.'

'I think it's amazing. I come here almost every day.'

'Every day?'

'Just for a bit.'

'I can see why you would.' She paused to look at Uma. 'It must be lonely for you here, in Ratnagiri. '

'Lonely?' Uma was taken aback. It hadn't occurred to her to use that word of herself. It was not as though she never met anyone, or that she was ever at a loss for things to do – the Collector made sure of that. Every Monday his office sent up a memorandum listing her engagements for the week – a municipal function, a sports day at a school, a prize-giving at the vocational college. She usually had only one appointment a day, not so many as to keep her uncomfortably busy nor so few as to make her days seem oppressively long. She went through the list carefully when it arrived at the beginning of the week, and then she put it on her dressing table, with a weight on it, so it wouldn't blow away. The thought of missing an appointment worried her, although there was little chance of that. The Collector's office was very good about sending reminders: a peon came up to the Residency about an hour before each new appointment to tell Kanhoji to bring the gaari round. She'd hear the horses standing under the porch; they'd snort and kick the gravel, and Kanhoji would click his tongue, tuk-tuk-tuk.

111

The nicest part of these appointments was the journey into town and back. There was a window between the coach and the driver's bench. Every few minutes Kanhoji would stick his tiny, wrinkled face into the window and tell her about the places around them – the Cutchery, the gaol, the college, the bazaars. There were times when she was tempted to get off so she could go into the bazaars and bargain with the fishwives. But she knew there would be a scandal; the Collector would come home and say: 'You should just have let me know so that I could have arranged some *bandobast*.' But the bandobast would have destroyed any pleasure she might have taken in the occasion: half the town would have gathered, with everyone falling over themselves to please the Collector. The shopkeepers would have handed over anything she so much as glanced at, and when she got home the bearers and the *khansama* would have sulked as though she'd dealt them a reproach.

'What about you, Dolly?' Uma said. 'Are you lonely here?'

'Me? I've lived here nearly twenty years, and this is home to me now.'

'Really?' It struck Uma that there was something almost incredible about the thought that a woman of such beauty and poise had spent most of her life in this small provincial district town.

'Do you remember anything of Burma?'

'I remember the Mandalay palace. Especially the walls.'

'Why the walls?'

'Many of them were lined with mirrors. There was a great hall called the Glass Palace. Everything there was of crystal and gold. You could see yourself everywhere if you lay on the floor.'

'And Rangoon? Do you remember Rangoon?'

'Our steamer anchored there for a couple of nights, but we weren't allowed into the city.'

'I have an uncle in Rangoon. He works for a bank. If I'd visited him I'd be able to tell you about it.'

Dolly turned her eyes on Uma's face. 'Do you think I want to know about Burma?'

'Don't you?'

'No. Not at all.'

'But you've been away so long.'

112

Dolly laughed. 'I think you're feeling a little sorry for me. Aren't you?'

'No,' Uma faltered. 'No.'

'There's no point in being sorry for me. I'm used to living in places with high walls. Mandalay wasn't much different. I don't really expect much else.'

'Do you ever think of going back?'

'Never.' Dolly's voice was emphatic. 'If I went to Burma now I would be a foreigner – they would call me a kalaa like they do Indians – a trespasser, an outsider from across the sea. I'd find that very hard, I think. I'd never be able to rid myself of the idea that I would have to leave again one day, just as I had to before. You would understand if you knew what it was like when we left.'

'Was it very terrible?'

'I don't remember much, which is a kind of mercy, I suppose. I see it in patches sometimes. It's like a scribble on a wall – no matter how many times you paint over it, a bit of it always comes through, but not enough to put together the whole.'

'What do you see?'

'Dust, torchlight, soldiers, crowds of people whose faces are invisible in the darkness . . .' Dolly shivered. 'I try not to think about it too much.'

After this, in what seemed like an impossibly short time, Dolly and Uma became close friends. At least once a week, and sometimes twice and even more, Dolly would come over to the Residency and they would spend the day together. Usually they stayed in, talking and reading, but from time to time Dolly would have an idea for an expedition. Kanhoji would drive them down to the sea or into the countryside. When the Collector was away touring the district, Dolly would stay over to keep Uma company. The Residency had several guest rooms and Uma assigned one of these exclusively to Dolly. They would sit up talking late into the night. Often they would wake up curled on one another's beds, having drifted off to sleep in mid-conversation.

One night, plucking up her courage, Uma remarked: 'One hears some awful things about Queen Supayalat.'

'What?'

'That she had a lot of people killed . . . in Mandalay.'

Dolly made no answer but Uma persisted. 'Doesn't it frighten you,' she said, 'to be living in the same house as someone like that?'

Dolly was quiet for a moment and Uma began to worry that she'd offended her. Then Dolly spoke up. 'You know, Uma,' she said in her softest voice. 'Every time I come to your house, I notice that picture you have, hanging by your front door . . .'

'Of Queen Victoria, you mean?'

'Yes.'

Uma was puzzled. 'What about it?'

'Don't you sometimes wonder how many people have been killed in Queen Victoria's name? It must be millions, wouldn't you say? I think I'd be frightened to live with one of those pictures.'

A few days later Uma took the picture down and sent it to the Cutchery, to be hung in the Collector's office.

Uma was twenty-six and had already been married five years. Dolly was a few years older. Uma began to worry: what was Dolly's future to be? Was she never to marry or have children? And what of the Princesses? The First Princess was twenty-three, the youngest eighteen. Were these girls to have nothing to look forward to but lifetimes of imprisonment?

'Why doesn't someone do something,' Uma said to the Collector, 'about arranging marriages for the girls?'

'It's not that no one's tried,' the Collector replied. 'It's the Queen who won't allow it.'

In his offices at the Cutchery, the Collector had found a thick file of correspondence chronicling his predecessors' attempts to deal with the question of the Princesses' futures. The girls were in the prime of their womanhood. If there were to be a scandal or an accident at Outram House the incumbent Collector would be held responsible: the Bombay secretariat had left no room for doubt on this score. In order to protect themselves, several previous Collectors had tried to find suitable grooms for the Princesses. One had even written to his colleagues in Rangoon, to make enquiries about eligible Burmese bachelors – only to learn that there were only sixteen such men in the whole country.

The custom of the ruling dynasties of Burma was to marry very closely within their houses. Only a man descended of Konbaung blood in both lines was eligible to marry into the Royal Family. It was the Queen who was to blame for the fact that there were now very few such pure-blooded princes left: it was she who had decimated her dynasty by massacring all of Thebaw's potential rivals. As for the few eligible men that there were, none found favour with the Queen. She announced that not a single one of them was a fit match for a true-born Konbaung Princess. She would not allow her daughters to defile their blood by marrying beneath themselves.

'But what about Dolly?' Uma said to the Collector. 'Dolly doesn't have to worry about finding a prince.'

'That's true,' said the Collector, 'but hers is an even stranger circumstance. She's spent her whole life in the company of the four Princesses. But she's also a dependant, a servant, of unknown family and origin. How would you set about finding a husband for her? Where would you start: here or in Burma?'

Uma had no answer for this. Neither she nor Dolly had ever broached the subject of marriage or children. With some of her other friends, Uma could talk of little else but of husbands, marriage, children – and of course, of remedies for her own childlessness. But with Dolly it was different: theirs was not the kind of friendship that was based on intimate disclosure and domesticity – quite the opposite. Both she and Dolly knew instinctively what could not be spoken of – Uma's efforts to conceive, Dolly's spinsterhood – and it was this that lent their meetings such an urgent wakefulness. When she was with Dolly, Uma felt as though a great burden had dropped from her mind, that she could look outside herself, instead of worrying about her own failings as a wife. Driving in the countryside for instance, she would marvel at the way in which people came running out of their houses to talk to Dolly, to hand her little odds and ends, fruits, a few vegetables, lengths of cloth. They would talk for a while, in Konkani, and when they were on their way again, Dolly would smile and say, in explanation, 'That woman's uncle [or brother or aunt]

115

used to work at Outram House.' Despite her shrugs of self-deprecation, Uma could tell that there was a depth to these connections that went far beyond the casual. Often Uma longed to know who exactly these people were and what they and Dolly were speaking of. But in these encounters it was she who was the outsider, the memsahib: to her, for once, fell the silence of exile.

Occasionally, when the crowds around them grew too large, Kanhoji would issue scoldings from his bench, telling the villagers to clear the way for the Collector's gaari, threatening to call the police. The women and children would glance at Uma; on recognizing the Collector's wife, their eyes would widen and they would shrink away.

'You see,' Dolly said once, laughing. 'The people of your country are more at home with prisoners than gaolers.'

'I'm not your gaoler.'

'What are you then?' Dolly said, smiling, but with a note of challenge audible in her voice.

'A friend. Surely?'

'That too, but by accident.'

Despite herself, Uma was glad of the note of scorn in Dolly's voice. It was a tonic restorative to the envy and obsequiousness she met with everywhere else, as the wife of the Collector and the district's pre-eminent memsahib.

One day, while driving out in the coach, Dolly had a sharp exchange of words with Kanhoji through the connecting window. They quickly became absorbed in their argument and Dolly seemed almost to forget Uma's presence. At intervals she made attempts to resume her normal manner, pointing at landmarks, and offering anecdotes about villages. But each time her anger got the better of her so that within moments she was at it again, whipping round to hurl a few more words at the coachman.

Uma was mystified: they were speaking in Konkani and she could understand nothing of what they said. What could they possibly be arguing about with their voices tuned to the intimately violent pitch of a family quarrel?

'Dolly, Dolly,' Uma shook her knee, 'what on earth is the matter?'

116

'Nothing,' Dolly said, pressing her lips primly together. 'Nothing at all. Everything is all right.'

They were on their way to the Bhagavati temple, which stood on the windswept cliffs above the bay, sheltered by the walls of Ratnagiri's medieval fort. As soon as the gaari came to a halt Uma took hold of Dolly's arm and led her towards the ruined ramparts. They climbed up to the crenellations and looked over: beneath them, the wall fell away in a straight line, dropping sheer into the sea a hundred feet below.

'Dolly, I want to know what the matter is.'

Dolly shook her head distractedly. 'I wish I could tell you but I can't.'

'Dolly, you can't shout at my coachman and then refuse to tell me what you were talking about.'

Dolly hesitated and Uma urged her again: 'You have to tell me, Dolly.'

Dolly bit her lip, looking intently into Uma's eyes. 'If I tell you,' she said, 'will you promise not to tell the Collector?'

'Yes. Of course.'

'You promise?'

'Solemnly. I promise.'

'It's about the First Princess.'

'Yes? Go on.'

'She's pregnant.'

Uma gasped, her hand flying to her mouth in disbelief. 'And the father?'

'Mohan Sawant.'

'Your coachman?'

'Yes. That's why your Kanhoji is so angry. He is Mohanbhai's uncle. Their family want the Queen to agree to a marriage so that the child will not be born a bastard.'

'But, Dolly, how could the Queen allow her daughter to marry a coachman?'

'We don't think of him as a coachman,' Dolly said sharply. 'He's Mohanbhai to us.'

'But what about his family, his background?'

Dolly flicked her wrist in a gesture of disgust. 'Oh, you Indians,' she said. 'You're all the same, all obsessed with your castes and

117

your arranged marriages. In Burma when a woman likes a man, she is free to do what she wants.'

'But, Dolly,' Uma protested, 'I've heard that the Queen is very particular about these things. She thinks there's not a man in Burma who's good enough for her daughters.'

'So you've heard about the list of husbands-to-be?' Dolly began to laugh. 'But you know, those men were just names. The Princesses knew nothing about them. To marry one of them would have been a complicated thing, a matter of state. But what's happened between Mohanbhai and the Princess is not a complicated thing at all. It's very simple: they're just a man and a woman who've spent years together, living behind the same walls.'

'But the Queen? Isn't she angry? The King?'

'No. You see, all of us are very attached to Mohanbhai – Min and Mebya most of all. In our different ways I think we all love him a little. He's been with us through everything, he's the one person who's always stood beside us. In a way it's he who's kept us alive, kept us sane. The only person who's really upset by this is Mohanbhai. He thinks your husband will send him to gaol when he finds out.'

'What about the Princess? How does she feel?'

'It's as though she's been reborn – rescued from a house of death.'

'And what of you, Dolly? We never talk of you or your future. What about your prospects of marriage, of having children of your own? Do you never think of these things?'

Dolly leant over the wall, fixing her eyes on the pounding sea. 'To tell you the truth, Uma, I used to think of children all the time. But once we learnt about the Princess's child – Mohanbhai's child – a strange thing happened. Those thoughts vanished from my mind. Now when I wake up I feel that the child is mine, growing inside me. This morning, I heard the girls asking the First Princess: "Has the child grown?" "Did you feel her move last night?" "Where are her heels this morning?" "Can we touch her head with our hands?" I was the only one who didn't need to ask her anything: I felt that I could answer every one of those questions myself; it was as though it were my own child.'

'But, Dolly,' Uma said gently, 'this is not your child. No matter how much it may seem your own, it is not, and never will be.'

'It must seem very strange to you, Uma. I can understand that it would, to someone like you. But it's different for us. At Outram House we lead very small lives. Every day for the last twenty years we have woken to the same sounds, the same voices, the same sights, the same faces. We have had to be content with what we have, to look for what happiness we can find. For me it does not matter who is bearing this child. In my heart I feel that I am responsible for its conception. It is enough that it is coming into our lives. I will make it mine.'

Glancing at Dolly, Uma saw that her eyes were brimming with tears. 'Dolly,' she said, 'don't you see that nothing will be the same after the birth of this child? The life you've known at Outram House will end. Dolly, you've got to leave while you can. You are free to go: you alone are here of your own will.'

'And where would I go?' Dolly smiled at her. 'This is the only place I know. This is home.'

Ten

When the timber-heavy streams of the monsoons debouched into the Irrawaddy the impact was that of colliding trains. The difference was that this was an accident continuously in the making, a crash that carried on uninterrupted night and day, for weeks on end. The river was by now a swollen, angry torrent, racked by clashing currents and pock-marked with whirlpools. When the feeder streams slammed head-on into the river, two-ton logs were thrown cartwheeling into the air; fifty-foot tree trunks were sent shooting across the water like flat-bottomed pebbles. The noise was that of an artillery barrage, with the sound of the detonations carrying for miles into the hinterland.

It was at these points, where the river intersected with its feeder streams, that the teak companies' profits were at greatest risk. So fast were the Irrawaddy's currents in this season, that the timber was as good as lost unless quickly brought to shore. It was here, of necessity, that the logs passed from their terrestrial handlers to the aquatic, from oo-sis and elephants to river-folk and raftsmen.

The streams' confluences were guarded by retrievers specialised in the capture of river-borne logs: for the sum of three annas per log these swimmers strung a human net across the river, wresting the logs from the currents and guiding them in to shore. At the start of the season whole villages moved location to take up stations along the river. Children kept watch along the banks, while their elders breasted the currents, darting between the giant trunks, treading water around churning whirlpools of teak. Some of these retrievers came back to shore lying prone on their captured logs while others sat astride them, legs dangling. A few rode in standing on their feet, guiding the spinning, moss-covered logs with prehensile toes: these were the monarchs of the river, the acknowledged masters of retrieval.

Once brought to the banks, the logs were anchored and moored. When enough had accumulated, skilled raftsmen bound them together into river-worthy craft. These rafts were all of the same size, the number of their logs being set, by the companies' ordinance, at an exact three hundred and sixty in each, a round sum of thirty dozen. At one ton or more per log this gave each raft the tonnage of a small battleship and a deck space that was many times larger, wide enough to accommodate a fair or a parade ground. At the centre of each of these immense floating platforms, there stood a small hut, built by the raftsmen as housing for the crew. Like the temporary dwellings of teak camps, these raft-borne huts were erected in a matter of hours. They were all exactly the same in plan, and yet always different in execution – one being marked by the trailed shoots of a quick-growing vine, another by a chicken coop or even a shelter for a pig or a goat. Each raft bore a tall mast and a pole with a handful of grass affixed to the top, an offering to the river's nats. Before being cut adrift the rafts were assigned numbers, to be displayed on their masts along with the flags of the companies that owned them. The rafts travelled only between dawn and dusk, covering some ten to fifteen miles a day, powered solely by the flow of the river, and guided only by oars. The journey to Rangoon from upcountry forests could take five weeks or even more.

Each season Rajkumar found one pretext or another to spend a few days on these rafts. There was something hypnotically pleasurable about the variable rhythms of life on these immense, rectangular platforms – in the contrast between the delectable languor of the daytime hours, when there was often nothing more to do than to watch a fish-hook trailing through the water, and the tense excitement of the sunset mooring, when ropes flew hissing between deck and shore, and everyone had to race to douse the smoking logs. Despite their immense size, the rafts were fragile in construction: running afoul of a shoal or sandbank, they could disintegrate in a matter of minutes. Solid in appearance, their surfaces were as deceptive as quicksand. Thousands of gaps constantly opened and closed between the logs, each a small but deadly ankle trap.

Many of the raftsmen were from Chittagong, and for Rajkumar there was a special satisfaction in being able to revert to the dialect of his boyhood; in savouring on his tongue the remembered heat of fish-head dals and fish-tail *jhols*, flecked with nigella seed and mustard; in watching once again, the changing flow of the river, slowing as it spread itself across a flood plain, and then abruptly speeding up again at the approach of a gorge; in observing the unexpected mutations of the landscape, now green and thickly wooded, and now a baked, red desert, dotted with the skeletal trunks of parched toddy palms.

Of all the river's sights the strangest was one that lay a little to the south of the great volcanic hump of Mount Popa. The Irrawaddy here described a wide, sweeping turn, spreading itself to a great width. On the eastern bank of the river, there appeared a range of low, foul-smelling mounds. These hillocks were covered in a thick ooze, a substance that would sometimes ignite spontaneously in the heat of the sun, sending streams of fires into the river. Often at night small, wavering flames could be seen in the distance, carpeting the slopes.

To the people of the area this ooze was known as earth-oil: it was a dark, shimmering green, the colour of bluebottles' wings. It seeped from the rocks like sweat, gathering in shiny green-filmed pools. In places, the puddles joined together to form creeks and rivulets, an oleaginous delta that fanned out along the shores. So strong was the odour of this oil that it carried all the way across the Irrawaddy: boatmen would swing wide when they floated past these slopes, this place-of-stinking-creeks – Yenangyaung.

This was one of the few places in the world where petroleum seeped naturally to the surface of the earth. Long before the discovery of the internal-combustion engine there was already a good market for this oil: it was widely used as an ointment, for the treatment of certain skin conditions. Merchants came to Yenangyaung from as far away as China to avail themselves of this substance. The gathering of the oil was the work of a community endemic to those burning hills, a group of people known as *twin-za*s, a tight-knit, secretive bunch of outcasts, runaways and foreigners.

122

Over generations twin-za families had attached themselves to individual springs and pools, gathering the oil in buckets and basins, and ferrying it to nearby towns. Many of Yenangyaung's pools had been worked for so long that the level of oil had sunk beneath the surface, forcing their owners to dig down. In this way, some of the pools had gradually become wells, a hundred feet deep or even more – great oil-sodden pits, surrounded by excavated sand and earth. Some of these wells were so heavily worked that they looked like small volcanoes, with steep, conical slopes. At these depths the oil could no longer be collected simply by dipping a weighted bucket: twin-zas were lowered in, on ropes, holding their breath like pearl divers.

Often, when moored within walking distance of Yenangyaung, Rajkumar would go over to watch the twin-zas at their work. Standing on the lip of a well he would look on as a man went down the shaft, rotating slowly on a sling. The rope would be attached, by way of a pulley, to his wife, family and livestock. They would lower him in by walking up the slope of the well, and when they felt his tug they would pull him out again by walking down. The lips of the wells were slippery from spills and it was not uncommon for unwary workers and young children to tumble in. Often these falls went unnoticed: there were no splashes and few ripples. Serenity is one of the properties of this oil: it is not easy to make a mark upon its surface.

After these visits to Yenangyaung, oil-soaked spectres would haunt Rajkumar's imaginings. What would it be like to drown in that ooze? To feel that green sludge, the colour of insects' wings, closing over your head, trickling into your ears and nostrils?

When he was about eighteen, Rajkumar came upon an unfamiliar sight at Yenangyaung. He noticed a couple of foreigners, white men, walking from well to well. From that time on, whenever he returned, there were more and more of these men around the slopes, armed with instruments and surveyors' tripods. They were from France, England and America, and they were said to be offering the twin-zas good money, buying up their pools and wells. Wooden obelisks began to rise on the hillocks, cage-like pyramids inside which huge mechanical beaks hammered ceaselessly on the earth.

On one of these visits to Yenangyaung Rajkumar's raft picked up a passenger. He was called Baburao and he was from Guntur, in India. Hair grew so thick upon his body that even when wearing a cotton vest he seemed to be coated in a fine wire mesh. He had a lot of money and dispensed liquor freely to the raftsmen, late into the night. He was a *maistry*, he said, a labour contractor: he had just transported forty-eight Cooringhees from eastern India to Yenangyaung. There was no quicker money to be made anywhere. Many foreign companies were busy digging for oil and they were desperate for labour. They needed workers and were willing to pay handsomely. It was hard to find workers in Burma: few Burmese were so poor as to put up with conditions like those of Yenangyaung. But back at home in India, Baburao said, there were uncountable thousands of people who were so desparate to leave that they would sign over many years' earnings. A young man like Rajkumar could grow rich quickly in this trade. What easier way to make money? All one needed was a few hundred rupees to pay one-way passages for the recruits.

Rajkumar wandered slowly to the edge of the moored raft and lit a cheroot, lying flat on his chest. His face was inches from the water, and schools of tiny riverbank fish rose to the surface to snap at his flaking ash. The encounter with the maistry had come at a time when the future was much on his mind. For the better part of the last year Saya John had been talking to him of planning ahead: 'Your days as a luga-lei are coming to their end, Rajkumar. The time has come when you have to make your own place in the world.'

What Rajkumar wanted most was to go into the timber business. Of this he was certain, for he knew he would never be so well acquainted with any other trade. But the problem was that he possessed none of the specialised skills that would have let him join a company's workforce as an oo-si or a raftsman. Nor did the prospect of earning a meagre twenty or thirty rupees a month hold any appeal. What then?

The best possible way to enter the teak business, Rajkumar had decided, would be through the acquisition of a timberyard. On his journeys downriver, Rajkumar stopped occasionally at the river port of Henzada. His old friend Doh Say lived there now, with his wife, Naw Da, and their two children. He worked in a small dockside yard, supervising a team of two elephants. Doh Say had suggested to Rajkumar that he set up a timberyard of his own: warehousing was a good way of entering the trade. 'You can start small,' he'd said. 'You can manage with just one elephant. I'll come and work with you, for half the usual salary, in exchange for a share of the business.' All that was needed was an outlay of capital.

It was Rajkumar's practice never to collect more than a part of his salary, banking the rest with Saya John. But after all these years his savings still amounted to no more than some two hundred rupees. The cost of setting up a timberyard amounted to several thousand – too much to ask from Saya John. To go to India with Baburao on the other hand would take not much more than he had already saved. And if he could persuade Saya John to lend him the rest, well then, within a few years he might have enough for his yard.

Back in Mandalay he waited for a good time to approach Saya John. 'All I need is a loan of a few hundred rupees,' he said quietly, taking care not to explain too much. 'And it'll come back to you many times over. Saya?'

Three months later Rajkumar left for India with Baburao. It took four days from Rangoon to Calcutta and another four to travel down the coast in the direction of Madras. Baburao rented two ox-carts at a small market town and had them tricked out in festive cloths. He bought several sacks of parched rice from the bazaar and recruited some half-dozen stick-wielding *lathiyals* to act as guards.

They headed into the countryside accompanied by drummers: it was as though they were a bridal procession, journeying to a wedding. On the way Baburao asked passers-by about the villages ahead. Were they rich or poor? Did the villagers own land or work for shares? What were the castes of the people who lived in them?

They stopped at a small hamlet, a shabby little cluster of huts huddled around an immense banyan tree. Baburao seated himself under the tree and told the drummers to start beating their instruments. At once all other activity came to a halt. Men came running in from the fields, leaving their oxen tethered to their ploughs. Children came floundering across the rice paddies. Women slipped out of their huts with their babies balanced on their hips.

Baburao welcomed everyone to the shade of the tree. Once the crowd was thick and deep he began to talk, his voice slowing to a chant in the reverential manner of a reciter of the *Ramayana*. He spoke of a land of gold, Burma, which the British Sarkar had declared to be a part of India. He pointed to the tasselled shawl that hung round his neck and invited his listeners to touch it with their fingers; he held up his hand so that everyone could see his gold and ruby rings. All of this, said Baburao, had come from Burma, the golden land. Before going there, he had had nothing, not even a goat or cow.

'And all these things can be yours too,' Baburao said to his listeners. 'Not in your next life. Not next year. Now. They can be yours now. All you need is an able-bodied man from your family to put his thumbprint on this sheet of paper.'

He took a handful of silver coins out of a velvet bag and let them fall back again, tinkling. 'Are there any here who have debts? Are there any who owe money to their landlords? You can settle your obligations right now, right here. As soon as your sons and brothers make their marks on these contracts, this money will be yours. In a matter of a few years they will earn back enough to free themselves of debt. Then they will be at liberty to return or stay in Burma as they choose.'

Fifteen men signed on in that village and twenty-three in the next: some rushed eagerly forward, some were pushed on by their relatives and some had their hands held forcibly to the paper by their fathers and brothers. Carrying tin boxes and cloth bundles, the recruits followed Baburao's ox-cart back to town. The lathiyals brought up the rear to make sure they kept in step. They stopped once every few hours, to eat parched rice and salt.

When they reached the coast, Baburao hired a country boat to take them to Calcutta. Many of the men had never been on the sea before. They were frightened by the waves and that night one of the men leapt overboard. Baburao jumped in after him, and pulled him back into the boat. The would-be runaway had swallowed a bellyful of water. He was limp and scrawny, with bones sticking out of his body. Baburao draped the man over the side of the boat, doubling him over the gunwale. Then he climbed on top of him, pinning his torso below with a bent knee. With a thrusting motion of his foot, he pushed the man against the beam, pumping his stomach until the water he had swallowed came dribbling out of his mouth, along with a spongy mass of parched rice and salt.

'Where did you think you were going?' Baburao crooned, almost tenderly, as though he were singing to a lover. 'And what about all the money I gave your father so he could pay off his debts? What use would your corpse be, to him or to me?'

At Calcutta they boarded the S.S. *Dufferin*, which was owned by a British company. Baburao had an arrangement with the steward of the ship: he was a valued customer because of the business he brought. He was given free passage, second class. Pocketing Rajkumar's fare he allowed him to sleep on the floor of his cabin. The thirty-eight men they had brought with them were sent below, to a holding space at the rear of the ship.

Some two thousand other would-be immigrants were there already. Most were men, but there were also some hundred and fifty women. At the back, jutting out over the ship's wake, there was a narrow wooden platform with four holes to serve as toilets. The passage was rough and the floor of the holding area was soon covered with vomit and urine. This foul-smelling layer of slime welled back and forth with the rolling of the ship, rising inches high against the walls. The recruits sat huddled on their tin boxes and cloth bundles. At the first sight of land, off the Arakan coast, several men leapt off the ship. By the third day of the voyage the number of people in the hold had dwindled by a few dozen. The corpses of those who had died on board were carried to the stern and dropped into the ship's churning wake.

On reaching the Rangoon docks, Baburao found that the voyage had cost him two men. He was not displeased. 'Two out of thirty-eight is not bad,' he told Rajkumar. 'On occasion I've lost as many as six.'

They travelled together to Yenangyaung and then Rajkumar told Baburao that he needed to go up to Mandalay. But this was a ruse. Rajkumar set off in a northerly direction, but once he'd put a little distance between himself and Baburao, he doubled back, heading straight for Rangoon. At a small shop on Mogul Street he bought a gold chain and a bright turquoise ring. Then he went down to the docks and boarded the *Dufferin*. During his last crossing, he had taken care to work out his own deal with the stewards of the ship: he was now welcomed as a maistry in his own right.

Rajkumar went back to the same district that he had visited with Baburao. He hired an ox-cart at the same market and employed the same lathiyals. He succeeded in indenturing fifty-five men and three women. On the way back to Calcutta, mindful of what had happened the last time, he sat up all night in his hired country boat, keeping watch over his recruits. Sure enough, one night, he spotted a man trying to slip silently overboard. Rajkumar was bigger and more alert than Baburao and had no need to jump in. He pulled the man out of the water by his hair and held him dangling in front of the others. He succeeded in bringing the whole group intact to Yenangyaung, and there he sold their indenture contracts to a local boss. The money was enough to pay off Saya John's loan.

Three years passed before Doh Say found a promising timberyard. By that time Rajkumar had made eight more trips to India. His accumulated savings now amounted to almost two-thirds of the asking price of the yard. Saya John lent him the rest.

The yard was in Rangoon, off Lower Kemendine Road. There were many sawmills in the area, and the air was always filled with the fragrance of sawdust. There was a Hindu cremation ground nearby, in Sanchaung, and sometimes, when the wind turned, clouds of ash would rise in circles above the funeral pyres. A brick wall ran most of the way round the compound, and at the back there was a narrow jetty, sticking like a tongue into the Rangoon river. At low tide the riverbank expanded into a vast shelf of cottony mud. In the front of the yard there were two small cabins, built of cast-off lumber and bamboo thatch. Rajkumar moved into the smaller of the two; the other went to Doh Say, Naw Da and their children, of whom there were now four.

On his first visit to the yard, Saya John ate a meal in the cabin where Doh Say and Naw Da lived. Saya John had not known that Doh Say was to be a partner in Rajkumar's business, but he was not particularly surprised to find that this was so. Rajkumar had always possessed a dogged kind of consistency – this was a quality quite different from loyalty, but no less enduring. The same shadows seemed to recur over and over again in his life, just as they did on puppet screens.

The following year Saya John went into semi-retirement and moved from Mandalay to Rangoon. The sale of his firm had made him a wealthy man. He set up a small office in Merchant Street, and bought a flat on Blackburn Lane. He bought a lot of furniture for his flat, hoping that his son, Matthew, would soon come home. But the boy was farther away than ever – a relative had taken him to San Francisco and he had written to say that he was studying in a Catholic seminary. There was no telling when he'd come back.

With time on his hands, Saya John began to take long walks, to air his pet birds. Rajkumar's timberyard was just a half-hour's stroll from his home and it became a ritual with him to stop by every morning, with a birdcage in his hand and a newspaper under his arm.

One morning he arrived to find Rajkumar waiting at the gate, hopping with impatience. 'You're late today, Saya.'

'Late? For what?'

'Late with your paper, Saya.' Rajkumar snatched the *Rangoon Gazette* out of Saya John's hands. 'Doh Say heard on the docks that an Indian railway company was going to put out a notice, asking for tenders for the supply of sleepers.'

'Tenders for the supply of sleepers!' The mynah inside Saya John's birdcage chirruped in imitation of its owner's chortling laugh. 'And what of it, Rajkumar? A contract with a railway company would mean the shipping of thousands of tons of teak. To supply timber on that scale you would need teams of oo-sis, pe-sis, raftsmen, agents, Assistants. All you have is Doh Say and one elephant. How do you think you would fulfil this contract?'

'This railway company is small and new, Saya, and it needs cheap supplies. I don't have to start by acquiring the timber: I'll start with the contract. Once I have it, the timber will follow automatically. You will see. There are dozens of yards here that are overstocked. Once they see that I'm offering down payments they'll all come to me.'

'And where will you get the money to make these down payments?'

'Why, Saya,' Rajkumar smiled, a little sheepishly, 'from you, of course. Why would I offer such an opportunity to anyone else?'

'But consider the risk, Rajkumar. The big English companies could destroy you, make you a laughing stock in Rangoon. You could be driven out of business.'

'But, Saya, look at what I have here now.' Rajkumar gestured at his rickety cabin and his half-empty yard. 'Saya, this is no better than a roadside teashop – I might as well still be working for Ma Cho. If I'm ever going to make this business grow, I'll have to take a few risks.'

'Think, Rajkumar, think. You're just starting out. You have no idea of how these deals are struck in Rangoon. All the big people here know each other. They go to the same clubs, eat at the same restaurants, put money on each other's horses . . .'

'It's not just the big people who always know everything, Saya,' Rajkumar said. 'If I could find out exactly how much the other companies are going to quote, then I might be able to put in a winning bid.'

'And how would you find out?'

'I don't know, Saya. But I think I have a way. We'll see.'

'But, Rajkumar, you can't even read English: how do you think you're going to make this bid?'

Rajkumar grinned. 'It's true that I can't read English, Saya, but I've learnt to speak it. And why do I need to read when you can do it for me? Saya?'

And so it fell to Saya John to deal with the paperwork for the bid. It was to him that Rajkumar went with the letter the company sent back.

Breaking open the florid seal, Saya John gave voice to an incredulous shout. 'Rajkumar! You've been asked to meet with the directors of the Chota-Nagpur Railway Company next week. They are coming to Burma to scrutinise the bids. You are to go to the offices of the Chartered Bank on the Strand at ten o' clock on Thursday.'

Saya John clicked his tongue incredulously as he looked up from the crackling sheet of paper in his hands. 'Rajkumar, I really never thought you would get this far.'

'I told you, Saya.' Rajkumar smiled. 'I found out what the other companies were offering and I made a better bid.'

'And how did you find out?'

Rajkumar smiled. 'That will be my secret, Saya.'

'Your secret isn't going to be of any help to you now. It's the meeting that will decide everything. That's what you've got to think about.' Saya John ran his eyes critically over Rajkumar's green longyi and scuffed pinni vest. 'For example: what are you going to wear? The Chartered Bank won't even let you past its doors if you're dressed like that.'

The next day Saya John came to the timberyard with a dapper young man. 'This is U Ba Kyaw,' he said to Rajkumar. 'He was a valet to an English planter in Maymyo. He can teach you many things, like how to eat at a European table with a knife and fork. Buy exactly what he says and do exactly as he tells you.'

On the morning of the meeting Saya John arrived at the timberyard in a hired coach, dressed in his best black suit and equipped with a fine malacca cane and a new hat. He stepped into Rajkumar's cabin to find him already clothed in his new trousers and shirt, standing rigidly still while U Ba Kyaw worked on his tie.

When Rajkumar's costuming had been completed, Saya John looked him over and decided that there was nothing to fault in his appearance: his suit was appropriately plain and black, and his tie neatly tied, the collar turned to just the right angle. It was true that his clothes were not quite as well tailored as they would have been in Singapore or Hong Kong, but for Rangoon they were more than adequate. In any event, no matter how costly Rajkumar's clothes or how well-fitting, it was a certainty that he would never be mistaken for a man who'd been born to wealth or office. There was a roughness to his face that was a surety against that.

'I'm coming with you, Rajkumar,' Saya John said. 'Just to bring you luck.'

At the Chartered Bank Saya John and Rajkumar were shown into an anteroom by a cashier, an Indian. Saya John saw to his surprise that Rajkumar was already acquainted with this man – D. P. Roy was his name. 'Everything is arranged,' Mr Roy said, in an undertone. 'The directors are in the boardroom now. They will call for you soon.'

The cashier left and they were on their own. The room was dark and cavernous, and its deep leather chairs smelt of cigar smoke. After a long wait a turbaned bearer came in to summon Rajkumar. Saya John rose to his feet too, with the intention of uttering a few words of encouragement and reassurance. But just as he was about to speak he stopped, his eyes resting on Rajkumar. It struck him that his one-time luga-lei was now so sure of himself, so confident, that there was nothing he could say that would not be superfluous. Saya John moved back a little, withdrawing a pace or two to observe him better. Suddenly, from that altered angle of vision he had the impression that he was looking at someone he had never seen before, a reinvented being, formidably imposing and of commanding presence. In that instant there flashed before Saya John's eyes a clear vision of that Mandalay morning when he had gone racing down an alley to rescue Rajku-mar – he saw him again as a boy, an abandoned kalaa, a rags-clad Indian who had strayed too far from home. Already then, the boy had lived a lifetime, and from the look of him now it was clear that he was embarking on several more.

Then Rajkumar did something he had never done before. Just as he was about to walk through the door, he stooped to touch Saya John's feet, in the Indian way.

'Give me your blessings, Saya.'

Saya John turned his head to hide the tears that had welled into his eyes. 'That which a man takes for himself no one can deny him. The contract will be yours, Rajkumar. I was wrong to doubt it.'

Eleven

The post came twice a week and was delivered directly to the Collector's office in the Cutchery. Uma's letters were usually picked out by the Collector and sent up to the Residency with a peon. Her mail was mostly from her parents but once or twice each month there was also a book or a magazine, posted by a Calcutta bookshop.

On maildays Uma spent hours daydreaming by the peepul tree. If she happened to have one of her official appointments she would be snappish and impatient, eager to get back to her letters. She'd think of her mother, at home in Calcutta, writing in bed, worrying about her inkwell and spills on the sheets.

One mailday morning the Collector's peon delivered a letter with an unusual postmark. The Collector had scrawled a note on the envelope: 'From Rangoon.' Uma turned the envelope over and saw her uncle's name on the back, D. P. Roy. She was surprised: it was years since she'd last heard from him. But after her marriage she'd grown accustomed to receiving letters from long-unseen relatives: the Collector wielded a lot of influence; he was a man who could get things done. She surmised that her uncle needed something.

She took the letter down to the peepul tree. Just as she'd expected, her uncle had written to ask a favour, on behalf of a friend – a Rajkumar Raha who was on his way to Bombay on business. The man had expressed a desire to come down to Ratnagiri for a quick visit. He was keen to pay his respects to the former King and Queen.

'I would be very grateful, Uma, if your husband could arrange

133

for Rajkumar-babu to call on the former King. Having somehow learnt of my connection with the Collector, he expressly sought me out to request my help in this matter. I might add that I am indebted to Rajkumar-babu for several good turns – indeed many members of our Bengali community in Rangoon have benefited from his assistance in one way or another.'

Rajkumar-babu, the letter continued, had lived in Rangoon many years but for much of that time he had had no contact with the other Bengalis of the city. Then suddenly one morning, he had dropped down like a hailstone from the sky, right into the Durga temple on Spark Street, the gathering-place of the city's Hindu Bengalis. He had come perfectly costumed for the occasion, in a starched white dhoti and a gold-buttoned *punjabi*. To ease his entry he had taken the precaution of bringing along a substantial donation for the *purohit*.

It turned out that Mr Raha was in the timber trade. He was planning to make a bid for a major contract and had come to ask the purohit to pray for him. Like all his kind the purohit had the intuition of a famished tiger when it came to the judging of potential prey. He did much more than offer a blessing. At the temple there were several employees of the big European banks and timber companies: the purohit made it his business to introduce Rajkumar-babu to all these men.

Over the next few days messages had flown back and forth between Spark Street and Merchant Street, between the Kalibari and the offices of the timber companies. Finally, when the directors of the Chota-Nagpur Railway Company announced their decision, it was learnt that one Mr Rajkumar Raha, a name then unknown in the world of teak, had succeeded in underbidding all the major companies.

On that contract alone Rajkumar-babu had netted a profit of eight lakh rupees – a fortune. Out of gratitude he'd virtually rebuilt the temple, paving its floors in marble, gilding the walls of the shrine and erecting a beautiful new dwelling for the purohit and his family. Since that time he had had several other successes and had risen to eminence within the business community. And all this at the age of thirty, before he had even had time to marry.

You will understand what I mean, Uma, when I say that our Rajkumar-babu is not the kind of person to whose society you are accustomed. You may well find him somewhat rough and even uncouth in his manner. You will no doubt be astonished to learn that although he speaks several languages fluently, including English and Burmese, he is for all practical purposes, an illiterate, barely able to sign his own name.

At home in India a man like Rajkumar-babu would stand little chance of gaining acceptance in the society of people like ourselves. But here in Burma our standards are a little more lax. Some of the richest people in the city are Indians, and most of them began with nothing more than a bundle of clothes and a tin box.

I fully understand that in India a man of Rajkumar-babu's station could scarcely hope to be entertained – or even received – by a District Collector. But you must consider that he has lived in Burma so long that he is now more Burmese than Indian and may well be counted as a foreigner. I hope you will make allowance for this, recalling that I for one would certainly be very grateful for your condescension in this matter.

Also associated with maildays was a special treat: fresh ice, shipped out from Bombay on the steamer. On mailday evenings the Collector liked to sit out in the garden, on a wicker chair, with an iced drink. Uma waited until the Collector had been served his whisky before she started reading him her uncle's letter. At the end of her recital the Collector took the sheet of paper from her and read it through himself.

He handed the letter back with a gesture of regret. 'If it were within my power,' he said, 'I would have liked to oblige your uncle. But unfortunately it's out of the question. The Government's instructions are quite clear. Their Highnesses are not to have visitors.'

'But why not?' Uma cried. 'You're the Collector. You could let him come if you wanted to. No one needs to know.'

The Collector placed his glass abruptly on the small peg table that stood by his chair. 'It's impossible, Uma. I'd have to forward the request to Bombay and from there it would be sent on to the Colonial Secretary in London. It could take months.'

'Just for a visit to Outram House?'

'Our teachers,' the Collector began – it was a running joke with him to speak of his British colleagues as *amader gurujon* – 'our teachers don't want political trouble in Burma. It's their richest province and they don't want to take any risks. The King is the one person who could bring the country together, against them. There are more than a dozen different tribes and peoples there. The monarchy is the only thing they have in common. Our teachers know this and they want to make sure that the King is forgotten. They don't wish to be cruel; they don't want any martyrs; all they want is that the King should be lost to memory – like an old umbrella in a dusty cupboard.'

'But what difference could a single visitor make?'

'He might get back and talk. Something could get into the newspapers. The Colonial Office won't even allow the King to be photographed for fear that the picture could get back to Burma. The other day I had a letter from a photographer, a Parsee woman. She's out on a picture-taking tour and wanted to stop by to take some photographs at Outram House. I forwarded her request to Bombay and heard back within the week: no pictures of the Royal Family are to be allowed. Government policy.'

'But that's monstrous,' Uma cried.

'Not at all.' The Collector's eyes narrowed. 'It's merely judicious. Do you think Burma would be well served by political trouble? Do you think this man Raha would have been able to get rich if Thebaw were still ruling? Why, if it were not for the British, the Burmese would probably have risen up against these Indian businessmen and driven them out like sheep.'

Uma knew she would not be able to best the Collector in an argument. She lowered her voice and placed a hand on his arm.

'You know,' she said, 'it's not for the King's sake, or even my uncle's that I'm asking you this.'

'Then why?'

Uma hesitated.

'Tell me.'

'It's because of Dolly.'

'Dolly?'

'She's lived here all her life, as a virtual prisoner, and she can't imagine anything other than the life she has. But she'll have to leave Outram House some day, and where is she to go? She's forgotten about Burma and I think she needs to talk to people who can remind her of it.'

'Dolly can go back to Burma whenever she wants.'

'But she doesn't have any family in Burma and she doesn't know anyone there. That's exactly why she needs to meet people who live there.'

The Collector fell silent and Uma sensed that he was beginning to relent. 'It's such a small thing,' she prompted. 'I'm sure there's a solution.'

'All right then,' he said at last, on a note of exasperation. 'Since it means so much to you I suppose there is one thing I could do.'

'What?'

'I could invite this Raha here as my personal guest. I could say he's a relative by marriage. And then, if he were to pay a visit to Outram House, it would be just a private visit – nothing official . . .'

'I'd be so glad . . .'

The very next morning a telegram was dispatched to Uma's uncle in Rangoon, to tell him that his friend, Mr Raha, was welcome to visit Ratnagiri; he would be received as the Collector's personal guest.

Twelve

Within moments of the steamer's arrival, word went out along the waterfront that there was a rich prince on board, one Rajkumar, a foreigner who was very free with his money. An uproar ensued: coolies and porters laid siege to the gangplank; idlers drifted in from the shaded shoreline and gathered on the beach.

Rajkumar was still asleep in his cabin when the steamer docked. It was U Ba Kyaw who woke him. It was Rajkumar's practice to bring a number of his people with him, when he was travelling abroad. This was his way of protecting himself from the pitfalls of his new circumstances. This particular journey had induced apprehensions of a novel kind and as a result his retinue was even larger than usual. Along with a stenographer and an accountant he had also brought U Ba Kyaw, his most trusted employee.

Rajkumar sent U Ba Kyaw ahead to distract the crowd and then slipped quickly off the steamer. There were two carriages waiting at the far end of the jetty: one was from the Residency. The Collector was out of town that morning, but he had left careful instructions on how the visitor was to be received. Kanhoji was to drive him to the Dak Bungalow where he was to stay. In the evening he was to dine at the Residency.

The other carriage at the jetty was the Outram House phaeton. Along with Kanhoji, Sawant was leaning on a rail, watching the uproar on the jetty. Both men were taken by surprise when Rajkumar was pointed out to them. Of all the party he looked the least likely to be the man whom Kanhoji had been sent to meet.

After dropping Rajkumar at the Dak Bungalow, Kanhoji headed

back to the Residency to give Uma a full account of the uproar at the jetty. His report was unsparingly detailed: he told Uma about the half-chewed cheroot in Rajkumar's mouth, the dishevelled untidiness of his attire, his crumpled longyi, his greasy vest and his uncombed hair. Uma was left with a sense of lingering unease. Was it prudent to invite someone like this to dinner? What exactly did he eat?

In a striking departure from custom, the Collector had entrusted the organising of the evening's meal to Uma. Usually it was he who oversaw the Residency's entertaining. Although otherwise uninterested in domestic matters, he was very particular about his dinner parties: he liked to examine the table and the place settings personally, tweaking the flowers and pointing out the plates and glasses that needed another round of polishing. It was to him that the servants went for their instructions on what to serve and which dinner service to use.

That morning when the khansama came to enquire about the menu, Uma had been taken by surprise. Thinking quickly, she told him to serve exactly what he had served the week before, when the Director of Public Education came to dinner. She remembered shepherd's pie and fried fish and blancmange.

'I want all of that tonight,' she'd told the cook, *'ekdum woh hi cheez.'* Then, on an impulse she wrote a note to the Anglo-Indian Superintendent of Police, Mr Wright, asking him to come to dinner, with his wife. She had already asked Mr Justice Naidu and Mrs Naidu – an elderly couple, unfailingly pleasant, undemanding. And of course Dolly was to come too: that had been arranged long before.

As evening approached, Uma tried to recall everything the Collector did before a dinner party. For once, she told herself, she would be a good memsahib. She went to the dining room and fussed with the plates and forks and flowers. But when the Collector came home, she discovered that she might as well have spared herself the effort. The Collector was plainly unimpressed. After stepping into the dining room to inspect her handiwork, he emerged with an unspoken rebuke on his face.

'The fish-knives weren't in the proper place,' he said. 'And there was dust on the wine glasses . . .' He made her go back

139

to rearrange everything. 'I'll come back again later to check.'

Waiting for the guests to arrive, Uma sat by a window, her hands folded in her lap like a chastened schoolgirl. Perhaps it was a mistake, this dinner party, inviting Dolly to meet this stranger. Perhaps even her own presence here was a mistake. This was a thought that had never occurred to her before, but its chill shadow lengthened quickly in her mind. Was this what they called a premonition?

'Madame . . .'

It was the Naidus, grey-haired, tall, brimming with soft-voiced goodwill. 'How nice . . .' And then in came the Wrights, with Dolly following a few minutes later.

Rajkumar was the last to arrive. Rising to greet him, Uma found that her first impressions were unexpectedly favourable. Looking over her folded hands, she noted that he had gone to some trouble to dress neatly and plainly, in 'English' clothes: a sober black suit, a carefully knotted tie. His pumps were polished to a fine sheen and in his hands he was carrying a malacca cane with a handle of delicately carved jade. He looked much older than she'd expected: his face was weathered with hard use and his lips were heavy and richly coloured, very red against his dark skin. Along the line of his jaw there was a fold of flesh that hinted at jowls to come. He was far from good-looking, but there was something arresting about him, a massiveness of construction, allied with an unlikely mobility of expression – as though life had been breathed into a wall of slate.

Glancing over her shoulder, Uma spotted Dolly sitting half-hidden behind the scrolled arm of a chaise-longue. She was wearing a mauve htamein and an aingyi of white silk. A lily glowed like a light against the black sheen of her hair.

'Dolly!' Uma made a gesture of introduction in Rajkumar's direction. 'This is Mr Raha; I don't believe you've met . . .'

He recognized her at once, at first glance, beyond the remotest possibility of doubt. It was not that she looked the same, because she didn't: her face was much longer than he remembered, and around the corners of her eyes and mouth there was a fine, almost invisible, filigree of lines, like the tracings of a goldsmith's awl. What he remembered was something else – an element of her expression, a kind of forlornness in her eyes. It was this that had held him that night at the Glass Palace and now it held him again.

'Mr Raha –' there was a note of concern in Uma's voice – 'is something the matter?'

'No.' He looked down to find that he was holding his cane suspended in midair. 'No. Not at all. Nothing is the matter.'

To prevent himself from leaving the room, he sat down heavily in the nearest chair. It was too soon: he had not expected to see her here. There was nothing he hated more than to be taken unawares. He had expected to prepare himself for this encounter in slow, measured steps. It had been difficult enough to walk into this house. Even now, after two years of dinners and parties, he found it hard to cope with this atmosphere of constrained enactment.

'Did you have a pleasant journey, Mr Raha?'

It was his hostess, the Collector's wife: there was a look on her face that told him that she was trying to draw him out. He nodded and tried to smile. He could feel his gaze straying towards the chaise-longue and he quickly dropped his eyes. There were others approaching, he could feel them hovering at his shoulder. What was he to say to them? He had never so much wanted to be left alone.

'Dinner. Shall we . . . ?'

On the way to the dining room Uma found herself momentarily alone with Dolly. 'What do you think of our guest?' she said quickly, under her breath.

'He's not what I expected: not at all like a big magnate.'

'Because he's so quiet, you mean?'

'He doesn't seem to be much at ease, does he?'

'Have you noticed how he keeps looking at you? It's almost as though he's seen you somewhere before.'

Dolly's eyes widened. 'That's such a strange thing to say, Uma. I wonder what could have made you say that?'

The Residency's dining room was too large to be properly lit. Its long mahogany table floated adrift in an island of darkness.

There were several enormous candlestands on the table but because of the hand-pulled punkah overhead, the candles in the silver branches could not be lit. As a result the diners' faces were half-obscured, never quite visible, even to their neighbours.

Uma had seated Rajkumar on her right and Mr Wright, the Superintendent of Police, on her left. Dolly was at the other end of the table, sitting next to the Collector. Along the walls, at a distance of some half-dozen paces from the table, there stood a line of bearers, one behind each chair. As was the custom, the diners had each brought their own bearer, all except Dolly, who was as good as a member of the household. The Naidus' bearers were local men, Mr Wright's a Sikh. Behind Rajkumar's chair stood U Ba Kyaw, in a pink gaung-baung and a purple longyi: everyone else was drab by comparison.

Presently, the Collector laid down his napkin, and looked across the table at Rajkumar. 'Burma, Mr Raha,' he said in his ironical way. 'You have told us very little about it. What took you there in the first place?'

'Accident,' Rajkumar said shortly.

'What kind of accident carries a man to another country?'

'I was working on a boat and found myself stranded in Mandalay. This was at the start of the British invasion. The river was closed to traffic.'

'An eventful time.'

'A strange time, sir.'

'Indeed? How so?'

Dolly was watching him from across the table. Hers was the only face he could see: the others were all wrapped in shadow.

'The British fleet took two weeks to move up the river,' Rajkumar said. 'And through most of that time Mandalay was very quiet. I was only a boy then, but I was one of the few in the city who seemed to be aware that trouble was on its way.'

At this juncture there occurred an odd little incident. The fish having just been served, Rajkumar glanced impatiently at the knives and forks that surrounded his plate. Then, as though in exasperation at the profusion of cutlery, he held up his right hand and snapped his fingers. Even before he had completed the gesture U Ba Kyaw had appeared at his side, to hand him the appropriate utensil. This took no more than an instant, but everyone in the room took startled notice. Only Rajkumar himself seemed to be unmindful of the interruption. He resumed his narrative as though nothing had happened.

'One morning we heard cannon-shots somewhere in the distance. When the noise stopped, everything went on again, just as usual. It was only when the foreign soldiers marched into the city that people understood what had happened: that the King had been defeated, the city conquered. Towards evening we saw troops marching out of the fort with sacks of loot. Palace workers too. A crowd gathered around the walls of the fort. I had never been past the walls. When I saw people crossing the moat, I went to join them. We went running in. At the walls of the palace we found a breached gateway. We broke through, hundreds of us. I suppose you could say it was a kind of riot. None of us knew what we were doing, everyone was following someone else. We went running into the rear of the palace: the women's section. The most valuable objects were already gone, but to us what was left seemed to be of an unimaginable sumptuousness, precious beyond imagining. People fell upon everything that was within reach, everything in sight, breaking the furniture, digging stones from the floor. After a while I left the main hallway and turned into an anteroom. There was a woman inside. She was small and slight of figure, and even though I had never seen her before I knew at once that she was Queen Supayalat.'

'The Queen?'

'Yes. Her Majesty herself. I imagine she had come there to salvage whatever was left of her possessions. She was without guards, without an escort. She should have been frightened, but she was not. She shouted at us, threatened us. But what was still more remarkable was that everyone who came into the room fell instantly to the floor, to shiko to the Queen. Imagine how strange this was: there they were, looting the palace and at the same time paying homage to their Queen! I was mesmerised: I sat in a corner, watching. And when I had been there a while I realised that the Queen was not alone. She had two children with her, and some attendants, a group of young girls. Of the children the older was perhaps three. I took her to be a Princess, from the style of her clothes. Standing beside the Princess was an attendant, also a child, perhaps a year or two younger than me, perhaps more, I could not be sure, for this was a child like none I had ever seen before – beautiful beyond belief, beyond comprehension. She was like the palace itself, a thing of glass, inside which you could see everything of which your imagination was capable. All around us there was noise, the sound of knives, axes, running feet. It was evident that the girl was frightened, and yet, at the same time, she was perfectly calm. I could not take my eyes off her. I knew I was watching something I would never forget.'

'Who was she?' Uma broke in. 'This girl – who was she? Did you ever find out?'

'To tell you the truth . . .' Rajkumar was about to go on, when Dolly cut him short.

'It would seem,' she said curtly, addressing the Collector, 'it would seem that this was all a great sport for Mr Raha.'

'No.' Rajkumar's voice grew louder. 'Not at all.'

Dolly kept her gaze away from him. 'Mr Raha,' she said, 'appears to have enjoyed himself thoroughly.'

'No. That was not what I meant.'

Glancing at Rajkumar, Uma saw a look of inexpressible dismay cross his face. Suddenly she was sorry for him: Dolly was being needlessly cruel, unfair; anyone could see that the man had not intended any disrespect.

'Mr Raha . . .' Uma put out her hand to tap him on his wrist, to bring him back to the present and remind him that he was in company. But her elbow brushed accidentally against the table as she was reaching out. A fork slipped off her plate and fell tumbling to the floor. The sound was very small, thinly metallic, but within the confines of that space, it achieved the amplitude of an explosion. Two bearers leapt simultaneously from their places at the wall: one snatched the fallen utensil from the floor while the other proffered a napkin-wrapped replacement.

'Ah, Madame . . .'

The Collector's voice was expansive and loud, filled with mirthful irony. At the sound of it she shrank into her chair, in mortification. She had come to dread this note of derision, this inflexion that so often accompanied his comments on her small acts of

144

clumsiness. She knew the incident would be mentioned many times that evening; there would be innumerable jokes, references, arch asides: these would constitute her punishment.

'Ah, Madame,' the Collector continued, 'may I urge you once again to refrain from juggling with the Government's silver?'

She shivered, her eyes fixed on her plate. How was it possible to endure this? She looked at the new fork, lying on her plate, and as though of its own accord her hand began to move. Her wrist snapped up, sending the fork cartwheeling into the air.

Just before the utensil had completed its arc, Rajkumar shot out a hand and snatched it out of the air. 'There,' he said, slapping it down on the tablecloth. 'No harm done.'

Across the table the Collector was watching in astonishment. 'Uma!' he cried, the note of irony gone from his voice. 'Uma! What is the matter with you today?'

There followed an instant of silence in which they heard the sound of a carriage, rumbling up to the Residency's gate. '*Kaun hai?*' came the sentry's shouted challenge. The reply was muffled and indistinct but Dolly started at once to her feet. 'It's Mohanbhai. Something must have happened at Outram House.'

A bearer came in, bowing, and presented the Collector with an envelope. 'Urgent, sir.'

Slitting the envelope the Collector took out a sheet of embossed notepaper. He read the letter through and looked up, smiling gravely. 'I'm afraid I must leave these revels. A summons. Her Highness wants me at Outram House. At once.'

'Then I should go too.' Dolly pushed back her chair.

'By no means.' The Collector gave her hand a pat. 'Stay and enjoy yourself. It's me she wants. Not you. '

Dolly and Uma exchanged glances: they both knew at once that the Queen had summoned the Collector in order to announce the Princess's pregnancy. Dolly could not decide whether it would be better to go back to Outram House or to stay away.

'Stay, Dolly,' Uma urged.

'All right,' Dolly nodded. 'I'll stay.'

The complicity of the two women was not lost on the Collector. He looked from Uma to Dolly and back again. 'What exactly is going on at Outram House?' he said. 'Does either of you have any idea?'

'No.' Uma was quick to answer, her voice a note higher than usual. 'Whatever it is, I'm sure it won't require Dolly's presence.'

'All right then.' The Collector moved quickly around the table, saying his goodbyes. 'I'll be back when Her Highness sees fit. Do keep yourselves amused . . .'

The suddenness of the Collector's departure set the others astir. The Naidus and the Wrights rose whispering to their feet. 'It's very late . . .' 'Ought to be on our way . . .' There was a flurry of leave-taking and handshakes. Following her guests to the door, Uma stopped to whisper to Dolly: 'I'll be back after I see them off. Wait for me . . .'

Dolly went dazedly into the drawing room and opened one of the French windows. Stepping out into the garden, she stopped to listen to the voices of the departing guests. They were saying their goodbyes. 'Thank you . . .' 'So nice . . .' One of the voices was Uma's, but it seemed very far away. She couldn't think clearly right now: everything seemed a little blurred. It struck her that she should shut the French window to keep the insects out of the house. But she let it pass: there was too much to think about.

Right now, at this very moment, at Outram House, the Princesses were probably sitting by their windows looking down the road, waiting for the sound of the Collector's carriage. Downstairs, the reception room was probably open already, the lamps lit, just two, to save on oil. The Queen would soon be on her way down, in her patched crimson htamein; in a moment she would seat herself with her back to the door. And there she would wait until the Collector was shown in.

This was how the accustomed world of Outram House would end: they'd known this, all along, she and the Princesses. This was exactly how it would happen: one day, suddenly, the Queen would decide the time had come. The Collector would be sent for immediately, not a minute to waste. The next day everyone would know: the Governor, the Viceroy, all of Burma. Mohanbhai would be sent away; perhaps the Princesses too. Only she, Dolly, would remain, to bear the blame.

'Miss Dolly.'

She recognised the voice. It was that man, the visitor from Burma.

146

'Miss Dolly.'

She turned on him, her temper rising. 'How did you know my name?'

'I heard . . .' He stopped to correct himself. 'The truth is that it was you who told me your name.'

'Impossible.'

'You did. Do you not remember? That night, in the Glass Palace. You were the girl with the Princess. You must remember. I spoke to you, asked you your name.'

Dolly clapped her hands over her ears. 'It's a lie. Every word of it. You've made it all up. Everything, every last word. There was not a line of truth in anything you said tonight. Min and Mebya were gods to the people of Mandalay. No one would have dared do the things you described . . . People cried when we were taken away.'

'They did. That is true. But this too is true: the mob, the palace. I was there, and so were you. You must recall – that night in the palace, someone had snatched something from you – a box. I found it and gave it back. That was when you told me your name: Dolly. I can still hear your voice.'

She averted her face. 'And you are here because of this? Because of what you saw that night at the palace?'

'Yes.'

'You've made a mistake, Mr Raha.' Her voice rose to a cry of plaintive denial. 'It wasn't me you saw. It was someone else. Children change as they grow. I have no memory of what you describe. I was not there. There were many of us – girls working in the palace. Perhaps it was someone else. I don't know. It wasn't me. I was not there.'

'I remember what I saw.'

'How can you be sure? I remember nothing of that time. I have never wanted to. And you yourself were a boy, a child.'

'But I still remember.'

'And for that you came here looking for me?'

'Miss Dolly, I have no family, no parents, no brothers, no sisters, no fabric of small memories from which to cut a large cloth. People think this sad and so it is. But it means also that I have no option but to choose my own attachments. This is not easy, as you can see. But it is freedom of a kind, and thus not without value.'

'And what did you expect to find? Did you come here thinking to find me still a child? Someone who could take you back to your boyhood?'

'I came because I could. Expecting nothing.'

Dolly fanned her face with her hands. She could smell the evening's fallen frangipani dying on the grass around her. 'Mr Raha.' She was calmer now, breathing more evenly. 'You are a rich man, I am told – a successful man. You have evidently lived a colourful life. I am at a loss to understand what it is exactly that has brought you here. I should tell you that, as far as I am concerned, this is my home and I have no other. I have spent twenty years here. I lead a very simple, practical life. There is nothing in me or the life I lead that can be of the remotest interest to someone like yourself.'

'I would like to say, with respect, that that is not for you to judge.'

'Mr Raha, it is best that you leave now.'

'I could not bring myself to leave without telling you that you had misunderstood me tonight at the dinner table. That is why I doubled back on my way out. I have come a long way. I could not leave on that note.'

A shadow appeared in the distance, framed against the drawing room's open window. It was Uma, calling out through cupped hands. 'Where are you, Dolly? In the garden?'

Dolly lowered her voice. 'Mr Raha, I am sorry if I said anything unjust or unkind. I am sure you meant no harm. But your coming here was a mistake and you would do best to put it behind you as quickly as possible. It is a pity that you have wasted so much time and effort.'

'It was not a waste.'

'There is nothing more to say Mr Raha.' Dolly joined together the palms of her hands. 'I must go now. I do not think we shall meet again, but I wish you well. *Namaste.*'

*   *   *

The Queen received the Collector, as always, seated in her ornate black armchair, with her back to the door. Her face was a painted mask, her lips a sunburst of red. Her ivory skin seemed almost translucent in the dim candlelight. She was dressed in a htamein of red silk and her stockinged feet were enclosed in black slippers, embroidered with fraying threads of gold.

Gesturing to the Collector to seat himself, she began without preamble, speaking in Hindustani. 'It is His Majesty the King's wish, Collector-sahib, that you be informed that our eldest daughter, Princess Ashin Hteik Su Myat Phaya Lat, is pregnant and that her confinement is perhaps just a week or two away. We would be grateful if you would convey the good news to your superiors in the Government of India.'

The Collector's first instinct was to correct her. 'But Your Highness this cannot be, for the Princess has no husband.'

'Not to your knowledge perhaps.'

'This is not a matter of opinion,' said the Collector. 'I have not issued a licence for the Princess's marriage. Therefore she cannot be legally married.'

The Queen was silent for a moment and then a slight smile appeared on her face.

'Collector-sahib, you keep yourself so well informed. I'm surprised that none of your spies have ever thought to tell you that children can be born without a licence.'

'So you mean the child . . .'

'Yes. By your laws, the child will be a bastard.'

'And the father?'

'You've met him often.' She fixed him with an unwavering gaze. 'He is our coachman, a fine young man.'

It was only now that the Collector began to grasp the full import of what she had said. 'But what am I to report? What am I to tell the Government?'

'You will convey what you have been told: you will say that our daughter is soon to have a child and that the father is our coachman, Sawant.'

'But, Your Highness,' the Collector said, 'consider the Princess's reputation, consider your standing in society.'

'Our standing? And what exactly is that, Collector-sahib?'

'Your husband is the King of Burma, albeit deposed. Your daughter is a Princess.'

'I assure you, Collector-sahib, that you of all people need not trouble to remind us of this.'

He could feel the sweat breaking out on his forehead. There was still time, he told himself: the matter could be handled discreetly, without any inkling of it reaching the public. The young man could be persuaded to go quietly back to his village and family. If he made trouble, Mr Wright and his policemen would deal with him.

'Your Highness, I beg you to reflect. Is it appropriate that a Princess of Burma should link herself to a household employee, a servant?'

A tiny, trilling laugh escaped the Queen's lips. 'Collector-sahib, Sawant is less a servant than you. At least he has no delusions about his place in the world.'

The Collector stared at her. 'I am frankly amazed,' he said, 'that Your Highness should choose to make light of such a scandal.'

'Scandal?' The Queen's eyes hardened as she repeated the English word. 'You have the insolence to come here and speak to us of scandals? There is no scandal in what my daughter has done. The scandal lies in what you have done to us; in the circumstances to which you have reduced us; in our very presence here. What did my daughters ever do, Collector-sahib, that they should have to spend their lives in this prison? Did they commit a crime? Were they tried or sentenced? We have heard so many lectures from you and your colleagues on the subject of the barbarity of the Kings of Burma and the humanity of the Angrez; we were tyrants you said, enemies of freedom, murderers. The English alone understand liberty, we were told; they do not put kings and princes to death; they rule through laws. If that is so, why has King Thebaw never been brought to trial? Where are these laws that we hear of? Is it a crime to defend your country against an invader? Would the English not do the same?'

The Collector knew that the appropriate response was to make a gesture of protest, a show of indignation. But under the Queen's hard-eyed scrutiny he was unable to find the right words.

'Your Highness,' he said at last, 'I am not your enemy. On the contrary I have acknowledged to you many times that I believe your grievances to be well-founded. The matter unfortunately is not in my hands. Please believe me when I say that I have only your best interests at heart. It is solely out of concern for you and your family that I am requesting you to reconsider your decision to accept this man – this coachman – into your family. I implore you, Your Highness, to think of how the public will view this – of the damage to your family's reputation.'

The Queen tilted her head. 'We are not public servants, Collector-sahib. To us the opinions of people at large are a matter of utter indifference.'

'I see your mind is made up.'

'Shame on you, Collector-sahib, that you should presume to judge the conduct of my children; shame on you that you should have the effrontery to come into this house and speak to me of scandal.'

The Collector rose to his feet. 'Your Highness, may I mention one last consideration? I do not expect it to weigh very greatly with you, but I feel that I have the right none the less, to bring it to your attention. You should be aware that if this matter becomes public, as your custodian-in-chief it is I, in all likelihood, who will bear the blame. Indeed it would almost certainly mean the end of my tenure here as Collector.'

'I assure you, Collector-sahib,' – the Queen laughed – 'we are well aware of this.' She laughed again, raising a tiny hand to cover her mouth. 'I am sure you will find a way to preserve yourself. Public officials usually do. If not you'll have only yourself to blame.'

There was nothing more to say. With a few mumbled words of regret the Collector excused himself from the Queen's presence. On his way out, he spotted Sawant coming out of the gatehouse. He could hear a woman's voice, calling out from within. Walking past the door, eyes discreetly averted, he caught a whiff of the hot, damp air inside. He quickened his pace. Was this where they cohabited then, the coachman and the First Princess, in that tiny hutch of a room? A profusion of images welled up before his eyes: Sawant, leaning on the doorpost, stroking his oiled moustache, beckoning to the girl with a smile; the Princess, stealing in through

151

an unlatched door while the rest of the household lay asleep; the rank little room, reeking of sweat and echoing to their muffled cries; the creaking of a *charpai*.

He hurried into his gaari, calling impatiently to Kanhoji, '*Chalo! Jaldi chalo, jaldi*, to the Residency, quickly.' He leant out of the gaari's window, breathing hard, but even the cool night air could not clear his nostrils of the smell of that room. Was this love then: this coupling in the darkness, a princess of Burma and a Marathi coachman; this heedless mingling of sweat?

And the Queen, with her snapping black eyes? He had heard it said once that she had always really loved Thebaw. But what could they possibly know of love, of any of the finer sentiments, these bloodthirsty aristocrats, these semi-illiterates who had never read a book in all their lives, never looked with pleasure upon a painting? What could love mean to this woman, this murderer, responsible for the slaughter of scores of her own relatives? And yet it was a fact that she had chosen captivity over freedom for the sake of her husband, condemned her own daughters to twenty years of exile. Would Uma do the same for him? Would anyone? He shivered, stretching out his arms to steady himself against the sides of the carriage.

At the Residency, Uma was waiting up. She came running to the door to let him in, waving the servants away. 'What happened? What did she say? Tell me.'

'Where's Dolly?' the Collector asked.

'She was tired. She went straight to bed.'

'Come.'

The Collector led her to their bedroom and shut the door.

'You knew. Didn't you?'

'About what?'

'Uma, whatever I am, I'm not a fool. I'm talking about the Princess's pregnancy.'

Uma sat down on the edge of their mosquito-netted bed, averting her gaze.

'So you knew, didn't you?'

'Yes.'

'Dolly told you?'

'Yes.'

'And it never occurred to you to tell me? That this might be a matter of some importance? That it would have consequences for me?'

'How could I tell you? I promised not to.'

He came to stand beside her, looking down at her lowered head.

'And your promise to Dolly meant more than the bond between us, you and me?' He reached for her hands and took them gently into his own. 'Look at me, Uma. Why could you not trust me? Have I ever betrayed you, in any way? Did you think I would not be discreet?'

'I promised.'

He stared at her in bemusement. 'You've known of this for days, perhaps months. We were together all that time. Did you never once feel the desire to talk of this with me? Not as the Collector of Ratnagiri, not even as your husband, but just as a companion, someone in whose company you spend your days?'

She pulled her hands free of his grip. What did he want of her? She did his bidding in all things: she went to the Club when he told her to; she went to all her appointments. What more was there to give?

She began to sob, covering her face with her hands. The wifely virtues she could offer him he had no use for: Cambridge had taught him to want more; to make sure that nothing was held in abeyance, to bargain for a woman's soul with the coin of kindness and patience. The thought of this terrified her. This was a subjection beyond decency, beyond her imagining. She could not bring herself to think of it. Anything would be better than to submit.

Thirteen

It seemed to Uma that she had only just drifted off, after many long hours of sleeplessness, when she heard a voice at her bedside: 'Memsahib! Memsahib!'

She stirred drowsily, pushing her pillows back against the polished headboard. 'Memsahib!' It was an ayah, her face veiled by the cloudy gauze of the mosquito net. 'Get up, memsahib! Get up!' The windows were open and the ceiling was bathed in reflected sunlight. There was a smell of freshly mown grass in the air. She heard scythes hissing in the garden and remembered that she'd told the *malis* to mow the lawn.

'Memsahib, wake up. A gentleman is waiting in the *baithak-khana*.'

'A gentleman? Who?'

'The one who was here for dinner yesterday – the *bahaarka* gentleman.'

'Mr Raha?' Uma sat up with a start. 'What is he doing here?'

'He asked to see you. And Dolly memsahib.'

'Have you told her this?'

'Dolly memsahib isn't here. She left early this morning.'

'When?'

'Very early. Kanhoji took her back to Outram House.'

The mosquito net had somehow worked its coils around Uma: she couldn't get the webbing off her face.

'Why wasn't I told?'

'Collector-sahib said not to wake you.'

She scratched impatiently at the net with clawed fingers. There was a tearing sound and a gap opened suddenly in front of her.

154

She climbed through the rent, swinging her legs off the bed.

It wasn't like Dolly to leave in such a hurry, without a word.

'Send some tea to the baithak-khana,' she said to the ayah. 'And tell the gentleman I'll be out soon.'

She dressed quickly and went hurrying down the corridor. She took the ayah with her into the drawing room, and left her squatting by the door for propriety.

'Mr Raha?'

He was on the far side of the room, blowing smoke through an open window. At the sound of her voice, he spun round, flicking away his cheroot. He was wearing 'English' clothes – a white linen suit.

'Madame Collector, I am sorry to have disturbed you . . .'

'No. Not at all.' She began to cough. The room was foggy with acrid tobacco smoke.

'I'm sorry.' He dispelled a cloud of smoke with an apologetic wave. 'I came to thank you . . . for last night.' There was a pause in which she heard him swallow as though he were trying to collect himself to say something. 'And I wanted to thank Miss Sein too, if I could.'

'Dolly? But she isn't here. She's gone back to Outram House.'

'Oh.' He fell into a chair, his lips working silently, as though he were saying something to himself. She noticed that his hair was dishevelled and his eyes bleary from lack of sleep.

'May I ask if she is likely to return here today?'

'Mr Raha,' said Uma quietly, 'I have to say that I am a little surprised that you should concern yourself so much with someone you hardly know.'

He looked up at her. 'Madame Collector . . .'

'Yes?'

'There is something I should tell you.'

'Go on.'

'I have not been entirely frank with you. Or your uncle.'

'How so?'

'This was not my first meeting with Miss Sein. The truth is that it is because of her that I am here. I came in search of her.'

'What?' Uma tried to laugh. 'There must be some mistake, Mr Raha. You are surely thinking of someone else. You could not

155

have met Dolly before this. Dolly has lived here all her life. I can assure you of that. She hasn't left Ratnagiri since she was ten years old.'

'The girl I spoke of last night – the girl in the Glass Palace?'

'Yes?'

'That was her – Dolly, Miss Sein.'

Uma felt the breath rushing out of her body. She rose unsteadily to her feet, and stepped through one of the French windows into the garden. 'Come, Mr Raha.' Without waiting for him, she set off across the freshly cut lawn. The malis were busy sweeping the cut grass to take home to their cows and goats; they looked up and salaamed as she swept by.

Rajkumar caught up with her at the bottom of the garden, just as she was opening the wicket gate. 'This must seem very strange to you.'

'Yes. It does.'

She led him to the earthen seat beneath the peepul tree. The Kajali river shone like glass in the valley below. 'Please sit down, Mr Raha.'

'I didn't know I would find her here,' Rajkumar said. 'Not for sure. This was just a place to begin – a way of settling a score with myself. As long as there existed a place where I could make enquiries, I had to come. I had no choice. I was sure that I'd find the matter settled: she would be married, I thought, or carrying someone else's child. Or dead, or turned into something unrecognisable. That would be that, the sight of her would wash the memory from my mind, set me free. Then I walked into your house last night, and there she was. I knew her at once: her face, her expression. And then the matter was indeed out of my hands, but not in the way I expected.'

'And you'd only seen her that one time?'

'Twice. In Mandalay. But if I had met her a thousand times it would have been no different. I know that. I am sure of that. When I was very young, I used to work on a boat, a Chittagong sampan. This was a long time ago, even before I went to Mandalay. One day we were caught in a storm. We were on the open sea and the storm came up very suddenly, as they do off the coast of Bengal. Water began to pour into the boat, over the stern. I was roped to a mast and given a bucket to bale with. Soon the sky grew so dark that my surroundings became invisible, except by lightning. During one of those flashes, I noticed something. It was an animal, a small, green-backed turtle. It had been washed aboard by a wave and had somehow got itself caught in some netting. It was just beyond my reach, and the waves were hitting the boat so hard I didn't dare undo my rope. We were both bound in our places, the turtle and I. At every flash of lightning, I looked up and there he was. And so it went, through that long, long night: the animal and I, watching one another, through the waves and the wind. Towards dawn the storm abated. I undid my ropes and unloosed the turtle from the net. I can see it clearly to this day. If you were to set a thousand turtles in front of me now, they would not be as real to me as that one animal.'

'Why are you telling me this, Mr Raha?'

'Who else can I tell?'

'Tell Dolly.'

'I tried to. Last night. I saw her going into the garden and I doubled back after leaving you.'

'What did she say?'

'She was determined to be angry – just as she was at dinner. She found fault with everything I said. She told me to go back. She would not see me again. I stayed up all night, thinking what do I do next? In any other place, I would have had people to turn to: my friends would have learnt her mind from her friends. I would have asked someone to speak to her family. Then I would have gone myself to meet her father. We would have discussed money, settlements. Things like that. I would have had some help. People to speak for me.'

'Yes.' Uma nodded. 'There would have been intermediaries. Go-betweens. People who can explain us better than we can ourselves.'

He was right, she knew – that was how these things happened: someone carried word from one mouth to another and so it went, whispers travelling like tendrils along hothouse trellises. That was exactly how it had happened in her own case: one night, a gaari had come clattering into the paved courtyard of their family home in Calcutta – the house to which her father had given the name Lankasuka. There was a loud banging on the front door,

157

downstairs. It was late, after dinner. Her father was in his study, busy working on his treatise on temple architecture. Her mother was preparing to go to bed. 'Someone must have died,' her mother had declared. 'There's only ever bad news at this time of night.'

Uma and her little brother had gone running to the veranda that overlooked the courtyard. One of their aunts was standing by the door downstairs. 'Has someone died?' Uma had shouted.

'Died?' Her aunt had burst into laughter. 'No, you silly girl. Let me in.'

Uma and her brother had listened at the door while their mother conferred with the visitor. They heard them mention the Collector's name and recognised it: they'd read about him recently, in newspapers and magazines. He was known to be a brilliant man. As a student, he'd done so well at Calcutta University that the well-to-do families of his neighbourhood had pooled their resources together to send him to Cambridge. He'd returned a minor hero, having been accepted into the grandest and most powerful imperial cadre, the Indian Civil Service.

It transpired that he had seen Uma at a *puja*: she'd been sixteen at the time, a schoolgirl. On his return from Cambridge, he'd made enquiries about her. His family was none too pleased: they'd had proposals from all over the city and thought they could do much better. But he persisted, insisting that he didn't want a conventional marriage. He'd be working with Europeans: it wouldn't do to have a conservative, housebound wife. He needed a girl who would be willing to step out into society; someone young, who wouldn't be resistant to learning modern ways.

'And he's asking about my Uma?'

Her mother's incredulous shriek had resounded through the house. Uma was by no means the best-looking or the most accomplished girl in her circle: she could neither sing nor sew; her hair wasn't quite straight and she was thought to be too tall to be graceful.

'My Uma?'

Her brother had backed away from her, his mouth falling open in disbelief. 'You!' To tease him she'd said: 'Well, he can hardly marry *you*.' He'd burst into tears, as though that were exactly what he'd been hoping for.

'Why me?' Uma had asked the question over and over again, of all the usual intermediaries and go-betweens. 'Why me?' The most that anyone had been able to tell her was: 'He thinks you'll be quick to learn.'

Their wedding was unlike any other. The Governor came, and many English civil servants and army officers. Instead of a *shehnai* there was a military band from Fort William.

When they were alone, in the flower-hung bedroom of the first night, they'd both sat a long while silent on the bed, held still by shyness, he no less than she. They'd listened to the voices of their friends and relatives, clustered round the closed door, laughing, making the usual ribald jokes. At last, to her relief, he'd begun to talk: he'd told her about Cambridge, about the cobbled streets and stone bridges, about concerts he'd attended. He'd hummed a tune: it was by his favourite composer, he said. She liked the liveliness of the tune and asked: what is it called? He was pleased that she'd asked.

'It's from "The Trout",' he explained, 'by Schubert.'

'It's nice. Hum it again.' She'd drifted off to sleep, waking hours later to his touch. The pain was not as terrible as she'd been told – not much worse than going to the doctor – and the room was very dark, which made it easier. When her mother asked the next day, she was embarrassed that she didn't have a fearsome story to tell, like everyone else.

'He was kind, gentle.'

'What more could anyone ask?' her mother had said. 'Treasure your good fortune, Uma. Don't let a day go by without being grateful for what you've got.'

A month later, in a train, the Collector had asked suddenly if she remembered the name of the tune he'd hummed that night. Her mind had gone empty. They were heading through the stark flatness of Western Rajputana and she was entranced by the land-scape. 'I don't remember,' she'd said. He had turned abruptly away, his face lengthening into a downcurl of disappointment. She had felt a tremor of dismay creeping slowly through her body like palsy. There would be more of this, she knew: these small episodes of disappointment would follow quickly on each other, in a long leaden chain.

Rajkumar's voice startled her back to the present: 'Will you help me then, Madame? You are the only person through whom I can reach Dolly now. There is no one else I can turn to.'

She tried to picture Dolly through the eyes of the man who was sitting beside her, this virtual stranger. Suddenly she felt her heart brimming over with tenderness, with love. Whose was it, this love? Was it his? Or her own? Or perhaps both? What would she do if Dolly left? Such brightness as there was in her life came from Dolly, although by rights, it should have been the other way round. It was Dolly who was the prisoner, after all: she was the lucky one, Mrs Uma Dey, of whom everyone always said, what more could you ask? But now, thinking of what it would be like in Ratnagiri without Dolly, she felt tears flooding into her eyes. She reached for the edge of the earthen bench to steady herself and her hand brushed against his.

'Madame? Mrs Dey?' He was peering at her, frowning in concern. 'Mrs Dey, are you all right?'

'Yes, yes.' She snatched her hand away. 'Just a little dizzy. I don't know what the matter is.'

'Shall we go back inside?'

'Yes.' She rose to her feet. 'Mr Raha, you still haven't told me. What is it that you expect of me?'

'Perhaps you could speak to her.'

'You must speak to her yourself, Mr Raha. Things never turn out well when there are go-betweens.'

He looked at her closely and then, suddenly, taking her by surprise, he said: 'The Collector is a fine man, Mrs Dey, a good man. Men like him are worth many –'

'Yes, of course,' she interrupted him quickly. 'Yes. Come let us go in.'

The ayah led Dolly to the drawing room and showed her the open window. 'Madame went into the garden – just a few minutes ago.'

Dolly nodded: of course, at this time of the day Uma was always to be found under the peepul tree. She went hurrying down the lawn, past the salaaming malis, to the wicket gate. Just as she was

160

fumbling with the latch, she heard voices. Before she could turn back, Uma and Rajkumar appeared before her, stepping suddenly out of the peepul's gnarled grey beard. They stood staring at each other, all three of them.

Uma was the first to speak. 'Mr Raha,' she said quietly, 'I hope you will not take it amiss if I ask you to leave us for a minute? I would like to talk to Dolly – just a few words. Perhaps you could wait for us here by the garden gate?'

'Of course.'

Uma took Dolly's arm. 'Come, let's go and sit under the tree for a bit.'

As they were picking their way through the labyrinth of roots beneath the peepul tree, Dolly whispered: 'What was he doing here, Uma? What does he want?'

'He was talking. About you.'

'What did he say?'

'I think he was trying to tell me that he's in love with you.' Uma seated herself under the tree and pulled Dolly down beside her.

'Oh, Uma.' Dolly buried her face in her hands. 'Last night, in your garden, he said so many things to me. It was so strange, so upsetting. I couldn't sleep, I kept thinking of home – Mandalay, the palace, the walls of glass.'

'He said you had no memory of him.'

'I thought not.'

'Do you then?'

'I'm not sure Uma. I remember someone, a boy, very dark; I remember being given a little packet of food; I remember Evelyn saying, take it, take it. But nothing is clear. It was so long ago, and whenever I think of it, I am frightened.'

'I think he really is in love with you, Dolly.'

'He's in love with what he remembers. That isn't me.'

'What about you, Dolly? What do you feel?'

'I'm frightened, Uma. I've made such terrible mistakes in the past. I promised myself I would never allow myself to make another.'

'What mistakes?'

'I've never told you this Uma, but many years ago, I thought I was in love with Mohanbhai – our coachman. Then the Princess found out. She threatened us. I suppose she was already in love with him herself.'

'Did you want to marry him?'

'I don't know, Uma. I was very young, and I didn't really understand what was happening. During the day I would keep him out of my mind. But at night I would dream of him and then I would wake up and think: Why can't we run away? Why can't I just wrap my things in a bundle right now, and go down to him and wake him up and say: "Mohanbhai, let's go, there's nothing for us here at Outram House"? But where could we have gone? And what would we have done? His family is very poor and they depend on him. In my heart I knew that even if I had begged him he would not have left. And this was the worst part of it, the humiliation. I would think, to myself, have I too become a servant, in my heart, as he has?'

'Did you ever tell him?'

'No. We never spoke, except of everyday matters. And after a while the dreams stopped and I thought, I am free of him now, it's all right at last. But last night, when I was sleeping in that room of yours, I began to dream again. I was at Outram House, in my bed. There was a mango tree beside my window. I got out of my bed and tied my things together, in a bundle, and slung it over my back. I climbed down and went running through the compound to the gatehouse. The door was open and I went in. It was dark and all I could see of him was his white langot, knotted tightly between his legs, rising and falling with his breath. I put my hand on his body. My knuckle fitted perfectly into the hollow at the base of his throat. He woke up and he looked at me and touched my face. And then he said: Shall we go? We went outside, and when we were in the moonlight I saw that it was not Mohanbhai.'

'Who was it?'

'It was him.' She inclined her head in the direction of the gate, where they had left Rajkumar.

'And then?'

'I woke up. I was terrified. I was in your house, in that bedroom. I couldn't bear to stay another moment. I went and woke Kanhoji.'

'Dolly. I think you have to tell him.'

'Whom?'

'Mr Raha.'

'No.' Dolly began to sob with her head on Uma's shoulder. 'No. Uma, all I can think of now is the birth of my child. There is no space in my head for anything else.'

Gently, Uma ran her hand over Dolly's head. 'The child is not yours, Dolly.'

'But it could have been.'

'Dolly, listen to me.' Putting her hands on Dolly's shoulders, Uma propped her up so she could look into her face. 'Dolly, will you believe me if I tell you that I love you like I've never loved anyone before? I was just a girl before I met you. You've shown me what courage is, what human beings can endure. I can't bear to think of being without you. I don't think I could remain here a single day if you weren't here. But I know this too, Dolly: you must go if you can. You must go now. The birth of this child will drive you out of your mind if you stay on at Outram House.'

'Don't say that, Uma.'

'Dolly, listen to me. This man loves you. I am convinced of it. You must at least allow yourself to listen to him.'

'Uma, I can't. Not now. Not with the child coming. If it was last year . . .'

'Then you must tell him that yourself. You owe him that.'

'No. Uma, no.'

Uma rose to her feet. 'I'm going to send him here. It'll only take a minute.'

'Don't leave, Uma. Please.' She clutched at Uma's hands. 'Please don't.'

'This is something that has to be done, Dolly. There is no way round it. I'll send him here. Then I'll go to the house. I'll be waiting. Come and tell me what happens.'

Rajkumar spotted her as he was picking his way round the tree: Dolly was sitting erect on the earthen bench, her hands folded neatly in her lap. He threw away his dying cheroot and put

163

another to his lips. His hand was shaking so hard that it took him several tries to light a match.

'Miss Dolly.'

'Mr Raha.'

'My name is Rajkumar. I would be glad if you would call me that.'

She mouthed the syllables hesitantly. 'Rajkumar . . .'

'Thank you.'

'Uma wanted me to speak to you.'

'Yes?'

'But the truth is I have nothing to say.'

'Then let me –'

She held up a hand to stop him. 'Please. Let me finish. You must understand. It's impossible.'

'Why is it impossible? I would like to know. I am a practical man. Tell me and I will try to do something about it.'

'There is a child.'

'A child?' Rajkumar removed the cheroot from his mouth. 'Whose child? Yours?'

'The First Princess is with child. The father works in Outram House. I too was once in love with him – the father of the Princess's child. You should know this. I am not the nine-year-old girl I was in Mandalay.'

'Are you in love with him now?'

'No.'

'Then the rest is immaterial to me.'

'Mr Raha, you must understand. There are things you cannot change no matter how much money you have. Things might have been different for us in another time, another place. But it's too late now. This is my home. I have lived all my life here. My place is here at Outram House.'

Now, at last, the hopes that had sustained him this far began slowly to leak away. He had said all he could. He could think of no other way to plead with her, and she silenced him before he could begin.

'Please. I beg you, do not say anything more. You will merely cause unnecessary pain. There are things in this world that cannot be, no matter how much we may want them.'

'But this can be . . . could be, if only you would allow yourself to think of it.'

'No. Please say no more. I've made up my mind. There is only one thing I want to ask of you now.'

'What is that?'

'I ask that you leave Ratnagiri as soon as you can.'

He flinched, then bowed his head.

'I can see no reason to refuse.' Without another word, he turned and walked away, into the shadows of the bearded peepul.

Fourteen

'Sawant.'

Removing his binoculars from his eyes, the King pointed in the direction of the bay. A boat stood moored at the jetty, a large country craft of a type known locally as a hori: a deep-hulled catamaran with a single outrigger.

'Sawant, he is leaving.'

'Min?' It was very early and Sawant had brought the King the cup of tea he liked to drink at daybreak.

'The man who arrived the other day on the Bombay steamer. He is leaving. They are loading his luggage at the jetty.'

'Min, there is no steamer today.'

'He's hired a boat.' At this time of year, soon after the departure of the monsoons, there was a change in the prevailing currents and the waters round the mouth of the bay became, for a short while, exceptionally hazardous. During these weeks horis were the only sailing craft that would brave the swirling undertow that swept the coast.

'Min.' Sawant placed the pot of tea beside the King's chair and backed quickly out of the room.

Apart from the King and Sawant himself, the house was still asleep. The anteroom where Dolly slept was just a couple of doors down the corridor. Dolly had the suite to herself now, for the First Princess rarely came upstairs any more, preferring mainly to stay in the gatehouse, with Sawant.

Pushing Dolly's door open, Sawant slipped inside. She was asleep, lying on the same narrow cot that she had used for the last twenty years. Her hair had come loose during the night and lay fanned across her pillow. In repose her skin looked almost translucent, and her face had the serene beauty of a temple carving. Standing over her bed, watching the slow rhythms of her breath, Sawant hesitated.

Yesterday, on his way to his village on the estuary, Sawant had met a goatherd who was returning from the direction of the Residency. They had talked for a while, about the peepul tree, about the Collector's memsahib, about the rich prince from Burma and how he was besotted with Dolly.

It was impossible to think of Outram House without Dolly; impossible to imagine Ratnagiri emptied of her presence. But better that than to see her waste away before his eyes. No, he owed her this. He kneeled beside her and raised his hand.

She was wearing a crumpled night-time sari. The cloth was white and it hung like a veil over her long slender limbs. He thought of the time when they'd sat together on his sagging rope bed, with his blood-stained langot draped over their interlocking limbs. Just as he was about to wake her, his hand froze. To think of being without Dolly: it was madness! He began to back away. But then again he stopped. No, he owed her this.

Suddenly she opened her eyes. 'You!' She sat upright, folding her arms over her chest.

He put a finger to his lips. 'Quiet. Everyone's asleep. Quick. Get dressed.'

'Why?'

'He's leaving. Your man.'

Her eyes widened, in dismay. 'So soon?'

'Yes.'

'But there's no steamer. And at this time of year, I didn't think he would be able to go.'

'He's hired a hori.'

'But isn't it too late now?'

'No. They won't be able to leave until the light's better. Quick. You have to stop him. Too much has gone wrong for you, Dolly. Not again. Come. Quick.'

'How?'

'I'll harness the trap and take you down to Mandvi. Quick.'

By the time she was dressed, the trap was outside, ready to go.

167

Sawant had harnessed it to his fastest horse, a grey mare. He held out a hand to help Dolly in and then flicked the tip of his whip over the mare's head. The trap lurched forward, and they went rattling down the hill, past the police lines, the gaol, the Cutchery. At the Jhinjhinaka bazaar, a pack of guard dogs ran howling after them as they went racing past. From a long way off they saw the hori, casting off its moorings and pulling away, under oar, into the bay.

'Mohanbhai!'

He cracked his whip. 'I can go no faster, Dolly.'

When they reached the jetty the boat was a long way gone, approaching the mouth of the bay. 'Run, Dolly, run!' Sawant leapt off and gripped the mare's bit. 'Run! Run!'

She ran down the jetty, waving: in the distance the boat was trying to manoeuvre its bows so that it would be able to slip through the shoals and currents ahead. Its stern bucked furiously as it approached the pounding waters of the open sea. In a few minutes it would be out of the bay. She waved again and just as she was about to give up the hori's bows began to turn, away from the bay's mouth. Circling all the way around the bay the heavy craft came back to the waterfront, pulling up at the end of the jetty. The hori sat high in the water and Rajkumar easily vaulted the distance between the boat and the jetty's outermost plank.

He walked up to her puffing on his cheroot. 'Yes?'

She could feel herself flushing, the blood rising to her face. 'Mr Raha,' she said, picking her words with care. 'The currents are dangerous at this time of year and the Dak Bungalow has been booked for a week. There is no reason to leave in such a hurry.'

'But it was you who said –'

'Yes, but there is sometimes a difference between what one says and what one means . . .'

Rajkumar took the cheroot from his mouth with a hand that was moving very slowly, as though in stunned disbelief. Then he uttered a shout of laughter and threw his cheroot high into the air. They stood looking at it, side by side, laughing, watching as it rose circling above them. Suddenly the glowing tip disintegrated and a shower of sparks came floating down. It was as though fireworks were raining down from the heavens.

The Collector gave the appearance of being delighted when Uma told him that Rajkumar and Dolly were to be married. 'Splendid!' he said. 'Splendid!'

Uma explained that Dolly wanted to have a very quiet ceremony: she was sure that the Queen would do her best to stop the marriage if she got to know of it.

In the spirit of the moment the Collector offered several suggestions. Why not have the ceremony at the Residency? He would issue the licence himself and preside over their marriage in person. Afterwards, perhaps champagne; just for the four of them – Uma must make sure to be careful in husbanding the last batch of ice from Bombay . . . The enthusiasm in his voice was such that Uma couldn't help feeling that her husband was delighted by the prospect of seeing the last of Dolly.

The day came and Uma provided two garlands, of marigolds and jasmine. She wove them herself, with flowers picked from the garden. At the end of the civil ceremony, in the Collector's 'camp office', Uma and Rajkumar garlanded each other, smiling like children.

The plan was for the couple to spend their wedding night at the Dak Bungalow where Rajkumar was staying. Dolly had smuggled a few belongings and a bagful of clothes out of Outram House with the help of the First and Second Princesses. The First Princess had given her a pair of earrings and the Second a jade bracelet. They were happy for her and they were sure the other girls would be too. But for the moment in order to keep the news a secret, they hadn't told the two younger Princesses. Later, when everything was safely signed and sealed, Dolly could go back to Outram House with her new husband to pay her respects.

Everything went as planned until it came time for Dolly and Rajkumar to sign the register. Uma was the only available witness and Dolly balked at asking the bearers. But just then, quite miraculously, Mrs Khambatta, a lady photographer from Bombay, drew up in a gaari, toting her bags and her camera. Rajkumar went running out to rope her in. She readily agreed to be a witness and afterwards they all went out to the garden. The Collector called for champagne. A gentle breeze was blowing in from the sea. The light was mellow and golden.

Mrs Khambatta's camera was an instrument of superb craftsmanship: a 1901 Graflex single-lens reflex, with a cube-like body, a bellows extension and a four-sided hood. It was fitted with a Globe wide-angle lens which proved perfect for the panorama deployed before the shutter. Before exposing her first plate, Mrs Khambatta spent a full half-hour working with a Hurter and Driffield Actinograph Exposure Calculator, peering at its slide rule and calibrating its rotary cylinder for the present time and latitude. Then, signalling her readiness with an upraised hand, she exposed several plates in quick succession, standing back from her camera to squint at the group before squeezing the bulb of her Guery Flap-Shutter.

At dusk Rajkumar and Dolly gathered up their belongings. Uma lent them Kanhoji's gaari. On the way to the Dak Bungalow Dolly changed her mind.

'Let's go to Outram House now,' she said to Rajkumar. 'Let's talk to the Queen. Let's get it over with.'

It was dark by the time they got there. A lamp was shining in the King's room and another in Sawant's by the gate. The Princesses would be downstairs, Dolly thought, sitting around a single light, to save oil. How surprised they would be!

The gates were locked, so she told Kanhoji to use the knocker. He banged hard for a full five minutes but there was no answer.

Dolly went to the gatehouse window and knocked on the wooden shutters. 'Mohanbhai,' she called out. 'Open the gates. It's me, Dolly. I've come to say goodbye. Open the gates.'

The lights in the room went out and a minute or two later, she heard Sawant's voice, whispering: 'Dolly?'

'Where are you Mohanbhai?'

'Here. By the gatepost.' He was peering through the crack between the wall and the gate. 'Dolly, Mebya knows. She's told me not to let you in, not to open the gates.'

Dolly gasped. How could she leave Ratnagiri without saying

goodbye to Min and Mebya, to the Princesses? 'But, Mohanbhai, it's me, Dolly. Let me in.'

'I can't, Dolly. You know I would if I could. But Mebya is in one of her rages. You know how angry she gets.'

There was a pause and then a cloth bundle appeared at the top of the gate.

'Mebya had us pack some of your things,' said Sawant. 'She told me to make sure you got this.'

Dolly let the bundle drop to the ground.

'Mohanbhai, let me in.' She was pleading now. 'Just for a few minutes. Just to say goodbye.'

'I can't, Dolly. I really can't. Mebya said she would sack me if I did; she said we couldn't ever say your name again in this house.'

Dolly began to sob, knocking her head against the gatepost.

'Don't cry, Dolly.' Sawant looked through the crack. 'We'll miss you, all of us. Look, the girls are waving to you from up there.'

The four Princesses were standing close together, at one of the windows upstairs. They waved and she tried to wave back too, but her legs buckled under her. She fell to her knees, sobbing. Rajkumar rushed to lift her off the ground. Holding her up with one arm, he picked up her bundled clothes with his free hand.

'Come, Dolly. Let's go. There's nothing to be done.' He had to lift her bodily off the ground to get her inside the gaari.

'Chalo, chalo, jaldi chalo.'

When they were trotting past the police-barracks, near the parade ground, some of the constables' wives and children came out to wave. They all seemed to know that Miss Dolly was going away.

She waved back, wiping the tears fiercely from her eyes. She would not allow herself to be robbed of this last glimpse of the lane: the leaning coconut palms, the Union Jack, flapping above the gaol on its crooked pole, the rickety teashop at the entrance to the lane. This was home, this narrow lane with its mossy walls of laterite. She knew she would never see it again.

She sat bent over in her seat, hugging her old clothes. A cloth bundle, once again: only this time she wasn't carrying it on her head.

*   *   *

With her hand raised to knock, Uma noticed that the door of the Collector's study was slightly ajar. She could see him through the crack. He was sitting upright in his straight-backed chair. His glasses were dangling around his neck and he was staring into space.

He turned with a start when she knocked. 'Come in.'

She seated herself opposite him, in a chair that had no arms. This was where his stenographer sat, she guessed, little Mr Ranade, with a pad on his knees, taking dictation. They looked at each other silently across the broad, leather-covered expanse of the desk. A letter lay open in front of him; she noted, in passing, that it was sealed with a florid rosette of red wax. She was the first to drop her eyes and it was only then that he spoke.

'You have come to tell me that you want to go home,' he said. 'Am I right?'

She nodded. 'Yes.'

'May I ask why?'

'I am useless here. There's nothing I can do for you that you cannot do better for yourself. And with Dolly gone . . .'

He cleared his throat, cutting her short. 'And may I ask when you will be coming back?'

She made no answer, looking silently down at her lap.

'Well?'

'You deserve better than me.'

He turned his face away abruptly, so that she could see only one side of his face.

'You can marry again,' she said quickly, 'take another wife. I will see that my family makes no objection.'

He raised a finger to silence her.

'Could you tell me,' he said in a coldly formal voice. 'What did I do wrong? Did I mistreat you? Behave badly?'

'No. Never.' The tears welled up in her eyes, blinding her. 'You have been nothing but kind and patient. I have nothing to complain of.'

'I used to dream about the kind of marriage I wanted.' He was speaking more to himself now than to her. 'To live with a woman as an equal, in spirit and intellect: this seemed to me the most wonderful thing life could offer. To discover together the world

172

of literature, art: what could be richer, more fulfilling? But what I dreamt of is not yet possible, not here, in India, not for us.' He ran his fingers over the letter in front of him, picking idly at the the heavy wax seal.

'So you'll go back to live with your parents then?'

'Yes.'

'You've picked a good time.' He gave her his thin, ironic smile. 'You would have had to pack your things soon enough anyway.'

'Why?' She was suddenly alert. 'What are you talking about?'

He picked the letter off his desk and tapped it with his gold-rimmed glasses. 'This is from the Chief Secretary, in Bombay. It came today. A reprimand, as it were. The Princess's pregnancy has awoken our teachers suddenly to the enormity of what they have done to this family. All the letters that I and my predecessors wrote had no effect whatever. But the smell of miscegenation has alarmed them as nothing else could have: they are tolerant in many things, but not this. They like to keep their races tidily separate. The prospect of dealing with a half-caste bastard has set them rampaging among their desks. I am to be the scapegoat for twenty years of neglect. My tenure here is terminated and I am to return to Bombay.'

He brought his fingertips together and smiled across the desk in his thinly ironic way.

'As I said, you've chosen a good time to leave.'

In the Ratnagiri boathouse there was one craft that was rarely used. This was the double-oared racing scull that had once belonged to Mr Gibb, the rowing legend.

It was the Collector's practice to go down to the Ratnagiri boathouse a couple of times each week. He had done a little rowing at Cambridge and would have done more if he had not been so busy studying for the Civil Service examinations. He enjoyed the focused concentration of the sport, the sense of moving ahead at a regulated pace, quick but unhurried. Besides, he had an almost religious belief in the importance of exercise.

Today, as he was walking into the boathouse, the Collector's eyes fell on Mr Gibb's racing shell. The elderly *chowkidar* who looked after the boathouse talked often of Mr Gibb. He was a rowing blue, Mr Gibb, and a skilled sailor besides. In the history of the Ratnagiri Club he was the only person who was known to have taken the slim, fragile craft out into the open sea and come back to tell the tale.

On his departure Mr Gibb had donated his shell to the boathouse. Since that time the boat had turned into a monument of sorts, a reliquary of Mr Gibb. It lay at one end of the shed and was never used. The Collector said to the chowkidar: 'How about this one?'

'That was Mr Gibb's boat,' came the answer. 'It was in that boat that Gibb-sahib used to row out to sea.'

'Is it usable?'

'Yes, sahib. Of course.' The chowkidar was proud of his job and worked hard to keep his boats in good repair.

'Well then, perhaps I'll take it out today.'

'You, sahib?' The chowkidar gasped. 'But Mr Gibb was very experienced –'

The Collector bridled at his tone. 'I think I can manage it,' he said coldly.

'But, sahib –'

'Please do as you're told.'

The boat was carried out to the water and the Collector climbed in and picked up the oars. He rowed once across the bay and turned round. He felt oddly exhilarated. The gap between the two arms of the bay began to beckon.

For several weeks now, he'd been thinking of trying the sea channel. He'd watched the local fishermen when they were slipping out of the bay, marking in his mind the precise point of their exit, the route through which they led their crafts into the open sea.

One day, he'd told himself, one day . . . He would start with a short, experimental foray, to test the waters, as it were. One day. But there were no more days now. Next week he would be in Bombay, in a windowless office, dealing with municipal taxation.

He scarcely noticed that his craft had veered from its trajectory; that its nose had turned westwards, pointing towards the opening

174

of the bay. It was as though the shell had been reclaimed by the spirit of some other, departed official, as though it were steering itself.

He felt strangely reassured, at peace. It was best to leave these things to men like Mr Gibb: you would always be safe with them, looked after, provided for.

There was no reason to hurry back to the Residency. No one was waiting for him there. The sea seemed warm and inviting and the scull seemed to know its own way.

High above the bay, in Outram House, the King was on his way to the balcony, with his father's gilded glasses clasped in one hand. He had lain awake much of the night and was up even earlier than usual. Dolly's departure had created an unquietness in the house. He was sensitive to these things; they upset him. It wasn't easy to cope with change at his age. He'd found it hard to sleep.

He lifted the glasses to his eyes. The light was not good. The fishermen of Karla village were not out of the estuary yet. Then he spotted the thin, long shape of a racing shell arrowing across the dark water. The oarsman was rowing in a strong, steady rhythm, almost touching his knees with his forehead before straightening out again.

He was taken aback. It was a long time since he had last seen the shell steering for the open sea – not since Mr Gibb, and that was a long time ago, more than ten years now. And even Mr Gibb had never ventured out on the sea during the monsoons: he wouldn't have thought of it, he knew about the cross-currents that swept the shore during the rains.

He watched in surprise as the streamlined craft shot forward in the direction of the foaming white line that separated the calm waters of the bay from the pounding monsoon sea. Suddenly the boat buckled and its nose shot out of the water. The oarsman flung up an arm, and then the undertow took hold of him and sucked him down, beneath the surface. The King started to his feet, in shock. Gripping the balcony's rails, he leant over the balustrade. He began to shout: 'Sawant! Sawant!'

It was early in the morning and his voice had grown prematurely feeble. Sawant was asleep in the gatehouse, on his string bed, with one arm thrown protectively over the First Princess.

175

'Sawant, Sawant!'

It was the Queen who heard his shouts. She too had been up all night – thinking of Dolly, remembering how she'd come to her as a child, of how she'd been the only person in the palace who could quiet the Second Princess; of how she had stayed on when the others left.

'Sawant.'

She climbed slowly out of bed and went over to see what the King wanted.

The King pointed to a few bits of wreckage, drifting in the distance, at the mouth of the bay. 'The Collector!'

She took a long look with his gilded binoculars.

'Is he dead?'

'I think so.'

If it were not for that man Dolly would still be at Outram House: Dolly, whom she'd adopted and brought up and loved like her own child. But Dolly was gone now, and it was right that he should pay. She leant over the balustrade and spat into the garden, in commemoration of her gaoler's death.

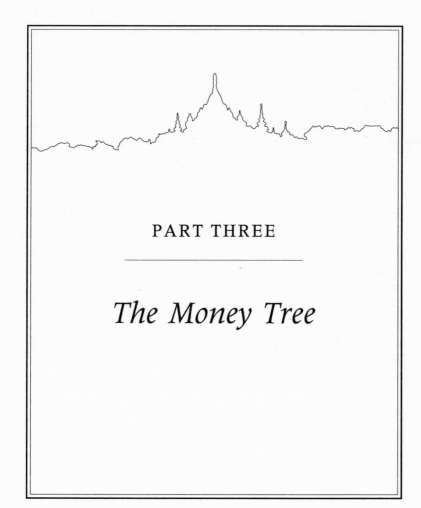

PART THREE

The Money Tree

Fifteen

Rangoon's Barr Street Passenger Jetty was something of a curiosity. It was built to resemble a floating pavilion, with fine woodwork and a peaked roof, like that of an Alpine cottage. Saya John held on to one of its carved posts as he leant over the jetty's side, scanning the river for the *Nuwara Eliya*, the steamer in which Rajkumar was returning to Rangoon with Dolly. When at last he spotted the ship, it was still a long way off, just approaching the mouth of the Pazundaung Creek, fighting the powerful currents that tore at the river's mud-brown surface.

It had been decided that Rajkumar and Dolly would stay initially with Saya John, at his spacious second-floor flat on Blackburn Lane – such accommodation as there was at Rajkumar's Kemendine compound was too rudimentary for the two of them to inhabit together. Saya John had sent a telegram to Rajkumar to let him know that he and Dolly were welcome to stay at Blackburn Lane until such time as they were able to build a habitable home.

The Pazundaung Creek was the wide inlet that marked the southern boundary of the city. Many of Rangoon's sawmills and rice mills were concentrated along the shores of this waterway – among them also the timberyard that was Rajkumar's principal place of business. When the steamer drew abreast of the creek, Rajkumar, watching from the *Nuwara Eliya*'s bows, caught a brief glimpse of the raised teakwood cabin that served as his office. Then the whole Rangoon waterfront opened up in front of him: the Botataung Pagoda, the stately buildings of the Strand, the golden finial of the Shwe Dagon in the distance.

Rajkumar turned impatiently away and headed for his cabin.

Since early that morning he had been trying to persuade Dolly to step outside: he was eager to show her this vista of Rangoon from the river; eager also to see whether she remembered any of it from her journey out, twenty-five years before. But over the last three days, as their ship approached Burma, Dolly had grown increasingly withdrawn. That morning she had refused to step out on deck; she'd said that she was seasick; that she would come out later, when she felt better; for the time being she wanted only to rest and collect herself.

But now there was no time at all. They would be at the jetty in a matter of minutes. Rajkumar burst into the cabin, his voice loudly exuberant: 'Dolly – we're home. Come on – outside . . .' When she didn't answer he broke off. She was sitting on the bed, curled up, with her forehead resting on her knees, dressed in the red, silk htamein that she'd changed into for the occasion.

'What's the matter Dolly?' He touched her shoulder to find that she was shivering. 'What's happened?'

'Nothing.' She shrugged his hand off. 'I'm all right. I'll come later; just let me sit here until everyone else is off the ship.'

He knew better than to make light of her apprehensions. 'All right,' he said. 'I'll come back for you in twenty minutes.'

'Yes. I'll be ready then.'

Dolly stayed as she was, with her head resting on her knees, trying to calm herself. She felt a jolt as the steamer docked and then she heard the voices of coolies and porters ringing through the gangways. Rippling patterns of opalescent light were dancing on the ceiling, shining in through a porthole, off the river's silt-dark surface. In a while, the cabin door squeaked open, and she heard Rajkumar's voice: 'Dolly . . .'

She looked up to see Rajkumar ushering someone into the cabin: a small, portly, owlish man, dressed in a grey suit and a felt hat. The visitor doffed his hat and smiled, so broadly that his eyes almost disappeared into the creases of his deeply lined face. This had to be Saya John, she knew, and the knowledge of this made her more apprehensive than ever. This was the meeting she had most dreaded: Rajkumar had talked of his mentor at such length that Saya John had become the equivalent of a father-in-law in her mind, to be either feared and propitiated, or else to be resisted and fought with – she had no idea how things would turn out between the two of them. Now, faced with him in person, she found herself folding her hands together, in the Indian way, unconsciously, through the force of long habit.

He laughed and came quickly across the cabin. Addressing her in Burmese, he said, 'Look, I have something for you.' She noticed that his accent was thickly foreign.

He reached into his pocket and took out a filigreed gold bracelet, wrapped in tissue paper. Taking hold of her wrist, he slipped the bracelet over her knuckles. 'It belonged to my wife,' he said. 'I put it aside for you.'

She spun the bracelet around her wrist. The polished gold facets gleamed in the dappled light that was shining in through the portholes. He put his arm around her and under the pressure of his hand, she felt her apprehensions seeping away. She glanced at him shyly and smiled. 'It's beautiful, Saya. I'll treasure it.'

Rajkumar, watching from the doorway, saw a lightening in the mists that had gathered around her over the last few days. 'Come,' he said quickly. 'Let's go. The gaari is waiting.'

On the way to Blackburn Lane, in the carriage, Saya John reached into his pocket once again. 'I have something for you too, Rajkumar.' He took out a small, spherical object, also wrapped in tissue paper. He handed it carefully to Rajkumar.

Undoing the tissue paper, Rajkumar found himself holding a spongy ball, made of whitish-grey strings that were tangled around each other, like wool. He raised the ball to his face, wrinkling his nose at the unfamiliar odour. 'What is it?'

'Rubber.' Saya John used the English word.

'Rubber?' Rajkumar recognised the word, but had only a dim awareness of what it referred to. He handed the ball to Dolly and she sniffed it, recoiling: its smell was more human than botanical, the scent of a bodily secretion, like sweat.

'Where did you get this, Saya?' Rajkumar said, in puzzlement.

'In my hometown – Malacca.'

Saya John had been travelling too, while Rajkumar was away in India: he had gone east, to Malaya, visiting friends and looking up his relatives by marriage. He'd stopped at Malacca, to visit his wife's grave. It was some years since he'd last been back, and he'd noticed immediately that something had changed in the interim, something new was afoot. For years, ever since he could remember, Malacca had been a town that was slowly dying, with its port silted up and its traders moving away, either northwards to Penang, or southwards to Singapore. But now, suddenly, Malacca was a changed place; there was a palpable quickening in the muddied veins of the sleepy old city. One day a friend took him to the outskirts of the town, to a place that he, John Martins, remembered from his childhood, an area that had once been home to dozens of small spice gardens, where pepper plants grew on vines. But the vines were all gone now, and in their place there were long straight rows of graceful, slender-trunked saplings.

Saya John had looked hard at the trees and had not been able to name them. 'What are they?'

'Rubber.'

Some nine years before, Mr Tan Chay Yan, scion of a well-known Peranakan Chinese family of Malacca, had converted his pepper garden into a rubber plantation. In 1897 this had seemed like a mad thing to do. Everyone had advised against it: rubber was known to be a risk. Mr Ridley, the curator of the Singapore Botanical Gardens, had been trying for years to interest British planters in giving rubber a try. The imperial authorities in London had spent a fortune in arranging to have seed stocks stolen from Brazil. But Mr Ridley was himself the first to admit that it might take as many as ten years for a rubber plantation to become productive. Malaya's European planters had backed away on learning this. But Mr Tan Chay Yan, persevering undeterred, had succeeded in milking rubber from his trees in three short years. Now everyone, even the most timid British corporation, was following his lead, planting rubber; money had been pouring into the city. The B. F. Goodrich company had sent representatives all the way from Akron, Ohio, urging the planters of Malaya to plant this new crop. This was the material of the coming age; the next generation of machines could not be made to work without this indispensable absorber of friction. The newest motor cars had dozens of rubber parts; the markets were potentially bottomless, the profits beyond imagining.

Saya John had made enquiries, asking a few knowledgeable

people about what was involved in planting rubber. The answers were always short: land and labour were what a planter needed most; seed and saplings were easily to be had. And of the two principal necessities, land was the easier to come by: of labour there was already a shortage. The British Colonial Government was looking to India to supply coolies and workers for the plantations.

Saya John had begun to toy with the idea of buying some land for Matthew, his son. He'd quickly discovered that land prices around Malacca had risen steeply; he was advised to travel north, in the direction of the Siam border. He'd set off, not quite convinced still. He was too old to start up a vast new project, this he knew; but there was Rajkumar to be counted on – he would know what to do about building a workforce – and of course there was always Matthew, who had been away in America many years. No one knew exactly what Matthew was doing there; the last he'd heard, the boy had travelled east, to New York. There had been a letter a while back; he'd said something about looking for a job – nothing at all about coming home. Perhaps this was exactly what was needed to bring the boy home: a huge new enterprise to which he could dedicate himself: something that would be his own; something that he could build up. He could see himself growing old, living with Matthew – the boy would have a family, children; they'd live together in a quiet place, surrounded by trees and greenery.

These ideas were still forming in his mind, when he glimpsed the perfect place, from the deck of a ferry boat: the south-facing slope of a mountain, an extinct volcano that reared out of the plain like the head of some fantastic beast. The place was a wilderness, a jungle; but at the same time, it was within easy distance of the island of Penang and the port of Butterworth.

'I've got land there now,' Saya John said to Rajkumar, 'and it's waiting for the day when Matthew comes back.'

Rajkumar, newly married and eager in his anticipation of the pleasures of domestic life, was not disposed to take his mentor seriously. 'But, Saya, what does Matthew know about rubber or plantations?'

'It doesn't matter. He'll find out. And of course, he'll have you

183

to help him. We'll be partners, the three of us: you, me, Matthew.'

Rajkumar shrugged. 'Saya, I know even less about this than Matthew does. My business is timber.'

'Timber is a thing of the past, Rajkumar: you have to look to the future – and if there's any tree on which money could be said to grow then this it – rubber.'

Rajkumar felt Dolly's hand, pressing against his own, in anxious enquiry. He gave her a reassuring nudge as though to say: it's just one of the old man's fancies; there's no need to worry.

In the immediate aftermath of her widowhood, Uma returned to Lankasuka, her parents' house, in Calcutta. Hers was a small family: she had only one brother, who was much younger than herself. Their house was spacious and comfortable, although not grand: it had two storeys, with a semi-circular balcony on each. The rooms were airy and bright with high ceilings and stone floors that stayed cool even in the hottest of summers.

But Uma's homecoming was not a happy one. Her father was an archaeologist and a scholar: he was not the kind of man to insist on all the customary observances of a Hindu widowhood, but nor was he so enlightened as to be wholly impervious to the strictures of his neighbours. Within his lights he did what he could to mitigate the rigours of his daughter's situation. But as a widow living at home, Uma's life was still one of rigid constraints and deprivation: her hair was shaved off; she could eat no meat nor fish and she was allowed to wear nothing but white. She was twenty-eight and had a lifetime ahead of her. As the months dragged by it became clear that some other solution would have to be thought of.

Uma was now a woman of independent means, the beneficiary of a very substantial pension. During his lifetime the Collector had held one of the most lucrative jobs in the Empire, and on his death it was discovered that he had made many astute investments, several of them in Uma's name. With her livelihood assured, and no children to care for, there was nothing to hold her at home and every reason to leave. The matter was decided when she received a letter from Dolly, inviting her to visit Rangoon. It was evident that the best possible solution was for her to go abroad.

On the journey over, Uma kept her head covered, with a shawl to hide her shaven head. Dolly and Rajkumar met her at the Barr Street Jetty and the moment she stepped off, Dolly tore away her shawl.

'Why are you hiding your face?' she said. 'I think you look nice like that.'

Dolly and Rajkumar brought Uma directly to their new home in Kemendine: they had only recently moved in and the house was still under construction. Having been very rapidly erected, the house was a haphazard, old-fashioned structure – two floors of interconnected rooms, grouped around a square courtyard. The floors were of polished red stone and the courtyard was lined with corridor-like balconies. The balustrades were of spindly wrought-iron. Along the walls of the compound there were a number of small outhouses. These were inhabited by watchmen, gardeners and other household employees.

Rangoon was almost as much a foreign city to Dolly as it was to Uma, and the two of them began to explore it together: they climbed the steps of the Shwe Dagon pagoda; they visited Uma's uncle in kalaa-basti, the Indian quarter; they attended the pony races at the Kyaikasan racecourse; they went walking in the narrow streets of Syriam, across the river, they promenaded around the Royal Lakes and went for drives around the Cantonment. Everywhere they went, Dolly was courted, sought after, besieged by armies of acquaintances, asked endless questions about the King and Queen and their life abroad. This was a subject of universal interest in Burma, and Dolly's sharing of the Royal Family's exile made her something of a celebrity herself.

Uma's time passed very pleasantly. She was often invited out with Dolly and was never at a loss for things to do. But as the weeks passed she found herself growing ever more painfully aware of the distance between Dolly's ebullient happiness and her own circumstances. In the past, Uma had often wondered about Dolly's marriage: had she married Rajkumar in order to escape the imprisonment of Outram House? Or was it just that she had fallen in love – that and nothing else? Now, watching them together, Uma saw that these reasons were not exclusive of each other: that each of these motives had played a part in creating a wholeness, as in the fitting together of the misshapen pieces of a puzzle. She saw also that this was a completeness that she, who had always prided herself on knowing her own mind in all things, had never known and perhaps would never know, because it was not within her to yield to the moment, in Dolly's way.

Dolly and Rajkumar seemed to have little knowledge of one another's likes and dislikes, preferences and habits, yet the miracle was – and this too Uma could see clearly – that far from weakening their bond, their mutual incomprehension served rather to strengthen it. Between herself and the Collector, on the other hand, every eventuality had been governed by clearly defined rules and meanings. Whenever there was a question about what either of them might like or want, all they had to do was to refer implicitly to usage and etiquette. Now, thinking back, she saw that she herself had come to resemble the Collector more closely than she had ever thought to admit; that she too had become a creature of rules and method and dogged persistence, and was in this sense utterly unlike Dolly.

As the days passed, she became conscious of a gathering grief, an emotion more powerful than any she had ever known. In the light of hindsight, she realised that those words that people had always used of the Collector – *he's a good man* – were true; that he indeed had been a good man, an honest man – a man of great intelligence and ability who happened to have been born into a circumstance that could not offer him an appropriate avenue for the fulfilment of his talents. He had wielded immense power as a District Collector, yet paradoxically, the position had brought him nothing but unease and uncertainty; she recalled the nervous, ironic way in which he had played the part of Collector; she remembered how he'd watched over her at table, the intolerable minuteness of his supervision, the effort he had invested in mould-ing her into a reflection of what he himself aspired to be. There seemed never to be a moment when he was not haunted by the fear of being thought lacking by his British colleagues. And yet it seemed to be universally agreed that he was one of the most successful Indians of his generation; a model for his countrymen. Did this mean that one day all of India would become a shadow of what he had been? Millions of people trying to live their lives in conformity with incomprehensible rules? Better to be what Dolly had been: a woman who had no illusions about the nature of her condition; a prisoner who knew the exact dimensions of her cage and could look for contentment within those confines. But she was not Dolly and never would be; some part of her was irretrievably the Collector's creation, and if nothing was to be served by mourning this disfigurement, then it was her duty to turn her abilities to the task of seeking a remedy.

One day, Rajkumar said to her: 'Everything we have we owe to you. If there's anything you should ever need, we would want to be the first to be asked.'

She smiled. 'Anything?'

'Yes, of course.'

She took a deep breath. 'Well then, I am going to ask you to book me a passage, to Europe . . .'

As Uma's ship made its way westwards, a wake of letters and postcards came drifting back, to wash up at Dolly's door in Kemendine. From Colombo there was a picture of the sea at Mount Lavinia, with a note about how Uma had met a family friend on board her ship, a Mrs Kadambari Dutt – one of the famous Hatkhola Dutts of Calcutta, a cousin of Toru Dutt, the poetess and a relative of the distinguished Mr Romesh Dutt, the writer and scholar. Mrs Dutt was a good deal older than herself and had lived a while in England; she was very experienced and knowledgeable about things – the perfect person to have on board, a godsend really. They were enjoying themselves together.

From Aden there was a postcard with a picture of a narrow channel, flowing between two immense cliffs. Uma wrote that she'd been delighted to discover that this waterway – which formed the link between the Indian Ocean and the Red Sea – was known in Arabic as the *Bab al-Mandab*, 'the gateway of lamentation'. Could there possibly be a better-chosen name?

From Alexandria there was a picture of a fortress, with a few wry remarks about how much friendlier the Europeans on the ship had become once they were past the Suez Canal. She, Uma, had been taken aback, but Mrs Dutt had said that it was always like this: there was something about the air of the Mediterranean that seemed to turn even the most haughty colonialists into affable democrats.

From Marseilles, Uma sent her first long letter: she and her newfound friend, Mrs Dutt, had decided to spend a few days in that city. Mrs Dutt had changed into a European skirt before going ashore; she'd offered to lend Uma one, but Uma had felt awkward and had refused; she'd stepped off the ship in a sari. They hadn't gone far before Uma was mistaken – of all things! – for a Cambodian; dozens of people had gathered around her, asking if she was a dancer. It turned out that King Sisowath of Cambodia had recently visited the city, with a troupe of dancers from his palace. The dancers had enjoyed a great success; the whole city was mad for them; the great sculptor, Mr Rodin, had come down from Paris, just to draw their likenesses. Uma had almost wished that she did not have to disappoint everyone by explaining that she was an Indian, not Cambodian.

They'd had a wonderful time, the two of them, she and Mrs Dutt; they'd walked around town and gone sightseeing and even ventured into the countryside. It had been strange, heady, exhilarating – two women travelling alone, unmolested, drawing nothing more than the occasional curious stare. She'd asked herself why it was not possible to do the same at home – why women could not think of travelling like this in India, revelling in this sense of being at liberty. Yet it was troubling to think that this privilege – of being able to enjoy this sense of freedom, however momentary – had become possible only because of the circumstances of her marriage and because she now had the money to travel. She had talked of this at length with Kadambari – Mrs Dutt: Why should it not be possible for these freedoms to be universally available, for women everywhere? And Mrs Dutt had said that of course, this was one of the great benefits of British rule in India; that it had given women rights and protections that they'd never had before. At this, Uma had felt herself, for the first time, falling utterly out of sympathy with her new friend. She had known instinctively that this was a false argument, unfounded and illogical. How was it possible to imagine that one could grant freedom by imposing subjugation? that one could open a cage by pushing it inside a bigger cage? How could any section of a people hope to achieve freedom where the entirety of a populace was held in subjection? She'd had a long argument with Mrs Dutt and in the end she had succeeded in persuading her friend that hers was the correct view. She'd felt this to be a great triumph – for of course Mrs Dutt was much older (and a good deal better educated) and until then it was always she who was telling her, Uma, how she ought to think of things.

Dolly was in bed when she read this letter. She was drinking a pungent concoction prescribed by a midwife and trying to rest. Some weeks earlier she had begun to suspect that she was pregnant and this intuition had been recently confirmed. As a result she'd been put on a regimen that required many different medicinal infusions and much rest. But rest was not always easy to come by in a household as busy and chaotic as her own. Even as she sat reading Uma's letter, there were frequent interruptions – with the cook and U Ba Kyaw and the master-bricklayers bursting in to ask for instructions. In between trying to guess what was to be prepared for dinner and how much money U Ba Kyaw would have to be advanced for his next visit home, she tried to think of Uma, revelling in the freedom of being able to walk out alone, in Europe. She understood intuitively why Uma took such pleasure in this, even though she herself would not have cared for it at all. Her mind seemed to have no room for anything but the crowded eventlessness of her everyday life. It struck her that she rarely gave any thought to such questions as freedom or liberty or any other such matters.

When she picked up a pen to write back to Uma, she could think of nothing to say; there was something incommunicable about the quotidian contentments of her life. She could try, for instance, to write about how her friend Daw Thi had stopped by last Wednesday and how they'd gone to look at the new furniture at Rowe and Co.; or else she could describe her last visit to the Kyaikasan racecourse and how Rajkumar had won almost one thousand rupees and had joked about buying a pony. But none of this seemed worth putting down on paper – certainly not in response to such concerns as Uma had expressed. Or else she could write about her pregnancy, about Rajkumar's happiness, about how he'd immediately started to think of names (the child was to be a boy of course). But she was superstitious about these things: neither she nor Rajkumar was telling people yet and wouldn't do so until it was unavoidable. Nor did she want to write to Uma about this subject: it would be as though she were flaunting her domesticity in her friend's face; underscoring her childlessness.

Two months passed without any further communication from Uma. As the days went by Dolly found herself less and less able to sleep. Shooting abdominal pains made her double over in bed at night. She moved into a room of her own, so as not to disturb Rajkumar. The midwife told her that everything was proceeding normally, but Dolly was not persuaded: she was increasingly sure that something had gone wrong. Then, late one night, the now-familiar pains changed suddenly into convulsions that shook the whole of her lower body. She realised that she was miscarrying and shouted for Rajkumar. He roused the household and sent people off in every direction – to fetch doctors, nurses, midwives. But it was too late and Rajkumar was alone with Dolly when the stillborn foetus was ejected from her body.

Dolly was still convalescing when Uma's next letter arrived. The letter bore a London address and opened with profuse apologies and an implied reproach. Uma wrote that she was saddened to think that they had allowed so many months to pass without an exchange of letters. She herself had been very busy in London, she said. Mrs Dutt had helped her find accommodation – as the paying guest of an elderly missionary lady who'd spent much of her life in India. The arrangement had worked out well and Uma had not lacked for company. Shortly after her arrival, people had begun to seek her out: mainly former friends and colleagues of the Collector's, most of them English. Some of them had known her late husband at Cambridge, others had worked with him in India. They had all been very kind, showing her around the city, taking her to events of the sort the Collector had liked to attend – concerts, plays, lectures at the Royal Academy. After a while, Uma had begun to feel as though the Collector were with her again; she would hear his voice describing Drury Lane or Covent Garden, pointing to the notable features; telling her what was in good taste and what was not.

Fortunately, she'd also kept up her connection with her ship-board friend, Mrs Dutt. It turned out that Mrs Dutt knew every Indian living in London, or almost. Through her she'd met many interesting people, most notably a lady by the name of Madame Cama. A Parsee from Bombay, Madame Cama seemed, at first glance, more European than Indian – in clothes, manner and appearance. Yet she, Uma, had never known anyone who spoke more truthfully or forthrightly on matters concerning India. She'd been kind enough to introduce Uma into her circle. Uma had never met such people – so interesting and idealistic, men and women whose views and sentiments were so akin to her own. Through these people Uma had begun to understand that a woman like herself could contribute a great deal to India's struggle from overseas.

Lately Madame Cama had been urging her, Uma, to visit the United States. She had friends among the Irish in New York, many of whom, she said, were sympathetic to India's cause. She thought it important for Uma to meet these people and felt that she might like living in that city. Uma was thinking the matter over quite seriously. Of this she was certain at any rate: that she would not long remain in England. In London she was haunted by the notion that the whole city was conspiring to remind her of her late husband.

Exhausted by the effort of reading this letter, Dolly dropped it on her bedside table. Later that day, when Rajkumar came home, he saw it lying there and picked it up.

'From Uma?'

'Yes.'

'What does she say?'

'Read it.'

Rajkumar smoothed down the page and read the letter through, slowly, following Uma's cramped handwriting with his forefinger, asking for Dolly's help with such words as he could not follow. At the end, he folded the pages and put them back on Dolly's bedside table.

'She's talking of going to New York.'

'Yes.'

'That's where Matthew is.'

'Yes. I'd forgotten.'

'You should send her his address. If she goes there, Matthew could help her settle in.'

'That's true.'

'And if you write to her you could also say that Saya John is worried about Matthew. He's been writing to Matthew to come home – but Matthew hasn't answered. Sayagyi can't understand why he won't come back. Perhaps Uma will be able to solve the puzzle.'

Dolly nodded. 'All right,' she said. 'It'll give me something to write about.' She spent a week composing a letter, writing out the paragraphs one at a time. She made no mention of her condition. Having said nothing about her pregnancy, it seemed out of place to refer to a miscarriage. She wrote mostly about Saya John and Rajkumar and posted the letter to Uma's London address.

By the time Dolly heard back, Uma had already crossed the Atlantic; she was in New York, and had been there several weeks already. Again, she was full of apologies for not having written earlier – there was so much to write about that she did not know where to start. New York had proved to be all that she had hoped – a kind of haven for someone like herself, except that the shelter it afforded consisted not of peace and quiet but the opposite. It was the kind of place where one could lose oneself in the press of people. She had decided to remain here for the time being: even on the way over, she had known that this was a place that would be to her taste because so many of the other passengers were people who were tired of the ruthless hypocrisies of Europe, just as she was.

But she also had something important to report, on the very subject that Dolly had written to her about. She had met Matthew

192

Martins soon after her arrival in America; he had come to see her, at the Ramakrishna Mission in Manhattan, where she was staying temporarily. He was not at all the person she had expected; his resemblance to his father was very slight. He was athletic in build and very good-looking, extremely urbane in manner. She had quickly discovered that he had a great passion for motor cars; it had been instructive to walk down the streets with him, for he would point here and there and announce, like a magician: 'there goes a brand-new new 1908 Hutton'; or 'there's a Beeston Humber' or 'that's a Gaggenau . . .'

As for the 'mystery' of his reluctance to leave New York, that had been very quickly solved. It turned out that he had an American fiancée, a woman by the name of Elsa Hoffman. He'd introduced her to Elsa and Uma had thought her to be a very pleasant woman: her demeanour was briskly good-natured, in the American way, and she was fine-looking too, with a gentle, heart-shaped face and long black hair. They'd quickly become friends, she and Elsa, and one day Elsa had confided that she was secretly engaged to Matthew. She hadn't told her family because she knew they'd disapprove and was afraid that they might try to send her away. And Matthew too was uncertain of how his father would respond – what with Elsa being a foreigner and a Protestant as well. Uma's feeling was that this was all that prevented Matthew from returning. If only Saya John were to drop Matthew a hint, that he had nothing to fear on this score, then it was quite likely that he would change his mind about staying in America . . .

By the time this letter was delivered to her, Dolly was perfectly recovered. She was so excited by Uma's report that she decided to go immediately to Rajkumar's timberyard, to give him the news. A hired gaari took her rattling down the dusty, village-like roads of Kemendine, to the black macadam of the Strand, where cargo ships stood moored along the wharves, past the Botataung Pagoda, with its goldfish-filled pools, across the railway crossing, and through the narrow lanes of Pazundaung to the walled compound that marked the premises of Rajkumar's yard. Inside, a team of elephants was hard at work, stacking logs. Dolly spotted Rajkumar standing in the shade of the raised wooden cabin that served as his office. He was dressed in a longyi and vest, smoking a cheroot, his face and head powdered with sawdust.

'Dolly!' He was startled to see her at the yard.

'I have news.' She waved the letter at him.

They climbed the ladder that led up to Rajkumar's office. She stood over him while he read Uma's letter and when he reached the end, she said: 'What do you think, Rajkumar? Do you think Sayagyi would disapprove – about Matthew's fiancée not being Catholic, and all that?'

Rajkumar laughed out loud. 'Sayagyi's no missionary,' he said. 'He keeps his religion to himself. In all the years I worked for him he never once asked me to go to church.'

'But still,' said Dolly, 'you have to be careful when you tell him . . .'

'I will be. I'll go and see him today. I think he'll be relieved to know that this is all it is.'

Soon after this, Dolly learnt that she was pregnant again. She forgot about Matthew and Elsa and even Uma: all her energies went into making sure that nothing went wrong again. Seven months went quickly by and then, on the doctors' advice, she was moved to a mission hospital on Dufferin Road, not far from Kemendine.

One day, Saya John came to see her. He seated himself beside her bed and took her hand, pressing it between his. 'I've come to thank you,' he said.

'For what, Sayagyi?'

'For giving me back my son.'

'What do you mean, Sayagyi?'

'I had a letter from Matthew. He's coming home. He's already making the arrangements. I know it's you who's to be thanked. I haven't even told Rajkumar yet. I wanted you to be the first to know.'

'No, Sayagyi – it's Uma who's to be thanked. It's all because of her.'

'Because of the both of you.'

'And Matthew? Is he coming alone?'

Saya John smiled, his eyes shining. 'No. He's bringing home a bride. They're going to be married by special licence, just before they leave, so that they can travel together.'

'So what will this mean, Sayagyi?'

'It means that it's time for me to move too. I'm going to sell my properties here. Then I'm going to go to Malaya, to get things ready for them. But there's plenty of time yet. I'll be here for the birth of your child.'

Six weeks later Dolly was delivered of a healthy, eight-pound boy. To celebrate, Rajkumar shut down his yards and announced a bonus of a week's wages for his employees. An astrologer was called in to advise them on the child's names: he was to have two, as was the custom among Indians in Burma. After deliberations that lasted for several weeks, it was decided that the boy's Burmese name would be Sein Win; his Indian name was to be Neeladhri – Neel for short. The names were decided on just in time for Saya John to hear of them before leaving for Malaya.

Four years later, Dolly had a second child, another boy. Like Neel he was given two names, one Burmese and one Indian: they were, respectively, Tun Pe and Dinanath. The latter was quickly shortened to Dinu, and it was by this name that he was known at home.

Soon after Dolly's delivery Rajkumar had a letter from Saya John: by coincidence Elsa too had just had a baby, her first. The child was a girl and had been named Alison. What was more, Matthew and Elsa had decided to build a house for themselves, on the plantation: the land had already been cleared and a date fixed for the ground-breaking ceremony. Saya John was very keen that Rajkumar and Dolly attend the ceremony, along with their children.

In the years since Saya John's departure from Rangoon, Rajkumar had spent a great deal of his time travelling between Burma, Malaya and India. As a partner in the plantation he had been responsible for ensuring a steady supply of workers, most of them from the Madras Presidency, in southern India. Rajkumar had kept Dolly abreast of the plantation's progress, but despite his pleas, she had not accompanied him on any of his trips to Malaya. She was not a good traveller, she had said. It had been hard enough to leave Ratnagiri to come to Burma; she was not in a hurry to go anywhere else. As a result, Dolly had never met Matthew and Elsa.

Rajkumar showed Dolly Saya John's letter, with the comment: 'If you're ever going to go there then this is the time.'

After she'd read the letter Dolly agreed: 'All right; let us go.'

From Rangoon, it was a three day voyage to the island of Penang in northern Malaya. On their last day at sea, Rajkumar showed Dolly a distant blue blur on the horizon. This grew quickly into a craggy peak that rose like a pyramid out of the sea. It stood alone, with no other landfall in sight.

'That's Gunung Jerai,' Rajkumar said. 'That's where the plantation is.' In years past, he said, when the forest was being cleared, the mountain had seemed to come alive. Travelling to Penang, Rajkumar would see great black plumes of smoke rising skywards from the mountain. 'But that was a long time ago: the place is quite changed now.'

The steamer docked at Georgetown, the principal port on the island of Penang. From there it was a journey of several hours to the plantation: first they took a ferry to the road- and rail-head of Butterworth, across a narrow channel from Penang. Then they boarded a train that took them northwards through a landscape of lush green paddies and dense coconut groves. Looming ahead, always visible through the windows of the carriage, was the soaring mass of Gunung Jerai, its peak obscured by a cloudy haze. It rose steeply out of the plain, its western slopes descending directly into the sparkling blue waters of the Andaman Sea. Dolly, now habituated to the riverine landscapes of southern Burma, was struck by the lush beauty of the coastal plain. She was reminded of Ratnagiri, and for the first time in many years, she missed her sketchbook.

This leg of their journey ended at Sungei Pattani, a district town on the leeward side of the mountain. The rail-track was newly laid and the station consisted of not much more than a length of beaten earth and a tiled shed. Dolly spotted Saya John as their train was pulling in; he looked older and a little shrunken; he was peering shortsightedly at a newspaper as the train chugged into the station. Standing beside him were a tall, khaki-clothed man and a woman in an ankle-length black skirt. Even before Rajkumar pointed them out, Dolly knew that they were Matthew and Elsa.

Elsa came up to Dolly's window when the train stopped. The first thing she said was: 'I'd have known you anywhere; Uma described you perfectly.'

Dolly laughed. 'And you too – both of you.'

Outside the rudimentary little station, there was a large compound. In its centre stood a thin sapling, not much taller than Dolly herself.

'Why,' Dolly said, startled, 'that's a padauk tree, isn't it?'

'They call them angsana trees here,' Elsa said. 'Matthew planted it, soon after Alison was born. He says that in a few years it's going to grow into a huge umbrella, casting its shade over the whole station.'

Now Dolly's eyes were drawn to a startling new sight: a motor-car – a gleaming, flat-topped vehicle with a rounded bonnet and glittering, twelve-spoked wheels. It was the only car in the compound and a small crowd had gathered around to marvel at its brass lamps and shining black paint.

The car was Matthew's. 'It's an Oldsmobile Defender,' he announced. 'Quite a modest car really, but mint-new, this year's model, a genuine 1914. It rolled out of the factory in January and was delivered to me six months later.' He spoke like an American, Dolly noticed, and his voice bore no resemblance to his father's.

Theirs was a sizeable party: there was an ayah for Dinu and Neel as well as a man to help with the luggage. The car was not large enough for all of them. After Dolly, Elsa and the children had been seated there was room only for the ayah and Matthew, who was driving. The others were left behind to follow in a buggy.

They drove through Sungei Pattani, along wide streets that were lined with tiled 'shophouses' – storefronts whose facades were joined together to form long, graceful arcades. Then the town fell away and the car began to climb.

'When was the last time you heard from Uma?' Dolly said to Elsa.

'I saw her last year,' said Elsa. 'I went to the States for a holiday and we met in New York.' Uma had moved into an apartment of her own, Elsa said. She'd taken a job, as a publisher's proof-reader.

But she was doing other things too; she seemed to keep herself very busy.

'What else is she doing exactly?'

'Political things mainly, I think,' Elsa said. 'She talked about meetings and speeches and some magazine that she's writing for.'

'Oh?' Dolly was still thinking about this when Elsa pointed ahead. 'Look – the estate. That's where it starts.'

They were climbing steeply, driving along a dirt road that was flanked on both sides by dense forest. Looking ahead, Dolly saw a wide gateway, with a sign that arched across the road. There were three words inscribed on the sign, in enormous gold lettering; Dolly read them out aloud, rolling them over her tongue: 'Morningside Rubber Estate.'

'Elsa named it,' Matthew said.

'When I was a child,' Elsa explained, 'I used to live near a park called Morningside. I always liked the name.'

At the gate, there was a sudden rent in the tangled curtain of greenery that covered the mountainside: ahead, stretching away as far as the eye could see, there were orderly rows of saplings, all of them exactly alike, all of them spaced with precise, geometrical regularity. The car went over a low rise and a valley appeared ahead, a shallow basin, cupped in the palm of a curved ridge. The basin had been cleared of trees and there was an open space in the middle. Grouped around this space were two ramshackle tin-roofed buildings, little more than huts.

'These were meant to be the estate's offices,' Elsa said apologetically. 'But we're living in them for the time being. It's very basic I'm afraid – which is why we need to build ourselves a habitable place.'

They settled in and later in the day, Elsa took Dolly for a walk through the rubber trees. Each tree had a diagonal slash across its trunk, with a halved coconut shell cupped underneath. Elsa swirled her forefinger through one of these cups, and dug out a hardened crescent of latex. 'They call these cup-lumps,' Elsa said, handing the latex to Dolly. Dolly raised the spongy grey lump to her nose: the smell was sour and faintly rancid. She dropped it back into the coconut-shell cup.

'Tappers will come by to collect the lumps in the morning,' Elsa said. 'Not a drop of this stuff can be wasted.'

They headed through the rubber trees, walking uphill, facing the cloud-capped peak of Gunung Jerai. The ground underfoot had a soft, cushioned feel, because of the carpet of dead leaves shed by the trees. The slope ahead was scored with the shadows of thousands of trunks, all exactly parallel, like scratches scored by a machine. It was like being in a wilderness, but yet not. Dolly had visited Huay Zedi several times and had come to love the electric stillness of the jungle. But this was like neither city nor farm nor forest: there was something eerie about its uniformity; about the fact that such sameness could be imposed upon a landscape of such natural exuberance. She remembered how startled she'd been when the car crossed from the heady profusion of the jungle into the ordered geometry of the plantation. 'It's like stepping into a labyrinth,' she said to Elsa.

'Yes,' said Elsa. 'And you'd be amazed how easy it is to lose your way.'

They entered a large clearing and Elsa came to a stop. 'This,' she said, 'is where Morningside House is going to be.'

Turning around, Dolly saw that the spot offered spectacular views on every side. To the west the mountain sloped gently into the reddening sunset sea; to the north rose the forested peak of Gunung Jerai, looking directly down on them.

'It's a wonderful spot,' Dolly said. But even as she was saying the words it struck her that she would not have wanted to live there, under the scowling gaze of the mountain, in a house that was marooned in a tree-filled maze.

'It's beautiful, isn't it?' Elsa said. 'But you should have seen what it looked like before it was cleared.'

She'd been horrified, she said, when she first came out to Gunung Jerai. The place was beautiful beyond imagining, but it was jungle – dense, towering, tangled, impassable jungle. Matthew had led her a little way in, on foot, and it was like walking up a carpeted nave, with the tops of the trees meeting far above, forming an endless, fan-vaulted ceiling. It was hard, almost impossible, to imagine that these slopes could be laid bare, made habitable.

Once the clearing of the forest started, Matthew had moved out to the land and built himself a small cabin, where the estate office now stood. She had lived away from him in a rented house, in

Penang. She would have preferred to be with Matthew, but he wouldn't let her stay. It was too dangerous, he said, like a battle-field, with the jungle fighting back every inch of the way. For a while Saya John had stayed with Matthew too, but then he'd fallen ill, and had had to move to Penang. Even though the plantation was his own idea, he'd had no conception of what would be involved in laying it out.

Several months went by before Elsa had been allowed to visit the location again and she understood then why Matthew had tried to keep her away. The hillside looked as though it had been racked by a series of disasters: huge stretches of land were covered with ashes and blackened stumps. Matthew was thin and coughed incessantly. She caught a glimpse of the workers' shacks – tiny hovels, with roofs made of branches and leaves. They were all Indians, from the south: Matthew had learnt to speak their language – Tamil – but she couldn't understand a word they said. She'd looked into the mud-walled hut where they went to be treated when they fell ill: the squalor was unimaginable, the floors covered with filth. She'd wanted to stay and work as a nurse, but Matthew had refused to let her remain. She'd had to go back to Penang.

But when she next returned, the transformation was again so great as to appear miraculous. The last time around she had felt as though she were entering a plague site; now the sensation was of walking into a freshly-laid garden. The ashes had been washed away by the rain, the blackened tree-stumps had been removed and the first saplings of rubber had begun to grow.

For the first time, Matthew had allowed her to stay over, in his cabin. At daybreak she'd looked out of the window and seen the morning pouring down the side of the mountain, lying on their land like a sheet of gold.

'That was when I told Matthew,' Elsa said, 'that there could only ever be one name for this place: Morningside.'

Later, back where they were staying, Elsa showed Dolly her sketches for Morningside House. She wanted it to look like the grand Long Island houses of her memory; it was to have a turret-like tower, steep gables and a veranda that went all the way around, to take advantage of the spectacular views. The one Eastern touch was to be the roof, which would be red, with carved, upcurling eaves.

While the women were poring over the sketches, Saya John was going through the newspaper that he had bought at the railway station: it was the previous day's edition of the *Straits Times*, published from Singapore. Suddenly he glanced up and beckoned to Matthew and Rajkumar, from across the room.

'Look at this,' he said.

Folding the paper in half, he showed them a report about the assassination of the Grand Duke Ferdinand in Sarajevo. Rajkumar and Matthew read through the first couple of paragraphs and then looked at each other and shrugged.

'"Sarajevo"?' said Rajkumar. 'Where's that?'

'A long way away.' Matthew laughed.

No more than anyone else in the world, did either of them have any inkling that the killing in Sarajevo would spark a world war. Nor did they know that rubber would be a vital strategic material in this conflict: that in Germany the discarding of articles made of rubber would become an offence punishable by law; that submarines would be sent overseas to smuggle rubber; that the commodity would come to be valued more than ever before, increasing their wealth beyond their most extravagant dreams.

Sixteen

Even when Neel and Dinu were very young, it was evident that they each took after a single parent. Neel looked very much like Rajkumar: he was big and robust, more Indian than Burmese in build and colouring. Dinu, on the other hand, had his mother's delicate features as well as her ivory complexion and fine-boned slimness of build.

Every year, around December, Dolly and Rajkumar took the boys to Huay Zedi. Doh Say and Naw Da had returned to their old village some years before. The expansion of their business had made Doh Say a wealthy man, and he owned several houses in and around the village: one of these was earmarked for Dolly and Rajkumar's annual visits. It seemed to Dolly that the boys enjoyed these trips, especially Neel, who had been befriended by one of Doh Say's sons, a sturdy thoughtful boy by the name of Raymond. Dolly, too, looked forward to these annual visits: since her trip to Morningside she had begun sketching again, and would spend hours by Huay Zedi's stream, with her sketchbook open on her lap and Dinu playing nearby.

One year, while they were at Huay Zedi, Dinu fell suddenly ill. Dolly and Rajkumar were not particularly alarmed. Dinu was prone to bouts of sickness and it was a rare week when he was entirely free of colds, coughs and fevers. But Dinu was also gifted with an innate resilience that made him actively combat his ill health, and his fevers rarely lasted for more than a day or two at a time. Knowing how well he fought off his fevers, Dolly and Rajkumar were certain that he would recover quickly. They decided to remain at Huay Zedi.

The house they were staying in was very much like a teak camp's tai, standing some six feet off the ground on massive timber posts. It was set at a slight remove from the rest of the village, a little distance up the thickly forested slope that served as a back-drop for the village. The jungle rose like a cliff behind the tai, skirting it on three sides. Just visible from the balcony was Huay Zedi's pebbled stream and the soaring bamboo steeple of its church.

As in all tais, the rooms were arranged in a row, one leading into another. Because of Dinu's illness, Dolly decided to change their usual sleeping arrangements. She took the child into her bed for the night, and dispatched Rajkumar to one of the inner rooms. With Dinu sleeping beside her, Dolly drifted into a dream. She saw herself lifting up her mosquito net, climbing out of bed and going to sit in a chair on the balcony. The tai was in darkness but the night was alive with cicadas and fireflies. Two doors away she could hear Rajkumar breathing heavily in his sleep. She saw her-self sitting awhile in the chair and then, after some time had passed, someone spoke, in a voice that was well known to her: it was Thebaw. He was saying something to her with great urgency. As so often in dreams, she could not tell the words apart, but she understood exactly what he was trying to communicate.

She screamed.

Rajkumar stumbled out with a candle and found her sitting in a chair, on the veranda, rocking back and forth, hugging herself with shaking arms.

'What's happened?'

'We have to leave,' she said. 'We have to get Dinu to a hospital in Rangoon.'

'Why?'

'Don't ask me now. I'll tell you later.'

They left Huay Zedi while it was still dark. Doh Say provided them with two ox-carts and escorted them personally to Pyin-mana. They arrived in Rangoon late the next night. Dinu was taken immediately to hospital.

After a long examination, the doctors took Dolly and Rajkumar aside. The boy had polio, they said; but for Dolly's promptness in bringing him to hospital, they might well have lost the child.

'I knew I had to bring him,' said Dolly.

'How did you know?'

'I was told.'

'By whom?'

'It doesn't matter. What matters is that we came.'

Dolly stayed the night in hospital and next morning, a nurse brought her breakfast on a tray. 'Did you hear, ma'am?' the nurse said. 'The old King is dead. He died in India.'

The breakfast tray slipped from Dolly's lap. 'When did it happen?' she asked the nurse.

'Let's see . . .' The nurse counted off the dates on her fingers. 'I think it must have happened the night before you came.'

It was Dolly's old charge, the Second Princess, who took the blame for the King's death. One bright December day in 1916, she eloped with a Burmese commoner and hid herself in the Residency. This was the beginning of the end.

By this time much had changed in Ratnagiri. The First Princess had had her baby, a girl (this was an event that Dolly had missed by only a few weeks). The child was nicknamed Baisu, Fatty, and to everyone's surprise, she had quickly become a favourite of the Queen's.

Soon after the birth of the child, the District Administration had discovered itself to be in possession of monies sufficient to build the King his long promised palace. A mansion had appeared on the hillside that faced the Residency. It came complete with a durbar hall, a gallery, outhouses, running water and a garage to accommodate the two cars that had recently been provided for the King and Queen (one a Ford, the other a De Dion). All of Ratnagiri turned out to celebrate the move. Cheering crowds lined the roads as the Royal Family drove out of Outram House for the last time. But as with all moves, the new place was quickly discovered to possess certain drawbacks. Its upkeep was found to require a small army: twenty-seven gatekeepers, ten peons, six *hazurdaars* and innumerable other attendants, cleaners, sweepers and ayahs – a total of one hundred and sixty-one in all. In addition, there were now more visitors from Burma and many more hangers-on. How to feed them? How to provide for them? Without Dolly no one knew how to manage.

And then, one morning the Second Princess disappeared. Enquiries revealed she had run away with a young man and taken refuge in the Residency. The King gave Sawant a note to take to his daughter, asking her to return to the palace. Standing at a window, he trained his binoculars on the De Dion as it made its journey across the hill. When the car turned around to come back he saw that his daughter was not in it. The binoculars dropped from his hands. He fell to the floor, clutching his left arm. The doctor arrived within the hour and pronounced him to have suffered a heart attack. Ten days later the King died.

The Queen let it be known that the Second Princess would never again be permitted to enter her presence.

And the funeral, Dolly, *the First Princess wrote in the first of several clandestine letters*. It was such a sad and miserable affair that Her Majesty flatly refused to attend. The Government was represented by a mere Deputy Collector! You would have wept to see it. No one could believe that this was the funeral of Burma's last King! We wanted the coffin stored in such a way that we could transport the remains to Burma some day. But when the authorities learnt of this they had the coffin forcibly removed from us. They are afraid that the King's body might become a rallying point in Burma! They built a monument on his grave, almost overnight, to make it impossible for us ever to take him back! You should have been here with us, Dolly. We all missed you, even Her Majesty, though of course she could not say so, since it was she who forbade us ever to utter your name.

Through the duration of Dinu's convalescence, Dolly never once left the premises of the hospital. She and Dinu had a room to themselves – large and sunny and filled with flowers. From the window they could see the majestic, shining hti of the Shwe Dagon. Rajkumar did everything in his power to ensure their comfort. U Ba Kyaw drove over at mealtimes, bringing fresh-cooked food in an enormous brass tiffin-carrier. The hospital was prevailed upon to relax its rules. Friends dropped by at all times of day and Rajkumar and Neel stayed late into the evenings, leaving only when it was time for Dinu to go to bed.

Dinu endured his month-long stay in hospital with exemplary stoicism, earning accolades from the staff. Although he had partially lost the use of his right leg, the doctors promised that he would recover to the point where a slight limp would be the only lasting trace of his illness.

On their return home, after Dinu's discharge, Dolly tried hard to revert to her normal domestic routines. She put Dinu into a room of his own, under the care of an ayah. For the first few days, he made no complaint. Then, late one night, Dolly woke suddenly, at the touch of his breath on her face. Her son was standing beside her, propped up on the edge of the bed. He had left his ayah snoring in his room, and crawled down the corridor, dragging his right leg behind him. Dolly took him into her bed, hugging his bony body to her chest, breathing in the soft, rain-washed smell of his hair. She slept better that night than she had at any time in the last several weeks.

During the day, as Dinu began trying to walk again, Dolly hovered over him, darting to move stools and tables out of his way. Watching him as he struggled to regain his mobility, Dolly began to marvel at her son's tenacity and resilience – at the strength of will that made him pick himself up, time and time again, until he was able to hobble just a step or two farther than before. But she could see also that this daily struggle was changing him. He was more withdrawn than she remembered, and seemed years older in maturity and self-possession. With his father and brother he was unresponsive and cold, as though he were self-consciously discouraging their attempts to include him in their exuberant games.

Dolly's absorption in Dinu's convalescence became so complete as to claim the entirety of her mind. She thought less and less about her circle of friends and the round of activities that had occupied her before – the gatherings, the tea-parties, the picnics. When occasionally a friend or an acquaintance dropped by, there were awkward silences: she would feign interest in their stories, without contributing a word of her own. When they asked what she did with her time, she found it hard to explain. So small was the span by which Dinu's successes were measured – an extra step or two at a time, a couple more inches – that it was impossible to communicate either the joy or the crestfallen emptiness that attended upon the passing of each day. Her friends would nod politely as they listened to her explanations and when they left she knew that it would be a long time before she saw them again. The odd thing was that far from feeling any regret, she was glad.

One weekend, Rajkumar said: 'You haven't been out in months.' He had a horse running for the Governor's Cup, at the Rangoon Turf Club: he insisted that she go with him to the races.

She went through the motions of dressing for the races as though she were performing a half-forgotten ritual. When she went down to the driveway, U Ba Kyaw bowed her into their car as though he were welcoming her home after a long absence. The car was a Pic-Pic – a Swiss-manufactured Piccard-Pictet – a commodious, durable machine with a glass pane separating the driver's seat from the interior cabin.

The Pic-Pic circled around the Royal Lake, driving past the Chinese burial grounds and passing within sight of the Rangoon Club. Now Dolly too began to feel that she'd been away a long time. All the familiar sights seemed new and startling – the reflection of the Shwe Dagon, shimmering on the lake; the long, low-slung building of the Boat Club, perched on the shore. She found herself leaning forward in her seat, with her face half out of the window, as though she were looking at the city for the first time. The roads around the racecourse had been sealed off by the police, but the Pic-Pic was recognised and they were waved through. The stands looked festive with pennants and flags fluttering above the terraces. On the way to Rajkumar's box, Dolly found herself waving to a great number of people whose names she had forgotten. Once they were seated, dozens of friends and acquaintances stopped by to welcome her back. She noticed, after a while, that

Rajkumar was whispering their names to her, under cover of his programme, to remind her who they were – 'U Tha Din Gyi, he's a Turf Club steward; U Ohn, the handicapper, Mr MacDonald, the totalizator . . .'

Everyone was kind. Old Mr Piperno, the bookmaker, sent one of his sons to ask if she wanted to place any bets. She was touched and chose a couple of horses at random, from her programme. The band of the Gloucestershire Regiment came marching out and played a serenade from Friedemann's *Lola*. Then they started on another piece, with a great flourish, and Rajkumar gave her arm a sudden tug.

'It's "God Save the King",' he hissed.

'I'm sorry,' she said, rising quickly to her feet. 'I wasn't paying attention.'

At last, to her relief, the races started. There was a long wait before the next race and another after it was over. Just as everyone around her was becoming more and more excited, Dolly's mind began to wander. It was weeks since she'd been away from Dinu for this long – but of course he probably hadn't even noticed that she was gone.

A sudden outburst of applause jolted her back to her surroundings. Sitting next to her was Daw Thi, the wife of Sir Lionel Ba Than, who was one of the stewards of the Turf Club. Daw Thi was wearing her famous ruby necklace, idly fingering the thumbnail-sized stones. Dolly saw that she was looking at her expectantly.

'What's happened?' said Dolly.

'Lochinvar has won.'

'Oh?' said Dolly.

Daw Thi gave her a long look, and burst into laughter. 'Dolly, you silly thing,' she said, 'have you forgotten? Lochinvar is your husband's horse!'

In the car, on the way back, Rajkumar was unusually quiet. When they were almost home, he leant over to slam shut the window that separated the driver's seat from the rear. Then he turned to look at her a little unsteadily. He'd been plied with champagne after his visit to the winner's paddock, and was slightly drunk.

'Dolly?' he said.

'Yes?'

'Something's happened to you.'

'No.' She shook her head. 'No. Nothing's happened.'

'You're changing . . . You're leaving us behind.'

'Who?'

'Me . . . Neel . . .'

She flinched. She knew it was true that she'd neglected her elder son lately. But Neel was filled with energy, boisterousness and loud-voiced goodwill and Rajkumar doted on him. With Dinu on the other hand, he was nervous and tentative; frailty and weakness worried him, puzzled him: he had never expected to encounter these in his own progeny.

'Neel doesn't need me,' Dolly said, 'in the way that Dinu does.'

He reached for her hand. 'Dolly, we all need you. You can't disappear into yourself. You can't leave us behind.'

'Of course not.' She laughed uneasily. 'Where would I go if I left you behind?'

He dropped her hand and turned away. 'Sometimes I can't help feeling that you've already gone away – shut yourself behind a glass wall.'

'What wall?' she cried. 'What are you talking about?' She looked up to see U Ba Kyaw watching her, in the Pic-Pic's rear-view mirror. She bit her lip and said nothing more.

This exchange came as a shock. She couldn't make sense of it at first. After a day or two she decided that Rajkumar was right, she ought to go out more, even if it was just to the Scott Market, to look round the shops. Dinu was already more self-sufficient; soon it would be time for him to start school. She would have to get used to being without him, and besides, it wasn't healthy to be always shut away behind the walls of the house.

She began to schedule little expeditions for herself. One morning she found herself stuck in one of the most crowded parts of the city, near Rangoon's Town Hall. Just ahead, at the intersection of Dalhousie Street and Sule Pagoda Street there lay a busy round-about. An ox-cart had collided with a rickshaw; someone was hurt. A crowd had gathered and the air was full of noise and dust.

The Sule Pagoda was at the centre of this roundabout. It had been freshly whitewashed, and it rose above the busy streets like a rock rearing out of the sea. Dolly had driven past the pagoda countless times but had never been inside. She told U Ba Kyaw to wait nearby and stepped out of the car.

She made her way carefully across the crowded roundabout and climbed a flight of stairs. Removing her shoes, she found herself standing on a cool, marble-paved floor. The noise of the street had fallen away and the air seemed clean, free of dust. She spotted a group of saffron-robed monks, chanting in one of the small shrines that ringed the pagoda's circular nave. She stepped in and knelt behind them, on a mat. In a raised niche, directly ahead, there was a small gilded image of the Buddha, seated in the *bhumisparshamudra*, with the middle finger of his right hand touching the earth. Flowers lay heaped below – roses, jasmine, pink lotuses – and the air was heady with their scent.

Dolly closed her eyes, trying to listen to the monks, but instead it was Rajkumar's voice that echoed in her ears: 'You're changing. . . leaving us behind.' In the tranquillity of that place, those words had a different ring: she recognised that he was right, that the events of the recent past had changed her no less than they had Dinu.

In hospital, at night, lying in bed with Dinu, she'd found herself listening to voices that were inaudible during the day: the murmurs of anxious relatives; distant screams of pain; women keening in bereavement. It was as though the walls turned porous in the stillness of the night, flooding her room with an unseen tide of defeat and suffering. The more she listened to those voices, the more directly they spoke to her, sometimes in tones that seemed to recall the past, sometimes in notes of warning.

Late one night she'd heard an old woman crying for water. The voice had been feeble – a hoarse, rasping whisper – but it had filled the room. Although Dinu had been fast asleep, Dolly had clapped a hand over his head. For a while she'd lain rigid on her side, clutching her child, using his sleeping body to shut out the sound. Then she'd slipped out of bed and walked quickly down the corridor.

A white-capped Karen nurse had stopped her: 'What are you doing here?'

'There was a voice,' Dolly had said, 'someone crying for water . . .' She'd made the nurse listen.

'Oh yes,' the nurse had said, offhandedly, 'that's from the malaria ward below. Someone's delirious. Go back to your room.' The moans had stopped soon afterwards but Dolly had stayed up all night, haunted by the sound of the voice.

Another time she had stepped out of the room to find a stretcher in the corridor. A child's body had been lying on it, covered with a white hospital sheet. Although Dinu had been no more than a few feet away, sleeping peacefully, Dolly had not been able to quell the panic that surged through her at the sight of the shrouded stretcher. Falling to her knees in the corridor, she had torn away the sheet that covered the corpse. The child had been a boy, of Dinu's age, and not unlike him in build. Dolly had begun to cry, hysterically, overwhelmed as much by guilt as relief. A nurse and an orderly had had to lift her up to take her back to bed.

Again that night, she had not been able to sleep. She'd thought of the child's body; she'd thought of what her life would be like in Dinu's absence; she'd thought of the dead boy's mother. She'd begun to cry – it was as though her voice had merged with that of the unknown woman; as though an invisible link had arisen between all of them – her, Dinu, the dead child, his mother.

Now, kneeling on the floor of the Sule Pagoda, she recalled the voice of King Thebaw, in Ratnagiri. In his later years the King had seemed more and more to dwell on the precepts he had learnt as a novice, in the palace monastery. She remembered a word he'd often used, *karuna* – one of the Buddha's words, Pali for compassion, for the immanence of all living things in each other, for the attraction of life for its likeness. A time will come, he had said to the girls, when you too will discover what this word karuna means, and from that moment on, your lives will never again be the same.

Shortly after King Thebaw's funeral, the Queen wrote to her gaolers asking for permission to move back to Burma. Her request was denied, on grounds of security, because of the war in Europe: it was felt that her presence might prove inflammatory at a delicate moment for the Empire. It was only after the end of the war that the Queen and her daughters were allowed to return to their homeland.

The First Princess now occasioned a fresh crisis. Was she to leave Ratnagiri to go to Burma with her mother? Or was she to stay with Sawant?

The Princess made a promise to her husband: she told him that she would travel with her mother to Burma and then return once Her Majesty had been safely installed in her new home. Sawant took her at her word and made no objection. But it was with a heavy tread that he walked down to the jetty at Mandvi, on the day of the royal party's departure. For all he knew this was the last time that he or his children would ever see the Princess.

The Queen's party made its way slowly across the subcontinent, travelling eastwards from Bombay by rail. In Calcutta the Queen's entourage stayed at the Grand Hotel. It so happened that the Second Princess was now also living in Calcutta, with her husband: she could scarcely ignore the presence of her mother and sisters. One evening the disowned Princess gathered her resolve and went over to the Grand Hotel to call on her mother.

The Queen flatly refused to receive either her daughter or her son-in-law. The Princess, knowing her mother all too well, retreated in good grace – not so her husband, who summoned the temerity to venture uninvited into Her Majesty's presence. This assault was quickly repulsed: with a single enraged shout the Queen sent her errant son-in-law fleeing down the Grand's marble staircase. It was his misfortune to be shod in smooth-soled leather pumps. His feet slipped and sent him flying into the lobby, where a chamber ensemble was serenading an audience of assembled guests. He flopped into their midst like a leaping trout. A cello splintered and a viola twanged. Seated nearby was the Third Princess, whose nerves had been sadly strained by her recent travels. She broke into hysterics and could not be calmed. A doctor had to be sent for.

On April 16, 1919, the Queen and her party boarded the R.M.S. *Arankola*. They arrived in Rangoon four days later and were spirited quietly off to a bungalow on Churchill Road. A fortnight went by in a flurry of activity. Then the First Princess took everybody aback by announcing that she was ready to go back to Sawant. The family's advisors wrung their hands. It was suggested that the Princess, as the eldest daughter, had a duty to remain with her mother – promises were, after all, frequently allowed to lapse in the interests of good sense and decency. No one doubted that a means could be found for discreetly closing the door on Sawant.

It was now that the First Princess showed herself to be a true daughter of her dynasty, every inch a Konbaung – her love for her family's former coachman proved just as unshakable as her mother's devotion to the late King. Defying her family, she went back to Sawant and never left Ratnagiri again. She lived the rest of her life with her husband and her children in a small house on the outskirts of town. It was there that she died twenty-eight years later.

The Second Princess and her husband lived in Calcutta for several years before moving to the hill-station of Kalimpong, near Darjeeling. There the Princess and her husband opened a dairy business.

So it happened that of the four Princesses, the two who'd been born in Burma both chose to live on in India. Their younger sisters, on the other hand, both born in India, chose to settle in Burma: both married and had children. As for the Queen, she spent her last years in her house on Rangoon's Churchill Road. Such money as she could extract from the colonial authorities, she spent on religious charities and on feeding monks. She never wore anything but white, the Burmese colour of mourning.

After the Queen's arrival in Rangoon, Dolly wrote her several letters, entreating to be allowed to call at her residence. None was ever answered. The Queen died in 1925, six years after her return from Ratnagiri. Even though she'd been cloistered for so many years, there was a sudden surge of sentiment in the city and people poured out to mourn. She was buried near the Shwedagon Pagoda in Rangoon.

Seventeen

In 1929, after a gap of several years, Dolly received a letter from New York. It was from Uma and she was writing to say that she was leaving America. Uma was fifty now and had been away from India for more than twenty years. In her absence her parents had died, leaving her the ground floor of their house, Lankasuka (the upper floor had gone to her brother, who was now married and the father of three children). She had decided to go home, to Calcutta, to settle.

Because of various engagements in Tokyo, Shanghai and Singapore, Uma wrote, she would be sailing across the Pacific rather than the Atlantic. One of the advantages of this route was that it would also enable her to visit friends – Matthew and Elsa in Malaya, and of course, Dolly and Rajkumar in Rangoon. She was writing now to propose that she and Dolly meet at Morningside and spend a fortnight there: it would be a pleasant holiday and afterwards they could travel back to Burma together – after so many years, there was a lot of catching up to be done. What would be better still was if Dolly came with Neel and Dinu: it would give her an opportunity to get to know the boys.

Dolly was oddly shaken by this letter. Although happy to hear from her friend, she was more than a little apprehensive. To resume a friendship that had been so long dormant was no easy matter. She could not help admiring Uma for her forthrightness; she knew that she herself had drawn away from the world, become increasingly reclusive, unwilling to travel or even go out. She was content leading the life she did, but it worried her that the boys had seen very little of the world – of India or Malaya or any other country. It wasn't right that they should never know any place other than Burma: no one could predict what lay ahead. Even through the shuttered windows of her room she could feel an unquietness in the land.

Dolly had not been back to Morningside in fifteen years, ever since her first visit; nor had the boys. It was unlikely, she knew, that Rajkumar would consent to go. He was working harder than ever at his business and there were whole weeks when she hardly saw him. When she mooted the idea to him, he shook his head brusquely, just as she had known he would: no, he was too busy, he couldn't go.

But for her own part, Dolly found herself increasingly drawn to the idea of meeting Uma at Morningside. It would be interesting to see Matthew and Elsa again: the Martinses had come to stay with them once, in Burma, with their two children – after Alison, they'd had a boy, Timmy. The children were all very young then and had got on well together, even Dinu who was withdrawn by nature and very slow to make friends. But that was a long time ago: Dinu was fourteen now, a student at St James's School, one of the best-known in Rangoon. Neel was eighteen, brawny and outgoing, reluctantly engaged in pursuing a course of studies at Rangoon's Judson College: he was eager to get into the timber business but Rajkumar had said that he would not take him into the family firm until his studies were finished.

When Dolly sounded Neel out about going to Morningside, he was immediately enthusiastic, keen to be off. She was not really surprised; she knew that he was always on the lookout for ways of getting out of attending his classes. Dinu proved to be much less keen but said he was willing to strike a bargain: he would go, he said, if she bought him a Brownie camera from Rowe and Co. She agreed; she liked to encourage his interest in photography – partly because she believed it to have grown out of his childhood habit of looking over her shoulder while she sketched; and partly because she felt that she ought to encourage any activity that would draw him out of himself.

The arrangements were quickly set in motion, with letters shooting back and forth between Burma, Malaya and the United States (Rangoon had recently acquired an air mail service, and this made communications much quicker than before). In April the next year, Dolly boarded a Malaya-bound steamer with her two sons. Rajkumar came to see the family off, and after Dolly had boarded, she looked over the side to find that he was waving to her from the jetty, gesticulating wildly, trying to draw her attention to something. She looked at the vessel's bows and discovered that she was on the *Nuwara Eliya*, the same vessel that had brought her to Rangoon immediately after her marriage. It was an odd coincidence.

Matthew and his family were waiting at the Georgetown docks when the *Nuwara Eliya* pulled in. It was Dinu who spotted them first, through the viewfinder of his Brownie. 'There . . . over there . . . look.'

Dolly leant over the gunwale, shading her eyes. Matthew looked very distinguished, with a thick frosting of grey around his head. Elsa had grown a little matronly since their last meeting, but in a regal and quite imposing way. Timmy was standing beside her, tall for his age and as thin as a string bean. Alison was there too, wearing a schoolgirl's frock, her hair braided into long pigtails. She was an unusual-looking girl, Dolly thought, her face an arresting blend of elements taken from both her parents: she had Matthew's cheekbones and Elsa's eyes; his silky hair and her upright carriage. It was clear that she would grow into a real beauty one day.

Matthew came on board and escorted them off the ship. They were all to spend the night in Georgetown and he had booked rooms in a hotel. Uma was due to arrive the next day and they were to drive to Morningside together. Matthew had brought two cars and a chauffeur: they were waiting at Butterworth, on the mainland.

The next morning, after breakfast, they walked together to the port, all seven of them. At the pier, they found themselves caught in a noisy throng. A large number of people had already gathered there, most of them Indians. Many were armed with flowers and garlands. At the head of this crowd stood two flamboyant and colourful figures, one a saffron-robed sadhu and the other a Sikh Giani, with a flowing beard and bushy white eyebrows. Neel, burly and assertive beyond his twenty years, pushed his way into the crowd to find out what the fuss was about. He came back looking puzzled.

216

'I asked them what they were doing here and they said: we've come to greet Uma Dey.'

'Do you think they mean our own Uma?' Dolly said incredulously, to Elsa.

'Yes, of course. There can't be two Uma Deys on the same ship.'

Then the ship came into view and a cheer erupted from the crowd: '*Uma Dey zindabad, zindabad* – long live, long live, Uma Dey.' This was followed by other shouts and slogans, all in Hindustani: '*Inquilab zindabad*' and '*halla bol, halla bol!*' When the ship docked the crowd's leaders went swarming up the gangplank, with garlands and marigolds. Then Uma appeared, at the head of the gangplank, and was met by a wild outburst of cheering: '*Uma Dey zindabad, zindabad!*' For a while there was complete confusion.

Watching from the far end of the pier, Dolly could tell that Uma had been taken by surprise: she was evidently unprepared for the reception that had been accorded her and didn't quite know how to respond. She was scanning the crowd, as though she were looking for someone in particular. Dolly raised an arm and waved. The gesture caught Uma's eye and she waved back worriedly, sketching a gesture of helplessness. Dolly made a sign to reassure her – don't worry, we'll wait.

Then Uma was ushered down the gangplank and garlanded again. Several people made speeches while everyone stood sweating under the hot sun. Dolly tried hard to concentrate on what was being said, but her eyes kept straying back to her friend. She saw that Uma had grown gaunt and her eyes had retreated into deep hollows, as though in protest against a hectic and uncertain life. But at the same time, there was a new assurance about the way she carried herself. It was clear that she was accustomed to being listened to and when it was her turn to speak, Dolly noticed, with dawning awe, that Uma seemed to know exactly what to say and how to handle the crowd.

Then, abruptly, the speeches were over, and Uma was pushing her way through the crowd. Suddenly, she was standing in front of Dolly, her arms thrown open: such a long time! such a long time! They laughed and hugged and held on to each other while the children looked quizzically on, standing a little apart.

'How well you look, Elsa! And your daughter – she's a beauty!'

217

'You look well too, Uma.'

Uma laughed. 'You don't have to lie to me. I look twice my age . . .'

Dolly broke in, jogging her friend's arm: 'Who are these people, Uma? We were so surprised . . .'

'They belong to a group I've been working with,' Uma said quickly. 'A group called the Indian Independence League. I hadn't told them I was coming here, but I suppose the word got out . . .'

'But what do they want, Uma? Why were they here?'

'I'll tell you later.' Uma took hold of Dolly's hand and stuck an arm through Elsa's. 'There's so much to talk about and I don't want to run out of time . . .'

In the afternoon they took the ferry to Butterworth where Matthew's cars were waiting at the port, one of them longer than any that Dolly had ever seen, almost the size of a railway carriage. This was a Duesenberg Model J Tourster, Matthew explained. It had a hydraulic braking system and a 6.9 litre, straight-8 engine. It had chain-driven overhead camshafts and could do up to 90 m.p.h. in second gear. In top gear it could cruise at 116.

Matthew was keen to show the Duesenberg off to Neel and Dinu so they rode with him, along with Timmy and Alison. Dolly and Elsa followed more sedately, in the car that Matthew had given Elsa for her fiftieth birthday – a magnificent tan-and-gold Isotta-Fraschini Tipo 8A Berlina Transformabile with power-assisted brakes. The coachwork was by Castagna and the upholstery was of Florentine leather.

The Isotta-Fraschini headed north with the sun dipping low over the Andaman Sea and by the time they reached Sungei Pattani, it was almost dark. They began to climb the slopes of Gunung Jerai with the Isotta-Fraschini's headlights shining into a fog of dust. Passing under the estate's arched gateway they went speeding up a red, dirt track. Then the car turned a corner, and a mansion appeared ahead, springing dramatically out of the slope, with lamps blazing through its windows and doorways. A rounded turret formed the fulcrum of the house. Built around this were wide, sweeping verandas and a roof that curved gently upwards, in the Chinese style.

'Morningside House,' announced Elsa.

Dolly was dazzled. In the inky darkness, it looked as though an unreal brightness were pouring out of the house; that the light was welling up from some interior source of illumination, spilling out of the mountain on which it stood.

'It's magnificent, Elsa,' Uma said. 'There's no other word for it. I think it's possibly the most beautiful house I've ever seen . . .'

Inside, the house was aglow with the rich warmth of polished wood. On their way down to dinner, both Dolly and Uma went astray in the long corridors, distracted by the many fine details of the interior: the floor was of intricate parquetry, and the walls were panelled with rich, fine-grained woods. Elsa came up to look for them and found them tapping the banister of the great stairway that wound through the centre of the house.

'How beautiful this is.'

'Do you like it?' Elsa's face lit up with pleasure. 'When we were building Morningside, Matthew said one day: Everything I have, I owe to trees of one kind or another – teak, rubber. And I thought to myself, why that's it: Morningside will be a monument to wood! I made Rajkumar send me the best teak from Burma; I sent people to the Celebes and Sumatra. You'll notice that each room has wood of a different kind . . .'

Elsa led them downstairs and ushered them into the dining room, which was very large, with a long, polished hardwood table running down the middle. The walls were lined with knitted bamboo and the lights that hung from the ceiling were set inside glowing nests of rattan. As they stepped in, Saya John rose from the table and came up to Dolly and Uma, walking slowly, with the help of a cane: he seemed smaller than before, and more gnome-like as though his body had shrunk in proportion to his head.

'Welcome, welcome.'

At dinner, Uma and Dolly sat between Matthew and Saya John. The men worked hard at keeping their plates filled with food.

'That's gulai tumis, fish cooked with pink ginger buds, bunga kuntan.'

'And this?'

'Prawns roasted in pandanus leaves.'

'Peanut crumpets.'

'Nine-layered rice cakes.'

'Chicken with blue flowers – bunga telang.'

'Pickled fish with turmeric leaves and lime leaves and leaves of purple mint.'

'A salad of shredded squid and polygonum and duan kado, a creeper that smells like a spice-garden.'

With every morsel their mouths were filled with new tastes, flavours that were as unfamiliar as they were delicious. Uma cried: 'What is this food called? I thought I'd eaten everything in New York, but I've never tasted anything like this.'

Saya John smiled: 'So you like Nyonya cooking then?'

'I've never eaten anything so wonderful. Where is it from?'

'From Malacca and Penang,' Elsa said smiling. 'One of the world's last great secrets.'

Replete at last, Uma pushed her plate away and sat back. She turned to Dolly who was sitting beside her.

'So many years.'

'Twenty-three, almost to the day,' said Dolly, 'since I last saw you in Rangoon.'

After dinner Dolly accompanied Uma to her bedroom. She sat on the bed, cross-legged, while Uma combed her hair at the dressing table.

'Uma,' Dolly said shyly, 'you know I'm still wondering . . .'

'About what?'

'Your reception at the port today – all those people . . .'

'Oh, you mean the League?' Uma put her comb down and smiled at Dolly, in her mirror.

'Yes. Tell me about it.'

'It's such a long story, Dolly. I don't know where to begin.'

'Never mind. Just start.'

It went back to New York, Uma said. That was where she had first joined the League, inducted by friends, other Indians living in the city. The Indians there were few in number but closely connected; some had come to seek shelter from the surveillance of the Empire's intelligence services; others had been drawn there because of the relative affordability of the education. Almost without exception they were passionately political; it was impossible, in that circumstance of exile, to remain aloof. At Columbia there was the brilliant and intense Dadasaheb Ambedkar; there was Taraknath Das, gentle in manner but stubborn in spirit. Midtown, there was the Ramakrishna Mission, housed in a tiny, loft-like apartment and manned by a single, saffron-robed *sant* and scores of American sympathisers; downtown, in a tenement south of Houston Street, there was an eccentric Raja who believed himself to be India's Bolivar. It was not that America was hospitable, either to them or their enterprise: it was merely oblivious, uninterested, but indifference too provided shelter of a certain kind.

Soon Uma's apartment had became one of the nodes in this small but dense net of Indian connections. She and her compatriots were like explorers or castaways; watching, observing, picking apart the details of what they saw around them, trying to derive lessons for themselves and their country. Witnessing the nascency of the new century in America, they were able to watch at first hand the tides and currents of the new epoch. They went to visit mills and factories and the latest mechanised farms. They saw that new patterns of work were being invented, calling for new patterns of movement, new ways of thought. They saw that in the world ahead literacy would be crucial to survival; they saw that education had become a matter of such urgency as to prompt every modern nation to make it compulsory. From those of their peers who had travelled eastwards they learnt that Japan had moved quickly in this direction; in Siam too education had become a dynastic crusade for the royal family.

In India on the other hand, it was the military that devoured the bulk of public monies: although the army was small in number it consumed more than sixty per cent of the Government's revenues, more even than was the case in countries that were castigated as 'militaristic'. Lala Har Dayal, one of Uma's most brilliant contemporaries, never tired of pointing out that India was, in effect, a vast garrison and that it was the impoverished Indian peasant who paid both for the upkeep of the conquering army and for Britain's eastern campaigns.

What would become of India's population when the future

they had glimpsed in America had become the world's present condition? They could see that it was not they themselves, nor even their children who would pay the true price of this Empire: that the conditions being created in their homeland were such as to ensure that their descendants would enter the new epoch as cripples, lacking the most fundamental means of survival; that they would truly become in the future what they had never been in the past, a burden upon the world. They could see too that already time was running out, that it would soon become impossible to change the angle of their country's entry into the future; that a time was at hand, when even the fall of the Empire and the departure of their rulers would make little difference; that their homeland's trajectory was being set on an unbudgeable path that would thrust it inexorably in the direction of future catastrophe.

What they saw and thought, seared them, burned them: they were all to some degree mutilated by the knowledge of the evil that was their enemy. Some became a little unhinged, some went mad, others simply gave up. Some turned communist, some took to religion, searching the scriptures for imprecations and formulae, to apply on themselves, like balm.

Among Uma's Indian contemporaries in New York there were many who took their direction from a newsletter published from the University of California, in Berkeley, by Indian students. This publication was called *Ghadar*, after the Hindustani word for the uprising of 1857. The people who were involved with the magazine were known as the Ghadar Party. Much of their support came from the Indians who'd settled on the Pacific coast in the late nineteenth and early twentieth centuries. Many of these immigrants were Sikhs – former soldiers of the British Indian army. The experience of living in America and Canada served to turn many of these former loyalists into revolutionaries. Perceiving a link between their treatment abroad and India's subject status, they had become dedicated enemies of the Empire they had once served. Some of them concentrated their efforts on trying to convert such of their friends and relatives as were still serving in the British Indian army. Others looked for allies abroad, developing links with the Irish resistance in America.

The Indians were, comparatively, novices in the arts of sedition. It was the Irish who were their mentors and allies, schooling them in their methods of organisation, teaching them the tricks of shopping for arms to send back home; giving them instruction in the techniques of fomenting mutiny among those of their countrymen who served the Empire as soldiers. On St Patrick's Day in New York a small Indian contingent would sometimes march in the Irish parade, with their own banners, dressed in sherwanis and turbans, dhoties and kurtas, angarkhas and angava-strams.

After the start of the First World War, under pressure from the British intelligence services, the Ghadar Party had gone under-ground, metamorphosing slowly into a number of different groups. Of these the Indian Independence League was the most important, with thousands of partisans among overseas Indians: it was their offices that Uma had been visiting in eastern Asia.

Here, Dolly, who had been growing increasingly puzzled, broke in. 'But, Uma,' she said, 'if what you're telling me is true, then why have I never heard of the League? The papers are always full of Mahatma Gandhi, but no one ever speaks of your group.'

'The reason for that, Dolly,' said Uma, 'is that Mr Gandhi heads the loyal opposition. Like many other Indians he's chosen to deal with the Empire's velvet glove instead of striking at its iron fist. He cannot see that the Empire will always remain secure while its Indian soldiers remain loyal. The Indian army will always put down opposition wherever it occurs – not just in India, but also in Burma, Malaya, East Africa, no matter where. And of course, the Empire does everything possible to keep these soldiers in hand: only certain castes of men are recruited; they're completely shut off from politics and the wider society; they're given land and their children are assured jobs.'

'What do you hope to do then?' Dolly asked.

'To open the soldiers' eyes. It's not as difficult as you might think. Many of the League's leaders are old soldiers. Giani Amreek Singh for instance – do you remember him? He was the distin-guished Sikh Giani who came to the pier today, remember?'

'Yes.'

'I'll tell you a story about him. I first met him in California, many years ago. He's an old military man himself: he'd risen to the rank of a junior NCO in the British Indian army before deserting. The first time I heard him speak, he talked about the necessity of opening the eyes of Indian soldiers. After a while I said to him: "But Gianiji, you served in this army yourself; why did it take you so long to understand that you were being used to conquer others like yourself?"'

'And what did he say?' Dolly asked.

'He said: "You don't understand. We never thought that we were being used to conquer people. Not at all: we thought the opposite. We were told that we were freeing those people. That is what they said – that we were going to set those people free from their bad kings or their evil customs or some such thing. We believed it because they believed it too. It took us a long time to understand that in their eyes freedom exists wherever *they* rule."'

Dolly acknowledged this with a smile and a nod. 'But what else, Uma? Did you ever meet anyone? A man? Did you never talk of anything but politics with your revolutionaries?'

Uma gave her a wan smile. 'I met many men, Dolly. But we were always like brothers and sisters – that's how we spoke to one another, *bhai* and *bahen*. As for me, because they knew that I was a widow, I think the men looked to me to be a kind of ideal woman, a symbol of purity – and to tell you the truth, I didn't much mind. That's the thing about politics – once you get involved in it, it pushes everything else out of your life.'

Eighteen

Uma woke the next morning to find that breakfast had been served on a veranda that looked down the slope of the mountain, towards the brilliant blue of the Andaman Sea. Neel and Timmy were leaning on the balcony's rail, talking about cars. Alison and Dinu were listening without joining in. Looking at them, it occurred to Uma that even until the day before, she would not have known them if she'd passed them in the street. Yet now, in their faces, she could see inscribed the history of her friendships and the lives of her friends – the stories and trajectories that had brought Elsa's life into conjuction with Matthew's, Dolly's with Rajkumar's, Malacca with New York, Burma with India.

'The children' – here they were, standing in front of her: a day had gone by and she had not said a single word to any of them. In San Francisco, before boarding, she'd gone into a shop to buy presents and had ended up wandering off in the direction of the baby clothes and rattles and silver cups. It was with a jolt that she'd recalled that 'the children' were almost adults now – that Neel was twenty or thereabouts, that Dinu and Alison were sixteen and Timmy just two years younger. It occurred to her that if she'd had children of her own, they would have been of the same age, they would all have been friends – the canvas of a lifetime's connections would have acquired the patina of another generation. But that was not to be, and now, listening to her friends' children as they bantered in the shorthand of their youth, Uma felt oddly shy: trying to think of things to say to them, she realised that she had no idea what they did with their time, the things they thought about, the books they read.

She felt herself slipping into a silence that would become, she knew, irremediable if it were allowed to persist. So, because she was the kind of person she was, she did exactly what she would have done at a political meeting: rising to her feet, she called them to order: 'I have something to say, so please listen. I feel I must talk to each of you on your own, or I'll never know what to say to any of you . . .'

Their eyes widened as they turned to look at her. She thought to herself: what have I done? I've scared them off; I've lost them for ever. But then, as the meaning of what she'd said dawned on them, they began to smile; she had the impression that no adult had ever spoken to them like this before; no grown-up had ever thought to seek them out for their company.

'All right then, Alison, let's go for a walk.'

From then on, it was easy: they seemed to want to show her round the estate, to go with her for walks. They called her 'Auntie' and this was oddly pleasing too. Soon they were not just 'the children' any more; each was someone she could recognise: Timmy was the confident one, who knew exactly what he intended to do: he wanted to go to America, to study, just as Matthew had, and then he wanted to go into business, on his own. Neel was a blunter and softer version of Rajkumar: she could see his father in him, quite clearly, but overlaid by a generation of wealth and comfort. Alison was a bit of an enigma, sometimes quiet and moody, but on occasion, wildly exuberant, full of laughter and sharp, intelligent conversation.

Dinu was the only one who left Uma feeling at a complete loss. Every time she tried to talk to him he seemed sullen, dour, and such observations as he occasionally had to offer were usually tart to the point of sourness. When he spoke, it was in odd staccato bursts, swallowing half his words and shooting out the rest: a manner of speech that made her afraid of saying anything, for fear that she might appear to be interrupting him. It was only when Dinu had a camera in his hands that he seemed to relax a little: but of course it was impossible to talk to someone who had no mind for anything but his viewfinder.

One morning, Alison said to Uma, 'There's something I want to show you. Can I take you for a drive?'

'By all means.'

Dinu was well within earshot and the invitation was extended in such a way as clearly to include him. But Alison's offer seemed to cast the boy into an agony of shyness. He began to back away, making a great show of dragging his right foot behind him.

'Dinu, won't you come with us?' Alison said.

'I don't know . . .' He went pale and began to mumble in confusion.

Uma was watching him closely and she knew suddenly that the boy was secretly infatuated with Alison. She was tempted to smile. Nothing would come of it, she could tell: they were as different as could be, he a creature of the shadows, she an animal that craved the spotlight. He would spend his life nurturing unuttered yearnings. Uma was tempted to grip him by the shoulders, to shake him awake.

'Come on, Dinu,' she ordered in a sharp, peremptory voice. 'Don't be a child.'

'Yes, do come,' Alison said brightly. 'I think you'll enjoy it.'

'Can I bring my camera?'

'Of course.'

They went down the sweeping, mahogany staircase, out into the gravelled driveway where a small, cherry-red roadster stood parked under the porch. The car was a 6-litre Paige Daytona, a three-seater, with a single rear seat that pulled out like a drawer, resting on the running board. Alison pulled the rear seat out for Dinu and then clicked open the passenger door for Uma.

'Alison!' Uma's voice rose in surprise. 'Does your father let you drive his cars?'

Alison grinned. 'Only this one,' she said. 'He won't hear of us driving the Duesie or the Isotta.' She gunned the engine and the car rocketed forward, shooting a shower of pebbles back into the porch.

'Alison!' Uma cried, clinging to her door. 'You're going far too fast.'

'This isn't half as fast as I'd like to go.' Alison laughed and tossed her head. The wind caught her hair and carried it out behind her, like a sail. Roaring through the gate at the bottom of the garden, they plunged abruptly into the hushed gloom of the plantation, with slender, long-leafed trees arching high above them on either side. The trees were ranged in lines that stretched as far as the eye could follow, dwindling into long, straight tunnels: the effect was giddying as they flashed past, thousands upon thousands of them. It was like staring at stripes on a fast-moving screen: Uma felt herself growing dizzy and had to lower her eyes.

Suddenly the trees ended and a small shantytown appeared, with rows of shacks lining the road – hutches of brick and mortar, sheltered under steepled sheets of tin. The shacks were exactly similar in design and yet each was defiantly distinctive in appearance: some were neat, with little curtains fluttering at their front windows, while other were hovels, with pyramids of filth piled at their doors.

'The coolie lines,' said Alison, slowing briefly. In a moment they were past and then the car picked up speed again. Once again, a tunnel of arched tree trunks closed around them, and they disappeared into a tube of kaleidoscopic lines.

The road ended at a stream. A ribbon of water was flowing down the face of a tilted sheet of rock, its surface braided with tiny ripples. On the far side, the mountain climbed steeply upwards, blanketed in a dense tangle of forest. Alison ran the car into a sheltered clearing and snapped her door open.

'The estate ends here,' she said. 'Now we have to walk.'

Taking Uma's hand, Alison helped her pick her way slowly over the stream. On the other side was a path that led directly into the jungle, heading up the slope of Gunung Jerai. The climb was steep and Uma soon ran out of breath.

'Do we have a long way to go?' she called ahead to Alison.

'No. We're almost there.'

'Where?'

Suddenly Dinu came up to stand beside her. 'Look.'

Following the direction of his pointing finger, Uma glanced up. Through a tangle of vines and bamboo, she caught a glimpse of a line of red masonry. 'Why,' she said, 'it appears to be a ruin of some kind.'

Dinu went ahead, hurrying in excitement after Alison. Uma caught up with them at a spot where the slope levelled out into a flat, rocky ledge. Directly ahead of her were two cenotaph-like structures, placed on square plinths: walled chambers of simple design, each with a doorway that led into a small enclosure. Their stone walls were mossy with age and their roofs had caved in.

'I was hoping you'd be able to tell us what they are, Auntie Uma.'

'Why me?'

'Well your father was an archaeologist, wasn't he?'

'Yes but . . .' Uma shook her head slowly. 'I didn't learn much from him . . .'

The sight was as evocative as any she'd ever seen: the crumbling red stone juxtaposed against the tangled greenery of the jungle, with the mountain rising serenely above, a halo of cloud around its peak. Dinu was absorbed in photographing the ruins, moving round the structures as fast as his foot would let him. Uma felt a sudden pang of envy: if I were his age, this would have taken hold of me too, it would have changed my life; I would have come back here again and again; I wouldn't rest until I'd had my fill of it; I'd want to dig them up and take them with me . . .

'Auntie Uma,' Dinu called to her, across the clearing, 'what are they – these ruins?'

She ran the edge of her thumb over the spongy stone. 'I think these were what my father used to call *chandis*,' she said softly. 'Shrines.'

'What sort of shrine?' said Dinu. 'Who built them?'

'I'd say they're either Hindu or Buddhist shrines.' She threw up her hands, in frustration at her own ignorance. 'I wish I could tell you more.'

'Do you think they're old?' Dinu said.

'Yes,' said Uma. 'I'm sure of that. Just look how weathered the stone is. I would say these chandis are very old indeed.'

'I knew they were old,' Alison said triumphantly. 'I knew it. Daddy doesn't believe me. He says nothing here can be old because there was only jungle when he first came.'

Dinu turned to Alison, in his abrupt way: 'And how did you find this place?'

'My father sometimes takes us shooting in the jungle,' Alison said. 'One day we stumbled upon this place.' She took Dinu's hand. 'Let me show you something,' she said. 'Come.'

229

She led him into the larger of the two structures. Stopping at the plinth, she pointed to an image on a pedestal, a weathered Ganesh, carved in moss-covered stone.

'We found the image lying on the floor,' said Alison, 'and we put it back – it seemed to belong there.'

Uma caught a glimpse of Dinu and Alison, standing framed in the ruined doorway, next to each other. They looked very young, more children than adolescents. 'Give me your camera,' she called out to Dinu. 'I'll take a picture of the two of you together.'

She took the Brownie from him and stepped back, with her eye to the viewfinder. It gave her a start to see them framed together. Suddenly she understood why people arranged marriages for their children: it was a way of shaping the future to the past, of cementing one's ties to one's memories and to one's friends. Dinu and Alison – if only they were better suited to each other; how wonderful it might be, the bringing together of so many stories. Then she recollected what she was supposed to be doing and was annoyed with herself for thinking about things that were none of her business. She clicked the shutter and handed the camera back to Dinu.

The day began very early at the plantation. Every morning, well before dawn, Uma was woken by Matthew's footsteps, going down the grand staircase and out to his car. From her window she would see his headlamps streaking down the slope, in the pre-dawn darkness, heading in the direction of the estate office.

One day she said to Matthew: 'Where do you go, so early in the morning?'

'To Muster.'

'What's that?'

'We have an assembly ground near the estate office. The tappers come there in the morning and the contractors give them their jobs for the day.'

She was intrigued by the jargon: muster, contractors, tappers. 'Can I come?'

'Certainly.'

The next morning Uma drove down to the office with Matthew, along shortcuts that went corkscrewing down the slope. Scores of tappers were converging in front of the plantation's tin-roofed offices by the light of blazing kerosene lamps: they were all Indians, mainly Tamils; the women were dressed in saris and the men in sarongs.

The ceremony that followed was part military parade and part school assembly. It was presided over by the estate's manager, Mr Trimble, a portly Eurasian. The tappers fell into straight lines, facing a tall flagpole that stood at the far corner of the assembly ground. Mr Trimble hoisted the Union Jack and then stood at attention beneath the flagpole, saluting stiffly, with two rows of Indian overseers lining up behind him – these were the 'conductors'.

Mr Trimble kept attentive watch as the conductors took attendance. His manner varied between that of a strict headmaster and a snappish sergeant. Occasionally he would dart into the ranks, with his rattan cane tucked under his arm. For some of the tappers he had a smile and a quick word of encouragement; with others, he made a great show of losing his temper, gesticulating and pouring out obscenities, in Tamil and English, singling out the object of his wrath with the tip of his pointing cane: 'You dog of a coolie, keep your black face up and look at me when I'm talking to you . . .'

Uma was disturbed by this spectacle: she had the feeling of watching something archaic, a manner of life that she had believed to be fortunately extinct. In the car Matthew asked what she had thought of 'Muster' and she had difficulty in keeping her voice under control.

'I don't know what to say, Matthew. It was like watching something that no longer existed: I was put in mind of the American South before the Civil War, of *Uncle Tom's Cabin*.'

'Oh, come on, aren't you exaggerating a bit? Our tappers are well fed and well looked after. And they're a lot better off than they would be if they were back where they came from.'

'Isn't that what masters have always said about slaves?'

Matthew raised his voice. 'They're not slaves, Uma.'

'No, of course not.' Uma reached out to touch his arm, in

231

apology. 'No. But did you see the terror on their faces when that man – the manager – shouted at them?'

'He's just doing his job, Uma. It's a very hard job and he does it very well. It's no easy thing to run a plantation you know. To look at, it's all very green and beautiful – sort of like a forest. But actually it's a vast machine, made of wood and flesh. And at every turn, every little piece of this machine is resisting you, fighting you, waiting for you to give in.'

He brought the car to a sudden halt. 'Let me show you something.' Opening his door, he led the way into a stand of rubber. 'Come. Over here.'

It was first light now and dawn was descending on the peak of Gunung Jerai. This was the one time of day when the mountain's heights were always visible, unclouded by the haze that rose later from the heated plain. On the slopes above them, the jungle was coming slowly to life, with flocks of birds rising from the forest canopy, and unseen troops of monkeys sailing through the tree-tops, leaving wakes of tossing leaves.

Under the rubber trees, there was a slow dripping of dew. Matthew leant against a tree trunk and pointed up. 'Look at this tree,' he said, 'and look at the others around it. Wouldn't you say they're all exactly the same?'

'Yes,' Uma nodded, 'it struck me the other day: even their limbs branch off at the same height, and in exactly the same way.'

'And so they should. An enormous amount of human ingenuity has been invested in making these trees exactly similar. They're called clones, you know, and scientists have been working on them for years. Most of our trees are of a clonal variety called Avros – developed by the Dutch in Sumatra in the twenties. We pay a lot of money to make sure that we get reliable clonal seed. But let me show you something.'

He pointed into a coconut-shell cup that was fastened in the tree's trunk, beneath a long, spiral slash in the bark. 'See how much latex this tree has produced overnight? The cup is half full, which is about right. If you walked down this row of trees, you'd find that most of them had yielded roughly the same amount of latex. But now look over here.'

He led the way to another tree. 'Look at this cup.'

232

Uma looked in and saw that the cup he was pointing to was almost empty. She asked: 'Is something wrong with this tree then?'

'Not that I can tell,' Matthew said. 'It looks all right – no different from the others. Think of all the human effort that has gone into making it the same as the rest. And yet . . .' – he pointed into the almost-empty cup, '. . . there you are.'

'So what do you think the matter is?'

'Botanists will tell you one thing and geologists will tell you another and soil specialists will tell you something else again. But if you ask me, the truth is quite simple.'

'What is it?'

'It's fighting back.'

Uma gave an astonished laugh. 'You can't really believe that.'

'I planted this tree, Uma. I've heard what all the experts say. But the tappers know better. They have a saying, you know – "every rubber tree in Malaya was paid for with an Indian life". They know that there are trees that won't do what the others do, and that's what they say – this one is fighting back.'

Through the surrounding tree trunks, the plantation's offices were visible in the distance, on the slope below. Matthew pointed to them, making a sweeping gesture with his hand.

'This is my little empire, Uma. I made it. I took it from the jungle and moulded it into what I wanted it to be. Now that it's mine I take good care of it. There's law, there's order, everything is well run. Looking at it, you would think everything here is tame, domesticated, that all the parts have been fitted carefully together. But it's when you try to make the whole machine work that you discover that every bit of it is fighting back. It has nothing to do with me or with rights and wrongs: I could make this the best-run little kingdom in the world and it would still fight back.'

'And what's the reason for that?'

'It's nature: the nature that made these trees and the nature that made us.'

'So are you saying then . . .' – Uma began to laugh, 'that some of your trees are rebels by instinct?'

'Not in so many words.'

'But, Matthew,' Uma laughed again, 'what on earth are you

233

going to do if your tappers decide to take a lesson from your trees?'

Now it was Matthew's turn to laugh. 'Let's hope it never comes to that.'

Unable to sleep past daybreak, Uma began to go for long walks in the rubber groves. It was years now since she had risen this early: dawn was a discovery. There were days when teams of rubber tappers would loom suddenly out of the golden early morning mist, with tendrils of fog clinging to their saris and sarongs. They would pass within inches of her, oblivious of her presence, utterly absorbed in keeping pace with each other, their scythe-like knives glinting in the half-light as they peeled slivers of bark from the tree trunks.

On one of these early morning walks, Uma became aware that she was being followed. She looked over her shoulder, and saw a figure slipping out of view: it was either a boy or a man, she couldn't tell. It was easy to lose sight of things in the rubber groves, especially in the half-light of dawn. The arrangement of the trees was such that things would slip away, from one line of sight into another, and you'd have no idea where they were in relation to yourself.

The next day, hearing the crackle of leaves behind her, it was she who hid herself. This time she was able to catch a glimpse of him in the distance: it was a boy, thin, lanky and dark. He was dressed in a shirt and checked sarong. She took him to be one of the worker's children.

'You, there . . .' she called out, her voice echoing through the tunnels of foliage. 'Who are you? Come here.' She caught a glimpse of the whites of his eyes, flaring suddenly in the darkness. Then he disappeared.

Back at the house, Uma described the boy to Alison. 'Do you know who he might be?'

'Yes.' Alison nodded. 'His name is Ilongo. He's from the coolie lines. Was he following you?'

'Yes.'

234

'He does that sometimes. Don't worry; he's completely harm-less. We call him Morningside's village idiot.'

Uma decided to befriend the boy. She set about it carefully, taking little gifts with her each morning, usually fruit, rambutans, mangoes or mangosteens. On catching sight of him she'd stop and call out, 'Ilongo, Ilongo, come here.' Then she'd put her offering down on the ground and walk away. Soon, he became confident enough to approach her. The first few times, she made no attempt to talk. She set down her gifts and watched him retrieve them, from a distance. He was about ten, but tall for his age, and very thin. His eyes were large and very expressive: looking into them, she could not believe that he was a simpleton.

'Ilongo,' she said to him one day, in English, 'why do you follow me around?' When he didn't answer she switched to Hindustani, asking the same question again.

This produced an immediate effect: spitting out an orange seed, he suddenly began to speak.

'After my mother leaves for Muster, I don't like to stay in the house, all by myself.'

'Are you alone at home then?'

'Yes.'

'What about your father?'

'My father isn't here.'

'Why? Where is he?'

'I don't know.'

'Have you never met him?'

'No.'

'Do you know where he lives?'

'No. But my mother has a picture of him: he's an important man, my mother says.'

'Can I see the picture?'

'I'll have to ask my mother.' Then something startled him and he vanished into the trees.

A couple of days later, walking past a line of rubber tappers, Ilongo pointed to a woman with a strong, square face and a silver nose ring. 'That's my mother,' he said. Uma made as though to approach her and the boy panicked. 'No. She's working now. The conductor will fine her.'

'But I'd like to talk to her.'

'Later. At our house. Come here at five, and I'll take you.'

That evening, Uma walked with Ilongo to the line of shacks where he lived. Their dwelling was small but neat and bare. Ilongo's mother had changed into a bright, peacock-green sari in anticipation of Uma's visit. She sent the boy out to play and set a pot of water on the fire, for tea.

'Ilongo said you had a picture of his father.'

'Yes.' She handed over a piece of fading newsprint.

Uma recognised the face at first glance. She realised now that she'd known all along, without wanting to acknowledge it to herself. She shut her eyes and turned the picture over so that she wouldn't have to look at it. It was Rajkumar.

'Do you know who this man is?' she said at last.

'Yes.'

'Do you know that he's married?'

'Yes.'

'How did it happen? Between you and him?'

'They sent me to him. On the ship, when I was coming over. They called me out of the hold and took me up to his cabin. There was nothing I could do.'

'That was the only time?'

'No. For years afterwards, whenever he was here he'd send for me. He wasn't so bad, better than some others. One time, I saw a picture of his wife and I said to him, she's so beautiful, like a princess – what do you want with a woman like me?'

'What did he say?'

'He told me that his wife had turned away from the world; that she'd lost interest in her home and her family, in him . . .'

'And when was the last time you saw him?'

'Many years ago. He stopped coming after I told him I was pregnant.'

'Did he not want to have anything to do with the boy – with Ilongo?'

'No. But he sends money.'

'Why haven't you spoken to his wife? Or to Mr or Mrs Martins? They could do something. What he's done is very wrong: he can't be allowed to abandon you like this.'

236

Ilongo's mother glanced at her visitor and saw that her face was flushed with indignation on her behalf. Now a note of anxiety entered the matter-of-fact tone of her voice. 'Madame, you won't speak of this to anyone?'

'You can be sure that I will,' Uma retorted. 'This is a shameful business. I'll go to the police if I need to . . .'

At this the woman panicked. She came quickly across the room and sank to her knees at Uma's feet. 'No,' she said, shaking her head vehemently. 'No. No. Please understand. I know you mean to help me but you are an outsider. You do not know how things are here.'

'What do you want then?' Uma rose angrily to her feet. 'Do you want that I should just let this pass? That he should get away with it?'

'This is my business. You have no right to speak of this to anyone . . .'

Uma was breathing heavily, her chest heaving in anger. 'I don't understand,' she said. 'This man should be punished for what he has done to you – to you and to his own wife and family. Why do you want to keep this matter hidden?'

'Because it will not help me to see him punished: it will only make things worse for everyone. The money will stop; there'll be trouble. I am not a child: it is not for you to take this decision on my behalf . . .'

Tears of frustration welled up in Uma's eyes. She'd often railed against women who allowed themselves to be trapped within labyrinths of fear – but now, confronted with this circumstance she was helpless, herself a part of the maze.

'. . . Madame, I want you to give me your word that you will not speak of this: I will not let you leave until you have.'

There was nothing Uma could do but produce a forced nod of assent.

Nineteen

From that point on, Uma's journey began to acquire an involuntary, dream-like quality, with impressions and events following scattershot on each other, like hailstones battering against a netted screen.

At Morningside, on the last day of her stay, Uma had a conversation with Dinu that took her completely by surprise. She'd noticed that Dolly spent an inordinate amount of time on her own, staying in her room all morning and rarely making an appearance downstairs before noon.

Succumbing to curiosity, Uma asked Dinu: 'Why doesn't Dolly have breakfast with us? Why does she come down so late?'

Dinu gave her a glance of surprise: 'Don't you know? She does her *te-ya-tai* in the morning.'

'What's that?'

'I don't know how to explain . . . I suppose you could say she meditates.'

'Oh.' Uma paused to digest this. 'And when did this start?'

'I don't know. She's been doing it ever since I can remember . . . Was there a time when she didn't?'

'I don't remember . . .'

Uma changed the subject abruptly and didn't touch on it again.

The next stop on Uma's itinerary was none other than Rangoon. Her trip had been so planned as to allow her to make the journey over from Malaya in the company of Dolly, Neel and Dinu. She was to stay with Dolly and Rajkumar for one month, before sailing on to Calcutta. While planning the trip, it was this leg of the journey that Uma had most looked forward to: she had imagined herself and Dolly spending hours together during the voyage, talking as they once had. Now, the prospect filled her with dread.

But once they were on board, the constraints of the last few days disappeared almost magically. Gradually, the old intimacy returned, to the point where Uma could even bring herself to comment on Dolly's daily periods of seclusion.

One morning, when they were both out on deck, Uma said, 'You know, Dolly, after we talked that first night, at Morningside, I thought it would be just like the old days. Do you remember, Dolly, at Ratnagiri, how we would talk through the night, and then when we woke up, we would start again, as though falling asleep were just an interruption? At Morningside, every morning, I'd say to myself, today I'll go for a walk with Dolly and we'll sit under a tree and look at the sea. But you were never there; you were never even down for breakfast. So one morning, I asked Dinu and he told me why you stayed so late in your room . . .'

'I see.'

'I tried so hard to tell you about my life and you never said a word about yours; nothing about what's on your mind or what you do with your time.'

'What could I say, Uma? If I'd been better with words, perhaps I could have. But I didn't know what to say. And especially to you . . .'

'Why especially me?'

'With you I feel that I have to account for myself – provide an explanation.'

Uma saw that this was not untrue. 'Perhaps you're right, Dolly. Perhaps I would have found it hard to understand. It's true that I'm not religious myself – but I would have tried to understand, simply because of you. And I'll still try, Dolly, if you'll let me.'

Dolly was silent for a moment. 'It's hard to know where to start, Uma. You'll remember that I wrote to you about Dinu's illness? After it was over, I found that something had changed in me. I couldn't go back to the life I'd led before. It wasn't that I was unhappy with Rajkumar, or that I no longer felt anything for him: it was just that the things I did no longer filled my time or occupied my mind. It was the feeling that you get when your day is empty and there's nothing to do – except that it went on, day after day. Then I heard about an old friend – we used to call her Evelyn. I heard she was at Sagaing, near Mandalay, and that she had become the head of a *thi-la-shin-kyaung* – what do you call it? – a Buddhist nunnery. I went up to see her, and I knew at once that that was where I wanted to be – that this would be my life.'

'Your life!' Uma stared at her, in shock. 'But what about the boys?'

'It's because of them – and Rajkumar – that I haven't gone yet. I want to see them settled first – in India perhaps, somewhere away from Burma, at any rate. Once they're safe, I'll feel free to go to Sagaing . . .'

'Safe? But aren't they safe where they are?'

'Things have changed in Burma, Uma. I feel frightened now. There's a lot of anger, a lot of resentment, and much of it is aimed at Indians.'

'But why?'

'Money, politics –' Dolly paused – 'so many different things, who's to say? Indian moneylenders have taken over all the farmland; Indians run most of the shops; people say that the rich Indians live like colonialists, lording it over the Burmese. I don't know what the wrongs and rights of it are, but I know that I feel frightened for the boys – even for Rajkumar. Some time ago, Dinu was shouted at, on the streets: they called him *Zerbadi* – which is a swear word, for people who're half-Indian, half-Burmese. And the other day in Rangoon, a crowd surrounded the car and shook their fists at me. I said to them: "Why are you doing this? What have I done to you?" Instead of giving me an answer, they began to chant *Amyotha Kwe Ko Mayukya Pa Net* . . .'

'What does that mean?'

'It's a political song: the gist of it is that it's wrong for Burmese to marry foreigners – that women like me, who're married to Indians, are traitors to their own people.'

'Did you say anything to them?'

'Yes I did. I was very angry. I said: "Do you know that I spent twenty years of my life in exile, with Burma's last king? Over here you forgot all about us. What little joy we had came from Indians."'

'And what did they say to that?'

'They looked sheepish and went away. But another time – who knows what they would do?'

'Have you told Rajkumar – that you want the family to leave Burma?'

'Yes. But of course, he won't listen. He tells me: "You don't understand. The economy wouldn't work without Indian businessmen; the country would collapse. These protests about Indians are the work of agitators and troublemakers who're just trying to incite the public." I've tried to tell him that it's he who doesn't understand; that the Burma of today is not the Burma he came to when he was eleven. But of course he pays no attention . . .' She broke off. 'You'll see what it's like when we get there . . .'

The next day, they reached Rangoon. The steamer was man-oeuvring itself into position beside the floating pavilion of the Barr Street Passenger Jetty, when Uma spotted Rajkumar standing in the shade of the ornamental eaves. He gave her a broad smile and waved. His hair was greying brightly at the temples and he seemed larger and bulkier than ever, with an immense, bellows-like chest. Uma gritted her teeth and forced a smile on to her face.

They drove to Kemendine in Rajkumar's new car, a grey 1929 Packard saloon. On the way Rajkumar pointed out the changes in their surroundings. The city seemed transformed beyond recognition to Uma. There were stately hotels, enormous banks, fashionable restaurants, arcaded department stores and even nightclubs. The one landmark that seemed to be proof against these changes was the Shwe Dagon Pagoda. It was exactly as Uma remembered, its graceful, gilded hti rising above the city like a benediction.

The Kemendine house had changed too: it still had its haphazard improvised look, but it was much larger now, with added-on floors above and sprawling wings at its side. Everywhere Uma looked there were caretakers, gardeners, chowkidars.

'How much your house has grown!' Uma said to Dolly. 'You could have an army in here if you wanted.'

'Rajkumar wants it to be large enough for the boys to live in,' Dolly said. 'They're each to have a floor of their own. He sees himself ruling over one of those vast joint families, growing larger with every generation . . .'

'It doesn't look,' said Uma, 'as if you're going to have a very easy time persuading him to leave.'

'No. It's going to be very hard . . .'

Later in the day, Dinu brought a Burmese school-friend to see her. His name was Maung Thiha Saw and he was a gawky, eager-looking boy with a great mass of shiny black hair and thick, smudged spectacles. He was as talkative as Dinu was reserved, and he peppered Uma with unexpected questions about America and the Depression.

The day was unnaturally still and airless and it was very hot inside the house. 'Come,' said Uma, 'let's talk outside – it may be a little cooler.'

They went downstairs and stepped out to walk round the compound. A tall electricity pole stood by the front gate and as they were approaching it, Uma noticed that it had begun to tilt. She came abruptly to a stop and ran a hand over her eyes. Then suddenly her feet grew unsteady. She felt as though her legs were going to pitch her forward.

'Dinu,' she cried, 'what's happening?'

'Earthquake!' Dinu put a hand on her shoulders and they huddled together with their arms round each other. It seemed like a very long time before the heaving in the earth came to a stop. Warily they let go of each other and looked around, taking stock. Suddenly Maung Thiha Saw shouted, his eyes fixed on the horizon.

'No!'

Uma spun round, just in time to see the great golden hti of the Shwe Dagon toppling over.

Soon after this, Uma made arrangements to travel round Burma with fellow-members of the Indian Independence League. From Rangoon she went eastwards to Moulmein and then turned north to go to Taunggyi, Toungoo, Meiktila and Mandalay. Everywhere she went she could see signs of a widening rift between Indians

242

and their Burmese neighbours. Amongst students and nationalists an agitation was under way to separate Burma's administration from that of British India. Many Indians saw this as a cause for alarm, believing that their safety would be threatened by a separation.

Uma was riven by this controversy: she sympathized with the fears of the Indian minority and yet it troubled her that they believed their safety lay in what she saw as the root cause of the problem – the pattern of imperial rule and its policy of ensuring its necessity through the division of its subjects. On returning to Rangoon, Uma was quick to offer Dolly an apology: 'Dolly, I hope you'll forgive me for treating your fears so lightly. I can see now that there's a lot to worry about. Frankly I feel utterly confused . . .'

A few days before her departure for Calcutta, Uma went for an early morning drive with Dolly in the grey Packard. They went first to Rangoon's Churchill Road, to look at the house where Queen Supayalat had died, a few years before.

'Did you ever see her again, Dolly?' Uma asked.

'No.' Dolly slowly shook her head. 'As far as she was concerned, I was in the same boat as the Second Princess: banished for ever from her presence . . .'

On the way back, they drove past the Sule Pagoda and found the streets unusually quiet for that time of day. 'I wonder why there are no rickshaws, no hawkers . . .' Dolly paused to look around. 'How odd: I can't see a single Indian on the street.'

In the distance, at a street corner there was a long line of men. As the Packard rolled past, they saw that the men were queueing to have tattoo-like designs painted on their chests. Dolly's reaction was instantaneous. She leant over to shake U Ba Kyaw's shoulder.

'Dolly – what's the matter? What's happening?'

'We have to turn round. We have to go back – back to the house.'

'Because of those men? Why? Does it have something to do with those tattoos?'

'Those weren't tattoos, Uma. Those designs were for soldiers who're going to war . . .' Dolly began to drum her fist distractedly on her knees. 'I think there's going to be some kind of trouble.

We have to find out where the boys are – where Rajkumar is. If we're quick maybe we'll be able to stop them leaving the house.'

Some twenty yards ahead of the Packard, a man leapt off a footpath and ran into the street. Uma and Dolly noticed him when he appeared in one corner of the Packard's wide, curved windscreen. He was an Indian, a rickshaw-puller, dressed in a tattered vest and a longyi. He was running hard and beads of sweat were flying off his arms. One of his hands was clawing the air, and the other was holding up his longyi, keeping it from getting entangled in his legs. His face was dark and his eyes very white and bulbous. Two steps carried him from the edge of their windscreen to its middle; he turned to glance over his shoulder and his eyes started in his head. Now they saw that he was being closely pursued by a man who was just two steps behind him. This man was bare-bodied and a black design was painted over his chest. He was carrying something but they couldn't see what it was, because it was hidden beneath the edge of their windscreen. Then, all of a sudden, the pursuer swung his shoulders and drew his arms back, in the manner of a tennis player preparing to make a stroke. They saw now that the instrument in his hands was a da, a long, glinting blade with a short handle, part sword, part axe. They sat transfixed in their seats as the da scythed through the air in a circular motion. The rickshaw-puller had almost reached the far end of their windscreen when suddenly his head toppled over like a lopped-off branch, hanging down over his spine, held on by a thin flap of skin. But the body did not fall instantly to the ground: for a fraction of a second the decapitated trunk stayed upright. They saw it advance by one more step before crashing to the pavement.

Uma's first impulse was to reach for the door handle.

'What are you doing?' Dolly screamed. 'Stop.'

'We have to help, Dolly. We can't just leave him on the street . . .'

'Uma, have you gone mad?' Dolly hissed. 'If you get out of the car now, you'll be killed too.' She gave Uma a push, thrusting her on to the floor of the car. 'You have to hide, Uma. We can't run the risk of your being seen.' She made Uma lie flat and then ripped the cloth covers off the Packard's back seat. 'I'm going to cover you with these. Lie still and don't say a word.'

Uma put her head down on the floor-mat and closed her eyes. The rickshaw-puller's face appeared in front of her: she saw his head once again, toppling backwards. In that instant when the decapitated body had still been upright, still moving forward, she had caught a glimpse of those white eyes, hanging down over his spine: their gaze had appeared to be directed into the car, right at her. Uma felt her gorge rise and then vomit came pouring of her mouth and her nose, fouling the floor-mat.

'Dolly.' Just as she was beginning to raise her head, Dolly gave her a sharp nudge. The car came to a sudden stop and she froze, with her face inches from the vomit-covered mat. Somewhere above Dolly was talking to someone – a group of men – she was explaining something in Burmese. The conversation took just a minute or two, but an eternity seemed to pass before the car moved on again.

The riots lasted several days and the casualties numbered in the hundreds. The toll would have been higher still, if it had not been for the many Burmese who had rescued Indians from the mob and sheltered them in their homes. It was discovered later that the trouble had started with a clash between Indian and Burmese workers at the docks. Many Indian- and Chinese-owned businesses were attacked, among them one of Rajkumar's timberyards. Three of his workers were killed and dozens were injured.

Rajkumar was at home when the trouble broke out. Neither he nor anyone else in the family suffered any personal injury. Neel happened to be safely out of town when the riots started, and Dinu was taken home from school by his friend, Maung Thiha Saw.

Despite his losses Rajkumar was now more adamant than ever about remaining in Burma: 'I've lived here all my life; everything I have is here. I'm not such a coward as to give up everything I've worked for at the first sign of trouble. And anyway, what makes you think that we'll be any more welcome in India than we are here? There are riots in India all the time – how do you know that the same thing wouldn't happen to us there?'

Uma saw that Dolly was near collapse and she decided to stay on in Rangoon, to help her cope. A week became a month and then another. Every time she spoke of leaving Dolly asked her to stay on a little longer: 'It's not over yet – I can feel something in the air.'

As the weeks passed, there was a deepening of the sense of unease that had settled on the city. There were more strange events. There was talk of trouble at the Rangoon Lunatic Asylum, where several thousand homeless Indians had been accommodated after the riots. In the city gaol a mutiny erupted among the prisoners and was suppressed at the cost of many lives. There were whispers of an even greater upheaval in the offing.

One day a stranger stopped Dolly on the street: 'Is it true that you worked in the Mandalay palace, in the time of King Thebaw?' When Dolly answered in the affirmative the stranger gave her a smile. 'Prepare yourself: there is soon to be another coronation. A prince has been found who will liberate Burma . . .'

A few days later they learnt that there had indeed been a coronation of sorts, not far from Rangoon: a healer by the name of Saya San had had himself crowned King of Burma, with all the traditional observances. He'd gathered together a motley band of soldiers and told them to avenge the capture of King Thebaw.

These rumours reminded Uma of the events that preceded the outbreak of the Indian uprising of 1857. Then too, well before the firing of the first shot, signs of trouble had appeared on the north Indian plains. Chapatis – those most unremarkable of everyday foods – had begun to circulate from village to village, as though in warning. No one knew where they came from or who had put them in motion – but somehow people had known that a great convulsion was on its way.

Uma's premonition was proved right. The uprising started in the interior of Tharawaddy district, where a forest official and two village headmen were killed; the next day rebels stormed a railway station. A company of Indian troops was sent to hunt down the insurgents. But suddenly the rebels were everywhere: in Insein, Yamthin and Pyapon. They appeared like shadows from the forest, with magical designs painted on their bodies. They fought like men possessed, running bare-chested into gunfire, attacking aeroplanes with catapults and spears. Thousands of rural folk declared their allegiance to the King-in-waiting. The colonial authorities fought back by sending more Indian reinforcements to root out the rebellion. Villages were occupied, hundreds of Burmese were killed and thousands wounded.

For Uma, the uprising and the means of its suppression were the culmination of a month-long nightmare: it was as though she were witnessing the realisation of her worst fears; once again, Indian soldiers were being used to fortify the Empire. Nobody in India seemed to know of these events; no one seemed to care. It seemed imperative that someone should take on the task of letting the people of her country know.

It so happened that KLM, the Dutch airline, had recently started a plane service linking a chain of cities between Batavia and Amsterdam. There were now regular flights between Rangoon's new airstrip at Mingaladon and Calcutta's Dum Dum. The journey from Rangoon to Calcutta took some six hours – a fraction of the sailing time. Uma was by now too distraught to undertake the four-day steamship voyage: Rajkumar bought her a ticket on KLM.

In the Packard, on the way out to the airstrip at Mingaladon, Uma became tearful. 'I can't believe what I've seen here – the same old story, Indians being made to kill for the Empire, fighting people who should be their friends . . .'

She was interrupted by Rajkumar: 'Uma, you're talking nonsense.'

'What do you mean?'

'Uma, have you for one moment stopped to ask yourself what would happen if these soldiers weren't used? You were here during the riots: you saw what happened. What do you think these rebels would do to us – to me, to Dolly, to the boys? Don't you see that it's not just the Empire those soldiers are protecting, it's also Dolly and me?'

The anger that Uma had held contained since Morningside came welling up. 'Rajkumar, you're in no position to offer opinions. It's people like you who're responsible for this tragedy. Did you ever think of the consequences when you were transporting people here? What you and your kind have done is far worse than the worst deeds of the Europeans.'

As a rule Rajkumar never challenged Uma on political matters. But he was on edge too now, and something snapped. 'You have so many opinions, Uma – about things of which you know nothing. For weeks now I've heard you criticising everything you see: the state of Burma, the treatment of women, the condition of India, the atrocities of the Empire. But what have you yourself ever done that qualifies you to hold these opinions? Have you ever built anything? Given a single person a job? Improved anyone's life in any way? No. All you ever do is stand back, as though you were above all of us, and you criticise and criticise. Your husband was as fine a man as any I've ever met, and you hounded him to his death with your self-righteousness –'

'How dare you?' Uma cried. 'How dare you speak to me like that? You – an animal, with your greed, your determination to take whatever your can – at whatever cost. Do you think nobody knows about the things you've done to people in your power – to women and children who couldn't defend themselves? You're no better than a slaver and a rapist, Rajkumar. You may think that you will never have to answer for the things you've done, but you're wrong.'

Without a further word to Uma, Rajkumar leant over to U Ba Kyaw and told him to stop the car. Then he stepped out on the road and said to Dolly: 'I'll find my own way back to the city. You see her off. I don't want anything to do with her.'

At Mingaladon, Uma and Dolly found the plane waiting on the airstrip. It was a trimotor Fokker F-VIII, with a silver fuselage and wings that were held up by struts. Once they were out of the car, Dolly said in hushed voice: 'Uma, you're very angry with Rajkumar and I suspect I know why. But you should not judge him too harshly, you know; you must remember that I too bear some of the guilt . . .'

They were at the gates; Uma held Dolly fast.

'Dolly, will this change everything – for us, you and me?'

'No. Of course not. I'll come to see you in Calcutta, whenever I can. It'll be all right – you'll see?'

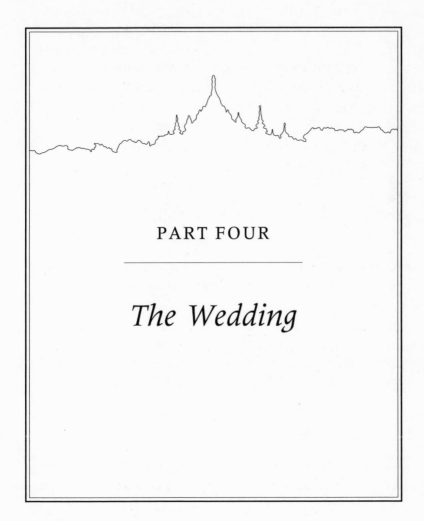

PART FOUR

The Wedding

Twenty

At the other end of the Bay of Bengal, in Calcutta, Uma's brother and his family were waiting to receive her at the Dum Dum airstrip.

Her brother was a quiet and somewhat colourless man who worked in the accounts department of a shipping company. His wife was a severe asthmatic who rarely left the house. Of their children, Bela, a girl, was the youngest, at six. Her siblings were twins and they were a full seven years older. The older twin was a boy, Arjun; the younger was a girl and she went by her family nickname, Manju. Her given name – marvellous to recount – was 'Brihannala', which proved obdurately resistant to everyday use.

For the twins, Uma's arrival in Calcutta was an event of unparalleled significance. This was not just because of who she was: it was at least partly because no one in the family had ever had occasion to go to Dum Dum before. It was just ten years since an aeroplane was first seen in Calcutta: in 1920, a Handley Page had been received at the racecourse by cheering crowds. Since then, planes belonging to Imperial Airways and Air France had also touched down in the city. But it was KLM that had started the first regular passenger service and the drama of its recently instituted comings and goings had held the city in thrall for months.

On the day of Uma's arrival the excitement in the house was such that the family went to the unprecedented step of hiring a car, a new 1930 Austin Chummy. But the twins' expectations were dashed on their arrival at the Dum Dum airstrip: there was nothing there but a stretch of tarmac, bordered by rice fields and coconut palms. This was too new a means of travel to have developed the trappings of ceremony. There was none of the pomp that accompanied an expedition to the docks: no uniformed sailors or peaked caps or beribboned harbourmasters. The terminal was a tin-roofed shed and the personnel consisted of foul-mouthed mechanics in grease-blackened overalls. What there was of a sense of occasion derived from the presence of the crowd of supporters who'd come to welcome Uma.

The waiting area consisted of a small, unroofed pen, fenced in with wire. The family, thoroughly intimidated, found itself pushed further and further back by Uma's exuberant well-wishers. They heard the Fokker F-VIII while it was still hidden by clouds. Arjun was the first to spot it when it broke through, its squat silver body glinting between its double wings. Its silver fuselage wobbled above the palm trees as it came in to land.

There was a long wait in the sun before Uma was cleared. When the people ahead began to cheer they knew Uma was through. And then, suddenly, there she was, in person, very simply dressed, in a white cotton sari.

To the twins Uma was a creature of legend: the firebrand aunt who had dedicated herself to a life of politics instead of accepting the usual lot of the Hindu widow. On finding themselves in her presence they were awed into silence: it seemed incredible that their heroine should be a frail-looking woman, with greying hair and a haggard face.

On the way back to Lankasuka, they sat crowded together in the Austin, exchanging news, catching up. Then Uma did something that took her relatives completely by surprise: unaccountably, for no reason that they could understand, she began to cry. They stared in horror as she sobbed into her sari. Intimidated by her legend, they could not bring themselves to reach out to her. They sat in silence, fidgeting, no one daring to say a word.

When the ride was almost over, Uma collected herself. 'I don't know what came over me,' she said, addressing no one in particular. 'These last few months have been very hard. I feel as if I'm waking from a terrible dream. In Rangoon, just before I left there was a terrible quarrel. I must try to forget some of these things . . .'

*   *   *

It was a while before the family saw anything of Uma again. In the following months, she devoted all her energies to bringing the Burmese rebellion to the knowledge of the Indian public. She sent articles to Calcutta's *Modern Review* and wrote letters to major newspapers; she made every effort to alert her compatriots to the part that Indian soldiers were being made to play in the suppression of the uprising. Her writings had no perceptible effect. The Indian public was consumed with the preoccupations of local politics and had little time to spare for Burma.

One day, opening a Bengali newspaper, she saw a grisly illustration of sixteen decapitated heads lined up on a table. The accompanying article said: *These are the heads of Burmese rebels who fell in an encounter with Imperial troops in Prome District in Burma. It was believed that they were displayed at the military headquarters at Prome for the purpose of striking terror into the hearts of those who might be rebelliously inclined.*

Uma tore the article out with shaking hands. She took it to her desk, intending to put it in the file where she kept her clippings. As she was putting it away, her eyes fell on the folder that held the remains of her KLM ticket: it had been lying forgotten on a corner of her desk ever since her arrival.

Looking at it now, she thought of the city she had flown out of in the silver Fokker; she thought of the businessmen – the timber merchants and oilmen – who were her fellow-passengers; she thought of how they had all congratulated themselves on being present at the dawn of a new era, an age when aviation would make the world so small that the divisions of the past would disappear. She too had joined in: looking down from above, on the foaming waves of the Bay of Bengal, it seemed impossible not to believe that the shrunken world that had built this aircraft was a better one than those that preceded it.

And now, a few months later, here was this picture – of sixteen severed heads, put on display by the ruling power – as starkly medieval an image as could be imagined. She recalled that Prome was the site of the Shwesandaw Pagoda, almost equal in veneration to Rangoon's Shwe Dagon: she remembered a story that one of her fellow-passengers, a big, swarthy oilman, had told her. On the day of the earthquake he'd been sitting in the English Club at Prome, right beside the Shwe Sandaw Pagoda. Right before his eyes, the pagoda had been rent by the movement of the earth. A great part of it had come crashing down in the grounds of the club.

Uma's eyes filled with remembered images: of the terrible sight she'd witnessed, framed in the windscreen of Dolly's Packard; of Rajkumar and his chain of betrayals; of the quarrel in the car on the way to the airport; and now of the deaths of those sixteen rebels and their gruesome decapitation.

That day marked the beginning of a change in Uma that was no less profound than the upheaval that had followed upon the death of the Collector. With the defeat of Burma's Saya San rebellion, she started to rethink her political ideas in their entirety. It was precisely on an uprising such as this that she and her political associates in the Ghadar Party had once pinned their hopes. But she saw now that a popular insurrection, inspired by legend and myth, stood no chance of prevailing against a force such as the Empire – so skilful and ruthless in its deployment of its overwhelming power; so expert in the management of opinion. In retrospect it became clear that disarmed, technologically back-ward populations such as those of India and Burma could not hope to defeat by force a well-organised and thoroughly modern military power; that even if such an effort were to succeed it would be at the cost of unimaginable bloodshed – a Saya San rebellion magnified many hundreds of times – that it would pit Indians against one another in such a way as to make victory just as undesirable as defeat.

In the past, she had been dismissive of Mahatma Gandhi's politi-cal thinking: non-violence, she had thought, was a philosophy of wish-fulfilment. She saw now that the Mahatma had been decades ahead of her in his thinking. It was rather the romantic ideas of rebellion that she had nurtured in New York that were pipe dreams. She remembered the words of the Mahatma, which she had often read and always disregarded: that the movement against colonialism was an uprising of unarmed Indians against those who bore arms – both Indians and British – and that its chosen instruments were the weapons of the weaponless, its very weak-ness its source of strength.

Once she had made up her mind, she was quick to act. She wrote to the Mahatma offering her services, and he, in return, invited her to his ashram at Wardha.

Twenty-one

Even when they were very young, Uma's nephew and older niece, the twins, were celebrated for their good looks. Manju and Arjun shared a feature that gave them an unusual charm: a dimple that appeared when they smiled, but only on one cheek, the left for Manju and the right for Arjun. When they were together it was as though a circuit had been completed, a symmetry restored.

The attention that her looks brought her made Manju self-conscious about her appearance from an early age. She grew up with a keen awareness of the impression she made on people. In this one regard Arjun was her opposite: he was easy-going to the point of slovenliness and liked nothing better than to lounge around the house in a threadbare vest, with a longyi knotted around his waist.

Arjun was the kind of boy of whom teachers complain that their performance is incorrigibly below their potential. Everybody knew that he had the intelligence and ability to do well in school but his interests appeared to be directed only towards ogling girls and reading novels. At mealtimes, long after everyone else was done, he would linger lazily over his plate, chewing on fish bones and sucking the last bits of dal-sodden rice from his fingers. As he grew older, Arjun became a cause of increasing concern to everyone in the family. People began to shake their heads, saying, 'Is that boy ever going to make anything of himself?'

Then one hot April day, Lankasuka's afternoon torpor was shattered by the sound of Arjun's voice uttering wild whoops and cries. Everyone in the house went running to the back balcony to look down into the courtyard.

'Arjun, what do you think you're doing?' his mother said.

'I've got in! I've got in!' Arjun was dancing around the court-yard, dressed in his usual dirty vest and torn longyi, waving a letter in one hand.

'Got into what?'

'The Indian Military Academy in Dehra Dun.'

'Idiot boy. What are you talking about?'

'Yes; it's true.' Arjun came running up the stairs, his face flushed, his hair falling over his eyes. 'They've accepted me as an officer cadet.'

'But how could this happen? How did they even know who you are?'

'I sat for an examination, Ma. I went with –' he named a school-friend – 'and I didn't tell you because I didn't think I'd get in.'

'But it's impossible.'

'Look.'

They passed the letter from hand to hand, marvelling at the fine stiff notepaper and the embossed emblem in the top right-hand corner. They could not have been more astonished if he'd announced that he'd sprouted wings or grown a tail. In Calcutta at that time, to join the army was almost unheard of. For genera-tions, recruitment into the British Indian army had been ruled by racial policies that excluded most men in the country, including those from Bengal. Nor was it possible, until quite recently, for Indians to enter the army as commissioned officers. The founding of the Indian Military Academy in Dehra Dun dated back only five years and the fact that some of its seats were open to public examination had gone largely unnoticed.

'How could you do this, Arjun? And without saying anything to us?'

'I'm telling you, I never thought I'd get in. Besides, everyone's always saying that I'll never amount to anything – so I thought all right, let's see.'

'You wait till your father gets home.'

But Arjun's father was not at all displeased by the news: on the contrary, he was so glad that he immediately organised an expedition of thanksgiving to the temple at Kalighat.

'The boy's settled now and there's nothing more for us to worry about . . .' Relief was plainly visible on his face. 'This is a ready-made career: whether he does well or not he'll be pushed up the ladder. At the end, there'll be an excellent pension. So long as he makes it through the academy, he's taken care of for the rest of his life.'

'But he's just a boy, and what if he gets injured? Or worse still?'

'Nonsense. The chances are very slight. It's just a job like any other. Besides, think of the status, the prestige . . .'

Uma's response came as even more of a surprise. Since the time when she'd visited Mahatma Gandhi, at his ashram in Wardha, she had changed her political affiliations. She had joined the Congress Party and had started working with the women's wing. Arjun had expected that she would try to argue him out of signing up. But what she said instead was: 'The Mahatma thinks that the country can only benefit from having men of conscience in the army. India needs soldiers who won't blindly obey their superiors . . .'

Manju's career took a very different turn from her twin's. At the age of twenty-one she came to the attention of a prominent film personality – a director whose niece happened to be her classmate in college. A man of formidable reputation, the director was then engaged in a very public search for a lead actress. The story of his hunt had caused huge excitement in Calcutta.

Manju was spotted, unbeknownst to herself, while at college: the first she knew of it was when she was handed an invitation to a screen test. Manju's instinct was to refuse: she knew herself to be shy and self-conscious and it was hard for her to imagine that she could ever enjoy acting. But when she returned to Lankasuka that afternoon, she found that the invitation was not quite so easily disposed of as she had imagined. She began to have doubts.

Manju's bedroom had a large window: it was usually while sitting on the sill that she and Arjun had talked in the past. She'd never before had to decide on anything entirely on her own; she had always had Arjun to confer with. But Arjun was now many hundreds of miles away, at his battalion headquarters in Saharanpur, in northern India.

She sat on the sill alone, braiding and unbraiding her hair and watching the afternoon's bathers splashing in the nearby lake. Presently she rose and went to fetch the Huntley and Palmer's biscuit tin in which she kept Arjun's letters. The earliest ones dated back to his days as a 'gentleman-cadet' and the notepaper was embossed with the emblem of the Indian Military Academy. The pages crackled between her fingers. How well he wrote – in proper sentences and paragraphs. When they were together they always spoke Bengali, but the letters were in English – an unfamiliar, idiomatic English, with words of slang that she didn't recognise and couldn't find in the dictionary. He'd gone to a restaurant 'in town' with another cadet, Hardayal Singh – known as 'Hardy' to his friends – and they'd eaten 'lashings' of sandwiches and drunk 'oodles' of beer.

His latest letter had arrived just a few days ago. The notepaper was different now and it bore the insignia of his new regiment, the 1st Jat Light Infantry.

> It's quiet here, because we're at our home station in Saharanpur. You probably think we spend all our time marching about in the sun. But it's nothing like that. The only difficult thing is getting up early to go to the parade ground for P.T. with the men. After that it's pretty quiet; we stroll around taking salutes and watching the NCOs as they put the men through their drills and their weapons training. But this takes only a couple of hours, and then we change for breakfast, which is at nine (stacks of eggs, bacon and ham). Then some of us go off to wait in the orderly room just in case any of the men are brought in. Once in a while the signals officers take us through the latest field codes, or else we get lessons in map-reading or double-entry book-keeping – that kind of thing. Then there's lunch – and beer and gin if you want it (but no whisky!) – and after that you're free to go off to your room. Later there's

259

usually time for a game of football with the men. At about 7.30 we drift off towards the mess lawn for a few whiskies before dinner. We call the mess the Nursery, as a joke, because potted plants die the moment they're brought in – no one knows why. Some of the chaps say it's because of the Dust of Colonels Past. We laugh about the Nursery but I tell you, sometimes halfway through dinner, or when we're drinking a toast, I look around and even now, after all these months here, I just can't believe my luck . . .

The last time Manju had had a long talk with Arjun was on this very windowsill. It was a little more than a year ago, just after he graduated from the academy. She'd kept wanting to call him Second Lieutenant Arjun – partly to tease him, but also because she'd liked the sound of the words. She'd been disappointed that he didn't wear his uniform more but he'd laughed at her when she told him this.

'Why can't you show me off to your friends as I am?'

The truth was that most of her friends at college were in love with him already. They'd badger her for news of him, and when they were over at the house they'd go to amazing lengths to ingratiate themselves with the family – hoping, of course, that someone would remember them when it came time to find a bride for Arjun.

Before he left for the academy, she'd never quite understood why her friends thought him so good-looking: to her he was just Arjun, his face a brother's. Then he came back for that visit and it was as though she were seeing him for the first time. She'd had to admit that he'd made quite an impression, with his moustache coming along nicely and his hair cut short. She'd been jealous, afraid that he wouldn't want to spend time with her. But he'd been quick to put her fears at rest. He'd sat on the sill every day, dressed in his usual vest and scruffy old longyi. They'd chatted for hours and she'd peeled him oranges or mangoes or lychees – he was just as hungry as he'd ever been.

He'd talked endlessly about the 1st Jat Light Infantry. He'd applied to half a dozen other regiments but right from the start there was only one that he really wanted – and that was the 1st Jats. Part of the reason was that his friend Hardy had applied to the 1st Jats too, and was almost certain to get in. He came from an old army family and his father and grandfather had both served in the regiment. But, of course, it was different for Arjun – he had no army connections – and he had prepared himself for a disappointment. As a result he was overjoyed when he heard that the regiment had accepted him:

> The night when I was formally dined into the regiment was probably the happiest of my life. Even as I'm writing this, I realize that this will probably seem strange to you, Manju. But the thing of it is that it's true: you have to remember that the regiment is going to be my home for the next fifteen to twenty years – perhaps even more, if things don't go too well with my career and I never get a staff appointment (God forbid!).
>
> What I'm really chuffed about, though, is my battalion. This'll probably surprise you, for civilians always think that the regiment is the most important thing about the army. But actually, in the Indian army, a regiment is just a collection of symbols – colours, flags, and so on. We're proud of our regiments of course, but they're not operational units and just about the only time when all the battalions of a regiment get together is when there's a Changing of the Colours – and it takes donkey's years for that to happen.
>
> The rest of the time you live and work with your battalion and that's what really matters: your life can be hell if you find yourself thrown in with the wrong sort of crowd. But once again I've been hellishly lucky – Hardy pulled a couple of his *'fauji'* strings and made sure we were both in the same battalion – the First. Officially, we're the 1/1 Jat Light Infantry, but everyone just calls us the 1/1 Jats – except that every now and again you'll come across some ancient Colonel Walrus who'll still use our old name, which was 'the Royal'. The story is that the battalion fought so well in the

Mahratta Wars that when Lord Lake reached the coast, he honoured us with a special title: *The Royal Battalion*.

Yesterday Hardy and I were looking at the battalion's battle honours, and I swear to you, Manju, the list was as long as my arm. During the Mutiny our troops stayed loyal – one of our companies was in the column that captured the old Emperor, Bahadur Shah Zafar, at his hidy-hole at Humayun's tomb. I noticed something that I bet would interest Dinu and Neel – the Royal was in Burma during General Prendergast's advance on Mandalay and it fought so well that it came to be known as *'Jarnail-sahib ki dyni haat ki paltan'* – the general's right-hand battalion.

To tell you the truth, Manju, it's just a little overwhelming even to think of all this. You should see the list of our medals: a Victoria Cross from the Somme; two Military Crosses for putting down the Arab rebellion in Mesopotamia in '18; a half-dozen DSOs and OBEs from when we fought the Boxer rebels in China. Sometimes when I wake up in the morning, I still find it hard to believe that I really belong with these men. It makes one so proud, but also humble, to think that one has all this to live up to. What makes me prouder still is the thought that Hardy and I are going to be the first Indian officers in the 1/1 Jats: it seems like such a huge responsibility – as though we're representing the whole of the country!

To top it all, we have an absolutely spiffing CO – Lieutenant-Colonel Buckland – whom everybody calls Bucky. To look at you'd think he's not a soldier at all, more like a professor. He came to lecture at the academy a couple of times: he was so good that he even managed to make Military History interesting. He's also an operations wizard and the men love him. His family's been with the 1/1 Jats since the time when we were called the Royal Battalion, and I don't think there's a man on the base whose name he doesn't know. And it's not just their names either – he knows which village they're from and who's married to whose daughter and how much dowry they paid. Of course, I'm so junior I can't be sure he even knows I exist.

It's Guest Night at the Nursery tonight, so I'd better go. My new batman is busy ironing my cummerbund, and I can tell from the way he's looking at me that it's time to get into my dinner jacket. His name is Kishan Singh and I just got him a few weeks ago. He's a weedy, earnest-looking fellow and at first I didn't think he'd do, but he's turned out quite well. Do you remember that book Uma-pishi sent me – the O. Henry stories? You'll never believe it, but I'd left it by my bed and one night I walked in and found him with his nose stuck in it. He had a puzzled frown on his face, like a bear clawing at a wireless set. He was scared half out of his mind at being found looking into my book – just stood there like a statue. So I told him the story about the lost necklace. You should have seen him, standing there as though he were at a court-martial, staring at the wall, while I went through the pages, translating into Hindustani. At the end of it, I barked at him, in my best parade-ground voice: 'Kishan Singh! What do you think of this *kahani*?'

And he said: 'Sahib, it's a very sad story . . .' I could have sworn there were tears in his eyes. They're very sentimental, these faujis, despite their moustaches and bloodshot eyes. It's true what the Britishers say: at heart they're very unspoilt; the salt of the earth – you can depend on them to be faithful. Just the kind of men you'd want by your side in a tight spot.

It was Arjun's letter that made Manju reconsider the idea of a screen test. There was her twin, hundreds of miles away, drinking whisky, eating at the officers' mess and getting his batman to iron his dinner jacket. And here she was in Calcutta, in the same room she'd been in all her life, braiding her hair into pigtails as she'd done since she was seven. The awful thing was that he hadn't even made a pretence of missing home.

She was on her own now, and she would have to think about what she was going to do with herself. So far as her mother was concerned, Manju knew, her future had already been decided: she would leave the house as someone's wife and not a day sooner. The mothers of two prospective grooms had already come calling to 'see' Manju. One of them had given her hair a discreet tug to make sure she wasn't wearing a wig; the other had made her bare her teeth as though she were a horse, pushing apart her lips with her fingers, and making faint clucking sounds. Her mother had been apologetic afterwards, but she'd made it clear that it wasn't in her power to ensure that these incidents would not be repeated: this was a part of the process. Manju knew that many more such ordeals probably lay ahead.

Manju looked again at the director's invitation. The studio was in Tollygunge, at the end of the number 4 tram line, which she took to college every day. All she'd have to do was head in the other direction. It wouldn't take long to get there. She decided to go – just to see what it was like.

But now a host of practical problems came suddenly to the surface. What was she to wear, for instance? Her 'good' Benarasi silk, the sari she wore to weddings, was locked in her mother's *almirah*. If she were to ask for it her mother would wring the truth out of her in a matter of minutes and that would be the end of the screen test. Besides, what would people say if she stepped out of the house bedecked in a crimson and gold Benarasi at eleven in the morning? Even if she succeeded in slipping past her mother, the whole neighbourhood would be in an uproar before she got to the end of the street.

She decided that the director wouldn't have gone looking for a college girl if he wanted a fancily dressed-up actress. She settled upon the best of her white cottons, the one with small green checks. But as soon as this was resolved, a dozen new dilemmas seemed to follow. What about make-up? Powder? Lipstick? Perfume?

The morning came and predictably everything went wrong. The sari she'd decided on wasn't back from the dhobi's; she had to choose another one, much older, with a sewn-over tear in the

264

anchal. Her hair wouldn't stay in place, and no matter how hard she tucked in her sari, the hem kept creeping down and tripping her. On her way out, she stepped into the puja room to say a prayer – not because she so badly wanted to be chosen, but just so that she would be able to get through the next few hours without making a fool of herself.

Sure enough, her mother spotted her coming out of the puja room. 'Manju, is that you? What were you doing in the puja room? Are you in some kind of trouble?' She peered suspiciously into Manju's face: 'And why've you got powder all over you? Is that any way to dress when you're going to college?'

Manju slipped away under the pretence of going to the bathroom to wipe her face. She walked quickly down the road to the tram stop. Keeping her face down, she looped her sari over her head, hoping that the neighbours wouldn't notice that she was waiting for the wrong tram. Just when she thought she'd managed to get by without drawing attention to herself, old Nidhu-babu came running out of the Lake Road Pharmacy.

'Is that really you, Manju-*didmoni*?' He hitched up his dhoti and bent double so that he could look up into her sari-shrouded face. 'But why are you waiting on the wrong side of the street? This way you'll end up in Tollygunge.'

Quelling her panic, she managed to invent a story about going to visit an aunt.

'Oh?' said the pharmacist, scratching his head. 'But then, you must come and wait in the shop. You shouldn't be standing out in the sun.'

'I'm all right, really,' she pleaded. 'Don't worry about me. I'll be all right. You should go back to your shop.'

'As you say.' He wandered off, scratching his head, but minutes later, he was back again, with an assistant who was carrying a chair. 'If you must wait here,' the old pharmacist said, 'at least you should sit down.' His assistant placed the chair at the tram stop and wiped it clean with a flourish.

It seemed easier to give in than to resist. Manju allowed herself to be enthroned on the chair, right beside the dusty tram stop. But within minutes, her worst fears were realised: a crowd gathered round to stare at her.

'The Roys' daughter,' she heard the pharmacist explaining to the crowd. 'Lives down the road – in that house over there. Going to visit her aunt in Tollygunge. Skipping college.'

Then, to her relief, the tram finally arrived. The pharmacist and his assistant held the others back so that Manju could be the first to step in. 'I'll send a note to your mother,' the old man shouted after her, 'to let her know that you got off safely to Tollygunge.'

'No,' pleaded Manju, wringing her hands and leaning out of the window. 'There's really no need . . .'

'What's that?' The pharmacist raised a hand to his ear. 'Yes, I said I'll send someone to your mother with a note. No, it's no trouble, none at all . . .'

Already shaken by this inauspicious start, Manju was even more put out when she arrived at the studio. She had expected something glamorous – like the Grand Hotel or the Metro Cinema, or the restaurants on Park Street, with their bright lights and red awnings. But instead she found herself walking into a building that looked like a warehouse or a factory, a big shed, with a roof of tin. Carpenters and *mistries* were hard at work inside, hoisting canvas backdrops and erecting bamboo scaffolding.

A chowkidar led her to a make-up room, a small, windowless cabin, with wooden walls made from sawn-up tea chests. Two women were lounging inside, sprawled in tilted chairs, chewing paan, their gauzy saris shining in the brightly lit mirrors behind them. Their eyes narrowed as they looked Manju over, their jaws moving in perfect unison.

'Why's this one dressed like a nurse?' one of them muttered to the other.

'Maybe she thinks she's going into hospital.'

There were cackles of laughter and then a sari was thrust into Manju's hands, a length of deep purple chiffon with a bright pink border.

'Go on. Get changed.'

'Why this?' Manju ventured in protest.

'Suits your colour,' snapped one of the women, cryptically. 'Put it on.'

Manju glanced around the room, looking for a place to change. There was none.

'What are you waiting for?' the women scolded. 'Be quick. The director's got an important guest coming today. Can't be kept waiting.'

In all her adult life Manju had never undressed in front of anyone, not even her mother. When it dawned on her that she would have to strip under the appraising scrutiny of these two paan-chewing women, her legs went numb. The courage that had brought her thus far began to seep away.

'Go on,' the women hurried her. 'The director's bringing a businessman who's going to put up money for the film. He can't be kept waiting. Everything's got to be tip-top today.' One of them snatched the sari out of Manju's hands and set about changing her clothes. Somewhere nearby a car drew up. This was followed by a patter of welcoming voices. 'The guest's arrived,' someone shouted through the door. 'Quick, quick, the director will want her any minute now.'

The two women ran to the door to peek at the newly-arrived personage.

'Doesn't he look important, with that beard and all?'

'And look at his suit – all dressed up like that . . .'

The women came back giggling and thrust Manju into a chair. 'Just one look and you can tell how rich he is . . .'

'Oh, if he'd only marry me . . .'

'You? Why not me?'

Manju stared into the mirror in an uncomprehending daze. The faces of the two women seemed monstrously large, their smirking lips grotesque in their size and shape. A sharp fingernail scraped her scalp, and she cried out in protest: 'What are you doing?'

'Just checking for lice.'

'For lice?' Manju cried in outrage. 'I don't have lice.'

'The last one did. And not just on her head.' This was followed by peals of laughter.

'How do you know?' Manju challenged them.

'The sari was crawling after she'd worn it.'

'The sari!' With a shriek Manju leapt out of the chair, clawing at the sari they'd given her, trying to tear it off.

The two women were helpless with laughter. 'Just a joke.' They were almost choking on their giggles. 'It was a different sari. Not this one.'

Manju began to sob. 'I want to go home,' she said. 'Please let me go. Don't send me out in front of them.'

'Everyone who comes here says that,' the women reassured her. 'Then they stay for ever.'

They took hold of her arms and led her out on to the brilliantly lit studio floor. Manju was now completely distraught, her nerves frayed and on edge. To keep herself from crying, she kept her gaze fixed on the floor, with her sari slung over her head. Presently a pair of polished black shoes edged into her circle of vision. She heard herself being introduced to the director. She put her hands together and whispered a *nomoshkar* without looking up. Then she saw a second pair of shoes approaching her, across the floor.

'And this here is my good friend,' the director's voice intoned. 'Mr Neeladhri Raha of Rangoon . . .'

She looked up. If she hadn't heard the name she would not have known who it was. She'd met both Neel and Dinu many years ago. They were visiting with their mother, staying down-stairs, in her aunt Uma's flat. But he looked completely different now, with his trimmed black beard and his suit.

'Neel?'

He was staring at her, his mouth agape, his tongue locked above an unuttered exclamation. It was not that he had recognised her: the reason he was unable to speak was because she was, without a doubt, the most beautiful woman he'd ever spoken to.

'Neel, is that you?' said Manju. 'Don't you remember me? I'm Manju – Uma Dey's niece.'

He nodded, in slow disbelief, as though he'd forgotten the sound of his own name.

She flew at him and threw her arms round his chest.

'Oh, Neel,' she said, wiping her eyes on his jacket. 'Take me home.'

The dressing room was a different place when Manju went back to reclaim her own clothes. The two make-up women were now almost worshipful in their attentiveness.

'So you know him then?'

'But why didn't you tell us?'

Manju wasted no time on explanations. She changed quickly and went hurrying to the door. Neel was outside, waiting beside the passenger-side door of a new 1938 Delage D8 Drophead. He opened the door for her and she stepped in. The car smelt of chrome and new leather. 'What a beautiful car,' she said. 'Is it yours?'

'No.' He laughed. 'The dealer offered to let me borrow it for a few days. I couldn't resist.'

Their eyes met for a moment and they both looked quickly away.

'Where would you like to go?' he said. He turned the ignition key and the Delage responded with a purr.

'Let's see . . .' Now that she was seated in the car, she no longer felt quite so pressed to get home.

He started to say something: 'Well . . .'

She could tell that they were both thinking along similar lines. 'Perhaps . . .' A sentence that had begun promisingly in her head died unfinished on her tongue.

'I see.'

'Yes.'

Somehow this terse exchange succeeded in conveying everything they wanted to communicate. Neel started the car and they drove out of the studio. They both knew that they were going nowhere in particular, just enjoying the sensory pleasure of sitting in a moving car.

'I was so surprised to see you in that studio,' Neel said with a laugh. 'Do you really want to be an actress?'

Manju felt herself changing colour. 'No,' she said. 'I just wanted to see what it was like. Things are so dull at home . . .'

Having said this much, she couldn't stop. She found herself telling him things she hadn't told anyone else: how much she missed Arjun; how his letters from the Military Academy had filled her with despair about her own future; about what a curse it was for a woman to live vicariously through a male twin. She even told him about the matches her mother had tried to arrange for her; about the mothers of the prospective grooms and how they had tugged her hair and inspected her teeth.

He didn't say much but she understood that his silence was

caused principally by a habitual lack of words. His face was hard to read behind the heavy black beard but she had a feeling that he was listening sympathetically, taking everything in.

'And what about you?' she said at last. 'Are you really a big film producer?'

'No!' The word burst out of his mouth with the force of an expletive. 'No. It wasn't my idea at all. It was Apé – my father – who suggested it . . .'

What he really wanted, he said, was to work in the timber trade. He'd asked to be allowed to join the family business – only to be turned down by his father. Rajkumar had suggested that he think of other lines of work: the timber business wasn't for everyone, he'd said, especially a city-bred boy like Neel. When Neel persisted, he'd given him a sum of money and told him that he should come back after he'd doubled his capital. But how? Neel had asked. Rajkumar's response was: Go and put it in films – anything. Neel had taken him at his word. He'd looked around for a film to invest in and hadn't been able to find one in Rangoon. He had decided to travel to India instead.

'How long have you been here then?' Manju said. 'And why didn't you come to see us? You could have stayed with Uma-pishi, downstairs.'

Neel scratched awkwardly at his beard. 'Yes,' he said, 'but you know, the trouble is . . .'

'What?'

'My father doesn't get along with your aunt.'

'That doesn't matter,' Manju said. 'Your mother often comes. I'm sure your father wouldn't mind if you did too.'

'Maybe not – but I wouldn't want to anyway.'

'Why not?'

'Well,' Neel scratched his beard again. 'It wouldn't be right . . .'

'What wouldn't be right?'

'I don't know if I can explain.' He gave her a bemused glance and she saw that he was struggling to find words for a thought that he'd never articulated before, even to himself.

'Go on.'

'You see,' he said, almost apologetically, 'it's just that I'm the only one who's on his side.'

270

Manju was startled. 'What do you mean?'

'That's just how I feel,' Neel said. 'That I'm the only one on his side. Take my brother Dinu, for example – I sometimes think he really hates Apé.'

'Why?'

'Maybe – because they're opposites.'

'And you're alike?'

'Yes,' he said. 'At least, that's what I would like to think.'

He turned his eyes away from the road to grin at her.

'I don't know why I'm telling you all this,' he said. 'I feel like an idiot.'

'You're not – I know what you're trying to say . . .'

They went on driving, more or less at random, down one street and another, backing out of blind alleys, and making U-turns on the wider avenues. It was almost dark by the time he dropped her off. They agreed that it would be better if he didn't come in.

They met again the next day and the day after that. He extended his stay and after a month had gone by he sent a telegram to Burma.

One day Dolly presented herself at Uma's office door.

'Dolly? You here?'

'Yes. And you'll never believe why . . .'

Twenty-two

The wedding was like a force of nature, changing everything it touched. In a matter of days Lankasuka was transformed into a huge, noisy fairground. Up on the roof a team of *pandal*-makers was at work, erecting an immense awning of coloured cloth and bamboo. In the tree-shaded yard at the back, a small army of hired cooks had pitched tents and dug pits for cooking fires. It was as though a carnival had moved in.

Bela was the youngest in the house: at fifteen, she was a thin, gawky girl, blossoming into a late and awkward adolescence. She was alternately apprehensive and exhilarated, unsure of whether to throw herself into the festivities or to hide in her bed.

As the wedding approached a whirlwind of telegrams – until then so rare and so dreaded – blew through Lankasuka, rattling its shuttered doors and windows. Not a day went by without Bela spotting a postman, running up the stairs with a pink envelope. Arjun was to arrive by rail, accompanied by his batman, Kishan Singh. Dolly, Dinu and Rajkumar were flying in two days before, on one of KLM's brand-new DC3s.

The excitement reached its pitch the day the Rangoon party was to arrive. Providentially, the family had just that year decided to buy a car, with the expenses shared equally between Uma and her brother. The car was delivered just as the arrangements were getting under way, a brand new 1939 model, a modest, 8 horse-power Jowett, with a long bonnet and beautiful oval grille. In addition to this, the wedding party also had the use of the Delage Drophead, which Neel had once again succeeded in borrowing from the dealer.

They arrived at Dum Dum airport to find it completely changed since the time of Uma's return to India. The old airstrip was now a fully-fledged airport, with customs facilities of its own. A hundred and fifty acres of land had been cleared and three new runways built. There was a fine three-storeyed administration building with a glass-paned control tower and radio room. The visitors' area had changed too: they found themselves entering a large, brightly lit gallery with fans whirring energetically overhead. At one end of the gallery there was a radio tuned in to the news; at the other there was a counter selling tea and snacks.

'Look!' Bela went running to the windows and pointed to a plane that was circling above. They watched the DC3 as it came into land. The first to come out was Dinu. He was wearing a longyi and a loose shirt, and his clothes flapped against his lean, compact frame as he stood on the tarmac, waiting for his parents.

Dolly and Rajkumar were among the last to emerge. Dolly was wearing a striped green longyi and as always there was a white flower in her hair. Rajkumar was walking very slowly, leaning on Dolly a little. His hair was covered with a thick frosting of white and the lines of his face had sagged into tired, drooping curves.

Rajkumar was now in his mid-sixties. He had recently suffered a minor stroke and had left his bed against his doctor's wishes. His business, wounded by the Depression, was no longer as profitable as it had once been. The teak industry had changed over the last decade, and old-fashioned timbermen like Rajkumar had become anachronisms. Rajkumar was saddled with huge debts and had been forced to sell off many of his properties.

But so far as the arrangements for Neel's wedding were concerned, Rajkumar was determined to put aside his financial difficulties. Everything that everybody else did he wanted to do on a larger and grander scale. Neel was his favourite and he was determined to make his boy's wedding an occasion to compensate for all the missed celebrations of his own life.

*   *   *

Dinu was a favourite of Bela's: she liked the way he looked, with his thin, bony cheeks and his wide forehead; she liked his seriousness and his manner of listening to people with an attentive frown, as though he were worrying about what they'd said; she even liked the way he talked, in explosive little bursts, as though his thoughts were spurting out of him in jets.

The day they went to Howrah station to get Arjun, Bela made sure that she was sitting next to Dinu. She noticed that he had a leather bag in his lap.

'What have you got in there?' she asked.

He opened the bag and showed her. It was a new camera, a kind she'd never seen before.

'It's a Rolleiflex,' he said. 'A twin-lens reflex . . .' He took it out of the bag and showed her how it worked; it opened like a hinged box, with its hood flipping back so that you had to look down on it from above.

'I've got a tripod for it,' he said. 'You can look through it . . . when I set it up . . .'

'Why're you taking it to the station?' she asked.

He shrugged vaguely. 'I saw some pictures recently,' he said. 'Railyard shots by Alfred Stieglitz . . . they made me wonder . . .'

The camera caused a stir when Dinu set it up at Howrah. The station was crowded and many people gathered round to stare. Dinu adjusted the tripod's height to suit Bela. 'Here, come . . . look.'

The platform was a long one, and it was topped with a steepled roof of corrugated steel. The late afternoon sunlight was filtering in from under the roof's scalloped skirt, creating a stark, back-lit effect. In the foreground there were great numbers of people: red-jacketed porters, hurrying tea-boys, and waiting passengers with mountains of luggage.

Dinu pointed out the details to Bela. 'I think this is even better than the pictures I had in mind,' he said, 'because of all the people . . . and the movement . . .'

Bela looked in again, and suddenly, as if by magic, Arjun appeared in the frame. He was hanging out of a carriage, holding on to the steel bar of the open doorway. He jumped off when he spotted them and the momentum of the still-moving train gave him a running start. He came racing out of the opaque white fog that was pouring from the engine's steaming smoke-stack, laughing as he dodged the vendors and porters who were swarming across the platform. The tunic of his khaki uniform was drawn tight around his waist and his cap was tilted back on his head. He swept down on them with his arms outspread, laughing, and lifted Manju off her feet and swung her round and round.

Bela stepped away from the camera, hoping to conceal herself until the first flush of Arjun's homecoming exuberance was spent. But just then he spotted her. 'Bela!' He swooped down to fling her up, over his head, ignoring her cries of protest. As she flew upwards, with the tumult of the station whirling around her head, her eyes fastened on a soldier who had approached unseen and was standing just a step behind Arjun. He looked younger than Arjun and was smaller in build; she noticed that he was carrying Arjun's luggage.

'Who is that?' she whispered into Arjun's ear.

He threw a glance over his shoulder, to see whom she was looking at. 'That's Kishan Singh,' he said, 'my batman.'

He put her down and went on ahead, with the others, talking excitedly. Bela followed behind, keeping pace with Kishan Singh. She stole a glance: he was nice-looking, she thought; his skin had a sheen like dark velvet, and although his hair was very short she could tell that it was fine and straight; she liked the way it made a pattern along the edges of his forehead. His eyes were fixed ahead of him, as though he were a moving statue.

It was only when they were about to get into the car that she knew without a doubt that he was aware of her presence. His eyes met hers for an instant and there was a fleeting change in his expression, a slight smile. Bela's head reeled: she had never known that a smile could have a physical impact – like a blow from a flying object.

As she was about to step into the car Bela heard Dinu say to Arjun: 'Have you heard? Hitler's signed a pact with Mussolini . . . there could be another war.'

But her brother's answer was lost to her. All the way home, she didn't hear a word that anybody said.

Twenty-three

Although Dinu and Arjun had known each other a long time they had never been friends. Dinu tended to think of Arjun on the analogy of a friendly and bumbling pet – a large dog perhaps, or a well-trained mule – a creature of unfailing, tail-wagging goodwill, but incurably indolent and barely capable of coherent utterance. But Dinu was not so arrogant as to be unwilling to correct himself. At Howrah station, on the day when he photographed Arjun running across the platform, he saw immediately that this was a significantly changed person from the boy he had known. Arjun had lost his somnolence, and his patterns of speech were no longer so garbled and indistinct as they had once been. This itself was an interesting paradox, for Arjun's vocabulary seemed now to consist mainly of jargon intermixed with assorted bits of English and Punjabi slang – everyone was now either a 'chap' or a *'yaar'*.

But on the way home from the station Arjun did something that astonished Dinu. In reminiscing about a tactical exercise, he launched into a description of a feature of topography – a hill. He listed its ridges and outcrops, the exact nature of its vegetation and the cover it afforded, he quoted the angle of the slope's incline and laughed about how his friend Hardy had got it wrong so that his results 'wouldn't play'.

Dinu understood words and images and the bridge of metaphor that linked the two – these were not languages with which he had ever thought to associate Arjun. Yet, by the end of Arjun's description, Dinu felt that he could see the hill, in his head. Of those who listened to Arjun's account, he alone was perhaps fully aware of the extreme difficulty of achieving such minuteness of

276

recall and such vividness of description: he was awed, both by the precision of Arjun's narrative and by the off-handed lack of self-consciousness with which it was presented.

'Arjun,' he said, fixing him with his dour, unblinking stare. 'I'm amazed . . . you described that hill as though you'd remembered every little bit of it.'

'Of course,' said Arjun. 'My CO says that, under fire, you pay with a life for every missed detail.'

This too made Dinu take notice. He'd imagined that he knew the worth of observation, yet he'd never conceived that its value might be weighed in lives. There was something humbling about the thought of this. He'd regarded a soldier's training as being, in the first instance, physical, a matter of the body. It took just that one conversation to show him that he had been wrong. Dinu's friends were mainly writers and intellectuals: he had never met a serviceman in all his life. Now suddenly, in Calcutta, he found himself surrounded by soldiers. Within hours of his arrival, Arjun had filled the house with his friends. It turned out that he knew a couple of officers at the Fort William cantonment in Calcutta. Once he'd made contact, his friends began to turn up at all times of day, in jeeps and occasionally even in trucks, their arrival signalled by booming klaxons and noisy boots.

'This is how it always happens in the army, yaar,' one of them said, by way of apologetic explanation. 'Where one fauji goes, the whole *paltan* follows . . .'

In the past Dinu's attitude towards the army had varied between outright hostility and amused indifference. Now he found himself more puzzled than antagonistic, increasingly interested in the mechanisms that made them tick. He was astonished by the communal nature of their lives; by the pleasure that Arjun, for instance, took in 'mucking in' with the others. This was a way of thinking and working that was the antithesis of everything that Dinu stood for and believed in. He himself was always happiest when he was on his own, His friends were few and even with the best of them there was always a residue of unease, an analytic guardedness. This was one of the reasons why he derived so much pleasure from photography. There was no place more solitary than a dark room, with its murky light and fetid closeness.

Arjun, on the other hand, seemed to find immense satisfaction in working on the details of plans that had been dictated by others – not necessarily people either, but manuals of procedure. Once, speaking of his battalion's move from one cantonment to another, he described their 'entrainment' routines with as much pride as though he had personally guided every soldier into the station. But at the end it emerged that his part had consisted of nothing more than standing at the door of a carriage and filling in a roster. Dinu was astonished to note that it was precisely from this that his satisfaction derived: the slow accumulation of small tasks, a piling up of rosters that culminated in the movement of a platoon and then a battalion.

Arjun was often at pains to explain that in the army, it was a vital necessity for 'the chaps' to possess a thorough and exhaustive understanding of one another; to know exactly how each of them would respond in certain circumstances. Yet, there was a paradox here that did not escape Dinu: when Arjun and his friends spoke of one another, their assessments were so exaggerated that they seemed to be inventing versions of themselves for collective consumption. In the fantastic bestiary of their table-talk, Hardy was the Spit-and-Polish perfectionist, Arjun a Ladies' Man, another a Pukka Sahib and so on. These paper-thin portraits were a part of the collective lore of their camaraderie – a fellowship in which they took immense pride, investing it with metaphors that sometimes extended even beyond mere kinship. Usually they were just 'brothers' but at times they were also much more, even the 'First True Indians'. 'Look at us –' they would say, – 'Punjabis, Marathas, Bengalis, Sikhs, Hindus, Muslims. Where else in India would you come across a group such as ours – where region and religion don't matter – where we can all drink together and eat beef and pork and think nothing of it?'

Every meal at an officers' mess, Arjun said, was an adventure, a glorious infringement of taboos. They ate foods that none of them had ever touched at home: bacon, ham and sausages at breakfast; roast beef and pork chops for dinner. They drank whisky, beer and wine, smoked cigars, cigarettes and cigarillos. Nor was this just a matter of satisfying appetites: every mouthful had a meaning – each represented an advance towards the evolution of a new, more complete kind of Indian. All of them had stories to tell about how their stomachs had turned the first time they had chewed upon a piece of beef or pork; they had struggled to keep the morsels down, fighting their revulsion. Yet they had persisted, for these were small but essential battles and they tested not just their manhood, but also their fitness to enter the class of officers. They had to prove, to themselves as well as to their superiors, that they were eligible to be rulers, to qualify as members of an elite: that they had vision enough to rise above the ties of their soil, to overcome the responses instilled in them by their upbringing.

'Look at us!' Arjun would say, after a whisky or two, 'we're the first modern Indians; the first Indians to be truly free. We eat what we like, we drink what we like, we're the first Indians who're not weighed down by the past.'

To Dinu this was profoundly offensive. 'It's not what you eat and drink that make you modern: it's a way of looking at things . . .' He'd fetch reproductions that he'd cut out of magazines, of photographs by Stieglitz, Cunningham and Weston.

Arjun would shrug these off with a laughing retort: 'To you the modern world is just something you read about. What you know of it you get from books and newspapers. We're the ones who actually live with Westerners . . .'

Dinu understood that it was through their association with Europeans that Arjun and his fellow-officers saw themselves as pioneers. They knew that to most of their compatriots the West was a distant abstraction: even though they might know themselves to be ruled by England, very few Indians had ever actually set eyes on an Englishman and fewer still had had occasion to speak to one. The English lived in their own enclaves and followed their own pursuits: most of the day-to-day tasks of ruling were performed by Indians. In the army, on the other hand, Indian officers were a band of the elect; they lived in a proximity with Westerners that was all but unknown to their compatriots. They shared the same quarters, ate the same food, did the same work: in this their situation was unlike that of any of the Empire's other subjects.

'We understand the West better than any of you civilians,' Arjun liked to say. 'We know how the minds of Westerners work. Only when every Indian is like us will the country become truly modern.'

Meals with Arjun's friends were boisterous events, accompanied by 'lashings' of beer, loud laughter and a great deal of acerbic joke-making, mainly by the officers, at each other's expense. This they described as 'ragging' and most of it was good-natured. But there was an occasion once when the flow of the meal was ruptured by an odd little incident. Seeing a dish of hot, steam-puffed chapatis, one of the officers said, in a loud, derisory 'ragging' voice: 'Hardy should have been here: he's the one who really loves chapatis . . .' These words, apparently innocuous, had a startling effect; the noise died abruptly and the officers' faces turned suddenly grave. The lieutenant who'd spoken changed colour, as though in acknowledgement of a collective rebuke. Then, as if to remind his friends of the presence of outsiders – Dinu, Manju and Neel, in other words – Arjun loudly cleared his throat and the conversation turned instantly to another subject. The interruption lasted no longer than a moment and passed unnoticed by everyone but Dinu.

Later that night, Dinu stopped by Arjun's room and found him sitting in bed, with a book against his knees and a brandy in his hand. Dinu lingered.

'You want to tackle me, don't you?' Arjun said. 'About what happened this evening?'

'Yes.'

'It was nothing really.'

'All the more reason to tell me . . .'

Arjun sighed: 'It was about a good friend of mine, Hardy. Odd to think he wasn't even here.'

'What were they talking about?'

'It's a long story. You see Hardy was in a row last year. It'll sound idiotic to you . . .'

'What happened?'

'Are you sure you want to know?'

'Yes.'

'Hardy's a *sardar*,' Arjun said, 'a Sikh – from a family that's been in the army for generations. You'd be surprised how many of the

280

chaps are from that kind of family. I call them the real faujis. Fellows like me, who have no army connections, are the exception . . .'

Hardy had grown up at the battalion's depot in Saharanpur, Arjun said. His father and grandfather had both served in the 1st Jats. They had joined as private soldiers and worked their way up to the rank of Viceroy's Commissioned Officer – which was the highest an Indian could rise in those days, somewhere between an NCO and an officer. Hardy was the first in his family to join the army as a commissioned officer, and he'd set his heart on getting into the 1/1 Jats. He used to joke that his dream was to be called 'Sahib' by his father's old colleagues.

But between the lives of officers and the other ranks there was a difference that Hardy had not reckoned with. The other ranks were served Indian food in their messes, prepared according to the precise dietary prescriptions of their various religions. The officers' mess, on the other hand, served 'English' food – and the trouble with Hardy was that he was one of those chaps who, no matter how hard they tried, simply could not get by without his daily dal-roti. He dutifully ate whatever was served in the mess but at least once a day, he'd find a pretext to leave the cantonment so that he could eat his fill somewhere in town. This was a commonplace enough occurrence among Indian officers, but Hardy crossed an unseen line: he started visiting the other ranks' messes. He enjoyed these little visits: he'd called some of the men 'uncle' as a child and he assumed that they would afford him the same indulgence and affection that he remembered from the past. They would keep his visits a secret, he thought. After all many of them were from the same village, the same extended family. Many had known his father.

It turned out that he could not have been more wrong. Far from being pleased at serving under Hardy, his father's old colleagues were deeply offended by his presence in the battalion. They were of the first generation of Indian soldiers to serve under Indian officers. Many of them were uneasy about this: their relationship with their British officers was the source of their pride and prestige. To serve under Indians was a dilution of this privilege.

281

A day came when the battalion's Commanding Officer, Lieutenant-Colonel 'Bucky' Buckland, recommended that Hardy be given command of C Company. So far as the company's NCOs were concerned, this was the last straw. Some of them knew Lieutenant-Colonel Buckland well; they had served with him for many years and it was part of their job to keep him informed about the happenings in the unit. They formed a delegation and went to see him. They told him: this boy, Hardayal Singh, to whom you've given charge of C Company, his father is known to us, his sisters are married to our brothers, his home is in the village next to ours. How can you expect us to treat this boy as an officer? Why, he cannot even stomach the food that officers eat. He steals secretly into our messes to eat chapatis.

Lieutenant-Colonel Buckland was deeply disturbed by these complaints: it was impossible not to be repelled by the murkiness of these sentiments. If there was an implicit self-hatred in trusting only your own, then how much deeper was the self-loathing that led a group of men to distrust someone for no reason other than that he was one of them?

Lieutenant-Colonel Buckland gave the NCOs a sharp reprimand: 'You are living in the past. The time has come when you will have to learn to take orders from Indians. This man is the son of your former colleague: do you really want to shame him in public?'

The NCOs held fast, despite this berating. In the end, it was the Lieutenant-Colonel who had had to yield. There had always been an unspoken compact between the men and their English officers: on certain matters it was understood that their wishes had to be taken into account. The Lieutenant-Colonel was left with no choice but to send for Hardy – to tell him that his appointment couldn't go through just yet. This proved to be the most difficult part of the whole affair. How were the charges to be explained to Hardy? How does a soldier defend himself against the accusation of being, as it were, a covert chapati-eater? What does this do to his self-respect?

Lieutenant-Colonel Buckland dealt with the situation as tactfully as anyone could have, and Hardy emerged from the interview without showing any visible signs of discomfiture. Only his closest friends knew how deeply he'd been wounded; how hard it had been for him to face those NCOs the next day. And, of course, the army being a small, tight institution, word always got around and from time to time even friends would say the wrong thing, just as they had that night.

'Do all of you face this then?' Dinu asked Arjun. 'Is it hard for you to be accepted as officers by your own men?'

'Yes and no,' Arjun replied. 'You always have the feeling that they're looking at you more closely than they would if you were a Britisher – especially me, I suppose, since I'm just about the only Bengali in sight. But you also have a sense that they're identifying with you – that some of them are urging you on, while others are just waiting to see you fall. When I'm facing them I can tell that they're putting themselves in my place, crossing a barrier that has become a great divide in their minds. The moment they imagine themselves past that line, something changes. It can't be as it was before.'

'What do you mean?'

'I'm not sure I can explain, Dinu. I'll tell you a story. Once, an old English colonel visited our mess. He was full of tales about the Good Old Days. After dinner I happened to hear him talking to Bucky – our CO. He was huffing and puffing and blowing through his whiskers. His view was that this business of making officers out of Indians would destroy the army; everyone would be at each other's throats and the whole thing would fall apart. Now Bucky's just about as fair and decent as a man can be and he wasn't going to put up with this. He defended us stoutly and said his Indian officers were doing a very good job and all the rest of it. But you know, the thing of it was that in my heart I knew that Bucky was wrong and the old codger was right.'

'Why?'

'It's simple. Every institution has its own logic, and the British Indian army has always functioned on the understanding that there was to be a separation between Indians and Britishers. It was a straightforward system: they stayed apart, and obviously

283

both sides felt that this was to their benefit. It's no easy thing you know, to make men fight. The Britishers found a way of doing it, and they made it work. But now, with us being inside the officers' mess, I don't know that it can go on.'

'Why not?'

Arjun got up to pour himself another brandy. 'Because it's true what the old codger said: we're at each other's throats.'

'Who?'

'Indians and Britishers.'

'Really? Why? What about?'

'Most of it is just little things. In the mess for instance, if a Britisher turns the radio to a broadcast in English, you can be sure that minutes later an Indian will tune it to Hindi film songs. And then someone will turn it back, and so on until all you can do is hope that it gets switched off altogether. Things like that.'

'You sound like . . . squabbling schoolchildren.'

'Yes. But there's something important behind it, I think.'

'What?'

'You see we all do the same work, eat the same food and so on. But the chaps who're trained in England get paid a lot more than we do. For myself I don't mind so much, but chaps like Hardy care very much about these things. To them this is not just a job as it is for me. You see, they really believe in what they're doing; they believe that the British stand for freedom and equality. Most of us when we hear big words like that tend to take them with a pinch of salt. They don't. They're deadly serious about these things, and that's why it's so hard for them when they discover that this equality they've been told about is a carrot on a stick – something that's dangled in front of their noses to keep them going, but always kept just out of reach.'

'Why don't they complain?'

'They do sometimes. But usually there's nothing in particular to complain about. Take the case of Hardy's appointment: who was to blame? Hardy himself? The men? It certainly wasn't the CO. But that's how it always is. Whenever one of us doesn't get an appointment or a promotion, there's always a mist of regulations that makes things unclear. On the surface everything in the army appears to be ruled by manuals, regulations, procedures:

284

it seems very cut and dried. But actually, underneath there are all these murky shadows that you can never quite see: prejudice, distrust, suspicion.'

Arjun tossed his brandy back and paused to pour himself another. 'I'll tell you something,' he said, 'something that happened to me while I was at the academy. One day a group of us went into town – Hardy, me, a few others. It started to rain and we stepped into a shop. The shopkeeper offered to lend us umbrellas. Without thinking about it I said, yes, of course, that'll be a help. The others looked at me as though I'd gone mad. "What are you thinking of?" Hardy said to me. "You can't be seen with an umbrella." I was puzzled. I said: "But why not? Why can't I be seen with an umbrella?" Hardy's answer was: "Have you ever seen an Indian soldier using an umbrella?" I thought about it and realised I hadn't. I said: "No."

'"Do you know why not?"

'"No."

'"Because in the old days in the East, umbrellas were a sign of sovereignty. The British didn't want their sepoys to get over-ambitious. That's why you'll never see umbrellas at a cantonment."

'I was amazed. Could this possibly be true? I felt sure there were no regulations on the subject. Can you imagine a rule that said: "Indians are not to keep umbrellas in their barracks"? It's inconceivable. But at the same time, it was also true that you never saw anyone with an umbrella at a cantonment. One day I asked the adjutant, Captain Pearson. I said: "Sir, why do we never use umbrellas, even when it rains?" Captain Pearson is a short, tough, bull-necked fellow. He looked at me as though I were a worm. Nothing could have shut me up quicker than the answer he gave me. He said: "We don't use umbrellas, Lieutenant, because we're not *women*."'

Arjun began to laugh. 'And now,' he said, 'I would rather do anything than be seen with an umbrella – I'd rather drown in the rain.'

Twenty-four

That year it seemed as though the monsoons had broken over Lankasuka well before the first clouds had appeared in the skies. Manju's wedding was in late June, just before the coming of the rains. The days were very hot, and in the park in front of the house, the lake fell to a level where boats could no longer be taken out on the water. It was the time of year when even the rotation of the earth seem to slacken in speed, in anticipation of the coming deluge.

But within Lankasuka the wedding created the semblance of a strange climatic anomaly: it was as though the compound was awash in a flood, its inhabitants swirling hectically downriver, carried along by great tides of disparate things – people, gifts, anxiety, laughter, food. In the courtyard at the back, cooking fires burnt all day long and on the roof, under the bright tented awnings that had been erected for the wedding, there seemed never to be a moment when several dozen people were not sitting down to a meal.

The days went by in a storm of feasting and observances: the solemn familial commitments of the *paka-dekha* led inexorably to the yellowed turmeric-anointing of the *gaye-holud*. Slowly, much as the rising water of the monsoons overwhelms the chequerboard partitions of a paddy field, so did the steady progression of the wedding sweep away the embankments that divided the lives of the people in the house. Uma's white-saried political associates pitched in to help, as did a great many khaki-clad Congress workers; Arjun's friends at Fort William sent auxiliary detachments of cooks, mess-boys, waiters and even, on occasion, entire marching bands, complete with wrap-around brass and uniformed bandmasters; much of Manju's college came pouring in, and so did a colourful throng of Neel's acquaintances from the film studios of Tollygunge – directors, actors, students, playback singers, even the two terrifying make-up women who had dressed Manju on the day of her fateful audition.

Dolly too had a hand in stirring the mix. Through her years of visiting Uma in Calcutta, she had developed a close connection with the city's Burmese temple. Small though this temple was, its past was not without lustre. Many great Burmese luminaries had spent time there, including the famous activist monk, U Wisara. By way of Dolly's links, Manju's wedding came to be attended by a substantial part of the city's Burmese community – students, monks, lawyers and even a few hulking sergeants of Calcutta's police force (many of whom were Anglo-Burmese in origin).

Considering how oddly assorted these groups were, disagreements were relatively few. But in the end it proved impossible to shut out the powerful winds that were sweeping the world. On one occasion a friend of Uma's, an eminent Congressman, arrived dressed in the manner of Jawaharlal Nehru, in a khaki cap and a long black *sherwani*, with a rose in his buttonhole. The elegant politician found himself standing next to a friend of Arjun's, a lieutenant dressed in the uniform of the 14th Punjab Regiment. 'And how does it feel,' the politician said, turning to the soldier with a sneer, 'for an *Indian* to be wearing that uniform?'

'If you must know, sir,' Arjun's friend snapped back, matching sneer for sneer, 'this uniform feels rather warm – but I imagine the same could be said of yours?'

Another day, Arjun found himself facing off against a strangely assorted crowd of Buddhist monks, Burmese student-activists and Congress Party workers. The Congressmen had bitter memories of their confrontations with Indian soldiers and policemen. They began to berate Arjun for serving in an army of occupation.

Arjun recalled that it was his sister's wedding and he managed to keep his temper. 'We aren't occupying the country,' Arjun said, as lightly as he could. 'We are here to defend you.'

287

'From whom are you defending us? From ourselves? From other Indians? It's your masters from whom the country needs to be defended.'

'Look,' said Arjun, 'it's a job and I'm trying to do it as best I can . . .'

One of the Burmese students gave him a grim smile: 'Do you know what we say in Burma when we see Indian soldiers? We say: there goes the army of slaves – marching off to catch some more slaves for their masters.'

It was with a great effort that Arjun succeeded in keeping control of himself: instead of getting into a fight, he turned round and marched away. Later, he went to complain to Uma and found her wholly unsympathetic. 'They were just telling you what most people in the country think, Arjun,' Uma said bluntly. 'If you're strong enough to face enemy bullets, you should be strong enough to hear them out.'

For the duration of his stay in Lankasuka, Kishan Singh had been allotted a small room that was tucked away at the rear of the house. At other times this room was generally used for storage, mainly food. Along the walls stood great, stone martabans, packed with pickles; in the corners were piles of ripening mangoes and guavas; hanging from the rafters, beyond the reach of ants and cats, were the rope-slung earthen pots in which the household's butter and ghee were stored.

One afternoon, Bela was sent to the storeroom on an errand, to fetch some butter. The wooden door was slightly warped and could not be properly closed. Looking through the crack, Bela saw that Kishan Singh was inside, lying on a mat. He'd changed into a longyi for his siesta, and his khakis were hanging on a peg. He was sweating in the June heat, bare-bodied but for the ghostly shadow of the army singlet that was singed on to his chest.

From the pumping motion of his ribs Bela could tell that he was fast asleep. She slipped into the room and tiptoed around his mat. She was on her knees, undoing the strings of the earthen butter pot, when Kishan Singh suddenly woke up.

He jumped to his feet and pulled on his khaki tunic, his face turning red with embarrassment.

'My mother sent me . . .' she said quickly, 'to fetch this . . .' She pointed at the earthen pot.

With his tunic on, he seated himself cross-legged on the mat. He gave her a smile. Bela smiled shyly back. She felt no inclination to leave; she hadn't spoken to him till then and it occurred to her now that there were many things she wanted to ask him.

The first question she blurted out was the one that was uppermost in her mind. 'Kishan Singh,' she said, 'are you married?'

'Yes,' he said gravely. 'And I have a little son. Just one year old.'

'How old were you when you were married?'

'It was four years ago,' he said. 'So I must have been sixteen.'

'And your wife,' she said, 'what is she like?'

'She's from the village next to mine.'

'And where is your village?'

'It's up north – a long way from here. It's near Kurukshetra – where the great battle of the Mahabharata was fought. That is why the men of our district make good soldiers – that's what people say.'

'And did you always want to be a soldier?'

'No.' He laughed. 'Not at all – but I had no choice.'

The men in his family had always lived by soldiering, he explained. His father, his grandfather, his uncles – they had all served in the 1/1 Jats. His grandfather had died at Passchendaele, in the Great War. The day before his death he had dictated a letter that was to be sent to his family, filled with instructions about the crops in the fields and what was to be planted and when they were to sow and when to harvest. They next day he had gone over the top of his trench, to save his wounded *afsar*, an English captain whose batman he had been for five years and whom he honoured above all men. For this he had been awarded, posthumously, the Indian Distinguished Service Medal, which his family had kept, in their *haveli*, in a glass box.

'And to this day the afsar's family send us money – not because we ask, nor from charity, but out of love of my grandfather, and to honour what he did for their son . . .'

Bela hung upon his words, drinking in every movement of the muscles of his face. 'Go on.'

His father had served in the army too, he said. He had been wounded in Malaya, at the time of a rebellion. A stab wound had ripped open his side and pierced his colon. The army doctors had done what they could for him, but the wound had burdened him with chronic, crippling stomach pains. He'd travelled far afield, visiting experts in Ayurveda and other systems of medicine; the expense had forced him to barter away his share of the family land. He hadn't wanted a fate like that for his Kishan Singh; he'd wanted his son to go to college and understand things; he himself had travelled the world – Malaya, Burma, China, East Africa – and had understood nothing.

Kishan Singh too would have liked to go to college, but when he was fourteen his father died. After that the option of school was no longer open: the family had needed money. His relatives urged him to report to the local recruitment office; they said that he was lucky to have been born into a caste that was allowed to enroll in the English sarkar's army.

'That was why you joined?'

He nodded. 'Yes.'

'And the women in your village,' she said, 'what are they like?'

'Not like you.'

She was hurt by this. 'Why? What do you mean?'

'In a way,' he said, 'they are soldiers too. From the time they are little they begin to learn what it means to be widowed early; to bring up children without their men; to spend their lives with husbands who are maimed and crippled . . .'

Just then she heard her mother calling her name, and went running out of the room.

For the duration of the wedding, Rajkumar and his family were staying at the Great Eastern Hotel. (It was unthinkable, in light of their past hostilities, for Rajkumar to stay with Uma, as Dolly usually did.) It had been agreed upon, however, that Neel and

290

Manju would spend their wedding night – their last in Calcutta – in Lankasuka, in Uma's flat.

When the day came, Uma and Dolly prepared the bridal bedroom themselves. They went early to the flower market at Kalighat and came back with dozens of loaded baskets. They spent the morning draping the wedding bed with garlands of flowers – hundreds of them. While working, they reminisced about their own weddings and how very different they'd been. In the afternoon they were joined by the Second Princess, who'd made a special trip from Kalimpong: this completed the circle.

It was hot and they were quickly drenched in sweat. 'I've had enough,' said Dolly. 'My wedding was easier.'

'Remember Mrs Khambatta – with the camera?'

They sat on the floor, laughing at the memory.

As the day progressed, a hundred minor crises accumulated. Mainly they concerned odds and ends that someone had forgotten to buy: yet another dhoti for the purohit; a fresh handful of *durba* grass; a sari for a forgotten aunt – small but essential items. In the late afternoon Arjun was told to organise a quick shopping expedition in the family Jowett. Dinu, Uma and Bela were to go with him, each armed with a shopping list.

Arjun brought the Jowett into the courtyard and the others climbed in.

'Where exactly are we going?' Uma asked.

'To the market at Kalighat,' Arjun said.

'Well, you'll have to be quick then,' said Uma.

'Why?'

'There's a big demonstration today – we could get cut off.'

'A demonstration?' Arjun was taken by surprise. 'What on earth is it about this time?'

This annoyed Uma. 'Don't you ever read the papers, Arjun?' she said. 'It's an anti-war march. We in the Congress believe that in the event of another war Britain can't expect our support unless they're willing to provide a guarantee of Indian independence.'

'Oh I see.' Arjun shrugged. 'Well, we're safe then – it'll take them a long time to get through all of that . . .'

Dinu laughed.

It took just fifteen minutes to get to the market, and within half an hour their shopping was done. They were on their way back, when they turned into a wide avenue and spotted the first of the demonstrators, approaching from a distance.

'Nothing to worry about,' Arjun said calmly. 'We're a long way ahead. They won't box us in.' But even as he was speaking the Jowett's engine had begun to splutter. And then suddenly the car went dead.

'Do something, Arjun!' Uma snapped. 'We can't stop here.'

'The spark plug,' Arjun muttered incredulously. 'I knew I should have cleaned it this morning.'

'Can't you fix it?'

'It's going to take a few minutes.'

'A few minutes!' Uma said. 'But they'll be all around us. Arjun, how could you allow this?'

'These things happen . . .'

Dinu and Arjun went around to the front and propped the hood open. The Jowett had been idling a good while in the courtyard and the engine was very hot. By the time the plug was fixed, the demonstration had closed around them. Marchers were flowing past on every side, some of them breaking ranks to stare at the stalled car and the two men standing beside the open hood. Arjun and Dinu got back into the car: there was nothing to do but sit and wait until the last demonstrators were past.

A marcher dropped a pamphlet through the car window. Arjun picked it up and glanced down at the front page. There were quotations from Mahatma Gandhi and a passage that said: 'Why should India, in the name of freedom, come to the defence of this Satanic Empire which is itself the greatest menace to liberty that the world has ever known?'

Arjun was extremely irritated by this time and he made an angry, spitting noise. 'Idiots,' he said. 'I wish I could stuff this down their throats. You'd think they'd have better things to do than march about in the hot sun . . .'

'Watch what you say, Arjun,' Uma said sharply, from the back seat. 'I hope you know that I was meant to be in that march too. I don't think you should be calling them idiots. After all what do you know about these things?'

'Oh, well . . .' Arjun was about to shrug this off when Dinu spoke up, unexpectedly, in his defence.

'I think Arjun's right,' he said. 'Those people *are* idiots . . .'

'What?' said Uma. 'What are you talking about, Dinu?'

'I'm talking about Fascism,' Dinu said, 'and why the most important thing right now is to fight it. Because if war does break out, it won't be like any other war . . . Hitler and Mussolini are among the most tyrannical and destructive leaders in all of human history . . . They're grotesque, they're monsters . . . If they succeed in imposing their will on the world, we'll all be doomed. Look at what they believe in . . . their whole ideology is about the superiority of certain races and the inferiority of others . . . Look at what they're doing to Jews . . . And if they have their way they'll destroy the working-class movement everywhere in the world . . . Their rule will be the most violent and despotic you can imagine, with some races at the bottom and some at the top . . . And don't imagine for a moment that India and Burma will be better off if the British are defeated . . . The Germans' plan is simply to take over the Empire and rule in their place . . . And think of what'll happen in Asia . . . The Japanese are already aspiring to an Empire, like the Nazis and Fascists . . . Last year, in Nanking, they murdered hundreds of thousands of innocent people . . . The last we heard from Saya John, he said that many of his wife's relatives had been killed . . . Lined up against walls and shot . . . Men, women, children . . . Do you think that if the Japanese army reached India they wouldn't do the same thing here? If you do, you're wrong . . . They would . . . They're imperialists and racialists of the worst order . . . If they succeed, it'll be the worst catastrophe in all of human history.'

Uma responded calmly. 'Dinu,' she said, 'you must not think for one moment that I, or anyone in the Congress, has an iota of sympathy for the Nazis and Fascists. Absolutely not: they are exactly what you say – monstrous, grotesque. As Mahatma Gandhi has said, many times, they represent the exact opposite of everything we stand for. But as I see it, we are caught between two scourges: two sources of absolute evil. The question for us is, why should we pick one over the other? You say that Nazism will rule through violence and conquest, that it will institutionalise racialism, that it will commit unspeakable atrocities. All of this is true: I don't dispute it for a moment. But think of the evils you have listed: racialism, rule through aggression and conquest. Is the Empire not guilty of all of this? How many tens of millions of people have perished in the process of this Empire's conquest of the world – in its appropriation of entire continents? I don't think there could ever be an accounting of the numbers. Worse still, the Empire has become the ideal of national success – a model for all nations to aspire to. Think of the Belgians, racing off to seize the Congo – they killed ten or eleven million people there. And what was it they wanted, other than to create a version of this Empire? Isn't that what Japan and Germany want today – empires of their own?'

Bela leant over the seat, trying to break in. 'We have to get back,' she cried. 'We can't just sit here, arguing. It's Manju's wedding night.'

The last of the demonstrators were now past. Arjun started the car and turned it round. They went speeding down the road, towards Lankasuka.

But the argument was not over so far as Dinu was concerned. He turned round in his seat. 'Aunt Uma,' he said, 'you're always talking about the evils of Empire and what the British have done to India . . . But do you think that terrible things weren't happening here before they came? Look at the way women are treated even today, look at the caste system, untouchability, widow-burning . . . all these terrible, terrible things.'

Uma retorted sharply: 'Let me be the first to admit the horrors of our own society – as a woman I assure you that I am even more aware of them than you are. Mahatma Gandhi has always said that our struggle for independence cannot be separated from our struggle for reform. But having said this, let me add that we must *not* be deceived by the idea that imperialism is an enterprise of reform. Colonialists would like us to believe this, but there is a simple and clear refutation. It is true that India is riven with evils such as those you describe – caste, the mistreatment of women, ignorance, illiteracy. But take the example of your own country, Burma – they had no caste system there. On the contrary the Burmese were very egalitarian. Women had a high standing –

probably more so than in the West. There was universal literacy. But Burma was conquered too, and subjugated. In some ways they fared even worse than we did at the hands of the Empire. It is simply mistaken to imagine that colonialists sit down and ponder the rights and wrongs of the societies they want to conquer: that is not why empires are built.'

Dinu gave a hoarse laugh. 'Here you are, so full of indignation about the British. And yet you use the English language more often than not . . .'

'That's neither here nor there,' Uma shot back. 'Many great Jewish writers write in German. Do you think that prevents them from recognising the truth?'

From the driver's seat, Arjun gave a shout: 'Hold on!' He threw the car into a steep turn, taking it through the gates of Lankasuka. As they were getting out, they were met by the sound of ululations and the trumpeting of conch-shells. They went racing upstairs to find Neel and Manju walking around the fire, his dhoti joined to her sari by a knot.

From under the hood of her sari, Manju had been peering about the room, looking everywhere for Arjun. When she finally saw him walking in, dressed in his grease-blackened clothes, her head snapped up, throwing off the hood. Everyone in the room froze, astonished by the sight of an unveiled bride. Just then, a moment before Manju had pulled her sari back in place, Dinu's flash went off. Later, everyone was to agree that this was by far the best picture of the wedding.

The night was unbearably hot. Bela's bed was drenched with sweat, despite the whirring of the electric fan overhead. She couldn't sleep; she kept smelling the scent of flowers – the heady fragrances of the last, hottest nights before the breaking of the rains. She thought of Manju, in her flower-strewn bed downstairs, with Neel. It was strange how heat had the effect of heightening the scent of flowers.

Her throat was dry, as parched as sand. She got out of bed and went into the hall outside. The house was dark and for the first time in weeks, there was no one about. The silence seemed almost unnatural, especially after the tumult of the last few days. She tiptoed through the hall to the veranda at the back of the house. There was a full moon, and its light lay on the floor glinting like silver foil. She glanced at the door of the room where Kishan Singh slept. It was, as always, slightly ajar. She wondered if she should shut the door. Stepping across the veranda, she went up to the door and looked in. She could see him lying on his mat, with his longyi tucked between his legs. A gust of wind blew the door a little further open. It seemed cooler inside. She slipped through and seated herself in a corner, with her chin on her knees.

Suddenly he stirred and sat up. 'Who is it?'

'It's me – Bela.'

'Bela?'

She heard a note of apprehension in his voice and she understood that it had more to do with Arjun than with herself; that he was afraid of what might happen if she was found in his room – an officer's sister, a girl who'd just turned fifteen and was still unmarried. She didn't want him to be afraid. She pushed herself across the floor and touched his hand. 'It's all right, Kishan Singh.'

'And what if . . . ?'

'Everyone's asleep.'

'But still . . .'

She saw that he was still afraid, so she stretched out her legs and lay down beside him. 'Tell me Kishan Singh,' she said, 'when you were married – what was it like, your first night with your wife?'

He laughed softly. 'It was strange,' he said. 'I knew that my friends and relatives were at the door listening and laughing.'

'And your wife? Was she scared?'

'Yes, but I was too – even more than her in some ways. Later, when we talked of it with others, we learnt that that is how it always is . . .'

He could have made love to her then and she would have let him, but she understood that he wouldn't, not because he was afraid, but because of some kind of innate decency, and she was glad of this because it meant that it was all right to be there. She

296

was happy just to be lying beside him, aware of his body, knowing that he was aware of hers. 'And when your son was born,' she said, 'were you there?'

'No. She was in the village and I was at the base.'

'What did you do when you heard the news?'

'I bought sweets from a *halwai* and I went to your brother and said: Sah'b, here is some *mithai*. He looked at me and asked: Why? So I said, Sah'b, I have a son.'

She tried to think of Arjun, in his uniform, talking to Kishan Singh. The picture wouldn't come to life. 'My brother – what is he like? As a soldier, I mean?'

'He's a good officer. The men, we like him.'

'Is he hard on you?'

'Sometimes. Of all the Indians in our battalion, he's the one who's the most English. We call him the "Angrez".'

She laughed: 'I must tell him.'

Suddenly he clapped a hand over her mouth. 'Shh.' There was a sound, of someone stirring downstairs. He sat up in alarm. 'They're flying to Rangoon today,' he said. 'They'll all be up early. You must go.'

'Just a little longer,' she pleaded. 'It's still night.'

'No.'

He pulled her to her feet and led her to the door. Just as she was about to slip out, he stopped her. 'Wait.' With a hand under her chin, he kissed her, very briefly, but full on the lips.

When Neel shook her awake, Manju could not believe that it was already time.

'Just a little longer,' she pleaded. 'Just a few more minutes.'

He put his chin against her cheek and tickled her with his beard. 'Manju, the plane leaves at 4 a.m.,' he said. 'We haven't got time . . .'

It was still dark when the chaos of departure got fully under way. Keyrings were found and forgotten; suitcases were sat upon and strapped with buckled belts; doors and windows were locked and checked and locked once again. A final round of tea was served and then, with the neighbourhood fast asleep, their luggage was loaded into a car. The family stood around the courtyard, waving: Uma, Bela, Arjun, their parents. Kishan Singh looked on from upstairs. Manju cried a little but there was no time for long goodbyes. Neel hurried her into the car and shut the door.

'We'll be back next year . . .'

It was so early that the roads were empty and it took just half an hour to drive to the Willingdon Air Base, on the banks of the Hooghly river. A few minutes later, Dolly, Rajkumar and Dinu arrived. At exactly 4 a.m. they were led to a jetty, where a sleek, grey motor-launch was waiting. The launch's engine started with a roar and they went shooting upriver, with the decks tilted backwards at a rakish angle. It was very dark, and all Manju could see of her surroundings was the muddy circle of water that was illuminated by the launch's powerful spotlight.

The launch slowed and the roar of its engine dwindled to a gentle whine. Its bows dropped back into the water and its spotlight roamed the waters ahead. Suddenly two immense white pontoons loomed out of the water and then the light climbed higher, illuminating the aircraft that was to take them to Rangoon. The plane was enormous, an eighteen-and-a-half-ton flying boat. The logo of the airline was painted on the plane's tail and a name was written in large letters across its nose – *Centaurus*.

'It's a Martin C-130 seaplane,' Neel whispered into Manju's ear. 'It's the kind that does the Pacific run for PanAm.'

'Like Humphrey Bogart's plane, in *China Clipper*?'

'Yes.' He laughed. 'And there was one in *Flying Down to Rio* too, remember, with Fred Astaire and Ginger Rogers?'

It was when she stepped through the hatch that the full extent of the plane's size became evident to Manju. The interior was as spacious as a ship's lounge, with deep, well-padded seats and glowing brass light fixtures. Manju pressed her nose to the window and saw the propellers starting to spin. Flecks of white froth appeared on the churning brown water below and then the shuddering fuselage began to advance, and the wake of its bow wave fanned out towards the invisible shore, rocking the little islands of water hyacinth that were floating downriver. A gurgling, sucking sound issued from the pontoons as the plane fought the

298

water's grip, gathering speed. Suddenly the *Centaurus* shot forward, as though catapulted by the beat of wind upon water. Manju saw the wind-drummed waters of the Hooghly falling away as the aircraft rose slowly above the river's steep embankments. Soon the lights of the city were gone and there was only darkness below: they were now flying over the mangrove swamps of the Sunderbans, heading towards the Bay of Bengal.

Shortly afterwards a steward took Manju and Neel on a tour of the plane. They went straight through to the navigating bridge, where the captain and the first officer sat side by side, behind identical controls. The first officer explained that the Calcutta–Rangoon flight was only one leg of a fortnightly, eleven-thousand-mile round trip that took the *Centaurus* from Southampton to Sydney and back.

Behind the bridge lay the cabins of the main deck. There was an area for the stewards, a midship cabin, a smoking cabin and a promenade deck – an area that was kept free of seats, so that passengers could stretch their legs in mid-flight. Well appointed as everything was, it was the ingenious design of the kitchen and pantry that took Manju's breath away. In an area that was no larger than the average closet, space had somehow been found for all the amenities of a first-rate restaurant – crockery, linen, silverware and even fresh flowers.

With dawn approaching the steward advised Manju and Neel to go to the promenade deck to watch the sunrise. They stepped through the arched entrance just in time to see the dark expanse of the Sunderbans yielding to the metallic glint of the Bay of Bengal. In the distance a sliver of colour had appeared on the horizon, like light leaking through a doorway. The dark skies turned quickly mauve and then a shimmering translucent green, shot with streaks of crimson and yellow.

While Dinu was attempting to photograph the sunrise, Manju and Neel crossed the aisle to look in the other direction. Manju cried out loud: to the west lay a stupefying view. The horizon was obscured by a mass of darkness, a bank of cloud that was as vast as a mountain range. It was as though the Himalayas had been magically transported across the sea. So heavy were the cloudbanks that their flat bottoms seemed almost to touch the waves while their peaks towered far, far above the plane – great Everests of cloud reaching tens of thousands of feet into the sky.

'The monsoons,' Neel said incredulously. 'We've run straight into the incoming rains.'

'Is it going to be dangerous?' Manju asked.

'In some other aircraft perhaps,' Neel said confidently. 'But not in this one.'

They went back to their seats and soon sheets of rain were whiplashing against the windows with a force that made Manju flinch from the glass. Yet, the starkly visible violence of the weather had almost no effect upon the plane – the speedometer in the cabin showed the *Centaurus* to be flying at a steady 200 miles per hour. But a while later the captain announced that the *Centaurus* would make a change of altitude to ride out the storm. It would descend from its present cruising height of 3,000 feet to a few hundred feet above sea level.

Manju fell into a doze and was jolted awake only when a ripple of excitement ran through the plane. Land had been spotted on the starboard side: a picture-book island ringed with beaches. Huge waves were disintegrating into sheets of white foam on the sand. At the centre of the island there stood a striped black and white tower.

'Ladies and gentlemen,' the captain announced, 'what we have here is the lighthouse of Oyster Reef. You should have your first glimpse of Burma very shortly. Watch out for the Arakan coast . . .'

Then there it was – close enough to touch – a densely clotted carpet of mangrove, veined with thin creeks and silver rivulets. As Manju sat looking through the window, Neel whispered into her ear, telling her the story of how his grandmother – Rajkumar's mother – had died somewhere below, on a sampan that was moored in one of those branching inlets.

The town of Akyab, the capital of the Arakan, was their first stop. 'This,' said Neel proudly, 'was where my father was born.' The airline's base lay in a natural sea-lane, a good distance from the town. All they saw of Akyab as the *Centaurus* came down was a clock-tower in the far distance. After a quick refuelling the plane was in the air again. The rain stopped and in the bright daylight the waters of the coast were revealed to be lined with miles of reef and great floating forests of seaweed – all clearly visible from above, as stains on the sparkling sea. Rangoon now lay due east, and the *Centaurus* soon turned inland, flying over a stretch of uninhabited countryside. The steward came by, handing out voluminous leather-bound menus.

At the end of her breakfast, Manju found herself looking down on a vista of square paddy fields. Some were already green and others were in the process of becoming so, with lines of workers advancing through the mud, transplanting seedlings. The workers stood up as the plane flew over, throwing their heads back and waving huge conical hats.

Manju caught sight of a river, curving across the landscape. 'Is that the Irrawaddy?' she asked Neel.

'No,' said Neel. 'That's the Rangoon river – the Irrawaddy doesn't flow past the city.'

Then a glint of sunlight drew her eye to an immense structure, far in the distance – a gilded mountain that tapered into a spire of gold. 'What's that?'

'That's the Shwe Dagon Pagoda,' Neel whispered in her ear. 'We're home.'

Manju glanced at her watch and saw that the journey had lasted exactly five and a half hours. It seemed impossible that less than a day had passed since her wedding night, since the time when Neel had shut the door of their flower-bedecked bedroom. She thought of how frightened she'd been and she wanted to laugh. It was only now, circling above the city that was to be her home, that she acknowledged how completely she was in love. He was her present, her future, the entirety of her existence. Time and being held no meaning without him. She slipped her hand into his and looked down again on the great muddy river and the spire of gold. 'Yes,' she said. 'I'm home.'

PART FIVE

Morningside

Twenty-five

Manju and Neel had not been married quite three months when the British Prime Minister, Neville Chamberlain, declared war on Germany, on behalf of Britain and her Empire. With the start of the war, an Air Raid Precautions scheme was prepared for Rangoon. The city was divided into sections and an ARP committee was formed for each. Medical officers were taught to deal with gas injuries; wardens were shown how to identify incendiary bombs; fire-fighting parties were formed and first-aid centres were set up. Rangoon's water table was too high to allow the building of underground shelters, but slit trenches were dug at strategic points around the city. Periodically there were 'blackouts'; trains entered and left the Rangoon railway station with darkened windows; wardens and civic guards stayed on duty through the night.

There was nothing unsatisfactory about the conduct of these exercises: the city's inhabitants followed their instructions good-humouredly and disturbances were few. But there was no denying the fact that a Rangoon blackout had more the feel of a performance than a drill: the public seemed to be going through the motions without being persuaded either of the imminence of war, or of its possible bearing on their lives. Certainly, in Burma, as in India, public opinion was deeply divided: in both places many important personages had expressed their support of the colonial Government. But many could also be heard to voice bitter condemnation of Britain's declaration of war on their behalf, without any binding guarantees of eventual independence. The mood among Burma's student activists was summed up in a slogan coined by a charismatic young student leader, Aung San:

Colonialism's difficulty, he said, was Freedom's opportunity. One day, Aung San disappeared: a rumour circulated that he was on his way to China to seek the support of the Communists. Later it came to be known that he had gone instead to Japan.

But these concerns were relatively distant from the life of the streets, where people seemed mainly to regard the ARP exercises as a species of entertainment, a mass diversion. Merrymakers strolled blithely through the darkened thoroughfares; young people flirted unseen in the parks; filmgoers flocked to see Ernst Lubitsch's *Ninotchka* at the Metro; *When Tomorrow Comes* had a long run at the Excelsior, and Irene Dunne was enshrined as one of the city's idols. At the Silver Grill on Fytche Square, cabarets and dancing continued as usual.

Dinu and his friend, Thiha Saw, were among the few who dedicated themselves wholeheartedly to the Air Raid Precautions scheme. At this time, both Dinu and Thiha Saw were deeply involved in student union politics. They were on the far left of the political spectrum and were involved in the publication of an anti-Fascist magazine. Participating in civil defences seemed a natural extension of their political work.

Dinu still lived at the Kemendine compound, in a couple of rooms at the top of the house. But at home, he made no mention of the work he was doing as an ARP warden – partly because he knew that Neel would tell him that he was wasting his time and needed to do some real work, and partly also because experience had led him to assume that his opinions would always be violently at odds with his father's. This was why he was taken completely by surprise at an ARP warden's meeting when he found himself suddenly face-to-face with none other than his father.

'You?'

'You!' There was no telling which of them was the more astonished.

After this encounter, there developed – for the first time ever – a brief bond between Rajkumar and Dinu. The outbreak of war had brought them through opposite routes to a shared position: Rajkumar had come to be convinced that in the absence of the British Empire, Burma's economy would collapse. Dinu's support for the Allied war effort was rooted in other kinds of soil: in his leftist sympathies; in his support for the resistance movements in China and Spain; in his admiration of Charlie Chaplin and Robert Capa. Unlike his father, he was not a believer in colonialism – indeed his antipathy to British rule was surpassed only by his loathing of European Fascism and Japanese militarism.

Whatever the reasons, this was an instance when father and son were in agreement – a situation that was without precedent in the memories of either. For the first time in their lives, they were working together – attending meetings, discussing such matters as the necessity of importing gas masks and the design of wartime posters. So novel was this experience that they both relished it in silence, speaking of it neither at home nor anywhere else.

One night an ARP blackout was accompanied by a thunderstorm. Despite the rain Rajkumar insisted on accompanying the wardens on their rounds. He was drenched when he got home. The next morning he woke up shivering. A doctor came and diagnosed pneumonia. Rajkumar was taken to hospital in an ambulance.

For the first few days, Rajkumar was barely conscious, unable to recognise Dolly, Dinu or Neel. His condition was judged to be serious enough for the doctors to bar all visitors. For several days he lay in a near-coma.

Then, slowly, the fever began to recede.

In his periods of lucidity Rajkumar took stock of his surroundings. It so happened that chance had brought him to a familiar place: the hospital room that Dolly and Dinu had occupied twenty-four years before. Looking around his bed, Rajkumar recognised the view from the window: the Shwe Dagon was framed exactly as he remembered. The blue and white curtains were slightly faded but still spotless and crisply starched; the tiled floors were, as ever, sparkling clean; and the dark, heavy furniture was recognisably the same, with inventory numbers stencilled on the varnished wood, in white paint.

When at last he was well enough to sit up, Rajkumar saw that the room had two additions. One was a Carrier air conditioner and the other a bedside radio – a 7-valve Paillard, with a 'magic eye', a metal cabinet, and chromium-plated mountings. The air conditioner Rajkumar had no use for, but the radio intrigued him. He flipped a switch and found himself listening to a station in Singapore: a newsreader's voice was recounting the latest developments in the war, describing the evacuation of British troops from Dunkirk.

After this, Rajkumar kept the radio on most of the time. Each night the nurse would turn it off when she was extinguishing the lights; Rajkumar would wait for her footsteps to die away before turning it on again. He would lie on his side and spin the knob, coasting from station to station. Twenty-four years before, at the time of Dolly's stay in that room, Europe had been convulsed by another war. Dolly too had stayed awake in this room, listening to the sounds of the night. But the whispers she'd heard had come from within the hospital: now, the room was filled with voices from around the world – London, New Delhi, Chungking, Tokyo, Moscow, Sydney. The voices spoke with such urgency and insistence that Rajkumar began to feel that he had lost touch with the flow of events; that he had become one of those men who sleepwalk their way to disaster by failing to note the significance of what was happening round them.

For the first time in many years, he allowed himself to think about the way he had been running his businesses. Day after day, month after month, he'd tried to handle every decision, review all the daily accounts, visit each location, every mill, every yard and outlet. He had been running his company as though it were a food-stall in a bazaar, and in the process he had blinded himself to the wider context.

Neel had long been pushing for a bigger role in the running of the business; Rajkumar had responded by trying to shut him out. He'd handed him money and told him to go and put it in films – as though he were buying off a child with packets of sweets. The ploy had worked, if only because Neel was too much in awe of him to challenge his authority. Now, the business was foundering. This was a fact that he'd refused to face. He'd suppressed hints from his accountants and managers, shouted at them when they tried to give him warning. And the stark fact was that he had no one to blame but himself: he had simply lost sight of what he was doing, and why.

308

As he lay listening to the radio's crackling voices, remorse settled on Rajkumar like a damp, stifling quilt. The doctors pronounced him to be well on the way to a complete recovery but his family could see no sign of an improvement, in either his manner or his appearance. He was in his mid-sixties at this time, but looked much older: his eyebrows had turned grey and bushy and his cheeks had begun to sag into overlapping dewlaps and jowls. He seemed scarcely to register the presence of the people who came to his room to see him; often when they tried to speak to him, he would silence them by turning up the radio.

One day Dolly unplugged the radio and shut the door. 'Rajkumar, what's on your mind? Tell me.'

At first he wouldn't speak but she prodded him until he answered.

'I've been thinking, Dolly.'

'What about? *Tell me.*'

'Do you remember how you and Dinu were in this room, that time . . . ?'

'Yes. Of course.'

'That night, at Huay Zedi, when Dinu was ill and you said we had to get him to a hospital – I thought you were hysterical. I went along just for your sake . . .'

She smiled: 'Yes. I know.'

'But you were right.'

'It was just luck – a premonition.'

'That's what you say. But when I look back now, I can see that you often are right. Even though you live so quietly, shut away in the house, you seem to know more about what's happening in the world than I do.'

'What do you mean?'

'I've been thinking about what you've been saying these many years, Dolly.'

'What exactly?'

'That we should leave.'

With a long sigh of relief, Dolly reached for his hand. 'So you've been thinking of that at last?'

'Yes. But it's hard, Dolly – it's hard to think of leaving: Burma has given me everything I have. The boys have grown up here:

they've never known any other home. When I first came to Mandalay the nakhoda of my boat said: This is a golden land – no one ever starves here. That proved true for me, and despite everything that's happened recently, I don't think I could ever love another place in the same way. But if there's one thing I've learnt in my life, Dolly, it is that there is no certainty about these things. My father was from Chittagong and he ended up in the Arakan; I ended up in Rangoon; you went from Mandalay to Ratnagiri and now you're here too. Why should we expect that we're going to spend the rest of our lives here? There are people who have the luck to end their lives where they began them. But this is not something that is owed to us. On the contrary, we have to expect that a time will come when we'll have to move on again. Rather than be swept along by events, we should make plans and take control of our own fate.'

'What are you trying to say, Rajkumar?'

'Just that it doesn't matter whether I think of Burma as home or not. What matters is what people think of us. And it's plain enough that men like me are now seen as the enemy – on all sides. This is the reality and I have to acknowledge it. My job now is to find a way of making sure that Dinu and Neel are provided for.'

'Surely they're provided for already?'

Rajkumar paused before answering. 'Dolly, I think you're aware that the business hasn't been doing well lately. But you probably don't know the full extent of it.'

'And how bad is that?'

'It's not good, Dolly,' he said quietly. 'There are debts – many of them.'

'But, Rajkumar, if we sold the house, the yards, our share in Morningside – surely something would be left so that the boys could make a start somewhere else?'

Rajkumar began to cough. 'That wouldn't work, Dolly. As things stand at this minute, even if we sold everything it still wouldn't be enough. As for Morningside, Matthew has troubles of his own, you know. Rubber was very badly hit by the Depression. We can't rush into this, Dolly – that way we're sure to run into disaster. This has to be done very, very carefully. We have to give it time . . .'

'I don't know, Rajkumar.' Dolly began to pick worriedly at the end of her htamein. 'Things are happening so fast now – people say that the war may spread; that Japan may get into it; that they could even attack Burma.'

Rajkumar smiled. 'That's impossible, Dolly. You just have to look at a map. To get here the Japanese would have to come across Singapore and Malaya. Singapore is one of the most heavily defended places in the world. The British have tens of thousands of troops there. There are thirty-six-inch guns all along the shore. We can't be chasing after smoke, Dolly, we can't do things in a panic. If this is to work, we have to be realistic, we have to make careful plans.'

Dolly leant over him to fluff up the pillows on his bed. 'So do you have a plan then?'

'Not yet, but I've been thinking. Whatever we do, it'll take time – at least a year, maybe more. You have to prepare yourself. I want to make it possible for us to leave Burma with enough so that the boys can settle comfortably somewhere – in India, or wherever they want to go.'

'And after that?'

'The two of us will be free.'

'To do what?'

'Well, you've already decided – you want to live in Sagaing.'

'And what about you?'

'Perhaps I'll come back too, Dolly. I sometimes think of living quietly in Huay Zedi – I'm sure Doh Say would have a place for me – and it wouldn't be so far from you.'

Dolly laughed. 'So you're going to sell everything, uproot all of us, go through all this, just to come back and live quietly in Huay Zedi?'

'It's not for myself that I'm thinking of doing this, Dolly – it's for the boys.'

Rajkumar smiled and allowed his head to fall back against his pillows. Once before in his life, he had known himself to be at a crossroads – that was when he was trying to get his first contract, for the Chota-Nagpur Railway. He'd thought hard and come up with a plan that had worked, laying the foundations of his future success. This time too he would have to think of something, a plan that would work: this would be his last challenge, the last hill to cross. After that he would rest. There was no shame in growing old and seeking rest.

The first months of the war found Arjun and his battalion on the frontiers of Afghanistan. Arjun was on garrison duty, at a small outpost called Charbagh, near the Khyber Pass. The border was quiet – unusually so, the older officers said – and the conflict in Europe seemed very far away. Charbagh was manned by a single company of soldiers, Arjun being the sole officer. The surroundings were spectacularly beautiful: craggy, ochre mountains, streaked with great slashes of brilliantly coloured rock. There was little to do apart from daily drills, barracks inspections and occasional marches with training columns. Arjun spent long hours reading and soon ran out of books.

At regular fortnightly intervals, the battalion's Commanding Officer, Lieutenant-Colonel 'Bucky' Buckland, stopped by on tours of inspection. The CO was a tall, professorial-looking man with a ruff of wiry hair clinging to the base of his high-domed, balding head.

'And what do you do with your time, Lieutenant?' the CO asked offhandedly on one of his visits. 'Do you shoot at all? I've heard there's plenty of game to be had here.'

'Actually, sir,' Arjun said quietly, 'I read books . . .'

'Oh?' The CO turned to look at him with new interest. 'I didn't take you for a reader. And may I ask what you read?'

Their tastes proved to be complementary: the CO introduced Arjun to Robert Graves and Wilfred Owen. Arjun lent him his copies of H. G. Wells's *War of the Worlds* and Jules Verne's *Twenty Thousand Leagues Under the Sea*. These exchanges became a pleasurable part of Arjun's life at Charbagh and he began to look forward to the CO's visits. In between there were long days when nothing happened. There was little to do apart from talking to the occasional traveller.

Late in the summer, Arjun's friend Hardy stopped by on his way to his own post, atop the Khyber Pass. Hardy was a quiet, clear-eyed man of medium height and average build. Whether in or out of uniform he was always neatly dressed – with the folds of his turban layered in precise order and his beard combed tight against his chin. Despite his soldiering background, Hardy did not in any way resemble the Sikh warriors of military lore – he was soft-spoken and slow-moving, with an expression of habitual sleepiness. He had a good ear for a tune and was usually the first in the mess to learn the latest Hindi film songs. It was his habit – annoying to some and entertaining to others – to hum these melodies under his breath as he went about his work. These quirks sometimes brought him a little more than his fair share of 'ragging' – yet his friends knew that there were certain limits beyond which he could not be goaded: although generally slow to take offence, Hardy was inflexible when roused and had a long memory for grudges.

Hardy had just spent a period of leave in his village. On his first night at Charbagh he told Arjun about some odd rumours that he'd heard during his stay. Most of his neighbours had relatives in the army, and some of them had spoken of incidents of unrest: troops were said to be resisting transfer orders abroad. In Bombay, a Sikh unit – a squadron of the Central India horse – was said to have mutinied. They had lain down their weapons and refused to board the ship that was to take them to North Africa. Two men had been executed. A dozen others had been exiled to the prisons of the Andaman Islands. Some of these men were from Hardy's own village: there could be no doubt about the reliability of these reports.

Arjun was astonished to hear this. 'You should tell Bucky,' he said. 'He should know.'

'He must know already,' Hardy said. 'And if he hasn't said anything to us, it must be for a reason . . .' They looked at each other uneasily and dropped the subject: neither of them mentioned these stories to anyone else.

A few months later the 1/1 Jats moved back to their battalion's base at Saharanpur, near Delhi. With the descent into the plains the rhythms of their life underwent a dramatic change. The army was now expanding at a furious pace: regiments were raising new battalions and headquarters was looking everywhere for experienced personnel. Like every other battalion in the regiment, the 1/1 Jats were milked of several officers and NCOs. Suddenly they found themselves struggling to fill the gaps in their ranks. Newly recruited companies were sent up from the battalion's training centre and a fresh batch of officers arrived, as replacements for those who'd left. The new officers consisted mainly of expatriate British civilians with Emergency Commissions – men who had until recently held jobs as planters, businessmen and engineers. They had little experience of the Indian army and its intricate customs and procedures.

Arjun and Hardy were both full lieutenants now and they were among the few regular army officers left in the unit. Lieutenant-Colonel Buckland began to depend on them more and more for the day-to-day running of the battalion.

First he saddled them with the job of forming a new administrative platoon. Then, sooner than anyone had expected, the battalion's motorised transport was brought up to authorised strength. Three dozen fifteen-hundredweight trucks arrived, along with a dozen smaller lorries. It was discovered that the battalion had mule-trainers aplenty, but lacked drivers. Arjun was taken off the administrative platoon and appointed Motor Transport Officer. It fell to him to teach the new drivers the tricks of threading heavyweight trucks through Saharanpur's narrow alleys and bazaars.

Even as the battalion was adjusting to its new vehicles, a shipment of armaments was sent up from New Delhi: 3-inch mortars, tommy guns and Vickers-Berthier light machine guns. Then came three Bren guns, with their carriers, six medium machine guns and five Boye's anti-tank rifles, one for each company. Hardy was given the responsibility of running weapons training courses for the men.

Just as Hardy and Arjun were settling cheerfully into their new jobs, the CO turned everything upside down again. He pulled both Arjun and Hardy from their assignments and set them to work on preparing a unit mobilisation scheme.

By this time, most of Arjun and Hardy's classmates from the Military Academy had already been sent abroad. Some were serving in North Africa, some in Eritrea (where one had won a Victoria

Cross), and some in the East – Malaya, Hong Kong and Singapore. Arjun and Hardy assumed that they too would soon be going abroad to join other units of the Indian army. When the CO asked them to draft a mobilisation plan, they took it as a sign that their departure was imminent. But a month went by without any further news, and then another. On New Year's Eve, they saw 1941 in with a wan celebration. Despite the ban on shop talk at the mess, the conversation kept returning to the question of where they would be sent, east or west – to North Africa or towards Malaya.

Opinion was evenly divided.

Rajkumar was discharged from hospital with strict orders to remain in bed for at least a month. On returning home, he insisted on being moved up to a room at the top of the house. A bed was brought up and placed by a window. Neel bought a radio, a Paillard just like the one in the hospital, and placed it on a table, beside the bed. When everything was exactly as he wanted, Rajkumar lay down, with a wall of pillows against his back, positioning himself so that he'd be able to look across the city, towards the Shwe Dagon.

As the days passed the outlines of a plan began to take shape, very slowly, before his eyes. During the last war the price of timber had soared. The profits he had made then had sustained him for a decade afterwards. It was not too far-fetched to imagine that something similar might happen again. The British and the Dutch were reinforcing their defences throughout the East – in Malaya, Singapore, Hong Kong, Java, Sumatra. It stood to reason that they would need materials. If he could build up a stockpile of timber in his yards, it was possible that he'd be able to sell at a good price next year. The problem was liquidity: he would have to sell or mortgage all his assets to find cash – he would have to get rid of the yards, the mills, the timber concessions, even the Kemendine house. Perhaps he could persuade Matthew to buy him out of Morningside: there might be some cash there.

The more he thought of it, the more plausible the plan seemed.

315

The risks were huge of course, but they always were when anything important was at stake. But the rewards too could be very great; enough to clear his debts and finance a new beginning for Neel and Dinu. And there would be other advantages to arranging things in this way: all his assets would have been disposed of by the time he made his final move. After that he'd be free to leave – nothing to hold him back, nothing more to worry about.

One afternoon, when Dolly brought him his meal, he sketched his plan for her. 'I think it could work, Dolly,' he concluded. 'I think it's our best chance.'

Dolly had many objections.

'How is all this to be done, Rajkumar? In your state of health, you can't be up and about, travelling to Malaya and all that.'

'I've thought of that,' he said. 'Neel and Dinu will do the travelling – not me. I'll tell them what they have to do. One of them can go upcountry; the other can go over to dispose of our part of Morningside.'

Dolly shook her head. 'Dinu won't agree. He's never wanted to have anything to do with the business – you know that.'

'He doesn't really have a choice, Dolly. If I were to die today, he would find himself paying off my debts whether he liked it or not. All I'm asking is a few months of his time. After that he'll be free to follow his own interests.'

Dolly fell silent, and Rajkumar reached out to jog her arm. 'Say something, Dolly – tell me what you think.'

'Rajkumar,' Dolly said quietly, 'this plan of yours – you do know what they call this kind of thing?'

'What?'

'Hoarding – war-profiteering.'

Rajkumar scowled.

'Hoarding applies to essential commodities, Dolly. That's not what I'll be dealing in. There's nothing illegal about my plan.'

'I'm not talking about the law . . .'

Rajkumar's tone grew impatient. 'Dolly, there's nothing else to be done. We have to take this chance – don't you see?'

Dolly rose to her feet. 'Does it really matter what I think, Rajkumar? If this is what you're set upon, then this is what you'll do. It is not important what I think.'

Late that night, when the whole house was asleep, the telephone began to ring in a hallway downstairs. Dolly got out of bed and ran to pick it up before it woke Rajkumar. She heard an operator's voice, crackling down the line, telling her she had a trunk call. The instrument seemed to go dead for a moment, and then she heard Alison's voice; it was very faint as though she were shouting across a crowded room.

'Alison?' She heard a sound that was like a sob. She raised her voice. 'Alison, is that you?'

'Yes.'

'Alison – is everything all right?'

'No . . . there's bad news.'

'Is it Sayagyi?'

'No.' There was a sob again. 'My parents.'

'Alison. I'm so sorry. What happened?'

'They were on holiday. Driving. In the Cameron Highlands. The car went over an embankment . . .'

'Alison, Alison . . .' Dolly couldn't think of what she was going to say next. 'Alison, I'd come myself, if I could, but Rajkumar isn't well. I can't leave him. But I'll send someone – one of the boys, probably Dinu. It may take a few weeks but he'll be there. I promise you . . .' The line went dead before she could say anything else.

Twenty-six

The day before Arjun's twenty-third birthday he and Hardy borrowed a jeep and drove down to Delhi for the weekend. Walking through the arcades of Connaught Circus, they ran into an acquaintance, Kumar, a debonair and famously fun-loving contemporary of theirs from the academy.

Kumar belonged to the 14th Punjab Regiment and his battalion was currently stationed in Singapore. He was in India only briefly, attending a signals training course. Kumar appeared distracted and preoccupied, very different from his usual high-spirited self. They went out for lunch, and Kumar told them about a very strange incident – something that had caused a lot of unease at headquarters.

At Singapore's Tyersall Park Camp an Indian soldier had inexplicably shot an officer and then committed suicide. On investigation it was discovered that this was no simple murder-suicide: there were undercurrents of unrest within the battalion. Certain officers of this battalion had been heard to say that Indians should refuse to participate in this war: that this was a competition for supremacy among nations who believed it to be their shared destiny to enslave other peoples – England, France, Germany. There was much concern at headquarters: more than half the troops in Malaya were Indian and it was clear that the colony could become indefensible if unrest were to spread. Despite the incendiary nature of these rumours, the high command had decided on a judicious and measured response. All that was done by way of disciplinary action was to send one of the battalion's junior officers back to India.

318

It so happened that the officer who was singled out for censure was a Muslim. When news of his punishment reached his battalion, a company of Muslim soldiers proceeded to lay down their weapons, in a show of sympathy. The next day many of the battalion's Hindu soldiers also laid down their arms.

At this point the incident assumed a new gravity. For generations, the British Indian army had operated on the principle of maintaining a careful balance between the troops. Every battalion was constituted of companies drawn from different castes and religions – Hindus, Muslims, Sikhs, Jats, Brahmins. Each company had its own mess, run strictly according to the dietary rules of the group from which the troops had been recruited. As an additional safeguard, infantry divisions were so composed that Indian troops were always balanced by a certain number of Australian or British units.

That Hindu and Muslim troops could act together to support an Indian officer came as a shock to the High Command. No one needed to be reminded that nothing of this kind had happened since the Great Mutiny of 1857. At this point half-measures were dispensed with. A platoon of British soldiers from the Argyll and Sutherland Highlanders was sent in to surround the mutinous Indians.

Thus far into the story Kumar had told them neither the name of the battalion concerned nor that of the officer who was to be punished. When at last he mentioned these, it became clear that Kumar, like the good raconteur that he was, had been saving his punchline for the last. It turned out that the battalion in question was a brother unit of the 1/1 Jats – a part of a Hyderabad infantry regiment. The officer who was being sent home was someone they had all known well at the academy.

Kumar concluded the story with an offhand observation: 'Going overseas has disturbing effects on the troops,' he said, shrugging his shoulders. 'On officers too. You'll see.'

'Perhaps it won't happen to us,' Hardy said hopefully. 'There's no certainty that we'll be sent abroad. They'll need forces here too, after all . . .'

Arjun was quick to challenge this. 'And what would that do for us?' he said. 'For you and me? We'll sit out the war and our careers will be dead on their feet. I think I'd rather take my chances abroad.'

They walked away in silence, not knowing what to make of this conversation. There was something about Kumar's story that defied belief. They both knew the officer who'd been punished – he was a quiet kind of man, from a middle-class family. He needed his job if nothing else. What had made him do what he'd done? It was hard to understand.

And if the story was true – and they were by no means sure of this – then the incident had other implications too. It meant for example that the other ranks were now taking their cues from their Indian officers rather than the High Command. But this was worrying – to them no less than to the High Command – for if the men were to lose faith in the structure of command, then the Indian officers too would eventually be rendered redundant. Only by making common cause with their British counterparts could they hope to prevent this. What would happen if there really were to be a fissure? How would the men respond? There was no telling.

Disquieting as the subject was, Arjun felt oddly exhilarated: it was an uncommon responsibility to be faced with such questions at the age of twenty-three.

That night they changed into *kurtas* and *churidar* pyjamas and went to a dancer's *kotha* near Ajmeri Gate. The dancer was in her forties and her face was painted white, with eyebrows that were as thin as wires. At first glance she looked stony and unattractive, but when she stood up to dance the hardness in her face melted away: her body was supple and lithe and there was a marvellous lightness in her feet. As the tabla's tempo increased she began to spin, whirling in time to the beat. Her gauzy knee-length *angarkha* corkscrewed around her, in tight spirals. The aureoles of her breasts stood outlined against the thin, white cloth. Arjun's throat went dry. When the tabla sounded its climactic stroke, her index finger came to rest on Arjun's forehead. She beckoned to him to follow her.

Arjun turned to Hardy in astonishment and his friend smiled and gave him a nudge. 'Go, yaar, it's your birthday isn't it? Jaa.'

Arjun followed the dancer up a flight of narrow stairs. Her room was small, with a low ceiling. She undressed him slowly, picking at the drawstring of his cotton churidar pyjamas with her nails. When he reached for her she pushed his hand away with a laugh.

'Wait.'

She made him lie face down on the bed and massaged a handful of oil into his back, her fingertips tripping over the knuckles of his spine in imitation of the rhythms of a dancer's feet. When at last she lay down beside him she was still fully clothed. He reached for her breasts and she pushed his hand away: 'No, not that.' She undid her drawstring and guided him into her body, watching with a smile, as he lay on her. When he was done she slipped quickly away, and it was as though nothing at all happened: even her drawstring seemed instantly back in place.

She put a finger under his chin and tipped his head back, puckering her lips as though she were looking at a beautiful child.

'So young,' she said. 'Just a boy.'

'I'm twenty-three,' he said proudly.

She laughed. 'You look sixteen.'

When Alison first broke the news of her parents' deaths to Saya John, his response had consisted of nothing more than a slight smile. A series of questions had followed, asked almost playfully, as though the situation that was under discussion was at best a remote possibility – an imaginative hypothesis that Alison had propounded in order to explain her parents' prolonged absence from the dinner table.

Alison had been so afraid of the impact the news might have on her grandfather that she had gone to great lengths to compose herself, caking make-up over the discolourations of her face and tying a scarf over her disarranged hair. Every eventuality that she could think of she had tried to prepare herself for. But the sight of her grandfather's childlike smile proved beyond her bearing. She got up and ran out of the room.

Saya John was now in his late eighties. His lifelong regimen of early-morning exercise had served him well, and he was in relatively sound health. His hearing had not deteriorated greatly and although his eyesight had never been good, he was still able to see his way round the house and grounds. Before the accident his advancing age had occasionally betrayed itself in a tendency towards confusion. He would often forget things that had been said to him minutes before, while still being able to recall, in minute detail, events that had occurred forty or fifty years before. The accident greatly accelerated this tendency: Alison could see that contrary to his pretence, the news of her parents' deaths had indeed registered on her grandfather's mind. But his response was not unlike that of a child's reaction to unwelcome noise: he had figuratively stopped his ears with his fingers, in order to shut out what he did not wish to know. With each passing day he spoke less and less. He would come down to eat with Alison, but he'd sit at the hardwood table in blank silence. Such sentences as he addressed to Alison, would begin, almost invariably, with observations like: 'When Matthew comes back . . .' or, 'We must remember to tell Elsa . . .'

In the beginning Alison responded to these remarks with undisguised fury, slamming her hands on the polished table, and repeating several times over: 'Matthew is *not* coming back . . .' At the time nothing seemed more important than that he should make proper acknowledgement of what had happened. In this she envisaged, if not a lessening of her own grief, then at least a sharing of its burden. But he would smile through her outbursts, and at the end he would carry on where she had interrupted him: '. . . and when they come back . . .'

It seemed somehow indecent, even obscene – a profanation of parenthood – that he should respond so blandly to so great a loss. But she saw that her insistence and her banging of tables made no difference: that short of hitting him, she had no means of forcing a rupture in the protective blanket of confusion that he had drawn around himself. She forced herself to gain control of her anger, but this came at the cost of acknowledging a further loss – that of her grandfather. She and her Baba, as she called him, had always been very close. Now it was as though she were being forced to accept that he was no longer a sentient presence in her life; that the comforts of the companionship they had shared had ceased for ever; that he who had always been an unfailing source of support had now, in the hour of her greatest need, chosen to become a burden. Of all the betrayals he could have perpetrated, this seemed the most terrible – that he should become a child in this moment of her utter abandonment. She could never have imagined it.

These weeks would have been unendurable, but for a single fortuitous circumstance. Some years before, acting on a whim, Saya John had adopted one of the plantation workers' children – 'that boy who's always hanging around the house' – Ilongo. The boy had continued to live with his mother, but Saya John had paid for his schooling in the nearby town of Sungei Pattani. Later he had sent him to a technical institution in Penang and Ilongo had qualified as an electrician.

Ilongo was now twenty, a dark, curly-haired youth, slow-moving and soft-spoken, but of imposing height and build. On finishing his electrician's course, Ilongo had returned to the vicinity of Morningside – his mother now lived in a small, tin-roofed house on the outskirts of the estate.

In the aftermath of the accident, Ilongo came often to see Saya John at Morningside House. Gradually, and without an unduly intrusive display of concern, he took over many of the daily functions of caring for the old man. His was an unobtrusive yet quietly reliable presence, and Alison soon found herself looking to him for help in running the plantation's offices. Ilongo had grown up on Morningside and knew every worker on the estate. They in turn accorded him an authority unlike that of anyone else on the plantation. He had come of age on the estate, but he'd also stepped outside its boundaries, learnt to speak Malay and English, acquired an education. He had no need to raise his voice or utter threats in order to gain respect: they trusted him as one of their own.

Saya John too found reassurance in his company. Every Sunday Ilongo would borrow a truck from the estate and drive him down to the Church of Christ the King, in Sungei Pattani. On the way they would stop at the shaded arcades of the red-tiled shophouses that lined the town's main street. Saya John would go into a small restaurant and ask for the proprietor, Ah Fatt, a large man with bright gold incisors. Ah Fatt had political connections in southern China, and Saya John had been a generous contributor ever since

323

Japan's invasion of Manchuria. Each week he would hand Ah Fatt a sum of money, in an envelope, to be sent on.

On those days when he was at Morningside House, it was Ilongo who answered the telephone. One day he came cycling down from the house to see Alison at the estate office.

'There was a call . . .'

'From whom?'

'Mr Dinu Raha.'

'What?' Alison was sitting at her desk. She looked up with a frown. 'Dinu? Are you sure?'

'Yes. He was calling from Penang. He's just arrived from Rangoon. He's coming to Sungei Pattani by train.'

'Oh?' Alison thought back to the letters that Dolly had written her in the weeks after her parents' deaths: she recalled a reference to an impending visit – but the letter had said that it would be Neel who'd be coming, not Dinu.

'Are you sure it was Dinu?' she asked Ilongo again.

'Yes.'

She glanced at her watch. 'Perhaps I'll go to the station to meet him.'

'He said there was no need: he'd find a taxi.'

'Oh? Well, I'll see. There's still time.' Ilongo left and she sat back in her chair, turning to face a window that looked out over the plantation, towards the distant blue of the Andaman Sea. It was a long time since she'd last had a visitor. Immediately after her parents' death, the house had been full. Friends and relatives had come from Penang, Malacca, Singapore – there had been piles of telegrams. Timmy had come all the way from New York, flying across the Pacific on PanAm's *China Clipper*. In the overwhelming bewilderment of that time, Alison had found herself praying that Morningside would be filled for ever with people: it was inconceivable that she should have to face, on her own, those rooms and corridors – the stairway where every join in the wood was a reminder of her mother. But a week or two had gone by and then the house had emptied just as suddenly as it had filled up. Timmy had left to go back to New York. He had his own business now and couldn't be too long away. In departing he had as good as handed Morningside over to her – to sell or run as she chose. In time, her sense of abandonment had yielded to the understanding that she could not look to the past to fill the gaps in her present; that she could not hope for the lingering traces of her parents' lives to serve as a buffer between herself and the aching isolation of Morningside – the crushing monotony, the solitude that resulted from being always surrounded by the same faces, the same orderly rows of trees, the inescapable sight of the same clouds hanging upon the same mountain.

And now here was Dinu, on his way to Morningside – strange old Dinu – so incorrigibly serious, so awkward and unsure of himself. She looked at her watch and at the window. Far in the distance, she could see a train making its way across the plain. She reached for her handbag and found the keys to the Daytona roadster. It would be a relief to get away, even if just for a couple of hours.

Twenty-seven

It was because of the war that Dinu's arrival at Morningside was so long delayed. The threat of submarine activity in the Bay of Bengal had forced steamship companies to cease publishing their schedules. Departures were now announced only hours before the time of sailing. This meant, in effect, that a constant vigil had to be maintained at the companies' offices. Dinu had considered himself lucky to get a berth at all and had not given any thought to wiring ahead.

The station at Sungei Pattani was as pretty as a toy: there was a single platform shaded by a low red-tiled awning. Dinu spotted Alison as the train was drawing in: she was standing in the shade of the tin awning, wearing sunglasses and a long, black dress. She looked thin, limp, wilted – a candlewick on whom grief burnt like a flame.

The sight of her induced a momentary rush of panic. Emotion of any kind inspired fear in him, but none so much as grief: for several minutes after the train pulled in he was literally unable to rise from his seat. It was not till the station master brandished his green flag that he started for the door.

Stepping out of the train, Dinu tried to recall the phrases of condolence he had rehearsed in preparation for this moment. But now, with Alison approaching across the platform, the idea of consolation seemed like an impossible impertinence. It would be kinder, surely, to behave as though nothing had happened?

'You shouldn't have come,' he said gruffly, dropping his eyes. 'I would have found a taxi.'

'I was glad to come,' she said. 'It's nice to have a break from Morningside.'

'Still.' Hefting his leather camera cases on his shoulders, he handed his suitcase to a porter.

She smiled. 'Is your father better?'

'Yes,' Dinu said stiffly. 'He's fine now . . . and Manju and Neel are expecting a baby.'

'That's good news.' She gave him a smile and a nod.

They stepped out of the station into a compound that was shaded by an immense, dome-like tree. Dinu stopped to look up. From the tree's moss-wrapped branches there hung a colourful array of creepers and wildflowers.

'Why,' said Dinu, 'isn't that a padauk tree?'

'We call them angsana trees here,' Alison said. 'My father planted this one the year I was born.' She paused. 'The year we were born I should have said.'

'Why yes . . . of course . . . we were born the same year.' Dinu smiled, hesitantly, surprised both by the fact that she'd remembered and that she'd chosen to comment on it.

The Daytona was parked nearby, with its hood pulled up. Alison slipped into the driver's seat, while Dinu saw to the loading of his luggage in the back. They drove out of the station and past the main marketplace with its long arcades of tiled shophouses. On the outskirts of town they passed a field that was ringed with barbed-wire fencing. At the centre of the field there stood several orderly rows of *attap* huts, roofed with sheets of corrugated iron.

'What's this?' Dinu asked. 'I don't remember any of this . . .'

'It's our new miltary base,' said Alison. 'Sungei Pattani has a big army presence now, because of the war. There's an airstrip in there and it's guarded by Indian soldiers.'

The road began to climb and Gunung Jerai reared up ahead, its peak obscured by the usual daytime heat haze. Dinu sank back in his seat, framing the mountain in an imaginary lens. Alison's voice took him by surprise.

'Do you know what the hard part is?'

'No – what is it?'

'Nothing has any shape.'

'What do you mean?'

'It's something you don't see until it's gone – the shapes that things have and the ways in which the people around you mould

327

those shapes. I don't mean the big things – just the little ones. What you do when you get up in the morning – the hundreds of thoughts that run through your head while you're brushing your teeth: "I have to tell Mummy about the new flowerbed" – that sort of thing. Over the last few years I'd started to take over a lot of the little things that Daddy and Mummy used to do at Morningside. Now, when I wake up in the morning those things still come back to me in just that way – I have to do this or that, for Mummy or for Daddy. Then I remember, No, I don't have to do any of those things; there's no reason to. And in an odd way, what you feel at those moments is not exactly sadness but a kind of disappointment. And that's awful too, for you say to yourself – is this the best I can do? No: this isn't good enough. I should cry – everyone says it's good to cry. But the feeling inside doesn't have an easy name: it's not exactly pain or sorrow – not right then. It feels more like the sensation you have when you sit down very heavily in a chair: the breath rushes out of your body and you find yourself gagging. It's hard to make sense of it – any of it. You want the pain to be simple, straightforward – you don't want it to ambush you in these roundabout ways, each morning, when you're getting up to do something else – brush your teeth or eat your breakfast . . .'

The car veered suddenly towards the side of the road. Dinu snatched at the wheel to steady it. 'Alison! Slow down – careful.'

She ran the car on to the grassy verge that flanked the road and stopped under a tree. Raising her hands, she touched her cheeks in a gesture of disbelief. 'Look,' she said. 'I'm crying.'

'Alison.' He wanted to reach for her, touch her shoulder, but it was not like him to be demonstrative. She lowered her forehead to the wheel, sobbing, and then suddenly his hesitations evaporated.

'Alison.' He drew her head to his shoulder, and felt the warmth of her tears dampening the thin cotton of his shirt. Her hair was silky against his cheek and smelt faintly of grapes. 'Alison, it's all right . . .'

He was struck by a deep astonishment at what he had done. It was as though someone had reminded him that gestures of this kind did not come naturally to him. The arm that was holding her cradled against his shoulder grew heavy and wooden and he found himself mumbling awkwardly: 'Alison . . . I know it's been hard . . .'

He was cut short by the roar of a fifteen-hundredweight truck, rolling down the road. Alison pulled quickly away and sat upright. Dinu turned as the truck rumbled by. A squad of Indian soldiers was squatting in the back of the truck, dressed in turbans and khaki shorts.

The sound of the truck faded away and the moment passed. Alison wiped her face and cleared her throat. 'Time to go home,' she said, turning the ignition key. 'You must be tired.'

It was mid-February when the long-awaited mobilisation orders finally arrived. Hardy was one of the first to know and he came running to Arjun's room.

'Yaar – have you heard?'

It was early evening and Hardy didn't bother to knock. He pushed the door open and looked in: 'Arjun, where are you?'

Arjun was inside the curtained dressing room that separated his bathroom from the living area. He had just finished washing off the dirt of a football match and his mud-caked shoes and shorts lay heaped on the floor. It was a Thursday – a night when, by tradition, dinner jackets were worn at the mess, this being the day of the week when the news of Queen Victoria's death had been received in India. Kishan Singh was at work in Arjun's bedroom, laying out his clothes for the evening – dinner jacket, dress trousers, silk cummerbund.

Hardy crossed the room quickly: 'Arjun? Did you hear? We've got the orders.'

Arjun pulled back the curtain, with a towel fastened around his waist.

'You're sure?'

'Yes. Heard from Adjutant-sah'b. '

They looked at each other without knowing what else to say. Hardy seated himself on the edge of the bed and began to crack his knuckles. Arjun started to button his starched dress shirt, flexing his knees, so that he could see himself in the mirror. He caught a glimpse of Hardy behind him, staring morosely at the floor. Trying to sound jocular, he said: 'At least we'll get to see if those

329

damned mobilisation plans that we drew up are any good or not . . .'

Hardy made no answer, and Arjun glanced over his shoulder. 'Aren't you glad the waiting's over? Hardy?'

Hardy's hands were clasped between his knees. He looked up suddenly. 'I keep thinking . . .'

'Of what?'

'Do you remember Chetwode Hall? At the Military Academy in Dehra Dun?'

'Of course.'

'There was an inscription which said: *The safety, honour and welfare of your country come first, always and every time. The honour, welfare and comfort of the men you command come next . . .*'

'*. . . And your own ease, comfort and safety come last, always and every time.*' Arjun laughed as he finished the quotation for Hardy. 'Of course I remember. It was inscribed on the podium – stared us in the face every time we entered Chetwode Hall.'

'Didn't it ever puzzle you – that inscription?'

'No. Why should it?'

'Well, didn't you ever think: this country whose safety, honour and welfare are to come first, always and every time – what is it? Where is this country? The fact is that you and I don't have a country – so where is this place whose safety, honour and welfare are to come first, always and every time? And why was it that when we took our oath it wasn't to a country but to the King Emperor – to defend the Empire?'

Arjun turned to face him. 'Hardy, what are you trying to get at?'

'Just this,' said Hardy. 'Yaar, if my country really comes first, why am I being sent abroad? There's no threat to my country right now – and if there were, it would be my duty to stay here and defend it.'

'Hardy,' Arjun said lightly, 'staying here wouldn't do much for your career . . .'

'Career, career.' Hardy clicked his tongue, in disgust. 'Yaar, don't you ever think of anything else?'

'Hardy.' Arjun gave him a look of warning, to remind him of Kishan Singh's presence.

Hardy shrugged and looked at his watch. 'All right, I'll shut up,' he said, standing up to go. 'I'd better change too. We'll talk later.'

Hardy left and Kishan Singh carried Arjun's trousers into the dressing room. Kneeling on the floor, he held them open, by the waistband. Arjun stepped into them gingerly, taking care not to shatter the fragile sharpness of their glassy creases. Rising to his feet, Kishan Singh began to circle around Arjun, tucking his shirt-tails into his trousers.

Kishan Singh's hand brushed against the small of Arjun's back and he stiffened: he was on the verge of snapping at his batman to hurry up, when he stopped himself. It annoyed him to think that after two years as a commissioned officer he had still not succeeded in training himself to be at ease with the enforced intimacies of military life. This was one of the many things, he knew, that set him apart from the real faujis, the born-and-bred army-wallahs like Hardy. He'd once watched Hardy going through this very process of dressing for Guest Night with his batman's help: he was oblivious of the man's presence in a way that he, Arjun, never was of Kishan Singh's.

Suddenly Kishan Singh spoke up, taking Arjun by surprise. 'Sah'b,' he said, 'do you know where the battalion is going?'

'No. Nobody does. We won't know till we're on the ship.'

Kishan Singh started wrapping Arjun's cummerbund around his waist. 'Sah'b,' he said, 'the NCOs have been saying that we'll be going east . . .'

'Why?'

'At first we were training for the desert and everyone said we would be going to North Africa. But the equipment we were sent recently was clearly meant for the rain . . .'

'Who's been telling you all this?' Arjun said in surprise.

'Everyone, sah'b. Even in the villages they know. My mother and my wife came to visit last week. They'd heard a rumour that we were about to leave.'

'What did they say?'

'My mother said, "Kishan Singh, when are you going to come back?"'

'And what did you tell her?'

Kishan Singh was kneeling in front of Arjun now, checking his fly buttons and smoothing down his trousers, pinching the creases to restore their edge. Arjun could see only the top of his head, and the whorled patterns of his close-cropped hair.

Suddenly, Kishan Singh looked up at him. 'Sah'b, I told her that you would make sure that I came back . . .'

Arjun, caught by surprise, felt the blood rushing to his face. There was something inexplicably moving about the sheer guilelessness of this expression of trust. He felt at a loss for words.

Once, during their conversations at Charbagh, Lieutenant-Colonel Buckland had said that the reward of serving in India, for Englishmen of his father's generation, lay in their bonds with 'the men'. This relationship, he had said, was of an utterly different kind from that of the regular British army, the mutual loyalties of Indian soldier and English officer being at once so powerful and so inexplicable that they could be understood only as a kind of love.

Arjun recalled how strange this word had sounded on the CO's reticent lips and how he had been tempted to scoff. It seemed that in these stories 'the men' figured only as abstractions, a faceless collectivity imprisoned in a permanent childhood – moody, unpredictable, fantastically brave, desperately loyal, prone to extraordinary excesses of emotion. Yet, he knew it to be true that even for himself there were times when it seemed as though the attributes of that faceless collectivity – 'the men' – had been conjured into reality by a single soldier, Kishan Singh: that the bond that had come into being between them really was a kind of love. It was impossible to know how far this was Kishan Singh's own doing and how far it was the product of the peculiar intimacy of their circumstances; or was it perhaps something else altogether, that Kishan Singh, in his very individuality, had become more than himself – a village, a country, a history, a mirror for Arjun to see refractions of himself?

For an eerie instant Arjun saw himself in Kishan Singh's place: as a batman, kneeling before a dinner-jacketed officer, buffing his shoes, reaching into his trousers to tuck in his shirt, checking his fly buttons, looking up from the shelter of his parted feet, asking for protection. He gritted his teeth.

Twenty-eight

The morning after his arrival, Dinu borrowed a bicycle and went to look for the ruined chandis of Gunung Jerai. Alison drew him a map and he followed it: the track ran uphill most of the way from Morningside House and he had to mount and dismount several times, wheeling his machine up the steeper inclines. He made a couple of wrong turns but eventually found his way to the very spot where Alison had parked her car the last time. The stream lay below and its surroundings were exactly as he remembered: there was a shallow ford, bridged by flat stones. A little lower down the slope, the stream widened into a pool, ringed by massive boulders. On the far side, a narrow path led into the jungle.

By this time his right leg was sore and aching. He hung his camera bags on a branch and stepped down to the pool. On the bank there was a boulder that was so shaped as to serve perfectly for a seat. Dinu kicked off his shoes, rolled his trousers up to his knees, and plunged his legs into the cool, rushing water.

He'd been hesitant about coming to Malaya, but now that he was here, he was glad to be away from Rangoon, glad to leave behind the tensions of the Kemedine house and all the constant worrying about the business. And it was a relief, too, to put a distance between himself and the political infighting that seemed to be consuming all his friends. He knew his father wanted Alison to sell Morningside – it would be too much for her to manage on her own, he'd said; the estate would lose money. But as far as he could tell Morningside was running smoothly enough and Alison seemed to be very much in control. He couldn't see that she had any need for his advice, but he was glad to be here anyway. It would give him a chance to think things over for himself: in Rangoon he was always too busy, with politics, with the magazine. He was twenty-eight now and this, if any, was the time to decide whether photography was going to be just a hobby or a career.

He lit a cigarette and smoked it down to the butt, before picking up his camera bag to cross the stream. The path was more over-grown than he remembered, and in places he had to beat down the undergrowth. When he came to the clearing, he was awed by the serene beauty of the place: the colours of the moss-covered chandis were even more vivid than he remembered; the vistas in the background even more sweeping. He wasted no time in setting up his tripod. He exposed two rolls and it was sunset by the time he got back to Morningside House.

He went back the next morning and the morning after that. The ride became a regular routine: he'd set off early, taking along a couple of rotis for lunch. When he got to the stream, he'd daydream for a while, sitting on his favourite rock, with his legs plunged deep in the water. Then he'd make his way to the clearing and set up his equipment. At lunchtime he'd take a long break and afterwards he'd have a nap, lying in the shade in one of the chandis.

One morning, instead of stopping at the chandis, he went a little further than usual. Pushing into the forest he spotted an overgrown mound a short distance ahead. He beat a path through the undergrowth and found himself confronted with yet another ruin, built of the same materials as the two chandis – laterite – but of a different design: this one was roughly octagonal and shaped like a stepped pyramid or ziggurat. Despite the monumen-tal design, the structure was modest in size, not much taller than his head. He climbed gingerly up the mossy blocks and at the apex he found a massive square stone, with a rectangular opening carved in the centre. Looking down, he found a puddle of rain-water trapped inside. The pool had the even shape and metallic glint of an antique mirror. He took a picture – a snapshot – and then sat down to smoke a cigarette. What was the opening for? Had it once been a base for a monumental sculpture – some gigantic, smiling monolith? It didn't matter: it was just a hole now, colonised by a family of tiny green frogs. When he looked down on his rippling reflection the frogs croaked at him in deep affront.

That evening, back at the house, he said to Alison: 'Did you know that there was another ruin – a kind of pyramid – a little farther into the jungle?'

She nodded. 'Yes, and there are others too. You'll find them if you go deep enough.'

The next day proved her right. Pushing a little further up the slope Dinu stumbled, quite literally, on a ten-foot-square platform made of laterite blocks – apparently the foundation of a small shrine. The plan of the temple was clearly visible on the floor, laid out like an architect's sketch, with a line of square embrasures indicating the placement of a row of columns. A day or so later he found another, much stranger ruin: a structure that had the appearance of being suspended within an explosion, like a prop in a photographic illusion. A banyan had taken root within the temple, and in growing, had pushed the walls apart, carrying away adjoining blocks of masonry. A doorway had been split in two, as though a bomb had exploded on the threshold. One stone post had been knocked over, while another had been carried off, coiled in a tangle of greenery, to a distance of several feet off the ground.

Sometimes, stepping into the ruins, Dinu would hear a rustle or a prolonged hiss. Occasionally the surrounding treetops would stir as though they'd been hit by a gust of wind. Dinu would look up to see a troop of monkeys examining him warily from the branches. Once he heard a sawing cough that could have been a leopard.

As his intimacy with the ruins deepened, Dinu began to find that his eye would go directly to the place where the temple's principal image would once have stood: his hands would reach automatically for the niches where offerings of flowers would have been laid; he began to recognise the limits beyond which he could not step without removing his shoes. When he crossed the stream, after bicycling through the estate, it was no longer as though he were tiptoeing into a place that was strange and unfamiliar, where life and order yielded to darkness and shadow. It was when he crossed back into the monochrome orderliness of the plantation that he felt himself to be passing into a territory of ruin, a defilement much more profound than temporal decay.

Late one afternoon, while standing at his tripod, he was alerted to the sound of a car by a commotion among the jungle's birds. He made his way quickly down the path to a vantage point where a gap in the greenery permitted a view of the stream below. He spotted Alison's red Daytona approaching on the far side. He left his tripod standing where it was and went hurrying down the path.

Dinu had seen very little of Alison since the day of his arrival. She left the house before dawn, in order to be present at Muster, and when she came back, he was usually out on the mountainside taking pictures. They generally met only at dinnertime, when conversation was inevitably constrained by Saya John's vacant silences. She seemed not to know how to fit a visitor into the fixed routines of her life on the plantation, and Dinu, for his part, was burdened by the knowledge of the task with which he had been entrusted. He knew that he would have to find a way of telling her that his father wanted to dispose of his share of Morningside and this seemed impossible at a time when she was so preoccupied, both with the grief of her parents' death, and with the daily anxieties of keeping the plantation afloat.

By the time Dinu reached the end of the path Alison had crossed the stream. Finding himself face to face with her now, he couldn't think of what to say and began to fumble in his pockets for a cigarette.

'Going back to the house?' he said at last, through his teeth, while striking a match.

'I thought I'd come by and see how you were getting on.'

'I was just setting up my camera . . .' He walked with her to the clearing, where his tripod was placed in front of one of the chandis.

'Can I watch you take pictures?' she asked brightly.

He hesitated, raising the cigarette to his mouth, squinting into the smoke. As though sensing a reluctance, Alison said: 'Would you mind? Would I be bothering you?'

'No,' he said. 'It's not that . . . you wouldn't be bothering me exactly . . . It's just that when I'm shooting I have to concentrate very hard . . . or it's a waste . . . It's like any other kind of work, you know . . . it's not easy to do if you're being watched.'

'I see.' The hollow sound of her voice indicated that she'd read this as a rebuff. 'Well, I'll go then.'

'No,' he said quickly, 'please stay . . . but then, if you're going to be here, could I take a few pictures of you . . . ?'

She was quick to deal out a rebuff of her own. 'No. I'm not really in the right frame of mind to become a part of your – your work.' She turned on her heel and headed down the path, towards the stream.

Dinu knew himself to be stranded unwittingly in a quarrel.

'Alison . . . I didn't mean . . .' He hurried after her, but she was walking fast and his leg put him at a disadvantage. 'Alison . . . please stay.' He caught up with her at the edge of the stream. 'Alison . . . I was just telling you what it's like . . . when I make a picture . . . I didn't mean to put you off . . . won't you stay?'

'Not now,' she glanced at her watch. 'Not today.'

'Then you'll come back?'

She'd already started across the ford. In mid-stream, without turning round, she raised a hand to wave.

Just before the battalion's departure from Saharanpur, new war equipment tables arrived. This meant that Arjun and Hardy had to stay up all night, revising their carefully-prepared Unit Mobilisation Scheme. But in the end all was well: the CO was pleased and the battalion was able to go ahead with its entrainment as planned. The train left for Bombay on schedule.

At Ajmer there was a slight delay. The 1/1 Jats were shunted aside so that a trainload of Italian prisoners of war could pass by. The Italians and Indians stared at each other in silence across the platform, through the barred windows of their respective carriages. This was their first glimpse of the enemy.

Next morning, they arrived at Bombay's Victoria terminus. They were told that their troop ship, the H.M.T. *Nuwara Eliya*, was waiting at the harbour. They drove to the Sassoon docks to find that their embarkation orders had already been issued.

The docks proved to be unexpectedly congested. It turned out that a British battalion was boarding another ship at exactly the same time. Soon the two battalions' baggage and equipment were hopelessly entangled with each other. NCOs began to shout, spreading panic among the dockworkers. Hardy was thrown into the midst of the confusion: he was the baggage officer for the 1/1 Jats and it fell on him to try and restore order.

Looking in Hardy's roster, Arjun learnt that he had been allotted a cabin to himself. He had never been on a ship before and was barely able to contain his excitement. He went hurrying up the gangplank to look for his cabin, with Kishan Singh following close behind, carrying his luggage.

They were the first to board and the ship was empty, but for its crew. Everything seemed new and startling: the white gunwales and narrow catwalks, the yawning hatches and the rounded frames of the portholes.

As they were stepping on to the upper deck, Kishan Singh happened to glance over the side. 'Sah'b – look!' He pointed, drawing Arjun's attention to an altercation on the docks below. Arjun saw that Hardy had got himself into a shouting match with a hulking British sergeant. They were standing toe to toe, with Hardy shaking a sheaf of papers under the sergeant's nose.

'Stay here.'

Arjun went racing down the way he had come. He arrived on the scene just a moment too late. Another officer from their battalion had got there before him – Captain Pearson, the adjutant, a bluff, stocky Englishman, with a booming voice and a quick temper.

Watching from a few paces away, Arjun saw Hardy turning to Captain Pearson. It was clear that Hardy was relieved to see the adjutant, fully confident that his senior would back him up – out of loyalty to a fellow-member of the battalion, if nothing else. But Captain Pearson had never made a secret of his belief that Hardy was 'difficult' and 'overly sensitive'. Instead of supporting him,

338

he let his annoyance show: 'Lieutenant, have you got yourself into a row again . . . ?'

Arjun saw the look on Hardy's face change from relief to seething outrage. It was painful to stand there as a silent witness to his friend's humiliation. He turned and slipped away.

Later that day, Hardy came to his cabin.

'We've got to teach that bastard Pearson a lesson,' he said. 'That bloody sergeant called me a stinking nigger in front of the men. Pearson let him get away with it. Yaar, would you believe it, the bugger blamed me! The only way we can stop this kind of thing is by sticking together.'

'What exactly do you mean?'

'I think we should boycott him.'

'He's the adjutant, Hardy,' Arjun said. 'How can we boycott him? Be reasonable.'

'There are ways of getting a message across,' Hardy said angrily. 'But that can happen only when you know which side you're on.' Rising abruptly to his feet, he left Arjun's cabin.

For two days the *Nuwara Eliya* waited offshore, while nine other ships assembled in the harbour. There was a rumour that a German submarine was lurking nearby and the ships were assigned an escort of two destroyers, an armed merchantman and a light cruiser. When the convoy finally departed, it was in a westerly direction, heading towards the setting sun. Their destination was still unknown; they had no idea whether they were to go east or west.

In Bombay, the CO had been handed a sealed envelope that was to be opened exactly twenty-four hours after their departure. When the time came, Arjun and the other officers gathered in a dining room on the *Nuwara Eliya*'s upper deck. The CO opened the envelope in his usual deliberate way, prising the seal off the paper with a knife. The officers waited in expectant silence. Arjun could feel a clammy dampness welling up in the palms of his hands.

Then at last, the CO looked up with a thin smile. He held the sheet of paper in front of him and read out aloud: 'This ship is headed for Singapore.'

Arjun stepped out on deck and found Hardy already there,

leaning over the gunwale, humming softly under his breath. Behind them the white ribbon of the ship's wake had already begun to describe a curve as the convoy slowly changed direction.

Twenty-nine

Manju had never been happier than she was in the first months of her pregnancy. She relished every reminder of her changing condition: the often imaginary twitches and movements; the pangs of hunger that could never be properly satisfied; even the nausea that woke her every morning and the acid tingling of her teeth.

The Kemendine house had changed greatly in the two years she'd been in Rangoon. Dinu was gone of course, and his apartment upstairs lay empty. Neel and Rajkumar were often away, arranging for the disposal of the family's properties or buying new stocks of teak. For much of the time Manju and Dolly had the house to themselves. The compound had grown unkempt; where there had once been a lawn the grass now stood knee-high. Many rooms and outhouses were locked up; much of the furniture had been sold. The dozens of employees who had once populated the place were gone – the servants, watchmen, gardeners and their families. Even U Ba Kyaw, the chauffeur, had gone back to his village. The Packard was one of the few disposable possessions that Rajkumar had retained, but it was now driven mainly by Neel.

Neither Manju nor Dolly regretted the emptying of the house. On the contrary, it was as though an enormous accumulation of cobwebs had been swept away, allowing them new and unaccustomed freedoms. In the past Dolly had often seemed remote and unapproachable to Manju, but now they became allies, colleagues, team-mates, working together for the family's renewal. Between the two of them they had little difficulty in managing the house.

On waking in the morning, Manju would find Dolly on her knees, dressed in a frayed old longyi, wiping the floors with tattered shreds of cloth. They would work together, going through a couple of rooms each day, breaking off when the monks came by for their daily visits.

For Manju these mid-morning breaks were the best-loved aspect of daily life in Rangoon. She'd always known that Buddhist monks lived by collecting alms, but it came as a surprise to observe the ways in which this tenet, more or less abstract, came to be translated into the mundane mechanics of everyday life – into the workaday reality of a tired-looking group of young men and boys, walking down a dusty street in saffron robes, with their baskets balanced on their hips. There was something magical about the fact that this interruption came always at a time of day when the tasks of the household were at their most pressing; when there was scarcely room in one's head but to think about what had to be done next. And in the midst of all that – to open the door and see the monks standing there, waiting patiently, with the sun beating down on their shaven heads: what better way could there be of unbalancing everyday reality?

Calcutta seemed very far away now. The flow of letters from India had suffered disruptions because of the threat of submarines in the Bay of Bengal. Steamer traffic between Calcutta and Rangoon had become so irregular that letters tended to arrive in bunches.

One such bunch brought news both of Arjun's impending departure and of his arrival in Malaya. Dolly was very glad to hear of this development: 'Perhaps Arjun could find out what's become of Dinu,' she said. 'It's a long time since we last heard from him.'

'Yes, of course. I'll write . . .'

Manju sent a letter to the address her father had provided – via army headquarters in Singapore. Many weeks went by without an answer.

'Don't worry,' Manju said to Dolly. 'I'm sure Dinu's fine. We'd have heard if anything was wrong.'

'You're probably right.' But a month passed and then another and Dolly seemed to become resigned to her son's continuing silence.

The baby was now kicking urgently against the walls of Manju's stomach and she had no attention to spare for anything other than her own condition. With the approach of the monsoons, the days grew hotter and the effort of carrying the child grew very much greater. Sooner than they had expected, the festival of Waso was upon them. Dolly took Manju on a drive into the countryside in a taxi rented for the day. They stopped in a wooded area off the Pegu road, and collected armloads of fragrant yellow padauk flowers. They were on their way back to Rangoon when Manju had a dizzy spell and fainted on the back seat.

After this episode the doctor confined Manju to bed. Dolly became her nurse, bringing her food, helping with her clothes, occasionally leading her around the compound. The days went by in a kind of trance; Manju would lie dreamily in bed, with a book beside her, open but unread. Hours would pass while she did nothing but listen to the sound of the pouring rain.

They were now well into Thadin – the annual three-month period of reflection and abstinence. Often Dolly would read to Manju, mainly from the scriptures – from such translations as she could find, since Manju knew neither Pali nor Burmese. One day Dolly chose a discourse by the Buddha, addressed to his son, Rahula.

She read: *Develop a state of mind like the earth, Rahula, for on the earth all manner of things are thrown, clean and unclean, dung and urine, spittle, pus and blood, and the earth is not troubled or repelled or disgusted . . .*

Manju watched her mother-in-law as she read: Dolly's long, black hair was slightly flecked with grey and her face was etched with a webbing of lines. Yet, there was a youthfulness in her expression that belied these signs of age: it was hard to believe that this was a woman in her mid-sixties.

. . . develop a state of mind like water, for in the water many things are thrown, clean and unclean, and the water is not troubled or repelled or disgusted. And so too with fire, which burns all things, clean and unclean, and with air, which blows upon them all, and with space, which is nowhere established . . .

Dolly's lips seemed hardly to move, and yet every word was perfectly enunciated: Manju had never before known anyone who

343

could appear to be in repose when she was actually at her most intently wakeful, her most alert.

When Manju reached the eighth month of her pregnancy Dolly banned Neel from any further travels. He was at home when Manju's labour started. He helped her into the Packard and drove her to the hospital. They could no longer afford the private suite that Dolly and Rajkumar had taken before, and instead Manju went into the general maternity ward. The next evening she was delivered of her child – a healthy, sharp-voiced girl, who began to suckle the moment she was put to Manju's breast. The baby was given two names – Jaya was to be her Indian name and Tin May the Burmese.

Exhausted by her labour Manju fell asleep. It was dawn when she woke up. The baby was in her bed again, rooting hungrily for her feed.

Holding her daughter to her breast, Manju remembered a passage that Dolly had read to her just a few days before: it was from the Buddha's first sermon, delivered at Sarnath, two thousand and five hundred years before: . . . *birth is sorrow, age is sorrow, disease is sorrow, death is sorrow; contact with the unpleasant is sorrow, separation from the pleasant is sorrow, every wish unfulfilled is sorrow* . . .

The words had made a great impression on her at the time, but now, with her newborn daughter beside her, they seemed incomprehensible: the world had never seemed so bright, so replete with promise, so profligate in its rewards, so generous in its joys and fulfilments.

For their first few weeks in Singapore the 1/1 Jats were based at the Tyersall Park camp. This was the very place that Arjun's friend Kumar had talked about – where a soldier had shot an officer and then committed suicide. In New Delhi the story had sounded unlikely and far-fetched – an extreme situation – like a report of a mother lifting up a car to save her children. But now that they were in Singapore themselves, with India half a continent away, nothing seemed improbable any more – everything appeared to be turned on its head. It was as though they no longer knew who they were, no longer understood their place in the order of things. Whenever they ventured beyond the familiar certainties of the battalion, they seemed to lose themselves in a labyrinth of hidden meanings.

It so happened that Kumar was in Singapore when the 1/1 Jats first arrived. One afternoon he took Arjun and Hardy to an exclusive club, for a swim. The pool was very crowded, filled with European expatriates and their families. It was a hot sticky day and the water looked cool and inviting. Following Kumar's lead, Arjun and Hardy jumped in. Within a few minutes they found themselves alone: the pool had emptied as soon as they entered the water.

Kumar was the only one who was not taken aback. His battalion had been in Malaya more than a year and he had travelled all round the colony.

'I should have warned you about this,' Kumar said, with a mischievous smile. 'It's like this everywhere in Malaya. In smaller towns, the clubs actually put up signs on their doors saying, "No Asiatics allowed". In Singapore they let us use the pool – it's just that everyone leaves. Right now they've had to relax the colour bar a little because there are so many Indian army units here. But you may as well get used to it because you'll come across it all the time – in restaurants, clubs, beaches, trains.' He laughed. 'We're meant to die for this colony – but we can't use the pools.' Ruefully shaking his head he lit a cigarette.

Soon their battalion was sent north. The Malayan countryside was a revelation to the Indian officers. They had never seen such prosperity, such beautiful roads, such tidy, well-laid-out little towns. Often, when they stopped, the local Indian residents would invite them to their houses. These were usually middle-class people with modest jobs – provincial lawyers and doctors, clerks and shopkeepers. But the signs of affluence in their homes were such as to amaze Arjun and his fellow-soldiers. It seemed that in Malaya even ordinary people were able to afford cars and refrigerators: some even had air conditioners and telephones. In India only Europeans and the richest of rich Indians could afford such things.

Driving along rural roads, the officers discovered that in Malaya the only people who lived in abject, grinding poverty were plantation labourers – almost all of whom were Indian in origin. They were astonished at the difference between the plantations' ordered greenery and the squalor of their coolie lines. Hardy once remarked on the starkness of the contrast and Arjun responded by pointing out that in India, they would have taken such poverty for granted; that the only reason they happened to notice it now was because of its juxtaposition with Malaya's prosperous towns. This thought made them both cringe in shame. It was as though they were examining their own circumstances for the first time, in retrospect; as though the shock of travel had displaced an indifference that had been inculcated in them since their earliest childhood.

Other shocks awaited. Out of uniform, Arjun and his friends found that they were often mistaken for coolies. In markets and bazaars shopkeepers treated them offhandedly, as though they were of no account. At other times – and this was worse still – they would find themselves being looked upon with something akin to pity. Once, Arjun got into an argument with a shopkeeper and found himself being called *Klang* – to his puzzlement. Later, enquiring about the meaning of this word, he discovered that it was a derogatory reference to the sound of the chains worn by the earliest Indian workers who were brought to Malaya.

Soon it seemed as though there was not a man in the battalion who had not found himself embroiled in an unsettling encounter of one kind or another. One evening, Kishan Singh was oiling Arjun's revolver, squatting on the floor, when he looked up suddenly. 'Sah'b,' he said to Arjun, 'can I ask you the meaning of an English word?'

'Yes. What is it?'

'*Mercenary* – what does it mean?'

'*Mercenary?*' Arjun started in surprise. 'Where did you hear this word?'

Kishan Singh explained that during one of their recent moves, their convoy of trucks had stopped at a roadside tea-stall, near the town of Ipoh. There were some local Indians sitting in the tea-stall. They had announced themselves to be members of a political group – the Indian Independence League. Somehow an argument had started. The civilians had told them that they – the 1/1 Jats – weren't real soldiers; they were just hired killers, mercenaries. A fight would have broken out, if the convoy hadn't got under way again. But later, when they were back on the road, they had begun to argue again – with each other this time – about the word mercenary and what it meant.

Arjun's instinct was to bark an order at Kishan Singh, telling him to shut up and get on with what he was doing. But by now he knew his batman well enough to be aware that an order would not deter him from looking for an answer to his question. Thinking quickly Arjun embarked on an explanation: mercenaries were merely soldiers who were paid for their work, he said. In this sense all soldiers, in all modern armies, were mercenaries. Hundreds of years ago soldiers had fought out of religious belief, or because of allegiance to their tribes, or to defend their kings. But those days were long past: now soldiering was a job, a profession, a career. Every soldier was paid and there was none who was not a mercenary.

This seemed to satisfy Kishan Singh, and he asked no more questions. But it was Arjun himself who now came to be troubled by the answer he had given his batman. If it was true (and it undoubtedly was) that all contemporary soldiers were mercenaries, then why did the word have the sting of an insult? Why did he feel himself smarting at its use? Was it because soldiering was not just a job after all, as he had taught himself to believe? That to kill without conviction violated some deep and unalterable human impulse?

One night he and Hardy stayed up late, discussing this subject over a bottle of brandy. Hardy agreed that it was hard to explain why it was so shameful to be called a mercenary. But it was he who eventually put his finger on it: 'It's because a mercenary's hands obey someone else's head; those two parts of his body have no connection with each other.' He paused to smile at Arjun: 'Because, yaar, in other words, a mercenary is a *buddhu*, a fool.'

Arjun refused to be drawn into Hardy's jocularity. He said: 'So are we mercenaries, do you think?'

Hardy shrugged. 'All soldiers are mercenaries today,' he said.

'In fact, why just stop with soldiers? In one way or another we're all a little like that woman you went to in Delhi – dancing to someone else's tune, taking money. There's not that much difference.' He tipped back his glass, with a laugh.

Arjun found an opportunity to take his doubts to Lieutenant-Colonel Buckland. He told him about the incident at the tea-stall and recommended that the other ranks' contacts with the local Indian population be more closely supervised. Lieutenant-Colonel Buckland heard him out patiently, interrupting only to nod assent: 'Yes, you're right, Roy, something must be done.'

But Arjun came away from this conversation even more disturbed than before. He had a feeling that the lieutenant-colonel could not understand why he was so outraged at being described as a 'mercenary'; in his voice there had been an undertone of surprise that someone as intelligent as Arjun could take offence at something that was no more than a statement of fact. It was as though the lieutenant-colonel knew something about him, that he, Arjun, either did not know or was not willing to recognise. Arjun was embarrassed now to think that he'd allowed himself to go off at the deep end. It was as though he were a child who'd taken umbrage at the discovery that he'd spoken prose all his life.

These experiences were so peculiar, so provocative of awkward emotions, that Arjun and the other officers could rarely bring themselves to speak of them. They had always known their country to be poor, yet they had never imagined themselves to be part of that poverty: they were the privileged, the elite. The discovery that they were poor too came as a revelation. It was as though a grimy curtain of snobbery had prevented them from seeing what was plainly before their eyes – that although they had never been hungry, they too were impoverished by the circumstances of their country; that such impressions as they'd had of their own wellbeing were delusions, compounded out of the unimaginable extremity of their homeland's poverty.

The strange thing was that even more than Arjun, it was the real faujis – the second- and third-generation army-wallahs – on whom these experiences had the most powerful effect. 'But your father and grandfather were here,' Arjun said to Hardy. 'It was they who helped in the colonisation of these places. They must

348

have seen some of the things that we've seen. Did they never speak of all this?'

'They didn't see things as we do,' Hardy said. 'They were illiterate yaar. You have to remember that we're the first generation of educated Indian soldiers.'

'But still, they had eyes, they had ears, they must occasionally have talked to local people?'

Hardy shrugged. 'The truth is yaar, they weren't interested; they didn't care; the only place that was real to them was their village.'

'How is that even possible . . . ?'

In the following weeks Arjun thought often of this: it was as though he and his peers had been singled out to pay the price of a monumental inwardness.

With every day that he spent on the mountainside Dinu could feel his pictures changing. It was as though his eyes were adjusting to unaccustomed lines of sight; as though his body were adapting to new temporal rhythms. His earliest pictures of the chandis were angular and densely packed, the frames filled with sweeping vistas. He saw the site as being replete with visual drama – the jungle, the mountain, the ruins, the thrusting vertical lines of the tree trunks juxtaposed against the sweeping horizontals of the distant sea – he laboured to cram all these elements into his frames. But the more time he spent on the mountain, the less the background seemed to matter. The vastness of the landscape had the effect of both shrinking and enlarging the forest-enclosed clearing in which the chandis stood: it became small and intimate, but saturated with a sense of time. Soon he could no longer see either the mountains or the forest or the sea. He found himself moving closer and closer to the chandis, following the grain of the laterite and the pattern of the moss that covered its surface; trying to find a way of framing the curiously voluptuous shapes of the toadstools that grew within the joins of the stone.

The rhythms of his work changed in ways that he could not fully control. Hours would go by before he made a single exposure; he would go back and forth dozens of times, between his camera and his subject; he began to stop his lens further and further down, experimenting with aperture settings that required exposures of several minutes at a time, even as much as half an hour. It was as though he were using his instrument to mimic the pinprick eyes of the lizards that sunned themselves on the chandis' floors.

Many times each day, inexplicable perturbations would sweep through the surrounding forests. Flocks of birds would rise screaming from the surrounding trees and go boomeranging through the skies, only to settle back in exactly the same spots from which they had risen. To Dinu each of these disturbances now seemed like an augury of Alison's arrival, and in listening for their causes – sometimes the backfiring of a truck on the estate, sometimes a plane coming in to land at the nearby airstrip – his senses came to achieve an uncannily close attunement to the sounds of the forest. Every time the trees were shaken alive, he would break away from his work, straining to catch the sound of the Daytona. Often he would go running down the path to the gap where he could look down on the ford. As the disappointments mounted, he grew steadily more impatient with himself: it was plain idiocy to imagine that she'd drive out this way again, considering the last time. And in any event, why come all the way here, when she would see him in the house at dinnertime?

But then one day there really was a glimmer of red on the far side of the stream and the Daytona really could be seen to be standing under a tree, half-obscured by a tangle of greenery. Dinu looked once more, incredulously, and spotted Alison. She was dressed in a dark-blue cotton frock, with a wide belt tied around her waist. But instead of making her way to the ford, she was heading downstream, to the very rock where he sat every morning, dangling his legs in the pool. He could tell from the practised way in which she seated herself – swinging her feet up and then pivoting around to plunge them into the water – that this was a familiar place, a spot where she often came to be alone.

As her feet slid beneath the water, her fingers picked at the hem of her skirt and pulled it back. The water rose past her ankles, to her knees, and with it her skirt rose too, slowly climbing the long line of her thigh. Now, to his surprise, he made the discovery that he was no longer looking at her directly, but through the

350

ground glass of his viewfinder, so that the image was partitioned from its surroundings and endowed with a startling clarity and vividness. The lines were clean, pure, beautiful – the curve of her thigh crossing his viewfinder diagonally, describing a gentle ellipsis.

She heard the click and looked up, startled, her fingers instantly loosening their grip on her skirt so that the fabric dropped into the water and ballooned around her, swirling in the current.

'Dinu?' she called out. 'Is that you?'

He had only this one chance now, he knew that, and he was powerless to stop himself. He stepped away from the gap and began to walk down the path, moving with the slow deliberation of a sleepwalker, holding his camera immobile in front of him.

'Dinu?'

He didn't try to answer but kept on moving, concentrating on the placing of one foot in front of the other, until he was clear of the greenery. From the far side of the pool, she looked into his eyes and swallowed back the words of greeting she'd been about to utter.

Dinu kept on walking. He dropped his camera on the grass and walked straight down the sandy bank, into the pool, directly across from the spot from where she sat. The water rose to his knees as he waded in, then to his groin, his hips, almost to his chest. The current began to tug at his clothes and his thin canvas shoes filled with sand and grit. He slowed to keep his footing, and then he saw her feet, hanging in the water, rippling in the current. He kept his eyes fixed on the shimmering flow and when his hands made contact with her legs he felt a deep breath rising from his lungs. It was the water that made this possible, he was sure of that; it was the stream that had washed away the barriers of fear and hesitation that had chained his hands before. He began to move his fingers, up the curve of her ankle, along the fine edge of her shin bone. Then his hands began to move on their own, pulling him behind them, between her parted knees, until suddenly her thighs were level with his face. It seemed the most natural thing in the world to follow his hands with his mouth, to move his lips along the elliptical line of her thigh, all the way along its length until the line parted. There he came to a stop, his face buried in her, his arms raised to shoulder height, holding her around her waist.

'Alison.'

She slid off the rock and stood neck deep in the water beside him. Taking his hand, she led him back through the pool, exactly the way he had come, to the other bank. They walked hand in hand, fully clothed and dripping wet, up the path that led to the ruined chandis. She took him through the clearing, up to a stone floor where a bed of moss lay thick on the laterite.

Then she reached for his hand and pulled him down.

Thirty

Neither Arjun nor anyone else in the 1/1 Jats knew quite what to expect when they arrived at Sungei Pattani. Before their departure from Ipoh they had been briefed – sketchily – on the problems they might encounter there. They knew that a mutiny had been narrowly averted just a few months before, but they were still unprepared for the cloud of disquiet that shrouded the base.

The troops at the Sungei Pattani base belonged to the 1st Bahawalpur Regiment. There had been a lot of friction between the battalion's officers and their English CO. Their CO had taken no pains to disguise his low opinion of his Indian officers: he'd been known to call them 'coolies' and to threaten them with his swagger stick. On one infamous occasion he had even kicked an officer. Things had got so bad that the GOC of the 11th Division had had to intervene personally; the CO had been relieved of his command and a number of officers had been sent home to India.

At their briefing the 1/1 Jats had been given to understand that these measures had substantially altered the situation; that the difficulties of the past had been resolved. But within a day of their arrival at Sungei Pattani it was evident that the troubles of the Bahawalpurs were far from over. Through the whole two hours of their first meal at the Bahawalpurs' mess hardly a word was exchanged between their British and Indian officers. And if the tensions in the Bahawalpurs' mess were clearly visible to Hardy and Arjun, they were certainly no less so to Lieutenant-Colonel Buckland. Over the next two days the Lieutenant-Colonel made a point of speaking to his officers individually, to let them know that fraternisation with the 1st Bahawalpurs would not be encouraged. In a way Arjun was glad. He knew this to be the right approach under the circumstances, and was more than ever grateful to have a commanding officer of the calibre and good sense of Lieutenant-Colonel Buckland. But the knowledge of this did not ease any of the small difficulties that arose in trying to avoid the Bahawalpurs' officers – some of whom were acquaintances from the academy.

Arjun had a room to himself, like all the officers of the 1/1 Jats. Their quarters, men and officers alike, consisted of attap huts – wooden barracks with palm-thatched roofs. These structures were mounted on pilings that were designed to keep out termites and damp. Yet, both insects and moisture figured large in the experience of living inside these barracks. The beds were frequently preyed upon by swarms of ants; after nightfall mosquitoes were so numerous that to climb out of bed for even a minute meant having to restring the whole mosquito net; the roofs often dripped and at night the rustling palm thatch seemed to come alive with rats and snakes.

Lieutenant-Colonel Buckland wanted the 1/1 Jats to use their time at Sungei Pattani on combat training, but circumstances conspired to confute all his plans. When they ventured into the surrounding rubber plantations the planters protested. Their attempts to acquaint the men with the terrain had to be called off. Then the medical corps began to complain about rising rates of malaria. As a result their plans for night training had to be cancelled. Frustrated in his more imaginative schemes, the CO set the battalion to a monotonous regimen of constructing fortifications around the base and the airstrip.

The airfield at Sungei Pattani consisted of just a single concrete runway and a few hangars, but it was still one of the few bases in north-western Malaya that boasted an operational air-squadron. The airmen at the base could on occasion be persuaded to provide joy-rides in their heavy-bellied Blenheims and Brewster Buffaloes. Arjun went on several of these rides, circling above the slopes of Gunung Jerai, looking down on the rubber plantations, swooping low over the grand houses and villas. At the summit of the mountain there stood a small lodge that served as a popular destination for holiday-makers. The pilots would often buzz the lodge, passing so close that the joy-riders could wave to the diners sitting at the tables on the veranda.

Through his first few weeks at Sungei Pattani Arjun had no idea that Dinu was living nearby. He was dimly aware that the Rahas owned shares in a rubber estate in Malaya, but he had no idea of where this plantation was. The first he knew of it was when he received a letter from Manju, posted in Rangoon.

Manju was unaware of her twin's exact location and knew only that he was somewhere in Malaya. She wrote to say that she was well and that her pregnancy was proceeding smoothly enough. But Neel and his parents were worried about Dinu: he'd gone over to Malaya several months before and hadn't been heard from for a while. They would be glad if Arjun would look him up. He was probably staying at the Morningside Estate with Alison, who had recently lost her parents. She provided a postal address.

Later in the day Arjun borrowed an Alvis staff car and drove into Sungei Pattani. He went to a Chinese restaurant where he and Hardy had eaten a couple of times. He asked for Ah Fatt, the proprietor, and showed him the address.

The proprietor took him outside into the shaded arcade and pointed across the street to a red roadster. That was Alison's car, he told Arjun, everyone in town knew it by sight. She had gone to her hairdresser's and would be out in a few minutes.

'There she is.'

She was wearing a *cheongsam* of black silk, with a slit that ran from her instep to her knee. Her hair framed her face like a polished helmet, its deep black sheen contrasting brightly with the soft glow of her skin.

It was several weeks since Arjun had spoken to a woman, and a very long time since he had beheld such a strikingly attractive face. He removed his cap and began to turn it over in his hands. He was just about to cross over, to introduce himself, when the red car pulled away from the shop and disappeared down the road.

*   *   *

Now the periodic disturbances of the mountainside did indeed become auguries of Alison's arrival. The rising of the birds from the canopy was a sure sign for Dinu to go hurrying down to the gap to look below – and often enough it really was Alison, dressed in one of the sombre black dresses that she wore to the office. Knowing that he'd be there, she'd look up and wave, and even as she was crossing the stream she'd begin to unbutton her blouse and unfasten her belt. Her clothes would be gone by the time she stepped into the clearing and he would be waiting, with his shutter primed.

It seemed that the hours he had spent attuning his eye to the mountainside had been an unconscious preparation for this – for Alison. He would spend long stretches of time thinking of where to place her, against which wall, or which part of the plinth; he'd imagine her seated upright, leaning against a lintel, one leg stretched straight in front of her and another bent back at the knee. In the gap between her legs he would glimpse a striation in the pitted surface of the laterite, or a soft mound of moss, as visual echoes of her body's fissures and curves. But the materiality of her presence would quickly disarrange these carefully imagined schemes. Once her body was placed where he wanted it, something would prove to be not quite right; he would frown into his square canvas of ground glass and go back to kneel beside her, sinking his fingertips softly into the tensile firmness of her thighs, teasing out minute changes in the angles of her limbs. Coaxing her legs further apart – or closer together – he would run a finger through the triangular swell of her pubis, sometimes combing the curls down, sometimes raking them back. Framed within the unnatural clarity of his viewfinder, these details seemed to assume a monumental significance: kneeling between her legs, he would wet his forefinger to draw a thin trail of moisture, a glistening hairline.

She would laugh at the intent seriousness with which he executed these intimate caresses, only to go hurrying back to his camera. When the reel was done, she would stop him before he could load another. 'No. Enough. Come here now.'

She would tug impatiently at his clothes – the shirt that was tucked carefully into his waistband, the undershirt beneath it.

'Why don't you just take these off when you come here – as I do?'

He would turn gruff. 'I can't, Alison . . . it's not my way . . .'

She would make him sit on the stone plinth and then peel away his shirt. Pushing him back, she would make him lie prone upon the stone. He would shut his eyes and knot his fingers under his head while she knelt between his legs. When his head cleared he would see her smiling at him, like a lioness looking up from a kill, mouth glistening. The lines were as perfect as any that could be imagined, the horizontal planes of her forehead, her eyebrows and her mouth, perfectly balanced by the verticals of her black, straight hair, and the translucent filaments that hung suspended from her lips.

She would see, reflected in his eyes, exactly what he beheld. Laughing out loud, she would say: 'No. This is a picture you'll never see anywhere but in your own head.'

Then afterwards, quickly but methodically, he would dress himself again, tucking his shirt carefully into his trousers, fastening his belt, kneeling to tie the laces of his canvas shoes.

'Why bother?' she'd challenge him. 'You'll just have to take them off again.'

He'd answer seriously, unsmiling: 'I have to, Alison . . . I have to be dressed when I work.'

Sometimes she would grow bored with the length of sitting. Often she would talk to herself while he was adjusting his camera, throwing in words of Malay, Tamil and Chinese, reminiscing about her mother and father, thinking aloud about Timmy.

'Dinu,' she cried one day in exasperation, 'I feel I have more of your attention when you're looking into your camera than when you're lying here with me.'

'And what's wrong with that?'

'I'm not just a thing, for your camera to focus on. Sometimes it's as if you have no other interest in me but this.'

He saw that she was upset and he left his tripod to sit with her. 'I see more of you in this way than I would in any other,' he said. 'If I were to talk to you for hours I wouldn't know you better. I don't say this is better than talking . . . it's just my way – my way of understanding . . . You mustn't think this is easy for me . . . I never do portraits; they frighten me . . . the intimacy . . . being in someone's company that long – I've never wanted to do them . . . nudes even less. These are my first and it's not easy.'

'Should I be flattered?'

'I don't know . . . but I feel my pictures have helped me know you . . . I think I know you better than I've ever known anyone.'

She laughed. 'Just because you've taken some pictures?'

'Not just that.'

'Then?'

'Because this is the most intimate way that I can know anyone . . . or anything.'

'Are you saying you wouldn't have known me if it weren't for your camera?'

He looked down at his hands, frowning. 'I can tell you this. If I hadn't spent this time with you, here, taking pictures . . . I wouldn't be able to say, with such certainty . . .'

'What?'

'That I'm in love with you.'

She sat up, startled, but before she could speak, Dinu continued, '. . . And I also know . . .'

'What?'

'That I want you to marry me.'

'Marry you!' She rested her chin on her knees. 'What makes you think I'd want to marry someone who can only talk to me through a camera?'

'Don't you then?'

'I don't know, Dinu.' She shook her head impatiently. 'Why marriage? Isn't this good enough?'

'Marriage is what I want – not just this.'

'Why spoil everything, Dinu?'

'Because I want it . . .'

'You don't know me, Dinu.' She smiled at him, running a hand over the back of his head. 'I'm not like you. I'm wilful, I'm spoilt: Timmy used to call me wayward. You'd hate me in a week if you were married to me.'

'I think that's for me to judge.'

'And what would we be marrying for? Timmy isn't here

358

and nor are my parents. You've seen how unwell my grand-father is.'

'But what if . . . ?' He leant over to place a hand on her belly. 'What if there's a child?'

She shrugged. 'We'll see then. For now – let's just be content with what we have.'

Without a single word being said on the subject, Dinu understood, soon after the time of their first meeting, that between himself and Ilongo there existed some sort of connection – a link that was known to Ilongo but of which he himself was unaware. This understanding arose gradually, out of their conversations, nur-tured by a pattern of questions and occasional oblique asides – by Ilongo's curiosity about the Raha house in Rangoon, by his interest in family photographs, by the manner in which his references to 'Your father' slowly metamorphosed so that the pronoun dis-appeared.

Dinu understood that he was being prepared, that when Ilongo judged it right he would let him know about whatever it was that lay between them. This awareness evoked strangely little curiosity in Dinu – and this was not merely because his attention was wholly claimed by Alison. It was also because of Ilongo himself – because there was something about him that was so transparently trustworthy that it caused Dinu no anxiety to concede to him his superior knowledge.

Except for Alison, Dinu saw more of Ilongo than of anyone else at Morningside: he was dependent on him for many small things – posting letters, cashing cheques, borrowing bicycles. When he decided to set up his own dark room, it was Ilongo who helped him find second-hand equipment in Penang.

One Sunday, Dinu accompanied Ilongo on his weekly trip to Sungei Pattani, with Saya John. They visited Ah Fatt's restaurant, where Saya John handed over an envelope, as always. 'I do it for my wife,' he told Dinu. 'She was Hakka you know, on both sides. She always said that I was Hakka too, except that no one could tell for sure, since I never knew my parents.'

Afterward Dinu and Ilongo drove Saya John to the Church of Christ the King, on the outskirts of town. The church was bright and cheerful-looking with a soaring white-washed steeple and a facade that was ornamented with polished wooden rails. Under the shade of a flowering tree, a colourfully-dressed congregation had gathered. A white-robed Irish priest led Saya John away, clapping him on the back: 'Mr Martins! And how are you today?'

Dinu and Ilongo went to the morning show at the cinema and saw Edward G. Robinson in *I am the Law*. On the way back, after collecting Saya John, they stopped at Ilongo's mother's house, for a bowl of noodles.

Ilongo's mother was near-sighted and prematurely bent. When Ilongo introduced him, Dinu could tell that she already knew exactly who he was. She asked him to come closer and touched his face with fingers that were cracked and callused. She said, in Hindustani, 'My Ilongo looks much more like your father than you do.'

In some region of his consciousness Dinu understood exactly what she was saying, but he responded to her words as though to a pleasantry. 'Yes, that's true. I can see the resemblance.'

Apart from this one charged moment, the visit went well. Saya John seemed unusually alert, almost his old self. They all ate several helpings of noodles and at the end of the meal, Ilongo's mother served thick, milky tea in glass tumblers. When they left, they were all aware – in a manner that was not in the least uncomfortable – that a visit that had begun as a meeting between strangers, had somehow changed, in tone and texture, to a family reunion.

On the way back to the house they sat three abreast in the truck, with Ilongo driving and Saya John in the middle. Ilongo looked visibly relieved, as though some sort of hurdle had been crossed. But Dinu found it hard to give shape to the thought that Ilongo might be his half-brother. A brother was what Neel was – a boundary to mark yourself off against. This was not what Ilongo was. If anything, Ilongo was an incarnation of his father – as he'd been in his youth, a far better man than the one whom he, Dinu, had known. There was some consolation in this.

It was on this night that Dinu mentioned his suspicions to Alison for the first time. She'd slipped into his room after dinner, as she sometimes did after settling her grandfather in his bed. At midnight she woke to see Dinu sitting by the window, smoking a cigarette. 'What's the matter, Dinu? I thought you were asleep.'

'Couldn't sleep.'

'Why not?'

Dinu told her about his visit to Ilongo's mother and what she had said. Then he looked straight into her eyes and asked: 'Tell me, Alison . . . am I imagining all this – or is there something to it?'

She shrugged and took a puff of his cigarette, without answering the question. So he asked again, more insistently: 'Is there any truth to this, Alison? You should tell me if you know . . .'

She said: 'I don't know, Dinu. There were always rumours. But nobody's ever said anything directly – not to me anyway. You know how it is – people don't talk about these things.'

'And you? Do you believe these . . . these rumours?'

'I didn't used to. But then Grandfather said something that made me change my mind.'

'What?'

'That your mother had asked him to look after Ilongo.'

'So she knows – my mother?'

'I think so.'

He lit another cigarette, in silence. Alison knelt beside him and looked into his face: 'Are you upset? Angry?'

He smiled, stroking her naked back. 'No. I'm not upset . . . and no angrier than I've always been. That's the strange thing really – knowing the kind of man my father is, it comes as no surprise. It just makes me want never to go back home . . .'

A few days later Alison sent up a letter that had just arrived. Dinu was working in his dark room and he broke off to look at the envelope: it was from Rangoon, from his father. Without another thought, he tore it up and went back to work.

That evening, after dinner, Alison asked: 'Dinu, did you get the letter?'

He nodded.

'It was from your father, wasn't it?'

'I suppose so.'

'Didn't you read it?'

'No. I tore it up.'

'Didn't you want to know what he was writing about?'

'I know what he was writing about.'

'What?'

'He wants to sell his share of Morningside . . .'

She paused and pushed her plate away. 'Is that what you want too, Dinu?'

'No,' he said. 'As far as I'm concerned, I'm going to be here for ever . . . I'm going to set up a studio in Sungei Pattani, and make a living from my camera. It's what I've always wanted to do – and this is as good a place as any to do it.'

Thirty-one

The night Ilongo brought Arjun to Morningside House, Dinu, Alison and Saya John were in the dining room, sitting at the long mahogany table. On the walls glowed the bamboo-shelled sconces that Elsa had designed. The room was filled with a rich, warm light.

Ilongo was smiling broadly, in anticipation of Dinu's surprise. 'Look who I've brought with me.' Then Arjun walked through the door, dressed in uniform, with his cap in his hands. His Sam Browne glistened in the golden glow of the bamboo sconces.

'Arjun?'

'Hello.' Arjun walked around the table and patted Dinu on the shoulder. 'Nice to see you, old chap.'

'But, Arjun . . .' Dinu stood up. 'What are you doing here?'

'I'll tell you soon enough,' Arjun said. 'But won't you introduce me first?'

'Oh yes. Of course.' Dinu turned to Alison. 'This is Arjun. Neel's brother-in-law – Manju's twin.'

'I'm so glad you came.' Alison leant over to Saya John and spoke softly into his ear. 'Grandfather, this is Dinu's brother-in-law,' she said. 'He's posted at the army base in Sungei Pattani.'

Now it was Arjun's turn to be surprised. 'How did you know I was posted at Sungei Pattani?'

'I saw you in town the other day.'

'Really? I'm amazed that you noticed.'

'Of course I noticed.' She threw back her head to laugh. 'In Sungei Pattani a stranger stands out.'

Dinu broke in. 'You didn't say anything to me, Alison . . .'

'I just saw a man in a uniform.' Alison laughed. 'How was I to know he was your brother-in-law?'

'I knew,' Ilongo said. 'I knew the moment I saw him.'

'He did.' Arjun nodded. 'I walked into the estate office to ask for Dinu. And before I'd even opened my mouth he said: "Aren't you Mister Neel's brother-in-law?" You could have knocked me over with a feather. I said: "How did you know?" and he said: "Mr Dinu showed me a picture – from your sister's wedding."'

'So I did.'

Dinu recalled that it was two years since he and Arjun had last met – in Calcutta. Arjun seemed to have grown in the meanwhile – or was it just that he had filled out his uniform? Even though Arjun had always been tall, Dinu could not remember ever feeling dwarfed in his presence as he did now.

'Well,' said Alison brightly. 'You must have something to eat – both you and Ilongo.'

The table was spread with dozens of small, colourful china bowls. Most of them still had their contents intact.

Arjun eyed the food with longing. 'A real meal, at last . . .'

'Why?' said Alison. 'Don't they feed you at your base?'

'They do their best I suppose.'

'There's plenty here for both of you,' Alison said. 'So sit down – Ilongo, you too. The cook's always complaining that we send the food back untouched.'

Ilongo shook his head. 'I can't stay . . .'

'Are you sure?'

'Yes. My mother will be waiting.'

Ilongo left and another place was laid at the table, next to Alison's. Arjun seated himself and Alison began to pile his plate with food.

'We call this *ayam limau purut* – chicken with lime leaves and tamarind; and here's some prawn sambal with screwpine leaves; and these are belacan brinjals; and over there is some chinchalok with chillies – shrimps, pickled in lime juice; and this here is fish steamed with ginger buds . . .'

'What a feast! And this was just an everyday dinner?'

'My mother was always very proud of her table,' Alison said. 'And now it's become a habit of the house.'

Arjun ate with gusto. 'This food is wonderful!'

'Your aunt Uma loved it too. Do you remember, Dinu? That time?'

'Yes I do.' Dinu nodded. 'I think I even have pictures.'

'I've never eaten anything like this,' Arjun said. 'What is it called?'

'It's Nyonya food,' Alison said. 'One of the world's last great secrets, my mother used to say.'

Suddenly Saya John spoke up, catching them all by surprise.

'It's the flowers that make the difference.'

'The flowers, Grandfather?'

Saya John looked at Arjun with eyes that were fleetingly clear. 'Yes – the flowers in the food. Bunga kentan and bunga telang – ginger flowers and blue flowers. They're what give the food its taste. That's what Elsa always says.'

A shadow passed over his face and his eyes grew cloudy again. He turned to Alison. 'We must remember to send Matthew and Elsa a telegram,' he said. 'They should stop in Malacca on the way back.'

Alison rose quickly from her chair. 'You must excuse us,' she said to Arjun. 'My grandfather is tired. I should take him up to bed.'

'Of course.' Arjun stood up.

Alison helped Saya John to his feet and led him slowly across the room. At the door, she turned to look back at Arjun. 'It's nice to have a visitor who likes our food – the cook's always saying that Dinu doesn't eat at all. She'll be delighted you enjoyed her cooking. You must come again.'

'I will.' Arjun grinned. 'You can be sure of that.'

There was a warmth and lightness in Alison's voice that Dinu hadn't heard before. Watching her from his place at the table, he was conscious of a sudden rush of jealousy.

'Well old chap,' said Arjun, in a booming, hearty voice, 'did you know that you've got everyone worried at home?'

'No.' Dinu flinched. 'And there's really no need to shout.' It was a struggle to muster the self-control to go on talking to Arjun.

'I'm sorry.' Arjun laughed. 'Didn't mean to put you out . . .'

'I'm sure you didn't.'

'I had a letter from Manju, you see – that's how I knew where to find you.'

'I see.'

'She said they hadn't heard from you in a while.'

'Oh?'

'What would you like me to tell them?'

Dinu raised his head with great deliberation. 'Nothing,' he said flatly. 'I'd like you to tell them nothing . . .'

Arjun raised an eyebrow. 'Can I ask why?'

'It's not very complicated.' Dinu shrugged. 'You see . . . my father sent me here because he wants to sell our share of Morningside.'

'And?'

'Now that I'm here . . . I've decided it wouldn't be a good idea.'

'You've grown to like the place I suppose?'

'It's not just that.' Dinu looked Arjun straight in the eye. 'It's Alison really.'

'What do you mean?'

'Well, you've met her . . .'

'Yes.' Arjun nodded.

'You probably know what I mean.'

'I think you're trying to tell me something, Dinu.' Arjun pushed his chair back from the table. 'Let me guess: are you saying you've fallen for her?' He laughed.

'Something like that.'

'I see. And do you think she's keen on you too?'

'I think so.'

'Hasn't she told you so?'

'Not . . . in so many words.'

'Hope you're right then.' Arjun laughed again and the light sparkled on his perfect teeth. 'I have to say I don't know if she's right for a chap like you – a woman like that.'

'It doesn't really matter, Arjun . . .' Dinu tried to smile. 'In my case it's something I have to believe . . .'

'And why is that?'

'You see – I'm not like you, Arjun. It's never been easy for me to get on with people – especially women. If something went wrong . . . between me and Alison, that is . . . I don't know how I'd cope . . .'

'Dinu, am I right to think that you're warning me – telling me to stay away?'

'Perhaps I am.'

'I see.' Arjun pushed his plate away. 'There's really no need, you know.'

'Good.' Dinu felt a smile returning to his face. 'Well, that's out of the way then.'

Arjun looked at his watch and stood up. 'Well, you've certainly made yourself clear. So perhaps I should be off. You'll make my excuses to Alison?'

'Yes . . . of course.'

They went together to the front door. Arjun's Ford V8 staff car was parked outside, under the porch. Arjun opened the door and held out his hand. 'It was nice to see you, Dinu,' he said. 'Even if briefly.'

Dinu was suddenly ashamed of his lack of generosity. 'I don't mean to send you away, Arjun . . .' he said guiltily. 'Please don't think that you're not welcome. You must come back . . . Soon . . . I'm sure Alison would like that.'

'And you?'

'Yes. Me too.'

Arjun appraised this with a frown. 'Are you sure?'

'Yes, of course. You must . . . you must come back.'

'I will then, if you don't mind, Dinu. It would be nice to get away from the base every now and again.'

'Why? Is something wrong?'

'Not wrong exactly – but it's not always as pleasant as it might be . . .'

'Why?'

'I don't know how to explain, Dinu. Ever since we've got to Malaya nothing's been the same.'

Arjun's entry into their lives was like a turning of the seasons. He dropped by almost daily, often bringing Hardy or some other friends with him. Sungei Pattani had now become the head-quarters of the 11th Division, and Arjun had linked up with many old acquaintances and friends. In the evenings he would gather them together and drive up from the base, in whatever vehicle was at hand – sometimes an Alvis staff car, sometimes a Ford V8, sometimes, even, a Harley-Davidson motorcycle. Usually they came after nightfall, driving up with their headlights blazing, sounding triumphal flurries on their horns.

'They're here!' Alison would run down to the kitchen to warn the cook.

It was evident that she enjoyed these visits; Dinu could tell that it delighted her to see the house filled with people again. She produced clothes that he did not know she possessed: until then he'd seen her only in the plain dresses she wore to the office, and an occasional silk cheongsam. Now richly coloured, beautifully tailored clothes poured out of her closets – elegant hats and gowns that her mother had ordered from Paris, in Morningside's heyday.

Almost every evening the house echoed to the sound of parade-ground voices and loud laughter. They seemed never to stop laughing, these young officers – the smallest joke would set them roaring, pounding each other on the back. They usually brought bottles of whisky, gin or rum from their mess. Sometimes Kishan Singh came with them to serve them their drinks. They would sit out on the veranda, sipping *stengahs* and gin slings. As if by magic, vast quantities of food would appear on the dining-room table. Alison would lead them in and then Arjun would take over, show-ing his friends round the table, explaining the dishes in minute detail: 'Look over here, this is duck – it's cooked in sugar-cane juice, you've never tasted anything like it. And here, see, these prawns? They're made with flowers – ginger buds – that's what gives them that amazing taste . . .'

Dinu would look on, like a spectator at a circus: he knew that the part of host should have been his own to play. But with each of these evenings he could feel his presence in the house diminishing, shrinking. It didn't seem to matter whether Arjun came alone or was accompanied by a troop of his friends. He seemed to have a way of filling the house, even when he was on his own. There was no denying that there was something magnetic about him – a self-confidence, a habit of command, an exuberant abundance of appetites. Dinu knew he could not hope to keep up with him.

At the end of each meal, Arjun would crank up the gramophone and clear the rugs off the hardwood floors. He and his friends would take turns dancing with Alison. It was a revelation to Dinu to discover how well she danced – better than anyone he'd ever known, just as well as dancers in the movies – with flair and rhythm and an energy that seemed inexhaustible. Amongst the men, Arjun was the best dancer by far. At the end of each night, he would put on his favourite record – Tommy Dorsey's band playing 'I'm Getting Sentimental Over You'. Everyone else would pull back to make space for them, and when the record came scratching to a stop the room would fill with applause. At the end of these evenings Alison seemed scarcely to remember that he, Dinu, still existed.

Once in a while Arjun would announce that he had succeeded in scrounging some extra petrol from the 'pilot chappies' at the airstrip. They would set out on an expedition, sometimes just the three of them, sometimes as a part of a much larger crowd. One such foray took them to the lodge that sat atop the summit of Gunung Jerai. A group of pilots had commandeered the place for a party; they were to be Arjun's guests.

They went in a Ford V8 staff car. To get to the summit they had to circle around the mountain driving past quiet *kampongs* with palm-shaded mosques. Children waved at them from ricefields, standing on tiptoe to reach above the grain-heavy stalks. It was a cloudy late November day and there was a cool breeze blowing in from the sea.

The road that led to the summit was not much better than a dirt track. It tacked back and forth across the slope, rising steeply. The mountainside was thickly forested and the track wound through dense patches of jungle. It was several degrees cooler than in the plain, and the sun was blocked by a constant, quick-moving blanket of cloud. At the top the vegetation ended abruptly and the lodge appeared – it looked a little like an English cottage, except that it was surrounded by a balcony that provided dramatic views of the coast and the surrounding plains.

The balcony was crowded with servicemen in grey, blue, khaki and bottle-green. Scattered among the uniforms were a few women dressed in brightly printed cottons. Somewhere inside the lodge a band was playing.

Arjun and Alison went off into the lodge to dance and Dinu was left to himself. He walked round the balcony, past tables that were draped in flapping white cloths. The view of the plain was hindered by a mantle of clouds blowing in from the sea. But every so often the wind would tear the cloud-cover apart, providing spectacular glimpses of the plain: he caught sight of Sungei Pattani, at the foot of the mountain, with hundreds of acres of rubber stretching away from it in all directions. In the distance, he spotted the craggy peaks of the island of Penang and the finger-like wharfs of the port of Butterworth. The north–south highway ran like a great stripe across the landscape, approaching from the southern end of the plain and disappearing towards the north, where the border lay. Along the west lay the Andaman Sea, alight with the bright colours of the sunset.

On the next clear day, Dinu promised himself, he would bring his cameras to the lodge. For the first time in his life, he regretted never having learned to drive: for this view alone, the effort would have been worthwhile.

The next day Arjun was back at Morningside again, at an unusual hour – at eleven in the morning. He was driving a motor-cycle, a wasp-waisted, pigeon-breasted Harley-Davidson, painted a dull, military green. It had a sidecar attached. Arjun drove up to the house from the plantation office with Alison sitting in the sidecar.

Dinu was in his dark room when Arjun shouted up from the porch: 'Dinu! Come down here. I've got some news.'

Dinu went running downstairs. 'Well . . . ?'

Arjun laughed, punching his shoulder. 'You're an uncle, Dinu – and so am I. Manju's had a baby – a girl.'

'Oh . . . I'm glad . . .'

'We're going to celebrate. Come with us.'

'Where are you going?'

'Down to the sea,' said Arjun. 'Jump on. Behind me.'

Dinu glanced at Alison, who looked away. He felt his feet grow-

370

ing leaden. Over the last many days he had struggled to keep pace with the two of them, but he could not be what he was not. He did not want to be with her just so that his presence would weigh on her as a reminder – anything but that.

'I don't think you really want me with you,' Dinu said quietly.

They sounded a chorus of protests.

'Oh, Dinu. Rubbish!'

'Oh, come on, Dinu. Don't be an ass.'

Dinu turned on his heel. 'I have work to finish in the dark room. You go ahead. You can tell me about it when you get back.' He went back into the house and ran upstairs. He heard the coughing sound of the motorcycle's kick-starter and could not keep himself from looking down, from a window. The Harley-Davidson was speeding down the drive, heading into the estate. He caught a glimpse of Alison's scarf, fluttering like a pennant.

He went back into his dark room and found that his eyes were smarting. In the past he'd always been able to count on the ambience of the dark room for reassurance; its dim red glow had been an unfailing source of comfort. But now the light seemed too bright, unbearably so. He switched it off and sat crouched on the floor, hugging his knees.

His instincts had been true from the start. He'd known that Arjun could not be trusted – nor Alison, not with him. Yet what could he have done? They were adults, and he had no real claim on either of them.

In a while he touched his face and found that it was wet. He grew angry with himself: if there was any tenet on which he'd wanted to build his life, it was that of never giving in to self-pity – that was a road that would not end, he knew, once he had started down it.

He rose to his feet and walked around the room in the darkness, trying to recall its exact size and layout as well as the placement of every bit of furniture and every object. He counted his paces and every time he touched a wall or bumped against something, he started over again.

He came to a decision. He would leave. It was clear that Alison had lost interest in him and there was nothing to be gained from remaining at Morningside. He would pack his things and spend the night at Ilongo's mother's house. Tomorrow he would go to Penang, to wait for a steamer that would take him back to Rangoon.

The motorcycle headed due west, down a road that dwindled into a fraying ribbon of tarmac, fringed by dust and sand. They drove through a small town with a blue-domed mosque and then the sea appeared in front of them, sparkling blue. Waves were climbing gently up a long shelf of sand. The road turned left and they stayed on it, driving parallel to the beach. They came to a small hamlet and the road ended. The marketplace smelt of salt water and drying fish.

Alison asked: 'Should we leave the motorcycle here?'

'No.' Arjun laughed. 'We don't have to. We can take it with us. This Harley can go anywhere.'

The villagers gathered to stare as they drove through the marketplace, slipping through the gaps between the shacks. The motorcycle whined as it climbed over the dune that separated the hamlet from the sea. The sand was blindingly white in the noonday sun. Arjun kept to the edge of the beach, where the ground was held together by a thin carpet of weeds. He drove slowly, dodging between the windblown trunks of coconut palms.

They left the village far behind and came to a cove that was sheltered by screwpines. The beach consisted of a thin, white fingernail of sand. At the mouth of the cove, no more than a hundred yards from the shore, there was a tiny island. It was thickly wooded, with green bushes and dwarf pines.

'Let's stop here,' said Alison.

Arjun wheeled the motorcycle into a patch of shade and pulled it on to its kickstand. They took off their shoes and left them on the sand. Arjun rolled up his trouser cuffs and they ran across the burning sliver of beach, straight into the water. It was low tide and the sea was very calm, with gentle waves lapping at the shore. The water was so clear that it magnified the shifting patterns of the sea floor, giving them the appearance of coloured mosaics.

'Let's swim,' said Arjun.

'I didn't bring anything.'

'It doesn't matter.' Arjun began to unbutton his khaki shirt. 'There's no one here.'

Alison was wearing a workaday cotton dress. She'd been holding it up, keeping the hem above the water. Now she let it drop. The water soaked quickly into the cotton, rising towards her waist.

'Come on, Alison. We have the whole place to ourselves.' Arjun's shirt-tails were hanging loose, the buttons undone.

'No.' She laughed. 'It's December. You have to respect our winter.'

'It's not cold. Come on.' He reached for her hand, his tongue flicking over the sparkling line of his teeth.

She dug her toes into the sand. Through the clear water, she spotted the curved edge of a seashell, buried between her feet. Reaching into the water she dug it out. The shell was unexpectedly heavy, large enough to fill both her hands.

'What is it?' said Arjun, looking over her shoulder. His khaki trousers were wet almost to the waist.

'It's a nautilus,' she said.

The shell had an elliptical opening at one end, like a horn: the colour inside was a rich mother of pearl, tinged with silver highlights. Its body was coiled into an almost perfectly circular mound. A spiral line ran along the mound, ending in a tiny protrusion, not unlike a nipple.

'How do you know what it's called?' Arjun asked. She could sense his presence behind her. He was looking over her at the shell, his chin resting lightly on her head.

'Dinu showed me a photograph of a shell like this one,' she said. 'He thinks it's one of the greatest pictures ever made.'

His arms reached round her shoulders, encircling her body. His hands closed on the shell, his fingers dwarfing hers, his palms wet against the back of her hands. He ran his thumb along the edge of the mother of pearl mouth, over the line that encircled the swelling body, to the tiny nipple-like point that topped the mound.

'We should . . .' She felt the touch of his breath blowing through her hair. 'We should take this back for Dinu,' he said. His voice had gone hoarse.

He let his arms drop and stepped away from her. 'Let's go and

373

explore,' he said, pointing in the direction of the island that lay at the mouth of the cove. 'I bet we could walk over. The water's very low.'

'I don't want to get my dress wet.' She laughed.

'You won't,' he promised. 'If the water gets too high I'll carry you on my back.'

He took hold of her hand and pulled her deeper into the water. The ground dipped until the water was at waist-level. Then the sandy floor began to rise again, sloping up towards the island. Arjun began to move faster, pulling her with him. They were running when they reached the shore. They raced across the sun-baked fringe of sand, into the shaded interior of the island. Alison fell on her back, on the soft, sandy earth, and looked up at the sky. They were encircled by bushy screwpines, screened from the shore.

Arjun threw himself down beside her, on his stomach. She was still holding the shell and he prised it free of her grip. He laid it on her chest, and ran his finger along the shell's spiral edge, cupping its body with his palm.

'It's so beautiful,' he said.

She saw how badly he wanted her; there was something irresistible about the insistency of his desire. When his hand slipped off the shell, on to her body, she made no effort to stop him. From that moment on, when it was already too late, everything changed.

It was as though he wasn't really there and nor was she; as though their bodies had been impelled more by a sense of inevitability than by conscious volition; by an inebriation of images and suggestion – memories of pictures and songs and dances; it was as though they were both absent, two strangers, whose bodies were discharging a function. She thought of what it was like with Dinu; the intensity of his focus on the moment; the sense of time holding still. It was only against the contrast of this cohabiting of absences that she could apprehend the meaning of what it meant to be fully present – eye, mind and touch united in absolute oneness, each beheld by the other, each beholding.

When Arjun rolled off her she began to cry, pulling her dress down over her body, clasping her knees. He sat up, in consternation. 'Alison – what's the matter? Why're you crying?'

She shook her head, her face buried between her knees.

He persisted. 'Alison, I didn't mean ... I thought you wanted ...'

'It's not your fault. I'm not blaming you. Only myself.'

'For what, Alison?'

'For what?' She looked at him in disbelief. 'How can you look at me after this and ask me a question like that? What about Dinu?'

'Alison.' He laughed, reaching for her arm. 'Dinu doesn't need to know. Why tell him about this?'

She pushed his hand away. 'Please,' she said. 'Please. Don't touch me.'

Then they heard a voice, calling in the distance, just loud enough to carry over the lapping of the water.

'Sah'b.'

Arjun pulled on his wet uniform and stood up. He saw Kishan Singh standing on the beach; behind him was a helmeted motor-cyclist, on a Harley-Davidson just like the one Arjun had driven up from the base.

Kishan Singh was waving a piece of paper, snapping it urgently through the air.

'Sah'b.'

'Alison,' Arjun said, 'something's up. They've sent a messenger from the base.'

'You go ahead,' Alison said. All she could think of at that moment was of throwing herself into the water, to wash off the feel of his touch. 'I'll follow in a minute.'

Arjun walked into the water and waded over to the beach. Kishan Singh was waiting at the water's edge; his eyes held Arjun's for an instant. There was something in them that made Arjun check his pace and look again. But now Kishan Singh had snapped to attention, his hand raised in a salute, his eyes fixed in an unseeing gaze.

'What is it, Kishan Singh?'

Kishan Singh handed him an envelope. 'Hardy-sah'b sent this.'

Arjun tore the envelope open and unfolded Hardy's note. He was still frowning at it when Alison stepped out of the water and walked up to him.

'What is it?' she said.

'I have to get back,' Arjun said. 'Right now. It looks as if something big is under way. We're leaving Sungei Pattani – my battalion, that is.'

'You're going away?' Alison stared at him, as though she couldn't believe what she'd heard.

'Yes.' He glanced at her. 'And you're glad – aren't you?'

She walked off without answering and he followed her. When they were over the crest of the dune, out of Kishan Singh's sight, he turned her around with a sudden violence.

'Alison,' he said sharply, 'you didn't answer me.'

She narrowed her eyes. 'Don't take that tone with me, Arjun. I'm not your batman.'

'I asked you a question.'

'What was it?'

'Are you glad that I'm leaving?'

'If you really want to know,' she said flatly, 'the answer is yes.'

'Why?' His voice was halting and confused. 'You came here because you wanted to. I don't understand this: why are you so angry with me?'

'I'm not.' She shook her head. 'I'm not angry at all – you're wrong about that. It wouldn't make sense to be angry with you, Arjun.'

'What the hell are you talking about?'

'Arjun – you're not in charge of what you do; you're a toy, a manufactured thing, a weapon in someone else's hands. Your mind doesn't inhabit your body.'

'That's crap . . .' He cut himself short. 'The only reason you can get away with that,' he said, 'is because you're a woman . . .'

She saw that he was a hair's-breadth away from hitting her and this had the odd effect of making her suddenly sorry for him. And then she realised that she had always felt sorry for him, a little, and that was why she had come with him that morning to the beach. She saw that despite the largeness and authority of his presence, he was a man without resources, a man whose awareness of himself was very slight and very fragile; she saw that Dinu was much stronger and more resourceful, and she understood that that was why she'd been tempted to be cruel to

376

him; that that was why she had had to take the risk of losing him. The thought of this made her suddenly apprehensive.

She walked quickly to the Harley-Davidson. 'Come on,' she said to Arjun. 'Take me back to Morningside.'

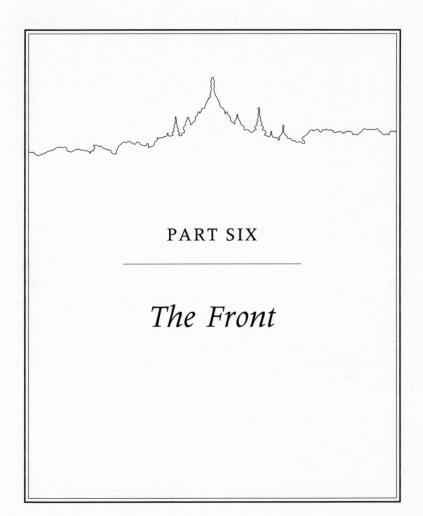

PART SIX

The Front

Thirty-two

It was early evening by the time the 1/1 Jats left Sungei Pattani. They drove out of their base in a convoy of trucks, heading north-wards, on the north–south highway. On reaching the town of Alor Star, they were deposited at the railway station and told to await further instructions. The men settled down at one end of the platform, the officers commandeered the other.

The station was the smallest and prettiest that Arjun had ever seen: it looked like a dolls' house version of the railway stations he'd known in India. There was a single, narrow platform, under a low, red-tiled awning. Potted palms hung in clusters from the beams and the wooden columns that lined the platform were wrapped in brightly-coloured bougainvillea bushes.

Lieutenant-Colonel Buckland had stayed on at divisional head-quarters and he arrived late. At midnight he called his officers together to brief them on the latest sitrep. There was to be a drastic change in tactics, he said. There were indications that the Japanese were about to enter the war: their forces were believed to be preparing to attack Malaya from the north. In order to forestall this a strike force was to thrust deep into Siam, to secure the eastern seaboard: this was intended to be a pre-emptive attack to deny a Japanese invasion force the potential landing grounds of the coast. The 1/1 Jats were to play a key part in this operation. The battalion's orders were to hold itself in readiness to entrain at a half-hour's notice. At dawn they would move northwards with the objective of occupying a beach-head near the coastal town of Singora. 'Jot these down.' Lieutenant-Colonel Buckland read out a string of map references while the officers took notes.

After the briefing Arjun spread a map on the station floor, under a naked lightbulb, brushing away the insects and moths that came to settle on the surface. He could feel his index finger shaking in excitement as he followed the thin red line of the road that led to the beach-head. This was it then: the proof of all these years of training; the waiting was over at last. Arjun glanced at the flower-bedecked platform: it struck him that this was a very unlikely place from which to launch a major operation.

It was hard to sleep. At about 3 a.m. Kishan Singh brought him a cup of tea in an enamel mug. Arjun took it gratefully, without asking where it had come from. Beside him Hardy was dozing peacefully in a long-armed chair, with his turban tipped back. Arjun stood up and strolled down the platform, picking his way past the huddled figures of the men. He noticed a light in the station master's office, and stepped in.

The station master was a Goan Christian. He was fast asleep, lying sprawled at his desk. There was a radio on a shelf. Arjun stepped round the desk and turned on the radio. He began to fiddle idly with the knobs. Presently, the crackling airwaves yielded a newsreader's voice: '. . . heavy fighting near Kota Baharu . . .'

Kota Baharu was in eastern Malaya: Arjun knew of it because of a friend who was stationed there. It was a small, out-of-the-way coastal town. Arjun turned up the volume and listened again: now the newsreader was talking of massive Japanese landings along the seaboard – he heard him mention Singora, the town they were meant to occupy the next day. Arjun turned and went sprinting down the platform to the waiting room where he had left the CO.

'Sir.'

The CO and Captain Pearson were dozing in armchairs.

'The balloon's up, sir: the Japs have landed.'

'Impossible, Lieutenant.' The CO sat up.

'It's on the radio, sir.'

'Where?'

Arjun led them to the station master's room. Along the platform the men were stirring now, aware that something was under way. Arjun pushed the station master's door open. The man was awake, groggily rubbing his fists in his eyes. Arjun stepped round him and turned up the volume. The newsreader's voice filled the room.

382

This was how they learnt that their pre-emptive strike had itself been pre-empted by an operation of unprecedented scale, involving synchronised attacks on targets thousands of miles apart – an air attack on Pearl Harbor and amphibious landings along the Malay peninsula. Singora, the town that was to have been their objective, was one of the first to have been occupied.

'Gentlemen.' Lieutenant-Colonel Buckland gave his officers a polite smile. 'If my knowledge of the army is any guide, I would suggest that you make yourselves comfortable here. It may be a while before we hear anything from HQ . . .'

There was something very comforting about the note of irony in his voice: listening to him, Arjun found it hard to imagine that anything could go seriously wrong.

There was a large airfield at Alor Star, and at first light a squadron of Blenheims took to the air. The 1/1 Jats cheered as the planes buzzed over the station. A couple of hours later, the Blenheims came circling back with empty fuel tanks. Within minutes of their return a flight of Japanese planes came humming over the horizon. They attacked the airport in close formation, at the precise moment when the refuelling Blenheims were at their most vulnerable. In a matter of minutes the planes were in flames. The timing of the raid was uncannily precise. There could be no doubt that the enemy had been tipped off by a spy or a local informer.

Later in the day Lieutenant-Colonel Buckland drove over to the airfield with a few of his officers. A medical centre had been hit and there was a powerful smell of chemicals. On the apron, the tar had liquefied around the Blenheims. In the distance there was a row of attap huts. These served as barracks for the Malay auxiliaries who guarded the airfield. The men were nowhere to be seen and Arjun was sent to look for them. He found their barracks in perfect order. The beds were all made and each had a kitbag hanging beside it. Rifles stood leaning against the wall, in neat rows, exactly as regulations demanded. But the men were gone. It was evident that after going through all the daily motions of tidying their quarters, the troops had quietly deserted.

*   *   *

383

Dinu had spent the night on a cot on the veranda of Ilongo's mother's house. He woke up early. Both Ilongo and his mother were still asleep. He looked at his watch. The train to Penang wasn't till midday; many long hours lay ahead.

He stepped outside and looked up at the mountain. The light had begun to change; the forest seemed to be coming alive. It struck him that he had never photographed the chandis at this time of morning. He spotted Ilongo's bicycle, standing inside a doorway. He decided to cycle up to the mountain with his cameras.

He put his equipment together quickly and cycled faster than usual. When he got to the stream he dispensed with his usual rituals: instead he went straight up to the clearing and set up his tripod. He was changing a roll when the first raiders flew over Gunung Jerai. At first he paid no attention, assuming that the planes were landing at the Sungei Pattani airbase. But minutes later, when the forest began to reverberate to the sound of explosions, he knew that something was wrong. When the next flight of bombers came by he looked more closely. The planes were flying quite low and there was no mistaking their markings. They were Japanese.

Dinu's first thought was for Alison. He hadn't seen her since she'd left for the beach, with Arjun, but he remembered that she had planned to go to Sungei Pattani that day – she had told him this the day before. She had errands to run.

It struck Dinu that she was probably still in town. He left his tripod standing where it was and hurried down to the bicycle. He went first to Morningside House where the cook confirmed that Alison had left the house very early that morning, in the Daytona. On his way out Dinu stopped to check on Saya John. He found him dozing peacefully in an armchair, on the veranda.

Cycling down to the office, Dinu noticed that a large number of people had collected on the parade ground. On approaching he saw that Ilongo was addressing the assembly, standing on a chair, speaking in Tamil. Dinu caught his eye and signalled to him to step aside for a quick word.

'What's happening, Ilongo?'

'Haven't you been listening to the radio?'

'No . . .'

'Japan's entered the war. The airstrip at Sungei Pattani has been bombed.'

Dinu took a moment to absorb this. 'Alison went to Sungei Pattani this morning . . .' he said. 'We have to go down there and see if she's all right . . .'

'I can't go right now.' Ilongo gestured at the people assembled on the parade ground. 'They're waiting . . .'

'Why – what do they want?'

'The managers of some of the neighbouring estates have abandoned their offices and driven off to Singapore. Our people here are worried. They want to make sure they'll get paid . . .' Breaking off to reach into his pocket Ilongo pulled out a set of keys. 'Here – you go yourself. Take the truck.'

Dinu pushed the keys back. 'I don't drive.'

'Then wait – I'll be done soon.'

Dinu watched from the balcony of the estate office while Ilongo addressed the assembly. The meeting seemed to last for ever: it was noon by the time the crowd began to disperse. Shortly afterwards Ilongo started up the truck, and they drove off in the direction of Sungei Pattani.

They soon ran into another crowd. The air raids had ended a good few hours before, but people were pouring down the road, heading away from town. Many were on foot; several families had their belongings slung over their shoulders, tied up in sheets; a boy was pushing a bicycle with a huge radio strapped to the carrier; two men were pulling an elderly woman behind them in a makeshift trolley. Nearer town the roads were clogged with honking cars. Sitting stalled in the truck, Ilongo began to ask questions, leaning out of the driver's window: he learnt that the air raid had taken the town by surprise; there had been no alarms, no warning. Now, everyone who had the option was heading into the countryside, to wait out the trouble.

They parked the truck behind a shop and walked into town. They checked all the places where Alison might conceivably have gone – the banks were empty and most of the shops had their shutters down. Alison's hairdresser was gone.

'Where could she be?'

'She'll be all right – don't worry.'

On the way back to the estate, they took a road that led them past the perimeter of the airstrip. The apron was littered with smoking heaps of metal but the runways were untouched. They came across an Indian – a caretaker who told them that there was a rumour that the Japanese bombers had been guided in by a spy, a traitor from the British forces.

'An Indian?' Dinu asked apprehensively.

'No – an Englishman. We saw him being led away, under arrest.'

Dinu was both shocked and relieved.

It was only when they were back at Ilongo's house that Dinu remembered that he'd been planning to leave for Penang. He decided to put off his departure for the time being: he couldn't leave without making sure that Alison was all right. He went up to Morningside and sat down to wait.

By the time Alison's car came up the driveway it was almost sunset. Dinu was at the door, waiting. The relief of seeing her unharmed had the effect of uncorking all the anxieties of the day. He began to shout as she stepped out of the roadster. 'Alison . . . where the hell have you been? You've been gone the whole damned day . . .'

She snapped back at him: 'And what about you? Where were you last night?'

'I was at Ilongo's,' he said defiantly. 'I'm going to leave . . . for Rangoon.'

She gave a hard little laugh. 'Good luck to you then. Let's see how far you get.'

'What do you mean?'

'I was in Butterworth this morning. There's chaos on the roads. I don't think you're going to get very far. '

'Butterworth? What were you doing in Butterworth?'

She raised an eyebrow and her voice went cold. 'It's none of your business.' She brushed past him and went up the stairs to her bedroom.

Dinu stood fuming in the porch for a few minutes and then followed her up the stairs. 'Alison . . .' He knocked at the door, his voice contrite. 'I'm sorry . . . I was just worried.'

She opened the door, wearing a white satin slip. Before he could say any more, she threw her arms around him. 'Oh, Dinu.'

'Alison . . . I was frantic . . . you being gone all day, with the bombing . . .'

'You shouldn't have worried. I was fine – nowhere near the bombs. They were hitting the port and I was on the other side of town.'

'But why did you go there anyway . . . ? All the way to Butter-worth? What for?'

She took his face between her hands and kissed him. 'I'll tell you later,' she said. 'Let's not talk about it now. Let's just be glad we're together and we're both all right.'

Thirty-three

Several hours passed without the 1/1 Jats receiving any word from divisional headquarters. Just after nightfall, a convoy of trucks arrived to move them to another location. They could tell they were travelling north but it was very dark and they could see nothing of the countryside.

At dawn Arjun discovered that they were encamped inside a rubber plantation. Beyond a few hundred yards the greenery seemed to solidify into a circular, bark-striped wall. Between the canopy of green leaves above and the carpet of dead foliage underfoot there seemed to be no direct light and no shadows. Sound appeared to travel and linger without revealing its point of origin. It was as though he had woken up to find himself inside an immense maze where the roof and the floor had been padded with cotton wool.

At the morning's briefing they learnt that the battalion was now positioned near the township of Jitra, very close to the northernmost tip of the Federated Malay States. Here the peninsula narrowed to a thin neck, forming a bridge between Malaya and Siam: any army advancing from the north would have to squeeze through this gullet and it was here that a southerly advance could best be throttled. The 1/1 Jats, along with several other battalions, had been concentrated along the north–south highway. It was along this road that the Japanese were expected to make their advance. Chance had thus thrust the 1/1 Jats into the first line of defence.

Arjun was commanding his battalion's C Company: they were positioned a few hundred yards to the left of the north–south highway. Hardy was with D Company, on the far side of the road.

They were flanked by the Leicestershire Regiment on one side and the 14th Punjab on the other.

The first job was to dig trenches, but here again the terrain proved deceptive. The soft loamy soil was easy to dig into, but hard to shore up. Ground water leaked in at unpredictable depths. The wireless sets began to malfunction and the problem was traced to the environment: the placement of the trees was found to interfere with the reception of radio waves. Even runners could not be relied upon. Disoriented by the geometrical maze of the plantation, they kept losing their way.

Then the rains broke. It dripped constantly and this too reinforced the impression of being locked inside a padded cage. Looking up, the soldiers would see rain pouring down from the sky. But by the time the water reached them, the showers had slowed to a steady drizzle. The dripping would continue long after the rain had stopped. They would look up to find that the skies had cleared; yet down where they were the rain kept falling, hour after weary hour. It was as though the leafy canopy were a wet mattress, emptying slowly under its own weight.

With the soil turning to mud, their jeeps and lorries began to slide out of control. The vehicles were found to have been equipped with sand-grip tyres, intended for use in the deserts of North Africa. Orders were issued banning them from entering the plantation: supplies now had to be carried in on foot.

On the afternoon of the second day, Hardy came running over and dropped into the trench. Arjun could tell from his face that he was ripe with news.

'What's happened?'

'Just heard a rumour.'

'What?'

'There was trouble with the 1st Hyderabads, at Kota Baharu.'

'What kind of trouble?'

'After the first Jap attack there was a panic at the airstrip. The airmen were Australians and apparently they left in a hurry. The Hyderabads' NCOs wanted to pull out too but the CO wouldn't let them. They mutinied, shooting a couple of officers. They've been disarmed and arrested. They're being sent to Penang, as a labour force.'

Arjun surveyed his trench, looking uneasily at the faces of his men. 'Better keep that to yourself, Hardy.'

'Just thought I'd let you know.'

The battalion's headquarters were deep inside the plantation, well to the rear of Arjun's company. Late on the second day, signals engineers laid a telephone line. The first call was from Captain Pearson.

'Contact?'

'Nothing yet,' said Arjun. The day had faded almost imperceptibly away, the gloom deepening slowly into a dripping, clammy darkness. At that very moment, the dark wall ahead was pierced by a red flash.

'Sniper!' said the *havildar*. 'Down, sah'b, down.' Arjun lunged face forward into the ankle-deep water at the bottom of the trench. There was another shot and then another. Arjun fumbled for the phone only to find that the line had gone dead.

Now the flashes of gunfire began to range through the surrounding darkness. The shots sounded at irregular intervals, punctuated by the dull thud of mortars and the spitting of light machine guns. To the right, from the direction of Hardy's emplacement, there came the sound of a Bren gun. This brought only a moment's relief, for Arjun noted suddenly, with an odd sinking feeling in his belly, that the Bren was rattling on too long: it was as though the men were too panicked to remember the ordered bursts that Hardy had tried to drill into them during weapons training.

Now the enemy snipers appeared to be on the move, pivoting freely around their position. As the hours passed the trench began to seem more a trap than a shelter: there was a peculiar defencelessness about being pinned into a stationary position by a mobile adversary. When they returned fire, it was as though they were letting fly randomly, in the way that a chained animal circles at the end of its leash, snapping at an unseen tormentor.

The dripping of the trees continued without interruption through the night. Soon after daybreak, they saw a Japanese spotter plane, circling overhead. A half-hour later another plane flew by, dipping low over their lines. It left behind a trail of paper that fluttered slowly down from the sky, like a great flight of butterflies.

Most of these sheets settled on the canopy above, but a few trickled through to the ground. Kishan Singh fetched some, handing one to Arjun and keeping a couple for himself.

Arjun saw that it was a pamphlet, written in Hindustani and printed in both Devanagari and Arabic script. It was an appeal directed to Indian soldiers, signed by one Amreek Singh of the Indian Independence League. The text began: *Brothers, ask your-selves what you are fighting for and why you are here: do you really wish to sacrifice your lives for an Empire that has kept your country in slavery for two hundred years?*

Arjun heard Kishan Singh reading the pamphlet aloud to the others and the blood rushed to his head. He shouted: 'Hand those to me.' Crumpling the pamphlets, he buried them deep under his heel, in the mud. 'Anyone who's found with these,' he said crisply, 'will be up for court martial.'

Minutes later, with a blast that was like a moving wall of sound, the Japanese heavy artillery opened up. The first shells went skimming over the tops of the trees, sending down showers of leaves and small branches. But then, slowly, the explosions began to move in their direction. The earth shook so violently as to send the water at the bottom of the trench shooting into their faces. Arjun saw a fifty-foot rubber tree rising gracefully from the earth and jumping several feet into the air before somersaulting towards them. They flattened themselves at the bottom of the trench just in time to get out of its way.

The bombardment continued without a break for hours.

Manju was in a deep sleep when Neel shook her awake. She rolled over, in a daze. It seemed as though weeks had gone by since she had last slept. Jaya was a colicky baby and often cried for hours. Nothing would stop her once she started. Even Woodward's Gripe Water had little effect: a tablespoonful would send her into a light doze but an hour or two later she'd be up again, crying harder than ever.

Manju glanced at Jaya's crib and saw that she was still asleep. She rubbed her eyes and turned away from Neel. She could not disguise her annoyance at being disturbed. 'What is it?' she said. 'Why did you wake me up?'

'I thought you'd want to know . . .'

'What?'

'The Japanese have entered the war.'

'Oh?' She still could not understand what this had to do with her being roused from her sleep.

'They've invaded Malaya.'

'Malaya?' Now everything was suddenly clear. She sat up. 'Arjun? Dinu? Is there any news?'

'No.' Neel shook his head. 'Nothing directly. But the radio said something about the 11th Division being involved in the fighting. Isn't that Arjun's division?'

She'd had a letter from Arjun just last week. He hadn't said very much about himself – just that he was well and thinking of her. Mostly, he'd asked about Jaya and her own health. He'd also mentioned that he'd met Dinu and he was fine – Dolly had been glad to hear that.

'Do you still have Arjun's letter?' Neel asked.

'Yes.' Manju jumped out of bed and went to fetch the letter.

'Does it say anything about his division?' Neel said.

The numeral 11 leapt at her almost at once, from the folds of the page. 'Yes,' she said. 'That's his division.' She looked at her husband and her eyes filled with tears.

Neel put his arm round her shoulders and held her tight. 'There's no reason to worry,' he said. 'As far as I can make out the 11th Division is headquartered very close to Morningside. Dinu will let us know what's going on.'

Then the baby woke up. Now, for the first time, Manju was grateful for Jaya's cantankerousness. Her ceaseless crying left her with no time to think of anything else.

Later that evening they were paid a visit by an eminent member of the Indian community in Rangoon – a lawyer by the name of Sahibzada Badruddin Khan. It so happened that the whole family was at home when the visitor dropped by.

Mr Khan was worried and he had come to give them some news. He had attended a meeting of some of the city's most prominent Indians. They had decided to form a Refugee Evacuation

Committee. It was felt that in the event of a Japanese advance into Burma the Indian population would be vulnerable on two fronts – they would be defenceless against hostile sections of the Burmese public and, what was more, as subjects of the British Empire, they would be treated as enemy aliens by the Japanese. Many members of the community had expressed fears of a coming catastrophe: the committee's intentions were to get as many Indians out of Burma as possible.

Rajkumar was amazed to learn of these measures. He was in an optimistic mood, despite the recent news. He had just discovered that a friend of his had secured a contract for a long stretch of the Burma–China road. He was now absolutely confident that he would be able to sell his stocks of timber at exactly the kind of price he had been hoping for.

'What?' Rajkumar broke into a disbelieving laugh. 'You mean you people are going to run away from Burma – because the Japanese have invaded Malaya?'

'Well, yes. People feel . . .'

'Nonsense, Khan.' Rajkumar slapped his friend on the back. 'You shouldn't be taken in by these scaremongers. Malaya's a long way from here.'

'Still,' said Mr Khan, 'there's nothing wrong with being prepared – especially where there are women and children involved . . .'

Rajkumar shrugged. 'Well, Khan, you must do what you think best. But as for myself I think this is a great opportunity –'

'Opportunity!' Mr Khan raised an eyebrow. 'How so?'

'There's no mystery to it, Khan. With America in the war, there'll be more money for defence preparations. Burma is crucial to the survival of the Chinese Government in Chungking: the north–south road will be their main supply line. I'm willing to bet that the road is going to be built faster than anyone ever expected.'

'And if there's an attack?'

Rajkumar shrugged. 'It's a question of nerve, Khan. I can understand why you'd want to leave. But for us it would be too soon. I've spent a long time preparing for this and I am not going to leave now.'

Manju was hugely reassured by Rajkumar's words. It was a great comfort to know that she did not have to think about going anywhere right now. Coping with Jaya was hard enough at home: she could not begin to imagine what it would be like in less favourable circumstances.

In the morning, a runner brought a message to Arjun's trench. It was from battalion headquarters: they were to fall back on the Asoon line – a string of defensive fortifications along a river, a few miles down the road. When Arjun gave the order to move there was a muted cheer. He felt like joining in himself – anything would be better than staying pinned in that trench.

They made their way through the plantation in good order but when they reached the road it became clear that the withdrawal was turning quickly into a headlong retreat. The men began to show signs of apprehension as truck after truck passed them by, packed with troops from other units. Arjun stayed with them long enough to see them into a truck and then he jumped into a jeep with Hardy.

'Yaar, did you hear?' Hardy said under his breath.

'What?'

'The Japs have sunk the *Prince of Wales* and the *Repulse*.'

'Impossible.' Arjun looked at him in disbelief. These were two of the most powerful battleships ever made, the pride of the British navy. 'It can't be true.'

'It *is* true – I ran into Kumar; he told me.' Suddenly a gleeful grin lit up his face. 'I can't wait to tell Pearson: I want to see the look on that bastard's face . . .'

'Hardy,' Arjun shouted, 'have you gone mad?'

'Why?'

'Have you forgotten that those ships were here to defend us? We're all on the same side, Hardy. A Jap bullet can't pick between you and Pearson . . .'

Hardy gave him a startled glance, and for a moment they looked at each other in mutual bewilderment. 'You're right,' said Hardy. 'Of course. But you know . . .'

'Let's drop it,' Arjun said quickly.

When they reached the Asoon river, the Japanese artillery fell unaccountably silent. Grateful for the respite, the 1/1 Jats took up positions beside the road, with their backs to the river. At this point, the north–south highway ran along a raised embankment, with thick stands of rubber on either side, leading as far as the eye could see. The whole battalion was now concentrated in one place, positioned to defend the approaches to the river. Their vehicles were lined up off the road, along the slopes of the embankment.

Arjun saw Hardy stepping out on the road and went to join him. Lieutenant-Colonel Buckland was just a few paces away, at the battalion's temporary command post. He was with Captain Pearson, who was fumbling with a map case.

Arjun stopped in the middle of the road to confer with Hardy. 'Why do you think they've stopped shelling?' he said.

'They seem to hold back at times,' Hardy said. 'It's hard to say why.'

'You don't think it's because their own armour is moving up, do you?'

Hardy scoffed at this. 'What armour? None of us has any tanks – neither them nor us. This isn't tank country.'

'That's what we were told. But . . .' Somewhere in the distance there was a rumbling sound. They both spun about on their heels to look down the road. It was now almost sunset. The clouds had cleared briefly and the sky had turned bright scarlet. The highway ran straight for a couple of hundred yards before disappearing around a bend: rubber trees rose above it on either side, almost coming together at the top to form an arch. The road was empty: there was nothing ahead.

Hardy breathed a sigh of relief. 'That gave me a fright . . .' He raised his sleeve to his forehead. 'I told you – this isn't tank country: that's the one thing we can be sure of, thank God.'

A moment later, with a great grinding of its metal treads, a tank turned the corner. On top of the turret, silhouetted against the sky, was a gunner's helmeted head. The turret swivelled in their direction until its gun became a single circular eye. Then the tank shuddered and its hollow eye turned a blazing red. At the bottom of the embankment, a petrol tank exploded and a half-ton truck did a little hop and burst into flames.

For an instant Arjun stood his ground. Nothing in his training had prepared him for this. A dim recollection of unfinished business urged him to turn and run back down the road, to his company, to rally them into throwing up the wall of fire that the CO had talked about at the last briefing. But the CO had said categorically that there would be no tanks – and anyway, the CO was gone now, rolling down the side of the embankment, along with Captain Pearson. On both sides of the highway, men were scattering into the plantation, running for cover.

'Run, Arjun!' The voice was Hardy's, and it jolted him awake. 'Run, run.'

He was stranded in the middle of the road, like a startled deer, and the first tank was almost upon him, so close that he could see the eyes of the man in the turret, darkened by a thick pair of goggles. He jumped, throwing himself over the side of the embankment, lunging sidewise to clear the CO's burning jeep. Then he picked himself up and ran for the trees: suddenly he was inside a long tunnel of greenery, his feet cushioned by a carpet of fallen leaves.

The lucidity that had possessed him momentarily as he was standing in the middle of the road had vanished now. Its place was taken by a blind, unseeing urgency. It was quite possible that he was heading straight towards a nest of Japanese guns. But even if he had known that to be so he would not have been able to stop himself. It was as though his breath and his blood had fused together to pound at his brain in unison, urging him on, pushing him to run in this direction.

He ran several yards without stopping. Then, leaning against a tree trunk, he turned, panting, to look back: the trees fell into a sightline at the end of which a small stretch of road was clearly visible, enclosed in a circular frame, as though he were looking through a telescope. He saw tank after tank rolling down the highway. By the sides of the embankment lay the vehicles of the 1/1 Jats. Some were upturned and some were on fire.

The sight was beyond comprehension. He could find no way of explaining what had happened, even to himself. Was this what was meant by the phrase 'put to rout' – this welter of fear and urgency and shame; this chaotic sensation of collapse in one's head, as though the scaffolding of responses implanted by years of training had buckled and fallen in?

Arjun had a sudden aching vision of their battalion's head-quarters in Saharanpur: he recalled the building they called 'the Nursery' – the long, low bungalow in which the officers' mess was housed. He thought of the heavy, gilt-framed paintings that hung on its walls, along with the mounted heads of buffalo and nilgai; the assegais, scimitars and feathered spears that his prede-cessors had brought back as trophies from Africa, Mesopotamia and Burma. He had learnt to think of this as home, and the battalion as his extended family – a clan that tied a thousand men together in a pyramid of platoons and companies. How was it possible that this centuries-old structure could break like an egg-shell, at one sharp blow – and that too, in this unlikeliest of battlefields, a forest planted by businessmen? Was the fault his own? Was it true then, what the older Englishmen said, that Indians would destroy the army if they became officers? This at least was beyond doubt: as a fighting unit the 1/1 Jats no longer existed. Every man in the battalion would now have to fend for himself.

He'd left his pack in the jeep, on the river: it hadn't occurred to him that he'd be running for his life within minutes of climbing out. All he had on him now was his .45 Webley, his water bottle and his belt with its small pack of odds and ends.

He looked around. Where was Hardy? Where were the CO and Captain Pearson? He'd caught glimpses of them earlier, as he was running into the plantation. But now in the gathering gloom it was hard to tell what lay ahead.

The Japanese infantry would almost certainly be mopping up behind their tanks, combing the plantations. It was possible that he was being watched even as he stood there, through any one of the hundreds of sightlines that converged on the precise spot on which he was standing.

What was he to do now?

Thirty-four

To drive to Gunung Jerai was Alison's idea. She and Dinu left the house well before sunset, in the Daytona, taking the road that circled around the mountain. The kampongs seemed deserted now, the daytime panic having yielded to a watchful quiet. In the markets there were hardly any people in sight. Alison was able to drive through at high speed.

They made good time and turned on to the summit road while there was still plenty of light. When they began to climb, the sound of the car rose to a shrill, steady whine. It was twilight on the slopes, because of the thick forest cover. Alison had to switch on her headlamps.

The turns on the road were very sharp. They came to a bend that switched back on itself, rising upwards at a steep angle. Alison had to stop and reverse the car in order to make the turn. As they were coming out of the corner, they both looked up at the same time. The sky above the northern horizon seemed to be darkened by a stain – a cloud of tiny, horizontal brushstrokes. Alison stopped dead, and they stared – several moments passed before they realised that they were looking at a flight of planes, heading directly towards them, from the north. They were facing the air-craft head-on and in profile the planes seemed stationary, their advance signalled only by a gradual thickening of their outlines.

Alison started the car again, and they went speeding up the road. The lodge loomed ahead, in the gathering darkness. It was empty, deserted. They parked under the porch and walked up to the veranda that ran around the building. Tables were placed along its length, draped in white cloth, weighted down with heavy ashtrays. Plates had been laid out, as though in expectation of a crowd of diners.

They could feel the roar of the approaching bombers under their feet, in the vibrating planks of the wood floor. The planes were very close now, flying at low altitudes. As they stood watching, the flight suddenly separated into two, parting round the mountain, like a stream flowing past a boulder. Banking steeply one wing veered off towards the seaward slope of the mountain, on a flight path set for Butterworth and Penang. The other wing headed for Sungei Pattani, on the landward side.

Alison reached for Dinu's hand and they began to walk along the balcony, making their way between the dining tables. The tablecloths were flapping in the breeze and the plates were covered with a thin film of dust.

There were no clouds today. Far below, in the dimming twilight, the island of Penang appeared as a dark shoal afloat on the sea; to the south-east lay Sungei Pattani, a small raft of habitation, marooned in an ocean of rubber trees. They could see roads and rail-lines, glimmering in the last flicker of daylight. The landscape was like a map, lying unfurled at their feet.

The planes were losing height in preparation for their bombing runs. Sungei Pattani was the nearest of the targets and it was the first to be hit. Bursts of flame appeared on the dark landscape, strung closely together in straight lines, like rows of bright stitches on an inky fabric.

They went around the veranda, picking at the tablecloths and running their fingers over the dust-filmed plates. They saw yet another cloud of planes approaching; on the seaward side, the bombers were diving low over the port of Fort Butterworth. Suddenly a great tower of orange flame shot up from the coast reaching hundreds of feet into the sky; the blast that followed was of such magnitude as to make itself felt all the way up the mountain.

'Oh my God!' Alison threw herself on Dinu. 'They've hit the oil-tanks at Butterworth.'

She buried her face in Dinu's chest, snatching at his shirt, bunching up the cloth in her fists. 'I drove past them, just that day.'

Dinu held her fast. 'Alison, you still haven't told me why you went . . .'

She wiped her face on his shirt and pulled away from him. 'Give me a cigarette.'

Dinu lit a cigarette and put it between her lips. 'Well?'

'I went to see a doctor, Dinu – a doctor who doesn't know me.'

'Why?'

'I thought I might be pregnant.'

'And?'

'I'm not.'

'And what if you had been pregnant, Alison,' Dinu said quietly. 'Would you have wanted the child to be Arjun's?'

'No.' She threw her arms round him, and he could feel her sobbing into his shirt.

'Dinu, I'm sorry. I'm so, so sorry.'

'About what?'

'About everything, Dinu. About going away that day – with Arjun. It was a mistake – a terrible, terrible mistake. If you only knew, Dinu . . .'

He silenced her by putting a finger over her lips. 'I don't want to know . . . Whatever happened . . . I don't want to know. It'll be better that way . . . for both of us. We don't need to talk about Arjun again.'

He was cut short by a flash of light, an explosion that illuminated the whole town of Sungei Pattani. A series of lesser explosions followed, one after the other, like a string of fireworks.

'The armoury,' Alison said. She lowered herself to her knees and stuck her head into a gap between the veranda's rails, holding on to the wooden bars with her fists. 'They must have hit the armoury.'

Dinu knelt beside her. 'Alison,' he said urgently, gripping her shoulders. 'One thing's for sure . . . You have to go away. With Japan and America at war, you're in danger here. Your mother was American . . . Your brother still lives there . . . There's no telling what would happen if the Japanese managed to push through. You've got to get away.'

'But where to?'

'To Singapore; you'll be safe there. It's very well defended.

We're too close to the border here . . . and you have to take your grandfather with you. You've got to leave.'

She shook her head, violently. 'I don't want to. I don't want to go.'

'Alison, you can't just think about yourself.'

'You don't understand, Dinu – I'm a territorial animal. I'd rather take a few of them with me than give up what's mine.'

'Alison, listen to me.' Dinu gripped her hands and shook them. 'You have to do it . . . For your grandfather's sake, if not your own.'

'And what about the estate?'

'Ilongo will run it while you're away . . . You'll see . . . You can trust him, you know that.'

'And you – you'll come with us, of course. Won't you?'

'Alison, I should go back, to Burma . . . My family . . . They might need me now.'

'But you could come to Singapore with us first; you could probably get a ship there. It might even be easier.'

Dinu paused to think. 'You may be right. Yes . . . I'll come.'

She reached for his hands. 'I don't think I could bear to go without you. Especially now.'

'Why now?'

She dug into his chest with her forehead. 'Because I think I'm in love with you, Dinu – or something like that at any rate. I didn't know it before, but I know it now.'

He pulled her closer. He did not care what had happened between her and Arjun; nothing mattered but this – that she loved him and he loved her. Nothing else was of any account, not the planes, not the bombs, nothing but this. This was what happiness was – he'd never known it before; this melting away, this exaltation, your guts spilling into your head, filling your eyes – your mind transformed into your body, your body instinct with the joy in your mind; this sensation of reality having met its end.

Although the sunset was still a few minutes away, under the rubber trees it was already dusk. Arjun had heard many

401

complaints about the terrain over the last few days, but it was only now that he became fully aware of the peculiar deceptiveness of his surroundings. He had a strange sense of having stepped into a picture that had been created with the express purpose of tricking the eye. At times the tunnels of foliage around him seemed still and empty, but moments later they appeared to be alive with movement. With every step, figures and shapes seemed to appear and disappear, as rows of trees fell into and out of alignment. Every gracefully arched tree held the promise of cover, yet there was no point that did not intersect with a perfect line of fire.

Arjun knew that many others had taken shelter in the plantation; at times he could sense their presence around him. Every now and again he'd hear whispers, or the sound of footsteps, echoing down the long, straight corridors that stretched away from him in every direction. Sometimes he'd hear a sound, somewhere close at hand. He'd spin around only to find that he'd stepped on a branch that was hidden under the carpet of dead leaves on the ground. It was impossible to distinguish form from shadow, movement from stillness – the real and the illusory seemed to have merged without seam.

Just as twilight was turning to darkness, he heard the click of a safety catch. A whisper followed, from somewhere nearby. '*Kaun hai?* Who is it?'

The voice sounded familiar, but Arjun waited until he heard the whisper again: '*Kaun?*'

This time he was certain. 'Kishan Singh?'

'Sah'b.'

Arjun took a couple of steps to his right and found himself face to face with his batman. 'How did you find me?' He acknowledged Kishan Singh's salute gravely, trying not reveal the full extent of his relief.

'Buckland-sah'b sent me,' Kishan Singh said.

'Where is he?'

'Over there.'

It turned out that Kishan Singh had escaped into the plantation with a dozen others from the battalion. They'd succeeded in keeping together through the confusion that had followed the Japanese tank attack. Eventually they'd met up with Hardy as well as

Lieutenant-Colonel Buckland. Captain Pearson was still missing. They were now keeping watch to see if they could intercept anyone else.

Lieutenant-Colonel Buckland was sitting with his back against a tree trunk, his right arm cradled in an improvised sling. He acknowledged Arjun's salute with a nod and a slight gesture of his left hand.

'Glad to have you back with us, Lieutenant.'

Arjun was elated to hear his wry voice again. He grinned. 'Glad to see you too, sir. How bad's your arm?'

'Just a graze – and it's been seen to. Fortunately we have a medical chap with us.' Lieutenant-Colonel Buckland gave Arjun a stiff-lipped smile. 'Do sit down, Roy. No need to stand on ceremony now.'

'Thank you, sir.' Arjun cleared a place for himself on the carpet of dead leaves.

'You'll be glad to know that Hardy made it too,' Lieutenant-Colonel Buckland said. 'I've sent him off to forage for water. We're very short.'

'It happened so fast, sir.'

'Yes, it did rather, didn't it?' Lieutenant-Colonel Buckland's voice faded away. When he spoke again, his voice was hoarse, rasping, almost unrecognisable.

'Tell me, Lieutenant,' he said, 'do you think I let the side down?'

There was something about his tone that moved Arjun. 'No, sir,' he said vehemently. 'There was nothing you could have done, sir.'

'There's always something one could have done.'

'But what could you have done, sir? We didn't have any air support. We didn't know about the tanks. It's not our fault, sir.'

'If you're in command it's always your fault.'

They were quiet again for a while. Presently the lieutenant-colonel said: 'Do you know what I've been thinking of, Roy?'

'Sir?'

'The Nursery – in Saharanpur. I remember when it was built. My father was CO at the time, you know – and the 1/1 Jats were still called the Royal Battalion. We were away in Simla for the summer and when we came back there it was – the building that

403

would come to be known as the Nursery. There was a ceremony and a *burra khana* for the men. My mother cut a ribbon. I remember how proud I was to see our colours hanging there – moth-holes and all. This was what got me started on military history. By the age of ten I knew our battle honours by heart. I could have told you exactly how Jemadar Abdul Qadir got his Victoria Cross. I was in my last year at school when the Royal Battalion went to the Somme. I came across something that Field Marshal Sir John French said in a speech and I cut it out.'

'What did he say, sir?'

'Something to the effect of: "The Jats will never be forgotten on the Western Front." '

'I see, sir.'

The lieutenant-colonel's voice dropped to a whisper. 'And what do you think they'll say about what happened to us today, Roy?'

Arjun replied quietly: 'I think they'll say we did what we could under the circumstances.'

'Will they? I can't help wondering. This was one of the finest units in one of the finest armies in the world. But today we were dispersed without being able to return fire. I will have to live with the knowledge of that for the rest of my life.'

'You can't blame yourself, sir.'

'Really?' Lieutenant-Colonel Buckland was quiet again. In the silence that followed Arjun became aware that it was raining and the canopy had begun to release its usual slow, unvarying drip.

'Sir.' Hardy stepped suddenly out of the darkness, taking them by surprise. He handed the CO a green bottle. 'Water, sir.'

'Where did you get it?'

'There was a small pond sir. We strained the water and used a few chlorine tablets. I think it's safe, sir.'

'All right then.' Lieutenant-Colonel Buckland's voice was businesslike again. 'You two had better get some rest. Tomorrow we'll head south-east. With any luck we'll be able to circle back towards our own lines.'

The rain continued without interruption, the moisture descending with the steady insistence they had all come to dread. Hardy commandeered a bedroll from one of the men, and he and Arjun sat leaning against a tree trunk, sitting at right-angles to each

other, keeping watch in the darkness. Mosquitoes buzzed incessantly and for once Arjun was grateful for his puttees. But there was
little he could do about his unprotected neck and face. He slapped
at the insects and thought with longing of the mosquito cream
he'd left behind at the Asoon river, tucked deep inside his pack.

'Sah'b.' Arjun was startled by the sound of Kishan Singh's voice.

'Kishan Singh?'

'Sah'b.'

Kishan Singh slipped something into his hand and was gone
before Arjun could say anything else.

'What is it?' Hardy said.

Arjun held his hand up to his nose. 'Why,' he said, 'I do believe
it's mosquito cream. He must have given me his own . . .'

'Lucky bloody *chootiya*,' Hardy said mournfully. 'My batman
would happily see me eaten alive before he parted with his. Let
me have some – there's a good chap.'

Sleep was impossible: there was nothing to do but to wait out
the night. At times Hardy hummed, under his breath, with Arjun
trying to guess the tunes. Intermittently they talked, in muted
voices, catching up on the events of the last few hours.

In a low whisper Hardy asked: 'What was Bucky saying to you
back there?'

'We were talking about what happened . . .'

'What did he say?'

'He was blaming himself.'

'But there was nothing he could have done.'

'That's not how he sees it. It was strange to listen to him – to
hear him talking about it in such a personal way, as though he
was responsible. I just hadn't thought of it like that.'

'Well, how could you?'

'Why couldn't I?'

'To us it makes no difference really, does it?'

'Of course it does. If it didn't we wouldn't be sitting here in the
rain.'

'Yes, but think about it, yaar Arjun – for example, what would
have happened if we'd held our position on the Asoon? Do you
think we – us Indians – do you think we would have been given
the credit?'

'Why not?'

'Think of those newspapers in Singapore – the ones that were writing about all the brave young soldiers who'd come to defend their colony. Do you remember?'

'Of course.'

'Remember how all those brave young soldiers were always Australian or Canadian or British?'

Arjun nodded. 'Yes.'

'It's as if we never existed. That's why what happened at Asoon doesn't matter – not to us, anyway. Whether we'd held our position or not, it would have been the same. Yaar, I sometimes think of all the wars my father and grandfather fought in – in France, Africa, Burma. Does anyone ever say – the Indians won this war or that one? It would have been the same here. If there had been a victory the credit for it would not have been ours. By the same logic the blame for the defeat can't be ours either.'

'It may not matter to others, Hardy,' Arjun said, 'but it matters to us.'

'Does it really, Arjun? I'll tell you what I felt when I was running into the plantation. Frankly I was relieved – I was glad that it was over. And the men, I'll bet most of them felt exactly as I did. It was as if some kind of charade had come to an end.'

'What charade, Hardy? There was nothing make-believe about those tanks.'

Hardy slapped at the mosquitoes that were buzzing around them. 'You know, yaar Arjun, over these last few days, in the trenches at Jitra – I had an eerie feeling. It was strange to be sitting on one side of a battle line, knowing that you had to fight and knowing at the same time that it wasn't really your fight – knowing that whether you won or lost, neither the blame nor the credit would be yours. Knowing that you're risking everything to defend a way of life that pushes you to the sidelines. It's almost as if you're fighting against yourself. It's strange to be sitting in a trench, holding a gun and asking yourself: who is this weapon really aimed at? Am I being tricked into pointing it at myself?'

'I can't say I felt the same way, Hardy.'

'But ask yourself, Arjun: what does it mean for you and me to be in this army? You're always talking about soldiering as being just a job. But you know, yaar, it isn't just a job – it's when you're sitting in a trench that you realise that there's something very primitive about what we do. In the everyday world when would you ever stand up and say – "I'm going to risk my life for this"? As a human being it's something you can only do if you know why you're doing it. But when I was sitting in that trench, it was as if my heart and my hand had no connection – each seemed to belong to a different person. It was as if I wasn't really a human being – just a tool, an instrument. This is what I ask myself, Arjun: in what way do I become human again? How do I connect what I do with what I want, in my heart?'

'Hardy – it doesn't do any good to think like that . . .'

They heard Lieutenant-Colonel Buckland's voice, somewhere nearby: 'Not so much talk, please . . .'

Arjun cut himself short.

Thirty-five

The offer, when it finally came, was so good, so much in excess of Rajkumar's highest hopes, that he made the messenger repeat it twice, just to make sure that he had got it right. On hearing confirmation, he looked down at his hands and saw that they had begun to shake. He could not trust himself to rise to his feet. He smiled at the messenger and said something that his pride would not otherwise have allowed him to say.

'Could you help me up?'

Leaning on the messenger's arm he went to the open window of his office and looked down into his timberyard to see if he could spot Neel. The yard was now stacked high with the stocks of timber he had accumulated over the last year. His son's bearded face was half-hidden behind an eight-foot pile of freshly milled planks.

'Neel.' Rajkumar's voice erupted from his chest in a joyful bellow. He shouted again. 'Neel.'

There was no reason to disguise his gladness: if ever in all his life he had had a moment of triumph, it was this.

'Neel!'

'Apé?' Neel turned his face up to his father, in surprise.

'Come up, Neel – there's good news.'

His legs were steadier now. Standing upright, he clapped the messenger on the back and handed him a coin. 'Just some tea money . . .'

'Yes, sir.'

The messenger smiled at the openness of Rajkumar's delight. He was a young clerk, sent to Rangoon by Rajkumar's contractor friend – the one who was working on the Burma–China road, up in the far north. Just as Rajkumar had foreseen, the building of the road had assumed a new strategic urgency with America's entry into the war. It was to be the principal supply line for the Government of Generalissimo Chiang Kai-Shek. New funds had become available and work was proceeding apace. The contractor now found himself in need of a very substantial amount of timber – hence the offer to Rajkumar.

The deal was not without its drawbacks. There was no advance of the kind that Rajkumar would have liked, and the exact date of payment was not guaranteed. But this was wartime after all, and every businessman in Rangoon had learnt to adapt. Rajkumar had no hesitation in accepting the offer.

'Neel!'

'Apé?'

Rajkumar observed his son's face closely as he told him the news. He was delighted when he saw Neel's eyes lighting up; he knew that Neel was glad not merely because of the concluding of a long-hoped-for deal but also because this would be a vindication of his almost childlike belief in his father. Looking into his son's shining eyes, Rajkumar could feel his voice going hoarse. He drew Neel to his chest and hugged him, holding him tight, squeezing the breath from his body, so that his son gasped and cried out aloud. Between the two of them there had always been a special bond, a particular closeness. There were no other eyes in the world that looked into Rajkumar's without reservation, without judgement, without criticism – not Dolly's, not Saya John's, Dinu's least of all. Nothing about this triumph was sweeter than the redemption of his boy's trust.

'And now, Neel –' Rajkumar gave his son's shoulder an affectionate punch – 'and now there's a lot to be done. You're going to have to work harder than you ever have.'

'Apé,' Neel nodded.

Thinking of all the arrangements that had to be made, Rajkumar's mind returned quickly to the matter at hand. 'Come on,' he said, starting down the ladder, 'let's try to get an idea of what we have to do and how much time we have.'

Rajkumar had sold off all his properties except for the

timberyard on the Pazundaung Creek. The creek's mouth lay at the intersection of the Rangoon and Pegu rivers and it provided quick access to the riverport. Many of the city's sawmills, warehouses, petroleum tanks and rice-mills were concentrated along the banks of this waterway. The yard itself consisted of not much more than an open space, crammed with timber and perpetually wreathed in a fog of sawdust. It was surrounded by a high perimeter wall and at its centre there stood a small cabin, elevated on stilts – a structure that vaguely resembled the tais of upcountry forests, except that it was built on a much smaller scale. The cabin served as an office for Rajkumar.

As he walked around the yard Rajkumar could not help congratulating himself on his foresight in concentrating all his stocks in one place – he'd known all along that the order, when it came, would have to be quickly executed: events had proved him right. But even then the job ahead would not be an easy one. Rajkumar saw that he would require large teams of oo-sis and elephants, coolies and trucks. His own elephants had long since been sold off and, with the exception of a couple of caretakers, all his regular employees had been dismissed. He had accustomed himself to managing with hired workforces.

There was a lot to be done and he wished he had more help. Rajkumar could tell that Neel was trying hard, but he was a town-boy, inexperienced in the timber business. Rajkumar knew that Neel was not to blame for this: it was his own fault for never having encouraged him to work in the timber business.

'I don't want to be working with strangers,' Rajkumar confided to Neel. 'I'd prefer to have Doh Say. He'd know exactly how to go about this.'

'But how are we to reach him in Huay Zedi?'

'We can reach him through Raymond.' This was Neel's old friend, Doh Say's son. He was now a student at Rangoon's Judson College. Rajkumar thought the matter over and nodded to himself. 'Yes, Raymond will be able to send him word. We must make sure to go and look for him this evening.'

When Rajkumar and Neel got back to Kemendine, the glow of victory was still bright on their faces. Dolly guessed at once that something was up. 'What is it? Tell me.'

410

Both Rajkumar and Neel began to talk at once, in voices that were loud enough to bring Manju running down the stairs, with the baby in her arms.

'Tell me too. Start again . . .'

Now for the first time in many weeks there was a lightening in the atmosphere of the house. Neither Arjun nor Dinu had yet been heard from – but this was an occasion when the anxieties of the war could legitimately be forgotten. Even Dolly, so long the sceptic, finally began to believe that Rajkumar's plans were about to pay off; as for Manju, she was overjoyed. The whole family piled into the Packard, with Manju holding the baby and Neel in the driver's seat. Laughing like children, they set off for Judson College, to find Doh Say's son, Raymond.

It was not long before Christmas now, and the central part of Rangoon was being readied for the festivities. This was the area that housed the big department stores, the fashionable restaurants, the clubs, bars and hotels. It was here too – within range of a few blocks of gabled, red-brick buildings – that most of the city's churches, schools and other missionary institutions were located. In December this quarter became one of the city's great seasonal attractions. People flocked in from other neighbourhoods – Kemendine, Kokine, Botataung, Kalaa Bustee – to promenade through the streets and admire the Christmas decorations.

This year the customary bright lights had been forbidden by the air-raid wardens. But otherwise the war had not greatly affected the spirits of the neighbourhood; on the contrary, the news from abroad had had the effect of heightening the usual Christmastime excitement. Among many of the city's British residents, the war had occasioned a renewed determination to carry on as usual. As a result the big shops and restaurants were just as brightly decorated as ever before. Rowe and Co. – the big department store – had put up its usual Christmas tree, a real pine, sent down, as always, from the Maymyo hills. The tree's base was surrounded by drifts of cottonwool and its branches were whitened with a frosting of Cuticura talcum powder. At Whiteway, Laidlaw – another large department store – the tree was even larger, with trimmings imported from England.

They stopped at the Scott Market and went to the Sun Cafe, to

411

sample the famous chocolate-covered Yule logs. On the way they passed a Muslim butcher who was tending a flock of live turkeys and geese. Many of the birds bore little wire tags – they had been reserved months in advance, by European families. The butcher was fattening them for Christmas.

Judson College was customarily one of the centres of Rangoon's Christmas festivities. The college was run by American Baptists and it was one of the best-known educational institutions in Burma.

Raymond was in the college's red-brick chapel. He was rehearsing Handel's *Messiah* with the choir. They sat down to wait, at the back of the chapel, and listened to the massed voices, surging through the arched rafters. The music was glorious and even the baby was lulled into silence.

At the end of the rehearsal Neel intercepted Raymond and brought him over. Raymond was a good-looking, sturdily-built young man with sleepy eyes and a doleful smile. He had been studying in Rangoon for three years, and was thinking of a legal career.

Raymond was delighted to see them and immediately undertook to send word to his father. He was confident that he would be able to get word to Huay Zedi within a few days, by means of a complicated network of telegrams and forwarders.

Rajkumar did not doubt for a moment that Doh Say would come immediately to Rangoon to help him out.

Next morning, Lieutenant-Colonel Buckland sent Arjun ahead with Kishan Singh and two other men. The men were armed with their usual Lee Enfield .303 rifles, while Arjun was issued their only Tommy gun.

Shortly before noon, Arjun came upon the plantation manager's house. It was a squat, two-storeyed bungalow with a tiled roof. It stood in the centre of a clearing that was almost perfectly square. The clearing was surrounded on all sides, by straight, orderly stands of rubber trees. A gravelled driveway snaked across a well-mowed lawn, leading to the front door. The garden was dotted with bursts of colour: the flowers were mostly English varieties – hollyhocks, snapdragons, hydrangeas. At the back there was a tall jacaranda tree with a wooden swing suspended from a branch. Beside it stood an elevated water storage tank. There were beds planted with vegetables – tomatoes, carrots, cauliflowers. A paved path led through the vegetable patch, to the back door. A cat was clawing at the door, crying to be let in.

Arjun circled around the clearing, keeping well within the shelter of the rubber trees. He followed the driveway a little distance down the slope: it could be seen winding through the plantation to join a tarred road, a half-mile or so away. No one was in sight.

Arjun put one of his men on watch and sent another to report back to Lieutenant-Colonel Buckland. Then, with Kishan Singh following close behind, he skirted round the house until he was facing the back door. He crossed the back garden at a run, taking care to keep his head down. The door was latched but gave way easily when he and Kishan Singh put their shoulders to it. The cat that was waiting outside went streaking into the house, through Arjun's feet.

Arjun stepped across the threshold and found himself standing in a large kitchen of European design. There was a wood-burning oven, made of iron, and windows that were draped with white lace curtains. Porcelain plates and bowls stood in rows in the wooden cabinets that lined the walls; the ceramic sink was scrubbed clean and the tin drainer beside it was stacked with glass tumblers and a row of freshly cleaned baby bottles. On the floor, there was a dog's feeding bowl. Where a refrigerator had once stood there was a rectangular discolouration, outlined against the whitewashed wall. On the kitchen table there lay heaps of eggs and bread, and a couple of half-used tins of Australian butter and processed cheese. It was evident that the refrigerator had been emptied in great haste before being carried away.

Although Arjun was now certain that there was no one in the house, he was careful to have Kishan Singh back him up as he went through the other rooms. The bungalow was littered with signs of a hasty departure. In the bedroom, drawers lay upturned, and brassieres and women's underclothing were strewn across the floor. In the living room, a piano stool stood forlornly by the wall. Half-hidden behind a door Arjun found a stack of framed photographs. He glanced at the pictures – a church wedding; children, a car and a dog – the photographs had been piled into a box, as though ready to be transported. Arjun had a sudden vision of the woman of the house making a last frantic run through the bungalow, looking for the box while her husband and family sat outside in a lorry that was piled high with strapped-down luggage; he imagined her rummaging in the cupboards while her husband gunned the engine and the dog barked and the children cried. He was glad that they'd got away when they had; annoyed, on their behalf, with whoever it was that had argued them out of leaving earlier.

He went back to the kitchen and switched on the overhead fan. To his astonishment it worked. On the table there stood a couple of bottles of water, still awash in the puddles of sweat that had formed around them when they were emptied from the refrigerator. He handed one to Kishan Singh and drained the other himself, almost at a gulp. The water had a dull, metallic taste as it coursed down his throat: it was only now that he remembered that it was a long time since he had last eaten.

Minutes later the others arrived.

'Plenty of food here, sir,' Arjun said.

Lieutenant-Colonel Buckland nodded. 'Good. Heaven knows, we need it. And I imagine we can clean up a bit as well.'

Upstairs there were two bathrooms, with fresh towels waiting in the racks. Lieutenant-Colonel Buckland used one bathroom while Arjun and Hardy took turns with the other. The water came from the shaded tank outdoors and was pleasantly cool. Before undressing Arjun stood his Tommy gun against the door. Then he filled a bucket and poured the cool water over his head. On the sink there lay a curled tube of toothpaste: he couldn't resist squeezing some on to his forefinger. With his mouth foaming he glanced out of the bathroom window. Kishan Singh and a couple of the other men were standing under the water tank, bare-bodied, sluicing water over their heads. Another man was keeping watch, smoking a cigarette, his hand resting loosely on his rifle.

They went back to the dining room and found it neatly laid, with plates and silverware. A meal had been prepared by a lance-

414

naik who had some experience of the officers' mess. There was a salad of tomatoes and carrots; eggs scrambled in butter and hot toast. Canned goods of many kinds had been found in the kitchen cupboards: there was duck-liver pâté, a plate of pickled herrings, thick slices of Dutch ham – all laid out nicely on porcelain plates.

In the sideboard that stood beside the dining table Arjun discovered a few bottles of beer. 'Do you think they would mind, sir?'

'Don't see why they should.' Lieutenant-Colonel Buckland smiled. 'I'm sure if we'd met them at the club they'd have told us to help ourselves.'

There was an interjection from Hardy. 'If *you* had met them at the club, sir,' he said quietly, offering a politely worded correction. 'The two of us wouldn't have been allowed in.'

Lieutenant-Colonel Buckland paused, with a tilted beer bottle in his grasp. Then he raised his glass and gave Hardy an ironic smile. 'To the clubs that won't have us, gentlemen,' he said. 'May they be for ever legion.'

Arjun raised a half-hearted cheer. 'Hear, hear.' He put his glass down and reached for the plate of ham.

Just as they were helping themselves, new cooking smells came wafting out of the kitchen: the fragrance of freshly rolled parathas and chapatis, of frying onions and chopped tomatoes. Hardy glanced down at his plate and its piles of ham and herring. Suddenly he stood up.

'Sir, may I be excused for a minute?'

'By all means, Lieutenant.'

He went into the kitchen and returned with a tray of chapatis and *ande-ka-bhujia* – eggs fried with tomatoes and onions. Glancing at his plate, Arjun found himself growing hungry all over again: to look away was an effort.

'It's all right, yaar.' Hardy was watching him with a smile. 'You can have some too. A chapati won't turn you into a savage, you know.'

Arjun sank back in his seat as Hardy shovelled chapatis and bhujia on to his plate: he lowered his gaze, in the sullen way of a child who is caught between warring parents. The weariness of the night before came on him again and he could barely bring himself to touch his food.

415

When they were done with eating Lieutenant-Colonel Buckland told Hardy to go outside, to check on the men who were guarding the bungalow's approach road.

Hardy saluted. 'Yes, sir.'

Arjun would have risen from the table too, but Lieutenant-Colonel Buckland stopped him. 'No hurry, Roy.' He reached for a beer bottle. 'Some more?'

'I don't see why not, sir.'

Lieutenant-Colonel Buckland poured beer into Arjun's glass and then filled his own.

'Tell me, Lieutenant,' he said presently, lighting a cigarette. 'How would you rate our morale at this moment?'

'After a lunch like this one, sir,' Arjun said brightly, 'I would say it couldn't be better.'

'It was a different story last night, eh, Lieutenant?' Lieutenant-Colonel Buckland smiled through a cloud of cigarette smoke.

'I don't know if I would say that, sir.'

'Well, you know I have ears of my own, Lieutenant. And while my Hindustani may not be as good as yours, I can assure you it's perfectly adequate.'

Arjun shot him a startled glance. 'I'm not sure I know what you're getting at, sir.'

'Well, none of us could sleep much last night, could we, Lieutenant? And whispers can carry a long way.'

'I don't quite take your meaning, sir.' Arjun felt his face growing hot. 'Are you referring to something I said?'

'It doesn't really matter, Lieutenant. Let's just say that there was a certain similarity of tone in all the voices around me.'

'I see, sir.'

'Lieutenant – I think you probably know that I – we – are not unaware of some of the tensions in our Indianised battalions. It's quite plain that many of our Indian officers feel strongly about public issues – particularly the question of independence.'

'Yes, sir.'

'I don't know what your own feelings are, Roy, but you should know that as far as the thrust of British public opinion goes, independence for India is just a matter of time. Everyone knows that the days of Empire are over – we're not fools, you know.

The last thing an ambitious young Englishman wants to do today is to go out to a backwater. The Americans have been telling us for years that we're going about this the wrong way. One doesn't have to keep up an Empire with all the paraphernalia of an administration and an army. There are easier and more efficient ways to keep a grip on things – it can be done at less expense, and with much less bother. We've all come to accept this now – even chaps like me who've spent our lives out east. The truth is that there's only one reason why England holds on any more – and that is out of a sense of obligation. I know this may be hard for you to believe but it's true. There's a feeling that we can't go under duress and we can't leave a mess behind. And you know as well as I do that if we were to pack our bags now, then you chaps would be at each other's throats in no time – even you and your friend Hardy, what with him being a Sikh and you a Hindu, a Punjabi and a Bengali . . .'

'I see, sir.'

'I'm telling you this, Lieutenant, only to alert you to some of the dangers of the situation in which we now find ourselves. I think we both know that our morale is not what it might be. But this is, of all times, the last in which anybody should waver in their loyalties. The reverses we've suffered are temporary – in a way they are a blessing in disguise. America's entry into the war makes it absolutely certain that we shall prevail, in time. In the meanwhile perhaps we should remind ourselves that the army has a very long memory when it comes to questions of allegiance and loyalty.'

The lieutenant-colonel paused to extinguish his cigarette. Arjun sat staring silently into his glass.

'You know, Roy,' Lieutenant-Colonel Buckland said quietly, 'my grandfather lived through the Mutiny of 1857. I remember that he bore very little rancour towards the civilians who'd got mixed up in the troubles. But as for the soldiers – the sepoys who'd led the Mutiny – that was another matter altogether. Those men had broken an oath: they were traitors, not rebels, and there is no traitor so contemptible as a soldier who reverses his allegiances. And if such a thing were to happen at a dodgy time, I think you would agree with me, wouldn't you, Roy, that it would be hard to conceive of anything quite so unspeakable?'

Arjun was about to answer when he was interrupted by the sound of racing footsteps. He turned to a window to see Hardy running across the front lawn.

'Sir,' Hardy came panting to the windowsill. 'Got to move, sir . . . Jap convoy heading up the road.'

'How many? Could we take them on?'

'No, sir . . . There're at least two platoons – maybe a company.'

Lieutenant-Colonel Buckland pushed his chair calmly back, dabbing his lips with a napkin. 'The main thing, gentlemen,' he said quietly, 'is not to panic. Take a moment to listen to me: this is what I want you to do . . .'

They left the house by the rear entrance with Arjun in the lead and Hardy and Lieutenant-Colonel Buckland bringing up the rear. On reaching the shelter of the first row of trees Arjun fell into a defensive position. With him was a detail composed of Kishan Singh and two other men. Their orders were to cover the others until everyone was clear of the grounds.

The first Japanese truck pulled into the compound just as Hardy and Lieutenant-Colonel Buckland were running across the back garden. For a moment Arjun allowed himself to believe that they had managed to escape unseen. Then a volley of gunfire erupted out of the back of the truck and Arjun heard a chorus of whistles shooting past, well over his head.

Lieutenant-Colonel Buckland and Hardy were almost abreast of him now. Arjun waited till they were clear before giving the order to return fire. '*Chalao goli.*' They fired indiscriminately, in the general direction of the bungalow. The only result was the immediate shattering of the kitchen's windows. In the meantime, the Japanese truck had swung round to take shelter on the far side of the house.

'*Piche. Chalo.*'

Arjun gave the order to fall back while staying in position himself, firing randomly, hoping to give Kishan Singh and the others time to regroup. He saw that the newly arrived Japanese soldiers were slipping into the trees one by one. He rose to his feet and began to run, holding his Tommy gun under his arm. Glancing over his shoulder, he encountered the now familiar sight of dozens of long files of trees, telescoping towards him – but with the difference that now, each tunnel offered a glimpse of a tiny grey-uniformed figure, somewhere in the far distance, running in pursuit.

Arjun began to run faster, breathing hard, watching out for the branches that lay hidden underneath the fallen leaves. A hundred feet or so ahead, the land fell away steeply. If he could get as far as that he might be able to lose the pursuing soldiers. He sprinted, shortening his steps as he neared the lip of the declivity. Just as he was going over the top he felt his right leg shooting out from beneath him. He fell, tumbling face first down the slope. The shock of the fall was compounded by confusion: he could not understand why he had fallen. He hadn't tripped and he hadn't lost his footing – he was sure of that. Grasping at the undergrowth he managed to bring himself to a halt. He tried to get back on his feet and found that he couldn't. He looked down and saw that his trouser leg was covered in blood. He could feel the wetness of the cloth against his skin yet he was not conscious of any pain. His pursuers' footsteps were closer now, and he glanced around himself quickly, looking at the carpet of dead leaves that stretched away in every direction.

Just then he heard a sound, a familiar whisper. 'Sah'b.'

He rolled over to find himself looking at Kishan Singh: his batman was lying prone, hidden inside a dark opening – a culvert or drainage pipe of some kind. The opening was blanketed by leaves and undergrowth. It was very well-hidden, almost invisible. The only reason that Arjun could see it at all was because he was lying flat on the ground.

Kishan Singh extended a hand and dragged him into the culvert. Then he crawled out to scatter leaves over the traces of Arjun's blood. Minutes later they heard the sound of footsteps racing past overhead.

The culvert was just wide enough for the two of them to lie side by side. Now, suddenly, Arjun's wound began to make itself felt, the pain welling out of his leg in waves. He tried to stifle a groan, not quite successfully. Kishan Singh threw a hand over his mouth and wrestled him into silence. Arjun realised that he was about to black out and he was glad: at that moment there was nothing he wanted more than oblivion.

Thirty-six

Even though he was following the news closely on the radio, Dinu had trouble understanding exactly what was under way in northern Malaya. The bulletins mentioned a major engagement in the region of Jitra but the reports were inconclusive and confusing. In the meantime, there were other indications of the way the war was going, all of them ominous. One of these was an official newspaper announcement, listing the closing of certain post offices in the north. Another was the increasing volume of southbound traffic: a stream of evacuees was pouring down the north–south highway in the direction of Singapore.

One day, on a visit to Sungei Pattani, Dinu had a glimpse of this exodus. The evacuees seemed to consist mainly of the families of planters and mining engineers. Their cars and trucks were filled with household objects – furniture, trunks, suitcases. He came across a truck that was loaded with a refrigerator, a dog and an upright piano. He spoke to the man who was driving the truck: he was a Dutchman, the manager of a rubber plantation near Jitra. His family were sitting crowded in the truck's cab: his wife, a newborn baby and two girls. The Dutchman said he'd managed to get out just ahead of the Japanese. His advice to Dinu was to leave as soon as possible – not to make the mistake of waiting until the last minute.

That night, at Morningside, Dinu told Alison exactly what the Dutchman had said. They looked at each other in silence: they had been over the subject several times before. They knew they had very few choices. If they went by road one of them would have to stay behind – the estate's truck was in no shape to make the long journey to Singapore and the Daytona would not be able to carry more than two passengers over that kind of distance. The only alternative was to go by train – but rail services had been temporarily suspended.

'What are we going to do, Alison?' Dinu said.

'Let's wait and see,' Alison said hopefully. 'Who knows? Perhaps we won't have to leave after all.'

Late that night they were woken by the crunch of bicycle wheels, rolling up the gravelled drive of Morningside House. A voice called out from below: 'Miss Martins . . .'

Alison got up and went to the window. It was still dark. Parting the curtains, she leaned out, peering down into the drive. Dinu glanced at a bedside clock and saw that it was four in the morning. He sat up: 'Alison? Who is it?'

'It's Ilongo,' Alison said. 'He has Ah Fatt with him – from the restaurant, in town.'

'At this time of night?'

'I think they want to tell me something.' Alison let the curtain drop. 'I'm going downstairs.' She pulled on a dressing gown and ran out of the room. A few minutes later, Dinu followed. He found Alison sitting in a huddle with the visitors. Ah Fatt was talking urgently, in rapid Malay, stabbing a finger in the air. Alison was biting her lip, nodding: Dinu could see a deepening anxiety in the crimped lines of her face.

In a while Dinu jogged her elbow. 'What are you talking about? Tell me.'

Alison stood up and took him aside.

'Ah Fatt says that Grandfather and I have to leave – for Singapore. He says it's going badly on the front. The Japanese may be able to push through in a day or two. He thinks the Kempeitai – their secret police – have information about us . . .'

Dinu nodded. 'He's right. It won't do to wait any longer. You've got to go.'

Tears started into Alison's eyes. 'I don't want to go, Dinu. Not without you. I really don't.'

'You have to, Alison. Think of your grandfather . . .'

'Miss Martins,' Ah Fatt interrupted, to let them know that he'd heard that a special evacuation train would be leaving from

Butterworth that morning. He wasn't sure that they'd be able to get on it – but it was worth trying.

Dinu and Alison exchanged smiles. 'We'll never get another chance like this,' Alison said.

'Let's wake your grandfather,' Dinu said. 'Let's not waste any time.'

They left early the next day in one of the estate's trucks. Ilongo drove and Dinu rode in the back with the luggage. Alison sat in front, with Saya John. There was little traffic, because of the time of day, and they arrived in Sungei Pattani in half the usual time. The town was silent: many of the shops and houses were locked or boarded up. Some had notices hanging outside.

A short way from town they picked up the main highway. The road's embankment was dotted with parked vehicles. Families could be seen to be sleeping in their cars, snatching a little rest before daylight. At intervals one-and-a-half-ton military trucks came barrelling down the highway, heading south. They would bear down very suddenly, pushing other traffic off the road, head-lights blazing, sounding their horns. Dinu caught occasional glimpses of soldiers, squatting in the trucks' tarpaulin-covered beds.

Approaching Butterworth, the road was jammed with cars and trucks. The railway station was right next to the ferry terminus that connected the mainland to the island of Penang. This area had taken several hits during the recent bombing raids and there was a great deal of confusion in the rubble-strewn streets. People could be seen heading towards the station on foot, carrying bags and suitcases.

Ilongo parked in a side street and left Alison, Dinu and Saya John in the truck while he went ahead to make inquiries. He came back an hour later to report that they had a long wait ahead. There were rumours that the train would not leave until after midnight. Penang was being evacuated too and a fleet of ferries was to be dispatched under cover of darkness. The train would not depart until the ferries had returned to Butterworth with the Penang evacuees.

Alison took a room in a hotel so that Saya John could rest. They spent the day taking it in turns to go out to make inquiries.

Night fell and at ten o'clock there was still no news. Then, a little after midnight, Ilongo came running into the hotel with the information that the ferries had been sighted, returning from Penang. Shortly afterwards a train was shunted into the platform of the railway station.

Alison woke Saya John and Dinu paid for the hotel room. They stepped out into the darkened street and joined the crowd that was hurrying toward the station. The entrance had been cordoned off and could only be approached through a defile that was packed with people and luggage.

A few yards from the entrance Ilongo decided to turn back. He put an arm around Saya John and gave him a big hug. 'Goodbye, Saya.'

Saya John gave him a blankly affectionate smile. 'Be careful how you drive, Ilongo.'

'Yes, Saya.' Ilongo laughed. He turned to Alison and Dinu but before he could say goodbye they were pushed ahead by the press of bodies. He shouted after them: 'I'm going to spend the night in the truck. You can find me there – just in case. Good luck.'

Dinu answered with a wave. 'And to you too . . . good luck.'

The entrance to the platform was manned by two guards, both Indian. They were dressed in green uniforms and had rifles slung over their shoulders. There were no tickets to be checked: the guards were looking the evacuees over and ushering them through.

They got to the gate with Saya John leaning heavily on Alison. Dinu was directly behind them, carrying their suitcases. Just as they were about to go through the entrance, a guard stopped Alison with an outstretched arm. There followed a hurried consultation between the two guards. Then the guards gestured to Dinu, Alison and Saya John to step aside. 'Please . . . Move away from the gate.'

'What's the matter?' Alison said to Dinu. 'What's happening?'

Dinu stepped up to face the guards. '*Kya hua*?' he said, addressing them in Hindustani. 'Why've you stopped us?'

'You can't go through.'

'Why not?'

'Don't you have eyes?' a guard said to him brusquely. 'Can't you see that this train's only for Europeans?'

'What?'

'You heard – it's only for Europeans.'

Dinu swallowed, trying to keep his composure. 'Listen,' he said carefully, 'that can't be true . . . This is wartime. We were told that this was an evacuation train. How can it be only for Europeans? There must be some mistake.'

The guard looked him in the eye, and gestured at the train with his thumb. 'You've got eyes of your own,' he said. '*Dekh lo* – take a look.'

Craning over the guard's shoulder, he looked up and down the platform, at the train's windows: he could not see a single face that looked Malay or Chinese or Indian.

'This is impossible . . . it's madness.'

'What? What's impossible?' Alison tugged at his arm. 'Dinu, tell me, what's going on?'

'The guards say this train is only for whites . . .'

Alison nodded. 'Yes. I had a feeling that it would be – that's how things are . . .'

'How can you say that, Alison?' Dinu was frantic now and sweat was pouring down his face. 'You can't put up with this stuff . . . Not now. Not when there's a war . . .'

Dinu spotted a uniformed Englishman, walking along the platform, checking a roster. Dinu began to plead with the guards: 'Listen – let me through – just for a minute . . . just to have a word with that officer over there . . . I'll explain to him; I'm sure he'll understand.'

'Not possible.'

Dinu lost his temper. He shouted into the guard's face. 'How can you stop me? Who's given you the right?'

Suddenly a third man appeared. He was dressed in a railway uniform and he too appeared to be Indian. He herded them away from the entrance, towards a flight of stairs that led back to the street. 'Yes please?' he said to Dinu. 'I am the station master – please tell me: what is the problem?'

'Sir . . .' Dinu made an effort to keep his voice even. 'They are not letting us through . . . They say the train is only for Europeans.'

The station master smiled apologetically. 'Yes – that is what we have been given to understand.'

'But how can that be? . . . This is wartime . . . This is an evacuation train.'

'What can I say? Why, in Penang, Mr Lim, the magistrate, was turned back even though he had an official evacuation letter. The Europeans would not let him board the ferries becuse of his being Chinese.'

'You don't understand . . .' Dinu began to plead. 'It's not just Europeans who are in danger . . . You can't do this . . . It's wrong . . .'

The station master pulled a face, shrugging dismissively. 'I do not see what is so wrong with it. After all it is common sense. They are the rulers; they are the ones who stand to lose.'

Dinu's voice rose. 'That's nonsense,' he shouted. 'If that's the way you look at it, then the war's already lost. Don't you see? You've conceded everything worth fighting for . . .'

'Sir,' the station master glared at him, 'there is no reason to shout. I am just doing my job.'

Dinu raised his hands and grabbed hold of the station master's collar. 'You bastard,' he said, shaking him. 'You bastard . . . it's you who're the enemy. People like you – just doing their jobs . . . you're the enemy.'

'Dinu,' Alison screamed. 'Look out!'

Dinu felt a hand closing on the back of his neck, wrenching him away from the station master. A fist slammed into his face, knocking him to the floor. His nostrils filled with the metallic smell of blood. He looked up to see the two guards glaring angrily down at him. Alison and Saya John were holding them off. 'Let him be. Let him be!'

Alison reached down and helped Dinu to his feet. 'Come on, Dinu – let's go.' She picked up their luggage and ushered Dinu and Saya John down the stairs. When they were back on the street, Dinu steadied himself against a lamp-post and put his hands on Alison's shoulders. 'Alison,' he said, 'Alison – maybe they'll let you on, by yourself. You're half-white. You have to try, Alison.'

'Shh.' She put a hand over his mouth. 'Don't say that, Dinu. I wouldn't think of it.'

Dinu wiped the blood from his nose. 'But you have to leave,

Alison . . . With your grandfather – you heard what Ah Fatt said. One way or another you have to go . . . You can't stay at Morningside any more . . .'

From inside the station there was a piercing whistle. All around them, people began to run, crowding into the station's entrance, pushing at the gates. Dinu, Alison and Saya John held on to each other's arms', anchoring themselves to the lamp-post.

At last they heard the train pulling away. 'It's gone,' said Saya John.

'Yes, Baba,' Alison said quietly. 'It's gone.'

Dinu stepped back and picked up a suitcase. 'Let's go and find Ilongo,' he said.

'Tomorrow morning we'll go back to Morningside.'

'To stay?'

Dinu shook his head. 'I'll stay there, Alison,' he said. 'They won't harm me – I don't have anything particular to be afraid of. But you and your grandfather – with your connections – American and Chinese . . . There's just no telling what they would do to you. You have to go . . .'

'But how, Dinu?'

At last Dinu said the words they'd both been dreading: 'The Daytona . . . It's the only way, Alison.'

'No.' She threw herself on him. 'Not without you.'

'It'll be all right, Alison.' He was careful to speak quietly, feigning a confidence that he was far from feeling. 'I'll join you soon . . . in Singapore, you'll see. We won't be long apart.'

It was dark when Arjun returned to consciousness. The sensation in his leg had subsided to a raw, throbbing pain. As his mind cleared Arjun realised that a stream of water was flowing past him and the culvert was resounding to a dull, drumming noise. It took him several minutes to understand that it was raining.

Just as he was beginning to stir, Arjun felt Kishan Singh's hand tightening on his shoulder, in warning. 'They're still around, sah'b,' Kishan Singh whispered. 'They've posted pickets in the plantation. They're waiting.'

'How close are they? Within earshot?'

'No. They can't hear us in the rain.'

'How long was I out?'

'More than an hour, sah'b. I bandaged your wound. The bullet passed cleanly through your hamstring. It'll be all right.'

Arjun touched his thigh gingerly. Kishan Singh had unwrapped his puttees, rolled up his trousers and applied a field dressing. He'd also made a kind of cradle to keep his leg out of the water, by propping two sticks against the sides of the culvert.

'What shall we do now, sah'b?'

The question confounded Arjun. He tried to look ahead but his mind was still clouded by pain and he could think of no clear plan. 'We'll have to wait them out, Kishan Singh. Tomorrow morning we'll see.'

'*Han*, sah'b.' Kishan Singh seemed relieved.

Lying motionless in the inches-deep water, Arjun became acutely aware of his surroundings: of the wet folds of cloth that were carving furrows into his skin, of the pressure of Kishan Singh's body, stretched out beside him. The culvert was filled with the smell of their bodies: the mildewed, rain-soaked, sweat-stained odour of their uniforms, the metallic smell of his own blood.

His mind strayed, disordered by the pain in his leg. He remembered suddenly the look that Kishan Singh had given him on the beach that day, when he came back from the island with Alison. Was it scorn that he'd seen in his eyes – a judgement of some kind?

Would Kishan Singh have done what he had? Allowed himself to make love to Alison; to prey upon her; to betray Dinu, who was both a friend and something more? He didn't know himself why he'd been driven to do it; why he'd wanted her so much. He'd heard some of the chaps saying that these things came on you in wartime – on the front. But Kishan Singh was on the front too – and it was hard to think of him doing anything like that. Was that part of the difference between being an officer and a *jawan* – having to impose yourself, enforce your will?

It occurred to him that he would have liked to talk about this. He remembered that Kishan Singh had once told him that he'd been married off at the age of sixteen. He would have liked to ask Kishan Singh: what was it like when you were married? Had you known your wife before? On the night of your wedding how did you touch her? Did she look you in the face?

He tried to form the sentences in his head and found that he did not know the right words in Hindustani; did not even know the tone of voice in which such questions could be asked. These were things he did not know how to say. There was so much that he did not know how to say, in any language. There was something awkward, unmanly even, about wanting to know what was inside one's head. What was it that Hardy had said the night before? Something about connecting his hand and his heart. He'd been taken aback when he said that; it wasn't on for a chap to say that kind of thing. But at the same time, it was interesting to think that Hardy – or anyone for that matter, even he himself – might want something without knowing it. How was that possible? Was it because no one had taught them the words? The right language? Perhaps because it might be too dangerous? Or because they weren't old enough to know? It was strangely crippling to think that he did not possess the simplest tools of self-consciousness – had no window through which to know that he possessed a within. Was this what Alison had meant, about being a weapon in someone else's hands? Odd that Hardy had said the same thing too.

Waiting for the minutes to pass he could feel his mind fixing on his wounded leg. The pain grew steadily, mounting in intensity until it saturated his consciousness, erasing all other sensation. He began to breathe in gasps, through gritted teeth. Then, through the fog of pain in his head, he became aware of Kishan Singh's hand, gripping his forearm, shaking his shoulder, in encouragement.

'*Sabar karo, sah'b*; it'll pass.'

He heard himself say: 'I don't know how long I can last, Kishan Singh.'

'You can last, sah'b. Just hold on. Be patient.'

Arjun had a sudden premonition of blacking out again, sinking face first into the rainwater, drowning where he lay. In panic he clutched at Kishan Singh, holding on to his arm as though it were a life raft.

'Kishan Singh, say something. Talk. Don't let me pass out again.'

'Talk about what, sah'b?'

'I don't care. Just talk, Kishan Singh – about anything. Tell me about your village.'

Hesitantly Kishan Singh began to speak.

'The name of our village is Kotana, sah'b, and it's near Kuruk-shetra – not far from Delhi . It's as simple a village as any, but there is one thing we always say of Kotana . . .'

'What is that?'

'That in every house in Kotana you will find a piece of the world. In one there is a hookah from Egypt; in another a box from China . . .'

Speaking through a wall of pain, Arjun said: 'Why is that, Kishan Singh?'

'Sah'b, for generations every Jat family in Kotana has sent its sons to serve in the army of the English sarkar.'

'Since when?'

'Since the time of my great-grandfather, sah'b – since the Mutiny.'

'The Mutiny?' Arjun recalled Lieutenant-Colonel Buckland's voice, speaking of the same thing. 'What does the Mutiny have to do with it?'

'Sah'b, when I was a boy, the old men of the village used to tell us a story. It was about the Mutiny. When the uprising ended and the British re-entered Delhi it came to be known that a great spectacle was to be held in the city. From Kotana a group of elders was deputed to go. They set off at dawn and walked, with hundreds of others, towards the southern postern of the old capital. When they were still far away they saw that the sky above the city was black with birds. The wind carried an odour that grew stronger as they approached the city. The road was straight, the ground level and they could see a long way into the distance. A puzzling sight lay ahead. The road seemed to be lined by troops of very tall men. It was as though an army of giants had turned out to stand guard over the crowd. On approaching closer, they saw that these were not giants, but men – rebel soldiers whose bodies had been impaled on sharpened stakes. The stakes were arranged in straight lines and led all the way to the city. The stench was terrible. When they returned to Kotana the elders gathered the villagers together. They said, "Today we have seen the face of defeat and it shall never be ours." From that day on, the families of Kotana decided that they would send their sons to the army of the English sarkar. This is what our fathers told us. I do not know whether this story is true or false, sah'b, but it is what I heard when I was a boy.'

In the confusion of his pain, Arjun had trouble following this. 'What are you saying then, Kishan Singh? Are you saying that the villagers joined the army out of fear? But that can't be: no one forced them – or you for that matter. What was there to be afraid of?'

'Sah'b,' Kishan Singh said softly, 'all fear is not the same. What is the fear that keeps us hiding here, for instance? Is it a fear of the Japanese, or is it a fear of the British? Or is it a fear of ourselves, because we do not know who to fear more? Sah'b, a man may fear the shadow of a gun just as much as the gun itself – and who is to say which is the more real?'

For a moment, it seemed to Arjun that Kishan Singh was talking about something very exotic, a creature of fantasy: a terror that made you remould yourself, that made you change your idea of your place in the world – to the point where you lost your awareness of the fear that had formed you. The idea of such a magnitude of terror seemed absurd – like reports of the finding of creatures that were known to be extinct. This was the difference, he thought, between the other ranks and officers: common soldiers had no access to the instincts that made them act; no vocabulary with which to shape their self-awareness. They were destined, like Kishan Singh, to be strangers to themselves, to be directed always by others.

But no sooner did this thought take shape in his mind than it was transformed by the delirium of his pain. He had a sudden, hallucinatory vision. Both he and Kishan Singh were in it, but transfigured: they were both lumps of clay, whirling on potters' wheels. He, Arjun, was the first to have been touched by the unseen potter; a hand had come down on him, touched him, passed over to another; he had been formed, shaped – he had become a thing unto itself – no longer aware of the pressure of

430

the potter's hand, unconscious even that it had come his way. Elsewhere, Kishan Singh was still turning on the wheel, still unformed, damp, malleable mud. It was this formlessness that was the core of his defence against the potter and his shaping touch.

Arjun could not blot this image from his mind: how was it possible that Kishan Singh – uneducated, unconscious of his motives – should be more aware of the weight of the past than he, Arjun?

'Kishan Singh,' he said hoarsely, 'give me some water.'

Kishan Singh handed him a green bottle and he drank, hoping that the water would dissipate the hallucinatory brilliance of the images that were passing before his eyes. But it had exactly the opposite effect. His mind was inflamed with visions, queries. Was it possible – even hypothetically – that his life, his choices, had always been moulded by fears of which he himself was unaware? He thought back to the past: Lankasuka, Manju, Bela , the hours he had spent sitting on the windowsill, the ecstatic sense of liberation that had come over him on learning that he had been accepted into the Military Academy. Fear had played no part in any of this. He had never thought of his life as different from any other; he had never experienced the slightest doubt about his personal sovereignty; never imagined himself to be dealing with anything other than the full range of human choice. But if it were true that his life had somehow been moulded by acts of power of which he was unaware – then it would follow that he had never acted of his own volition; never had a moment of true self-consciousness. Everything he had ever assumed about himself was a lie, an illusion. And if this were so, how was he to find himself now?

Thirty-seven

When they left for Morningside, the next day, the roads were even busier than on the way out. But theirs seemed to be the only vehicle going north: everyone else was heading in the opposite direction – towards Kuala Lumpur and Singapore. Heads turned to stare as they drove by; they were flagged down several times by helpful people who wanted to make sure they knew where they were going.

They passed dozens of army trucks, many of them travelling two abreast, with their klaxons blaring, crowding them off the road. Over long stretches they were forced to drive on the grassy verge, crawling along at speeds of fifteen to twenty miles an hour.

It was late afternoon when they came into Sungei Pattani: it was just a day since they'd last driven through, but the town already seemed a changed place. In the morning, they'd found it empty and ghostlike: most of its inhabitants had scattered into the countryside; its shops had been boarded and locked. Now Sungei Pattani was empty no longer: everywhere they looked there were soldiers – Australians, Canadians, Indians, British. But these were not the orderly detachments they had grown accustomed to seeing; these were listless, weary-looking men, bunched together in small groups and ragged little clusters. Some were ambling through the streets with their guns slung over their shoulders, like fishing rods; some were lounging in the shade of the shophouse arcades, eating out of cans and packets, scooping out the food with their fingers. Their uniforms were sweat-stained and dirty, their faces streaked with mud. In the town's parks and roundabouts – where children usually played – they saw groups

432

of exhausted men, lying asleep, with their weapons cradled in their arms.

They began to notice signs of looting: broken windows, gates that had been wrenched open, shops with battered shutters. They saw looters stepping in and out of the breaches – soldiers and locals were milling about together, tearing shops apart. There were no policemen anywhere in sight. It was clear that the civil administration had departed.

'Faster, Ilongo.' Dinu rapped on the truck's window. 'Let's get through . . .'

They came to a road that was blocked by a group of soldiers. One of them was pointing a gun at the truck, trying to wave it down. Dinu noticed that he was swaying on his feet. He shouted to Ilongo. 'Keep going; they're drunk . . .' Ilongo swerved suddenly, taking the truck over the median, into the other lane. Dinu looked back to see the soldiers staring after them, cursing: 'Fuckin' monkeys . . .'

Ilongo turned into an alley, then took the truck speeding down a side road, out of town. A few miles further on, he spotted an acquaintance standing by the roadside. He stopped to ask what was going on.

The man was a contractor on a rubber plantation not far from Morningside. He told them they were lucky that they were still in possession of their truck: on his estate, every single vehicle had been commandeered. An English officer had come through with a detachment of soldiers earlier in the day: they'd driven their trucks away.

They exchanged glances, all of them thinking immediately of the Daytona, back at its Morningside garage.

Dinu began to chew on his knuckles: 'Come on, let's not waste time . . .'

A few minutes later they drove past Morningside's arched gateway. It was as though they had entered another country; here there was no sign of anything untoward. The estate was tranquil and quiet; children waved at them as they drove up the unpaved road. Then the house appeared, far ahead on the slope: it looked majestic, serene.

Ilongo took the truck directly to the garage. He jumped down and pulled the door open. The Daytona was still inside.

433

Dinu and Alison stood looking at the car. Dinu took hold of her arm and nudged her into the garage: 'Alison . . . you should set off right now . . . there's so little time.'

'No.' Alison pulled her arm free and slammed shut the garage door. 'I'll leave later – at night. Who knows how long it'll be before we see each other again? I want to spend a few hours with you before I go.'

In the morning Kishan Singh went to investigate and found that the Japanese had withdrawn from the plantation, under cover of night. He helped Arjun crawl out of the culvert and propped him upright, on the leaf-carpeted ground. Then he eased off Arjun's wet clothes, wrung them out, and spread them in a sunlit spot.

Arjun's chest and stomach were puckered from their long immersion, but the pain in his leg had eased. He was relieved to see that the bandage on his thigh had done its work, stopping the flow of blood.

Kishan Singh found a branch that could be used as a crutch and they started off slowly with Arjun stopping every few paces to adjust his grip. Presently they arrived at a gravelled track. Keeping to the shelter of the treeline they followed the direction of the track. In a while they began to notice signs of approaching habitation – shreds of clothing, footprints, discarded eggshells that had been carried away by birds. Soon they saw curls of woodsmoke rising above the trees. They caught the familiar smells of rice and scorched mustard seeds. Then they spotted the plantation's coolie lines: twins rows of shacks, facing each other across the track. Large numbers of people were milling about in the open and it was clear, even from a distance, that something unusual was under way.

The shacks lay in a gentle depression, a basin, surrounded by higher land on all sides. With Kishan Singh's help Arjun climbed up a low ridge. Lying flat on their stomachs, they looked down into the basin below.

There were some fifty dwellings in the lines, arranged in parallel

434

rows. At one end there was a small Hindu temple – a tin-roofed shed surrounded by a wall that was painted red and white. Next to the temple there was a clearing with an open-sided shed, also roofed in tin. This was evidently a communal meeting place. It was this shed that was the focus of the excitement. Everyone in the hamlet was heading in its direction.

'Sah'b. Look.' Kishan Singh pointed to a black car standing half hidden beside the shed. There was a flag on the bonnet, affixed to an upright rod. The flag seemed very small from that distance and Arjun failed to recognise it at first glance. It was both familiar and unfamiliar; of a design that he knew well, but had not seen in a long time. He turned to Kishan Singh and found his batman watching him warily.

'Do you know that *jhanda*, Kishan Singh?'

'Sah'b, it is the *tiranga* . . .'

Of course – how could he have failed to recognise it? It was the flag of the Indian national movement: a spinning wheel, set against a background of saffron, white and green. He was still puzzling over the flag when there followed a second surprise. A familiar khaki-turbaned figure came out of the shed, walking towards the car. It was Hardy and he was deep in conversation with another man, a stranger – a white-bearded Sikh, dressed in the long, white tunic of a learned man, a Giani.

There was no reason to wait any longer. Arjun struggled to his feet. 'Kishan Singh, *chalo* . . .' Leaning heavily on his crutch he began to walk down the slope towards the shed.

'Hardy! *Oye*, Hardy!'

Hardy broke off his conversation and looked up. 'Yaar? Arjun?'

He came running up the slope, a grin spreading across his face. 'Yaar – we thought for sure the bastards had got you.'

'Kishan Singh came back for me,' Arjun said. 'I wouldn't be here now if it wasn't for him.'

Hardy clapped Kishan Singh on the shoulder. '*Shabash!*'

'Now tell me –' Arjun jogged Hardy's elbow – 'what's going on here?'

'No hurry, yaar,' Hardy said. 'I'll tell you, but we should get you cleaned up first. Where exactly were you hit?'

'Hamstring, I think.'

'Is it bad?'

'Better today.'

'Let's go somewhere where we can sit down. We'll get your wound dressed.'

Hardy beckoned to a soldier. '*Jaldi – M.O. ko bhejo.*' He led Arjun into one of the shacks and held the door open. 'Our HQ,' he said with a grin.

It was dark inside, the narrow windows being draped in ragged bits of cloth. The walls were of wood, covered with layers of soot, and there was a powerful smell of smoke. Beside one wall there stood a narrow string *charpoy*: Hardy led Arjun to the bed and helped him sit down.

There was a knock at the door and the medical orderly entered. He subjected Arjun's bandage to a careful examination and then ripped it off, in one quick movement. Arjun grimaced and Hardy handed him a glass of water.

'Drink up. You need it.'

Arjun drained the glass and handed it back. 'Hardy?' he said. 'Where's Bucky?'

'He's resting,' said Hardy. 'There's a vacant shed down the road. It was the only suitable place for him. His arm's been troubling him. We had to give him painkillers. He's been out all morning.'

The orderly began to swab Arjun's wound and he braced himself by gripping the edge of the bed.

'So tell me, Hardy,' he said, through gritted teeth. 'What's going on here?'

'I'll make it as short as possible,' said Hardy. 'It happened like this: last night, not long after we lost you, we came across a couple of rubber tappers. They were Indian and when we spoke to them they said we would be safe in the coolie lines. They brought us here. They were very welcoming: gave us food, beds. Showed us the shed where we put Bucky. We didn't know this then, but it turned out that some of them were members of the Indian Independence League. They sent word to their office and this morning Gianiji arrived, in a car – flying the flag. You can imagine how amazed we were. Turns out he's Giani Amreek Singh – recognise the name? His signature was on the pamphlets the Japs dropped on us at Jitra.'

436

'Yes,' said Arjun, drily. 'I know that name. What does he want?'

Hardy paused, humming a tune under his breath. Arjun knew that he was thinking carefully about what he was going to say next.

'Arjun, do you remember Captain Mohun Singh?'

'Yes. 1/14 Punjab, right? Wasn't he at Jitra too? I thought I saw him on the way to the Asoon line.'

'Yes. They took cover in the plantation and headed eastwards just as we did.'

'So what about Captain Mohun Singh?'

'Gianiji told me that he'd made contact with the Indian Independence League.'

'Go on.'

'Wait.' The orderly had finished dressing Arjun's wound. Hardy saw him out and then shut the door. He paused, running a finger through his beard. 'Look, Arjun,' he said, 'I don't know how you'll take this. I'm just telling you what I know . . .'

'Go on, Hardy.'

'Captain Mohun Singh has taken a big step.'

'What step?'

'He's decided to break with the Britishers.'

'What?'

'Yes,' said Hardy in a flat, even voice. 'He's going to form an independent unit – the Indian National Army. All the 14th Punjab officers are with him – the Indians I mean. Kumar, Masood, many others too. They've invited all of us to join . . .'

'So?' Arjun said. 'Are you thinking of doing it?'

'What can I say, Arjun?' Hardy smiled. 'You know how I feel. I've never made a secret of my views – unlike some of you chaps.'

'Hardy, wait.' Arjun stabbed a finger at him. 'Just think a minute. Don't be in a hurry. How do you know who this Giani is? How do you even know he's telling the truth about Captain Mohun Singh? How do you know he's not just a Japanese stooge?'

'Amreek Singh was in the army too,' Hardy said. 'He knew my father – his village isn't far from ours. If he is a Japanese stooge then there must be some reason why he became one. In any case, who are we to call him a stooge?' Hardy laughed. 'After all, aren't we the biggest stooges of all?'

437

'Wait.' Arjun tried to marshal his thoughts. It was a huge relief to be able to speak out at last, to bring into the open the long arguments that he had conducted with himself in the secrecy of his mind.

'So what does this mean?' Arjun said. 'That Mohun Singh and his lot will be fighting on the Japanese side?'

'Yes. Of course. For the time being – until the British are out of India.'

'But Hardy – let's think this thing through. What do the Japanese want with us? Do they care about us and our independence? All they want is to push the Britishers out so they can step in and take their place. They just want to use us: don't you see that?'

'Of course they do, Arjun,' Hardy shrugged his acquiescence. 'If it wasn't them it would be someone else. There'll always be someone trying to use us. That's why this is so hard, don't you see? This is the first time in our lives that we're trying to make up our own minds – not taking orders.'

'Hardy, look.' Arjun made an effort to keep his voice calm. 'That's how it may look to you right now, but just ask yourself: what are the chances that we'll be able to do anything for ourselves? Most likely we'll just end up helping the Japs to get into India. And what would be the point of exchanging the Britishers for the Japanese? As colonial masters go the British aren't that bad – better than most. Certainly a lot better than the Japanese would be.'

Hardy gave a full-throated laugh, his eyes shining. 'Yaar Arjun, think of where we've fallen when we start talking of good masters and bad masters. What are we? Dogs? Sheep? There are no good masters and bad masters, Arjun – in a way the better the master, the worse the condition of the slave, because it makes him forget what he is . . .'

They were glaring at each other, their faces no more than inches apart. Hardy's eyelid was twitching and Arjun could feel the heat of his breath. He was the first to pull away.

'Hardy, it won't help for us to fight each other.'

'No.'

Arjun began to chew his knuckles. 'Listen, Hardy,' he said. 'Don't think that I disagree with what you're saying. I don't. I think for the most part you're right on the mark. But I'm just trying to think about us – about men like you and me – about our place in the world.'

'I don't follow.'

'Just look at us, Hardy – just look at us. What are we? We've learnt to dance the tango and we know how to eat roast beef with a knife and fork. The truth is that except for the colour of our skin, most people in India wouldn't even recognise us as Indians. When we joined up we didn't have India on our minds: we wanted to be sahibs and that's what we've become. Do you think we can undo all of that just by putting up a new flag?'

Hardy shrugged dismissively. 'Look,' he said, 'I'm a simple soldier, yaar. I don't know what you're trying to get at. To me, it's a question of right and wrong – what's worth fighting for and what's not. That's all.'

There was a knock on the door. Hardy opened it to see Giani Amreek Singh standing outside.

'Everyone's waiting . . .'

'Gianiji, *ek minit* . . .' Hardy turned back to Arjun. 'Look, Arjun –' his voice was tired after the effort of the argument – 'I'll tell you what I'm going to do. Gianiji has offered to take us through the Jap lines, to Mohun Singh. For myself I've made up my mind already. I'm going to explain this to the men; I'm going to tell them why I think this is the right thing to do. They can decide for themselves. Do you want to come and listen?'

Arjun nodded. 'Yes.'

Hardy handed Arjun his crutch and they went together to the communal shed, walking slowly down the gravel track. The shed was full: the soldiers were at the front, squatting in orderly rows. Behind them were the inhabitants of the coolie lines: the men were in sarongs, the women in saris. Many of the tappers had children in their arms. At one end of the shed there stood a table and a couple of chairs. Hardy took his place behind the table while Arjun and Giani Amreek Singh seated themselves on the chairs. There was a lot of noise: people were whispering, talking, some of the children were giggling at the novelty of the occasion. Hardy had to shout to make himself heard.

Once Hardy began, Arjun realised, with some surprise, that he was a talented speaker, almost a practised orator. His voice filled the shed, his words echoing off the tin roof – *duty, country, freedom*. Arjun was listening intently when he became aware that a film of sweat was running down his face. He looked down and realised that he was dripping – sweat was pouring off his elbows and off his legs. He felt himself growing feverish as he had the night before.

Suddenly the shed rang to the sound of massed voices. The noise was deafening. Arjun heard Hardy bellowing into the crowd: 'Are you with me?'

There was another eruption; a huge burst of sound welled up to the roof and came echoing back. The soldiers were on their feet. A couple of them linked arms and began to dance the *bhangra*, shaking their shoulders and stamping their feet. Behind them the workers were shouting too – men, women, children – throwing things in the air, clapping, waving. Arjun looked at Kishan Singh and saw that his face was flushed, joyful, his eyes alight.

Arjun noted, in a detached and almost disinterested way, that since the time he'd entered the shed, everything seemed to have altered. It was as though the whole world had suddenly changed colour, assumed a different guise. The realities of a few minutes before now seemed like an incomprehensible dream: had he really been surprised to look over the bluff and see an Indian flag in the coolie lines? But where else would such a flag be? Was it really true that Kishan Singh's grandfather had won a decoration at Flanders? Was it true that Kishan Singh was the same man that he had always taken him to be – the most of loyal of soldiers, descended from generations of loyal soldiers? He looked at the dancing men: how was it possible that he had served with those men for so long and never had an inkling that their acquiescence was not what it seemed to be? And how was it possible that he had never known this even of himself?

Was this how a mutiny was sparked? In a moment of heedlessness, so that one became a stranger to the person one had been a moment before? Or was it the other way round? That this was when one recognised the stranger that one had always been to oneself; that all one's loyalties and beliefs had been misplaced?

But where would his loyalties go now that they were unmoored? He was a military man and he knew that nothing –

nothing important – was possible without loyalty, without faith. But who would claim his loyalty now? The old loyalties of India, the ancient ones – they'd been destroyed long ago; the British had built their Empire by effacing them. But the Empire was dead now – he knew this because he had felt it die within himself, where it had held its strongest dominion – and with whom was he now to keep faith? Loyalty, commonalty, faith – these things were as essential and as fragile as the muscles of the human heart; easy to destroy, impossible to rebuild. How would one begin the work of re-creating the tissues that bound people to each other? This was beyond the abilities of someone such as himself; someone trained to destroy. It was a labour that would last not one year, not ten, not fifty – it was the work of centuries.

'So, Arjun?' Suddenly Hardy was kneeling in front of him, looking into his face. He was beaming, glowing with triumph.

'Arjun? What are you going to do then? Are you with us or against us?'

Arjun reached for his crutch and pushed himself to his feet. 'Listen, Hardy. Before we think of anything else – there's something we have to do.'

'What?'

'Bucky, the CO – we have to let him go.'

Hardy stared at him, without uttering a sound.

'We have to do it,' Arjun continued. 'We can't be responsible for his being taken prisoner by the Japs. He's a very fair man, Hardy, and he's been good to serve under – you know that. We have to let him go. We owe him that.'

Hardy scratched his chin. 'I can't allow it, Arjun. He'd give away our position, our movements . . .'

Arjun interrupted him. 'It's not a question of what you'll allow, Hardy,' he said tiredly. 'You're not my senior, and I'm not yours. I'm not asking you. I'm letting you know that I'm going to give the CO some food and some water and then I'm going to let him find his way back across the lines. If you want to stop me you'll have a fight on your hands. I think some of the men would take my side. You decide.'

A thin smile crossed Hardy's face. 'Look at you, yaar.' His voice was acid with sarcasm. 'Even at a time like this you're a *chaploos*

441

– still thinking of sucking up. What are you hoping for? That he'll speak up for you if things don't turn out right? Take out a little insurance against the future?'

'You bastard.' Arjun lurched towards Hardy, reaching for his collar, swinging his crutch.

Hardy stepped away easily. 'I'm sorry,' he said gruffly. 'I shouldn't have said that. *Theek hai*. Do what you want. I'll send someone along to show you where Bucky is. Just be quick – that's all I ask.'

Thirty-eight

Alison and Dinu spent an hour clearing out the dark room. There was no electricity and they had to work by candlelight. They took down his enlarger, stacked his trays, packed away his prints and his negatives, wrapping them in old cloth and laying them in boxes. When they were done, Dinu snuffed out the candle. They stood still in the airless warmth of the cupboard-like room, listening to the night-time buzz of cicadas and the croaking of wet-weather frogs. Intermittently they could hear a distant, staccato sound, a kind of barking, as though a pack of dogs had been disturbed in a sleeping village.

'Guns,' she whispered.

Dinu reached for her in the darkness, pulling her towards him. 'They're very far away.'

He held her, his arms tightening round her body. He opened the palms of his hands and ran them over her hair, her shoulders, along the concave curve of her back. His fingers snagged in the strap of her dress and he peeled the fabric slowly away, picking it off her shoulders, tugging it back. Sinking to his knees, he ran his face down the length of her body, touching her with his cheek, his nose, his tongue.

They lay on the cramped floor, pushed up close, legs intertwined, thigh on thigh, arms extended, the flatness of their bellies imprinted on each other. Membranes of sweat hung cobwebbed between their bodies, joining them, pulling them together.

'Alison . . . what am I going to do? Without you?'

'And me, Dinu? What about me? What will I do?'

Afterwards, they lay still, pillowing each other's heads on their arms. He lit a cigarette and held it to her lips.

'One day,' he said, 'one day, when we're back here together, I'll show you the true magic of a dark room . . .'

'And what's that?'

'When you print by contact . . . when you lay the negative on the paper and watch them come to life . . . the darkness of the one becomes the light of the other. The first time I saw it happen I thought, what must it be like to touch like this? . . . with such utter absorption? . . . For one thing to become irradiated with the shadows of another?'

'Dinu.' She ran her fingertips over his face.

'If only I could hold you in that way . . . so that you were imprinted on me . . . every part of me . . .'

'Dinu, there'll be time.' She took his face between her hands and kissed him. 'We'll have the rest of our lives . . .' Rising to her knees she lit the candle again. Holding the flame in front of his face, she looked fiercely into his eyes, as though she were trying to bore into his head.

'It won't be long, Dinu?' she said. 'Will it?'

'No . . . not long.'

'Do you really believe that? Or are you lying – for my sake? Tell me the truth, Dinu: I'd rather know.'

He gripped her shoulders. 'Yes, Alison.' He spoke with all the conviction he could muster. 'Yes. We'll be back here before long . . . We'll be back at Morningside . . . Everything will be the same, except . . .'

'Except?' She bit her lip, as though she were afraid of hearing what he was going to say.

'Except that we'll be married.'

'Yes.' She burst into delighted laughter. 'Yes,' she said, tossing her head. 'We'll be married. We've left it too long. It was a mistake.'

She picked up the candle and ran out of the room. He lay still, listening to her footsteps: the house was quieter than he'd ever known it to be. Downstairs, Saya John was in bed, exhausted and asleep.

He got up and followed her through the dark corridors to her bedroom. Alison was unlocking closets, rummaging through drawers. Suddenly she turned to him, holding out her hand. 'Look.' Two gold rings glinted in the candlelight.

'They belonged to my parents,' she said. She reached for his hand and pushed one of the rings over the knuckle of his ring finger. *'With this ring I thee wed.'*

She laughed, placing the other ring in his palm. Then she extended a finger, holding her hand in front of her.

'Go on,' she challenged him. 'Do it. I dare you.'

He turned the ring over in his hands and then slipped it into place, on her finger.

'Are we married now?'

She tossed her head, laughing, and held her finger up to the candlelight. 'Yes,' she said. 'In a way. In our own eyes. When you're away you'll still be mine because of the ring.'

She shook free the mosquito net that hung down from the ceiling, draping it over the sides of her bed. 'Come.' She blew out the candle and drew him into the net.

An hour later, Dinu woke to the sound of approaching planes. He reached for her hand and found that she was already awake, sitting up with her back against the headboard. 'Alison . . .'

'Don't say it's time. Not yet.'

They held each other and listened. The planes were directly overhead, flying low. The windows rattled as they went past.

'When I was little,' Dinu said, 'my father once told me a story about Mandalay. When the king was sent into exile, the palace girls had to walk through the city, to the river . . . My mother was with them and my father followed, keeping to the shadows. It was a long walk and the girls were tired and miserable . . . My father put together all his money and bought some sweets . . . to lift their spirits. The girls were guarded by soldiers – foreigners, Englishmen . . . Somehow he – my father – managed to slip through the cordon . . . He gave my mother the packet of sweets. Then he ran back into the shadows . . . He watched her open the packet . . . He was amazed . . . The first thing she did was to offer some to the soldiers who were marching beside her. At first he was angry; he felt betrayed . . . Why was she giving them away . . . especially to these men, her captors? But then, slowly he

445

understood what she was doing and he was glad . . . He saw that this was the right thing to do – a way to stay alive. To shout defiance would have served no purpose . . .'

'I think you're trying to tell me something, Dinu,' she said quietly. 'What is it?'

'I just want you to be careful, Alison . . . not to be headstrong . . . not to be the woman you are, just for a while . . . to be cautious, quiet . . .'

'I'll try, Dinu.' She squeezed his hand. 'I promise. And you too: you have to be careful as well.'

'I will – it's in my nature. We're not the same in that way . . . That's why I worry about you.'

Another flight of planes went by. It was impossible to keep still any longer, with the windows rattling as though they would break. Alison swung her legs off the bed. She picked up the handbag in which she carried the Daytona's keys. It was unexpectedly heavy. She opened the clasp, looked inside and raised an eyebrow at Dinu.

'It's your father's revolver. I found it in a drawer.'

'Is it loaded?'

'Yes. I checked.'

She shut the clasp and slung the bag over her shoulder. 'It's time.'

They went down to find Saya John sitting on the veranda, in his favourite wing-chair. Alison dropped to her knees beside him and put an arm around his waist.

'I want your blessings, Grandfather.'

'Why?'

'Dinu and I are going to be married.'

His face broke into a smile. She saw to her delight that he had understood; that his eyes were clear and unclouded. He motioned to both of them to come closer and put his arms round their shoulders.

'Rajkumar's son and Matthew's daughter.' He swayed gently from side to side, holding their heads like trophies, under his arms. 'What could be better? The two of you have joined the families. Your parents will be delighted.'

They went outside and found that it had begun to rain. Dinu buckled down the Daytona's hood and held the door open for

446

Saya John. The old man gave him a pat on the back as he stepped in.

'Tell Rajkumar that it'll have to be a big wedding,' he said. 'I shall insist on having the Archbishop.'

'Yes.' Dinu tried to smile. 'Of course.'

Then Dinu went to Alison's side and knelt beside the window. She would not look at him.

'We won't say goodbye.'

'No.'

She started the car and he stepped back. At the bottom of the drive, the Daytona came to a stop. He saw her leaning out, her head silhouetted against the car's rain-haloed lights. She raised an arm to wave and he waved back. Then he ran up the stairs, racing from window to window. He watched the Daytona's lights until they disappeared.

The shed in which Lieutenant-Colonel Buckland had spent the night was a small red-brick structure, surrounded by trees. It was about a quarter of a mile from the coolie lines. Arjun was led there by a fast-talking young 'contractor', dressed in khaki shorts: it was he who carried the water bottle and the cloth bundle of food that had been prepared for the lieutenant-colonel.

The contractor showed Arjun a track that led southwards through a range of low hills. 'There's a town a couple of miles away,' he said. 'The last we heard it was still held by the British.' They came up to the steps that led into the building. The contractor handed over the water bottle and the bundle of food that he had been carrying.

'The colonel will be safe if he keeps to this track. It won't take him more than an hour or two to the town, even if he walks very slowly.'

Arjun went gingerly up the steps to the door. He knocked and when there was no answer, he used the tip of his crutch to push the door open. He found Lieutenant-Colonel Buckland lying on the cement floor, on a mattress.

'Sir.'

Lieutenant-Colonel Buckland sat up suddenly, peering around him. He said sharply: 'Who is it?'

'Lieutenant Roy. Sir.' Arjun saluted, leaning on his crutch.

'Oh, Roy.' Lieutenant-Colonel Buckland's voice warmed. 'I'm glad to see you.'

'I'm glad to see you too, sir.'

'You're wounded – what happened?'

'Bullet through the hamstring, sir. It'll be all right. And how's your arm?'

'Been acting up a bit.'

'Do you think you're well enough to walk, sir?'

Lieutenant-Colonel Buckland raised an eyebrow. 'Why?' He glanced sharply at the cloth bundle and the water bottle that Arjun was carrying in his hands. 'What have you got there, Roy?'

'Some food and water, sir. The Japanese are advancing down the north–south highway. If you head in the other direction you should be able to get across the lines.'

'Get across the lines?' Lieutenant-Colonel Buckland repeated this slowly to himself. 'Am I going alone then? What about you? And the others?'

'We're staying here, sir. For the moment.'

'I see.' Lieutenant-Colonel Buckland rose to his feet, holding his right arm stiffly across his chest. He took the water bottle from Arjun and examined it, turning it over in his hands. 'So you're going over, are you – to the Japs?'

'That's not how I would put it, sir.'

'I'm sure you wouldn't.' Lieutenant-Colonel Buckland looked at Arjun closely, frowning.

'You know, Roy,' he said at last. 'You, I never took for a turn-coat. Some of the others, yes – you could see where the possibility might lie. But you: you don't have the look of a traitor.'

'Some would say that I've been a traitor all along, sir.'

'You don't really believe that, do you?' Lieutenant-Colonel Buckland shook his head. 'In fact you don't believe any of it.'

'Sir?'

'You don't. Or else you wouldn't be here, bringing me food and water. Only an incompetent soldier would help an enemy escape. Or a fool.'

'I felt I had to, sir.'

'Why?'

'Because,' said Arjun, 'it's not your fault, sir. You've always been fair to us. You were the best CO we could have hoped for – under the circumstances.'

'I suppose you expect me to thank you for saying that?'

'I don't expect anything, sir.' Arjun held the door open. 'But if you don't mind, sir, there's not much time. I'll show you the way.'

Lieutenant-Colonel Buckland stepped out and Arjun followed him. They went down the steps and into the trees. When they were a little distance away, Lieutenant-Colonel Buckland cleared his throat. 'Look, Roy,' he said. 'It's not too late. You can still change your mind. Come away with me. We can give them the slip. We'll forget about this . . . this incident.'

A moment passed before Arjun answered. 'Sir, may I say something?'

'Go ahead.'

'Sir, do you remember when you were teaching at the academy – you once quoted someone in one of your lectures. An English general – Munro, I think his name was. You quoted something he'd said over a hundred years ago about the Indian army: *The spirit of independence will spring up in this army long before it is even thought of among the people . . .*'

Lieutenant-Colonel Buckland nodded: 'Yes. I remember that. Very well.'

'All of us in the class were Indians and we were a little shocked that you'd chosen to quote something like this to us. We insisted that Munro had been talking nonsense. But you disagreed . . .'

'Did I?'

'Yes. At the time I thought you were playing devil's advocate; that you were just trying to provoke us. But that wasn't true, was it, sir? The truth is you knew all along: you knew what we'd do – you knew it before we did. You knew because you made us. If I were to come away with you now no one would be more surprised than you. I think, in your heart, you would despise me a little.'

'That's rubbish, Roy. Don't be a fool, man. There's still time.'

449

'No, sir.' Arjun brought himself to a halt and held out his hand. 'I think this is it, sir. This is where I'm going to turn round.'

Lieutenant-Colonel Buckland looked at his hand and then at him. 'I'm not going to shake your hand, Roy,' he said quietly, in an even, emotionless voice. 'You can justify what you're doing to yourself in a thousand different ways, but you should make no mistake about the truth, Roy. You're a traitor. You're a disgrace to the regiment and to your country. You're scum. When the time comes you'll be hunted down, Roy. When you're sitting in front of a court-martial I'll be there. I'll see you hang, Roy. I will. You should have not a moment's doubt of that.'

Arjun dropped his hand. For the first time in many days he felt completely certain of his mind. He smiled.

'There's one thing you can be sure of, sir,' he said. 'On that day, if it comes, you'll have done your duty, sir, and I'll have done mine. We'll look at each other as honest men – for the first time. For that alone this will have been worthwhile.'

He saluted, balancing on his crutch. For an instant, Lieutenant-Colonel Buckland hesitated and then, involuntarily, his hand rose to acknowledge the salute. He turned on his heel and walked into the trees.

Arjun watched him leave and then he swung himself round on his crutch and went hobbling back to the coolie lines.

Alison had been driving for about an hour when she noticed that the Daytona's pedals were growing hot under her feet. She began to watch the bonnet and caught sight of leaking wisps of steam. She pulled off the road, and when her grandfather turned to look at her, she flashed him a reassuring smile. 'It's all right, Baba,' she said, 'don't worry. It'll just take a minute.' She left him sitting inside and climbed out.

With the car at a standstill, she could see steam leaking through the grille. The bonnet was too hot to touch. She wrapped her scarf around her hand and felt under the hood for the catch. A geyser of steam gushed into her face and she sprang back, coughing.

It was very dark. She reached through the window on the driver's side and turned the headlights on. She spotted a branch, lying on the ground, near her feet. She used it to lever up the hood and a cloud of steam welled out. She propped the bonnet open and went back to the driver's window to turn the headlights off.

'It won't be long, Baba,' she said. 'We'll just wait a while.'

To the north, she could see flashes of light. On the highway the flow of traffic had dwindled to an occasional speeding car. She had the feeling that she was among the last on the road; those who'd planned to leave were long gone and everyone else was waiting to see what would happen next.

The night was cool and it wasn't long before the steam from the radiator dissipated. She wrapped her hand in the scarf again and unscrewed the cap. Then she fetched a bottle and poured in some water: it boiled up almost immediately, frothing over the top. She splashed some water over the radiator and waited a while longer before pouring the rest in. Slamming the hood shut, she went back to the driver's seat.

She gave her grandfather a smile. 'It's all right now,' she said. 'We'll be fine.'

She turned the key and was hugely relieved when the engine responded. Switching on the headlamps she pulled on to the road again. No other cars had passed them in a while. With the road to herself, she was tempted to drive at high speed. She had to remind herself that she had to go slowly if the car was not to overheat.

They'd gone only a few miles when the engine started to knock. She knew now that there was no point trying to go any further. At the next turn she pulled off the main road. She was on a dusty side road, little more than a gravelled track. On both sides, there were stands of rubber: she felt obscurely grateful for this, glad to be in a familiar environment.

The best thing to do, she decided, was to stay close to the road: perhaps she'd be able to flag down some help in the morning. She took the car a short distance down the track and then turned into the trees, pulling up at a spot that was sheltered by a bush. She turned the engine off and opened her door.

'We'll stay here for a while, Baba,' she said. 'We can go on when the light's better.' She prised the bonnet open again and came back to the driver's seat. 'Go to sleep, Baba,' she said. 'There's no point staying awake. There's nothing we can do right now.'

She climbed out and walked around the car. With the headlights turned off, it was very dark: she could see no lights and no sign of habitation. She went back to the driver's seat and sat down again. Saya John was sitting up, looking intently at his hand. His fingers were spread out in front of him, as though he were counting something.

'Tell me, Alison,' he said. 'Today is Saturday – isn't it?'

'Is it?' She tried to think what day it was but she'd lost track. 'I don't know. Why do you ask?'

'I think it's Sunday tomorrow. I hope Ilongo remembers that I have to go to church.'

She stared at him. 'I'm sorry, Baba,' she said sharply. 'I'm afraid you're going to have to miss church tomorrow.'

He glanced at her like a disappointed child and she was suddenly contrite for having snapped at him. She reached for his hand. 'Just this once, Baba. We'll go to Mass in Singapore, next week.'

He gave her a smile and leaned back, resting his head against his seat. She looked at her watch. It was four in the morning. It would be dawn soon. Once it was light she'd go back to the highway and see if she could flag down a truck or a car: something was sure to come along. She let her head fall back against the seat: she was tired – not afraid, just tired. She could hear her grandfather, drifting off to sleep, breathing slowly and deeply. She shut her eyes.

She was woken by a shaft of sunlight, shining through the feathery canopy above. She stirred and her hand fell on the seat beside her. It was empty. She sat up, startled, rubbing her eyes. When she looked at the seat she saw that her grandfather was gone.

She opened the door and stepped out. 'Baba?' He'd probably gone into the trees to relieve himself. She raised her voice. 'Baba – are you there?' Shading her eyes, she turned all the way around, peering into the dim tunnels of rubber around her. He was nowhere to be seen.

Stepping around the car, she stumbled on his brown leather

suitcase. It was lying open on the ground, with clothes spilling out, scattered among the leaves. He'd been looking for something – but what? Glancing around, she spotted some clothes, lying on the ground, a few feet away. She went to investigate and found a pair of trousers and a shirt, the clothes her grandfather had been wearing the night before.

A thought struck her. She darted back to his suitcase and rummaged quickly through the rest of his clothes, looking for the dark suit that he liked to wear to church. It wasn't there: she was sure that he'd had it with him when they set out. It wasn't like him to go anywhere without it. That was what he'd changed in to; she was sure of it. He'd probably wandered off, along the highway, thinking that it would lead him to his church. She would have to hurry if she was to find him before he got into trouble.

She reached into the car and snatched her handbag off the seat. It occurred to her that she could try and follow in the car but she decided against it. There was no telling how much time she'd waste trying to start it. It would probably be quicker on foot. Slinging her handbag over her shoulder, she began to run towards the highway.

She could tell, even when she was a good distance away, that there was no traffic. The highway was very quiet. But when she was some twenty yards from the road she heard some distant voices. She stopped to look, glacing sidewise along a corridor of tree trunks. She spotted a group of bicyclists, in the distance: there were some half-dozen of them and they were cycling in her direction.

Her first reaction was relief; she knew that if she ran hard, she'd be able to reach the road just as the cyclists were going past. Maybe they'd be able to help. She took a couple of steps and then she stopped and looked again, sheltering behind the trunk of a tree. She realised now that the bicyclists were all wearing caps and that their clothes were all of exactly the same colour. Grateful for the shelter of the plantation, she slipped a little closer to the road, being careful to stay out of view.

When the cyclists were some twenty yards away, she saw that they were Japanese soldiers. They were unshaven and their grey uniforms were spattered with dust and mud, their tunics drenched in sweat. Some had caps with long neckcloths while others wore helmets, covered with nets. They were wearing tightly bound puttees and canvas shoes. The man who was in the lead had a sword attached to his belt: the scabbard was clattering rhythmically against his bicycle's mudguard. The others were carrying rifles, fitted with bayonets. Their bicycles creaked and squealed as they went past. She could hear them panting as they pedalled.

A short distance ahead, there was a corner where the highway described a sharp turn. The cyclists were still in view as they went around the bend: she heard one of them shout, raising his hand to point down the road. Suddenly she was seized by a sharp sense of misgiving. She'd thought that she'd find her grandfather heading back, in the direction of Sungei Pattani: but what if, instead, he'd headed in the other direction?

She glanced in both directions and saw that the highway was empty. Sprinting across the road, she slipped into the stands of rubber on the far side. Heading diagonally through the trees, she caught sight of the highway again: she saw the backs of the cyclists, pedalling along, pointing at a diminutive figure a long way ahead. It was a man, wearing a hat and a suit, ambling along by the side of the road. Alison knew that it was her grandfather. The soldiers were closing on him, pedalling hard.

She began to run, fast, dodging between the trees. She was still several hundred yards away when the soldiers caught up with Saya John. She saw them dismounting, letting their bicycles drop on the grass. They surrounded him and the sound of a voice came floating back to her: one of the soldiers was shouting, saying something she couldn't follow. She began to mumble to herself as she ran, 'Please, please . . .'

She could tell that her grandfather hadn't understood what the soldiers were saying. He touched his hat and turned away, trying to push past them. One of the soldiers put out a hand to stop him and he waved it aside. All the soldiers were shouting at him now, but he seemed not to hear anything. He was flicking his hand at them, as though trying to brush off street-corner loiterers. Then one of the soldiers struck him, slapping him hard across his face, knocking him off his feet. He fell heavily to the ground.

Alison came to a stop, panting, leaning her weight against a tree trunk, holding it with both hands. If only he would keep still, they would go away, she was sure of that. She began to mumble to herself, praying that he'd been knocked unconscious. They wouldn't bother with him: surely they'd see that he was just a confused old man; that he meant no harm.

But then her grandfather's prone body began to move again. He stirred and sat up with his legs spread out in front of him, like a child waking in the morning. He reached for his hat, put it on his head and pushed himself to his feet again. He looked at the soldiers with a bewildered frown, rubbing his face. And then he turned his back on them and began to walk away.

She saw one of the soldiers pulling his rifle off his back. He shouted something and cocked the gun so that the bayonet was pointing directly at the old man's back.

Almost without thinking, Alison reached for her handbag. She pulled out the revolver and dropped to one knee. Crossing her left arm in front of her, she steadied her wrist against her forearm, just as her father had taught her. She took aim at the man with the bayonet, hoping to drop him. But at exactly that moment, another soldier stepped across her line of fire; the bullet hit him in the ribs and he fell screaming to the ground. The man with the bayonet froze for an instant, but then, suddenly, as though triggered by a reflex, his arm moved, driving the blade in and out of Saya John's body, in one quick motion. Saya John toppled over, falling face first on the road.

She was perfectly calm now, breathing evenly. She took aim carefully, and fired again. This time she hit the man with the bayonet. He screamed and dropped his rifle, falling face first on the ground. Her third shot went wide, ploughing up a divot of grass on the roadside. The soldiers were flat on their stomachs now, and a couple of them were sheltering behind Saya John's inert body. Her targets were smaller now, and her fourth shot went wide. But with her fifth, she hit another soldier, sending him spinning on his side.

Then, suddenly, something slammed into her with great force, throwing her on her back. She could feel no pain, but she knew she'd been hit. She lay still, looking up at the arched branches of the rubber trees around her. They were swaying in the breeze, like fans.

She was glad that it would end like this; with her eyes resting on something familiar. She remembered what Dinu had said about his mother and the sweets she had shared with her captors. The memory made her smile; that wouldn't have suited her at all. She was glad that she'd made them pay; that she hadn't gone without striking back.

She could hear their footsteps now and knew that they were running towards her. She raised the gun to her temple and shut her eyes.

Thirty-nine

Doh Say, ever the loyal friend, forswore his family's Christmas celebrations in order to be of help to Rajkumar. He arrived in Rangoon on December 22. Just as Rajkumar had expected, he quickly took matters in hand, arranging for the hiring of a team of elephants and some half-dozen oo-sis. Neel had already organised the rental of two lorries. It was decided that the clearing of the Pazundaung timberyard would start the next day.

They left the house early in the morning – Doh Say, Raymond, Neel and Rajkumar. They went in the Packard, with Neel driving. Dolly and Manju waved them off. They got to the yard to find that the oo-sis had already arrived, along with their elephants. The rented lorries were there too. Rajkumar was relieved: he'd been hoping to get an early start. He'd worried that the teams might turn up late.

But then, an unexpected hitch arose. 'We would like to talk to you,' one of the lorry drivers said. A delegation came up to the small cabin that served as an office; it turned out that the oo-sis and lorry drivers wanted a part-payment at midday.

It was not uncommon, of course, for hired crews to make demands just as the day's work was getting started: that was exactly when they were in the best position to bargain. Rajkumar's original plan had been to go to the bank in the early afternoon, when the work was almost done. With the Christmas holidays beginning tomorrow, this was the last day in the week when the banks would be open. He'd taken the precaution of visiting the bank the day before to make sure that the money was ready and available. He could have taken it with him right then, but had thought better of it. It wasn't safe – especially now that they were alone at home, with no gatekeepers to keep watch. He'd decided to come back when the work was near completion.

This new development meant that Rajkumar would have to change his plans. He persuaded the men to start work, promising to have the money ready at midday. He went to the window of his office to watch them get started.

He smiled as he looked down on the yard, with its huge, neat stacks of timber. It was unnerving to think that this was the sum total of everything he possessed. He knew he ought to be on his way, but he couldn't help dawdling. Even now, after all these years, he could not resist the spectacle of watching elephants at work: once again he found himself marvelling at the sure-footedness with which they made their way through the narrow aisles, threading their great bodies between the timber stacks. There was something almost preternatural about the dexterity with which they curled their trunks around the logs.

He spotted Neel, darting between the elephants. It made Rajkumar nervous to see his son down there, with the animals.

'Neel,' Rajkumar called out. 'Be careful.'

Neel turned round, a wide smile on his bearded face. He waved.

'I'll be fine, apé. You should be on your way to the bank now. Don't leave it too late.'

Rajkumar looked at his watch. 'There's still time. The bank's not even open yet.'

Doh Say added his voice to Neel's. 'Yes, go now, Rajkumar. The sooner you get there, the sooner you'll be back. I'll take care of everything here – it'll be all right.'

Rajkumar walked out into the street and found a cycle-rickshaw. The driver pedalled hard and they soon found themselves nearing the centre of the city. The traffic was heavy and Rajkumar was afraid that he'd be held up. But the driver threaded deftly through the streets and brought him to the bank in good time.

Rajkumar paid off the driver and climbed a wide flight of stairs. The bank's main doors were closed: it was still a quarter of an hour to opening time. Some half-dozen men were already waiting at the door. Rajkumar joined the line. The morning was

458

exceptionally clear with scarcely a cloud in the sky. It was an unusually cool day for Rangoon and many passers-by were swathed in woollen shawls and cardigans.

The bank was situated at a busy intersection. The surrounding streets were jammed with the usual start-of-the-day rush-hour traffic. Buses were inching along the road, belching smoke; under looped awnings of wire, trams were rumbling by, their bells tinkling.

Suddenly, an air-raid siren started up, somewhere in the distance. Neither Rajkumar nor the people around him paid much attention. Air-raid warnings had sounded several times over the last few weeks – they had all proved to be false alarms. At the bottom of the bank's steps, a footpath hawker was frying baya-gyaw in a large, soot-blackened pot. She grimaced in irritation and went on with what she was doing. Rajkumar's response was much the same as hers: he was annoyed to think of the delays the sirens would cause.

The sirens sounded a second time and now people paid more attention. It was unusual to have two alarms going off in such quick succession. Heads appeared in the windows of the buses and trams; eyes turned towards the sky as though in search of rain.

Rajkumar spotted an air-raid warden in a tin hat. He was walking down the street, waving his arms at pedestrians. Rajkumar knew the warden: he was an Anglo-Burmese bookmaker, an acquaintance from his own racing days. He went hurrying down the steps to accost him.

The warden wasted no time on civilities. 'Better find a safe place, Mr Raha,' he said brusquely. 'The balloon is definitely up. They've passed the second warning system.' Cupping his hands around his mouth the warden began to shout at the passers-by: 'Get out of here; get to your shelters, go home . . .'

A few people stared but otherwise no one paid attention. The warden fumed, with his hands on his hips. 'Look at them; they think it's a bloody circus . . .'

There was a small patch of garden in front of the bank. Months before, slit trenches had been dug between the ornamental palms. But in the meantime evil-smelling pools of moisture had accumulated in the trenches, along with white-haired mango-pits and other bits of refuse. People balked at jumping in.

Rajkumar went back up the steps to see if the bank had opened. Just then the air-raid sirens went off, for the third time. Now everyone took notice. The traffic on the streets came to an abrupt halt. There was no panic and no running for shelter. Instead people climbed out of their trams and buses and stood on the streets in a half-disbelieving daze, looking skywards, shading their eyes against the light. Several men came up the stairs to stand beside Rajkumar: the bank's threshold commanded an excellent view of the surroundings.

'Listen.' A low steady droning became audible in the distance.

The sound lent a sudden and ominous credibility to the idea of an imminent air raid. There was a moment of uncertainty and then panic swept like a gale down the streets. People began to run. Some darted indoors, others hurried away, dodging through the stalled traffic. The foul-smelling trenches at the corner were filled in seconds.

Somewhere nearby, a woman let out a howl of pain. Spinning round, Rajkumar saw that the baya-gyaw cart had been upended at the bottom of the steps; the vendor's pot had tipped over, spattering her with boiling oil. She was running down the road, shrieking, clawing at her clothes with both hands.

Rajkumar decided not to brave the panicked crowd. Instead he braced himself against the bank's heavy doors. The distant drone changed into a loud rhythmic noise. Then the first planes came into view: tiny specks, approaching from the east. The city's anti-aircraft guns opened up with a dull, thudding sound. The guns were few and they were concentrated mainly in the vicinity of Mingaladon airport and the military cantonment. But there was something reassuring about the thought that the city's defences were operational. Even in the midst of the panic, many people could be heard to cheer.

The bombers changed formation as they approached the eastern peripheries of the city, dipping lower in the sky. Their fuselages opened and their cargo of bombs began to descend, trailing behind the craft like glinting, tinsel ribbons. It was as though an immense silver curtain had suddenly appeared over the eastern horizon.

The first bombs fell several miles away, the explosions following in evenly spaced rhythmic succession. Suddenly there was a booming sound, several times louder than all the preceding blasts. From somewhere in the eastern reaches of the city, a huge cloud of black smoke mushroomed up towards the sky, almost engulfing the bombers.

'They've hit the oil tanks,' someone said, 'on the Pazundaung Creek.'

Rajkumar knew at once that this was right. His stomach lurched. The city's main oil reservoirs were on the far side of the creek, well within sight of his timberyard. He looked up at the bombers and saw that they were making another run over the same area. He realised now that they were not bombing blindly: they were targeting the city's long waterfront, aiming for its mills, warehouses, tanks and railway lines.

Suddenly Rajkumar thought of the elephants, working in his yard. He recalled how unpredictable these animals were in their response to noise. It sometimes took just a single sharp sound to stampede a herd. Once, in the old days, at a teak camp, he had witnessed such a stampede; the echo of a gunshot had startled an old cow elephant into producing a distinctive trumpeting note; this had triggered an instinctive response in the herd. There had been a lot of damage and it had taken the oo-sis hours to regain control of their animals.

What would happen if a team of elephants were to panic inside the log-jammed confines of a timberyard? It was unthinkable.

Rajkumar could no longer bear to remain where he was. He set off on foot, in the direction of Pazundaung. The bombs were coming closer now, falling in curtains, floating towards the city's centre. Suddenly a bullock-cart appeared directly ahead, racing at him down the footpath. The runaway bullocks were foaming at the mouth, showing the whites of their eyes. The driver was screaming, holding on to the sides of the cart. Rajkumar jumped aside just in time to let it pass by.

A flight of planes was passing directly overhead. Rajkumar looked up into the bright, clear December sky. They swooped downwards and their bays opened. Strings of bombs appeared, falling sidewise, catching the light, sparkling like diamonds.

461

There were no trenches nearby. Rajkumar crouched in a door-way, holding his hands over his head. The air shook and he was aware of the sound of shattering glass.

He lost track of how long he stayed there. He stirred only when he felt a warmth at his back. Turning around he saw a dog, pushing against him, whimpering in fear. He thrust the dog aside and stood up. Columns of smoke were climbing into the sky from all around him. He thought of Dolly, Manju and Jaya, his grandchild. He glanced in the direction of Kemendine and was relieved to see that that part of the city was relatively unaffected. He started to walk in the other direction, towards his timberyard, in Pazundaung.

On Merchant Street a marketplace had been hit. Fruit and veg-etables lay scattered along the sides of the road. Already beggars and ragpickers were scratching through the debris. He noticed the burnt-out remains of a shop and recalled, almost with a sense of nostalgia, that this was his favourite place to buy tandoori chicken. A blast had driven a set of skewers through the clay walls of the oven, breaking it in half, like an eggshell. He heard a man's voice calling for help. He hurried on. He had no time: he had to get to his yard in Pazundaung.

He passed the storefront of Rowe and Co. The windows were shattered and there were gaping holes in the walls. Looters were climbing in through the gaps. He could see the store's Christmas tree lying aslant on the floor. There was an old woman work-ing busily beside it, her face white with talcum powder. She was picking cottonwool off the floor, stuffing it into a sack.

In front of the telegraph office a water main had been hit. A ten-foot-high jet was spraying into the sky. There was water everywhere, gathering in puddles, flowing down the road. A whirlpool was swirling around the mouth of the shattered main.

People had been crouching along the walls of the telegraph office when the water source was hit. Many had died. Dis-membered limbs could be seen in the pool that was spinning around the main: there was a child's arm, a leg. Rajkumar averted his eyes and walked on.

Approaching Pazundaung, he saw that both sides of the creek

462

were blanketed in flames. While still a good distance away he spotted the perimeter walls of his yard. They were shrouded in clouds of smoke.

Everything he owned was in that place, all that he had ever worked for; a lifetime's accumulation of labour stored as a single cache of wood. He thought of the elephants and the bombs falling around them; the flames leaping from the well-stacked wood; the explosions, the trumpeting.

It was he who had concentrated all his holdings in this one place – that too was a part of the plan – and now the bombs had claimed it all. But it didn't matter; nothing mattered so long as Neel was unharmed. The rest were just things, possessions. But Neel . . .

He turned into the alley that led to his yard and saw that it was filled with swirling clouds of smoke. On the skin of his face, he could feel the scorching heat of the fire that was raging through his yard. He shouted into the smoke: 'Neel.'

He saw a figure taking shape in the distance. He began to run. 'Neel? Neel?'

It was Doh Say. His lined, wrinkled face was blackened with smoke. He was weeping.

'Rajkumar . . .'

'Where's Neel?'

'Forgive me, Rajkumar.' Doh Say covered his face.'There was nothing I could do. The elephants ran wild. I tried to send your boy away but he wouldn't listen. The logs got loose and he fell under.'

Now Rajkumar saw that Doh Say had been dragging a body through the alley, pulling it away from the fire. He ran over to it and fell on his knees.

The body was almost unrecognisable, crushed by an immense weight. But despite the terrible disfigurement Rajkumar knew that this was his son and that he was dead.

Once, when she was still a girl, Manju had observed the shaving of a widow's head. This was at a neighbour's house in Calcutta:

a barber had been paid to do it and the women of the family had been round to help.

In her sewing box Manju came upon a pair of scissors. Seating herself at her dresser she looked into the mirror and tried the scissors on her hair. The blades were dull with use and her hair was strong, thick and black – a young woman's hair. The scissors were useless. She dropped them back into her sewing box.

The baby began to cry, so Manju shut the door on her. She went down the stairs to the kitchen – a dark, sooty, airless room, at the back of the house. She found a knife, a long, straight-bladed knife with a serrated edge and a wooden handle. She tried it on her hair but found that it was no more use than the scissors.

Casting around for a better instrument, Manju recalled the scythes that had once been used to cut the compound's grass. These scythes were very sharp: she remembered how the hissing of their blades had echoed through the house. The malis who'd tended the grounds were long gone, but the scythes remained. She knew where they were to be found: in an outhouse by the front gate.

She opened the front door and ran across the compound to the outhouse. The scythes were exactly where she had thought, piled in a heap with the other gardening implements. She stood in the knee-deep grass of the compound and held up her hair, drawing it away from her head. She raised the scythe and hacked at it, blindly, because her hand was behind her head. She saw a lock of hair falling on to the grass and this gave her encouragement. She sawed at another handful and then another. She could see the pile of hair growing in the grass around her feet. The one thing she could not understand was the pain: why should it hurt so much to cut one's hair?

She heard a voice, speaking softly, somewhere nearby. She turned around and saw that it was Raymond, standing beside her. He put out a hand, reaching for the scythe. She took a step away: 'You don't understand . . .' she said. She tried to smile, to let him know that she knew what she was doing and that it could not be done any other way. But suddenly his hands were on her wrist. He twisted her arm and the scythe fell from her grasp. He kicked it, sending it flying aside.

Manju was astonished at the strength of Raymond's grip; at the way he was restraining her with a wrestler's armlock. No one had ever held her in this way – as though she were a madwoman.

'What do you think you're doing, Raymond?'

He twisted her hands around so that they were in front of her face. She saw that her fingers were smeared with blood.

'You've cut yourself,' he said quietly. 'You've cut your scalp.'

'I didn't know.' She tried to jerk her arms free but this only made him tighten his hold. He led her into the house and made her sit in a chair. He found some cottonwool and swabbed her scalp. The baby began to cry: they could hear her downstairs. Raymond led her to the stairs and gave her a nudge.

'Go. The child needs you.'

She went up a few steps, and then she couldn't go any more. She couldn't bear to think of going into that room and picking up the child. It was pointless. Her breasts had run dry. There was nothing she could do. She buried her face in her hands.

Raymond came up the stairs and pulled her head back, gripping it by the remains of her hair. She saw him drawing his arm back and then his hand hit her across the cheek. She clutched her stinging face and looked at him. His gaze was steady and not unkind.

'You are the mother,' he said. 'You must go to the child. A child's hunger doesn't stop, no matter what . . .' He followed her to the room and kept watch until she picked the baby up and held her to her breast.

The next day it was Christmas and in the evening Doh Say and Raymond left the house to go to church. Shortly afterwards the sirens sounded and the bombers came back. The baby had been sleeping but the sirens woke her. She began to cry.

The day of the first raid, Manju and Dolly had known exactly what to do: they'd gone to a windowless room on the ground floor and waited until the sirens sounded the all clear. There had been such a sense of urgency then: but now none of it remained. It was as though the house were already empty.

Manju stayed in bed with the baby while the bombs fell. That night the infant's voice seemed louder than ever: louder than the sirens, the bombs, the distant explosions. After a while Manju could no longer bear the sound of the child's crying. She climbed out of bed and went down the stairs. She opened the front door and stepped into the compound. It was very dark except for distant flames and flashes of light shooting through the sky.

She saw another figure ahead of her and somehow, even in the darkness, she knew that it was Rajkumar. This was the first time that she'd seen him since Neel's death. He was still dressed in the clothes that he'd been wearing that morning: a pair of trousers and a shirt that was now blackened with soot. His head was thrown back and he was staring into the sky. She knew what he was looking for and she went to stand beside him.

The planes were far up in the sky, barely visible, like the shadows of moths. She longed for them to come closer; close enough to see a face. She longed to know what kind of being this was that felt free to unleash this destruction: what was it for? What sort of creature could think of waging war upon herself, her husband, her child – a family such as hers – for what reason? Who were these people who took it upon themselves to remake the history of the world?

If only she could find some meaning in this, she knew she would be able to restore order to her mind; she would be able to reason in accustomed ways; she would know when and why it was time to feed the baby; she would be able to understand why it was necessary to take shelter, to care for one's children, to think of the past and the future and one's place in the world. She stood with Rajkumar and looked into the sky. There was nothing to be seen but shadows far above and nearer at hand, flames, explosions and noise.

Doh Say and Raymond returned the next morning, after sheltering in a church through the night. The streets were mostly empty now, they said. The workers who serviced the city were mainly Indians and many of them had fled or gone into hiding. In some areas there was already a stench of uncleared nightsoil. At the port, ships were going up in flames, with their cargoes still intact in their holds. There were no stevedores left to do the unloading: they too were mainly Indian. The administration had opened the gates of the Rangoon lunatic asylum and the inmates were now wandering about trying to find food and shelter. There were looters everywhere, breaking into abandoned houses and apartments, carrying their trophies triumphantly through the streets.

Doh Say said that it was no longer safe to remain in Rangoon. The Packard had miraculously survived the bombing. Raymond had retrieved it and brought it to back to Kemendine. Dolly loaded the car with a few necessities – some rice, dal, milk powder, vegetables, water. Then Raymond took the wheel and they drove out of the house: the plan was that they would all go to Huay Zedi and remain there until conditions changed.

They took the Pegu road, heading northwards. The central areas of the city were eerily empty, yet many major thoroughfares were impassable and they had to circle round and round to find their way out of the city. Buses lay abandoned at intersections; trams had jumped off their tracks and ploughed into the tar; rickshaws lay sidewise across the road; electric cables and tramlines lay knotted across the footpaths.

They began to notice other people – a few scattered handfuls at first, then more and more and still more, until the roads became so thickly thronged that they could barely move. Everyone was heading in the same direction: towards the northern, landward passage to India – a distance of more than a thousand miles. They had their possessions bundled on their heads; they were carrying children on their backs; wheeling elderly people in carts and barrows. Their feet had stirred up a long, snaking cloud of dust that hung above the road like a ribbon, pointing the way to the northern horizon. They were almost all Indians.

There were cars and buses too, along with taxis, rickshaws, bicycles and ox-carts. There were open trucks, with dozens of people squatting in their beds. The larger vehicles kept mainly to the centre of the road, following each other slowly in a straight line. Cars went leapfrogging along this line, passing the buses and trucks with a great trumpeting of their horns. But the press of traffic was such that even they made very slow progress.

467

At the end of the first day the Packard had not quite left Rangoon behind. By the second day, they had worked their way towards the head of the column of refugees, and now they made better time. Two days later they found themselves looking across the river, towards Huay Zedi.

They made the crossing and stayed in Huay Zedi several weeks. But then it became clear that the Japanese advance was accelerating. Doh Say decided to evacuate the village and move its inhabitants deeper into the jungle. By this time Manju's behaviour had become very erratic: Dolly and Rajkumar decided that she had to be taken home. They elected to make one last effort to reach India.

An ox-cart took them to the river – Manju, Dolly, Rajkumar and the baby. They found a boat that took them upriver, through Meiktila, past Mandalay to the tiny town of Mawlaik, on the Chindwin river. There they were confronted by a stupefying spectacle: some thirty thousand refugees were squatting along the river-bank, waiting to move on towards the densely forested mountain ranges that lay ahead. Ahead there were no roads, only tracks, rivers of mud, flowing through green tunnels of jungle. Since the start of the Indian exodus, the territory had been mapped by a network of officially recognised evacuation trails: there were 'white' routes and 'black' routes, the former being shorter and less heavily used. Several hundred thousand people had already tramped through this wilderness. Great numbers of refugees were still arriving, every day. To the south the Japanese army was still advancing and there was no turning back.

They carried the baby in a shawl that was slung hammock-like over their shoulders. Every few hundred yards they would stop and switch loads, taking turns, all three of them, Manju, Dolly and Rajkumar. They would switch between the baby and the tarpaulin-wrapped packages in which they kept their clothes and their bundle of firewood.

Dolly was using a stick, limping heavily. On the instep of her right foot there was a sore that had first showed itself as an innocuous-looking blister. In three days it had grown into a huge inflammation, almost as wide as her foot. It leaked a foul-smelling pus and ate steadily through skin, muscle and flesh. They met a nurse who said that it was a 'Naga sore'; she said that Dolly was lucky that hers had not been invaded by maggots. She had heard of a case when a boy had developed such a sore in his scalp: when it was treated with kerosene, no fewer than three hundred and fifty maggots were taken out, each the size of a small worm. And yet the boy had lived.

Despite the pain Dolly called herself lucky. They met people whose feet had almost entirely rotted away, eaten by these inflammations: hers was not nearly so badly affected. It made Manju wince to watch her: not because of her obvious pain, but because of her willed imperviousness to it. They were so strong, the two of them, Dolly and Rajkumar, so tenacious – they clung so closely together, even now, despite their age, despite everything. There was something about them that repelled her, filled her with revulsion: Dolly even more than Rajkumar, with her maddening detachment, as though all of this were a nightmare of someone else's imagining.

There were times when she could see pity in Dolly's eyes, a sort of compassion – as though she, Manju, were somehow a sadder creature than she herself; as though it was she who had lost her hold on her mind and her reason. That look made her seethe. She wanted to hit Dolly, slap her, shout in her face: 'This is reality, this is the world, look at it, look at the evil that surrounds us; to pretend that it is an illusion will not make it go away.' It was she who was sane, not they. What could be better proof of their insanity than that they should refuse to acknowledge the magnitude of their defeat; the absoluteness of their failure, as parents, as human beings?

Their firewood was wrapped in big, furry, teak leaves, to keep the rain out. It was tied with a rope that Rajkumar had rolled, from a length of vine. Sometimes the rope would come loose and a stick or a bit of wood would fall out. Every piece that fell out disappeared instantly – being either snatched up by the people behind, or else trampled into the mud, too deep to retrieve.

The mud had a strange consistency, more like quicksand than

469

clay. It would suck you in, very suddenly, so that before you knew it, you were in thigh-deep. All you could do was keep still and wait, until somebody came to your help. It was worst when you stumbled, or fell on your face; it would cling to you like a hungry animal, fastening upon your clothes, your limbs, your hair. It would hold you so tight that you could not move; it would immobilise your legs and arms, sucking them tightly in place, in the way that glue holds insects.

Somewhere they'd passed a woman. She was a Nepali and she'd been carrying a child in the same way that they were, slung in a folded cloth. She'd fallen face-first in the mud and been unable to move; it was her bad fortune that this happened on an unfrequented trail. There was no one around to help; she'd died where she lay, held fast by the mud with her child tied to her back. The baby had starved to death.

Rajkumar would get very angry if they lost any part of their trove of firewood. It was he who collected most of it. He'd keep watch as they walked and every now and again he'd spot a branch or some twigs that had escaped the notice of the tens of thousands of people who had gone ahead of them, passed the same way, tramping the sodden earth into a river of mud. In the evenings, when they stopped he would walk into the jungle and come back carrying armloads of firewood. Most of the refugees were afraid of leaving the trail; there were persistent rumours of thieves and dacoits, keeping watch and picking off stragglers. Rajkumar went anyway; he said that they could not afford for him to do otherwise. The firewood was their capital, their only asset. At the end of each day it was this wood that Rajkumar bartered for food – there were always people who needed wood; rice and dal were no use without fires to cook them on. Wood bought food more easily than money or valuables. Money cost nothing here. There were people – rich Rangoon merchants – who would give away fistfuls of notes in exchange for a few packets of medicine. And as for valuables, they were just an extra weight. The trails were littered with discarded goods – radios, bicycle frames, books, a craftsman's tools. No one even stopped to look.

They came across a lady one day, dressed in a beautiful silk sari, a peacock-green Kanjeevaram. She looked to be from a wealthy family but she too had run out of food. She was trying to bargain with a group of people who were sitting by a fire. Suddenly she began to undress and when she'd stripped off her sari they saw that she had others on underneath, beautiful, rich silks, worth hundreds of rupees. She offered up one of these, hoping to exchange it for a handful of food. But no one had any use for it; they asked instead for kindling and wood. They saw her arguing vainly with them – and then, perhaps recognising finally the worthlessness of her treasured possession, she rolled the sari into a ball and put it on their fire: the silk burnt with a crackling sound, sending up leaping flames.

The firewood had splinters, which would work their way into your flesh, but Manju preferred carrying the wood to carrying her daughter. The baby cried whenever it came near her. 'She's just hungry,' Dolly would say. 'Give her your breast.' They would stop and she would sit, in the rain, with the baby in her arms. Rajkumar would rig a shelter above them, with leaves and branches.

A little bit further, they said. India isn't far now. Just a little bit more.

There was nothing in her body – Manju was certain of this – but somehow the baby would find a way of squeezing a few drops from her sore, chafing breasts. Then, when the trickle ran dry, she would begin to cry again – in an angry, vengeful way, as though she wanted nothing more than to see her mother dead. At times she would try to feed the baby other things – she would work a bit of rice into a paste and tuck it into a corner of the child's mouth. She seemed to relish the taste: she was a hungry girl, greedy for life; more her grandparents' child than her own.

One day Manju fell asleep sitting up with the baby in her arms. She woke to find Dolly standing over her, looking worriedly into her face. She could hear the buzz of insects, flying around her head. They were the shimmer-winged bluebottles that Rajkumar called 'vulture-flies' because they were always to be seen on people who were too weak to go on – or who were near death.

Manju heard the baby screaming in her lap, but for once the sound did not bother her. There was a restful numbness in her body: she wanted nothing more than to sit there as long she could, relishing the absence of sensation. But as always her tormentors were bearing down on her; Dolly was shouting at her: 'Get up, Manju, get up.'

'No,' she said. 'Please let me be. Just a little longer.'

'You've been sitting there since yesterday,' Dolly shouted. 'You have to get up, Manju, or you'll stay there for ever. Think of the baby; get up.'

'The baby's happy here,' Manju said. 'Let us be. Tomorrow we'll walk again. Not now.'

But Dolly wouldn't listen. 'We won't let you die, Manju. You're young; you have the baby to think of . . .' Dolly took the child out of her arms and Rajkumar pulled her to her feet. He shook her hard, so that her teeth rattled.

'You have to go on, Manju; you can't give up.'

She stood staring at him in the pouring rain, in her white widow's sari, her hair shorn. He was dressed in a tattered longyi, shod in mud-caked slippers. His belly was gone and his frame was wasted with hunger; his face was mottled with white stubble, his eyes blood-shot and red-rimmed.

'Why, old man, why?' she shouted at him. She called him *buro* in contempt; she no longer cared that he was Neel's father and that she'd always been in awe of him: now he was just her tormen-tor, who would not let her enjoy the rest that she had earned. 'Why do I have to go on? Look at you: you've gone on – and on and on and on. And what has it brought you?'

Then, to her surprise, tears welled up in his eyes and rolled down the cracks and fissures of his face. He seemed like a stricken child: helpless, unable to move. She thought for a moment she'd won at last, but then Dolly stepped in. She took his arm and turned him round so that he was looking ahead, to the next range of mountains. He stood where he was, his shoulders sagging, as though the truth of their condition had finally dawned on him.

Dolly pushed him on. 'You can't stop now, Rajkumar – you have to go on.' At the sound of her voice, some inner instinct seemed to take hold of him. He slung the bundle of firewood over his shoulders and walked on.

There were places where the trails converged and became bottlenecks. Usually these were on the banks of streams and rivers. At each of these crossings there would be thousands and thousands of people gathered together, sitting, waiting – moving through the mud with tiny, exhausted steps.

They came to a river that seemed very broad. It flowed with the speed of a mountain stream and its water was as cold as ice. Here, on a stretch of sandy bank, surrounded by steep jungle, there was the largest gathering of people they had yet come across: tens of thousands – a sea of heads and faces.

They joined this great mass of people and sat squatting, on the river's sandy bank. They waited, and in time, a raft arrived. It was unwieldy-looking and not very large. Manju watched it as it bobbed on the swollen river: it was the most beautiful craft that she had ever seen and she could tell that it was her saviour. It filled up in minutes and went away upstream, chugging slowly round a great bend. She did not lose faith; she was certain that it would return. And sure enough, in a while, the raft came back again. And again and again, filling up in minutes each time.

At last it was their turn and they climbed in. Manju handed the baby to Dolly and found herself a place by the raft's edge, where she could sit by the water. The raft started off and she watched the river rushing past; she could see its whirlpools and its swirling currents – the patterns of its flow and movement were etched on its surface. She touched the water and found that it was very cold.

Somewhere in the distance, she could hear the baby crying. No matter how loud the noise around her, no matter how many people she was surrounded by, she always knew her daughter's voice. She knew that Dolly would soon seek her out and bring the baby to her; that she would stand over her, watching, to make sure that the child was fed. She let her hand fall over the raft's edge and thrilled to the water's touch. It seemed to be pulling at her, urging her to come in. She let her arm trail a little, and then dipped her foot in. She felt her sari growing heavier, unfurling in the water, pulling away from her, tugging at her body, urging her to follow. She heard the sound of crying and she was glad that her daughter was in Dolly's arms. With Dolly and Rajkumar the child would be safe; they would see her home. It was better this way: better that they, who knew what they were living for, should have her in their care. She heard Dolly's voice, calling to her –

'Manju, Manju stop – be careful . . .' – and she knew the time had come. It was no effort at all to slip over, from the raft into the river. The water was fast, dark and numbingly cold.

PART SEVEN

The Glass Palace

Forty

Bela was eighteen when Dolly and Rajkumar crossed the mountains. The day when they arrived in Lankasuka was to live in her mind for ever.

This was in 1942, which was as terrible a year as any that Bengal had ever known. At the time, little was known in India about conditions in Burma and Malaya. Because of wartime security, news was sketchy and all the usual channels of communication had broken down. The year before, when the first evacuation ship from Rangoon arrived in Calcutta, Bela and her parents had gone to meet it at the docks. They had hoped to see Manju among the disembarking passengers. Instead they learnt that Rajkumar and his family had decided to stay on in Burma.

Then came the bombing of Rangoon and the great northwards exodus of the Indian population. When the first refugees arrived in Calcutta, Bela sought them out, asking for information, citing names, addresses. She learnt nothing.

It was also in 1942 that Mahatma Gandhi launched the Quit India movement. Uma was one of the many thousands of Congress workers who were imprisoned. Some were gaoled until the end of the war. Uma's stay was relatively short; she fell ill with typhoid and was allowed to return home.

Uma had been home a couple of months when, one afternoon, her elderly gatekeeper came to tell her that there were some destitutes outside, asking for her. This was only too common at the time; Bengal was in the throes of a famine, one of the worst in history. The city was full of starving migrants from the countryside; people were stripping the parks of grass and leaves, sifting through the sewers for grains of rice.

At Lankasuka, such spare food as there was was distributed to the poor once a day. On that particular day, the morning's food distribution was long over. Uma was busy at her desk when the chowkidar walked in to tell her about the destitutes. She said: 'Tell them to come back tomorrow, at the right time.'

The chowkidar went away, only to return shortly afterwards. 'They won't leave.'

Bela happened to be at hand. Uma said: 'Bela, go and see what the matter is.'

Bela stepped out into the courtyard and began to walk towards the gate. She saw a man and a woman holding the metal bars. Then she heard a voice, saying her name, in a hoarse whisper – 'Bela' – and she looked closely at their faces.

Uma heard a scream and ran out into the courtyard. She snatched the keys from the chowkidar's hands. She went running to the gate and threw it open.

'Look.'

Rajkumar was kneeling on the pavement. He held out his arms and they saw that he was holding a child, a baby – Jaya. Suddenly the baby's face turned a bright, dark red and she began to cry at the top of her voice. At that moment the world held no more beautiful sound than this utterance of rage: this primeval sound of life proclaiming its determination to defend itself.

It was not till the latter months of the next year, 1943, that the first rumours of the Indian National Army began to reach India – but this was not the same force that Arjun had joined, in northern Malaya. The first Indian National Army had not lasted long. About a year after its founding, its leader, Captain Mohun Singh, had disbanded it, fearing that the Japanese were trying to take it over. The army was resurrected by Subhas Chandra Bose, the Indian nationalist politician, who reached Singapore in 1943 by way of Afghanistan and Germany. Bose reinvigorated the Indian National Army, drawing tens of thousands of new recruits from the Indian

478

populations of South East Asia: Arjun, Hardy, Kishan Singh, Ilongo and many others joined.

At the end of the war thousands of members of the Indian National Army were brought back to India as prisoners of war. To the British they were JIFs – Japanese Inspired Fifth Columnists. They were regarded as traitors – both to the Empire, and to the Indian army, the bulk of which had continued to fight for the Allies, in North Africa, southern Europe, and finally in the British counter-invasion of Burma. The Indian public, however, saw the matter quite differently. To them imperialism and Fascism were twin evils, one being a derivative of the other. It was the defeated prisoners of the Indian National Army that they received as heroes – not the returning victors.

In December 1945 the colonial government chose to bring charges against three members of the Indian National Army – the famous 'Red Fort Three': Shah Nawaz Khan, Gurbakhsh Singh Dhillon and Prem Sahgal. The country erupted with protests and demonstrations; support committees were formed all over India, despite an official ban. General strikes shut down entire states; students held huge public meetings defying curfew orders. In the southern city of Madurai two people died after the police opened fire on a demonstration. In Calcutta tens of thousands of people poured into the streets. They took over the city for several days. Dozens were shot by the police. In Bombay, naval ratings mutinied. For the Congress Party the trial was a windfall. The party had lost the momentum it had gained in the pre-war years and it badly needed an issue that would serve to mobilise the country. The trial provided just such a cause.

Once the trial got under way, the prosecution quickly ran into problems. It was not able to produce any evidence to link the Indian National Army either with Japanese atrocities in South East Asia, or with the mistreatment of British and Australian prisoners of war. While it did prove that some Indian prisoners had indeed been mistreated, none of these cases had any link with the three defendants.

On December 1, 1945, Bhulabhai Desai, the chief defence lawyer, rose to make his concluding address. 'What is now on trial before this court,' he said, 'is the right to wage war with immunity on the part of a subject race.'

479

There was essentially only one charge against his clients, he argued, that of waging war against the King. All the other charges, he claimed, were derived from the first. It fell to Desai to demonstrate that international law recognised the right of subject peoples to wage war for their freedom and this he did by citing a series of precedents. He showed that the British Government had itself recognised this right, when expedient, in cases that dated back to the nineteenth century. They had, for example, supported the Greeks and a number of other nationalities in rebellions against the Ottoman Empire; more recently, they had supported the Polish National Army and Czechoslovak rebels; they had similarly insisted on the right of the French maquis to be treated as belligerents even though the Government of Marshal Pétain was at that time the *de jure* and *de facto* Government of France. The trial ended with all three defendants being found guilty of 'waging war against the King'. They were sentenced to transportation for life, but all three had their sentences commuted. They were set free and were received by tumultuous crowds.

Hardy was by this time a national figure (he was later to become an ambassador and a high-ranking official of the Indian Government). He came to see Jaya's grandparents in Calcutta in 1946. It was from him that they learnt that Arjun had died fighting in one the INA's last engagements – fought in central Burma, in the final days of the war.

At this point in the conflict, the Japanese were in retreat and the Allied Fourteenth Army, under the command of General Slim, was advancing rapidly southwards. The Indian units in central Burma were among the last to continue resisting. Their numbers were tiny and they were armed with obsolete weaponry, dating back to the early days of the war. The forces they were fighting against were often mirror-images of what they themselves had been at the start of the war: most were Indians, often from the same regiments, often recruited from the same villages and districts. It was not usual for them to be fighting their younger brothers and nephews.

The Indian National Army's resistance at this stage was largely symbolic, undertaken in the hope of inspiring a revolt in the Indian army. Although they were never a serious threat to the

480

victorious Fourteenth Army they were more than a minor irritant. Many fought and died with great courage, providing heros and martyrs for the movement. Arjun was among those who had died a hero, Hardy said. And so had Kishan Singh. That was all they knew about Arjun's death and they were content that it should be so.

For the next six years Dolly and Rajkumar stayed with Uma, in her flat. The legacy of Rajkumar's quarrel with Uma was forgotten and the baby, Jaya, became a bond linking every member of the household.

Dolly took a job with an army publications unit, translating wartime pamphlets into Burmese. Rajkumar did occasional supervisory work at sawmills and timberyards. In January 1948 Burma gained her independence. Soon after this Dolly decided that she and Rajkumar would return to Rangoon, at least for a while. In the meantime, Jaya was to be left in Calcutta, with her aunt Bela and her other grandparents.

Dolly's eagerness to go back to Burma was due largely to the fact that Dinu had not been heard from in seven years. Dolly believed that he was still alive and she was keen to find him. Rajkumar expressed his willingness to go with her and she booked passages for both of them.

But as the day approached, it became clear that Rajkumar was very far from being certain of his own mind. Over the last six years, he had grown very attached to his orphaned grandchild. More than anyone else in the house, it was he who undertook the responsibilities of her everyday care: he sat with her through her meals, walked with her in the park, told her stories at bedtime. Dolly began to wonder whether he would be able to sustain the pain of wrenching himself away from the child.

The question was settled when Rajkumar disappeared, two days before they were due to depart for Burma. He came back after the ship had sailed. He was contrite and full of apologies; he said he had no memory of where he had been or why he'd gone. He urged Dolly to make another booking; he promised it would not happen again. In the meanwhile, Dolly had decided that it would be better to leave Rajkumar where he was – both for his own sake and Jaya's. Uma for her part made no objection; she was content to have him stay on: he was very little trouble and often made himself useful round the house.

Dolly went back to the steamship company's office and booked a single, one-way passage to Rangoon. She knew that Rajkumar would feel obliged to accompany her if he learnt of her plans. She decided not to tell him. She went about her daily business as usual. On the morning of her departure she cooked *mohingya* noodles, Rajkumar's favourite dish. They went for a walk around the lake and afterwards Rajkumar fell asleep.

It had been arranged that Uma would go with Dolly to the Khidderpore docks. Neither of them said much on the way; there was a finality about this departure that they could not bring themselves to acknowledge. At the end, when Dolly was about to board her ship, she said to Uma: 'I know Jaya will be fine. There are many of you to care for her. It's Rajkumar that I'm worried about.'

'He'll be all right, Dolly.'

'Will you look after him, Uma? For my sake?'

'I will; I promise.'

At Lankasuka, Rajkumar woke to find a note on his pillow: it was written in Dolly's careful hand. He picked up the note and smoothed it down. It said: *Rajkumar – in my heart I know that Dinu is still alive and that I shall find him. After that I shall go to Sagaing as I have so long wanted to do. Know that nothing in this world will be harder to renounce than you and the memory of our love. Dolly.*

He never saw her again.

Forty-one

As the only child in the house, Jaya had the run of Lankasuka when she was growing up. Her aunt Bela lived upstairs, inheriting the flat after her parents' death. She never married and the every-day tasks of looking after Jaya fell mainly to her: it was in her flat that Jaya usually slept and ate.

But Rajkumar was never more than one flight of stairs away: after Dolly's departure, he continued to live on the ground floor, in Uma's flat. He had a small room of his own, next to the kitchen, furnished sparsely, with a narrow bed and a couple of bookshelves.

The only inessential object in Rajkumar's room was a radio – an old-fashioned Paillard with a wooden cabinet, and a textile-covered grille. Rajkumar always took his afternoon siesta with the radio on – it was Jaya who usually turned it off, after coming home from school. The silencing of the radio would often rouse Rajkumar from his nap. He would sit up, leaning back against his pillow, settling his granddaughter beside him. When he put his arm around Jaya's shoulders she would disappear into the crook of his elbow; his hands were huge, the skin very dark, marbled with lighter-coloured veins. The white hairs on his knuckles stood out in startling contrast. He would shut his eyes and the hollows of his face would fill with leathery creases. And then he would begin to talk; stories would come pouring out of him – of places that Jaya had never been to and never seen; of images and scenes that were so vivid as to brim over from the measuring cup of reality into an ocean of dreams. She lived in his stories.

Rajkumar's favourite haunt was a small Buddhist temple in the centre of the city, a place that Dolly had liked to visit too, in the past. This was where Calcutta's Burmese community for-gathered, and on special occasions Rajkumar would take Jaya there with him. The temple was on the fourth floor of a tumble-down old building, in an area where the streets were clogged with traffic and the air was dense with diesel smoke. They would make their way across town on a bus and get off at the stop for the Eden Hospital. They'd climb up the grimy marble stairs and when they reached the top, they would step into a hall that seemed a world away from its surroundings: full of light, perfumed with the scent of fresh flowers, its floors shining clean. On the floor there would be rush mats, woven in distinctive patterns: different from Indian mats, although at the same time, not dissimilar.

The temple was always at its liveliest during the great Burmese festivals – Thingyan, the water festival that inaugurated the Bur-mese New Year; Waso, which marked the beginning of Thadin, the annual three-month period of fasting and abstinence, and Thadingyut, the festival of light, which celebrated its end.

Once, when Jaya was ten, Rajkumar took her to the temple for Thadingyut. The temple was filled with people; women were bustling about in their longyis, preparing a feast; the walls glowed with the shimmering light of hundreds of lamps and candles. Suddenly, in the midst of the noise and the bustle, there was a hush. Whispers ran around the room: 'The Princess . . . the Second Princess, she's coming up the stairs . . .'

The Princess stepped in and there was a quickening of breath, a nudging of elbows; those who knew how performed the shiko. The Princess was wearing a scarlet *htamein* and a kind of sash; she was in her late sixties, with her greying hair tied at the back of her head in a severe little bun. She was tiny, with a kindly face and black, twinkling eyes. She too was living in India then, in the hill-station of Kalimpong. Her circumstances were known to be extremely straitened.

The Princess exchanged a few gracious pleasantries with the people around her. Then her eyes fell on Rajkumar and her face creased into a fond, warm smile. She broke off her conversations; the crowd parted and she made her way slowly across the room. Every eye in the temple was now on Rajkumar. Jaya could feel herself swelling with pride on her grandfather's behalf.

The Princess greeted Rajkumar warmly, in Burmese; Jaya couldn't understand a word of their conversation, but she watched both their faces carefully, studying their changing expressions, smiling when they smiled, frowning when they were grave. Then Rajkumar introduced her: 'And this is my granddaughter . . .'

Jaya had never met a princess before and didn't know what to do. But she was not without a certain resourcefulness; she recalled a movie she had recently seen – was it *Sleeping Beauty* or *Cinderella*? – and sketched the beginning of a curtsey, holding the edge of her dress pinched between finger and thumb. She was rewarded with a hug from the Princess.

Later, people gathered around Rajkumar, wondering why she had singled him out. 'What did Her Highness say?' they asked. 'How did she know you?'

'Oh, I've known her most of my life,' Rajkumar said off-handedly.

'Really?'

'Yes. The first time I saw her was in Mandalay and she was just six months old.'

'Oh? And how did that come about?'

And then Rajkumar would start at the beginning, going back to that day more than sixty years before, when he had heard the sound of English cannon rolling in across the plain to the walls of Mandalay's fort.

In a quiet corner of Lankasuka, there was a niche that served as a shrine to Jaya's parents and her uncle, Arjun. Two framed photographs stood in the niche: one of these was a picture of Manju and Neel, taken at their wedding – they'd been caught glancing up from the sacramental fire, in surprise. The hooded veil of Manju's sari had slipped momentarily from her head. They were smiling, their faces shining and radiant. The photograph of Arjun was taken at Howrah Station: he was in uniform, laughing. A second face was clearly discernible, over his shoulder: Bela told her niece that this was her uncle's batman, Kishan Singh.

Three times each year, Bela and Jaya would perform a small ceremony at their shrine. They'd garland the photographs and light incense. Bela would hand Jaya flowers, directing her to pay her respects to her mother, her father and Arjun, the uncle she had never known. But when Bela lit the *dhoop* sticks, there were always four bunches, not three. Without ever being told, Jaya knew that the extra one was for Kishan Singh: he too was among their dead.

It was only when Jaya was ten years old, already conscious of a growing interest in cameras and photographs, that it occurred to her to ask her aunt about the pictures and who had taken them.

Bela was surprised.' I thought you knew,' she said in puzzlement. 'They were taken by your uncle Dinu.'

'And who was that?' said Jaya.

This was how Jaya learnt that she had a second uncle, on her father's side – an uncle who had not been memorialised because his fate was unknown. In Lankasuka no one ever spoke of Dinu – neither Rajkumar, nor Uma nor Bela. No one knew what had become of him. He was known to have stayed on at Morningside until the last weeks of 1942. At some point after that he'd left for Burma. Nothing had been heard from him since. Privately everyone suspected that he had become yet another casualty of the war, but no one wished to be the first to voice this fear and, as a result, Dinu's name was never mentioned in the house.

Through the late 1940s, the shadows of the Second World war deepened over Burma. First there were protracted civil conflicts and a large-scale Communist uprising. Then, in 1962, General Ne Win seized power in a coup and the country became subject to the bizarre, maniacal whimsies of its dictator: Burma, 'the golden', became synonymous with poverty, tyranny and misgovernment. Dinu was among the many millions who had vanished into the darkness.

Until the day of her marriage Jaya lived in Lankasuka, with Bela, Uma and Rajkumar. She married young, at the age of seventeen. Her husband was a doctor, ten years older. They were very much in love and a year after the wedding, they had a son.

But when the boy was two years old, tragedy struck: his father was killed in a train accident.

Soon after this Jaya moved back to Lankasuka. With her aunt Bela's support, she enrolled at Calcutta University, took a degree and found a job as a college teacher. She worked hard to give her son a good education. He went to the city's best schools and colleges and at the age of twenty-two he won a scholarship and went abroad.

Now for the first time in years, Jaya had time on her hands. She resumed work on a long-delayed PhD thesis, on the history of photography in India.

In 1996 Jaya's college sent her to an art history conference at the University of Goa. On the way, while changing planes at Bombay airport, she was ambushed by one of the worst of all possible airport experiences: on arriving at the check-in counter she was told that her plane had been overbooked. If she wanted to be sure of a seat she would have to wait at least a couple of days; alternatively the airline would pay for a bus or a train.

Jaya went to another counter, brandishing her ticket. She found herself at the end of a long line of angry people; they were all shouting the same refrain at the desk-clerk: 'But we had reservations . . .'

Jaya was slightly built and of medium height. Her hair was wispy and grey and she looked very much what she was – an unassuming and rather withdrawn college professor who often had difficulty keeping order in class. She knew that there was no point in adding her voice to the chorus of indignation at the counter: where the others had been foiled, no one was less likely to prevail than someone such as herself. She decided to take the train.

Bombay was not a city that Jaya knew well. She collected a voucher and went to Shivaji station on a bus provided by the airline. She bought a railway timetable and learnt that the earliest train was not till several hours later. She got her ticket and then decided to go for a walk. She checked her suitcase into the left-luggage facility and stepped out of the station. It was late afternoon, the start of the rush hour; she allowed herself to be swept along by the surging crowds.

After a while she found herself standing beside the tinted doors of an air-conditioned art gallery. Her breath created a misty halo on the chilled green glass. There was a flyer on the door, announcing an exhibit of newly-discovered work by a pioneering photographer from the early years of the century, a hitherto unknown Parsee woman. At the top of the flyer there was a small graphic, a computer-shrunken reproduction of one of the photographs in the exhibition – a group portrait of four seated figures. There was something about the picture that caught Jaya's eye. She pushed the door open. The gallery was very cold and almost empty. There was the usual surly chowkidar perched on a stool, and behind a desk, a bored-looking woman in a silk sari and diamond nose-ring.

'Could you please show me the picture that's on this flyer?'

The woman must have heard a note of excitement in Jaya's voice for she rose quickly to her feet and led her to the far corner of the gallery. 'That one?'

Jaya nodded. The image was blown up to a great size, larger than a poster, whereas the version she remembered was no bigger than a postcard. She had known the picture all her life, but she was looking at it now as though for the first time. The picture was taken in the garden of the Collector's residence. Four chairs were placed in a semicircular arrangement on a finely trimmed lawn. Uma and her husband were at the centre of the group, and seated beside them, on either side, were Dolly and Rajkumar.

Behind them was a terraced garden, descending steeply down the side of a hill. A number of people were visible in shadowy outline in the middle distance, in carefully arranged postures – servants, grooms and gardeners, all equipped with the instruments of their various trades: sickles, hoes, whips. In the background, stretched across the top of the frame, was a landscape – so sweeping and dramatic that it looked like a painted backdrop: a river curled round a hill and broadened into an estuary, a line of cliffs jutted out into a frothing sea, a palm-fringed beach slid gently into a sun-washed bay.

488

The Collector was in the foreground, thin and dapper, dressed in a three-button linen suit. He was sitting perched on the edge of his chair like an alert bird, with his head cocked at a stiff and slightly distrustful angle. Uma, on the other hand, seemed very much at ease. There was a certain poise and self-assurance about her demeanour, about the way her hand rested lightly on her knees. She was wearing a plain, light-coloured sari, with an embroidered border; the end was draped shawl-like over her head. Her eyes were large and long-lashed, her face generous but also strong: Jaya remembered it well from her childhood. It was strange, in retrospect, to think how little Uma's appearance had changed over the course of her life.

The gallery owner interrupted these reflections. 'I take it you know this picture?' she said.

'Yes. The woman in the middle was my great-aunt. Her name was Uma Dey.'

And then Jaya noticed a detail. 'Look,' she said, 'look how she's wearing her sari.'

The gallery owner leaned over to examine the print. 'I don't see anything unusual in it. That's how everyone wears it.'

'Actually,' said Jaya, 'Uma Dey was one of the first women in India to wear a sari in this particular way.'

'Which way?'

'The way I'm wearing mine, for example – or you yours.'

The woman frowned. 'This is how saris have always been worn,' she said matter-of-factly. 'Saris are a very ancient garment.'

'Yes, they are,' Jaya said quietly, 'but not the ways of wearing them. The contemporary style of wearing a sari with a blouse and petticoat is not very old at all. It was invented by a man, in the days of the British Raj.'

Suddenly, across the years, she heard Uma's voice, explaining the evolution of sari-wearing. It gave Jaya a thrill, even after all those years, to recall how astonished she'd been when she'd first heard the story. She'd always imagined saris to be a part of the natural order of the Indian universe, handed down from immemorial antiquity. It had come as a shock to discover that the garment had a history, created by real people, through human volition.

On her way out of the gallery, Jaya stopped to buy a postcard reproduction of the picture. On the back there was a brief explanatory note: it said that Ratnagiri lay between Bombay and Goa. On an impulse, Jaya pulled her railway timetable out of her bag: she saw that her train was scheduled to stop at Ratnagiri on its way to Goa. It occurred to her that she could easily stop there for a night or two: the conference wasn't due to start until two days later.

Jaya walked out of the gallery and wandered into an Irani restaurant. She ordered some tea and sat down to think. She was suddenly possessed with the idea of going to Ratnagiri: she'd often thought of going and had always found reasons for putting it off. But perhaps the time was now: the photograph in the gallery seemed to be an indication of some kind – almost a sign. Ratnagiri was the place where her own, very particular, history had had its origins – but the thought of going there unsettled her, stirring up forgotten sediments of anxiety and disquiet.

She felt the need to talk to someone. She paid her bill and went outside. Bracing herself against the crowd, she walked up the street to a long-distance telephone booth. Stepping in, she dialled her own Calcutta number. After two rings her aunt answered. 'Jaya? Where are you?'

'Bombay . . .' Jaya explained what had happened. As she talked, she pictured her aunt, standing over the chipped black phone in her bedroom, frowning anxiously, her gold-rimmed reading glasses slipping down her long thin nose.

'I'm thinking of spending a couple of nights in Ratnagiri,' Jaya said. 'My train stops there, on the way to Goa.'

There was a silence. Then she heard Bela's voice, speaking quietly into the phone. 'Yes – of course you must go; you should have gone years ago . . .'

Ratnagiri's setting was every bit as spectacular as Jaya had imagined. But she quickly discovered that very little remained of the places that she had heard about as a child. The jetty at Mandvi was a crumbling ruin; the Bhagavati temple, once just a spire and a shrine, was now a soaring mass of whitewashed concrete; Outram

490

House, where King Thebaw and his entourage had lived for some twenty-five years, had been torn down and rebuilt. Ratnagiri itself was no longer the small, provincial town of Thebaw's time. It was a thriving city, with industries clustered thickly around it on all sides.

But the strange thing was that through all of this, the town had somehow succeeded in keeping King Thebaw and his memory vibrantly alive. *Thiba-Raja* was omnipresent in Ratnagiri: his name was emblazoned on signs and billboards, on street-corners, restaurants, hotels. The King had been dead more than eighty years, but in the bazaars people spoke of him as though they'd known him at first hand. Jaya found this touching at first, and then deeply moving – that a man such as Thebaw, so profoundly untransportable, should be still so richly loved in the land of his exile.

Jaya's first real find was the site of the Collector's residence – the place where Uma had lived. It turned out that it was right around the corner from her hotel, on the crest of a hill that overlooked the bay and the town. The compound was government property and it was surrounded by a massive, forbidding wall. The hillside – thickly forested in Uma's time – had since been cleared, with the result that the view was even more dramatic than before, a vast panorama of river, sea and sky. Ratnagiri lay spread out below, the perfect model of a colonial district town, with an invisible line separating its huddled bazaars from the 'Cutchery' – the red-brick Victorian compound that housed the district courts and offices.

Impatient for a glimpse of the Collector's residence, Jaya piled a few bricks against the compound's walls and climbed up to look inside. She found another disappointment lying in wait: the old bungalow was gone, with its Grecian portico and its sloping lawn and terraced gardens. The grounds had been split up to accommodate several smaller houses.

Jaya was about to jump down when she was accosted by an armed guard. 'Hey you,' he shouted. 'What are you doing? Get down from there.'

He came running up and fired off a volley of questions: Who was she? Where was she from? What was she doing there?

To distract him, she produced the postcard she had bought at the gallery in Bombay. It had exactly the effect she had hoped for. The guard stared at the picture and then led her down the road to a lookout point, on a tongue of land that hung poised above the valley.

'There's the Kajali river,' he said, pointing, 'and that over there's the Bhate beach.'

Then he began to ask questions about the people in the photograph – the Collector, Uma. When his finger came to Rajkumar, he laughed.

'And look at this fellow,' he said, 'he looks as though he owns the place.'

Jaya looked more closely at the picture. She saw that there was indeed a jaunty tilt to Rajkumar's head, although he looked otherwise quite solemn. His face was massive and heavy-jawed, his eyes grave; he appeared gigantic beside the slim, diminutive form of the Collector. He was dressed in dark trousers, a linen jacket and a round-collared shirt. His clothes were neither as elegant nor as finely cut as the Collector's, but he looked much more at ease; his legs were negligently crossed, and he had a slim silver cigarette case in one hand. He was holding it up as though it were an ace of trumps, pinched between finger and thumb.

'That was my grandfather,' Jaya said, by way of explanation.

The guard had already lost interest in Rajkumar. Through all this his eyes had kept straying to Dolly, seated in her corner beside Uma, her body half turned against the camera as though to defend herself from its gaze.

Dolly was dressed in a green silk longyi and a white blouse. Her face was long and slender, with a scaffolding of finely moulded bones standing outlined beneath her skin. Her hair was tied back, but a single strand had escaped, curling down from her temple. She was wearing no jewellery, but she had a spray of flowers, white-petalled frangipani, pinned above one of her ears. In her hands she was holding a garland of white jasmine.

'She's very beautiful,' said the guard.

'Yes,' said Jaya. 'Everybody said so . . .'

The next day was Jaya's last in Ratnagiri. In the late afternoon she hired a scooter-rickshaw and asked the driver to take her to the

Bhate beach. The scooter drove through the town, past the red-brick buildings of the high school and college, over the bridge that crossed the estuary, to a beach on the southern side of the bay. In the distance, the sun had swelled to fill the mouth of the bay, growing ever larger as it dipped towards the horizon. The sand was copper-coloured and it slipped beneath the water at a gentle incline. Coconut palms grew thick along the edge of the beach, their trunks leaning thirstily into the wind. Along the line where the sand changed into soil there was a densely tangled accumulation of grass and shells and dried seaweed.

It was there, hidden in the undergrowth, that Jaya found what she was looking for – a small stone memorial to her great-uncle, the Collector. The engraved lettering was worn thin by the combined action of wind, water and sand. There was just enough light to read the inscription. It said: 'To the memory of Beni Prasad Dey Esq., District Collector, 1905–1906.' Jaya stood up to look at the windswept beach, sloping gently down to the waves. The red sand had turned grey with the setting of the sun. Uma had told her, long ago, that if she were to walk from the memorial stone to the water, in a straight line, she would cross the very spot where the Collector's body had been found, along with the wreckage of his capsized boat.

Forty-two

On her return to Calcutta, Jaya began to look through the huge collection of documents and papers that Uma had left her, in her will. Jaya had occasionally toyed with the idea of writing a biography of her great-aunt; an important publisher had even offered her a contract once. Jaya knew that there had been a great revival of interest in Uma recently, as a pioneering political figure. There was bound to be a biography soon – she was loath to think that it would appear under someone else's name.

It took Jaya several days to sort through Uma's papers, many of which had been eaten into by insects. The strange thing was that the more she read, the more she found herself thinking of Rajkumar. It was as though in this one regard, childhood habits of associative reasoning had remained with her. Through all the years that she'd known him, her grandfather had lived downstairs, in a small anteroom in Uma's flat. There was no inference of conjugality in these living arrangements: Rajkumar's status in the household was understood to fall somewhere between that of poor relative and employee. But the geography of the house being what it was, it meant that for Jaya, to think of the one was to think of the other: to go down to see her grandfather meant also seeing her great-aunt.

Recollections came flooding back to Jaya. She remembered the particular tone of voice in which Rajkumar would say, several times each day: 'Ah, Burma – now Burma was a golden land . . .' She remembered how he'd liked to smoke Burmese-style cheroots – longer and thicker than bidis but not as dark nor as big as cigars. Cheroots of this kind were not easily to be had in India, but there were certain substitutes that Rajkumar deemed acceptable. Not far from Lankasuka there was a paan shop that stocked these cheroots. Jaya would sometimes walk to this shop with her grandfather. She remembered how he'd narrow his eyes when he was lighting a cheroot. Then he would blow out a huge cloud of grey smoke and begin: 'Ah, Burma – now . . .'

The paan-wallah who owned this shop was more irascible than most. She remembered an occasion when she'd heard him snap at Rajkumar: 'Yes, yes, no need to tell us again. Your Burma is so golden you can pluck nuggets out of people's farts . . .'

She remembered how she'd go with Rajkumar to visit the Burmese temple in north Calcutta. She remembered the people who'd gather there – many of them Indians, people who'd left Burma in 1942, just like Rajkumar. There were Gujaratis, Bengalis, Tamils, Sikhs, Eurasians. In the temple they would all speak Burmese. Some had done well after their departure. They'd built new businesses, made new homes for themselves; others had dedicated themselves to their children and grandchildren – in much the same way that Rajkumar had built his new life around Jaya. Not all the people who came to the temple were Buddhists, by birth or conviction. They came because this was the one place where they could be sure of meeting others like themselves; people to whom they could say, 'Burma is a golden land' knowing that their listeners would be able to filter these words through the sieves of exile, sifting through their very specific nuances. She recalled how they had thirsted for news of Burma – longed to hear word of those who had been left behind. She remembered the stir that greeted new arrivals; how they would be besieged with questions: 'And what about . . . ?' '. . . and did you hear about so-and-so?'

Rajkumar was always the noisiest of the questioners, taking advantage of his booming voice to shout questions – questions about someone with a Burmese name; someone whom she had not known to be her uncle until Bela told her at the age of ten – her uncle Dinu, whom she'd never met.

These memories provoked a new chain of thought. Jaya put away Uma's papers and pulled out a file of her own – of old clippings that she had compiled over the last nine years. She'd started the file in 1987, on reading about the birth of a democracy

495

movement in Rangoon. These events had rekindled a dormant interest in the land of her birth. She had tracked the emergence of the movement's leader, Aung San Suu Kyi, and had cut out many magazine and newspaper articles. In August 1988 when the military junta struck back, imprisoning Aung San Suu Kyi and unleashing a savage campaign of repression, Jaya had sat up nights, listening to the BBC. She had bought pamphlets that described the bloodshed that followed: the mass shootings, the imprisonments, the scattering of the activists.

Now, as she looked through the yellowing contents of her file, Jaya's attention was caught by a magazine photograph: a picture of Aung San Suu Kyi. It struck her that there was something different about the photograph; it had a quality that set it apart from most magazine illustrations. The photographer had caught Aung San Suu Kyi's fine-boned face in a moment of quiet reflection; there was something in the framing of the picture that reminded her of the silver-framed photographs that stood on Bela's dresser.

Jaya glanced at the line of fine print on the top edge of the picture. The photograph had been credited to one U Tun Pe. She said the name out loud and something stirred, deep within the settled sediments of her memory. She got up and went to Bela's room. 'Do you remember Dinu-kaka's Burmese name?'

'Let me see . . .' Bela paused, running her fingers through her short-clipped white hair. 'It was Tun – something. Of course, in Burma the prefix changes as you grow older. If you're a woman it goes from Ma to Daw and if you're a man, you're Maung and then Ko and then U. So if he were alive today, he would be U Tun . . . Something like that anyway.'

Jaya produced the picture and pointed to the credit line. 'Could it be this?'

Wrinkling her nose, Bela squinted through her gold-rimmed glasses. 'U Tun Pe? Let me see . . .' She mumbled under her breath: 'Ko Tun Pe . . . U Tun Pe . . . Why yes! That sounds right . . .' She turned the cutting over. 'But when was this picture taken?'

'Nineteen-eighty-eight.'

Bela pursed her lips. 'I know what you're thinking, Jaya. But don't get carried away. It could be someone else. In Burma thousands of people have the same name. And in any case, Dinu would have been seventy-four in 1988. That is to say, he'd be eighty-two if he were still alive. And he was never robust, what with his leg. It's very unlikely . . .'

'You're probably right,' Jaya said, taking the picture back. 'But I still have to find out. I have to know for sure.'

It was Bela who provided Jaya with her next lead. She gave her a name: Ilongo Alagappan. 'Try to find him – if anyone knows about Dinu it will be him.'

Over the last two years, in order to keep in touch with her son, Jaya had familiarised herself with e-mail and the Internet. She had an account at a commercial computer centre and the next time she went by, she bought herself a half-hour on the Web. First, she keyed in a search under the words: 'U Tun Pe'. Nothing turned up. She rested her fingers on the keyboard and took a deep breath. Then she typed in the words 'Ilongo Alagappan' and hit 'enter'.

The search engine quivered, like a hound that had sniffed a hot trail. For a long, nerve-racking minute, an icon winked on the monitor. Suddenly the screen quivered again and a message appeared: the list of entries under 'Ilongo Alagappan' ran to five hundred and sixty items. Jaya got up from her chair and went to the manager's desk. 'I think I'm going to need an extra hour. Maybe two . . .'

She went back to her seat and started with item number one. She began to copy paragraphs into a separate file. She discovered that Ilongo was a prominent figure in Malaysian politics; he'd been a minister in the Government and had been honoured with a title – 'Dato'. His career had started after the war, when plantation workers had begun to form trade unions. Many had become active in politics and Ilongo was one such; in a few short years he had become one of the most important trade-unionists in the country – something of a legend in the plantations. He had founded a co-operative and had raised enough money to buy the Morningside plantation. This was at a time when rubber prices had slumped and thousands of workers were losing their jobs. He had been responsible for transforming Morningside into one of the flagship enterprises of the co-operative movement. The plantation workers' unions had grown into an extraordinary success story: there were health-care systems, pensions, educational pro-gramme, worker-retraining projects.

One of the items on the screen listed a web page for the 'Morn-ingside Co-operative'. Jaya decided to take a chance. She logged in and left a message for Ilongo. She introduced herself and said that she was gathering material for a book – on her great-aunt Uma and her grandfather, Rajkumar. She very much wanted to interview him, she wrote; she would be grateful for the favour of a response.

The next day she got a phone call from the manager of the computer centre. He was very excited. 'Good news, didi! Message for you! From Malaysia! We are all so happy! Someone is sending you a plane ticket . . .'

So striking was Ilongo's resemblance to Rajkumar that when Jaya first set eyes on him, at the Sungei Pattani railway station, the hairs rose on the back of her neck. Like Rajkumar, Ilongo was built on a generous scale: he was tall, wide-shouldered, very dark, and he too had a substantial belly, of the kind that is produced not by lethargy but rather by an excess of energy – his stomach was like an extra fuel tank, strapped to the outside of a truck. His hair was white and rumpled and he had a great deal of it, all over him – his arms, his chest, his knuckles: its lightness was a startling contrast to the colour of his skin. His face, like Rajkumar's, was deeply creased, with heavy dewlaps and jowls; it was enormous, thorny, and it seemed to be constructed mainly of armature, as though nature had equipped it for survival in the deep seas.

Only his speaking voice came as a true surprise. He sounded nothing like Rajkumar, in either English or Hindustani. His English was distinctively Malaysian – soft, peppered with float-ing interrogatives – *la?* – a very engaging, congenial manner of speech.

498

They stepped out of the station and Ilongo led her to a boxy, four-wheel-drive Toyota Land Cruiser. The vehicle's doors bore the logo of the co-operative that owned Morningside. They climbed in and Ilongo took out a flat tin box and lit a cheroot. This added to the eerie resemblance to Rajkumar.

'So tell me about your book,' he said. 'What is it going to be about?'

'I'm not sure yet,' she said. 'Maybe after I've interviewed you, I'll have a better idea.'

On the way to Morningside, Ilongo told her a little about his career and about the making of the Morningside co-operative. Timothy Martins, Alison's brother, had served in the US army during the war, as an interpreter. He'd been in the Pacific Theatre and at the end of the war, he'd come to Sungei Pattani for a brief visit. Ilongo had gone to see him. 'Aren't you going to visit Morningside?' he'd asked. Timothy had answered with a flat 'No'. He had no wish to return; the estate was a living reminder of everything that he wished to erase from his memory – the death of his parents, his sister, his grandfather; he wanted nothing so much as to be rid of it. Besides he had no interest in running a plantation. It was clear that the future of rubber, as a commodity, was none too bright. The war had stimulated research; substitutes were on their way. 'I'm going to put Morningside up for sale,' Timothy had told Ilongo. 'You should let everyone know.'

The estate was on the market for almost two years. There were no buyers. Timothy was not the only businessman who could see that the demand for rubber had run its course. All over Malaya, thousands of plantation workers were out of work; investors were buying up estates and selling off the land in parcels. In the end Ilongo had decided to make matters into his own hands: it was either that, or seeing everyone thrown out. He'd gone around with a begging bowl – quite literally – and in the end the money had been found.

'There it is,' Ilongo said proudly, pointing ahead. 'Morningside.'

They drove under an arched sign. The legend *Morningside Estate* was emblazoned across it in fine but faded Gothic characters. Underneath, in brighter, but more simple lettering there appeared the words: *A property of the Malaysian Plantation Workers'*

Co-operative. Gunung Jerai lay directly ahead, its peak veiled by a dense curtain of cloud.

The road headed uphill, snaking through alternating tracts of rubber and a crop of another kind – a short, stubby palm. These were oil palms, Ilongo explained, currently a more profitable investment than rubber: the plantation was increasing the acreage of the one at the expense of the other.

Jaya was fascinated by the oil palms: clusters of yellowish-orange fruit hung from the stub-like trunks, each as big as a lamb. The air was very still and it seemed to have the texture of grease. Between the palms there were bird-houses elevated on poles. These were for owls, Ilongo explained: the oil-rich fruit attracted great quantities of rodents; the birds helped keep their numbers under control.

Then Morningside House appeared ahead. It was freshly painted and had a bright cheerful look: its roof and shutters were red, while the rest of the house was a pale lime-green. There were trucks and cars parked in front – under the porch and all along the driveway. People were bustling about all over the grounds.

'The house seems very busy,' Jaya said.

'It is,' said Ilongo. 'I like to feel that it's being put to good use. I and my family occupy just one part of it: the rest of it serves as the co-op's office. I didn't want the house to become a monument. It's better this way: it serves a useful function.'

They drove round the house to the rear entrance. Mrs Alagappan, Ilongo's wife was waiting for them. She was tall and grey-haired, dressed in a green silk sari. The two of them lived alone in their part of the house: their children were grown up, all of them 'well settled and doing fine'. One of their daughters was in the civil service; another was a doctor; their son was a business-man, based in Singapore.

'It's just the two of us now.'

Every year, in the winter, they took a holiday on a cruise ship. The house was filled with mementoes of visits to South Africa, Mauritius, Fiji, Australia; there was a picture of the two of them dancing in a ship's ballroom. She was in a silk sari; he in a grey safari suit.

Mrs Alagappan had prepared *idlis* and *dosas* in anticipation of

Jaya's arrival. After lunch she was shown up to the guest room. She walked through the door and found herself facing the mountain through an open window. The clouds had cleared from the peak. On a wall beside the window there hung a photograph of the same view.

Jaya came to a dead stop, looking from the picture to the mountain and back. Ilongo was standing behind her. She turned to him. 'Dato?' she said. 'Who took that picture?'

He smiled. 'Who do you think?'

'Who?'

'Your uncle – Dinu.'

'And do you have other photographs of his?'

'Yes – many. He left a huge collection here, with me. That's why I wanted you to come. I thought he would have wanted you to have them. I'm getting old now, and I don't want them to be forgotten. I wrote to Dinu to ask what I should do but I never heard back . . .'

'So you're in touch with him then?'

'I wouldn't put it like that – but I had news of him once.'

'When?'

'Oh, it was a while ago now . . .'

Some five years earlier, Ilongo said, the co-operative had decided to start a programme for migrant workers. Malaysia's increasing prosperity had begun to draw many migrants from all over the region. Some of these workers were from Burma (or Myanmar as it was now called). It was not very difficult to cross clandestinely from Myanmar to Malaysia: the borders of the two countries were separated only by a few hundred miles of coastline. Among the Myanmarese migrants, there were some who'd been active in the democracy movement. They'd been driven underground after the crackdown of 1988 and had later decided to flee across the border. Quite by chance, Ilongo had met an activist of Indian origin – a young student who'd known Dinu well. He'd said that when he'd last heard of him, Dinu was living alone in Rangoon – Yangon as it was now called.

For over thirty years, Ilongo learnt, Dinu had been married to a well-known Burmese writer. His wife, Daw Thin Thin Aye, had been closely involved with the democracy movement. After

501

the crackdown, both she and Dinu had been gaoled. They'd been let out after serving three years. But Daw Thin Thin Aye had contracted tuberculosis in prison and had died within a year of her release. That was four years ago, in 1992.

'I asked if there was any way I could contact him,' Ilongo said. 'The boy told me it wouldn't be easy – the junta has barred Dinu from having a phone or a fax. Even letters aren't safe, but that was the only way, he said. So I wrote, but I never heard back. I suppose someone kept the letter . . .'

'But you have an address for him then?' Jaya said.

'Yes.' Ilongo reached into his pocket and took out a sheet of paper. 'He has a small photo studio. Does portraits, wedding pictures, group photographs. That sort of thing. The address is for his studio: he lives right above it.'

He held the paper out to her and she took it. The sheet was smudged and crumpled. She peered at it closely, deciphering the letters. The first words that met her eyes were: *'The Glass Palace: Photo Studio.'*

Forty-three

A few months later, Jaya found herself walking down a quiet and relatively uncrowded street in one of the older parts of Yangon. The flagstones on the footpaths were buckled and broken and weeds were growing out of the cracks. The houses along the road had plaster walls, most of them patched and discoloured. She caught glimpses of courtyards with trees growing over the doors. It was mid-December, a clear, cool day. There was very little traffic; children were back from school, playing football on the road. Barred windows looked down on the street from either side: it occurred to Jaya that she was the only person in sight who was dressed in anything other than a longyi; women in saris were few, and trousers seemed to be worn almost exclusively by policemen, soldiers and men in uniform. She had the feeling that she was being observed by a great many eyes.

Jaya's visa allowed her just one week in Myanmar. This seemed a very short time in which to find someone. What if Dinu were away, visiting friends, travelling? She had nightmare visions of waiting in a dingy hotel, in a place where she knew no one.

Earlier, at the airport in Calcutta, she had found herself exchanging glances with her fellow-passengers. They'd all been trying to sum each other up: why was he or she going to Yangon? What sort of business would take a person to Myanmar? All the passengers were Indians, people like herself; she could tell at a glance that they were going for exactly the same reason that she was: to look for relatives and to explore old family connections.

Jaya had gone to some trouble to get a window seat on the plane. She had been looking forward to comparing her experiences of the journey to Yangon with all the accounts she had heard over the years. But once she was seated, a sense of panic set in. If she were to find Dinu, what was the surety that he would be willing to talk to her? The more she thought of it the more the imponderables seemed to mount.

Now here she was, on a street that bore the same name as the one on the address. The numbering of the houses was very confusing. There were numerals and fractions and complicated alphabetical demarcations. Small doorways led into courtyards that proved to be alleys. She stopped to ask directions at a pharmacy. The man behind the counter looked at her piece of paper and pointed her to the adjoining house. She stepped out to find herself looking at a pair of street-level doors that led to the outer room of a large old-style house. Then she noticed a small, hand-painted sign, hanging above the doorway. Most of the lettering was in Burmese, but at the bottom, almost as an afterthought, there were a few words in English: *The Glass Palace: Photo Studio*.

Clearly she was in the right place, but the door was locked and it was evident that the place was closed. She was about to turn away, in disappointment, when she saw that the man in the pharmacy was gesturing in the direction of an alley, right next to the Glass Palace. She looked round the corner and saw a door that seemed to be fastened from the inside. Beyond lay a courtyard and the threshold of an old warren of a house. Glancing over her shoulder, she saw that the pharmacist was signalling vigorously, apparently urging her to step through. She knocked and when there was no answer, she banged hard, thumping the wood with the heel of her palm. Suddenly the doors flew apart. She stepped through and found herself in a walled courtyard. A couple of women were squatting in a corner, tending a cooking fire. She went up to them and asked: 'U Tun Pe?' They nodded, smiling, and pointed to a spiral staircase that led to the second floor: evidently Dinu lived in an apartment that was situated directly above his studio.

Climbing the stairs, Jaya became aware of a voice speaking in Burmese. It was the voice of an old man, quavering and feeble: the speaker appeared to be delivering some kind of discourse – a lecture or a speech. He was speaking in staccato bursts, the sentences punctuated by coughs and pauses. She came to the landing that led to the apartment: dozens of pairs of slippers and rubber sandals lay on the floor. The doors of the apartment stood open, but the entrance was angled in such a way that she could not see in. It was clear, however, that large numbers of people were gathered inside and it occurred to her that she might have stumbled upon a political meeting, even a clandestine one; she began to wonder whether her presence would constitute an unwelcome intrusion. Then she had a surprise: she heard the speaker uttering some words that were not Burmese; they were names that were familiar to her from the history of photography – Edward Weston, Eugène Atget, Brassaï. At this point, curiosity triumphed over discretion. She kicked off her slippers and stepped up to the door.

Beyond lay a large room with a high ceiling: it was crammed full of people. A few were sitting on chairs but most were seated on mats, on the floor. The crowd was larger than the room could comfortably hold and despite the presence of several whirring table fans, the air was hot and close. At the far end of the room there were two tall windows with white shutters. The walls were a dank, patchy blue and parts of the ceiling were blackened with soot.

The speaker was sitting in a rattan armchair that was draped with a green antimacassar. His chair was so positioned that he was facing most of his listeners: she found herself looking at him directly, from across the room. His hair was neatly cropped and parted, grey only at the temples. He was wearing a dark purple longyi and a blue knit T-shirt, with some kind of logo embroidered on the chest. He was rail-thin and his forehead and cheeks were deeply scored, with creases and fissures that seemed to move with the fluidity of ripples on water. It was a very fine face, suffused with the enrichment of age: the mobility of its lines created the impression of a range of perception and feeling that exceeded the ordinary by several extra registers.

It struck Jaya for the first time that she had never seen a picture of her uncle Dinu: he'd always been behind the camera, never in front of it. Could this be he? Jaya saw no resemblance to Rajkumar: to her he looked completely Burmese – but then this was true of many people of Indian, or part-Indian parentage. Either way, she could not be sure.

Jaya noticed now that the speaker was holding something in his hands – a large poster. He appeared to be using it to illustrate his lecture. She saw that the picture was of a shell, closely photographed. Its voluptuously rounded tail curled into a trunk that seemed almost to rise out of the print's surface. She recognised it as a reproduction of a monumental Weston nautilus.

Jaya had been standing at the door a couple of minutes without being noticed. All of a sudden every eye in the room turned in her direction. There was a silence and the place seemed to fill, almost instantaneously, with a fog of fear. The speaker put away the poster and rose slowly to his feet. He alone seemed calm, unafraid. He reached for a cane and came limping up, dragging his right foot behind him. He looked into her face and said something in Burmese. Jaya shook her head and tried to smile. He saw that she was a foreigner and she could almost hear him breathing a sigh of relief.

'Yes?' he said quietly in English. 'May I help you?'

Jaya was about to ask for U Tun Pe when she changed her mind. She said: 'I'm looking for Mr Dinanath Raha . . .'

The creases of his face seemed to shimmer, as though a gust of wind had blown suddenly across a lake. 'How did you know that name?' he said. 'It's many, many years since I last heard it used.'

'I'm your niece,' she said. 'Jaya – your brother's daughter . . .'

'Jaya!'

Jaya realised that they had somehow switched languages and he was now speaking to her in Bengali. Letting his cane drop, he put a hand on her shoulder and looked at her closely, as though searching for a confirmation of her identity. 'Come and sit beside me,' he said, his voice falling to a whisper. 'I'll just be a few more minutes.'

Jaya helped him back to his chair and sat cross-legged on the floor while he resumed his lecture. She was facing Dinu's audience now and she saw that it consisted of a motley mix of people, old and young, girls and boys, men and women. They were all Burmese but some looked to be of Indian origin, some Chinese. Some were smartly dressed while others were wearing cast-offs.

There was a student in a black cap that said *Giorgio Armani*, and in one corner there sat a group of three monks in saffron robes. They were all listening to Dinu with intent attention; some were taking notes.

Rows of glass-fronted bookcases ringed the floor. On the walls there were dozens, perhaps hundreds of photographic reproductions that looked as though they had been cut out of books and magazines. Some were in wooden frames; some were pasted on cardboard. She recognised several of them; they were all reproductions of well-known photographs: there was a famous Weston image of a sea-shell; a print of Cartier-Bresson's veiled women, standing grouped on a Kashmir hilltop; there was a Raghubir Singh picture of an old house in Calcutta.

In one corner of the room there stood a brightly decorated table. A hand-painted banner hung above: it said: 'Happy Birthday'. On the table there were paper cups, snacks, presents wrapped in paper . . .

She wished she knew what was going on.

Dinu's talk ended in a wild outburst of cheering and laughter. He smiled and turned to her with apologies for keeping her waiting. 'You found me in the middle of my weekly session . . . I call it my *glass palace* day.'

'It was not a long wait,' she said. 'What were you talking about?'

'Pictures . . . photography . . . anything that comes to mind. I just start them off – then it's everyone else's turn. Listen.' He smiled, looking round the room: it was filled with the noise of a dozen different conversations. At the back, a handful of people were blowing up balloons.

'Is it a class?' she asked. 'A lecture course?'

'No!' He laughed. 'They just come . . . every week . . . some are new, some have been here before. Some are students, some are artists, some have aspirations to becoming photographers . . . Of course most of them cannot afford a camera – you know how poor we are in our *Myanmar*' – he laughed satirically as he said the word '– and even if they could, they would not be able to

507

pay for film or printing or developing . . . But some of them have money – perhaps their parents are smugglers or contractors or colonels . . . I don't ask . . . It's better not to know. They take pictures and bring them here . . . We pass them around and discuss them . . . Or else I show them copies of old photographs and we talk about why they are good or why they are not. The Glass Palace is the only place in Yangon where you can see things like this . . . works of contemporary art . . .' He lifted his cane and pointed to his bookcases. 'Books, magazines . . . these are very hard, almost impossible to find here, because of the censors. This is one of the few places where they are to be found. People know, so they come . . .'

'How did you acquire these books?' she asked.

'It was hard . . .' He laughed. 'I made friends with ragpickers and the people who sort through refuse. I told them what I wanted and they saved them for me. The foreigners who live in Yangon – the diplomats and aid-workers and so on – they tend to read a lot . . . there's not much else for them to do, you see . . . they're watched all the time . . . They bring books and magazines with them and from time to time they throw them away . . . Fortunately the military does not have the imagination to control their trash . . . These things find their way to us. All these bookcases – their contents were gathered one at a time, by ragpickers. I sometimes think how astonished the original owners would be if they knew . . . It took me a long time . . . Then word got around and people began to come . . . they came, they looked and often they couldn't understand what they saw, so they would ask me and I would give them my opinion. First it was just a few people, then there were more . . . and more. Now they come every week . . . Even when I'm away they come . . . someone else talks . . . they look at pictures . . . Those who can afford it make a contribution – for tea, sweets, snacks. Those who can't don't . . . no one's ever been turned away. Today it's someone's birthday . . .' He pointed across the room to a young man. 'His friends are having the party here. That happens often . . . here they feel free to enjoy themselves . . . I encourage them to say whatever they like . . . to speak freely, even of simple things – for them this is an adventure, a discovery . . .'

'What do you mean?'

'You have to understand,' he said, 'that all their lives they've been trained to obey . . . their parents, their teachers, the military . . . this is what their education teaches: the habit of obedience . . .'

He laughed, his eyes twinkling. 'When they come here . . . they find that no one will scold them for what they say . . . they can criticise even their parents if they wish . . . this is a very shocking idea for many of them . . . some of them never come back . . . but many do, again and again . . .'

'Do they talk about politics too?'

'Yes. All the time. It is impossible not to, in Myanmar . . .'

'Doesn't the military do anything? Don't they try to stop you? Send spies?'

'Yes, of course. They send spies . . . There are probably a few here right now – in Myanmar there are always spies, everywhere. But no one ever discusses organisational matters here; we talk only of ideas and they know, also, that I'm not directly involved in the movement any more . . . my body won't allow me . . . They look at me and they see a tired old cripple . . . in a way my body protects me . . . You have to understand that their brutality is of a strangely medieval ilk . . . they are not so advanced as to be able to perceive a threat in what we do in this room. They would never be able to understand the attraction that brings people here, even though some of them are their own children . . . nothing that interests them is here – no booze, no drugs, no conspiracy . . . that is what protects us. And when we talk of politics it is in such ways that they cannot follow . . . we don't say things they can pin down . . . in Myanmar nothing that is worth saying can be spoken in ordinary language . . . everyone learns other means of communication, secret languages. Today for example, I was talking about Edward Weston's theory of pre-visualisation . . . that you must see the truth of your subject in your mind . . . after that the camera is incidental, unimportant . . . If you know the truth of what you see, the rest is mere execution. Nothing can come between you and your imagined desire . . . No camera, no lens . . .' He shrugged, smiling. 'To that list I could have added: No band of criminals like this regime . . . But I did not have to tell them that in so many words . . . They understood what I was saying . . . they knew . . . you saw how they laughed and clapped . . . Here in the Glass Palace photography too is a secret language.'

At the other end of the room, the birthday party was getting under way. A clamour arose for Dinu's presence at the table. He got to his feet and went over, leaning heavily on his stick. There were dishes of fried savouries, a cake, and a couple of large plastic bottles of Coca-Cola. A large can of Canadian beer stood at the centre of the table, untouched and immaculate, like an ornamental epergne. Dinu explained that one of the Glass Palace regulars was the son of a top general. He attended in secret, without his family's knowledge. From time to time he brought along a few items that were otherwise available only to smugglers and the junta's top brass. The beer can had stood on the table for more than a year.

Someone began to strum a guitar. A chorus started up and the cake was cut. Dinu presided over the celebration with benevolent good humour and there was a great deal of joking and light-heartedness. Jaya remembered one of Rajkumar's favourite sayings: 'Nowhere do they have such a gift for laughter as they do in Burma . . .' Yet it was evident that the laughter here had a special edge, honed upon fears that were never quite absent. It was a greedy kind of merriment, as though everyone wanted to have their fill while they could.

In other parts of the room a number of arguments and discussions were under way. Occasionally Dinu would be appealed to by one group or another. After one such intervention he turned to Jaya, in explanation: 'They're arguing about the picture that I was talking about – Weston's nautilus . . . some of them see themselves as revolutionaries . . . they insist that aesthetic matters have no relevance to our situation . . .'

'And what was your answer?'

'I quoted Weston . . . Weston reflecting on Trotsky . . . that new and revolutionary art forms may awaken a people or disturb their complacency or challenge old ideals with constructive prophecies of change . . . It doesn't matter . . . every week this comes up . . . every week I say the same thing.'

Presently a couple of young men took up a collection and went out to get biryani from a nearby shop. They were back in a few minutes, loaded down with paper packets. Dinu filled a plate and handed it to Jaya: she was surprised by how good the biryani was.

Slowly, as the evening neared its end, everyone grew quieter. A subdued resignation seemed to set in, as though darkness were knocking at the windows, providing a reminder of the constancy of its vigil.

Shortly before nine, Dinu said to Jaya: 'Where are you staying?'

She told him: it was a small hotel, picked at random.

'I would ask you to stay here,' he said. 'I live alone and you could look after yourself . . . It would be easy . . . But unfortunately the procedure takes a long time.'

'Procedure for what?' She was startled.

'For guests,' he said apologetically. 'Don't forget that you are in Myanmar. Nothing is simple here . . . Every household has a registered list of members . . . Nobody else can spend the night there without permission. I know a woman who after three years of marriage has to apply every week to be included in her husband's family's "guest list" . . .'

'And where does this permission come from?'

'The Chairman of the Ward Council . . . there's one in each neighbourhood . . . they can make your life hell . . . everyone hates them . . . mine is especially bad. So, you see, I would ask you to stay, but . . . The police make regular checks, especially at night. You never know when they're coming . . .'

Dinu gave Jaya a pat on the back: 'You'd better go now . . . the others will walk you back to your hotel . . . you will have been seen coming here, you may be sure of that . . . Was there a man in the pharmacy next door? There you are . . . If he isn't there by any chance, wait till he's seen you going . . . If he doesn't see you leaving you can be sure that there will soon be a knock on my door. Come back tomorrow . . . early . . . I'll get some pictures ready. We'll talk for as long as you want . . . We'll do nothing but talk . . . Every day that you're here . . .'

Forty-four

Dinu left Malaya shortly after Alison's death. Following the Japanese occupation, there was turmoil on the rubber estates. Many hundreds of workers left Morningside to join the Indian Independence League and the Indian National Army. Ilongo was one of them, and it was through him that Dinu came to know that Arjun had been one of the first to join Captain Mohun Singh's INA. The movement gathered such force that Dinu was powerless against it. His own views on the war remained unchanged, however, and after the news of Alison's death reached Morningside, he decided to cross over clandestinely into Burma.

Dinu eventually left Malaya in a fishing boat. Sailing mainly by night, hopping from island to island, he managed to make his way along the Isthmus of Kra. The boat left him on a beach, a few miles short of Mergui, the southernmost town in Burma. Dinu had hoped to make his way to Rangoon by land, but the Japanese invasion of Burma was now fully under way. The routes to the north were cut off.

Accompanying the Japanese ground forces was a small group of Burmese volunteers – the Burma Independence Army. This group was led by an acquaintance of Dinu's from Rangoon, the student leader, Aung San. As the Japanese army advanced, there were bloody clashes between the student-led group and some of the peoples of the border area – especially the indigenous Christians, many of whom remained loyal to the British. The border region was thrown into turmoil and there was no question of travelling north. Dinu remained in Mergui for several months.

By the time Dinu made his way to Rangoon, it was June 1942

and the city was under Japanese occupation. Dinu went to Kemendine and found the house gutted: the compound had suffered a direct hit. Dinu went to look for Thiha Saw, his old friend. He learnt that Thiha Saw, along with many other leftists, had escaped to India; his family had dispersed into the countryside. Only Thiha Saw's grandmother was still in Rangoon: she was being looked after by a young relative, a girl by the name of Ma Thin Thin Aye. Thiha Saw's relatives took Dinu in and gave him shelter; it was from them that Dinu learnt of Neel's death and of his family's subsequent departure for Huay Zedi.

North of Rangoon there was still fierce fighting between the Japanese forces and the retreating British army. To travel through the countryside at this time was very nearly an impossibility: all road and rail traffic was strictly controlled, through an elaborate regimen of cards and permits. The Japanese had installed a new government in Rangoon, under the leadership of a Burmese politician, Dr Ba Maw. Aung San and many others from the Burma Independence Army were members of this government – among them several former friends and acquaintances of Dinu's from Rangoon University. One of them helped him procure a pass that allowed him to travel north.

Dinu arrived at Huay Zedi only to find his family gone and the village almost deserted. He discovered that the sympathies of the people of this region were firmly with the Allies: Raymond was one of many men from Huay Zedi who had been recruited into an Allied partisan group – Force 136.

On receiving word of Dinu's arrival, Raymond materialised suddenly, to welcome him back. Raymond was no longer the sleepy-eyed student of Dinu's memory: he was wearing a khaki tunic and carrying a gun. He explained that his father, Doh Say, had urged Rajkumar and Dolly to stay on and had promised to do everything he could to ensure their comfort and safety. But after Neel's death Manju had become increasingly erratic in her behaviour and, in the end, fearing for her sanity, Rajkumar and Dolly had decided to take her back to India. They had left several months before Dinu's arrival; he had no hope of catching up with them now. Dinu decided to remain with Doh Say and Raymond, in their camp deep inside the jungle.

In 1944, the Allies launched a counter-invasion of Burma, spearheaded by the Fourteenth Army, under the command of General Slim. Within a few months the Japanese were pushed back from the Indian frontier and by early 1945 they were in headlong retreat. They were dealt a final blow by General Aung San who dramatically reversed his allegiances: although the Burma Independence Army had entered the country with the aid of the Japanese, they had never been more than reluctant allies for the occupiers. In 1945 General Aung San issued a secret order to his followers to join the drive to push the Japanese out of Burma. After this it was clear that the Japanese occupation was almost at an end.

But the fighting was not over yet. One day in March 1945, Doh Say sent for Dinu; he explained that he had received some worrying news. There had been a great battle at the town of Meiktila, some hundred miles to the north. The Fourteenth Army had won a decisive victory and the Japanese were in precipitate retreat. But a few last diehards from the Indian National Army were still battling on in central Burma, harrassing the advancing Allied army. One of these units had strayed across the Sittang and was believed to be advancing in the direction of their camp. Doh Say was concerned that the soldiers might cause trouble for the villagers; he wanted Dinu to seek them out and intercede with them. His hope was that by virtue of his Indian connections, Dinu would be able to persuade them to stay away from their village.

Dinu set off the next morning. Raymond went with him, as a guide.

After a few days' wait, a meeting was arranged, through the head-man of a village. It was held at an abandoned teak camp, deep in the jungle. The camp was an old one, of the kind that Dinu had heard his father describe – with a teakwood tai standing at the centre of a large clearing. This camp had been abandoned for many years, since long before the war. Much of it had been reclaimed by the jungle; the clearing was covered in four-foot-high grass, and many of the oo-sis' huts had been blown over by wind and rain.

Only the tai was still standing, though its ladder was entwined with vines and parts of its roof had fallen in.

Dinu's instructions were to wait alone. Raymond led him to the edge of the clearing and then slipped back into the forest. Dinu stood in front of the tai, in a position where he could be observed from a distance. He was dressed in a brown longyi and a homespun, black-and-white Karen tunic. He had stopped shaving after his arrival at Huay Zedi and his beard had greatly altered his appearance. He had a red-and-white cloth tied around his neck and he was carrying a woven shoulder bag, with some food, water and tobacco.

There was a tree-stump directly in front of the tai, and Dinu seated himself on it. A gentle breeze started up, rustling the tall grass in the camp clearing. Beyond, wisps of mist were rising from the tops of the hundred-foot trees that surrounded the camp. The greenery was a dense, blank wall: Dinu knew that the Indian soldiers were somewhere beyond, watching him.

In his cloth shoulder bag Dinu had some packets of boiled rice, wrapped in banana leaves. He opened one, and began to eat. While eating he listened to the sounds of the forest: a commotion among a flock of parrots told him that the soldiers were approaching. He sat still and went on eating.

Presently, from the corner of his eye, he saw an Indian soldier stepping into the clearing. He rolled his banana leaf into a ball and tossed it away. The soldier's head was just visible: he was wading through the grass with a high-stepping motion, using his gun to sweep aside the undergrowth.

Dinu watched the man approach. His face was so gaunt that he looked almost wizened – although Dinu guessed, from his carriage and his build, that he was in his early twenties. His uniform was in tatters and his shoes were so badly worn that his toes were visible; the soles were tied to his foot with bits of string. The soldier stopped a couple of feet from Dinu and made a gesture with the tip of his rifle. Dinu stood up.

'I have no weapons,' he said in Hindustani.

The soldier ignored him. 'Show me what's in your bag,' he said.

Dinu opened the mouth of his cloth bag.

'What's inside?'

Dinu reached in and took out his water-container and a leaf-wrapped packet of boiled rice. There was a look in the soldier's eyes that gave him pause. He undid the strings of the packet and handed it to him.

'Here,' he said. 'Take it. Eat.'

The soldier held the packet to his mouth and wolfed the rice down. Dinu saw that his condition was even worse than he'd first thought: the whites of his eyes had a jaundiced tinge and he looked malnourished, with discolourations on his skin and blisters at the corners of his mouth. After watching him for a minute, it seemed to Dinu that there was something about the soldier that looked familiar. Suddenly he knew who it was. In a disbelieving voice he said, 'Kishan Singh?' The soldier looked at him uncomprehendingly, narrowing his yellow-flecked eyes. 'Kishan Singh – don't you remember me?'

The soldier nodded, still holding the rice to his mouth. His expression changed hardly at all: it was as though, by this time, he were too fatigued to make the effort of recognition.

'Kishan Singh,' Dinu said, 'is Arjun with you?'

Kishan Singh nodded again. Then he turned on his heel, tossed the leaf wrapper aside and went back into the trees.

Dinu reached into his cloth bag. He took out a cheroot and lit it with a shaking hand. He seated himself again on the tree-stump. In the distance, another figure had stepped into the clearing, followed by a group of some thirty men. Dinu stood up. For some reason he couldn't understand, his palms had begun to sweat, dampening his cheroot.

Arjun stopped a few paces away. He and Dinu stood facing each other across the tree-stump. Neither of them said a word. At length Arjun gestured at the tai. 'Let's go up there.'

Dinu nodded his agreement. Arjun set his men on guard round the tai, and he and Dinu climbed up the ladder, seating themselves on the rotting floor planks. Close up, Arjun looked to be in an even worse way that Kishan Singh. A part of his scalp had been eaten away by a sore; the wound extended from above his right ear, almost as far as his eye. His face was covered in lacerations and insect bites. His cap was gone and so were the buttons of his uniform; his tunic was missing a sleeve.

Dinu would not have come if he'd known that he would be

516

meeting Arjun. It was now more than three years since they had last met and so far as Dinu was concerned Arjun was guilty, by association, for much of the horror and devastation of those years. Yet now that they were face to face, Dinu felt neither anger nor revulsion. It was as though he were looking not at Arjun, but at his pounded remains, the husk of the man that he had once been. Dinu opened his cloth bag and took out his remaining packets of rice.

'Here,' he said. 'You look as if you need something to eat.'

'What is it?'

'Just some rice . . .'

Arjun raised the packets to his nose and sniffed them. 'That's good of you,' he said. 'The men will be grateful . . .'

He got up and went to the ladder. Dinu heard him telling his men to distribute the rice among themselves. When he came back, Dinu saw that he had given away all the packets. He understood that pride would not allow Arjun to accept food from him.

'What about a cheroot?' Dinu said. 'Can I give you one of those?'

'Yes.'

Dinu handed him a cheroot and struck a match. 'Why are you here?' Arjun said.

'I was asked to come,' Dinu said. 'I've been living in a village . . . not far from here. They heard that your men were heading in their direction . . . They were worried.'

'They have nothing to worry about,' Arjun said. 'We try to stay away from local people. We have no dispute with them. You can tell them they're safe – from us at any rate.'

'They'll be glad.'

Arjun drew on his cheroot, and blew the smoke out through his nose. 'I heard about Neel,' he said. 'I'm sorry – for you, for Manju . . .'

Dinu acknowledged this with a gesture.

'And what about your family?' Arjun said. 'Have you had any news – of Manju? The baby?'

'I haven't heard anything for the last three years,' Dinu said. 'They were here for a while . . . after Neel died . . . they were in the same place that I am now . . . with old family friends. Then

517

they went to Mawlaik, to try to cross over . . . They haven't been heard from since . . . my mother, my father . . . None of them . . .'

Dinu chewed on his thumbnail and cleared his throat. 'And did you hear about Alison . . . and her grandfather?'

'No.' Arjun's voice was a whisper. 'What happened?'

'They were heading south from Morningside . . . the car broke down and they ran into some Japanese soldiers . . . they were both killed . . . but she fought back . . .'

Arjun covered his face with his hands. Dinu could tell from the rhythmic tremor in his shoulders that he was sobbing. Dinu felt only pity for Arjun now. He reached across the floor and put an arm around his shoulders.

'Arjun . . . Stop . . . It won't help . . .'

Arjun shook his head, violently, as though he were trying to wake himself from a nightmare. 'Sometimes I wonder if it'll ever end.'

'But, Arjun . . .' Dinu was surprised by the gentleness in his own voice. 'Arjun . . . it was you . . . you who joined them . . . of your own free will. And you're still fighting on – now . . . even after the Japanese . . . Why? What for?'

Arjun's looked up, his eyes snapping. 'You see, Dinu – you don't understand. Not even now. You think I joined *them*. I didn't. I joined an Indian army that was fighting for an Indian cause. The war may be over for the Japanese – it isn't for us.'

'But, Arjun . . .' Dinu's voice was still gentle. 'You must see that you don't have a hope . . .'

At this, Arjun laughed.

'Did we ever have a hope?' he said. 'We rebelled against an Empire that has shaped everything in our lives; coloured everything in the world as we know it. It is a huge, indelible stain which has tainted all of us. We cannot destroy it without destroying ourselves. And that, I suppose, is where I am . . .'

Dinu put his arms round Arjun again. He could feel tears welling up in his eyes, yet there was nothing he could say; there was nothing to be said.

This is the greatest danger, he thought, this point at which Arjun has arrived – where, in resisting the powers that form us, we allow them to gain control of all meaning; this is their moment of victory: it is in this way that they inflict their final and most terrible defeat. For Arjun, now, he felt not pity but compassion: what must it be like to visualise defeat so accurately, so completely? There was a sort of triumph in this – a courage – the value of which he did not wish to diminish by arguing.

'I should go now,' Dinu said.

'Yes.'

They climbed down the vine-swathed ladder. At the bottom, they embraced again.

'Be careful, Arjun . . . be careful.'

'I'll be all right.' Arjun smiled. 'One day we'll laugh about this.' He waved and walked away into the shoulder-high grass.

Dinu leant against the tai's ladder and watched him go. Long after the soldiers were gone, he remained where he was. When Raymond appeared, out of the darkness, Dinu said: 'Let's stay here tonight.'

'Why?'

'I don't feel well enough to go.'

This encounter with Arjun left Dinu profoundly shaken: now, for the first time, he began to understand the irreducible reality of the decision that Arjun had made; he saw why so many others whom he'd known – men such as Aung San – had made the same choices. He began to doubt his own absolute condemnation of them. How does one judge a person who claims to act on behalf of a subordinated people, a country? On what grounds can the truth of such a claim be established or refuted? Who can judge a person's patriotism except those in whose name he claims to act – his compatriots? If the people of India chose to regard Arjun as a hero; if Burma saw Aung San as her saviour – was it possible for someone such as him, Dinu, to assume that there was a greater reality, a sweep of history, that could be invoked to refute these beliefs? He could no longer be confident that this was so.

Forty-five

Arjun's unit had initially numbered about fifty men: only twenty-eight now remained. Very few of these had been lost to hostile fire: most of the losses were due to desertion.

At the outset, the unit was evenly split between professional soldiers and volunteers. The professionals were those who'd been recruited in India, men like Kishan Singh, and Arjun himself. When Singapore fell, there were some fifty-five thousand Indian troops on the island. Of these more than half joined the Indian National Army. The volunteers were recruits from the Indian population in Malaya and most of them were Tamil plantation workers.

In the beginning some of Arjun's fellow-officers had been sceptical about the abilities and endurance of the new recruits. The army that had trained them, the British Indian army, had not recruited Tamils: they were counted as one of the many Indian groups that were racially unfit for soldiering. Being professional soldiers, Arjun's fellow-officers were steeped in the racial mythologies of the old mercenary army. Even though they knew those theories to be without foundation, they found it hard to rid themselves entirely of the old imperial notions about the kinds of men who made good soldiers and those who didn't. It was only under fire that they'd come to recognise how false those myths were: experience had demonstrated the plantation recruits to be, if anything, much hardier and more dedicated than the professionals.

In his own unit, Arjun found that there was a clear pattern to desertions: the men who'd melted away were almost all professionals; not a single plantation recruit had left. He'd been puzzled by this until Kishan Singh explained the reasons behind it. The professionals knew the men on the other side; the men they were fighting against were their relatives and neighbours; they knew that if they went over, they wouldn't be badly treated.

Arjun could tell that the plantation workers understood this too. They knew who the professional soldiers were and what class they came from; they knew exactly how their minds worked and why they deserted. Every time a few more 'professionals' went missing, Arjun would see a deepening contempt in their eyes; he knew that in private the plantation men laughed about the pampered lives the soldiers had been used to, about the way they'd been fed and fattened by their colonial masters. They – the plantation recruits – seemed to have recognised that in the end, theirs wasn't the same struggle as that of the professionals; in a way, they weren't even fighting the same war.

Not all the plantation recruits spoke Hindustani: Arjun often had difficulty in communicating with them. There was only one man with whom Arjun could converse fluently: his name was Rajan. He was a lean, wiry man, all muscle and bone, with red-flecked eyes and a thick moustache. Arjun had recruited him himself, at Sungei Pattani. He'd wondered at the time whether Rajan was suitable material. But after his recruitment, Rajan had become another person altogether: training had transformed him. He seemed to have developed an aptitude for soldiering and had emerged as the most forceful personality among the plantation recruits.

Once, going over a ridge, Rajan had asked Arjun to point in the direction of India. Arjun had shown him: it was to the west. Rajan stood a long time staring into the distance; so did many of the other men.

'Have you ever been to India?' Arjun asked.

'No, sir.' Rajan shook his head.

'What do you think you'll find there?'

Rajan shrugged: he didn't know and in a way, he didn't seem to care. It was enough that it was India.

Arjun discovered later that Rajan had been born in Malaya; his knowledge of India came solely from stories told by his parents. The same was true of all the plantation recruits: they were fighting for a country they had never seen; a country that had extruded their parents and cut them off. This made their fervour all the more remarkable. Why? What were their motivations? There was so much about their lives that he, Arjun, didn't know and could not fathom – the way they talked about 'slavery' for instance, always using the English word. At first Arjun had thought that they were using the term loosely, as a kind of metaphor – for after all, it wasn't true technically that they were slaves; Rajan knew that as well as Arjun did. What did he mean then? What was it to be a slave? When Arjun asked this question Rajan would always answer indirectly. He would begin to talk about the kind of work they'd done, on the plantation – every action constantly policed, watched, supervised; exactly so many ounces of fertiliser, pushed exactly so, in holes that were exactly so many inches wide. It wasn't that you were made into an animal, Rajan said – no, for even animals had the autonomy of their instincts. It was being made into a machine: having your mind taken away and replaced by a clockwork mechanism. Anything was better than that.

And India – what was India to them? This land whose freedom they were fighting for, this land they'd never seen, but for which they were willing to die? Did they know of the poverty, of the hunger their parents and grandparents had left behind? Did they know about the customs that would prevent them from drinking at high-caste wells? None of that was real to them; they had never experienced it and could not imagine it. India was the shining mountain beyond the horizon, a sacrament of redemption – a metaphor for freedom in the same way that slavery was a metaphor for the plantation. What would they find, Arjun wondered, when they crossed the horizon?

And it was in the act of posing this question that Arjun began to see himself through their eyes – a professional, a mercenary, who would never be able to slough off the taint of his past and the cynicism that came with it, the nihilism. He saw why they might think of him with contempt – as an enemy even – for it was true in the end, that he was not fighting their war; that he did not believe as they believed; that he did not dream their dreams.

*　　*　　*

It was Rajan who brought Kishan Singh back, with his hands tied, stumbling through the undergrowth. Kishan Singh's condition was such that he hadn't been able to get very far. Rajan had found him holed up under an overhang, hiding, shivering, praying.

Rajan gave Kishan Singh a push, and he fell on his knees.

'Get up,' Arjun said. He couldn't stand to look at Kishan Singh like this. '*Utho* – get up, Kishan Singh.'

Rajan took hold of Kishan Singh's collar and pulled him to his feet. Kishan Singh's frame was so wasted that he was like a stick-figure, a broken puppet.

Rajan had only contempt for Kishan Singh. He spoke to Arjun directly, looking him in the eyes: 'And what will you do with him now?'

There was no 'sir', no 'sahib', and the question wasn't 'what has to be done?' but, 'what will *you* do?' Arjun could see the challenge in Rajan's eyes; he knew what was in Rajan's mind – that the professionals would stick together, that he would find a way of letting Kishan Singh off. Time. He had to make time.

'We have to hold a court-martial,' Arjun said.

'Here?'

Arjun nodded. 'Yes. There's a procedure. We have to try and keep to it.'

'Procedures? Here?' The sarcasm was audible in Rajan's voice.

Arjun could tell that Rajan was trying to show him up in front of the other men. Using the advantage of his height, he went up to him and stared into his eyes,

'Yes,' said Arjun. 'Procedures. And we have to respect them. That's how armies are run – that's what make them different from street gangs.'

Rajan shrugged and ran his tongue over his lips. 'But where?' he said. 'Where are you going to find a place for a court-martial?'

'We'll go back to that teak camp,' Arjun said. 'It'll be easier there.'

'The camp? But what if we were followed?'

'Not yet. We'll go.' The camp was an hour away: it would buy a little time.

'Fall in.' Arjun took the lead. He didn't want to watch Kishan Singh being pushed along, with his hands tied behind his back.

It began to rain and they were drenched by the time they got to the camp. Arjun led the way across the clearing, to the tai. The area under the stilts was dry, sheltered from the rain by the structure above. Rajan let Kishan Singh go and he sank to the ground, squatting on his haunches, shivering.

'Here,' said Arjun. 'We'll hold the hearings here.'

Rajan fetched a chair from the tai and placed it in front of Arjun. 'For you, sir,' he said, with a mocking excess of politeness. 'Since you are the judge.'

Arjun ignored him. 'Let's begin.'

Arjun tried to prolong the ritual, asking questions, going over the details. But the facts were clear: there was no disputing them. When he asked Kishan Singh to speak in his own defence, all he could do was beg, clasping his hands together. 'Sah'b – my wife, my family . . .'

Rajan was watching Arjun, smiling. 'Any other procedures? Sir?'

'No.' Arjun saw that Rajan and the other men had formed a circle: he and Kishan Singh were at its centre. Arjun stood up. 'I've made my decision.' He turned to Rajan. 'I'm putting you in charge of the firing squad,' he said. 'Ask for volunteers. Do it quickly.'

Rajan looked straight back at him, shaking his head. 'No,' he said. 'None of us will volunteer. He's one of yours – one of your men. You will have to deal with him yourself.'

Arjun looked at the circle of men around him. They were all watching him; their faces were expressionless, their eyes unblinking. Arjun turned away; shreds of memory floated through his mind . . . this is how mutiny looks from the other end; you're alone, and the only thing you can fall back on is the authority of a distant chain of command; on threats of the army's justice, of eventual retribution once victory is won. But what do you do when you know that there will be no victory, when defeat is certain? How do you claim the validation of the future, knowing that it will not be yours?

'Come, Kishan Singh.' Arjun helped his former batman to his feet. His body was very light, almost weightless. Arjun could feel his hands growing gentle, as he took hold of Kishan Singh's arm.

It was strange to be touching him in this way, knowing what lay ahead.

'Come. Kishan Singh.'

'Sah'b.'

Kishan Singh stood up and Arjun took hold of his arm, pushing him forward, past the others, out of the tai's shelter, into the rain. They waded into the tall grass and Kishan Singh stumbled. Arjun put his arm round him and held him up. Kishan Singh was so weak that he could barely walk; he rested his head on Arjun's shoulder.

'Keep going, Kishan Singh.' His voice was soft, as though he were whispering to a lover. '*Sabar karo*, Kishan Singh – it'll be over soon.'

'Sah'b.'

When they came to the edge of the clearing, Arjun let him go. Kishan Singh dropped to his knees, holding himself upright by clinging to Arjun's leg.

'Sah'b.'

'Why did you do it, Kishan Singh?'

'Sah'b, I was afraid . . .'

Arjun unbuttoned his leather holster with one hand and took out his sidearm – the Webley that Kishan Singh had always polished and oiled for him.

'Why did you do it, Kishan Singh?'

'Sah'b – I couldn't go on . . .'

He looked down at the welts and jungle sores on Kishan Singh's head. He thought of another time when Kishan Singh had knelt between his feet, asking for his protection; he thought of his guile-lessness and trust and innocence, of how he had been moved by the histories that lay behind them – the goodness and strength he had seen in him; all the qualities that he himself had lost and betrayed – qualities that had never been his to start with, he who had sprung from the potter's wheel, fully made, deformed. He knew he could not allow Kishan Singh to betray himself, to become something other than he was – to become a creature like himself, grotesque, misshapen. It was this thought that gave him the strength to put his gun to Kishan Singh's head.

At the touch of the cold metal, Kishan Singh raised his eyes, looking up at him. 'Sah'b – remember my mother, my home, my child . . .'

Arjun took hold of Kishan Singh's head, curling his fingers through his matted hair. 'It's because I remember that I must do this, Kishan Singh. So that you cannot forget all that you are – to protect you from betraying yourself.'

He heard the shot and then he staggered away, towards a clump of trees. He reached for a branch to steady himself, and he saw, suspended in the branches, a dripping shred of flesh and bone. He could not tear his eyes from it: it was a part of Kishan Singh, of the head he'd just held in his hands. He took another step and fell to his knees. When he looked up Rajan and the other men were standing around him, watching. In their eyes there was a kind of pity.

There was rejoicing at the camp when Doh Say decided to move back to Huay Zedi. The march down the slope was a triumphal, joyful parade, complete with drums, flutes and elephants.

Doh Say gave Dinu a small place of his own, at the edge of the village. Dinu was just settling in when Raymond sought him out.

'Come with me,' Raymond said. 'I have something to tell you.'

They went down to the stream, and watched the village children shooting for fish in the shallows of Huay Zedi's stream, with their crossbows and bamboo darts.

'I have some news.'

'What?'

Arjun was dead, Raymond said. He'd been tracked down by a unit from Force 136; they'd caught up with him at the old teak camp.

'Was it you who led them there?' Dinu asked.

'No. A deserter. One of his own men – an old soldier.'

'But you were there?' Dinu said. 'At the end . . . ?'

'Yes.'

'What happened?'

'They'd called me in – the people who were hunting him. They'd heard that many of his men had left –'

'So was Arjun alone then?'

'Yes. Completely alone – he was back at the abandoned teak camp. The rest of his men had left, they were all gone – they'd taken off their uniforms, put on longyis and disappeared into the forest. I tried to track them – but it was impossible. They knew the jungle, those men – they'd vanished.'

'And Arjun?'

'There was an Indian colonel there. He tried to get Arjun to surrender, told him that it was over, he would be all right. But Arjun shouted back, calling them slaves and mercenaries. And then he stepped out, on the tai's veranda, shooting . . .'

Raymond stopped to toss a pebble into the stream.

'It was clear,' he said, 'that he did not want to live.'

Forty-six

In 1946, when it became apparent that Burma would soon become independent, Doh Say decided to leave Huay Zedi and move eastwards, into the mountainous regions of the Burma–Thailand border. The war had pitted the peripheries of the country against its centre: Doh Say was one of many who had deep misgivings about what the future held for Burma's minorities.

Most of Huay Zedi's population took Doh Say's advice, Dinu among them. The village was abandoned and its inhabitants settled in Loikaw, a small frontier town, deep in the Karenni hills, not far from the border of Thailand. For Dinu, there was one great advantage to being in Loikaw: he was once again able to find photographic materials – many of them smuggled across the Thai border. He set up a studio and became the only professional photographer within hundreds of miles. Even in difficult times, people married, had children – they needed records and were willing to pay, sometimes in cash but more often in kind.

In 1947, in preparation for the British departure, Burma's first national elections were held. They were won by General Aung San. It was widely believed that he alone would be able to ensure the country's unity and stability. But on 19 July, shortly before he was to assume office, Aung San was assassinated, along with several of his would-be colleagues. Within months of the assassination, a Communist-led insurgency broke out in central Burma. Some of the army's Karen units mutinied. The Karen were the country's largest ethnic group after the Burmans; a major Karen organisation took up arms against the Rangoon Government.

Other groups followed suit. In a short time, there were sixteen insurgencies raging in Burma.

One day, in Loikaw, a boy came running to Dinu's door. 'Ko Tun Pe – someone come looking for you.' Another child followed and then another. They stood in his doorway panting, watching in bright-eyed expectation. They all said the same thing. 'Ko Tun Pe – you have a visitor; she's walking up from the bus station.'

He ignored them; he stayed inside his studio, doing nothing, trying not to look out of the window. Then he heard more voices approaching – a procession appeared to be making its way towards his shack. He could hear people calling out: 'Ko Tun Pe – look who's here!' He saw a shadow on his threshold and looked up. It was Dolly.

It had taken Dolly several months to track Dinu to Loikaw. She had arrived in Burma late in 1948, just as the insurgencies were getting under way. On coming to Rangoon, she'd discovered that the authority of the elected Government did not extend far beyond the capital's municipal limits. Even the areas that bordered Mingaladon airport were in rebel hands. Much of Rangoon was in ruins, bombed to ashes by successive air campaigns. With the Kemendine house burnt to the ground, she had nowhere to stay; a friend gave her refuge.

One day Dolly heard that Dinu's old friend, Thiha Saw, was back in Rangoon, working for a newspaper. She went to see him to ask if he had any news of Dinu. It so happened that U Thiha Saw had recently attended a political conference where Raymond had also been present. U Thiha Saw told Dolly that Dinu was safe, living in Loikaw. Dolly had left Rangoon by boat the next day. After a journey of several weeks she had boarded a rattling old bus that was on its way to Loikaw.

Dolly and Dinu spent days talking. She told him about Neel's death and Manju's death; about the march across the mountains and how she and Rajkumar had made the journey from the Indian border, through Assam, to Calcutta; she explained why she had come back to Burma alone.

He took pictures of her. Dolly was very thin and the bones of her face could be seen as clearly as the ridges of a fluted cup. Her hair was tied tightly back at the nape of her neck: it was still dark and glossy, with only a few white streaks at the temple.

She urged him to write to his father: 'You should go and find him; you would not have the trouble with him that you had before. He is changed, a different man, almost a child. You should go to him; he needs you – he is alone.'

Dinu would make no promises. 'Maybe. Some day.'

He knew, without her telling him, that she had not come to stay. He was not surprised when she said: 'Next week I shall leave for Sagaing.'

He went with her. This was the first time he'd ventured into the plains since the end of the war. He was stupefied by the devastation. They travelled through territories that had been scorched not once but twice by retreating armies. River channels were blocked and railway lines lay mangled on their sleepers. From village to village a different group or party was in charge. Farmers ploughed round bomb-craters; children pointed out the places where mines lay unexploded. They took roundabout routes, skirting round those districts which were said to be particularly dangerous. They walked and hired ox-carts, and took an occasional bus or a river boat. At Mandalay they stopped a night. Much of the fort was in ruins; the palace had been destroyed by artillery fire; the pavilions that Dolly had known had burnt to the ground.

They walked the last few miles to Sagaing and took a ferry across the Irrawaddy. To their intense relief Sagaing was unchanged. The hills were tranquil and beautiful, dotted with thousands of white pagodas. Dolly began to walk faster as they approached the nunnery. At the entrance she held Dinu fast and then Evelyn led her in. The next day, when Dinu went to see her, her head was shaved and she was wearing a saffron robe. She looked radiant.

It was arranged that he would come back to see her again the next year. The time came and he went back, from Loikaw to Sagaing, making the long journey again. At the gates of the nunnery there was a long wait. At length Evelyn came down. She gave him a gentle smile.

'Your mother passed away a month ago,' she said. 'We could

not inform you because of the troubles. You'll be happy to know that it was very quick and she suffered no pain.'

In 1955 Doh Say died, in Loikaw. By this time, he had become a great patriarch and an influential leader. He was mourned by thousands. To Dinu, Doh Say had been almost as much a parent as a mentor: his death was a great blow. Shortly afterwards, Dinu decided to move to Rangoon.

The mid-1950s were a relatively quiet time in Burma. There was a stand-off in the insurgencies and the Government was a functioning democracy. U Thiha Saw had become the editor of one of the country's leading Burmese-language newspapers and wielded considerable influence in Rangoon.

On arriving in Rangoon, Dinu went to see his old friend: he had grown from a thin, tall boy into a portly, authoritative-looking man. He wore colourful longyis and floppy bush shirts, and almost invariably had a pipe in his hands. He gave Dinu a job as a photographer at his newspaper. Later, when Dinu found a suitable place for a studio, it was U Thiha Saw who loaned him the money to buy it.

Some of the best-known photographers of pre-war Rangoon had been Japanese. After the war many had closed down their studios and disposed cheaply of their equipment. In his years in Loikaw, Dinu had made himself an expert in repairing and restoring old and discarded photographic equipment: he was able to set up his studio at very little cost.

U Thiha Saw was one of the first visitors to Dinu's studio. He looked round it with approval. 'Very nice, very nice.' He stopped to puff on his pipe. 'But haven't you forgotten something?'

'What?'

'A signboard. Your studio has to have a name, after all.'

'I haven't thought of a name . . .' Dinu glanced around. Everywhere he looked, his eyes met glass: framed photographs, countertops, camera lenses.

'The Glass Palace,' he said suddenly. 'That's what I'll call it . . .'

'Why?'

531

'It was a favourite phrase of my mother's,' he said. 'Just something she used to say . . .'

The name stuck and Dinu's work quickly gained a reputation. The Fourth Princess was now living in Rangoon. Her husband was an artist. They were both regular visitors to the Glass Palace. Soon Dinu had more work than he could handle. He asked around for an assistant and U Thiha Saw recommended a relative, a young woman who was in need of a part-time job. This proved to be none other than Ma Thin Thin Aye – the young girl who'd helped to shelter Dinu when he'd passed through Rangoon in 1942. She was now in her mid-twenties, a student at Rangoon University. She was doing research in Burmese literature, writing a dissertation on *The Glass Palace Chronicles* – a famous nineteenth-century history, written in the reign of King Bodawpaya, an ancestor of King Thebaw's. The name of Dinu's studio struck Ma Thin Thin Aye as a happy coincidence. She took the job.

Ma Thin Thin Aye was slim, petite and neat in her movements. Every day, at four in the afternoon, she walked down the street, past the pharmacy, to the wooden door that led to the Glass Palace. Standing outside, she would sing out Dinu's name – 'U Tun Pe!' – to let him know that she'd come. At seven-thirty she and Dinu would close the studio: she'd walk away down the street and Dinu would lock up and go round the corner to climb the stairs to his room.

After a few weeks, Dinu discovered that Ma Thin Thin Aye's mornings were not spent solely on research. She was also a writer. Rangoon had a thriving culture of small literary magazines. One of these had published a couple of her short stories.

Dinu tracked down her stories. They took him by surprise. Her work was innovative and experimental; she was using the Burmese language in new ways, marrying classicism with folk usage. He was astonished by the wealth of allusion, by her use of dialect, by the intensity of her focus on her characters. It seemed to him that she had achieved much that he'd once aspired to himself – ambitions that he'd long abandoned.

Dinu was a little awed, and this made it hard for him to tell Ma Thin Thin Aye of his admiration for her work. Instead, he began to tease her, in his earnest, staccato way. 'That story of yours,' he said, 'the one about the street where you live . . . You say the people on the street are from many different places . . . from the coasts and the hills . . . Yet in your story they all speak Burmese. How is that possible?'

She was not at all put out.

'Where I live,' she said softly, 'every house on the street speaks a different language. I have no choice but to trust my reader to imagine the sound of each house. Or else I would not be able to write at all about my street – and to trust your reader is not a bad thing.'

'But look at Burma,' Dinu went on, still teasing. 'We are a universe on our own . . . Look at all our people . . . Karen, Kayah, Kachin, Shan, Rakhine, Wa, Pa-O, Chin, Mon . . . Wouldn't it be wonderful if your stories could contain each language, each dialect? If your reader could hear the vastness of the music? the surprise?'

'But they do,' she said. 'Why do you think they don't? A word on the page is like a string on an instrument. My readers sound the music in their heads, and for each it sounds different.'

At this point in his life, photography was no longer a passion for Dinu. He did only commercial work, making studio portraits and printing other people's negatives. He bestowed a great deal of care and attention on what he did, but took no particular pleasure in it: mainly he was grateful for possessing a skill that could be parlayed into a livelihood. When people asked him why he no longer photographed outside his studio, he told them that his eyes had lost the habit of looking; his vision had withered for lack of practice.

The photographs that he thought of as his real work, he rarely showed. These pictures were in, any case, very few in number. His early prints and negatives had been destroyed when the Kemendine house went up in flames; the work he'd done in Malaya was still at Morningside. All he possessed of his own work were a few pictures taken in Loikaw – of his mother, of Doh Say and Raymond and their families. Some of these he'd framed and hung on the walls of his apartment. He fought shy of inviting Ma Thin Thin Aye upstairs to see them. She was so young – more than ten years his junior. It mattered very much that she not think badly of him.

A year went by and every day Ma Thin Thin Aye left and entered the studio by the door that led to the street. One day she said: 'U Tun Pe, do you know what I find hardest in my writing?'

'What?'

'The moment when I have to step off the street and go into a house.'

He frowned. 'Why . . . ? Why that?'

She wrung her hands together in her lap, looking exactly like the serious student that she was. 'It is very hard,' she said. 'And to you it may seem like a small thing. But I do believe that it is this moment that marks the difference between classical and modern writing.'

'Of all things . . . ! How so?'

'You see, in classical writing, everything happens outside – on streets, in public squares and battlefields, in palaces and gardens – in places that everyone can imagine.'

'But that is not how you write?'

'No.' She laughed. 'And to this day, even though I do it only in my mind, nothing is more difficult for me than this – going into a house, intruding, violating. Even though it's only in my head, I feel afraid – I feel a kind of terror – and that's when I know I must keep going, step in, past the threshold, into the house.'

He nodded but made no comment. He gave himself a little time to think about what she'd said. One afternoon he bought biryani from Mughal Street and invited her up.

A few months later, they were married. The ceremony was a quiet one and they invited very few people. Afterwards, Ma Thin Thin Aye moved into Dinu's two rooms. She marked off a corner for herself and set up a desk. She began to teach literature at the university. In the afternoons, she still helped at the studio. They were happy, content with the smallness and privacy of their world. Their childlessness did not seem a great lack. Her work began to gain notice, even beyond literary circles. She became one of the select group of Burmese writers whose presence was regularly sought at festivals in the countryside.

534

One morning, Daw Thin Thin Aye was tutoring a promising young student at the university, when she heard a burst of gunfire close at hand. She went to the window and saw hundreds of young men and women running by, some covered in blood.

Her student pulled her away from the window. They hid under a desk. After a couple of hours they were found by one of Daw Thin Thin Aye's colleagues. There had been a coup, they learnt. General Ne Win had seized power. Dozens of students had been shot down, right inside the university.

Neither Dinu nor Daw Thin Thin Aye had ever been directly involved in politics. After the coup, they kept to themselves and waited for the winds to change. It was not until many years had passed that they realised that this was a storm that had come to stay.

U Thiha Saw was arrested and his newspaper was shut down. General Ne Win, the new dictator, began to juggle with the currency. Notes of certain denominations were declared to be valueless; overnight, millions of kyats became waste paper. Thousands of the country's brightest young people fled into the countryside. Rebellions multiplied and flourished. Raymond went underground with several hundred followers. In the east, on the Thai border, the insurgents gave a name to the territories under their control: they became a Karen Free State – Kwathoolei, with its capital at the riverbank town of Manerplaw.

With each year the generals seemed to grow more powerful while the rest of the country grew ever feebler: the military was like an incubus, sucking the life from its host. U Thiha Saw died at Insein gaol, in circumstances that were not explained. His body was brought home bearing marks of torture and the family was not permitted a public funeral. A new censorship regime developed, growing out of the foundations of the system that had been left behind by the old Imperial Government. Every book and magazine had to be presented to the Press Scrutiny Board, for the perusal of a small army of captains and majors.

One day Daw Thin Thin Aye was ordered to report to the

Scrutiny Board's office. The building was plain and functional, like a school, and its long corridors smelt of toilets and disinfectant. She went to an office with a plywood door and sat for several hours on a bench. When at last she was shown in, she found herself facing an officer who looked to be in his late twenties. He was sitting at a desk and the manuscript of one of her stories was lying in front of him. His hands were in his lap and he seemed to be toying with something – she could not tell what it was.

She stood at the desk, fidgeting with the hem of her blouse. He did not ask her to sit. He stared, looking her up and down. Then he jabbed a finger at the manuscript. 'Why have you sent this here?'

'I was told,' she said quietly, 'that that is the law.'

'The law is for writers,' he said. 'Not for people like you.'

'What do you mean?'

'You do not know how to write Burmese. Look at all these mistakes.'

She glanced at her manuscript and saw that it was covered with red pencil marks, like a badly filled schoolbook.

'I've wasted a lot of time correcting this,' he said. 'It's not my job to teach you people how to write.'

He got up from his chair and she saw that he was holding a golf club in his hands. It struck her now that the room was full of golfing paraphernalia – caps, balls, clubs. He reached for her manuscript and crumpled it into a ball, with one hand. Then he put it on the ground between his feet. He took many little steps, swinging the head of his club back and forth. He swung, and the ball of paper went sailing across the room. He held the pose for a moment, admiring his swing – the bent knee, the flexed leg. He turned to her. 'Pick it up,' he said. 'Take it home and study it. Don't send anything to this office again until you've learnt to write proper Burmese.'

In the bus, on the way home, she smoothed out the pages, one by one. His vocabulary, she realised, was that of a child; he was barely literate. He had run his pencil through everything he hadn't understood – puns, allusions, archaisms.

She stopped writing. Nothing could be published unless it had undergone the board's scrutiny. Writing was hard enough, even with nothing to deal with except yourself. The thought of another such encounter made those hours at the desk seem unendurable.

The newspapers were full of strident denunciations of imperialism. It was because of the imperialists that Burma had to be shut off from the world; the country had to be defended against neo-colonialism and foreign aggression.

These tirades sickened Dinu. One day he said to his wife: 'Look at the way in which these thugs use the past to justify the present. And they themselves are much worse than the colonialists; at least in the old days, you could read and write.'

Daw Thin Thin Aye smiled and shook her head in reproof. She said: 'To use the past to justify the present is bad enough – but it's just as bad to use the present to justify the past. And you can be sure that there are plenty of people to do that too: it's just that we don't have to put up with them.'

Their lives became very quiet and stunted: they were like plants whose roots had been trimmed to contain them inside tiny pots. They mixed with very few people, and were always careful about what they said, even with friends. They grew gnarled with age, inside and outside: they moved round their rooms with slow deliberation, like people who are afraid of knocking things over.

But all was not quiet around them. There were changes under way that they did not know about. Their lives were so quiet, so shut off that they didn't feel the first rumbles under the volcano. The eruption, when it came, took them by surprise.

It started with another of the general's crazed whims – another juggling of the currency. But this time people were not content to see their life's savings turned into waste paper. There were protests, quiet and hesitant at first. One day, in the university, there was a brawl in a teashop – a small, apparently innocuous event. But suddenly classrooms emptied, students came pouring out into the streets; leaders emerged and with astonishing speed, organisations developed.

One day Daw Thin Thin Aye was taken to a meeting. She went unwillingly, pushed on by her students. Afterwards, she helped write a pamphlet. When she picked up the pen her hand was shaking – she saw herself in the censor's office again. But as she began to write, a strange thing happened. With every sentence she saw her crumpled pages coming alive, rising off the floor and hitting back at the golf club, knocking it out of the major's hands.

She began to go to meetings all over town. She tried to get Dinu to come but he resisted. Then one day there was news of a new speaker: she was to address a huge gathering, near the Shwe Dagon – her name was Aung San Suu Kyi and she was the daughter of Dinu's old acquaintance from the university, General Aung San.

Dinu was seventy-four at the time; with age his right leg had grown stiffer and he walked with difficulty, but this new name had an energising effect on him. He went to the meeting and after that he was not able to stay at home again. He began to take pictures; he travelled with his camera, putting together a pictorial record of the movement in its headiest and most joyful days.

On August 8, 1988 Dinu woke up with a mild fever. Daw Thin Thin Aye made him a meal and told him to stay in bed. There was to be an important march in the city that day: she left early in the morning. Some three or four hours later, Dinu heard repeated volleys of gunfire in the distance. He was too ill to go out; he lay in bed and waited for his wife to come home. In the late afternoon there was a knock on the door. He dragged himself out of bed and threw the door open.

There were three or four uniformed policeman standing on the stairs. Behind them were several longyi-clad plain-clothes men.

'Yes?' said Dinu. 'What do you want?'

They pushed past him without a word. He looked on helplessly as they went through the flat, opening cupboards and closets, rifling through their possessions. Then a plain-clothes man pointed to a framed picture of Raymond. The others gathered around, whispering.

One of the policemen came over to Dinu, with the framed photograph in his hand. 'Do you know this man?' he said to Dinu.

'Yes.' Dinu nodded.

'Do you know who he is?'

Dinu picked his words carefully. 'I know his name.'

'Do you know that he's the leader of an insurgency? Did you know that he's one of the most wanted terrorists in the country?'

'No.' Dinu's answer was non-committal.

'Anyway – you will have to come with us.'

'Not right now,' said Dinu. 'I can't. I'm ill and I'm waiting for my wife.'

'Don't worry about her,' said the man in the uniform. 'She's already been taken to a place where she will be safe.'

Forty-seven

On Jaya's last day in Yangon, Dinu promised to take her to 38 University Avenue, to attend a public meeting at Aung San Suu Kyi's house.

The year 1996 marked the sixth of Aung San Suu Kyi's house arrest. Despite her confinement, Aung San Suu Kyi's compound was still the centre of the city's political life. Twice every week, on Saturdays and Sundays, she held a meeting at her house: people gathered outside and she addressed them from the gate. These meetings had become pilgrimages. A hush fell on Rangoon on weekend afternoons and thousands poured into the city from all round the country.

Dinu came to Jaya's hotel to pick her up. A friend of his had driven him there in car – a 1954 Czech-built Skoda. The car was making loud coughing noises as it idled on the street. As she was stepping in, Jaya noticed that the car's doors were all of different colours, all oddly misshapen, as though they'd been banged into shape with sledgehammers.

'What a strange-looking car,' she said.

Dinu laughed. 'Yes . . . this is a car that has been put together entirely from bits of other cars . . . The bonnet is from an old Japanese Ohta . . . one of the doors is from a Volga . . . It's a miracle that it runs at all . . .'

The backfiring of the Skoda's engine echoed through the streets as they drove away. The centre of the city was almost eerily quiet, emptier than Jaya had ever seen it before. But as they went northwards the traffic increased: there were cars, buses, small trucks. They came to a wide, tree-shaded avenue lined with large villas.

They parked a good distance away, and joined the many hundreds of people who were walking down the avenue.

They came to a house with a green and yellow fence. There was a large crowd outside. Not much was visible of the interior of the compound: the house was set well back from the road, surrounded by stands of tall bamboo. The gates were of metal, with spikes along the top. There were some ten thousand people gathered round them, most sitting patiently on the grassy verge that lined the avenue on both sides. The road was kept clear by volunteers and policemen, and traffic was flowing through, right past the gates, at a slow but steady pace.

The volunteers were wearing saffron tunics and green longyis: Jaya learnt that these were the colours of the democracy movement. Dinu was recognised by many of the volunteers. They waved him through to a vantage point that was quite close to the gates. The view was good and Jaya spent a long time looking at the people around her: there were many students and a fair sprinkling of Buddhist nuns and monks, but most of the people there seemed like ordinary folk. There were plenty of women, a large number being accompanied by children. The atmosphere was expectant but not tense; there were many food vendors making their way through the crowd, selling drinks and snacks.

Dinu nudged Jaya's elbow and pointed to a photographer and a couple of men in wire-rimmed sunglasses. 'M.I.,' he said with a chuckle. 'Military intelligence. They will film it all and take it back to their headquarters. Their bosses will watch it tomorrow.'

Jaya noticed that there were many Indians in the crowd. She commented on this to Dinu and he said, 'Yes, you can be sure this fact hasn't escaped the regime ... the official papers often describe these meetings as gatherings of evil Indians.' He laughed.

Suddenly there was a great uproar. 'There she is,' Dinu said. 'Aung San Suu Kyi.'

A slim, fine-featured woman stepped up. Her head was just visible above the gate. Her hair was dark black, and gathered at the neck. She was wearing white flowers above her hair. She was beautiful almost beyond belief.

Aung San Suu Kyi waved at the crowd and began to speak. She was using Burmese and Jaya could not understand what she was saying. But the delivery was completely unlike anything she'd ever heard. She laughed constantly and there was an electric brightness to her manner.

The laughter is her charisma, Jaya thought. She could hear echoes of Aung San Suu Kyi's laughter everywhere around her, in the crowd. Despite the swarming intelligence agents, the atmosphere was not heavy or fear-filled. There was a good-humouredness that seemed very much at odds with the deadened city beyond. Jaya understood why so many people had pinned their hopes on Aung San Suu Kyi; she knew that she herself would have been willing to do anything that was asked of her at that moment: it was impossible to behold this woman and not be half in love.

Both she and Dinu were silent as they walked back to the old Skoda. They got back inside, and presently Dinu said: 'It's strange . . . I knew her father . . . I knew many others who were in politics . . . many men who are regarded as heroes now . . . But she is the only leader I've ever been able to believe in.'

'Why?'

'Because she's the only one who seems to understand what the place of politics is . . . what it ought to be . . . that while misrule and tyranny must be resisted, so too must politics itself . . . that it cannot be allowed to cannibalise all of life, all of existence. To me this is the most terrible indignity of our condition – not just in Burma, but in many other places too . . . that politics has invaded everything, spared nothing . . . religion, art, family . . . it has taken over everything . . . there is no escape from it . . . and yet, what could be more trivial, in the end? She understands this . . . only she . . . and this is what makes her much greater than a politician . . .'

'But if that's true,' Jaya said hesitantly, 'doesn't it make it much harder for her to succeed – as a politician?'

Dinu laughed. 'But she has already succeeded . . . don't you see? She has torn the masks from the generals' faces . . . She has shown them the limits of what she is willing to do . . . and these limits have imprisoned them too . . . she haunts them unceasingly, every moment . . . She has robbed them of words, of discourse.

They have no defence against her but to call her an imperialist ... which is laughable ... when in fact, it is they who invoke the old imperial laws and statutes to keep themselves in power. The truth is that they've lost and they know this ... this is what makes them so desparate ... the knowledge that soon they will have nowhere to hide ... that it is just a matter of time before they are made to answer for all that they have done.'

Forty-eight

Dinu came to Jaya's hotel to take her to the airport. On the way, as they were driving through the city in the Skoda, Dinu said: 'You've been here seven days and we've never once spoken of my father.'

'That is true,' Jaya said guiltily.

'Tell me about his last days,' Dinu said. 'Were you with him?'

'Yes, I remember it very well. My great-aunt Uma had died just a few days before, you see. They were almost ninety, both of them . . .'

They died within a few weeks of each other. Uma was the first to go: she died in her sleep and it was Rajkumar who found her. The news caused a stir: she was given a state funeral and the Governor came. The family was pushed quietly to the background.

Rajkumar died of a heart attack, a month later. His funeral was as modest as Uma's had been grand. A few of his friends from the Burmese temple carried his body to the crematorium. Afterwards Jaya and Bela took his ashes to the river. Jaya scattered them in the water.

'I remembered how he'd always said that for him, the Ganges could never be the same as the Irrawaddy.'

Jaya glanced at Dinu and saw that he was crying, tears running down the creases of his face. She reached for his hand.

'You asked me about his last days,' she said, 'and the truth is that what I told you is quite different from what I remember.'

'What do you remember?'

'I remember a story my son told me.'

544

'Your son? I didn't know you had a son.'

'Yes, I do. He's grown up now. He's been living in America these last few years.'

'And what was his story?'

I was very young, maybe four or five. Lankasuka was my home too; I lived upstairs with my mother and my great-aunt, Bela. Rajkumar lived downstairs, in Uma's flat, in a small room next to the kitchen. In the morning, on waking up, the first thing I would do was to go down to look for him.

That morning I went to Rajkumar's room and found that his bed had not been slept in. I was alarmed. I went running across the flat to Uma's bedroom, to tell her that my great-grandfather was missing.

Although Rajkumar had lived in Uma's flat for some twenty years, there was never any ambiguity about their living arrangements or the nature of their relationship. It was understood by everyone that their connection was one of charity, founded on Uma's affection for Dolly. Uma was a benevolent benefactress; he a near-destitute refugee. His presence in the household did not in any way compromise Uma's reputation as a woman of icy self-containment, a widow who had mourned her dead husband for more than half a century.

The geography of Uma's flat mirrored their relationship. Uma slept in the master-bedroom, overlooking the park; Rajkumar's room was a converted pantry, near the kitchen. It was only in the afternoons that he was allowed into Uma's room and he always sat in the same place – a large divan that was ringed with cotton-stuffed bolsters. They had lived thus for twenty years.

But that morning when I ran into Uma's room, I found, to my surprise, that Rajkumar was in her bed. They were fast asleep, their bodies covered by a thin, cotton sheet. They looked peaceful and very tired, as though they were resting after some great exertion. Their heads were thrown back on a bank of piled pillows and their mouths were open. This was the very pose that we children used in games that required the figuring of death: head

545

bent back, mouth open, tongue protruding between the lips. That I should be confused was only natural.

I shouted: 'Are you dead?'

They woke up, blinking short-sightedly. They were both extremely short-sighted and there ensued a flurry of bed-slapping and pillow-turning as they fumbled for their eyeglasses. In the process, their covers slipped off and their bodies were revealed to be naked. Uma's skin looked very soft and was covered with a delicate tracery of tiny cracks; every single hair on Rajkumar's body had turned white, creating a startlingly elegant effect against his dark complexion.

'Why,' I said stupidly, 'your clothes are off . . .'

They found their glasses and snatched the covers back. Uma produced a loud gargling sound, a kind of volcanic mumble. Her mouth was strangely puckered, and on looking more closely I realised that both she and Rajkumar were without their teeth.

I was fascinated by dentures, as all children are, and I knew exactly where Uma put hers when she retired at night: to prevent them from being knocked over, they were placed out of reach of the bed, immersed in water, in a large glass tumbler.

In an effort to be helpful, I approached the tumbler, so that I could spare them the trouble and embarrassment of getting out of bed naked. But when I looked at the tumbler, I discovered that there was not one, but two sets of dentures inside. What was more, they had somehow become entangled, so that their jaws were interlocked, each reaching deep into the mouth of the other, each biting down on the other's teeth.

In a further effort to be helpful, I tried to pry the dentures apart. But Rajkumar had grown impatient and he snatched the tumbler from me. It was only after he had thrust his teeth into his mouth that he discovered that Uma's dentures were clamped within his. And then, as he was sitting there, staring in round-eyed befuddlement at the pink jaws that were protruding out of his own, an astonishing thing happened – Uma leant forward and fastened her mouth on her own teeth. Their mouths clung to each other and they shut their eyes.

I had never seen a kiss before. In India, in those days, such things were excised from sight by unseen censors, in real life as in film. Even though I did not know that this embrace had a name, I did realise that to remain in that room would be to violate something that was beyond my understanding. I slipped away.

What I saw that morning in my great-great-aunt Uma's bedroom remains to this day the most tender, the most moving sight I have ever seen, and from the day when I sat down to write this book – the book my mother never wrote – I knew that it was this that it would end.

Author's Notes

The seed of this book was brought to India long before my own lifetime by my father and my uncle, the late Jagat Chandra Datta of Rangoon and Moulmein – 'The Prince' as he was known to his relatives. But neither my father nor my uncle would have recognised the crop that I have harvested. By the time I started work on this book, the memories they had handed on to me had lost their outlines, surviving often only as patterns of words, moods, textures. In attempting to write about places and times that I knew only at second- and third-hand, I found myself forced to create a parallel, wholly fictional world. *The Glass Palace* is thus unqualifiedly a novel and I can state without reservation that except for King Thebaw, Queen Supayalat and their daughters, none of its principal characters bear any resemblance to real people, living or deceased.

Perhaps it was the very elusiveness of what I was trying to remember that engendered in me a near-obsessive urge to render the backgrounds of my characters' lives as closely as I could. In the five years it took me to write *The Glass Palace* I read hundreds of books, memoirs, travelogues, gazetteers, articles and notebooks, published and unpublished; I travelled thousands of miles, visiting and re-visiting, so far as possible, all the settings and locations that figure in this novel; I sought out scores of people in India, Malaysia, Myanmar and Thailand. In the process I amassed vast arrears in debts of gratitude – the one kind of insolvency that one may justly consider a form of riches – a roster so large indeed that I can, at best, hope only to make a few gestures of acknowledgement towards the most pressing of these debts.

Of the people who took the time to speak to me during my travels in 1995, 1996, 1997 and 1999, I would particularly like to record my gratitude to the following. In Malaysia: Janaki Bai Devadasan, G. Anthony Samy, E. R. Samikannu, Anjali Suppiah, A. V. Pillai, A. Ponnusamy, R. Chinamma Rangaswamy, S. P. Velusamy; Lt. K. R. Das, Abraham Muttiah, F. R. Bhupalan, M. Y. B. Abbas, M. Gandhinathan, Eva Jenny Jothi, Nepal Mukherjee, N. G. Choudhury, V. Irulandy, S. P. Narayanswamy, S. Natarajan and Y. B. Tan Sri Dato K. R. Somasundaram of the National Land Finance Co-operative Society Ltd. I would also like to thank D. Narain Samy and other members of the staff of the Bukit Sidim Estate for their hospitality during my stay. But I am beholden most of all to the storied Puan Sri Janaki Athinagappan of Kuala Lumpur, who introduced me to many of the above, and who has, over the years, taken me and my family into her own. In Singapore, my thanks go to Elizabeth Choy, Ranjit Das, Bala Chandran, Dr. N. C. Sengupta and particularly my friend Dr. Shirley Chew who opened many doors for me in that city. In Thailand, for their kindness in taking the time to talk to me, I would like to record my gratitude to: Pippa Curwen, U Aye Saung, Khun Kya Oo, Khun Kya Noo, Lyndell Barry, Sam Kalyani, Nyi Nyi Lwin, Abel Tweed, Aung Than Lay, Ma Thet Thet Lwin, Than Kyaw Htay, Oo Reh, Tony Khoon, David Saw Wah, Raymond Htoo, David Abel, Teddy Buri, and particularly Ko Sunny (Mahinder Singh). U Tin Htun (E. C. Nanabawa) also went out of his way to help me during my travels and I owe him many thanks.

In India I would like to thank: Aruna Chatterjee, Col. Chatterjee, Dr. Sugato Bose, Capt. Lakshmi Sahgal, Lt-Gen N. S. Bhagat, Capt. Khazan Singh, Capt. Shobha Ram Tokas, Shiv Singh, Hari Ram, Major Devinder Nath Mohan, Capt. A. Yadav, Barin Das, Tarit Datta, Arabinda Datta and Derek Munro. Mrs Ahona Ghosh kindly allowed me to consult her father's handwritten notes of the 1942 trek; I owe her many thanks. I am also deeply grateful to Nellie Casyab, of Calcutta, a survivor of that great trek which the historian Hugh Tinker calls the 'Forgotten Long March' of 1941. It was she who introduced me to the Burmese and Anglo-Burmese worlds of Calcutta and put me in touch with the few other remaining survivors of that terrible ordeal. I would also like to thank Albert Piperno, another survivor of the trek, for his efforts in recalling the bombing of Rangoon on December 23, 1941. I owe a very special debt to Lieutenant-Colonel Gurubakhsh Singh Dhillon, the last of the 'Red Fort Three', who met with me for several days and spent many hours recounting the events of December 1941.

I greatly regret that, for fear of reprisals against those concerned, I am unable to thank either my friends in Myanmar or those of their compatriots who went out of their way to speak to me, often at no little risk to themselves. I trust that, should any of them ever happen to read this, they will know who they are and understand the depth of my gratitude to each of them.

Sadly, circumstances permit me to acknowledge only one of my most salient debts in Yangon: to the late writer Mya Than Tint, who has been removed by his untimely death from the reach of the regime whose oppressions he had so long and so heroically endured. Mya Than Tint was, for me, a living symbol of the inextinguishable fortitude of the human spirit: although I knew him only briefly, I felt myself to be profoundly changed and deeply instructed by his vision of literature. Everyone who knew him will recognise at once the pervasiveness of his influence on this book.

In the course of writing this book I lost a close friend: Raghubir Singh, the photographer, who was my mentor and teacher in all things relating to photography. It is my great regret that I was unable to acknowledge the depth of my gratitude to him in his lifetime: if I do so now, it is not in the hope of making amends, but rather, in order to record an unrepayable debt. Naturally, neither he nor anyone else named above bears any responsibility for any aspect of the contents of this book, the onus of which rests on me alone.

Amongst published sources my greatest debt is to the monograph *Deposed King Thebaw of Burma in India, 1885–1916* (Bharatiya Vidya Series, Vol. 25, Bharatiya Vidya Bhavan, Bombay 1967) by Walter A. Desai. In his memoir, *The Changing of Kings* (Peter Owen, London, 1985), Philip Glass describes Desai as "a quiet old Indian historian from (Rangoon) University". I like to think of the 'quiet old Indian' living in India in his retirement, sifting through the archives of New Delhi and Bombay as an act of homage and restitution to the country he had lost. Desai's attempt to recover traces of this erased life is to me, in its slow careful unemphatic accumulation of detail, a deeply moving work; an affirmation that every life leaves behind an echo that is audible to those who take the trouble to listen.

Much of the travel and research for this book was supported by *The New Yorker*. I am grateful to many members of the staff of that magazine for their consistent support, and would like to thank, in particular, Tina Brown, Bill Buford, Alice Quinn, Peter Canby and Liesl Schillinger. Thanks also to Laura McPhee, for her help and advice, and to my old friend James Simpson, who has enriched this book immensely by his reading of the manuscript. I am deeply grateful to my editors Susan Watt, Ravi Dayal, Kate Medina and Rukun Advani. To Barney Karpfinger, my agent, who found me the time I needed to write this book and was a pillar of strength through its most difficult moments, my gratitude is beyond measure. To Debbie, my wife, for her unfailing support, and my children, Lila and Nayan, for their forbearance, I am, as ever, deeply beholden.

In the end my greatest debt is to my father, Lieutenant-Colonel Shailendra Chandra Ghosh. He fought in the Second World War as an officer of the 12th Frontier Force Regiment, a unit of the then British-Indian Army. He was in General Slim's Fourteenth Army during the Burma campaign of 1945 and was twice mentioned in dispatches: he was thus among those 'loyal' Indians who found themselves across the lines from the 'traitors' of the Indian National Army. He died in February 1998 and never saw any part of my manuscript. Only in his absence did I come to understand how deeply my book was rooted in his experience, his reflections on the war and his self-questioning: it is to his memory that I dedicate *The Glass Palace*.